# POSTAL

## COMPLETE COLLECTION

PUBLISHED BY TOP COW PRODUCTIONS, INC.
LOS ANGELES

# POSTAL™

## COMPLETE COLLECTION

### CREATED BY MATT HAWKINS

**BRYAN HILL**
**MATT HAWKINS**
WRITERS

FOR THIS EDITION COVER ART BY
**LINDA SEJIC**

**ISAAC GOODHART**
**RAFFAELE IENCO**
**ATILIO ROJO**
ARTISTS

ORIGINAL EDITIONS EDITED BY
**ELENA SALCEDO, RYAN CADY,**
**ASHLEY VICTORIA ROBINSON,**
**& BETSY GOLDEN**

**K. MICHAEL RUSSELL**
**BETSY GOLDEN**
COLORISTS

BOOK DESIGN & LAYOUT BY
**VINCENT VALENTINE**

**TROY PETERI**
LETTERER

For *Top Cow Productions, Inc.*
**Marc Silvestri** - CEO
**Matt Hawkins** - President & COO
**Elena Salcedo** - Vice President of Operations
**Vincent Valentine** - Vice President of Production
**Lisa Y. Wu** - Marketing Director

EDENVERSE

To find the comic shop
nearest you, call:
***1-888-COMICBOOK***

Want more info? Check out:
**www.topcow.com**
for news & exclusive Top Cow merchandis

**IMAGE COMICS, INC.** • **Robert Kirkman:** Chief Operating Officer • **Erik Larsen:** Chief Financial Officer • **Todd McFarlane:** President • **Marc Silvestri:** Chie Executive Officer • **Jim Valentino:** Vice President • **Eric Stephenson:** Publisher / Chief Creative Officer • **Nicole Lapalme:** Vice President of Finance • **Leann Caunter:** Accounting Analyst • **Sue Korpela:** Accounting & HR Manager • **Matt Parkinson:** Vice President of Sales & Publishing Planning • **Lorelei Bunjes:** Vic President of Digital Strategy • **Dirk Wood:** Vice President of International Sales & Licensing • **Ryan Brewer:** International Sales & Licensing Manager • **Alex Co**x Director of Direct Market Sales • **Chloe Ramos:** Book Market & Library Sales Manager • **Emilio Bautista:** Digital Sales Coordinator • **Jon Schlaffman:** Specialt Sales Coordinator • **Kat Salazar:** Vice President of PR & Marketing • **Deanna Phelps:** Marketing Design Manager • **Drew Fitzgerald:** Marketing Content Associat • **Heather Doornink:** Vice President of Production • **Drew Gill:** Art Director • **Hilary DiLoreto:** Print Manager • **Tricia Ramos:** Traffic Manager • **Melissa Gifford** Content Manager • **Erika Schnatz:** Senior Production Artist • **Wesley Griffith:** Production Artist • **Rich Fowlks:** Production Artist • **IMAGECOMICS.CO**M

POSTAL: THE COMPLETE COLLECTION TRADE PAPERBACK. April 2023. ISBN: 978-1-5343-9944-0

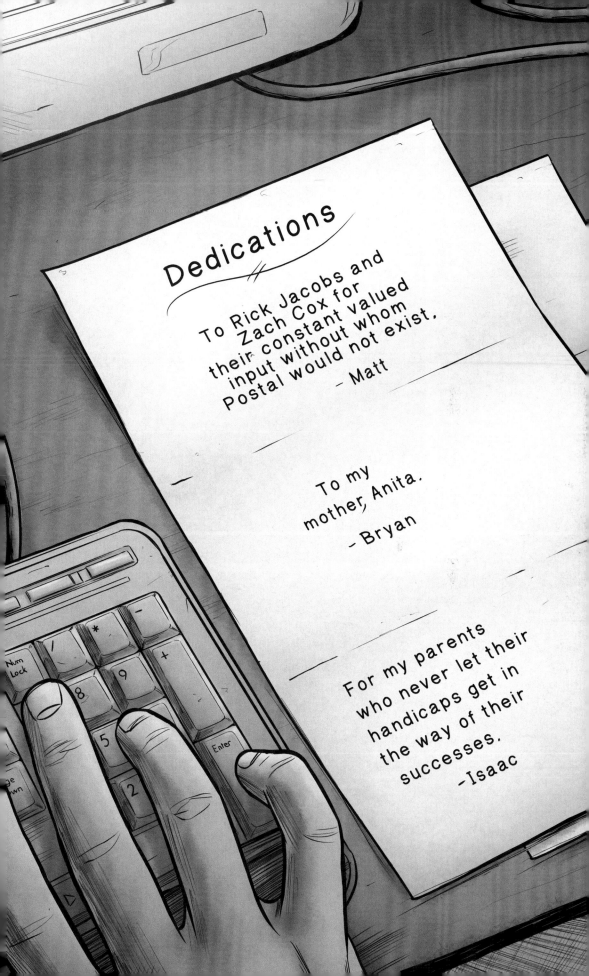

# Dedications

To Rick Jacobs and
Zach Cox for
their constant valued
input without whom
Postal would not exist,

— Matt

To my
mother, Anita.

— Bryan

For my parents
who never let their
handicaps get in
the way of their
successes.

—Isaac

# CHAPTER 1

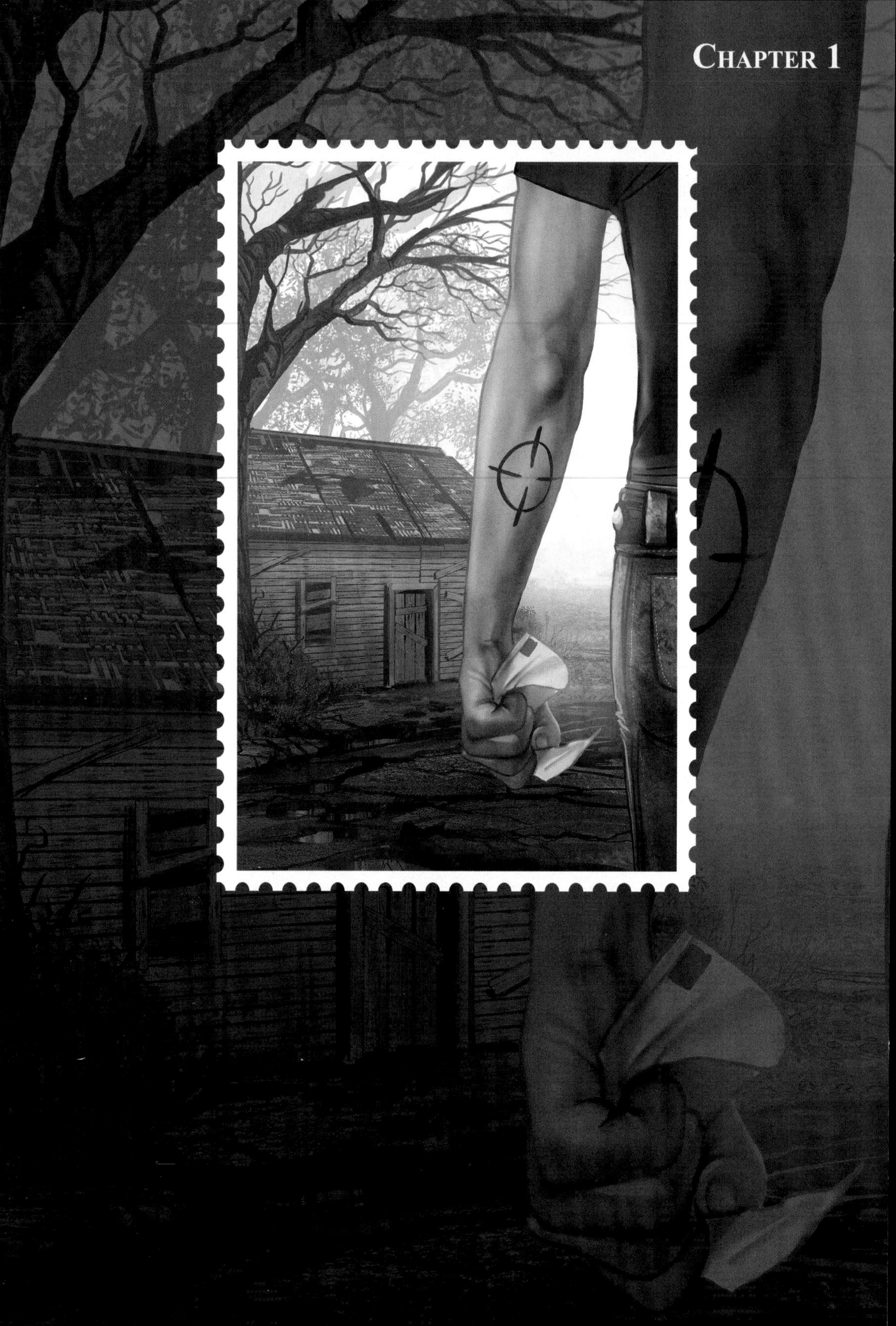

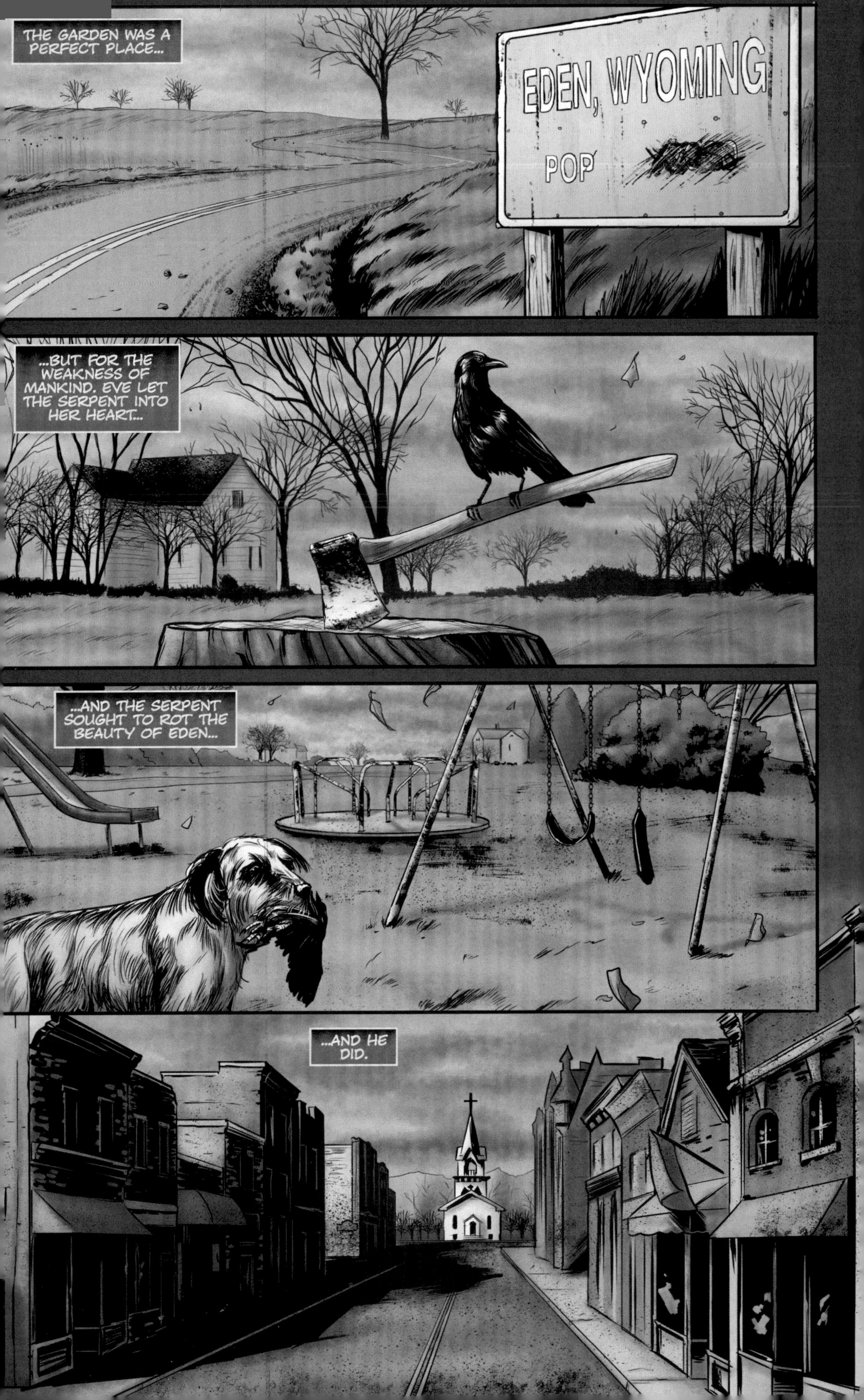
THE GARDEN WAS A PERFECT PLACE...
EDEN, WYOMING
POP
...BUT FOR THE WEAKNESS OF MANKIND. EVE LET THE SERPENT INTO HER HEART...
...AND THE SERPENT SOUGHT TO ROT THE BEAUTY OF EDEN...
...AND HE DID.

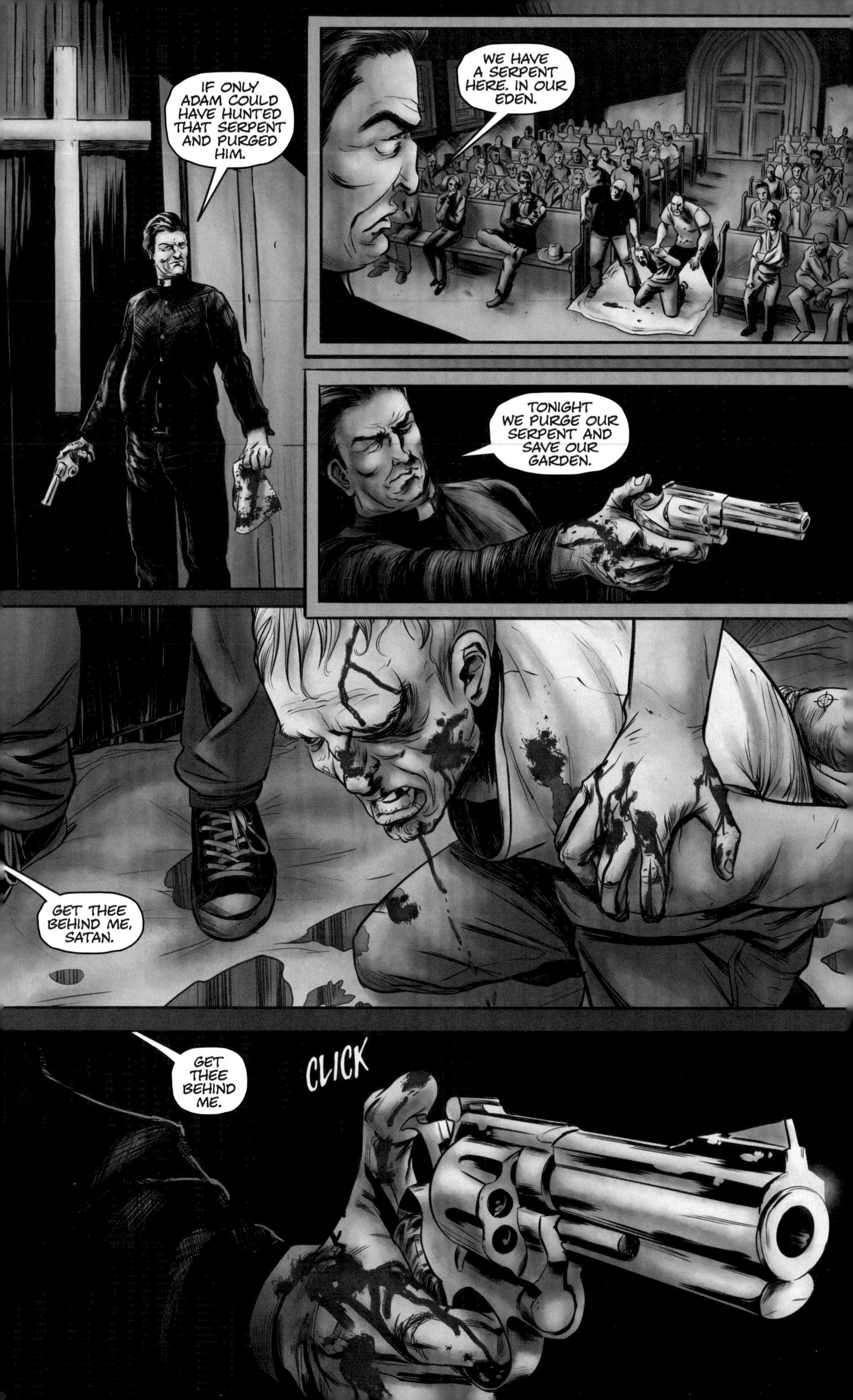
IF ONLY ADAM COULD HAVE HUNTED THAT SERPENT AND PURGED HIM.
WE HAVE A SERPENT HERE. IN OUR EDEN.
TONIGHT WE PURGE OUR SERPENT AND SAVE OUR GARDEN.
GET THEE BEHIND ME, SATAN.
GET THEE BEHIND ME.
CLICK

24 HOURS EARLIER.

EDEN POST OFFICE

THERE ARE 2,198 PEOPLE IN THIS TOWN.

I MANAGE THEIR MAIL.

INCOMING. OUTGOING.

EVERYTHING IN ITS RIGHT PLACE.

DAMAGED LETTERS GET TRANSCRIBED.

IT'S POLICY.

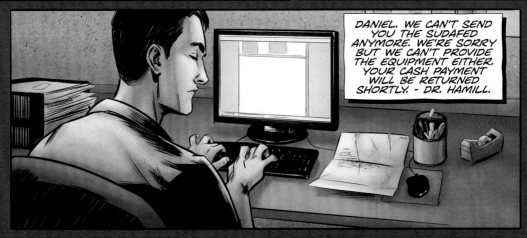

DANIEL. WE CAN'T SEND YOU THE SUDAFED ANYMORE. WE'RE SORRY BUT WE CAN'T PROVIDE THE EQUIPMENT EITHER. YOUR CASH PAYMENT WILL BE RETURNED SHORTLY. - DR. HAMILL.

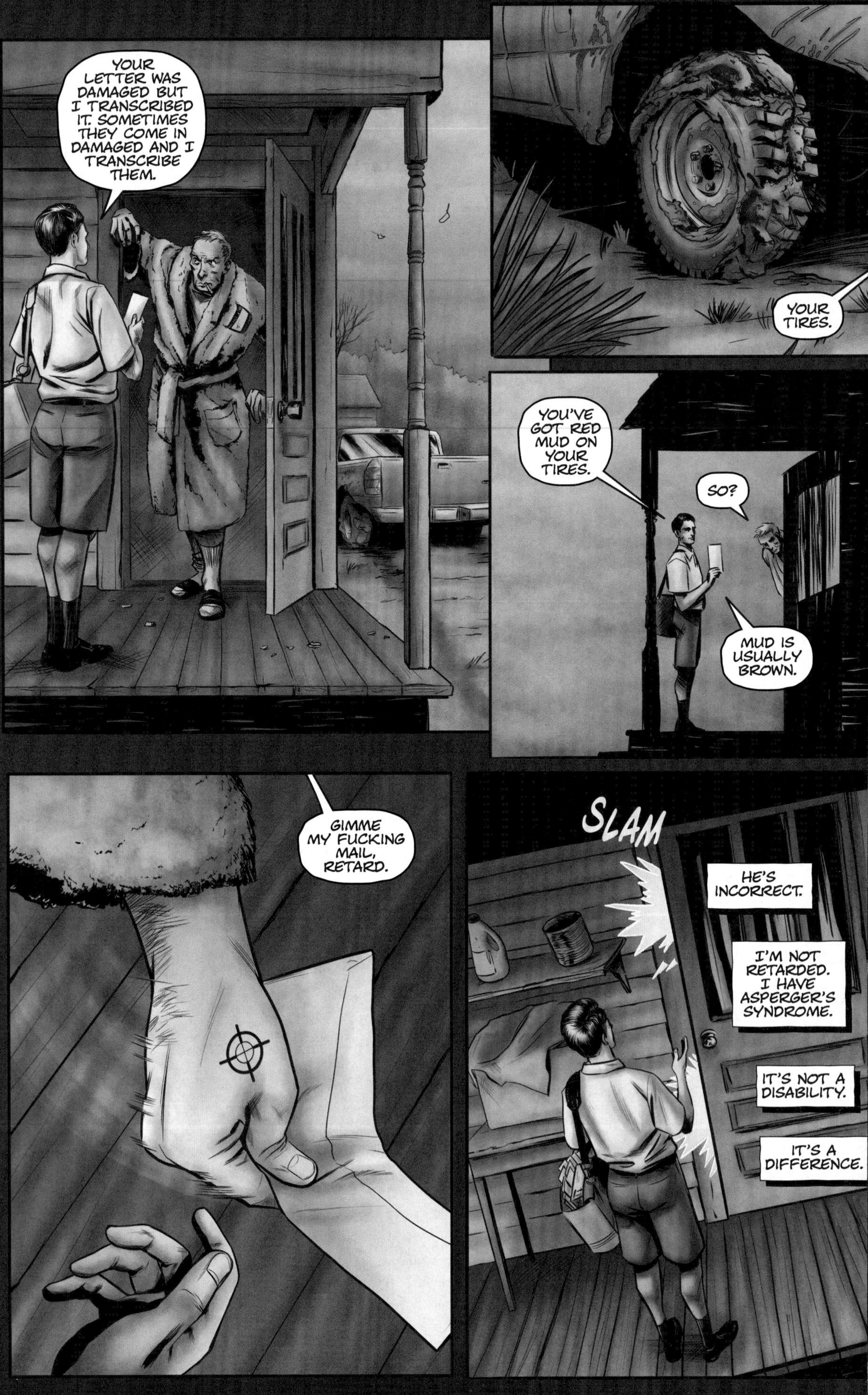
YOUR LETTER WAS DAMAGED BUT I TRANSCRIBED IT. SOMETIMES THEY COME IN DAMAGED AND I TRANSCRIBE THEM.
YOUR TIRES.
YOU'VE GOT RED MUD ON YOUR TIRES.
SO?
MUD IS USUALLY BROWN.
GIMME MY FUCKING MAIL, RETARD.
SLAM
HE'S INCORRECT.
I'M NOT RETARDED. I HAVE ASPERGER'S SYNDROME.
IT'S NOT A DISABILITY.
IT'S A DIFFERENCE.

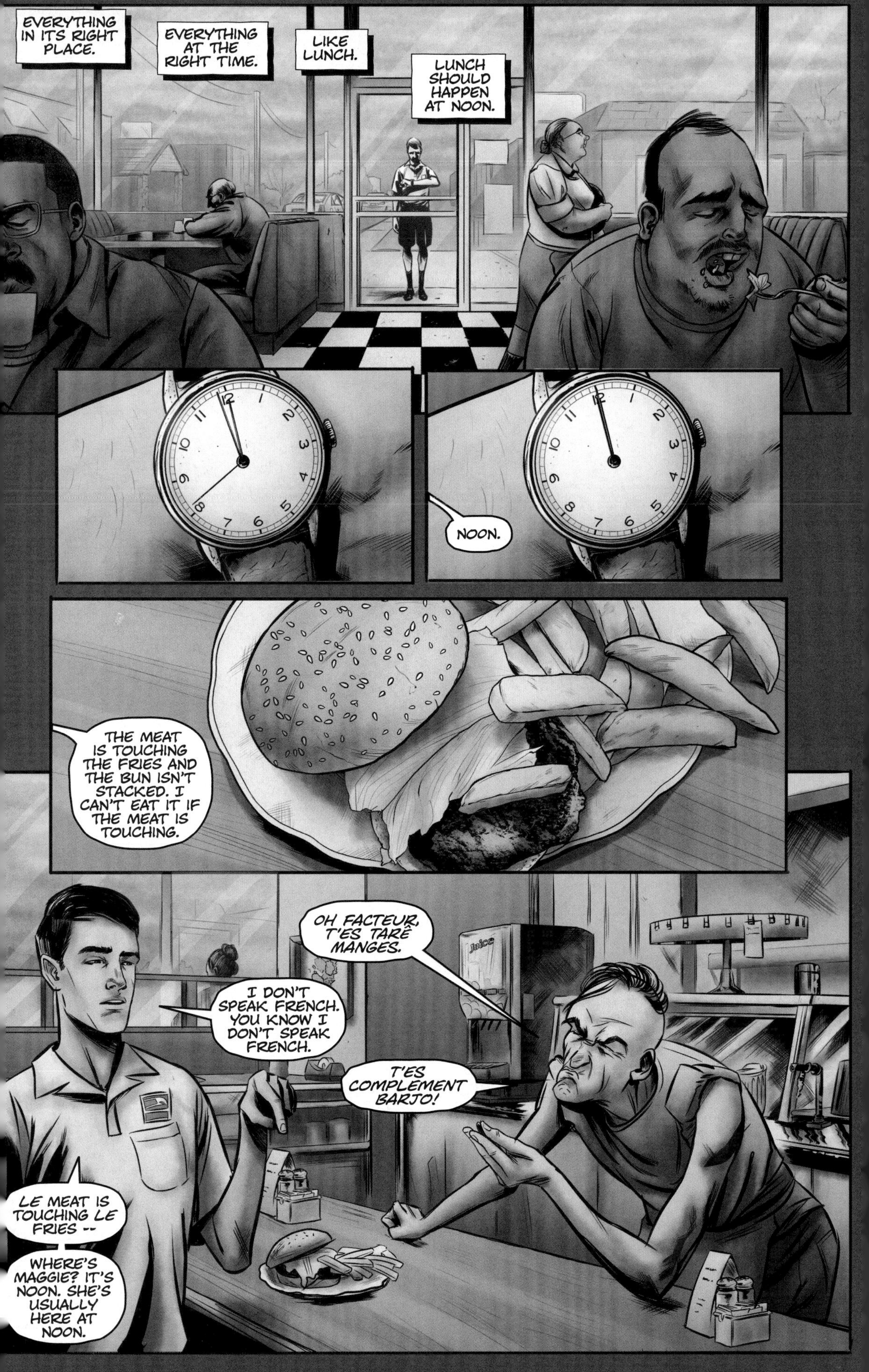
EVERYTHING IN ITS RIGHT PLACE.
EVERYTHING AT THE RIGHT TIME.
LIKE LUNCH.
LUNCH SHOULD HAPPEN AT NOON.
NOON.
THE MEAT IS TOUCHING THE FRIES AND THE BUN ISN'T STACKED. I CAN'T EAT IT IF THE MEAT IS TOUCHING.
OH FACTEUR, T'ES TARÊ MANGES.
I DON'T SPEAK FRENCH. YOU KNOW I DON'T SPEAK FRENCH.
T'ES COMPLEMENT BARJO!
LE MEAT IS TOUCHING LE FRIES --
WHERE'S MAGGIE? IT'S NOON. SHE'S USUALLY HERE AT NOON.

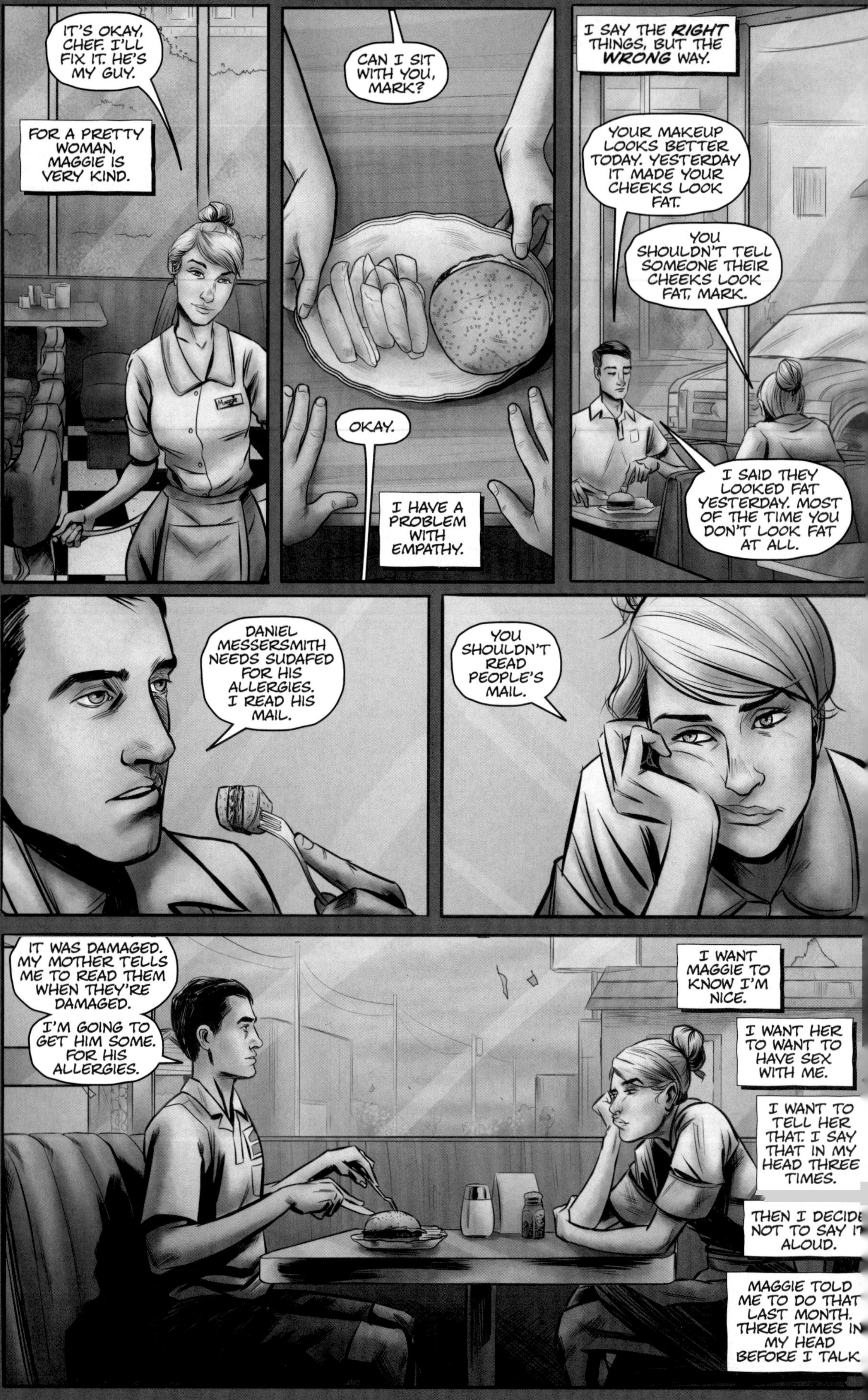
IT'S OKAY, CHEF. I'LL FIX IT. HE'S MY GUY.
FOR A PRETTY WOMAN, MAGGIE IS VERY KIND.
CAN I SIT WITH YOU, MARK?
OKAY.
I HAVE A PROBLEM WITH EMPATHY.
I SAY THE RIGHT THINGS, BUT THE WRONG WAY.
YOUR MAKEUP LOOKS BETTER TODAY. YESTERDAY IT MADE YOUR CHEEKS LOOK FAT.
YOU SHOULDN'T TELL SOMEONE THEIR CHEEKS LOOK FAT, MARK.
I SAID THEY LOOKED FAT YESTERDAY. MOST OF THE TIME YOU DON'T LOOK FAT AT ALL.
DANIEL MESSERSMITH NEEDS SUDAFED FOR HIS ALLERGIES. I READ HIS MAIL.
YOU SHOULDN'T READ PEOPLE'S MAIL.
IT WAS DAMAGED. MY MOTHER TELLS ME TO READ THEM WHEN THEY'RE DAMAGED.
I'M GOING TO GET HIM SOME. FOR HIS ALLERGIES.
I WANT MAGGIE TO KNOW I'M NICE.
I WANT HER TO WANT TO HAVE SEX WITH ME.
I WANT TO TELL HER THAT. I SAY THAT IN MY HEAD THREE TIMES.
THEN I DECIDE NOT TO SAY IT ALOUD.
MAGGIE TOLD ME TO DO THAT LAST MONTH. THREE TIMES IN MY HEAD BEFORE I TALK

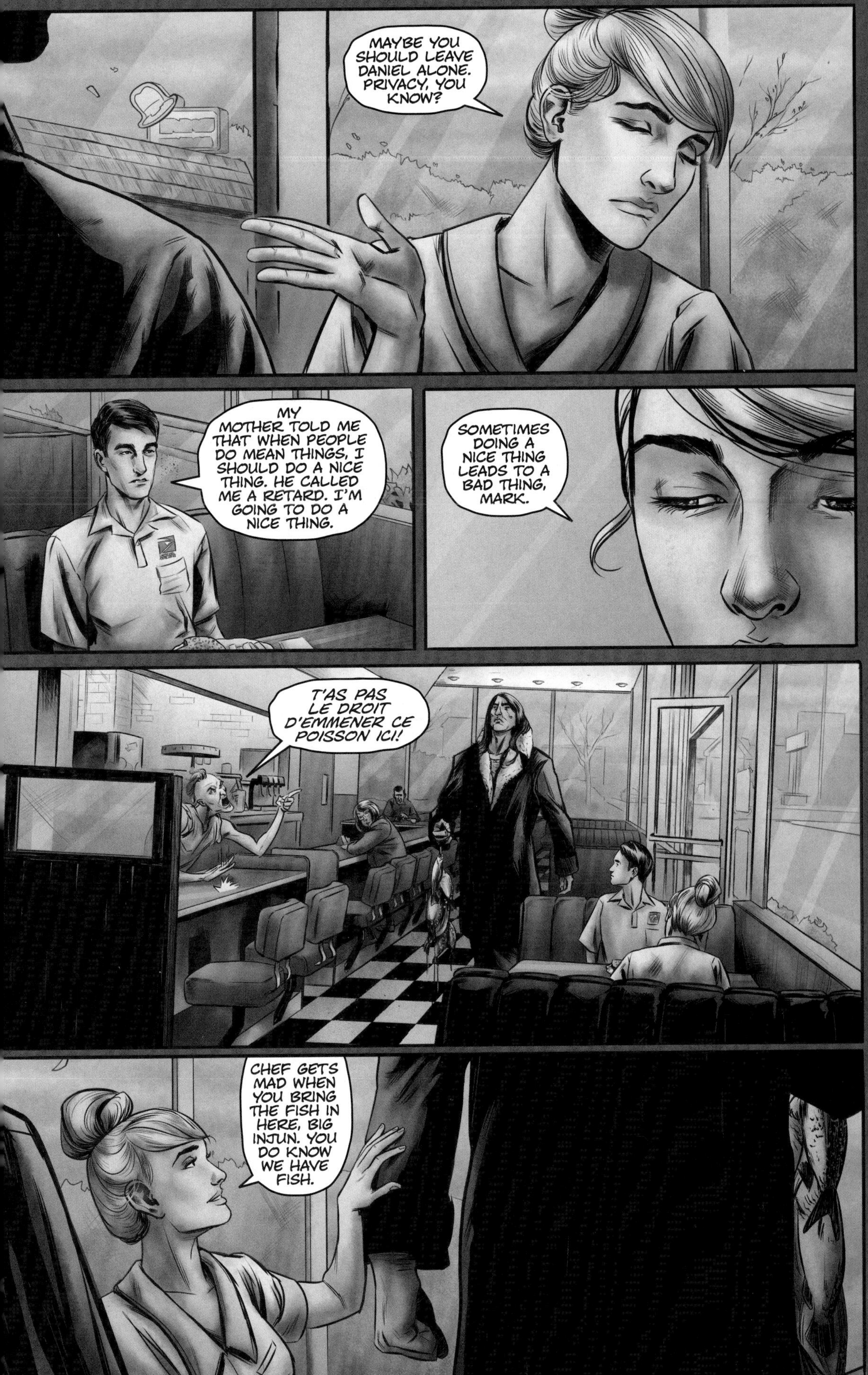
MAYBE YOU SHOULD LEAVE DANIEL ALONE. PRIVACY, YOU KNOW?
MY MOTHER TOLD ME THAT WHEN PEOPLE DO MEAN THINGS, I SHOULD DO A NICE THING. HE CALLED ME A RETARD. I'M GOING TO DO A NICE THING.
SOMETIMES DOING A NICE THING LEADS TO A BAD THING, MARK.
T'AS PAS LE DROIT D'EMMENER CE POISSON ICI!
CHEF GETS MAD WHEN YOU BRING THE FISH IN HERE, BIG INJUN. YOU DO KNOW WE HAVE FISH.

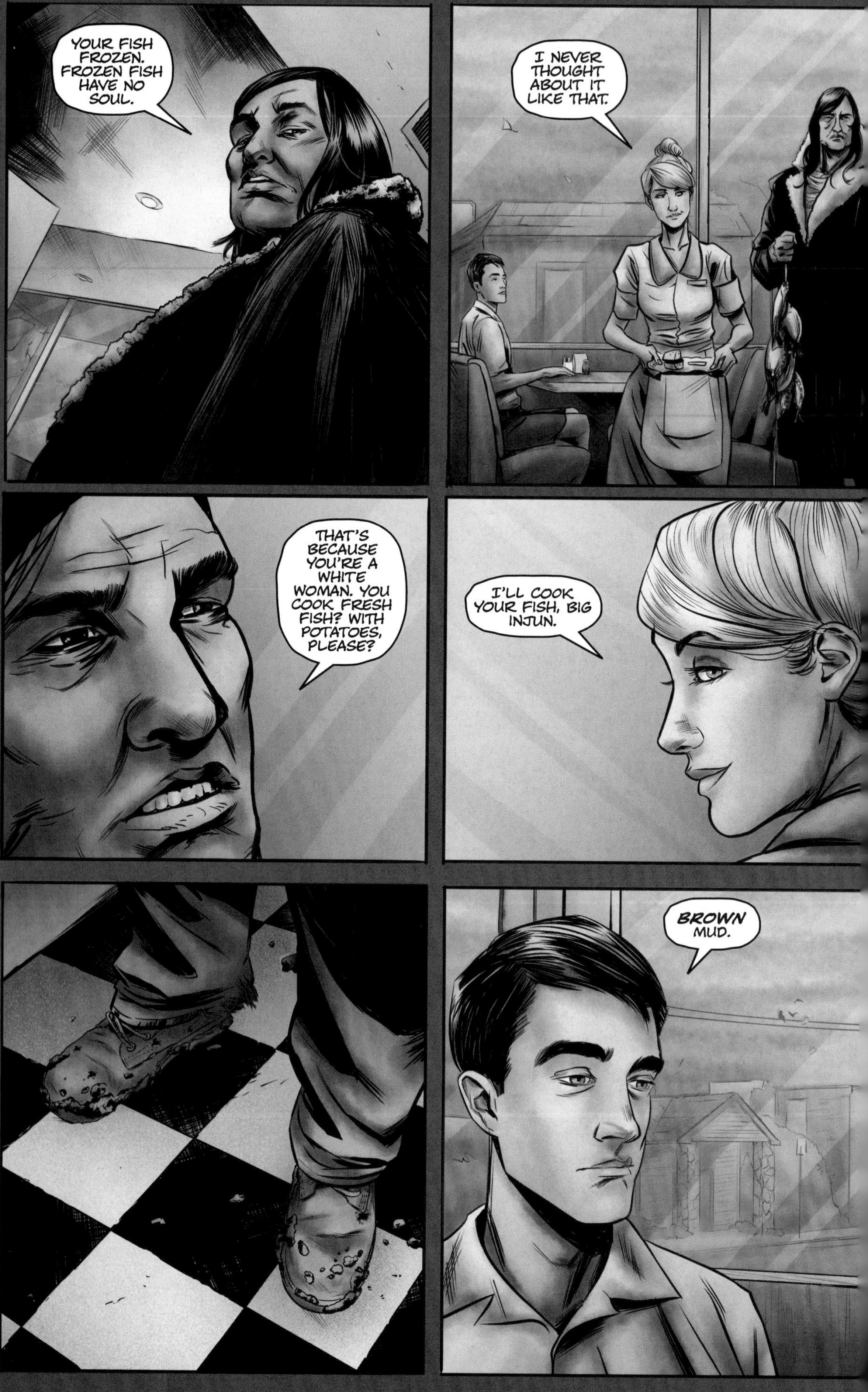
YOUR FISH FROZEN. FROZEN FISH HAVE NO SOUL.
I NEVER THOUGHT ABOUT IT LIKE THAT.
THAT'S BECAUSE YOU'RE A WHITE WOMAN. YOU COOK FRESH FISH? WITH POTATOES, PLEASE?
I'LL COOK YOUR FISH, BIG INJUN.
BROWN MUD.

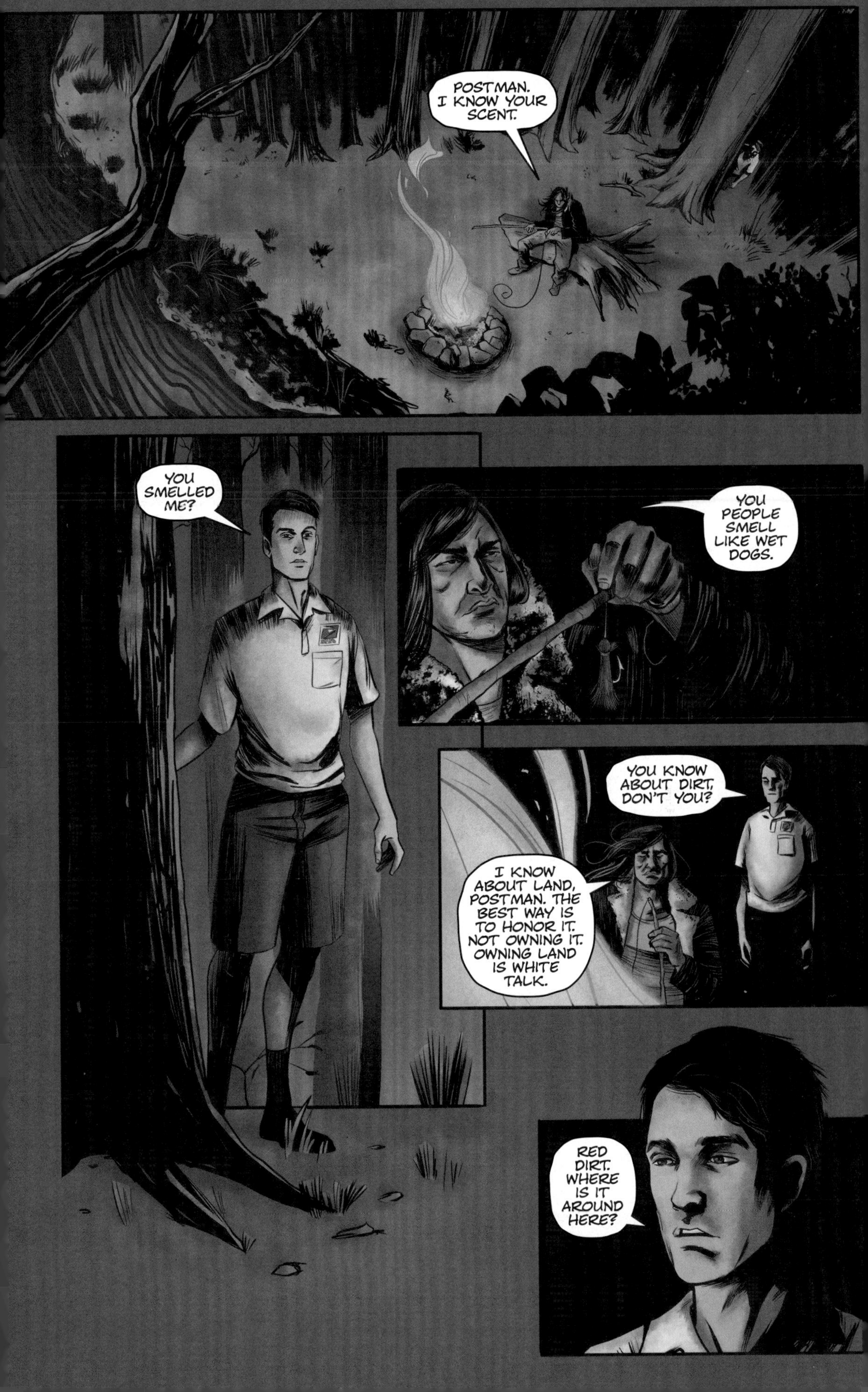
POSTMAN. I KNOW YOUR SCENT.
YOU SMELLED ME?
YOU PEOPLE SMELL LIKE WET DOGS.
YOU KNOW ABOUT DIRT, DON'T YOU?
I KNOW ABOUT LAND, POSTMAN. THE BEST WAY IS TO HONOR IT. NOT OWNING IT. OWNING LAND IS WHITE TALK.
RED DIRT. WHERE IS IT AROUND HERE?

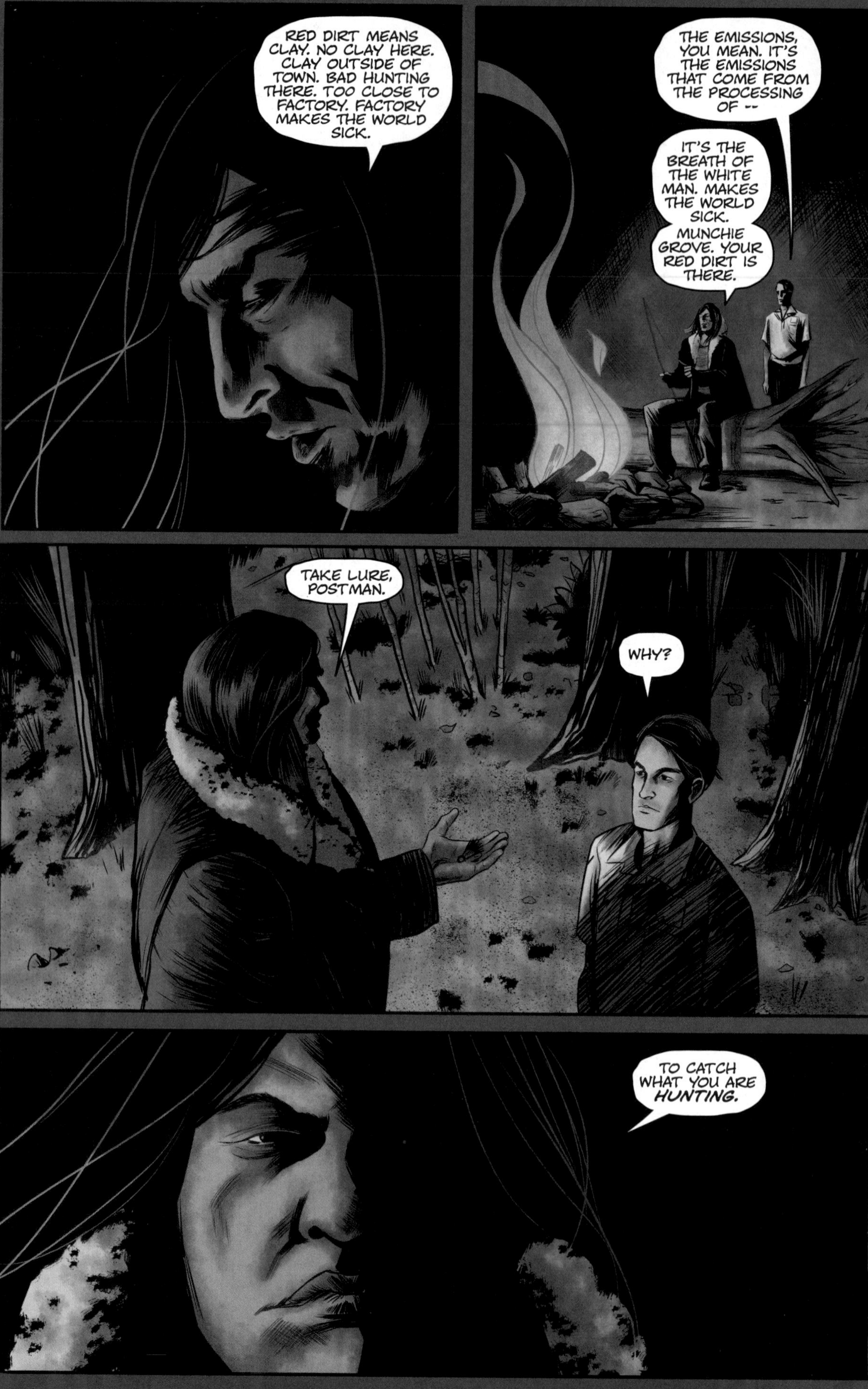
RED DIRT MEANS CLAY. NO CLAY HERE. CLAY OUTSIDE OF TOWN. BAD HUNTING THERE. TOO CLOSE TO FACTORY. FACTORY MAKES THE WORLD SICK.
THE EMISSIONS, YOU MEAN. IT'S THE EMISSIONS THAT COME FROM THE PROCESSING OF --
IT'S THE BREATH OF THE WHITE MAN. MAKES THE WORLD SICK.
MUNCHIE GROVE. YOUR RED DIRT IS THERE.
TAKE LURE, POSTMAN.
WHY?
TO CATCH WHAT YOU ARE *HUNTING.*

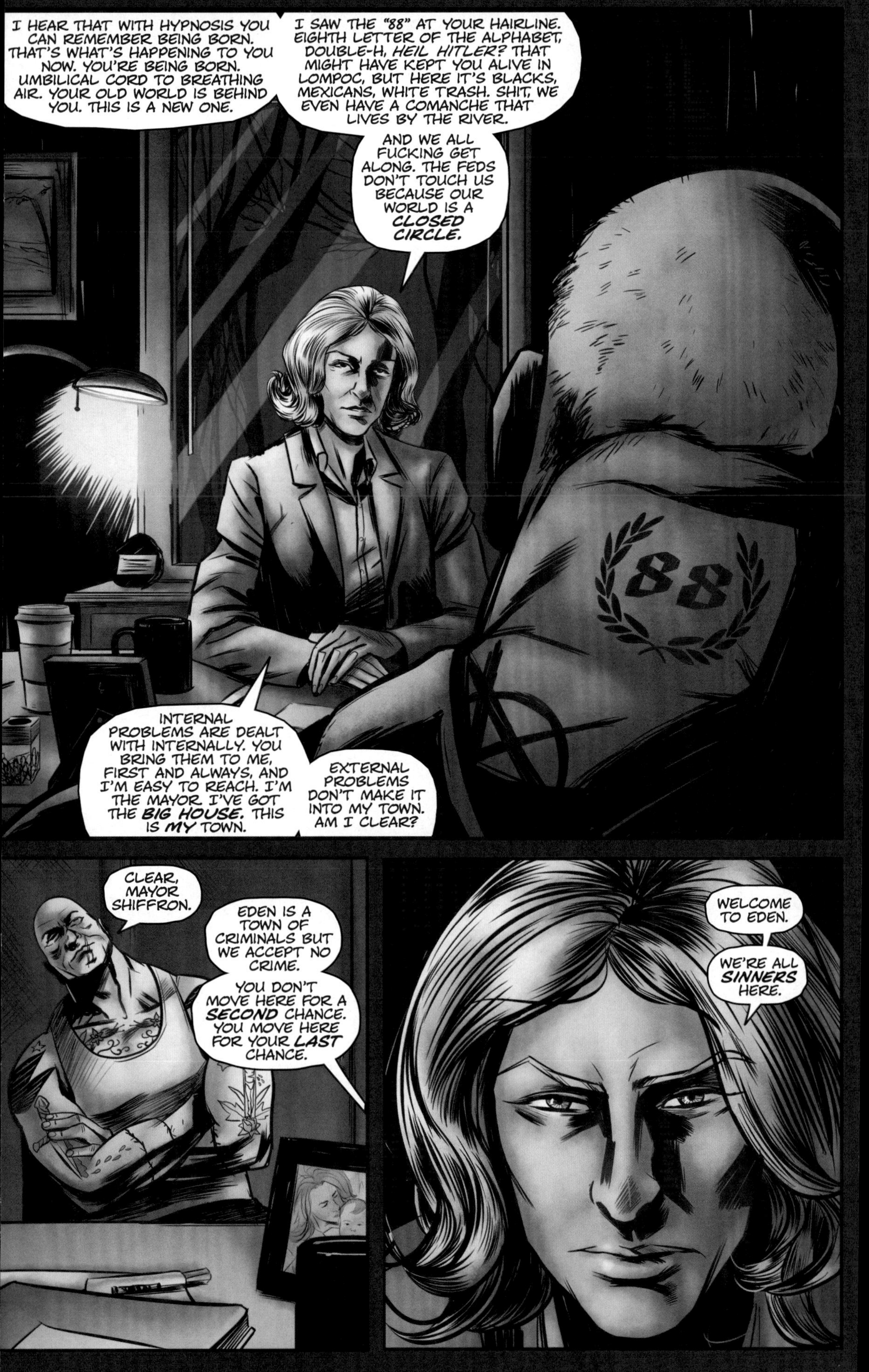

I HEAR THAT WITH HYPNOSIS YOU CAN REMEMBER BEING BORN. THAT'S WHAT'S HAPPENING TO YOU NOW. YOU'RE BEING BORN. UMBILICAL CORD TO BREATHING AIR. YOUR OLD WORLD IS BEHIND YOU. THIS IS A NEW ONE.
I SAW THE "88" AT YOUR HAIRLINE. EIGHTH LETTER OF THE ALPHABET, DOUBLE-H, *HEIL HITLER?* THAT MIGHT HAVE KEPT YOU ALIVE IN LOMPOC, BUT HERE IT'S BLACKS, MEXICANS, WHITE TRASH. SHIT, WE EVEN HAVE A COMANCHE THAT LIVES BY THE RIVER.
AND WE ALL FUCKING GET ALONG. THE FEDS DON'T TOUCH US BECAUSE OUR WORLD IS A ***CLOSED CIRCLE.***
88
INTERNAL PROBLEMS ARE DEALT WITH INTERNALLY. YOU BRING THEM TO ME, FIRST AND ALWAYS, AND I'M EASY TO REACH. I'M THE MAYOR. I'VE GOT THE ***BIG HOUSE.*** THIS IS ***MY*** TOWN.
EXTERNAL PROBLEMS DON'T MAKE IT INTO MY TOWN. AM I CLEAR?
CLEAR, MAYOR SHIFFRON.
EDEN IS A TOWN OF CRIMINALS BUT WE ACCEPT NO CRIME.
YOU DON'T MOVE HERE FOR A ***SECOND*** CHANCE. YOU MOVE HERE FOR YOUR ***LAST*** CHANCE.
WELCOME TO EDEN.
WE'RE ALL ***SINNERS*** HERE.

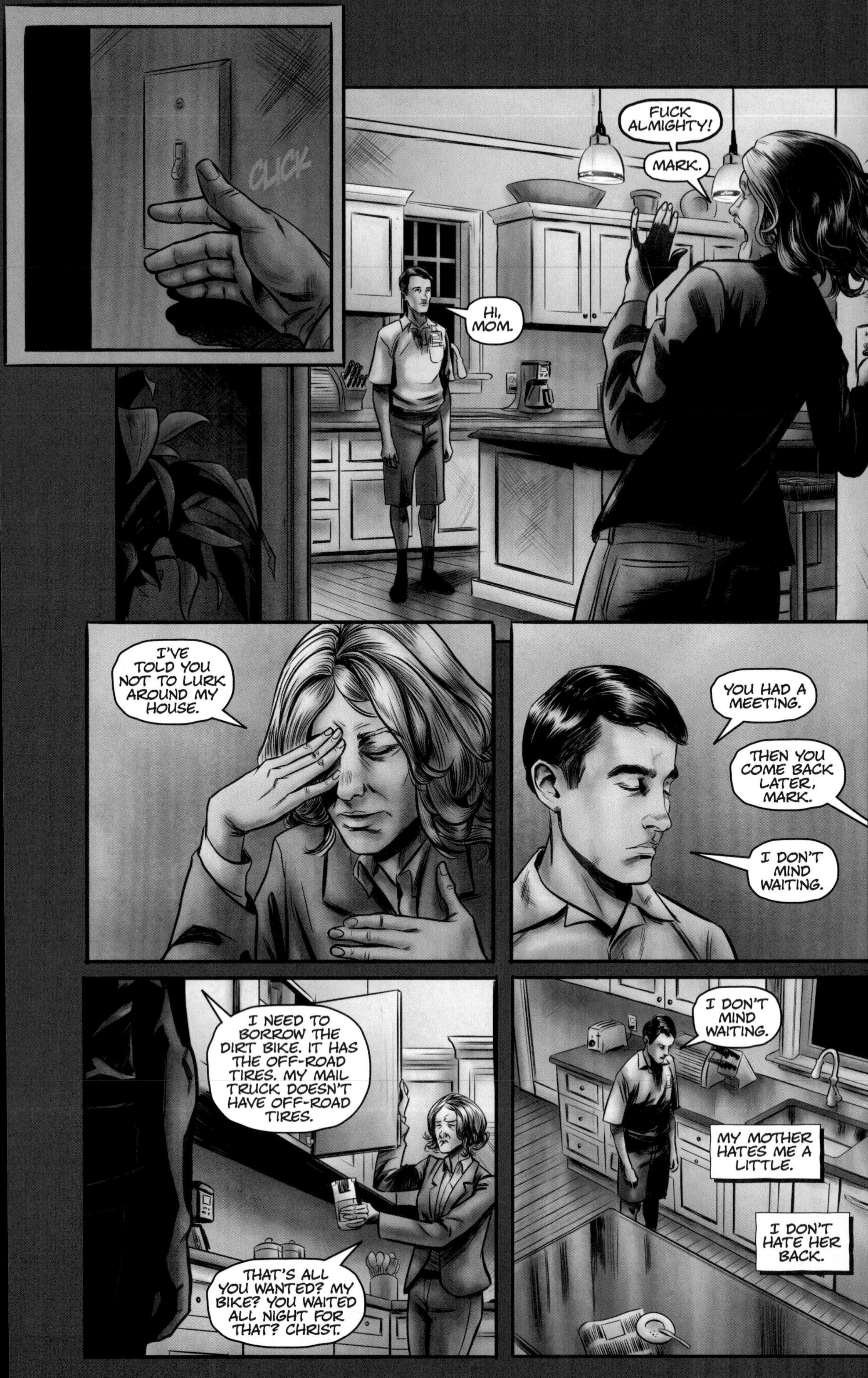
CLICK
FUCK ALMIGHTY!
MARK.
HI, MOM.
I'VE TOLD YOU NOT TO LURK AROUND MY HOUSE.
YOU HAD A MEETING.
THEN YOU COME BACK LATER, MARK.
I DON'T MIND WAITING.
I NEED TO BORROW THE DIRT BIKE. IT HAS THE OFF-ROAD TIRES. MY MAIL TRUCK DOESN'T HAVE OFF-ROAD TIRES.
THAT'S ALL YOU WANTED? MY BIKE? YOU WAITED ALL NIGHT FOR THAT? CHRIST.
I DON'T MIND WAITING.
MY MOTHER HATES ME A LITTLE.
I DON'T HATE HER BACK.

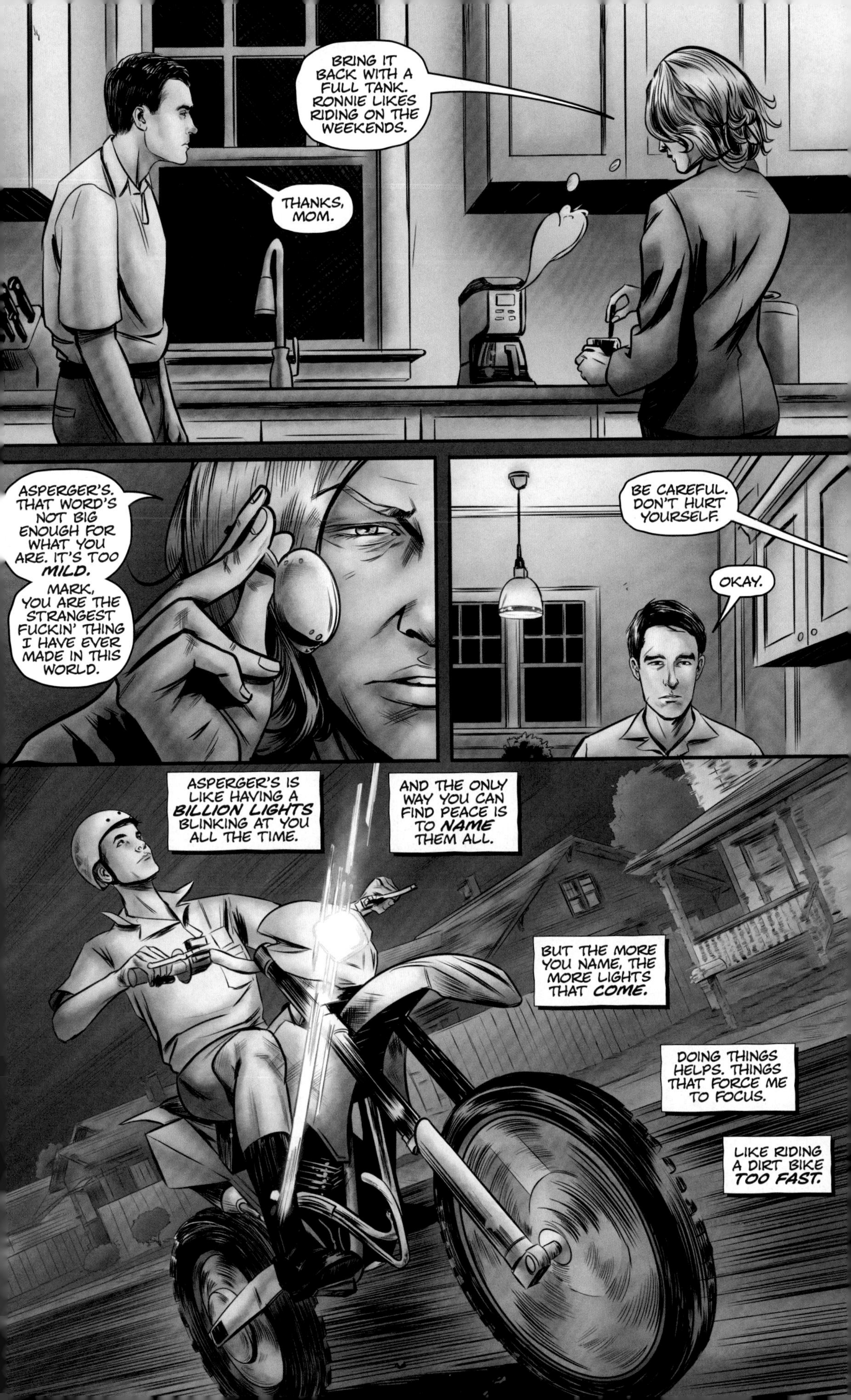
BRING IT BACK WITH A FULL TANK. RONNIE LIKES RIDING ON THE WEEKENDS.
THANKS, MOM.
ASPERGER'S. THAT WORD'S NOT BIG ENOUGH FOR WHAT YOU ARE. IT'S TOO *MILD.*
MARK, YOU ARE THE STRANGEST FUCKIN' THING I HAVE EVER MADE IN THIS WORLD.
BE CAREFUL. DON'T HURT YOURSELF.
OKAY.
ASPERGER'S IS LIKE HAVING A *BILLION LIGHTS* BLINKING AT YOU ALL THE TIME.
AND THE ONLY WAY YOU CAN FIND PEACE IS TO *NAME* THEM ALL.
BUT THE MORE YOU NAME, THE MORE LIGHTS THAT *COME.*
DOING THINGS HELPS. THINGS THAT FORCE ME TO FOCUS.
LIKE RIDING A DIRT BIKE *TOO FAST.*

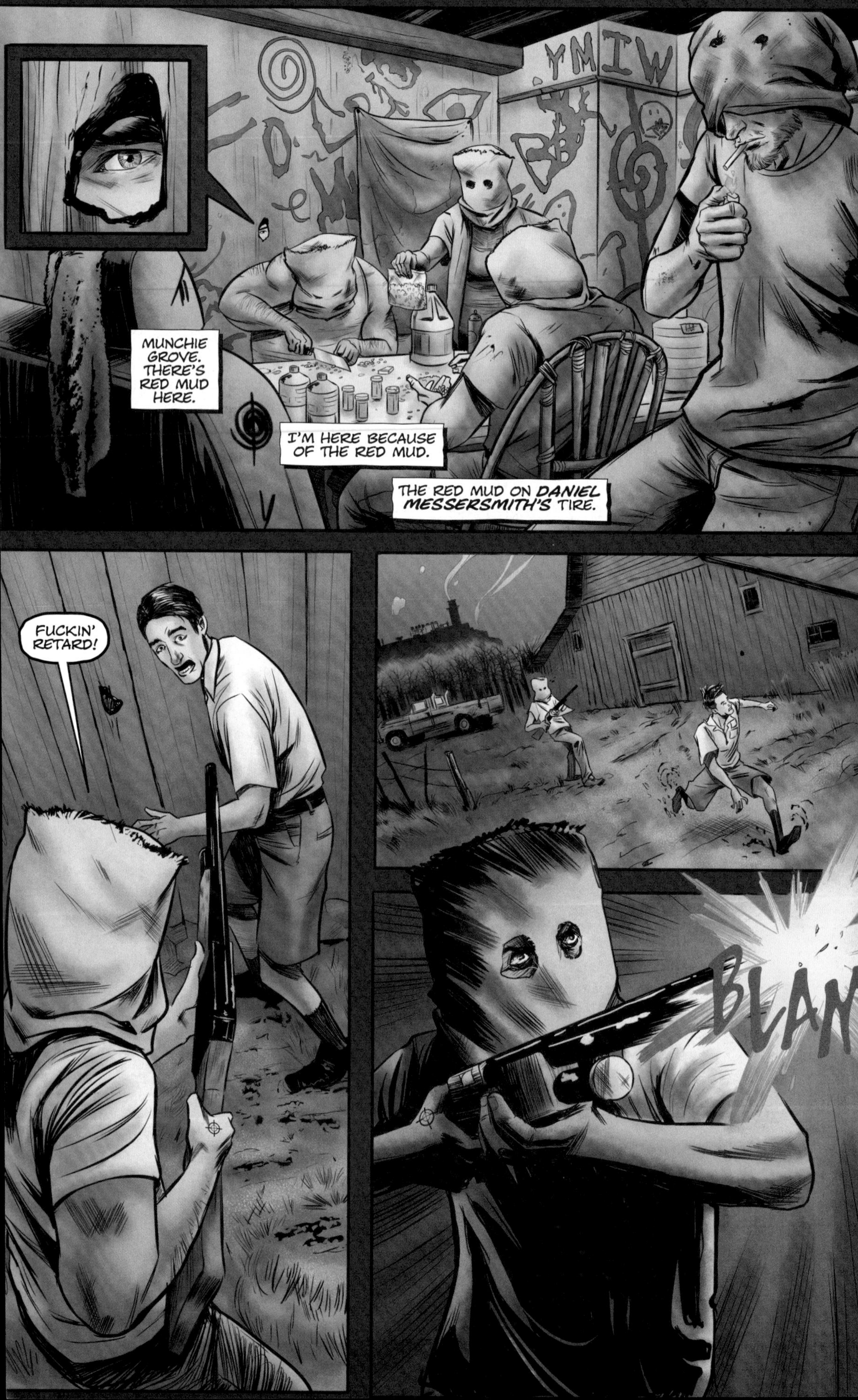
MUNCHIE GROVE. THERE'S RED MUD HERE.
I'M HERE BECAUSE OF THE RED MUD.
THE RED MUD ON *DANIEL MESSERSMITH'S* TIRE.
FUCKIN' RETARD!
BLAM

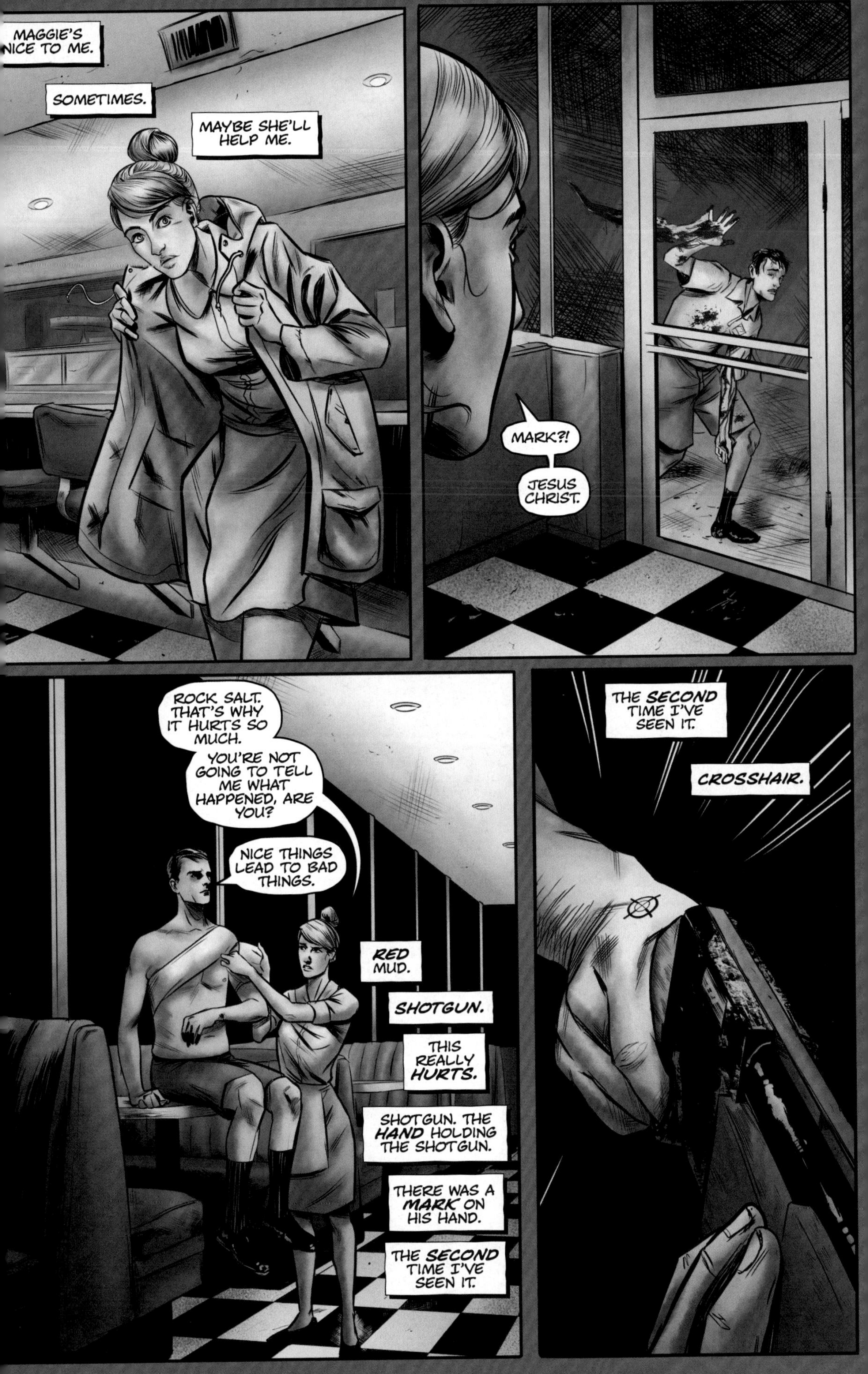
MAGGIE'S NICE TO ME.
SOMETIMES.
MAYBE SHE'LL HELP ME.
MARK?!
JESUS CHRIST.
ROCK SALT. THAT'S WHY IT HURTS SO MUCH.
YOU'RE NOT GOING TO TELL ME WHAT HAPPENED, ARE YOU?
NICE THINGS LEAD TO BAD THINGS.
RED MUD.
SHOTGUN.
THIS REALLY HURTS.
SHOTGUN. THE HAND HOLDING THE SHOTGUN.
THERE WAS A MARK ON HIS HAND.
THE SECOND TIME I'VE SEEN IT.
THE SECOND TIME I'VE SEEN IT.
CROSSHAIR.

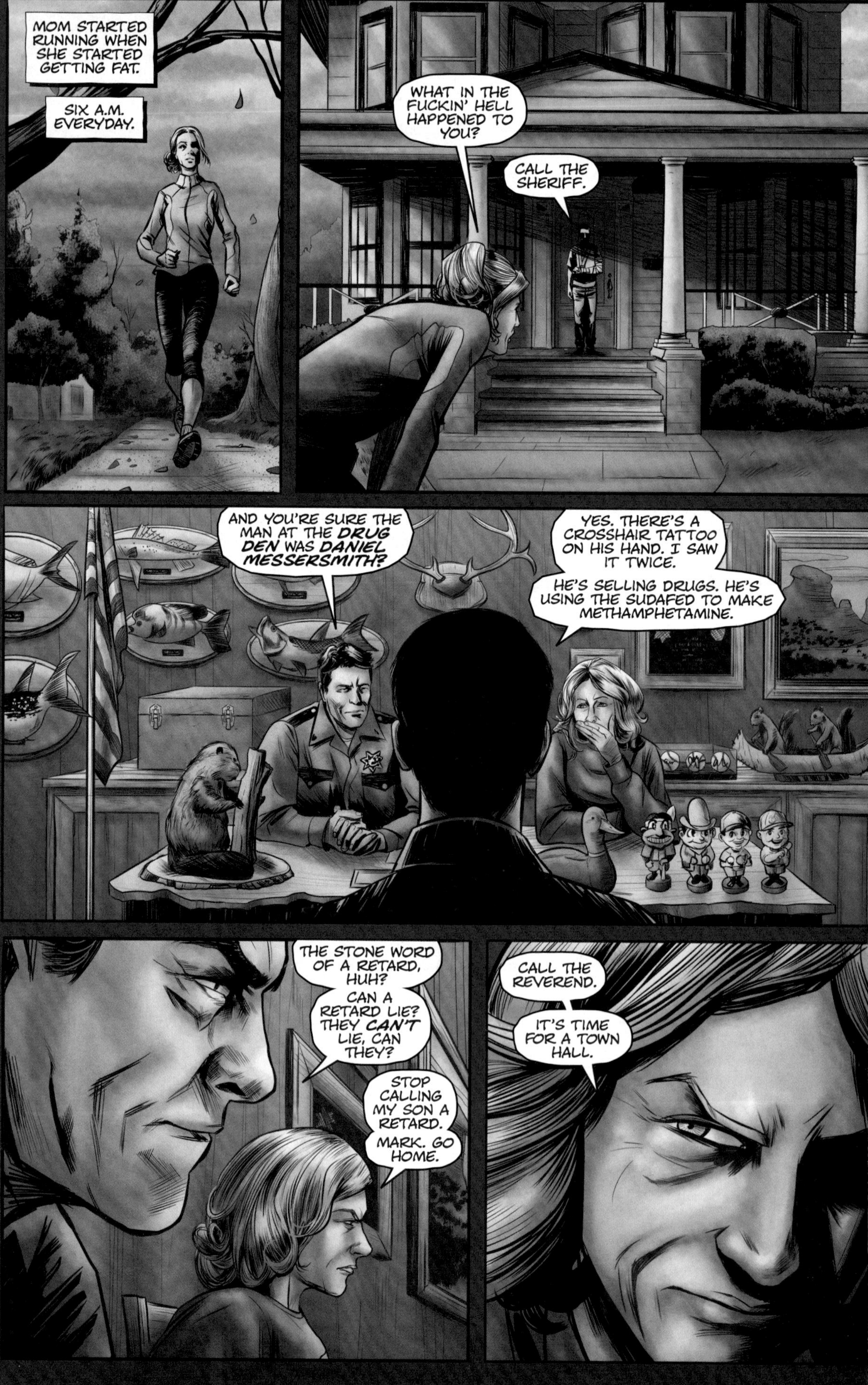
MOM STARTED RUNNING WHEN SHE STARTED GETTING FAT.
SIX A.M. EVERYDAY.
WHAT IN THE FUCKIN' HELL HAPPENED TO YOU?
CALL THE SHERIFF.
AND YOU'RE SURE THE MAN AT THE **DRUG DEN** WAS **DANIEL MESSERSMITH?**
YES. THERE'S A CROSSHAIR TATTOO ON HIS HAND. I SAW IT TWICE.
HE'S SELLING DRUGS. HE'S USING THE SUDAFED TO MAKE METHAMPHETAMINE.
THE STONE WORD OF A RETARD, HUH?
CAN A RETARD LIE? THEY *CAN'T* LIE, CAN THEY?
STOP CALLING MY SON A RETARD.
MARK. GO HOME.
CALL THE REVEREND.
IT'S TIME FOR A TOWN HALL.

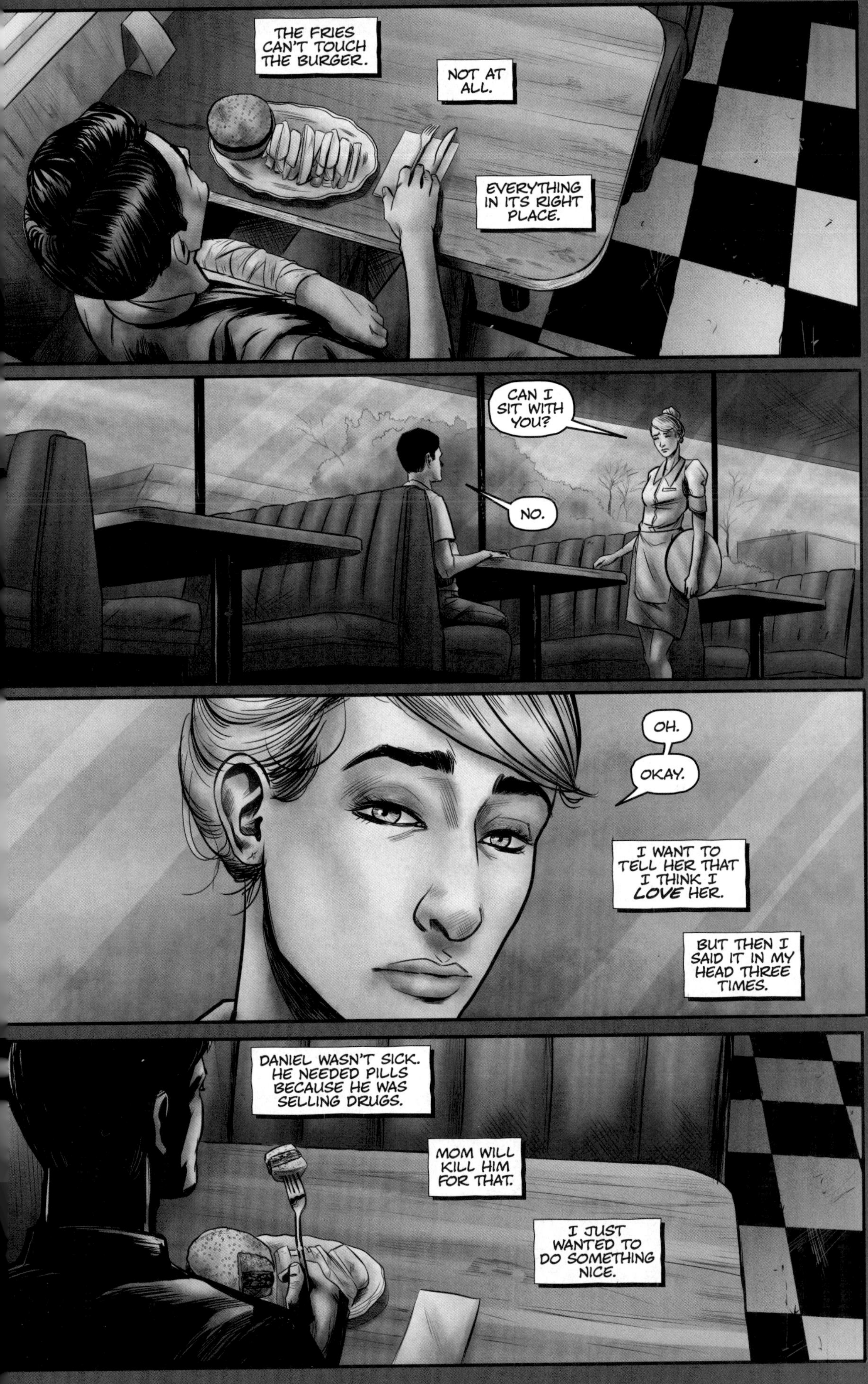
THE FRIES CAN'T TOUCH THE BURGER.
NOT AT ALL.
EVERYTHING IN ITS RIGHT PLACE.
CAN I SIT WITH YOU?
NO.
OH.
OKAY.
I WANT TO TELL HER THAT I THINK I LOVE HER.
BUT THEN I SAID IT IN MY HEAD THREE TIMES.
DANIEL WASN'T SICK. HE NEEDED PILLS BECAUSE HE WAS SELLING DRUGS.
MOM WILL KILL HIM FOR THAT.
I JUST WANTED TO DO SOMETHING NICE.

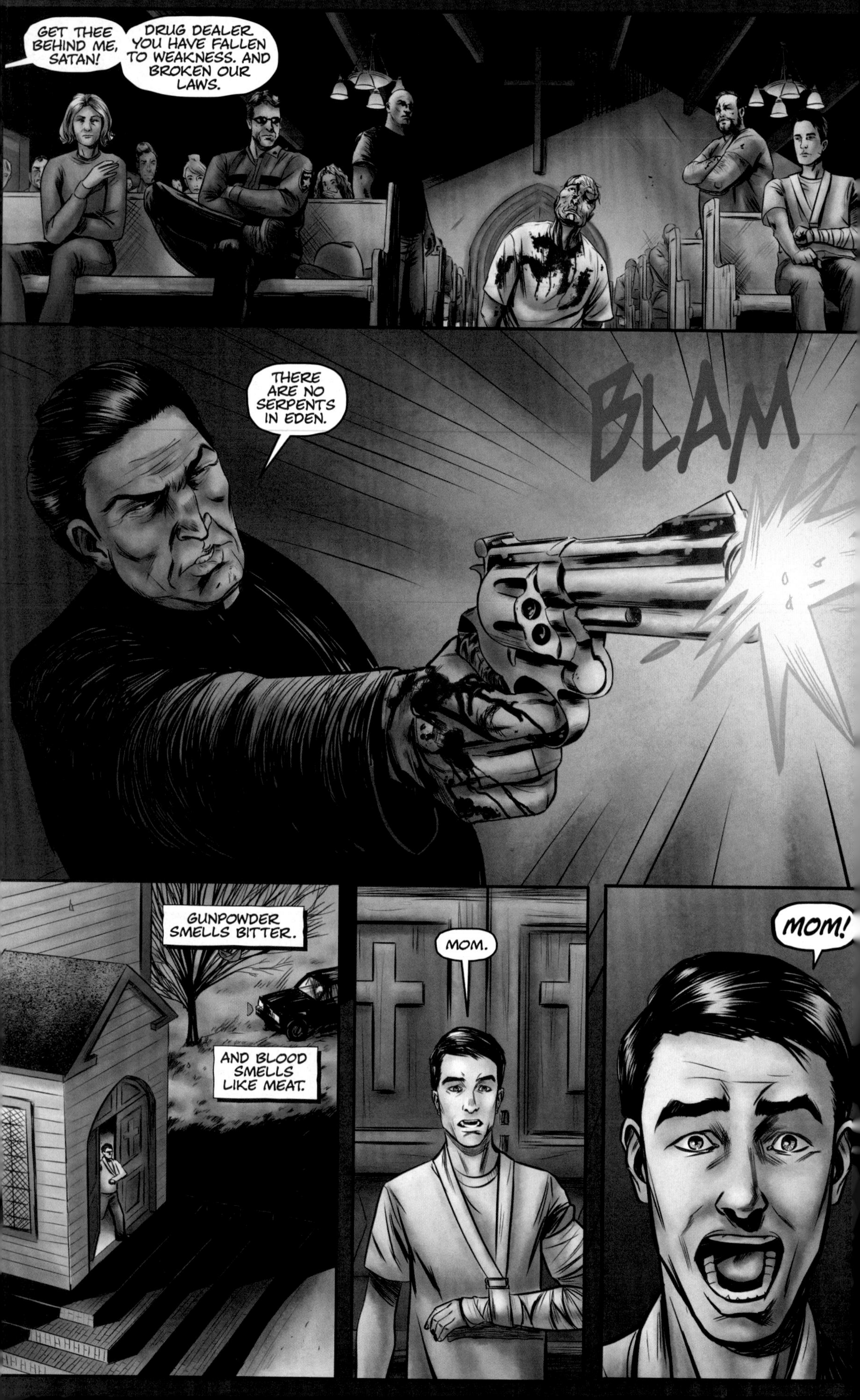
GET THEE BEHIND ME, SATAN!
DRUG DEALER YOU HAVE FALLEN TO WEAKNESS. AND BROKEN OUR LAWS.
THERE ARE NO SERPENTS IN EDEN.
BLAM
GUNPOWDER SMELLS BITTER.
AND BLOOD SMELLS LIKE MEAT.
MOM.
MOM!

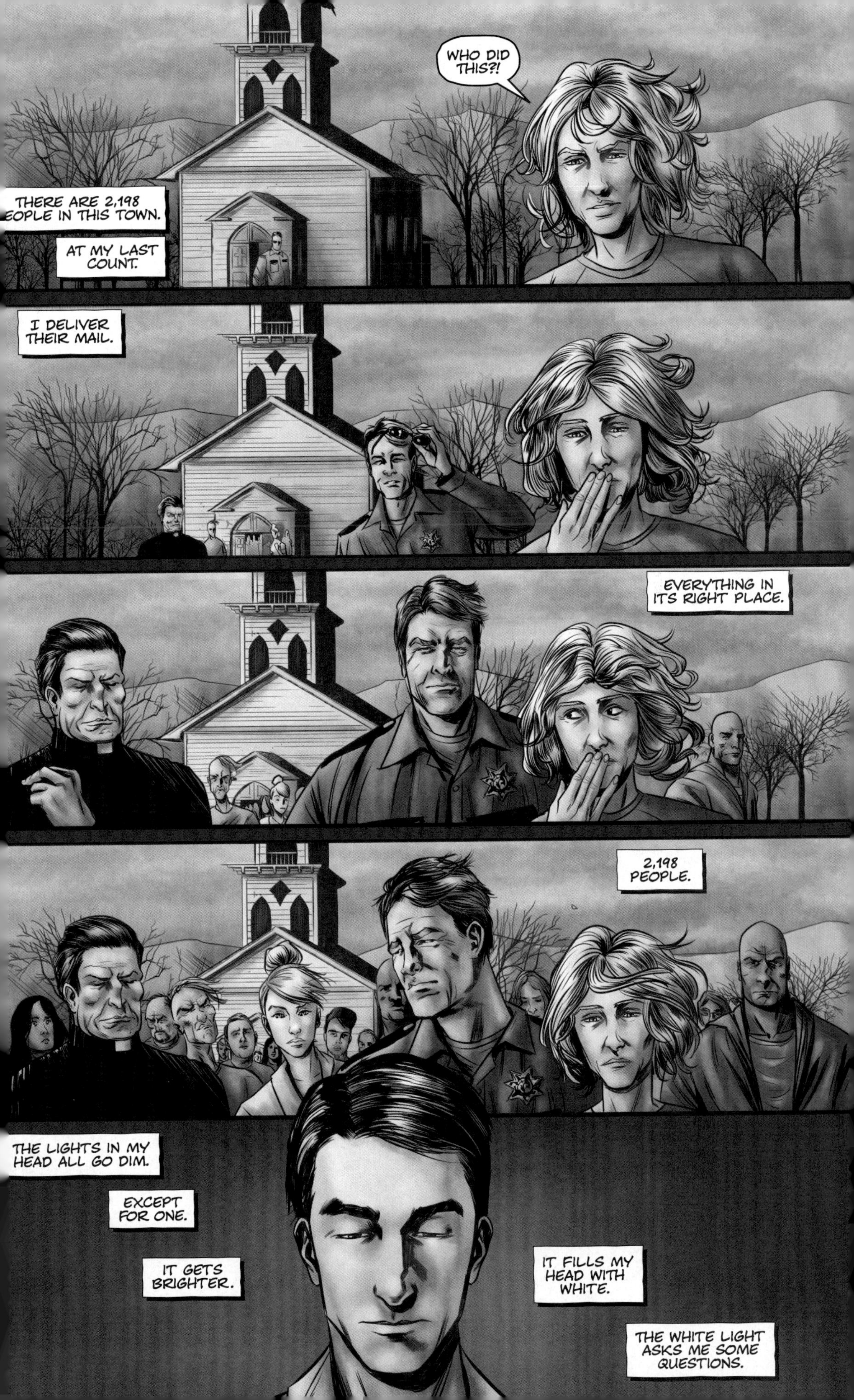
WHO DID THIS?!
THERE ARE 2,198 EOPLE IN THIS TOWN.
AT MY LAST COUNT.
I DELIVER THEIR MAIL.
EVERYTHING IN ITS RIGHT PLACE.
2,198 PEOPLE.
THE LIGHTS IN MY HEAD ALL GO DIM.
EXCEPT FOR ONE.
IT GETS BRIGHTER.
IT FILLS MY HEAD WITH WHITE.
THE WHITE LIGHT ASKS ME SOME QUESTIONS.

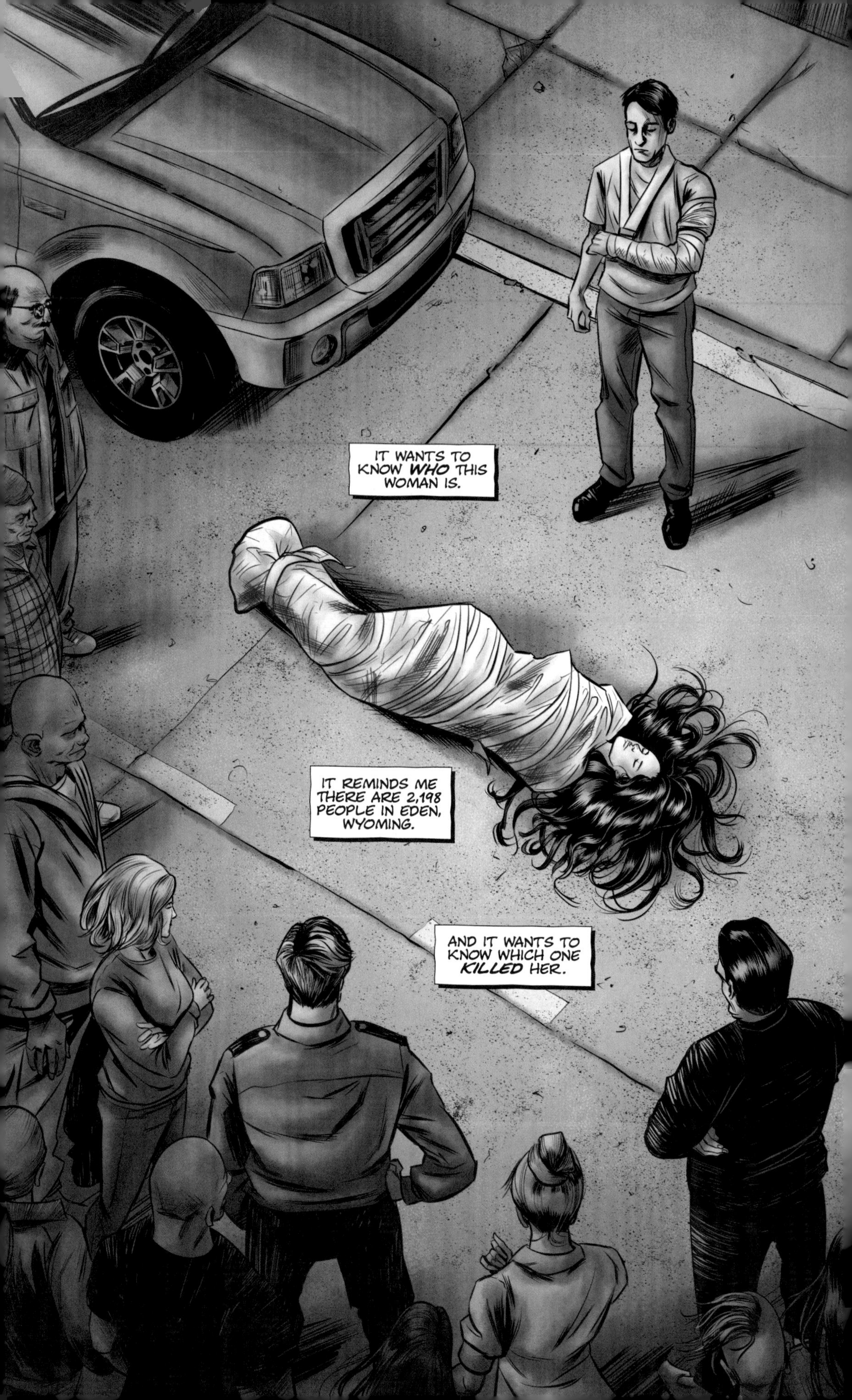
IT WANTS TO KNOW WHO THIS WOMAN IS.
IT REMINDS ME THERE ARE 2,198 PEOPLE IN EDEN, WYOMING.
AND IT WANTS TO KNOW WHICH ONE KILLED HER.

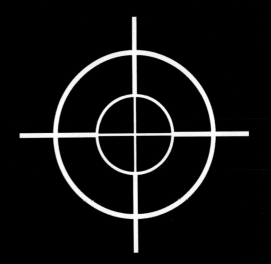

# Chapter 2

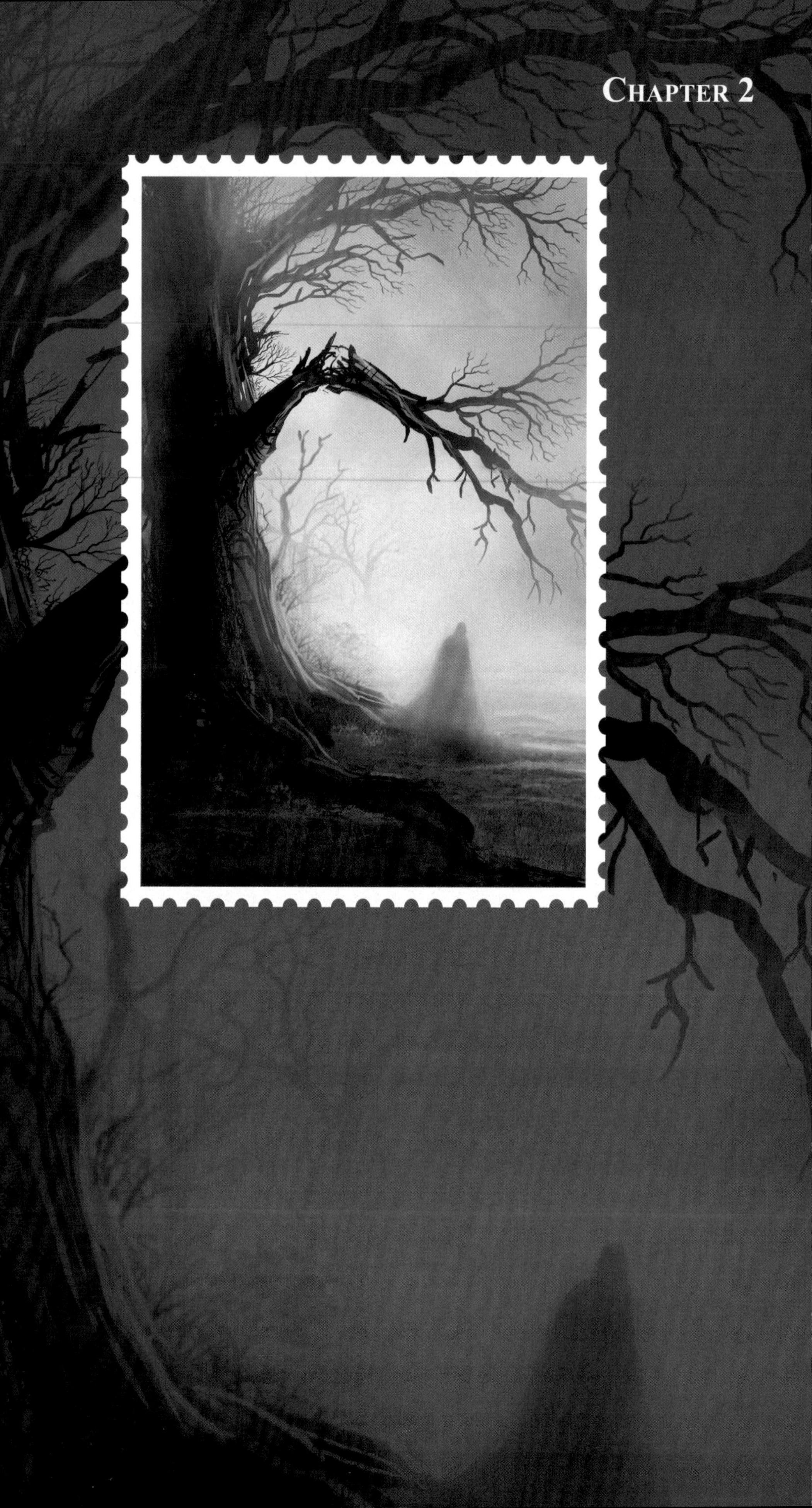

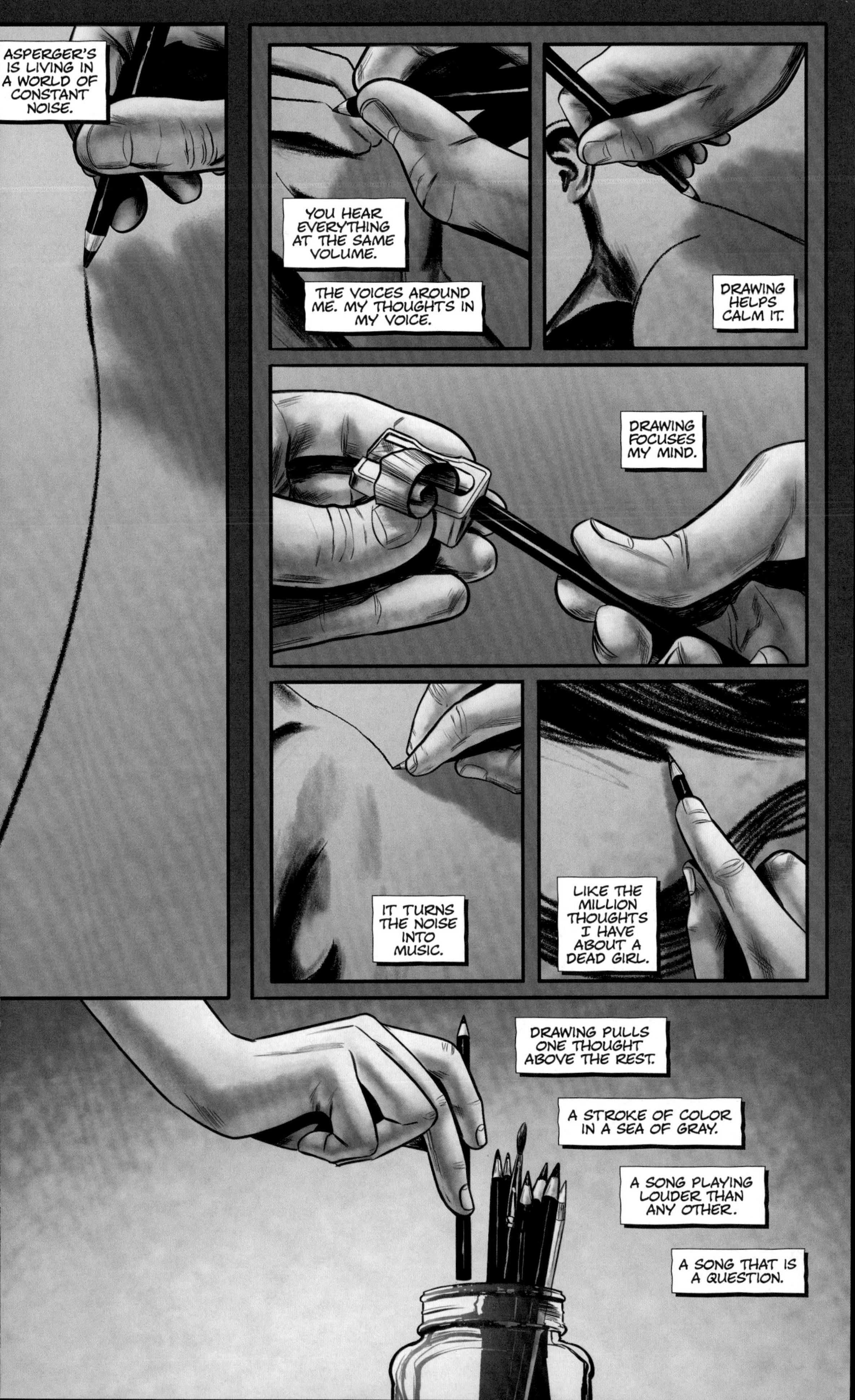
ASPERGER'S IS LIVING IN A WORLD OF CONSTANT NOISE.
YOU HEAR EVERYTHING AT THE SAME VOLUME.
THE VOICES AROUND ME. MY THOUGHTS IN MY VOICE.
DRAWING HELPS CALM IT.
DRAWING FOCUSES MY MIND.
IT TURNS THE NOISE INTO MUSIC.
LIKE THE MILLION THOUGHTS I HAVE ABOUT A DEAD GIRL.
DRAWING PULLS ONE THOUGHT ABOVE THE REST.
A STROKE OF COLOR IN A SEA OF GRAY.
A SONG PLAYING LOUDER THAN ANY OTHER.
A SONG THAT IS A QUESTION.

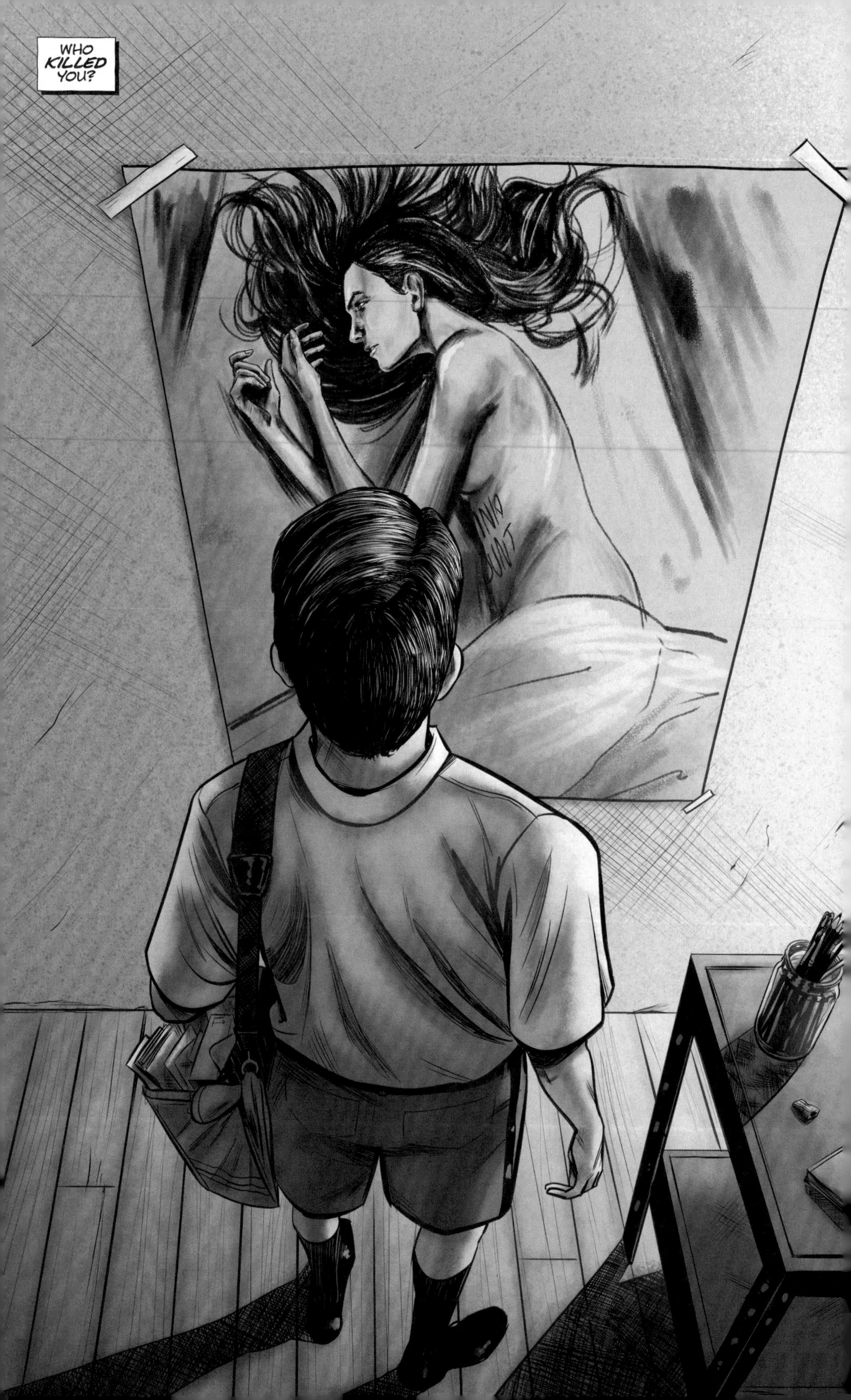
WHO KILLED YOU?

NATURE MAKES PERFECT THINGS ALL THE TIME.

LIKE THE EGG YOLK CIRCLE IN THE WHITE.

♪♪ WE SKIPPED THE LIGHT FANDANGOOO, TURNED CARTWHEELS 'CROSS THE FLOOOOOOR... ♪♪

THEN IT MAKES THINGS LIKE ME. IMPERFECT.

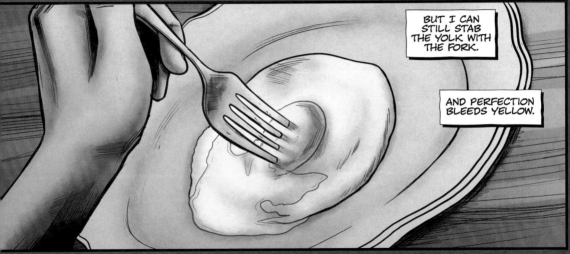

BUT I CAN STILL STAB THE YOLK WITH THE FORK.

AND PERFECTION BLEEDS YELLOW.

CAN I SIT DOWN WITH YOU?

OKAY.

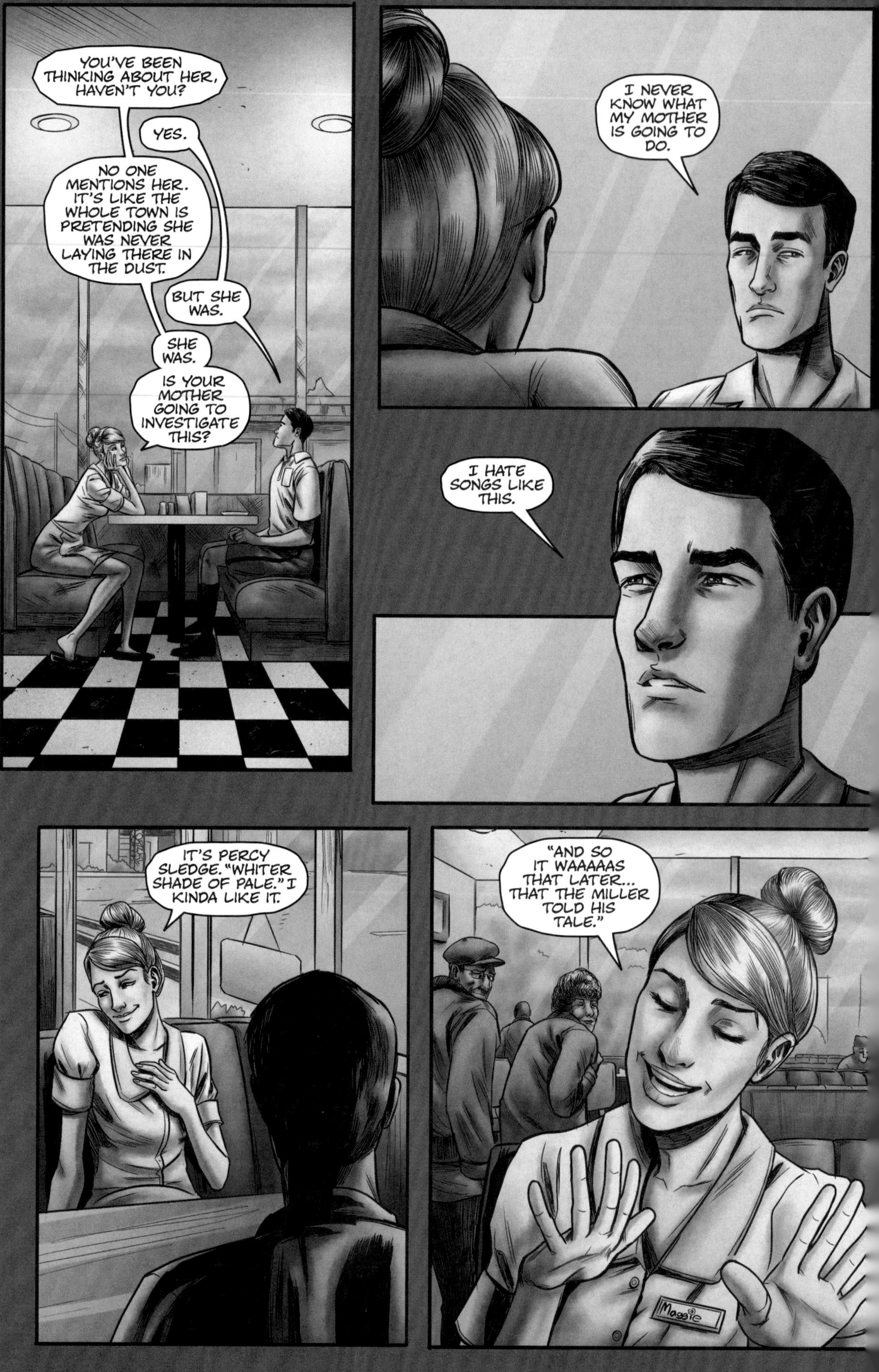
YOU'VE BEEN THINKING ABOUT HER, HAVEN'T YOU?
YES.
NO ONE MENTIONS HER. IT'S LIKE THE WHOLE TOWN IS PRETENDING SHE WAS NEVER LAYING THERE IN THE DUST.
BUT SHE WAS.
SHE WAS.
IS YOUR MOTHER GOING TO INVESTIGATE THIS?
I NEVER KNOW WHAT MY MOTHER IS GOING TO DO.
I HATE SONGS LIKE THIS.
IT'S PERCY SLEDGE. "WHITER SHADE OF PALE." I KINDA LIKE IT.
"AND SO IT WAAAAAS THAT LATER... THAT THE MILLER TOLD HIS TALE."
Maggie

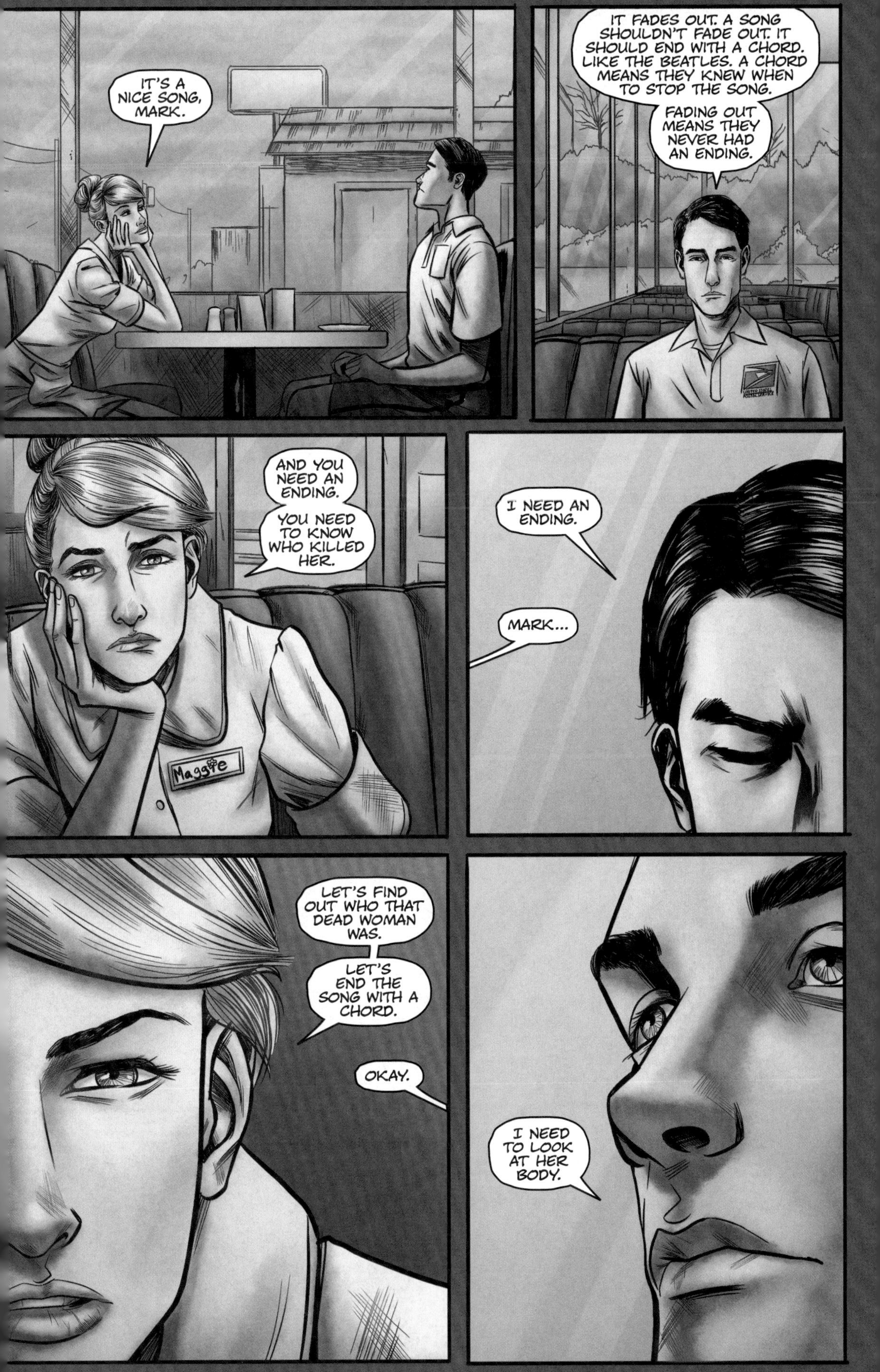
IT'S A NICE SONG, MARK.
IT FADES OUT. A SONG SHOULDN'T FADE OUT. IT SHOULD END WITH A CHORD. LIKE THE BEATLES. A CHORD MEANS THEY KNEW WHEN TO STOP THE SONG.
FADING OUT MEANS THEY NEVER HAD AN ENDING.
AND YOU NEED AN ENDING.
YOU NEED TO KNOW WHO KILLED HER.
Maggie
I NEED AN ENDING.
MARK...
LET'S FIND OUT WHO THAT DEAD WOMAN WAS.
LET'S END THE SONG WITH A CHORD.
OKAY.
I NEED TO LOOK AT HER BODY.

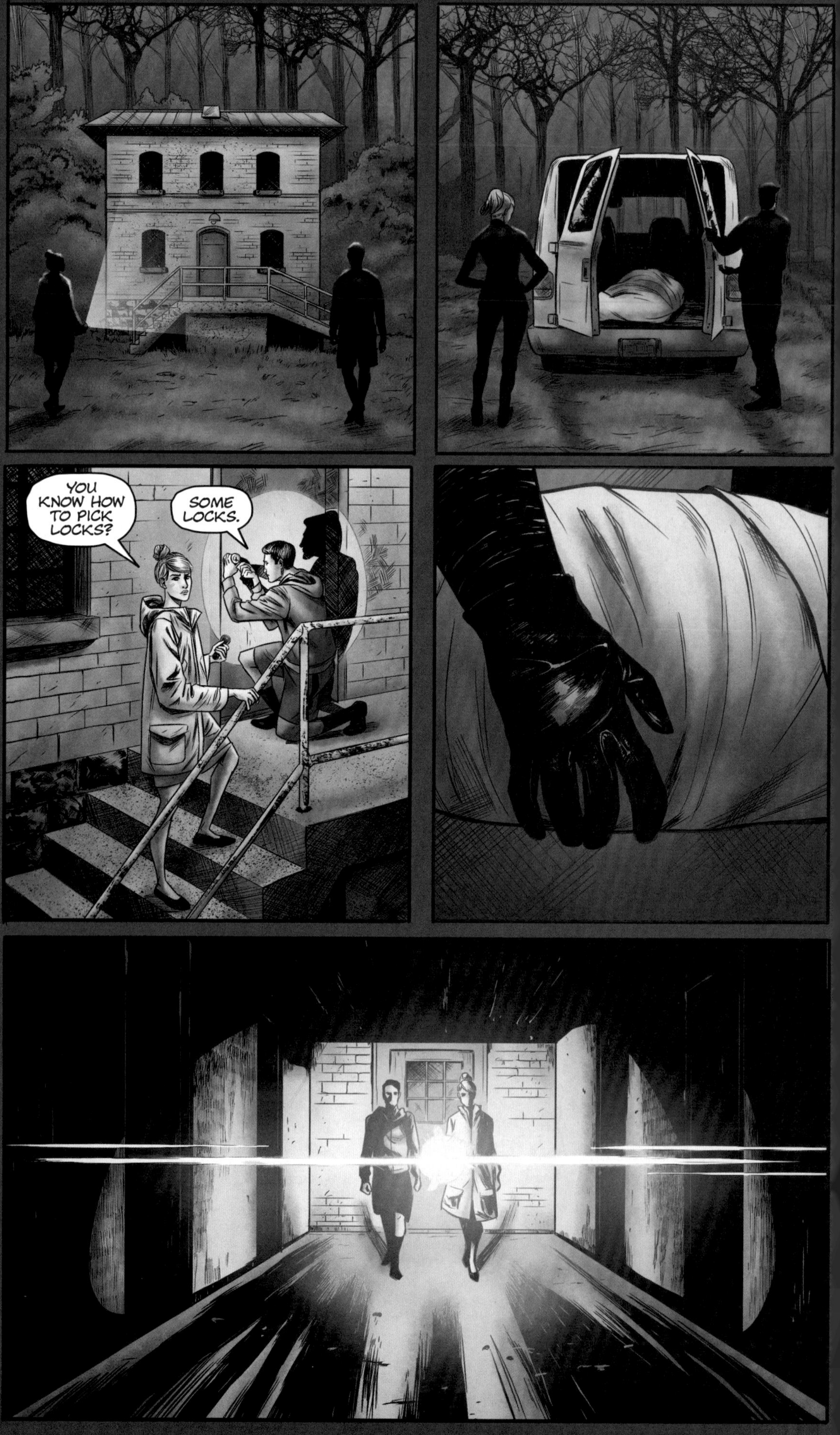
YOU KNOW HOW TO PICK LOCKS?
SOME LOCKS.

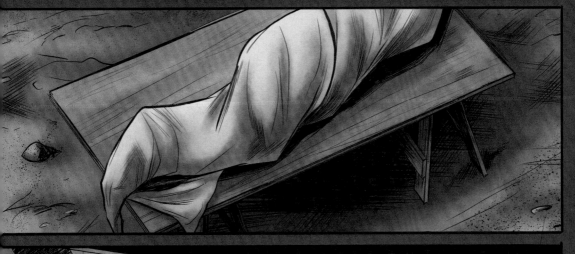

SHE SHOULD BE HERE.

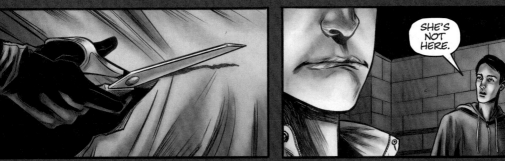

SHE'S NOT HERE.

YOU SMELL THAT?

SMELL WHAT?

UNDERNEATH THE FORMALDEHYDE. THE KIND OF AFTERSHAVE LOTION WITH A SHIP ON THE BOTTLE.

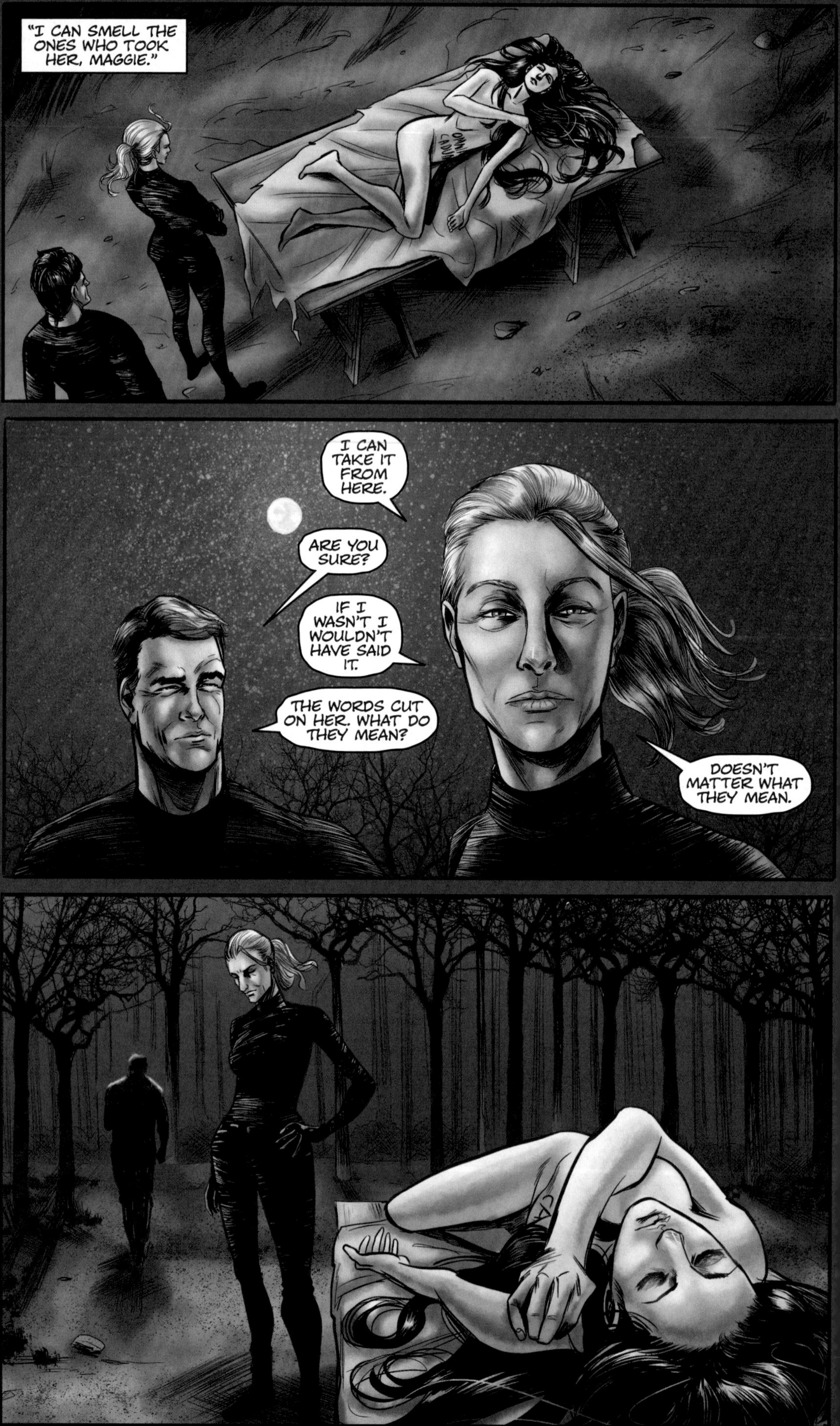
"I CAN SMELL THE ONES WHO TOOK HER, MAGGIE."
I CAN TAKE IT FROM HERE.
ARE YOU SURE?
IF I WASN'T I WOULDN'T HAVE SAID IT.
THE WORDS CUT ON HER. WHAT DO THEY MEAN?
DOESN'T MATTER WHAT THEY MEAN.

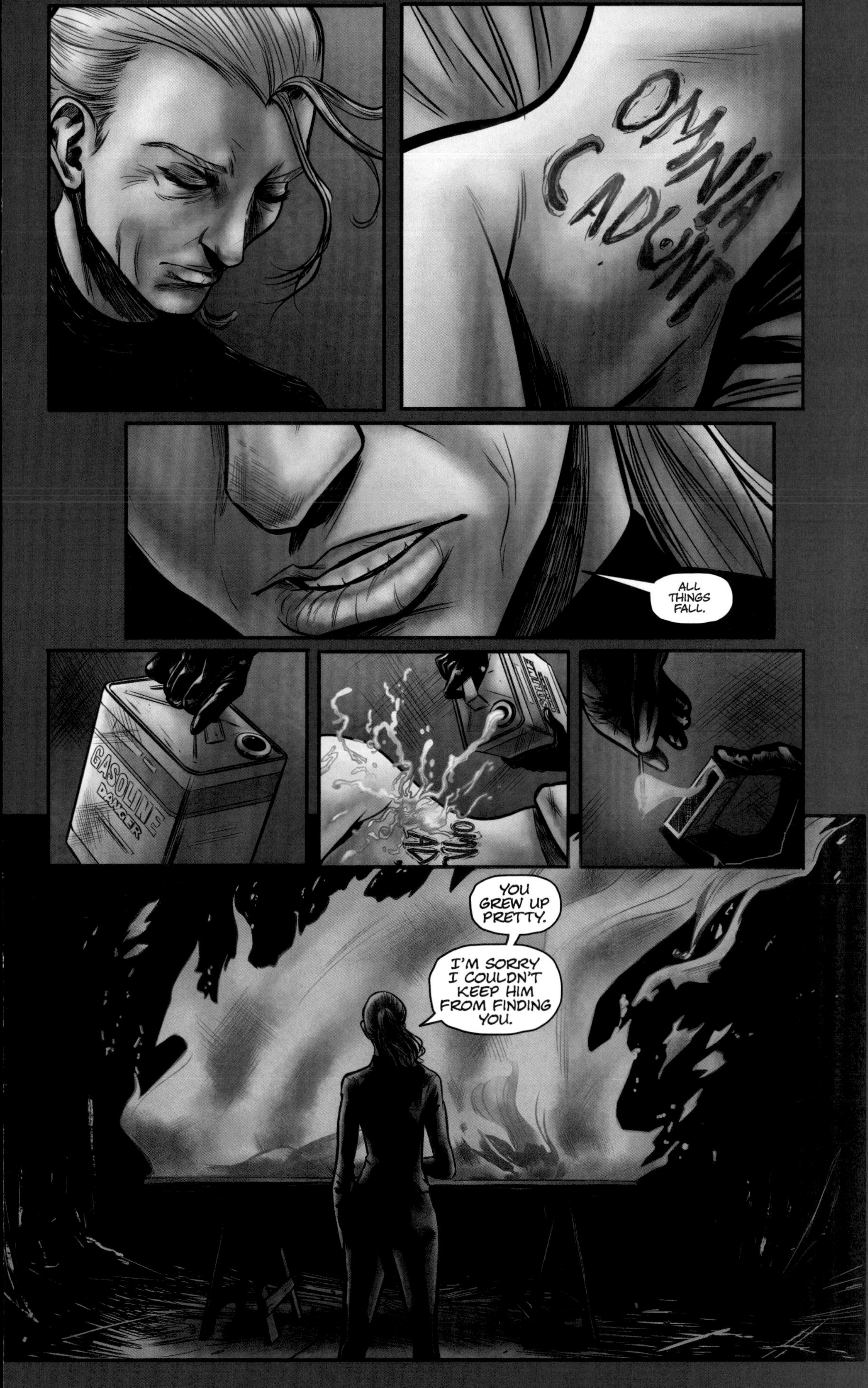
OMNIA CADUNT
ALL THINGS FALL.
GASOLINE
DANGER
YOU GREW UP PRETTY.
I'M SORRY I COULDN'T KEEP HIM FROM FINDING YOU.

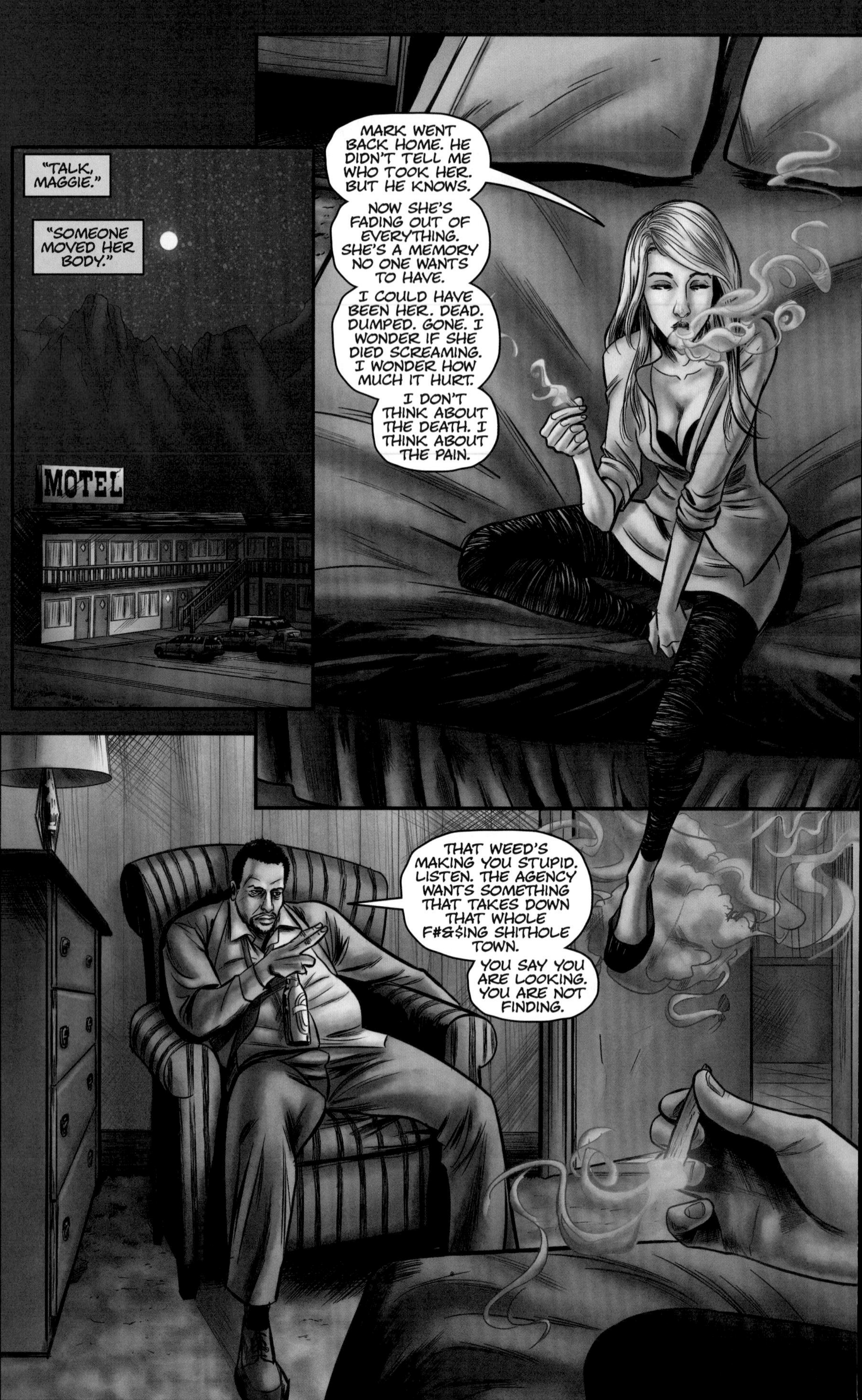
"TALK, MAGGIE."
"SOMEONE MOVED HER BODY."
MOTEL
MARK WENT BACK HOME. HE DIDN'T TELL ME WHO TOOK HER. BUT HE KNOWS.
NOW SHE'S FADING OUT OF EVERYTHING. SHE'S A MEMORY NO ONE WANTS TO HAVE.
I COULD HAVE BEEN HER. DEAD. DUMPED. GONE. I WONDER IF SHE DIED SCREAMING. I WONDER HOW MUCH IT HURT.
I DON'T THINK ABOUT THE DEATH. I THINK ABOUT THE PAIN.
THAT WEED'S MAKING YOU STUPID. LISTEN. THE AGENCY WANTS SOMETHING THAT TAKES DOWN THAT WHOLE F#&$ING SHITHOLE TOWN.
YOU SAY YOU ARE LOOKING. YOU ARE NOT FINDING.

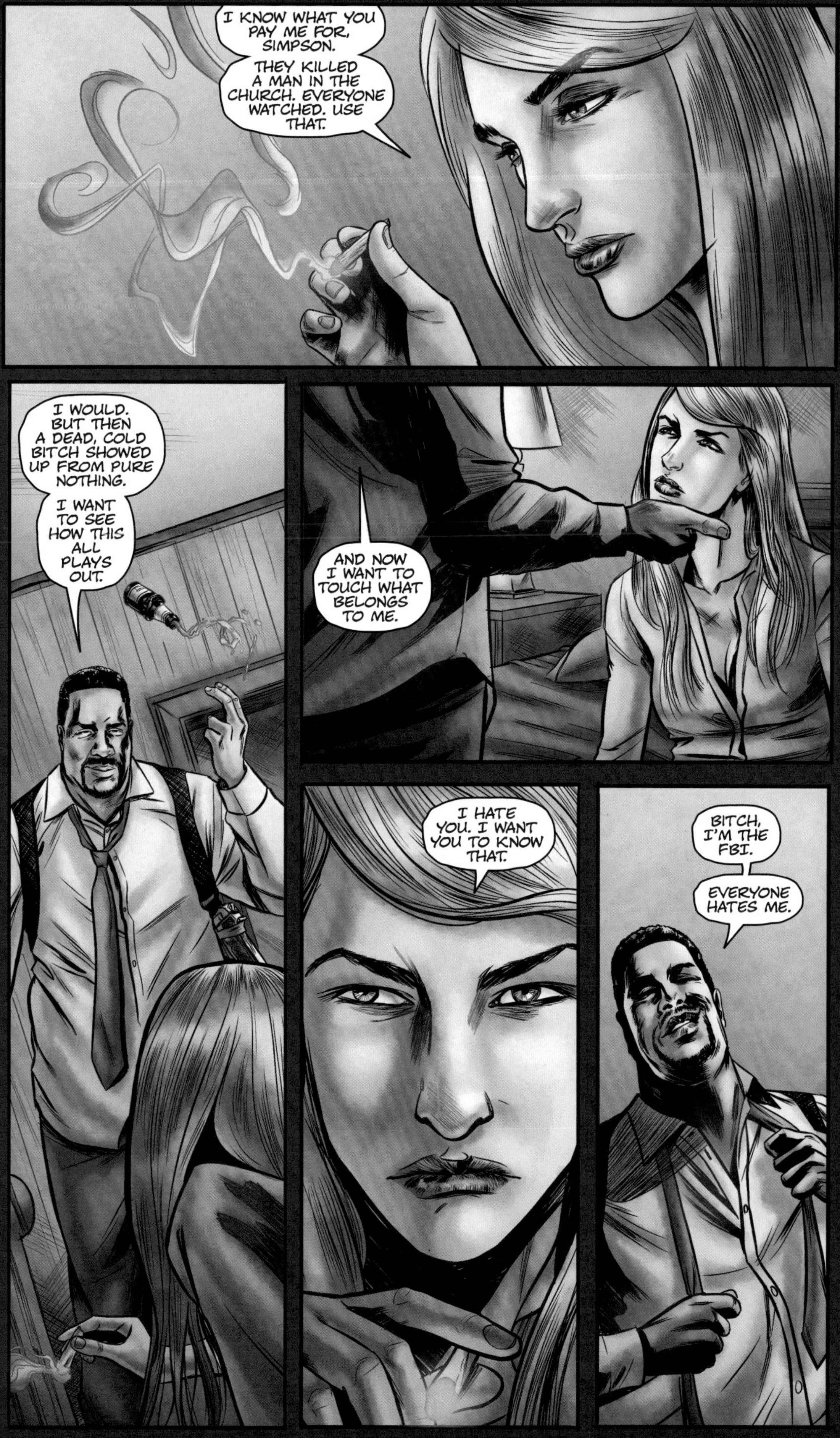
I KNOW WHAT YOU PAY ME FOR, SIMPSON.
THEY KILLED A MAN IN THE CHURCH. EVERYONE WATCHED. USE THAT.
I WOULD. BUT THEN A DEAD, COLD BITCH SHOWED UP FROM PURE NOTHING.
I WANT TO SEE HOW THIS ALL PLAYS OUT.
AND NOW I WANT TO TOUCH WHAT BELONGS TO ME.
I HATE YOU. I WANT YOU TO KNOW THAT.
BITCH, I'M THE FBI.
EVERYONE HATES ME.

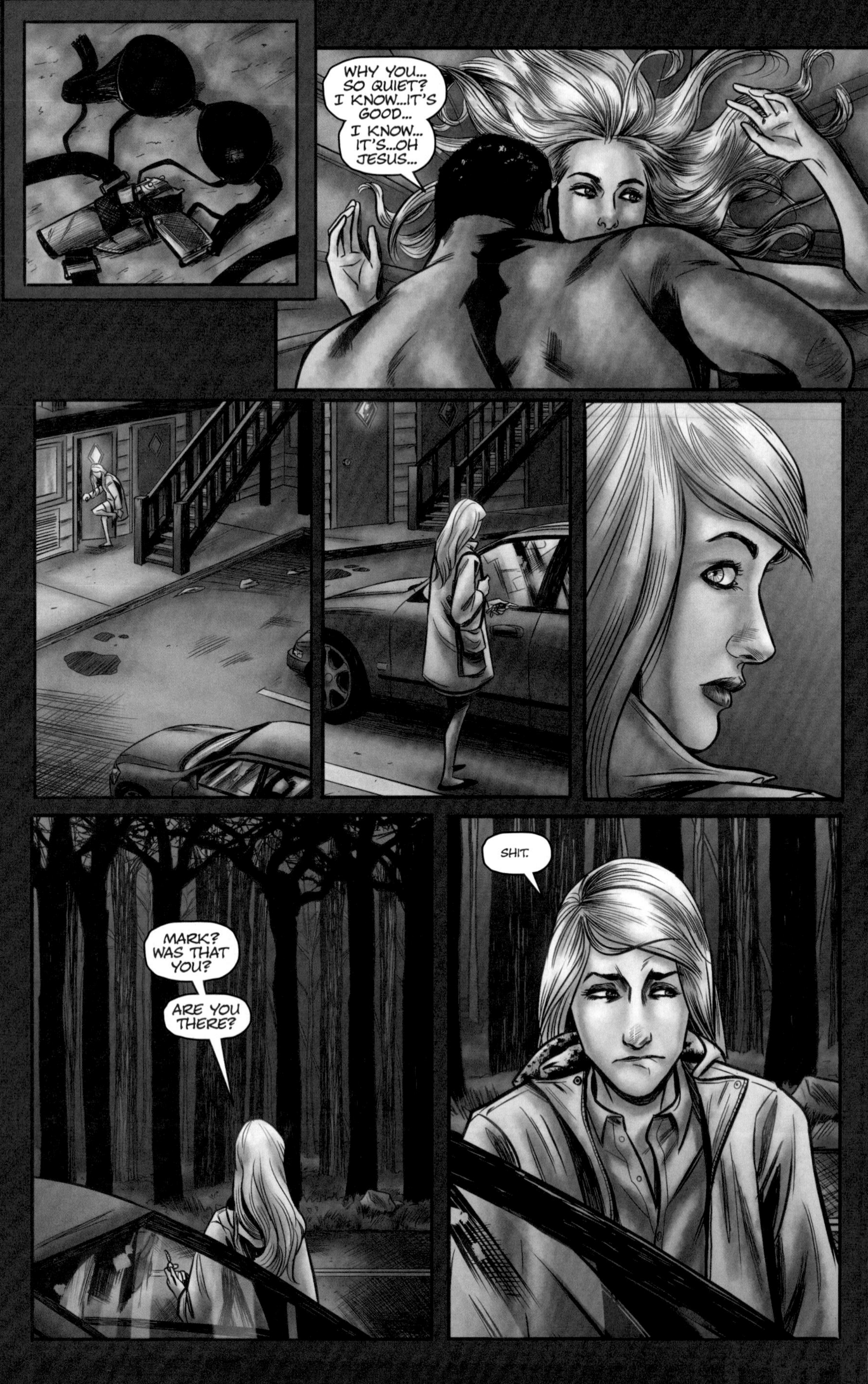
WHY YOU... SO QUIET? I KNOW...IT'S GOOD... I KNOW... IT'S...OH JESUS...
MARK? WAS THAT YOU?
ARE YOU THERE?
SHIT.

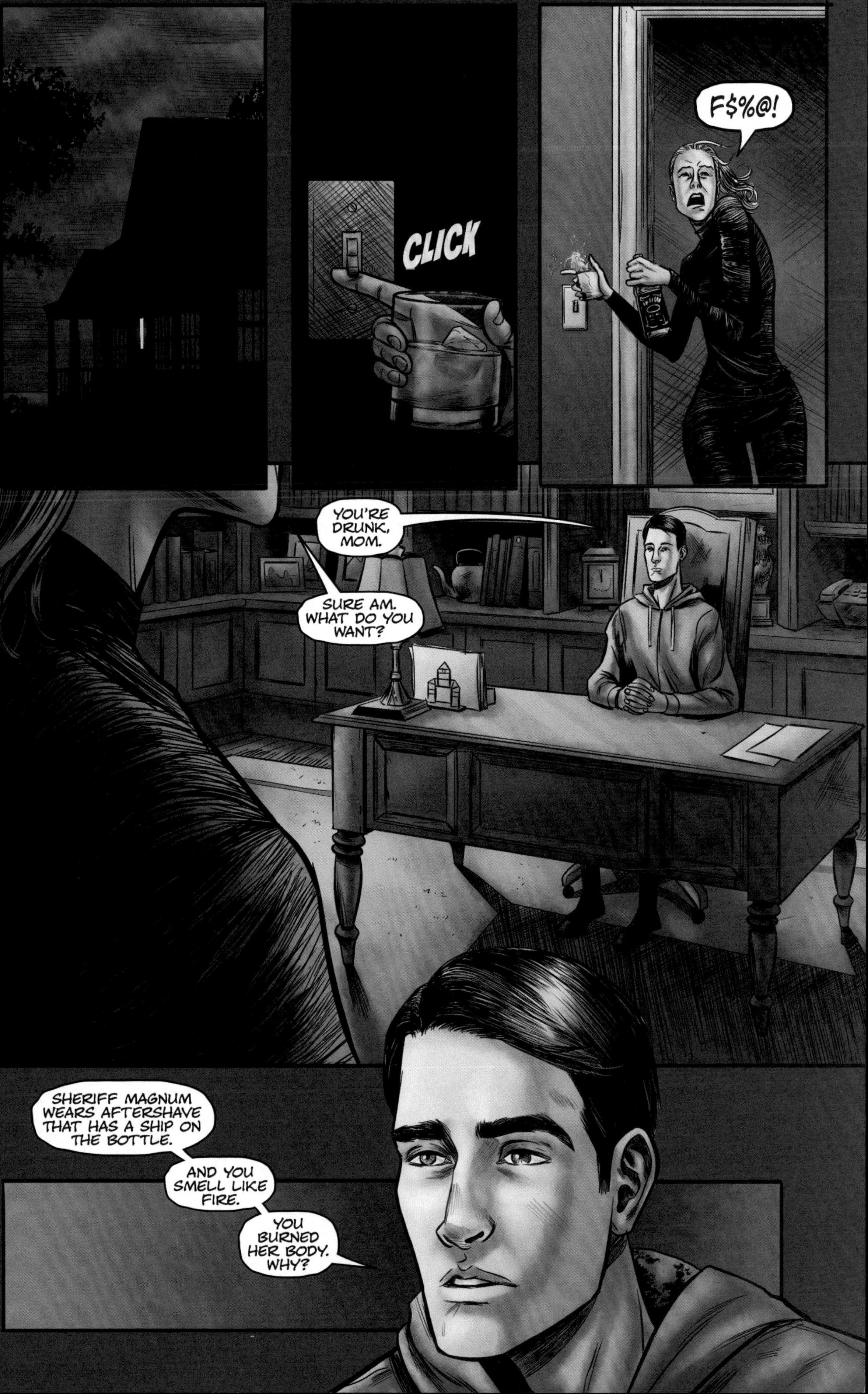
CLICK
F$%@!
YOU'RE DRUNK, MOM.
SURE AM. WHAT DO YOU WANT?
SHERIFF MAGNUM WEARS AFTERSHAVE THAT HAS A SHIP ON THE BOTTLE.
AND YOU SMELL LIKE FIRE.
YOU BURNED HER BODY. WHY?

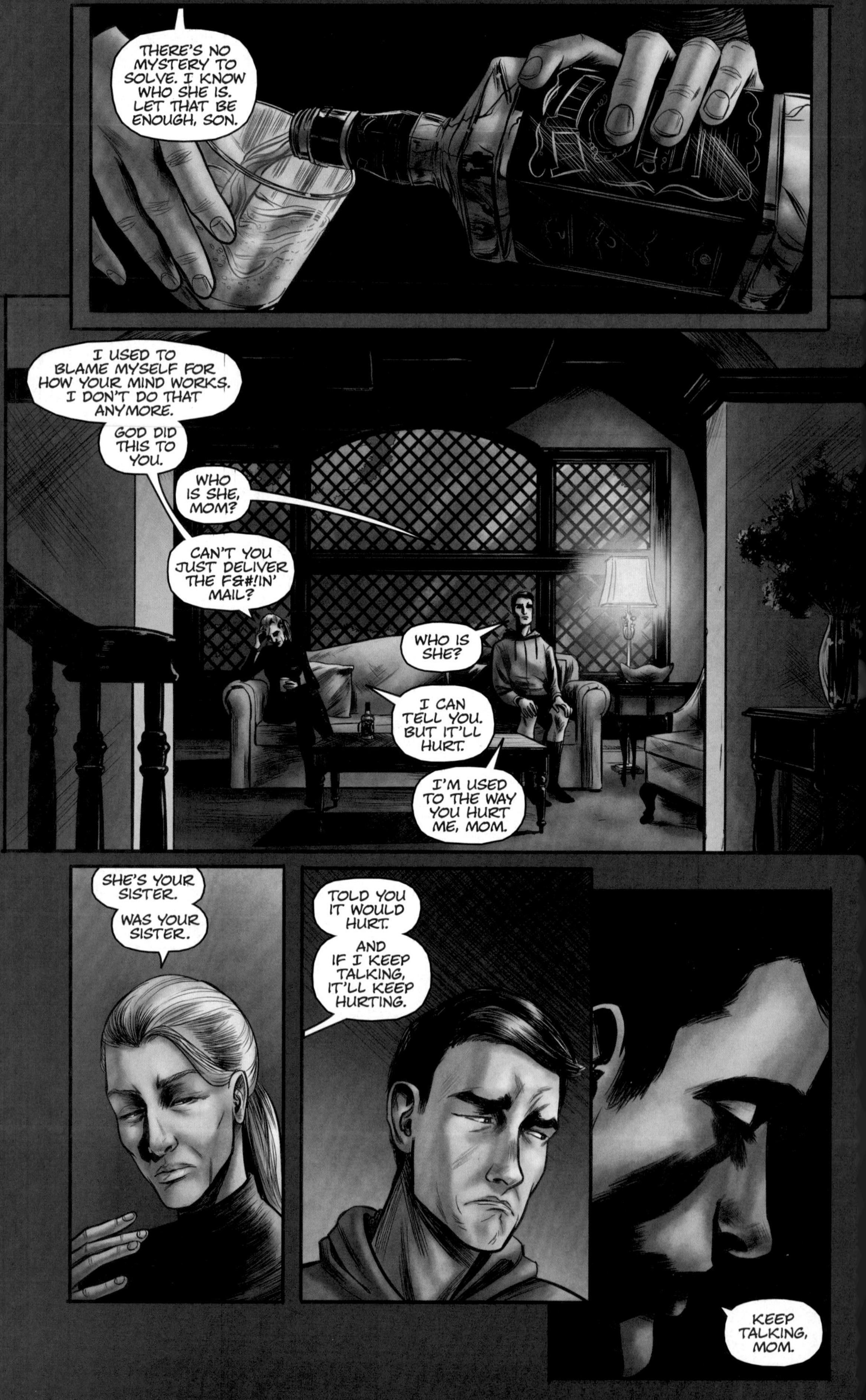
THERE'S NO MYSTERY TO SOLVE. I KNOW WHO SHE IS. LET THAT BE ENOUGH, SON.
I USED TO BLAME MYSELF FOR HOW YOUR MIND WORKS. I DON'T DO THAT ANYMORE.
GOD DID THIS TO YOU.
WHO IS SHE, MOM?
CAN'T YOU JUST DELIVER THE F&#!IN' MAIL?
WHO IS SHE?
I CAN TELL YOU. BUT IT'LL HURT.
I'M USED TO THE WAY YOU HURT ME, MOM.
SHE'S YOUR SISTER.
WAS YOUR SISTER.
TOLD YOU IT WOULD HURT.
AND IF I KEEP TALKING, IT'LL KEEP HURTING.
KEEP TALKING, MOM.

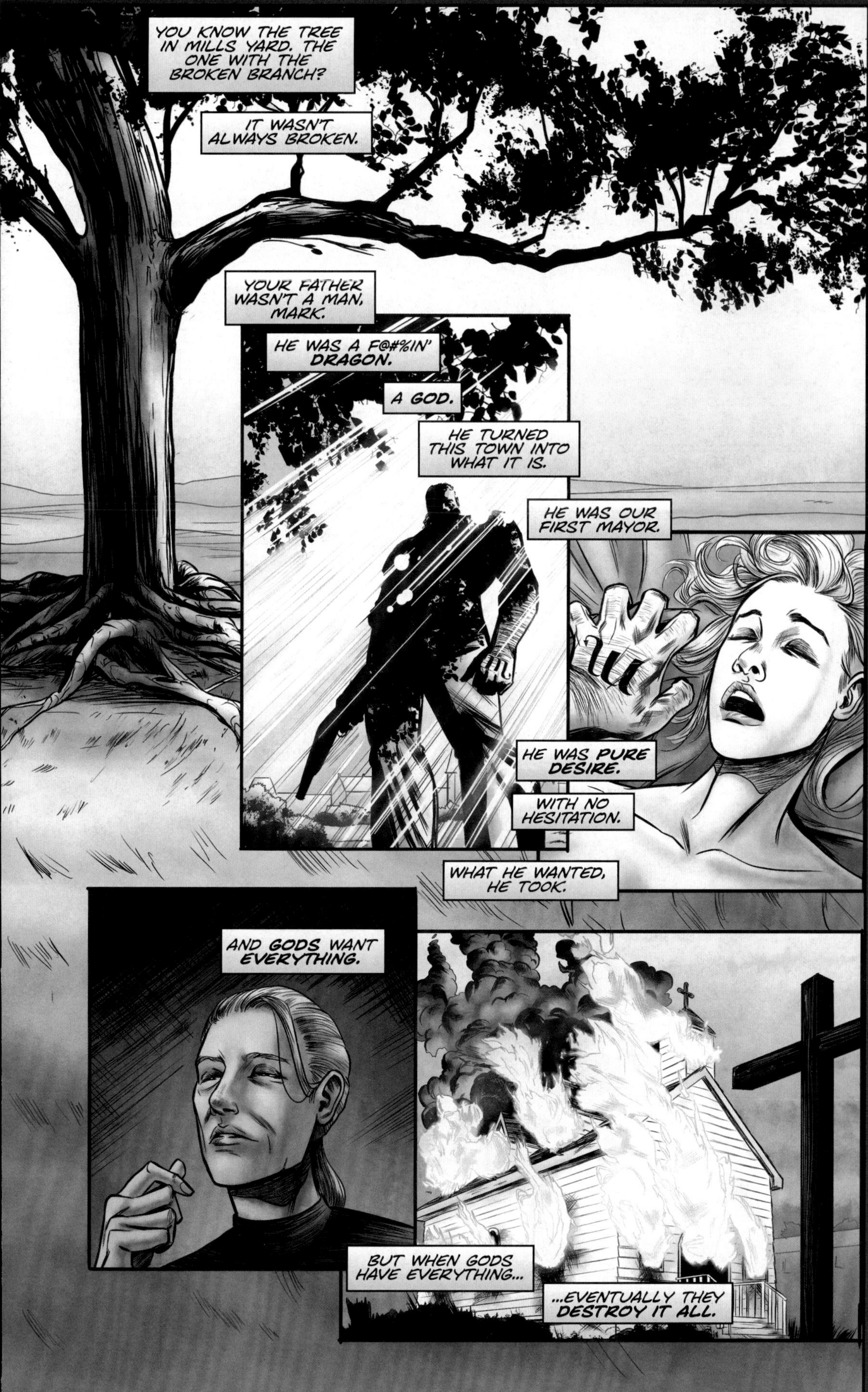
YOU KNOW THE TREE IN MILLS YARD. THE ONE WITH THE BROKEN BRANCH?
IT WASN'T ALWAYS BROKEN.
YOUR FATHER WASN'T A MAN, MARK.
HE WAS A F@#%IN' DRAGON.
A GOD.
HE TURNED THIS TOWN INTO WHAT IT IS.
HE WAS OUR FIRST MAYOR.
HE WAS PURE DESIRE.
WITH NO HESITATION.
WHAT HE WANTED, HE TOOK.
AND GODS WANT EVERYTHING.
BUT WHEN GODS HAVE EVERYTHING...
...EVENTUALLY THEY DESTROY IT ALL.

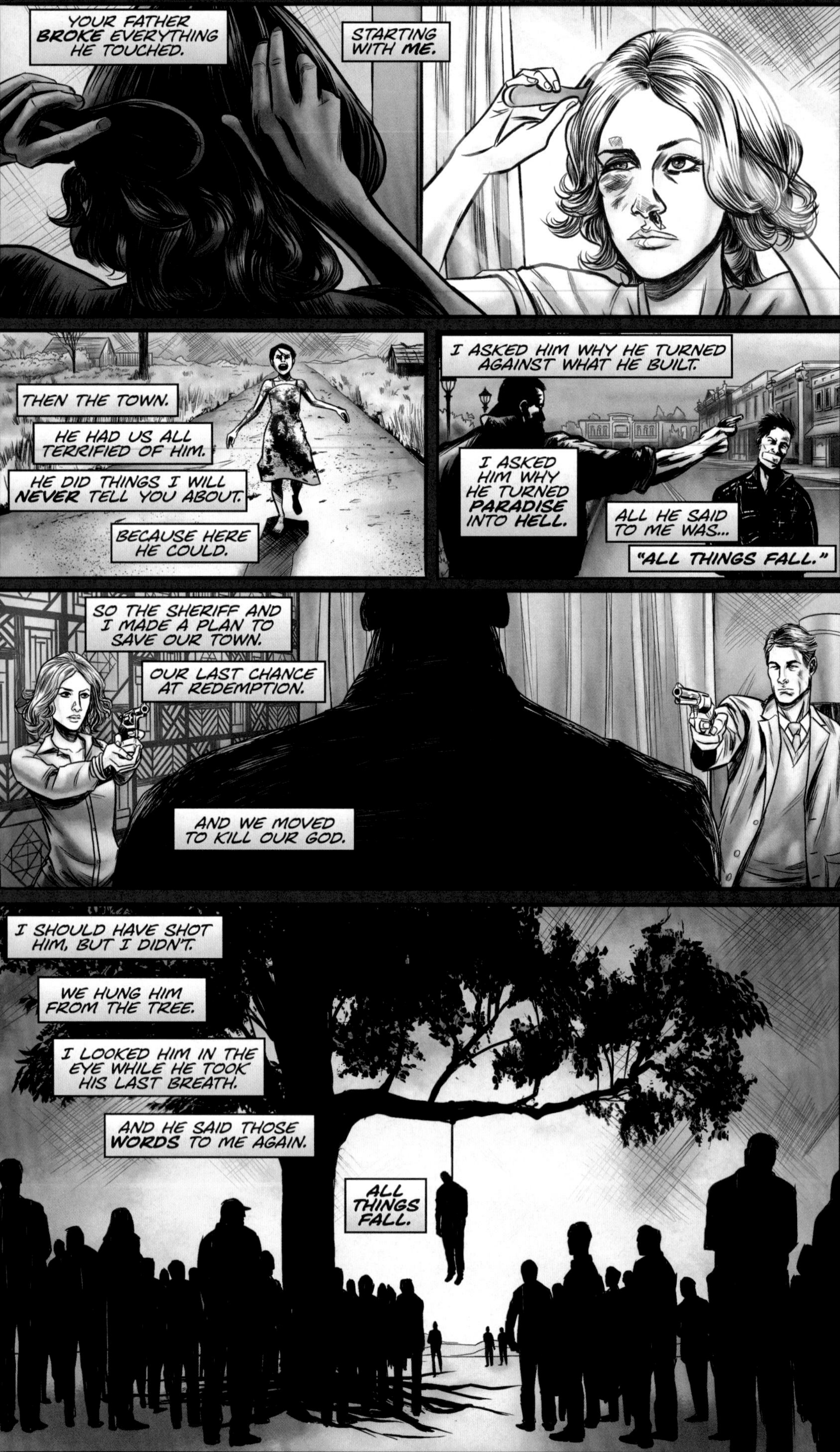
YOUR FATHER BROKE EVERYTHING HE TOUCHED.
STARTING WITH ME.
THEN THE TOWN.
HE HAD US ALL TERRIFIED OF HIM.
HE DID THINGS I WILL NEVER TELL YOU ABOUT.
BECAUSE HERE HE COULD.
I ASKED HIM WHY HE TURNED AGAINST WHAT HE BUILT.
I ASKED HIM WHY HE TURNED PARADISE INTO HELL.
ALL HE SAID TO ME WAS...
"ALL THINGS FALL."
SO THE SHERIFF AND I MADE A PLAN TO SAVE OUR TOWN.
OUR LAST CHANCE AT REDEMPTION.
AND WE MOVED TO KILL OUR GOD.
I SHOULD HAVE SHOT HIM, BUT I DIDN'T.
WE HUNG HIM FROM THE TREE.
I LOOKED HIM IN THE EYE WHILE HE TOOK HIS LAST BREATH.
AND HE SAID THOSE WORDS TO ME AGAIN.
ALL THINGS FALL.

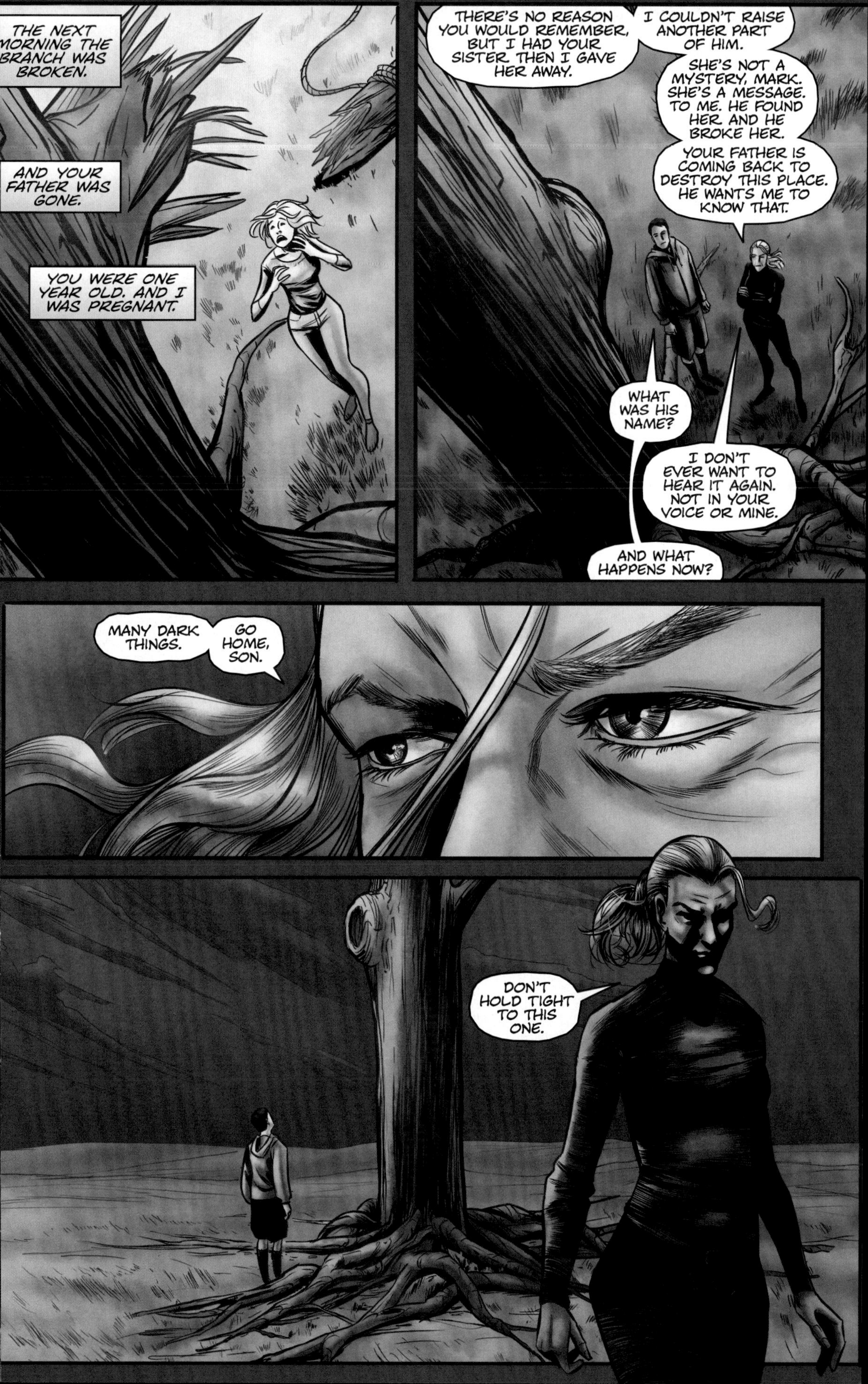
THE NEXT MORNING THE BRANCH WAS BROKEN.
AND YOUR FATHER WAS GONE.
YOU WERE ONE YEAR OLD. AND I WAS PREGNANT.
THERE'S NO REASON YOU WOULD REMEMBER, BUT I HAD YOUR SISTER. THEN I GAVE HER AWAY.
I COULDN'T RAISE ANOTHER PART OF HIM.
SHE'S NOT A MYSTERY, MARK. SHE'S A MESSAGE. TO ME. HE FOUND HER AND HE BROKE HER.
YOUR FATHER IS COMING BACK TO DESTROY THIS PLACE. HE WANTS ME TO KNOW THAT.
WHAT WAS HIS NAME?
I DON'T EVER WANT TO HEAR IT AGAIN. NOT IN YOUR VOICE OR MINE.
AND WHAT HAPPENS NOW?
MANY DARK THINGS.
GO HOME, SON.
DON'T HOLD TIGHT TO THIS ONE.

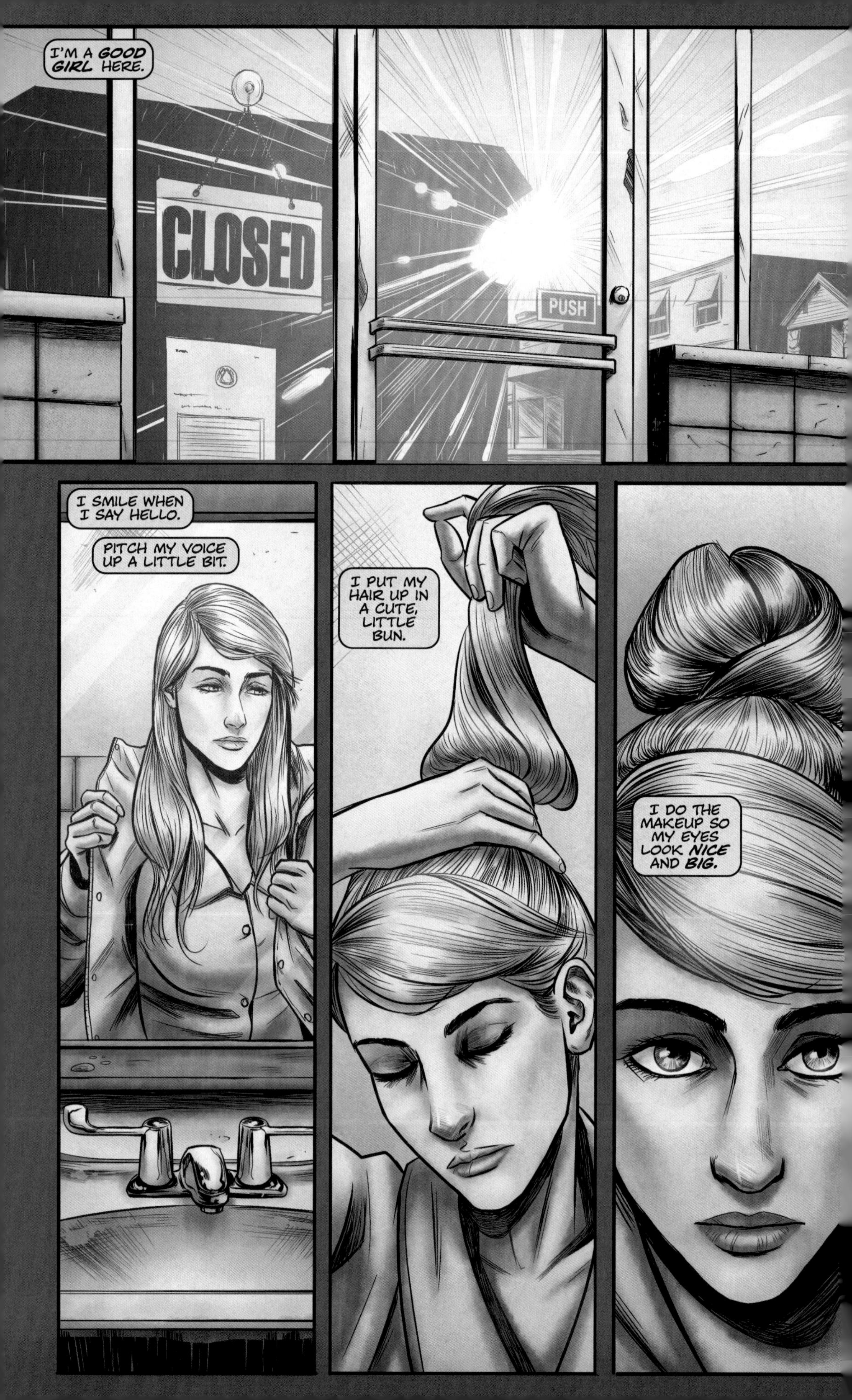
I'M A **GOOD GIRL** HERE.
CLOSED
PUSH
I SMILE WHEN I SAY HELLO.
PITCH MY VOICE UP A LITTLE BIT.
I PUT MY HAIR UP IN A CUTE, LITTLE BUN.
I DO THE MAKEUP SO MY EYES LOOK **NICE** AND **BIG.**

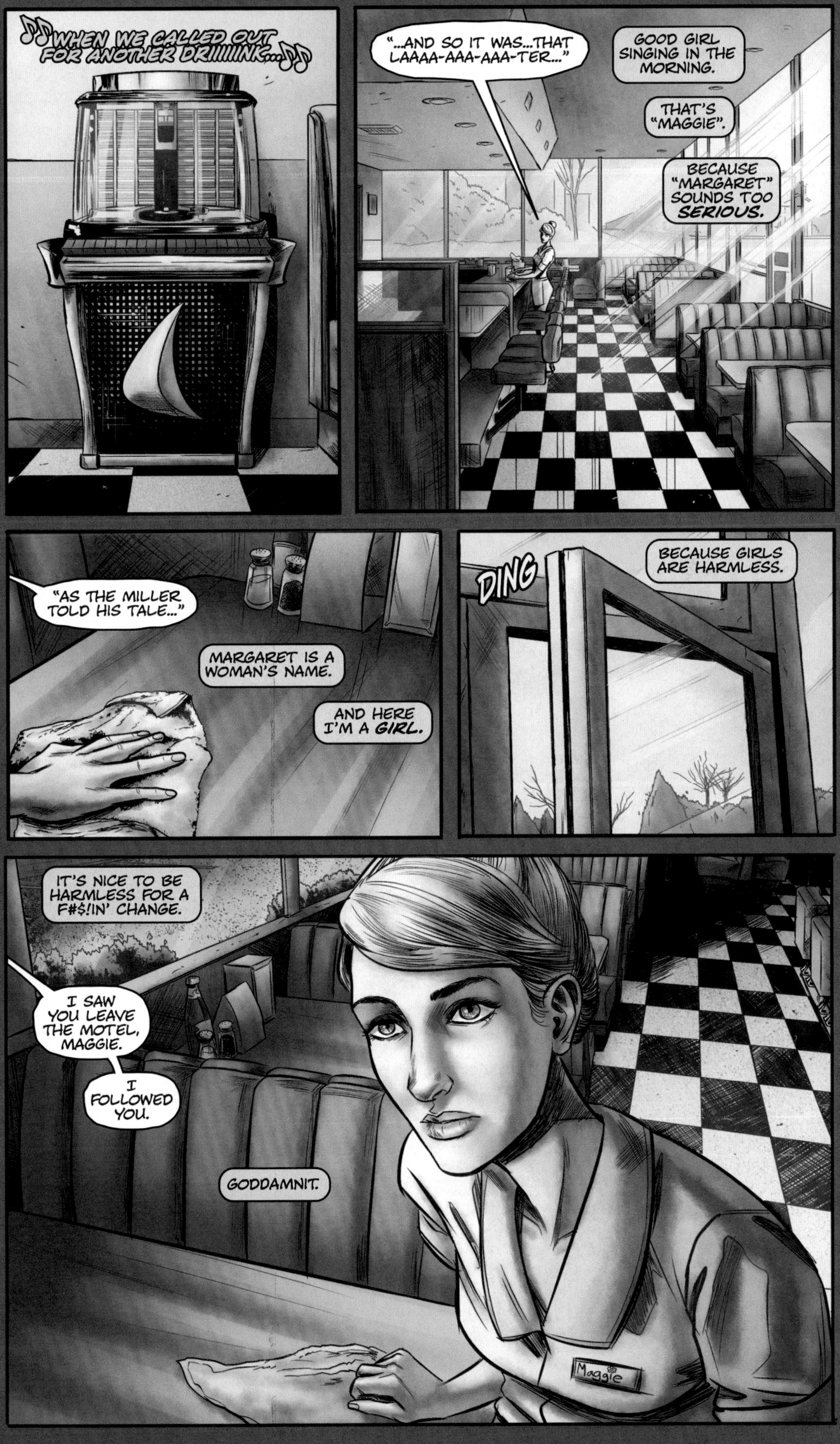
WHEN WE CALLED OUT FOR ANOTHER DRIIIIIINK...
"...AND SO IT WAS...THAT LAAAA-AAA-AAA-TER..."
GOOD GIRL SINGING IN THE MORNING.
THAT'S "MAGGIE".
BECAUSE "MARGARET" SOUNDS TOO SERIOUS.
"AS THE MILLER TOLD HIS TALE..."
MARGARET IS A WOMAN'S NAME.
AND HERE I'M A GIRL.
DING
BECAUSE GIRLS ARE HARMLESS.
IT'S NICE TO BE HARMLESS FOR A F#$!IN' CHANGE.
I SAW YOU LEAVE THE MOTEL, MAGGIE.
I FOLLOWED YOU.
GODDAMNIT.
Maggie

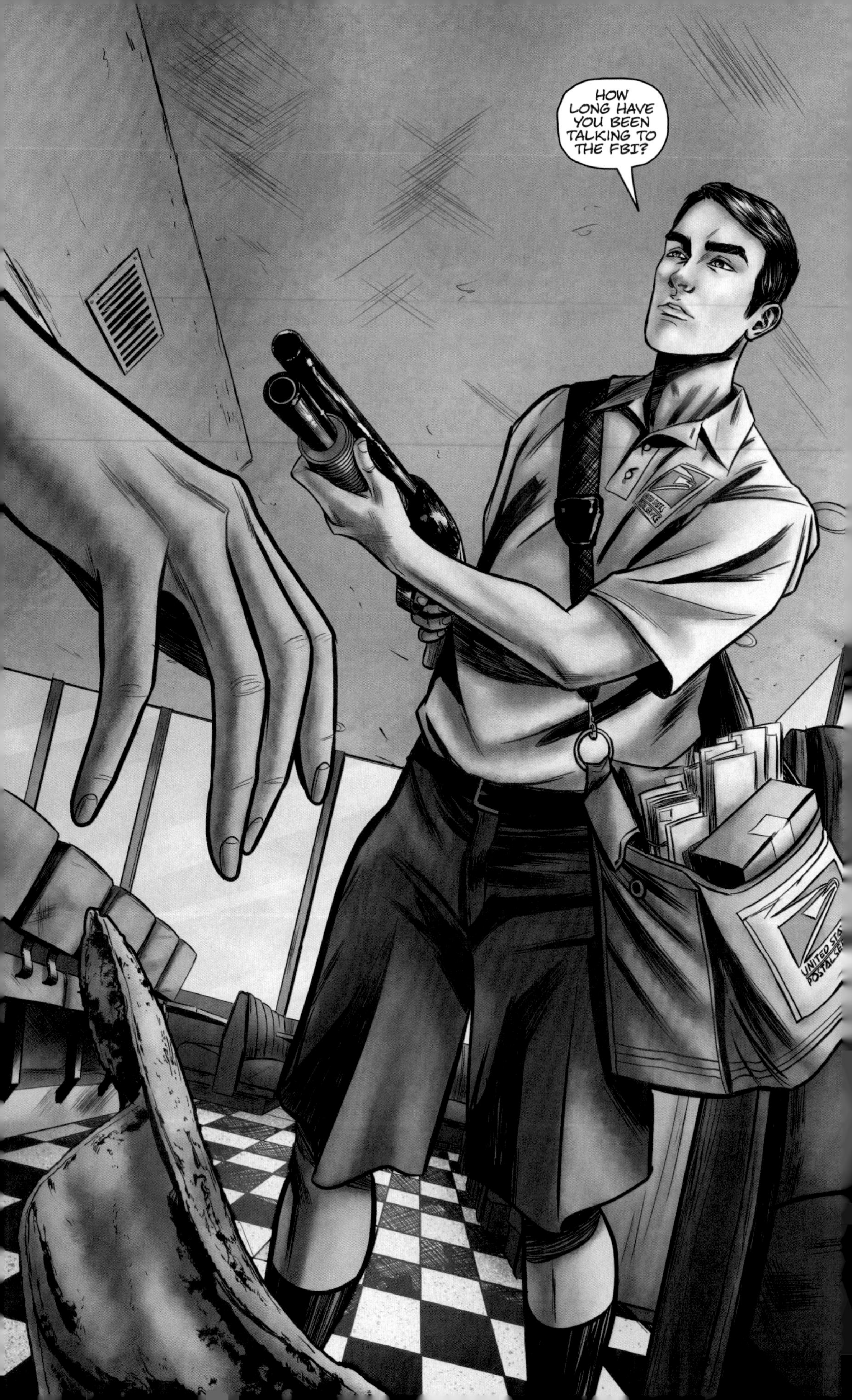
HOW LONG HAVE YOU BEEN TALKING TO THE FBI?
UNITED STATES POSTAL SERVICE

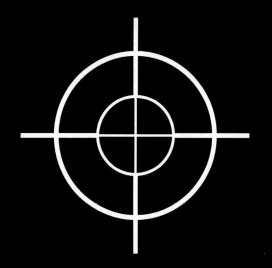

# Chapter 3

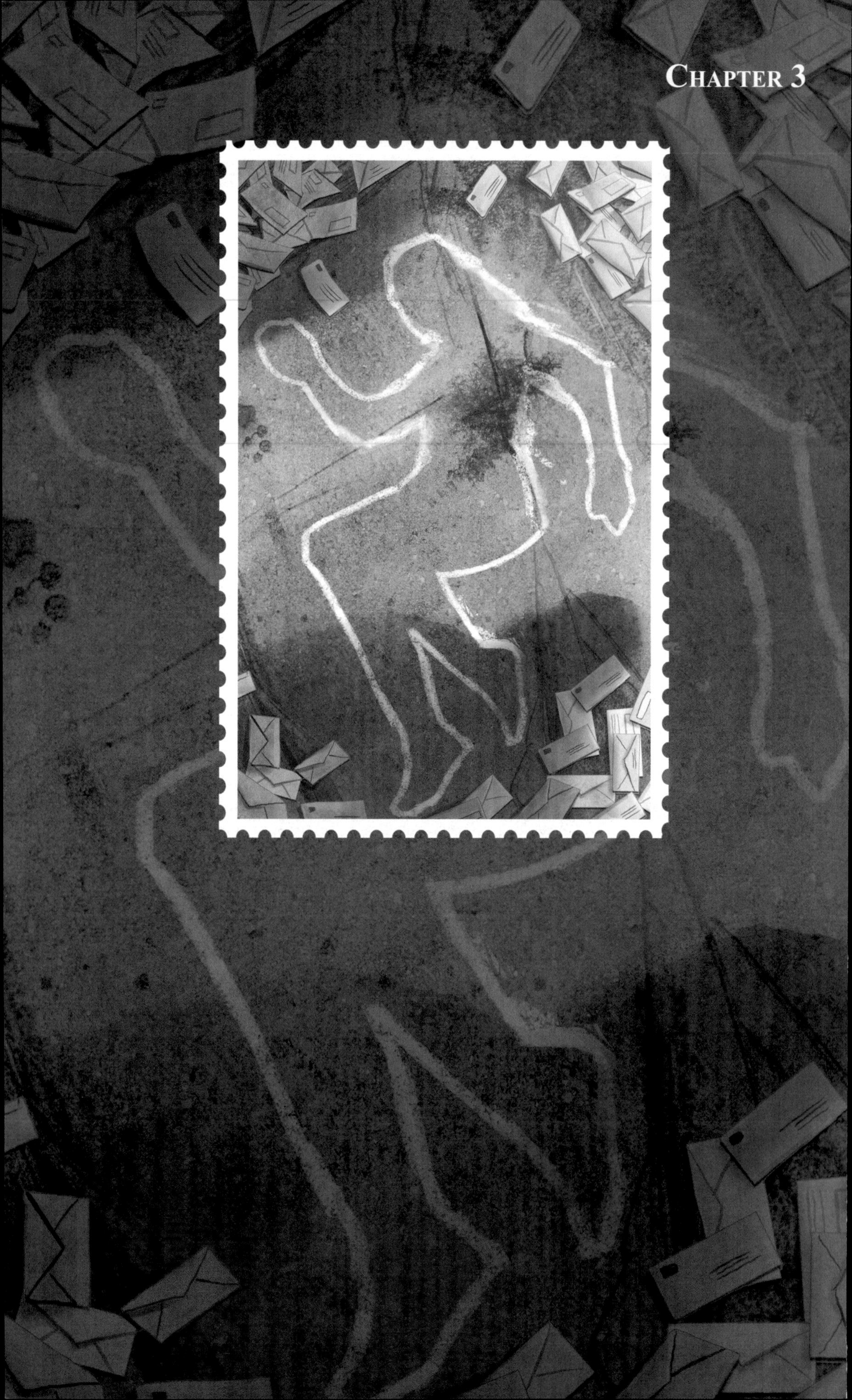

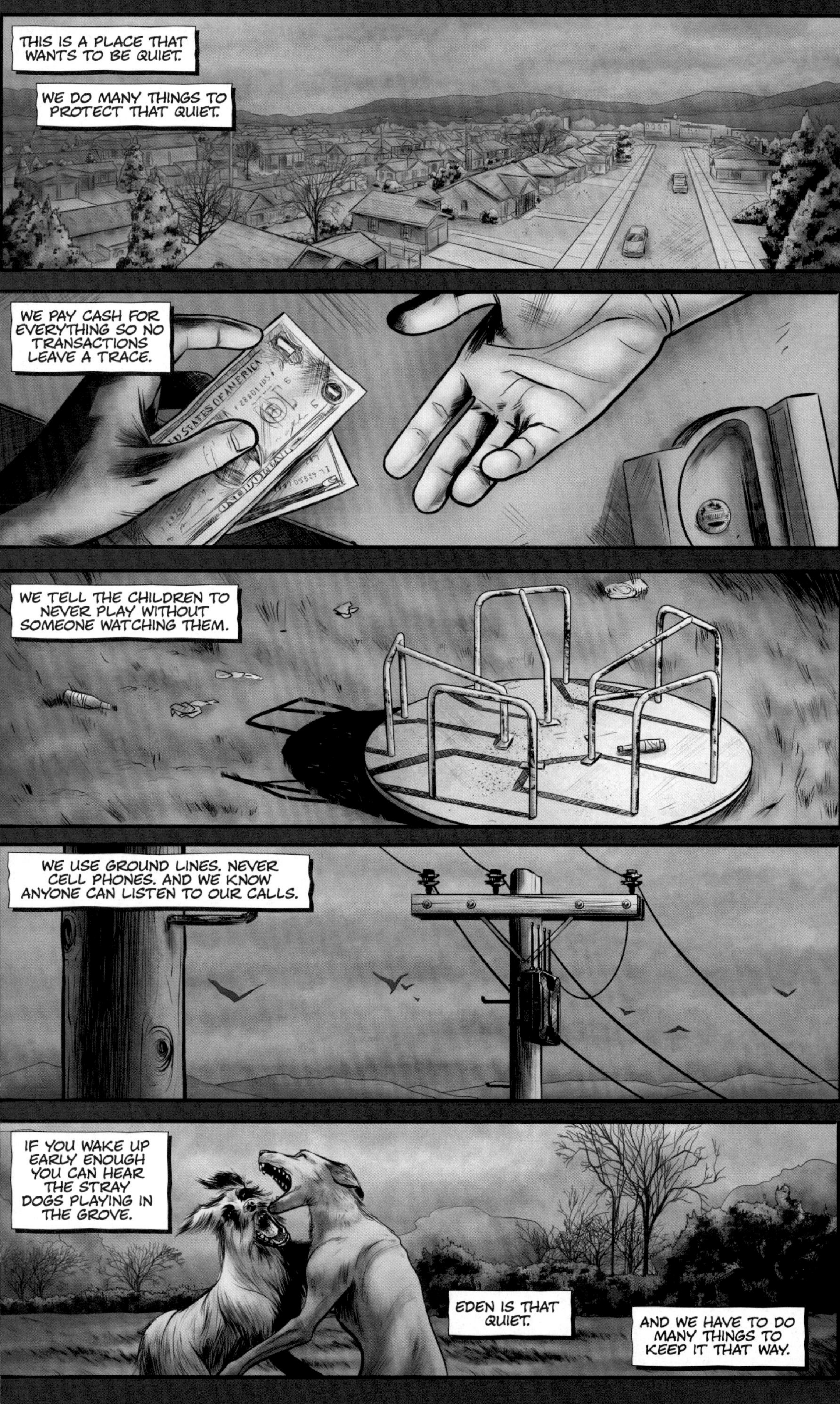
THIS IS A PLACE THAT WANTS TO BE QUIET.
WE DO MANY THINGS TO PROTECT THAT QUIET.
WE PAY CASH FOR EVERYTHING SO NO TRANSACTIONS LEAVE A TRACE.
WE TELL THE CHILDREN TO NEVER PLAY WITHOUT SOMEONE WATCHING THEM.
WE USE GROUND LINES. NEVER CELL PHONES. AND WE KNOW ANYONE CAN LISTEN TO OUR CALLS.
IF YOU WAKE UP EARLY ENOUGH YOU CAN HEAR THE STRAY DOGS PLAYING IN THE GROVE.
EDEN IS THAT QUIET.
AND WE HAVE TO DO MANY THINGS TO KEEP IT THAT WAY.

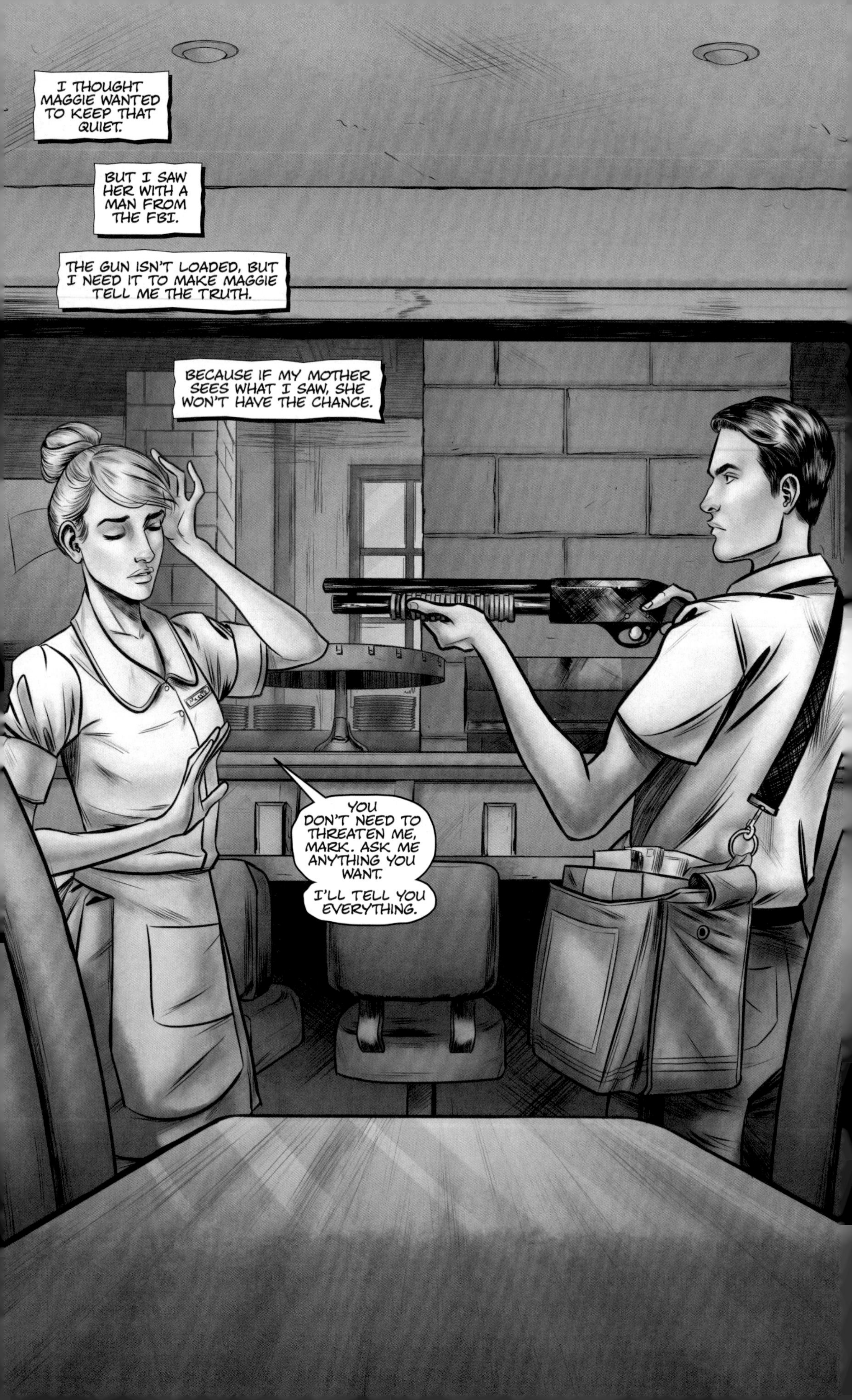
I THOUGHT MAGGIE WANTED TO KEEP THAT QUIET.
BUT I SAW HER WITH A MAN FROM THE FBI.
THE GUN ISN'T LOADED, BUT I NEED IT TO MAKE MAGGIE TELL ME THE TRUTH.
BECAUSE IF MY MOTHER SEES WHAT I SAW, SHE WON'T HAVE THE CHANCE.
YOU DON'T NEED TO THREATEN ME, MARK. ASK ME ANYTHING YOU WANT.
I'LL TELL YOU EVERYTHING.

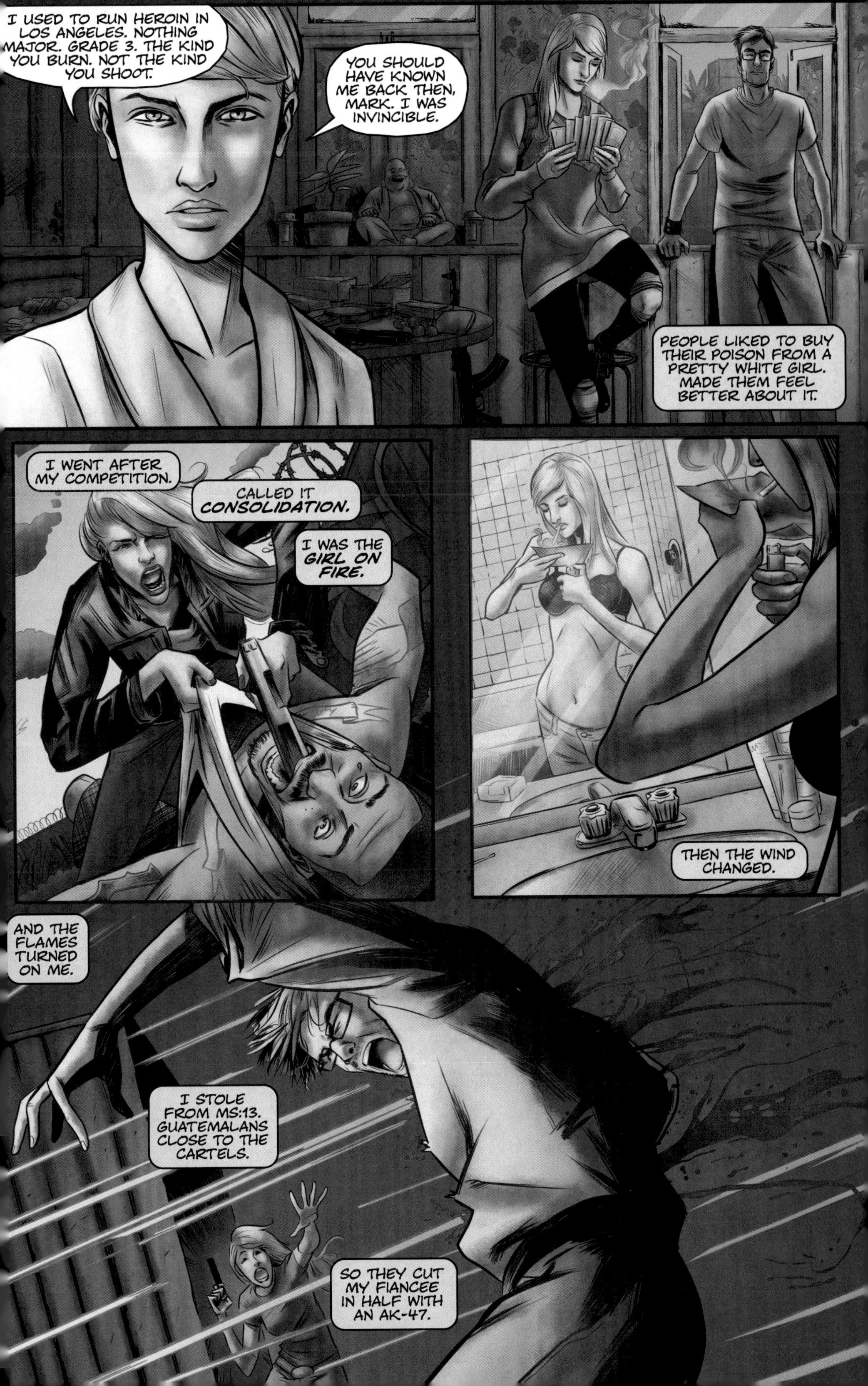
I USED TO RUN HEROIN IN LOS ANGELES. NOTHING MAJOR. GRADE 3. THE KIND YOU BURN. NOT THE KIND YOU SHOOT.
YOU SHOULD HAVE KNOWN ME BACK THEN, MARK. I WAS INVINCIBLE.
PEOPLE LIKED TO BUY THEIR POISON FROM A PRETTY WHITE GIRL. MADE THEM FEEL BETTER ABOUT IT.
I WENT AFTER MY COMPETITION.
CALLED IT CONSOLIDATION.
I WAS THE GIRL ON FIRE.
THEN THE WIND CHANGED.
AND THE FLAMES TURNED ON ME.
I STOLE FROM MS:13. GUATEMALANS CLOSE TO THE CARTELS.
SO THEY CUT MY FIANCEE IN HALF WITH AN AK-47.

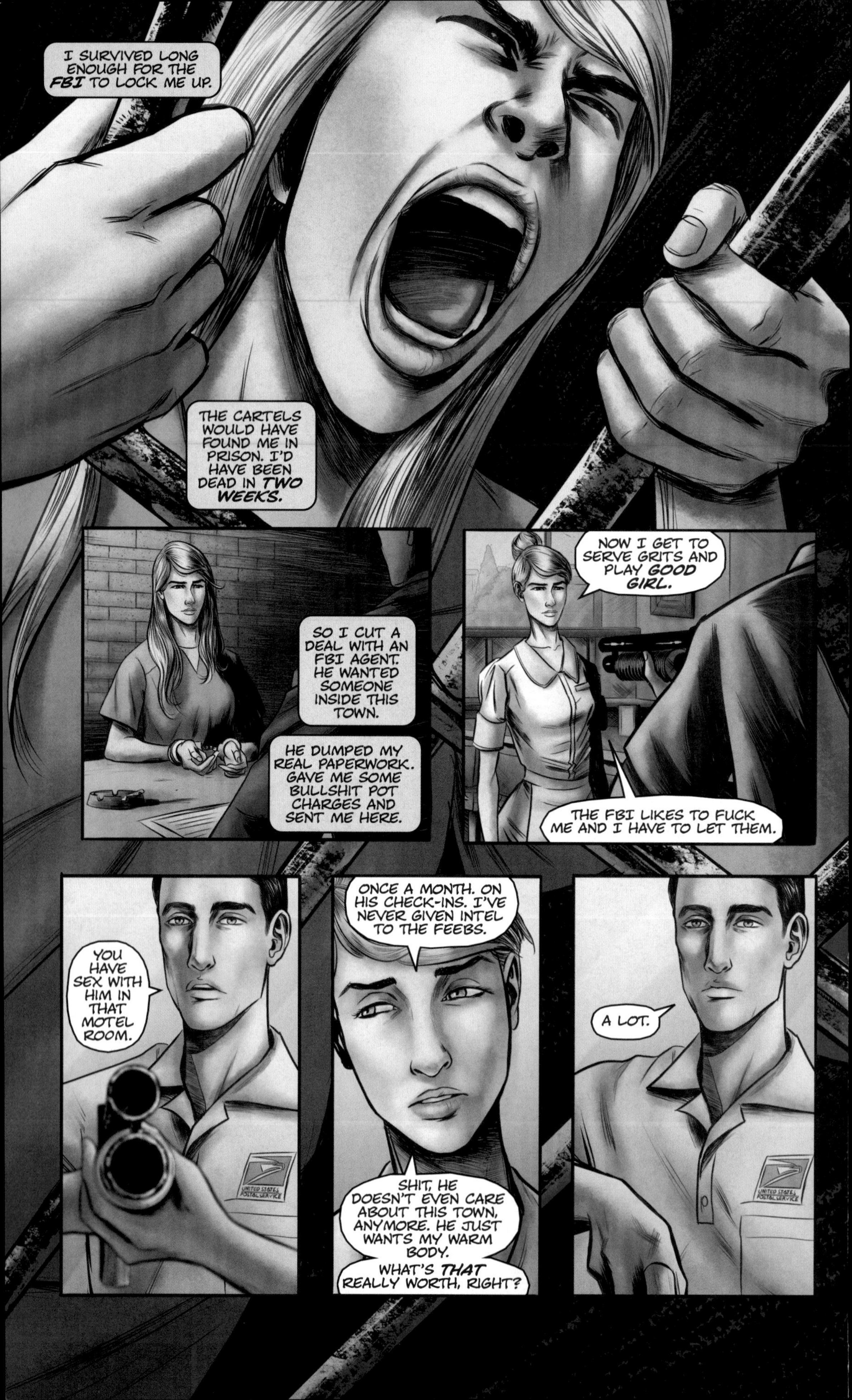
I SURVIVED LONG ENOUGH FOR THE FBI TO LOCK ME UP.
THE CARTELS WOULD HAVE FOUND ME IN PRISON. I'D HAVE BEEN DEAD IN TWO WEEKS.
SO I CUT A DEAL WITH AN FBI AGENT. HE WANTED SOMEONE INSIDE THIS TOWN.
HE DUMPED MY REAL PAPERWORK. GAVE ME SOME BULLSHIT POT CHARGES AND SENT ME HERE.
NOW I GET TO SERVE GRITS AND PLAY GOOD GIRL.
THE FBI LIKES TO FUCK ME AND I HAVE TO LET THEM.
YOU HAVE SEX WITH HIM IN THAT MOTEL ROOM.
ONCE A MONTH. ON HIS CHECK-INS. I'VE NEVER GIVEN INTEL TO THE FEEBS.
SHIT, HE DOESN'T EVEN CARE ABOUT THIS TOWN, ANYMORE. HE JUST WANTS MY WARM BODY.
WHAT'S THAT REALLY WORTH, RIGHT?
A LOT.
UNITED STATES POSTAL SERVICE
UNITED STATES POSTAL SERVICE

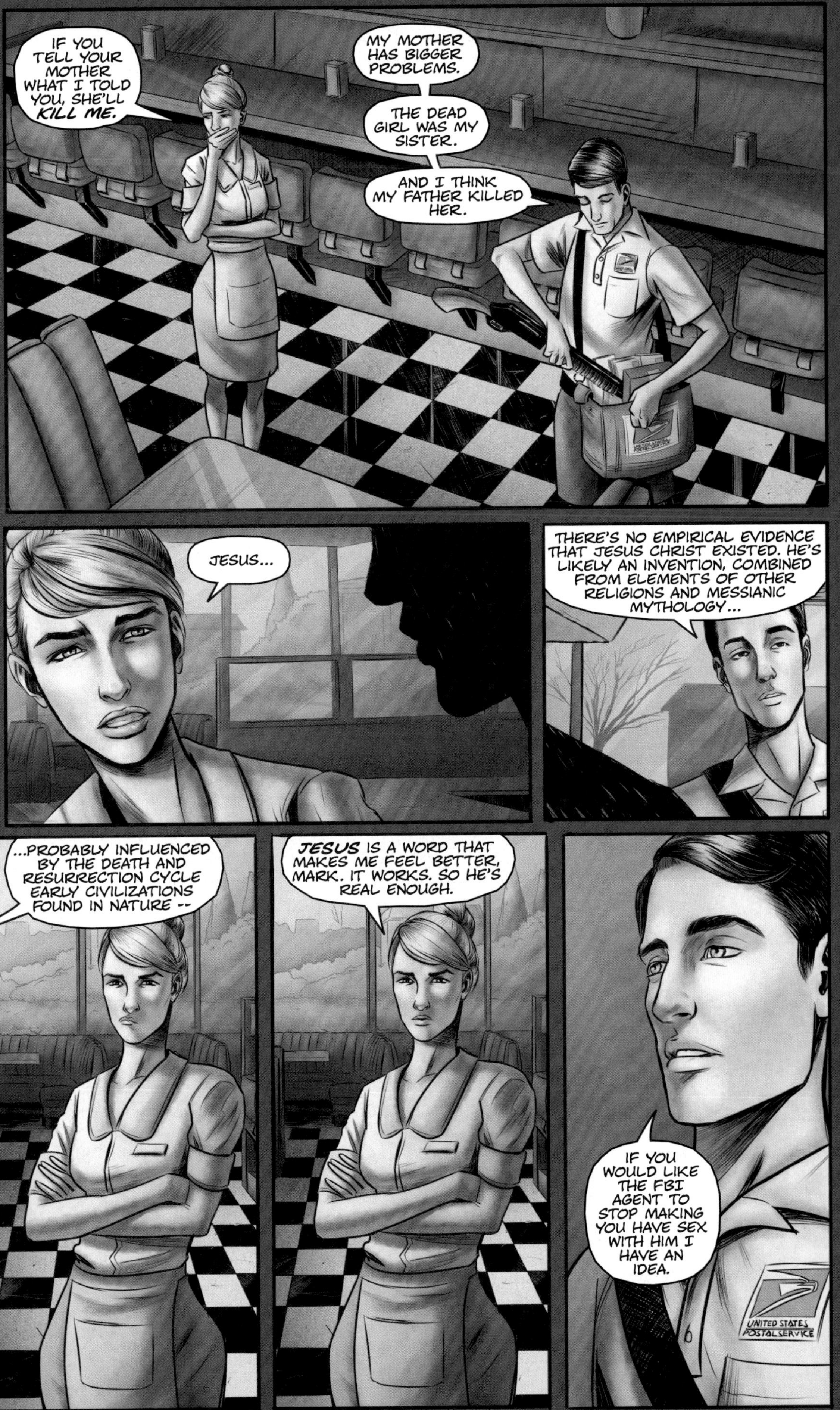
IF YOU TELL YOUR MOTHER WHAT I TOLD YOU, SHE'LL *KILL ME.*
MY MOTHER HAS BIGGER PROBLEMS.
THE DEAD GIRL WAS MY SISTER.
AND I THINK MY FATHER KILLED HER.
JESUS...
THERE'S NO EMPIRICAL EVIDENCE THAT JESUS CHRIST EXISTED. HE'S LIKELY AN INVENTION, COMBINED FROM ELEMENTS OF OTHER RELIGIONS AND MESSIANIC MYTHOLOGY...
...PROBABLY INFLUENCED BY THE DEATH AND RESURRECTION CYCLE EARLY CIVILIZATIONS FOUND IN NATURE --
*JESUS* IS A WORD THAT MAKES ME FEEL BETTER, MARK. IT WORKS. SO HE'S REAL ENOUGH.
IF YOU WOULD LIKE THE FBI AGENT TO STOP MAKING YOU HAVE SEX WITH HIM I HAVE AN IDEA.
UNITED STATES POSTAL SERVICE

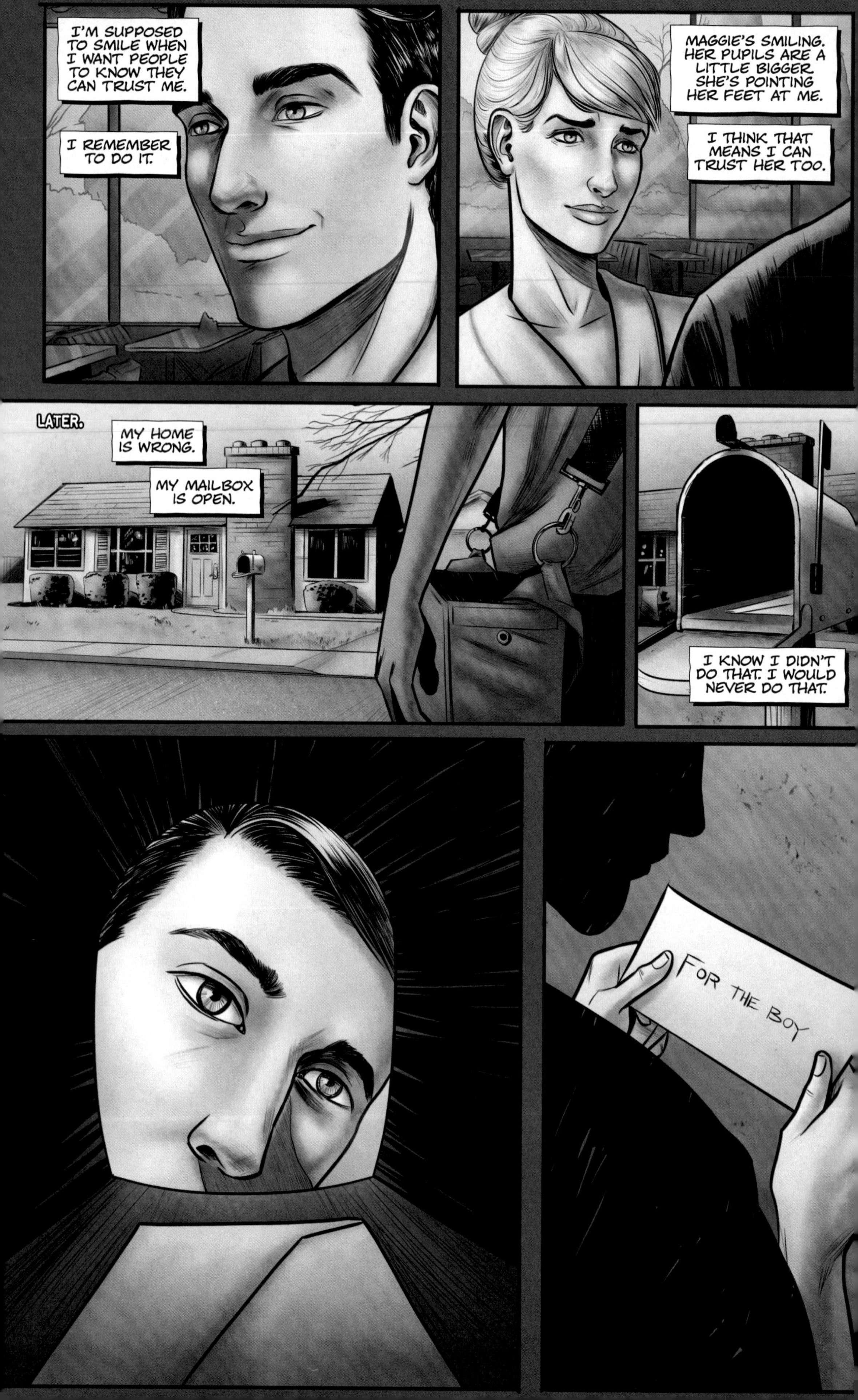
I'M SUPPOSED TO SMILE WHEN I WANT PEOPLE TO KNOW THEY CAN TRUST ME.
I REMEMBER TO DO IT.
MAGGIE'S SMILING. HER PUPILS ARE A LITTLE BIGGER. SHE'S POINTING HER FEET AT ME.
I THINK THAT MEANS I CAN TRUST HER TOO.
LATER.
MY HOME IS WRONG.
MY MAILBOX IS OPEN.
I KNOW I DIDN'T DO THAT. I WOULD NEVER DO THAT.
FOR THE BOY

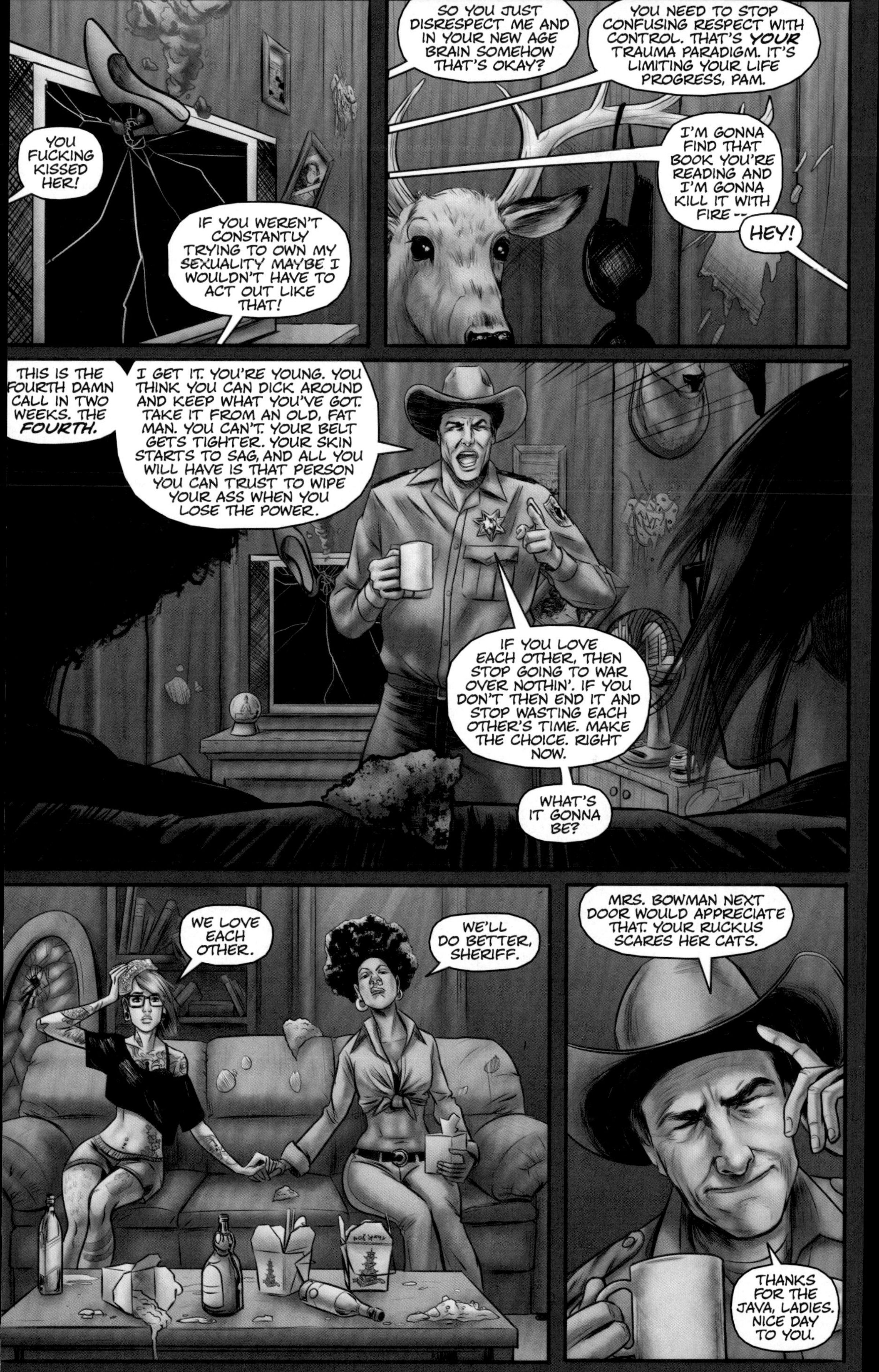
YOU FUCKING KISSED HER!
IF YOU WEREN'T CONSTANTLY TRYING TO OWN MY SEXUALITY MAYBE I WOULDN'T HAVE TO ACT OUT LIKE THAT!
SO YOU JUST DISRESPECT ME AND IN YOUR NEW AGE BRAIN SOMEHOW THAT'S OKAY?
YOU NEED TO STOP CONFUSING RESPECT WITH CONTROL. THAT'S YOUR TRAUMA PARADIGM. IT'S LIMITING YOUR LIFE PROGRESS, PAM.
I'M GONNA FIND THAT BOOK YOU'RE READING AND I'M GONNA KILL IT WITH FIRE --
HEY!
THIS IS THE FOURTH DAMN CALL IN TWO WEEKS. THE FOURTH.
I GET IT. YOU'RE YOUNG. YOU THINK YOU CAN DICK AROUND AND KEEP WHAT YOU'VE GOT. TAKE IT FROM AN OLD, FAT MAN. YOU CAN'T. YOUR BELT GETS TIGHTER. YOUR SKIN STARTS TO SAG, AND ALL YOU WILL HAVE IS THAT PERSON YOU CAN TRUST TO WIPE YOUR ASS WHEN YOU LOSE THE POWER.
IF YOU LOVE EACH OTHER, THEN STOP GOING TO WAR OVER NOTHIN'. IF YOU DON'T THEN END IT AND STOP WASTING EACH OTHER'S TIME. MAKE THE CHOICE. RIGHT NOW.
WHAT'S IT GONNA BE?
WE LOVE EACH OTHER.
WE'LL DO BETTER, SHERIFF.
MRS. BOWMAN NEXT DOOR WOULD APPRECIATE THAT. YOUR RUCKUS SCARES HER CATS.
THANKS FOR THE JAVA, LADIES. NICE DAY TO YOU.

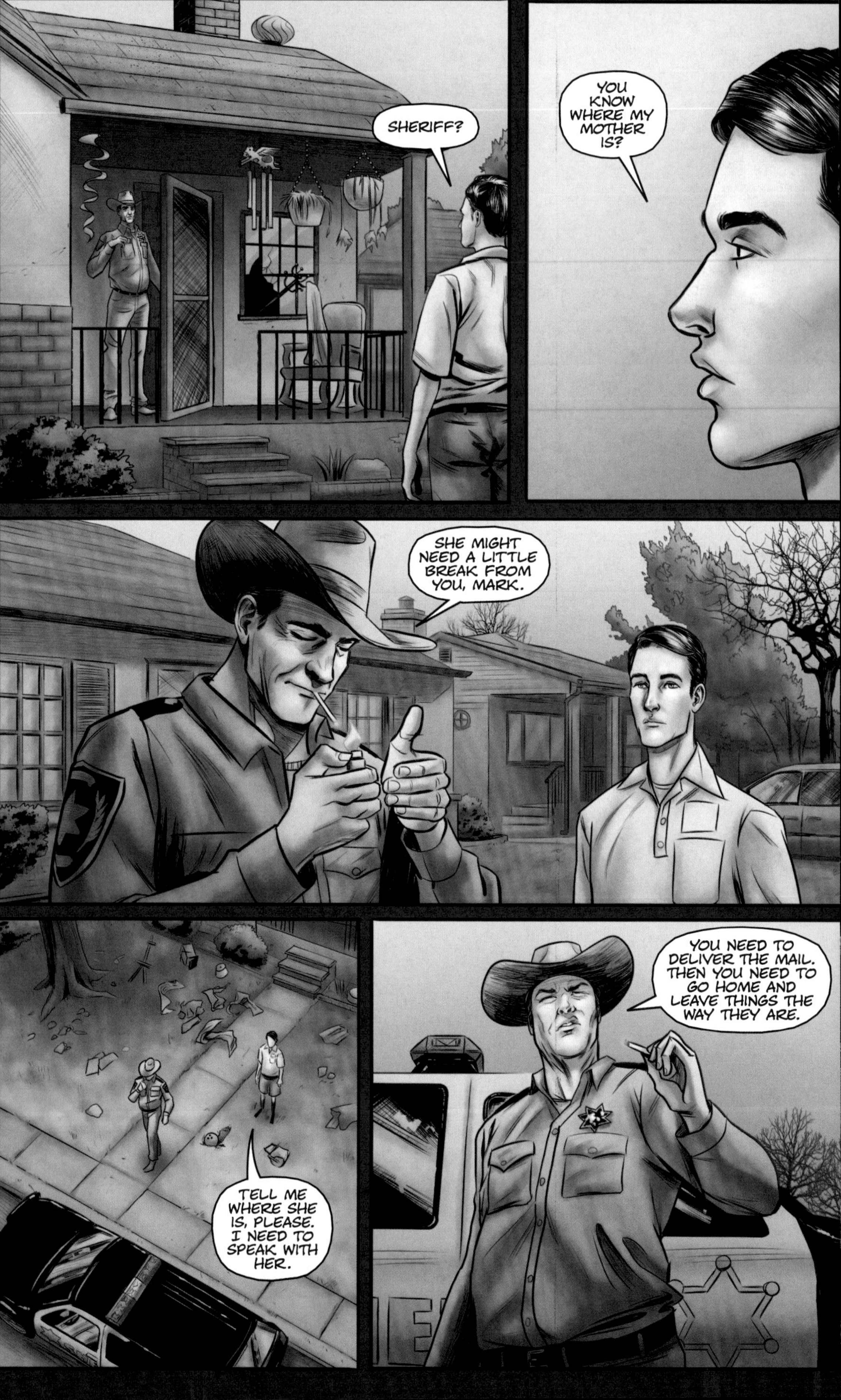
SHERIFF?
YOU KNOW WHERE MY MOTHER IS?
SHE MIGHT NEED A LITTLE BREAK FROM YOU, MARK.
TELL ME WHERE SHE IS, PLEASE. I NEED TO SPEAK WITH HER.
YOU NEED TO DELIVER THE MAIL. THEN YOU NEED TO GO HOME AND LEAVE THINGS THE WAY THEY ARE.

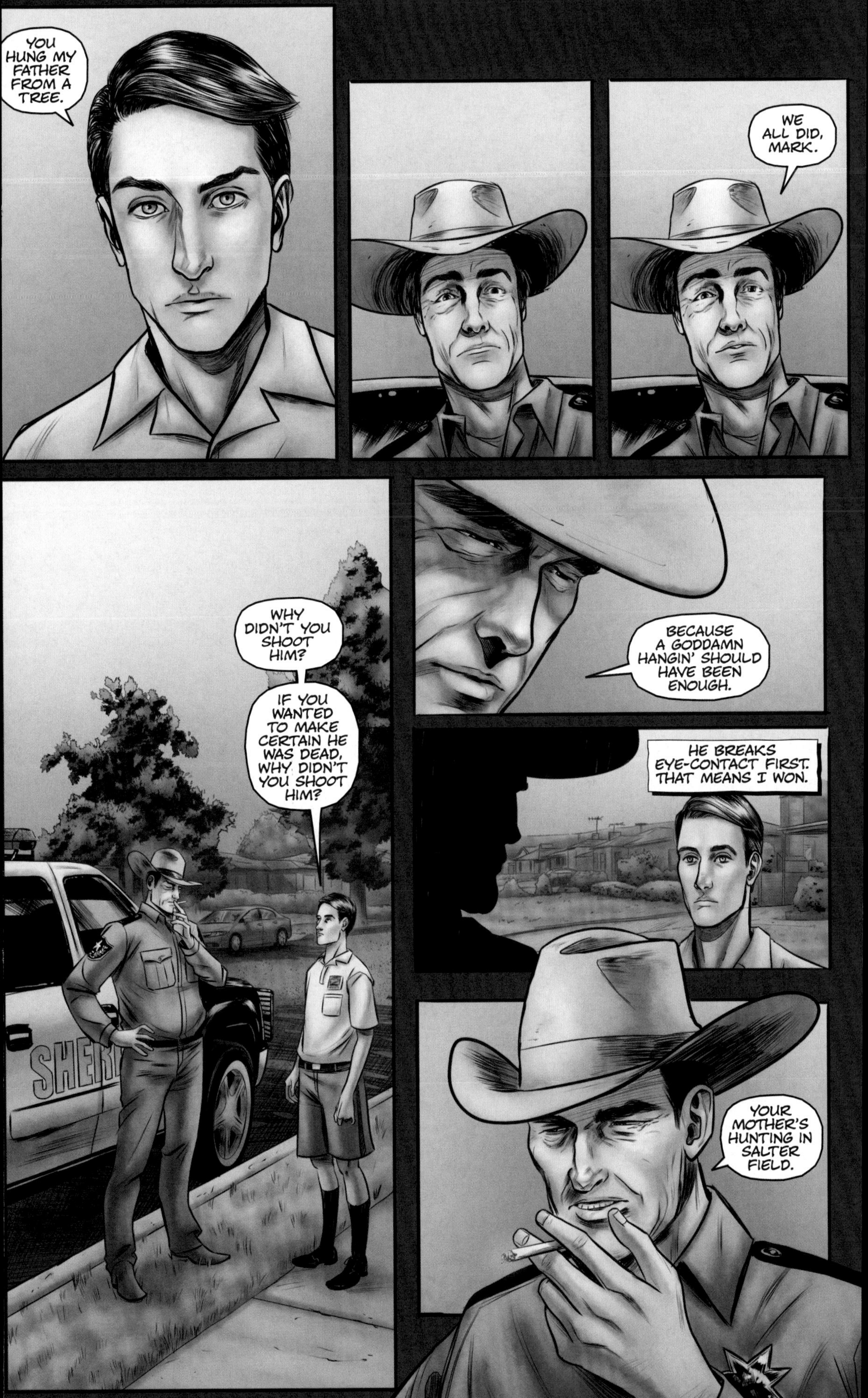
YOU HUNG MY FATHER FROM A TREE.
WE ALL DID, MARK.
WHY DIDN'T YOU SHOOT HIM?
IF YOU WANTED TO MAKE CERTAIN HE WAS DEAD, WHY DIDN'T YOU SHOOT HIM?
BECAUSE A GODDAMN HANGIN' SHOULD HAVE BEEN ENOUGH.
HE BREAKS EYE-CONTACT FIRST. THAT MEANS I WON.
YOUR MOTHER'S HUNTING IN SALTER FIELD.

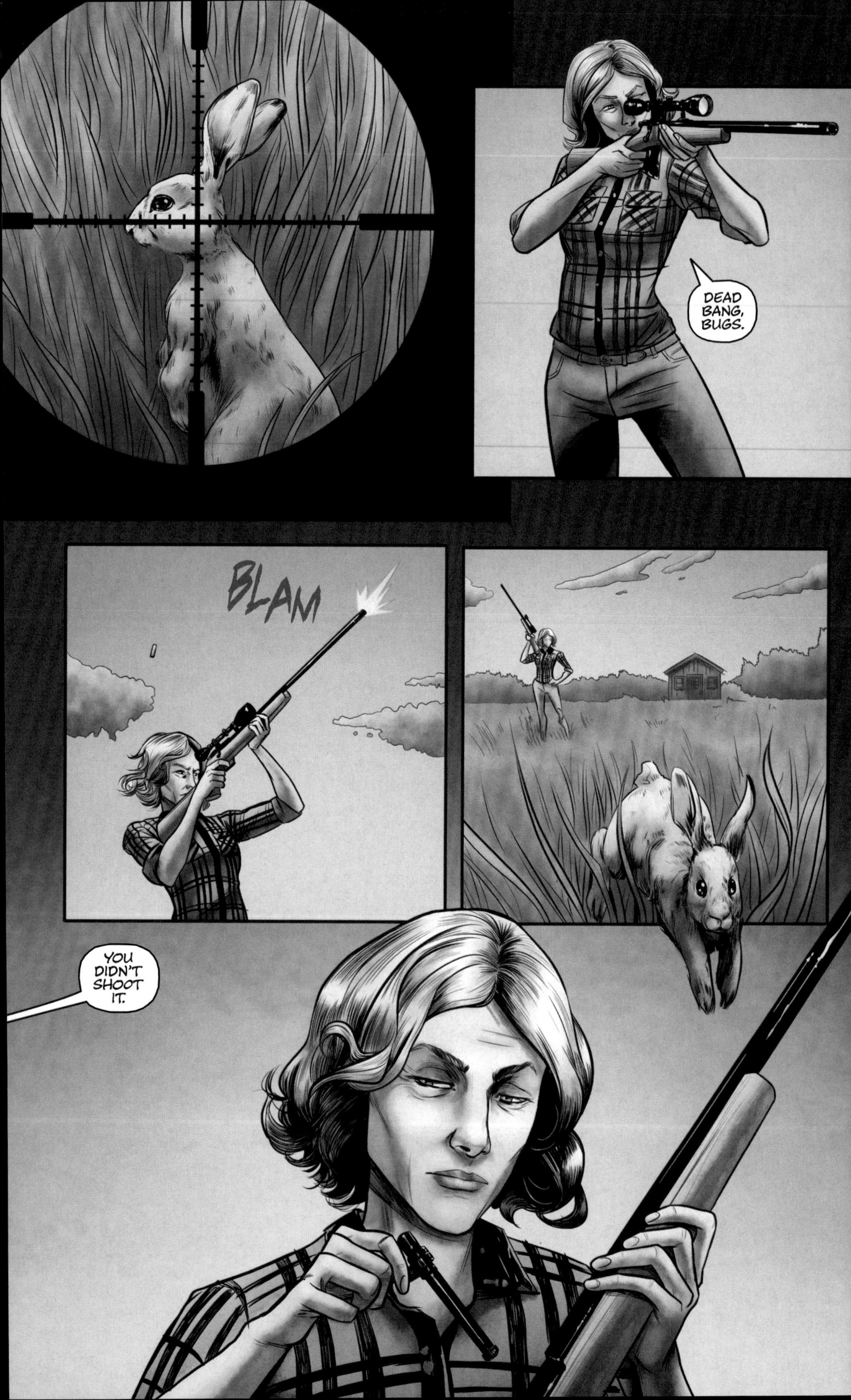
DEAD BANG, BUGS.
BLAM
YOU DIDN'T SHOOT IT.

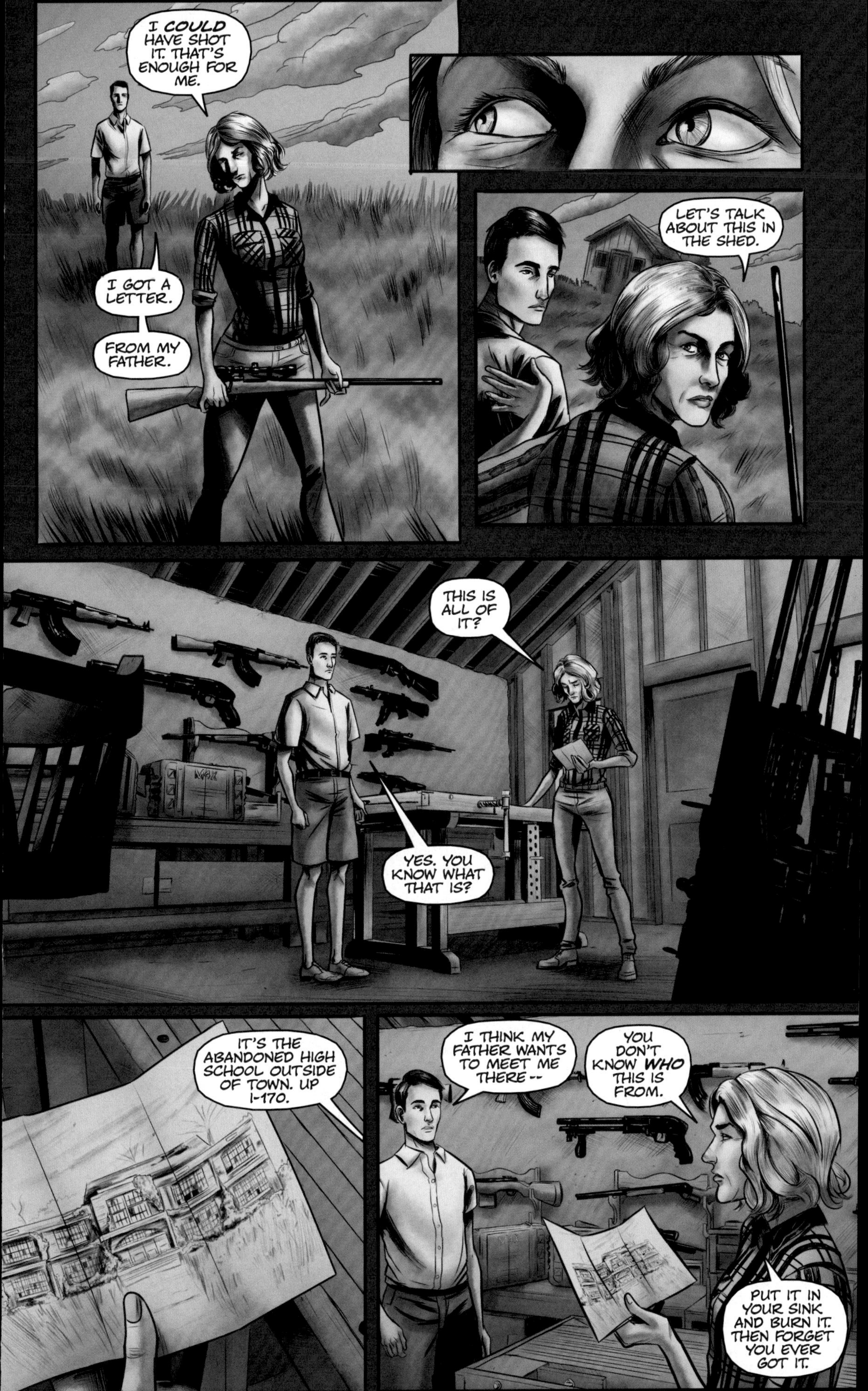
I COULD HAVE SHOT IT. THAT'S ENOUGH FOR ME.
I GOT A LETTER.
FROM MY FATHER.
LET'S TALK ABOUT THIS IN THE SHED.
THIS IS ALL OF IT?
YES. YOU KNOW WHAT THAT IS?
IT'S THE ABANDONED HIGH SCHOOL OUTSIDE OF TOWN. UP I-170.
I THINK MY FATHER WANTS TO MEET ME THERE --
YOU DON'T KNOW WHO THIS IS FROM.
PUT IT IN YOUR SINK AND BURN IT. THEN FORGET YOU EVER GOT IT.

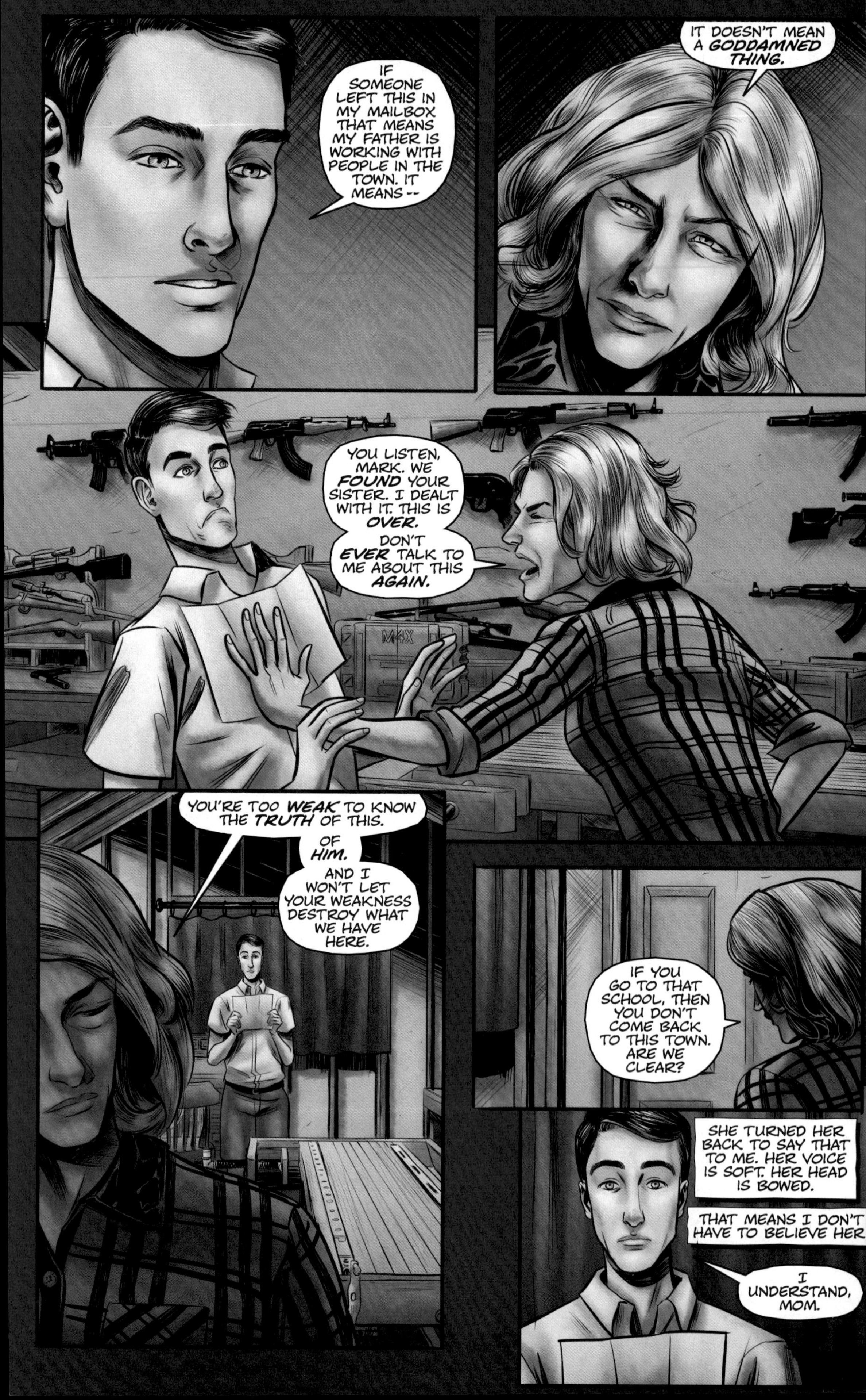
IF SOMEONE LEFT THIS IN MY MAILBOX THAT MEANS MY FATHER IS WORKING WITH PEOPLE IN THE TOWN. IT MEANS --
IT DOESN'T MEAN A GODDAMNED THING.
YOU LISTEN, MARK. WE FOUND YOUR SISTER. I DEALT WITH IT. THIS IS OVER.
DON'T EVER TALK TO ME ABOUT THIS AGAIN.
M4X
YOU'RE TOO WEAK TO KNOW THE TRUTH OF THIS.
OF HIM.
AND I WON'T LET YOUR WEAKNESS DESTROY WHAT WE HAVE HERE.
IF YOU GO TO THAT SCHOOL, THEN YOU DON'T COME BACK TO THIS TOWN. ARE WE CLEAR?
SHE TURNED HER BACK TO SAY THAT TO ME. HER VOICE IS SOFT. HER HEAD IS BOWED.
THAT MEANS I DON'T HAVE TO BELIEVE HER
I UNDERSTAND, MOM.

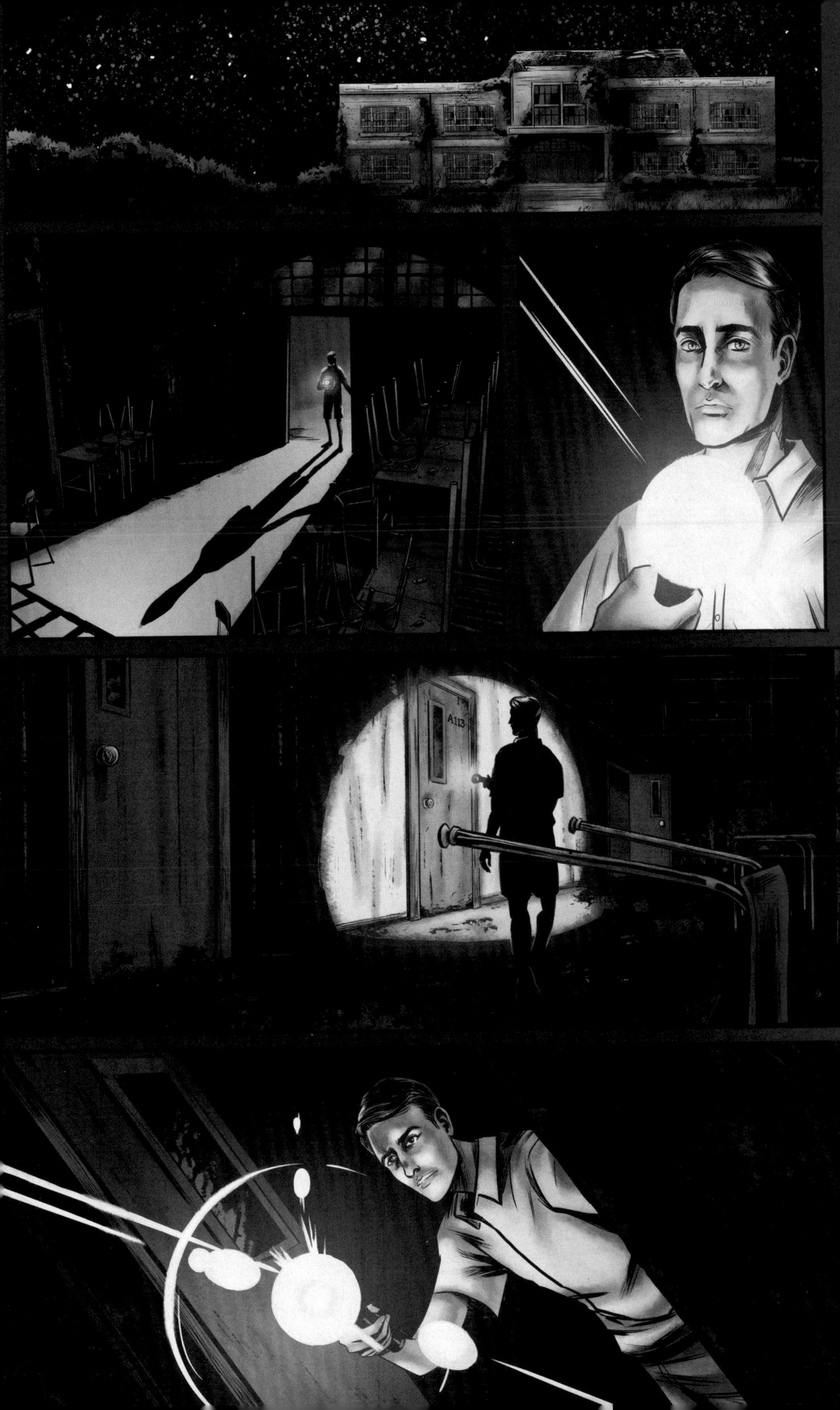
A113

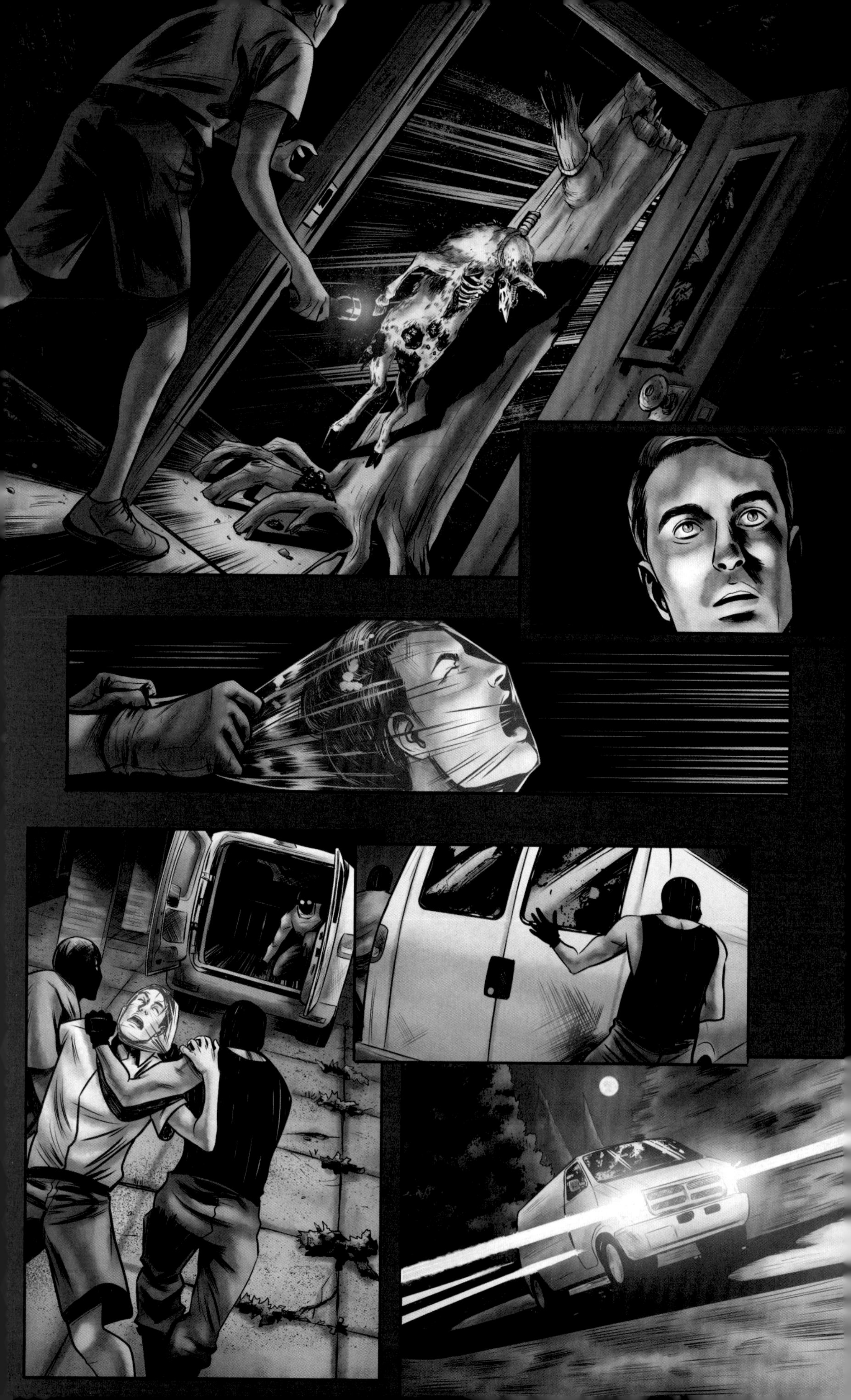

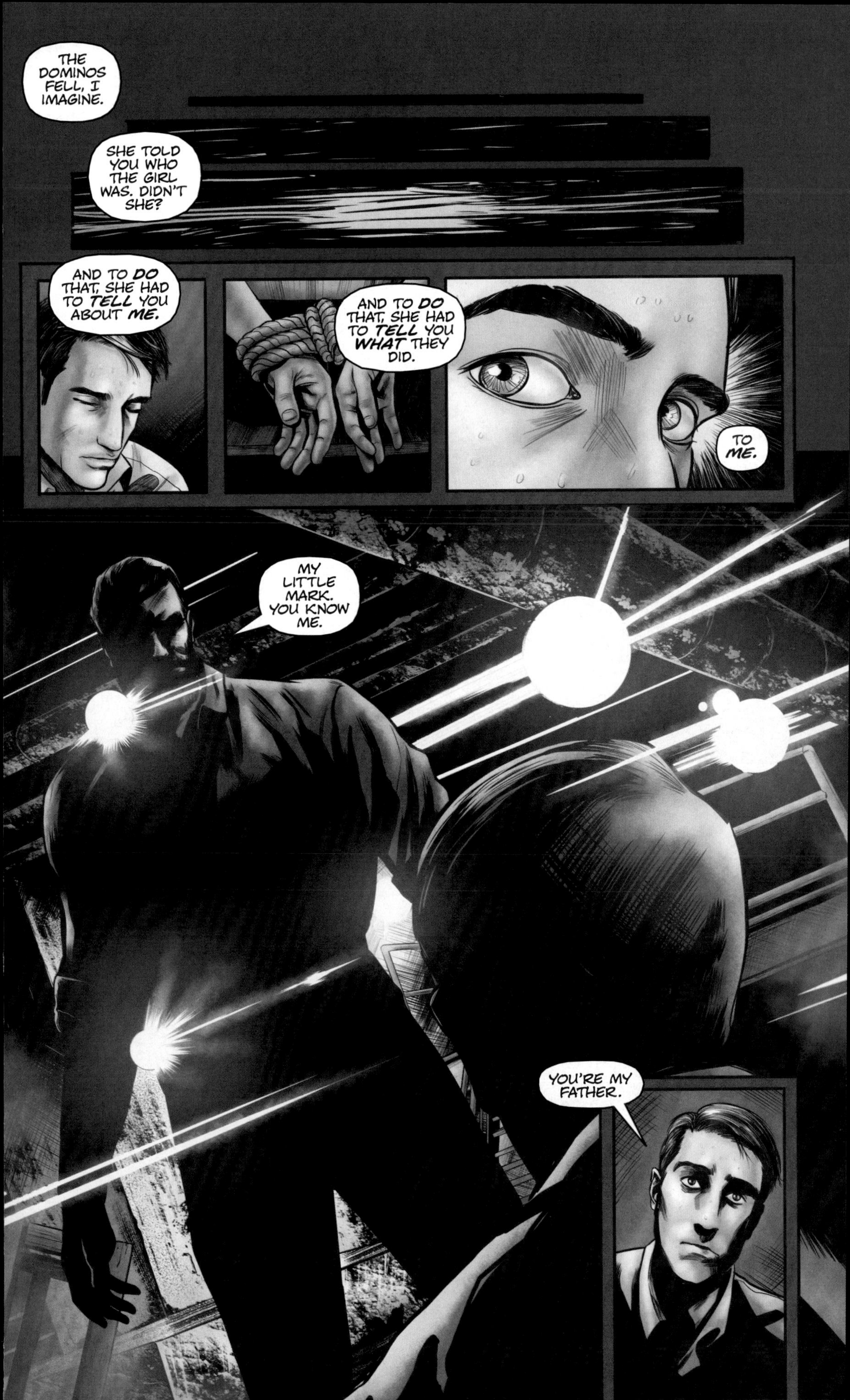
THE DOMINOS FELL, I IMAGINE.
SHE TOLD YOU WHO THE GIRL WAS. DIDN'T SHE?
AND TO DO THAT, SHE HAD TO TELL YOU ABOUT ME.
AND TO DO THAT, SHE HAD TO TELL YOU WHAT THEY DID.
TO ME.
MY LITTLE MARK. YOU KNOW ME.
YOU'RE MY FATHER.

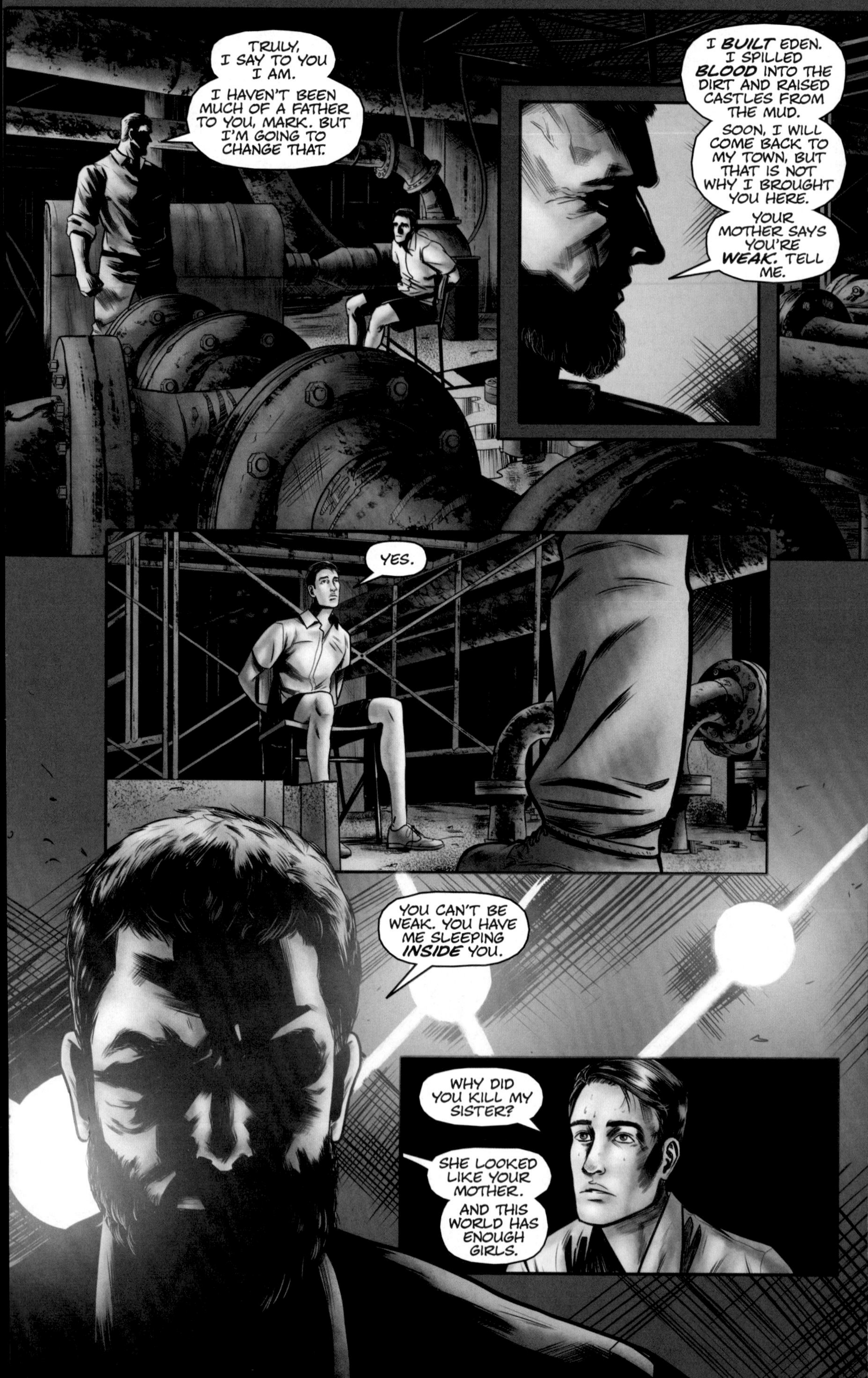
TRULY, I SAY TO YOU I AM.
I HAVEN'T BEEN MUCH OF A FATHER TO YOU, MARK. BUT I'M GOING TO CHANGE THAT.
I BUILT EDEN. I SPILLED BLOOD INTO THE DIRT AND RAISED CASTLES FROM THE MUD.
SOON, I WILL COME BACK TO MY TOWN, BUT THAT IS NOT WHY I BROUGHT YOU HERE.
YOUR MOTHER SAYS YOU'RE WEAK. TELL ME.
YES.
YOU CAN'T BE WEAK. YOU HAVE ME SLEEPING INSIDE YOU.
WHY DID YOU KILL MY SISTER?
SHE LOOKED LIKE YOUR MOTHER.
AND THIS WORLD HAS ENOUGH GIRLS.

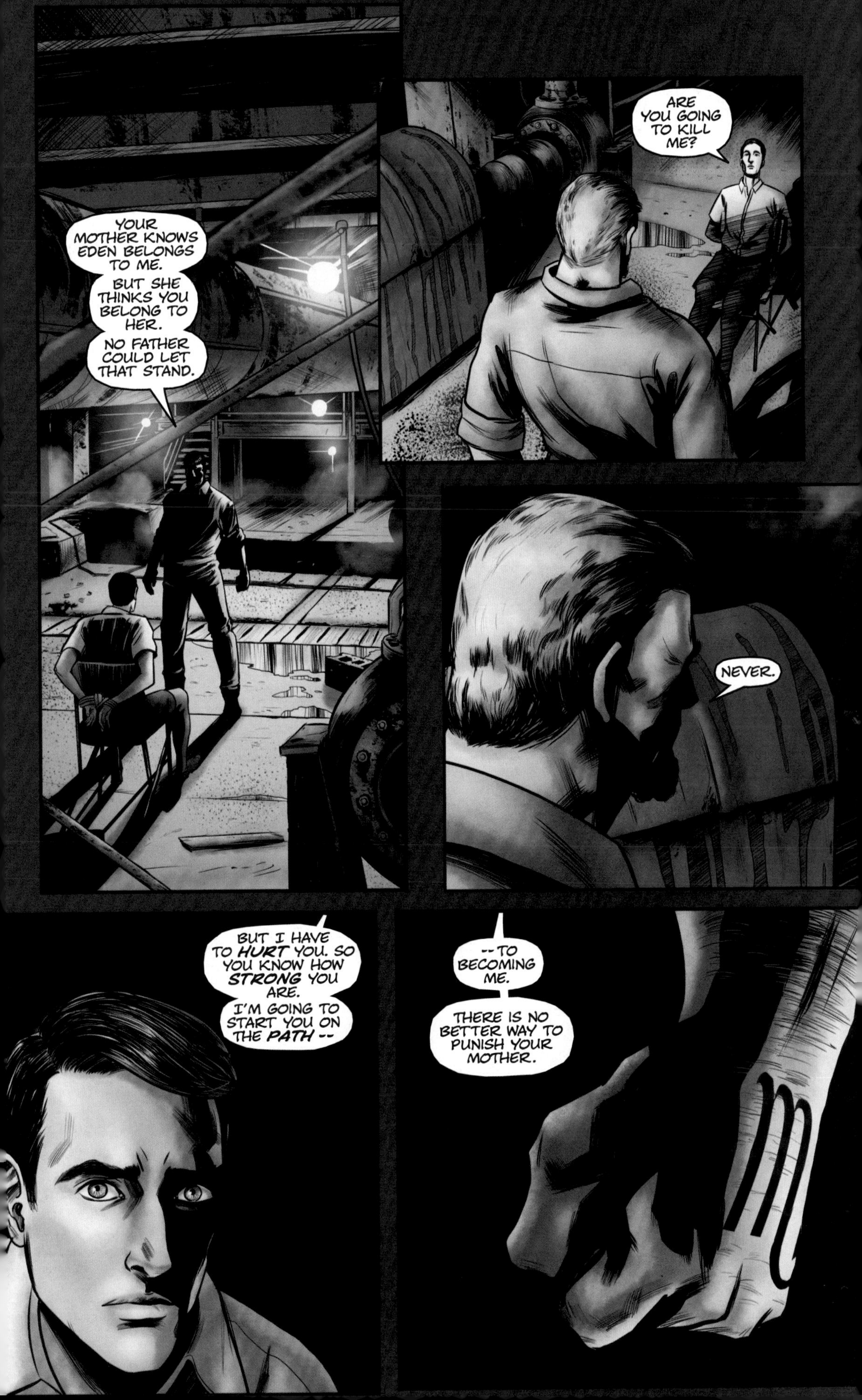
YOUR MOTHER KNOWS EDEN BELONGS TO ME.
BUT SHE THINKS YOU BELONG TO HER.
NO FATHER COULD LET THAT STAND.
ARE YOU GOING TO KILL ME?
NEVER.
BUT I HAVE TO *HURT* YOU. SO YOU KNOW HOW *STRONG* YOU ARE.
I'M GOING TO START YOU ON THE *PATH* --
--TO BECOMING ME.
THERE IS NO BETTER WAY TO PUNISH YOUR MOTHER.

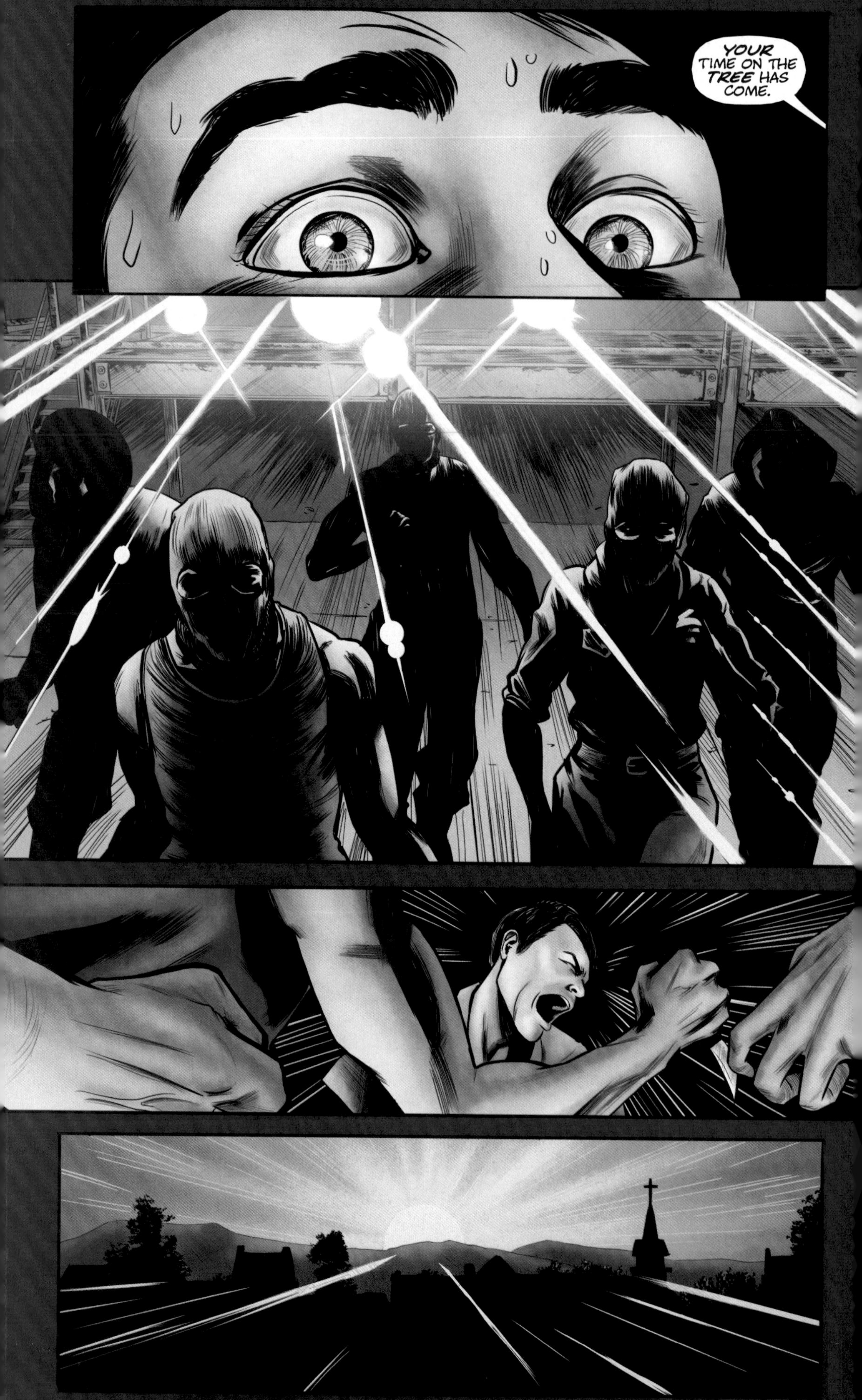
YOUR TIME ON THE TREE HAS COME.

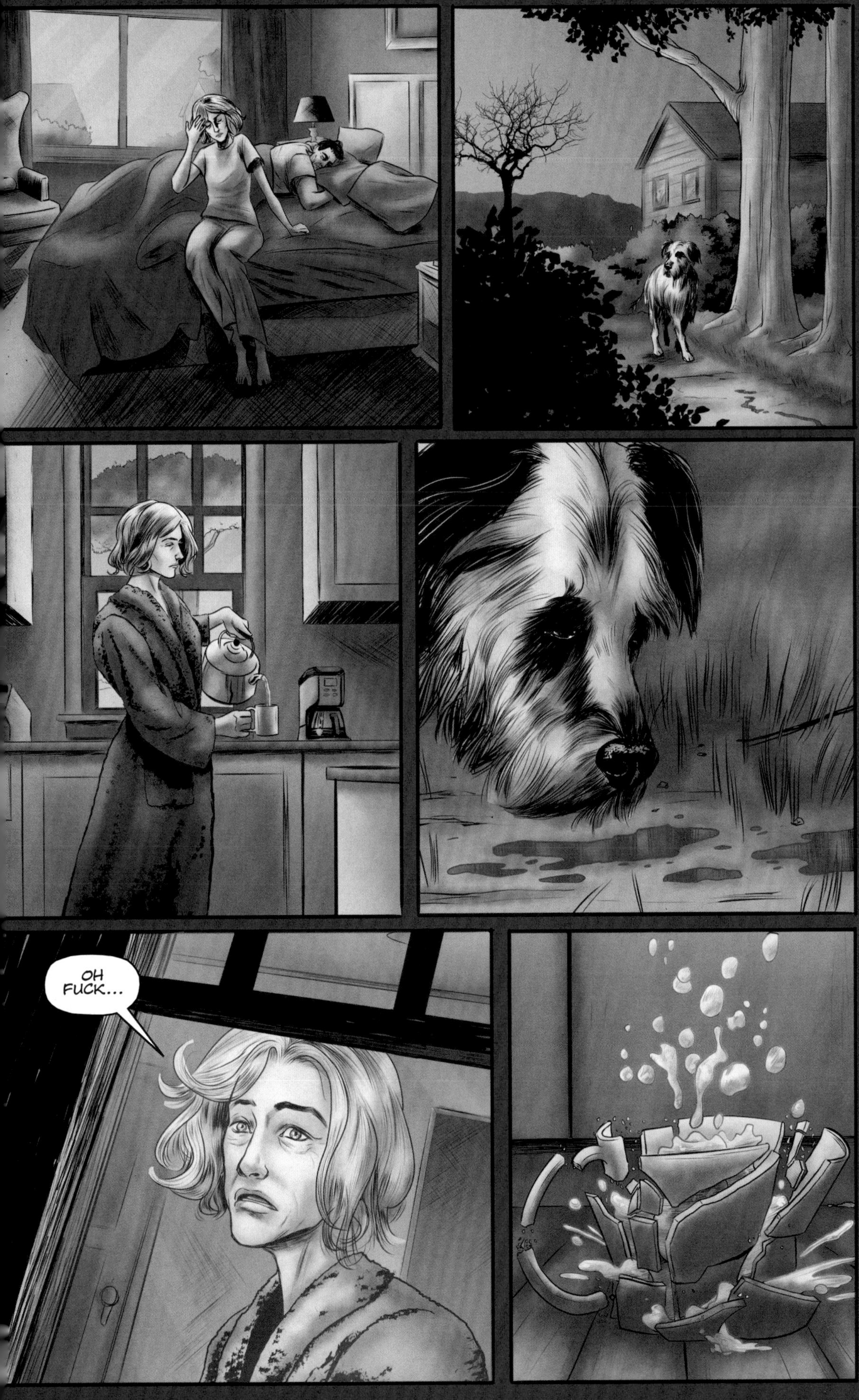
OH FUCK...

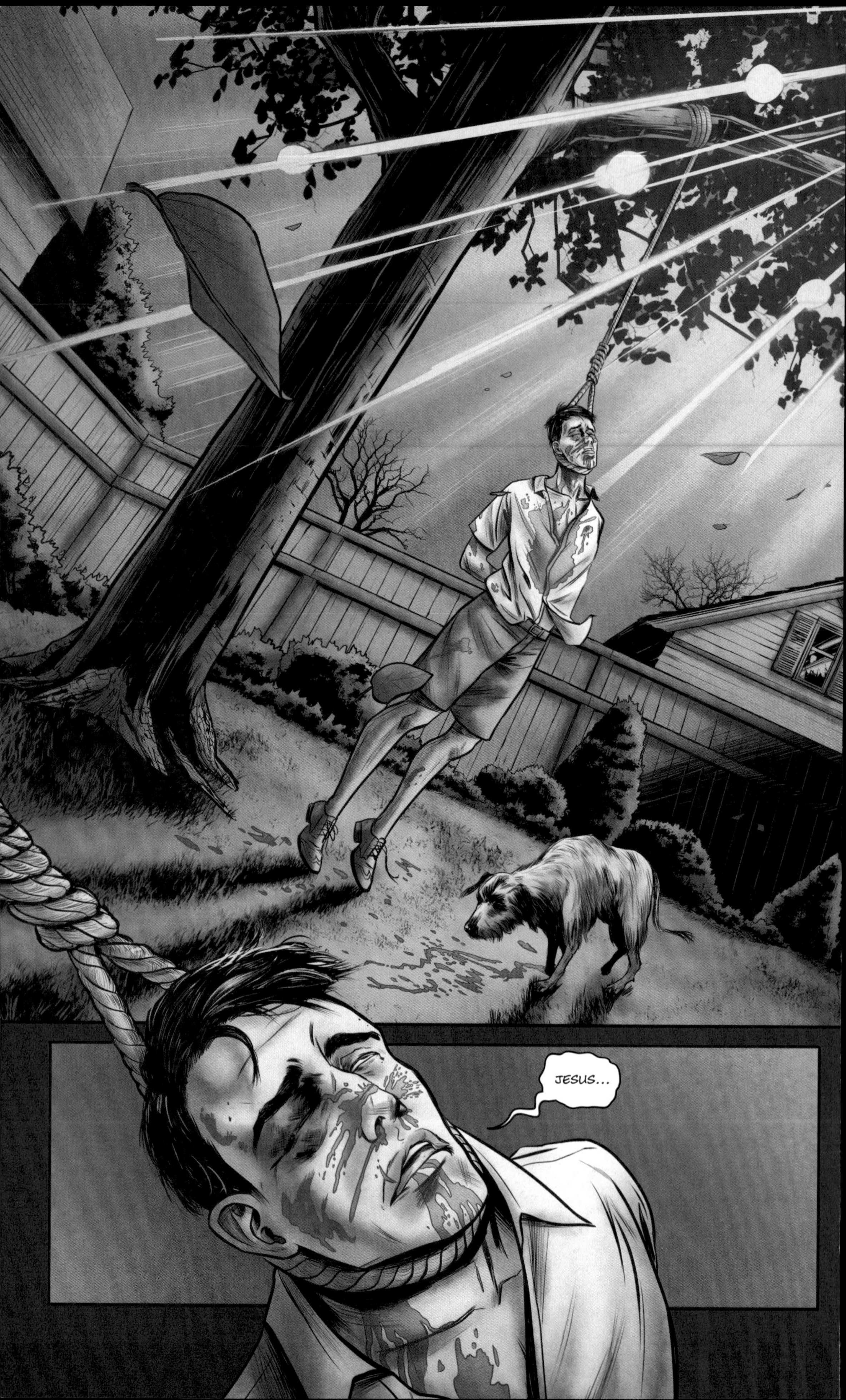
JESUS...

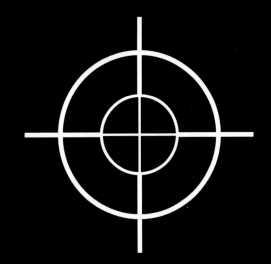

# CHAPTER 4

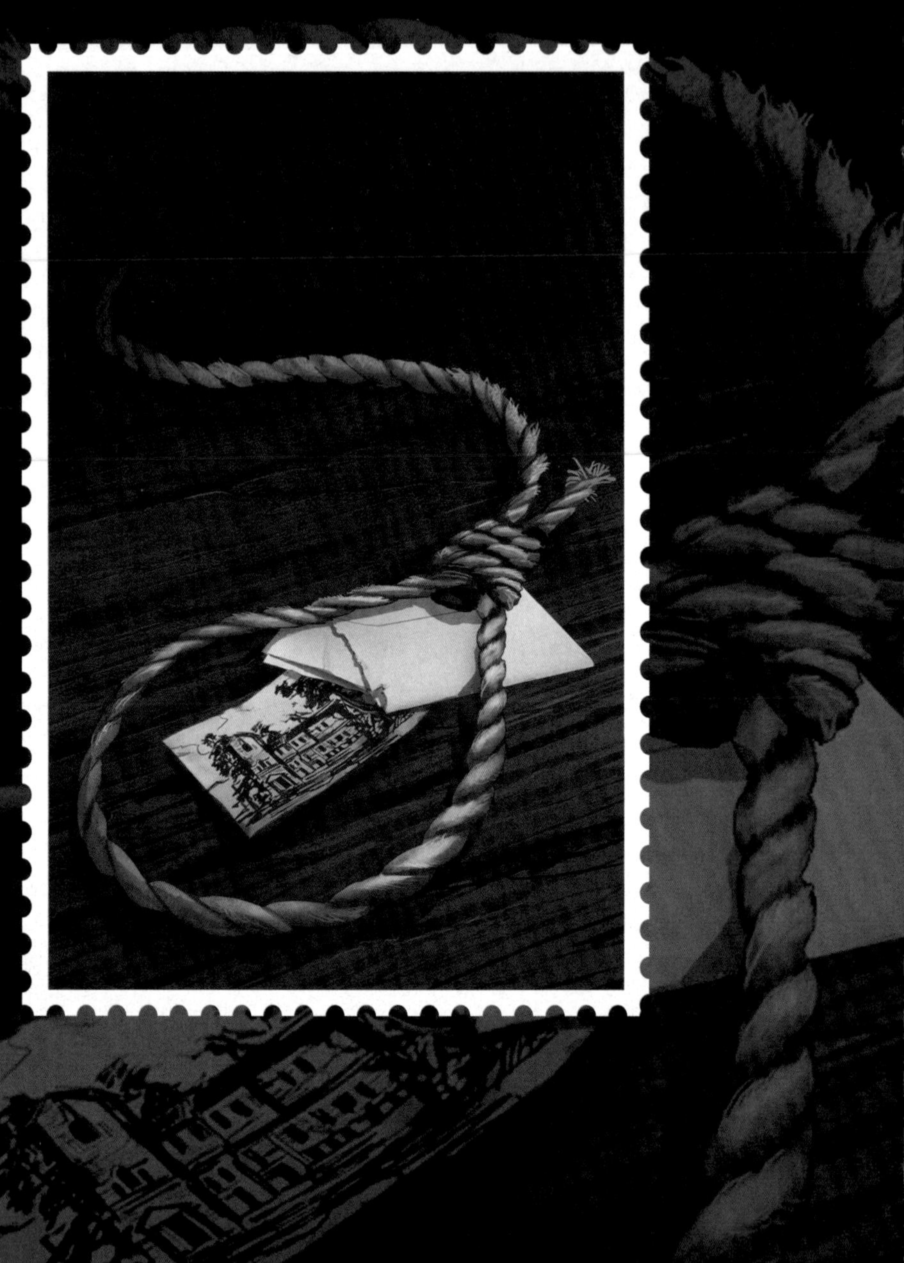

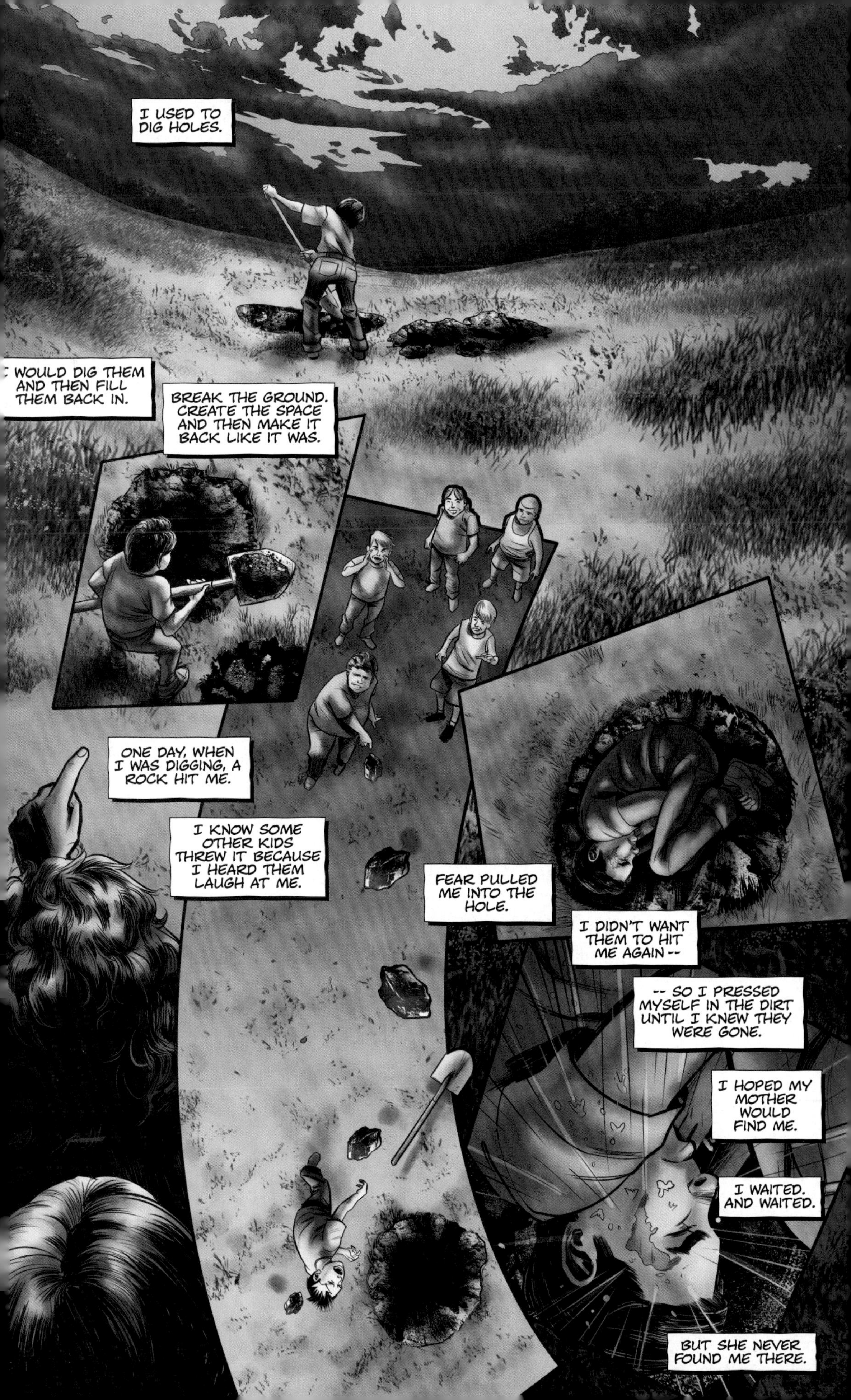
I USED TO DIG HOLES.
I WOULD DIG THEM AND THEN FILL THEM BACK IN.
BREAK THE GROUND. CREATE THE SPACE AND THEN MAKE IT BACK LIKE IT WAS.
ONE DAY, WHEN I WAS DIGGING, A ROCK HIT ME.
I KNOW SOME OTHER KIDS THREW IT BECAUSE I HEARD THEM LAUGH AT ME.
FEAR PULLED ME INTO THE HOLE.
I DIDN'T WANT THEM TO HIT ME AGAIN --
-- SO I PRESSED MYSELF IN THE DIRT UNTIL I KNEW THEY WERE GONE.
I HOPED MY MOTHER WOULD FIND ME.
I WAITED. AND WAITED.
BUT SHE NEVER FOUND ME THERE.

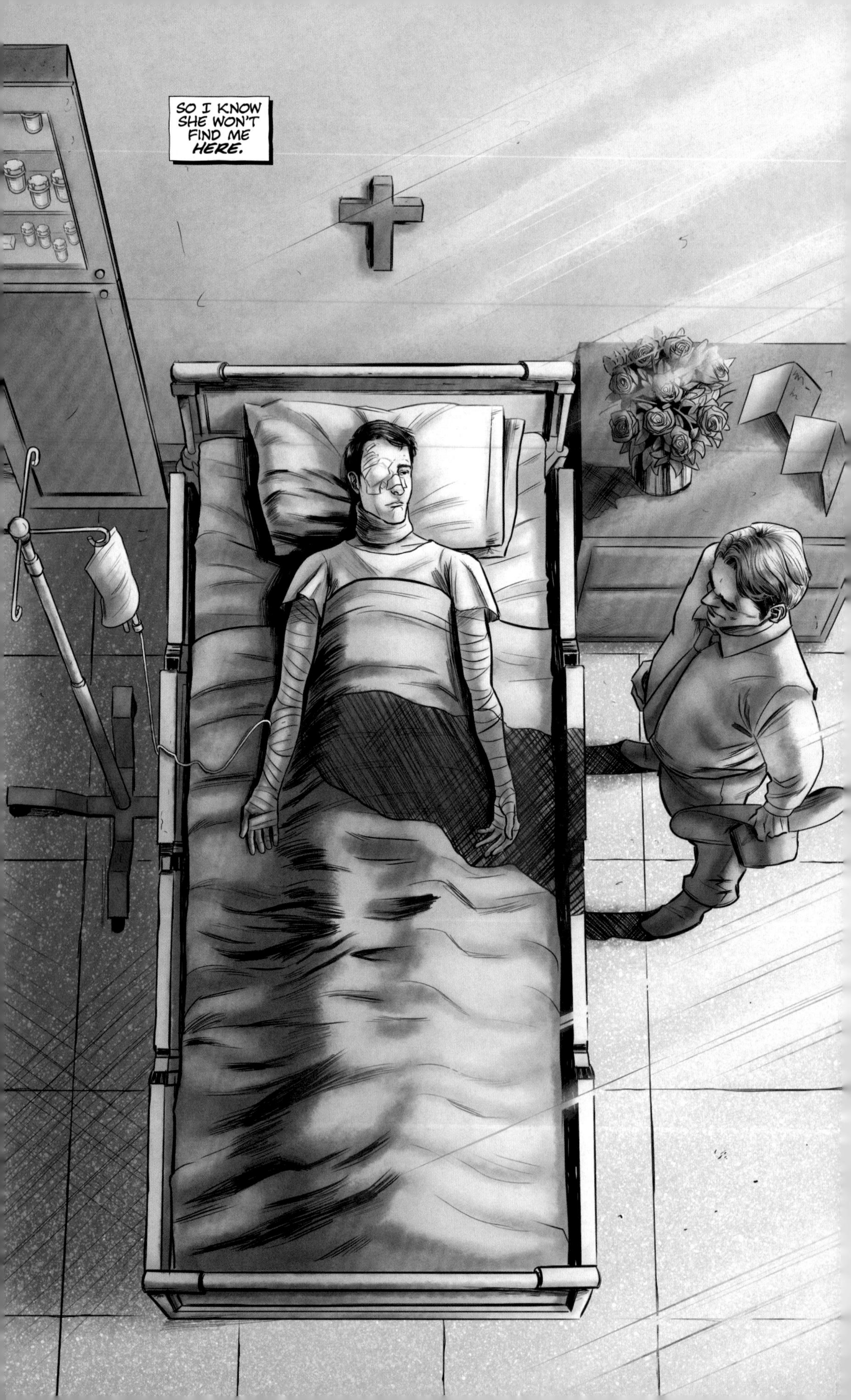
SO I KNOW SHE WON'T FIND ME *HERE.*

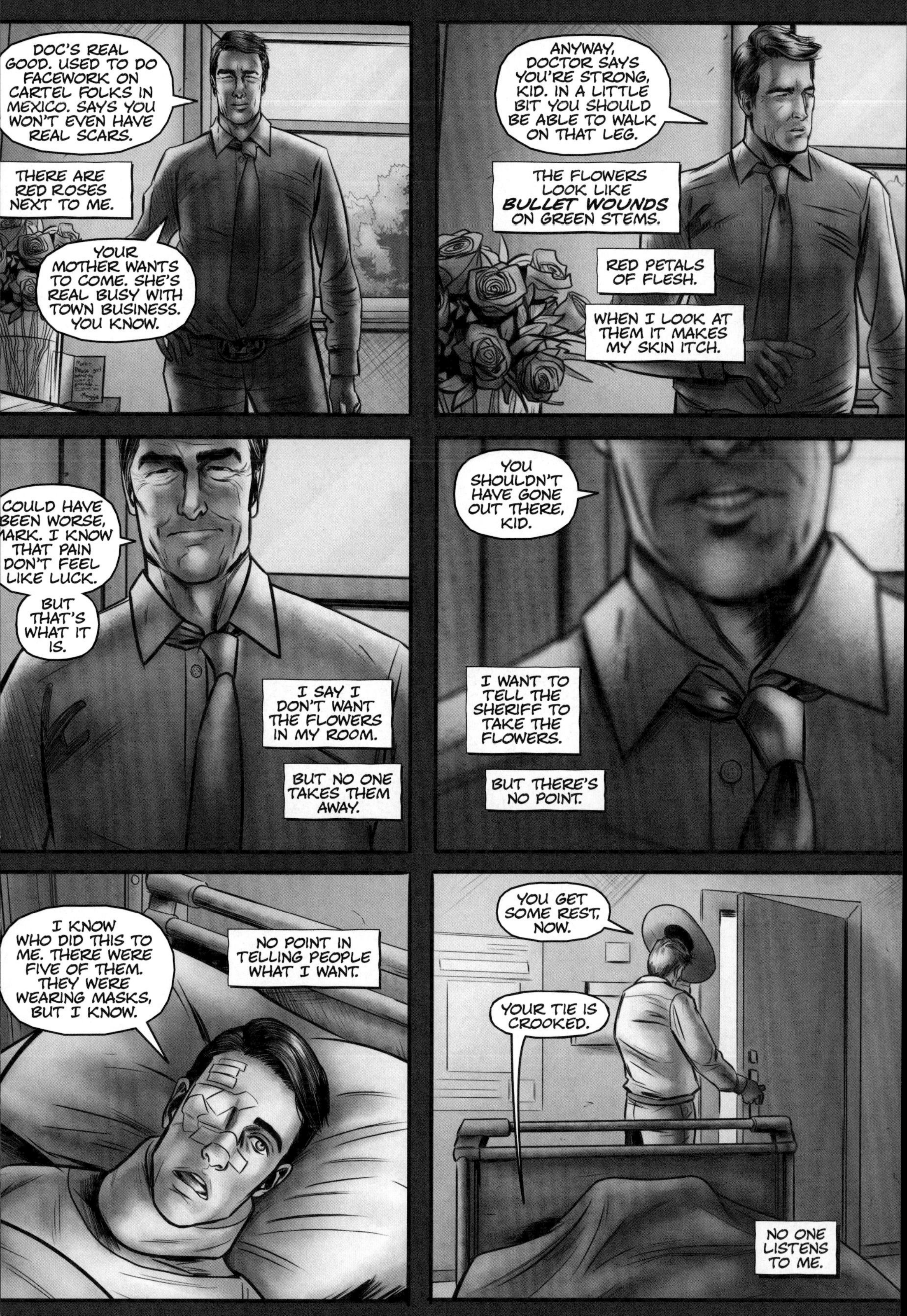
DOC'S REAL GOOD. USED TO DO FACEWORK ON CARTEL FOLKS IN MEXICO. SAYS YOU WON'T EVEN HAVE REAL SCARS.
THERE ARE RED ROSES NEXT TO ME.
YOUR MOTHER WANTS TO COME. SHE'S REAL BUSY WITH TOWN BUSINESS. YOU KNOW.
ANYWAY, DOCTOR SAYS YOU'RE STRONG, KID. IN A LITTLE BIT YOU SHOULD BE ABLE TO WALK ON THAT LEG.
THE FLOWERS LOOK LIKE ***BULLET WOUNDS*** ON GREEN STEMS.
RED PETALS OF FLESH.
WHEN I LOOK AT THEM IT MAKES MY SKIN ITCH.
COULD HAVE BEEN WORSE, MARK. I KNOW THAT PAIN DON'T FEEL LIKE LUCK.
BUT THAT'S WHAT IT IS.
I SAY I DON'T WANT THE FLOWERS IN MY ROOM.
BUT NO ONE TAKES THEM AWAY.
YOU SHOULDN'T HAVE GONE OUT THERE, KID.
I WANT TO TELL THE SHERIFF TO TAKE THE FLOWERS.
BUT THERE'S NO POINT.
I KNOW WHO DID THIS TO ME. THERE WERE FIVE OF THEM. THEY WERE WEARING MASKS, BUT I KNOW.
NO POINT IN TELLING PEOPLE WHAT I WANT.
YOU GET SOME REST, NOW.
YOUR TIE IS CROOKED.
NO ONE LISTENS TO ME.

THE DOCTOR SAID HE'S GOING TO BE FINE?

HE SAYS HE KNOWS WHO DID THIS TO HIM. SOMETHING ABOUT MASKS AND --

I DON'T CARE WHAT HE KNOWS.

YOU AREN'T GOING TO *DO* ANYTHING --

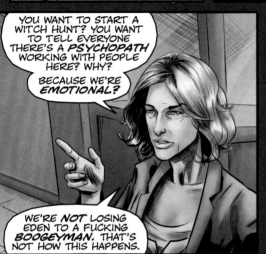

YOU WANT TO START A WITCH HUNT? YOU WANT TO TELL EVERYONE THERE'S A *PSYCHOPATH* WORKING WITH PEOPLE HERE? WHY?

BECAUSE WE'RE *EMOTIONAL?*

WE'RE *NOT* LOSING EDEN TO A FUCKING *BOOGEYMAN.* THAT'S NOT HOW THIS HAPPENS.

THIS IS A DANCE, MAGNUM. HE PUSHES US, WE PUSH BACK AND WE'RE DANCING.

BUT MARK'S FATHER IS PLAYING THE MUSIC, AND THAT MEANS HE'S LEADING. YOU KNOW WHAT HAPPENS IF WE FOLLOW HIM.

SO THEY ALL GET AWAY WITH *TORTURING* YOUR BOY?

IF YOU BELIEVE THAT, THEN YOU DON'T KNOW ME AT ALL.

WE WAIT. WE FIND OUT WHAT WE'RE DEALING WITH.

THEN *WE KILL EVERYTHING.*

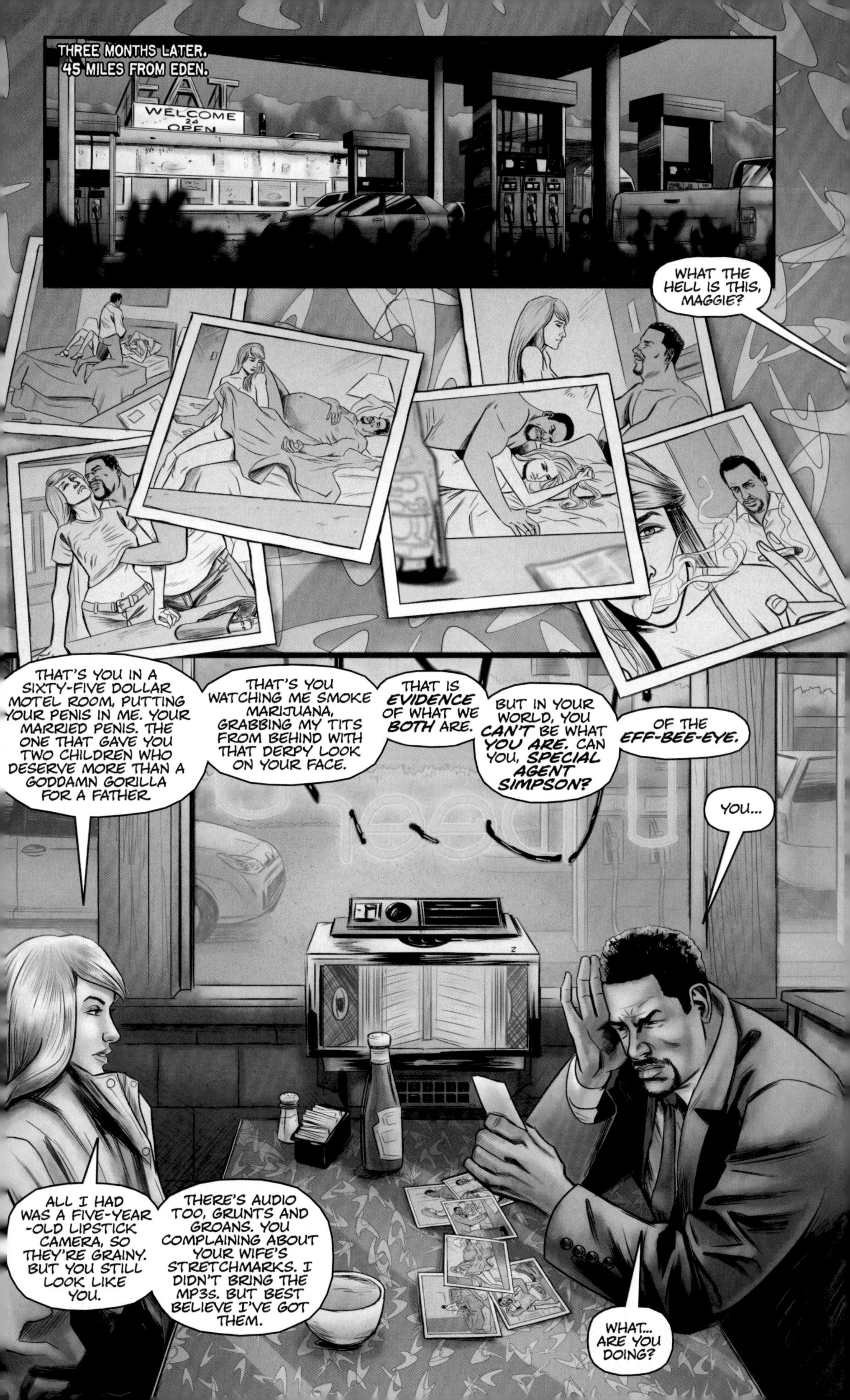
THREE MONTHS LATER. 45 MILES FROM EDEN.
EAT
WELCOME 24 OPEN
WHAT THE HELL IS THIS, MAGGIE?
THAT'S YOU IN A SIXTY-FIVE DOLLAR MOTEL ROOM, PUTTING YOUR PENIS IN ME. YOUR MARRIED PENIS. THE ONE THAT GAVE YOU TWO CHILDREN WHO DESERVE MORE THAN A GODDAMN GORILLA FOR A FATHER
THAT'S YOU WATCHING ME SMOKE MARIJUANA, GRABBING MY TITS FROM BEHIND WITH THAT DERPY LOOK ON YOUR FACE.
THAT IS EVIDENCE OF WHAT WE BOTH ARE.
BUT IN YOUR WORLD, YOU CAN'T BE WHAT YOU ARE. CAN YOU, SPECIAL AGENT SIMPSON?
OF THE EFF-BEE-EYE.
YOU...
ALL I HAD WAS A FIVE-YEAR-OLD LIPSTICK CAMERA, SO THEY'RE GRAINY. BUT YOU STILL LOOK LIKE YOU.
THERE'S AUDIO TOO, GRUNTS AND GROANS. YOU COMPLAINING ABOUT YOUR WIFE'S STRETCHMARKS. I DIDN'T BRING THE MP3S. BUT BEST BELIEVE I'VE GOT THEM.
WHAT... ARE YOU DOING?

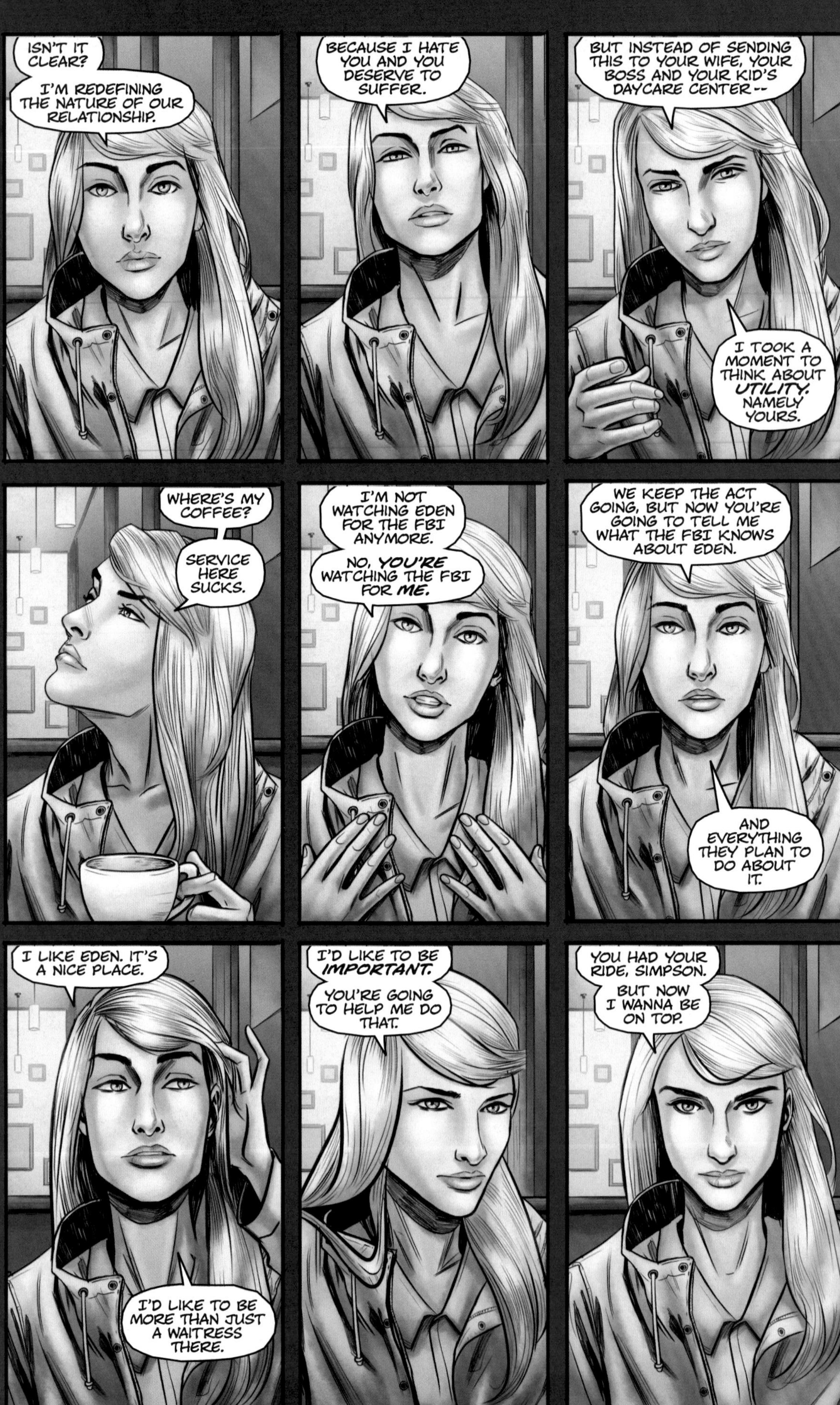
ISN'T IT CLEAR?
I'M REDEFINING THE NATURE OF OUR RELATIONSHIP.
BECAUSE I HATE YOU AND YOU DESERVE TO SUFFER.
BUT INSTEAD OF SENDING THIS TO YOUR WIFE, YOUR BOSS AND YOUR KID'S DAYCARE CENTER--
I TOOK A MOMENT TO THINK ABOUT *UTILITY.* NAMELY YOURS.
WHERE'S MY COFFEE?
SERVICE HERE SUCKS.
I'M NOT WATCHING EDEN FOR THE FBI ANYMORE.
NO, ***YOU'RE*** WATCHING THE FBI FOR ***ME.***
WE KEEP THE ACT GOING, BUT NOW YOU'RE GOING TO TELL ME WHAT THE FBI KNOWS ABOUT EDEN.
AND EVERYTHING THEY PLAN TO DO ABOUT IT.
I LIKE EDEN. IT'S A NICE PLACE.
I'D LIKE TO BE MORE THAN JUST A WAITRESS THERE.
I'D LIKE TO BE ***IMPORTANT.***
YOU'RE GOING TO HELP ME DO THAT.
YOU HAD YOUR RIDE, SIMPSON.
BUT NOW I WANNA BE ON TOP.

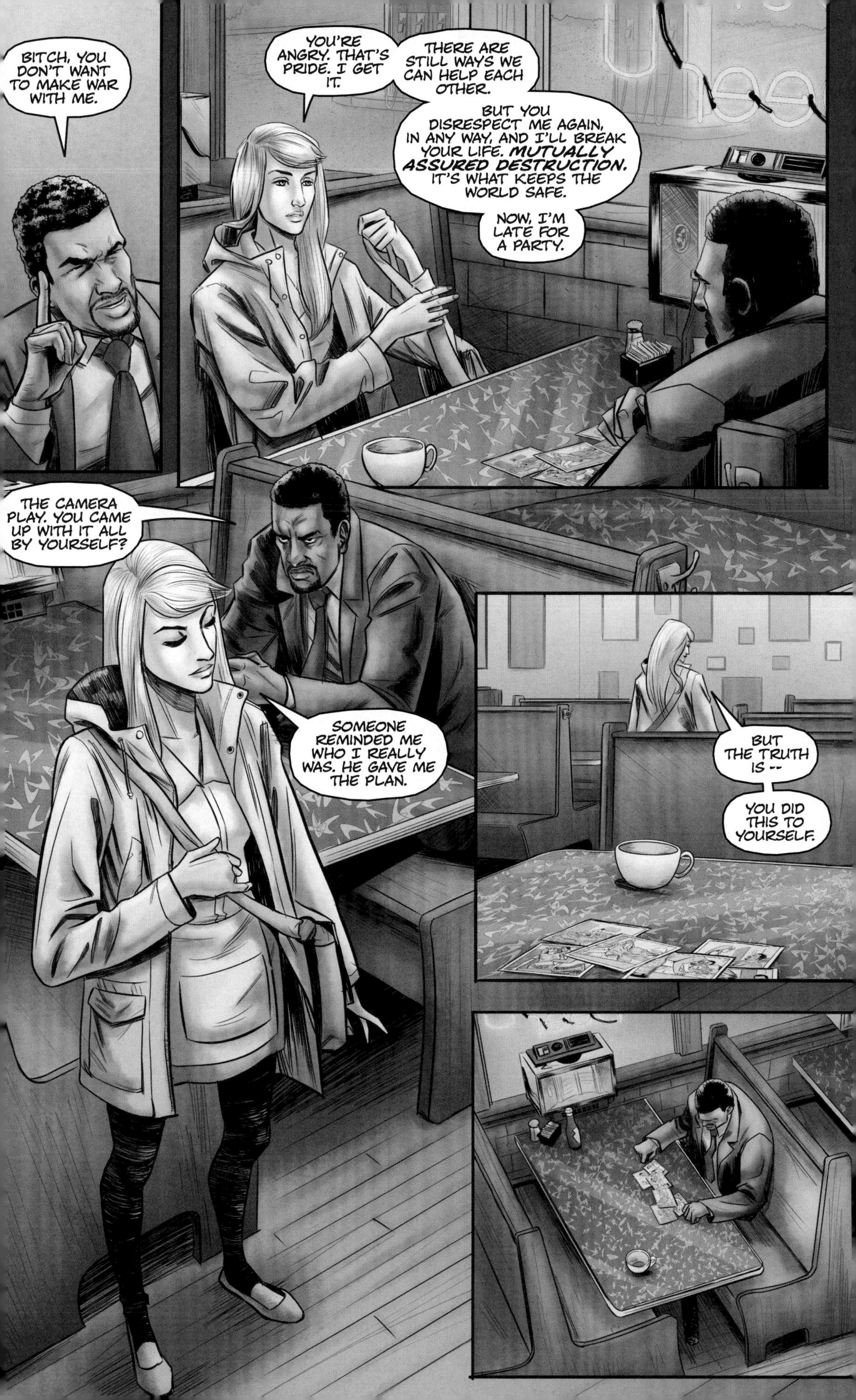

BITCH, YOU DON'T WANT TO MAKE WAR WITH ME.
YOU'RE ANGRY. THAT'S PRIDE. I GET IT.
THERE ARE STILL WAYS WE CAN HELP EACH OTHER.
BUT YOU DISRESPECT ME AGAIN, IN ANY WAY, AND I'LL BREAK YOUR LIFE. MUTUALLY ASSURED DESTRUCTION. IT'S WHAT KEEPS THE WORLD SAFE.
NOW, I'M LATE FOR A PARTY.
THE CAMERA PLAY. YOU CAME UP WITH IT ALL BY YOURSELF?
SOMEONE REMINDED ME WHO I REALLY WAS. HE GAVE ME THE PLAN.
BUT THE TRUTH IS --
YOU DID THIS TO YOURSELF.

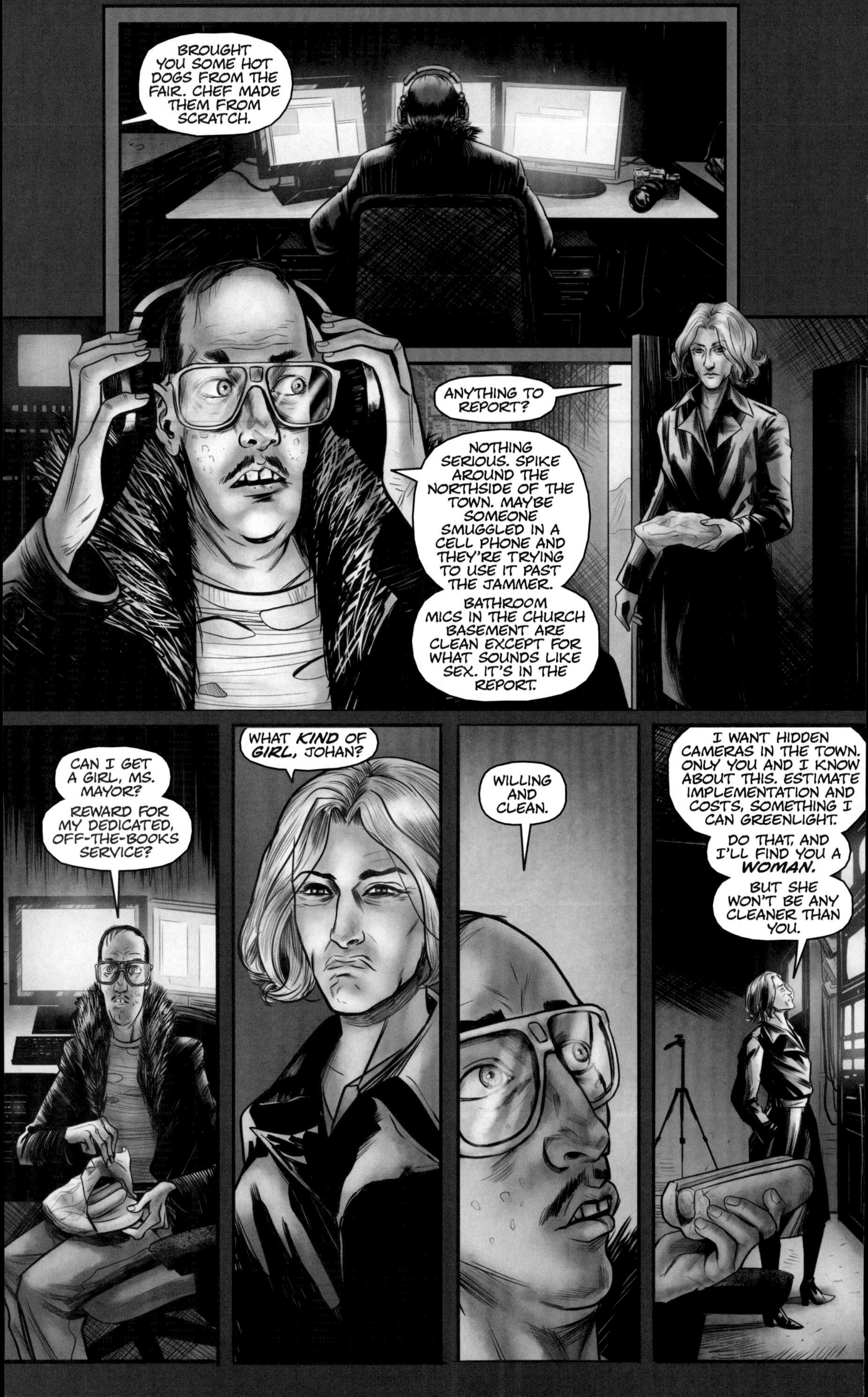
BROUGHT YOU SOME HOT DOGS FROM THE FAIR. CHEF MADE THEM FROM SCRATCH.
ANYTHING TO REPORT?
NOTHING SERIOUS. SPIKE AROUND THE NORTHSIDE OF THE TOWN. MAYBE SOMEONE SMUGGLED IN A CELL PHONE AND THEY'RE TRYING TO USE IT PAST THE JAMMER.
BATHROOM MICS IN THE CHURCH BASEMENT ARE CLEAN EXCEPT FOR WHAT SOUNDS LIKE SEX. IT'S IN THE REPORT.
CAN I GET A GIRL, MS. MAYOR?
REWARD FOR MY DEDICATED, OFF-THE-BOOKS SERVICE?
WHAT KIND OF GIRL, JOHAN?
WILLING AND CLEAN.
I WANT HIDDEN CAMERAS IN THE TOWN. ONLY YOU AND I KNOW ABOUT THIS. ESTIMATE IMPLEMENTATION AND COSTS, SOMETHING I CAN GREENLIGHT.
DO THAT, AND I'LL FIND YOU A WOMAN.
BUT SHE WON'T BE ANY CLEANER THAN YOU.

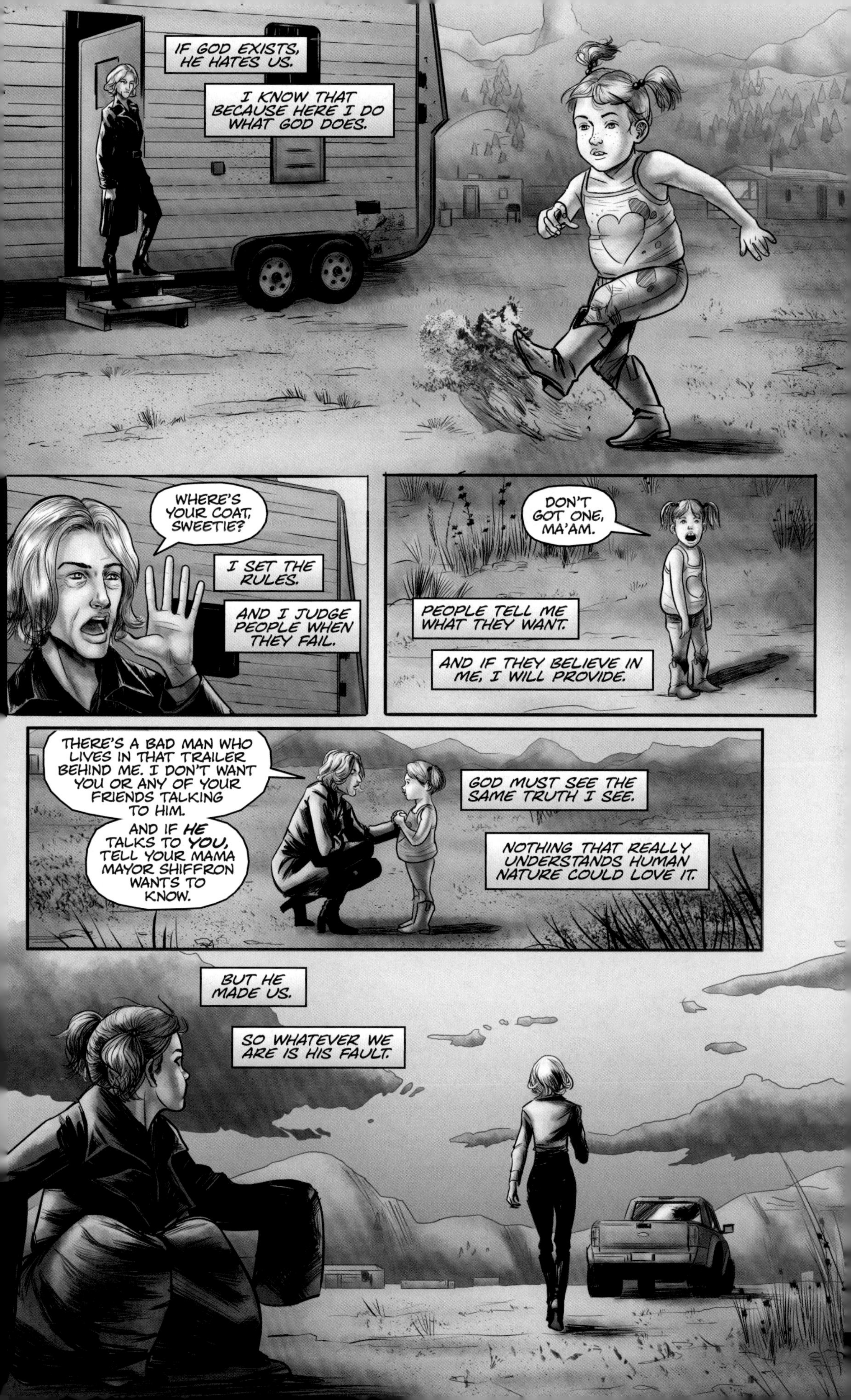
IF GOD EXISTS, HE HATES US.
I KNOW THAT BECAUSE HERE I DO WHAT GOD DOES.
WHERE'S YOUR COAT, SWEETIE?
I SET THE RULES.
AND I JUDGE PEOPLE WHEN THEY FAIL.
DON'T GOT ONE, MA'AM.
PEOPLE TELL ME WHAT THEY WANT.
AND IF THEY BELIEVE IN ME, I WILL PROVIDE.
THERE'S A BAD MAN WHO LIVES IN THAT TRAILER BEHIND ME. I DON'T WANT YOU OR ANY OF YOUR FRIENDS TALKING TO HIM.
AND IF HE TALKS TO YOU, TELL YOUR MAMA MAYOR SHIFFRON WANTS TO KNOW.
GOD MUST SEE THE SAME TRUTH I SEE.
NOTHING THAT REALLY UNDERSTANDS HUMAN NATURE COULD LOVE IT.
BUT HE MADE US.
SO WHATEVER WE ARE IS HIS FAULT.

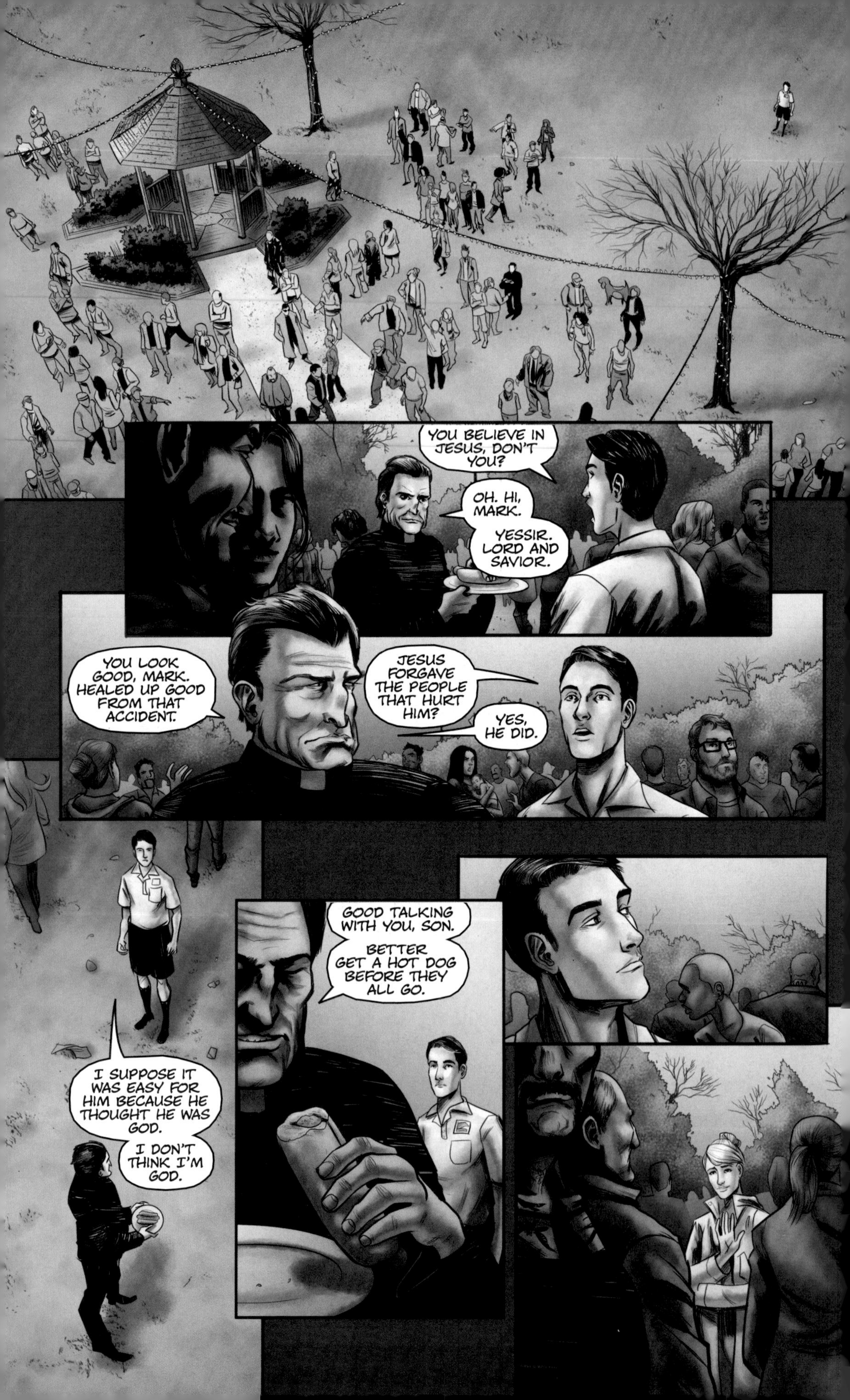
YOU BELIEVE IN JESUS, DON'T YOU?
OH. HI, MARK.
YESSIR. LORD AND SAVIOR.
YOU LOOK GOOD, MARK. HEALED UP GOOD FROM THAT ACCIDENT.
JESUS FORGAVE THE PEOPLE THAT HURT HIM?
YES, HE DID.
I SUPPOSE IT WAS EASY FOR HIM BECAUSE HE THOUGHT HE WAS GOD.
I DON'T THINK I'M GOD.
GOOD TALKING WITH YOU, SON.
BETTER GET A HOT DOG BEFORE THEY ALL GO.

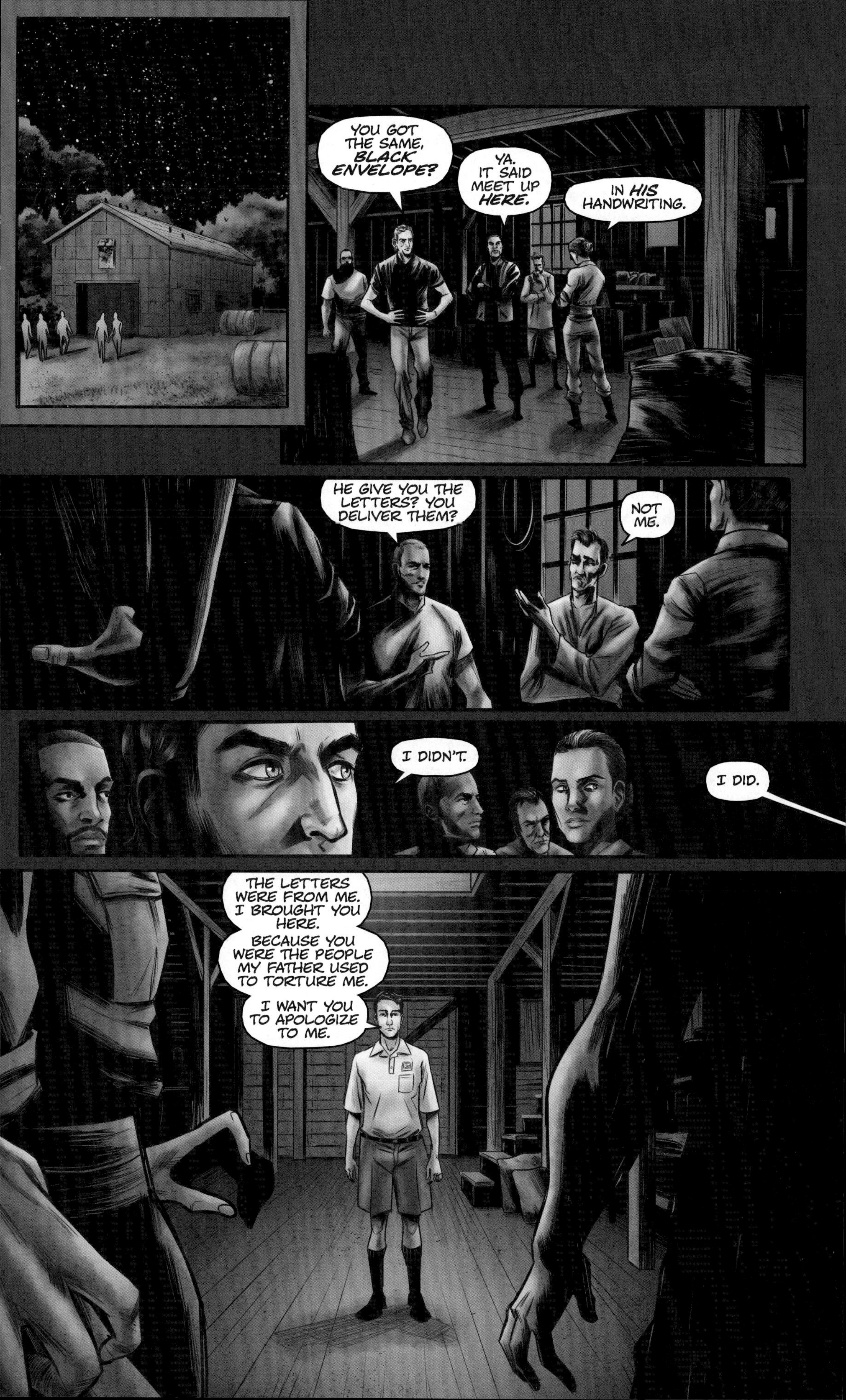
YOU GOT THE SAME, BLACK ENVELOPE?
YA. IT SAID MEET UP HERE.
IN HIS HANDWRITING.
HE GIVE YOU THE LETTERS? YOU DELIVER THEM?
NOT ME.
I DIDN'T.
I DID.
THE LETTERS WERE FROM ME. I BROUGHT YOU HERE.
BECAUSE YOU WERE THE PEOPLE MY FATHER USED TO TORTURE ME.
I WANT YOU TO APOLOGIZE TO ME.

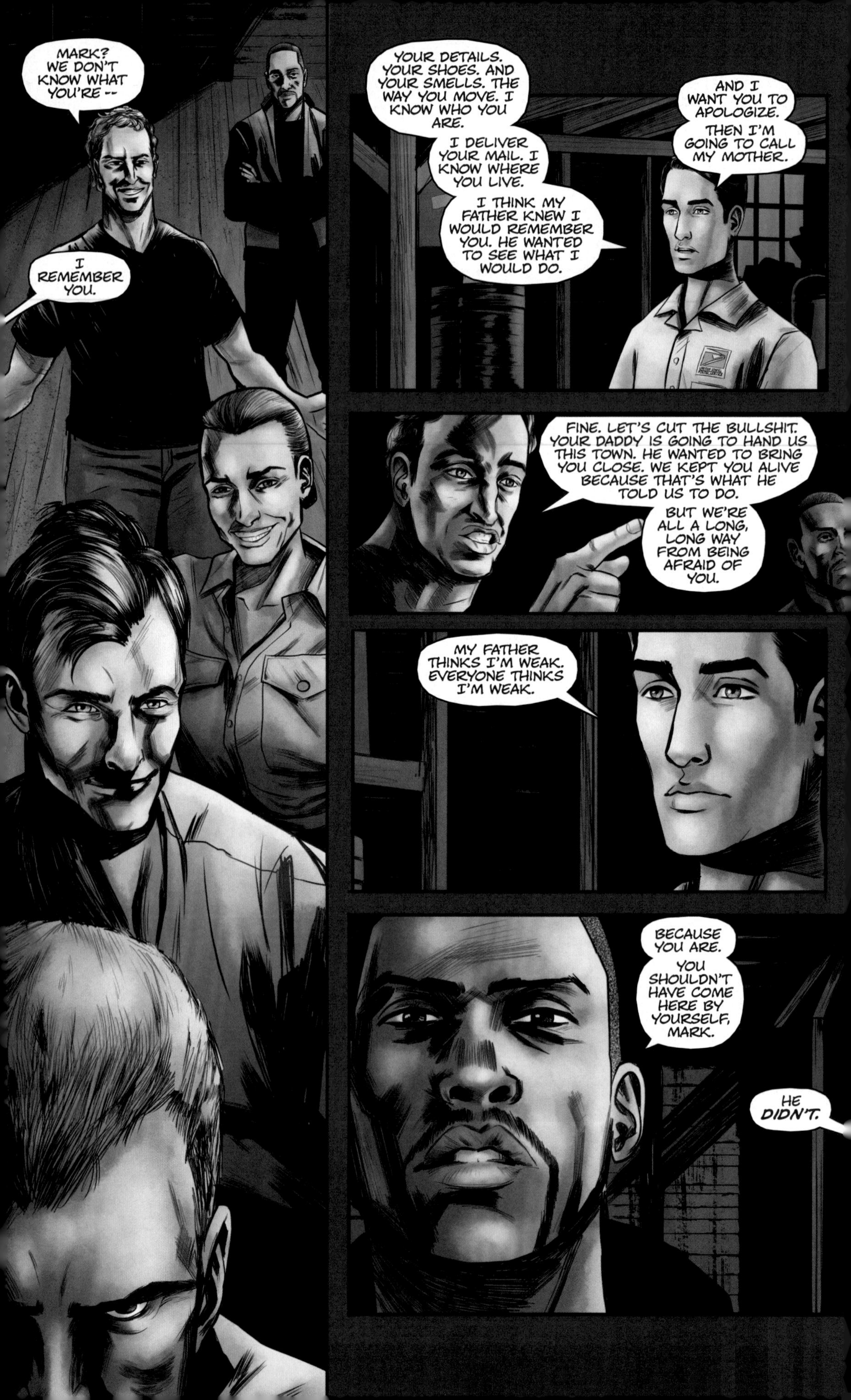
MARK? WE DON'T KNOW WHAT YOU'RE --
I REMEMBER YOU.
YOUR DETAILS. YOUR SHOES. AND YOUR SMELLS. THE WAY YOU MOVE. I KNOW WHO YOU ARE.
I DELIVER YOUR MAIL. I KNOW WHERE YOU LIVE.
I THINK MY FATHER KNEW I WOULD REMEMBER YOU. HE WANTED TO SEE WHAT I WOULD DO.
AND I WANT YOU TO APOLOGIZE.
THEN I'M GOING TO CALL MY MOTHER.
FINE. LET'S CUT THE BULLSHIT. YOUR DADDY IS GOING TO HAND US THIS TOWN. HE WANTED TO BRING YOU CLOSE. WE KEPT YOU ALIVE BECAUSE THAT'S WHAT HE TOLD US TO DO.
BUT WE'RE ALL A LONG, LONG WAY FROM BEING AFRAID OF YOU.
MY FATHER THINKS I'M WEAK. EVERYONE THINKS I'M WEAK.
BECAUSE YOU ARE.
YOU SHOULDN'T HAVE COME HERE BY YOURSELF, MARK.
HE *DIDN'T.*

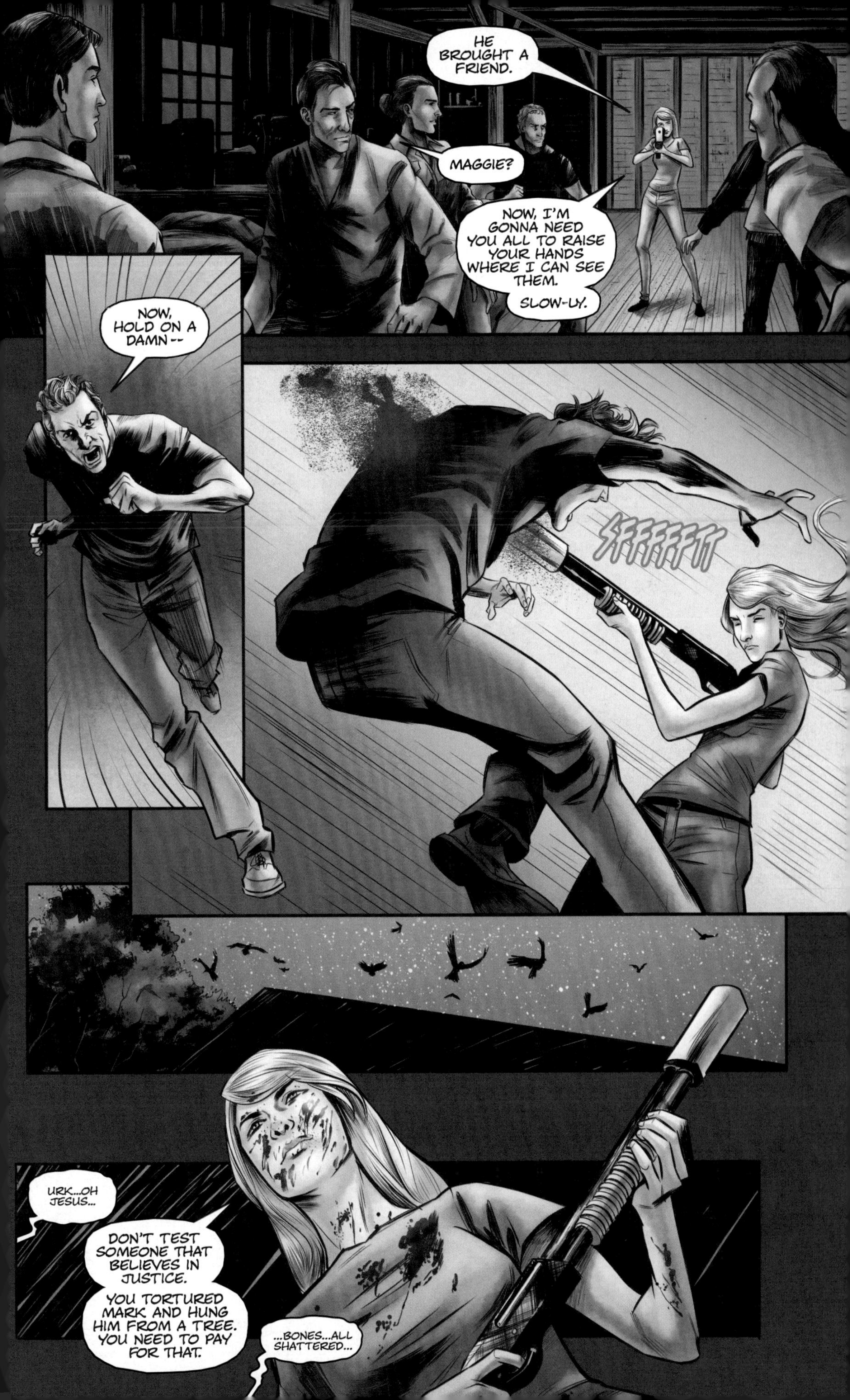
HE BROUGHT A FRIEND.
MAGGIE?
NOW, I'M GONNA NEED YOU ALL TO RAISE YOUR HANDS WHERE I CAN SEE THEM.
SLOW-LY.
NOW, HOLD ON A DAMN --
SFFFFFTT
URK...OH JESUS...
DON'T TEST SOMEONE THAT BELIEVES IN JUSTICE.
YOU TORTURED MARK AND HUNG HIM FROM A TREE. YOU NEED TO PAY FOR THAT.
...BONES...ALL SHATTERED...

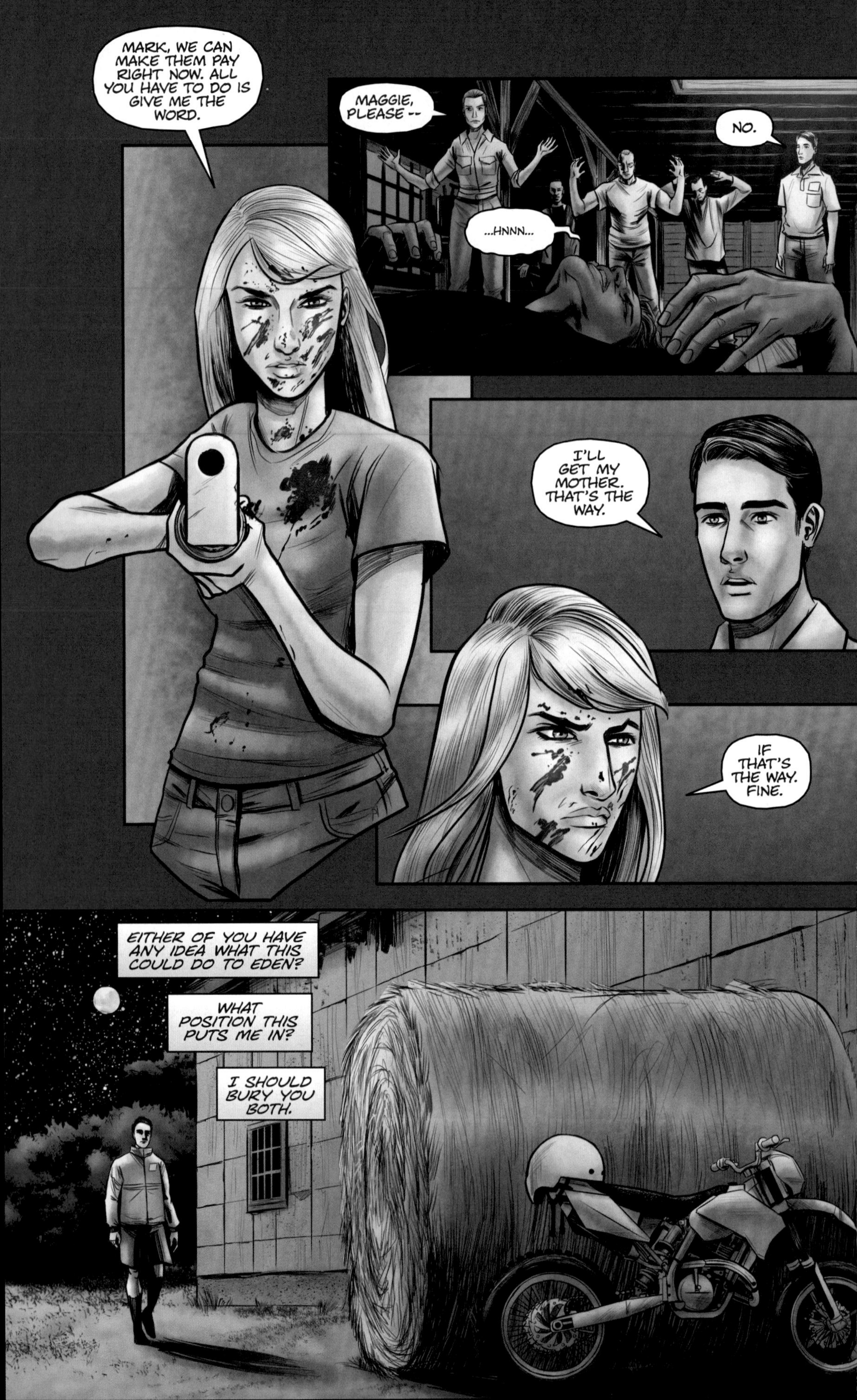
MARK, WE CAN MAKE THEM PAY RIGHT NOW. ALL YOU HAVE TO DO IS GIVE ME THE WORD.
MAGGIE, PLEASE --
NO.
...HNNN...
I'LL GET MY MOTHER. THAT'S THE WAY.
IF THAT'S THE WAY. FINE.
EITHER OF YOU HAVE ANY IDEA WHAT THIS COULD DO TO EDEN?
WHAT POSITION THIS PUTS ME IN?
I SHOULD BURY YOU BOTH.

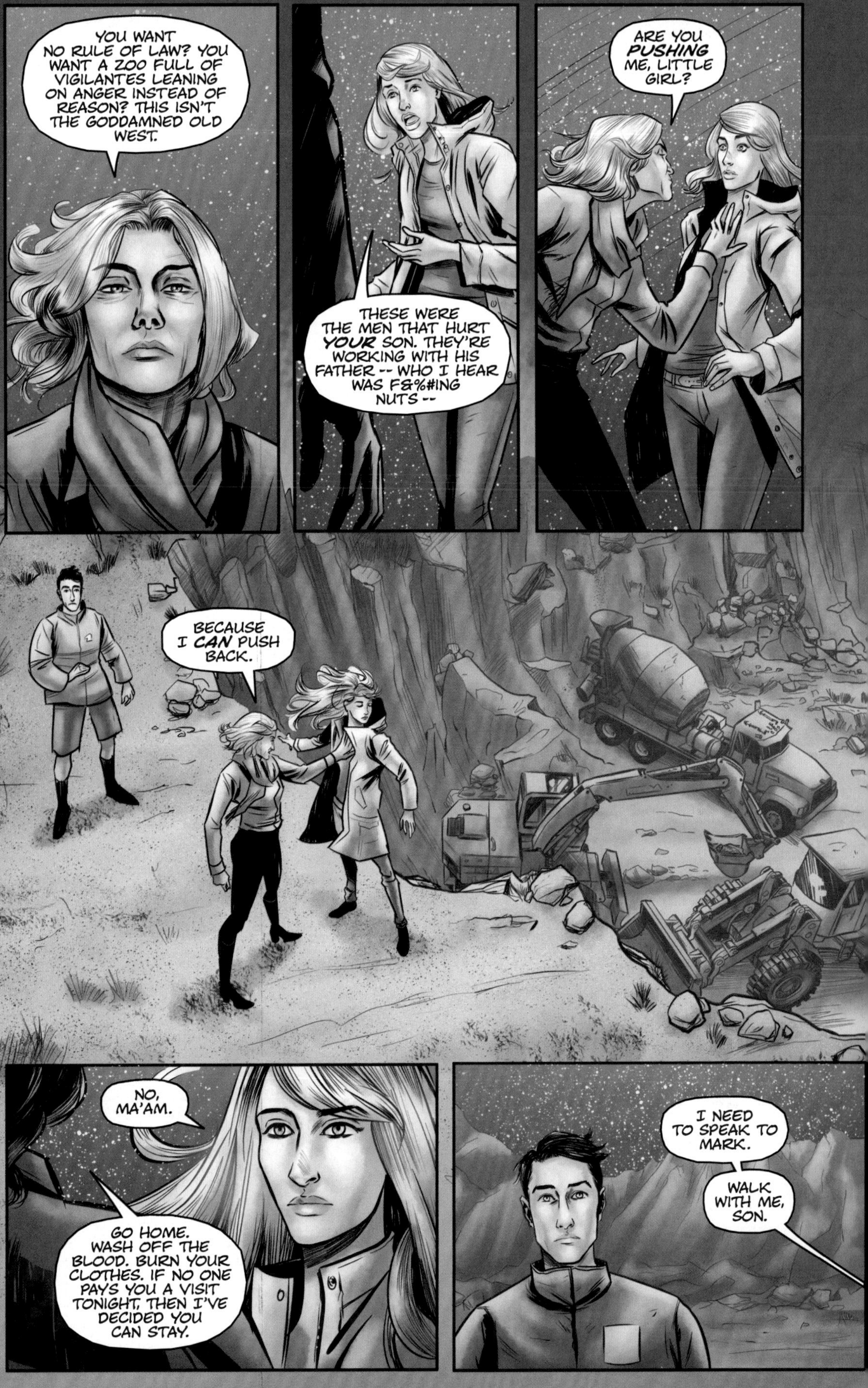
YOU WANT NO RULE OF LAW? YOU WANT A ZOO FULL OF VIGILANTES LEANING ON ANGER INSTEAD OF REASON? THIS ISN'T THE GODDAMNED OLD WEST.
THESE WERE THE MEN THAT HURT YOUR SON. THEY'RE WORKING WITH HIS FATHER -- WHO I HEAR WAS F&%#ING NUTS --
ARE YOU PUSHING ME, LITTLE GIRL?
BECAUSE I CAN PUSH BACK.
NO, MA'AM.
GO HOME. WASH OFF THE BLOOD. BURN YOUR CLOTHES. IF NO ONE PAYS YOU A VISIT TONIGHT, THEN I'VE DECIDED YOU CAN STAY.
I NEED TO SPEAK TO MARK.
WALK WITH ME, SON.

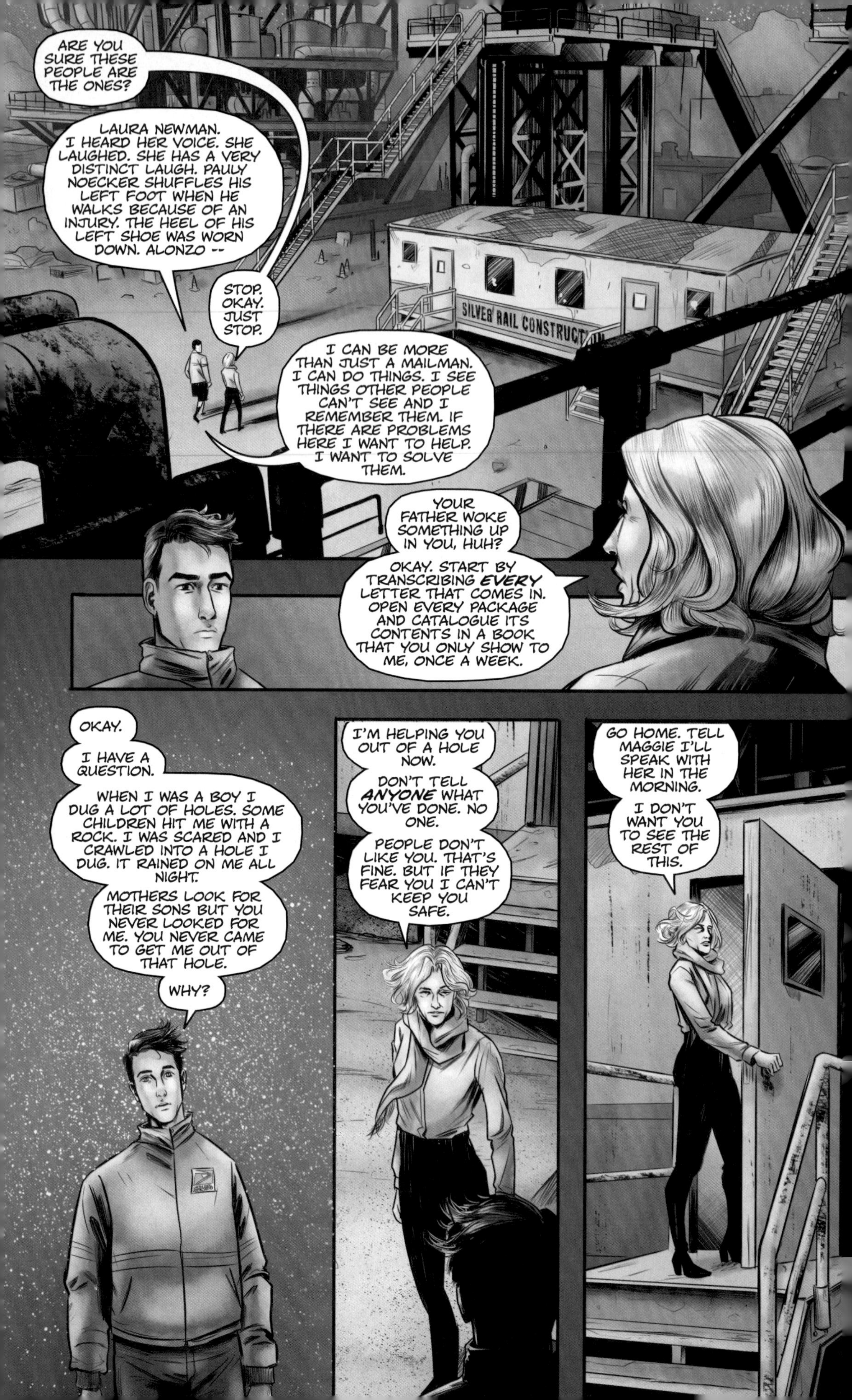

ARE YOU SURE THESE PEOPLE ARE THE ONES?
LAURA NEWMAN. I HEARD HER VOICE. SHE LAUGHED. SHE HAS A VERY DISTINCT LAUGH. PAULY NOECKER SHUFFLES HIS LEFT FOOT WHEN HE WALKS BECAUSE OF AN INJURY. THE HEEL OF HIS LEFT SHOE WAS WORN DOWN. ALONZO --
STOP. OKAY. JUST STOP.
SILVER RAIL CONSTRUCT
I CAN BE MORE THAN JUST A MAILMAN. I CAN DO THINGS. I SEE THINGS OTHER PEOPLE CAN'T SEE AND I REMEMBER THEM. IF THERE ARE PROBLEMS HERE I WANT TO HELP. I WANT TO SOLVE THEM.
YOUR FATHER WOKE SOMETHING UP IN YOU, HUH?
OKAY. START BY TRANSCRIBING ***EVERY*** LETTER THAT COMES IN. OPEN EVERY PACKAGE AND CATALOGUE ITS CONTENTS IN A BOOK THAT YOU ONLY SHOW TO ME, ONCE A WEEK.
OKAY.
I HAVE A QUESTION.
WHEN I WAS A BOY I DUG A LOT OF HOLES. SOME CHILDREN HIT ME WITH A ROCK. I WAS SCARED AND I CRAWLED INTO A HOLE I DUG. IT RAINED ON ME ALL NIGHT.
MOTHERS LOOK FOR THEIR SONS BUT YOU NEVER LOOKED FOR ME. YOU NEVER CAME TO GET ME OUT OF THAT HOLE.
WHY?
I'M HELPING YOU OUT OF A HOLE NOW.
DON'T TELL ***ANYONE*** WHAT YOU'VE DONE. NO ONE.
PEOPLE DON'T LIKE YOU. THAT'S FINE. BUT IF THEY FEAR YOU I CAN'T KEEP YOU SAFE.
GO HOME. TELL MAGGIE I'LL SPEAK WITH HER IN THE MORNING.
I DON'T WANT YOU TO SEE THE REST OF THIS.

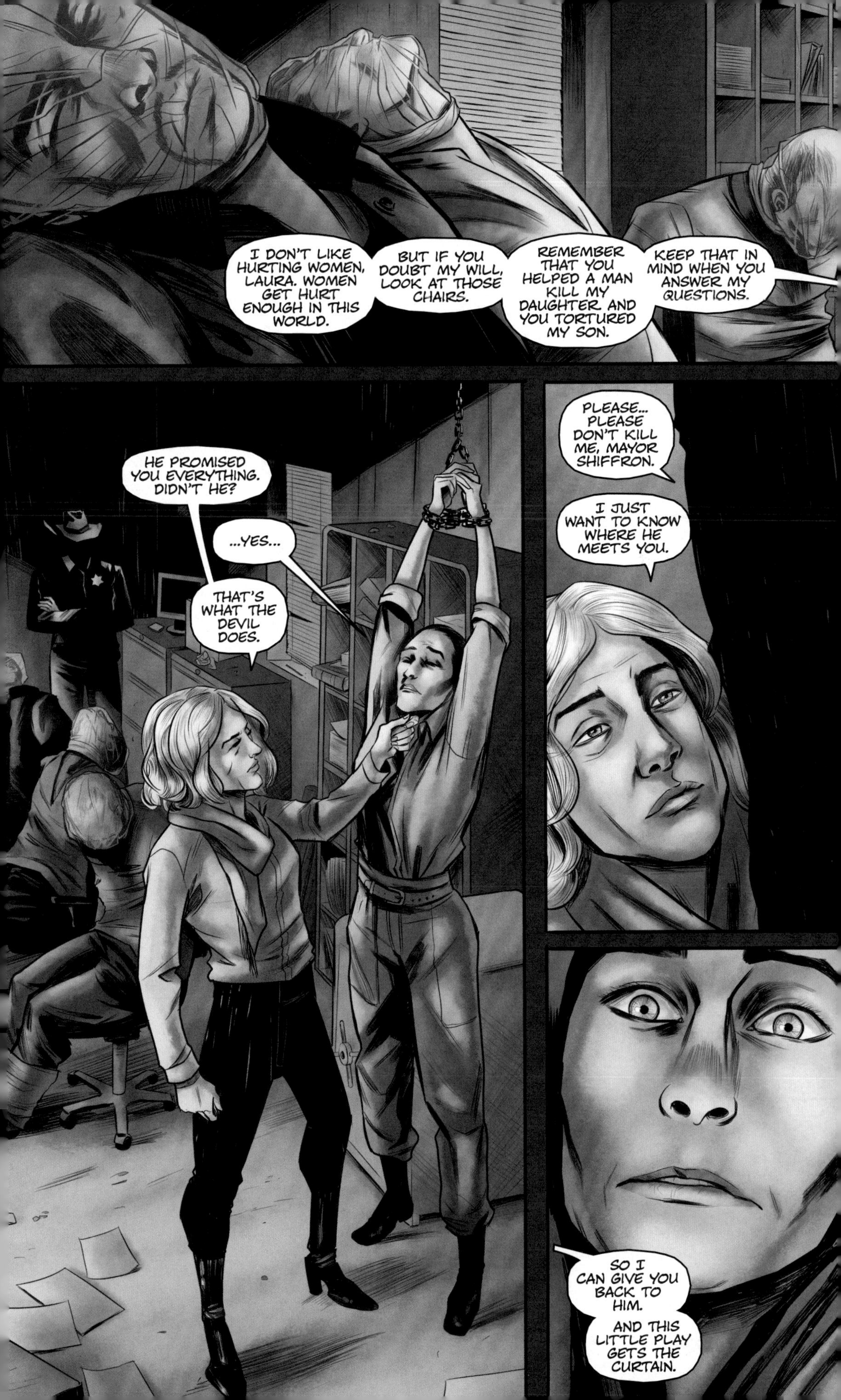
I DON'T LIKE HURTING WOMEN, LAURA. WOMEN GET HURT ENOUGH IN THIS WORLD.
BUT IF YOU DOUBT MY WILL, LOOK AT THOSE CHAIRS.
REMEMBER THAT YOU HELPED A MAN KILL MY DAUGHTER AND YOU TORTURED MY SON.
KEEP THAT IN MIND WHEN YOU ANSWER MY QUESTIONS.
HE PROMISED YOU EVERYTHING. DIDN'T HE?
...YES...
THAT'S WHAT THE DEVIL DOES.
PLEASE... PLEASE DON'T KILL ME, MAYOR SHIFFRON.
I JUST WANT TO KNOW WHERE HE MEETS YOU.
SO I CAN GIVE YOU BACK TO HIM.
AND THIS LITTLE PLAY GETS THE CURTAIN.

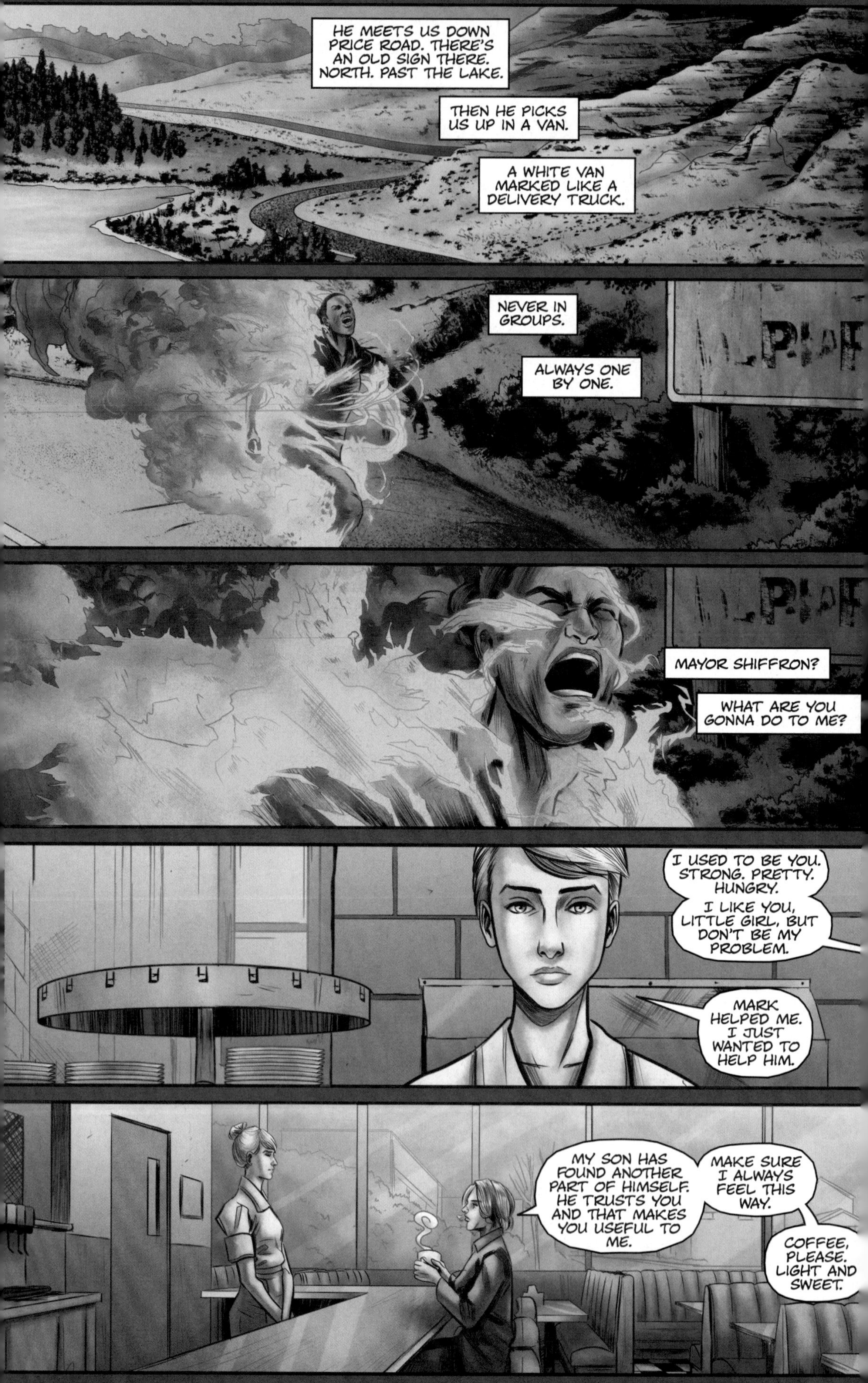
HE MEETS US DOWN PRICE ROAD. THERE'S AN OLD SIGN THERE. NORTH. PAST THE LAKE.
THEN HE PICKS US UP IN A VAN.
A WHITE VAN MARKED LIKE A DELIVERY TRUCK.
NEVER IN GROUPS.
ALWAYS ONE BY ONE.
MAYOR SHIFFRON?
WHAT ARE YOU GONNA DO TO ME?
I USED TO BE YOU. STRONG. PRETTY. HUNGRY.
I LIKE YOU, LITTLE GIRL, BUT DON'T BE MY PROBLEM.
MARK HELPED ME. I JUST WANTED TO HELP HIM.
MY SON HAS FOUND ANOTHER PART OF HIMSELF. HE TRUSTS YOU AND THAT MAKES YOU USEFUL TO ME.
MAKE SURE I ALWAYS FEEL THIS WAY.
COFFEE, PLEASE. LIGHT AND SWEET.

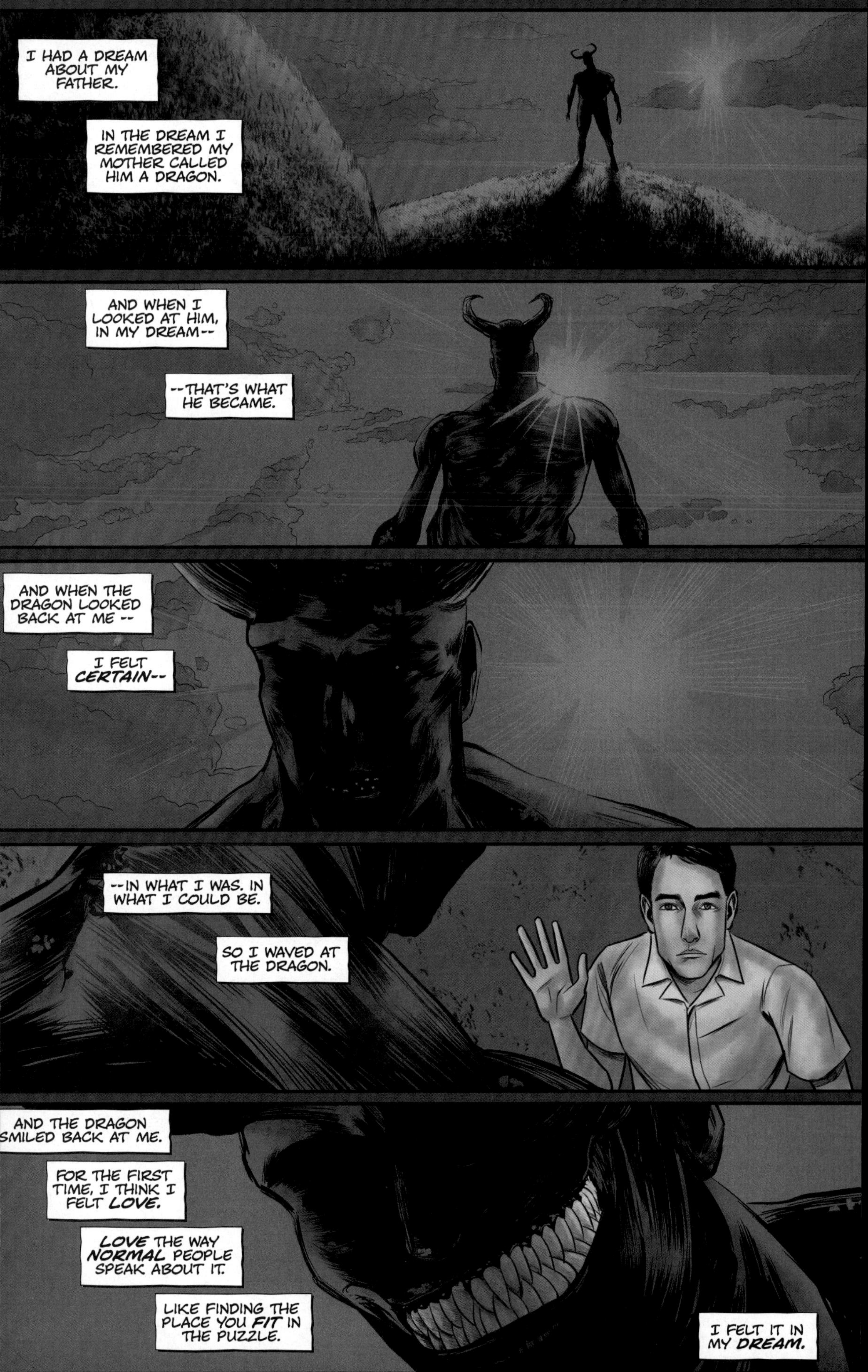
I HAD A DREAM ABOUT MY FATHER.
IN THE DREAM I REMEMBERED MY MOTHER CALLED HIM A DRAGON.
AND WHEN I LOOKED AT HIM, IN MY DREAM--
--THAT'S WHAT HE BECAME.
AND WHEN THE DRAGON LOOKED BACK AT ME --
I FELT CERTAIN--
--IN WHAT I WAS. IN WHAT I COULD BE.
SO I WAVED AT THE DRAGON.
AND THE DRAGON SMILED BACK AT ME.
FOR THE FIRST TIME, I THINK I FELT LOVE.
LOVE THE WAY NORMAL PEOPLE SPEAK ABOUT IT.
LIKE FINDING THE PLACE YOU FIT IN THE PUZZLE.
I FELT IT IN MY DREAM.

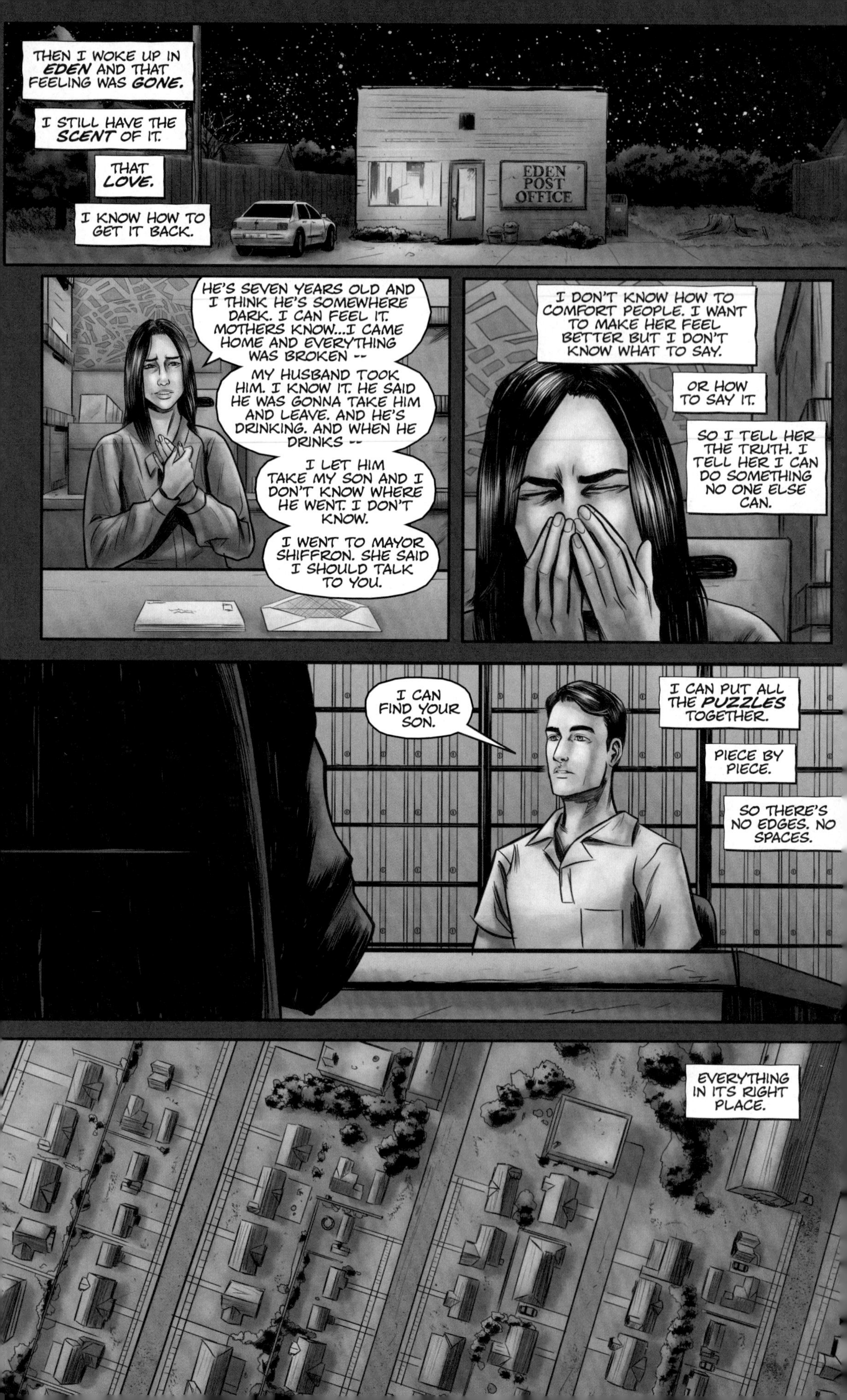
THEN I WOKE UP IN EDEN AND THAT FEELING WAS GONE.
I STILL HAVE THE SCENT OF IT.
THAT LOVE.
I KNOW HOW TO GET IT BACK.
EDEN POST OFFICE
HE'S SEVEN YEARS OLD AND I THINK HE'S SOMEWHERE DARK. I CAN FEEL IT. MOTHERS KNOW...I CAME HOME AND EVERYTHING WAS BROKEN --
MY HUSBAND TOOK HIM. I KNOW IT. HE SAID HE WAS GONNA TAKE HIM AND LEAVE. AND HE'S DRINKING. AND WHEN HE DRINKS --
I LET HIM TAKE MY SON AND I DON'T KNOW WHERE HE WENT. I DON'T KNOW.
I WENT TO MAYOR SHIFFRON. SHE SAID I SHOULD TALK TO YOU.
I DON'T KNOW HOW TO COMFORT PEOPLE. I WANT TO MAKE HER FEEL BETTER BUT I DON'T KNOW WHAT TO SAY.
OR HOW TO SAY IT.
SO I TELL HER THE TRUTH. I TELL HER I CAN DO SOMETHING NO ONE ELSE CAN.
I CAN FIND YOUR SON.
I CAN PUT ALL THE PUZZLES TOGETHER.
PIECE BY PIECE.
SO THERE'S NO EDGES. NO SPACES.
EVERYTHING IN ITS RIGHT PLACE.

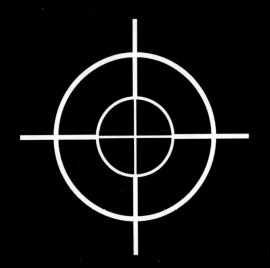

# CHAPTER 5

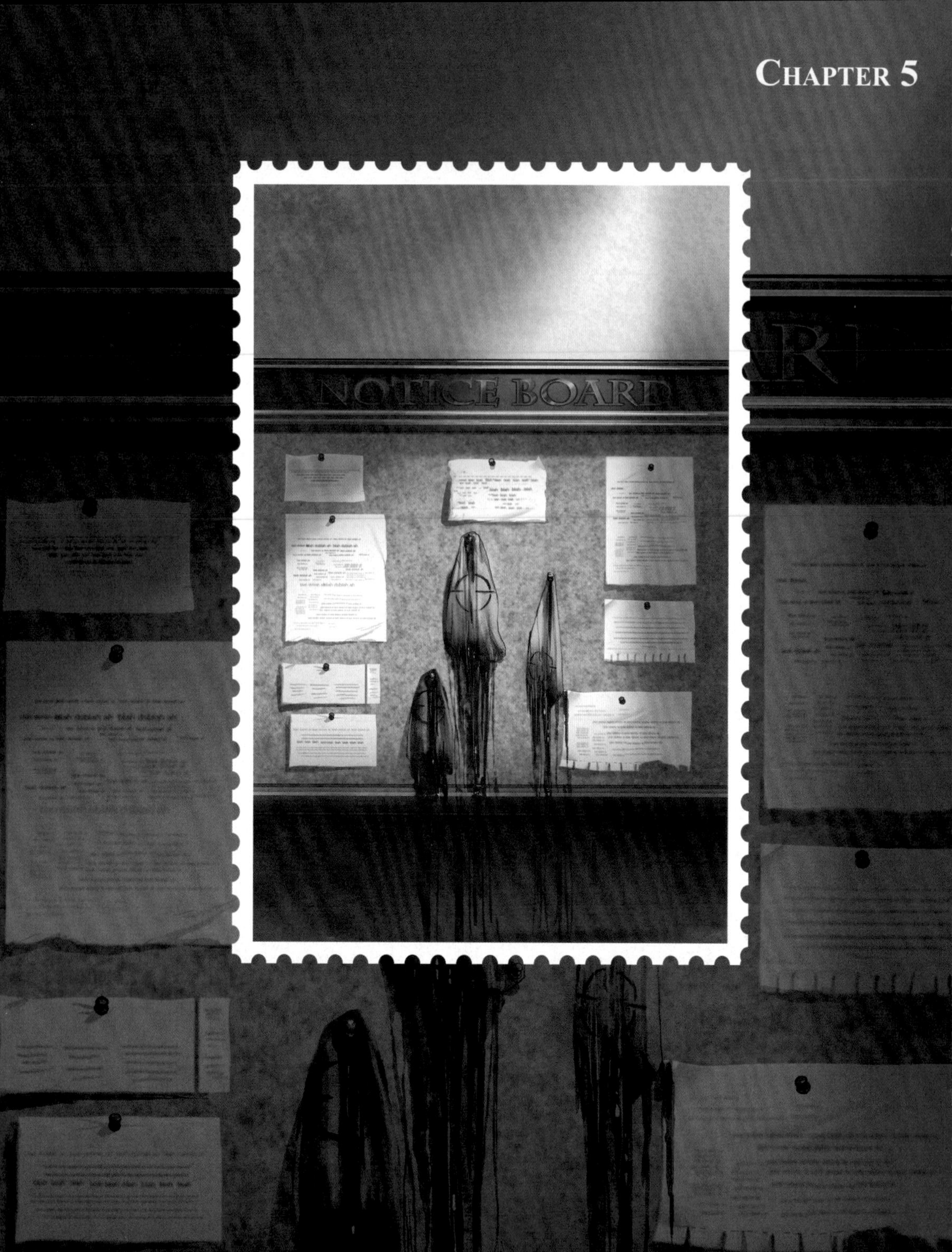
NOTICE BOARD

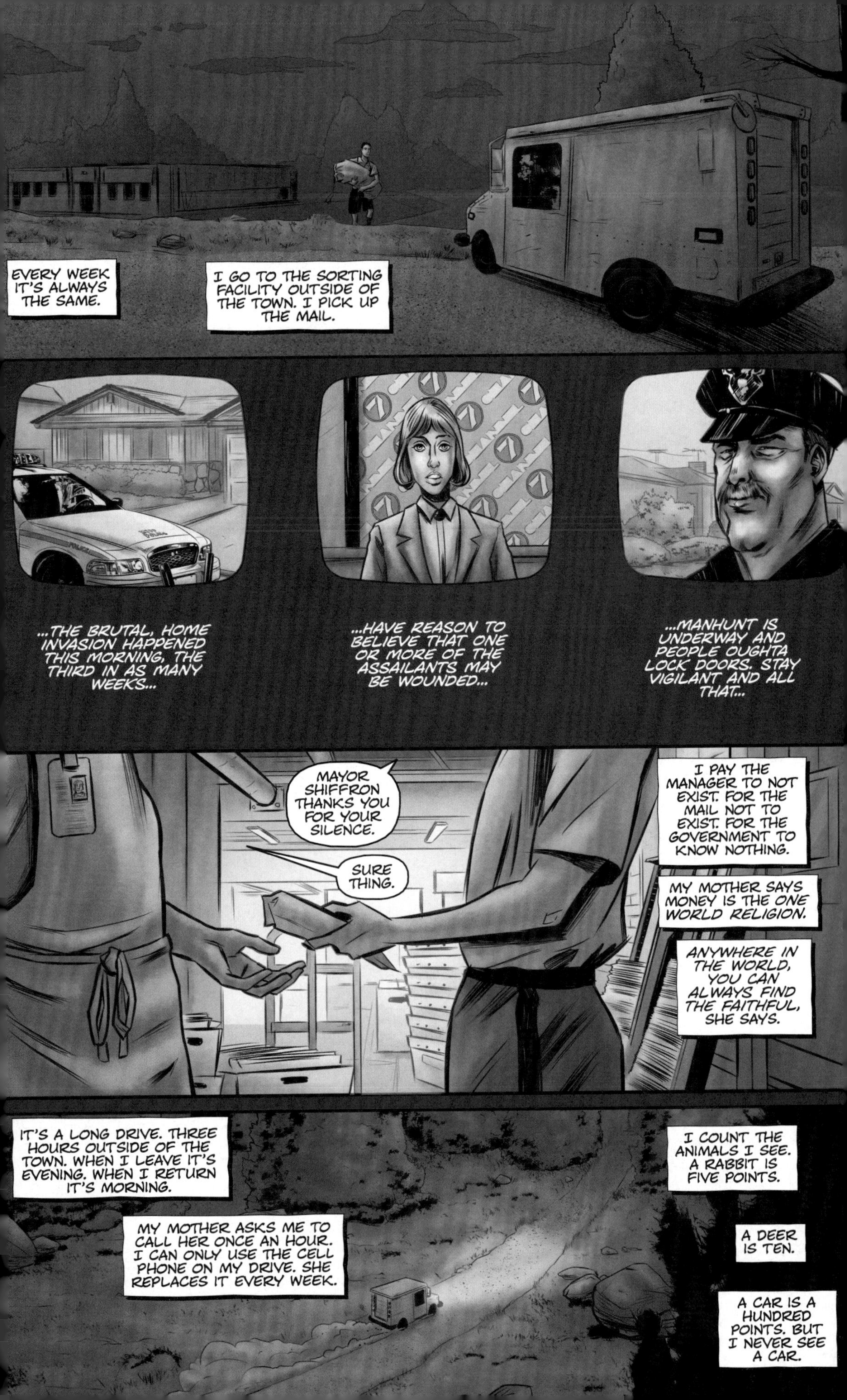
EVERY WEEK IT'S ALWAYS THE SAME.
I GO TO THE SORTING FACILITY OUTSIDE OF THE TOWN. I PICK UP THE MAIL.
...THE BRUTAL, HOME INVASION HAPPENED THIS MORNING, THE THIRD IN AS MANY WEEKS...
...HAVE REASON TO BELIEVE THAT ONE OR MORE OF THE ASSAILANTS MAY BE WOUNDED...
...MANHUNT IS UNDERWAY AND PEOPLE OUGHTA LOCK DOORS. STAY VIGILANT AND ALL THAT...
MAYOR SHIFFRON THANKS YOU FOR YOUR SILENCE.
SURE THING.
I PAY THE MANAGER TO NOT EXIST. FOR THE MAIL NOT TO EXIST. FOR THE GOVERNMENT TO KNOW NOTHING.
MY MOTHER SAYS MONEY IS THE ONE WORLD RELIGION.
ANYWHERE IN THE WORLD, YOU CAN ALWAYS FIND THE FAITHFUL, SHE SAYS.
IT'S A LONG DRIVE. THREE HOURS OUTSIDE OF THE TOWN. WHEN I LEAVE IT'S EVENING. WHEN I RETURN IT'S MORNING.
MY MOTHER ASKS ME TO CALL HER ONCE AN HOUR. I CAN ONLY USE THE CELL PHONE ON MY DRIVE. SHE REPLACES IT EVERY WEEK.
I COUNT THE ANIMALS I SEE. A RABBIT IS FIVE POINTS.
A DEER IS TEN.
A CAR IS A HUNDRED POINTS. BUT I NEVER SEE A CAR.

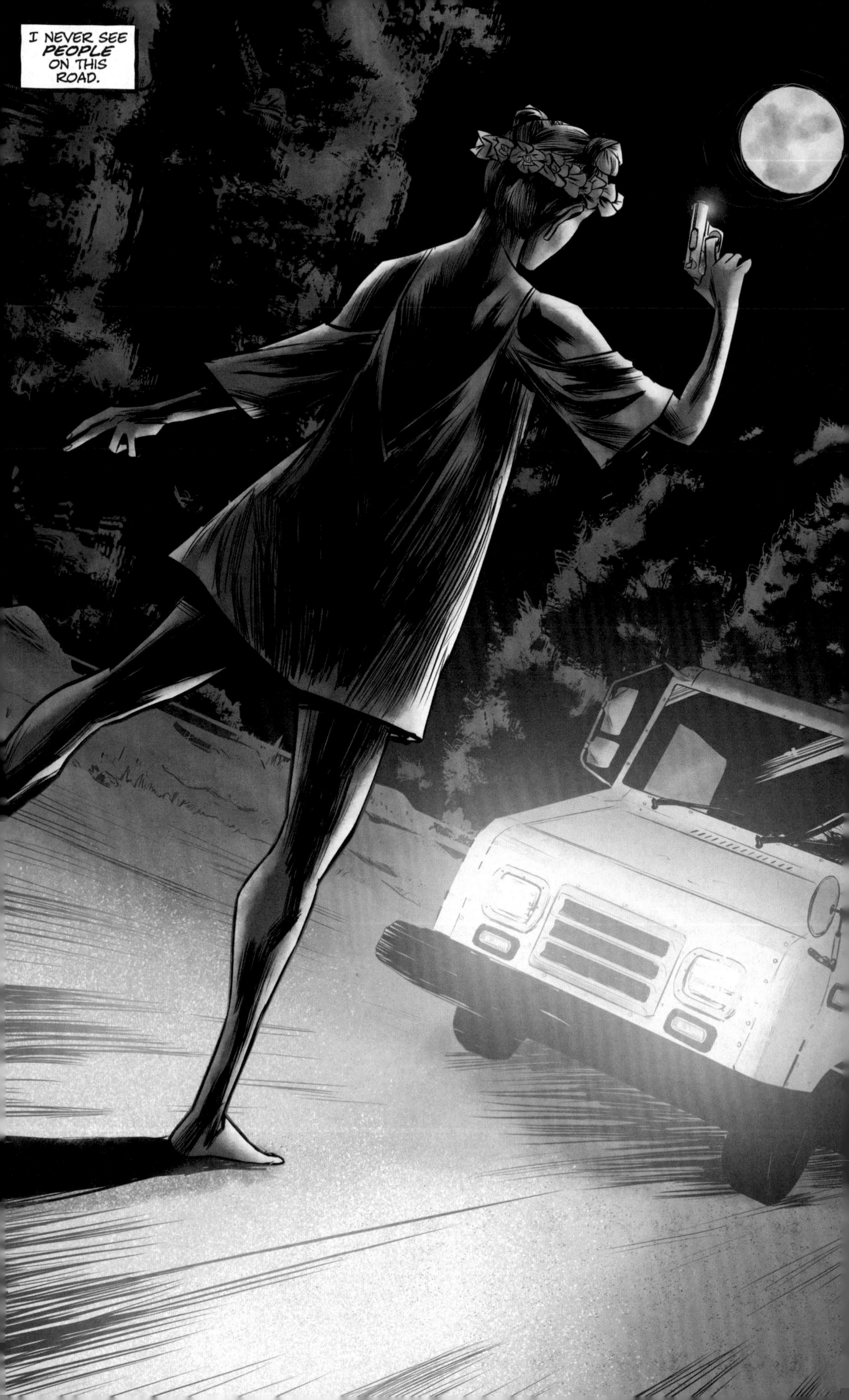
I NEVER SEE PEOPLE ON THIS ROAD.

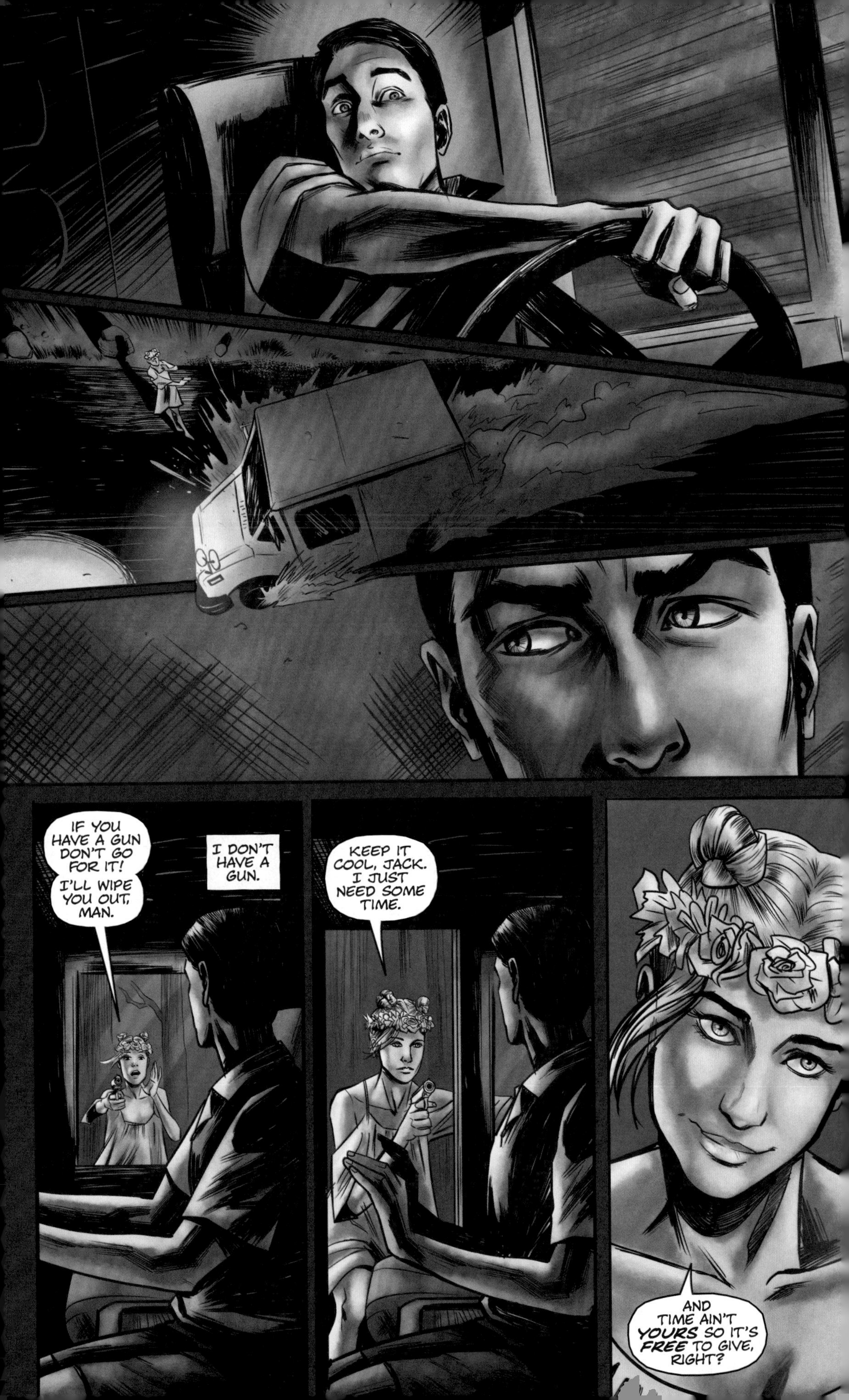
IF YOU HAVE A GUN DON'T GO FOR IT!
I'LL WIPE YOU OUT, MAN.
I DON'T HAVE A GUN.
KEEP IT COOL, JACK. I JUST NEED SOME TIME.
AND TIME AIN'T YOURS SO IT'S FREE TO GIVE, RIGHT?

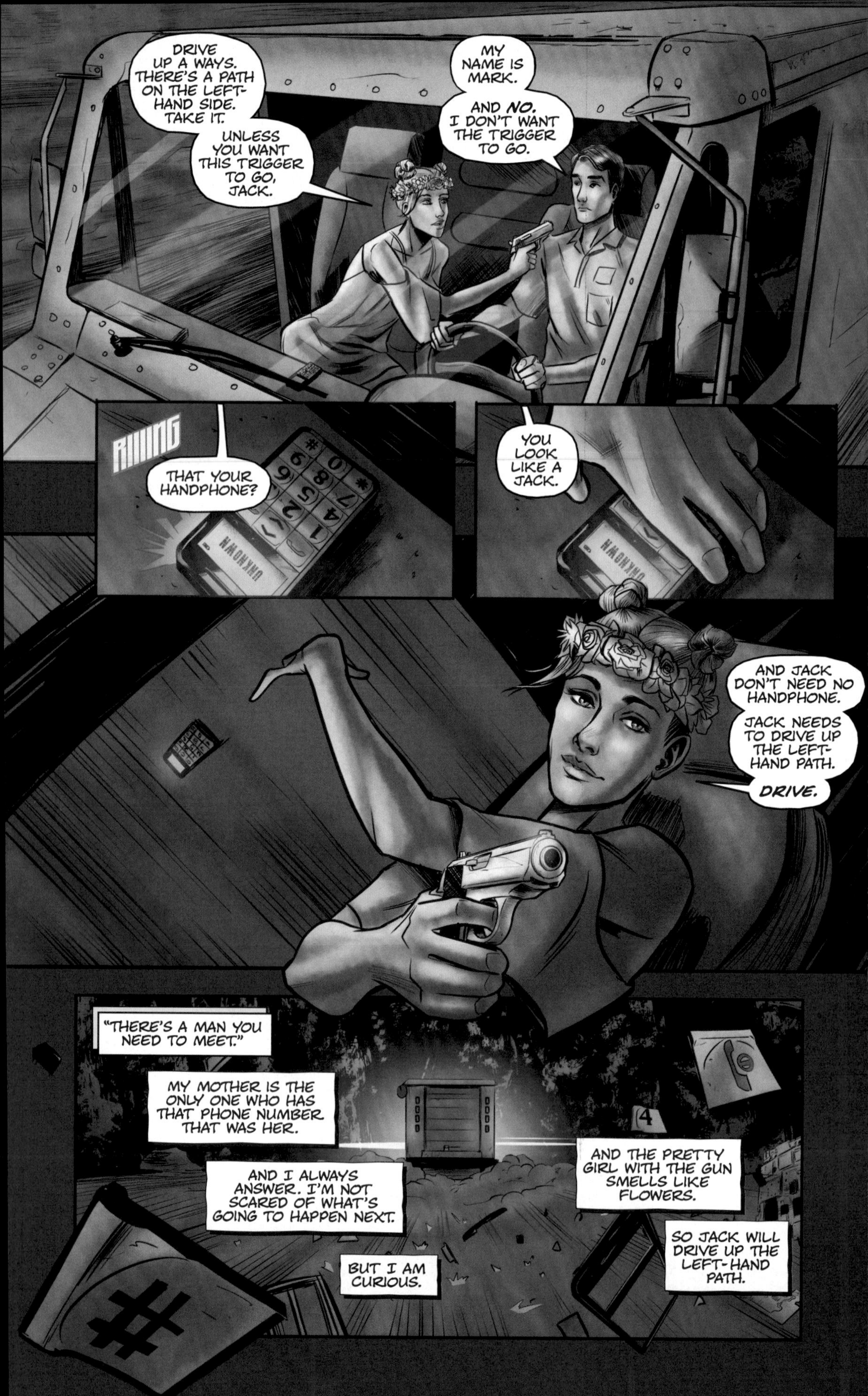
DRIVE UP A WAYS. THERE'S A PATH ON THE LEFT-HAND SIDE. TAKE IT.
UNLESS YOU WANT THIS TRIGGER TO GO, JACK.
MY NAME IS MARK.
AND NO. I DON'T WANT THE TRIGGER TO GO.
RIIIING
THAT YOUR HANDPHONE?
UNKNOWN
YOU LOOK LIKE A JACK.
AND JACK DON'T NEED NO HANDPHONE.
JACK NEEDS TO DRIVE UP THE LEFT-HAND PATH.
DRIVE.
"THERE'S A MAN YOU NEED TO MEET."
MY MOTHER IS THE ONLY ONE WHO HAS THAT PHONE NUMBER THAT WAS HER.
AND I ALWAYS ANSWER. I'M NOT SCARED OF WHAT'S GOING TO HAPPEN NEXT.
BUT I AM CURIOUS.
AND THE PRETTY GIRL WITH THE GUN SMELLS LIKE FLOWERS.
SO JACK WILL DRIVE UP THE LEFT-HAND PATH.

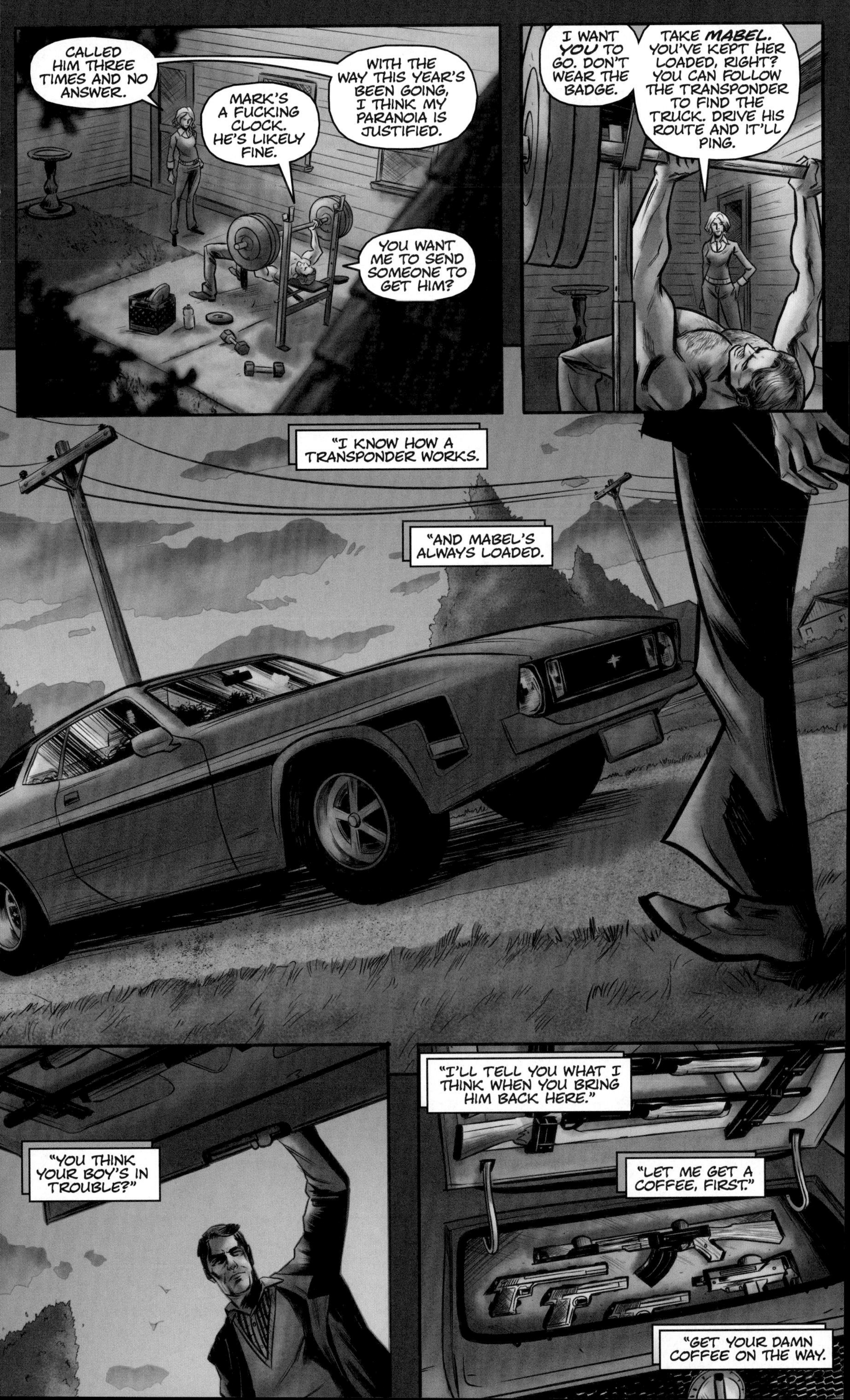
CALLED HIM THREE TIMES AND NO ANSWER.
MARK'S A FUCKING CLOCK. HE'S LIKELY FINE.
WITH THE WAY THIS YEAR'S BEEN GOING, I THINK MY PARANOIA IS JUSTIFIED.
YOU WANT ME TO SEND SOMEONE TO GET HIM?
I WANT YOU TO GO. DON'T WEAR THE BADGE.
TAKE MABEL. YOU'VE KEPT HER LOADED, RIGHT? YOU CAN FOLLOW THE TRANSPONDER TO FIND THE TRUCK. DRIVE HIS ROUTE AND IT'LL PING.
"I KNOW HOW A TRANSPONDER WORKS.
"AND MABEL'S ALWAYS LOADED.
"YOU THINK YOUR BOY'S IN TROUBLE?"
"I'LL TELL YOU WHAT I THINK WHEN YOU BRING HIM BACK HERE."
"LET ME GET A COFFEE, FIRST."
"GET YOUR DAMN COFFEE ON THE WAY.

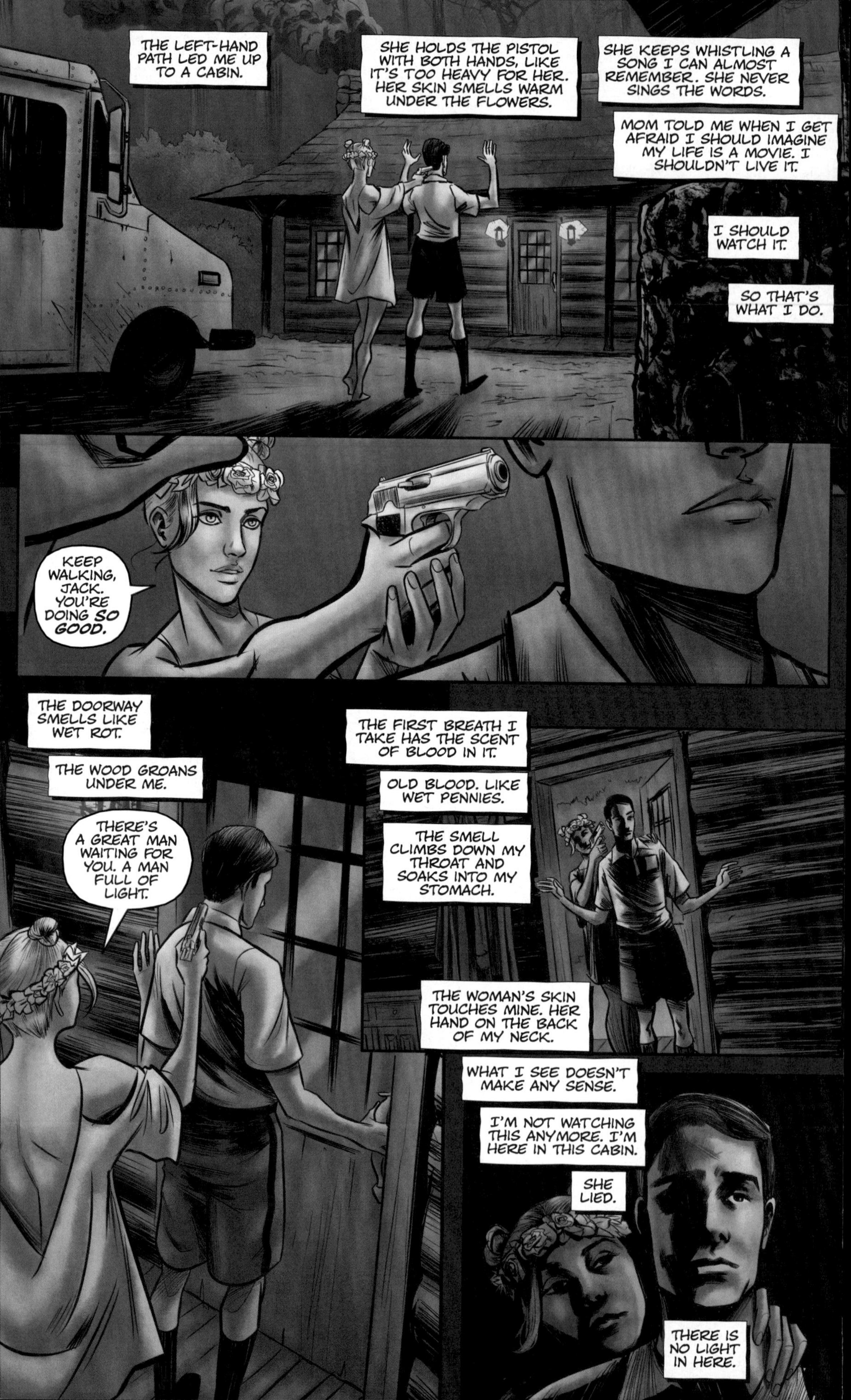

THE LEFT-HAND PATH LED ME UP TO A CABIN.
SHE HOLDS THE PISTOL WITH BOTH HANDS, LIKE IT'S TOO HEAVY FOR HER. HER SKIN SMELLS WARM UNDER THE FLOWERS.
SHE KEEPS WHISTLING A SONG I CAN ALMOST REMEMBER. SHE NEVER SINGS THE WORDS.
MOM TOLD ME WHEN I GET AFRAID I SHOULD IMAGINE MY LIFE IS A MOVIE. I SHOULDN'T LIVE IT.
I SHOULD WATCH IT.
SO THAT'S WHAT I DO.
KEEP WALKING, JACK. YOU'RE DOING SO GOOD.
THE DOORWAY SMELLS LIKE WET ROT.
THE WOOD GROANS UNDER ME.
THERE'S A GREAT MAN WAITING FOR YOU. A MAN FULL OF LIGHT.
THE FIRST BREATH I TAKE HAS THE SCENT OF BLOOD IN IT.
OLD BLOOD. LIKE WET PENNIES.
THE SMELL CLIMBS DOWN MY THROAT AND SOAKS INTO MY STOMACH.
THE WOMAN'S SKIN TOUCHES MINE. HER HAND ON THE BACK OF MY NECK.
WHAT I SEE DOESN'T MAKE ANY SENSE.
I'M NOT WATCHING THIS ANYMORE. I'M HERE IN THIS CABIN.
SHE LIED.
THERE IS NO LIGHT IN HERE.

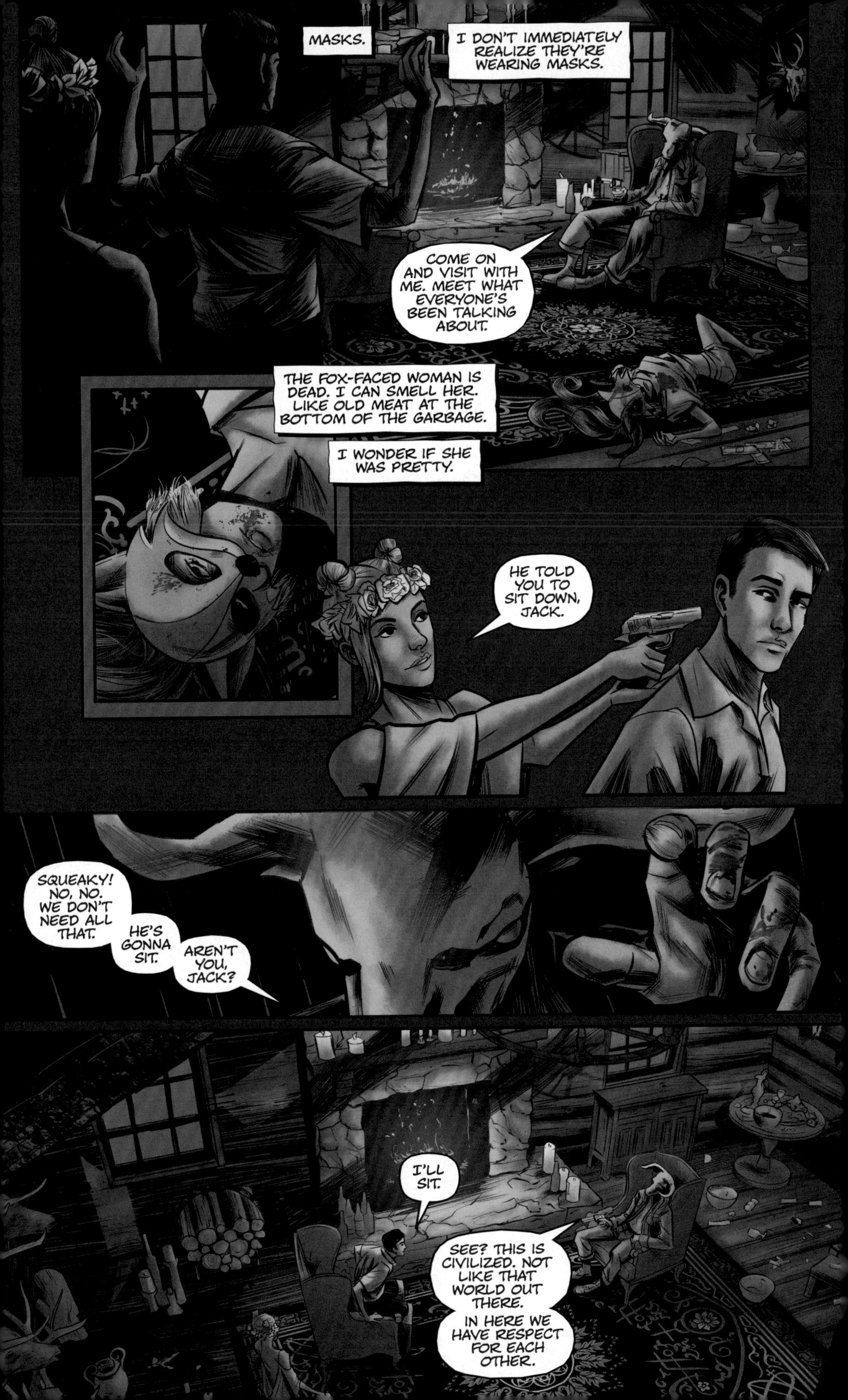
MASKS.
I DON'T IMMEDIATELY REALIZE THEY'RE WEARING MASKS.
COME ON AND VISIT WITH ME. MEET WHAT EVERYONE'S BEEN TALKING ABOUT.
THE FOX-FACED WOMAN IS DEAD. I CAN SMELL HER. LIKE OLD MEAT AT THE BOTTOM OF THE GARBAGE.
I WONDER IF SHE WAS PRETTY.
HE TOLD YOU TO SIT DOWN, JACK.
SQUEAKY! NO, NO. WE DON'T NEED ALL THAT.
HE'S GONNA SIT.
AREN'T YOU, JACK?
I'LL SIT.
SEE? THIS IS CIVILIZED. NOT LIKE THAT WORLD OUT THERE.
IN HERE WE HAVE RESPECT FOR EACH OTHER.

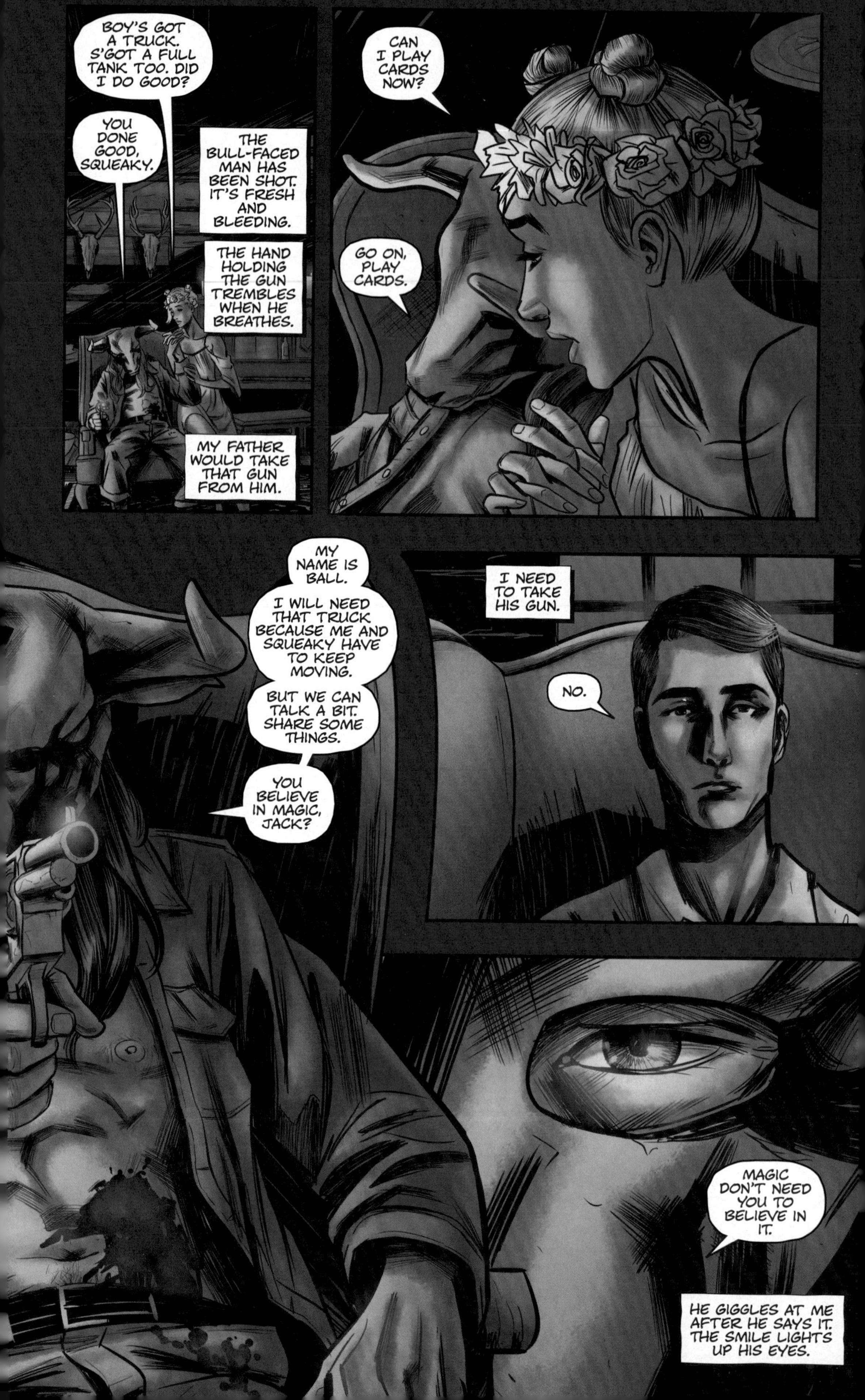
BOY'S GOT A TRUCK. S'GOT A FULL TANK TOO. DID I DO GOOD?
YOU DONE GOOD, SQUEAKY.
THE BULL-FACED MAN HAS BEEN SHOT. IT'S FRESH AND BLEEDING.
THE HAND HOLDING THE GUN TREMBLES WHEN HE BREATHES.
MY FATHER WOULD TAKE THAT GUN FROM HIM.
CAN I PLAY CARDS NOW?
GO ON, PLAY CARDS.
MY NAME IS BALL.
I WILL NEED THAT TRUCK BECAUSE ME AND SQUEAKY HAVE TO KEEP MOVING.
BUT WE CAN TALK A BIT. SHARE SOME THINGS.
YOU BELIEVE IN MAGIC, JACK?
I NEED TO TAKE HIS GUN.
NO.
MAGIC DON'T NEED YOU TO BELIEVE IN IT.
HE GIGGLES AT ME AFTER HE SAYS IT. THE SMILE LIGHTS UP HIS EYES.

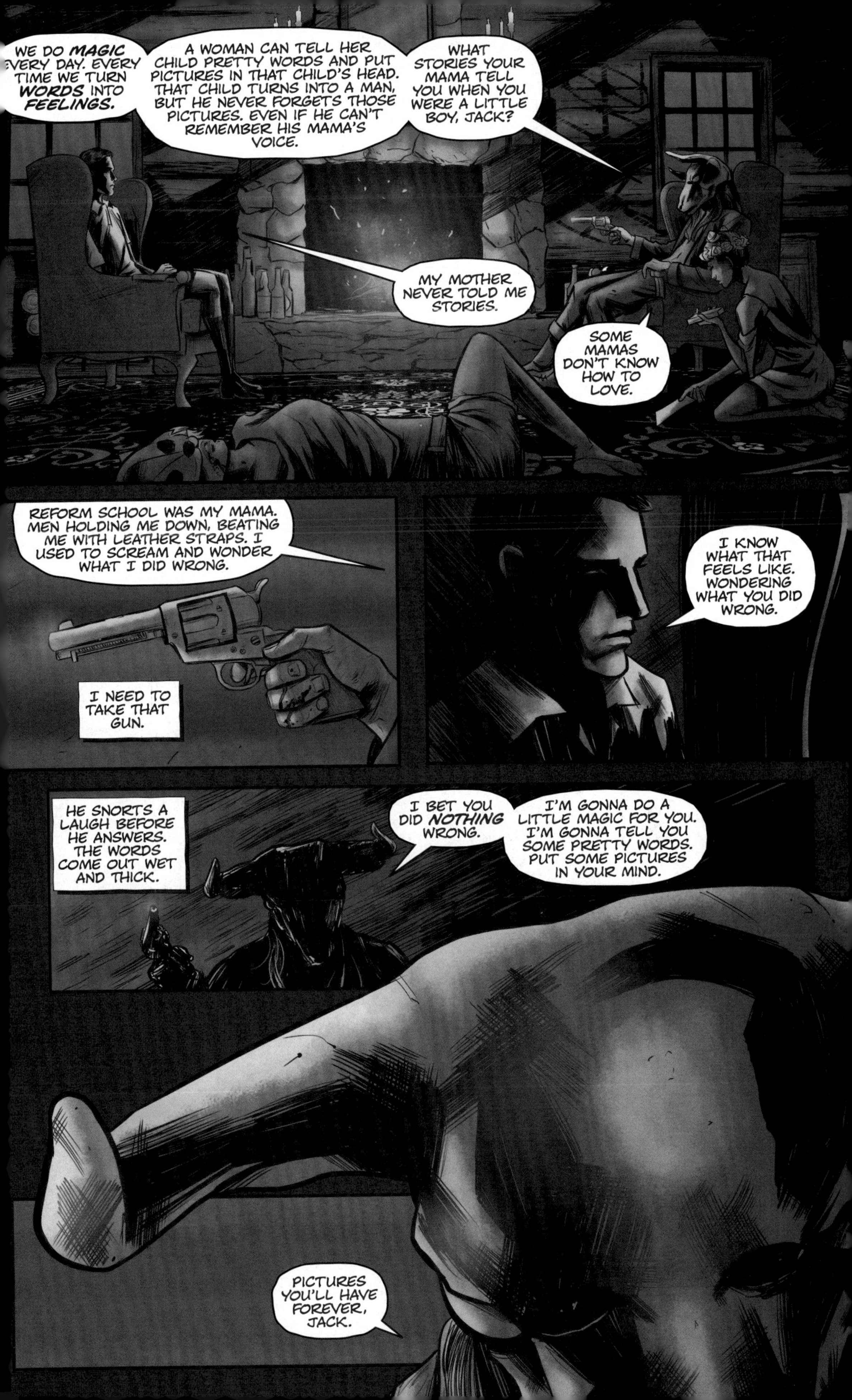
WE DO *MAGIC* EVERY DAY. EVERY TIME WE TURN *WORDS* INTO *FEELINGS.*
A WOMAN CAN TELL HER CHILD PRETTY WORDS AND PUT PICTURES IN THAT CHILD'S HEAD. THAT CHILD TURNS INTO A MAN, BUT HE NEVER FORGETS THOSE PICTURES. EVEN IF HE CAN'T REMEMBER HIS MAMA'S VOICE.
WHAT STORIES YOUR MAMA TELL YOU WHEN YOU WERE A LITTLE BOY, JACK?
MY MOTHER NEVER TOLD ME STORIES.
SOME MAMAS DON'T KNOW HOW TO LOVE.
REFORM SCHOOL WAS MY MAMA. MEN HOLDING ME DOWN, BEATING ME WITH LEATHER STRAPS. I USED TO SCREAM AND WONDER WHAT I DID WRONG.
I NEED TO TAKE THAT GUN.
I KNOW WHAT THAT FEELS LIKE. WONDERING WHAT YOU DID WRONG.
HE SNORTS A LAUGH BEFORE HE ANSWERS. THE WORDS COME OUT WET AND THICK.
I BET YOU DID *NOTHING* WRONG.
I'M GONNA DO A LITTLE MAGIC FOR YOU. I'M GONNA TELL YOU SOME PRETTY WORDS. PUT SOME PICTURES IN YOUR MIND.
PICTURES YOU'LL HAVE FOREVER, JACK.

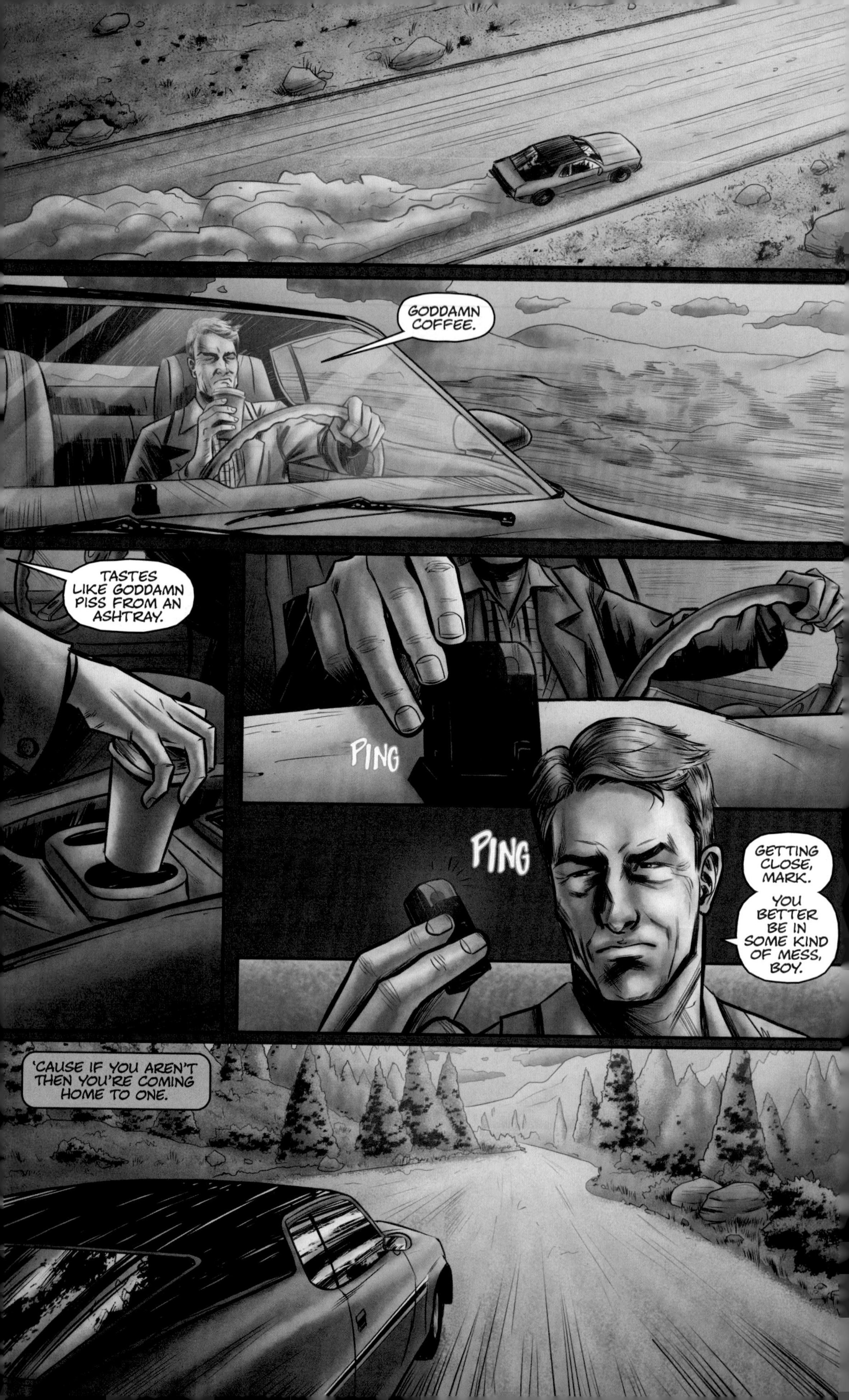
GODDAMN COFFEE.
TASTES LIKE GODDAMN PISS FROM AN ASHTRAY.
PING
PING
GETTING CLOSE, MARK.
YOU BETTER BE IN SOME KIND OF MESS, BOY.
'CAUSE IF YOU AREN'T THEN YOU'RE COMING HOME TO ONE.

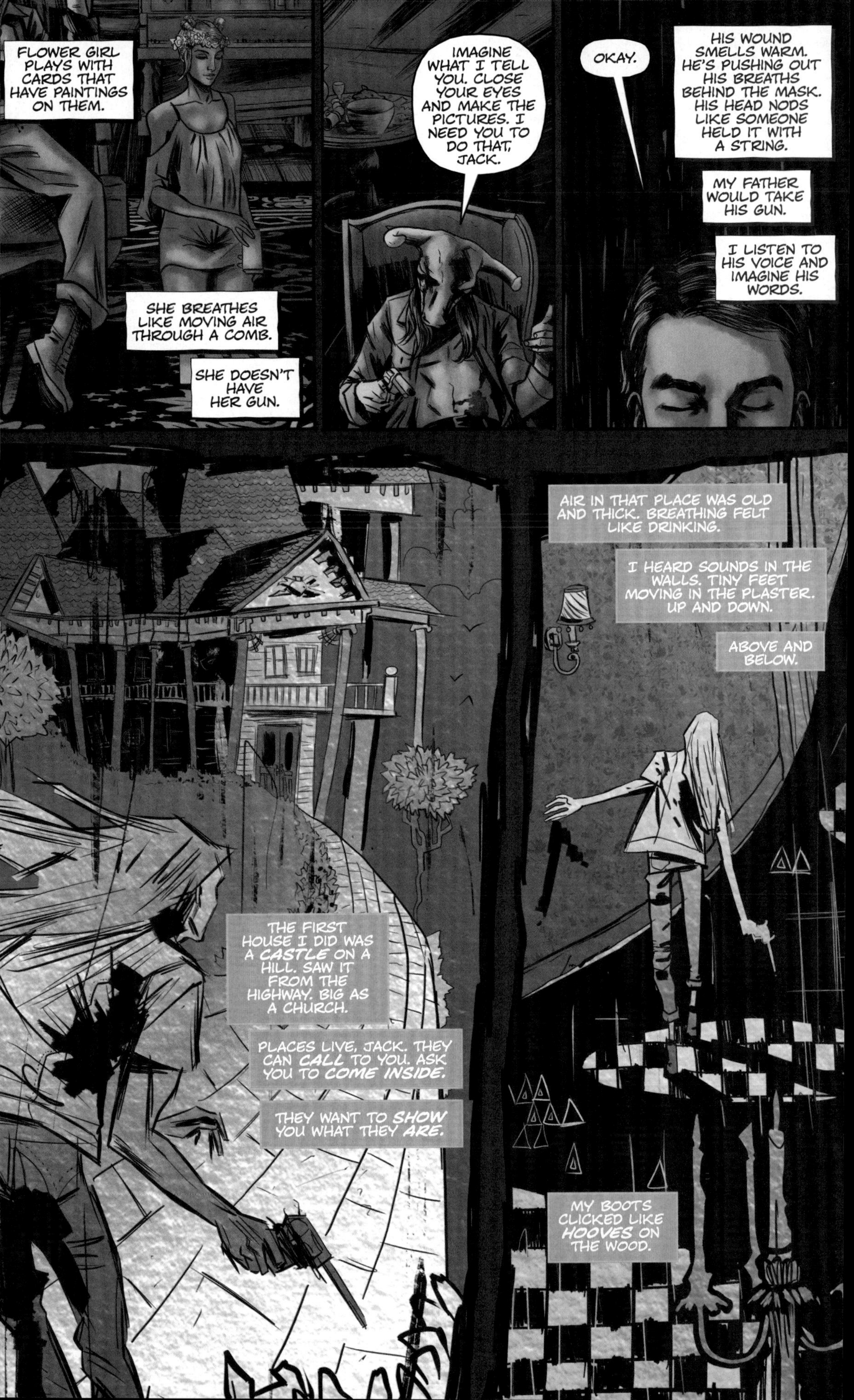
FLOWER GIRL PLAYS WITH CARDS THAT HAVE PAINTINGS ON THEM.
SHE BREATHES LIKE MOVING AIR THROUGH A COMB.
SHE DOESN'T HAVE HER GUN.
IMAGINE WHAT I TELL YOU. CLOSE YOUR EYES AND MAKE THE PICTURES. I NEED YOU TO DO THAT, JACK.
OKAY.
HIS WOUND SMELLS WARM. HE'S PUSHING OUT HIS BREATHS BEHIND THE MASK. HIS HEAD NODS LIKE SOMEONE HELD IT WITH A STRING.
MY FATHER WOULD TAKE HIS GUN.
I LISTEN TO HIS VOICE AND IMAGINE HIS WORDS.
THE FIRST HOUSE I DID WAS A CASTLE ON A HILL. SAW IT FROM THE HIGHWAY. BIG AS A CHURCH.
PLACES LIVE, JACK. THEY CAN CALL TO YOU. ASK YOU TO COME INSIDE.
THEY WANT TO SHOW YOU WHAT THEY ARE.
AIR IN THAT PLACE WAS OLD AND THICK. BREATHING FELT LIKE DRINKING.
I HEARD SOUNDS IN THE WALLS. TINY FEET MOVING IN THE PLASTER. UP AND DOWN.
ABOVE AND BELOW.
MY BOOTS CLICKED LIKE HOOVES ON THE WOOD.

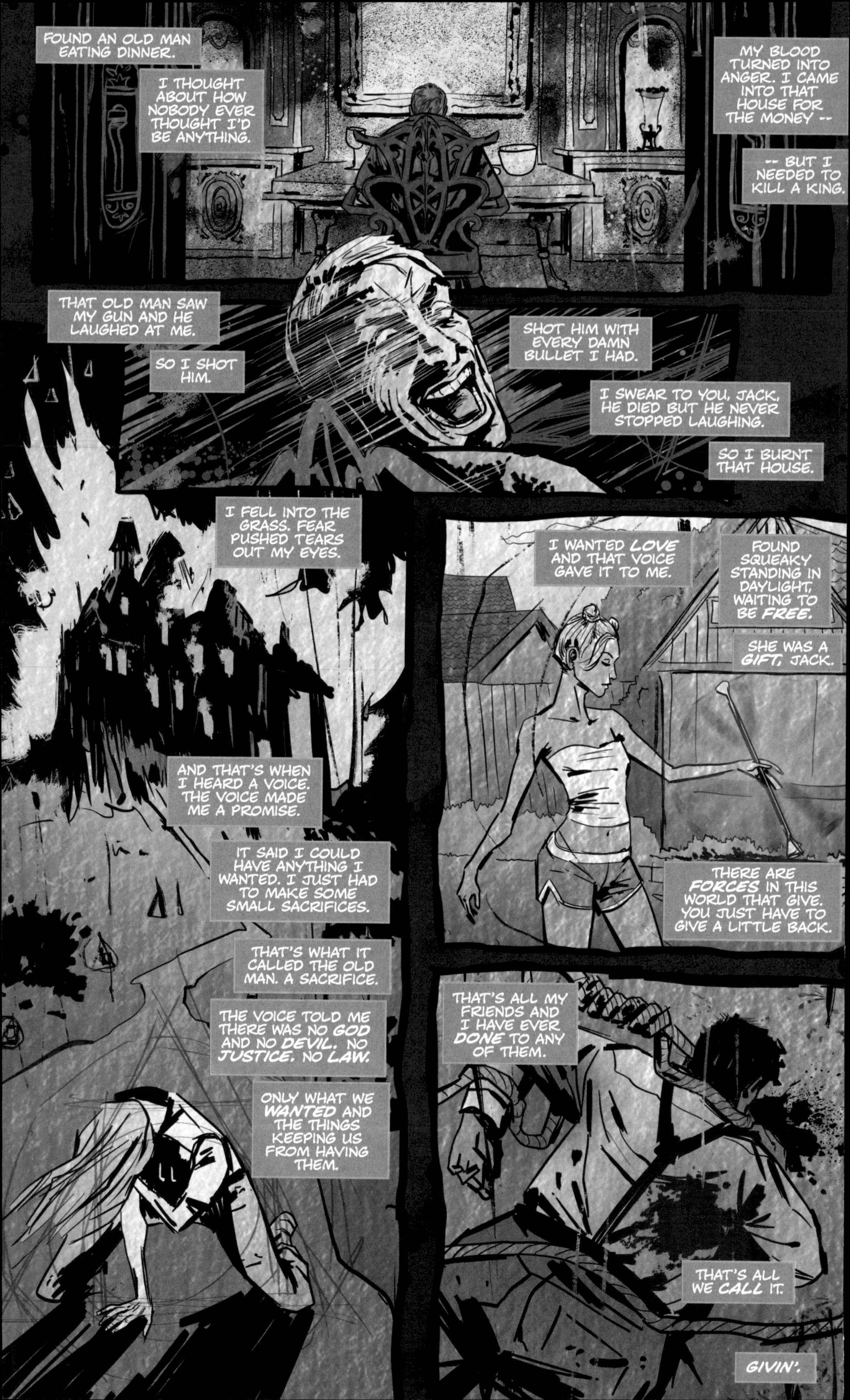
FOUND AN OLD MAN EATING DINNER.
I THOUGHT ABOUT HOW NOBODY EVER THOUGHT I'D BE ANYTHING.
MY BLOOD TURNED INTO ANGER. I CAME INTO THAT HOUSE FOR THE MONEY --
-- BUT I NEEDED TO KILL A KING.
THAT OLD MAN SAW MY GUN AND HE LAUGHED AT ME.
SO I SHOT HIM.
SHOT HIM WITH EVERY DAMN BULLET I HAD.
I SWEAR TO YOU, JACK, HE DIED BUT HE NEVER STOPPED LAUGHING.
SO I BURNT THAT HOUSE.
I FELL INTO THE GRASS. FEAR PUSHED TEARS OUT MY EYES.
AND THAT'S WHEN I HEARD A VOICE. THE VOICE MADE ME A PROMISE.
IT SAID I COULD HAVE ANYTHING I WANTED. I JUST HAD TO MAKE SOME SMALL SACRIFICES.
THAT'S WHAT IT CALLED THE OLD MAN. A SACRIFICE.
THE VOICE TOLD ME THERE WAS NO GOD AND NO DEVIL. NO JUSTICE. NO LAW.
ONLY WHAT WE WANTED AND THE THINGS KEEPING US FROM HAVING THEM.
I WANTED LOVE AND THAT VOICE GAVE IT TO ME.
FOUND SQUEAKY STANDING IN DAYLIGHT, WAITING TO BE FREE.
SHE WAS A GIFT, JACK.
THERE ARE FORCES IN THIS WORLD THAT GIVE. YOU JUST HAVE TO GIVE A LITTLE BACK.
THAT'S ALL MY FRIENDS AND I HAVE EVER DONE TO ANY OF THEM.
THAT'S ALL WE CALL IT.
GIVIN'.

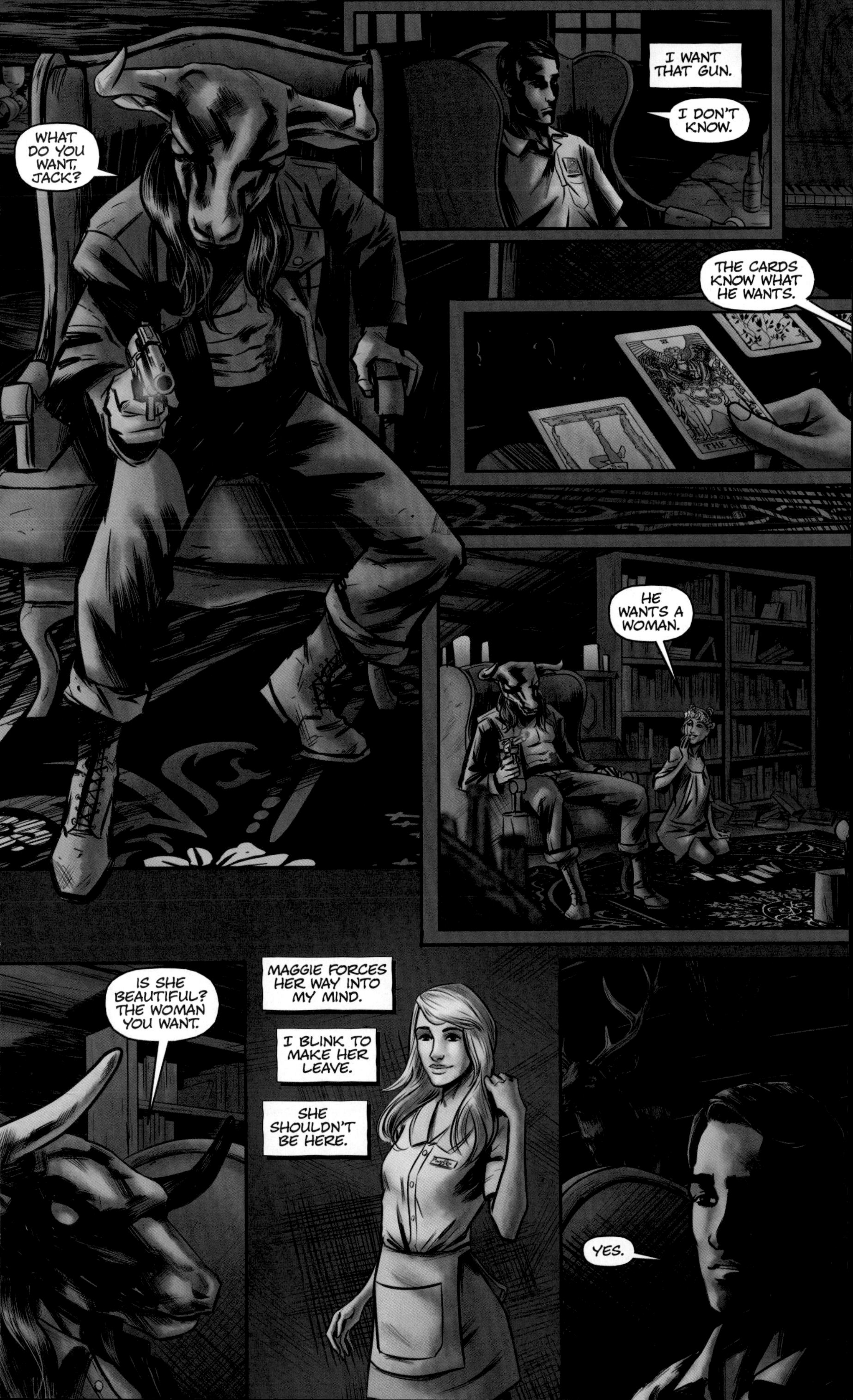
WHAT DO YOU WANT, JACK?
I WANT THAT GUN.
I DON'T KNOW.
THE CARDS KNOW WHAT HE WANTS.
HE WANTS A WOMAN.
IS SHE BEAUTIFUL? THE WOMAN YOU WANT.
MAGGIE FORCES HER WAY INTO MY MIND.
I BLINK TO MAKE HER LEAVE.
SHE SHOULDN'T BE HERE.
YES.

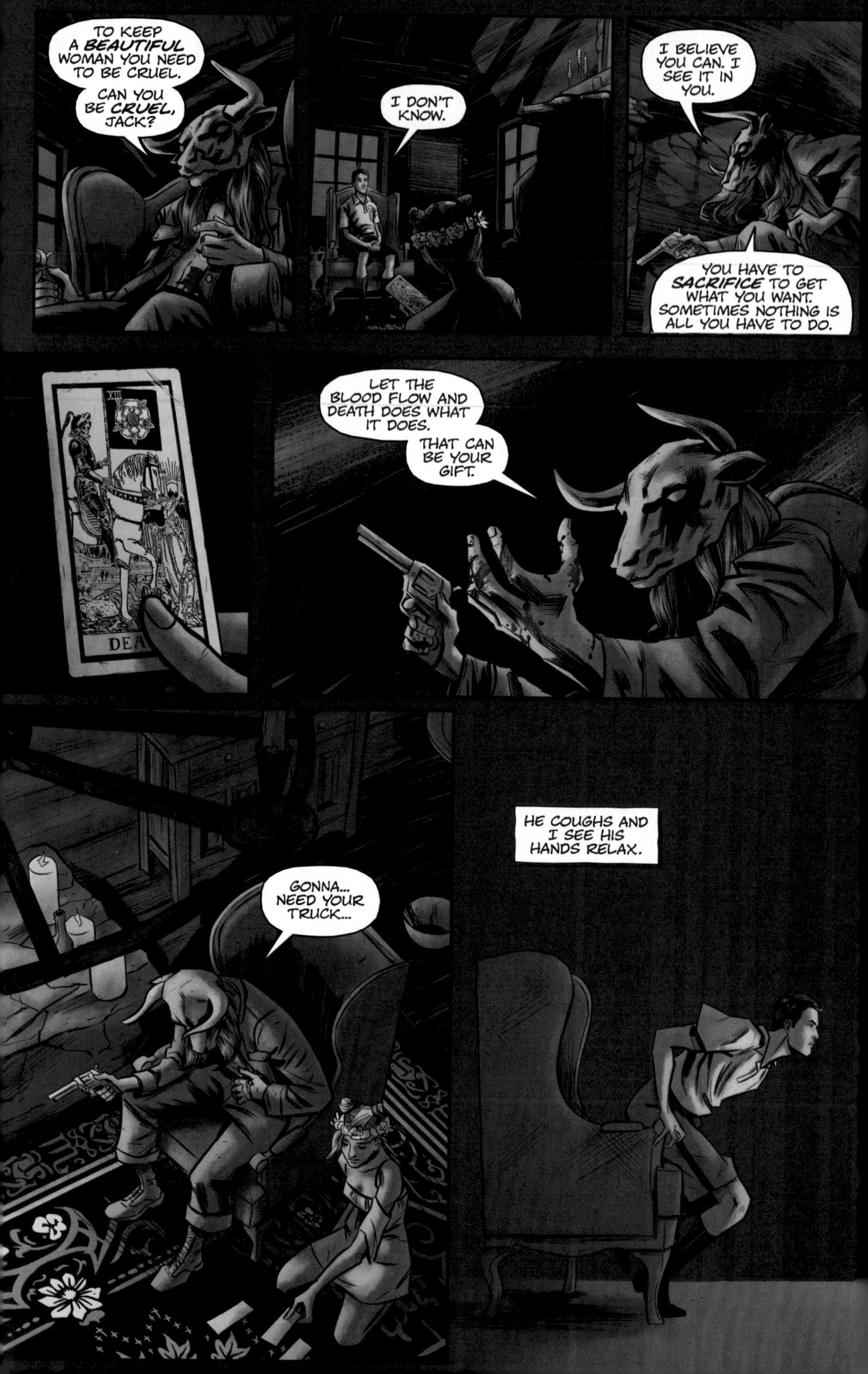

TO KEEP A BEAUTIFUL WOMAN YOU NEED TO BE CRUEL.
CAN YOU BE CRUEL, JACK?
I DON'T KNOW.
I BELIEVE YOU CAN. I SEE IT IN YOU.
YOU HAVE TO SACRIFICE TO GET WHAT YOU WANT. SOMETIMES NOTHING IS ALL YOU HAVE TO DO.
XIII
DEA
LET THE BLOOD FLOW AND DEATH DOES WHAT IT DOES.
THAT CAN BE YOUR GIFT.
GONNA... NEED YOUR TRUCK...
HE COUGHS AND I SEE HIS HANDS RELAX.

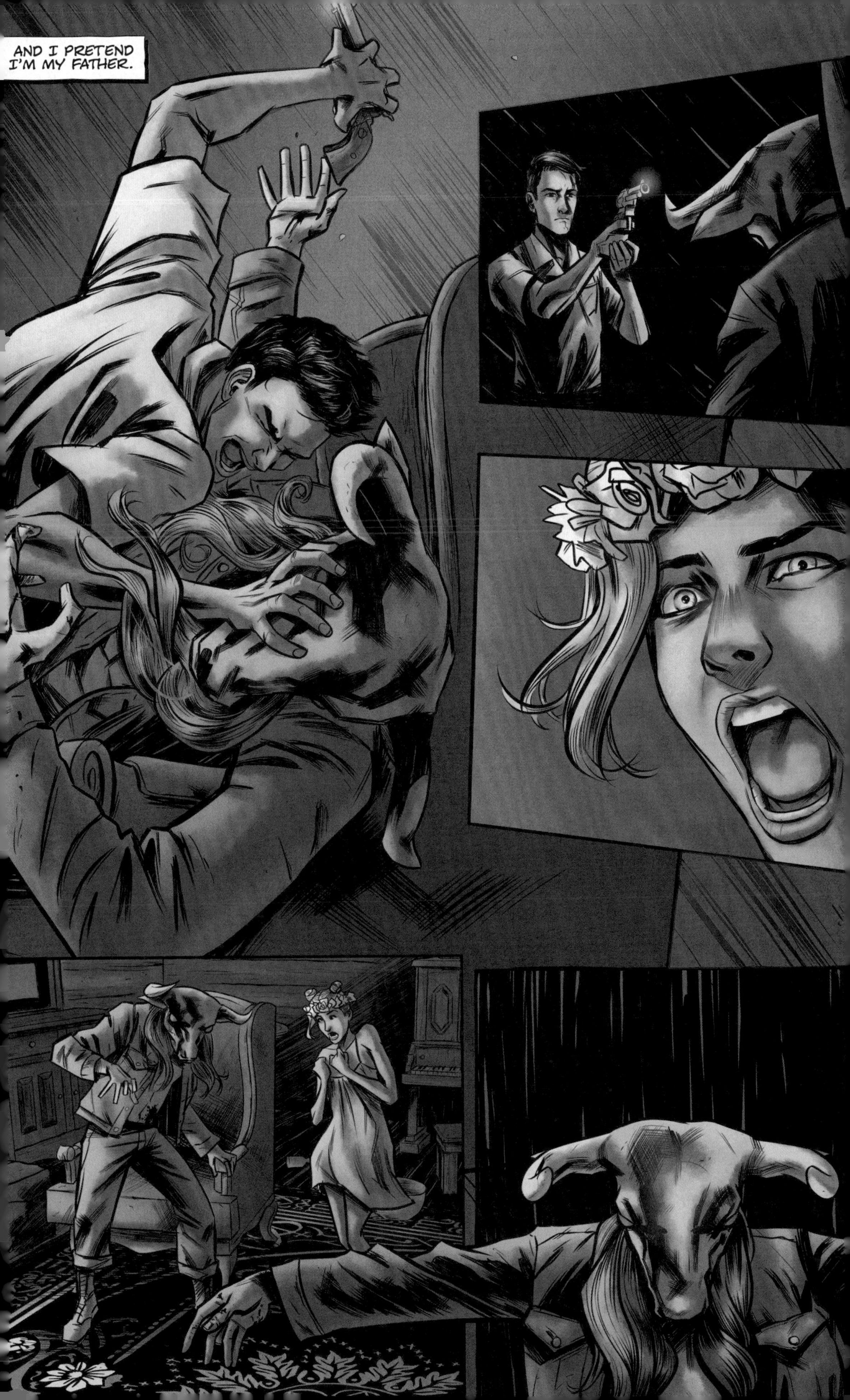
AND I PRETEND I'M MY FATHER.

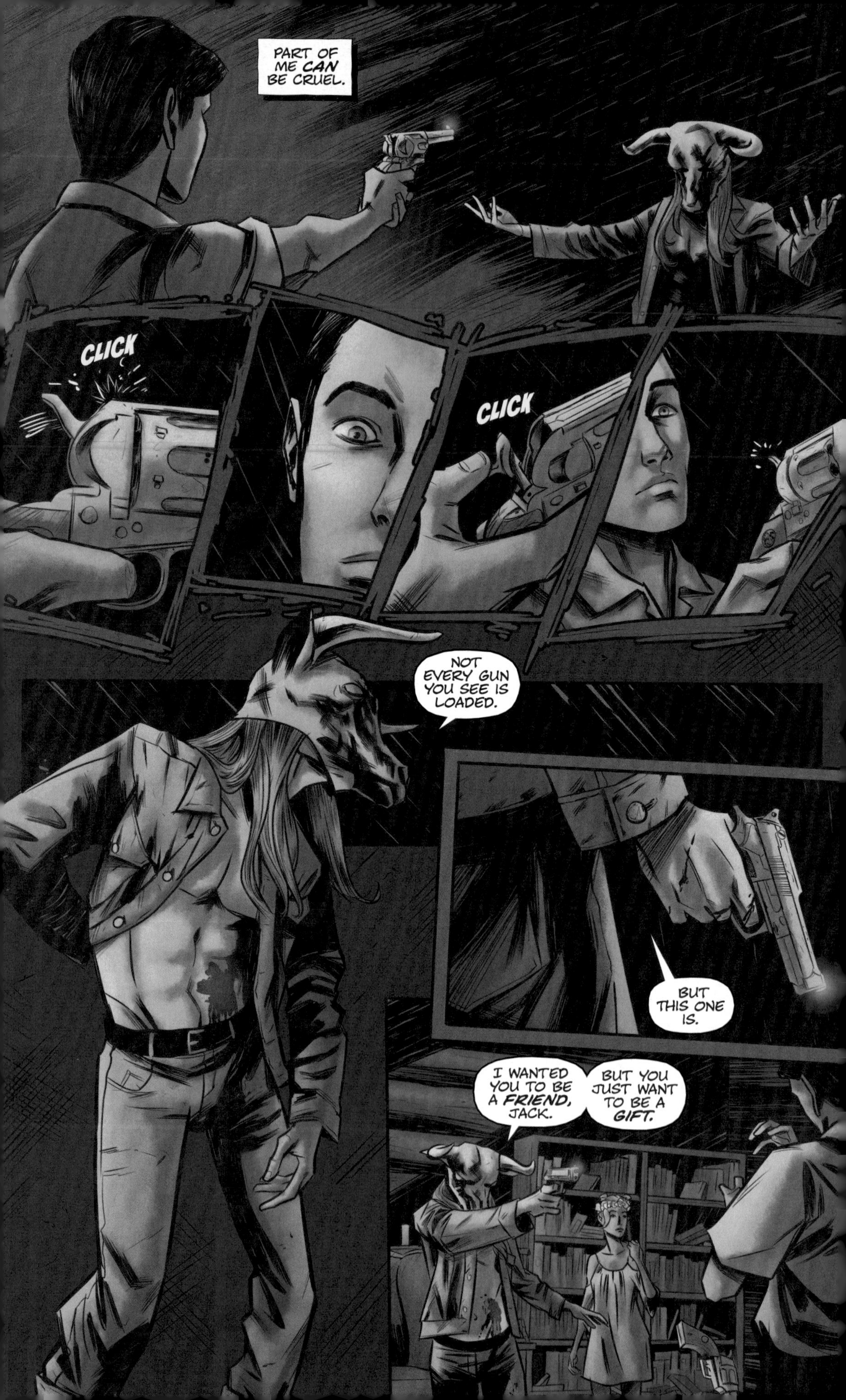
PART OF ME CAN BE CRUEL.
CLICK
CLICK
NOT EVERY GUN YOU SEE IS LOADED.
BUT THIS ONE IS.
I WANTED YOU TO BE A FRIEND, JACK.
BUT YOU JUST WANT TO BE A GIFT.

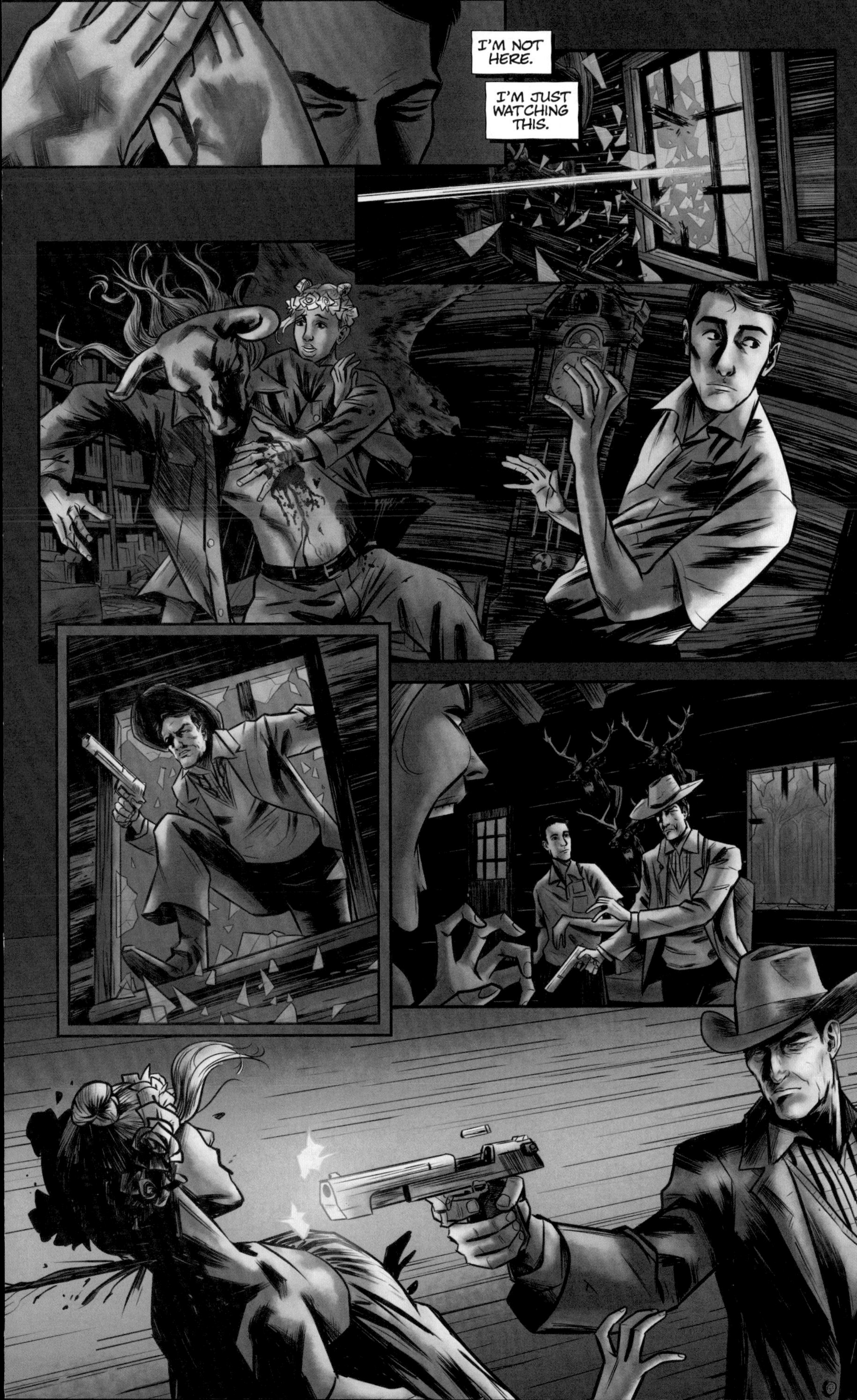
I'M NOT HERE.
I'M JUST WATCHING THIS.

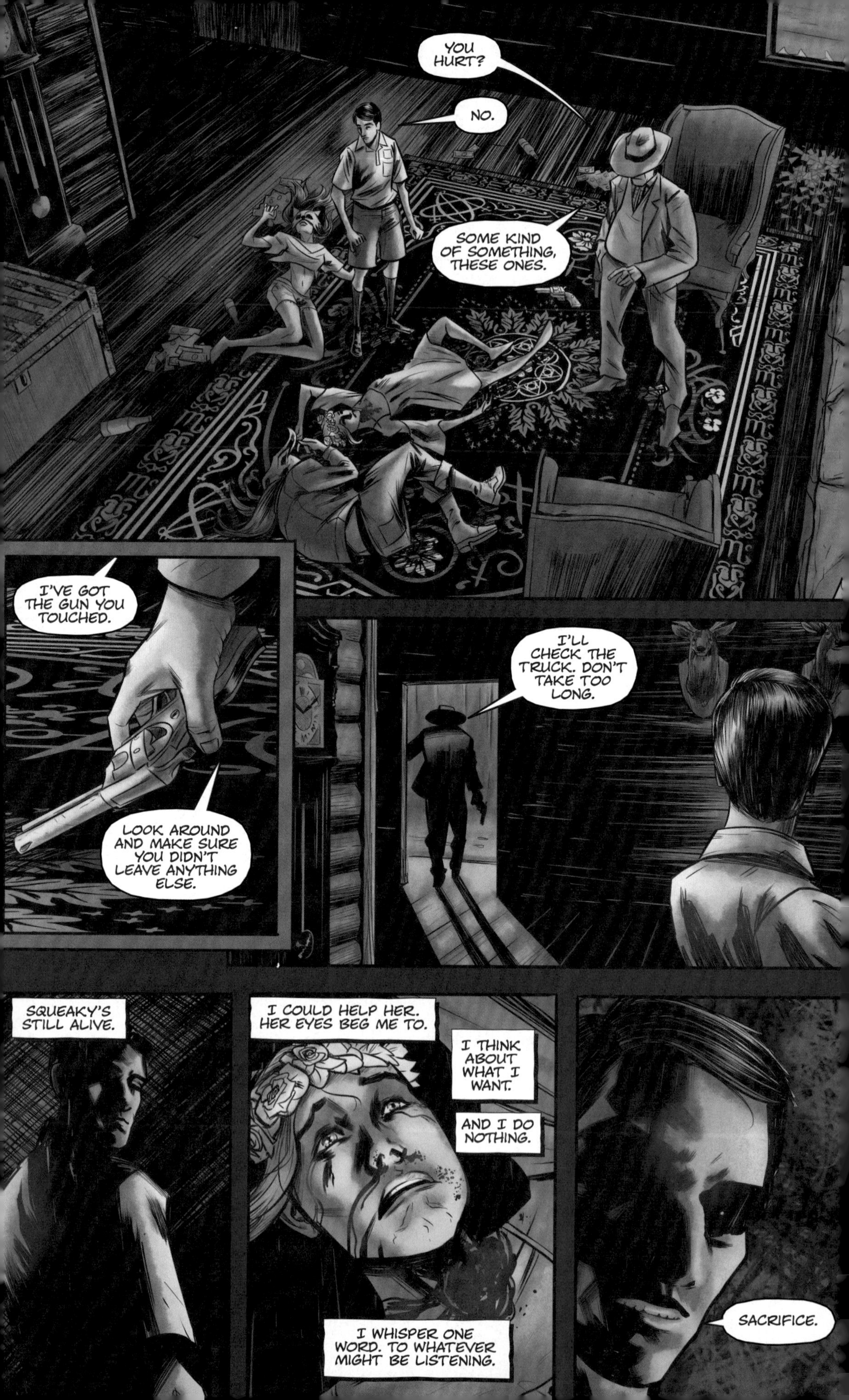
YOU HURT?
NO.
SOME KIND OF SOMETHING, THESE ONES.
I'VE GOT THE GUN YOU TOUCHED.
LOOK AROUND AND MAKE SURE YOU DIDN'T LEAVE ANYTHING ELSE.
I'LL CHECK THE TRUCK. DON'T TAKE TOO LONG.
SQUEAKY'S STILL ALIVE.
I COULD HELP HER. HER EYES BEG ME TO.
I THINK ABOUT WHAT I WANT.
AND I DO NOTHING.
I WHISPER ONE WORD. TO WHATEVER MIGHT BE LISTENING.
SACRIFICE.

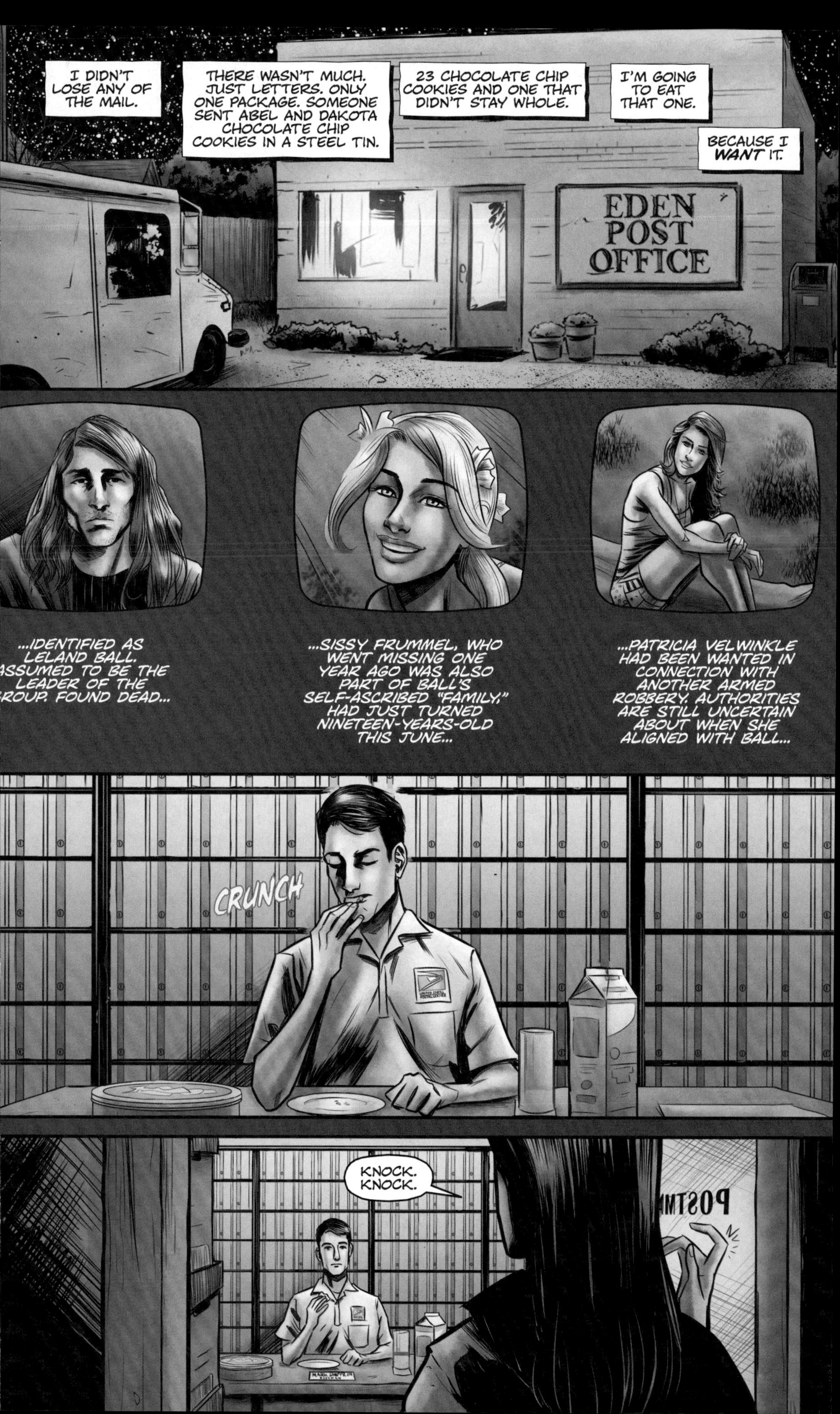

I DIDN'T LOSE ANY OF THE MAIL.
THERE WASN'T MUCH. JUST LETTERS. ONLY ONE PACKAGE. SOMEONE SENT ABEL AND DAKOTA CHOCOLATE CHIP COOKIES IN A STEEL TIN.
23 CHOCOLATE CHIP COOKIES AND ONE THAT DIDN'T STAY WHOLE.
I'M GOING TO EAT THAT ONE.
BECAUSE I *WANT* IT.
EDEN POST OFFICE
...IDENTIFIED AS LELAND BALL. ASSUMED TO BE THE LEADER OF THE ROUP. FOUND DEAD...
...SISSY FRUMMEL, WHO WENT MISSING ONE YEAR AGO WAS ALSO PART OF BALL'S SELF-ASCRIBED "FAMILY," HAD JUST TURNED NINETEEN-YEARS-OLD THIS JUNE...
...PATRICIA VELWINKLE HAD BEEN WANTED IN CONNECTION WITH ANOTHER ARMED ROBBERY. AUTHORITIES ARE STILL UNCERTAIN ABOUT WHEN SHE ALIGNED WITH BALL...
CRUNCH
KNOCK. KNOCK.

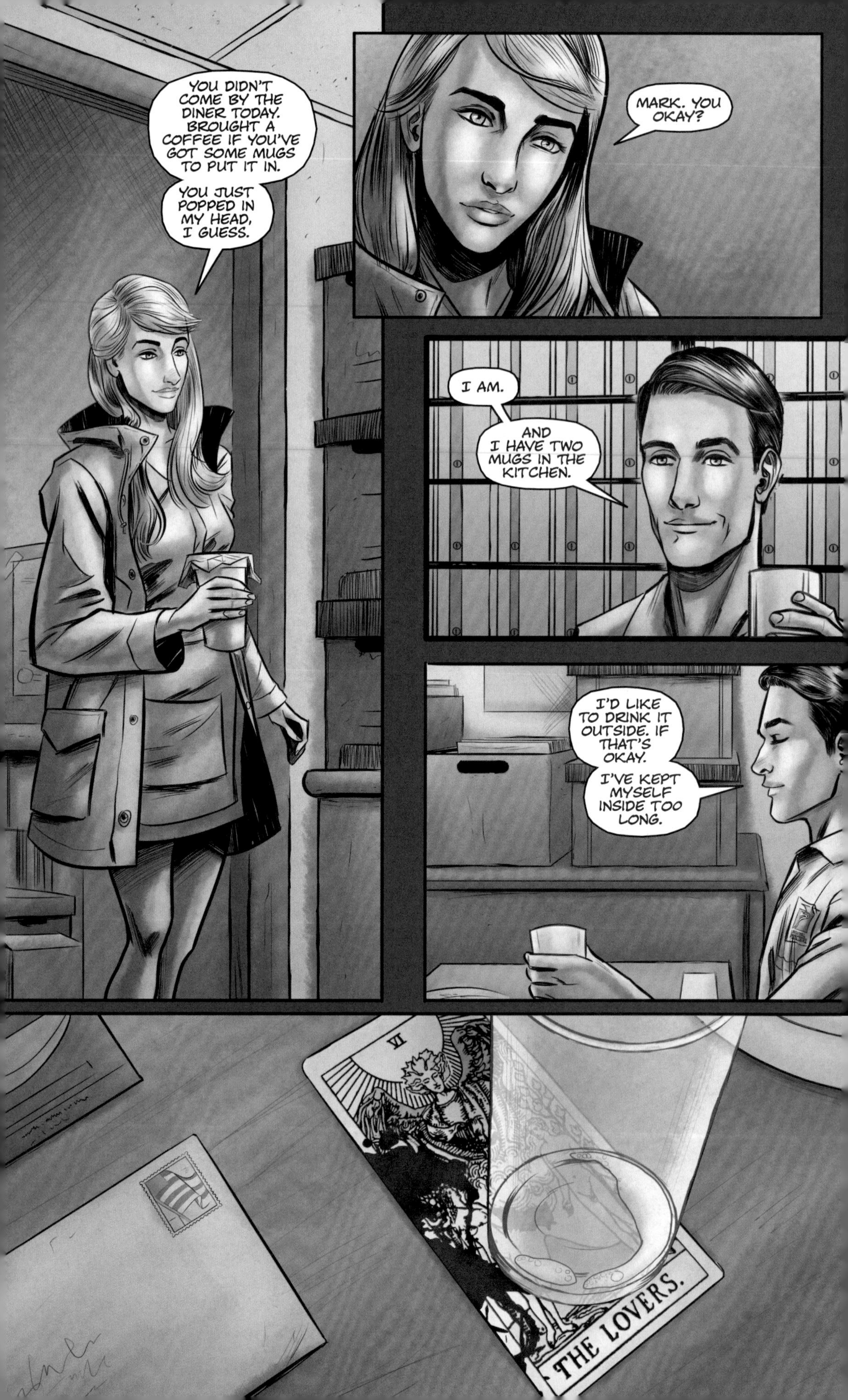
YOU DIDN'T COME BY THE DINER TODAY. BROUGHT A COFFEE IF YOU'VE GOT SOME MUGS TO PUT IT IN.
YOU JUST POPPED IN MY HEAD, I GUESS.
MARK. YOU OKAY?
I AM.
AND I HAVE TWO MUGS IN THE KITCHEN.
I'D LIKE TO DRINK IT OUTSIDE. IF THAT'S OKAY.
I'VE KEPT MYSELF INSIDE TOO LONG.
VI
THE LOVERS.

# MAIL CALL

I transcribe all the mail now. I take the letters and postcards in different fonts and sizes an make them all the same. Times New Roman, 12-point font, 8 ½" x 11", bright white paper I file them away for my mother.

Except for these three. These three are just for me.

Letter from Leland Ball, to Sissy "Squeaky" Frummel:

You wanna know what I see in you? What makes you special? You're a blossom, Squeaky. When I first came down from my pilgrimage of blood, I bore witness to your spectacle – a preparation for transformation. A display of potential. You showed me, with a twirl of baton, with the alchemic circle, symbol upon symbol, you proved your worth.

## Letter from Sissy Frummel, to her parents:

Let your daughter teach you, for you do not understand as I do. I have read your letters, childish scrawl, unlearned, concerned with the world I have abandoned. I ain't your "Sissy," I ain't your anything. I'm about something new. I'm about Ball, now, and His great work. He called me a "gift."

Watch me walking in the path of Jupiter, garland of flowers, guided by Him. When He found me, He saw the potential in me to become something more, to transform. And I have transformed and am still transforming. I'm prettier for Him than I was for you.

When I was with you I understood as a child, but I have set aside childish things – Ball has shown me better. Ball has shown me that truth is not a farmhouse or a high school dance or a lifetime working paycheck to paycheck. The truth is not my Sunday dress or the misunderstandings of the false prophets in your liar's churches. The truth, the real truth…that's a truth I can dig. Ball's truth. Your whole world was all show and no go. Ball's gonna teach me to tune it all out.

When you catch sight of me next, it will be as He sees me. Holy, wholly, light, and free – of the air and the beyond. It's gonna take blood to show me and to show you. It always does.

---

## Letter from Leland Ball, to Patricia Velwinkle:

That's a load of bull. Here's the heavy, friend – you can have anything you want if you're willing to give up what's necessary.

I can show you something more, if you want. I can show you a place where all the castles are kingless and all the moats are full of blood. I can teach you all about how they went and fucked the world with bombs and books. There was an old way of doing things. A right way. A path colored carmine, firelit, where a man made his own way and only hurt those that needed hurting.

Let me help you walk it. It ain't easy, but I can help you, if you'll let me. Won't you let me be a friend?

# POSTAL

# Patricia Velwinkle's Final Diary Entry

You know foxes eat their young? Ball taught me that. Ball taught me all kinds of stuff.

It's weird, ya know? I've been watching us on the news, folks always talking about us and what we do. I watched some chrome dome with a bad mustache asking you questions on the tube, and you said how you were just so afraid for me, and you were afraid I was gonna eat it once and for all.

But that's what you don't get – there's no such thing as once and for all. Permanency, transience, diamonds are forever – it's all bullshit. There's no start and no stop, and that's why it's okay. I saw you crying and I wanted to wipe off those tears and tell you that it was okay, no, better than okay.

It was good.

It was good when we broke into those people's homes and it was good when we gathered them and their families and cut them up and let them bleed. It was good of us to do that because that's how the cycle works. Ball taught me that, too, and at least we tried to teach those people before they bit it.

This body's hurting pretty bad. Ball says that the MEDIA will call this a suicide note, but that's so ignorant. That's so jacked and wrong. Because I'm not gonna die, man, I'm never gonna die. That's not what any of this is. There's blood everywhere but it's a good thing because I'm not dying.

I'm being born. Maybe as something new. Maybe as a fox – wouldn't that be rad? My new mama would eat me and I'd start fresh right away. Far out. I love you, Mama. I love you Dad. Almost as much as I loved Him.

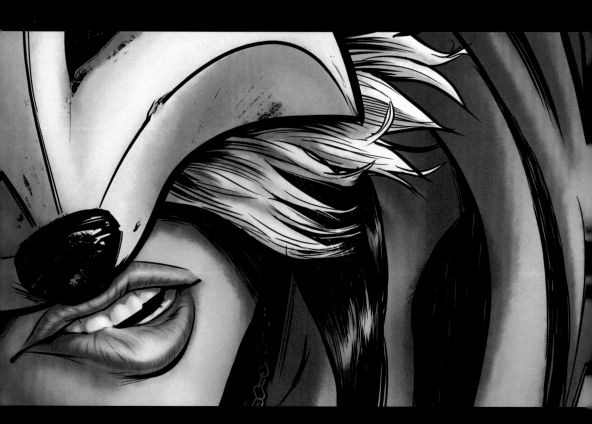

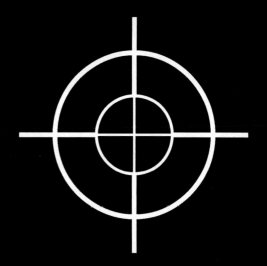

# Chapter 6

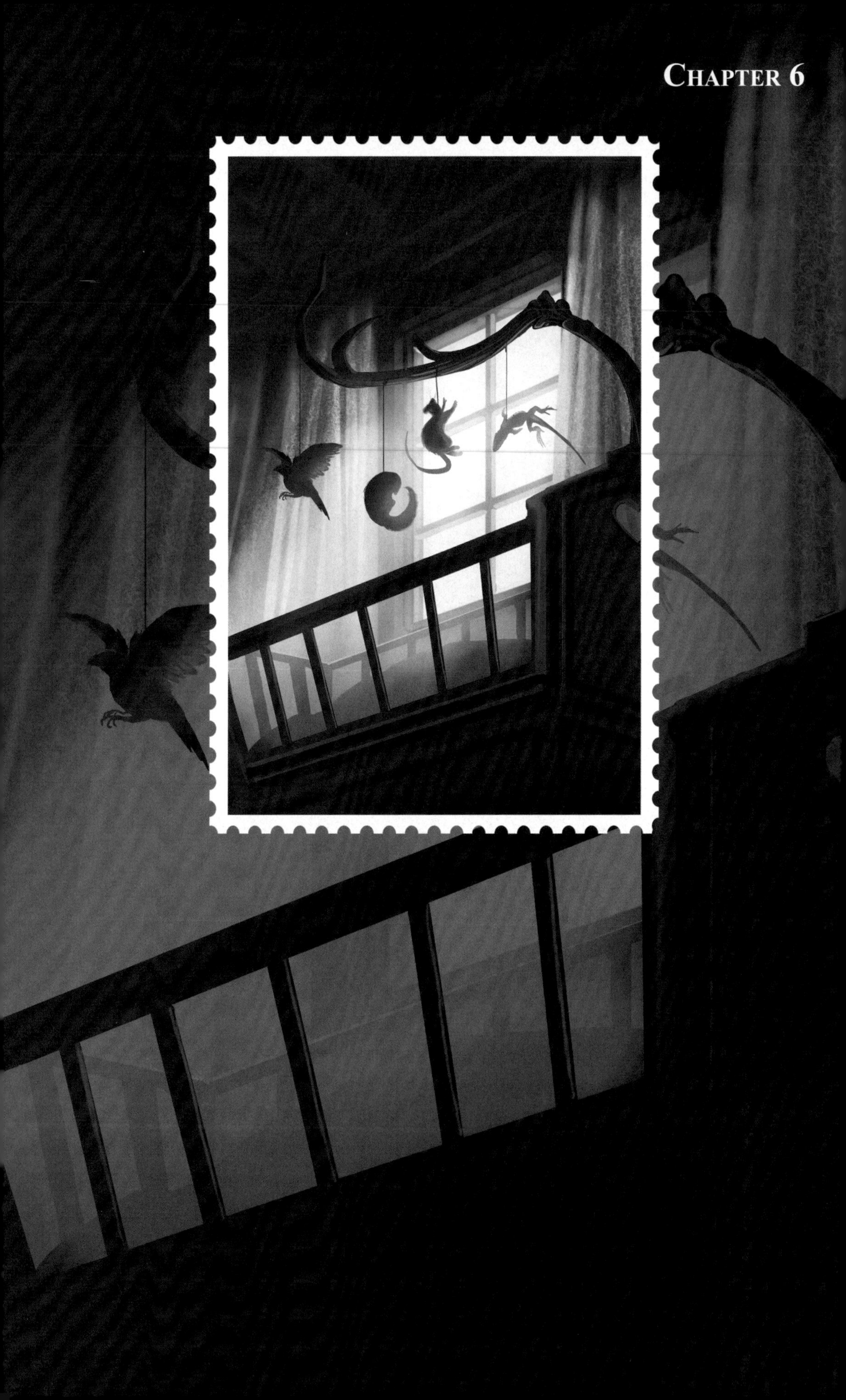

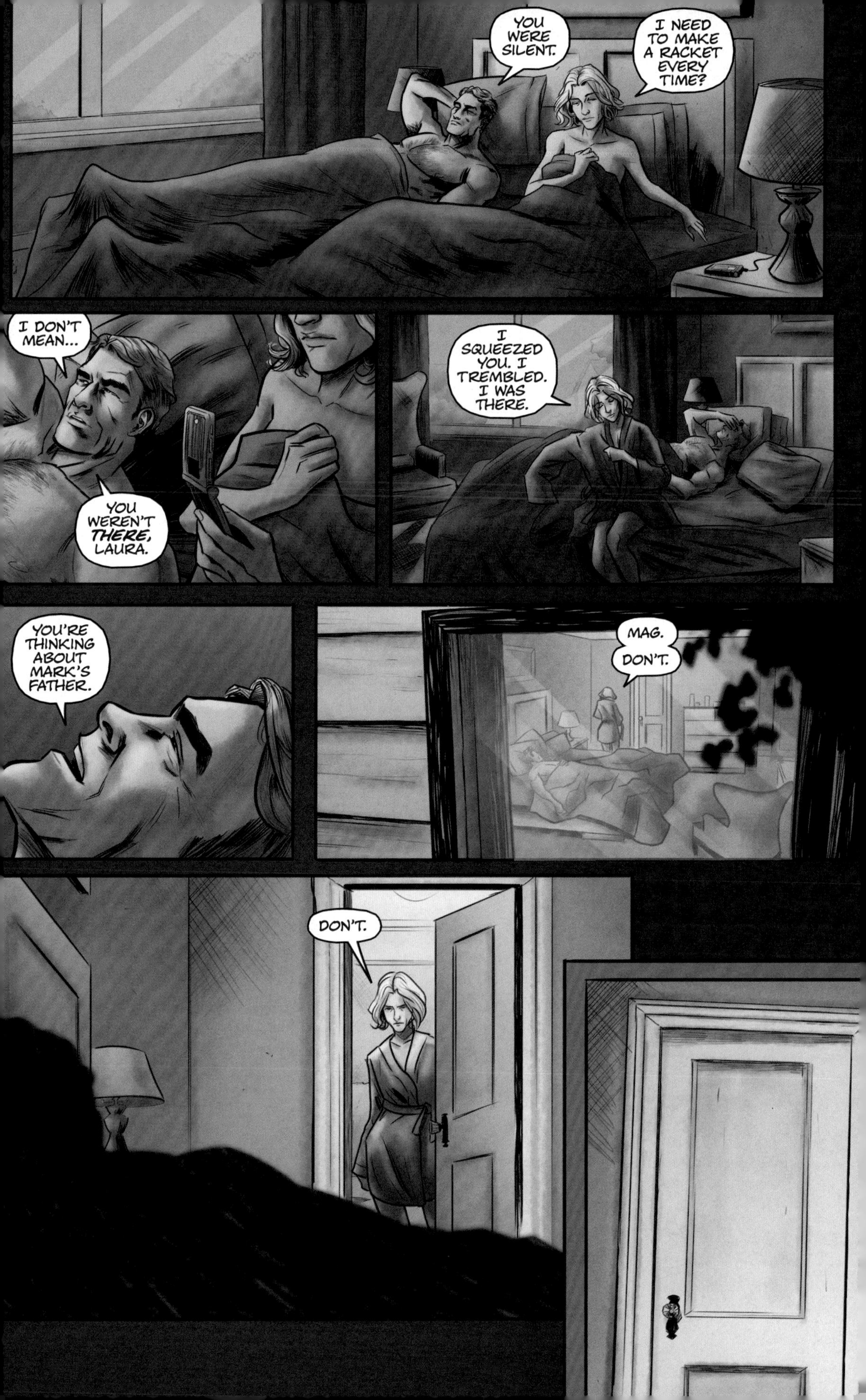
YOU WERE SILENT.
I NEED TO MAKE A RACKET EVERY TIME?
I DON'T MEAN...
YOU WEREN'T THERE, LAURA.
I SQUEEZED YOU. I TREMBLED. I WAS THERE.
YOU'RE THINKING ABOUT MARK'S FATHER.
MAG.
DON'T.
DON'T.

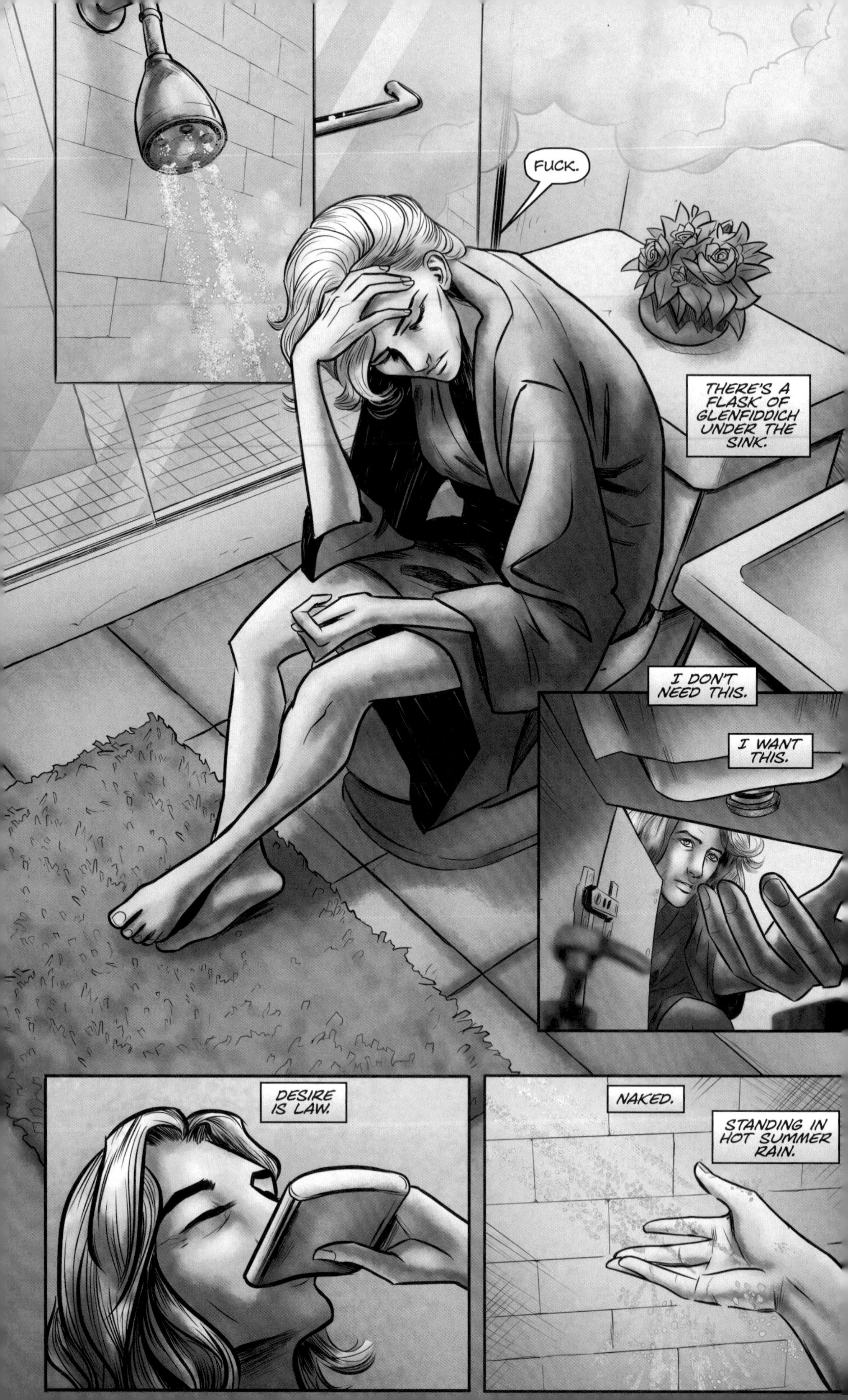

FUCK.
THERE'S A FLASK OF GLENFIDDICH UNDER THE SINK.
I DON'T NEED THIS.
I WANT THIS.
DESIRE IS LAW.
NAKED.
STANDING IN HOT SUMMER RAIN.

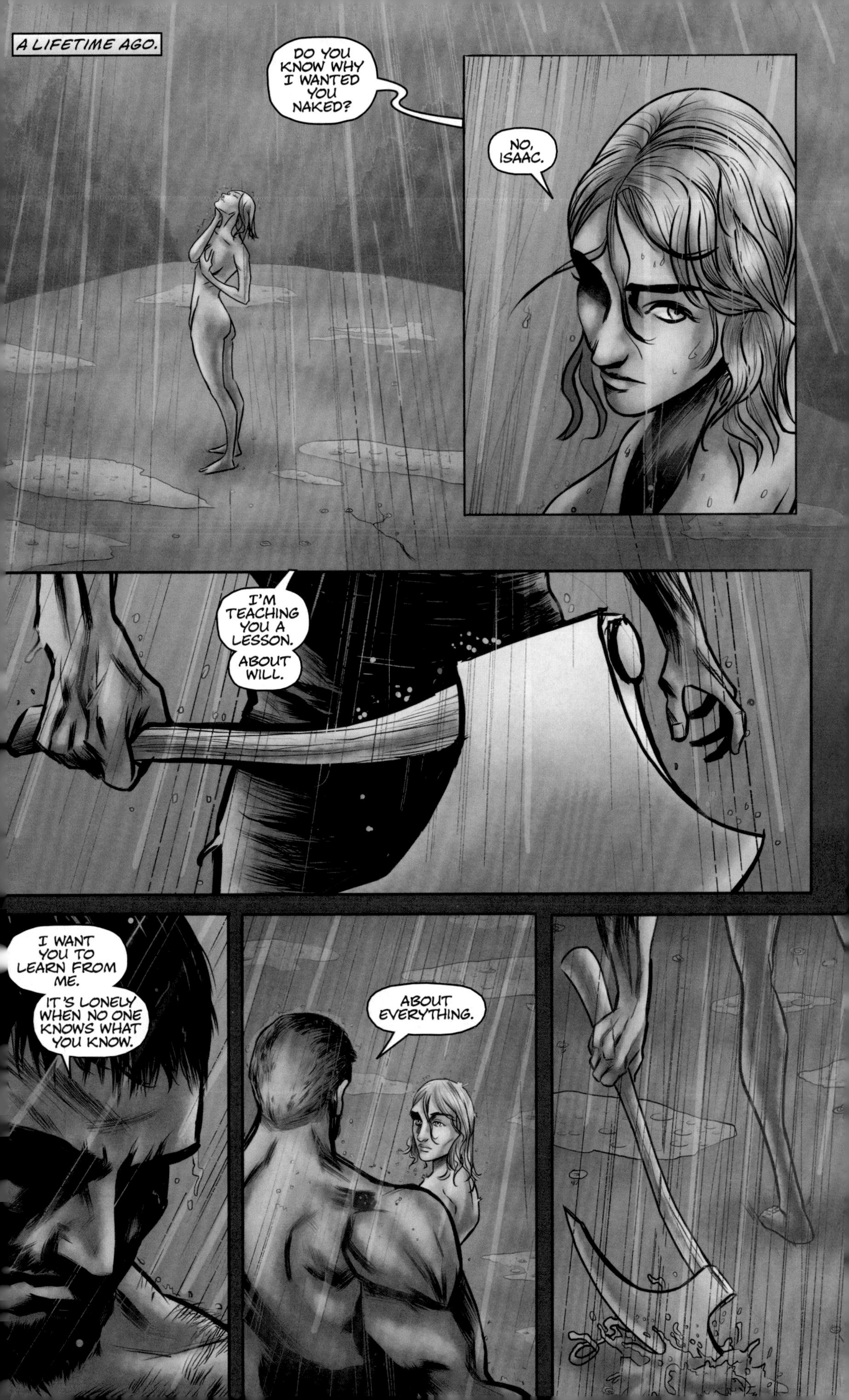
A LIFETIME AGO.
DO YOU KNOW WHY I WANTED YOU NAKED?
NO, ISAAC.
I'M TEACHING YOU A LESSON.
ABOUT WILL.
I WANT YOU TO LEARN FROM ME.
IT'S LONELY WHEN NO ONE KNOWS WHAT YOU KNOW.
ABOUT EVERYTHING.

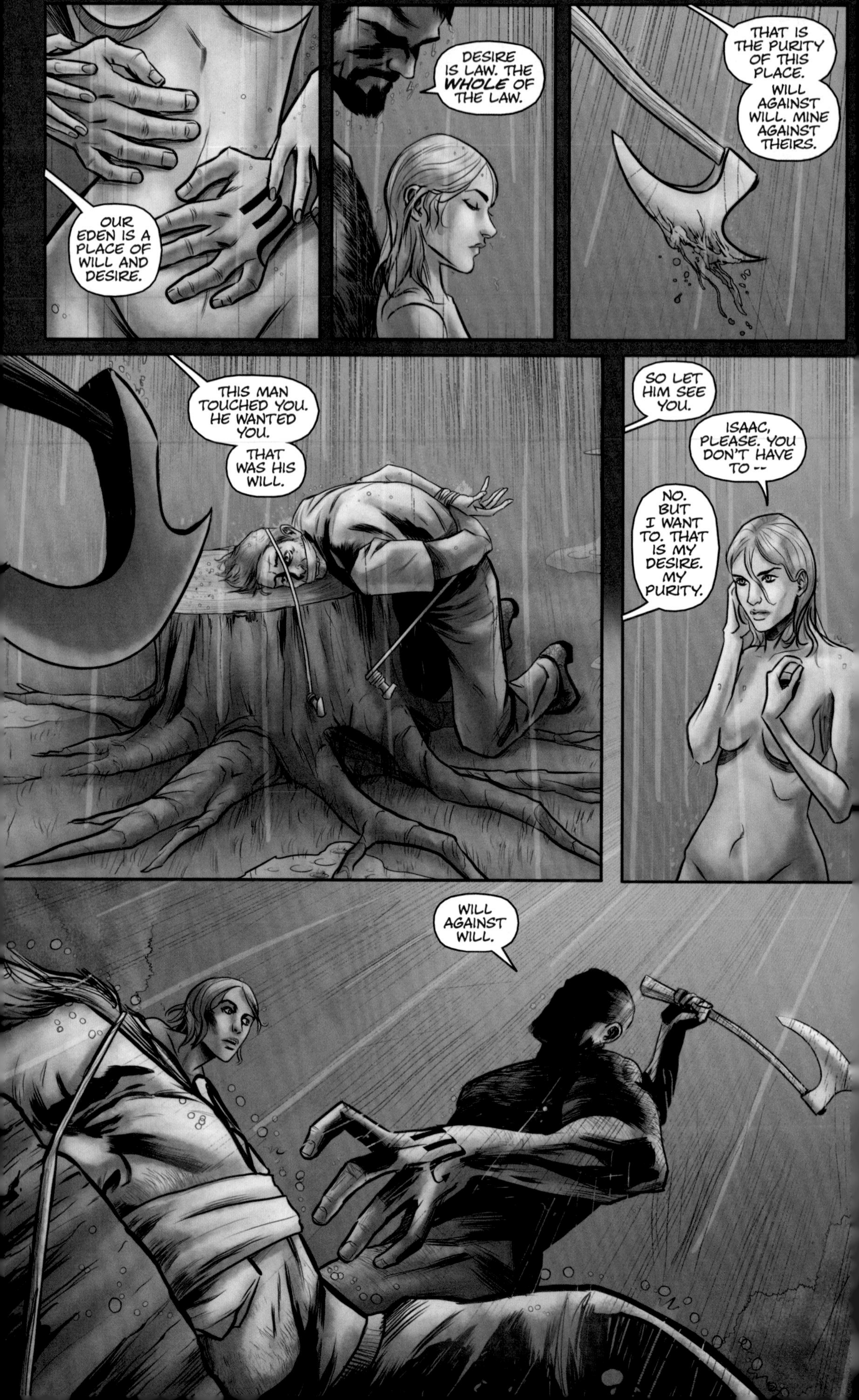
OUR EDEN IS A PLACE OF WILL AND DESIRE.
DESIRE IS LAW. THE **WHOLE** OF THE LAW.
THAT IS THE PURITY OF THIS PLACE.
WILL AGAINST WILL. MINE AGAINST THEIRS.
THIS MAN TOUCHED YOU. HE WANTED YOU.
THAT WAS HIS WILL.
SO LET HIM SEE YOU.
ISAAC, PLEASE. YOU DON'T HAVE TO --
NO. BUT I WANT TO. THAT IS MY DESIRE. MY PURITY.
WILL AGAINST WILL.

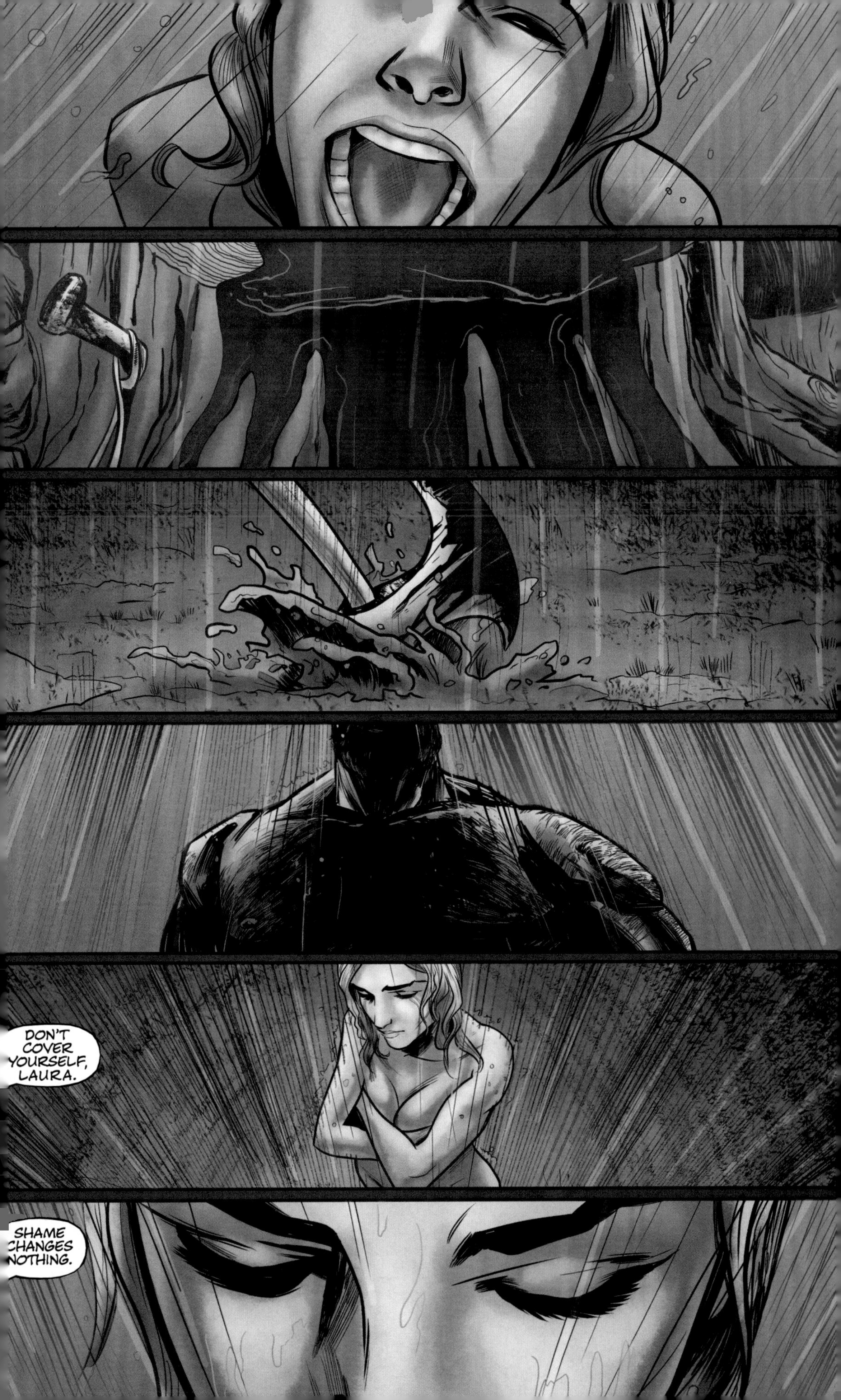
DON'T COVER YOURSELF, LAURA.
SHAME CHANGES NOTHING.

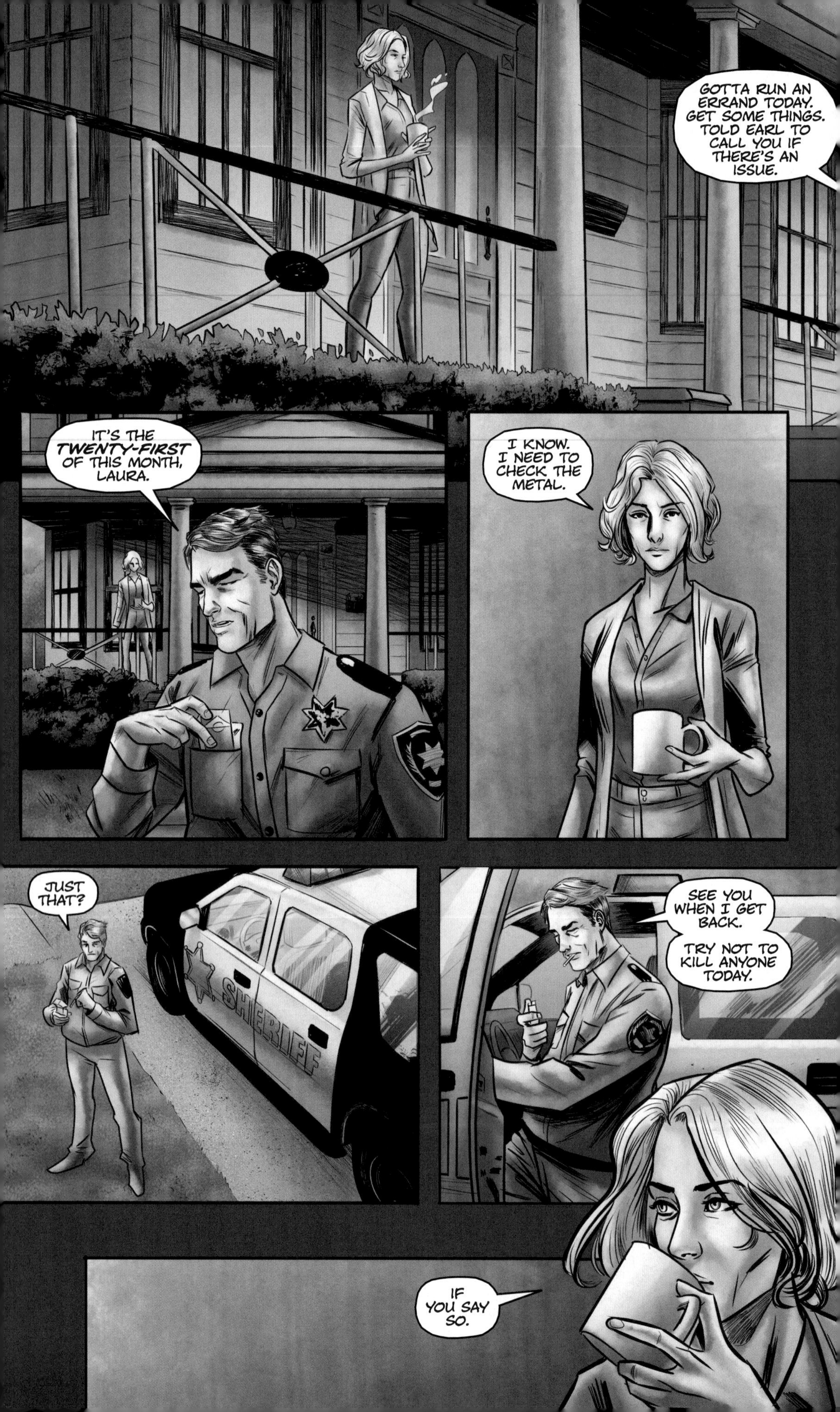
GOTTA RUN AN ERRAND TODAY. GET SOME THINGS. TOLD EARL TO CALL YOU IF THERE'S AN ISSUE.
IT'S THE *TWENTY-FIRST* OF THIS MONTH, LAURA.
I KNOW. I NEED TO CHECK THE METAL.
JUST THAT?
SEE YOU WHEN I GET BACK.
TRY NOT TO KILL ANYONE TODAY.
SHERIFF
IF YOU SAY SO.

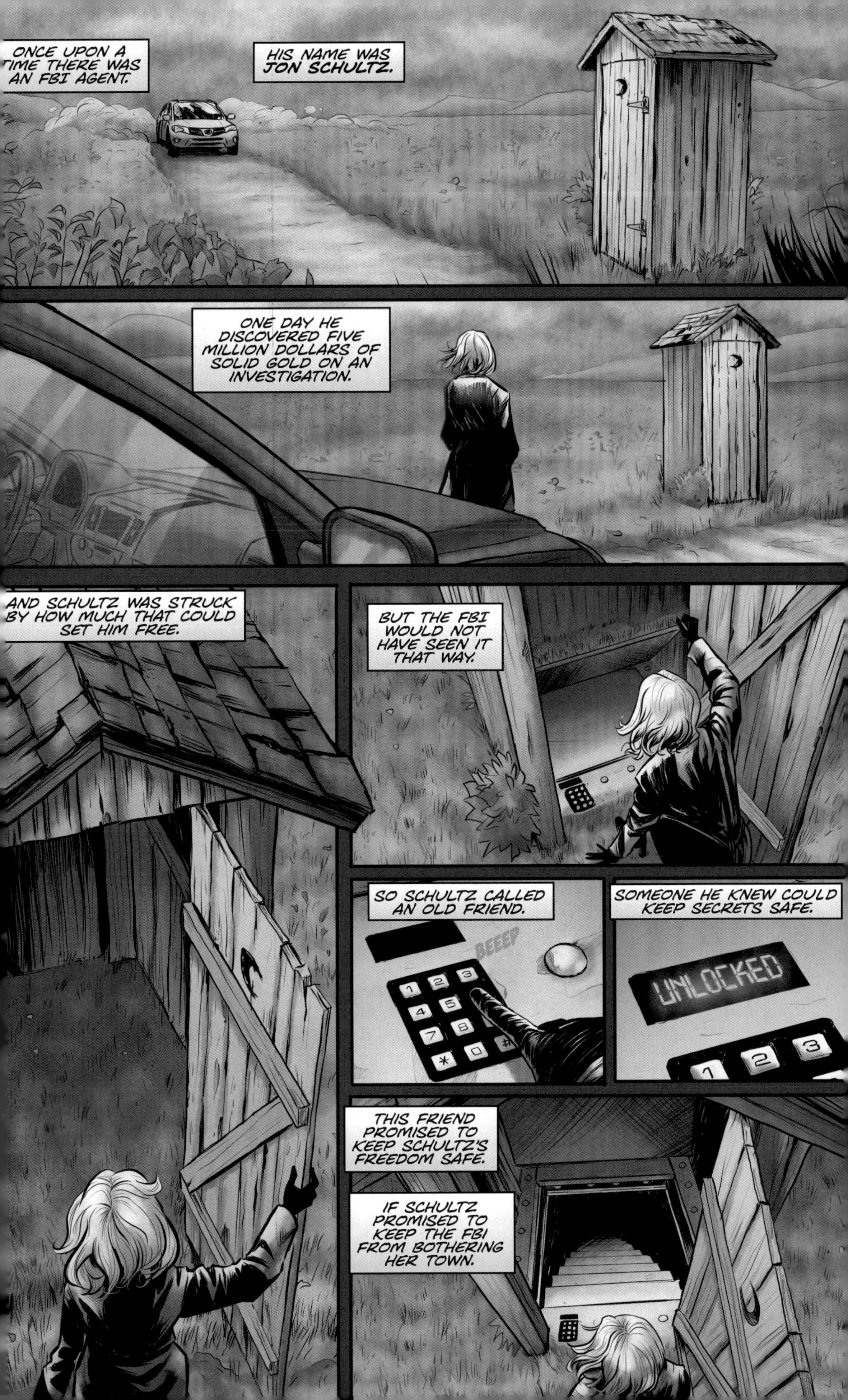
ONCE UPON A TIME THERE WAS AN FBI AGENT.
HIS NAME WAS JON SCHULTZ.
ONE DAY HE DISCOVERED FIVE MILLION DOLLARS OF SOLID GOLD ON AN INVESTIGATION.
AND SCHULTZ WAS STRUCK BY HOW MUCH THAT COULD SET HIM FREE.
BUT THE FBI WOULD NOT HAVE SEEN IT THAT WAY.
SO SCHULTZ CALLED AN OLD FRIEND.
BEEEP
SOMEONE HE KNEW COULD KEEP SECRETS SAFE.
UNLOCKED
THIS FRIEND PROMISED TO KEEP SCHULTZ'S FREEDOM SAFE.
IF SCHULTZ PROMISED TO KEEP THE FBI FROM BOTHERING HER TOWN.

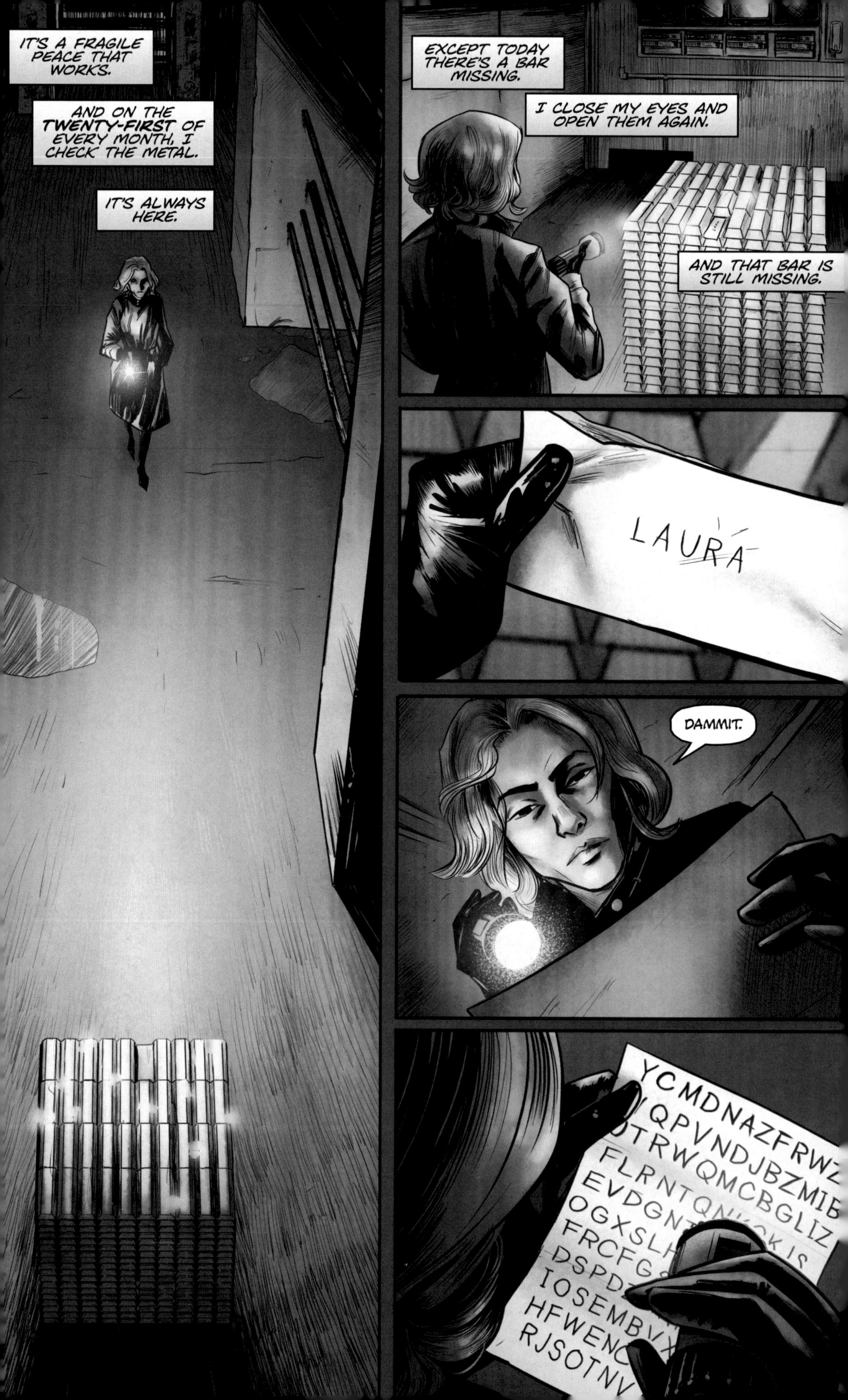
IT'S A FRAGILE PEACE THAT WORKS.
AND ON THE TWENTY-FIRST OF EVERY MONTH, I CHECK THE METAL.
IT'S ALWAYS HERE.
EXCEPT TODAY THERE'S A BAR MISSING.
I CLOSE MY EYES AND OPEN THEM AGAIN.
AND THAT BAR IS STILL MISSING.
LAURA
DAMMIT.

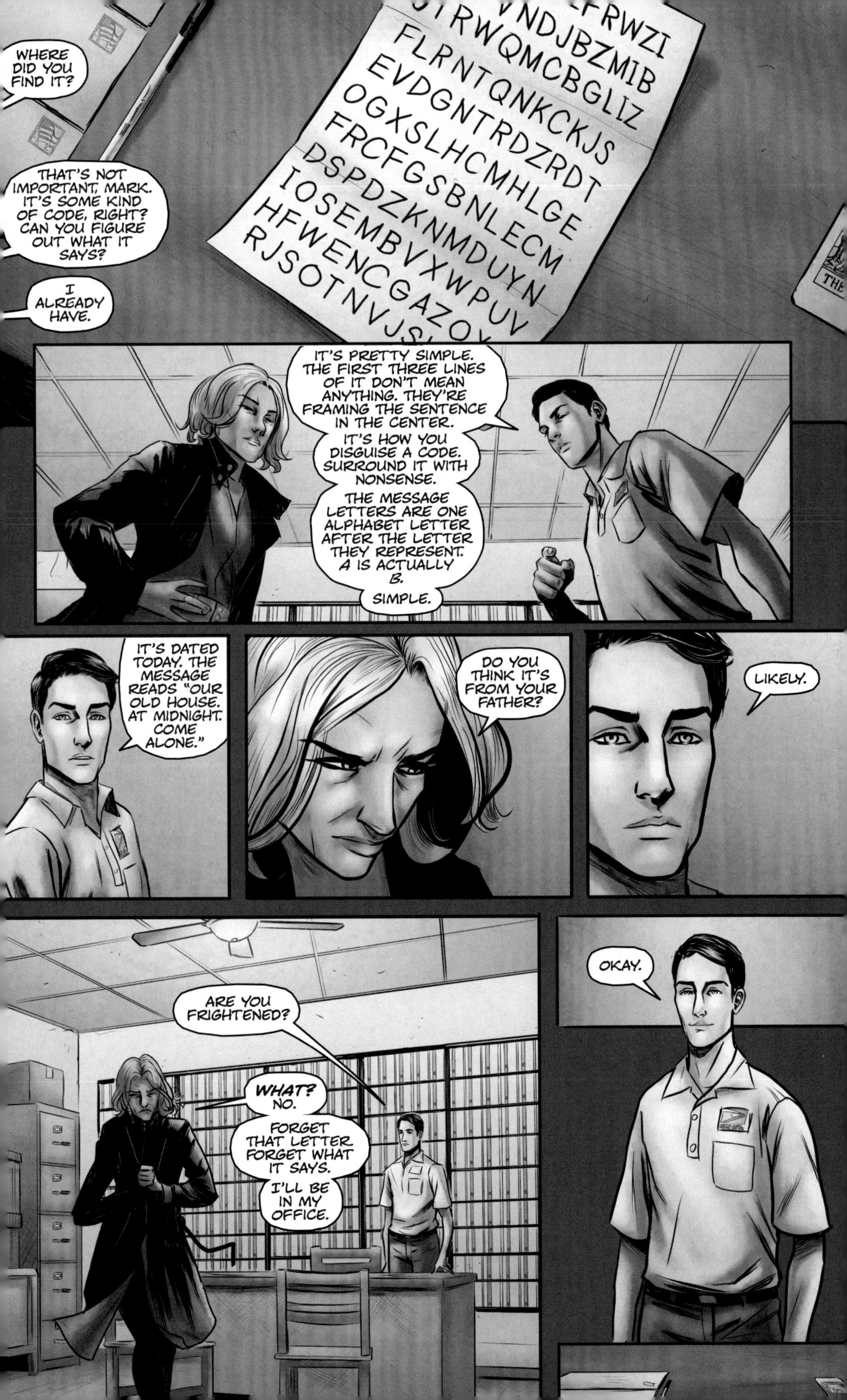

WHERE DID YOU FIND IT?
THAT'S NOT IMPORTANT, MARK. IT'S SOME KIND OF CODE, RIGHT? CAN YOU FIGURE OUT WHAT IT SAYS?
I ALREADY HAVE.
IT'S PRETTY SIMPLE. THE FIRST THREE LINES OF IT DON'T MEAN ANYTHING. THEY'RE FRAMING THE SENTENCE IN THE CENTER.
IT'S HOW YOU DISGUISE A CODE. SURROUND IT WITH NONSENSE.
THE MESSAGE LETTERS ARE ONE ALPHABET LETTER AFTER THE LETTER THEY REPRESENT. A IS ACTUALLY B.
SIMPLE.
IT'S DATED TODAY. THE MESSAGE READS "OUR OLD HOUSE. AT MIDNIGHT. COME ALONE."
DO YOU THINK IT'S FROM YOUR FATHER?
LIKELY.
ARE YOU FRIGHTENED?
WHAT? NO.
FORGET THAT LETTER FORGET WHAT IT SAYS.
I'LL BE IN MY OFFICE.
OKAY.

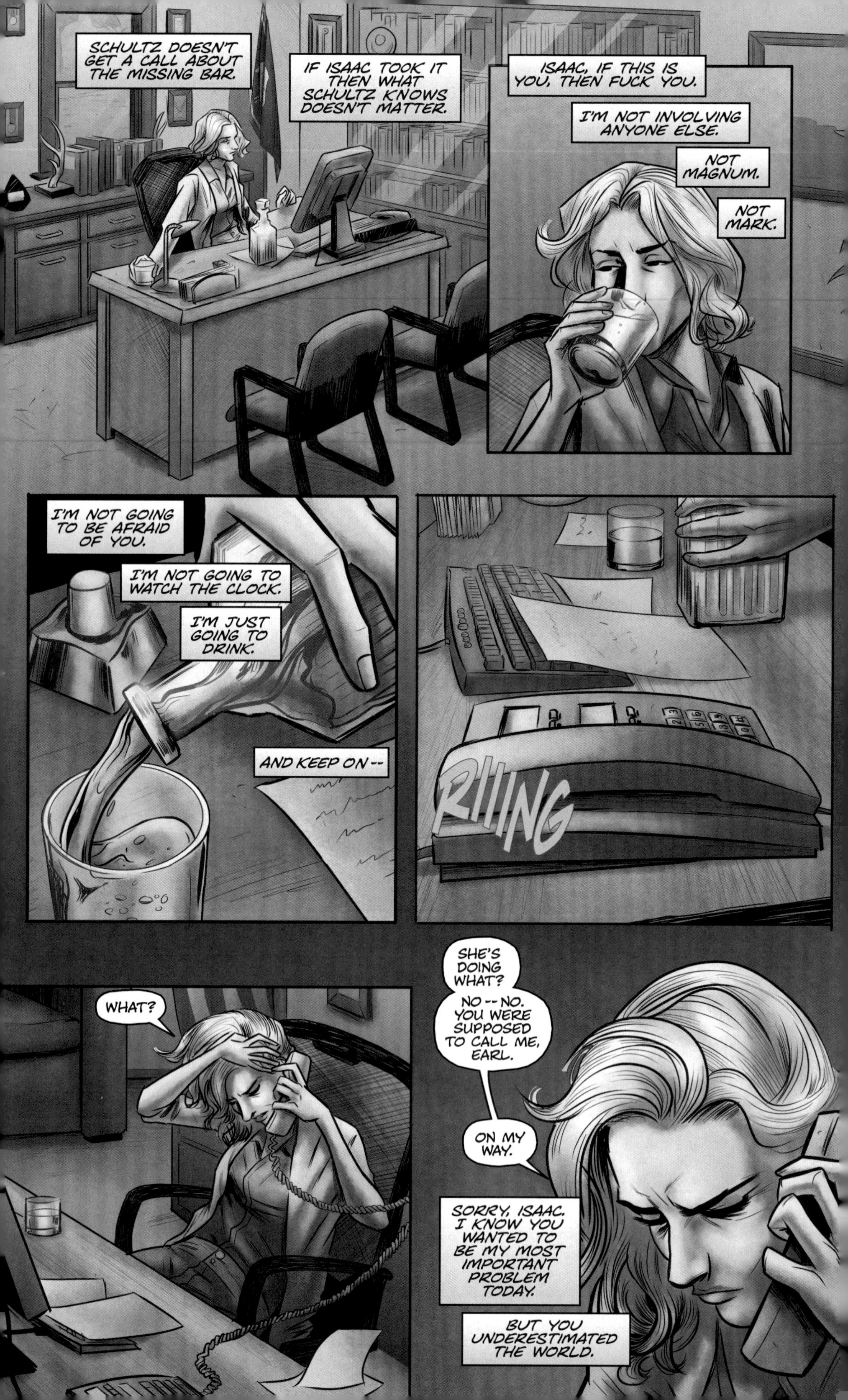
SCHULTZ DOESN'T GET A CALL ABOUT THE MISSING BAR.
IF ISAAC TOOK IT THEN WHAT SCHULTZ KNOWS DOESN'T MATTER.
ISAAC, IF THIS IS YOU, THEN FUCK YOU.
I'M NOT INVOLVING ANYONE ELSE.
NOT MAGNUM.
NOT MARK.
I'M NOT GOING TO BE AFRAID OF YOU.
I'M NOT GOING TO WATCH THE CLOCK.
I'M JUST GOING TO DRINK.
AND KEEP ON --
RIIING
WHAT?
SHE'S DOING WHAT?
NO -- NO. YOU WERE SUPPOSED TO CALL ME, EARL.
ON MY WAY.
SORRY, ISAAC. I KNOW YOU WANTED TO BE MY MOST IMPORTANT PROBLEM TODAY.
BUT YOU UNDERESTIMATED THE WORLD.

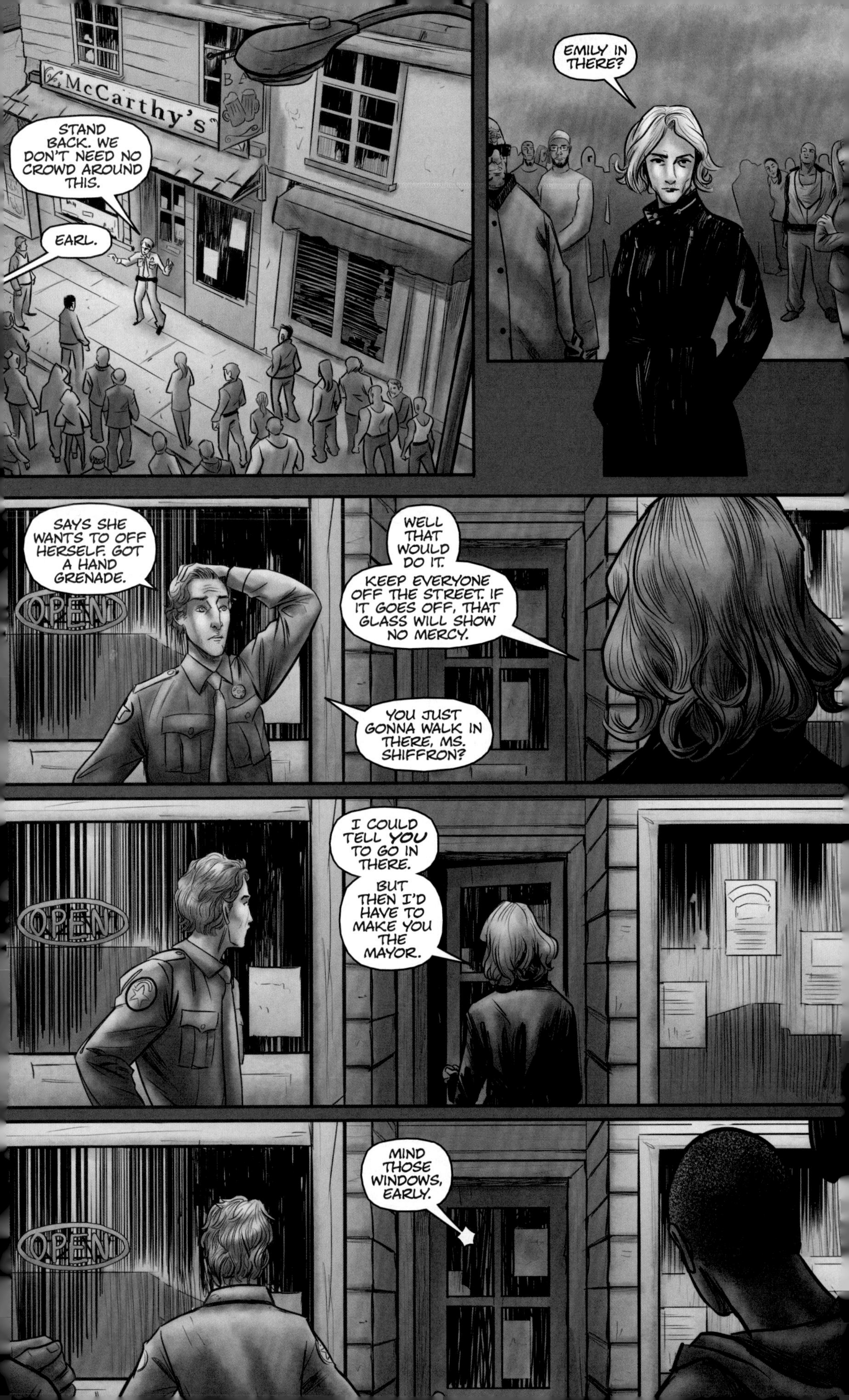
McCarthy's
STAND BACK. WE DON'T NEED NO CROWD AROUND THIS.
EARL.
EMILY IN THERE?
SAYS SHE WANTS TO OFF HERSELF. GOT A HAND GRENADE.
OPEN
WELL THAT WOULD DO IT.
KEEP EVERYONE OFF THE STREET. IF IT GOES OFF, THAT GLASS WILL SHOW NO MERCY.
YOU JUST GONNA WALK IN THERE, MS. SHIFFRON?
OPEN
I COULD TELL *YOU* TO GO IN THERE.
BUT THEN I'D HAVE TO MAKE YOU THE MAYOR.
OPEN
MIND THOSE WINDOWS, EARLY.

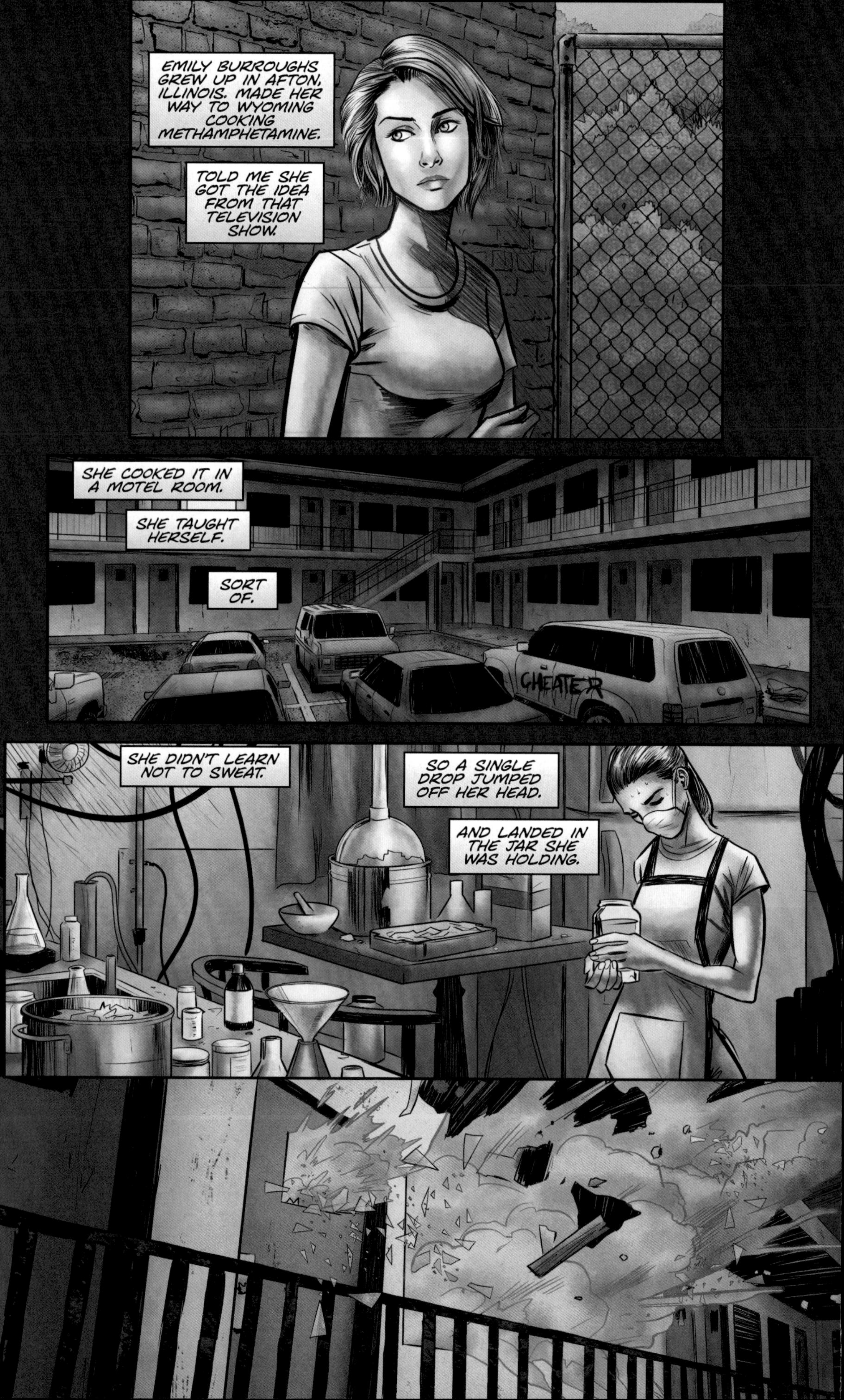
EMILY BURROUGHS GREW UP IN AFTON, ILLINOIS. MADE HER WAY TO WYOMING COOKING METHAMPHETAMINE.
TOLD ME SHE GOT THE IDEA FROM THAT TELEVISION SHOW.
SHE COOKED IT IN A MOTEL ROOM.
SHE TAUGHT HERSELF.
SORT OF.
CHEATER
SHE DIDN'T LEARN NOT TO SWEAT.
SO A SINGLE DROP JUMPED OFF HER HEAD.
AND LANDED IN THE JAR SHE WAS HOLDING.

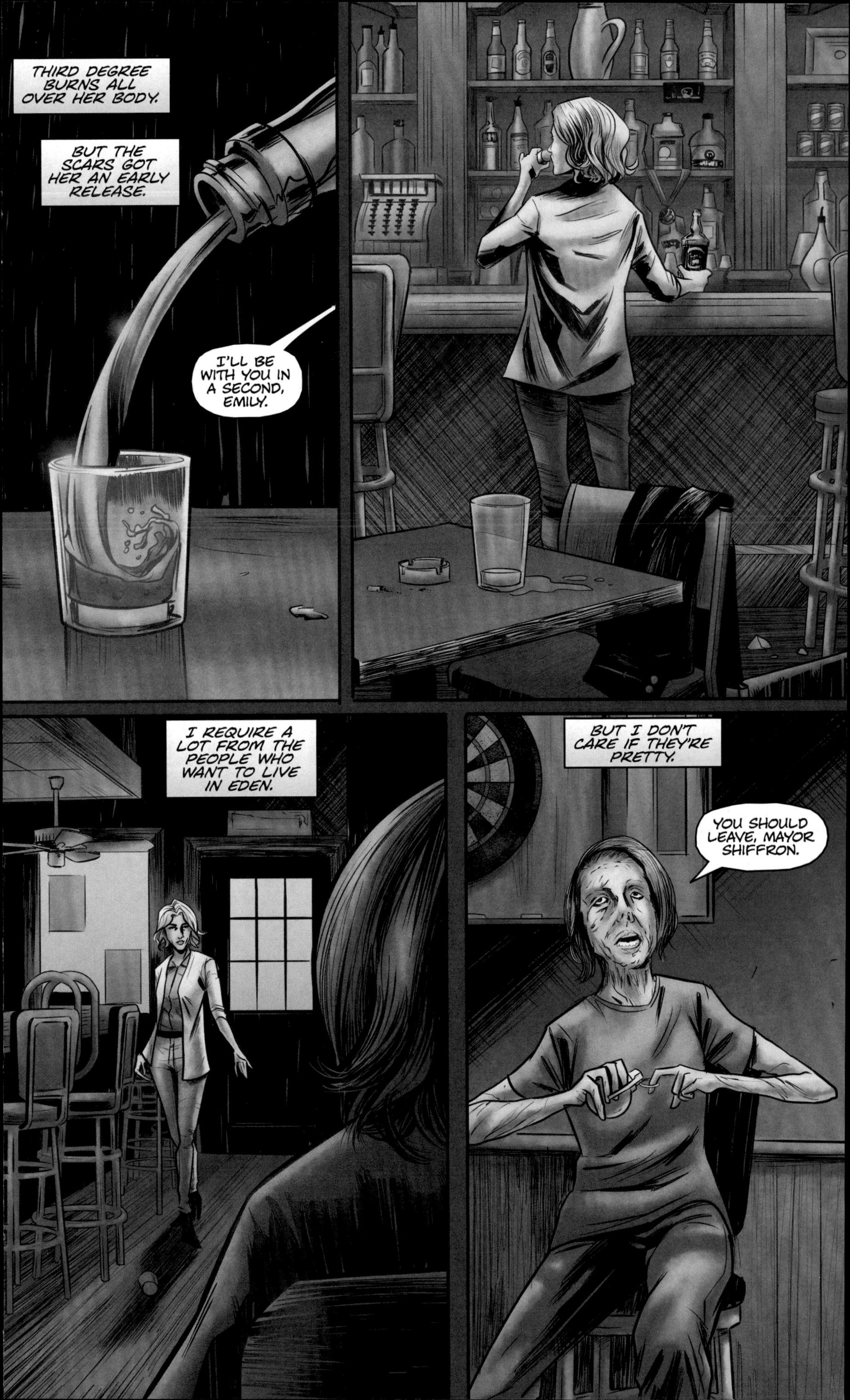
THIRD DEGREE BURNS ALL OVER HER BODY.
BUT THE SCARS GOT HER AN EARLY RELEASE.
I'LL BE WITH YOU IN A SECOND, EMILY.
I REQUIRE A LOT FROM THE PEOPLE WHO WANT TO LIVE IN EDEN.
BUT I DON'T CARE IF THEY'RE PRETTY.
YOU SHOULD LEAVE, MAYOR SHIFFRON.

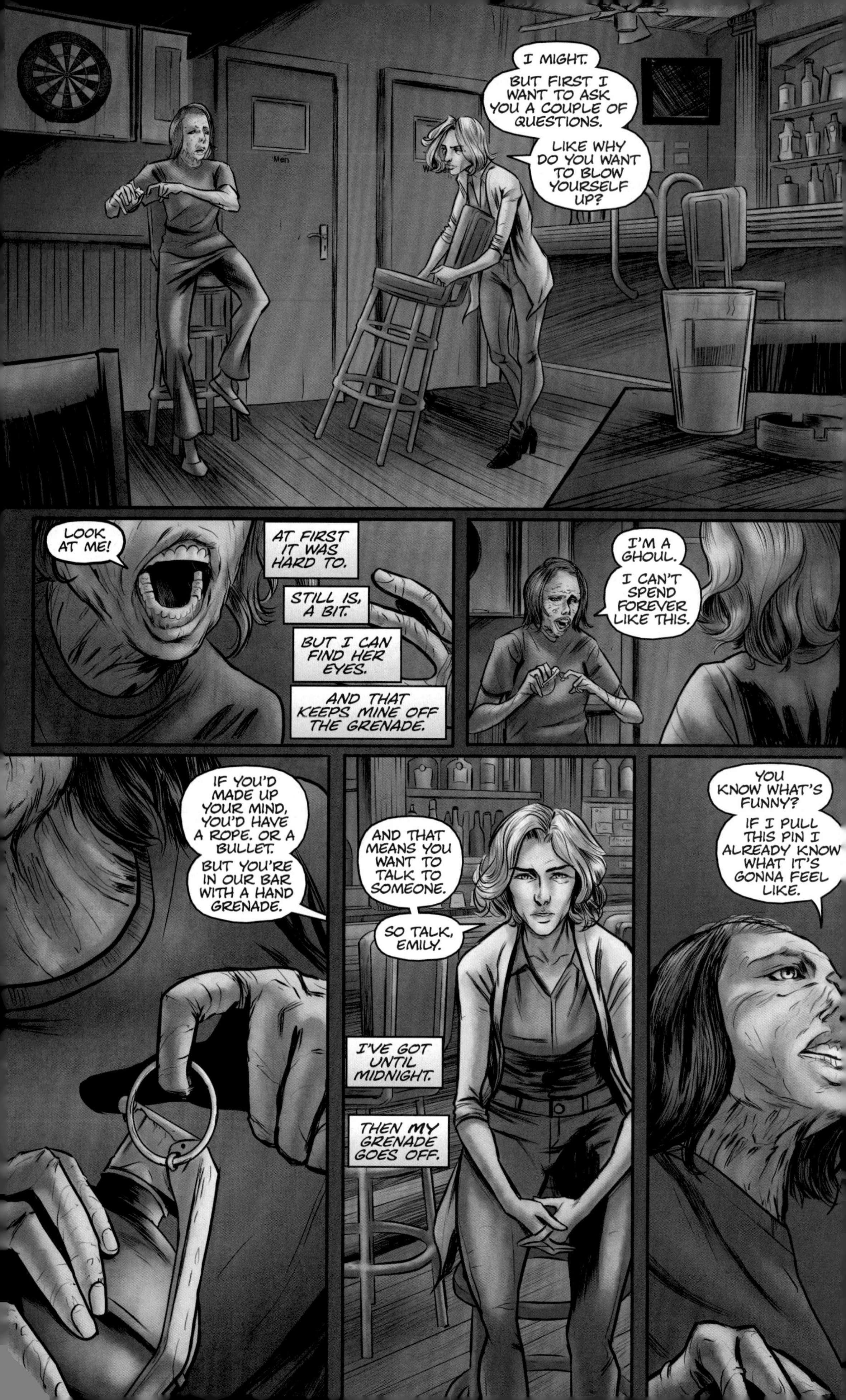
Men
I MIGHT.
BUT FIRST I WANT TO ASK YOU A COUPLE OF QUESTIONS.
LIKE WHY DO YOU WANT TO BLOW YOURSELF UP?
LOOK AT ME!
AT FIRST IT WAS HARD TO.
STILL IS, A BIT.
BUT I CAN FIND HER EYES.
AND THAT KEEPS MINE OFF THE GRENADE.
I'M A GHOUL.
I CAN'T SPEND FOREVER LIKE THIS.
IF YOU'D MADE UP YOUR MIND, YOU'D HAVE A ROPE. OR A BULLET.
BUT YOU'RE IN OUR BAR WITH A HAND GRENADE.
AND THAT MEANS YOU WANT TO TALK TO SOMEONE.
SO TALK, EMILY.
I'VE GOT UNTIL MIDNIGHT.
THEN MY GRENADE GOES OFF.
YOU KNOW WHAT'S FUNNY?
IF I PULL THIS PIN I ALREADY KNOW WHAT IT'S GONNA FEEL LIKE.

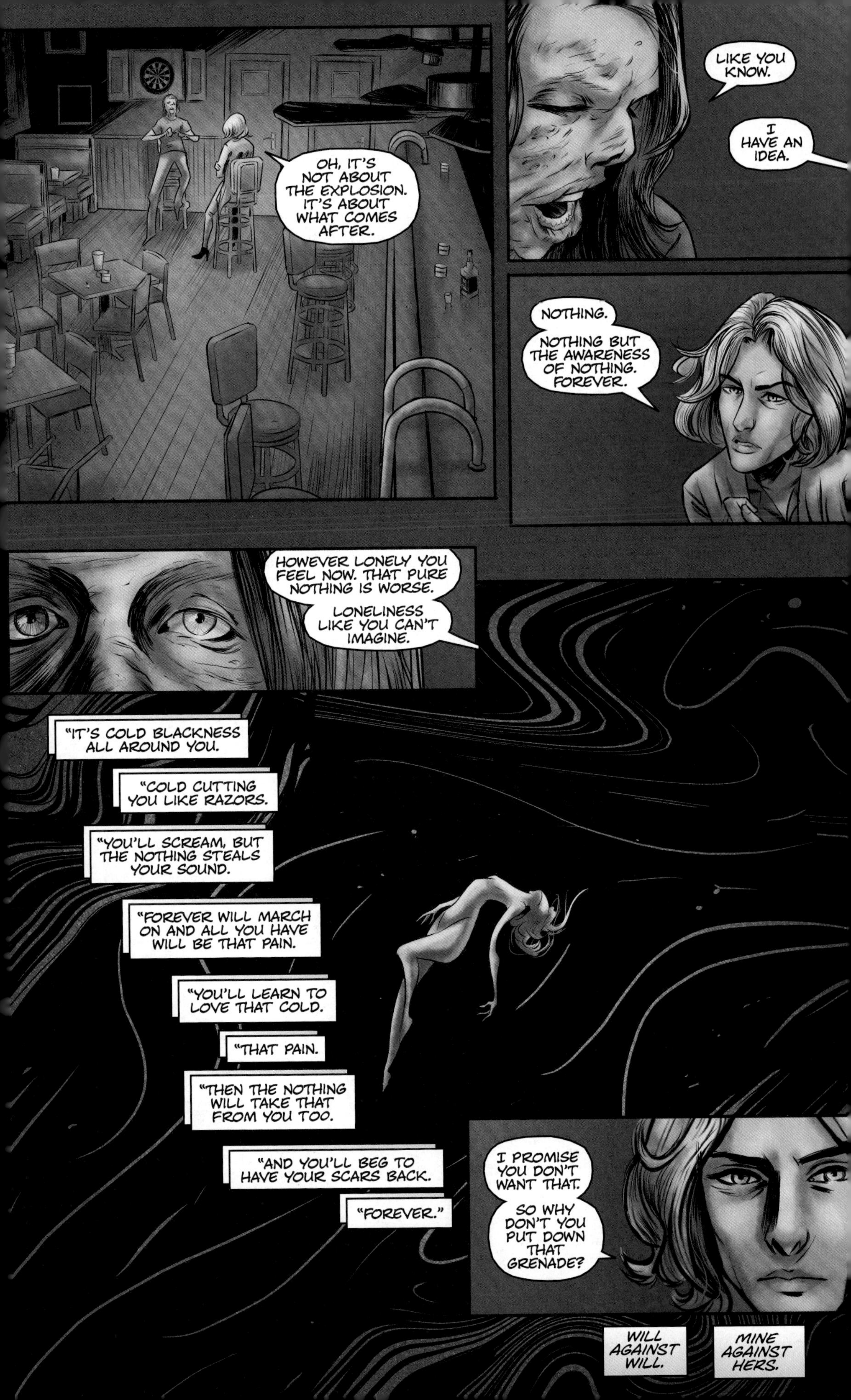
OH, IT'S NOT ABOUT THE EXPLOSION. IT'S ABOUT WHAT COMES AFTER.
LIKE YOU KNOW.
I HAVE AN IDEA.
NOTHING.
NOTHING BUT THE AWARENESS OF NOTHING. FOREVER.
HOWEVER LONELY YOU FEEL NOW. THAT PURE NOTHING IS WORSE.
LONELINESS LIKE YOU CAN'T IMAGINE.
"IT'S COLD BLACKNESS ALL AROUND YOU.
"COLD CUTTING YOU LIKE RAZORS.
"YOU'LL SCREAM, BUT THE NOTHING STEALS YOUR SOUND.
"FOREVER WILL MARCH ON AND ALL YOU HAVE WILL BE THAT PAIN.
"YOU'LL LEARN TO LOVE THAT COLD.
"THAT PAIN.
"THEN THE NOTHING WILL TAKE THAT FROM YOU TOO.
"AND YOU'LL BEG TO HAVE YOUR SCARS BACK.
"FOREVER."
I PROMISE YOU DON'T WANT THAT.
SO WHY DON'T YOU PUT DOWN THAT GRENADE?
WILL AGAINST WILL.
MINE AGAINST HERS.

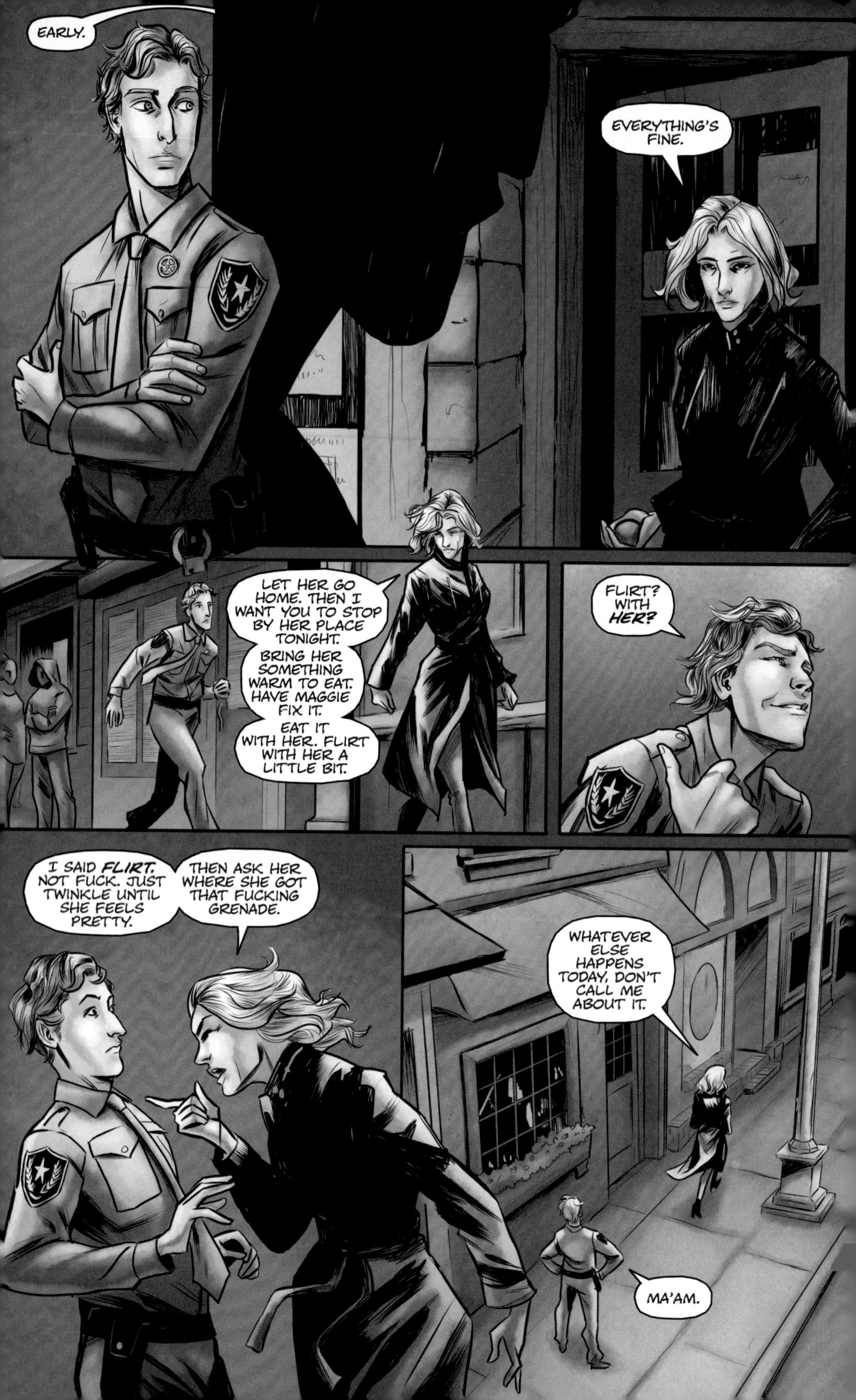
EARLY.
EVERYTHING'S FINE.
LET HER GO HOME. THEN I WANT YOU TO STOP BY HER PLACE TONIGHT.
BRING HER SOMETHING WARM TO EAT. HAVE MAGGIE FIX IT.
EAT IT WITH HER. FLIRT WITH HER A LITTLE BIT.
FLIRT? WITH *HER?*
I SAID *FLIRT.* NOT FUCK. JUST TWINKLE UNTIL SHE FEELS PRETTY.
THEN ASK HER WHERE SHE GOT THAT FUCKING GRENADE.
WHATEVER ELSE HAPPENS TODAY, DON'T CALL ME ABOUT IT.
MA'AM.

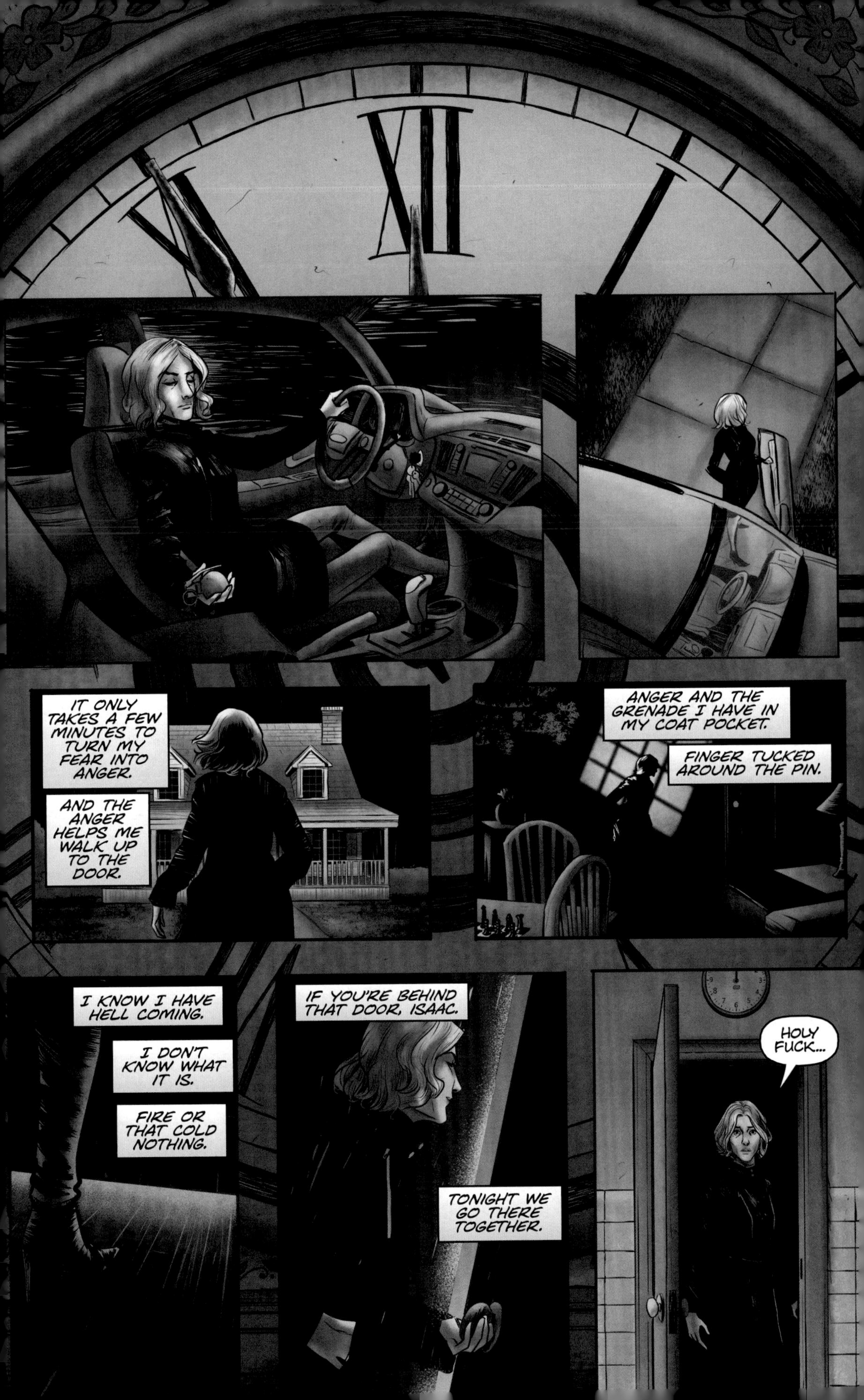

IT ONLY TAKES A FEW MINUTES TO TURN MY FEAR INTO ANGER.
AND THE ANGER HELPS ME WALK UP TO THE DOOR.
ANGER AND THE GRENADE I HAVE IN MY COAT POCKET.
FINGER TUCKED AROUND THE PIN.
I KNOW I HAVE HELL COMING.
I DON'T KNOW WHAT IT IS.
FIRE OR THAT COLD NOTHING.
IF YOU'RE BEHIND THAT DOOR, ISAAC.
TONIGHT WE GO THERE TOGETHER.
HOLY FUCK...

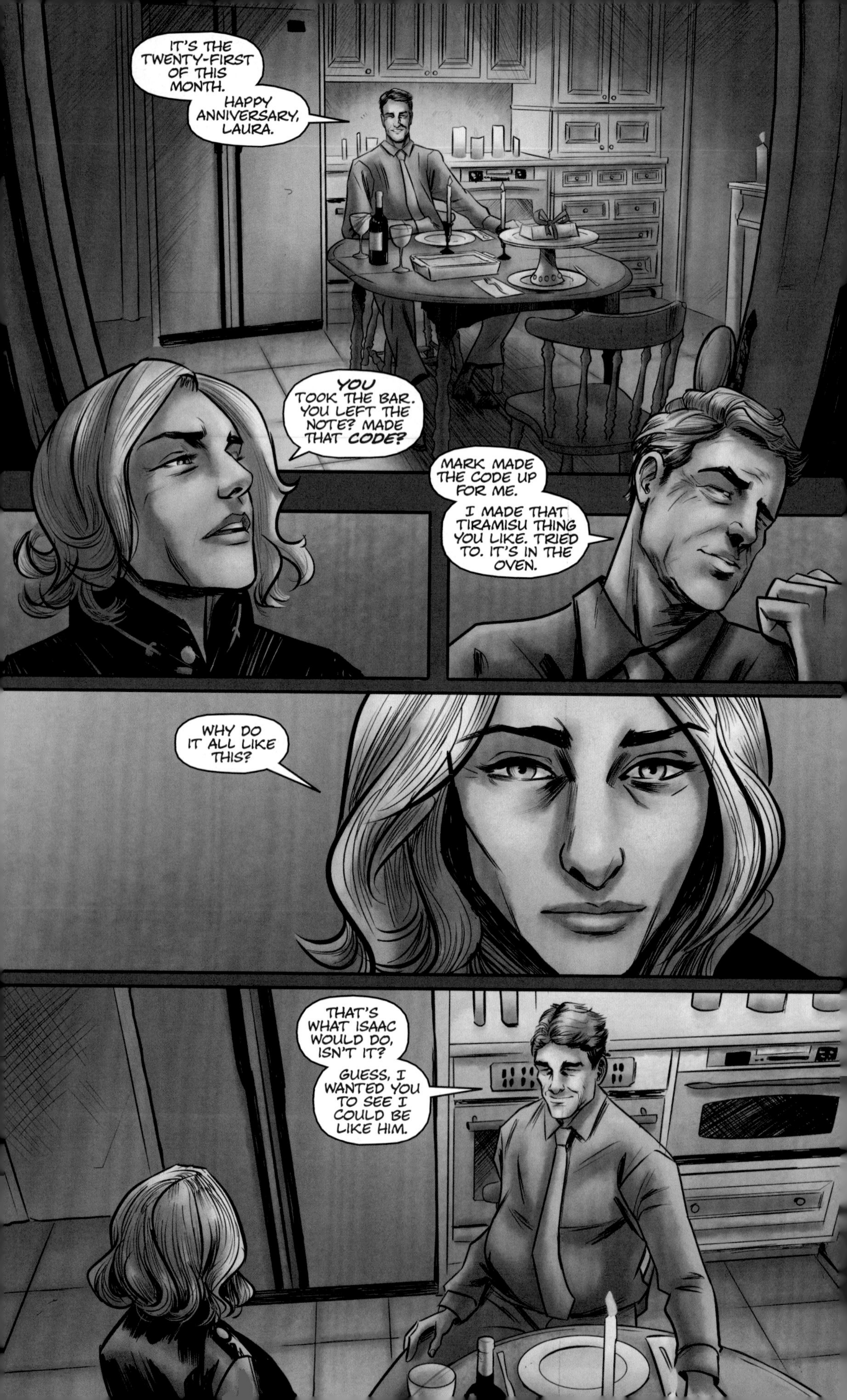
IT'S THE TWENTY-FIRST OF THIS MONTH.
HAPPY ANNIVERSARY, LAURA.
YOU TOOK THE BAR. YOU LEFT THE NOTE? MADE THAT CODE?
MARK MADE THE CODE UP FOR ME.
I MADE THAT TIRAMISU THING YOU LIKE. TRIED TO. IT'S IN THE OVEN.
WHY DO IT ALL LIKE THIS?
THAT'S WHAT ISAAC WOULD DO, ISN'T IT?
GUESS, I WANTED YOU TO SEE I COULD BE LIKE HIM.

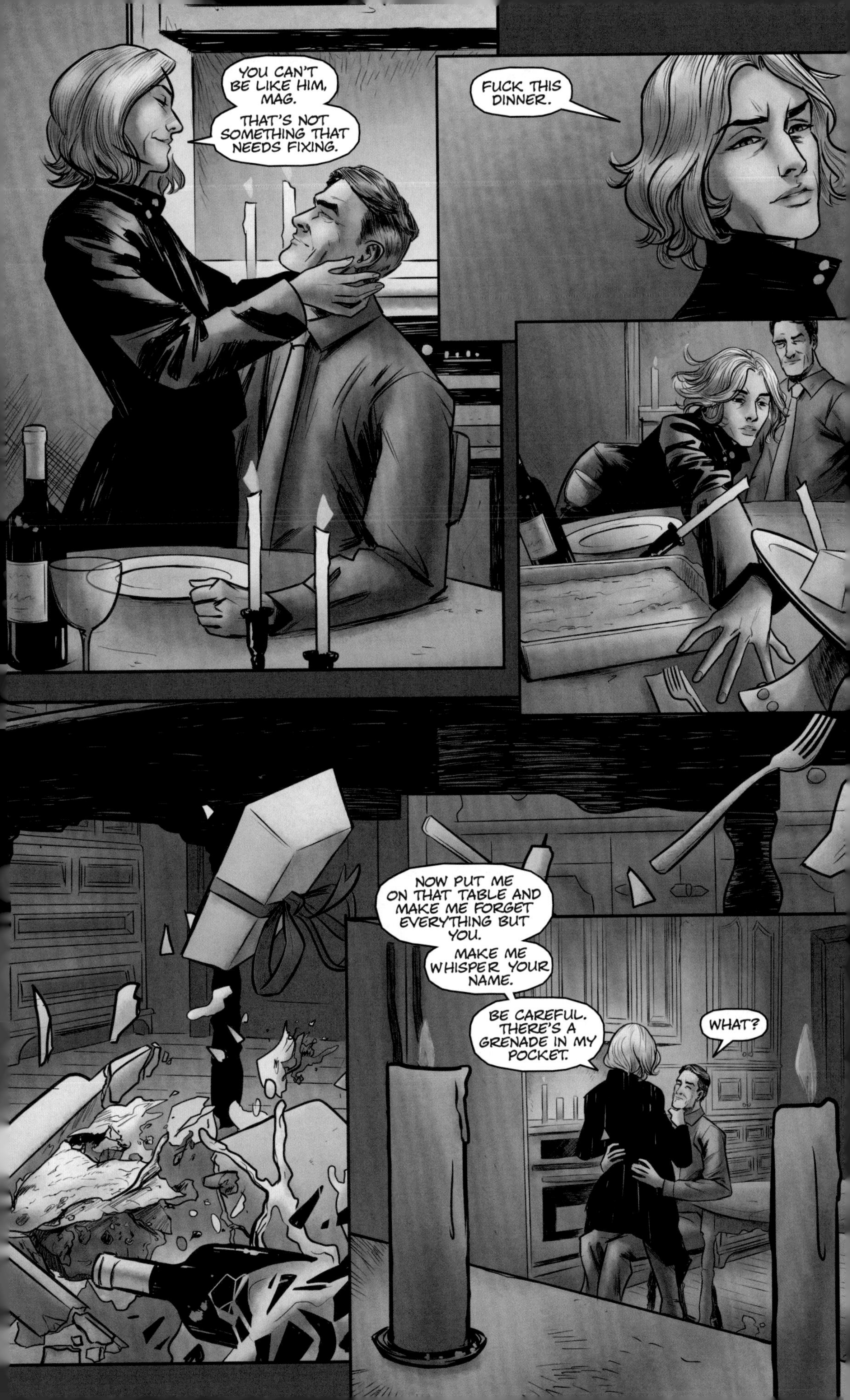
YOU CAN'T BE LIKE HIM, MAG.
THAT'S NOT SOMETHING THAT NEEDS FIXING.
FUCK THIS DINNER.
NOW PUT ME ON THAT TABLE AND MAKE ME FORGET EVERYTHING BUT YOU.
MAKE ME WHISPER YOUR NAME.
BE CAREFUL. THERE'S A GRENADE IN MY POCKET.
WHAT?

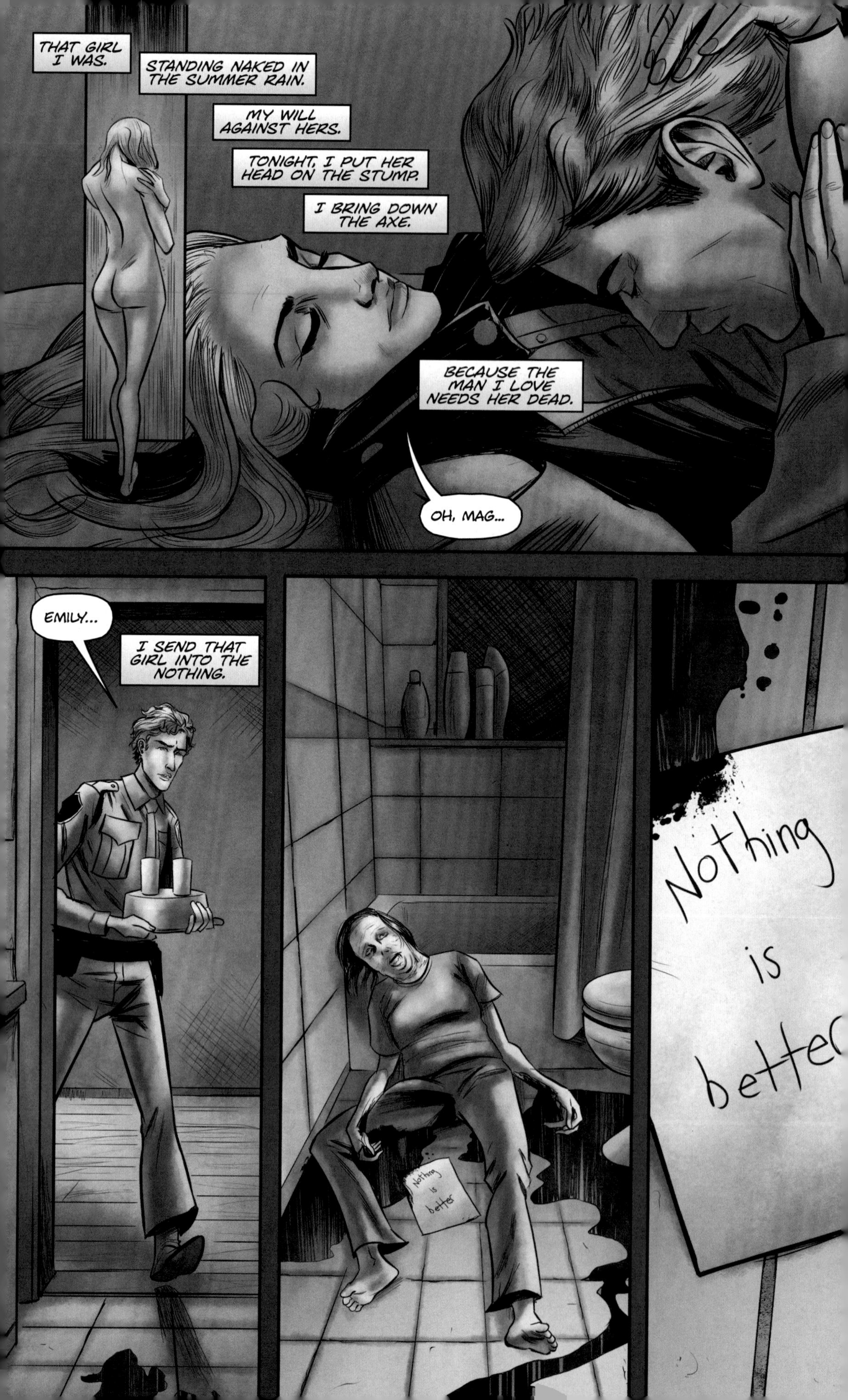
THAT GIRL I WAS.
STANDING NAKED IN THE SUMMER RAIN.
MY WILL AGAINST HERS.
TONIGHT, I PUT HER HEAD ON THE STUMP.
I BRING DOWN THE AXE.
BECAUSE THE MAN I LOVE NEEDS HER DEAD.
OH, MAG...
EMILY...
I SEND THAT GIRL INTO THE NOTHING.
Nothing is better
Nothing is bette

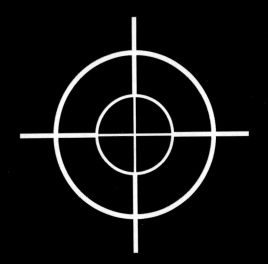

# CHAPTER 7

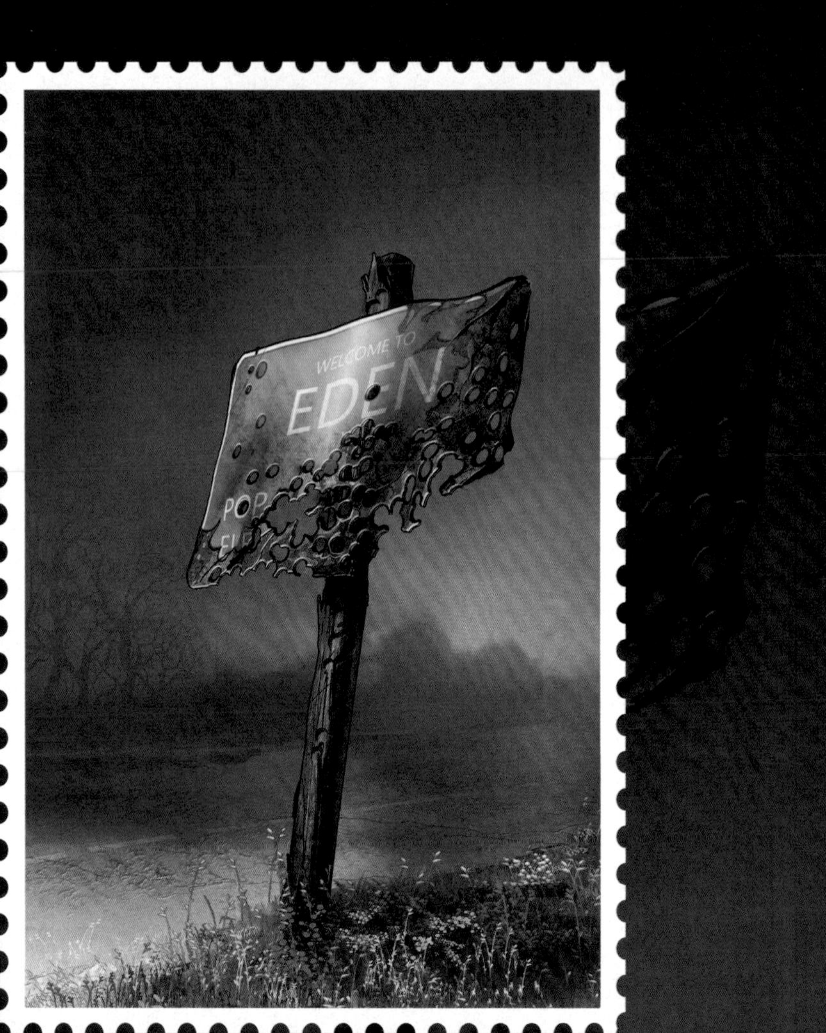
WELCOME TO
EDEN
POP

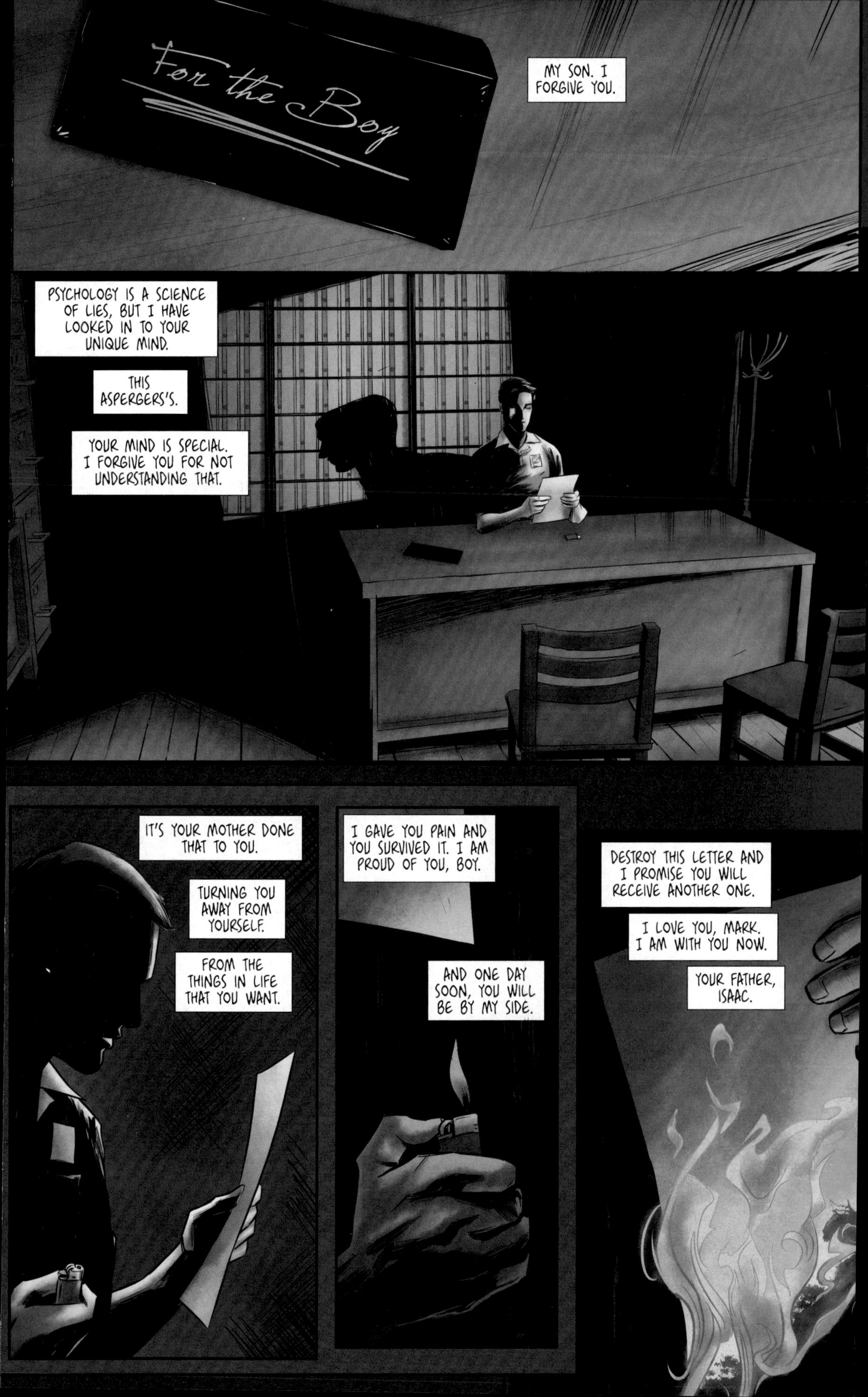
For the Boy
MY SON. I FORGIVE YOU.
PSYCHOLOGY IS A SCIENCE OF LIES, BUT I HAVE LOOKED IN TO YOUR UNIQUE MIND.
THIS ASPERGERS'S.
YOUR MIND IS SPECIAL. I FORGIVE YOU FOR NOT UNDERSTANDING THAT.
IT'S YOUR MOTHER DONE THAT TO YOU.
TURNING YOU AWAY FROM YOURSELF.
FROM THE THINGS IN LIFE THAT YOU WANT.
I GAVE YOU PAIN AND YOU SURVIVED IT. I AM PROUD OF YOU, BOY.
AND ONE DAY SOON, YOU WILL BE BY MY SIDE.
DESTROY THIS LETTER AND I PROMISE YOU WILL RECEIVE ANOTHER ONE.
I LOVE YOU, MARK. I AM WITH YOU NOW.
YOUR FATHER, ISAAC.

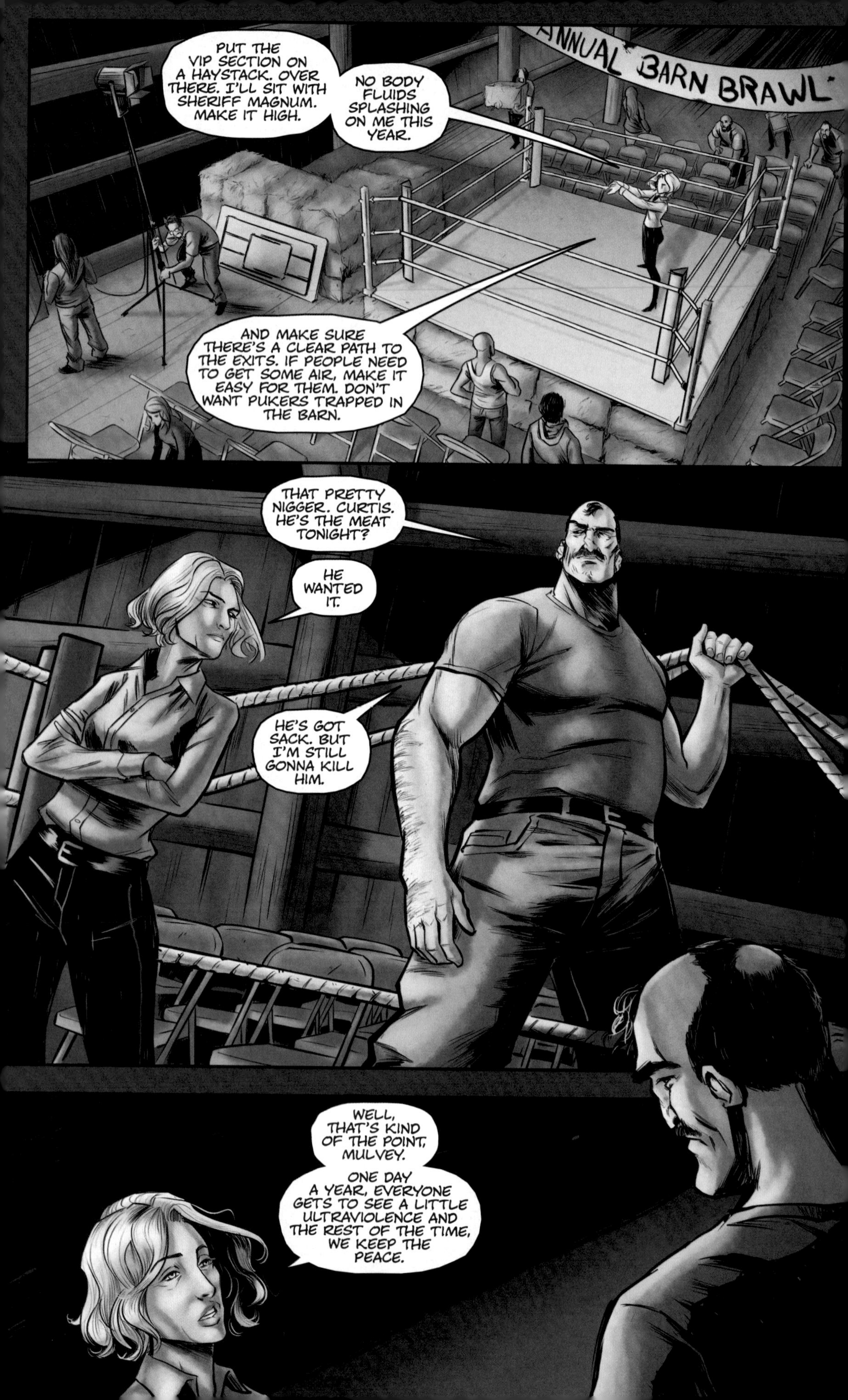
ANNUAL BARN BRAWL
PUT THE VIP SECTION ON A HAYSTACK. OVER THERE. I'LL SIT WITH SHERIFF MAGNUM. MAKE IT HIGH.
NO BODY FLUIDS SPLASHING ON ME THIS YEAR.
AND MAKE SURE THERE'S A CLEAR PATH TO THE EXITS. IF PEOPLE NEED TO GET SOME AIR, MAKE IT EASY FOR THEM. DON'T WANT PUKERS TRAPPED IN THE BARN.
THAT PRETTY NIGGER. CURTIS. HE'S THE MEAT TONIGHT?
HE WANTED IT.
HE'S GOT SACK. BUT I'M STILL GONNA KILL HIM.
WELL, THAT'S KIND OF THE POINT, MULVEY.
ONE DAY A YEAR, EVERYONE GETS TO SEE A LITTLE ULTRAVIOLENCE AND THE REST OF THE TIME, WE KEEP THE PEACE.

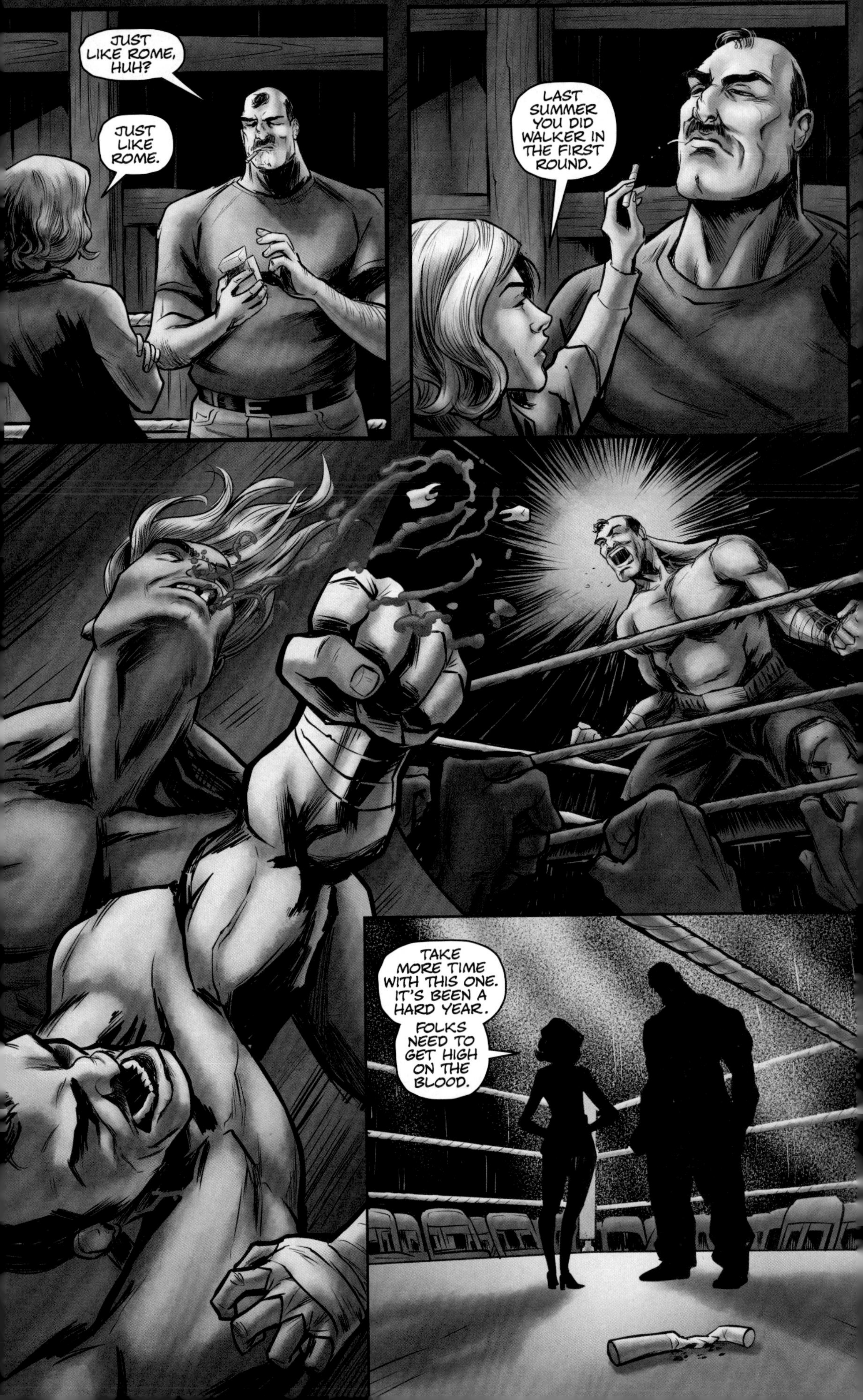
JUST LIKE ROME, HUH?
JUST LIKE ROME.
LAST SUMMER YOU DID WALKER IN THE FIRST ROUND.
TAKE MORE TIME WITH THIS ONE. IT'S BEEN A HARD YEAR.
FOLKS NEED TO GET HIGH ON THE BLOOD.

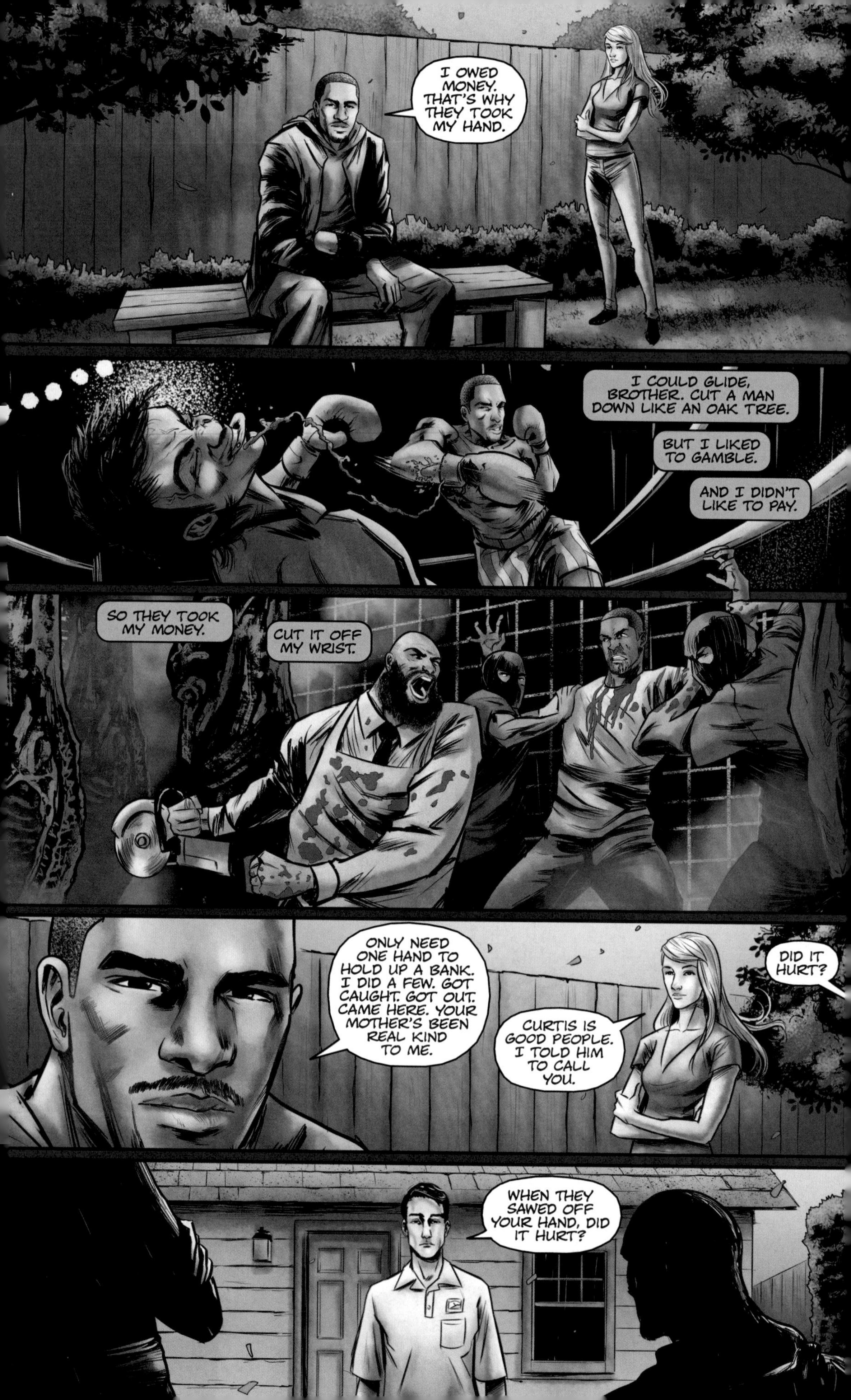
I OWED MONEY. THAT'S WHY THEY TOOK MY HAND.
I COULD GLIDE, BROTHER. CUT A MAN DOWN LIKE AN OAK TREE.
BUT I LIKED TO GAMBLE.
AND I DIDN'T LIKE TO PAY.
SO THEY TOOK MY MONEY.
CUT IT OFF MY WRIST.
ONLY NEED ONE HAND TO HOLD UP A BANK. I DID A FEW. GOT CAUGHT. GOT OUT. CAME HERE. YOUR MOTHER'S BEEN REAL KIND TO ME.
CURTIS IS GOOD PEOPLE. I TOLD HIM TO CALL YOU.
DID IT HURT?
WHEN THEY SAWED OFF YOUR HAND, DID IT HURT?

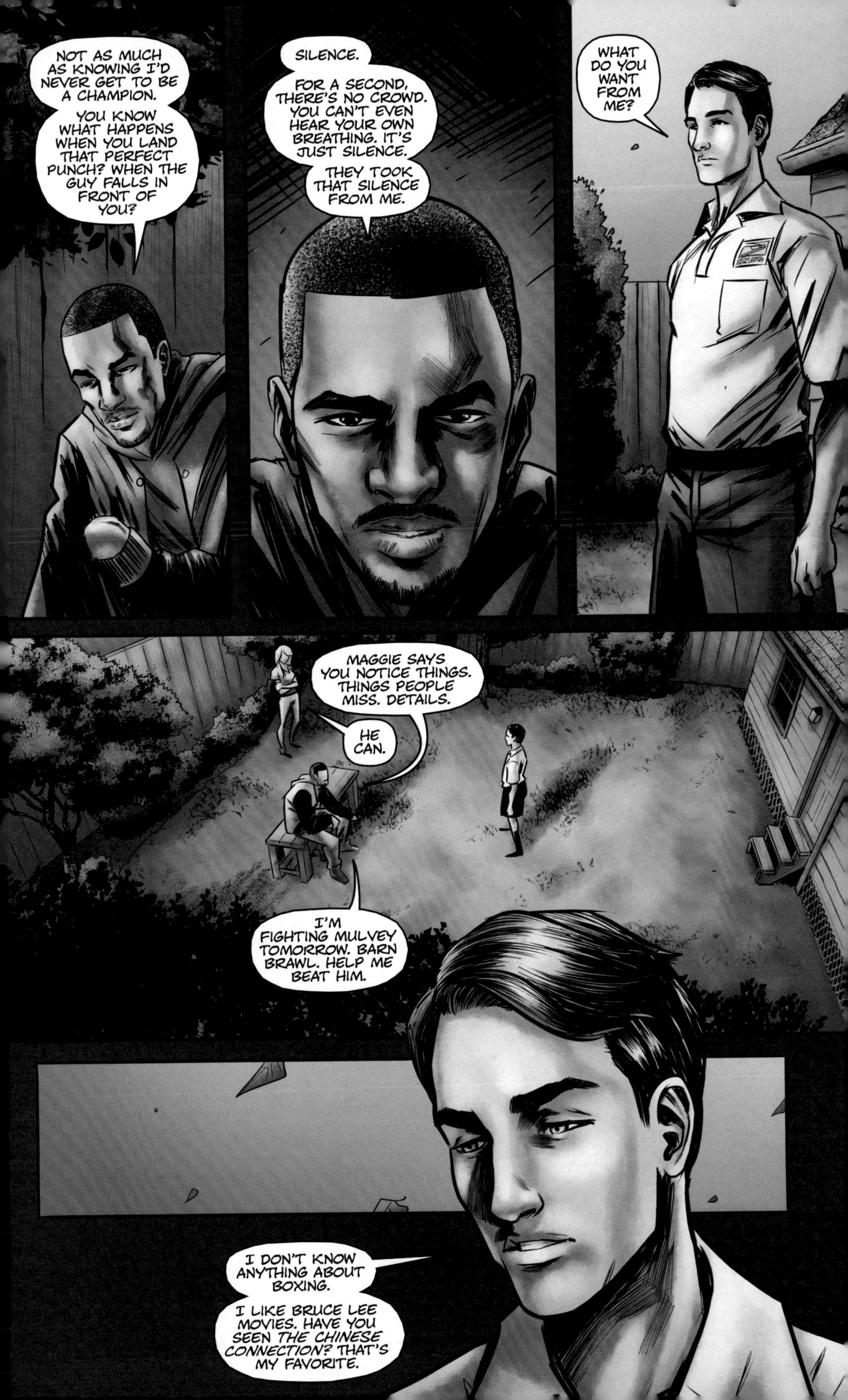
NOT AS MUCH AS KNOWING I'D NEVER GET TO BE A CHAMPION.
YOU KNOW WHAT HAPPENS WHEN YOU LAND THAT PERFECT PUNCH? WHEN THE GUY FALLS IN FRONT OF YOU?
SILENCE.
FOR A SECOND, THERE'S NO CROWD. YOU CAN'T EVEN HEAR YOUR OWN BREATHING. IT'S JUST SILENCE.
THEY TOOK THAT SILENCE FROM ME.
WHAT DO YOU WANT FROM ME?
MAGGIE SAYS YOU NOTICE THINGS. THINGS PEOPLE MISS. DETAILS.
HE CAN.
I'M FIGHTING MULVEY TOMORROW. BARN BRAWL. HELP ME BEAT HIM.
I DON'T KNOW ANYTHING ABOUT BOXING.
I LIKE BRUCE LEE MOVIES. HAVE YOU SEEN *THE CHINESE CONNECTION*? THAT'S MY FAVORITE.

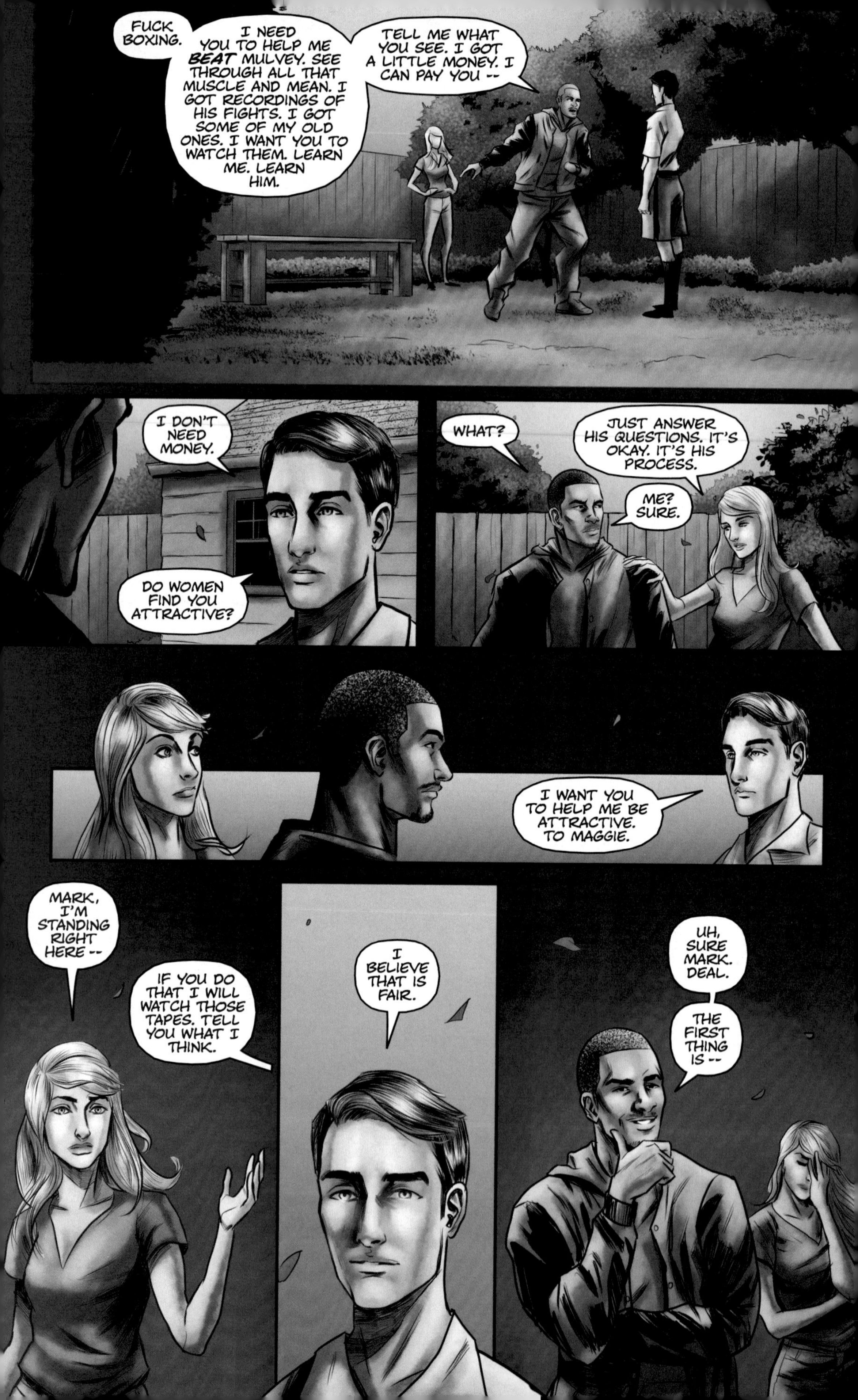
FUCK BOXING.
I NEED YOU TO HELP ME BEAT MULVEY. SEE THROUGH ALL THAT MUSCLE AND MEAN. I GOT RECORDINGS OF HIS FIGHTS. I GOT SOME OF MY OLD ONES. I WANT YOU TO WATCH THEM. LEARN ME. LEARN HIM.
TELL ME WHAT YOU SEE. I GOT A LITTLE MONEY. I CAN PAY YOU --
I DON'T NEED MONEY.
DO WOMEN FIND YOU ATTRACTIVE?
WHAT?
JUST ANSWER HIS QUESTIONS. IT'S OKAY. IT'S HIS PROCESS.
ME? SURE.
I WANT YOU TO HELP ME BE ATTRACTIVE. TO MAGGIE.
MARK, I'M STANDING RIGHT HERE --
IF YOU DO THAT I WILL WATCH THOSE TAPES. TELL YOU WHAT I THINK.
I BELIEVE THAT IS FAIR.
UH, SURE MARK. DEAL.
THE FIRST THING IS --

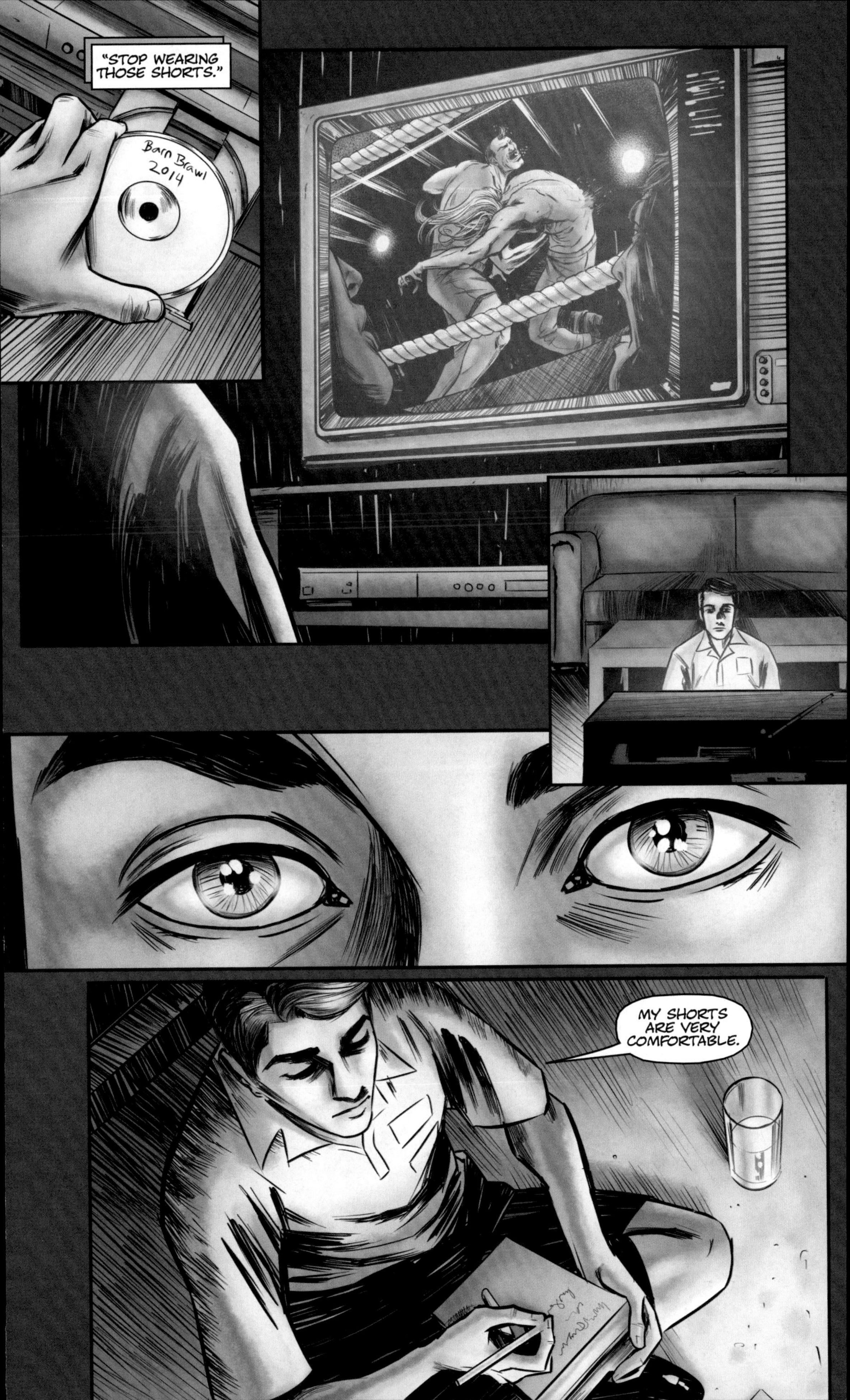
"STOP WEARING THOSE SHORTS."
Barn Brawl 2014
MY SHORTS ARE VERY COMFORTABLE.

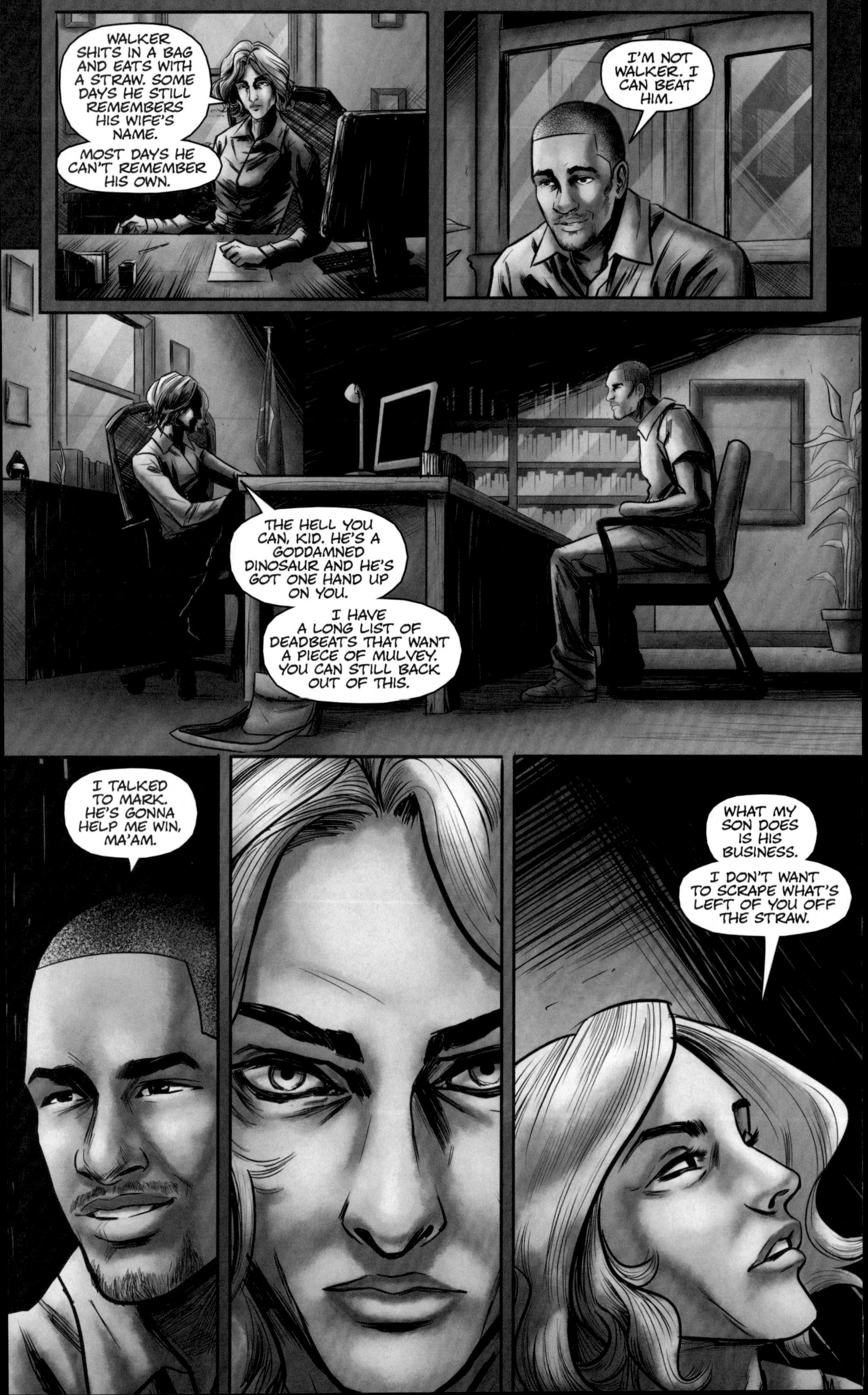
WALKER SHITS IN A BAG AND EATS WITH A STRAW. SOME DAYS HE STILL REMEMBERS HIS WIFE'S NAME.
MOST DAYS HE CAN'T REMEMBER HIS OWN.
I'M NOT WALKER. I CAN BEAT HIM.
THE HELL YOU CAN, KID. HE'S A GODDAMNED DINOSAUR AND HE'S GOT ONE HAND UP ON YOU.
I HAVE A LONG LIST OF DEADBEATS THAT WANT A PIECE OF MULVEY. YOU CAN STILL BACK OUT OF THIS.
I TALKED TO MARK. HE'S GONNA HELP ME WIN, MA'AM.
WHAT MY SON DOES IS HIS BUSINESS.
I DON'T WANT TO SCRAPE WHAT'S LEFT OF YOU OFF THE STRAW.

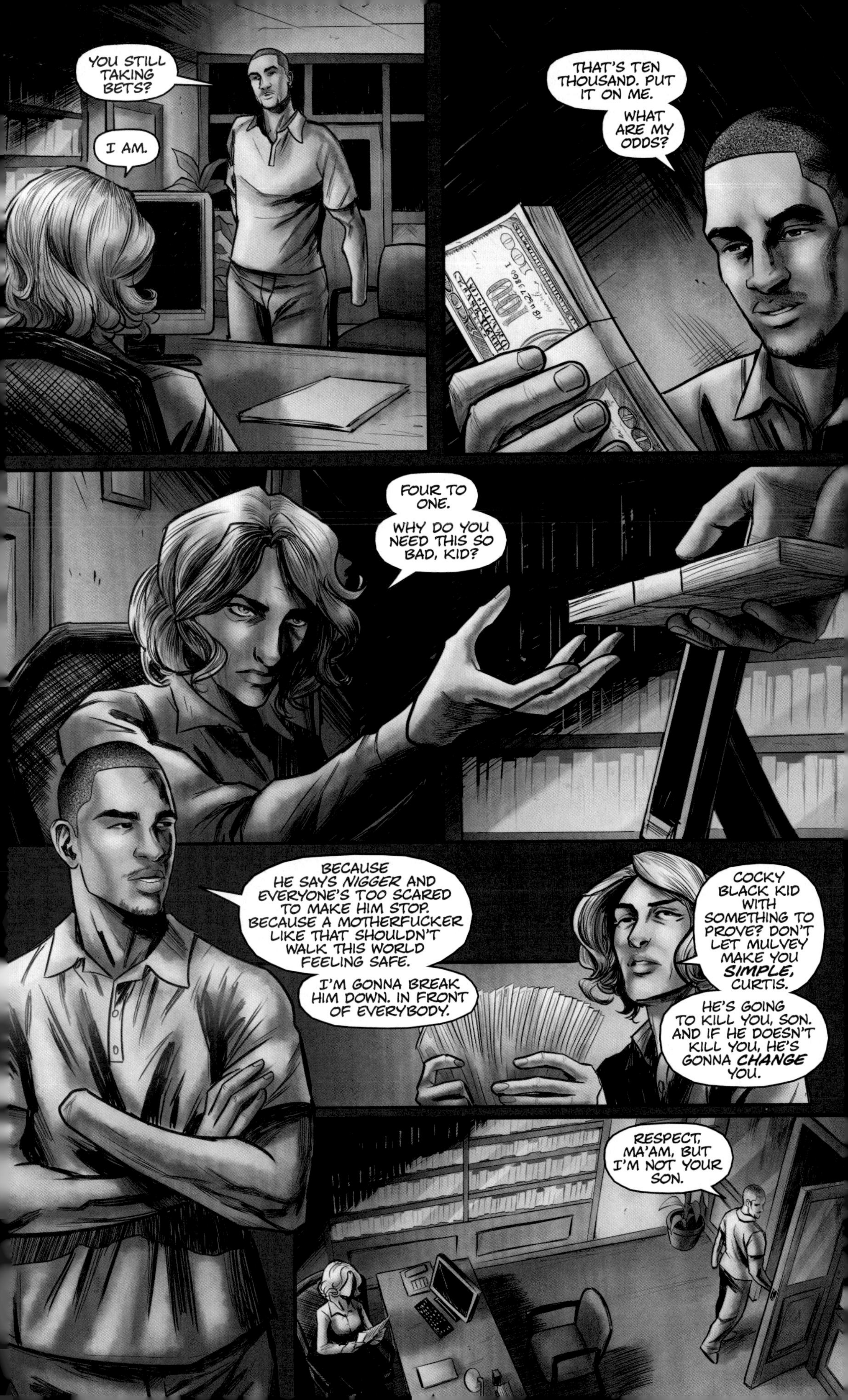
YOU STILL TAKING BETS?
I AM.
THAT'S TEN THOUSAND. PUT IT ON ME.
WHAT ARE MY ODDS?
FOUR TO ONE.
WHY DO YOU NEED THIS SO BAD, KID?
BECAUSE HE SAYS *NIGGER* AND EVERYONE'S TOO SCARED TO MAKE HIM STOP. BECAUSE A MOTHERFUCKER LIKE THAT SHOULDN'T WALK THIS WORLD FEELING SAFE.
I'M GONNA BREAK HIM DOWN. IN FRONT OF EVERYBODY.
COCKY BLACK KID WITH SOMETHING TO PROVE? DON'T LET MULVEY MAKE YOU ***SIMPLE,*** CURTIS.
HE'S GOING TO KILL YOU, SON. AND IF HE DOESN'T KILL YOU, HE'S GONNA ***CHANGE*** YOU.
RESPECT, MA'AM, BUT I'M NOT YOUR SON.

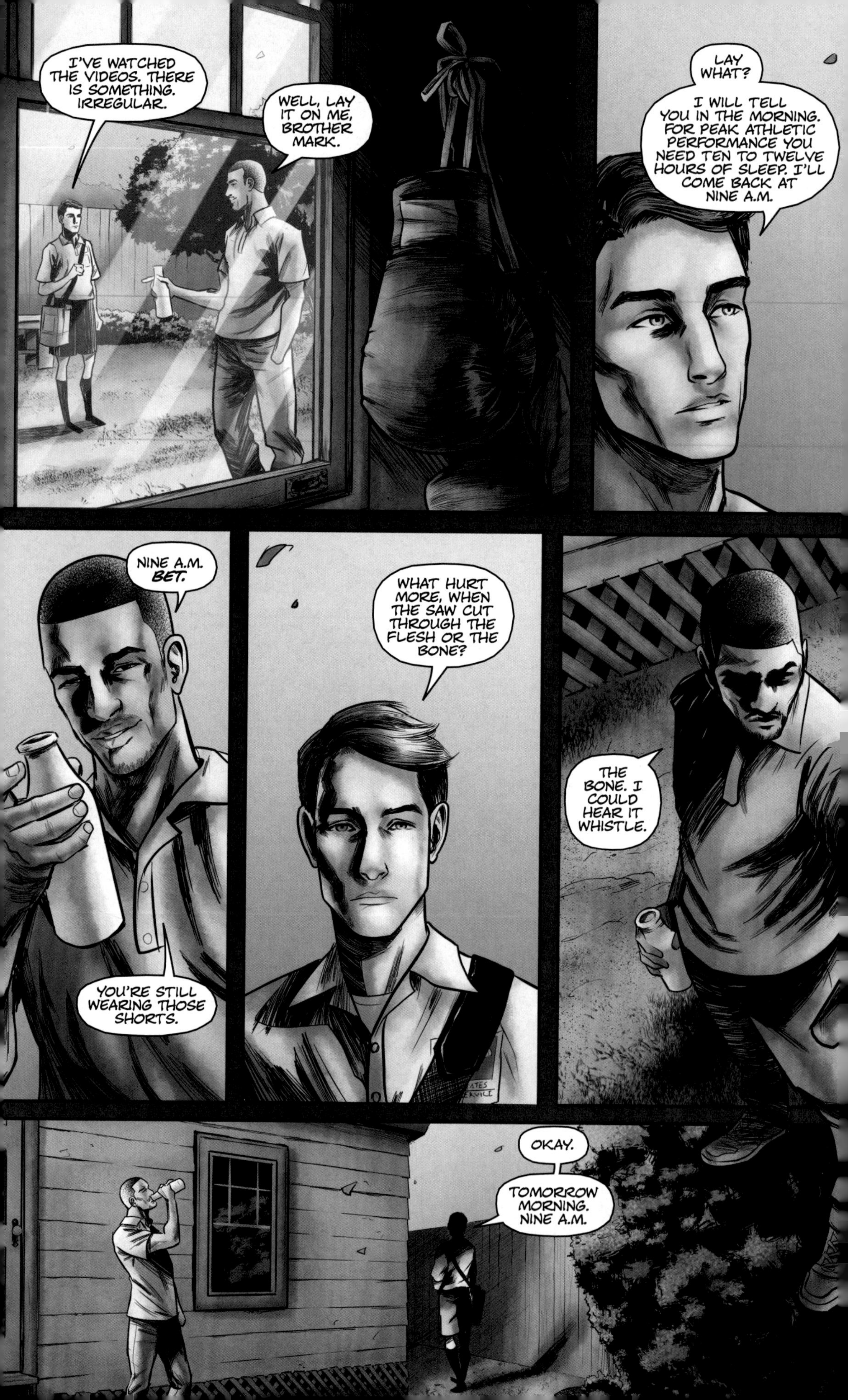
I'VE WATCHED THE VIDEOS. THERE IS SOMETHING. IRREGULAR.
WELL, LAY IT ON ME, BROTHER MARK.
LAY WHAT?
I WILL TELL YOU IN THE MORNING. FOR PEAK ATHLETIC PERFORMANCE YOU NEED TEN TO TWELVE HOURS OF SLEEP. I'LL COME BACK AT NINE A.M.
NINE A.M. BET.
YOU'RE STILL WEARING THOSE SHORTS.
WHAT HURT MORE, WHEN THE SAW CUT THROUGH THE FLESH OR THE BONE?
THE BONE. I COULD HEAR IT WHISTLE.
OKAY.
TOMORROW MORNING. NINE A.M.

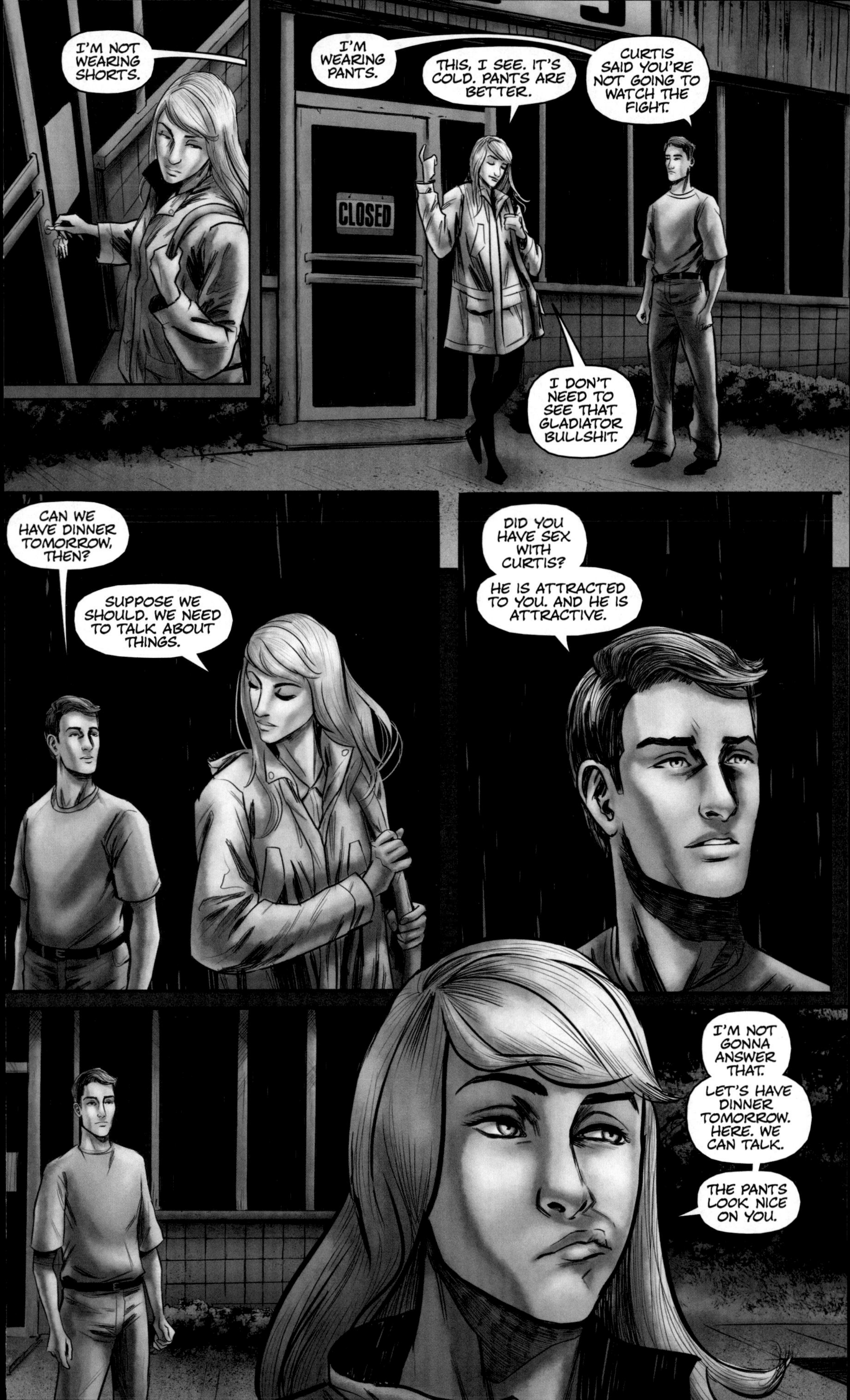
I'M NOT WEARING SHORTS.
I'M WEARING PANTS.
THIS, I SEE. IT'S COLD. PANTS ARE BETTER.
CURTIS SAID YOU'RE NOT GOING TO WATCH THE FIGHT.
CLOSED
I DON'T NEED TO SEE THAT GLADIATOR BULLSHIT.
CAN WE HAVE DINNER TOMORROW, THEN?
SUPPOSE WE SHOULD. WE NEED TO TALK ABOUT THINGS.
DID YOU HAVE SEX WITH CURTIS?
HE IS ATTRACTED TO YOU. AND HE IS ATTRACTIVE.
I'M NOT GONNA ANSWER THAT.
LET'S HAVE DINNER TOMORROW. HERE. WE CAN TALK.
THE PANTS LOOK NICE ON YOU.

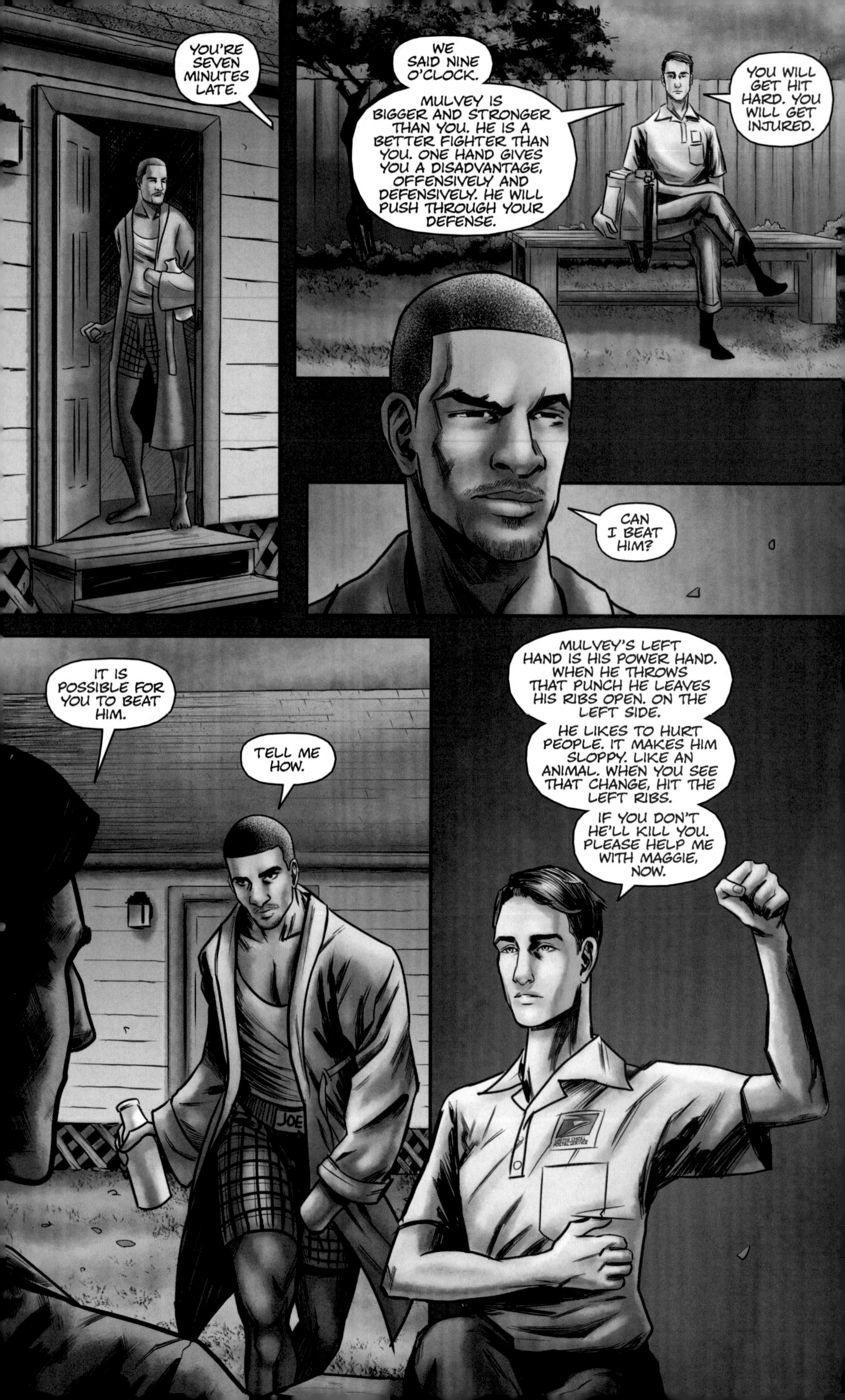
YOU'RE SEVEN MINUTES LATE.
WE SAID NINE O'CLOCK.
MULVEY IS BIGGER AND STRONGER THAN YOU. HE IS A BETTER FIGHTER THAN YOU. ONE HAND GIVES YOU A DISADVANTAGE, OFFENSIVELY AND DEFENSIVELY. HE WILL PUSH THROUGH YOUR DEFENSE.
YOU WILL GET HIT HARD. YOU WILL GET INJURED.
CAN I BEAT HIM?
IT IS POSSIBLE FOR YOU TO BEAT HIM.
TELL ME HOW.
MULVEY'S LEFT HAND IS HIS POWER HAND. WHEN HE THROWS THAT PUNCH HE LEAVES HIS RIBS OPEN. ON THE LEFT SIDE.
HE LIKES TO HURT PEOPLE. IT MAKES HIM SLOPPY. LIKE AN ANIMAL. WHEN YOU SEE THAT CHANGE, HIT THE LEFT RIBS.
IF YOU DON'T HE'LL KILL YOU. PLEASE HELP ME WITH MAGGIE, NOW.
JOE

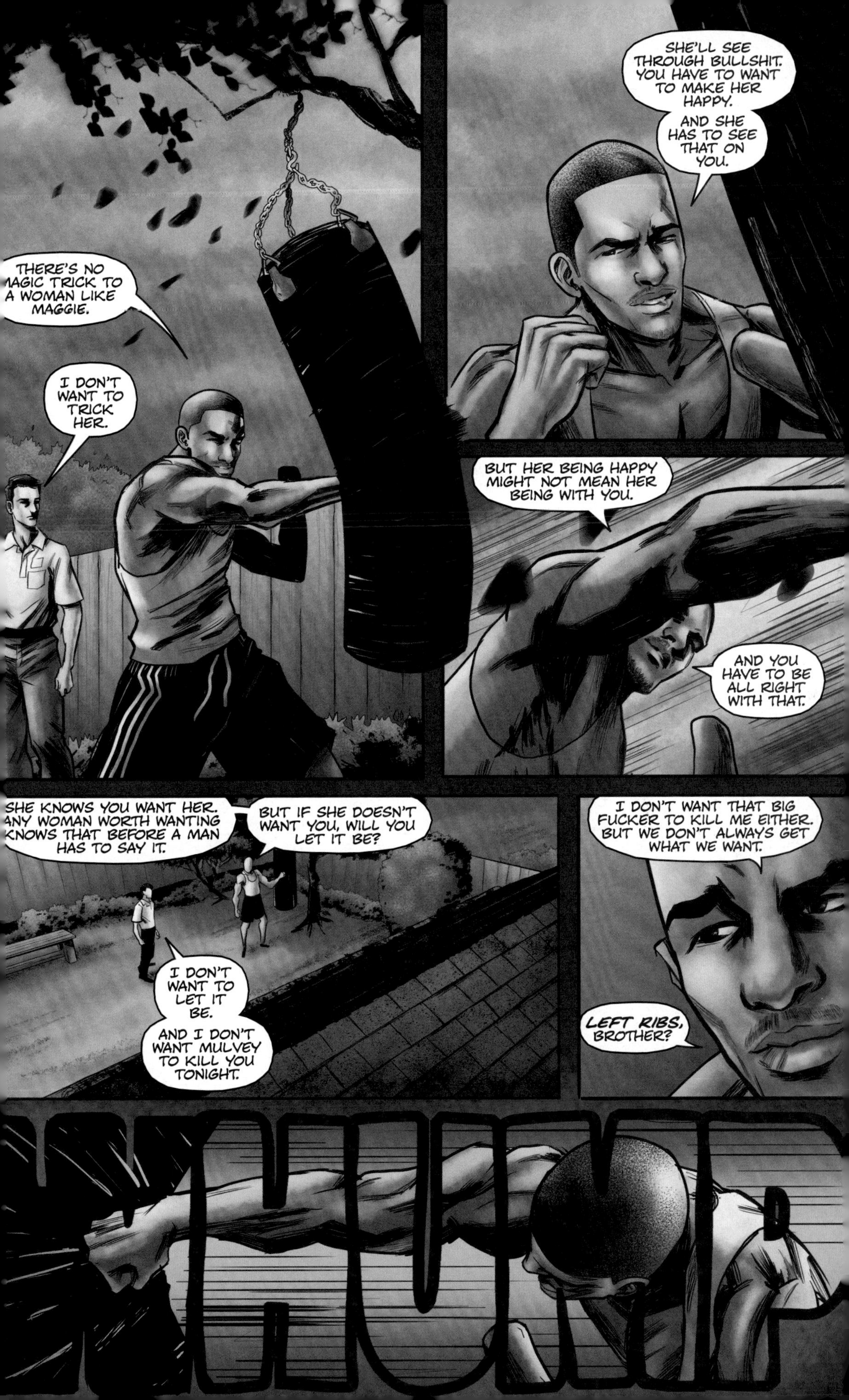
THERE'S NO MAGIC TRICK TO A WOMAN LIKE MAGGIE.
I DON'T WANT TO TRICK HER.
SHE'LL SEE THROUGH BULLSHIT. YOU HAVE TO WANT TO MAKE HER HAPPY.
AND SHE HAS TO SEE THAT ON YOU.
BUT HER BEING HAPPY MIGHT NOT MEAN HER BEING WITH YOU.
AND YOU HAVE TO BE ALL RIGHT WITH THAT.
SHE KNOWS YOU WANT HER. ANY WOMAN WORTH WANTING KNOWS THAT BEFORE A MAN HAS TO SAY IT.
BUT IF SHE DOESN'T WANT YOU, WILL YOU LET IT BE?
I DON'T WANT TO LET IT BE.
AND I DON'T WANT MULVEY TO KILL YOU TONIGHT.
I DON'T WANT THAT BIG FUCKER TO KILL ME EITHER. BUT WE DON'T ALWAYS GET WHAT WE WANT.
LEFT RIBS, BROTHER?

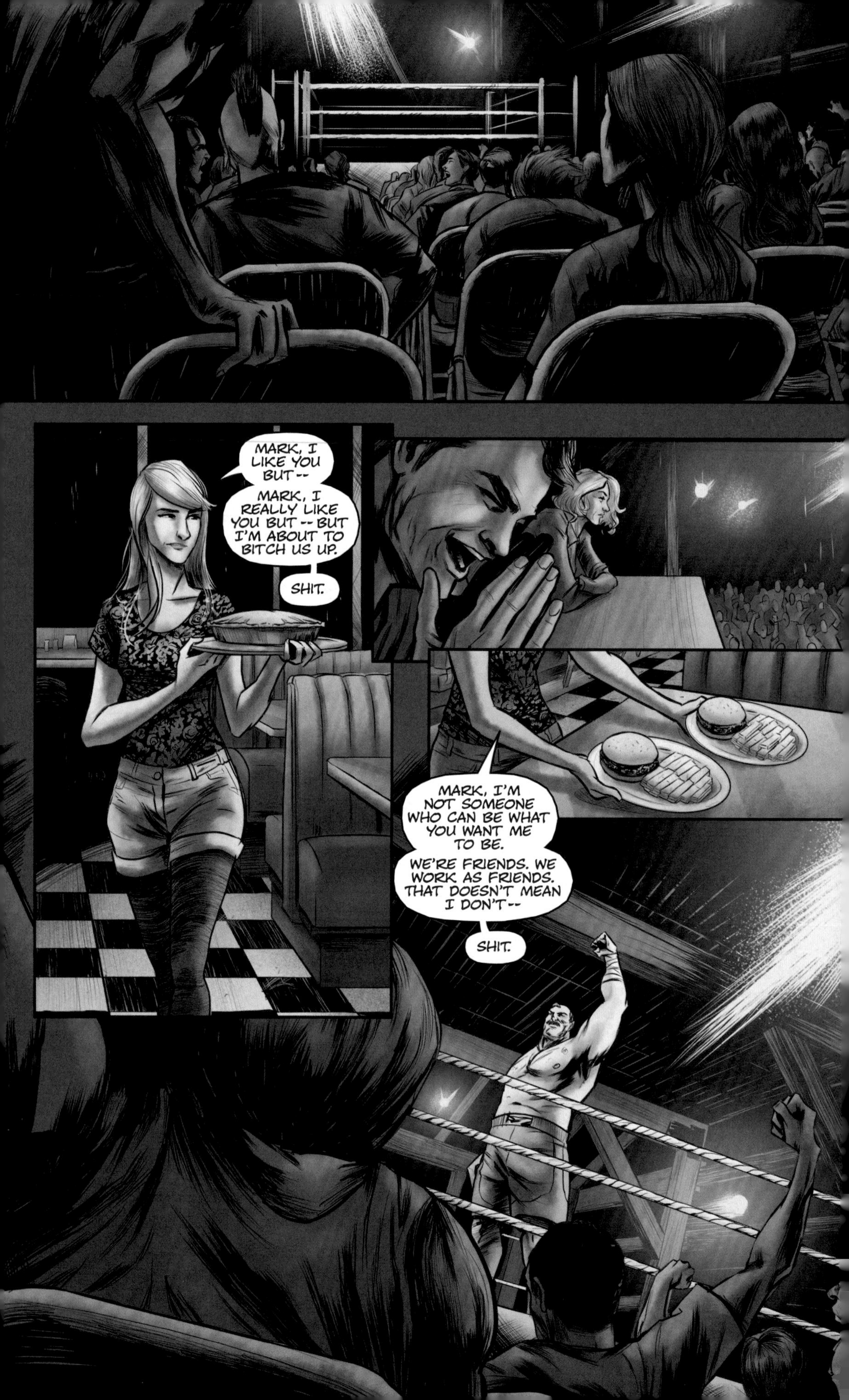
MARK, I LIKE YOU BUT--
MARK, I REALLY LIKE YOU BUT--BUT I'M ABOUT TO BITCH US UP.
SHIT.
MARK, I'M NOT SOMEONE WHO CAN BE WHAT YOU WANT ME TO BE.
WE'RE FRIENDS. WE WORK AS FRIENDS. THAT DOESN'T MEAN I DON'T--
SHIT.

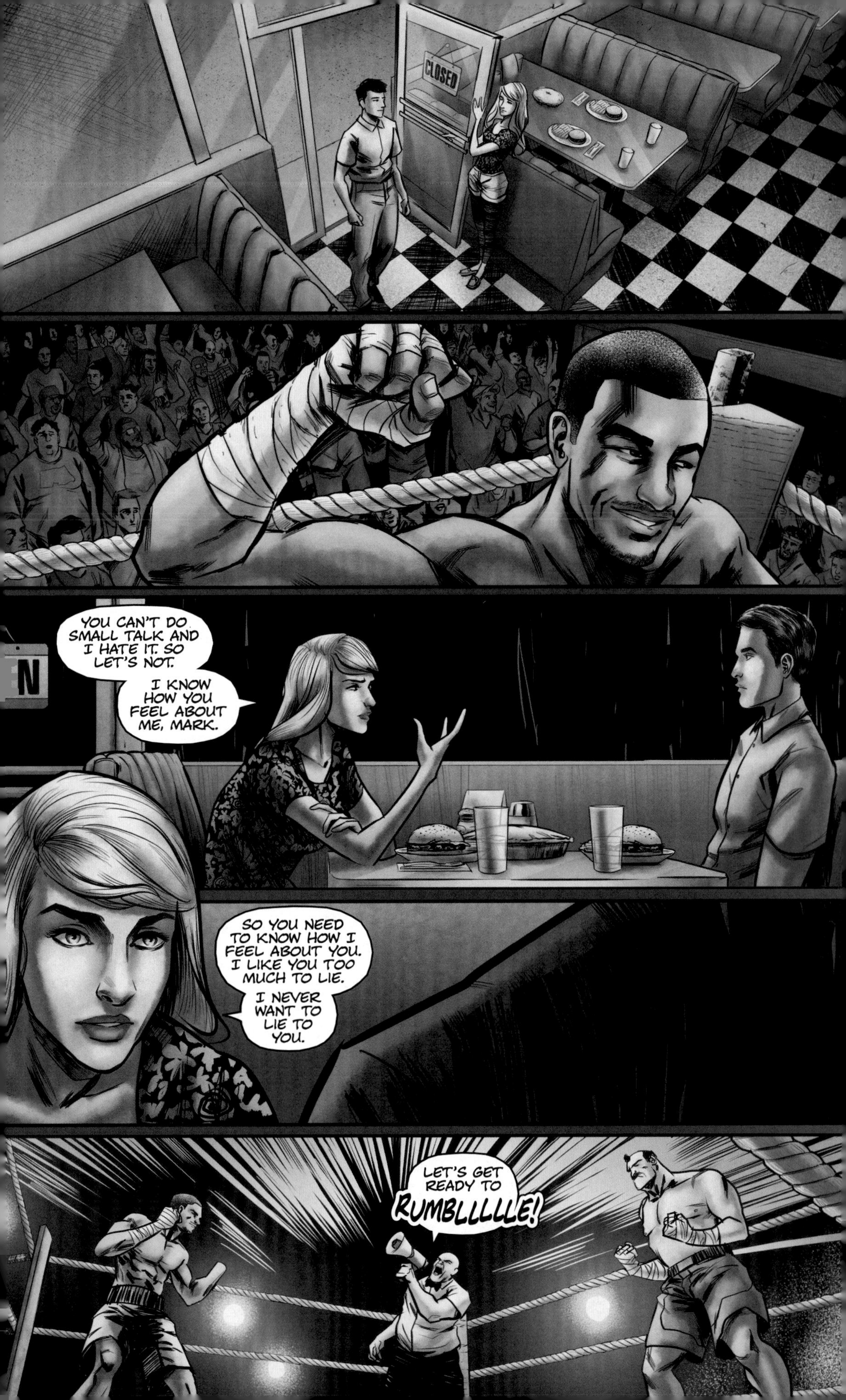
CLOSED
YOU CAN'T DO SMALL TALK AND I HATE IT. SO LET'S NOT.
I KNOW HOW YOU FEEL ABOUT ME, MARK.
SO YOU NEED TO KNOW HOW I FEEL ABOUT YOU. I LIKE YOU TOO MUCH TO LIE.
I NEVER WANT TO LIE TO YOU.
LET'S GET READY TO
RUMBLLLLLE!

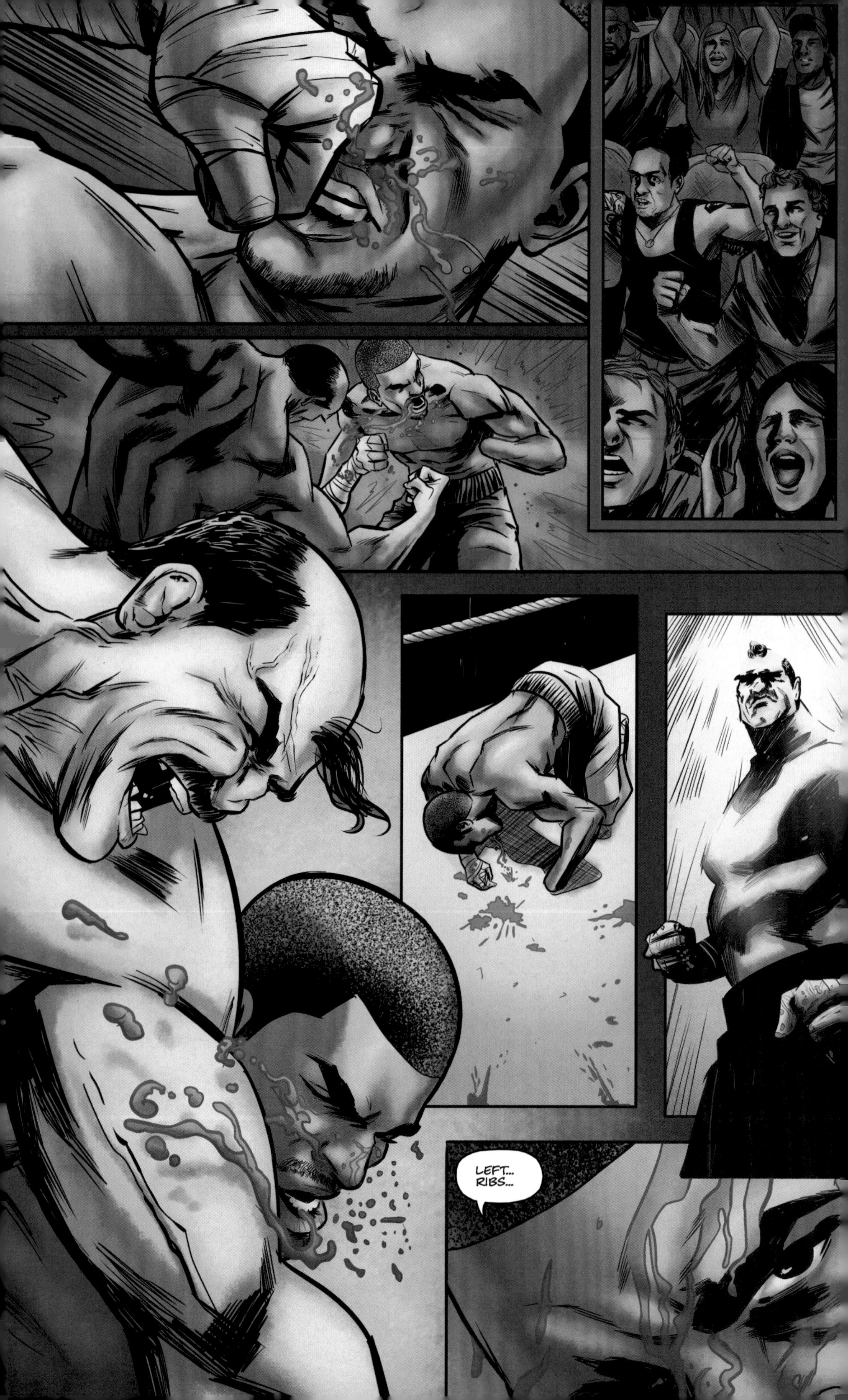
LEFT... RIBS...

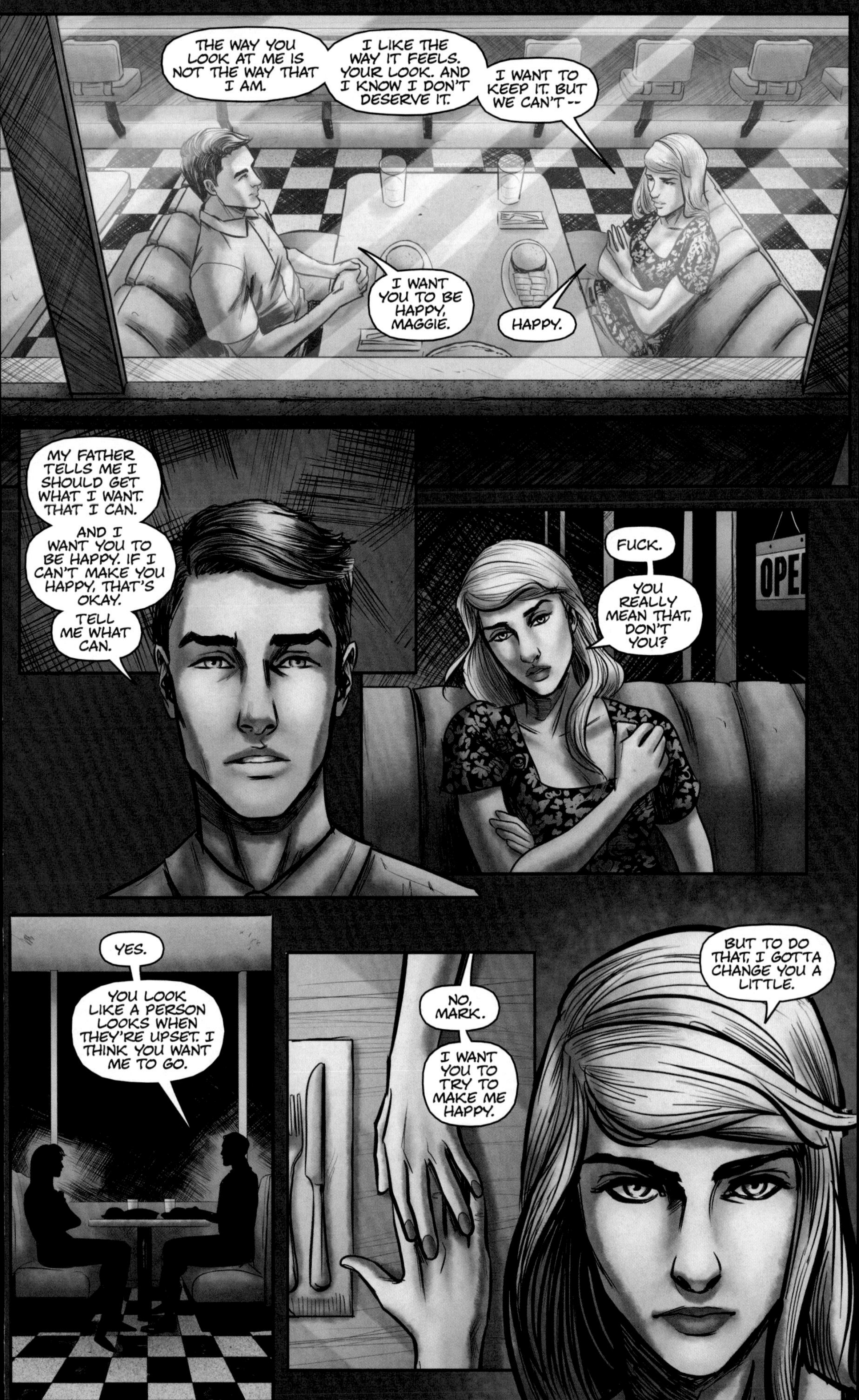
THE WAY YOU LOOK AT ME IS NOT THE WAY THAT I AM.
I LIKE THE WAY IT FEELS. YOUR LOOK. AND I KNOW I DON'T DESERVE IT.
I WANT TO KEEP IT. BUT WE CAN'T --
I WANT YOU TO BE HAPPY, MAGGIE.
HAPPY.
MY FATHER TELLS ME I SHOULD GET WHAT I WANT. THAT I CAN.
AND I WANT YOU TO BE HAPPY. IF I CAN'T MAKE YOU HAPPY, THAT'S OKAY.
TELL ME WHAT CAN.
FUCK.
YOU REALLY MEAN THAT, DON'T YOU?
OPE
YES.
YOU LOOK LIKE A PERSON LOOKS WHEN THEY'RE UPSET. I THINK YOU WANT ME TO GO.
NO, MARK.
I WANT YOU TO TRY TO MAKE ME HAPPY.
BUT TO DO THAT, I GOTTA CHANGE YOU A LITTLE.

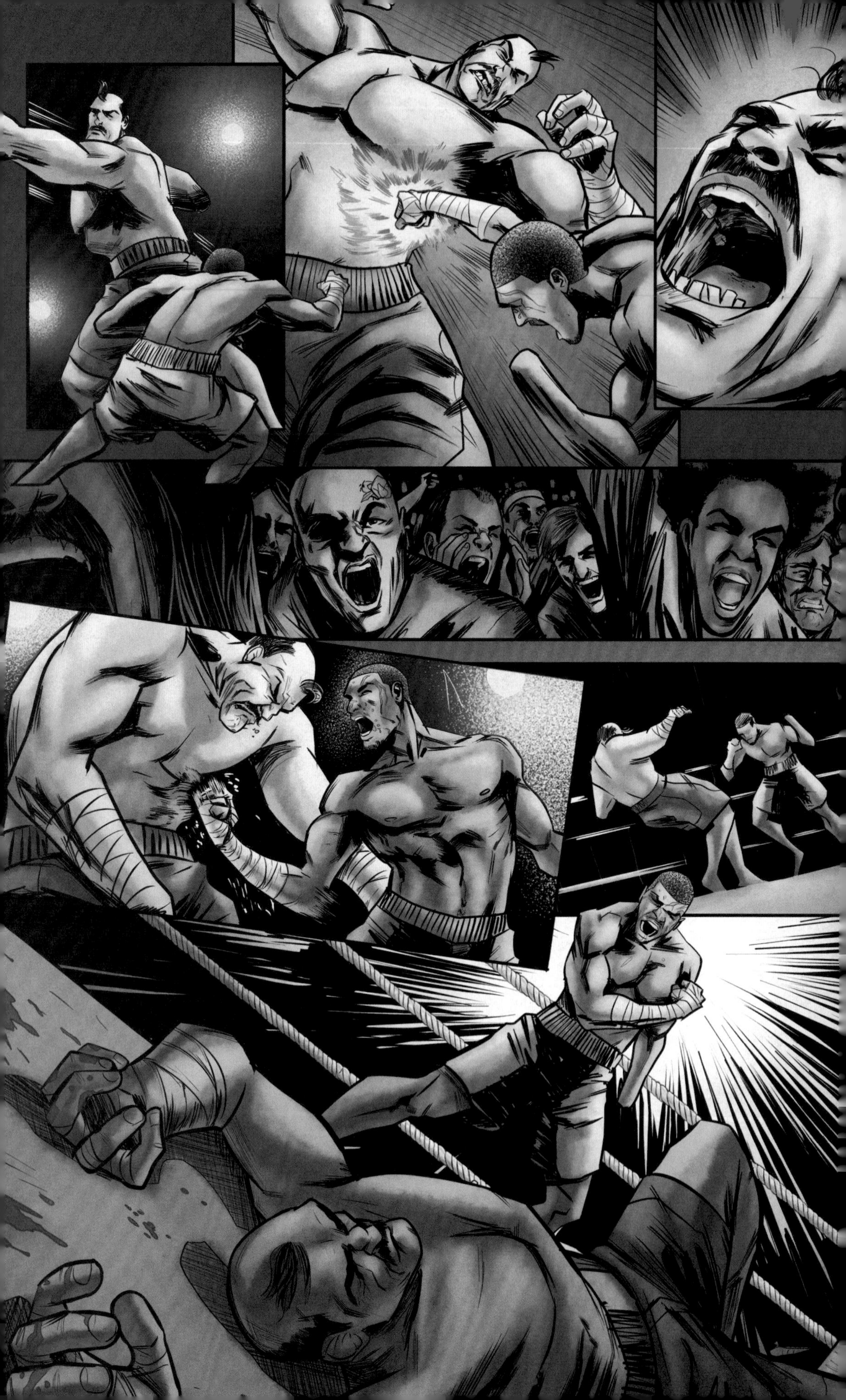

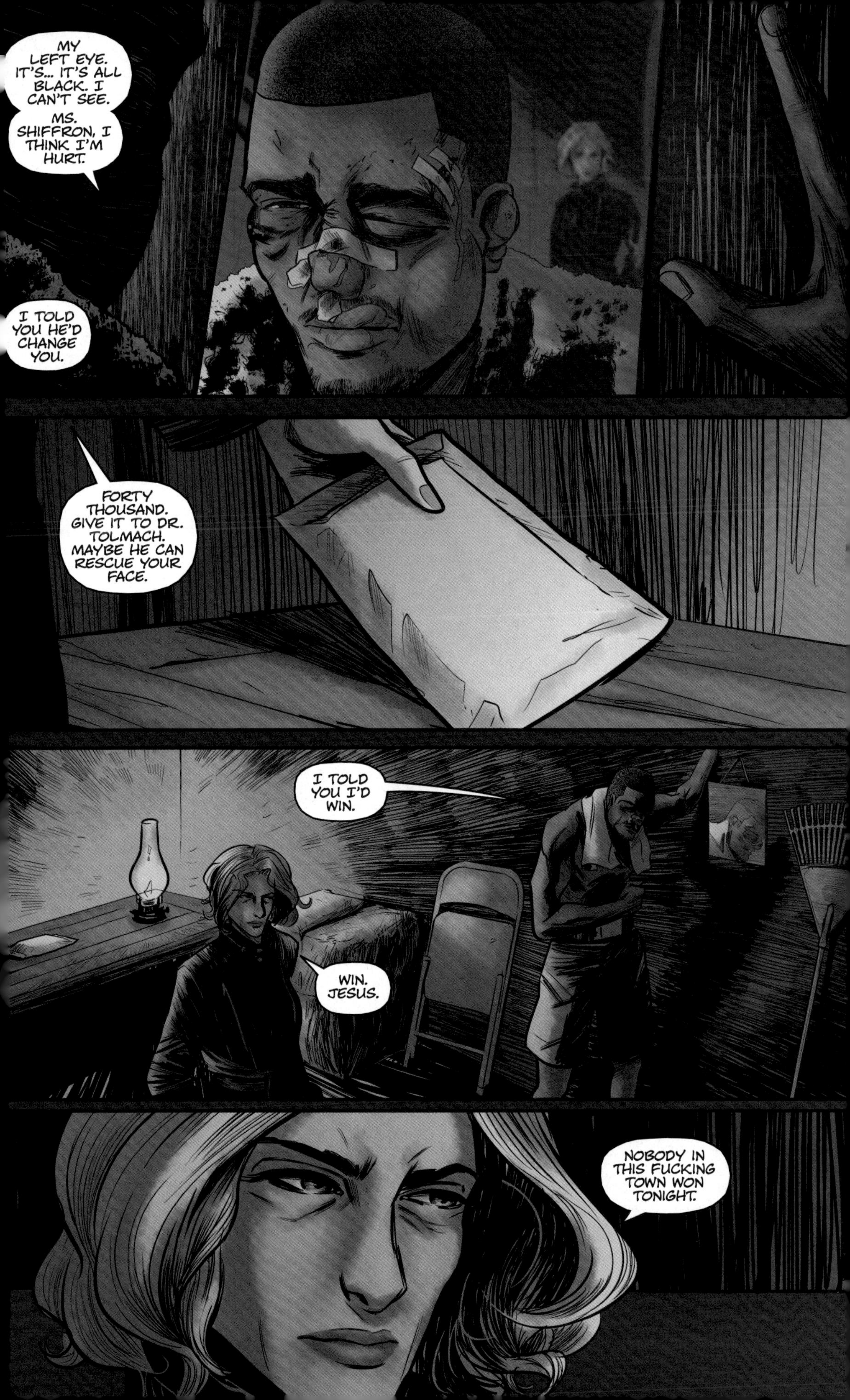
MY LEFT EYE. IT'S... IT'S ALL BLACK. I CAN'T SEE.
MS. SHIFFRON, I THINK I'M HURT.
I TOLD YOU HE'D CHANGE YOU.
FORTY THOUSAND. GIVE IT TO DR. TOLMACH. MAYBE HE CAN RESCUE YOUR FACE.
I TOLD YOU I'D WIN.
WIN. JESUS.
NOBODY IN THIS FUCKING TOWN WON TONIGHT.

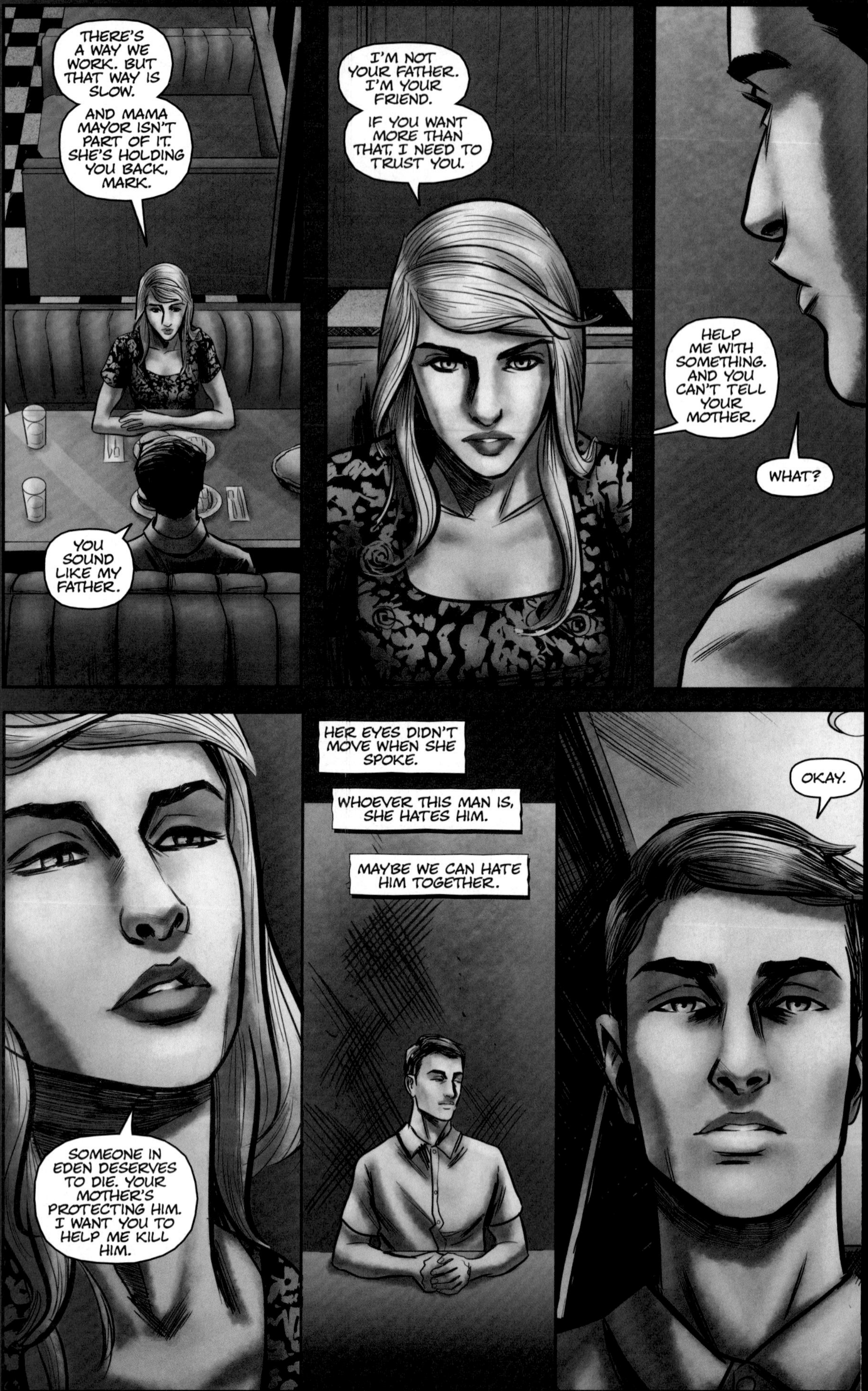
THERE'S A WAY WE WORK. BUT THAT WAY IS SLOW.
AND MAMA MAYOR ISN'T PART OF IT. SHE'S HOLDING YOU BACK, MARK.
YOU SOUND LIKE MY FATHER.
I'M NOT YOUR FATHER. I'M YOUR FRIEND.
IF YOU WANT MORE THAN THAT, I NEED TO TRUST YOU.
HELP ME WITH SOMETHING. AND YOU CAN'T TELL YOUR MOTHER.
WHAT?
SOMEONE IN EDEN DESERVES TO DIE. YOUR MOTHER'S PROTECTING HIM. I WANT YOU TO HELP ME KILL HIM.
HER EYES DIDN'T MOVE WHEN SHE SPOKE.
WHOEVER THIS MAN IS, SHE HATES HIM.
MAYBE WE CAN HATE HIM TOGETHER.
OKAY.

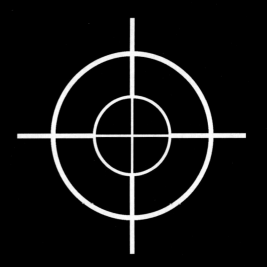

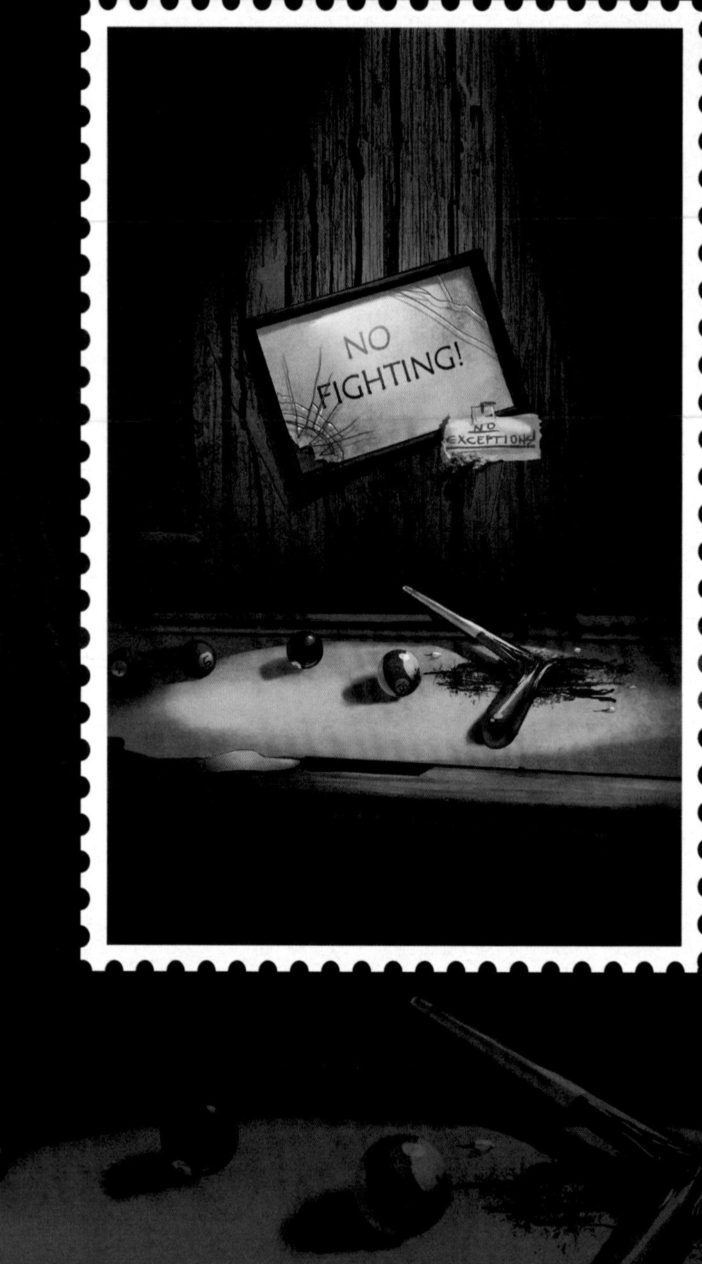
NO
FIGHTING!
NO
EXCEPTIONS!

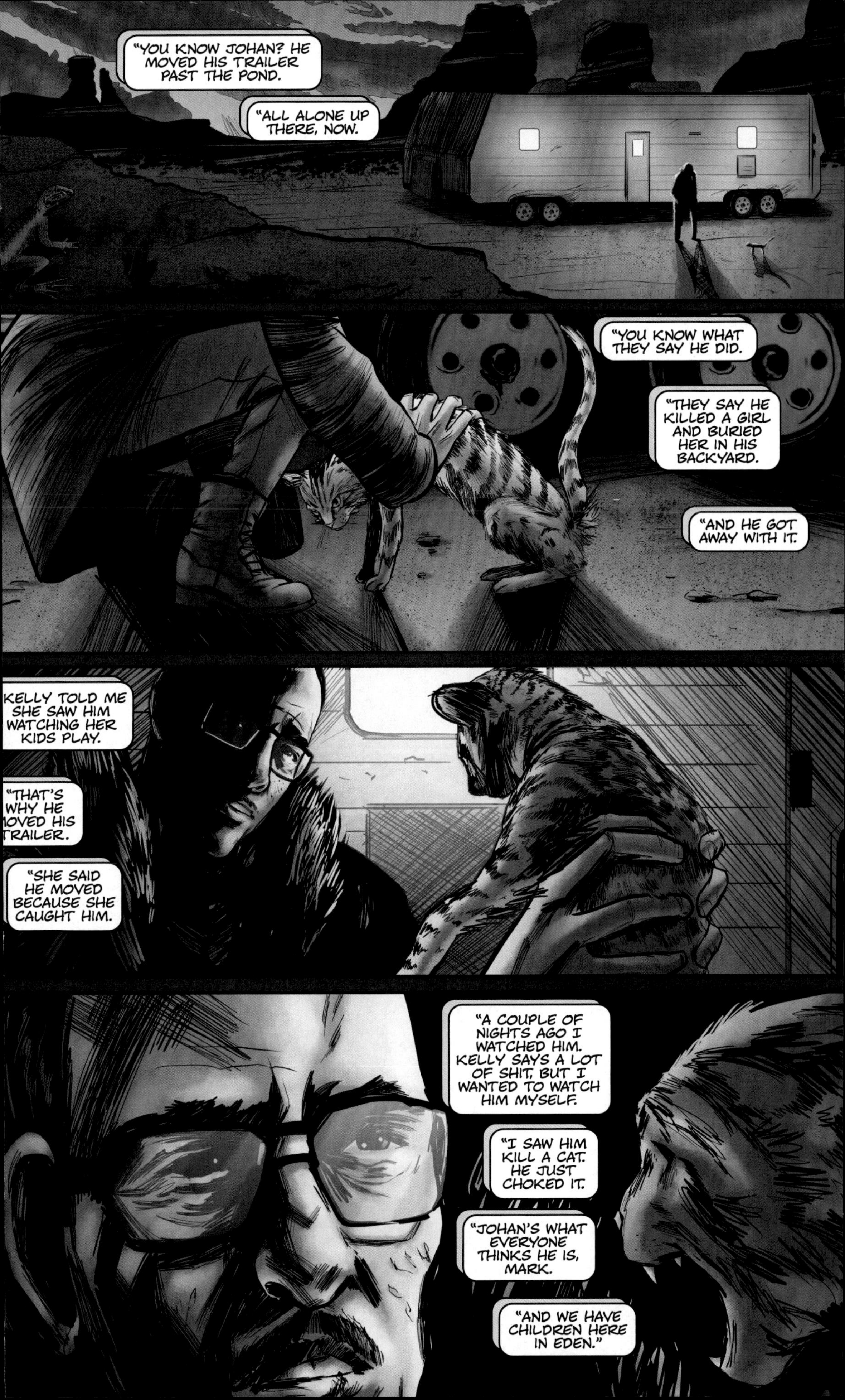
"YOU KNOW JOHAN? HE MOVED HIS TRAILER PAST THE POND.
"ALL ALONE UP THERE, NOW.
"YOU KNOW WHAT THEY SAY HE DID.
"THEY SAY HE KILLED A GIRL AND BURIED HER IN HIS BACKYARD.
"AND HE GOT AWAY WITH IT.
KELLY TOLD ME SHE SAW HIM WATCHING HER KIDS PLAY.
"THAT'S WHY HE MOVED HIS TRAILER.
"SHE SAID HE MOVED BECAUSE SHE CAUGHT HIM.
"A COUPLE OF NIGHTS AGO I WATCHED HIM. KELLY SAYS A LOT OF SHIT, BUT I WANTED TO WATCH HIM MYSELF.
"I SAW HIM KILL A CAT. HE JUST CHOKED IT.
"JOHAN'S WHAT EVERYONE THINKS HE IS, MARK.
"AND WE HAVE CHILDREN HERE IN EDEN."

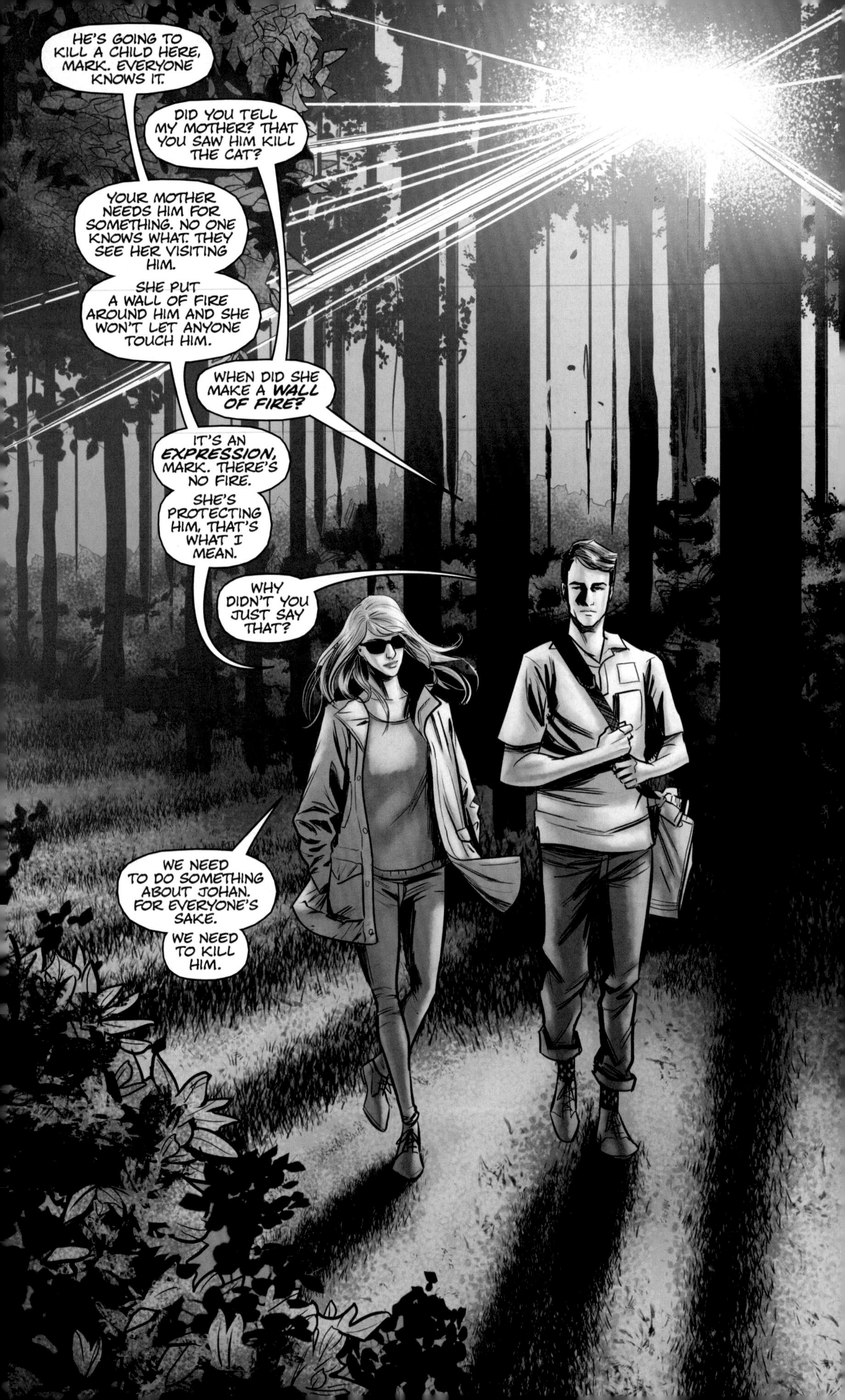

HE'S GOING TO KILL A CHILD HERE, MARK. EVERYONE KNOWS IT.
DID YOU TELL MY MOTHER? THAT YOU SAW HIM KILL THE CAT?
YOUR MOTHER NEEDS HIM FOR SOMETHING. NO ONE KNOWS WHAT. THEY SEE HER VISITING HIM.
SHE PUT A WALL OF FIRE AROUND HIM AND SHE WON'T LET ANYONE TOUCH HIM.
WHEN DID SHE MAKE A ***WALL OF FIRE?***
IT'S AN ***EXPRESSION,*** MARK. THERE'S NO FIRE.
SHE'S PROTECTING HIM, THAT'S WHAT I MEAN.
WHY DIDN'T YOU JUST SAY THAT?
WE NEED TO DO SOMETHING ABOUT JOHAN. FOR EVERYONE'S SAKE.
WE NEED TO KILL HIM.

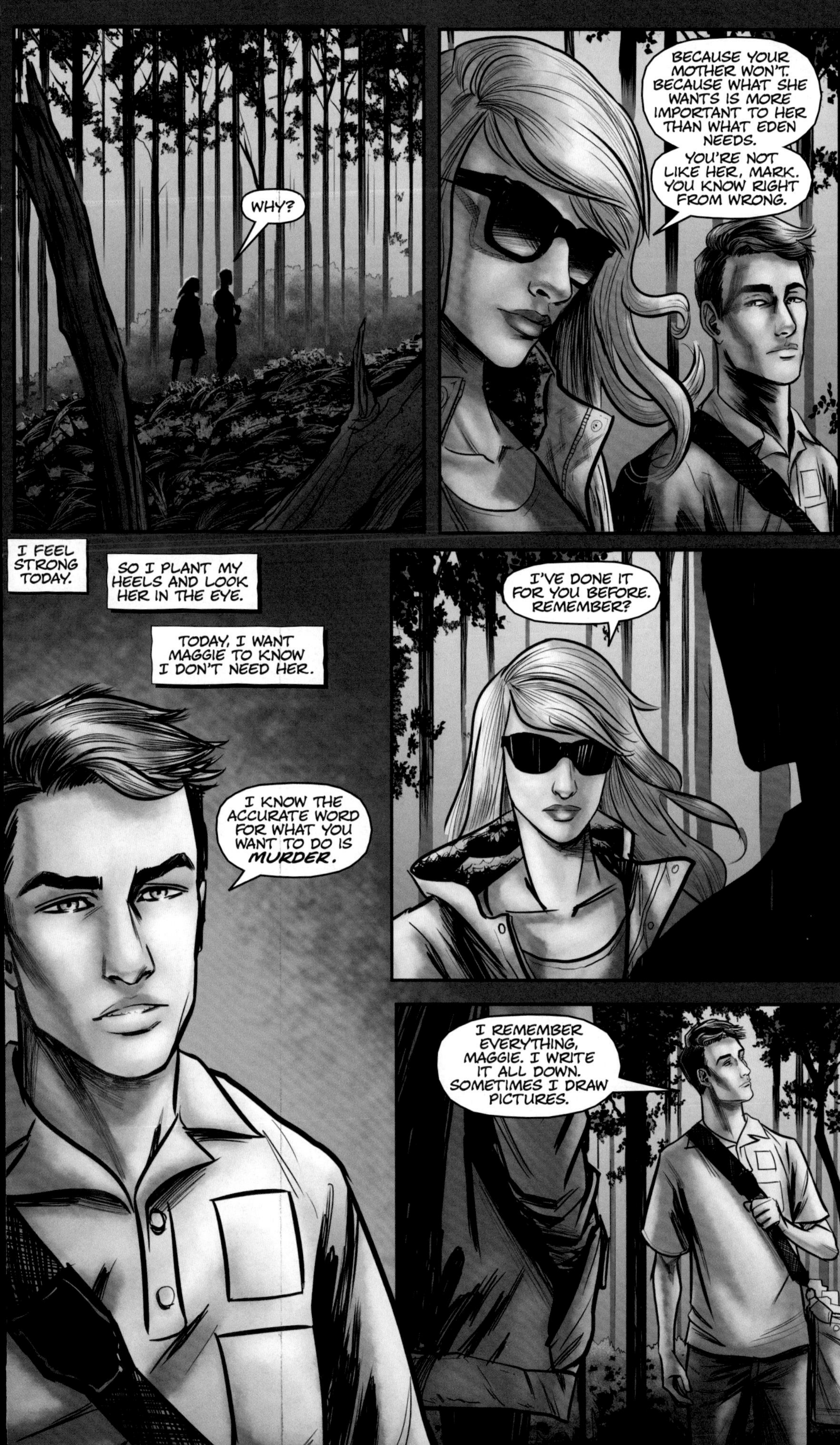
WHY?
BECAUSE YOUR MOTHER WON'T. BECAUSE WHAT SHE WANTS IS MORE IMPORTANT TO HER THAN WHAT EDEN NEEDS.
YOU'RE NOT LIKE HER, MARK. YOU KNOW RIGHT FROM WRONG.
I FEEL STRONG TODAY.
SO I PLANT MY HEELS AND LOOK HER IN THE EYE.
TODAY, I WANT MAGGIE TO KNOW I DON'T NEED HER.
I KNOW THE ACCURATE WORD FOR WHAT YOU WANT TO DO IS ***MURDER***.
I'VE DONE IT FOR YOU BEFORE. REMEMBER?
I REMEMBER EVERYTHING, MAGGIE. I WRITE IT ALL DOWN. SOMETIMES I DRAW PICTURES.

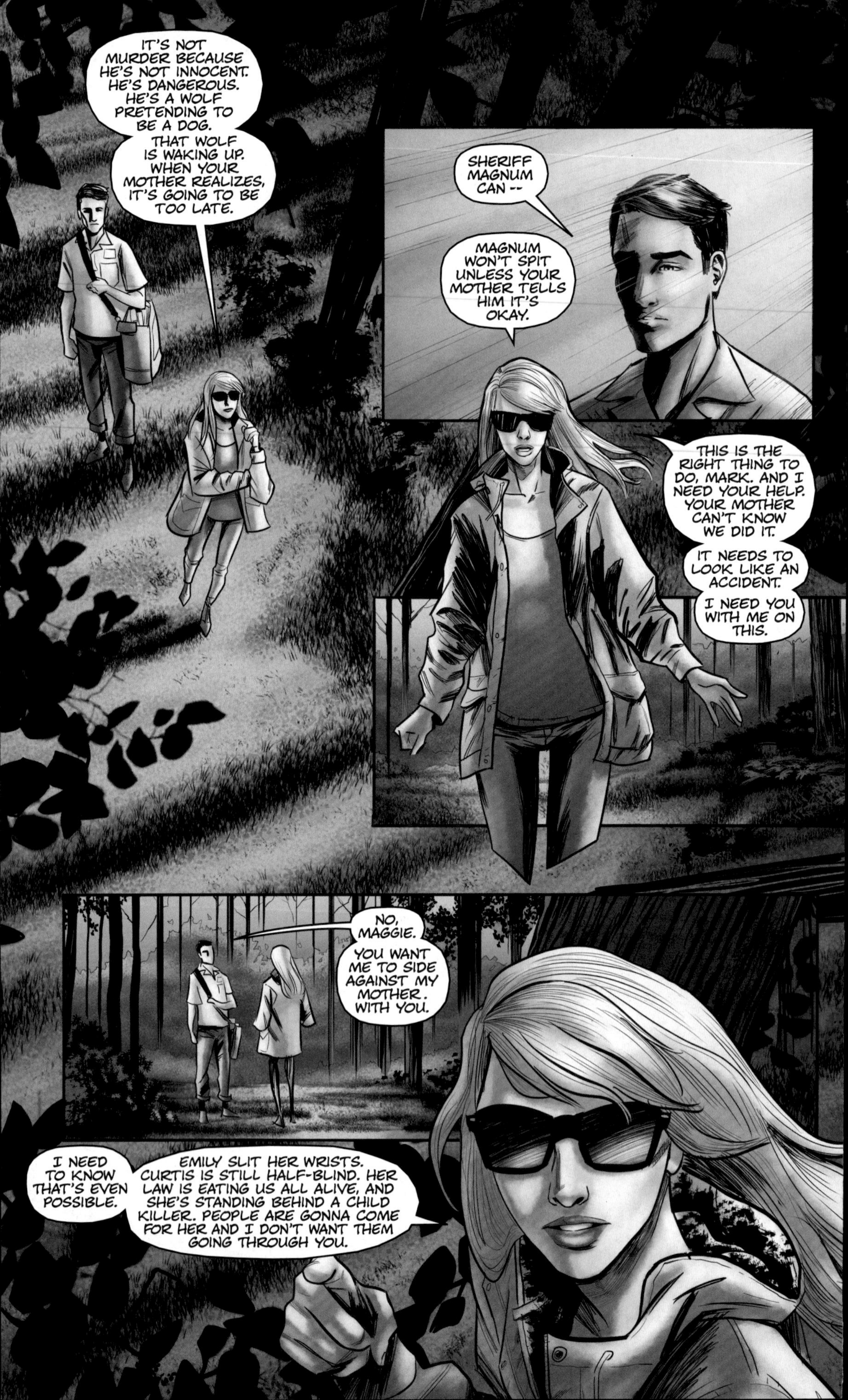
IT'S NOT MURDER BECAUSE HE'S NOT INNOCENT. HE'S DANGEROUS. HE'S A WOLF PRETENDING TO BE A DOG.
THAT WOLF IS WAKING UP. WHEN YOUR MOTHER REALIZES, IT'S GOING TO BE TOO LATE.
SHERIFF MAGNUM CAN --
MAGNUM WON'T SPIT UNLESS YOUR MOTHER TELLS HIM IT'S OKAY.
THIS IS THE RIGHT THING TO DO, MARK. AND I NEED YOUR HELP. YOUR MOTHER CAN'T KNOW WE DID IT.
IT NEEDS TO LOOK LIKE AN ACCIDENT.
I NEED YOU WITH ME ON THIS.
NO, MAGGIE.
YOU WANT ME TO SIDE AGAINST MY MOTHER. WITH YOU.
I NEED TO KNOW THAT'S EVEN POSSIBLE.
EMILY SLIT HER WRISTS. CURTIS IS STILL HALF-BLIND. HER LAW IS EATING US ALL ALIVE, AND SHE'S STANDING BEHIND A CHILD KILLER. PEOPLE ARE GONNA COME FOR HER AND I DON'T WANT THEM GOING THROUGH YOU.

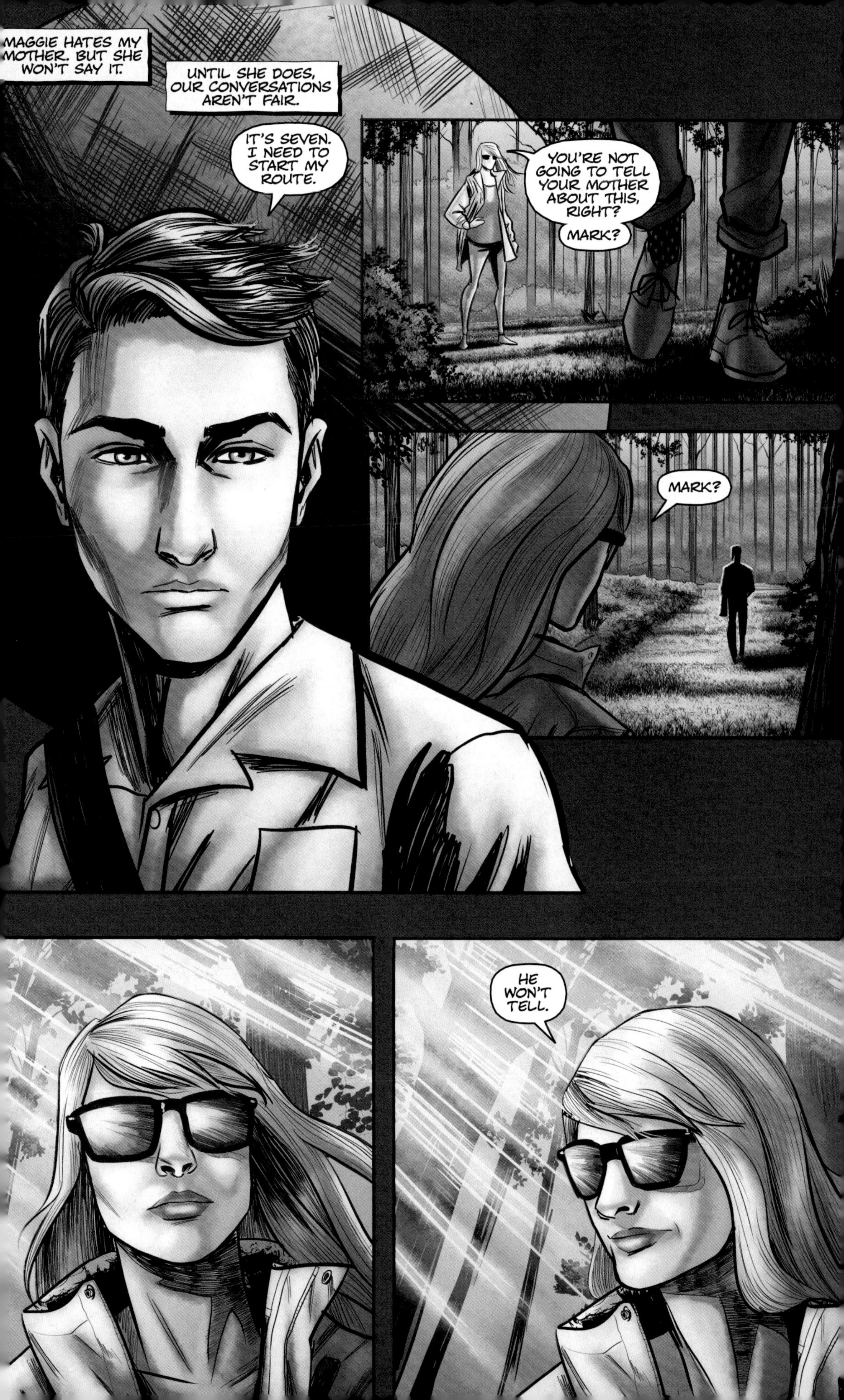
MAGGIE HATES MY MOTHER. BUT SHE WON'T SAY IT.
UNTIL SHE DOES, OUR CONVERSATIONS AREN'T FAIR.
IT'S SEVEN. I NEED TO START MY ROUTE.
YOU'RE NOT GOING TO TELL YOUR MOTHER ABOUT THIS, RIGHT?
MARK?
MARK?
HE WON'T TELL.

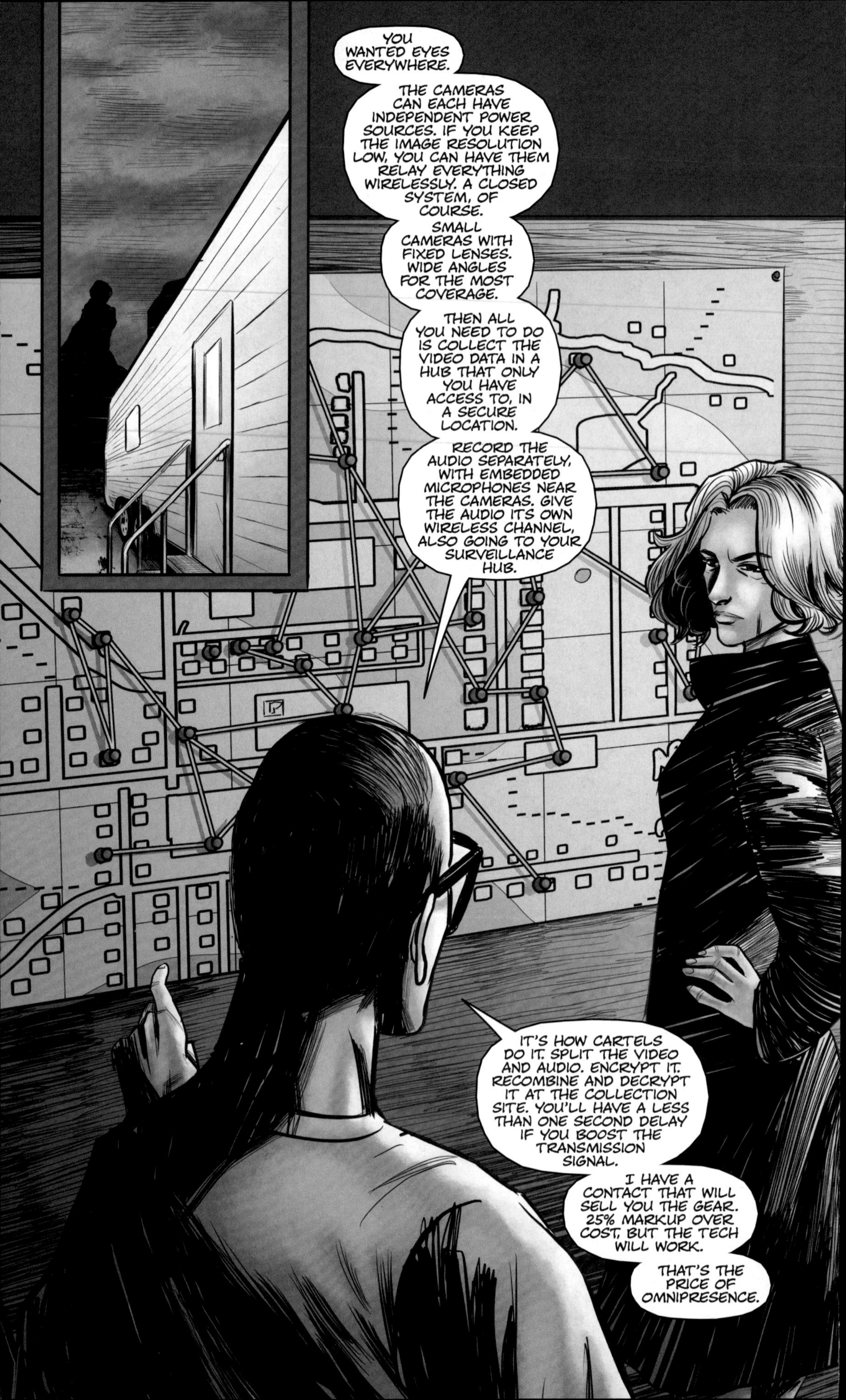
YOU WANTED EYES EVERYWHERE.
THE CAMERAS CAN EACH HAVE INDEPENDENT POWER SOURCES. IF YOU KEEP THE IMAGE RESOLUTION LOW, YOU CAN HAVE THEM RELAY EVERYTHING WIRELESSLY. A CLOSED SYSTEM, OF COURSE.
SMALL CAMERAS WITH FIXED LENSES. WIDE ANGLES FOR THE MOST COVERAGE.
THEN ALL YOU NEED TO DO IS COLLECT THE VIDEO DATA IN A HUB THAT ONLY YOU HAVE ACCESS TO, IN A SECURE LOCATION.
RECORD THE AUDIO SEPARATELY, WITH EMBEDDED MICROPHONES NEAR THE CAMERAS. GIVE THE AUDIO ITS OWN WIRELESS CHANNEL, ALSO GOING TO YOUR SURVEILLANCE HUB.
IT'S HOW CARTELS DO IT. SPLIT THE VIDEO AND AUDIO. ENCRYPT IT. RECOMBINE AND DECRYPT IT AT THE COLLECTION SITE. YOU'LL HAVE A LESS THAN ONE SECOND DELAY IF YOU BOOST THE TRANSMISSION SIGNAL.
I HAVE A CONTACT THAT WILL SELL YOU THE GEAR. 25% MARKUP OVER COST, BUT THE TECH WILL WORK.
THAT'S THE PRICE OF OMNIPRESENCE.

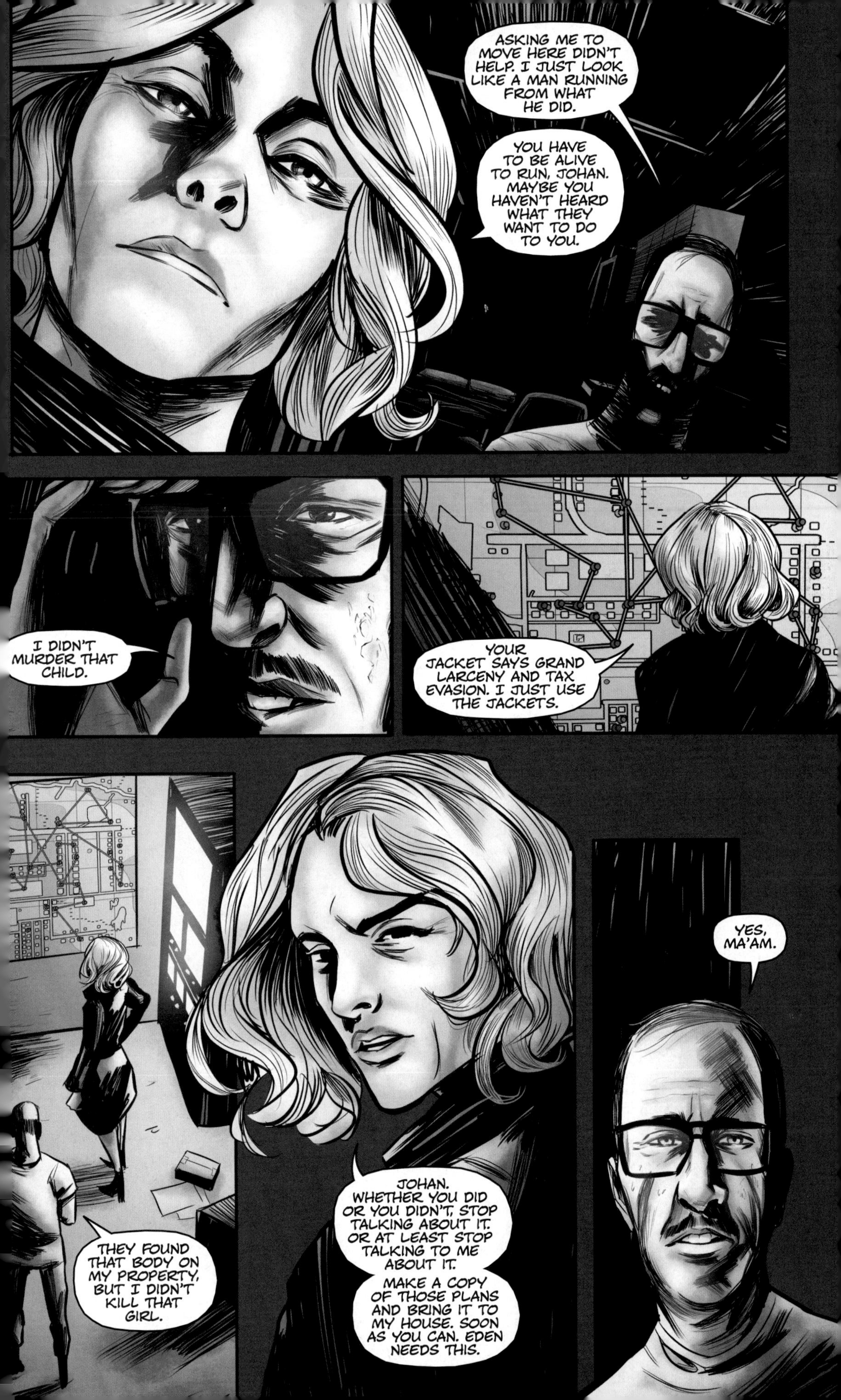
ASKING ME TO MOVE HERE DIDN'T HELP. I JUST LOOK LIKE A MAN RUNNING FROM WHAT HE DID.
YOU HAVE TO BE ALIVE TO RUN, JOHAN. MAYBE YOU HAVEN'T HEARD WHAT THEY WANT TO DO TO YOU.
I DIDN'T MURDER THAT CHILD.
YOUR JACKET SAYS GRAND LARCENY AND TAX EVASION. I JUST USE THE JACKETS.
THEY FOUND THAT BODY ON MY PROPERTY, BUT I DIDN'T KILL THAT GIRL.
JOHAN. WHETHER YOU DID OR YOU DIDN'T, STOP TALKING ABOUT IT. OR AT LEAST STOP TALKING TO ME ABOUT IT.
MAKE A COPY OF THOSE PLANS AND BRING IT TO MY HOUSE. SOON AS YOU CAN. EDEN NEEDS THIS.
YES, MA'AM.

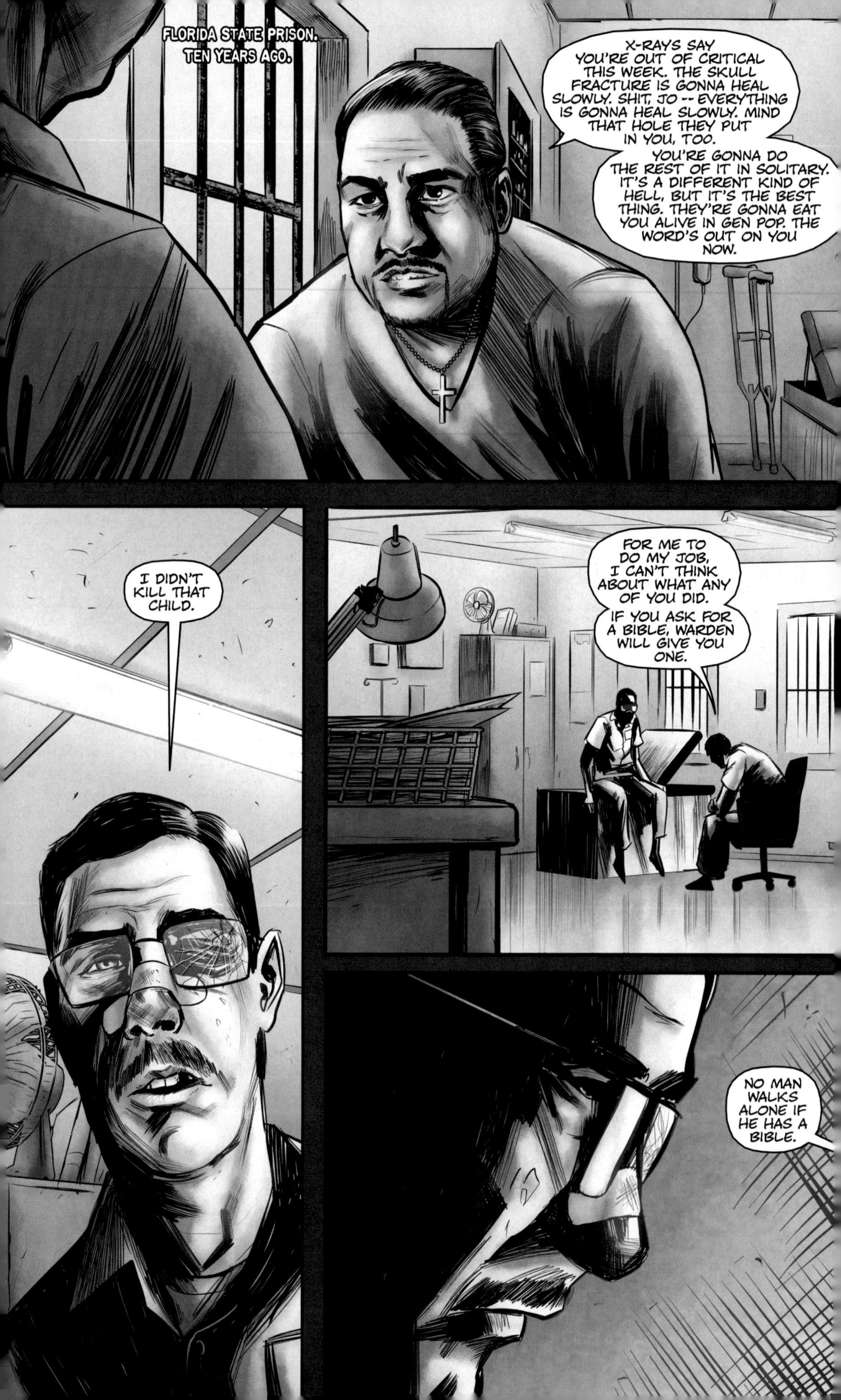
FLORIDA STATE PRISON. TEN YEARS AGO.
X-RAYS SAY YOU'RE OUT OF CRITICAL THIS WEEK. THE SKULL FRACTURE IS GONNA HEAL SLOWLY. SHIT, JO -- EVERYTHING IS GONNA HEAL SLOWLY. MIND THAT HOLE THEY PUT IN YOU, TOO.
YOU'RE GONNA DO THE REST OF IT IN SOLITARY. IT'S A DIFFERENT KIND OF HELL, BUT IT'S THE BEST THING. THEY'RE GONNA EAT YOU ALIVE IN GEN POP. THE WORD'S OUT ON YOU NOW.
I DIDN'T KILL THAT CHILD.
FOR ME TO DO MY JOB, I CAN'T THINK ABOUT WHAT ANY OF YOU DID.
IF YOU ASK FOR A BIBLE, WARDEN WILL GIVE YOU ONE.
NO MAN WALKS ALONE IF HE HAS A BIBLE.

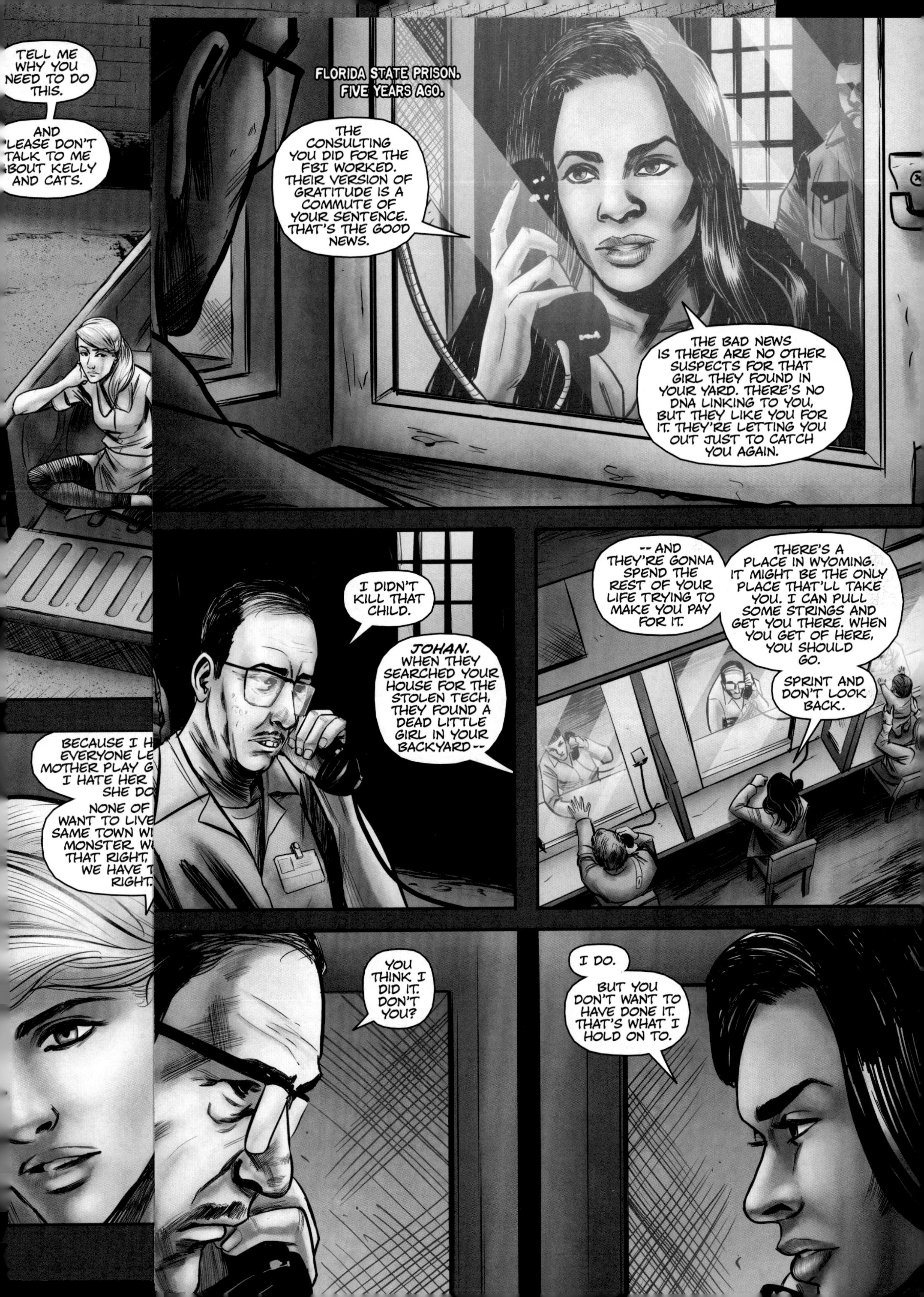

TELL ME WHY YOU NEED TO DO THIS.
AND 'LEASE DON'T TALK TO ME BOUT KELLY AND CATS.
FLORIDA STATE PRISON. FIVE YEARS AGO.
THE CONSULTING YOU DID FOR THE FBI WORKED. THEIR VERSION OF GRATITUDE IS A COMMUTE OF YOUR SENTENCE. THAT'S THE GOOD NEWS.
THE BAD NEWS IS THERE ARE NO OTHER SUSPECTS FOR THAT GIRL THEY FOUND IN YOUR YARD. THERE'S NO DNA LINKING TO YOU, BUT THEY LIKE YOU FOR IT. THEY'RE LETTING YOU OUT JUST TO CATCH YOU AGAIN.
I DIDN'T KILL THAT CHILD.
JOHAN. WHEN THEY SEARCHED YOUR HOUSE FOR THE STOLEN TECH, THEY FOUND A DEAD LITTLE GIRL IN YOUR BACKYARD--
--AND THEY'RE GONNA SPEND THE REST OF YOUR LIFE TRYING TO MAKE YOU PAY FOR IT.
THERE'S A PLACE IN WYOMING. IT MIGHT BE THE ONLY PLACE THAT'LL TAKE YOU. I CAN PULL SOME STRINGS AND GET YOU THERE. WHEN YOU GET OF HERE, YOU SHOULD GO.
SPRINT AND DON'T LOOK BACK.
YOU THINK I DID IT. DON'T YOU?
I DO.
BUT YOU DON'T WANT TO HAVE DONE IT. THAT'S WHAT I HOLD ON TO.

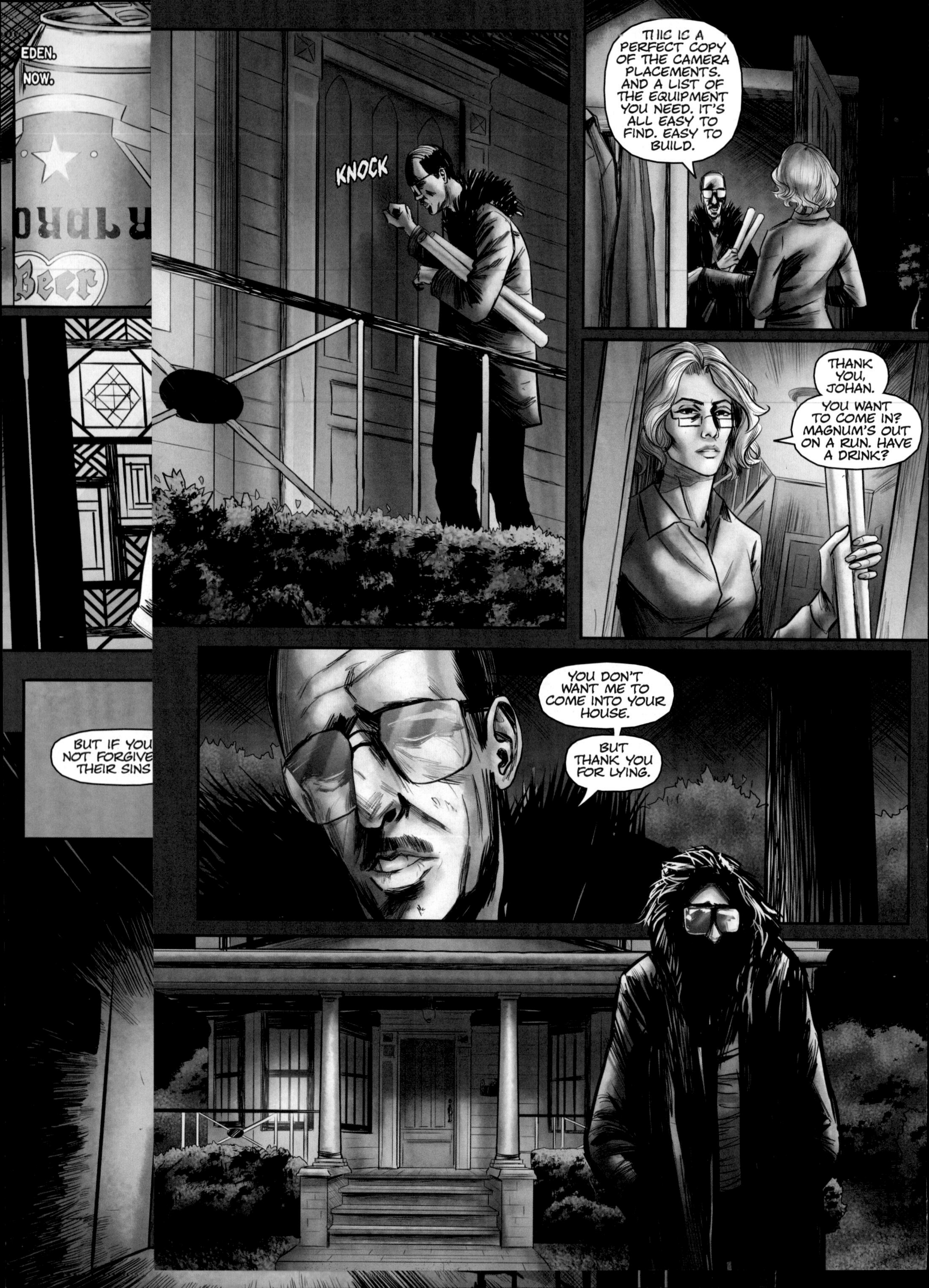
EDEN.
NOW.
KNOCK
THIS IS A PERFECT COPY OF THE CAMERA PLACEMENTS. AND A LIST OF THE EQUIPMENT YOU NEED. IT'S ALL EASY TO FIND. EASY TO BUILD.
THANK YOU, JOHAN.
YOU WANT TO COME IN? MAGNUM'S OUT ON A RUN. HAVE A DRINK?
YOU DON'T WANT ME TO COME INTO YOUR HOUSE.
BUT THANK YOU FOR LYING.
BUT IF YOU NOT FORGIVE THEIR SINS
Beer

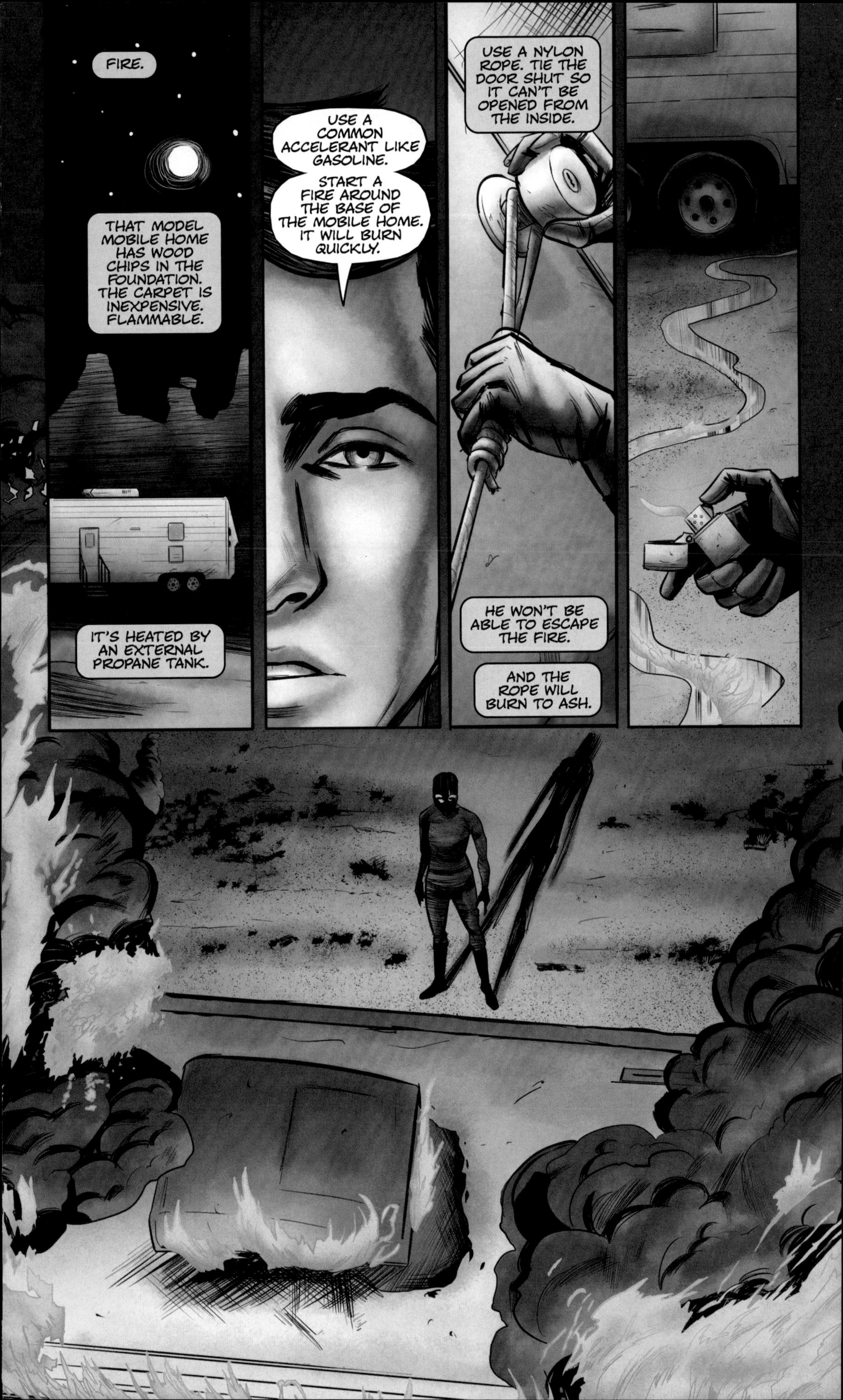
FIRE.
THAT MODEL MOBILE HOME HAS WOOD CHIPS IN THE FOUNDATION. THE CARPET IS INEXPENSIVE. FLAMMABLE.
IT'S HEATED BY AN EXTERNAL PROPANE TANK.
USE A COMMON ACCELERANT LIKE GASOLINE.
START A FIRE AROUND THE BASE OF THE MOBILE HOME. IT WILL BURN QUICKLY.
USE A NYLON ROPE. TIE THE DOOR SHUT SO IT CAN'T BE OPENED FROM THE INSIDE.
HE WON'T BE ABLE TO ESCAPE THE FIRE.
AND THE ROPE WILL BURN TO ASH.

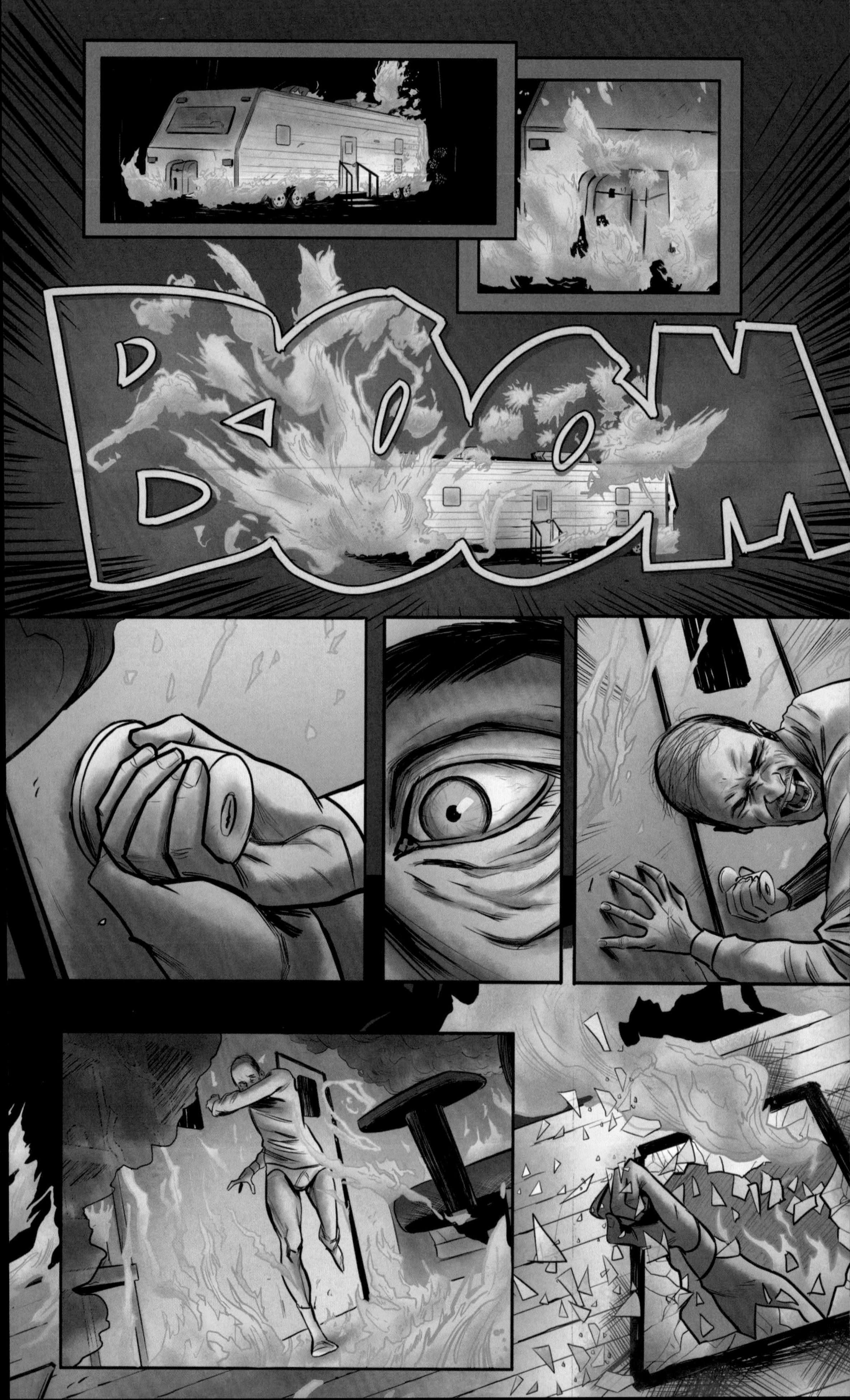
BADOOM

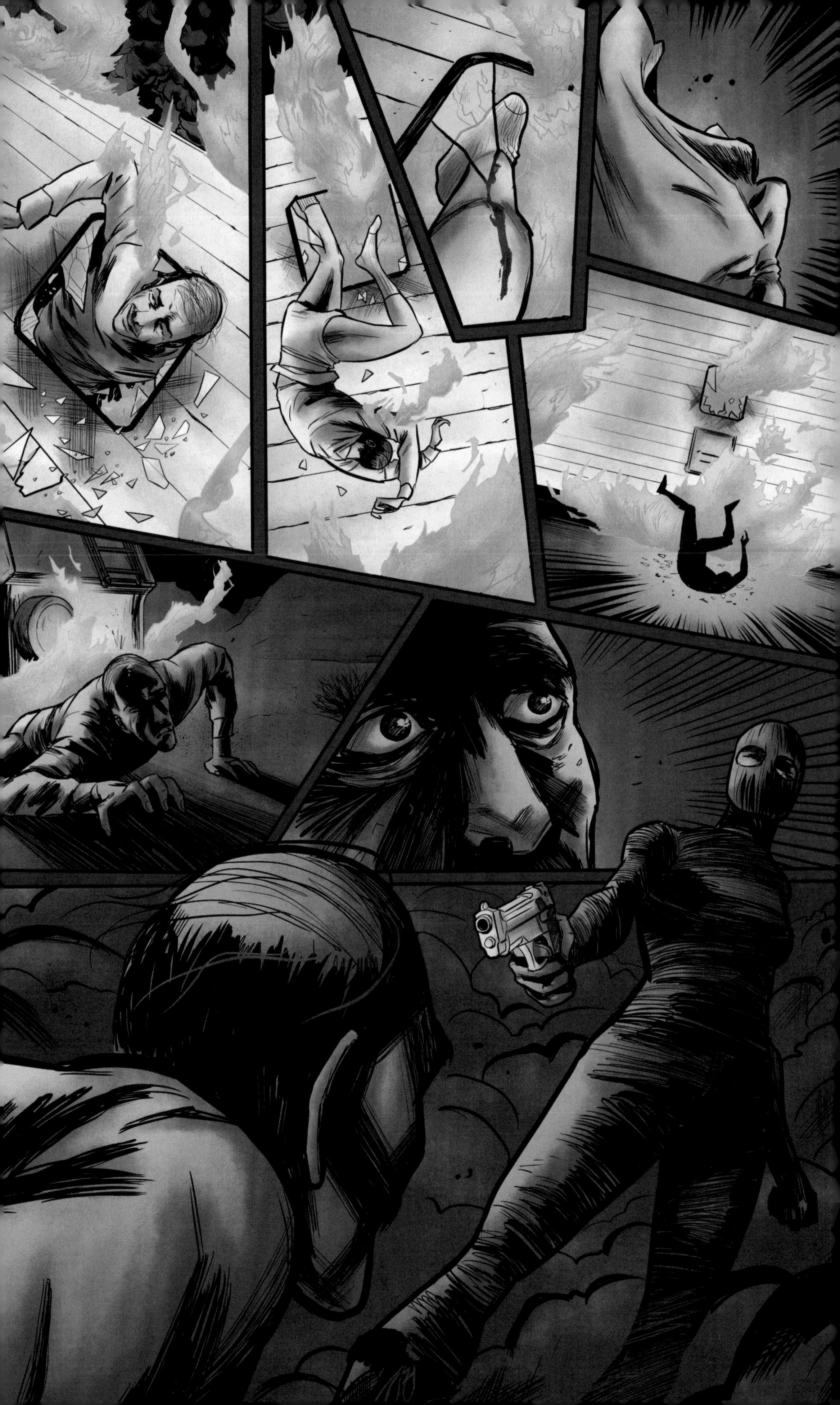

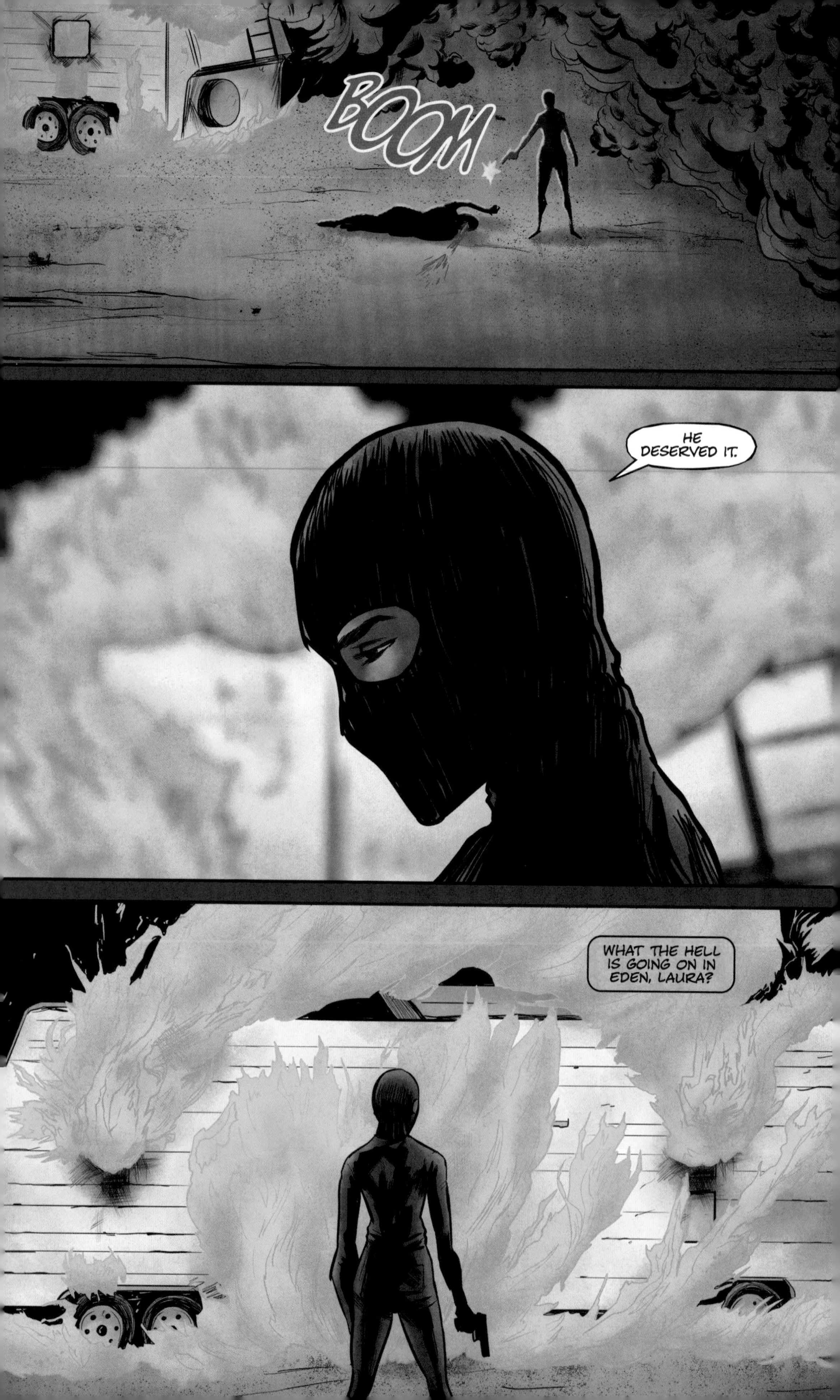
BOOM
HE DESERVED IT.
WHAT THE HELL IS GOING ON IN EDEN, LAURA?

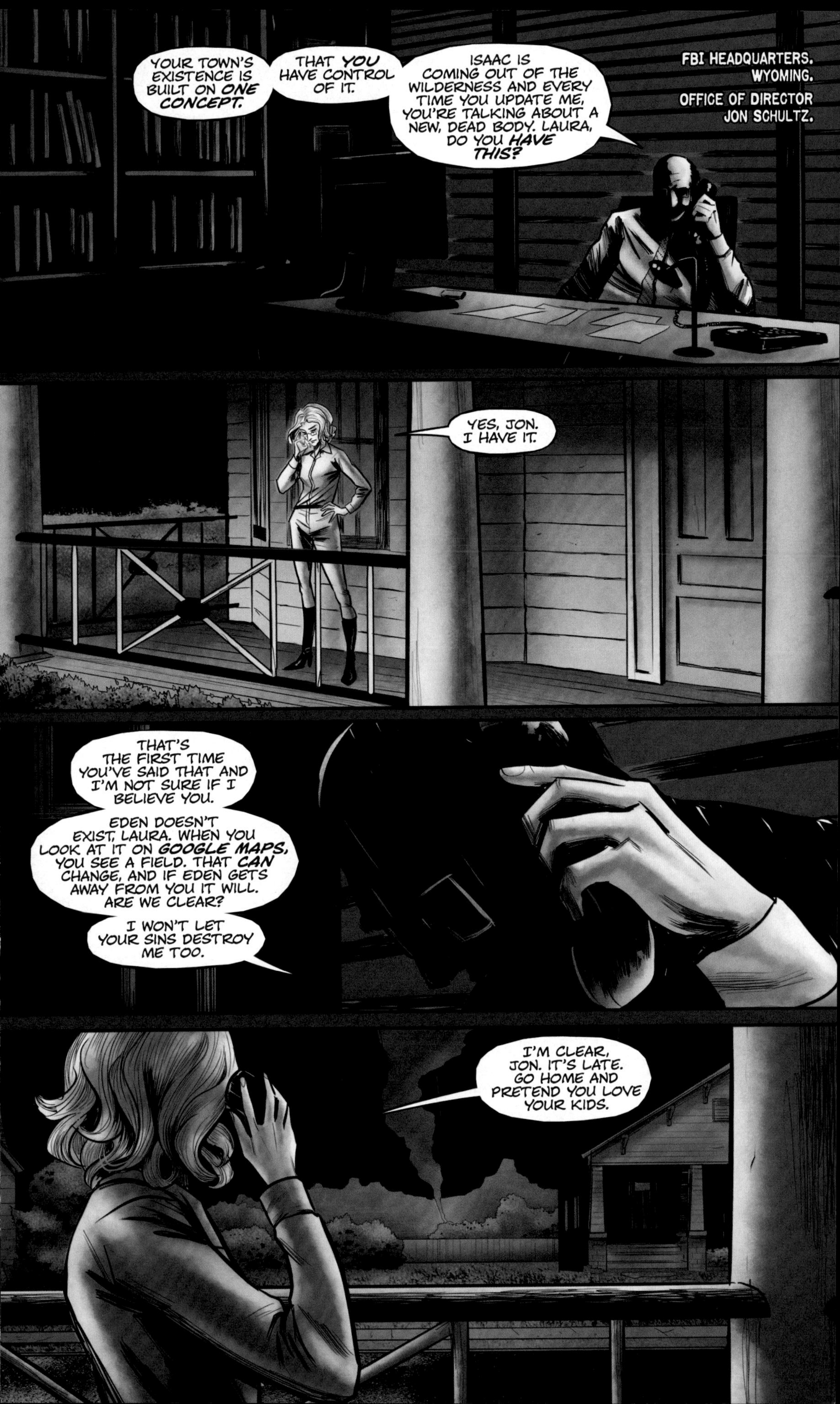
FBI HEADQUARTERS. WYOMING.
OFFICE OF DIRECTOR JON SCHULTZ.
YOUR TOWN'S EXISTENCE IS BUILT ON ONE CONCEPT.
THAT YOU HAVE CONTROL OF IT.
ISAAC IS COMING OUT OF THE WILDERNESS AND EVERY TIME YOU UPDATE ME, YOU'RE TALKING ABOUT A NEW, DEAD BODY. LAURA, DO YOU HAVE THIS?
YES, JON. I HAVE IT.
THAT'S THE FIRST TIME YOU'VE SAID THAT AND I'M NOT SURE IF I BELIEVE YOU.
EDEN DOESN'T EXIST, LAURA. WHEN YOU LOOK AT IT ON GOOGLE MAPS, YOU SEE A FIELD. THAT CAN CHANGE, AND IF EDEN GETS AWAY FROM YOU IT WILL. ARE WE CLEAR?
I WON'T LET YOUR SINS DESTROY ME TOO.
I'M CLEAR, JON. IT'S LATE. GO HOME AND PRETEND YOU LOVE YOUR KIDS.

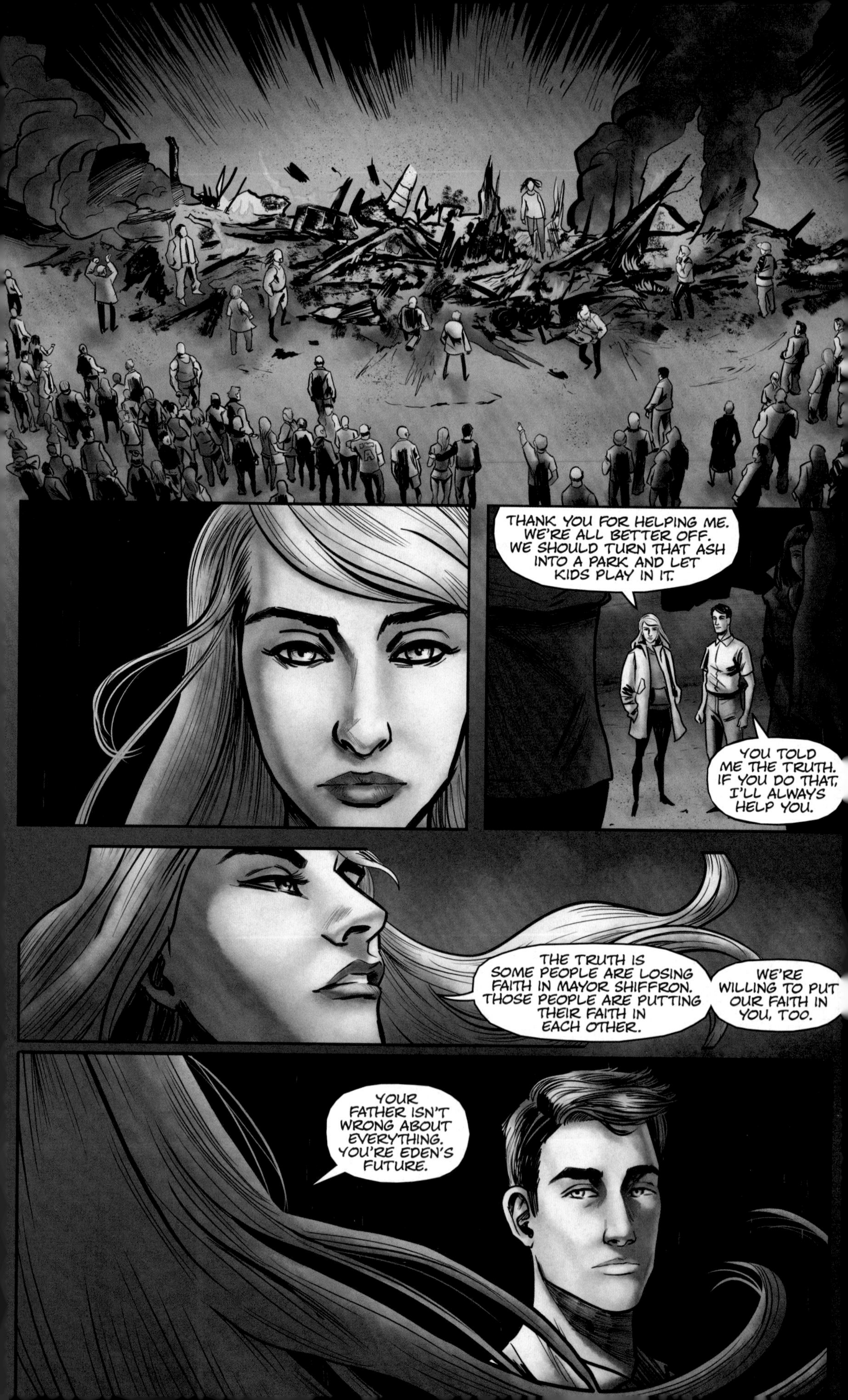
THANK YOU FOR HELPING ME. WE'RE ALL BETTER OFF. WE SHOULD TURN THAT ASH INTO A PARK AND LET KIDS PLAY IN IT.
YOU TOLD ME THE TRUTH. IF YOU DO THAT, I'LL ALWAYS HELP YOU.
THE TRUTH IS SOME PEOPLE ARE LOSING FAITH IN MAYOR SHIFFRON. THOSE PEOPLE ARE PUTTING THEIR FAITH IN EACH OTHER.
WE'RE WILLING TO PUT OUR FAITH IN YOU, TOO.
YOUR FATHER ISN'T WRONG ABOUT EVERYTHING. YOU'RE EDEN'S FUTURE.

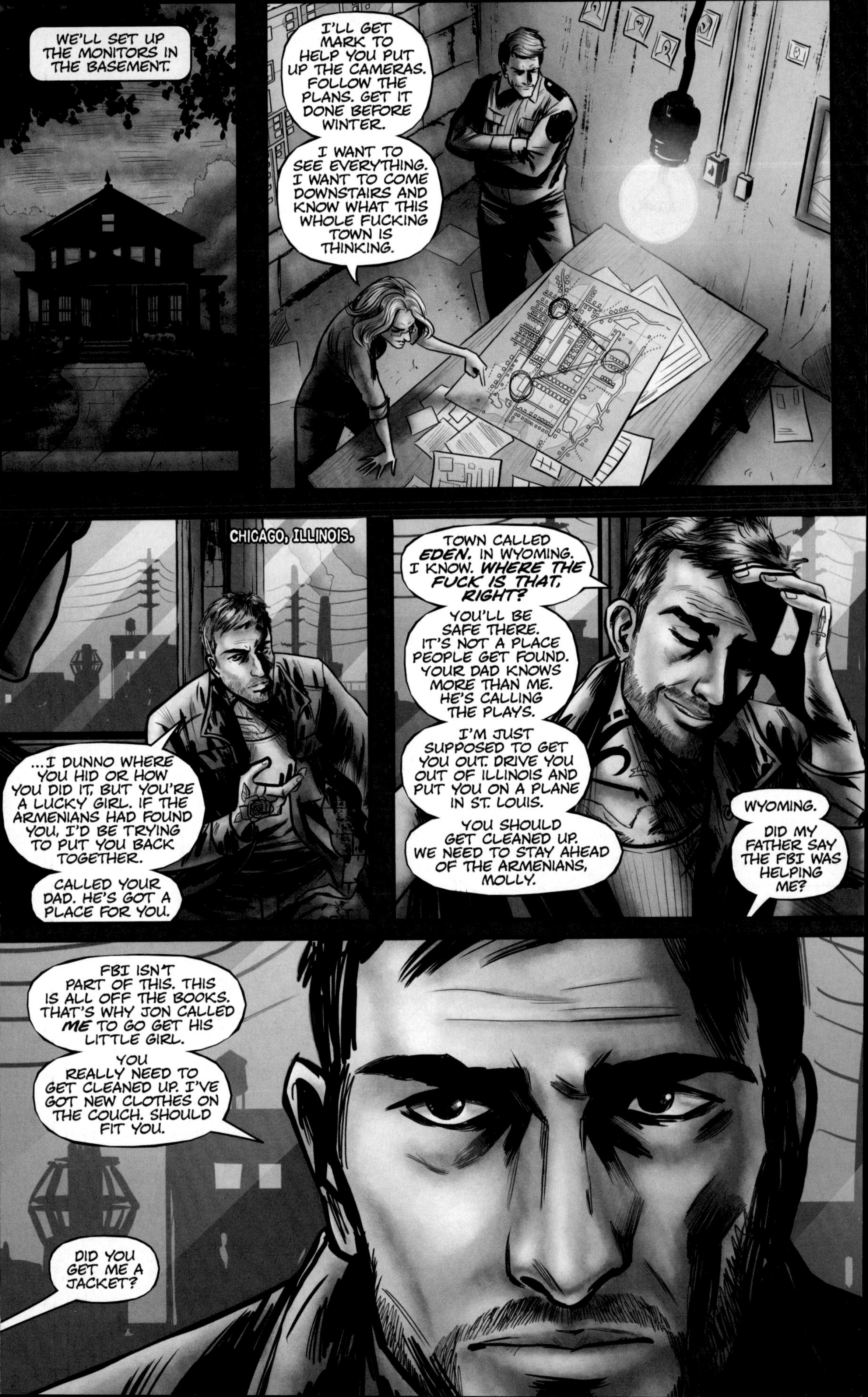
WE'LL SET UP THE MONITORS IN THE BASEMENT.
I'LL GET MARK TO HELP YOU PUT UP THE CAMERAS. FOLLOW THE PLANS. GET IT DONE BEFORE WINTER.
I WANT TO SEE EVERYTHING. I WANT TO COME DOWNSTAIRS AND KNOW WHAT THIS WHOLE FUCKING TOWN IS THINKING.
CHICAGO, ILLINOIS.
...I DUNNO WHERE YOU HID OR HOW YOU DID IT, BUT YOU'RE A LUCKY GIRL. IF THE ARMENIANS HAD FOUND YOU, I'D BE TRYING TO PUT YOU BACK TOGETHER.
CALLED YOUR DAD. HE'S GOT A PLACE FOR YOU.
TOWN CALLED *EDEN.* IN WYOMING. I KNOW. ***WHERE THE FUCK IS THAT, RIGHT?***
YOU'LL BE SAFE THERE. IT'S NOT A PLACE PEOPLE GET FOUND. YOUR DAD KNOWS MORE THAN ME. HE'S CALLING THE PLAYS.
I'M JUST SUPPOSED TO GET YOU OUT. DRIVE YOU OUT OF ILLINOIS AND PUT YOU ON A PLANE IN ST. LOUIS.
YOU SHOULD GET CLEANED UP. WE NEED TO STAY AHEAD OF THE ARMENIANS, MOLLY.
WYOMING.
DID MY FATHER SAY THE FBI WAS HELPING ME?
FBI ISN'T PART OF THIS. THIS IS ALL OFF THE BOOKS. THAT'S WHY JON CALLED *ME* TO GO GET HIS LITTLE GIRL.
YOU REALLY NEED TO GET CLEANED UP. I'VE GOT NEW CLOTHES ON THE COUCH. SHOULD FIT YOU.
DID YOU GET ME A JACKET?

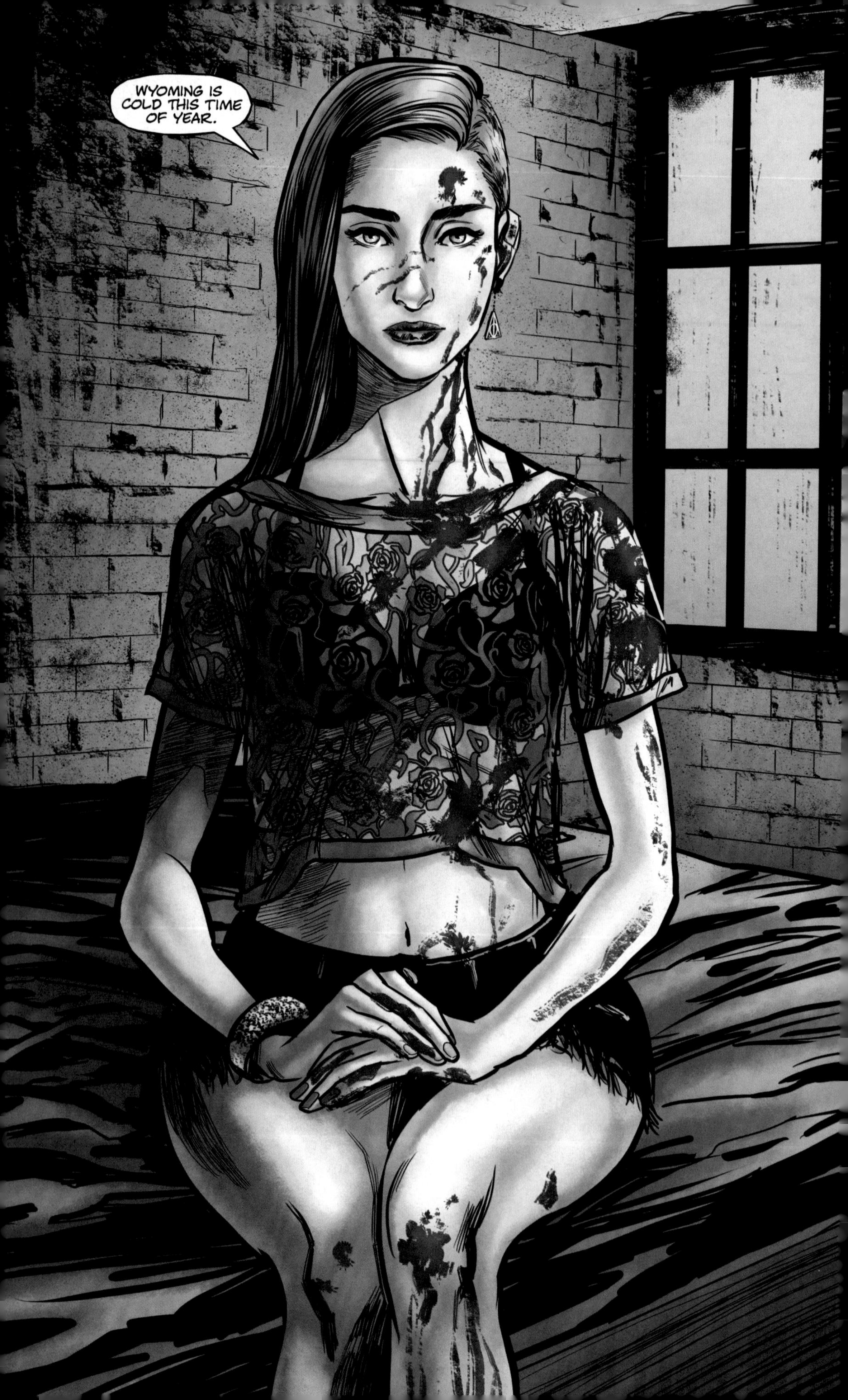
WYOMING IS COLD THIS TIME OF YEAR.

# Chapter 9

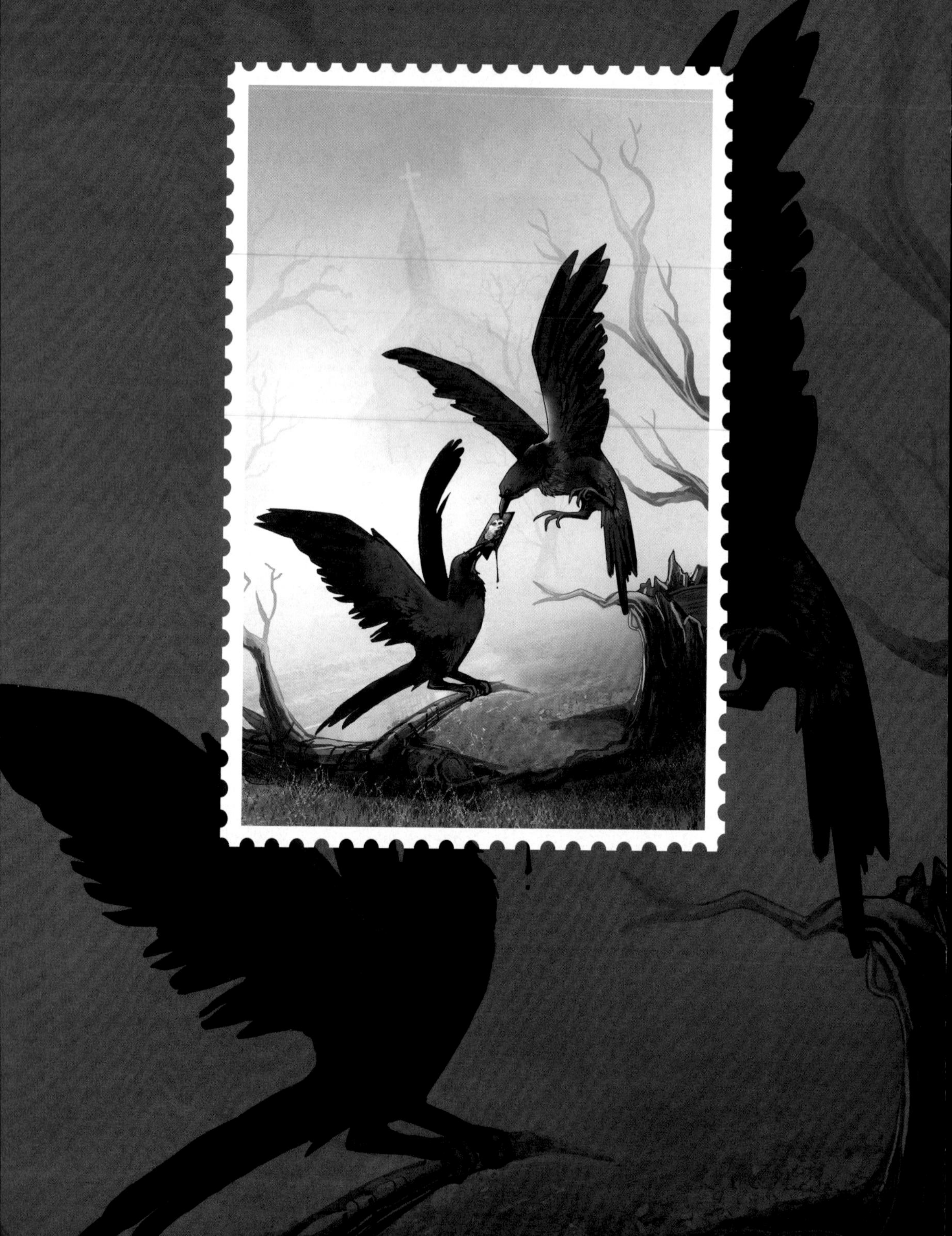

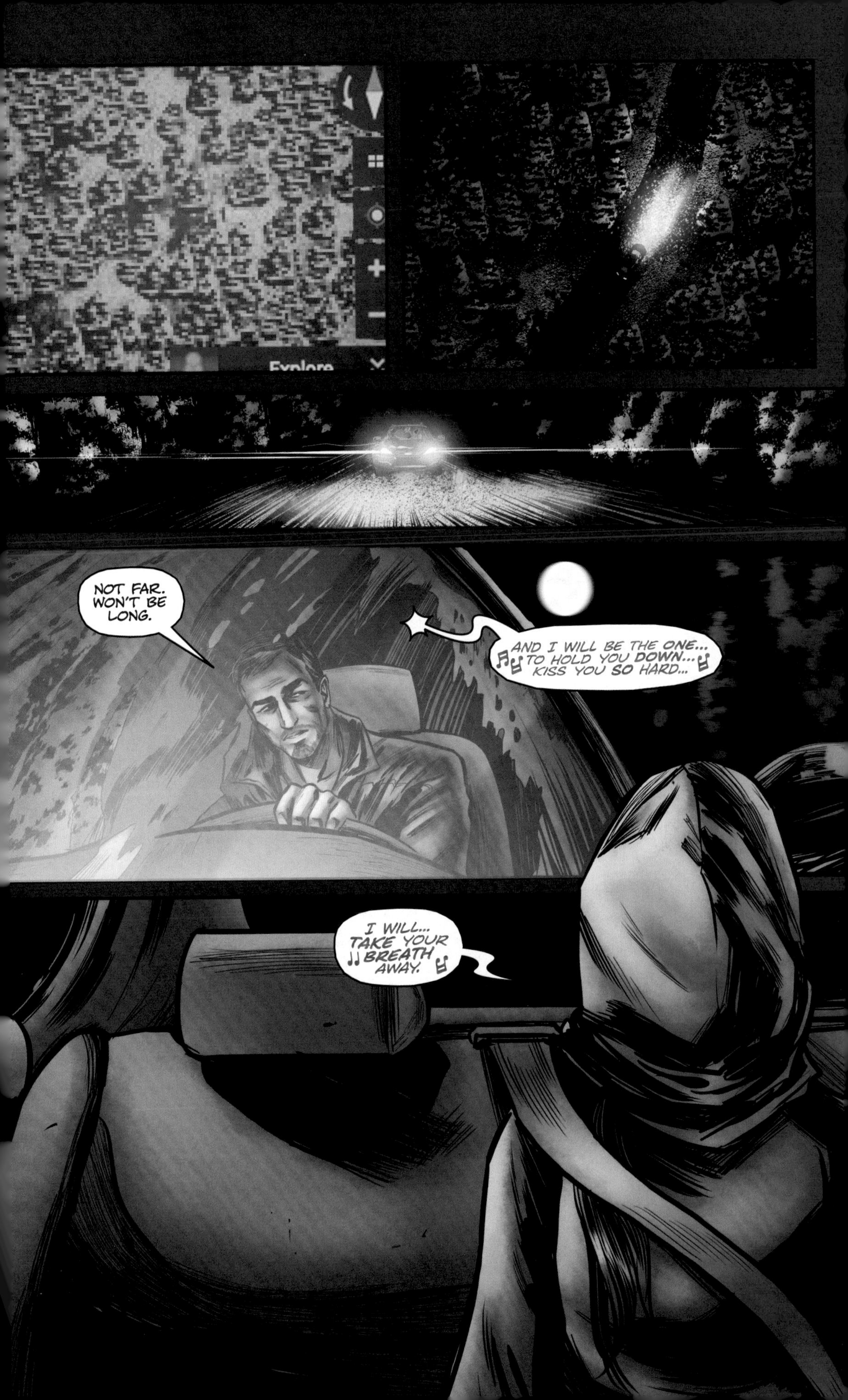
Explore
NOT FAR. WON'T BE LONG.
AND I WILL BE THE ONE... TO HOLD YOU DOWN... KISS YOU SO HARD...
I WILL... TAKE YOUR BREATH AWAY.

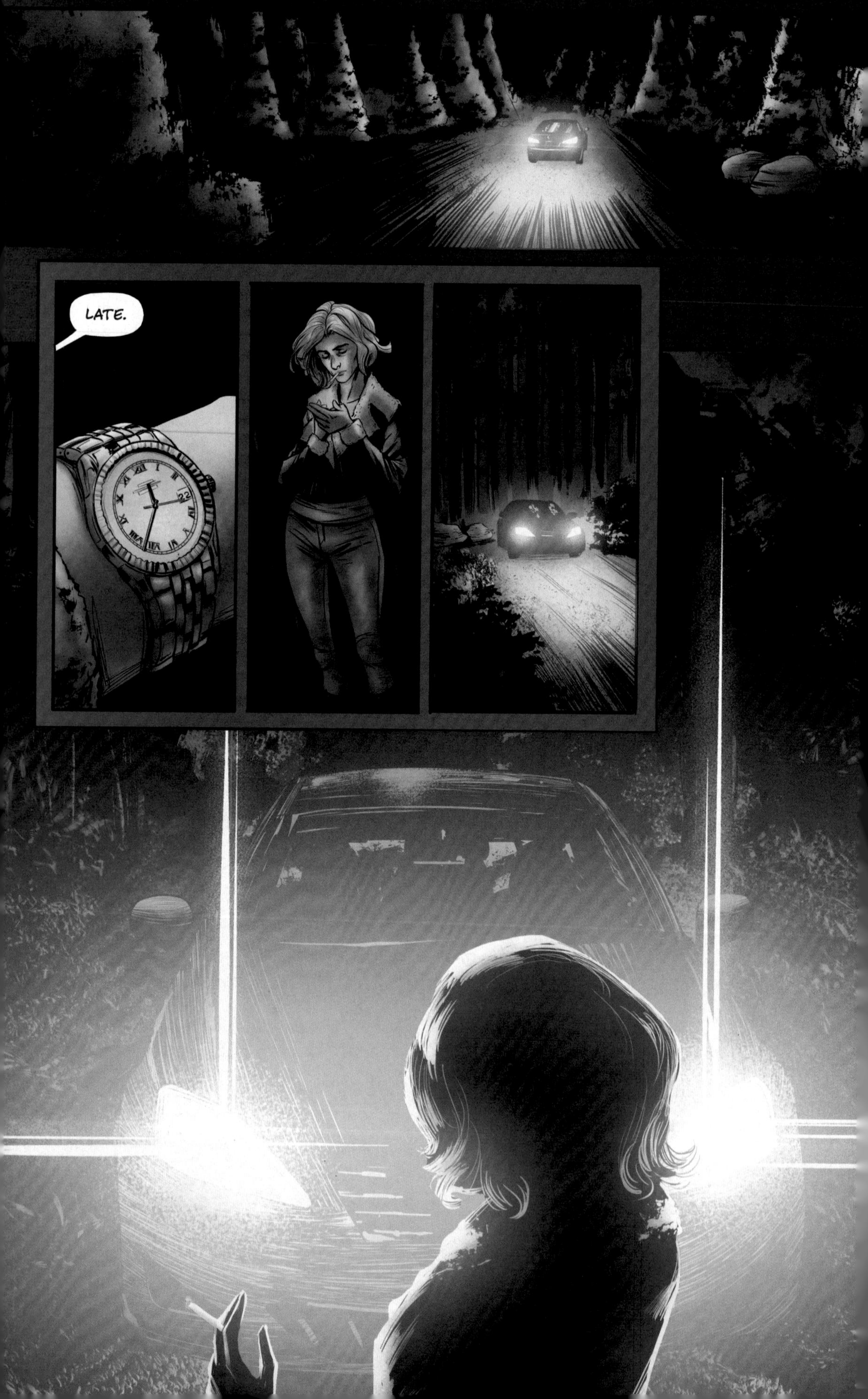
LATE.

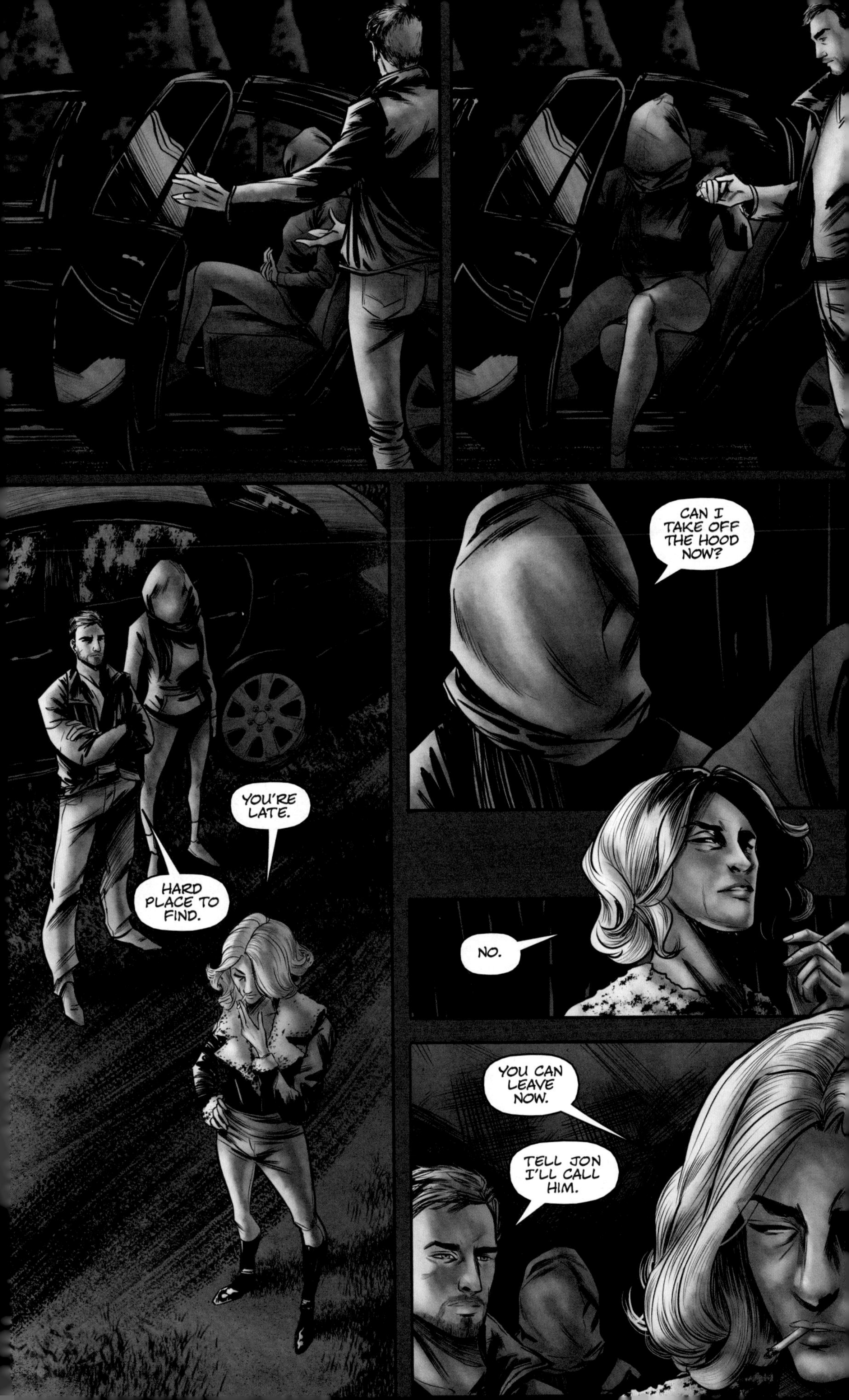
YOU'RE LATE.
HARD PLACE TO FIND.
CAN I TAKE OFF THE HOOD NOW?
NO.
YOU CAN LEAVE NOW.
TELL JON I'LL CALL HIM.

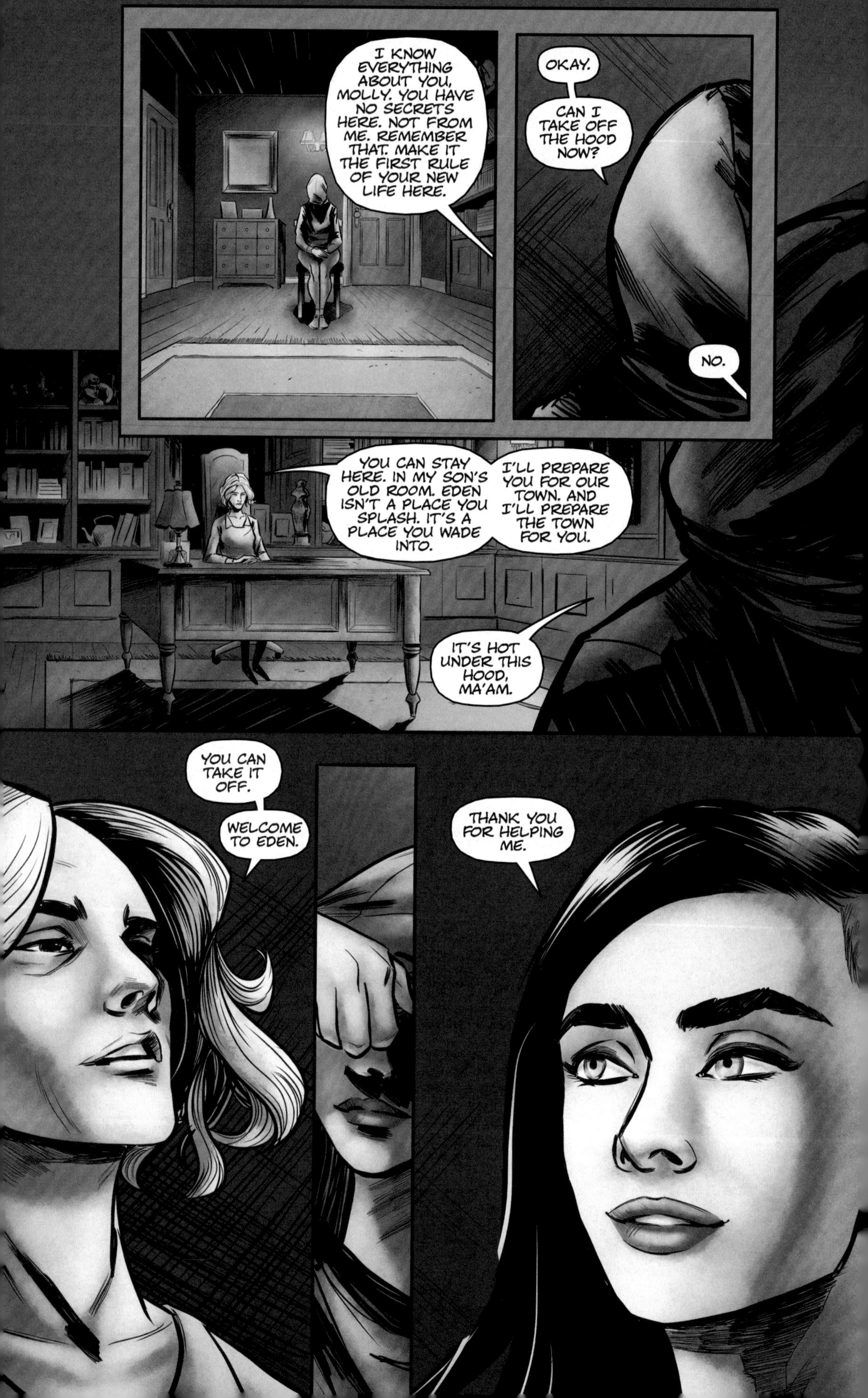
I KNOW EVERYTHING ABOUT YOU, MOLLY. YOU HAVE NO SECRETS HERE. NOT FROM ME. REMEMBER THAT. MAKE IT THE FIRST RULE OF YOUR NEW LIFE HERE.
OKAY.
CAN I TAKE OFF THE HOOD NOW?
NO.
YOU CAN STAY HERE. IN MY SON'S OLD ROOM. EDEN ISN'T A PLACE YOU SPLASH. IT'S A PLACE YOU WADE INTO.
I'LL PREPARE YOU FOR OUR TOWN. AND I'LL PREPARE THE TOWN FOR YOU.
IT'S HOT UNDER THIS HOOD, MA'AM.
YOU CAN TAKE IT OFF.
WELCOME TO EDEN.
THANK YOU FOR HELPING ME.

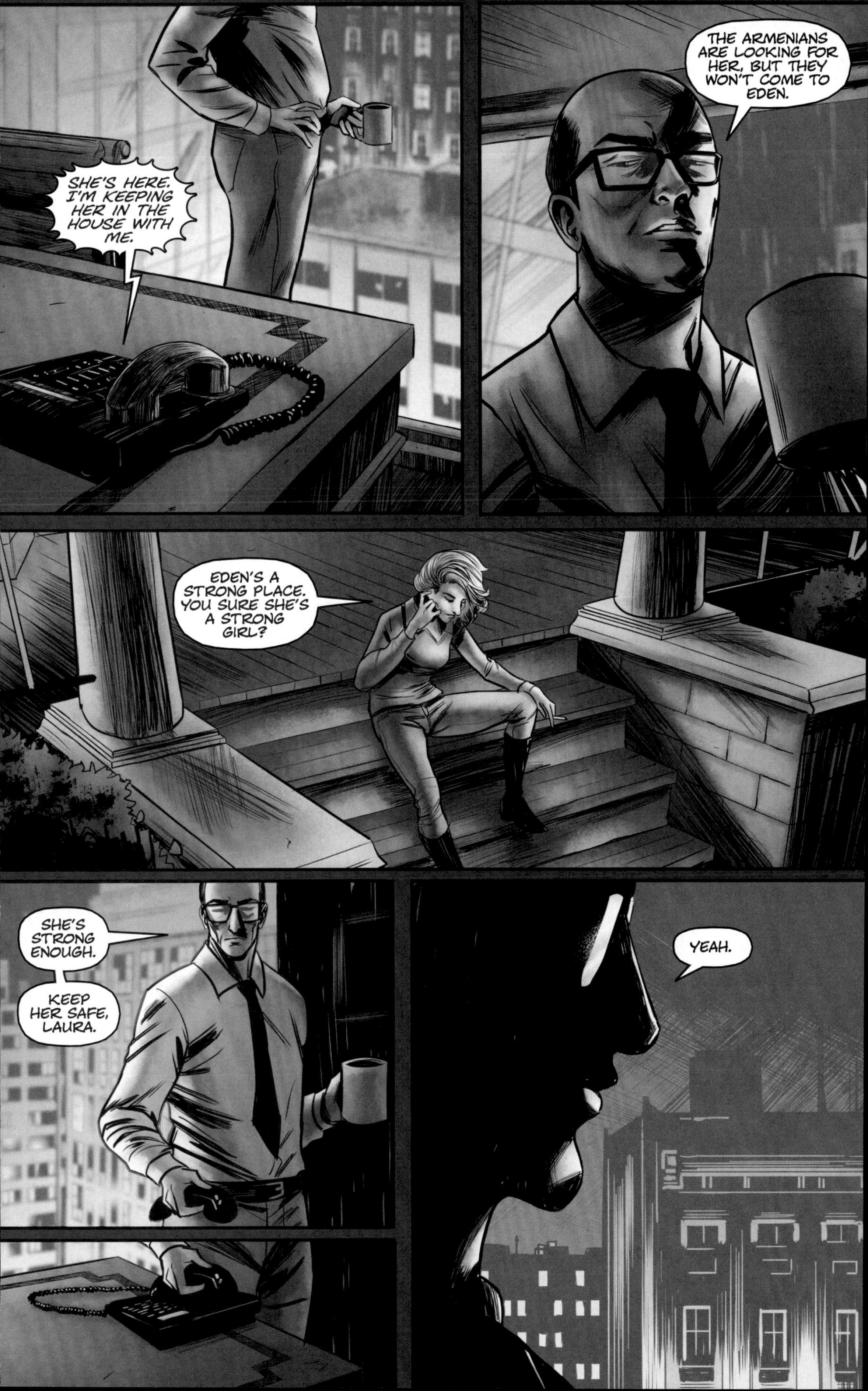
SHE'S HERE. I'M KEEPING HER IN THE HOUSE WITH ME.
THE ARMENIANS ARE LOOKING FOR HER, BUT THEY WON'T COME TO EDEN.
EDEN'S A STRONG PLACE. YOU SURE SHE'S A STRONG GIRL?
SHE'S STRONG ENOUGH.
KEEP HER SAFE, LAURA.
YEAH.

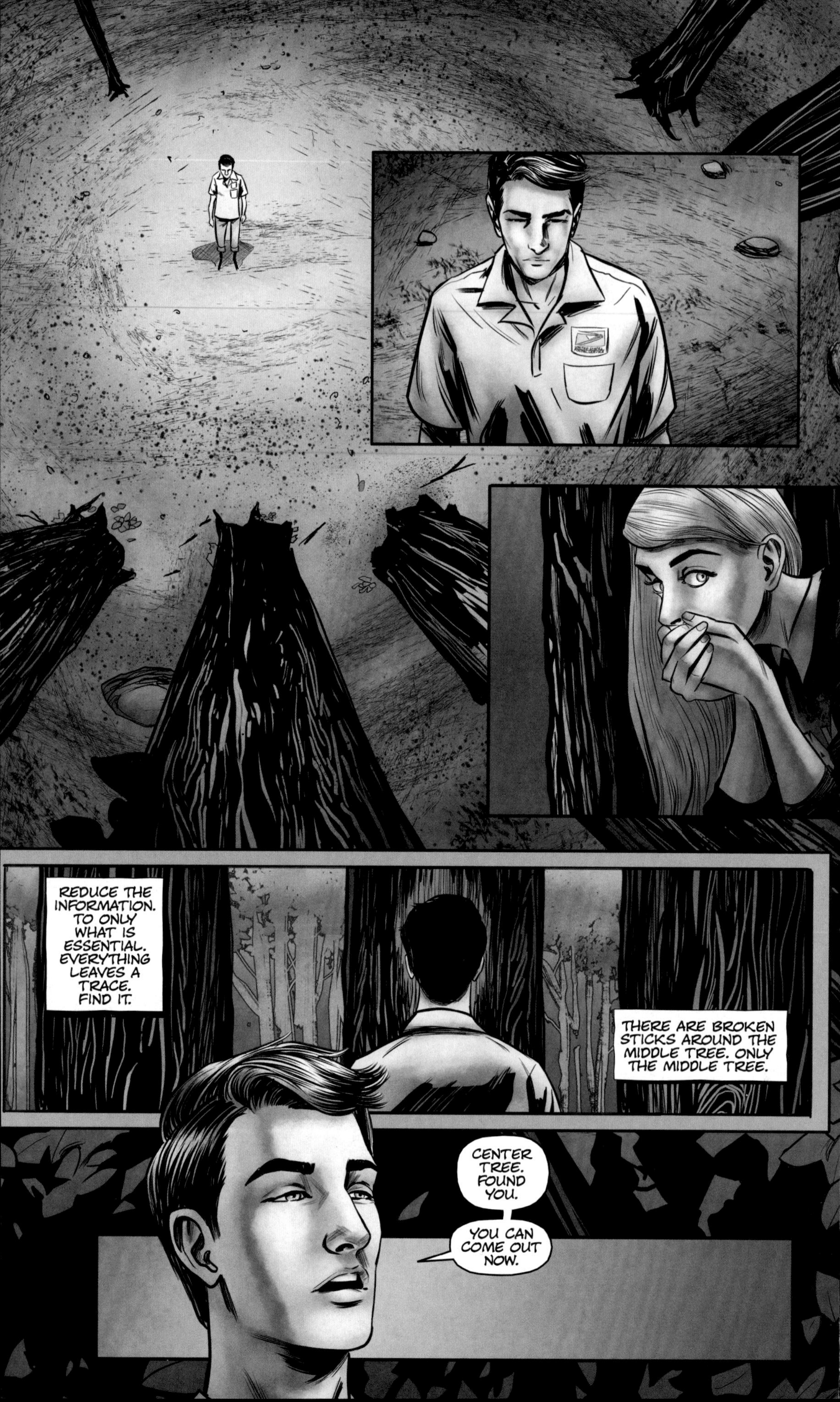
REDUCE THE INFORMATION. TO ONLY WHAT IS ESSENTIAL. EVERYTHING LEAVES A TRACE. FIND IT.
THERE ARE BROKEN STICKS AROUND THE MIDDLE TREE. ONLY THE MIDDLE TREE.
CENTER TREE. FOUND YOU.
YOU CAN COME OUT NOW.

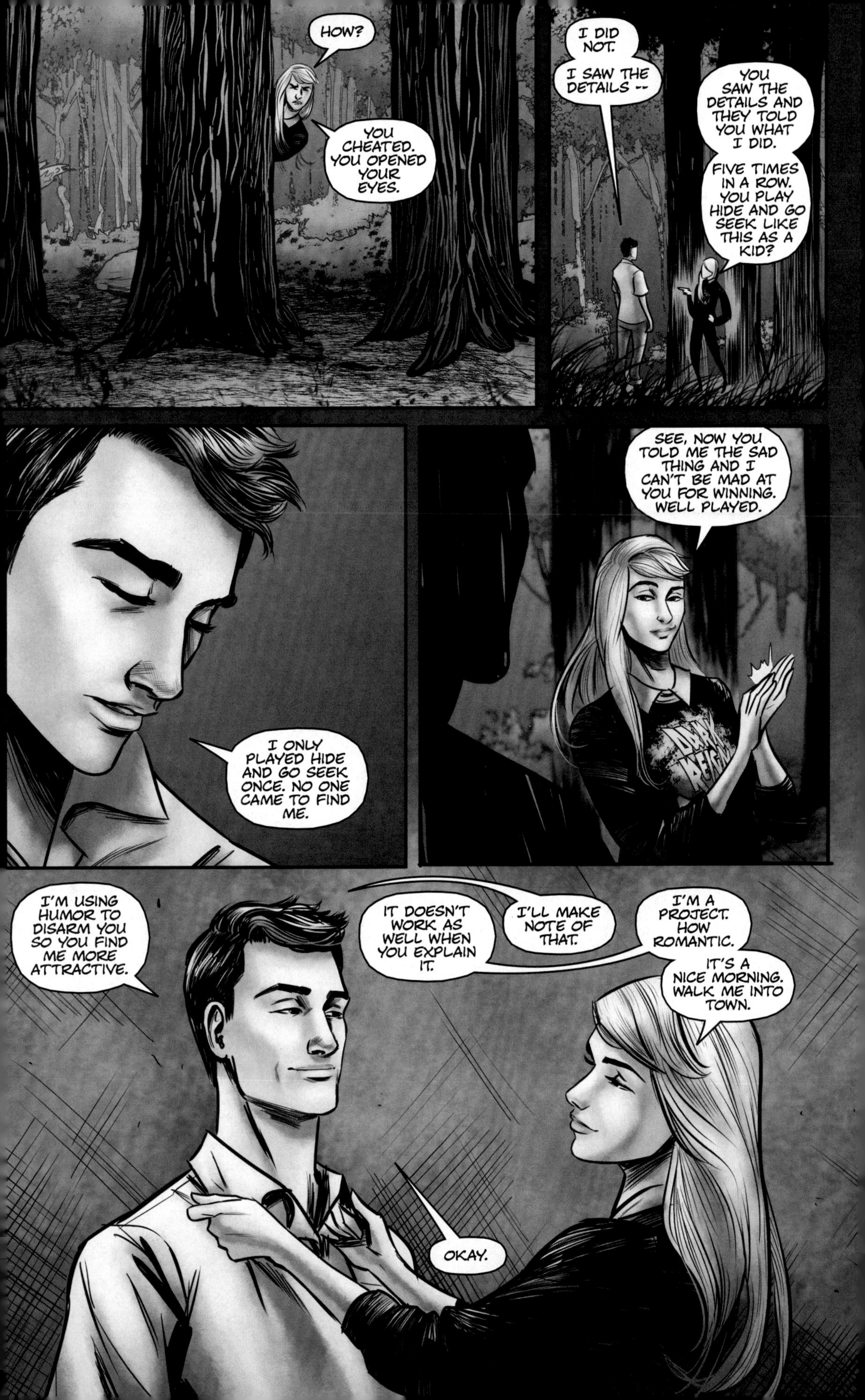
HOW?
YOU CHEATED. YOU OPENED YOUR EYES.
I DID NOT.
I SAW THE DETAILS --
YOU SAW THE DETAILS AND THEY TOLD YOU WHAT I DID.
FIVE TIMES IN A ROW. YOU PLAY HIDE AND GO SEEK LIKE THIS AS A KID?
I ONLY PLAYED HIDE AND GO SEEK ONCE. NO ONE CAME TO FIND ME.
SEE, NOW YOU TOLD ME THE SAD THING AND I CAN'T BE MAD AT YOU FOR WINNING. WELL PLAYED.
I'M USING HUMOR TO DISARM YOU SO YOU FIND ME MORE ATTRACTIVE.
IT DOESN'T WORK AS WELL WHEN YOU EXPLAIN IT.
I'LL MAKE NOTE OF THAT.
I'M A PROJECT. HOW ROMANTIC.
IT'S A NICE MORNING. WALK ME INTO TOWN.
OKAY.

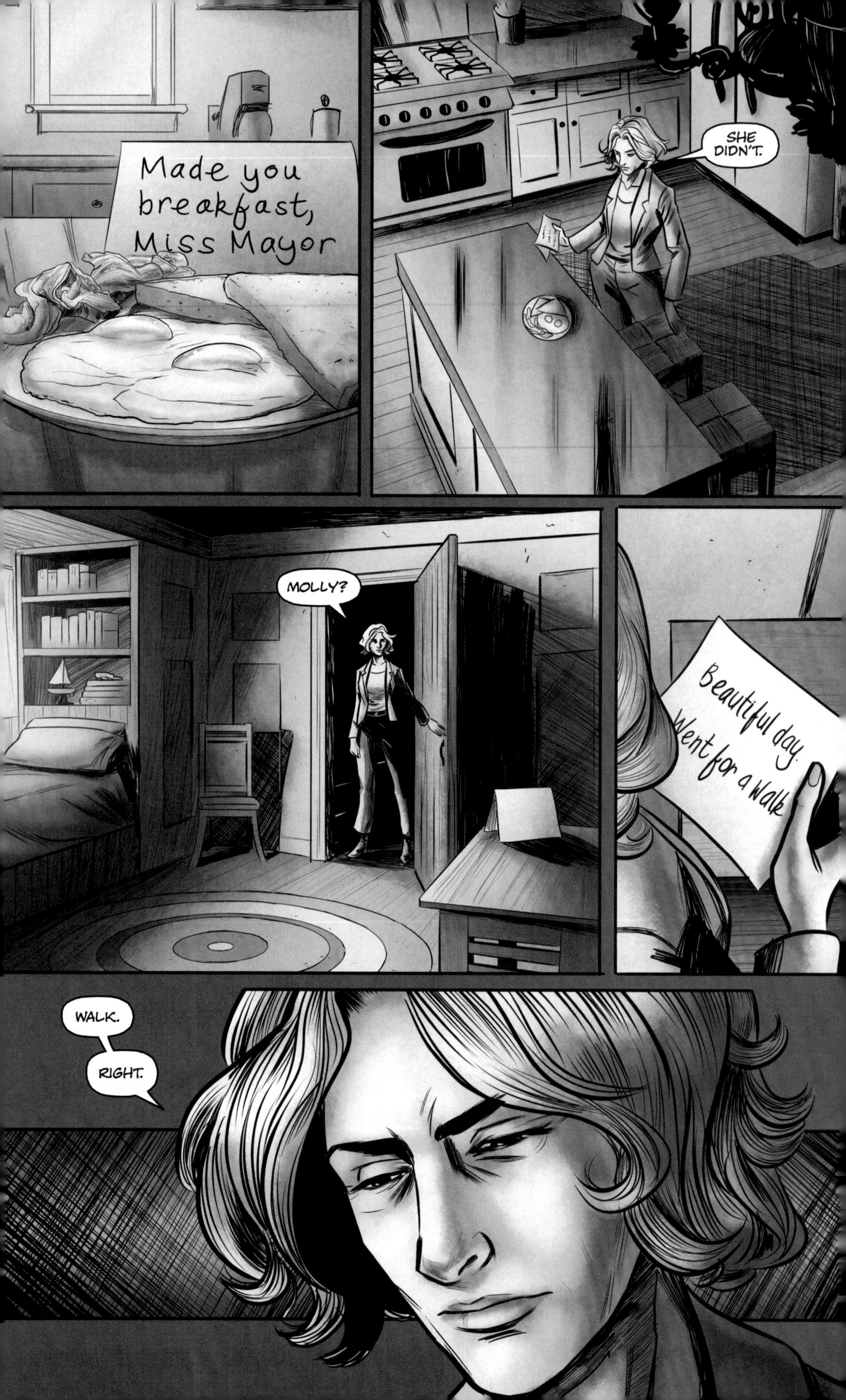
Made you breakfast, Miss Mayor
SHE DIDN'T.
MOLLY?
Beautiful day. Went for a walk
WALK.
RIGHT.

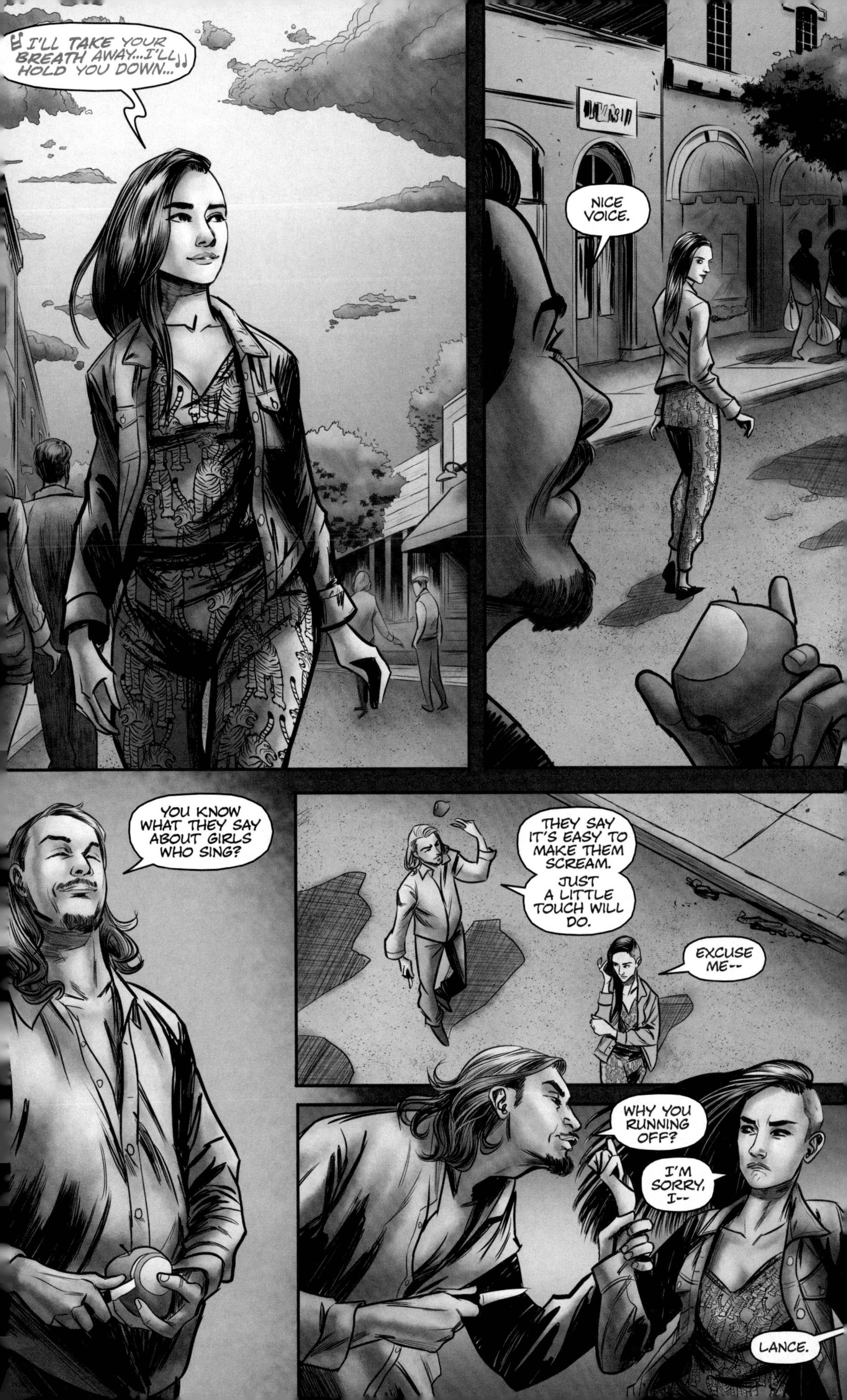
I'LL TAKE YOUR BREATH AWAY...I'LL HOLD YOU DOWN...
NICE VOICE.
YOU KNOW WHAT THEY SAY ABOUT GIRLS WHO SING?
THEY SAY IT'S EASY TO MAKE THEM SCREAM.
JUST A LITTLE TOUCH WILL DO.
EXCUSE ME--
WHY YOU RUNNING OFF?
I'M SORRY, I--
LANCE.

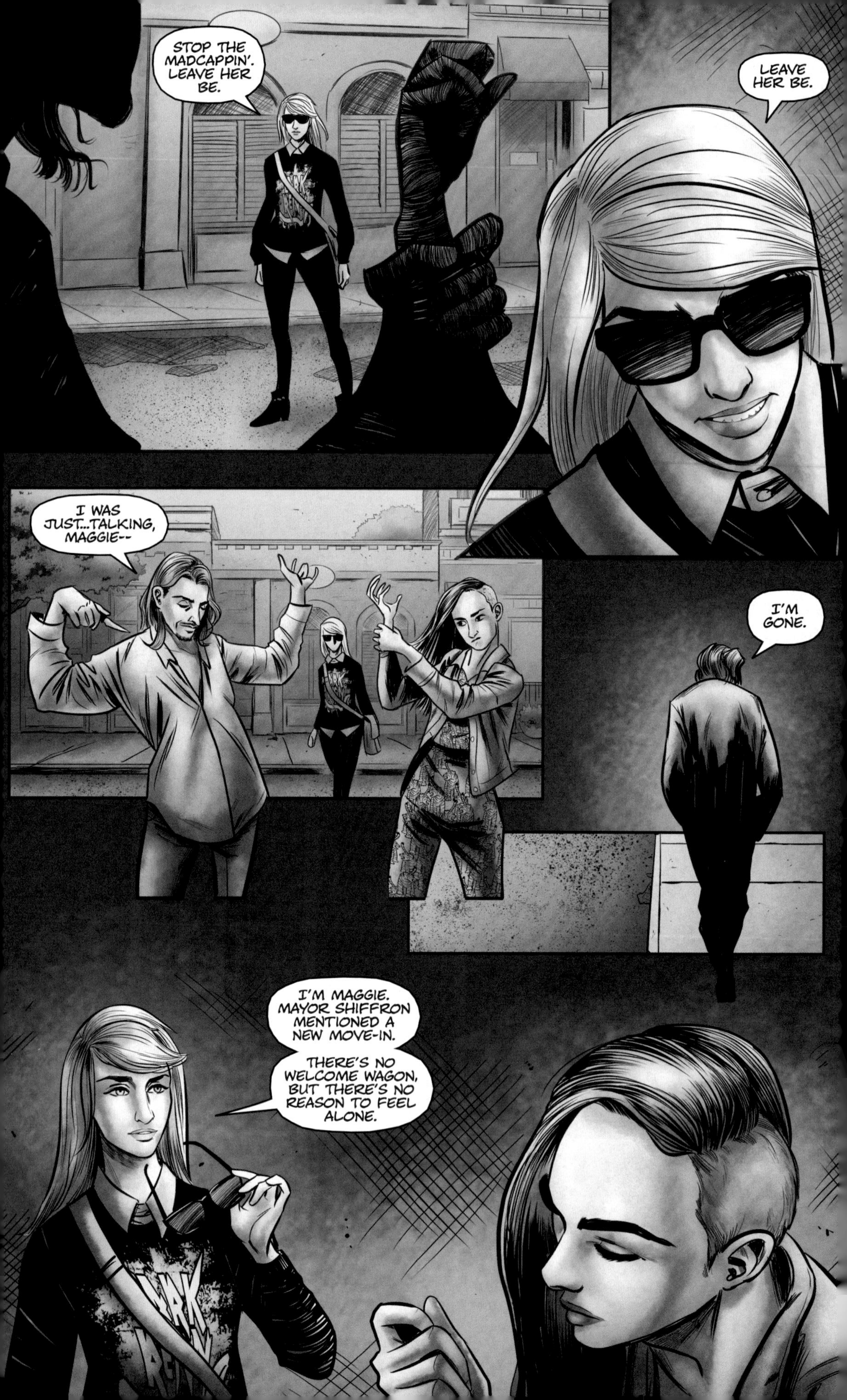
STOP THE MADCAPPIN'. LEAVE HER BE.
LEAVE HER BE.
I WAS JUST...TALKING, MAGGIE--
I'M GONE.
I'M MAGGIE. MAYOR SHIFFRON MENTIONED A NEW MOVE-IN.
THERE'S NO WELCOME WAGON, BUT THERE'S NO REASON TO FEEL ALONE.

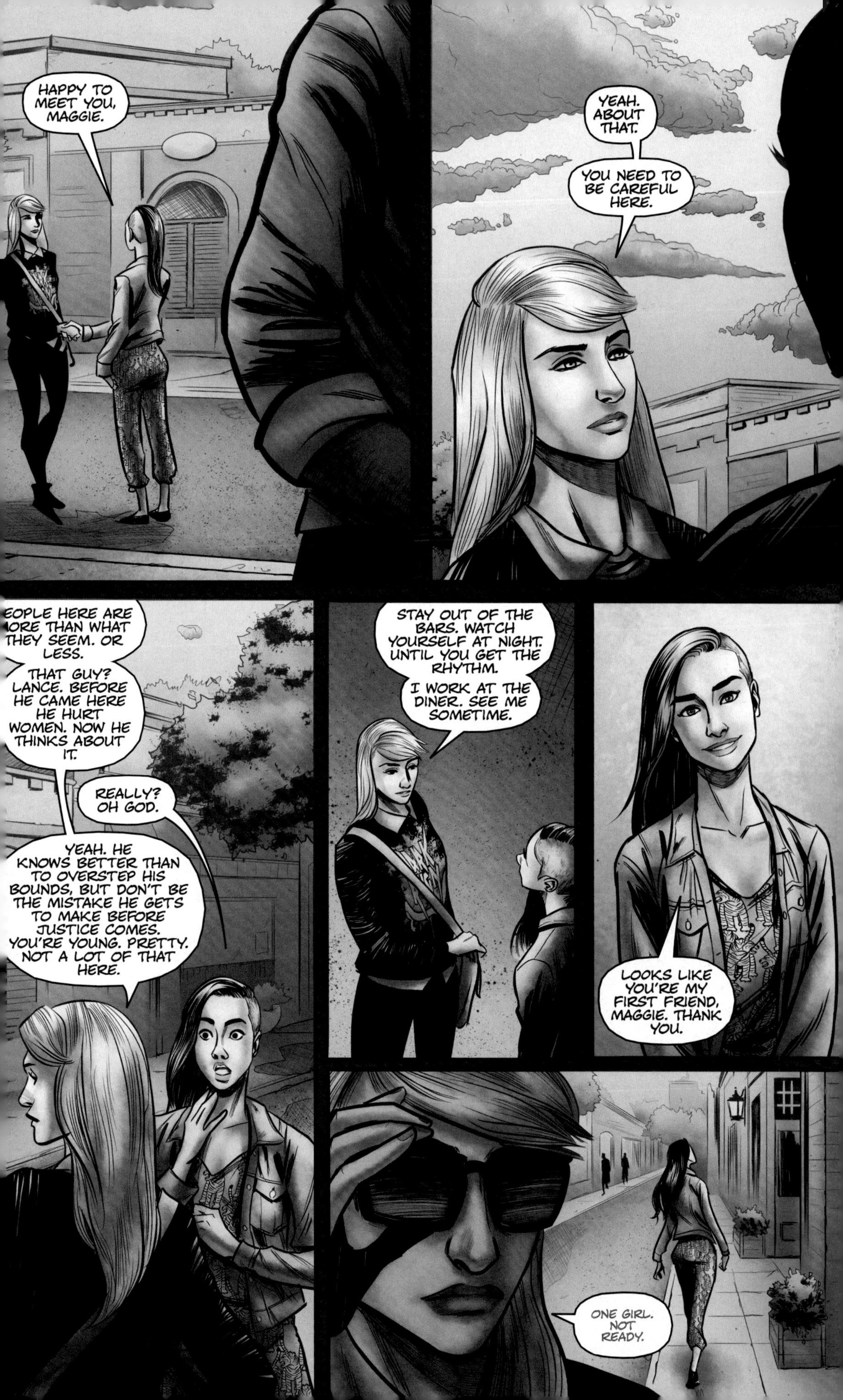
HAPPY TO MEET YOU, MAGGIE.
YEAH. ABOUT THAT.
YOU NEED TO BE CAREFUL HERE.
EOPLE HERE ARE ORE THAN WHAT THEY SEEM. OR LESS.
THAT GUY? LANCE. BEFORE HE CAME HERE HE HURT WOMEN. NOW HE THINKS ABOUT IT.
REALLY? OH GOD.
YEAH. HE KNOWS BETTER THAN TO OVERSTEP HIS BOUNDS, BUT DON'T BE THE MISTAKE HE GETS TO MAKE BEFORE JUSTICE COMES. YOU'RE YOUNG. PRETTY. NOT A LOT OF THAT HERE.
STAY OUT OF THE BARS. WATCH YOURSELF AT NIGHT. UNTIL YOU GET THE RHYTHM.
I WORK AT THE DINER. SEE ME SOMETIME.
LOOKS LIKE YOU'RE MY FIRST FRIEND, MAGGIE. THANK YOU.
ONE GIRL. NOT READY.

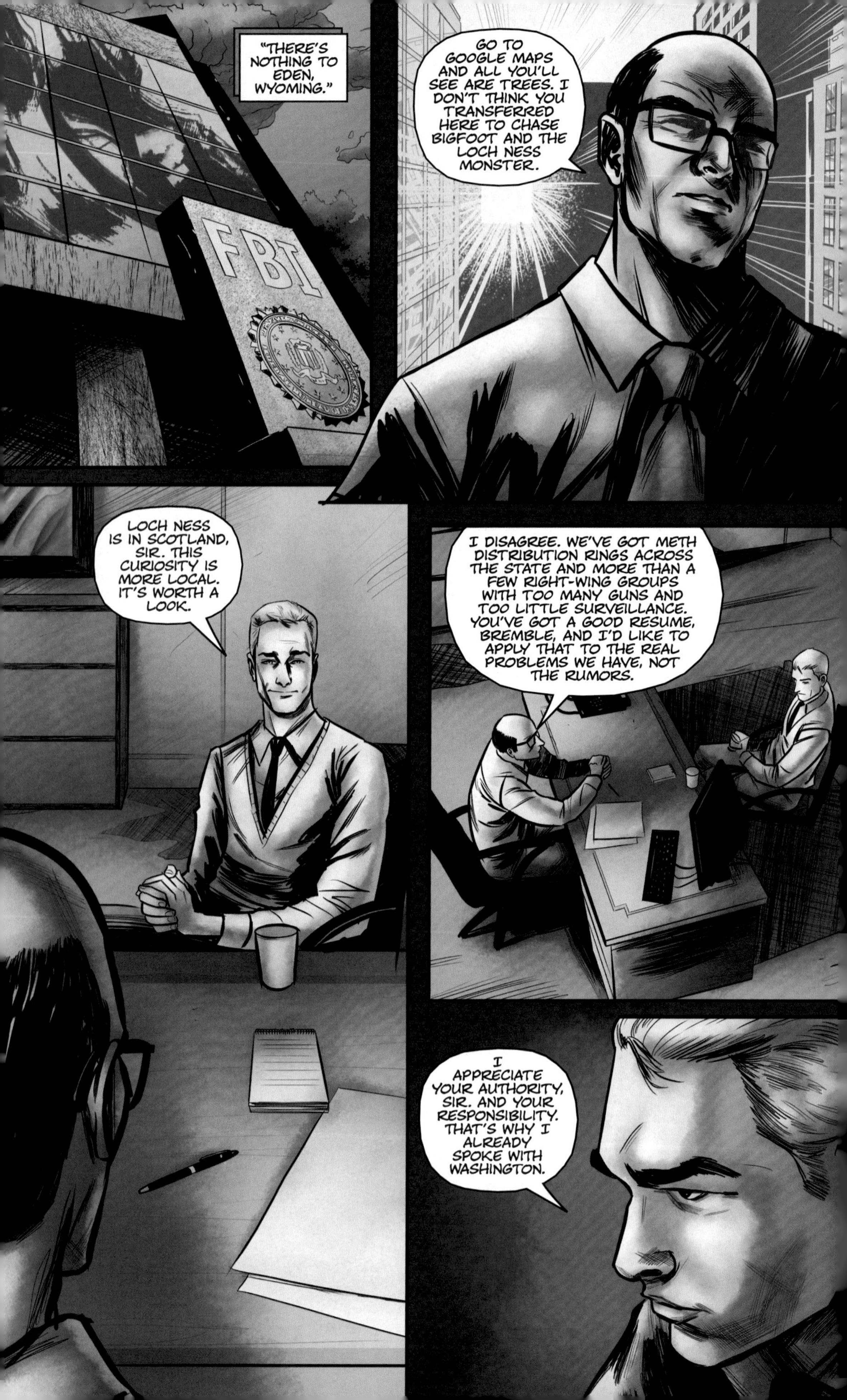
"THERE'S NOTHING TO EDEN, WYOMING."
FBI
GO TO GOOGLE MAPS AND ALL YOU'LL SEE ARE TREES. I DON'T THINK YOU TRANSFERRED HERE TO CHASE BIGFOOT AND THE LOCH NESS MONSTER.
LOCH NESS IS IN SCOTLAND, SIR. THIS CURIOSITY IS MORE LOCAL. IT'S WORTH A LOOK.
I DISAGREE. WE'VE GOT METH DISTRIBUTION RINGS ACROSS THE STATE AND MORE THAN A FEW RIGHT-WING GROUPS WITH TOO MANY GUNS AND TOO LITTLE SURVEILLANCE. YOU'VE GOT A GOOD RESUME, BREMBLE, AND I'D LIKE TO APPLY THAT TO THE REAL PROBLEMS WE HAVE, NOT THE RUMORS.
I APPRECIATE YOUR AUTHORITY, SIR. AND YOUR RESPONSIBILITY. THAT'S WHY I ALREADY SPOKE WITH WASHINGTON.

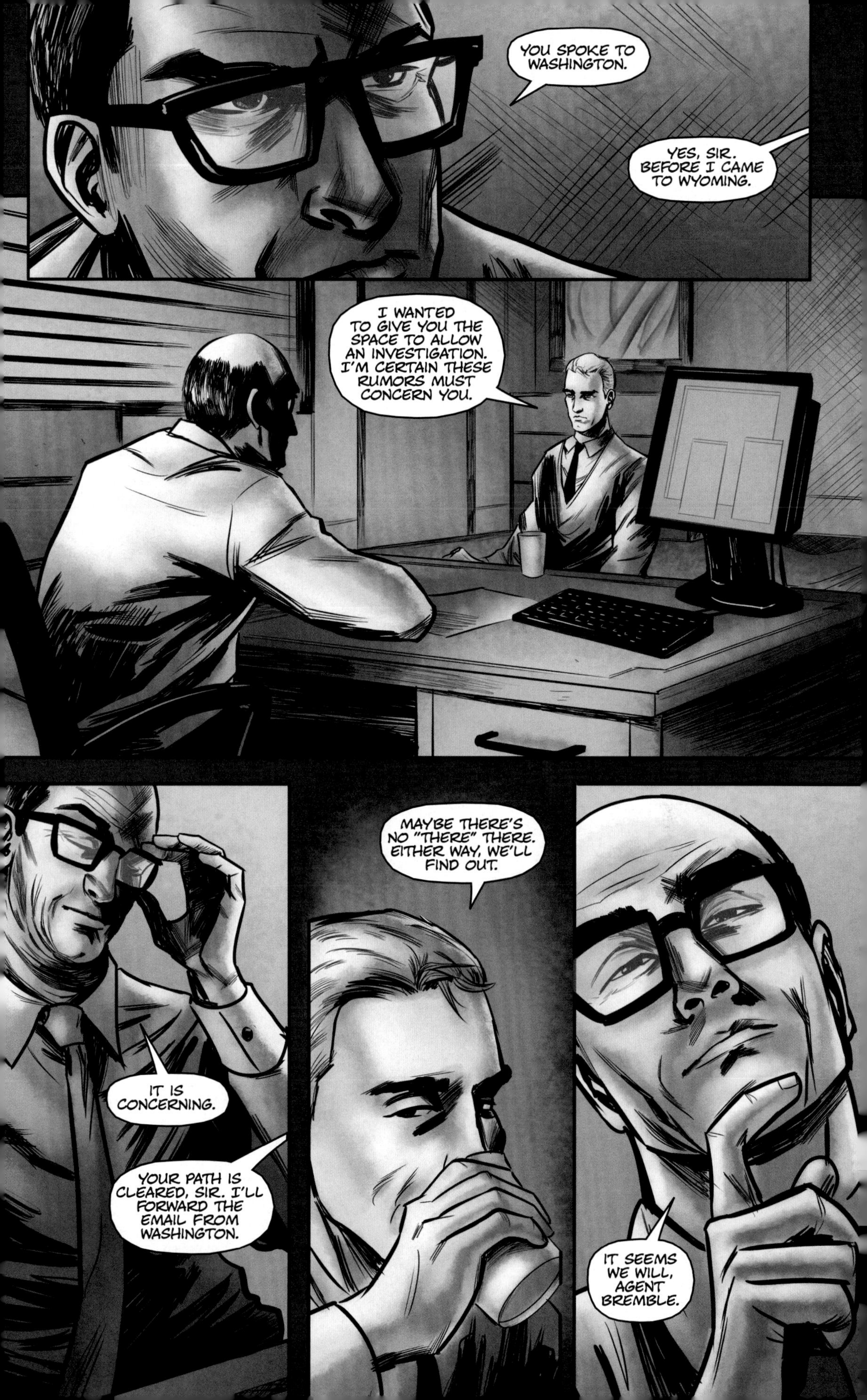
YOU SPOKE TO WASHINGTON.
YES, SIR. BEFORE I CAME TO WYOMING.
I WANTED TO GIVE YOU THE SPACE TO ALLOW AN INVESTIGATION. I'M CERTAIN THESE RUMORS MUST CONCERN YOU.
IT IS CONCERNING.
YOUR PATH IS CLEARED, SIR. I'LL FORWARD THE EMAIL FROM WASHINGTON.
MAYBE THERE'S NO "THERE" THERE. EITHER WAY, WE'LL FIND OUT.
IT SEEMS WE WILL, AGENT BREMBLE.

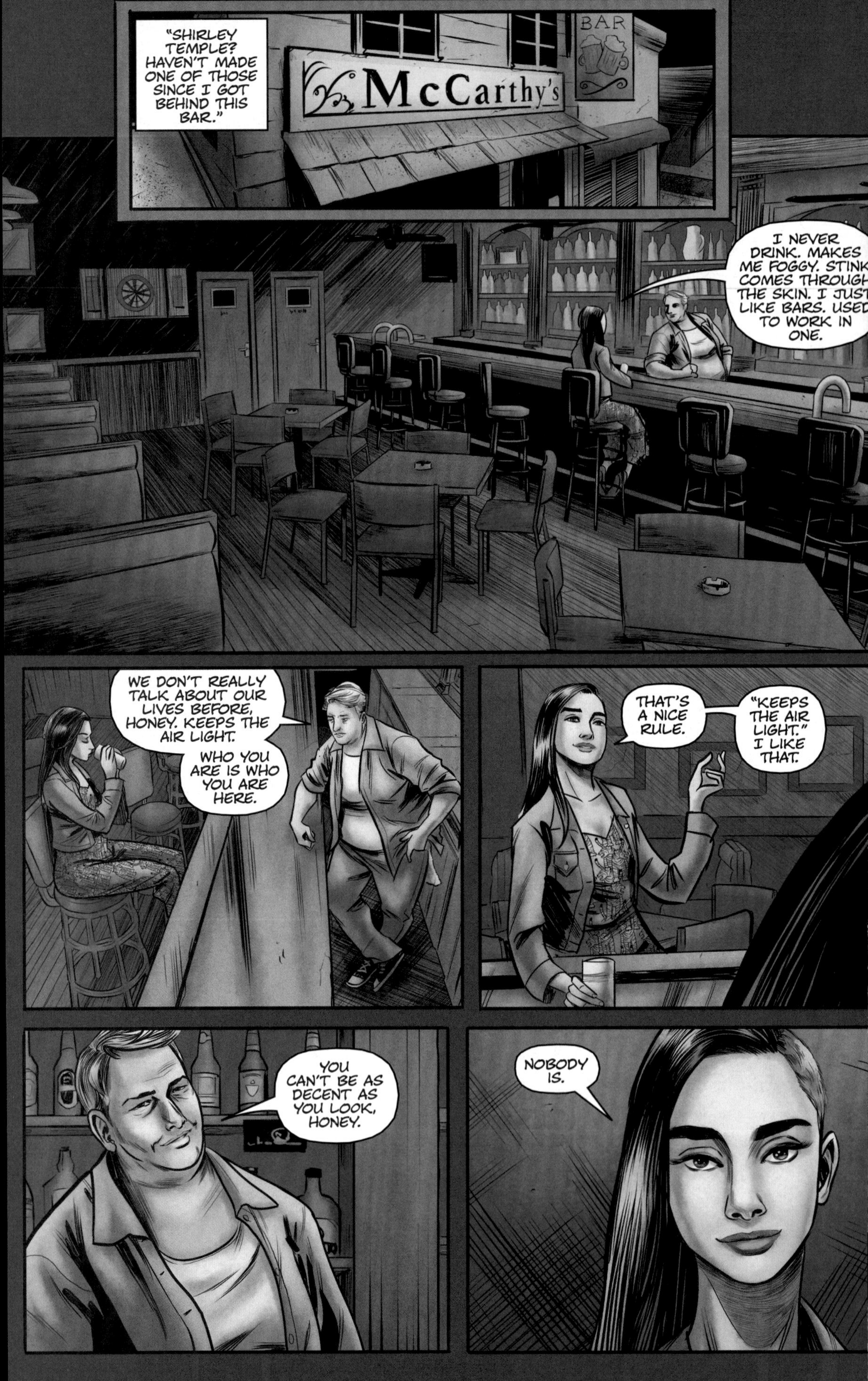
"SHIRLEY TEMPLE? HAVEN'T MADE ONE OF THOSE SINCE I GOT BEHIND THIS BAR."
BAR
McCarthy's
I NEVER DRINK. MAKES ME FOGGY. STINK COMES THROUGH THE SKIN. I JUST LIKE BARS. USED TO WORK IN ONE.
WE DON'T REALLY TALK ABOUT OUR LIVES BEFORE, HONEY. KEEPS THE AIR LIGHT.
WHO YOU ARE IS WHO YOU ARE HERE.
THAT'S A NICE RULE.
"KEEPS THE AIR LIGHT." I LIKE THAT.
YOU CAN'T BE AS DECENT AS YOU LOOK, HONEY.
NOBODY IS.

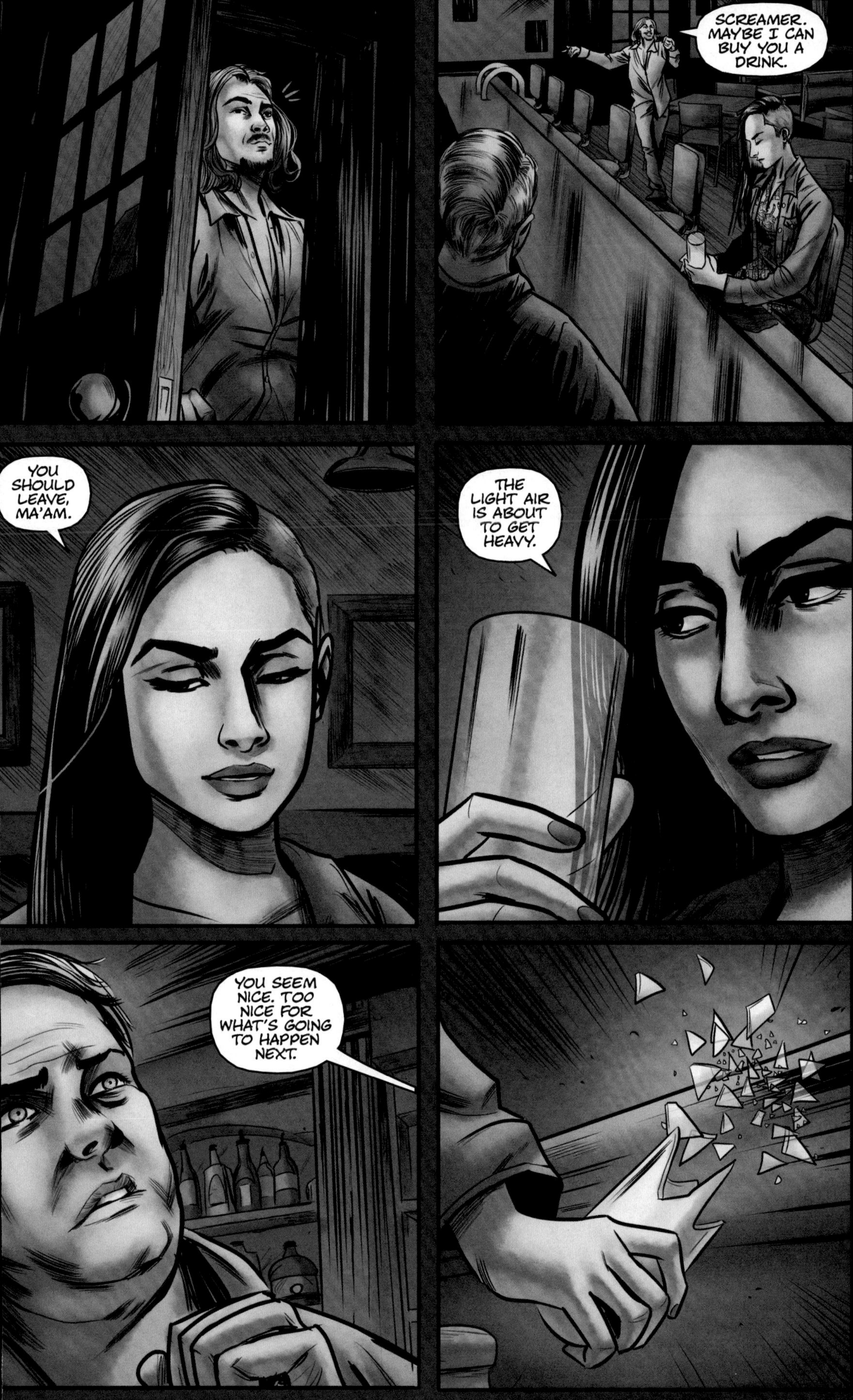
SCREAMER. MAYBE I CAN BUY YOU A DRINK.
YOU SHOULD LEAVE, MA'AM.
THE LIGHT AIR IS ABOUT TO GET HEAVY.
YOU SEEM NICE. TOO NICE FOR WHAT'S GOING TO HAPPEN NEXT.

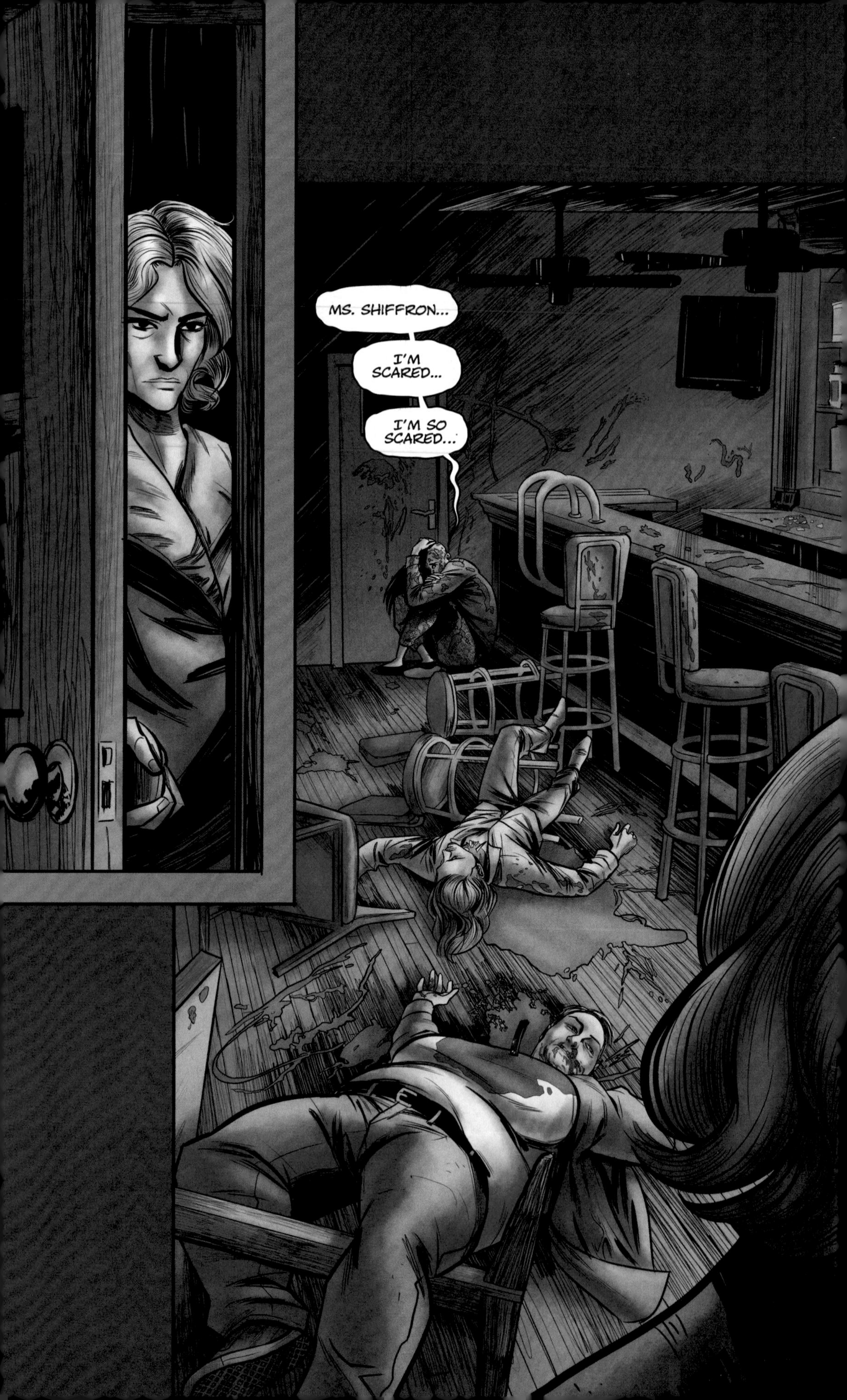
MS. SHIFFRON...
I'M SCARED...
I'M SO SCARED...

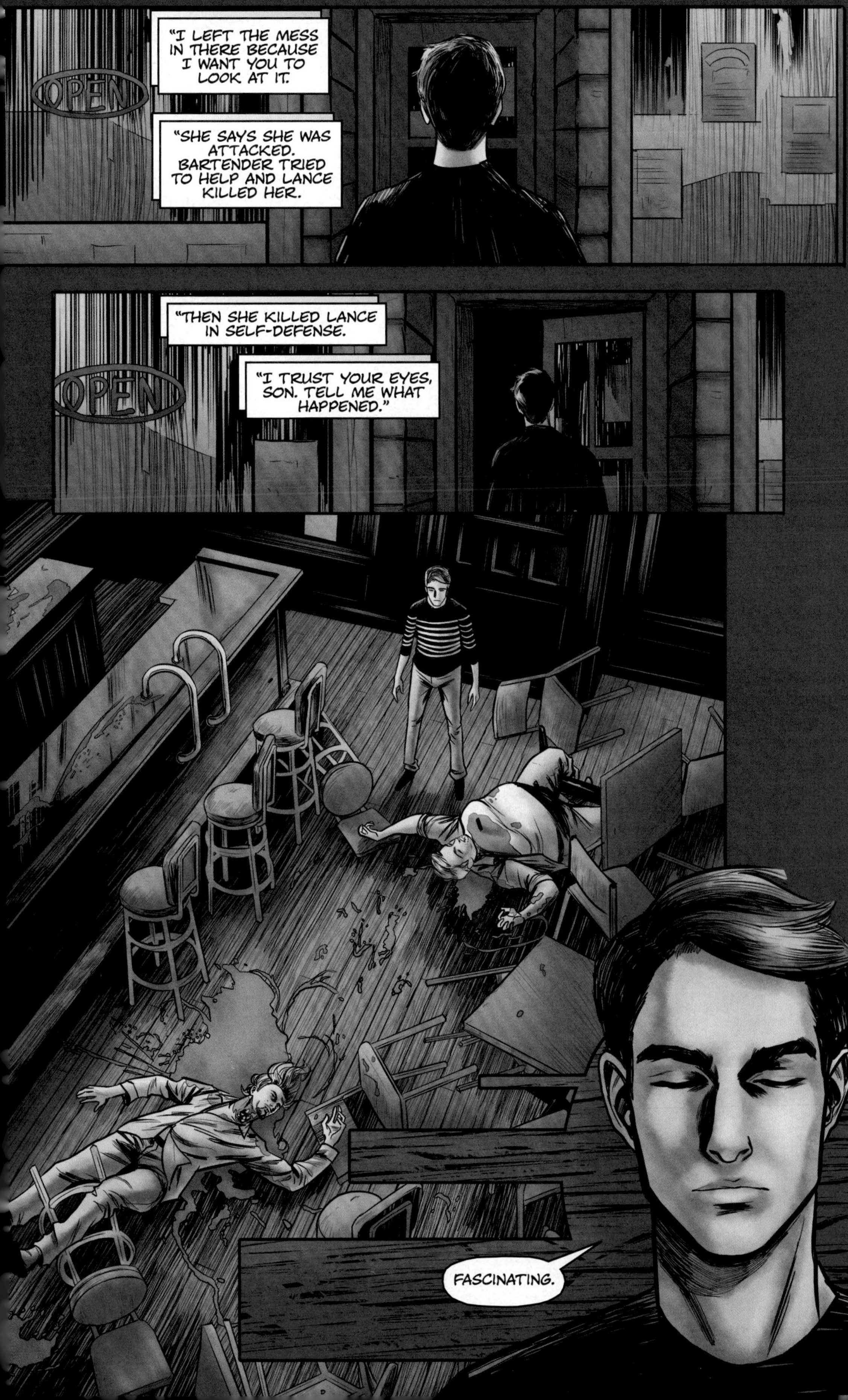
"I LEFT THE MESS IN THERE BECAUSE I WANT YOU TO LOOK AT IT.
"SHE SAYS SHE WAS ATTACKED. BARTENDER TRIED TO HELP AND LANCE KILLED HER.
OPEN
"THEN SHE KILLED LANCE IN SELF-DEFENSE.
"I TRUST YOUR EYES, SON. TELL ME WHAT HAPPENED."
OPEN
FASCINATING.

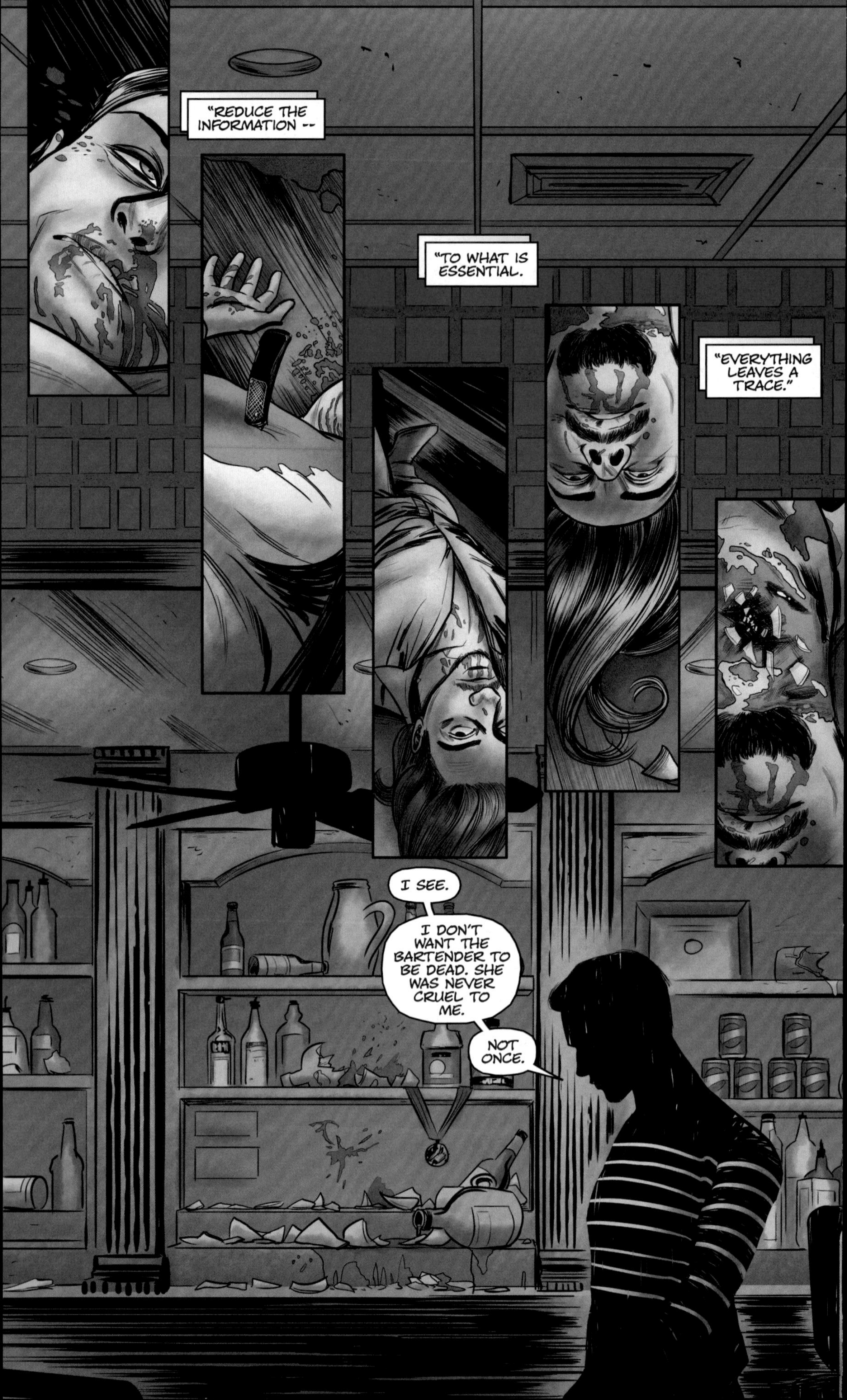
"REDUCE THE INFORMATION --
"TO WHAT IS ESSENTIAL.
"EVERYTHING LEAVES A TRACE."
I SEE.
I DON'T WANT THE BARTENDER TO BE DEAD. SHE WAS NEVER CRUEL TO ME.
NOT ONCE.

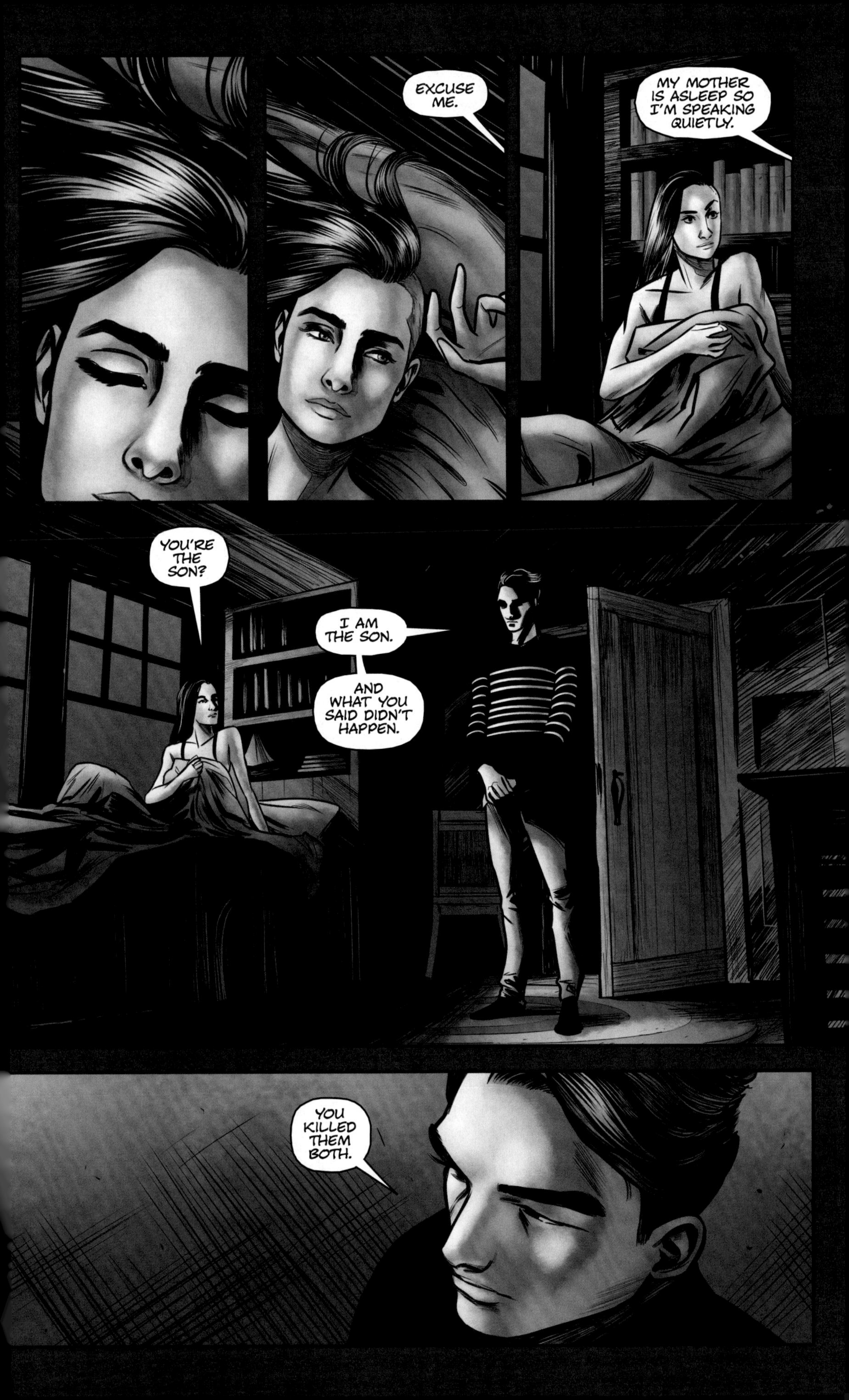
EXCUSE ME.
MY MOTHER IS ASLEEP SO I'M SPEAKING QUIETLY.
YOU'RE THE SON?
I AM THE SON.
AND WHAT YOU SAID DIDN'T HAPPEN.
YOU KILLED THEM BOTH.

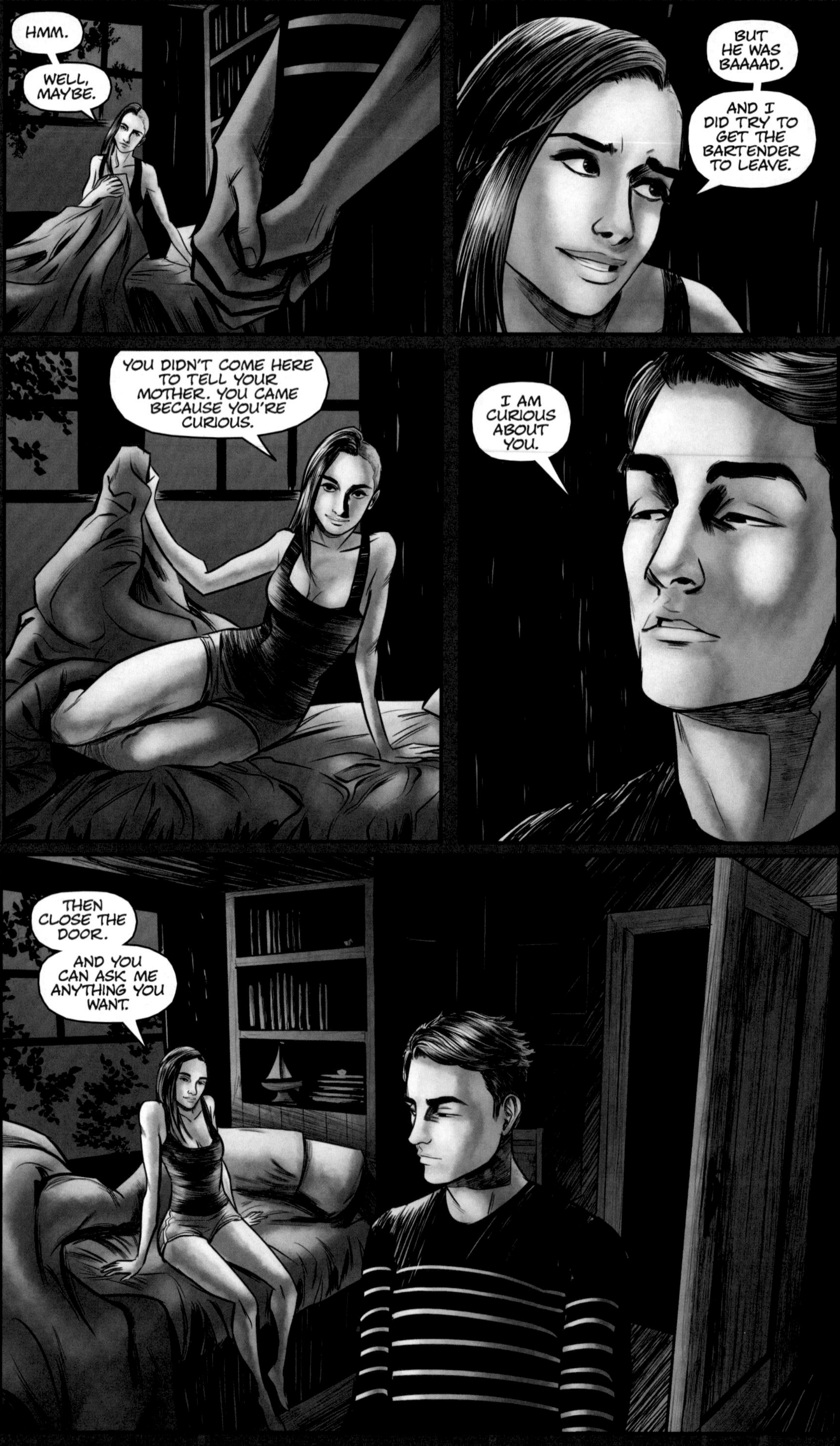
HMM.
WELL, MAYBE.
BUT HE WAS BAAAAD.
AND I DID TRY TO GET THE BARTENDER TO LEAVE.
YOU DIDN'T COME HERE TO TELL YOUR MOTHER. YOU CAME BECAUSE YOU'RE CURIOUS.
I AM CURIOUS ABOUT YOU.
THEN CLOSE THE DOOR.
AND YOU CAN ASK ME ANYTHING YOU WANT.

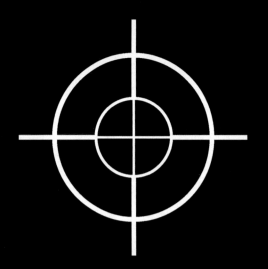

# Chapter 10

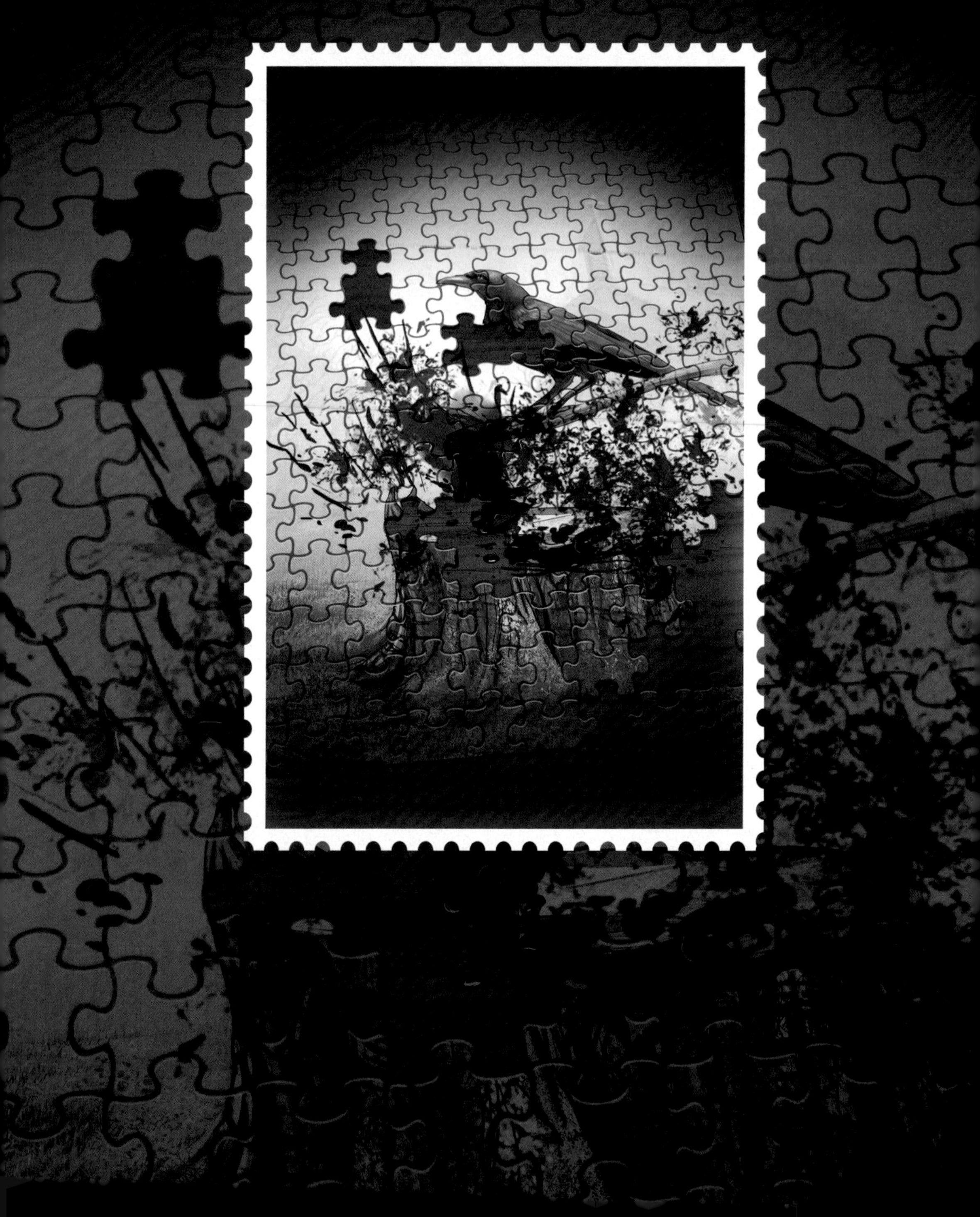

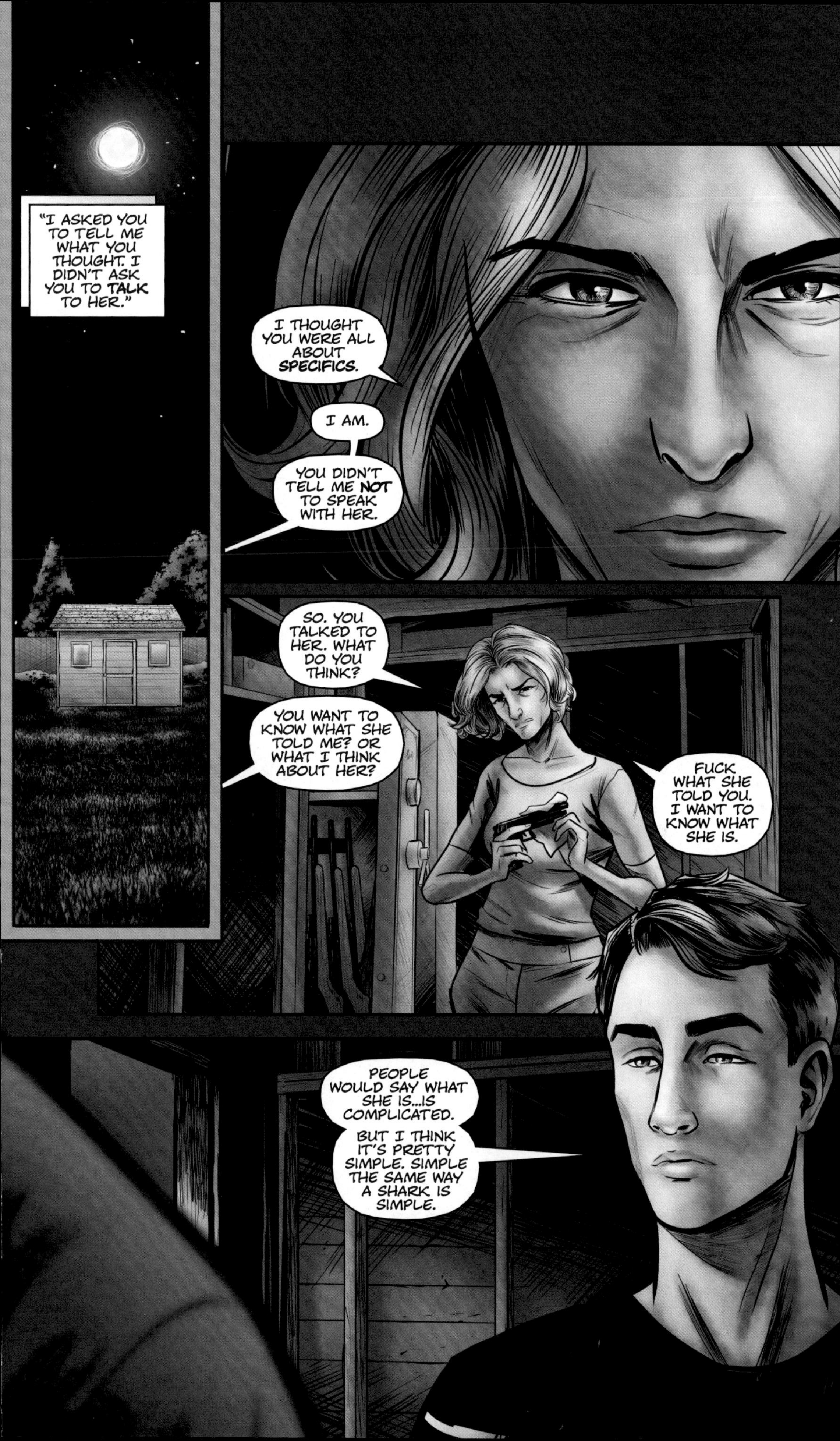
"I ASKED YOU TO TELL ME WHAT YOU THOUGHT. I DIDN'T ASK YOU TO TALK TO HER."
I THOUGHT YOU WERE ALL ABOUT SPECIFICS.
I AM.
YOU DIDN'T TELL ME NOT TO SPEAK WITH HER.
SO. YOU TALKED TO HER. WHAT DO YOU THINK?
YOU WANT TO KNOW WHAT SHE TOLD ME? OR WHAT I THINK ABOUT HER?
FUCK WHAT SHE TOLD YOU. I WANT TO KNOW WHAT SHE IS.
PEOPLE WOULD SAY WHAT SHE IS...IS COMPLICATED.
BUT I THINK IT'S PRETTY SIMPLE. SIMPLE THE SAME WAY A SHARK IS SIMPLE.

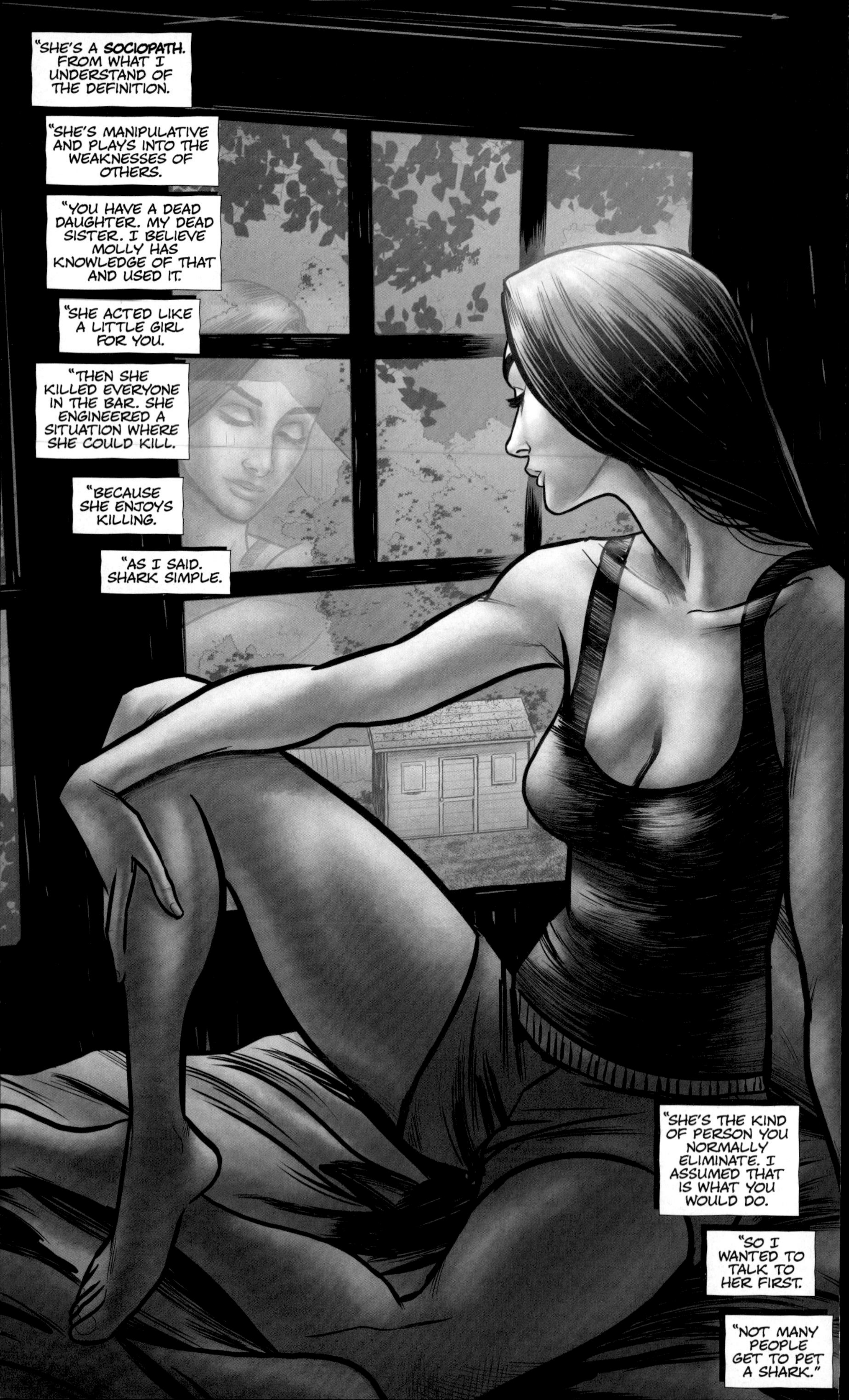
"SHE'S A SOCIOPATH. FROM WHAT I UNDERSTAND OF THE DEFINITION.
"SHE'S MANIPULATIVE AND PLAYS INTO THE WEAKNESSES OF OTHERS.
"YOU HAVE A DEAD DAUGHTER. MY DEAD SISTER. I BELIEVE MOLLY HAS KNOWLEDGE OF THAT AND USED IT.
"SHE ACTED LIKE A LITTLE GIRL FOR YOU.
"THEN SHE KILLED EVERYONE IN THE BAR. SHE ENGINEERED A SITUATION WHERE SHE COULD KILL.
"BECAUSE SHE ENJOYS KILLING.
"AS I SAID. SHARK SIMPLE.
"SHE'S THE KIND OF PERSON YOU NORMALLY ELIMINATE. I ASSUMED THAT IS WHAT YOU WOULD DO.
"SO I WANTED TO TALK TO HER FIRST.
"NOT MANY PEOPLE GET TO PET A SHARK."

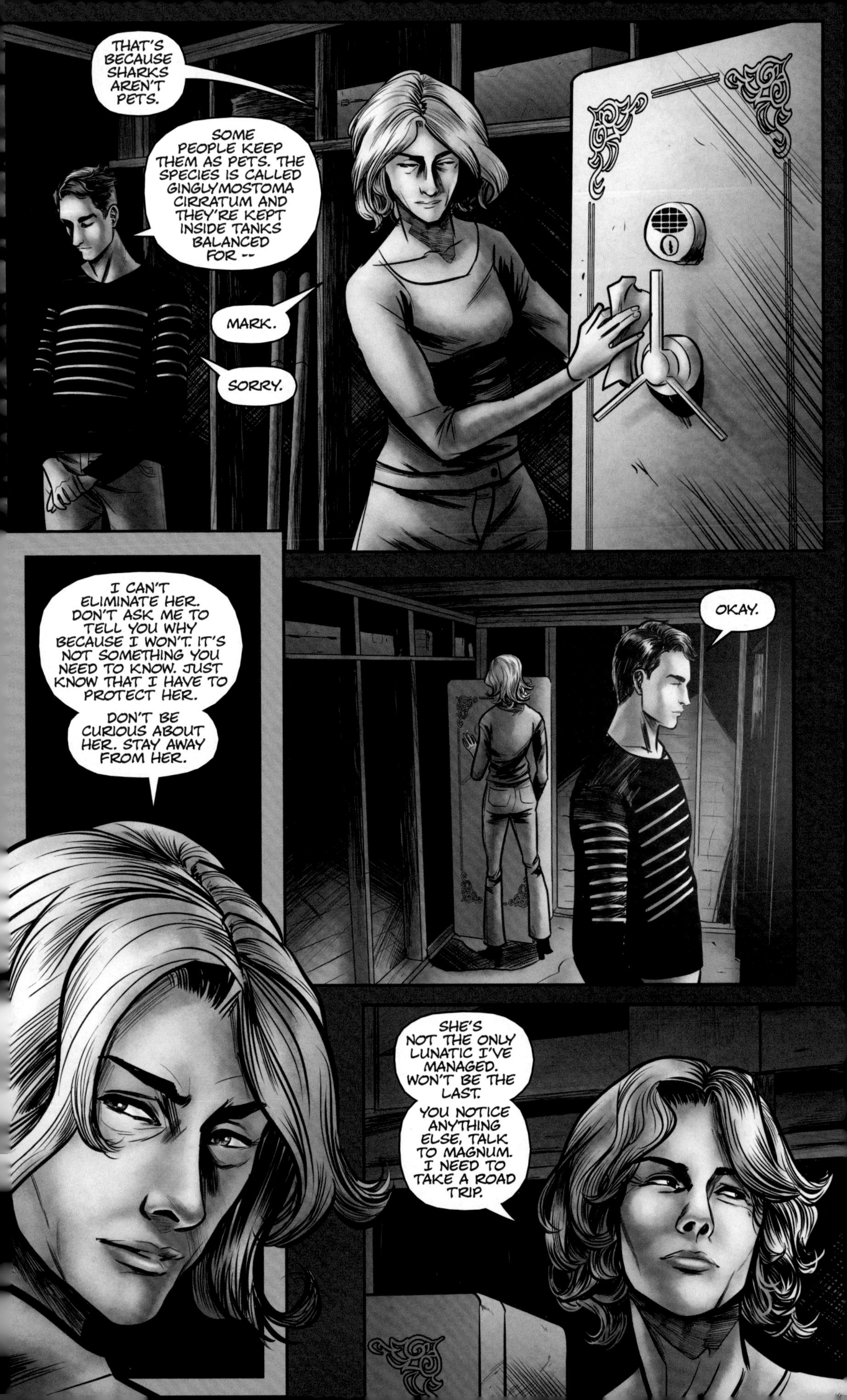
THAT'S BECAUSE SHARKS AREN'T PETS.
SOME PEOPLE KEEP THEM AS PETS. THE SPECIES IS CALLED GINGLYMOSTOMA CIRRATUM AND THEY'RE KEPT INSIDE TANKS BALANCED FOR --
MARK.
SORRY.
I CAN'T ELIMINATE HER. DON'T ASK ME TO TELL YOU WHY BECAUSE I WON'T. IT'S NOT SOMETHING YOU NEED TO KNOW. JUST KNOW THAT I HAVE TO PROTECT HER.
DON'T BE CURIOUS ABOUT HER. STAY AWAY FROM HER.
OKAY.
SHE'S NOT THE ONLY LUNATIC I'VE MANAGED. WON'T BE THE LAST.
YOU NOTICE ANYTHING ELSE, TALK TO MAGNUM. I NEED TO TAKE A ROAD TRIP.

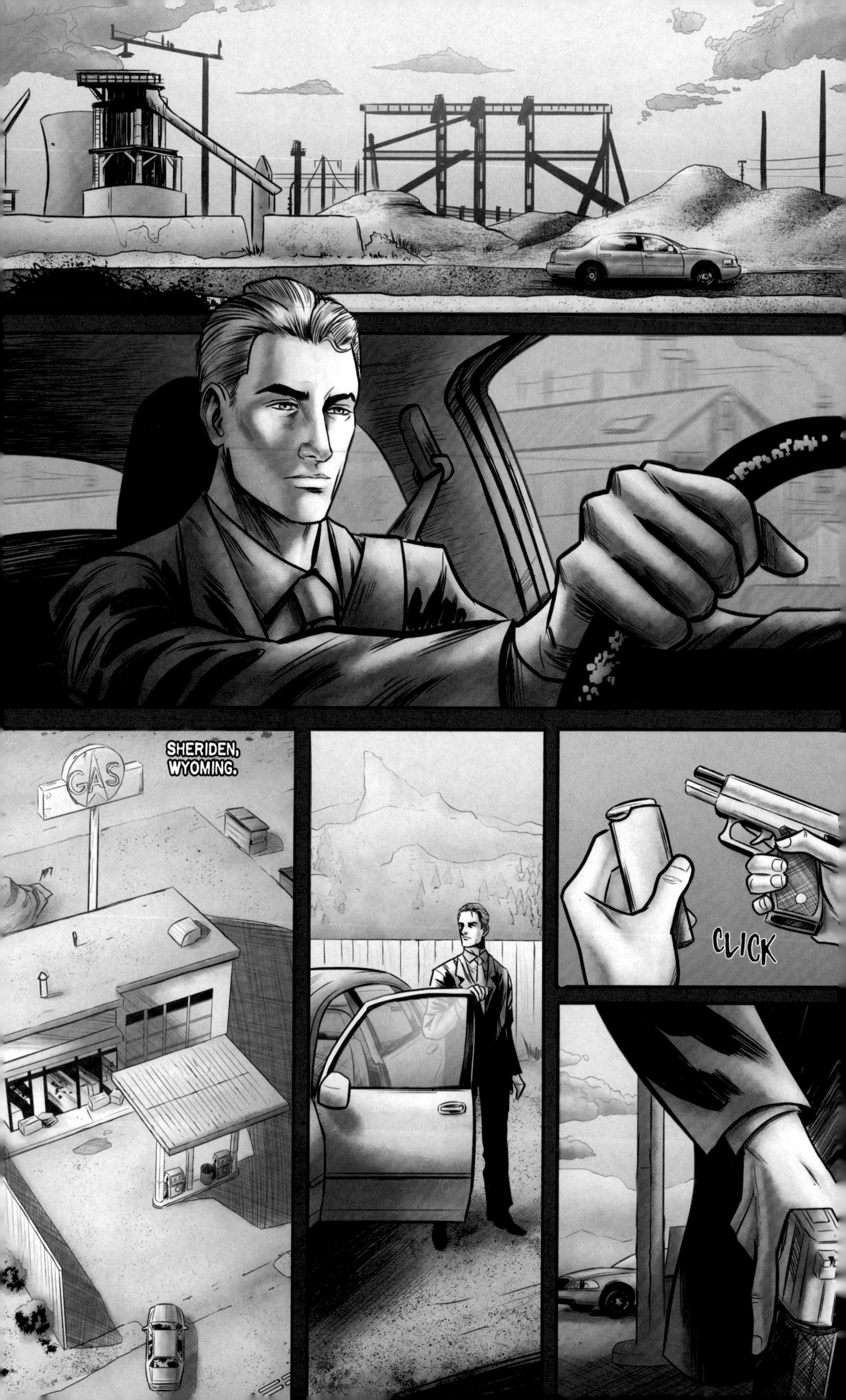
SHERIDEN, WYOMING.
GAS
CLICK

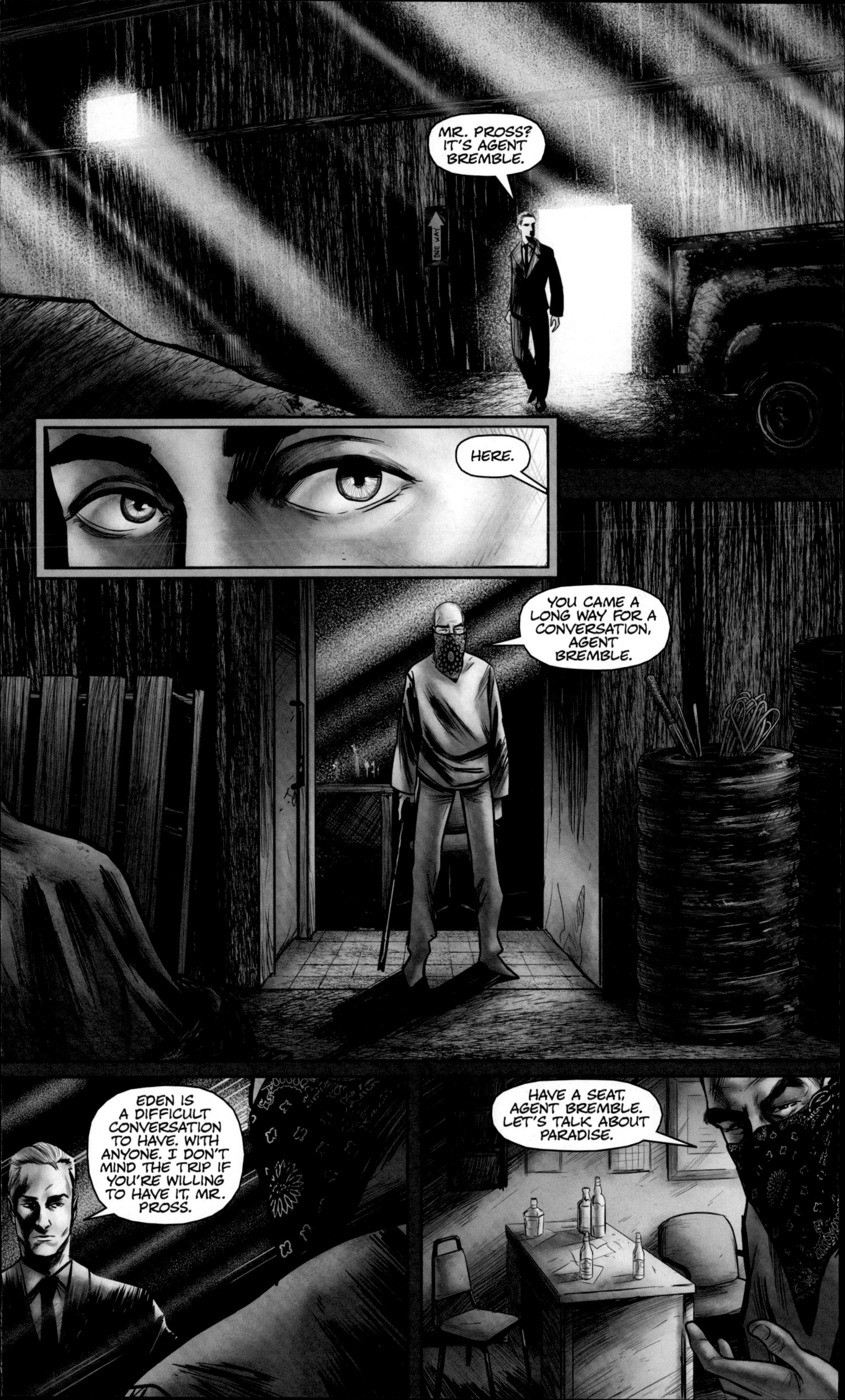
MR. PROSS? IT'S AGENT BREMBLE.
ONE WAY
HERE.
YOU CAME A LONG WAY FOR A CONVERSATION, AGENT BREMBLE.
EDEN IS A DIFFICULT CONVERSATION TO HAVE. WITH ANYONE. I DON'T MIND THE TRIP IF YOU'RE WILLING TO HAVE IT, MR. PROSS.
HAVE A SEAT, AGENT BREMBLE. LET'S TALK ABOUT PARADISE.

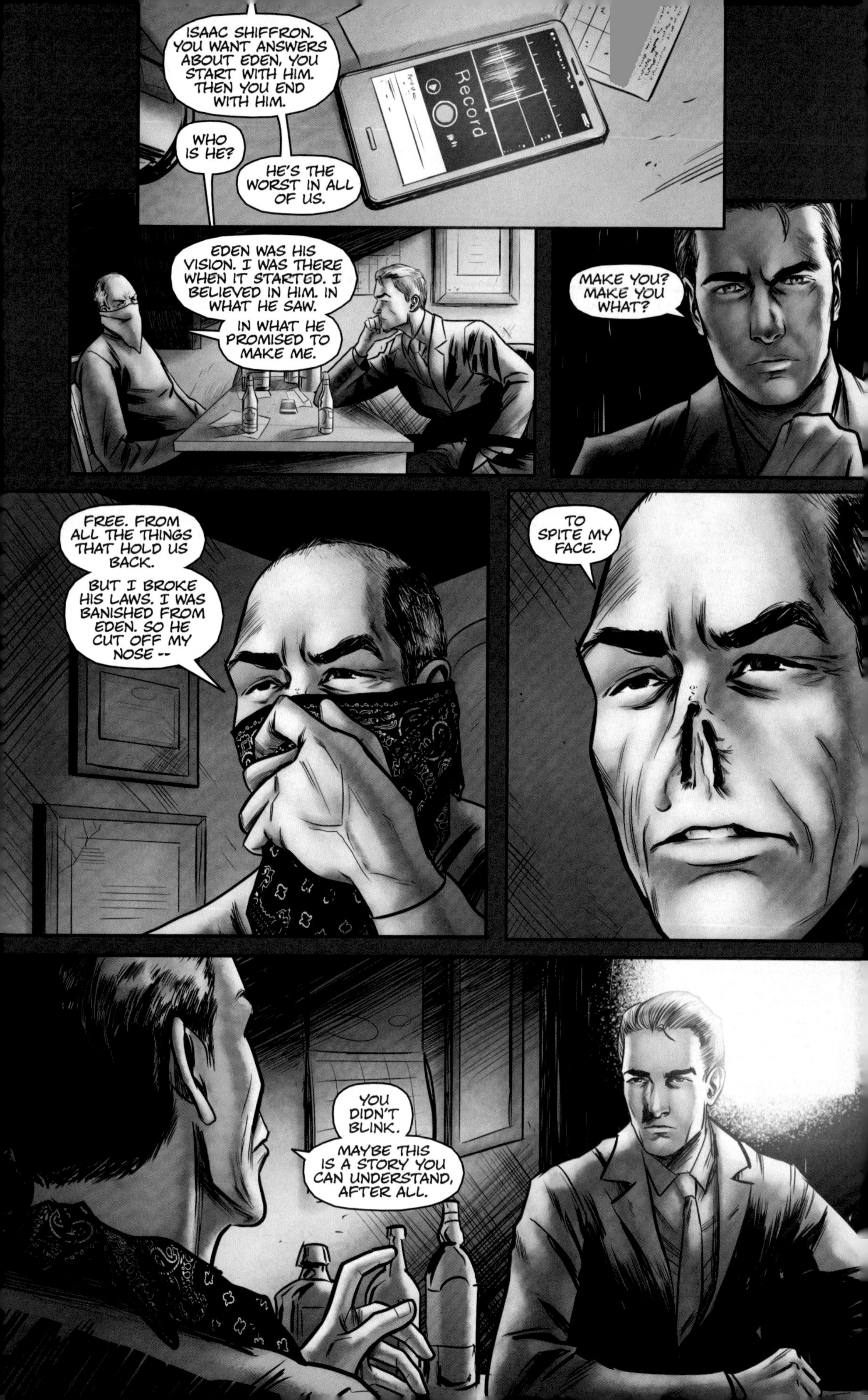

ISAAC SHIFFRON. YOU WANT ANSWERS ABOUT EDEN, YOU START WITH HIM. THEN YOU END WITH HIM.
WHO IS HE?
HE'S THE WORST IN ALL OF US.
Record
EDEN WAS HIS VISION. I WAS THERE WHEN IT STARTED. I BELIEVED IN HIM. IN WHAT HE SAW.
IN WHAT HE PROMISED TO MAKE ME.
MAKE YOU? MAKE YOU WHAT?
FREE. FROM ALL THE THINGS THAT HOLD US BACK.
BUT I BROKE HIS LAWS. I WAS BANISHED FROM EDEN. SO HE CUT OFF MY NOSE --
TO SPITE MY FACE.
YOU DIDN'T BLINK.
MAYBE THIS IS A STORY YOU CAN UNDERSTAND, AFTER ALL.

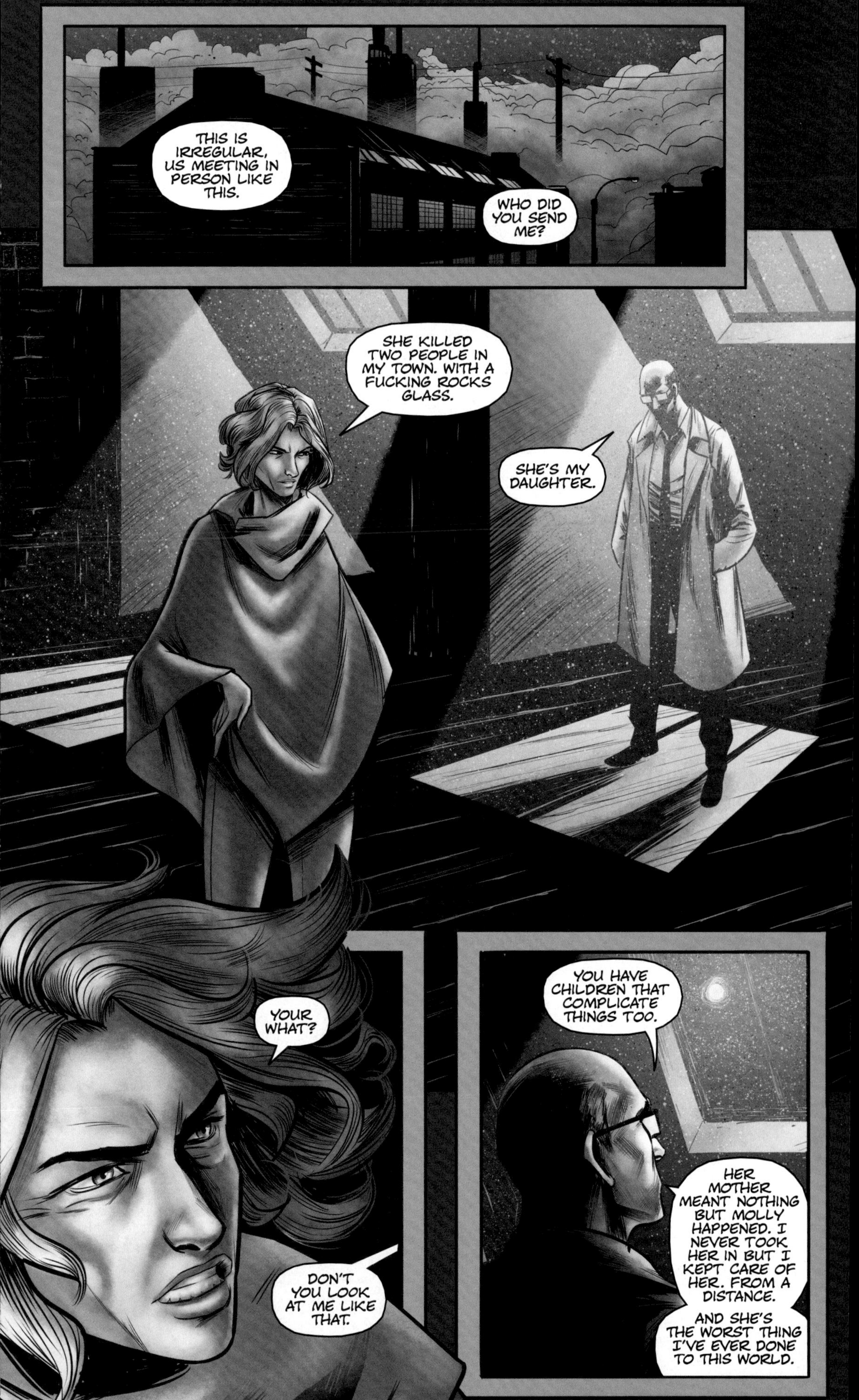
THIS IS IRREGULAR, US MEETING IN PERSON LIKE THIS.
WHO DID YOU SEND ME?
SHE KILLED TWO PEOPLE IN MY TOWN. WITH A FUCKING ROCKS GLASS.
SHE'S MY DAUGHTER.
YOUR WHAT?
DON'T YOU LOOK AT ME LIKE THAT.
YOU HAVE CHILDREN THAT COMPLICATE THINGS TOO.
HER MOTHER MEANT NOTHING BUT MOLLY HAPPENED. I NEVER TOOK HER IN BUT I KEPT CARE OF HER. FROM A DISTANCE.
AND SHE'S THE WORST THING I'VE EVER DONE TO THIS WORLD.

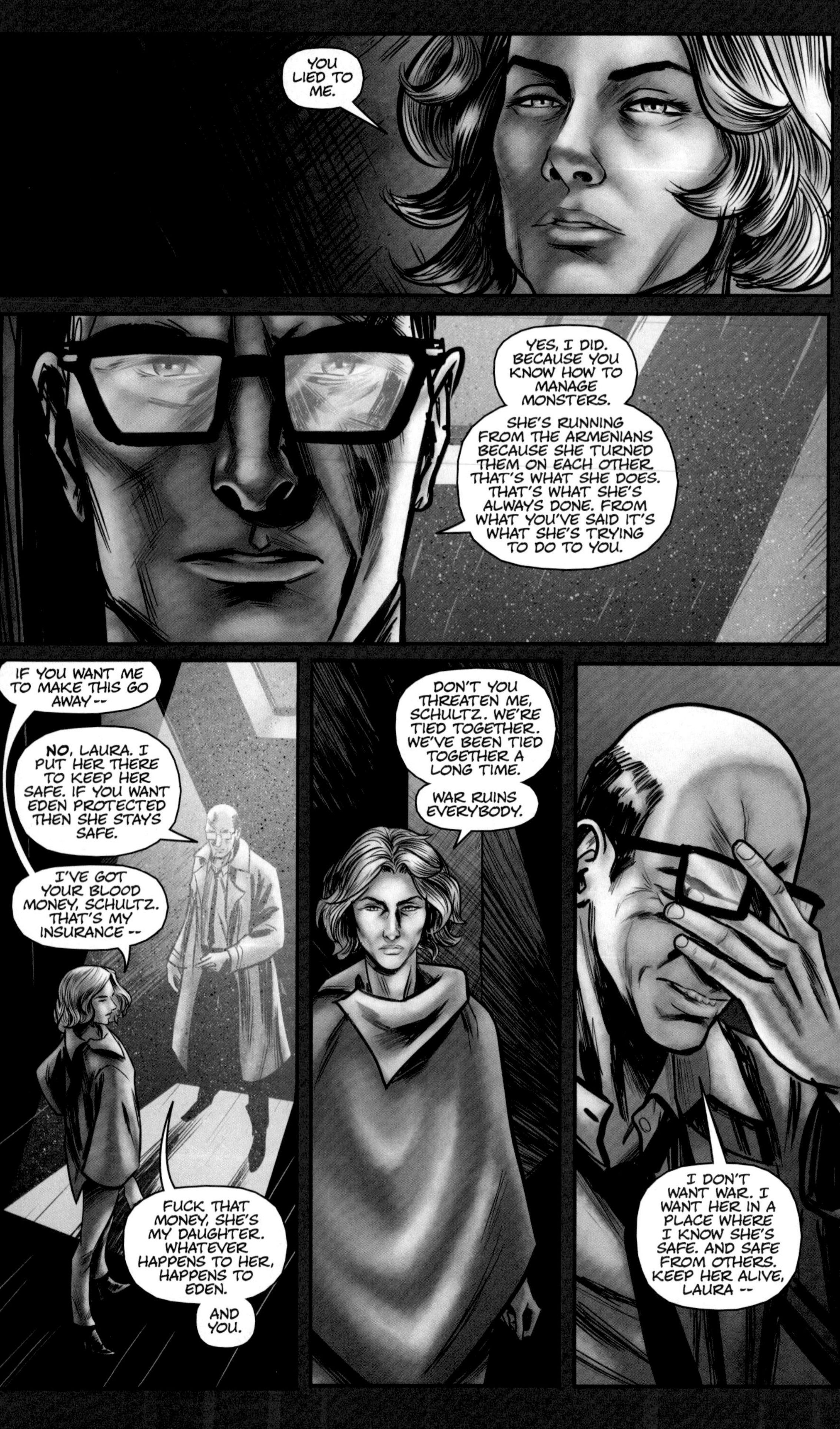
YOU LIED TO ME.
YES, I DID. BECAUSE YOU KNOW HOW TO MANAGE MONSTERS.
SHE'S RUNNING FROM THE ARMENIANS BECAUSE SHE TURNED THEM ON EACH OTHER. THAT'S WHAT SHE DOES. THAT'S WHAT SHE'S ALWAYS DONE. FROM WHAT YOU'VE SAID IT'S WHAT SHE'S TRYING TO DO TO YOU.
IF YOU WANT ME TO MAKE THIS GO AWAY--
NO, LAURA. I PUT HER THERE TO KEEP HER SAFE. IF YOU WANT EDEN PROTECTED THEN SHE STAYS SAFE.
I'VE GOT YOUR BLOOD MONEY, SCHULTZ. THAT'S MY INSURANCE --
FUCK THAT MONEY, SHE'S MY DAUGHTER. WHATEVER HAPPENS TO HER, HAPPENS TO EDEN.
AND YOU.
DON'T YOU THREATEN ME, SCHULTZ. WE'RE TIED TOGETHER. WE'VE BEEN TIED TOGETHER A LONG TIME.
WAR RUINS EVERYBODY.
I DON'T WANT WAR. I WANT HER IN A PLACE WHERE I KNOW SHE'S SAFE. AND SAFE FROM OTHERS. KEEP HER ALIVE, LAURA --

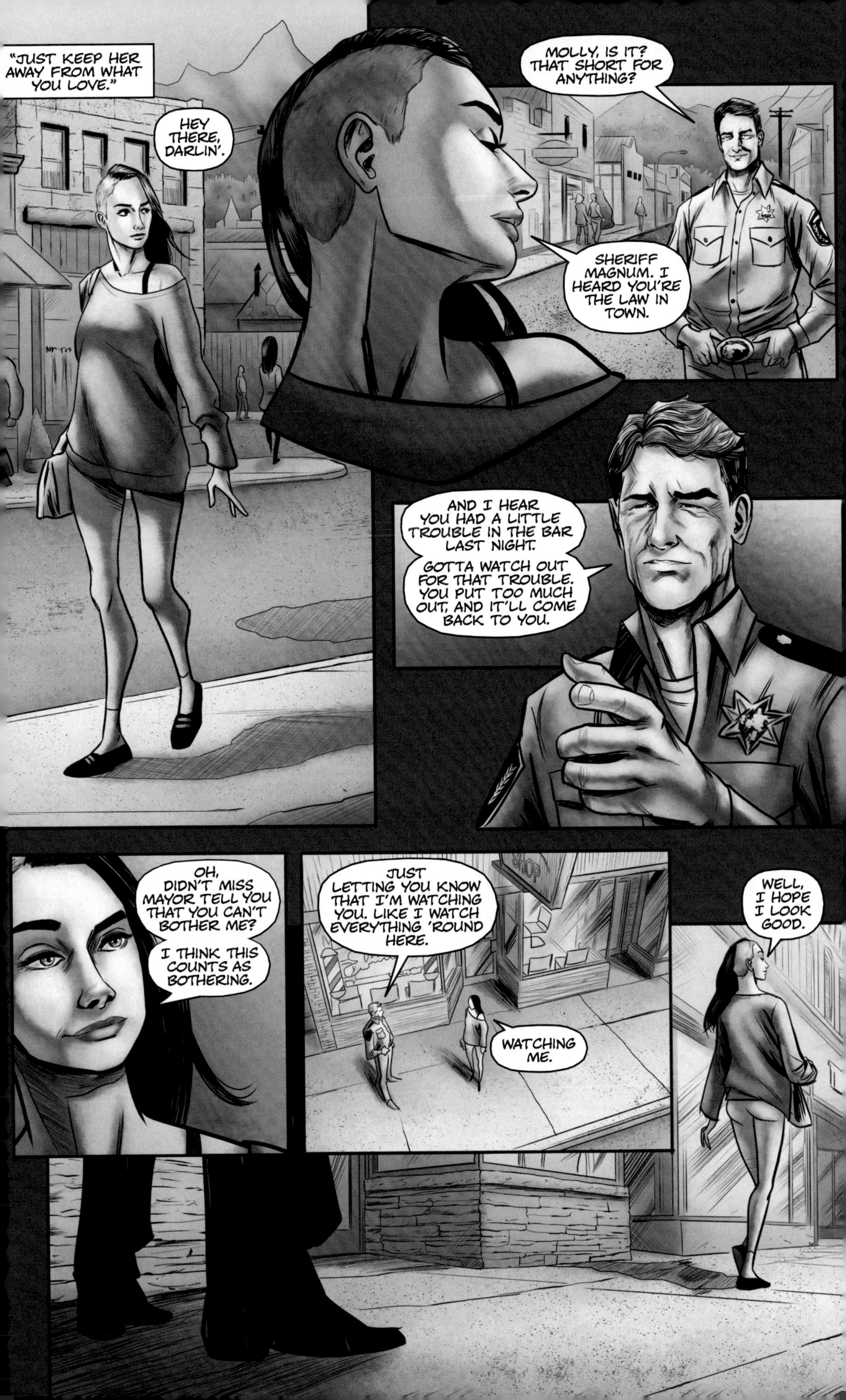
"JUST KEEP HER AWAY FROM WHAT YOU LOVE."
HEY THERE, DARLIN'.
MOLLY, IS IT? THAT SHORT FOR ANYTHING?
SHERIFF MAGNUM. I HEARD YOU'RE THE LAW IN TOWN.
AND I HEAR YOU HAD A LITTLE TROUBLE IN THE BAR LAST NIGHT.
GOTTA WATCH OUT FOR THAT TROUBLE. YOU PUT TOO MUCH OUT, AND IT'LL COME BACK TO YOU.
OH, DIDN'T MISS MAYOR TELL YOU THAT YOU CAN'T BOTHER ME?
I THINK THIS COUNTS AS BOTHERING.
JUST LETTING YOU KNOW THAT I'M WATCHING YOU. LIKE I WATCH EVERYTHING 'ROUND HERE.
WATCHING ME.
WELL, I HOPE I LOOK GOOD.

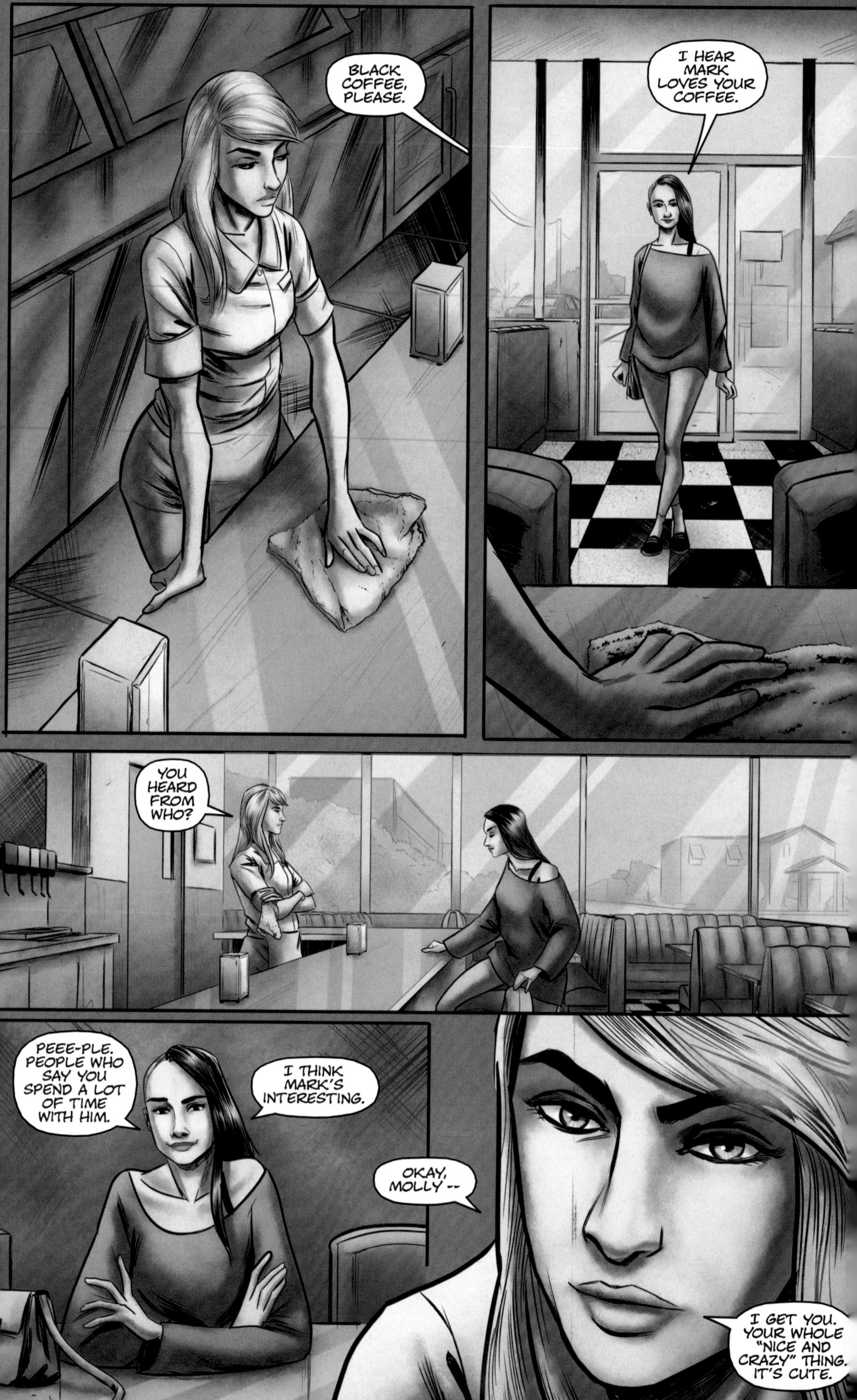
BLACK COFFEE, PLEASE.
I HEAR MARK LOVES YOUR COFFEE.
YOU HEARD FROM WHO?
PEEE-PLE. PEOPLE WHO SAY YOU SPEND A LOT OF TIME WITH HIM.
I THINK MARK'S INTERESTING.
OKAY, MOLLY --
I GET YOU. YOUR WHOLE "NICE AND CRAZY" THING. IT'S CUTE.

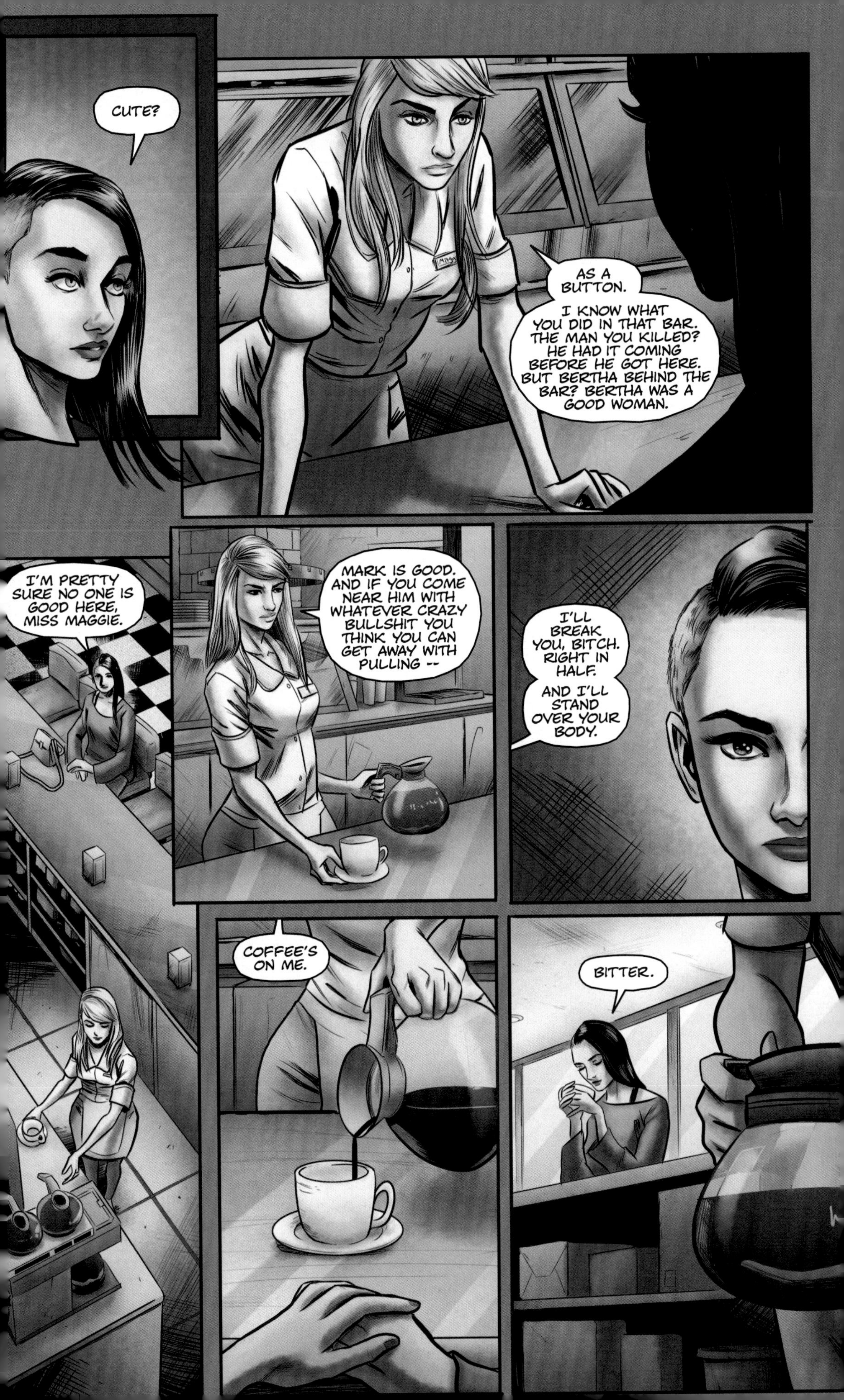
CUTE?
AS A BUTTON.
I KNOW WHAT YOU DID IN THAT BAR. THE MAN YOU KILLED? HE HAD IT COMING BEFORE HE GOT HERE. BUT BERTHA BEHIND THE BAR? BERTHA WAS A GOOD WOMAN.
I'M PRETTY SURE NO ONE IS GOOD HERE, MISS MAGGIE.
MARK IS GOOD. AND IF YOU COME NEAR HIM WITH WHATEVER CRAZY BULLSHIT YOU THINK YOU CAN GET AWAY WITH PULLING --
I'LL BREAK YOU, BITCH. RIGHT IN HALF.
AND I'LL STAND OVER YOUR BODY.
COFFEE'S ON ME.
BITTER.

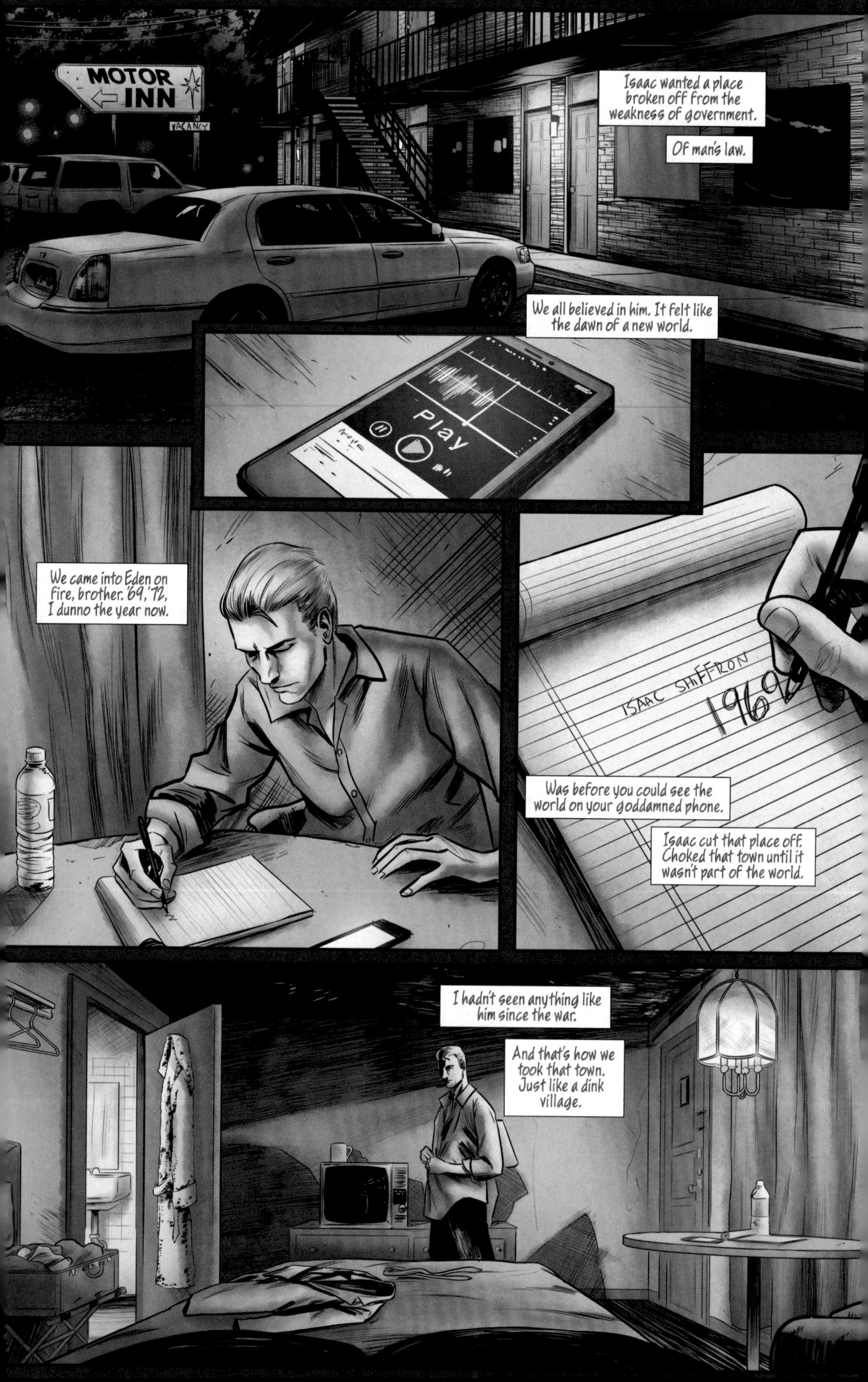
MOTOR INN
VACANCY
Isaac wanted a place broken off from the weakness of government.
Of man's law.
We all believed in him. It felt like the dawn of a new world.
Play
We came into Eden on fire, brother. '69, '72, I dunno the year now.
ISAAC SHIFFRON
1969
Was before you could see the world on your goddamned phone.
Isaac cut that place off. Choked that town until it wasn't part of the world.
I hadn't seen anything like him since the war.
And that's how we took that town. Just like a dink village.

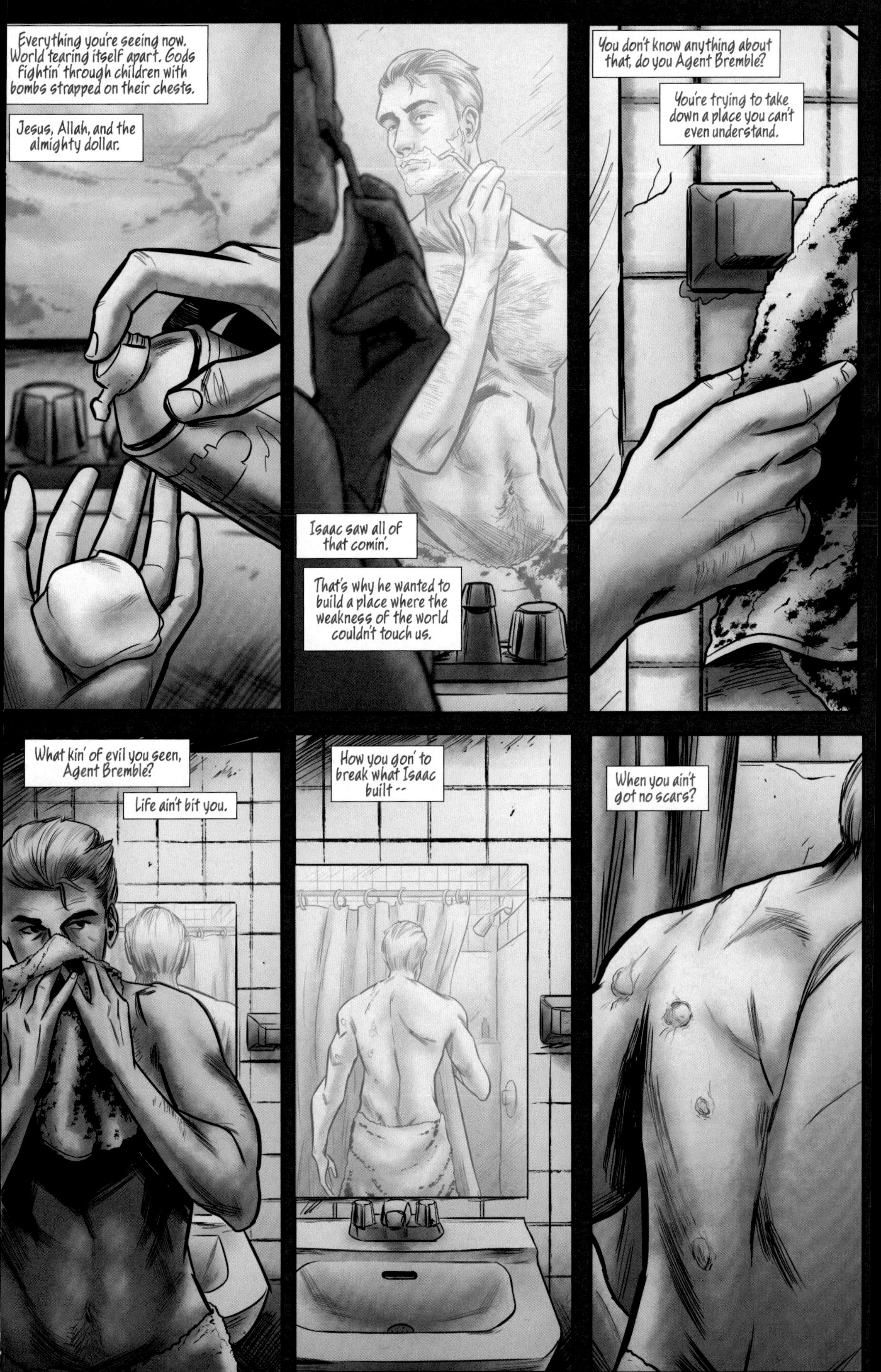
Everything you're seeing now. World tearing itself apart. Gods fightin' through children with bombs strapped on their chests.
Jesus, Allah, and the almighty dollar.
Isaac saw all of that comin'.
That's why he wanted to build a place where the weakness of the world couldn't touch us.
You don't know anything about that, do you Agent Bremble?
You're trying to take down a place you can't even understand.
What kin' of evil you seen, Agent Bremble?
Life ain't bit you.
How you gon' to break what Isaac built --
When you ain't got no scars?

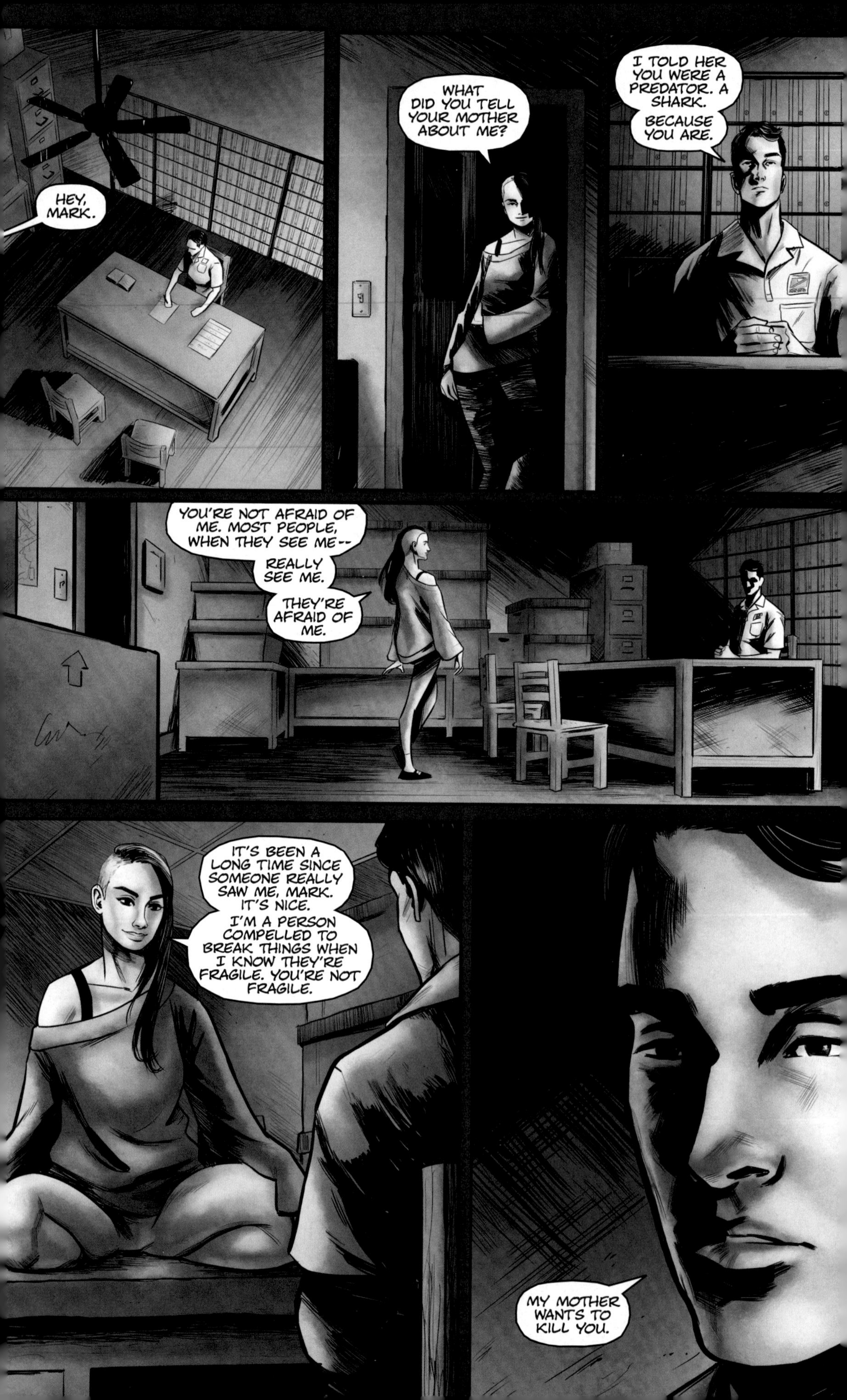
HEY, MARK.
WHAT DID YOU TELL YOUR MOTHER ABOUT ME?
I TOLD HER YOU WERE A PREDATOR. A SHARK.
BECAUSE YOU ARE.
YOU'RE NOT AFRAID OF ME. MOST PEOPLE, WHEN THEY SEE ME--
REALLY SEE ME.
THEY'RE AFRAID OF ME.
IT'S BEEN A LONG TIME SINCE SOMEONE REALLY SAW ME, MARK. IT'S NICE.
I'M A PERSON COMPELLED TO BREAK THINGS WHEN I KNOW THEY'RE FRAGILE. YOU'RE NOT FRAGILE.
MY MOTHER WANTS TO KILL YOU.

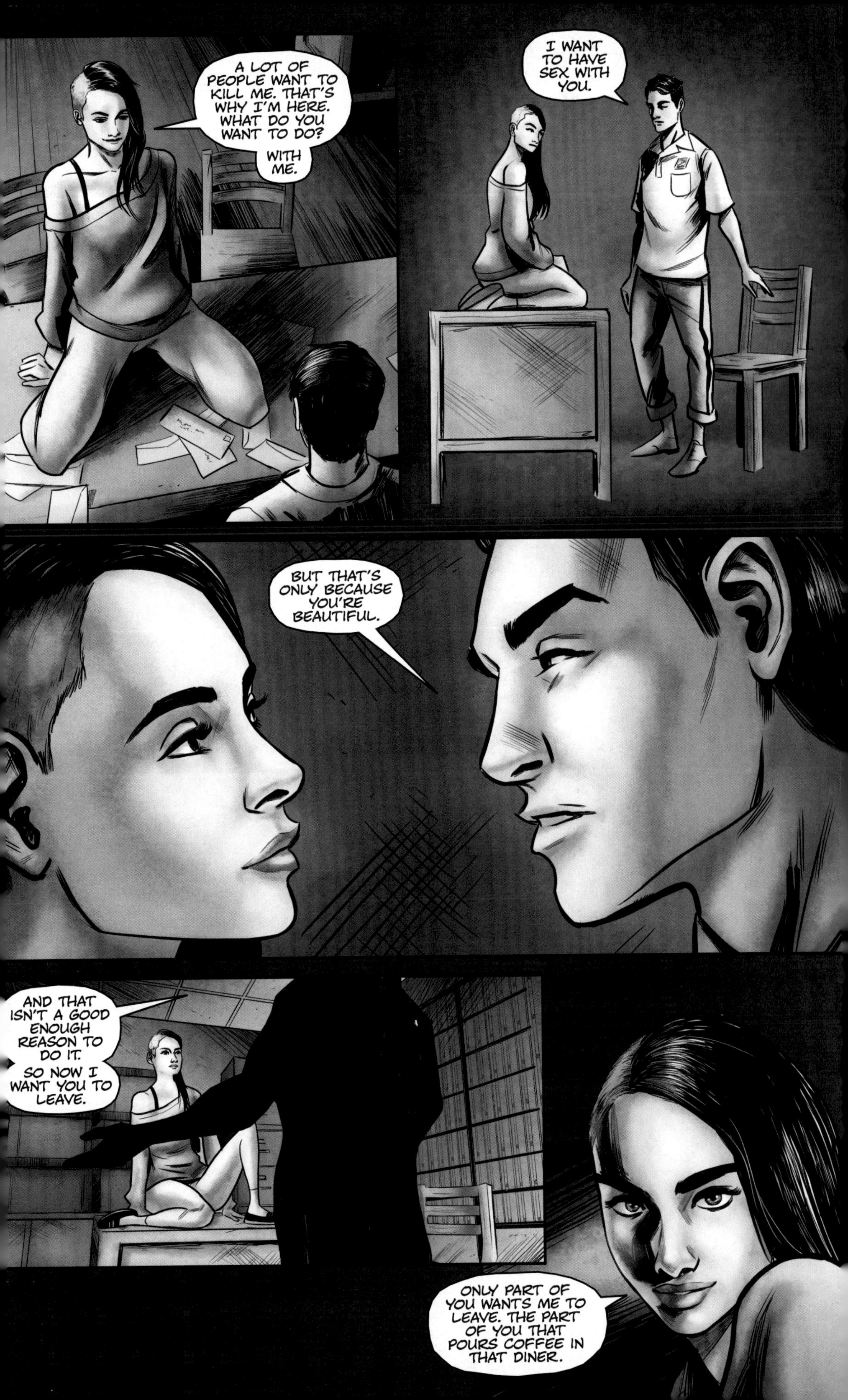
A LOT OF PEOPLE WANT TO KILL ME. THAT'S WHY I'M HERE. WHAT DO YOU WANT TO DO?
WITH ME.
I WANT TO HAVE SEX WITH YOU.
BUT THAT'S ONLY BECAUSE YOU'RE BEAUTIFUL.
AND THAT ISN'T A GOOD ENOUGH REASON TO DO IT.
SO NOW I WANT YOU TO LEAVE.
ONLY PART OF YOU WANTS ME TO LEAVE. THE PART OF YOU THAT POURS COFFEE IN THAT DINER.

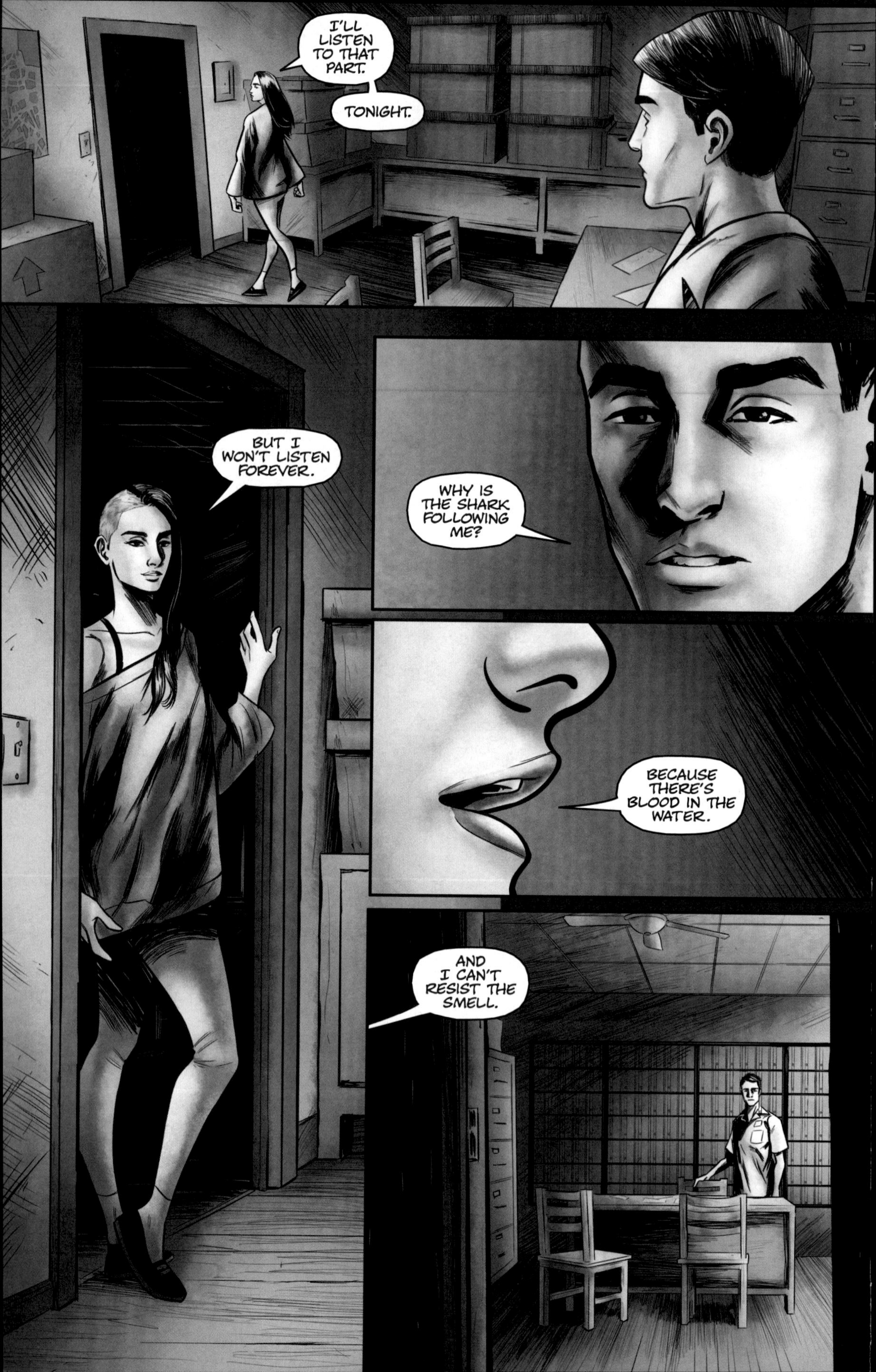
I'LL LISTEN TO THAT PART.
TONIGHT.
BUT I WON'T LISTEN FOREVER.
WHY IS THE SHARK FOLLOWING ME?
BECAUSE THERE'S BLOOD IN THE WATER.
AND I CAN'T RESIST THE SMELL.

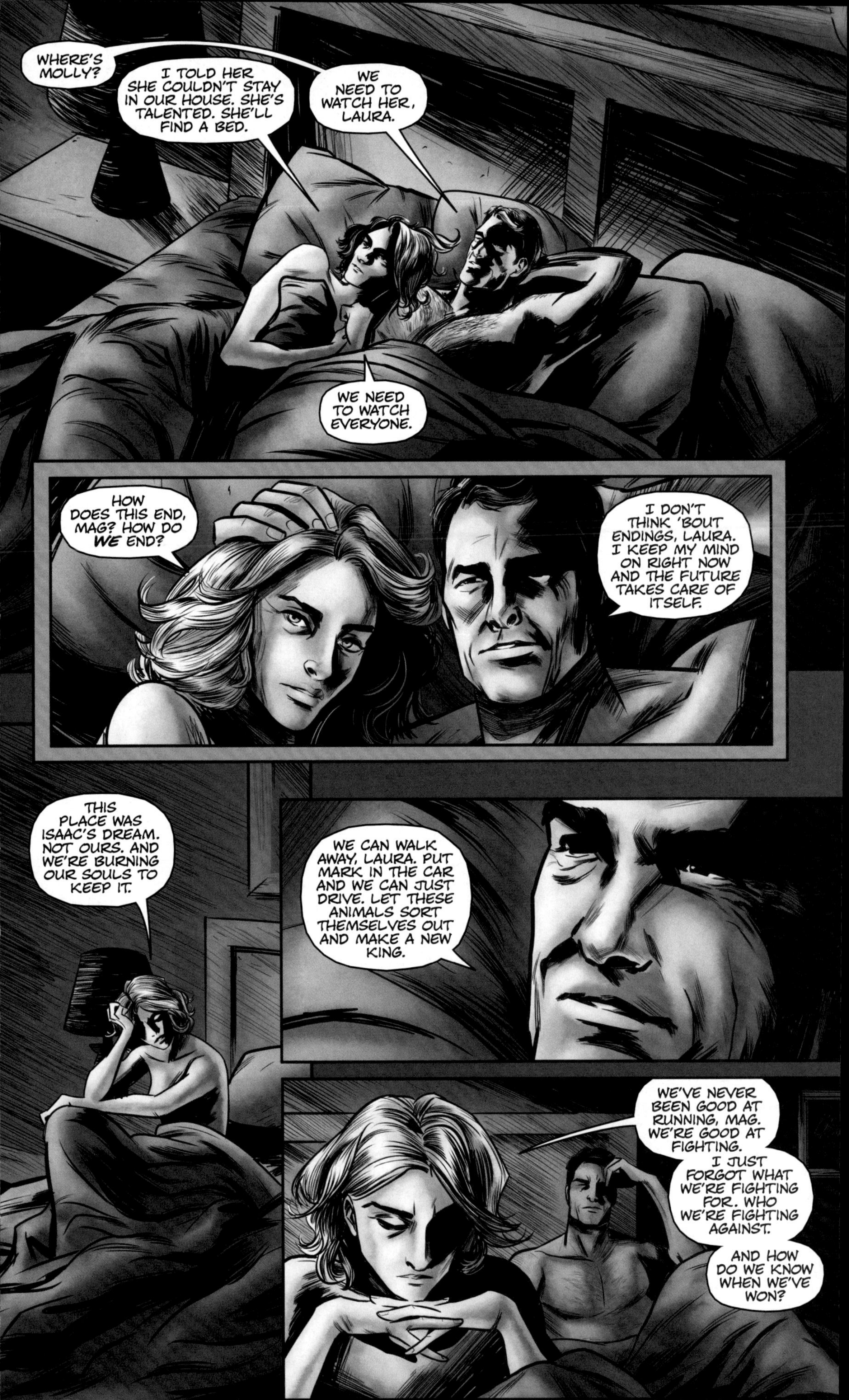
WHERE'S MOLLY?
I TOLD HER SHE COULDN'T STAY IN OUR HOUSE. SHE'S TALENTED. SHE'LL FIND A BED.
WE NEED TO WATCH HER, LAURA.
WE NEED TO WATCH EVERYONE.
HOW DOES THIS END, MAG? HOW DO *WE* END?
I DON'T THINK 'BOUT ENDINGS, LAURA. I KEEP MY MIND ON RIGHT NOW AND THE FUTURE TAKES CARE OF ITSELF.
THIS PLACE WAS ISAAC'S DREAM. NOT OURS. AND WE'RE BURNING OUR SOULS TO KEEP IT.
WE CAN WALK AWAY, LAURA. PUT MARK IN THE CAR AND WE CAN JUST DRIVE. LET THESE ANIMALS SORT THEMSELVES OUT AND MAKE A NEW KING.
WE'VE NEVER BEEN GOOD AT RUNNING, MAG. WE'RE GOOD AT FIGHTING.
I JUST FORGOT WHAT WE'RE FIGHTING FOR. WHO WE'RE FIGHTING AGAINST.
AND HOW DO WE KNOW WHEN WE'VE WON?

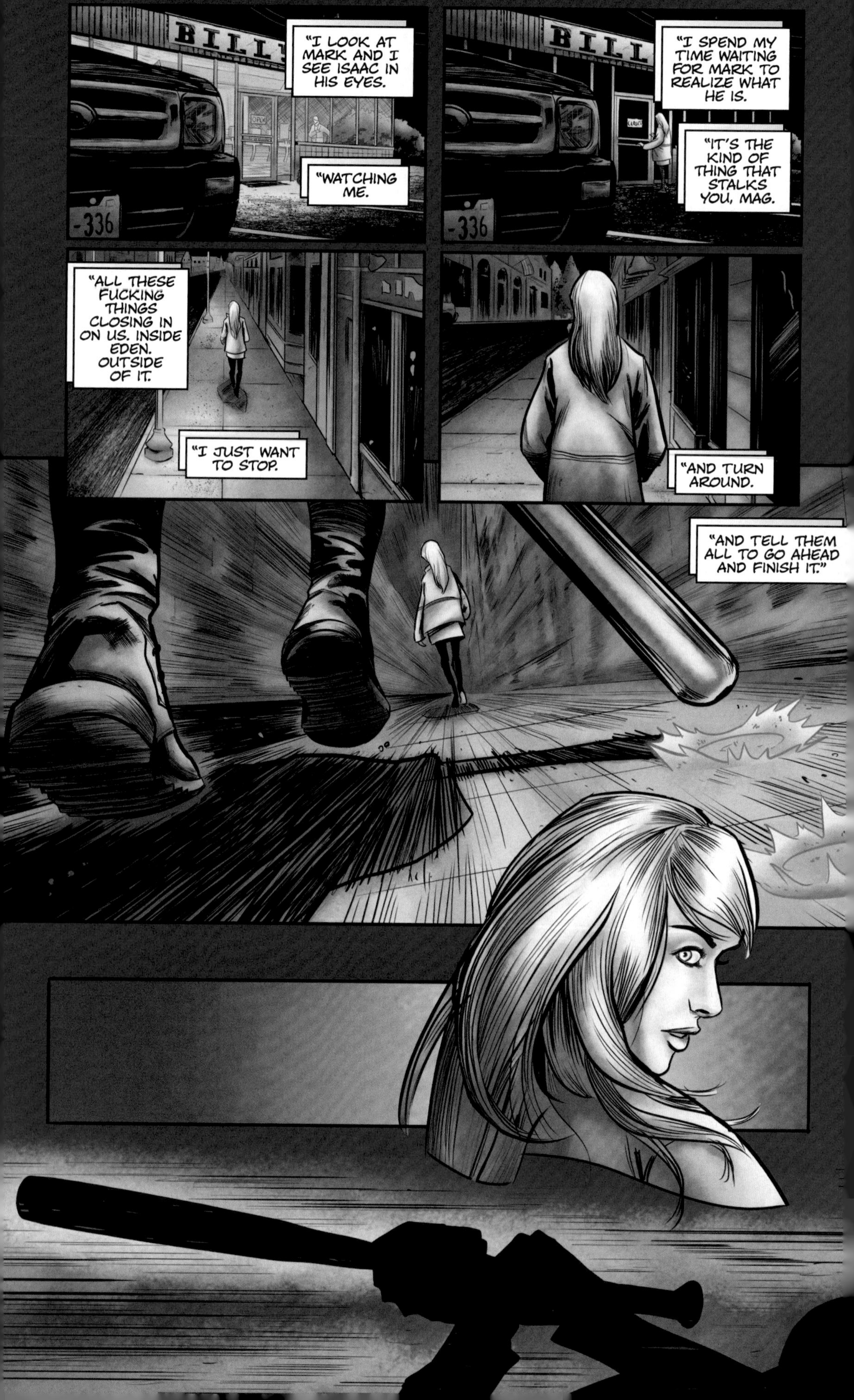
BILL
-336
"I LOOK AT MARK AND I SEE ISAAC IN HIS EYES.
"WATCHING ME.
BILL
-336
"I SPEND MY TIME WAITING FOR MARK TO REALIZE WHAT HE IS.
"IT'S THE KIND OF THING THAT STALKS YOU, MAG.
"ALL THESE FUCKING THINGS CLOSING IN ON US. INSIDE EDEN. OUTSIDE OF IT.
"I JUST WANT TO STOP.
"AND TURN AROUND.
"AND TELL THEM ALL TO GO AHEAD AND FINISH IT."

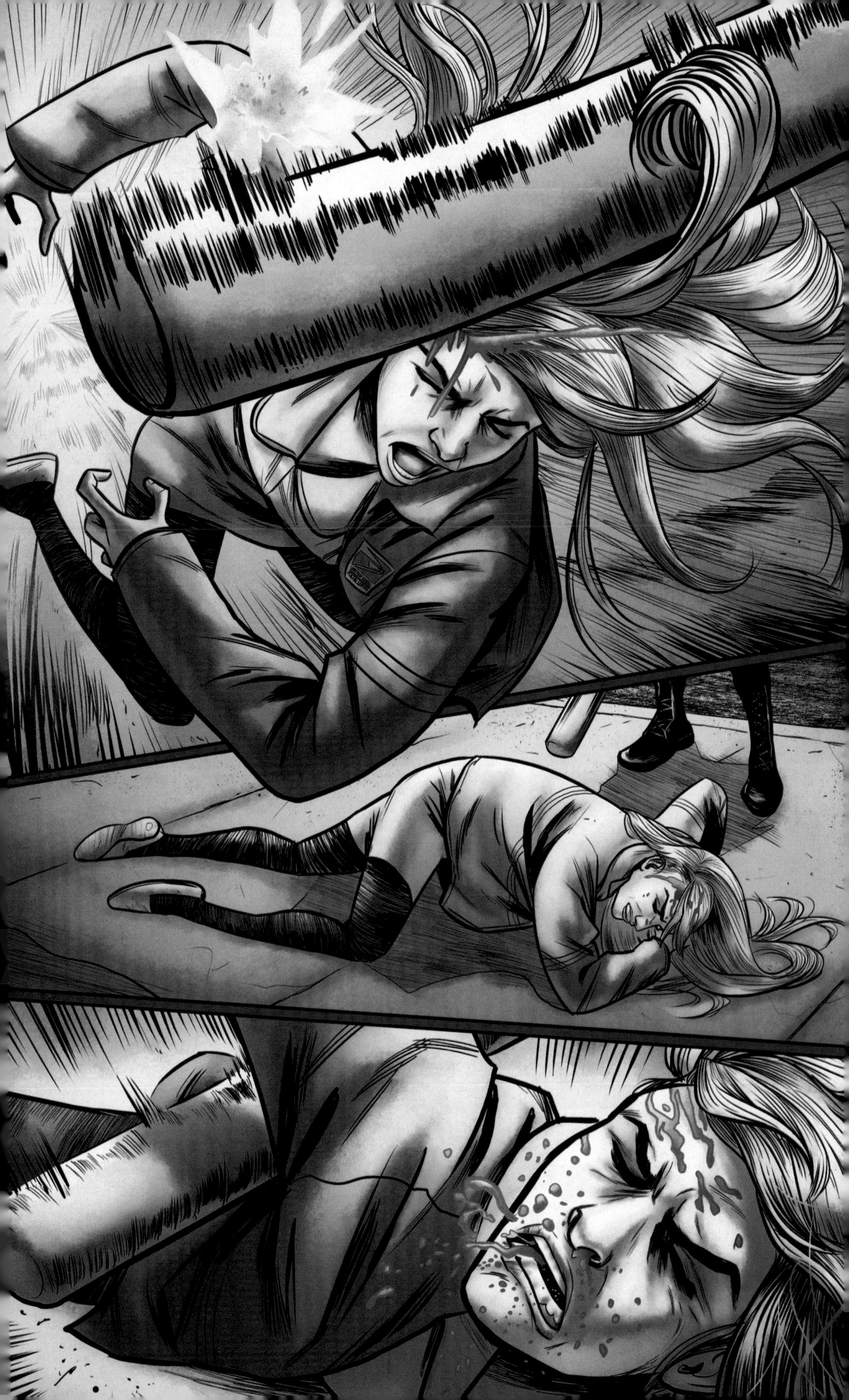

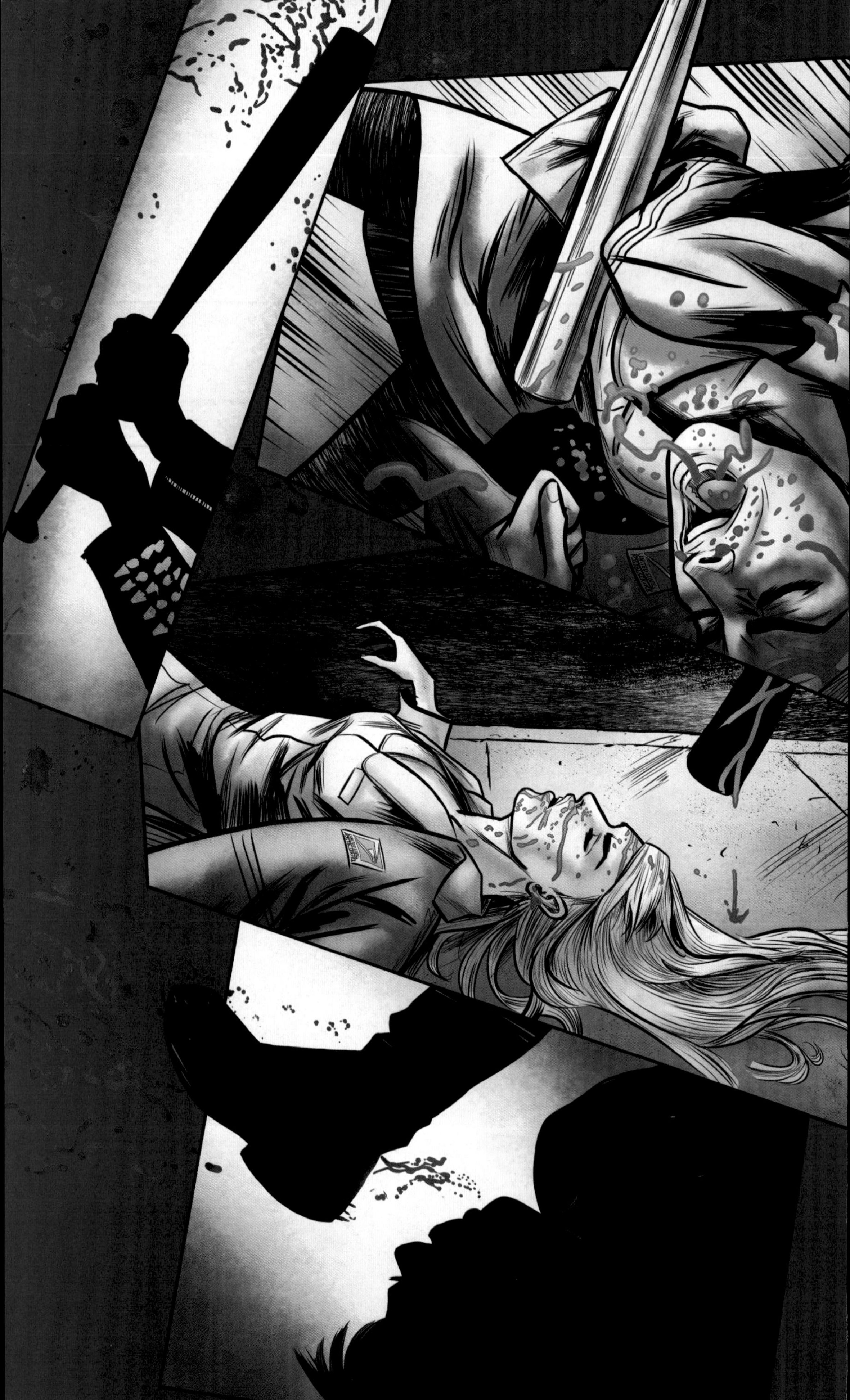

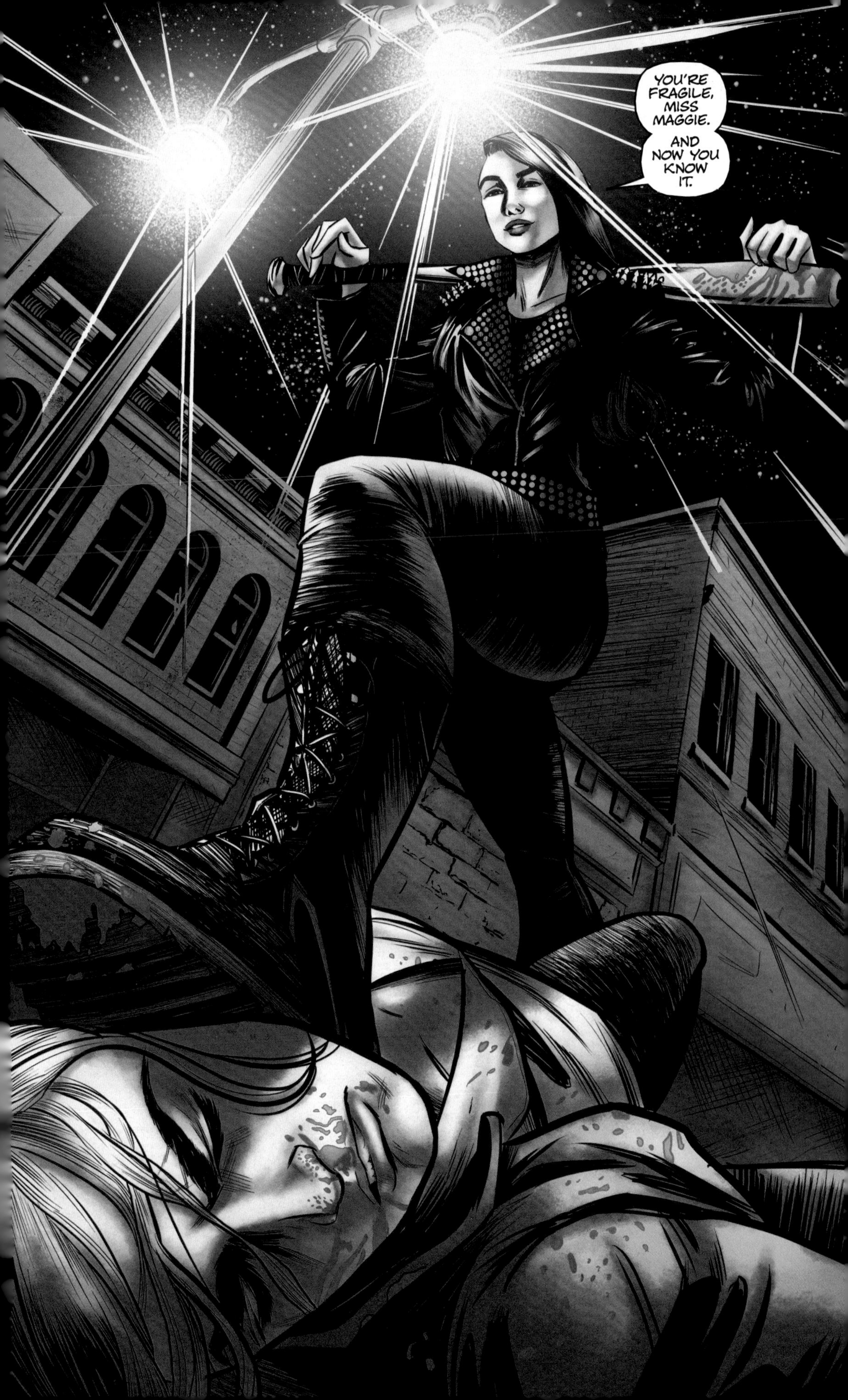
YOU'RE FRAGILE, MISS MAGGIE.
AND NOW YOU KNOW IT.

# Chapter 11

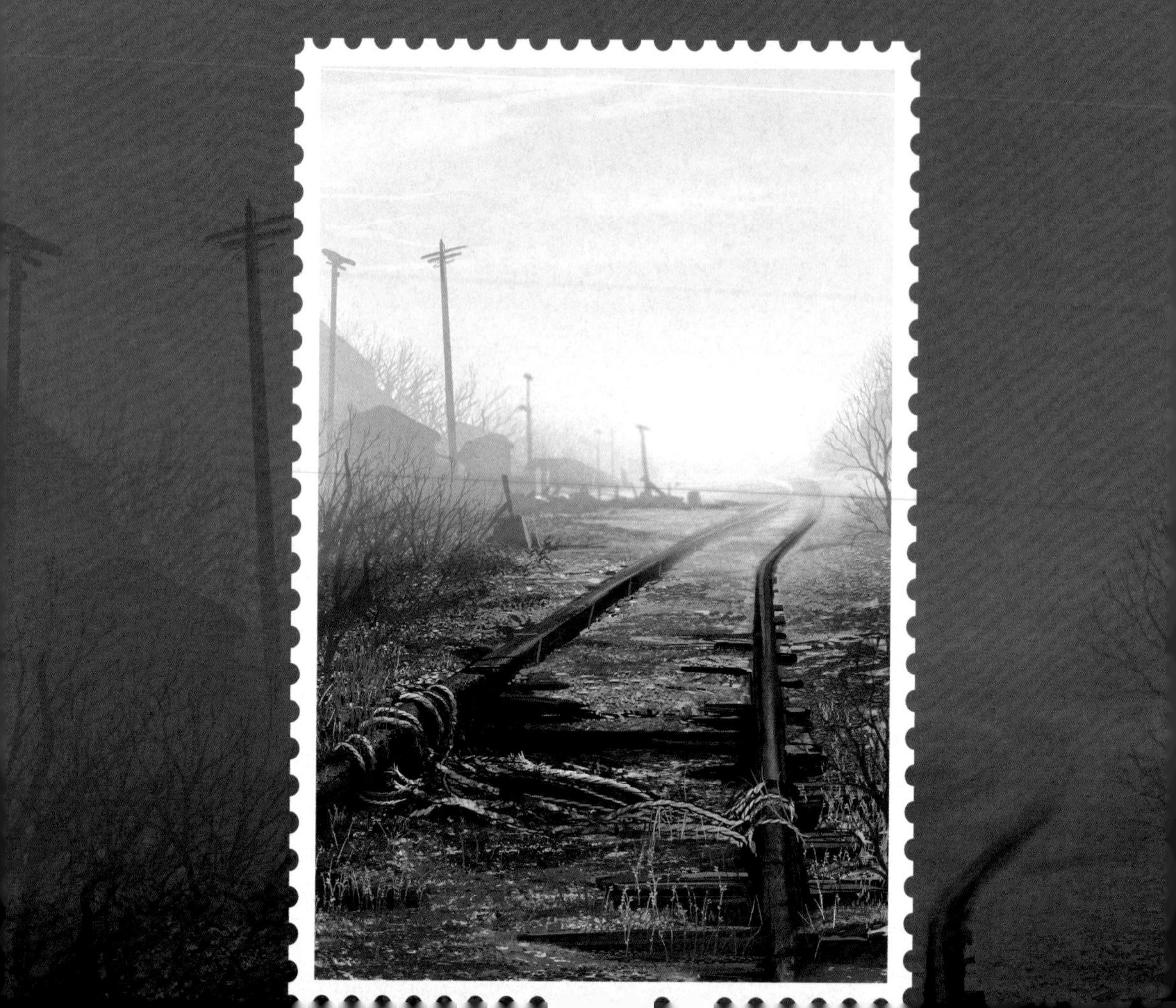

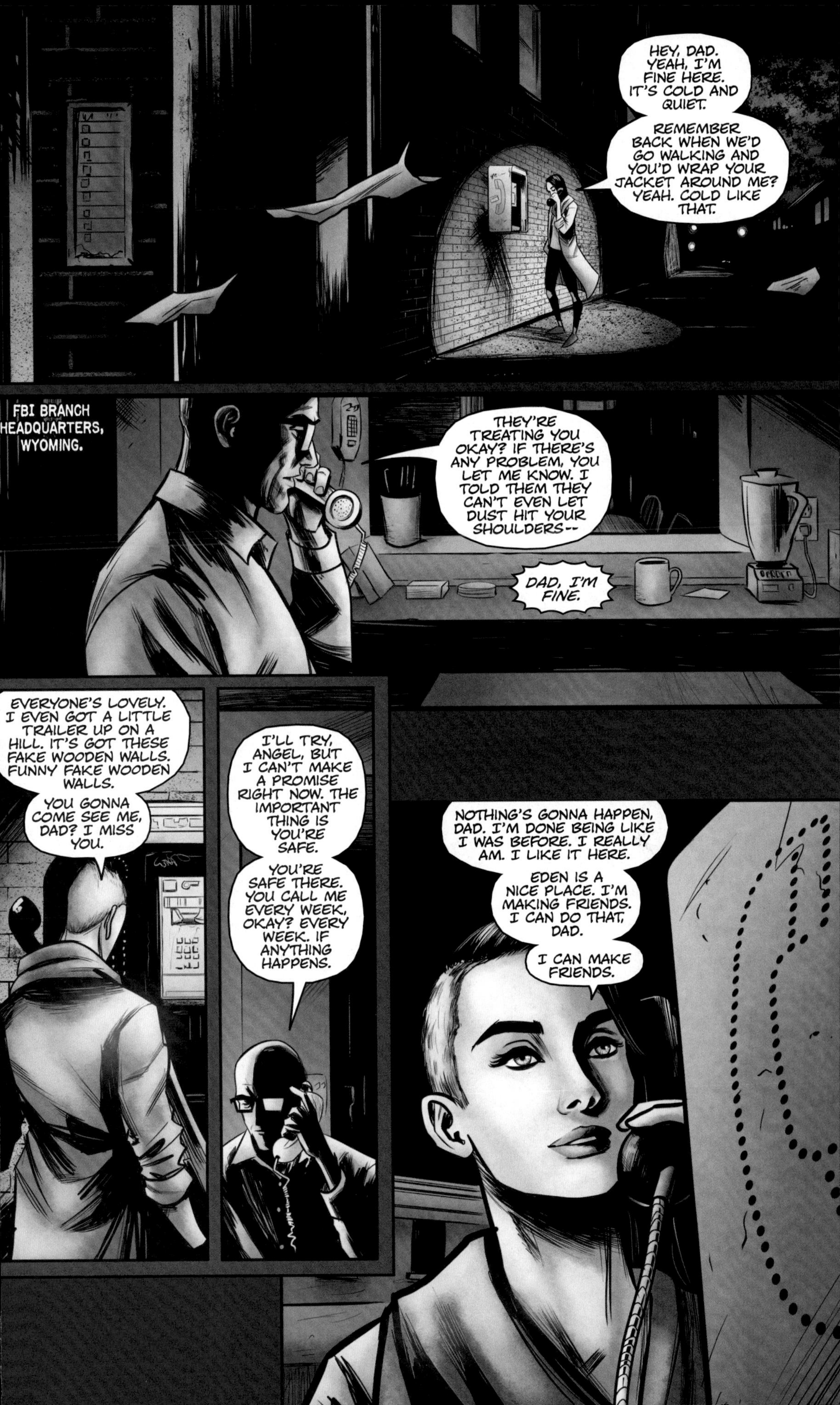
HEY, DAD. YEAH, I'M FINE HERE. IT'S COLD AND QUIET.
REMEMBER BACK WHEN WE'D GO WALKING AND YOU'D WRAP YOUR JACKET AROUND ME? YEAH. COLD LIKE THAT.
FBI BRANCH HEADQUARTERS, WYOMING.
THEY'RE TREATING YOU OKAY? IF THERE'S ANY PROBLEM, YOU LET ME KNOW. I TOLD THEM THEY CAN'T EVEN LET DUST HIT YOUR SHOULDERS--
DAD, I'M FINE.
EVERYONE'S LOVELY. I EVEN GOT A LITTLE TRAILER UP ON A HILL. IT'S GOT THESE FAKE WOODEN WALLS. FUNNY FAKE WOODEN WALLS.
YOU GONNA COME SEE ME, DAD? I MISS YOU.
I'LL TRY, ANGEL, BUT I CAN'T MAKE A PROMISE RIGHT NOW. THE IMPORTANT THING IS YOU'RE SAFE.
YOU'RE SAFE THERE. YOU CALL ME EVERY WEEK, OKAY? EVERY WEEK. IF ANYTHING HAPPENS.
NOTHING'S GONNA HAPPEN, DAD. I'M DONE BEING LIKE I WAS BEFORE. I REALLY AM. I LIKE IT HERE.
EDEN IS A NICE PLACE. I'M MAKING FRIENDS. I CAN DO THAT, DAD.
I CAN MAKE FRIENDS.

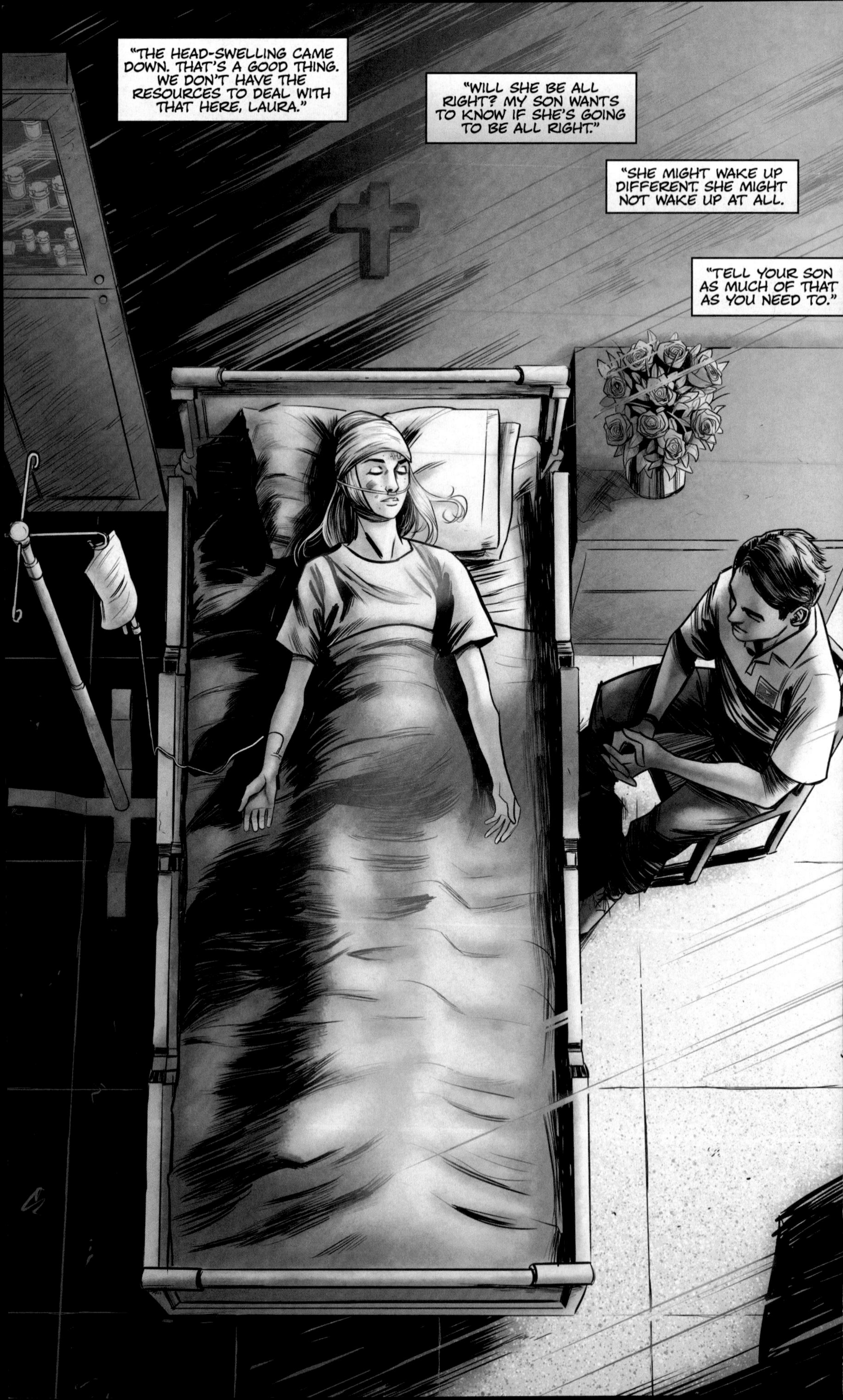
"THE HEAD-SWELLING CAME DOWN. THAT'S A GOOD THING. WE DON'T HAVE THE RESOURCES TO DEAL WITH THAT HERE, LAURA."
"WILL SHE BE ALL RIGHT? MY SON WANTS TO KNOW IF SHE'S GOING TO BE ALL RIGHT."
"SHE MIGHT WAKE UP DIFFERENT. SHE MIGHT NOT WAKE UP AT ALL.
"TELL YOUR SON AS MUCH OF THAT AS YOU NEED TO."

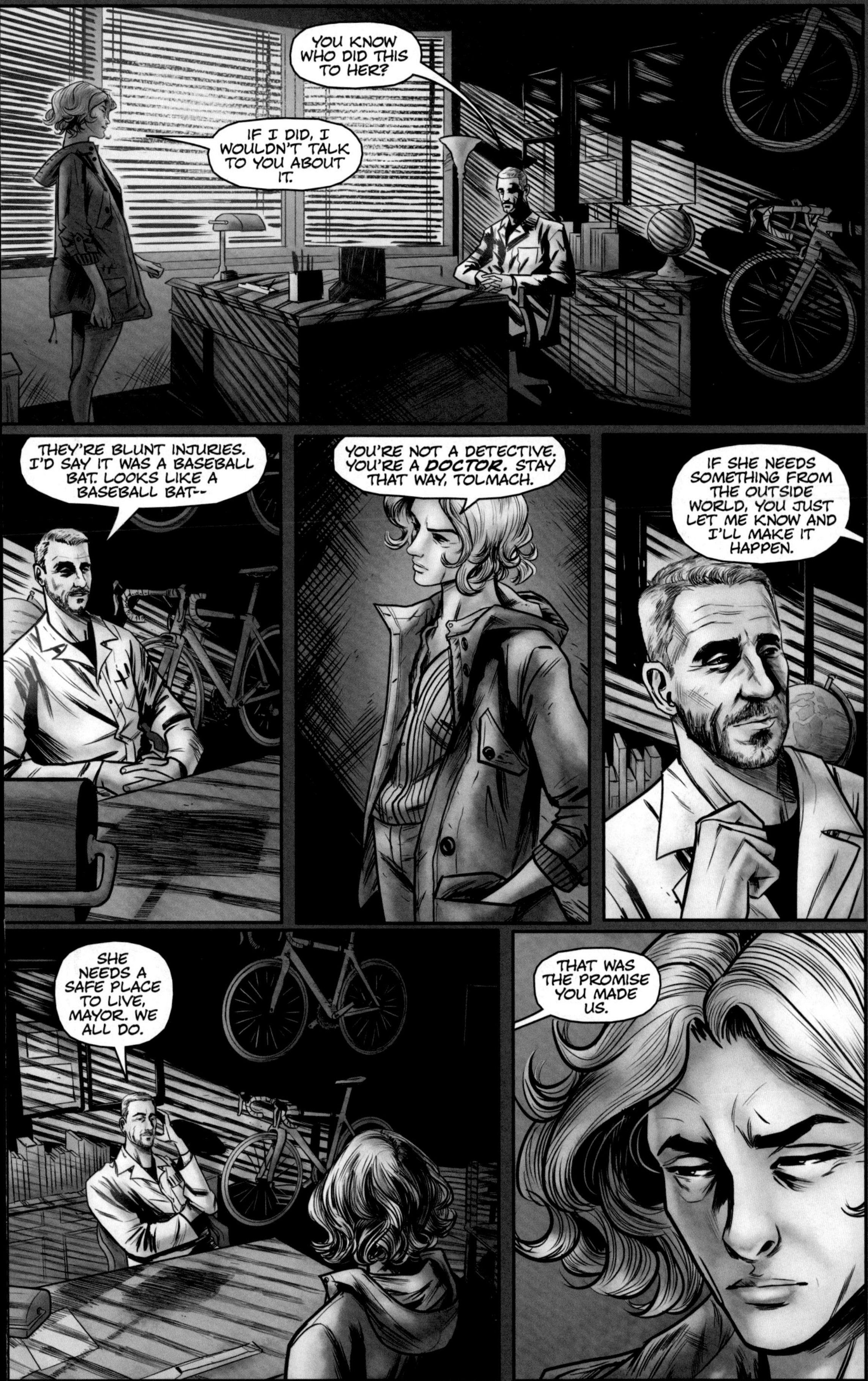
YOU KNOW WHO DID THIS TO HER?
IF I DID, I WOULDN'T TALK TO YOU ABOUT IT.
THEY'RE BLUNT INJURIES. I'D SAY IT WAS A BASEBALL BAT. LOOKS LIKE A BASEBALL BAT--
YOU'RE NOT A DETECTIVE. YOU'RE A DOCTOR. STAY THAT WAY, TOLMACH.
IF SHE NEEDS SOMETHING FROM THE OUTSIDE WORLD, YOU JUST LET ME KNOW AND I'LL MAKE IT HAPPEN.
SHE NEEDS A SAFE PLACE TO LIVE, MAYOR. WE ALL DO.
THAT WAS THE PROMISE YOU MADE US.

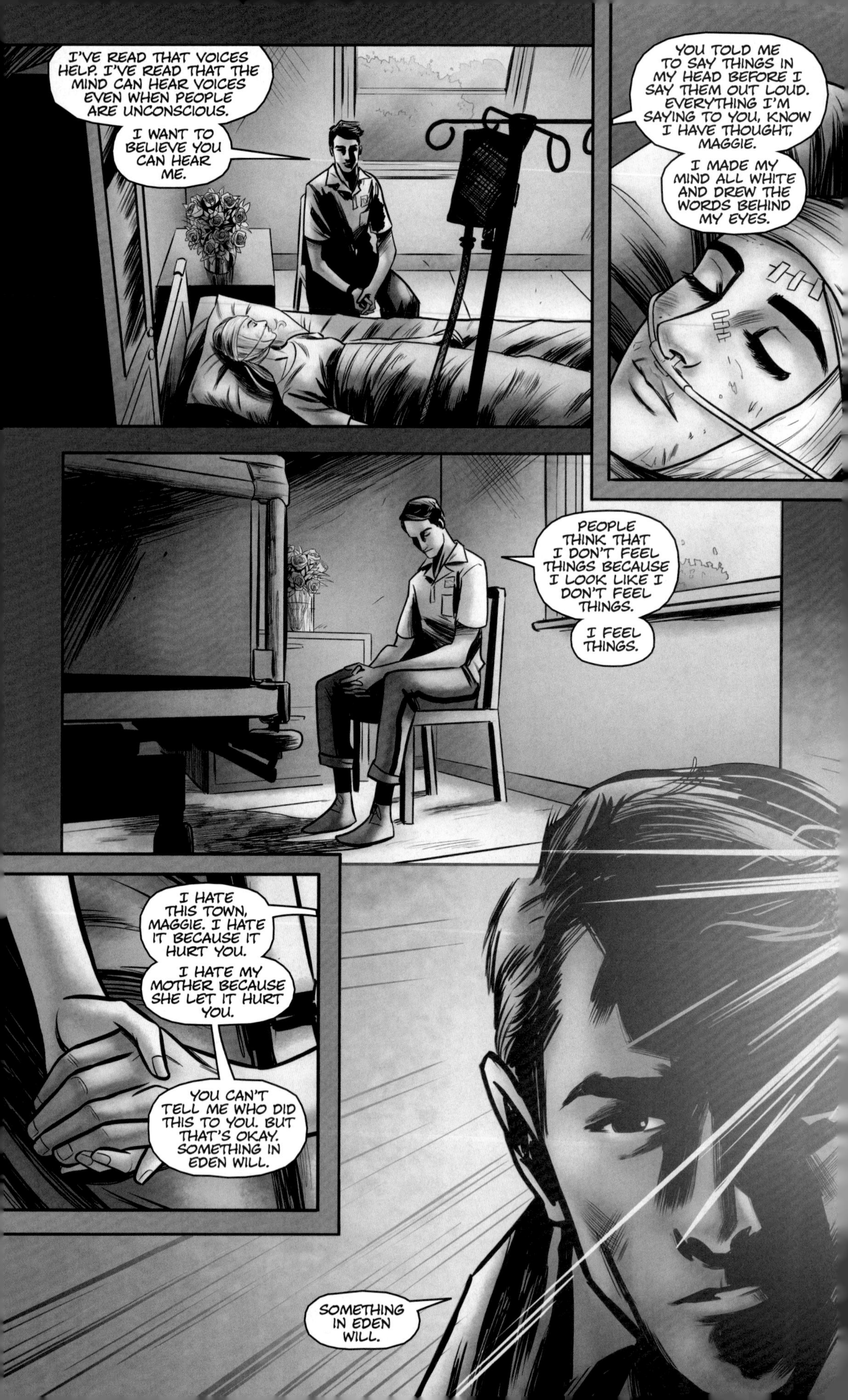
I'VE READ THAT VOICES HELP. I'VE READ THAT THE MIND CAN HEAR VOICES EVEN WHEN PEOPLE ARE UNCONSCIOUS.
I WANT TO BELIEVE YOU CAN HEAR ME.
YOU TOLD ME TO SAY THINGS IN MY HEAD BEFORE I SAY THEM OUT LOUD. EVERYTHING I'M SAYING TO YOU, KNOW I HAVE THOUGHT, MAGGIE.
I MADE MY MIND ALL WHITE AND DREW THE WORDS BEHIND MY EYES.
PEOPLE THINK THAT I DON'T FEEL THINGS BECAUSE I LOOK LIKE I DON'T FEEL THINGS.
I FEEL THINGS.
I HATE THIS TOWN, MAGGIE. I HATE IT BECAUSE IT HURT YOU.
I HATE MY MOTHER BECAUSE SHE LET IT HURT YOU.
YOU CAN'T TELL ME WHO DID THIS TO YOU. BUT THAT'S OKAY. SOMETHING IN EDEN WILL.
SOMETHING IN EDEN WILL.

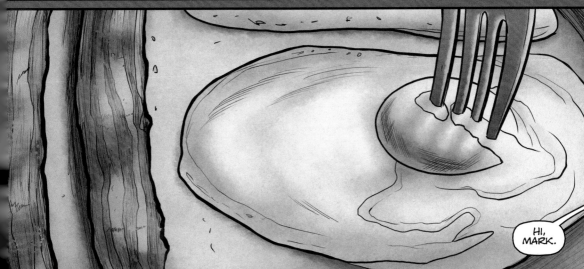

HI, MARK.

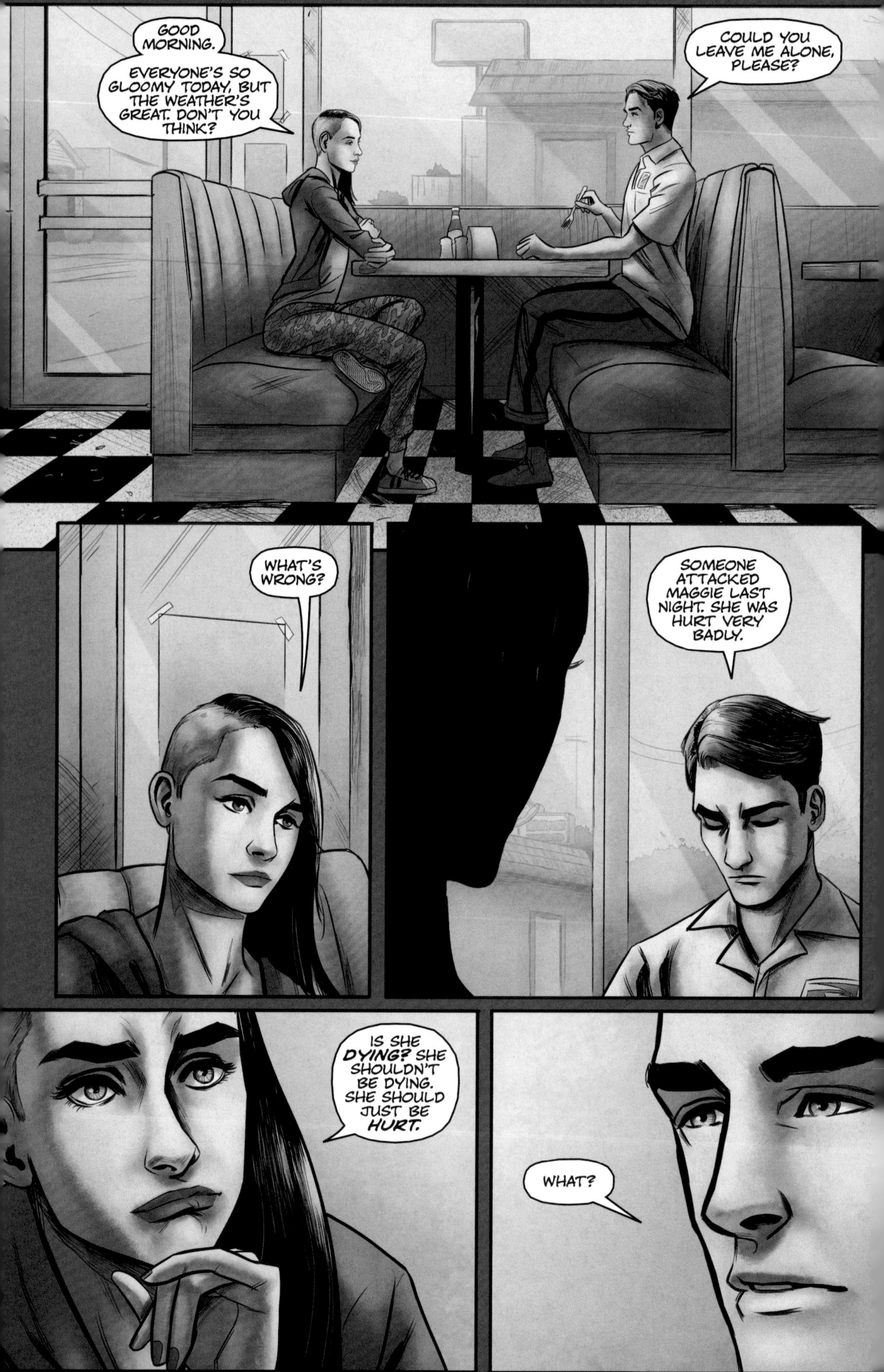
GOOD MORNING.
EVERYONE'S SO GLOOMY TODAY, BUT THE WEATHER'S GREAT. DON'T YOU THINK?
COULD YOU LEAVE ME ALONE, PLEASE?
WHAT'S WRONG?
SOMEONE ATTACKED MAGGIE LAST NIGHT. SHE WAS HURT VERY BADLY.
IS SHE DYING? SHE SHOULDN'T BE DYING. SHE SHOULD JUST BE HURT.
WHAT?

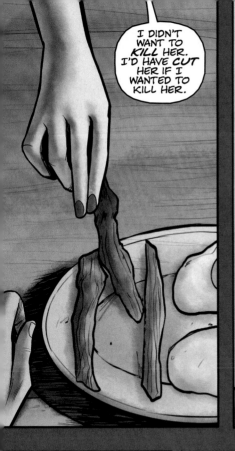

I DIDN'T WANT TO *KILL* HER. I'D HAVE *CUT* HER IF I WANTED TO KILL HER.

I JUST WANTED TO MAKE HER GO AWAY FOR A LITTLE WHILE.

WHY?

AH, I DUNNO. JUST HAD A FEELING SHE WAS GOING TO STOP US FROM GETTING TO KNOW EACH OTHER AND I'D LIKE TO GET TO KNOW YOU.

IS THAT HATE ON YOUR FACE? PEOPLE SAY YOU'RE A MANNEQUIN, THAT YOU NEVER SHOW EMOTION. THAT'S NOT TRUE.

I SEE PLENTY ON YOU.

THAT IS HATE ON MY FACE.

WELL, THAT BETTER *CHANGE*.

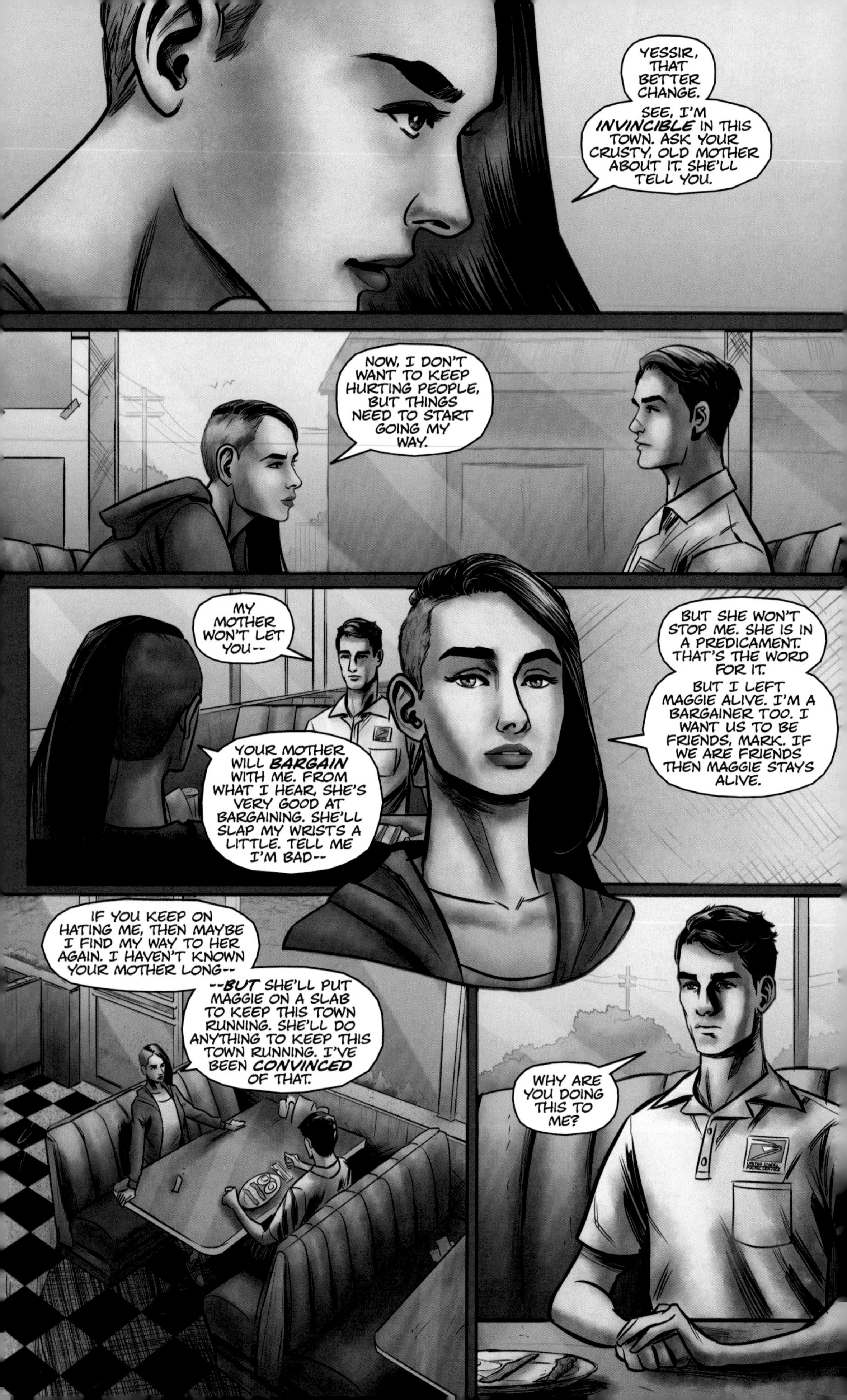
YESSIR, THAT BETTER CHANGE.
SEE, I'M INVINCIBLE IN THIS TOWN. ASK YOUR CRUSTY, OLD MOTHER ABOUT IT. SHE'LL TELL YOU.
NOW, I DON'T WANT TO KEEP HURTING PEOPLE, BUT THINGS NEED TO START GOING MY WAY.
MY MOTHER WON'T LET YOU--
YOUR MOTHER WILL BARGAIN WITH ME. FROM WHAT I HEAR, SHE'S VERY GOOD AT BARGAINING. SHE'LL SLAP MY WRISTS A LITTLE. TELL ME I'M BAD--
BUT SHE WON'T STOP ME. SHE IS IN A PREDICAMENT. THAT'S THE WORD FOR IT.
BUT I LEFT MAGGIE ALIVE. I'M A BARGAINER TOO. I WANT US TO BE FRIENDS, MARK. IF WE ARE FRIENDS THEN MAGGIE STAYS ALIVE.
IF YOU KEEP ON HATING ME, THEN MAYBE I FIND MY WAY TO HER AGAIN. I HAVEN'T KNOWN YOUR MOTHER LONG--
--BUT SHE'LL PUT MAGGIE ON A SLAB TO KEEP THIS TOWN RUNNING. SHE'LL DO ANYTHING TO KEEP THIS TOWN RUNNING. I'VE BEEN CONVINCED OF THAT.
WHY ARE YOU DOING THIS TO ME?

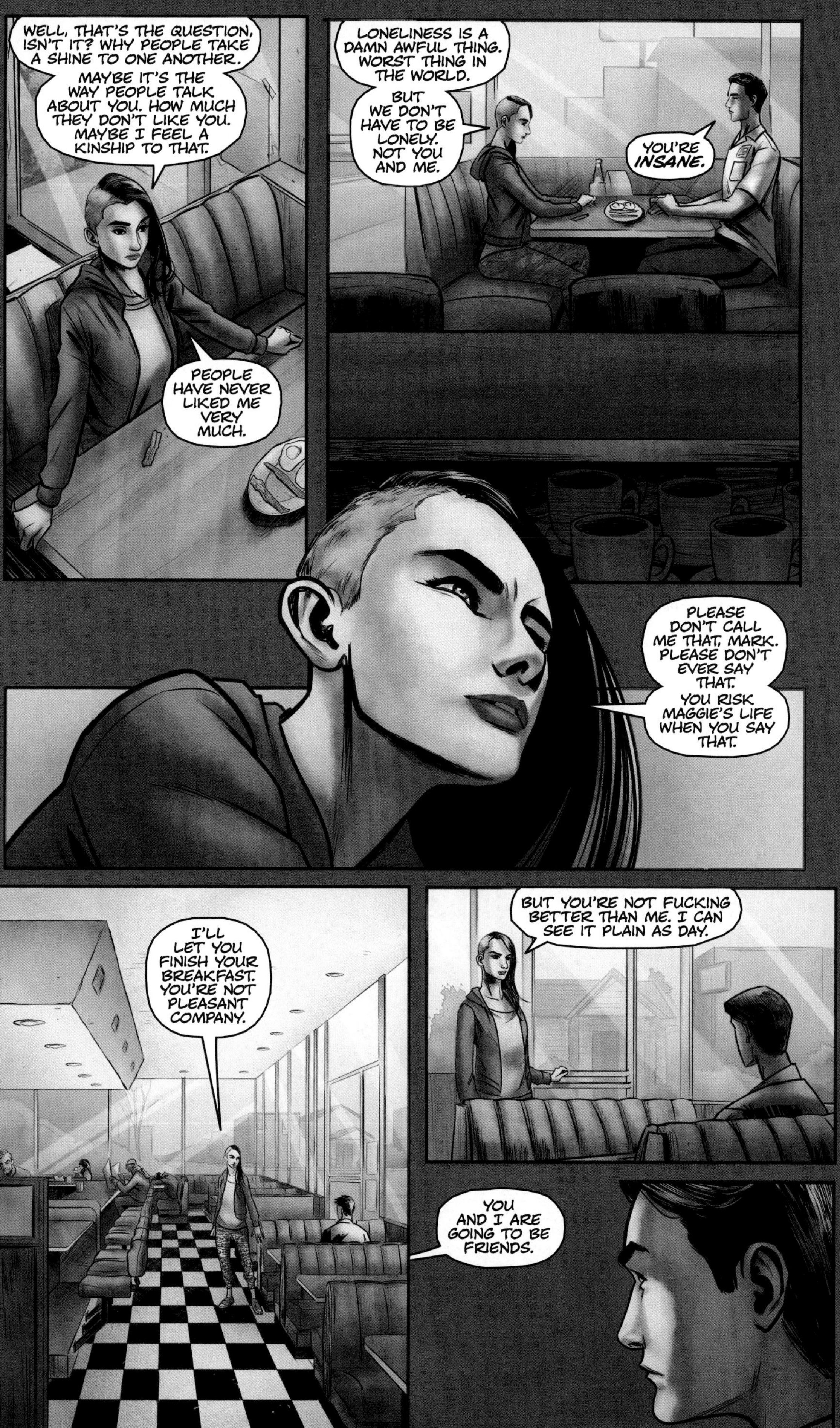
WELL, THAT'S THE QUESTION, ISN'T IT? WHY PEOPLE TAKE A SHINE TO ONE ANOTHER.
MAYBE IT'S THE WAY PEOPLE TALK ABOUT YOU. HOW MUCH THEY DON'T LIKE YOU. MAYBE I FEEL A KINSHIP TO THAT.
PEOPLE HAVE NEVER LIKED ME VERY MUCH.
LONELINESS IS A DAMN AWFUL THING. WORST THING IN THE WORLD.
BUT WE DON'T HAVE TO BE LONELY. NOT YOU AND ME.
YOU'RE INSANE.
PLEASE DON'T CALL ME THAT, MARK. PLEASE DON'T EVER SAY THAT.
YOU RISK MAGGIE'S LIFE WHEN YOU SAY THAT.
I'LL LET YOU FINISH YOUR BREAKFAST. YOU'RE NOT PLEASANT COMPANY.
BUT YOU'RE NOT FUCKING BETTER THAN ME. I CAN SEE IT PLAIN AS DAY.
YOU AND I ARE GOING TO BE FRIENDS.

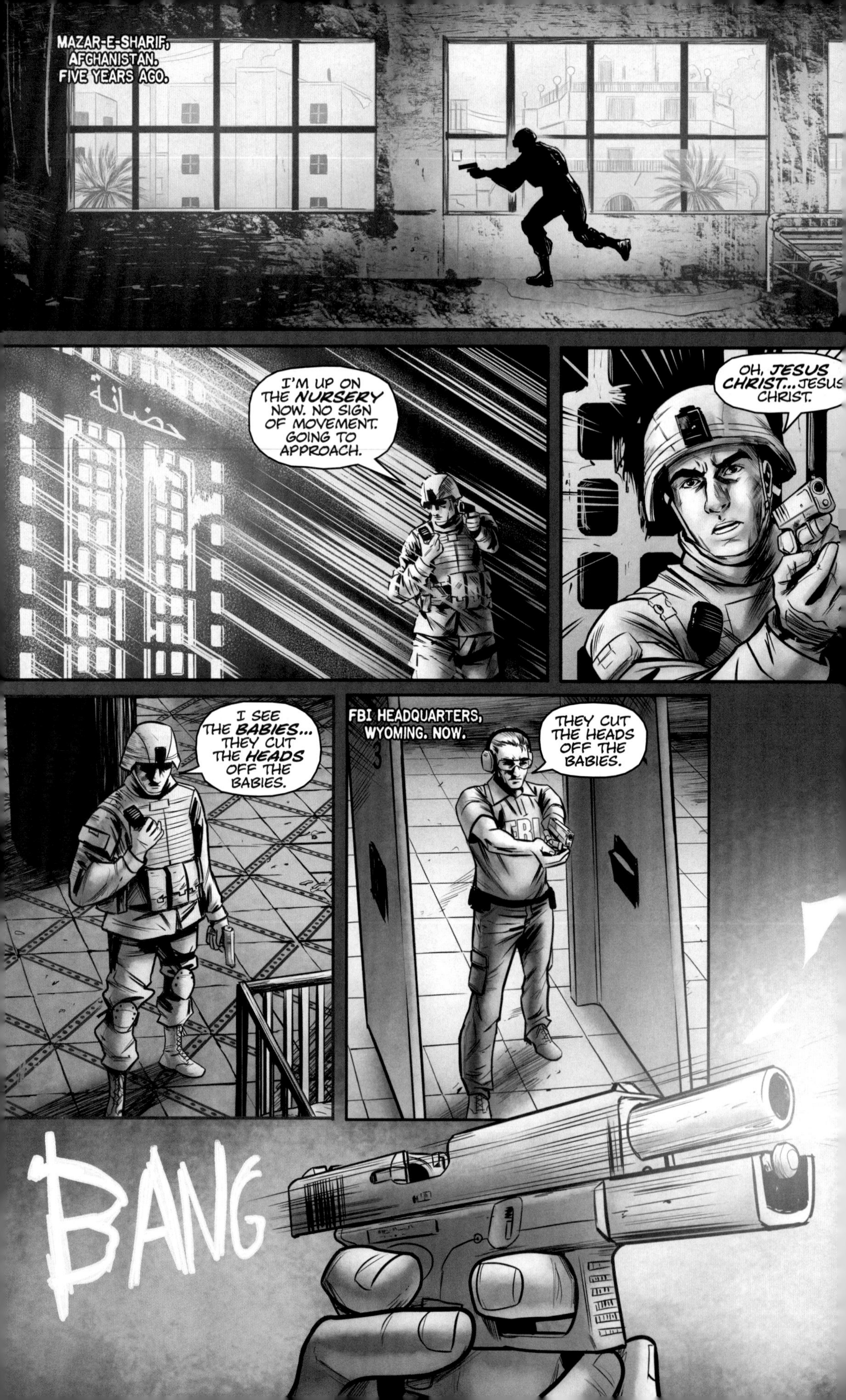
MAZAR-E-SHARIF, AFGHANISTAN. FIVE YEARS AGO.
حضانة
I'M UP ON THE NURSERY NOW. NO SIGN OF MOVEMENT. GOING TO APPROACH.
OH, JESUS CHRIST... JESUS CHRIST.
I SEE THE BABIES... THEY CUT THE HEADS OFF THE BABIES.
FBI HEADQUARTERS, WYOMING. NOW.
THEY CUT THE HEADS OFF THE BABIES.
FBI
BANG

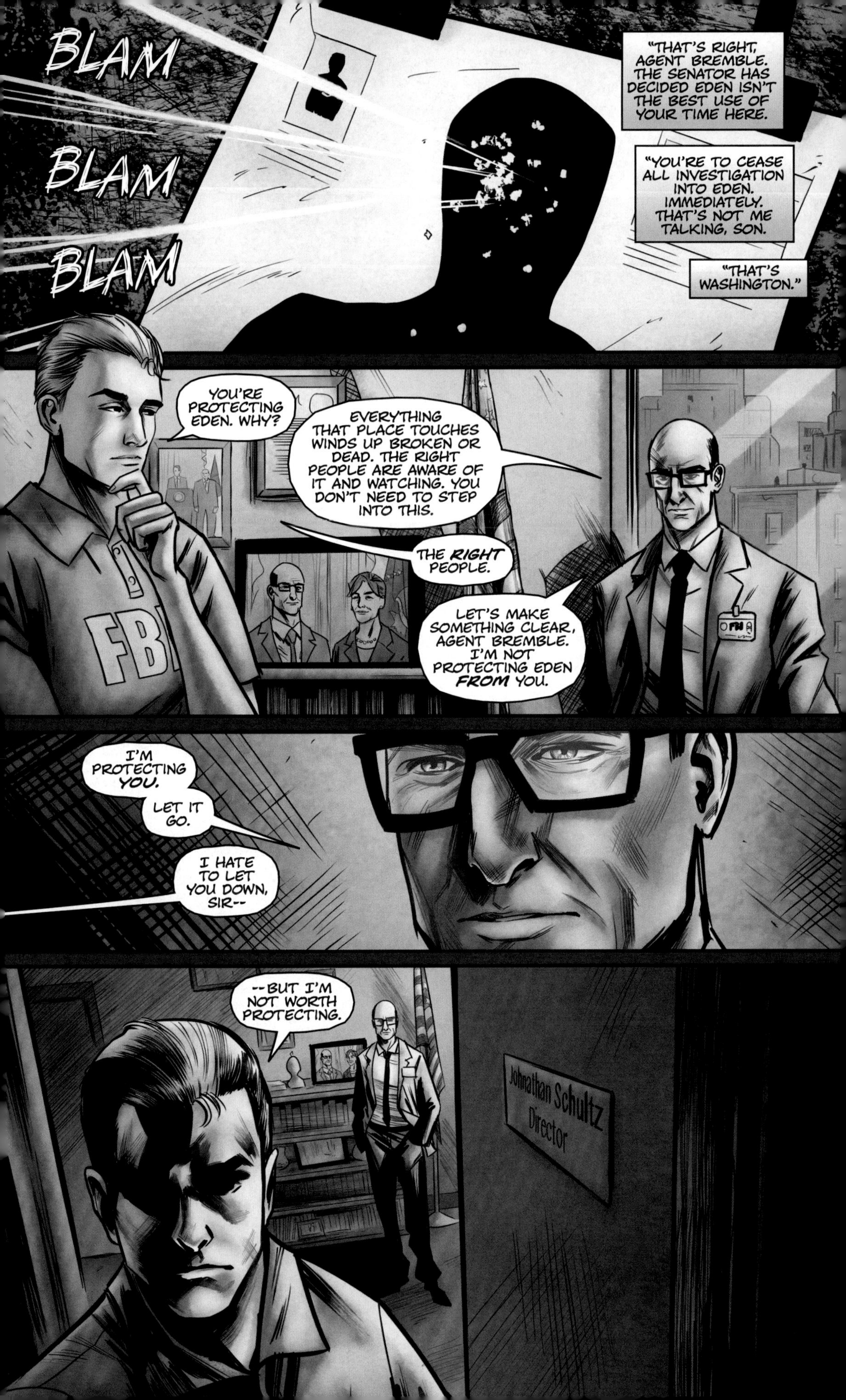
BLAM
BLAM
BLAM
"THAT'S RIGHT, AGENT BREMBLE. THE SENATOR HAS DECIDED EDEN ISN'T THE BEST USE OF YOUR TIME HERE.
"YOU'RE TO CEASE ALL INVESTIGATION INTO EDEN. IMMEDIATELY. THAT'S NOT ME TALKING, SON.
"THAT'S WASHINGTON."
YOU'RE PROTECTING EDEN. WHY?
EVERYTHING THAT PLACE TOUCHES WINDS UP BROKEN OR DEAD. THE RIGHT PEOPLE ARE AWARE OF IT AND WATCHING. YOU DON'T NEED TO STEP INTO THIS.
THE RIGHT PEOPLE.
LET'S MAKE SOMETHING CLEAR, AGENT BREMBLE. I'M NOT PROTECTING EDEN FROM YOU.
FBI
I'M PROTECTING YOU.
LET IT GO.
I HATE TO LET YOU DOWN, SIR--
--BUT I'M NOT WORTH PROTECTING.
Johnathan Schultz
Director

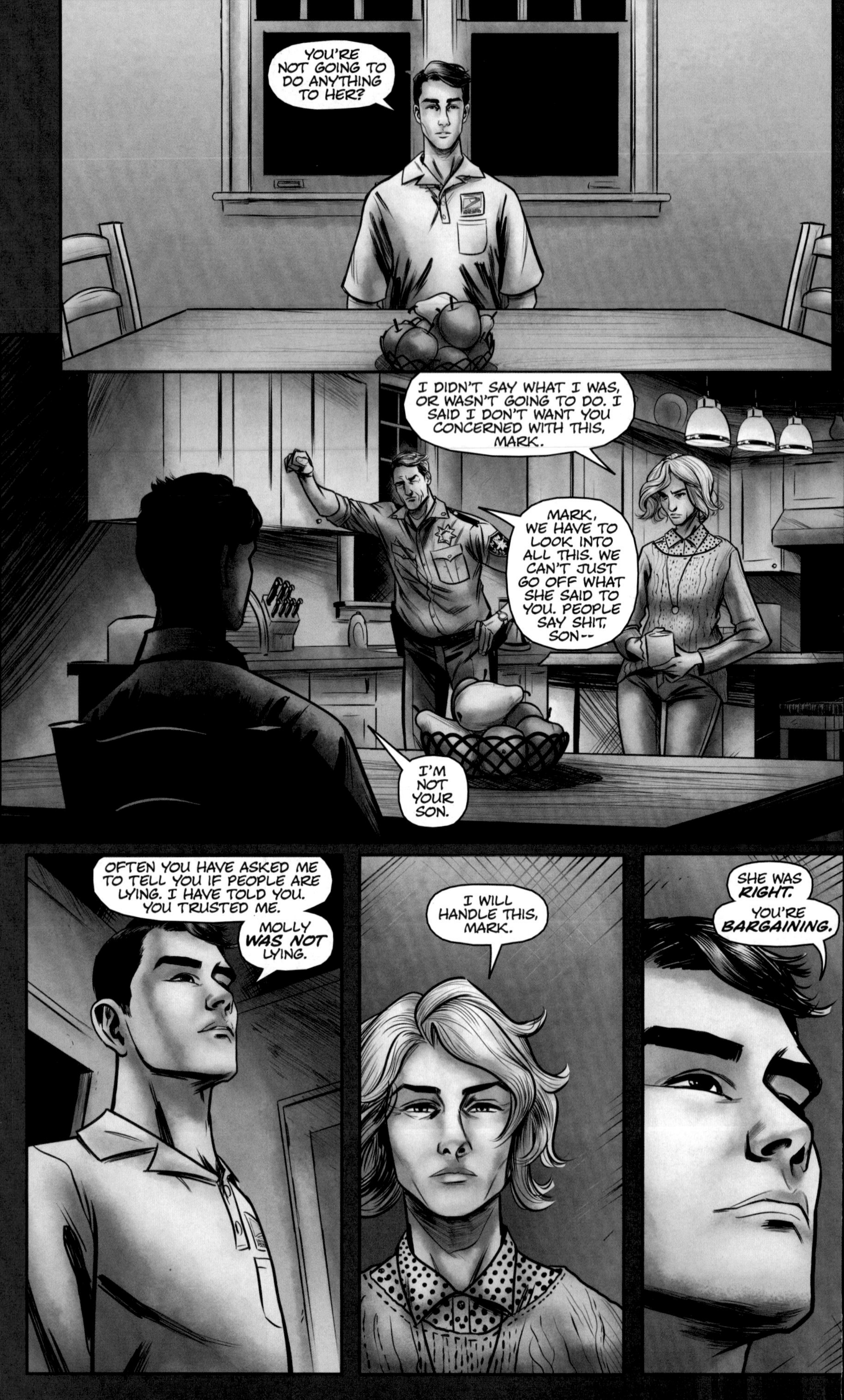
YOU'RE NOT GOING TO DO ANYTHING TO HER?
I DIDN'T SAY WHAT I WAS, OR WASN'T GOING TO DO. I SAID I DON'T WANT YOU CONCERNED WITH THIS, MARK.
MARK, WE HAVE TO LOOK INTO ALL THIS. WE CAN'T JUST GO OFF WHAT SHE SAID TO YOU. PEOPLE SAY SHIT, SON--
I'M NOT YOUR SON.
OFTEN YOU HAVE ASKED ME TO TELL YOU IF PEOPLE ARE LYING. I HAVE TOLD YOU. YOU TRUSTED ME.
MOLLY **WAS NOT** LYING.
I WILL HANDLE THIS, MARK.
SHE WAS **RIGHT.**
YOU'RE **BARGAINING.**

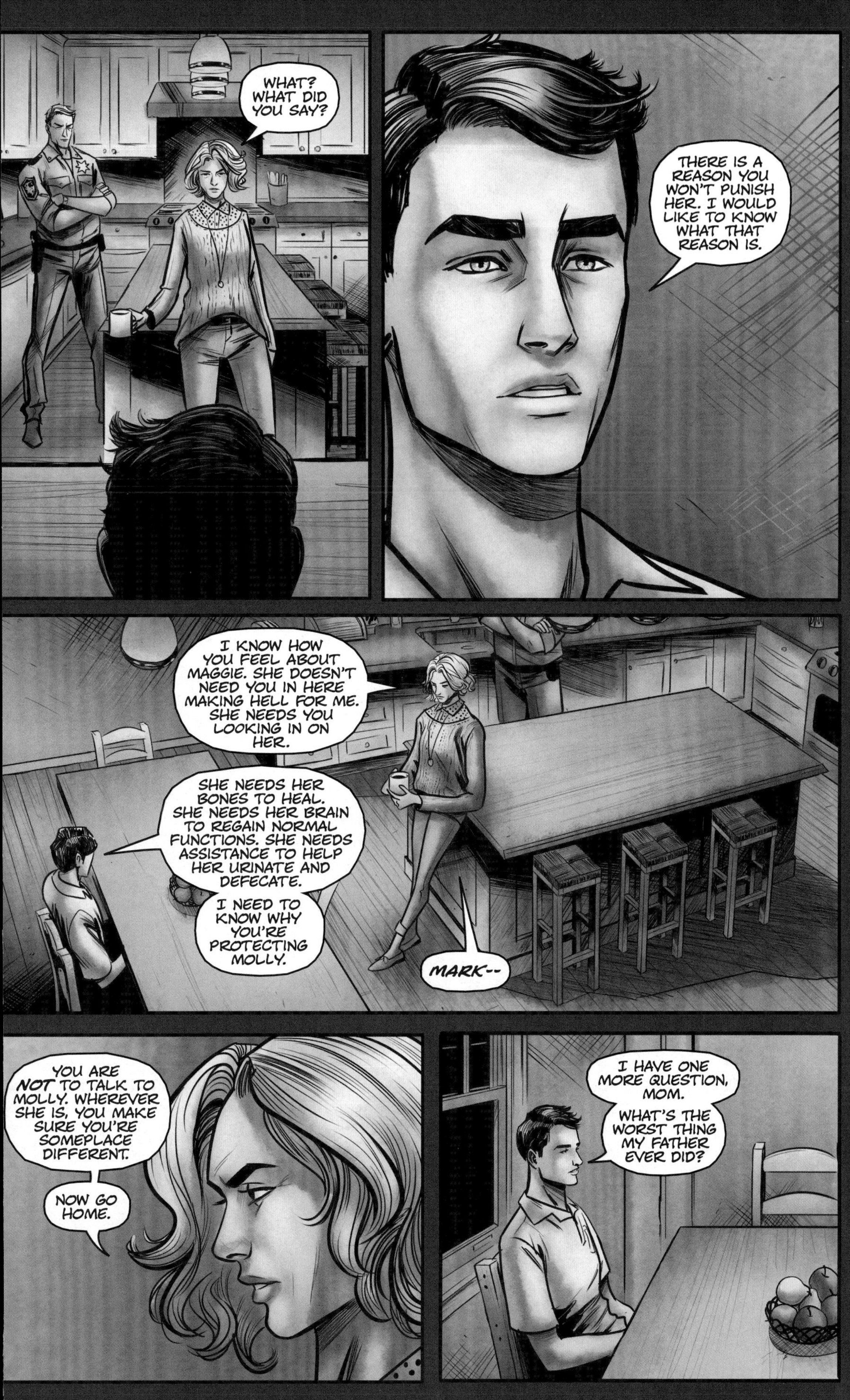
WHAT? WHAT DID YOU SAY?
THERE IS A REASON YOU WON'T PUNISH HER. I WOULD LIKE TO KNOW WHAT THAT REASON IS.
I KNOW HOW YOU FEEL ABOUT MAGGIE. SHE DOESN'T NEED YOU IN HERE MAKING HELL FOR ME. SHE NEEDS YOU LOOKING IN ON HER.
SHE NEEDS HER BONES TO HEAL. SHE NEEDS HER BRAIN TO REGAIN NORMAL FUNCTIONS. SHE NEEDS ASSISTANCE TO HELP HER URINATE AND DEFECATE.
I NEED TO KNOW WHY YOU'RE PROTECTING MOLLY.
MARK--
YOU ARE NOT TO TALK TO MOLLY. WHEREVER SHE IS, YOU MAKE SURE YOU'RE SOMEPLACE DIFFERENT.
NOW GO HOME.
I HAVE ONE MORE QUESTION, MOM.
WHAT'S THE WORST THING MY FATHER EVER DID?

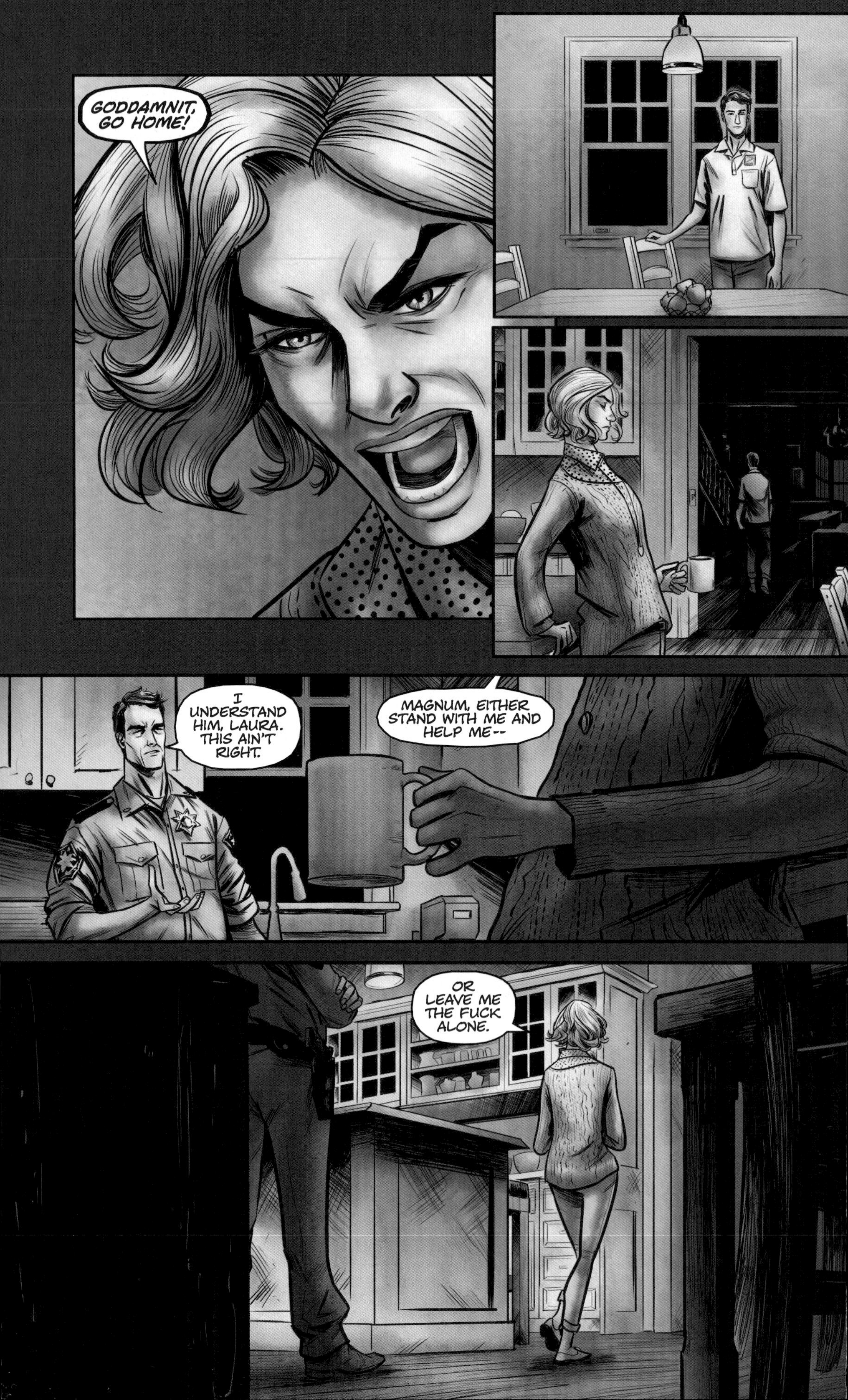
GODDAMNIT, GO HOME!
I UNDERSTAND HIM, LAURA. THIS AIN'T RIGHT.
MAGNUM, EITHER STAND WITH ME AND HELP ME--
OR LEAVE ME THE FUCK ALONE.

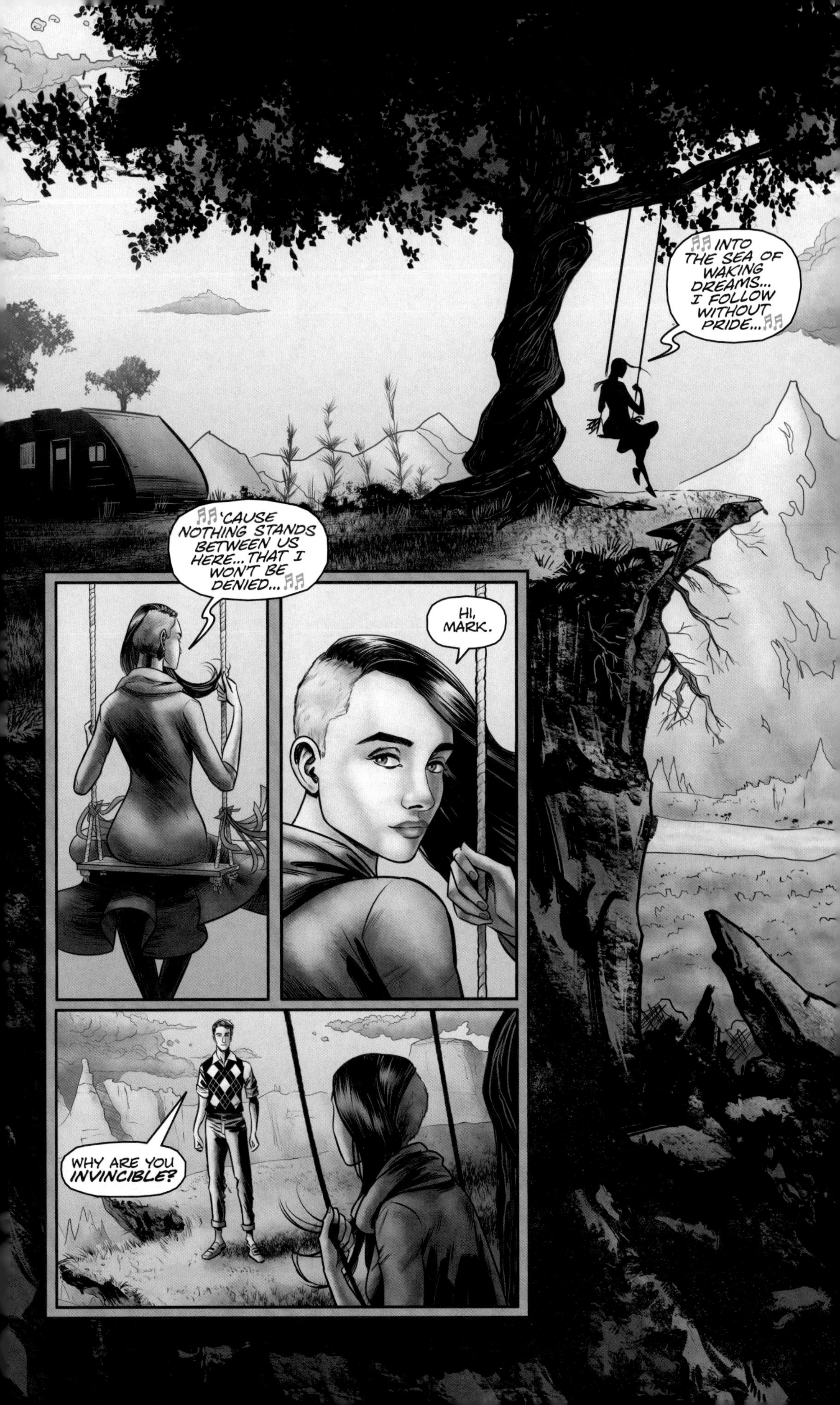
♬ INTO THE SEA OF WAKING DREAMS... I FOLLOW WITHOUT PRIDE... ♬
♬ 'CAUSE NOTHING STANDS BETWEEN US HERE... THAT I WON'T BE DENIED... ♬
HI, MARK.
WHY ARE YOU INVINCIBLE?

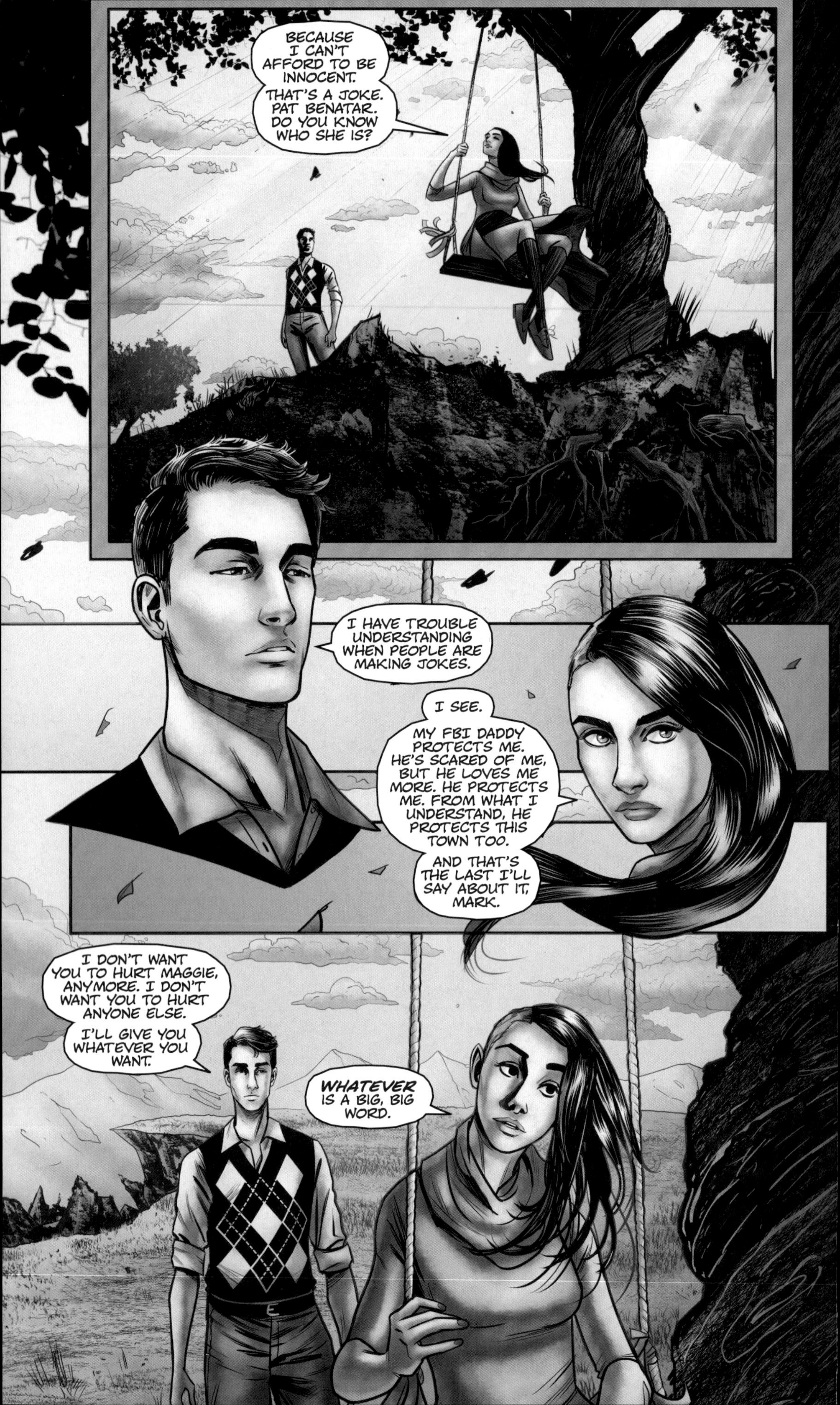
BECAUSE I CAN'T AFFORD TO BE INNOCENT.
THAT'S A JOKE. PAT BENATAR. DO YOU KNOW WHO SHE IS?
I HAVE TROUBLE UNDERSTANDING WHEN PEOPLE ARE MAKING JOKES.
I SEE.
MY FBI DADDY PROTECTS ME. HE'S SCARED OF ME, BUT HE LOVES ME MORE. HE PROTECTS ME. FROM WHAT I UNDERSTAND, HE PROTECTS THIS TOWN TOO.
AND THAT'S THE LAST I'LL SAY ABOUT IT, MARK.
I DON'T WANT YOU TO HURT MAGGIE, ANYMORE. I DON'T WANT YOU TO HURT ANYONE ELSE.
I'LL GIVE YOU WHATEVER YOU WANT.
*WHATEVER* IS A BIG, BIG WORD.

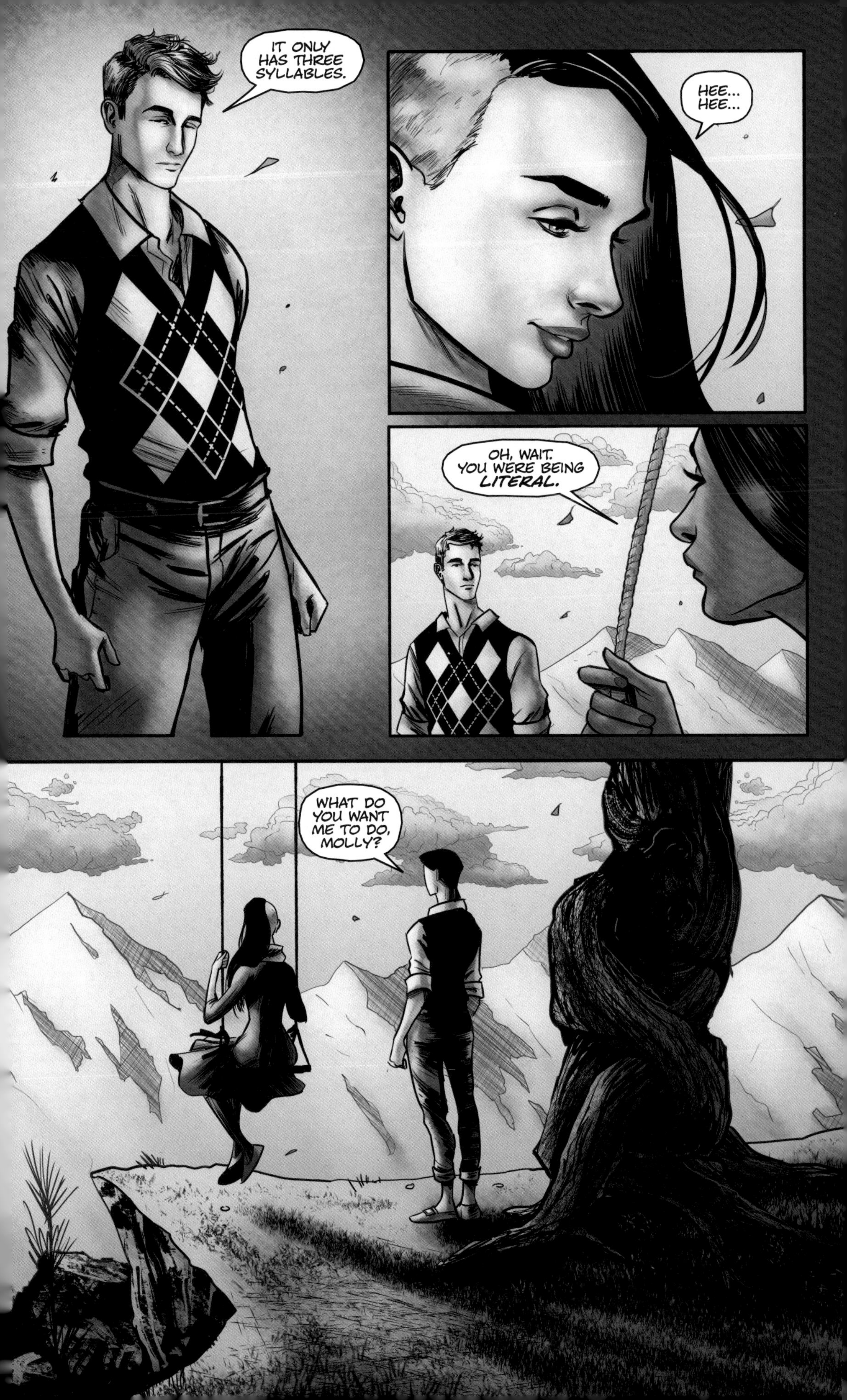
IT ONLY HAS THREE SYLLABLES.
HEE... HEE...
OH, WAIT. YOU WERE BEING *LITERAL.*
WHAT DO YOU WANT ME TO DO, MOLLY?

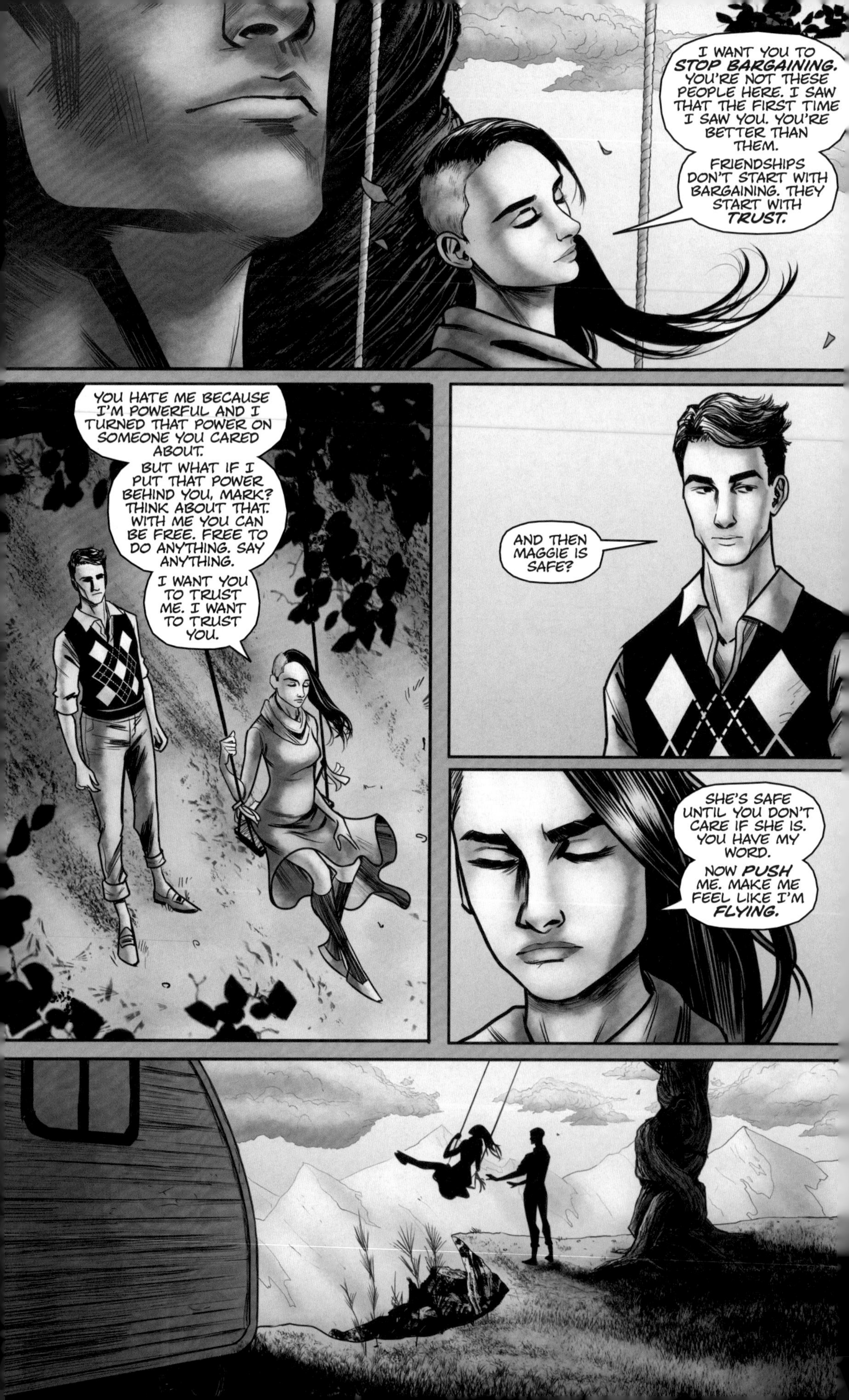
I WANT YOU TO STOP BARGAINING. YOU'RE NOT THESE PEOPLE HERE. I SAW THAT THE FIRST TIME I SAW YOU. YOU'RE BETTER THAN THEM.
FRIENDSHIPS DON'T START WITH BARGAINING. THEY START WITH TRUST.
YOU HATE ME BECAUSE I'M POWERFUL AND I TURNED THAT POWER ON SOMEONE YOU CARED ABOUT.
BUT WHAT IF I PUT THAT POWER BEHIND YOU, MARK? THINK ABOUT THAT. WITH ME YOU CAN BE FREE. FREE TO DO ANYTHING. SAY ANYTHING.
I WANT YOU TO TRUST ME. I WANT TO TRUST YOU.
AND THEN MAGGIE IS SAFE?
SHE'S SAFE UNTIL YOU DON'T CARE IF SHE IS. YOU HAVE MY WORD.
NOW PUSH ME. MAKE ME FEEL LIKE I'M FLYING.

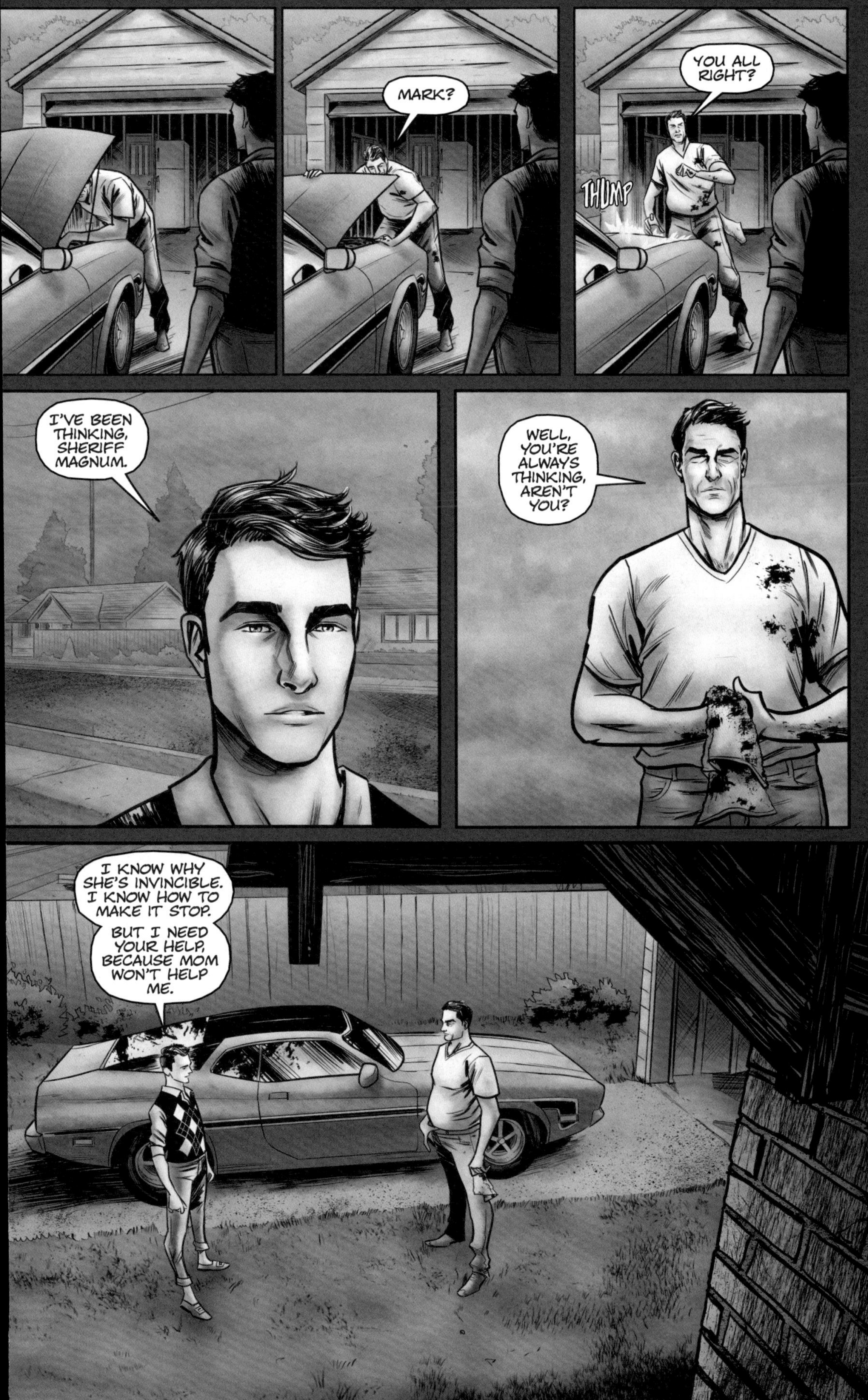
MARK?
YOU ALL RIGHT?
THUMP
I'VE BEEN THINKING, SHERIFF MAGNUM.
WELL, YOU'RE ALWAYS THINKING, AREN'T YOU?
I KNOW WHY SHE'S INVINCIBLE. I KNOW HOW TO MAKE IT STOP.
BUT I NEED YOUR HELP, BECAUSE MOM WON'T HELP ME.

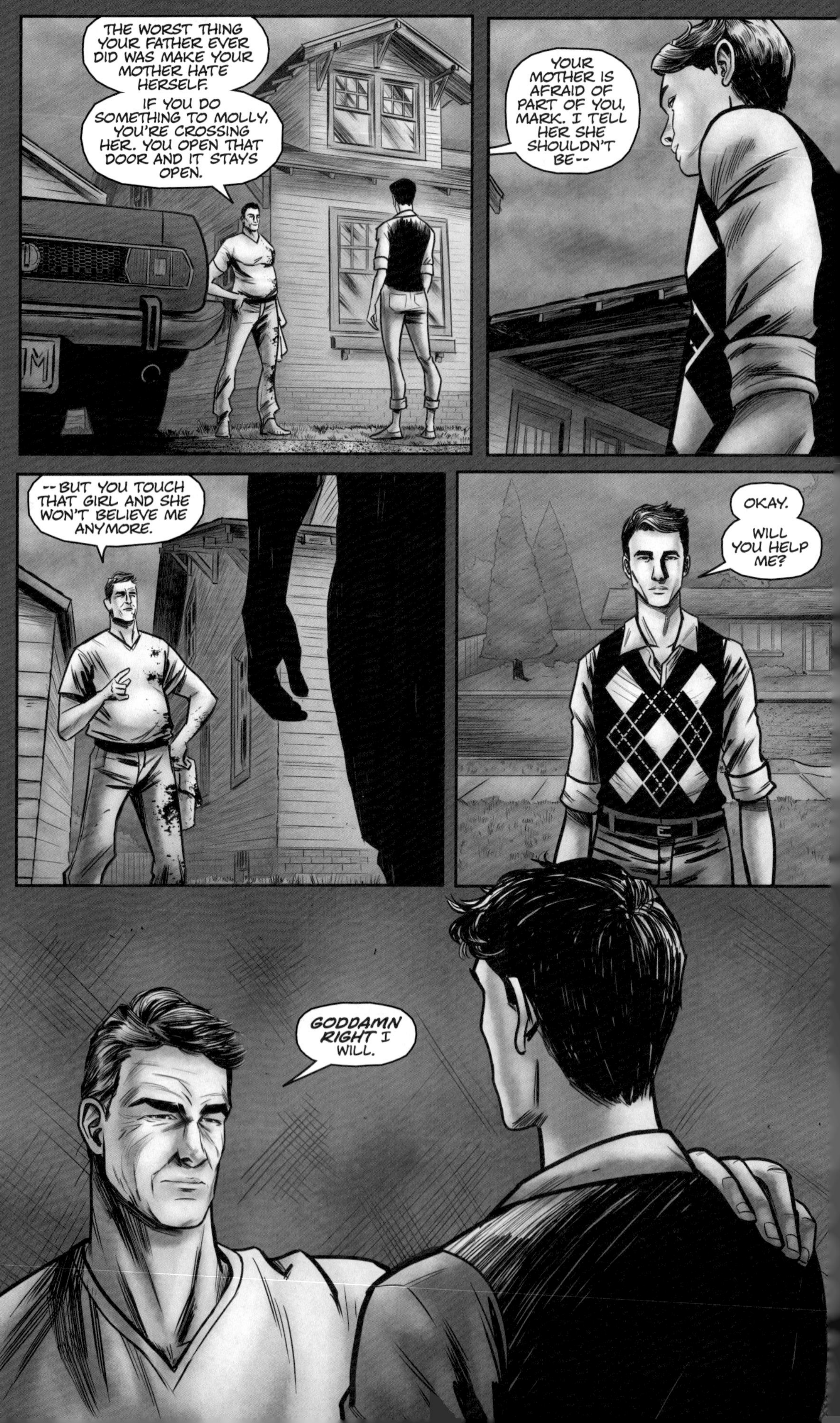
THE WORST THING YOUR FATHER EVER DID WAS MAKE YOUR MOTHER HATE HERSELF.
IF YOU DO SOMETHING TO MOLLY, YOU'RE CROSSING HER. YOU OPEN THAT DOOR AND IT STAYS OPEN.
YOUR MOTHER IS AFRAID OF PART OF YOU, MARK. I TELL HER SHE SHOULDN'T BE--
--BUT YOU TOUCH THAT GIRL AND SHE WON'T BELIEVE ME ANYMORE.
OKAY.
WILL YOU HELP ME?
GODDAMN RIGHT I WILL.

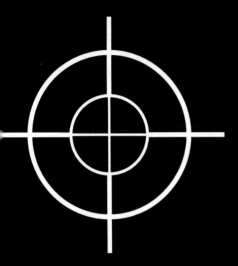

# CHAPTER 12

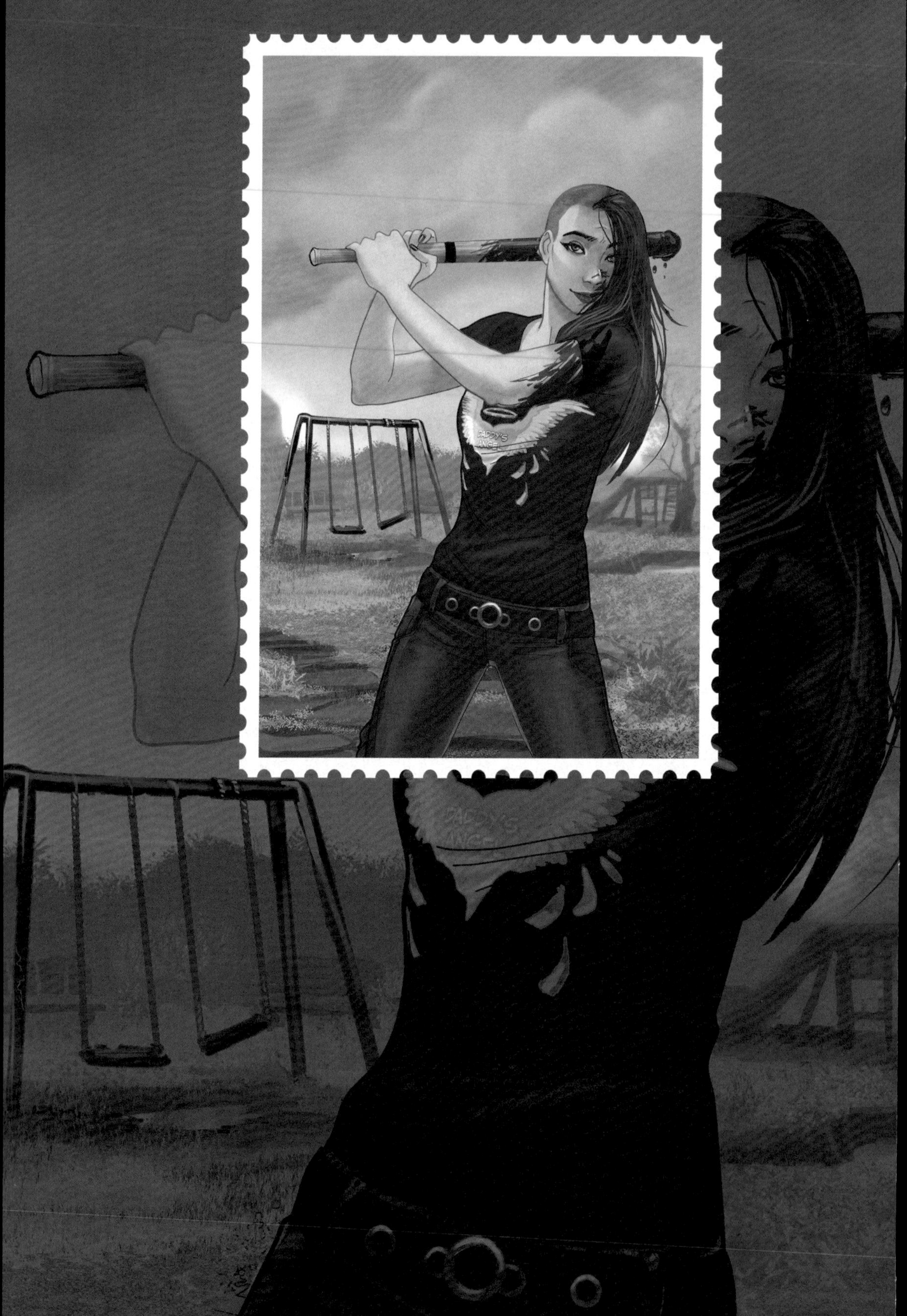
DADDY'S ANGEL

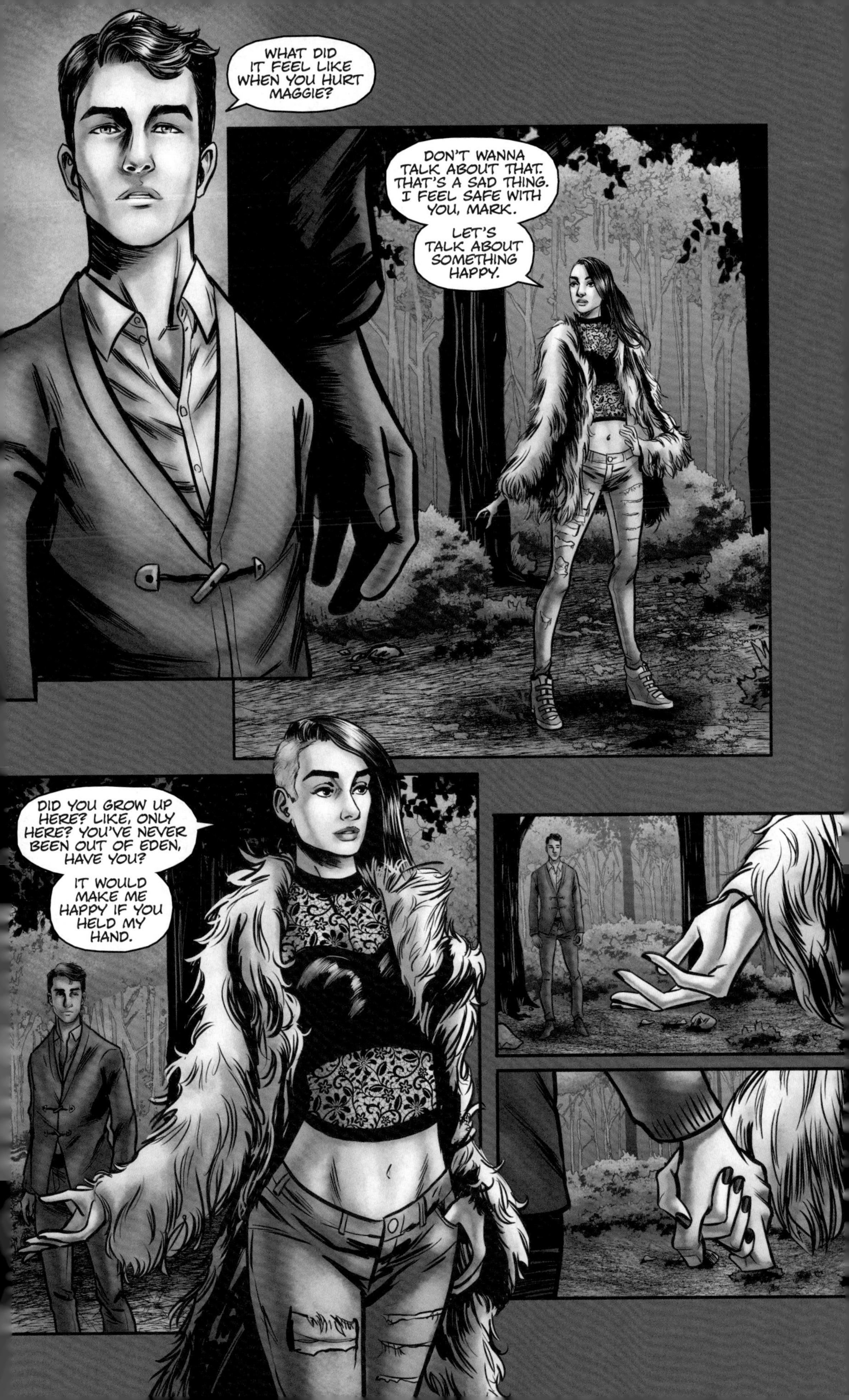
WHAT DID IT FEEL LIKE WHEN YOU HURT MAGGIE?
DON'T WANNA TALK ABOUT THAT. THAT'S A SAD THING. I FEEL SAFE WITH YOU, MARK.
LET'S TALK ABOUT SOMETHING HAPPY.
DID YOU GROW UP HERE? LIKE, ONLY HERE? YOU'VE NEVER BEEN OUT OF EDEN, HAVE YOU?
IT WOULD MAKE ME HAPPY IF YOU HELD MY HAND.

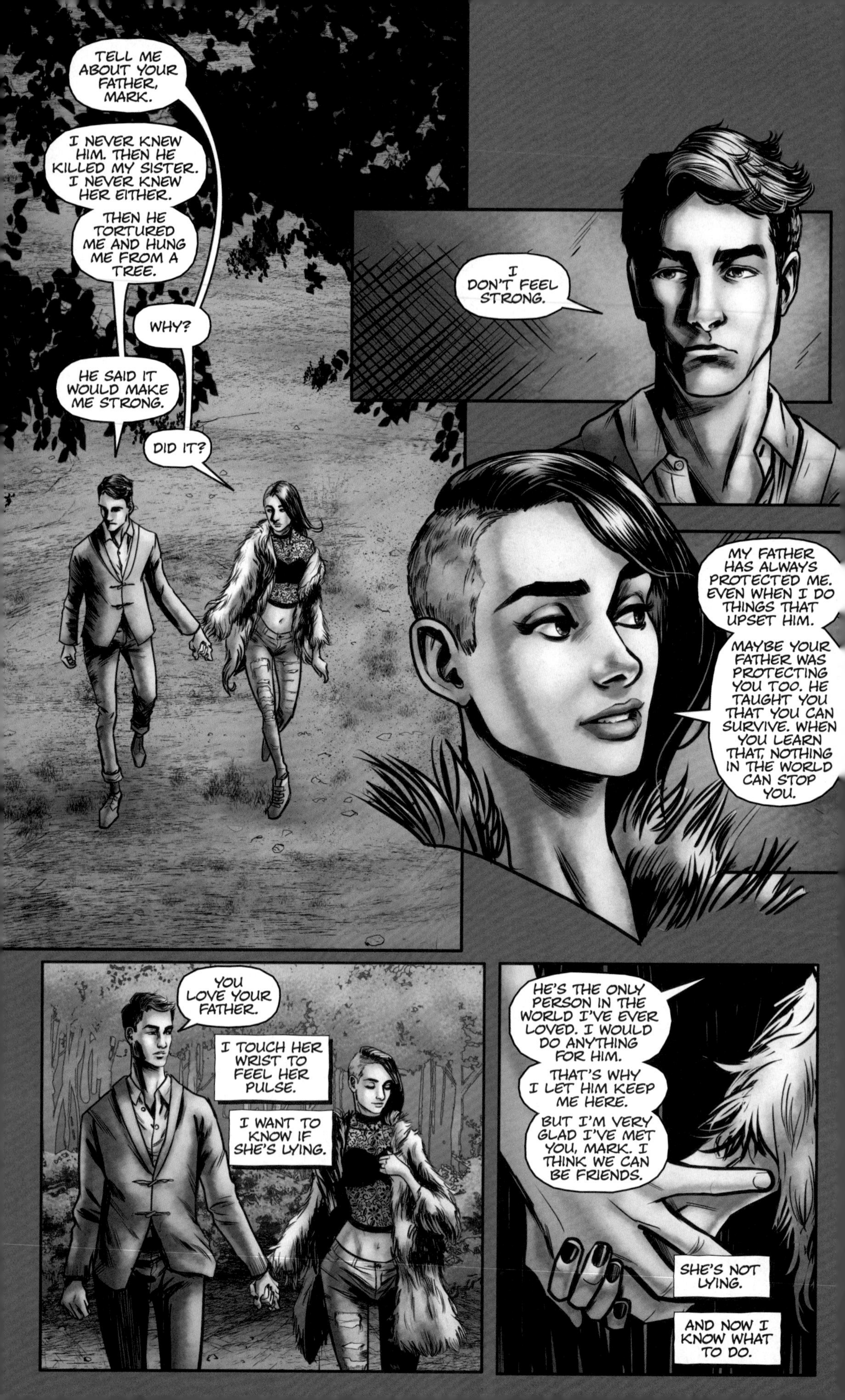
TELL ME ABOUT YOUR FATHER, MARK.
I NEVER KNEW HIM. THEN HE KILLED MY SISTER. I NEVER KNEW HER EITHER.
THEN HE TORTURED ME AND HUNG ME FROM A TREE.
WHY?
HE SAID IT WOULD MAKE ME STRONG.
DID IT?
I DON'T FEEL STRONG.
MY FATHER HAS ALWAYS PROTECTED ME. EVEN WHEN I DO THINGS THAT UPSET HIM.
MAYBE YOUR FATHER WAS PROTECTING YOU TOO. HE TAUGHT YOU THAT YOU CAN SURVIVE. WHEN YOU LEARN THAT, NOTHING IN THE WORLD CAN STOP YOU.
YOU LOVE YOUR FATHER.
I TOUCH HER WRIST TO FEEL HER PULSE.
I WANT TO KNOW IF SHE'S LYING.
HE'S THE ONLY PERSON IN THE WORLD I'VE EVER LOVED. I WOULD DO ANYTHING FOR HIM.
THAT'S WHY I LET HIM KEEP ME HERE.
BUT I'M VERY GLAD I'VE MET YOU, MARK. I THINK WE CAN BE FRIENDS.
SHE'S NOT LYING.
AND NOW I KNOW WHAT TO DO.

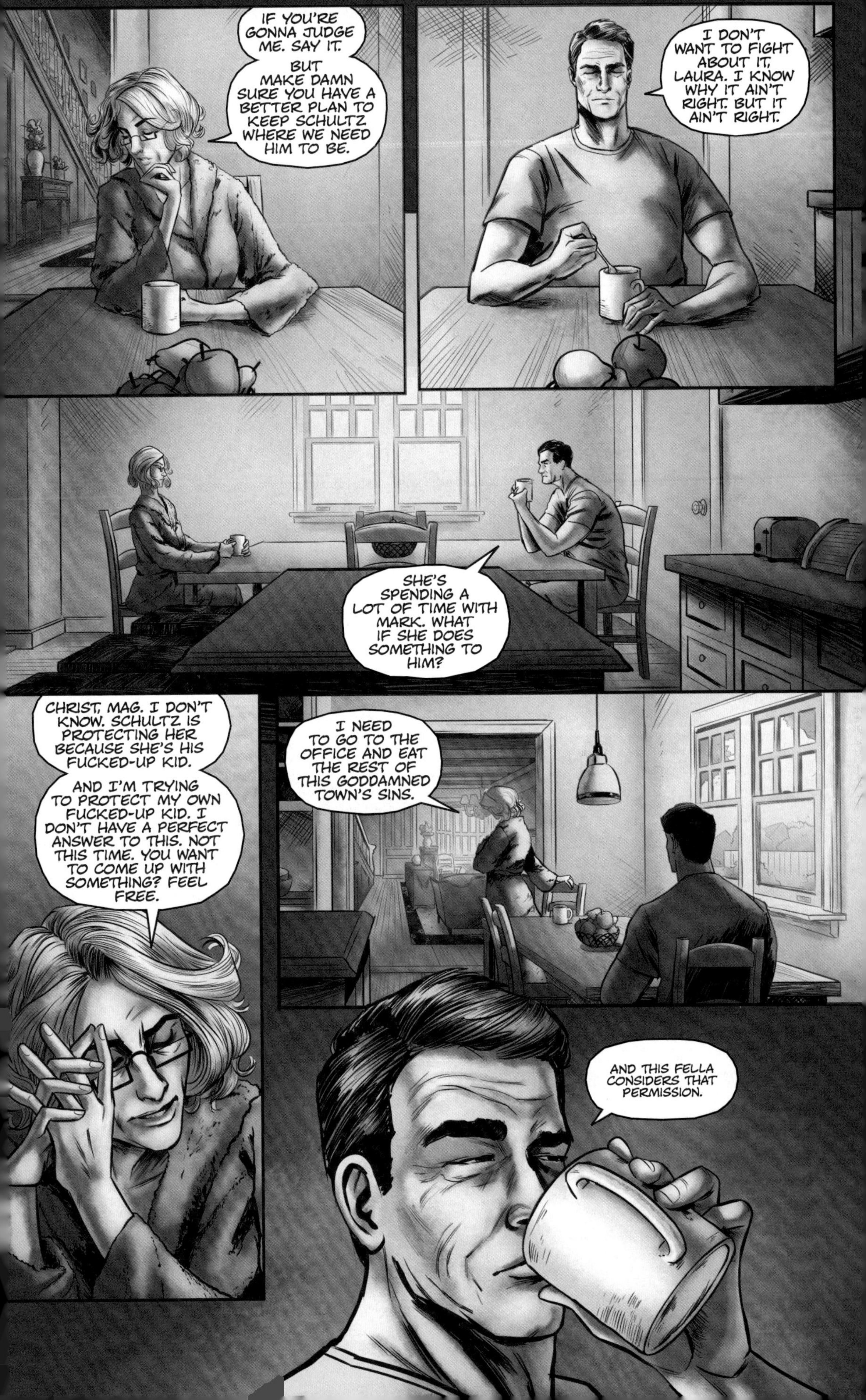
IF YOU'RE GONNA JUDGE ME. SAY IT.
BUT MAKE DAMN SURE YOU HAVE A BETTER PLAN TO KEEP SCHULTZ WHERE WE NEED HIM TO BE.
I DON'T WANT TO FIGHT ABOUT IT, LAURA. I KNOW WHY IT AIN'T RIGHT. BUT IT AIN'T RIGHT.
SHE'S SPENDING A LOT OF TIME WITH MARK. WHAT IF SHE DOES SOMETHING TO HIM?
CHRIST, MAG. I DON'T KNOW. SCHULTZ IS PROTECTING HER BECAUSE SHE'S HIS FUCKED-UP KID.
AND I'M TRYING TO PROTECT MY OWN FUCKED-UP KID. I DON'T HAVE A PERFECT ANSWER TO THIS. NOT THIS TIME. YOU WANT TO COME UP WITH SOMETHING? FEEL FREE.
I NEED TO GO TO THE OFFICE AND EAT THE REST OF THIS GODDAMNED TOWN'S SINS.
AND THIS FELLA CONSIDERS THAT PERMISSION.

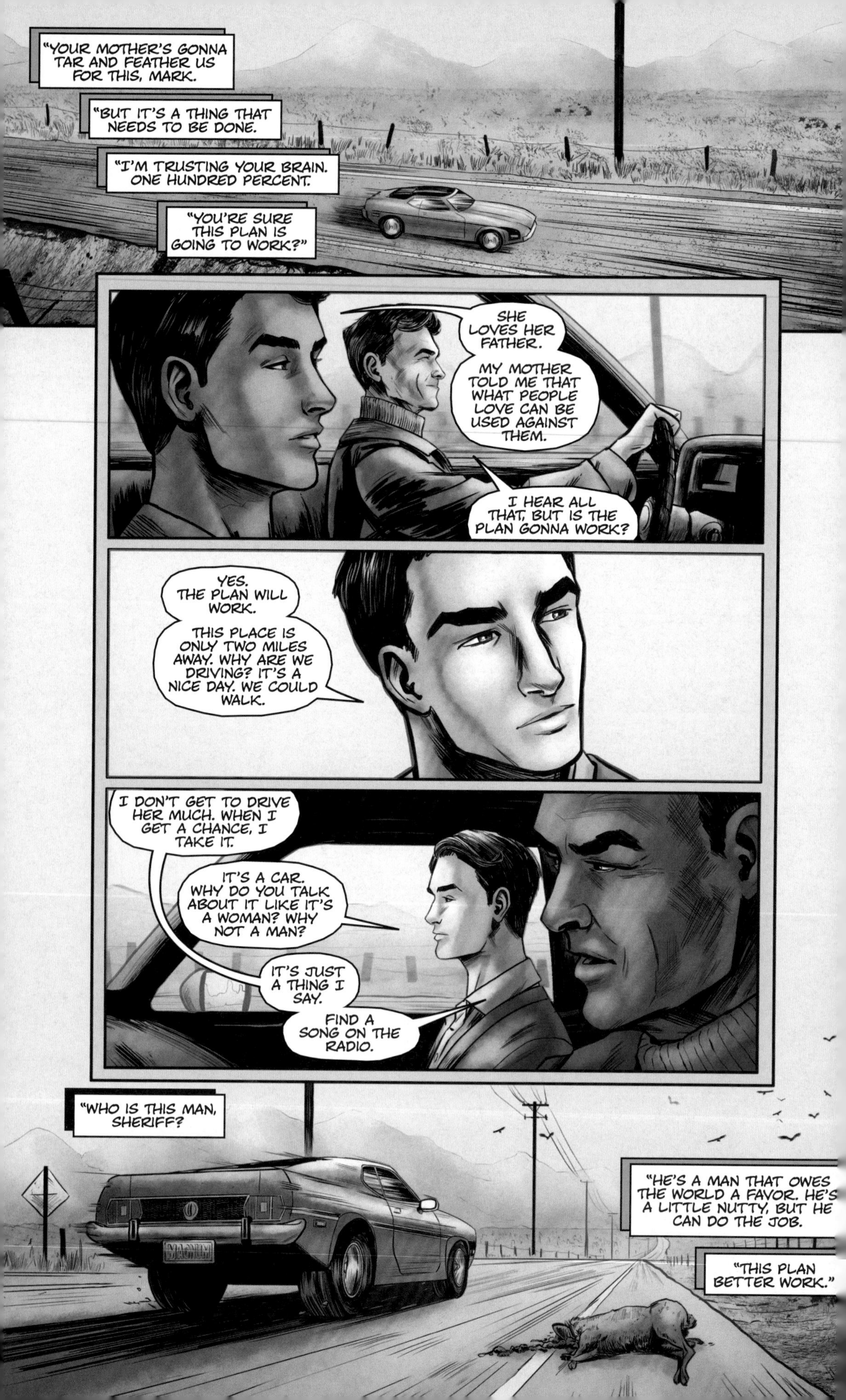
"YOUR MOTHER'S GONNA TAR AND FEATHER US FOR THIS, MARK.
"BUT IT'S A THING THAT NEEDS TO BE DONE.
"I'M TRUSTING YOUR BRAIN. ONE HUNDRED PERCENT.
"YOU'RE SURE THIS PLAN IS GOING TO WORK?"
SHE LOVES HER FATHER.
MY MOTHER TOLD ME THAT WHAT PEOPLE LOVE CAN BE USED AGAINST THEM.
I HEAR ALL THAT, BUT IS THE PLAN GONNA WORK?
YES. THE PLAN WILL WORK.
THIS PLACE IS ONLY TWO MILES AWAY. WHY ARE WE DRIVING? IT'S A NICE DAY. WE COULD WALK.
I DON'T GET TO DRIVE HER MUCH. WHEN I GET A CHANCE, I TAKE IT.
IT'S A CAR. WHY DO YOU TALK ABOUT IT LIKE IT'S A WOMAN? WHY NOT A MAN?
IT'S JUST A THING I SAY.
FIND A SONG ON THE RADIO.
"WHO IS THIS MAN, SHERIFF?
"HE'S A MAN THAT OWES THE WORLD A FAVOR. HE'S A LITTLE NUTTY, BUT HE CAN DO THE JOB.
"THIS PLAN BETTER WORK."

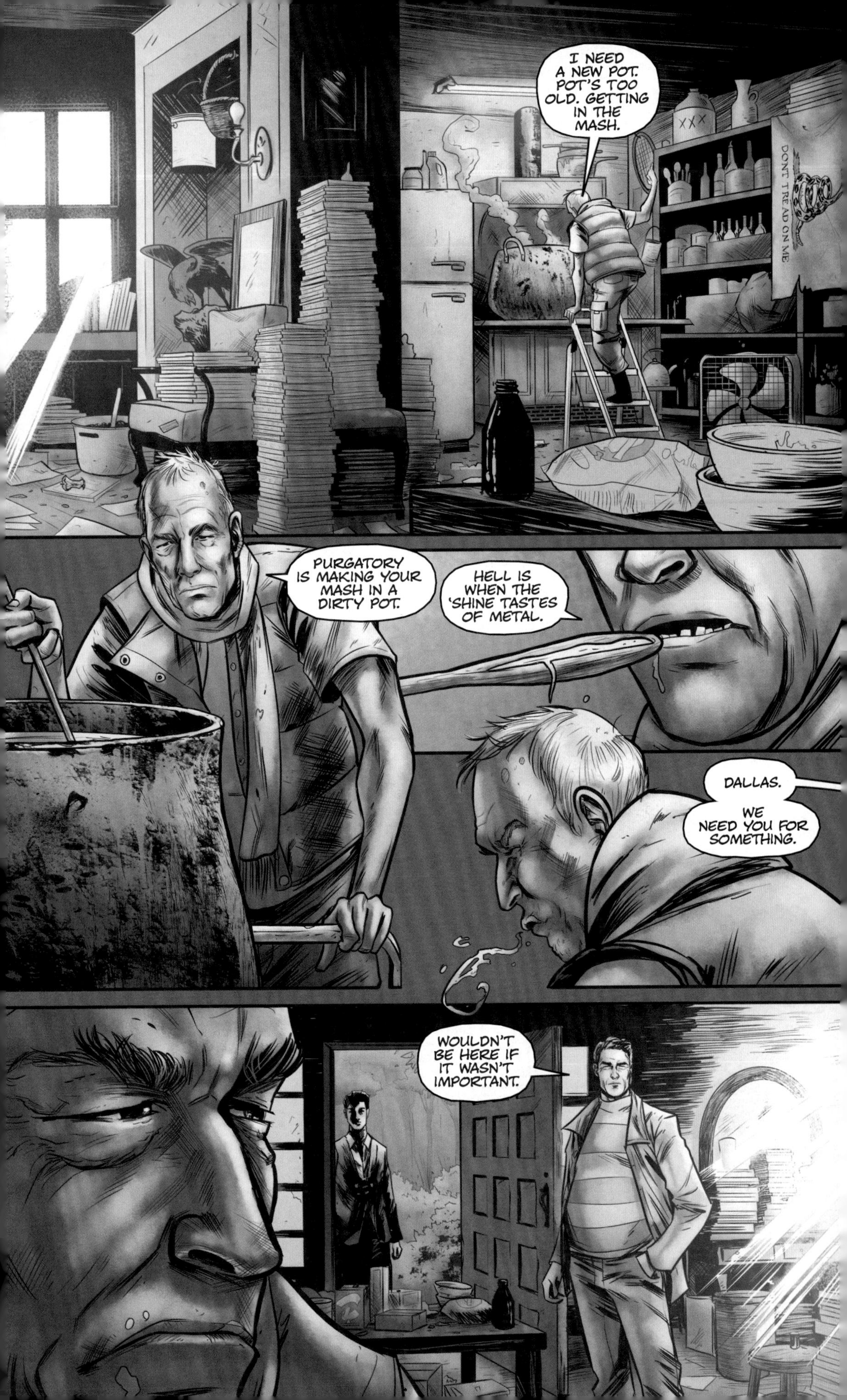
I NEED A NEW POT. POT'S TOO OLD. GETTING IN THE MASH.
DONT TREAD ON ME
PURGATORY IS MAKING YOUR MASH IN A DIRTY POT.
HELL IS WHEN THE 'SHINE TASTES OF METAL.
DALLAS.
WE NEED YOU FOR SOMETHING.
WOULDN'T BE HERE IF IT WASN'T IMPORTANT.

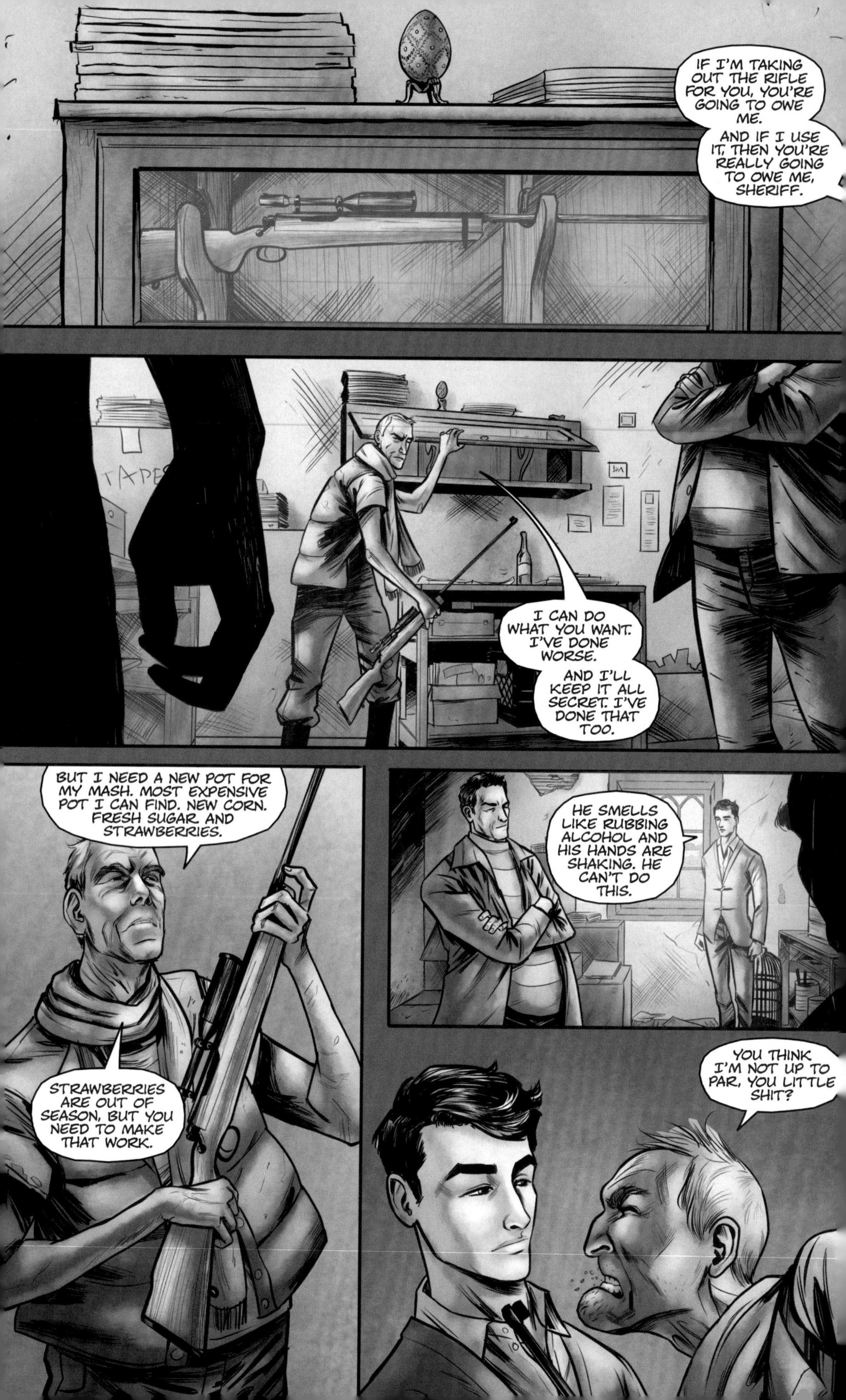
IF I'M TAKING OUT THE RIFLE FOR YOU, YOU'RE GOING TO OWE ME.
AND IF I USE IT, THEN YOU'RE REALLY GOING TO OWE ME, SHERIFF.
TAPES
I CAN DO WHAT YOU WANT. I'VE DONE WORSE.
AND I'LL KEEP IT ALL SECRET. I'VE DONE THAT TOO.
BUT I NEED A NEW POT FOR MY MASH. MOST EXPENSIVE POT I CAN FIND. NEW CORN. FRESH SUGAR AND STRAWBERRIES.
STRAWBERRIES ARE OUT OF SEASON, BUT YOU NEED TO MAKE THAT WORK.
HE SMELLS LIKE RUBBING ALCOHOL AND HIS HANDS ARE SHAKING. HE CAN'T DO THIS.
YOU THINK I'M NOT UP TO PAR, YOU LITTLE SHIT?

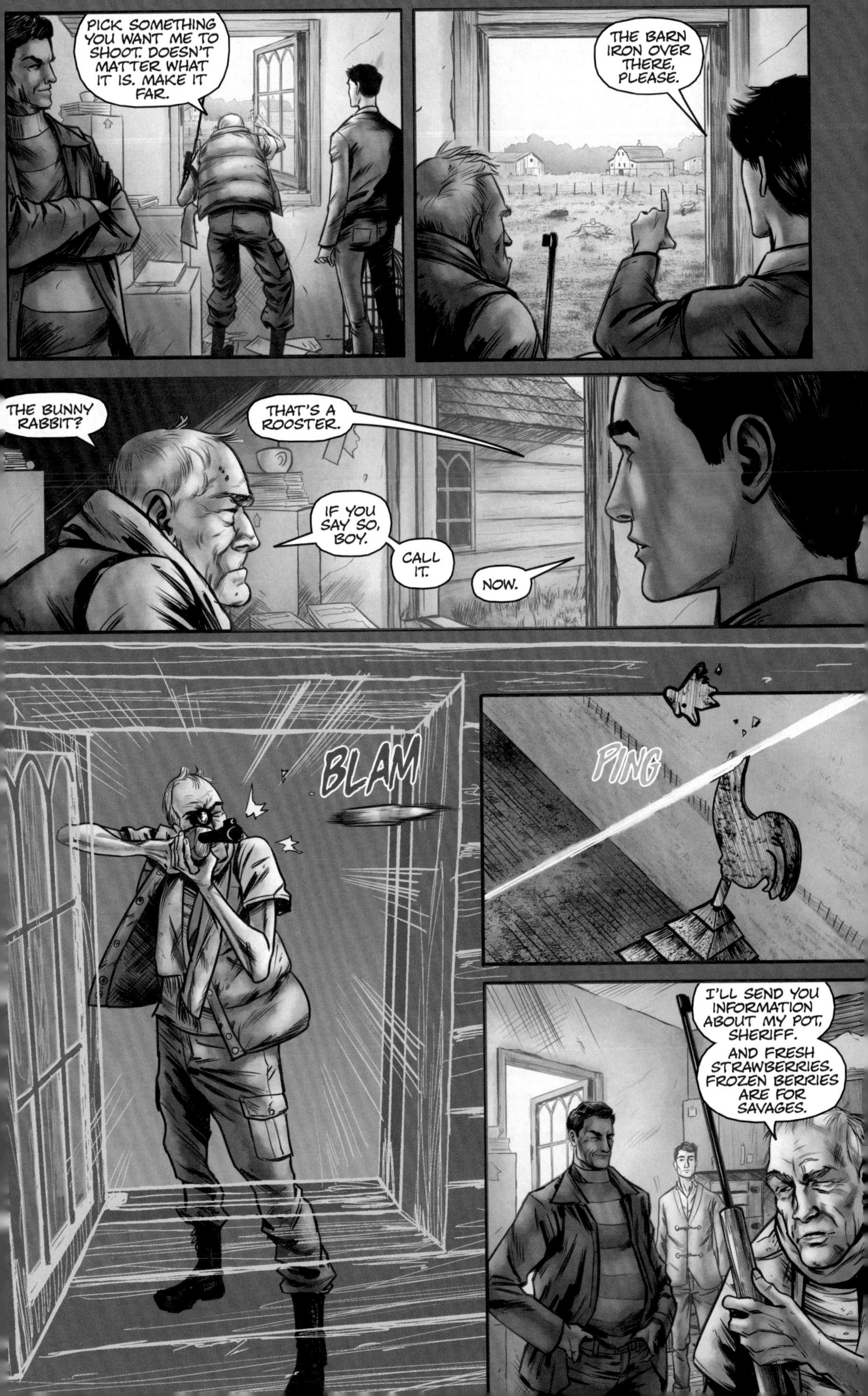
PICK SOMETHING YOU WANT ME TO SHOOT. DOESN'T MATTER WHAT IT IS. MAKE IT FAR.
THE BARN IRON OVER THERE, PLEASE.
THE BUNNY RABBIT?
THAT'S A ROOSTER.
IF YOU SAY SO, BOY.
CALL IT.
NOW.
BLAM
PING
I'LL SEND YOU INFORMATION ABOUT MY POT, SHERIFF.
AND FRESH STRAWBERRIES. FROZEN BERRIES ARE FOR SAVAGES.

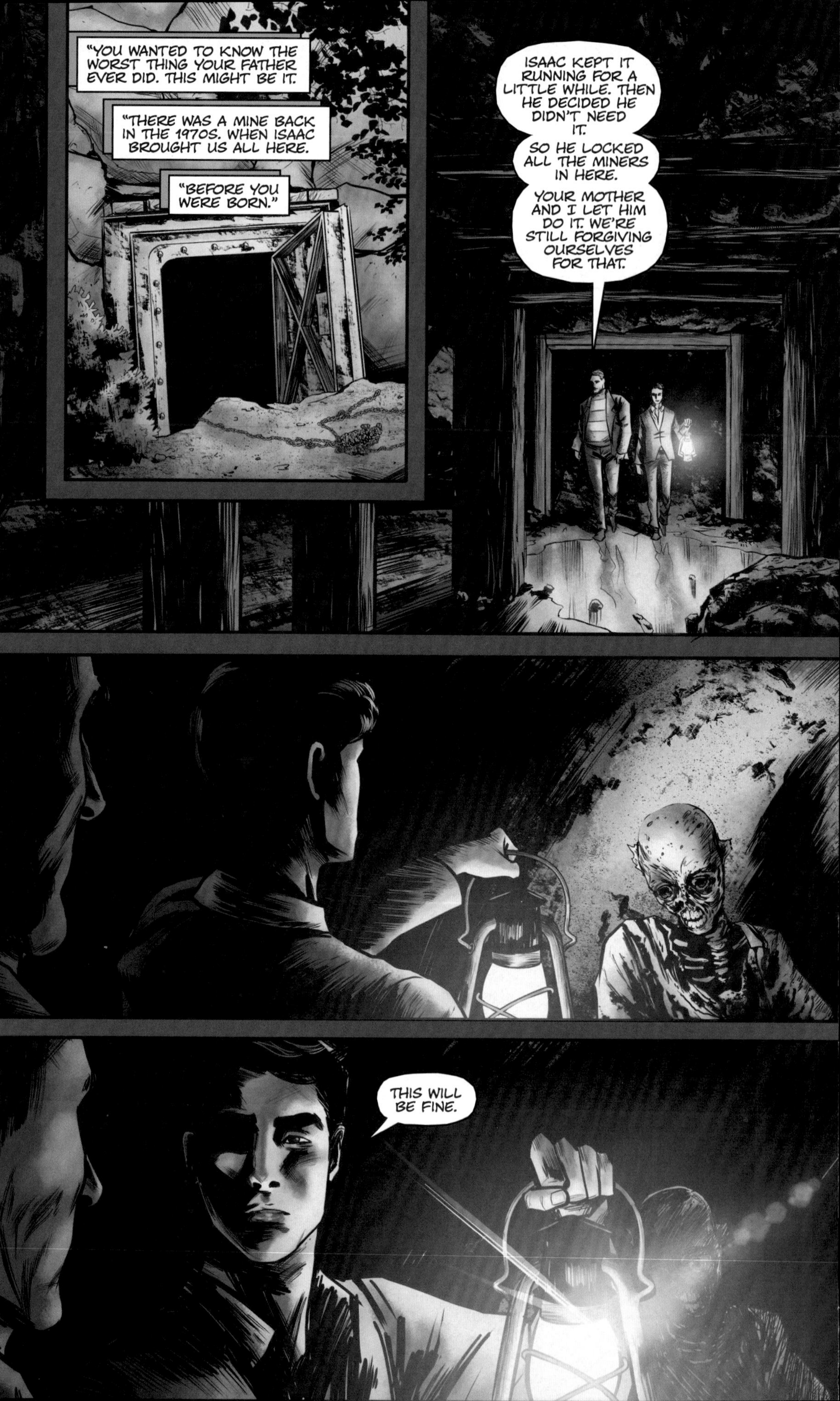
"YOU WANTED TO KNOW THE WORST THING YOUR FATHER EVER DID. THIS MIGHT BE IT.
"THERE WAS A MINE BACK IN THE 1970S. WHEN ISAAC BROUGHT US ALL HERE.
"BEFORE YOU WERE BORN."
ISAAC KEPT IT RUNNING FOR A LITTLE WHILE. THEN HE DECIDED HE DIDN'T NEED IT.
SO HE LOCKED ALL THE MINERS IN HERE.
YOUR MOTHER AND I LET HIM DO IT. WE'RE STILL FORGIVING OURSELVES FOR THAT.
THIS WILL BE FINE.

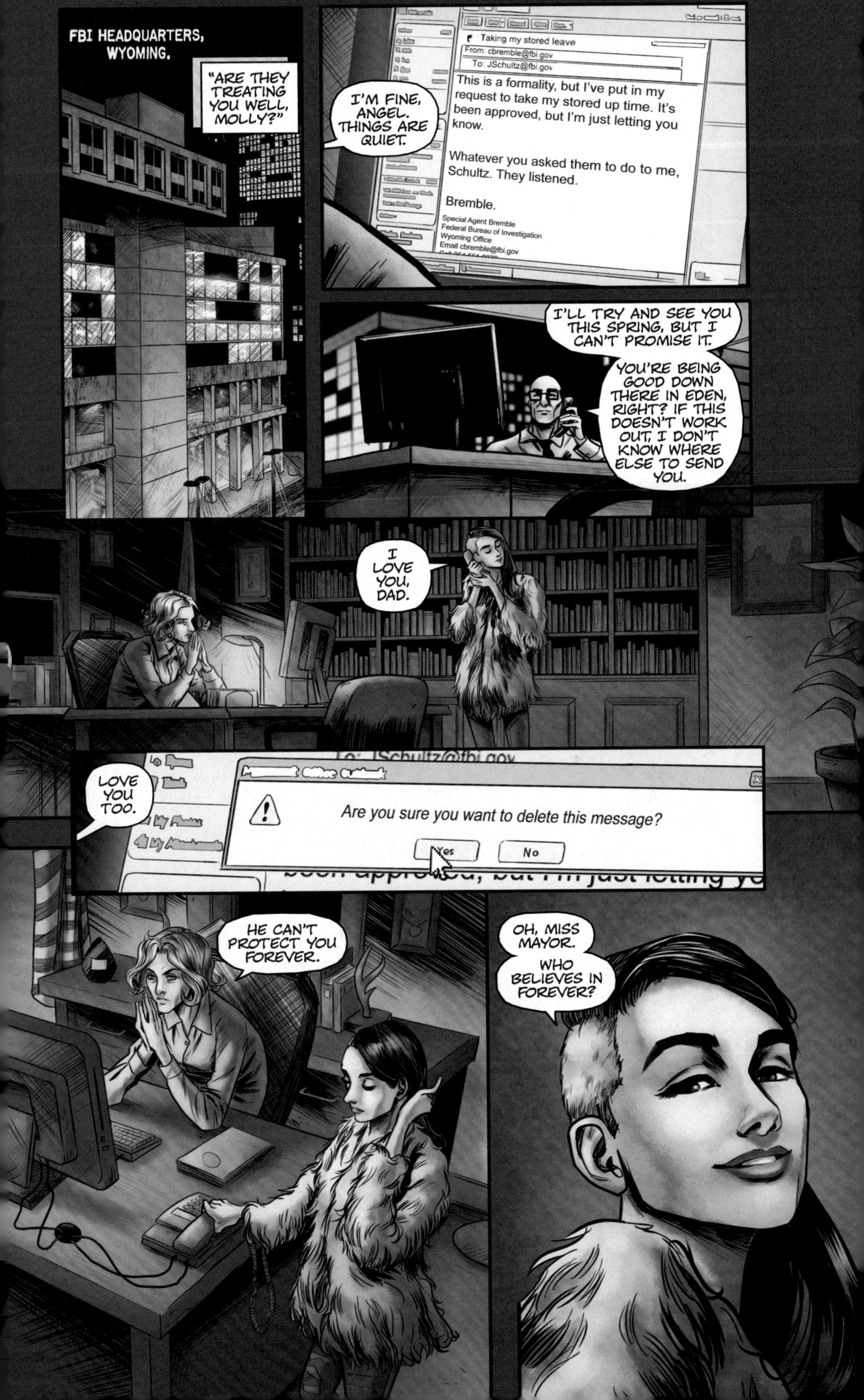

FBI HEADQUARTERS, WYOMING.
"ARE THEY TREATING YOU WELL, MOLLY?"
I'M FINE, ANGEL. THINGS ARE QUIET.
Taking my stored leave
From: cbremble@fbi.gov
To: JSchultz@fbi.gov
This is a formality, but I've put in my request to take my stored up time. It's been approved, but I'm just letting you know.
Whatever you asked them to do to me, Schultz. They listened.
Bremble.
Special Agent Bremble
Federal Bureau of Investigation
Wyoming Office
Email cbremble@fbi.gov
I'LL TRY AND SEE YOU THIS SPRING, BUT I CAN'T PROMISE IT.
YOU'RE BEING GOOD DOWN THERE IN EDEN, RIGHT? IF THIS DOESN'T WORK OUT, I DON'T KNOW WHERE ELSE TO SEND YOU.
I LOVE YOU, DAD.
LOVE YOU TOO.
Are you sure you want to delete this message?
Yes
No
HE CAN'T PROTECT YOU FOREVER.
OH, MISS MAYOR.
WHO BELIEVES IN FOREVER?

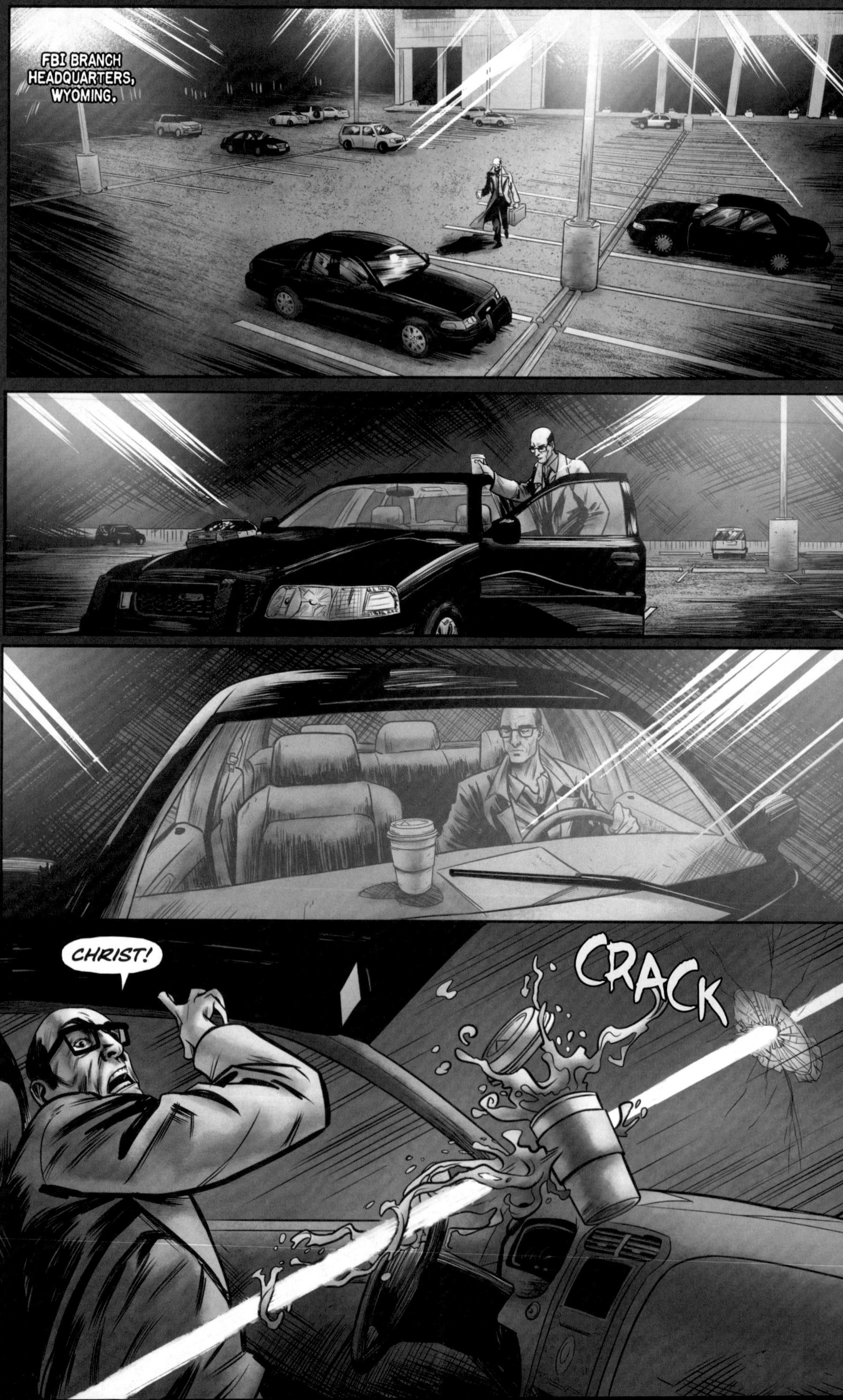
FBI BRANCH HEADQUARTERS, WYOMING.
CHRIST!
CRACK

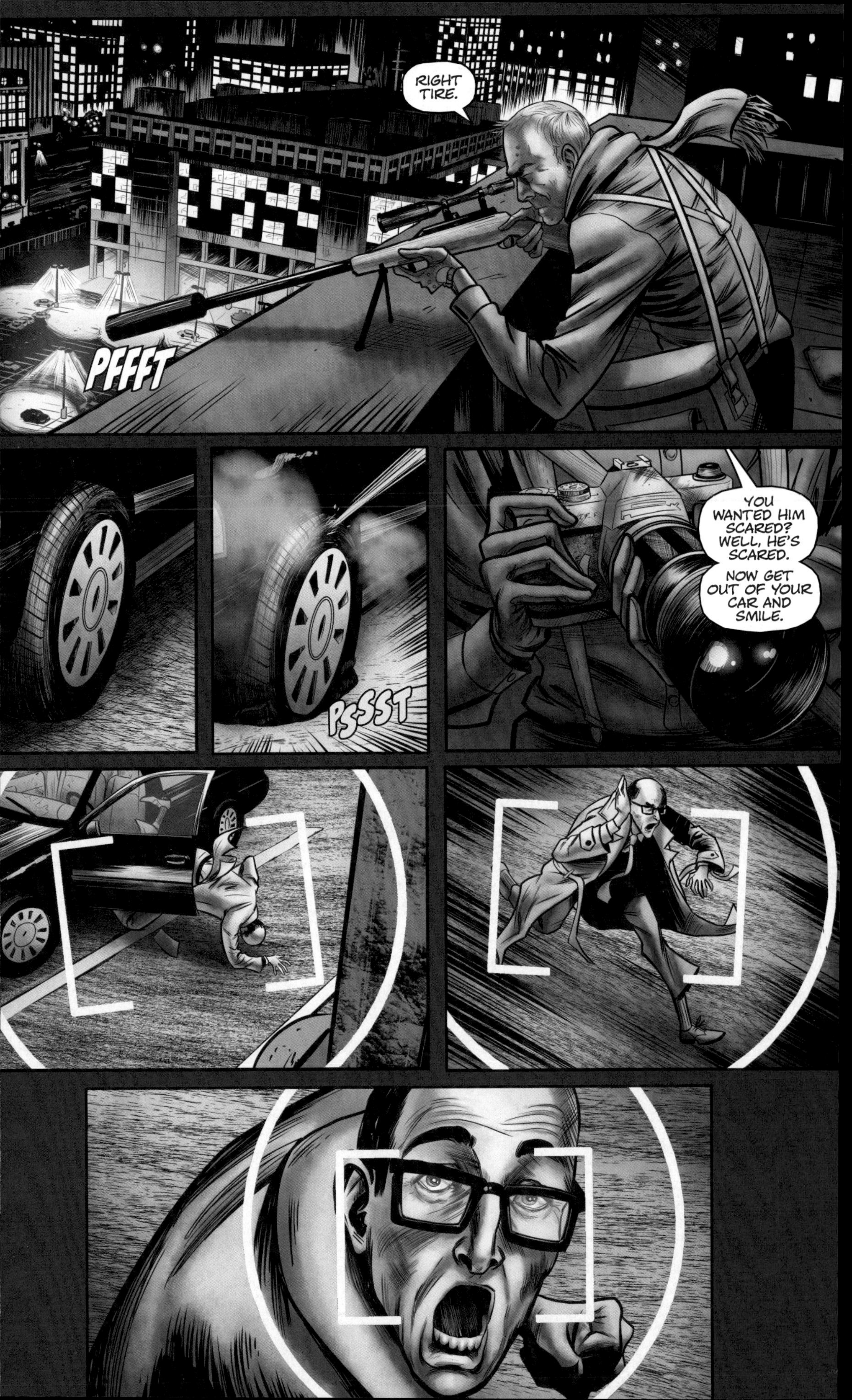
RIGHT TIRE.
PFFFT
PS-SST
YOU WANTED HIM SCARED? WELL, HE'S SCARED.
NOW GET OUT OF YOUR CAR AND SMILE.

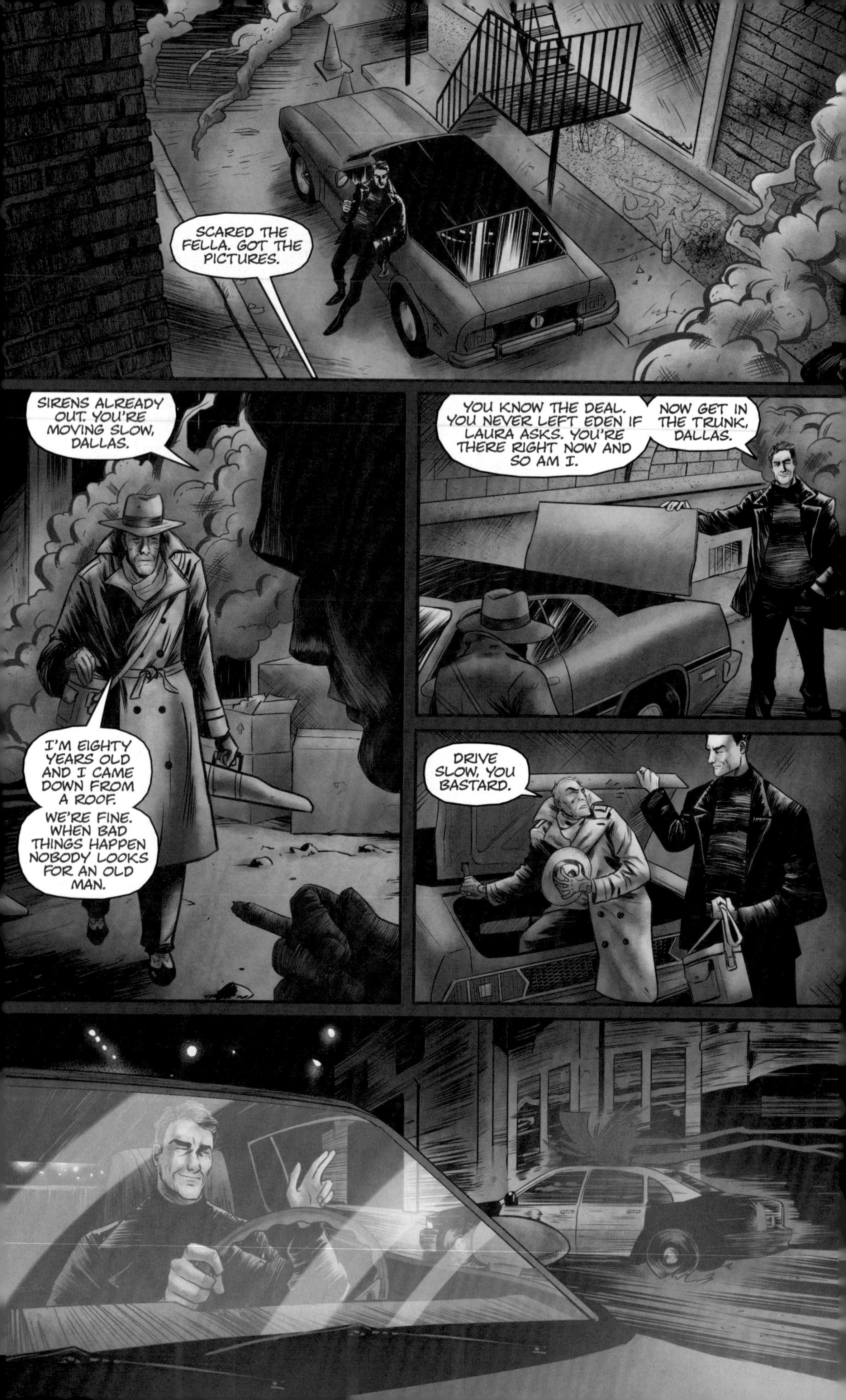
SCARED THE FELLA. GOT THE PICTURES.
SIRENS ALREADY OUT. YOU'RE MOVING SLOW, DALLAS.
I'M EIGHTY YEARS OLD AND I CAME DOWN FROM A ROOF.
WE'RE FINE. WHEN BAD THINGS HAPPEN NOBODY LOOKS FOR AN OLD MAN.
YOU KNOW THE DEAL. YOU NEVER LEFT EDEN IF LAURA ASKS. YOU'RE THERE RIGHT NOW AND SO AM I.
NOW GET IN THE TRUNK, DALLAS.
DRIVE SLOW, YOU BASTARD.

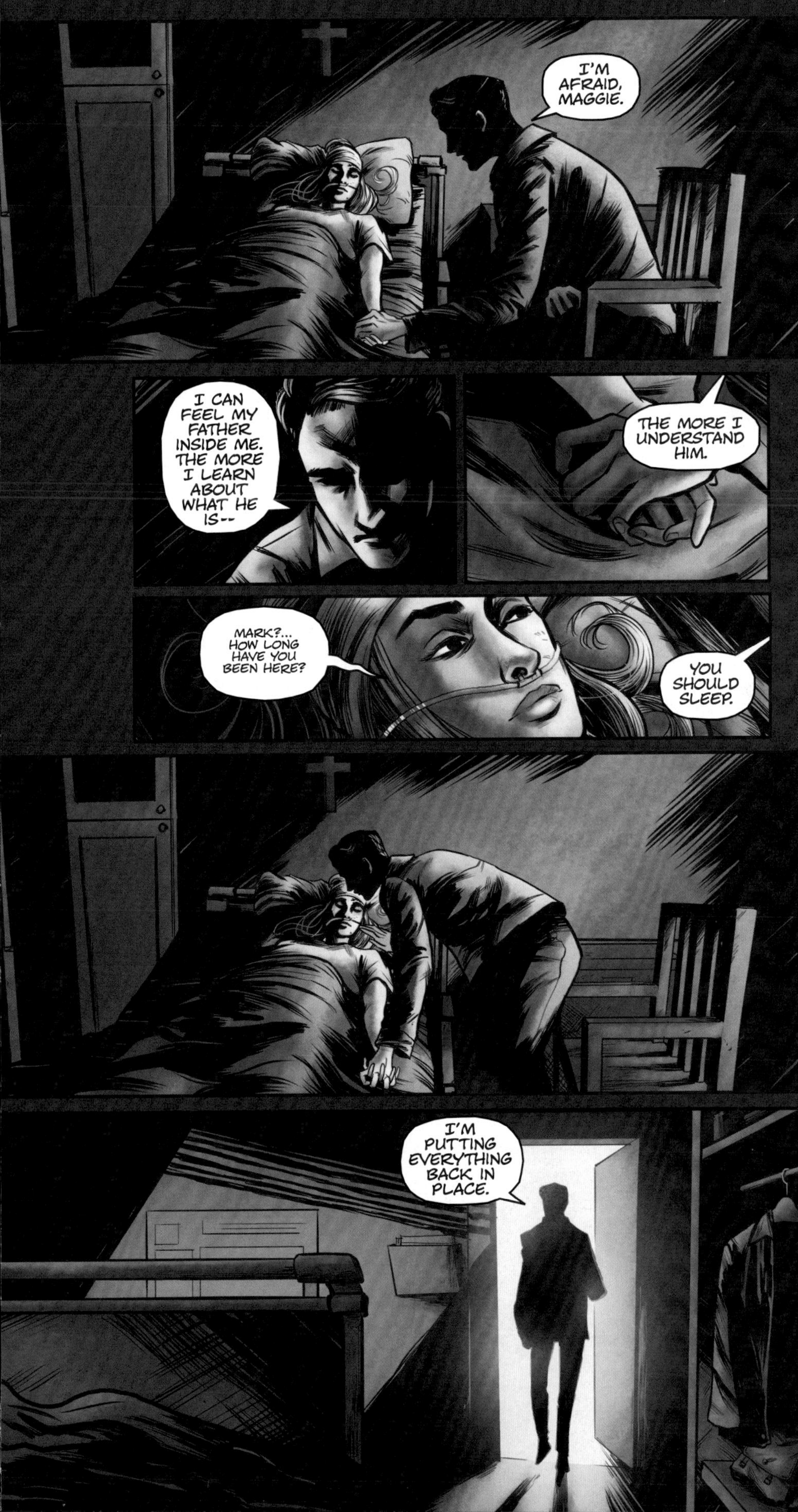
I'M AFRAID, MAGGIE.
I CAN FEEL MY FATHER INSIDE ME. THE MORE I LEARN ABOUT WHAT HE IS--
THE MORE I UNDERSTAND HIM.
MARK?... HOW LONG HAVE YOU BEEN HERE?
YOU SHOULD SLEEP.
I'M PUTTING EVERYTHING BACK IN PLACE.

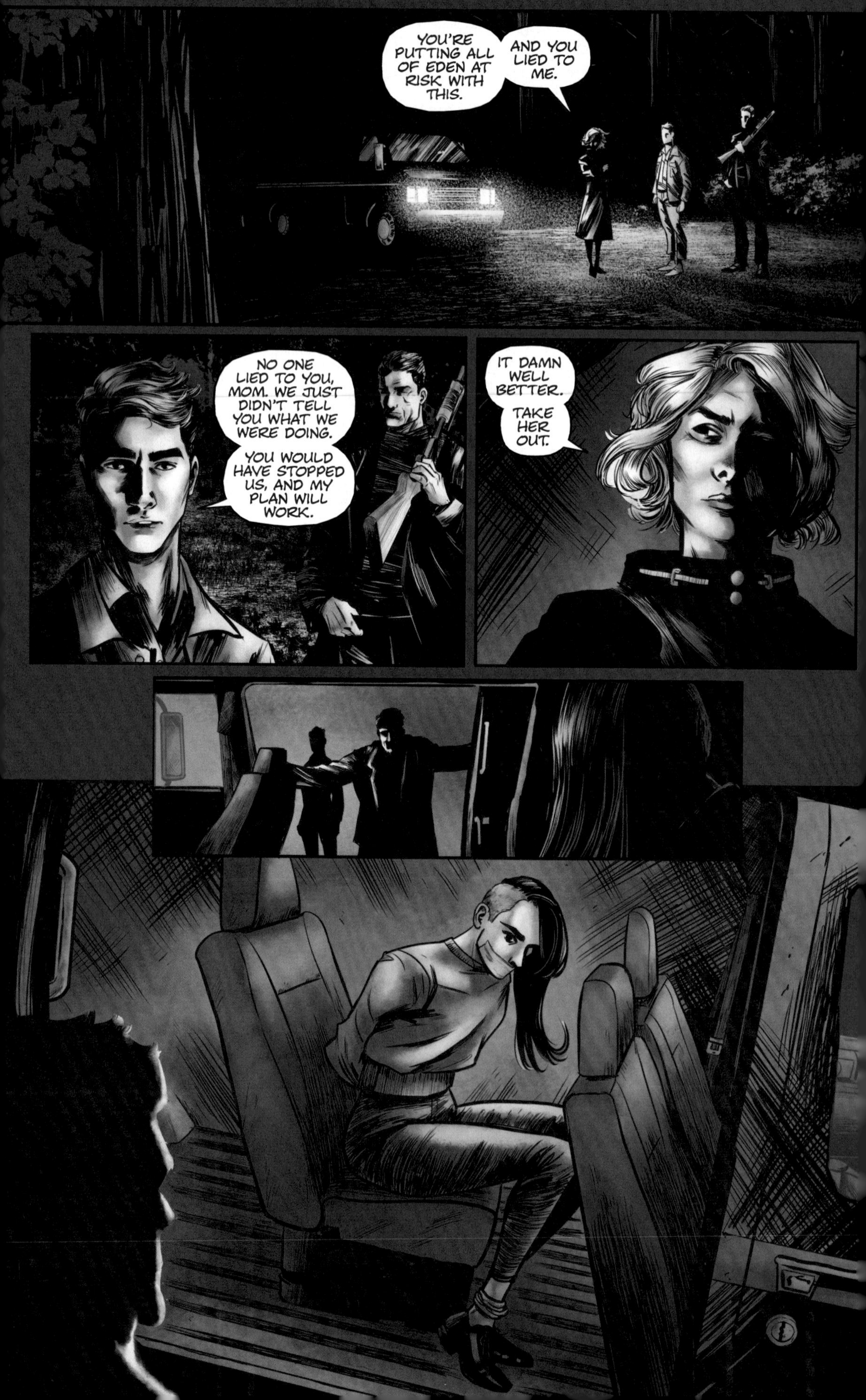

YOU'RE PUTTING ALL OF EDEN AT RISK WITH THIS.
AND YOU LIED TO ME.
NO ONE LIED TO YOU, MOM. WE JUST DIDN'T TELL YOU WHAT WE WERE DOING.
YOU WOULD HAVE STOPPED US, AND MY PLAN WILL WORK.
IT DAMN WELL BETTER.
TAKE HER OUT.

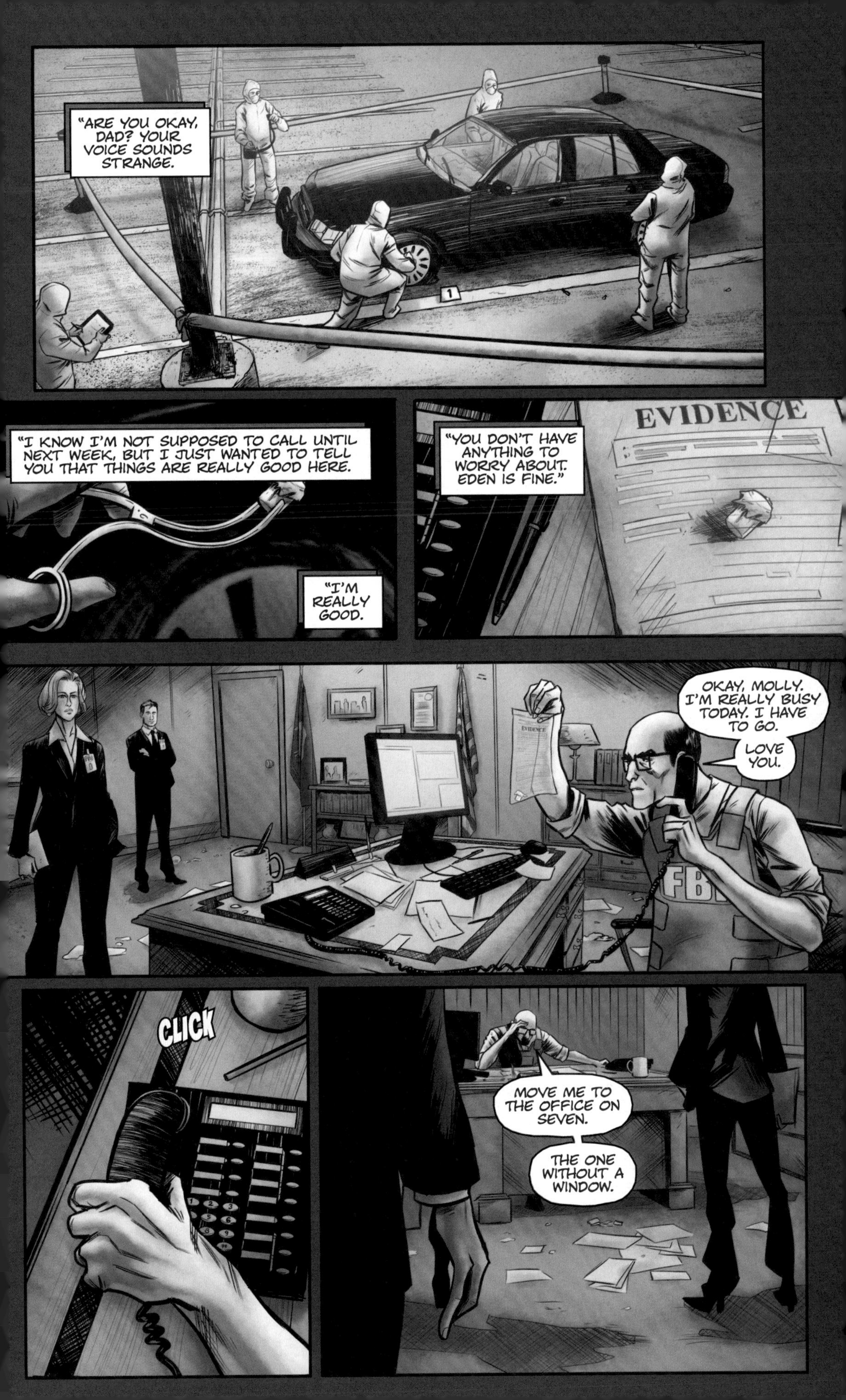
"ARE YOU OKAY, DAD? YOUR VOICE SOUNDS STRANGE.
1
"I KNOW I'M NOT SUPPOSED TO CALL UNTIL NEXT WEEK, BUT I JUST WANTED TO TELL YOU THAT THINGS ARE REALLY GOOD HERE.
"I'M REALLY GOOD.
"YOU DON'T HAVE ANYTHING TO WORRY ABOUT. EDEN IS FINE."
EVIDENCE
OKAY, MOLLY. I'M REALLY BUSY TODAY. I HAVE TO GO.
LOVE YOU.
EVIDENCE
FBI
CLICK
MOVE ME TO THE OFFICE ON SEVEN.
THE ONE WITHOUT A WINDOW.

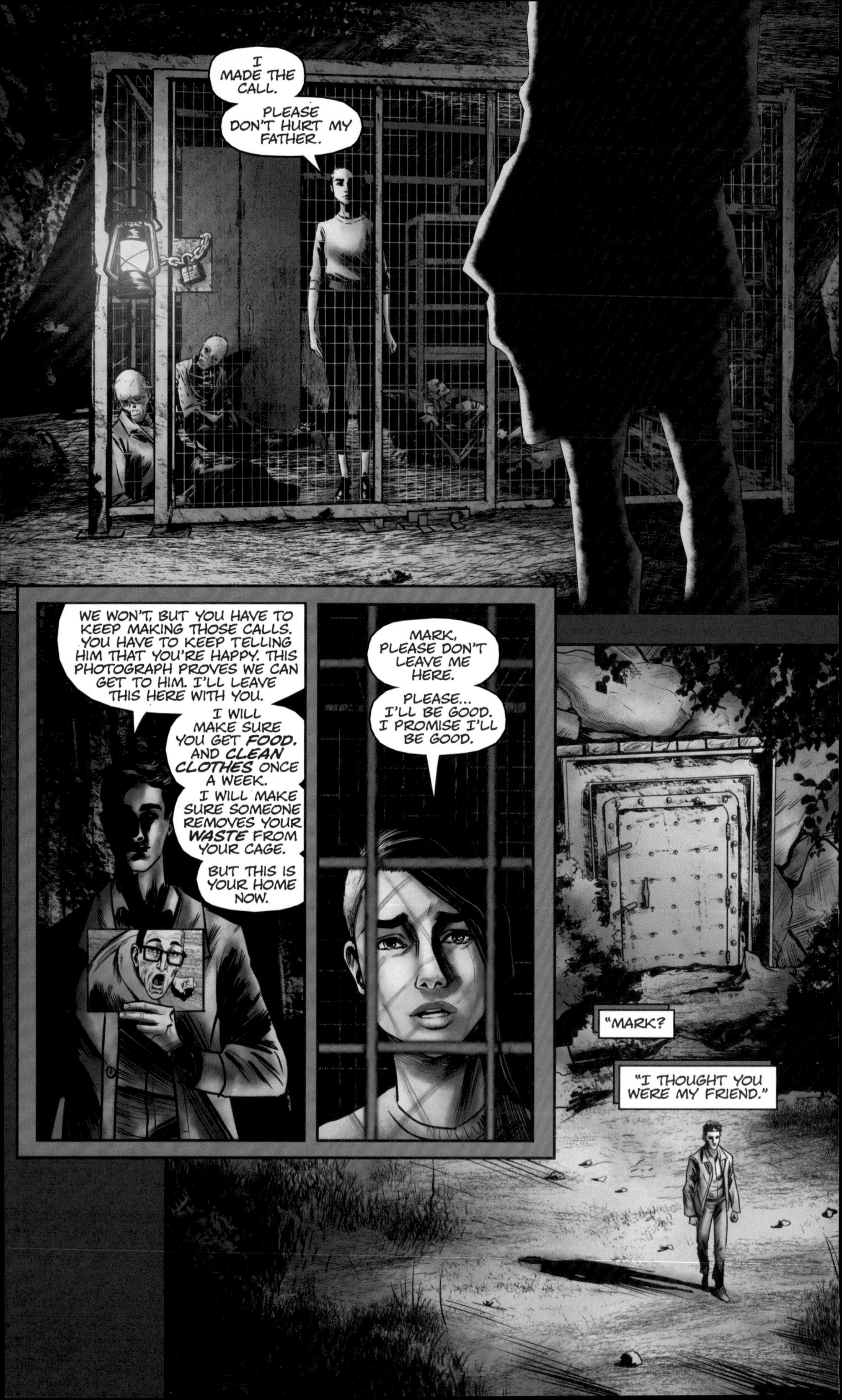
I MADE THE CALL.
PLEASE DON'T HURT MY FATHER.
WE WON'T, BUT YOU HAVE TO KEEP MAKING THOSE CALLS. YOU HAVE TO KEEP TELLING HIM THAT YOU'RE HAPPY. THIS PHOTOGRAPH PROVES WE CAN GET TO HIM. I'LL LEAVE THIS HERE WITH YOU.
I WILL MAKE SURE YOU GET FOOD. AND CLEAN CLOTHES ONCE A WEEK.
I WILL MAKE SURE SOMEONE REMOVES YOUR WASTE FROM YOUR CAGE.
BUT THIS IS YOUR HOME NOW.
MARK, PLEASE DON'T LEAVE ME HERE.
PLEASE... I'LL BE GOOD. I PROMISE I'LL BE GOOD.
"MARK?
"I THOUGHT YOU WERE MY FRIEND."

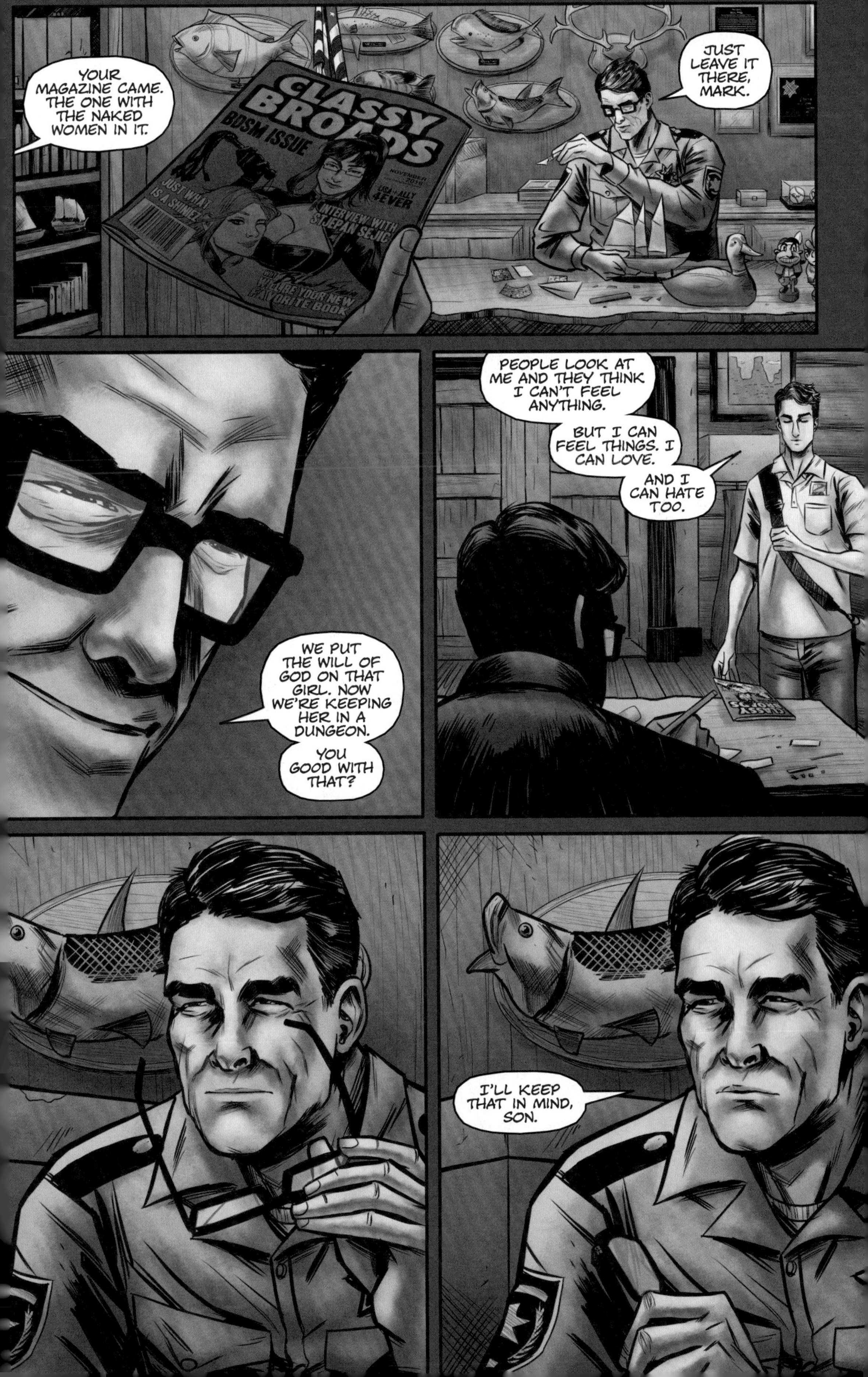
YOUR MAGAZINE CAME. THE ONE WITH THE NAKED WOMEN IN IT.
CLASSY BROADS
BDSM ISSUE
JUST WHAT IS A SHINEZ
INTERVIEW WITH STJEPAN SEJIC
4EVER
FAVORITE BOOK
JUST LEAVE IT THERE, MARK.
WE PUT THE WILL OF GOD ON THAT GIRL. NOW WE'RE KEEPING HER IN A DUNGEON.
YOU GOOD WITH THAT?
PEOPLE LOOK AT ME AND THEY THINK I CAN'T FEEL ANYTHING.
BUT I CAN FEEL THINGS. I CAN LOVE.
AND I CAN HATE TOO.
I'LL KEEP THAT IN MIND, SON.

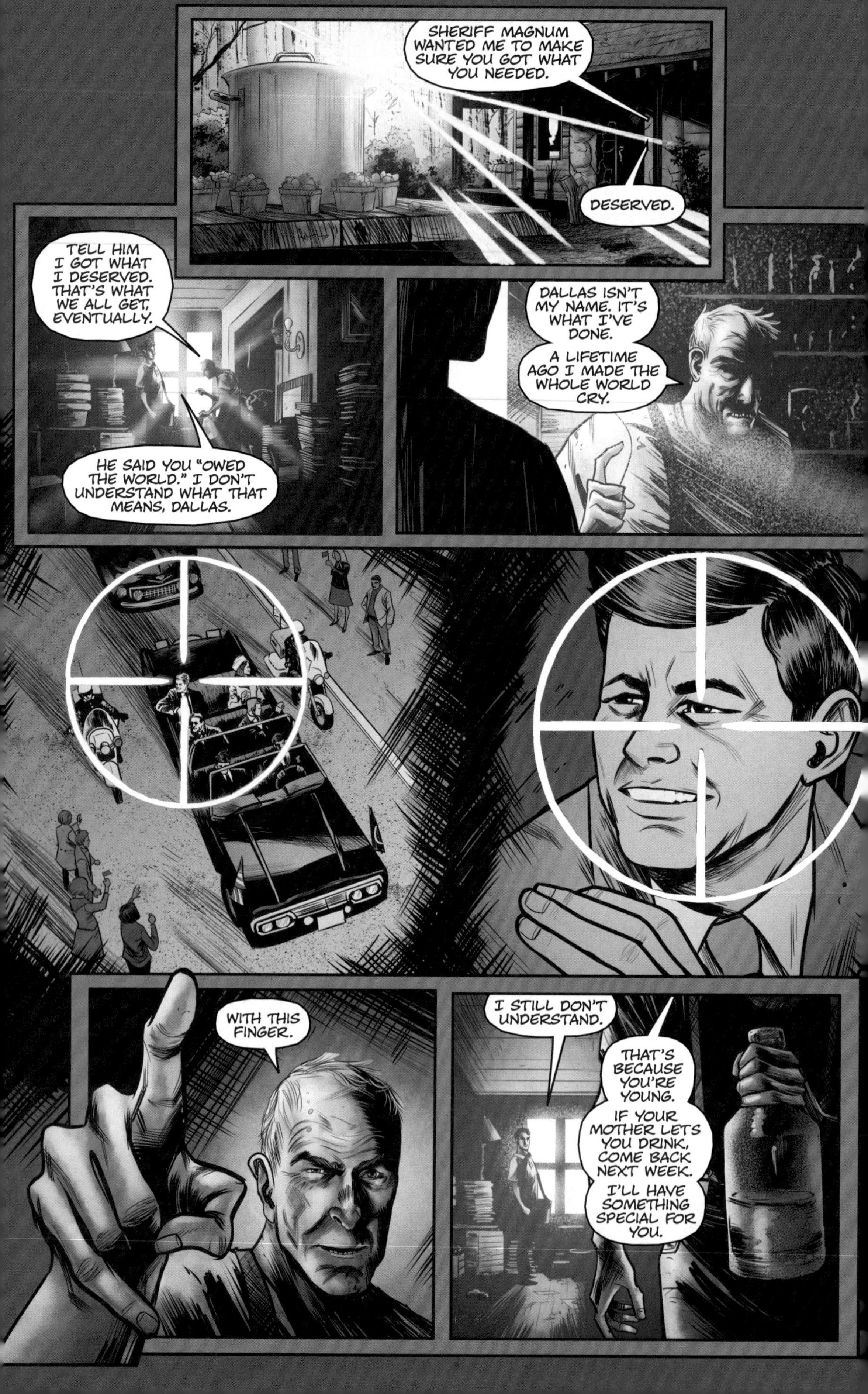
SHERIFF MAGNUM WANTED ME TO MAKE SURE YOU GOT WHAT YOU NEEDED.
DESERVED.
TELL HIM I GOT WHAT I DESERVED. THAT'S WHAT WE ALL GET, EVENTUALLY.
HE SAID YOU "OWED THE WORLD." I DON'T UNDERSTAND WHAT THAT MEANS, DALLAS.
DALLAS ISN'T MY NAME. IT'S WHAT I'VE DONE.
A LIFETIME AGO I MADE THE WHOLE WORLD CRY.
WITH THIS FINGER.
I STILL DON'T UNDERSTAND.
THAT'S BECAUSE YOU'RE YOUNG.
IF YOUR MOTHER LETS YOU DRINK, COME BACK NEXT WEEK.
I'LL HAVE SOMETHING SPECIAL FOR YOU.

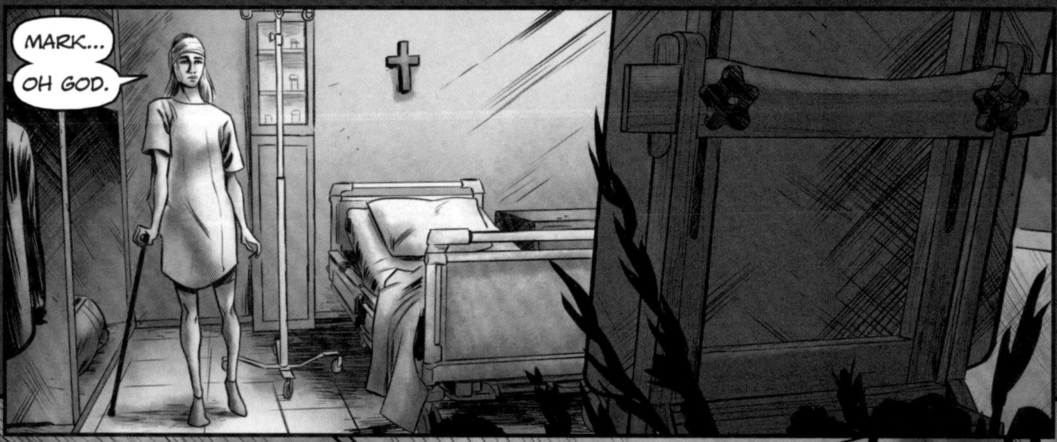
MARK...
OH GOD.
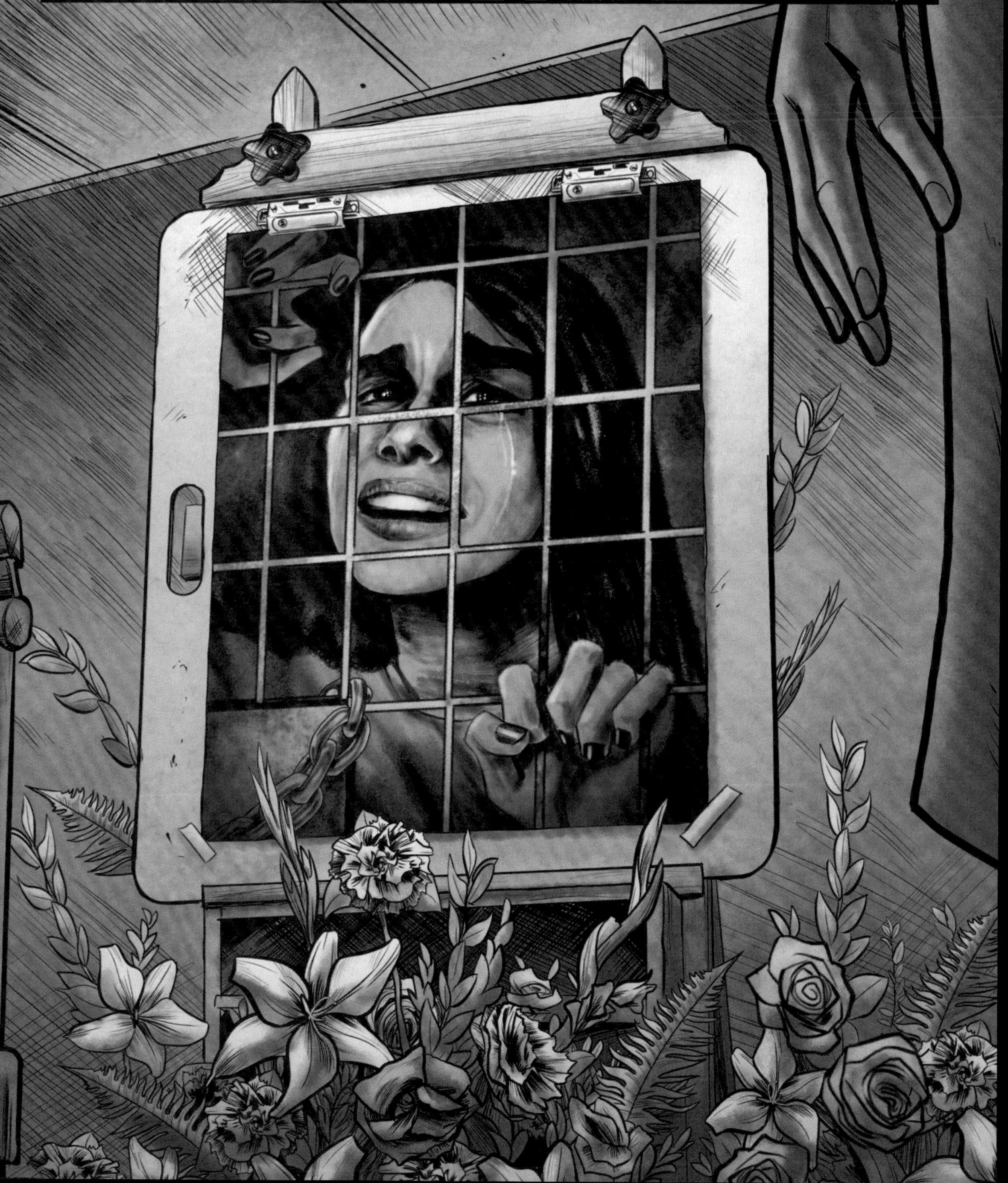

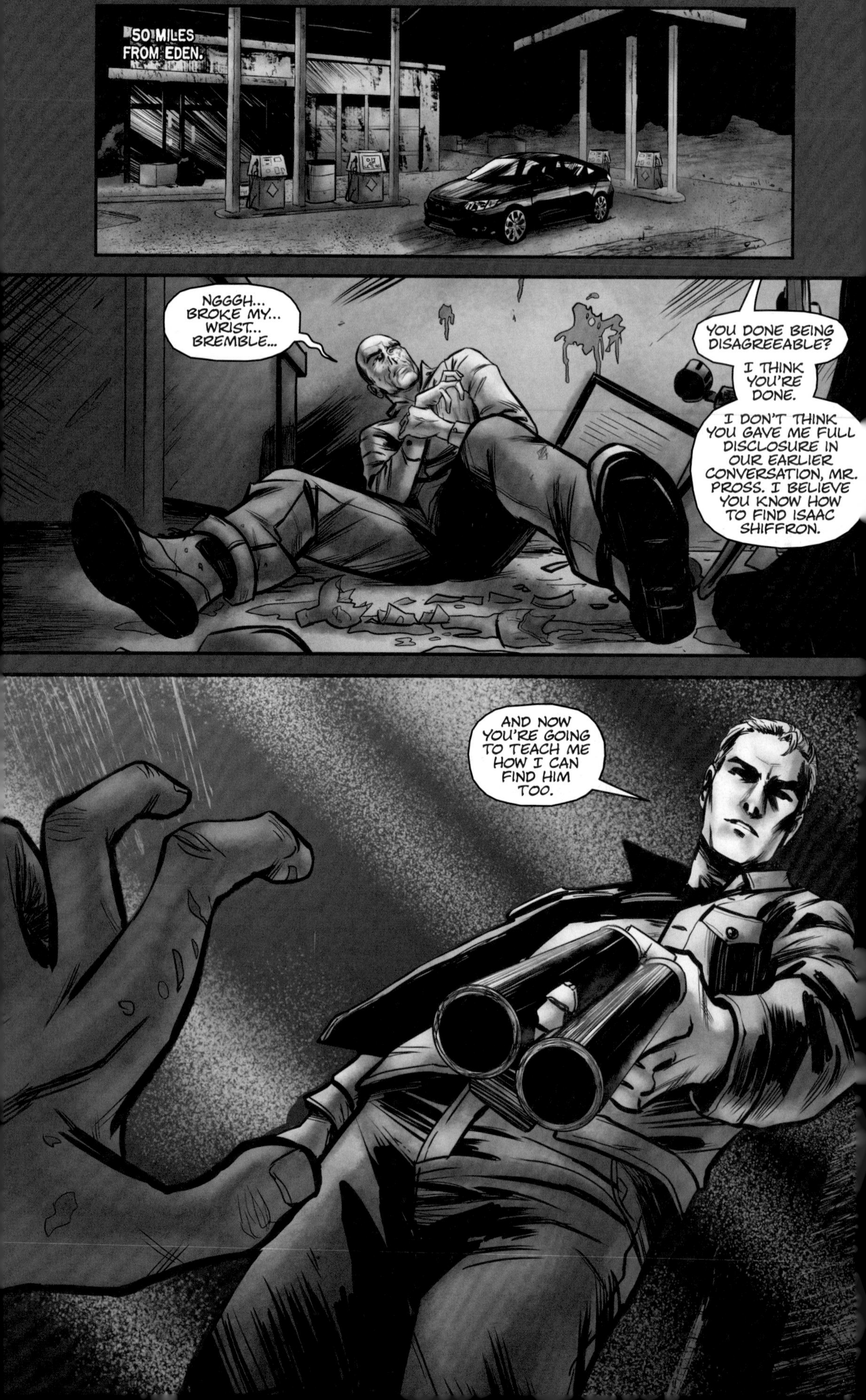
50 MILES FROM EDEN.
NGGGH... BROKE MY... WRIST... BREMBLE...
YOU DONE BEING DISAGREEABLE?
I THINK YOU'RE DONE.
I DON'T THINK YOU GAVE ME FULL DISCLOSURE IN OUR EARLIER CONVERSATION, MR. PROSS. I BELIEVE YOU KNOW HOW TO FIND ISAAC SHIFFRON.
AND NOW YOU'RE GOING TO TEACH ME HOW I CAN FIND HIM TOO.

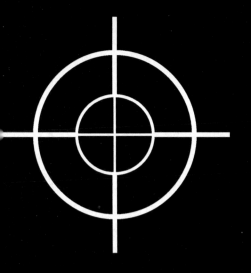

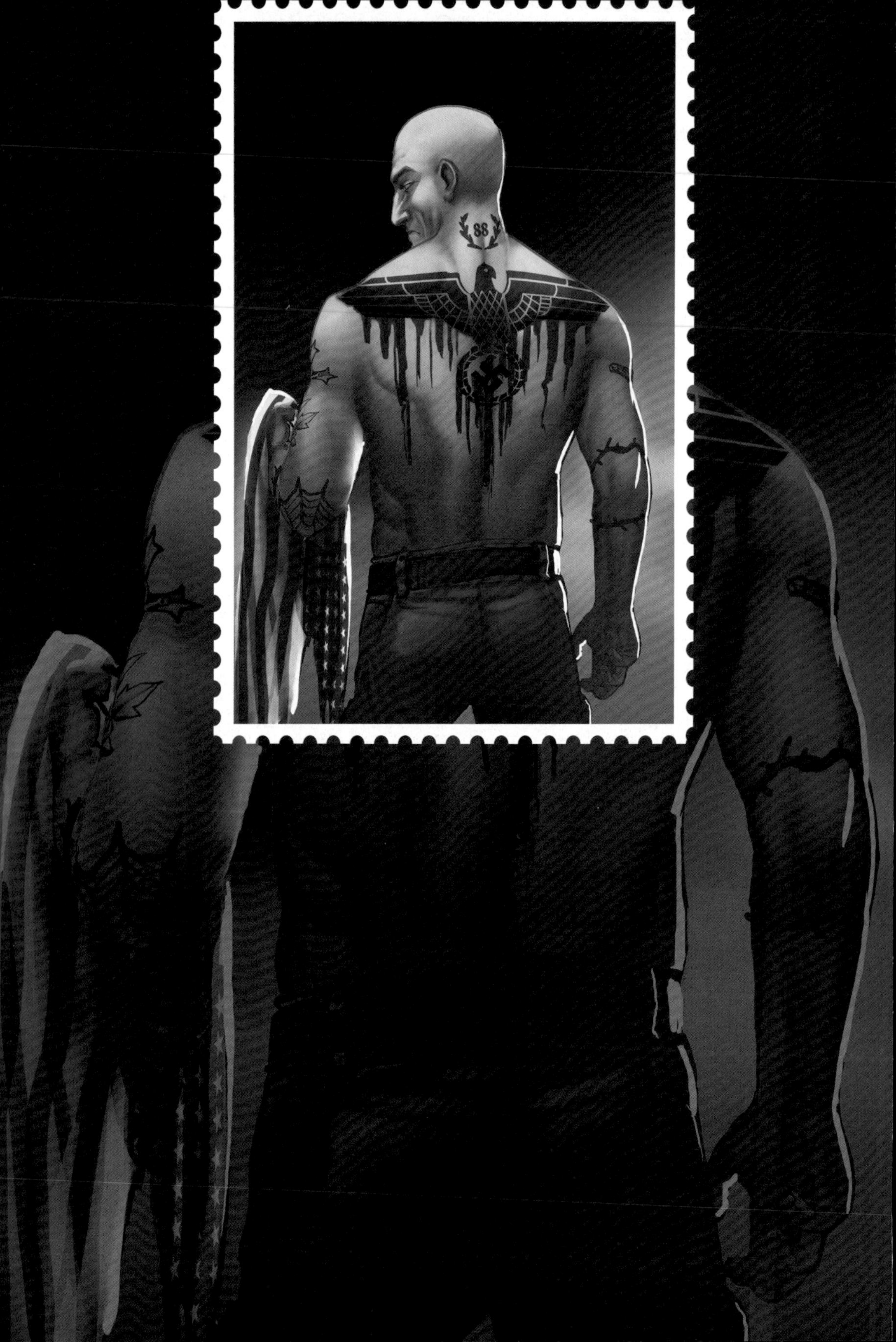
88

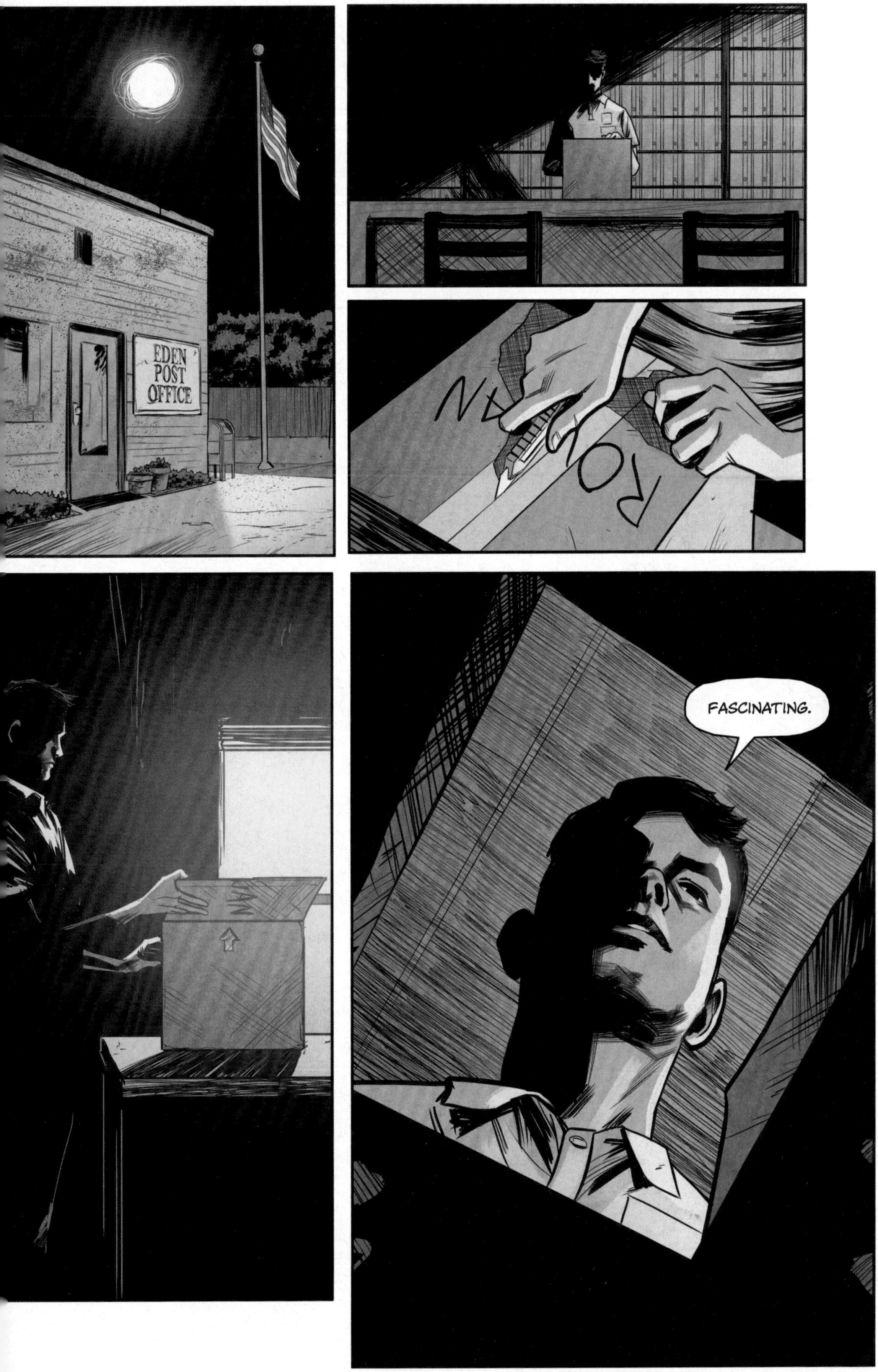
EDEN
POST
OFFICE
FASCINATING.

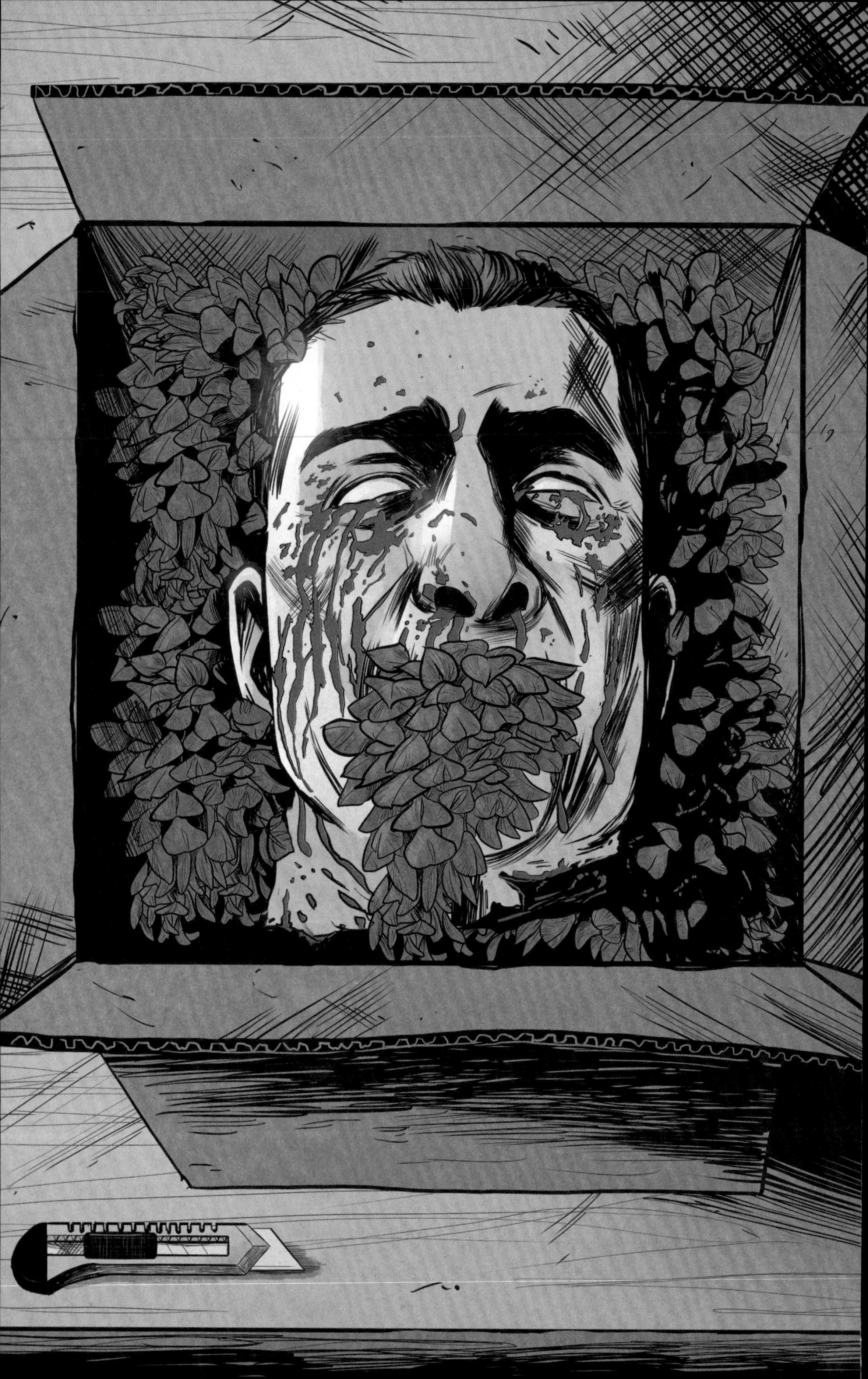

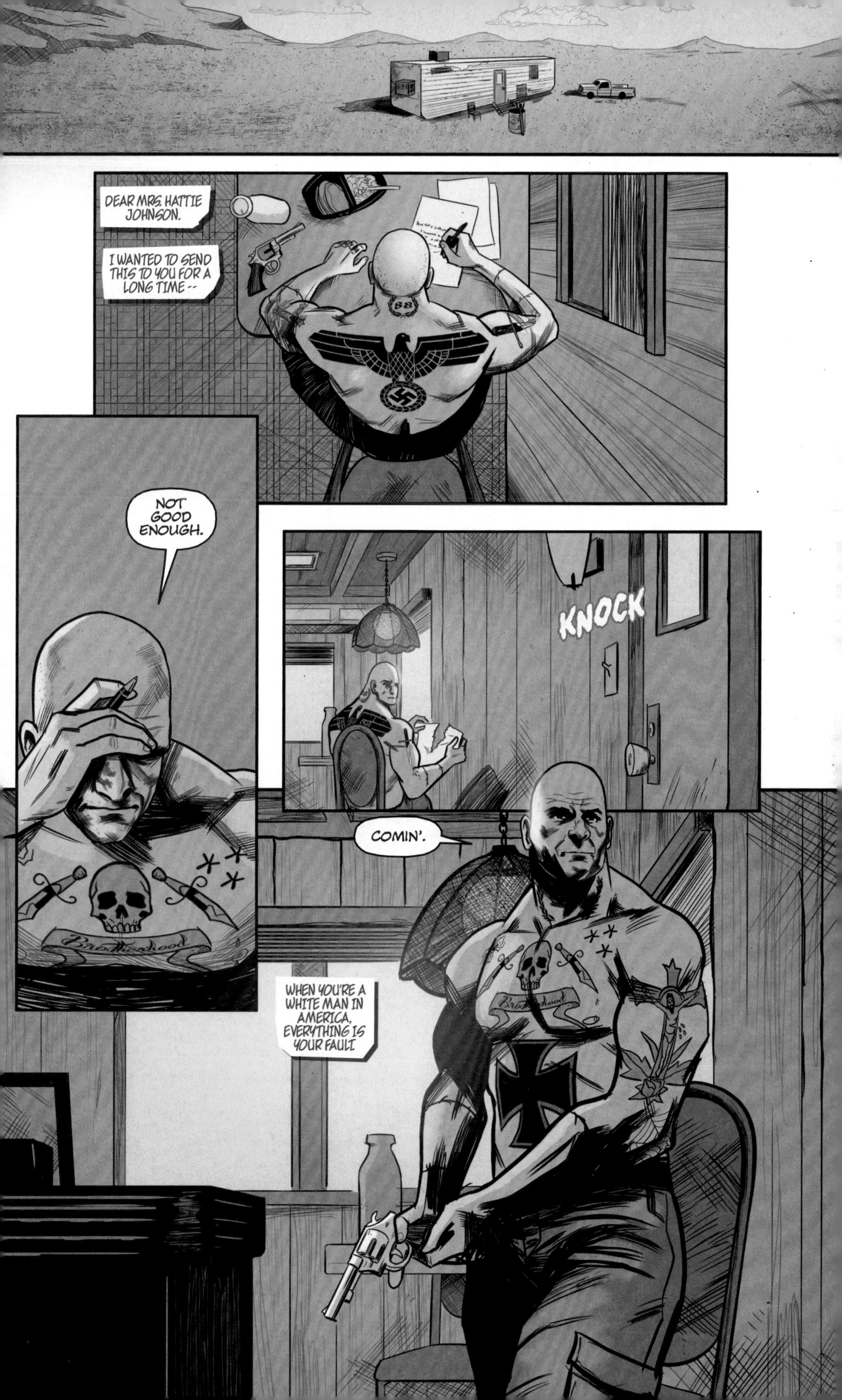
DEAR MRS. HATTIE JOHNSON.
I WANTED TO SEND THIS TO YOU FOR A LONG TIME --
NOT GOOD ENOUGH.
KNOCK
COMIN'.
WHEN YOU'RE A WHITE MAN IN AMERICA, EVERYTHING IS YOUR FAULT.

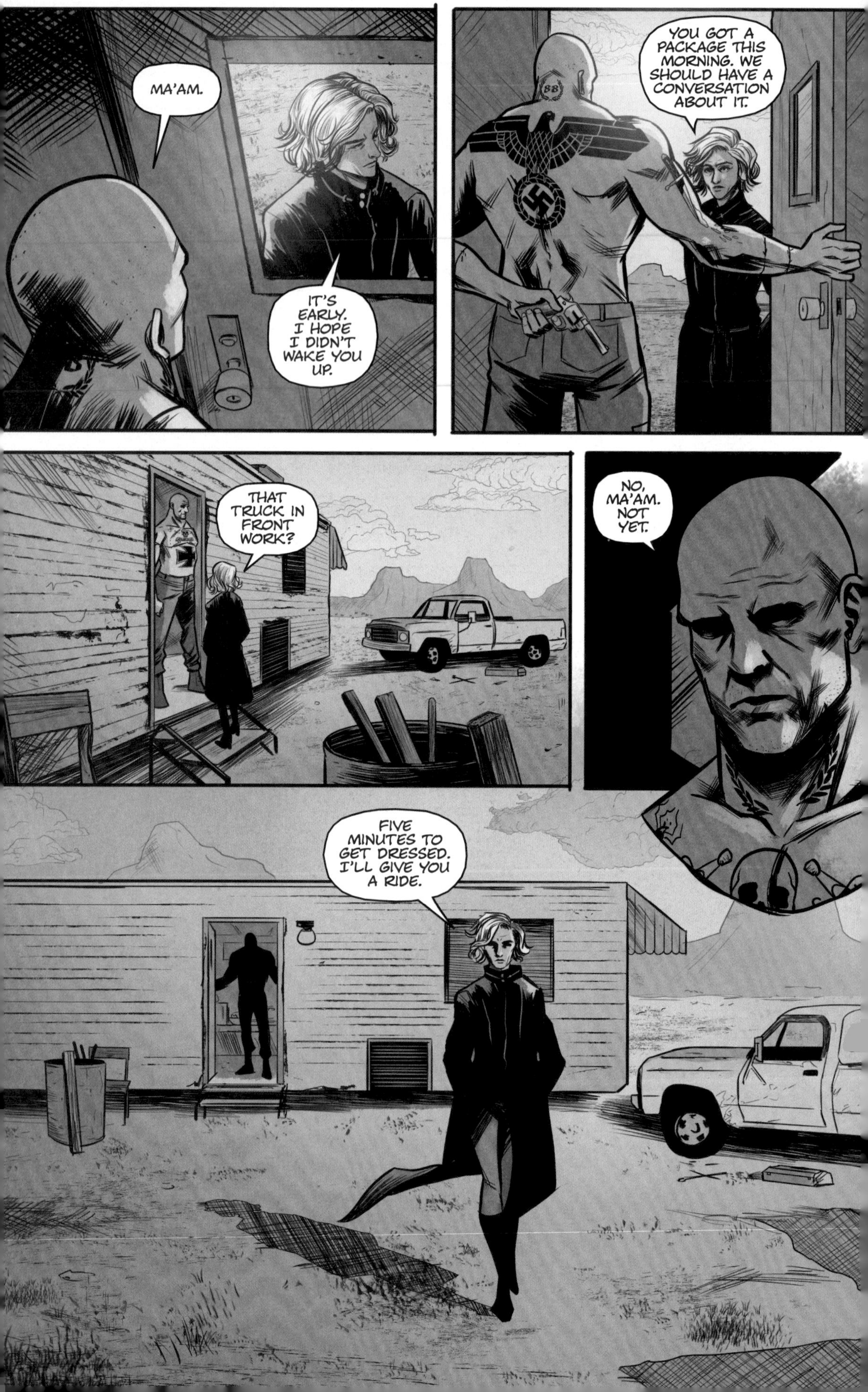

MA'AM.
IT'S EARLY. I HOPE I DIDN'T WAKE YOU UP.
YOU GOT A PACKAGE THIS MORNING. WE SHOULD HAVE A CONVERSATION ABOUT IT.
THAT TRUCK IN FRONT WORK?
NO, MA'AM. NOT YET.
FIVE MINUTES TO GET DRESSED. I'LL GIVE YOU A RIDE.

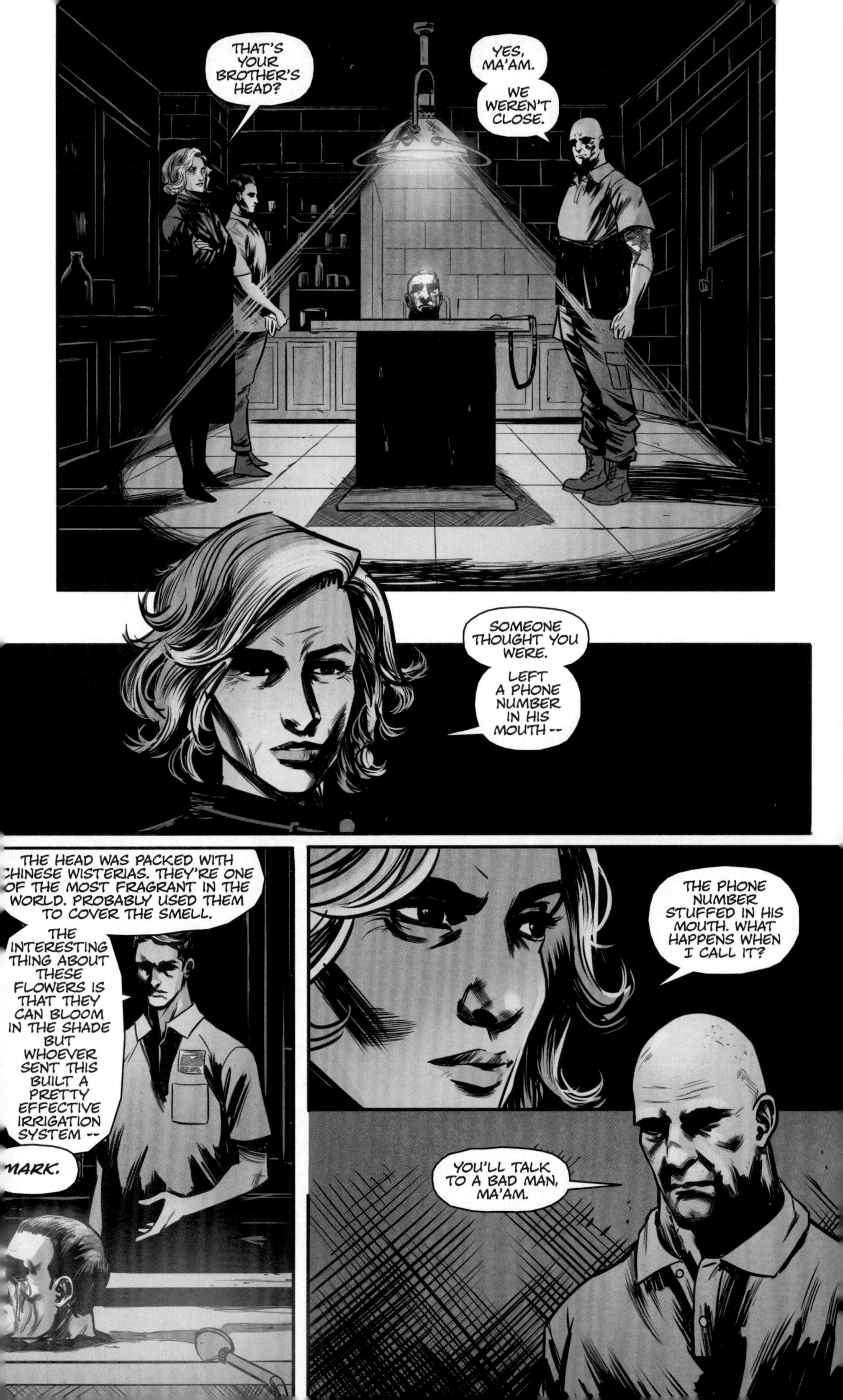

THAT'S YOUR BROTHER'S HEAD?
YES, MA'AM.
WE WEREN'T CLOSE.
SOMEONE THOUGHT YOU WERE.
LEFT A PHONE NUMBER IN HIS MOUTH --
THE HEAD WAS PACKED WITH CHINESE WISTERIAS. THEY'RE ONE OF THE MOST FRAGRANT IN THE WORLD. PROBABLY USED THEM TO COVER THE SMELL.
THE INTERESTING THING ABOUT THESE FLOWERS IS THAT THEY CAN BLOOM IN THE SHADE BUT WHOEVER SENT THIS BUILT A PRETTY EFFECTIVE IRRIGATION SYSTEM --
MARK.
THE PHONE NUMBER STUFFED IN HIS MOUTH. WHAT HAPPENS WHEN I CALL IT?
YOU'LL TALK TO A BAD MAN, MA'AM.

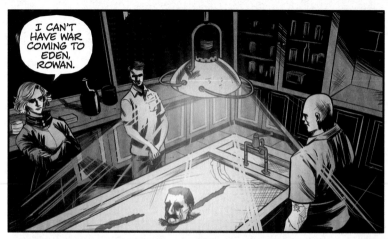

I CAN'T HAVE WAR COMING TO EDEN, ROWAN.

UNDERSTOOD.

THAT FARMHOUSE ON THE OUTSKIRTS OF TOWN. ON THE HILL. ANYONE LIVE THERE?

NO.

THEN I'LL CALL THAT NUMBER AND TELL THE BAD MAN THAT'S WHERE I'LL BE.

GOT A PHONE I CAN USE, MA'AM?

I DO. WHEN YOU'RE FINISHED, I WANT YOU TO COME WITH ME.

MIGHT HAVE SOME HELP FOR YOU.

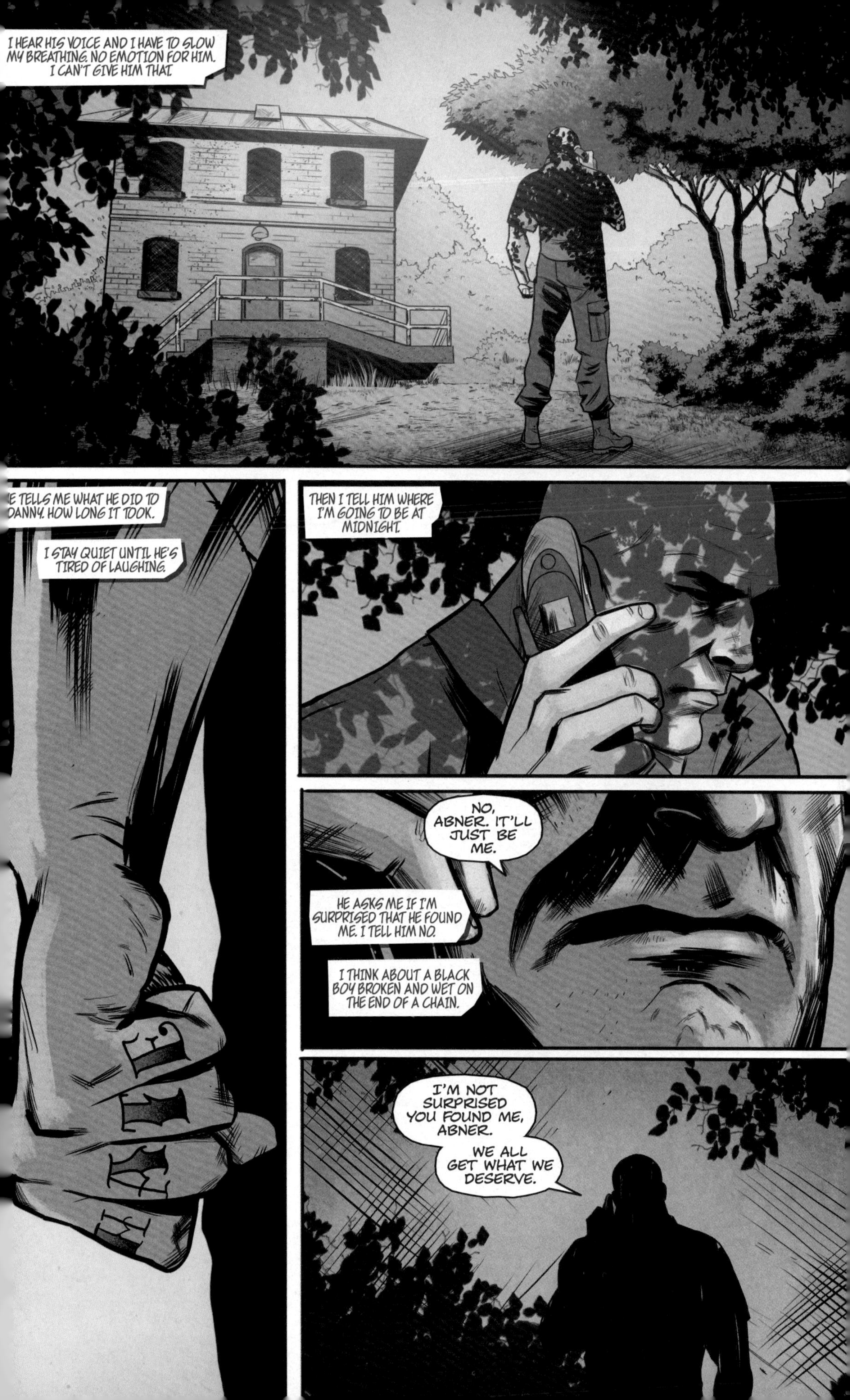
I HEAR HIS VOICE AND I HAVE TO SLOW MY BREATHING. NO EMOTION FOR HIM. I CAN'T GIVE HIM THAT.
E TELLS ME WHAT HE DID TO DANNY. HOW LONG IT TOOK.
I STAY QUIET UNTIL HE'S TIRED OF LAUGHING.
THEN I TELL HIM WHERE I'M GOING TO BE AT MIDNIGHT.
NO, ABNER. IT'LL JUST BE ME.
HE ASKS ME IF I'M SURPRISED THAT HE FOUND ME. I TELL HIM NO.
I THINK ABOUT A BLACK BOY BROKEN AND WET ON THE END OF A CHAIN.
I'M NOT SURPRISED YOU FOUND ME, ABNER.
WE ALL GET WHAT WE DESERVE.

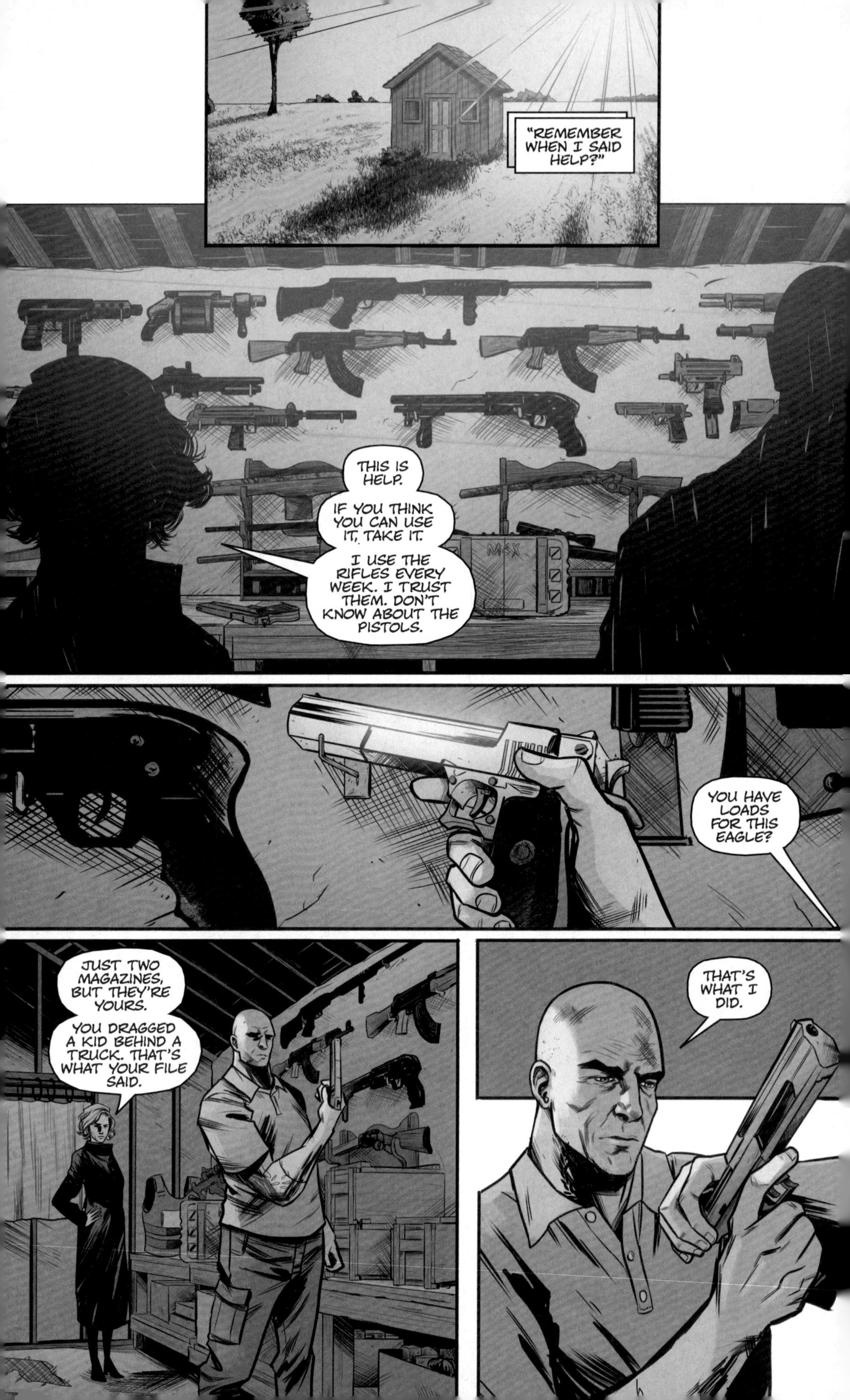
"REMEMBER WHEN I SAID HELP?"
THIS IS HELP.
IF YOU THINK YOU CAN USE IT, TAKE IT.
I USE THE RIFLES EVERY WEEK. I TRUST THEM. DON'T KNOW ABOUT THE PISTOLS.
YOU HAVE LOADS FOR THIS EAGLE?
JUST TWO MAGAZINES, BUT THEY'RE YOURS.
YOU DRAGGED A KID BEHIND A TRUCK. THAT'S WHAT YOUR FILE SAID.
THAT'S WHAT I DID.

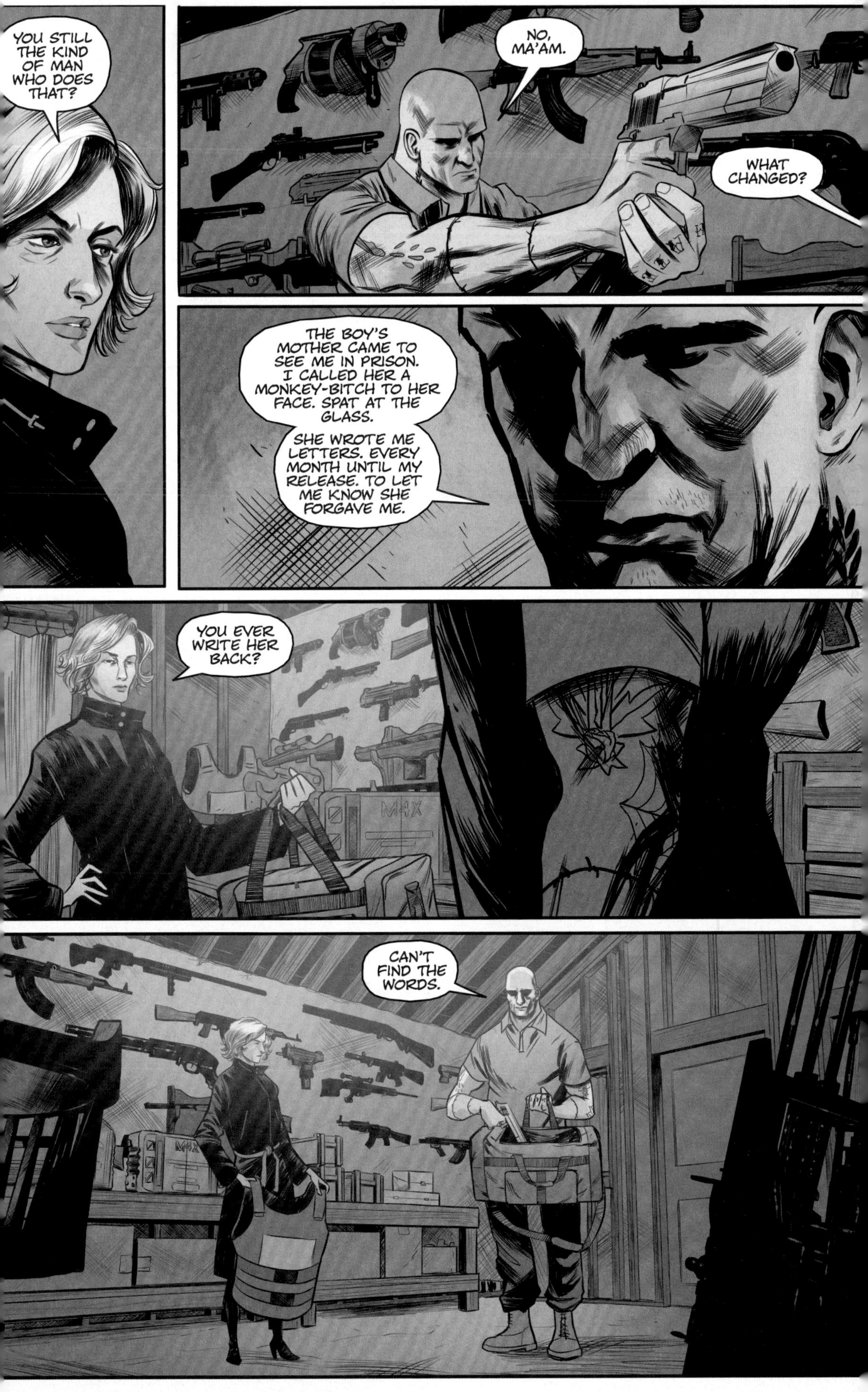
YOU STILL THE KIND OF MAN WHO DOES THAT?
NO, MA'AM.
WHAT CHANGED?
THE BOY'S MOTHER CAME TO SEE ME IN PRISON. I CALLED HER A MONKEY-BITCH TO HER FACE. SPAT AT THE GLASS.
SHE WROTE ME LETTERS. EVERY MONTH UNTIL MY RELEASE. TO LET ME KNOW SHE FORGAVE ME.
YOU EVER WRITE HER BACK?
CAN'T FIND THE WORDS.

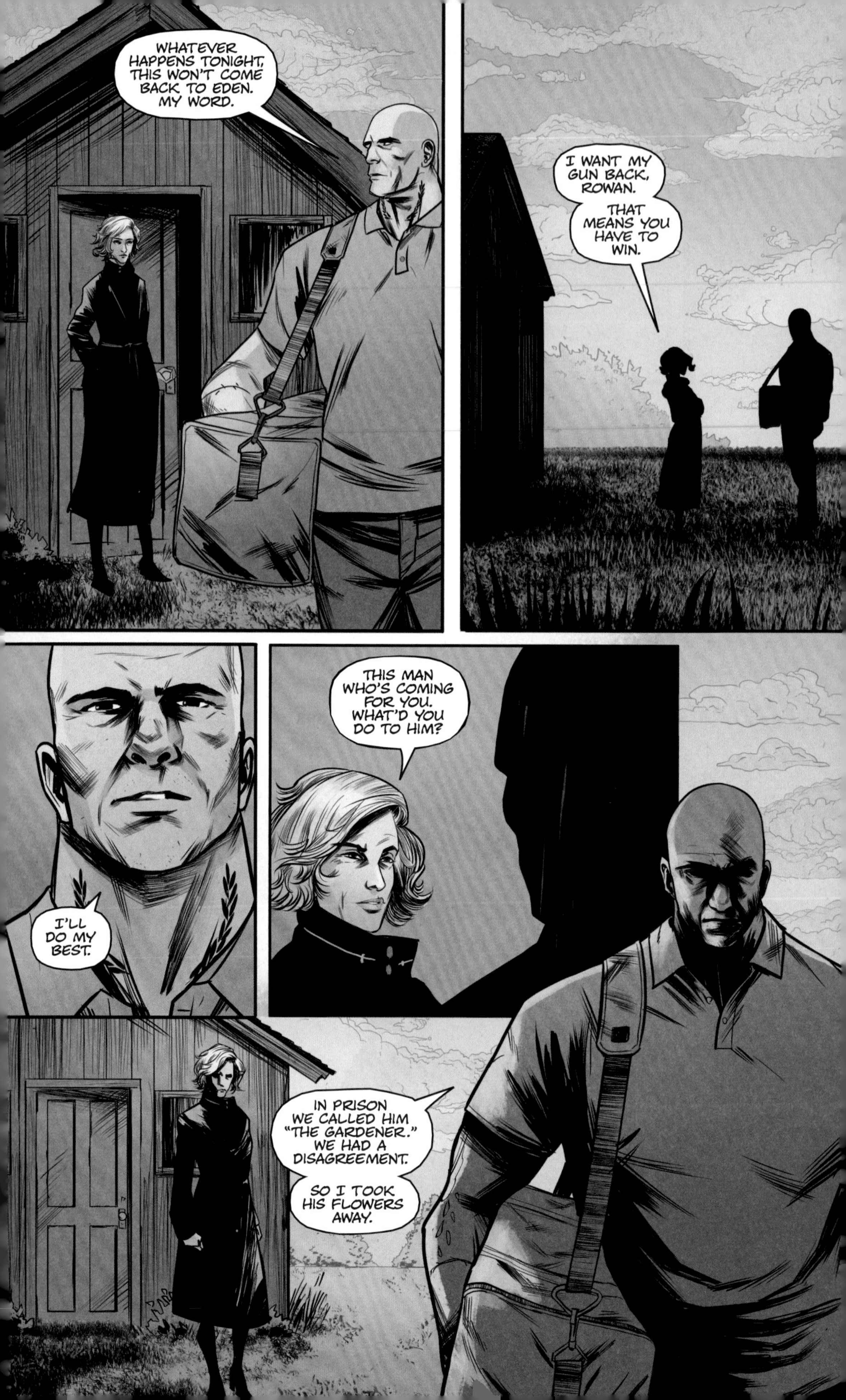
WHATEVER HAPPENS TONIGHT, THIS WON'T COME BACK TO EDEN. MY WORD.
I WANT MY GUN BACK, ROWAN.
THAT MEANS YOU HAVE TO WIN.
I'LL DO MY BEST.
THIS MAN WHO'S COMING FOR YOU. WHAT'D YOU DO TO HIM?
IN PRISON WE CALLED HIM "THE GARDENER." WE HAD A DISAGREEMENT.
SO I TOOK HIS FLOWERS AWAY.

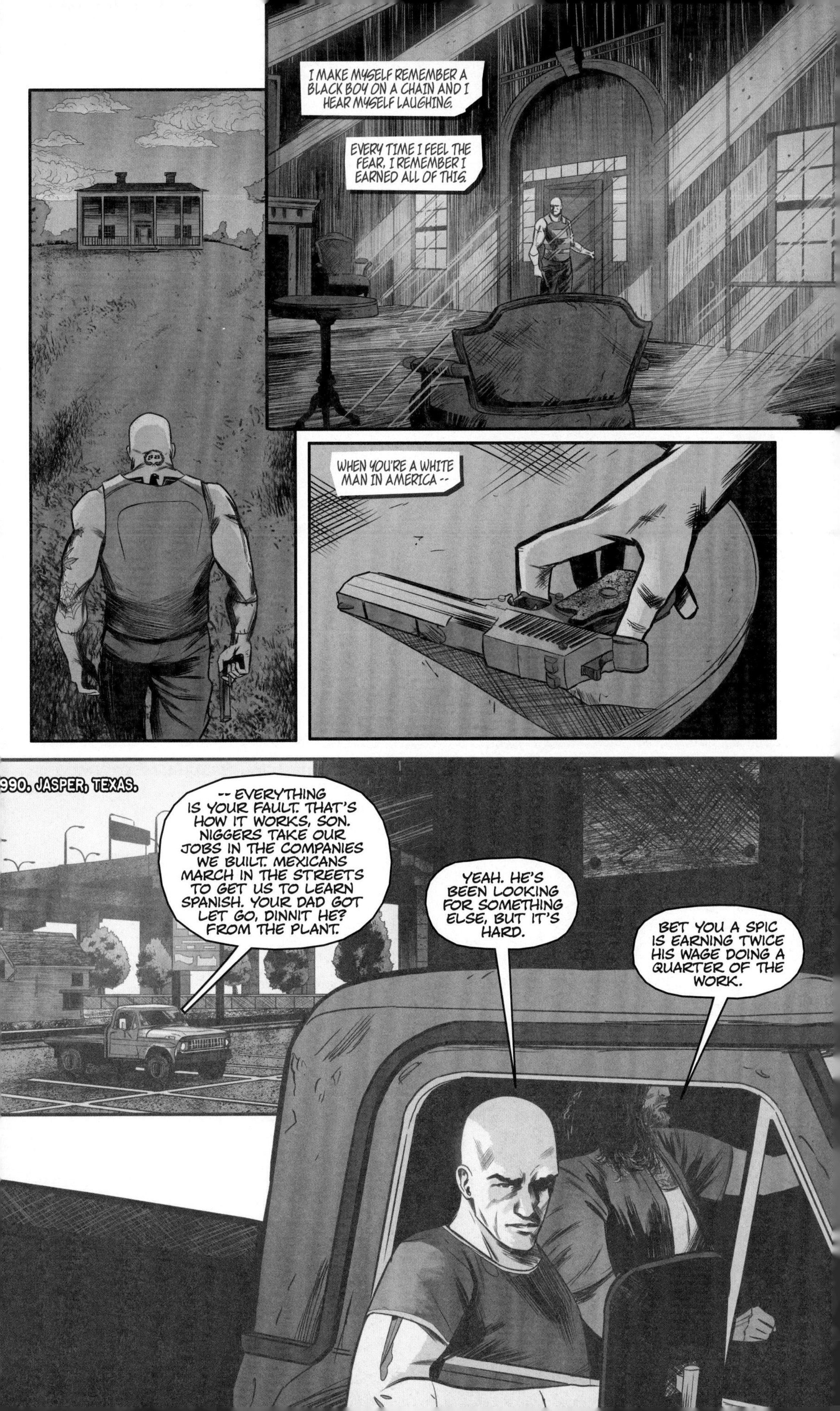
I MAKE MYSELF REMEMBER A BLACK BOY ON A CHAIN AND I HEAR MYSELF LAUGHING.
EVERY TIME I FEEL THE FEAR, I REMEMBER I EARNED ALL OF THIS.
WHEN YOU'RE A WHITE MAN IN AMERICA --
990. JASPER, TEXAS.
-- EVERYTHING IS YOUR FAULT. THAT'S HOW IT WORKS, SON. NIGGERS TAKE OUR JOBS IN THE COMPANIES WE BUILT. MEXICANS MARCH IN THE STREETS TO GET US TO LEARN SPANISH. YOUR DAD GOT LET GO, DINNIT HE? FROM THE PLANT.
YEAH. HE'S BEEN LOOKING FOR SOMETHING ELSE, BUT IT'S HARD.
BET YOU A SPIC IS EARNING TWICE HIS WAGE DOING A QUARTER OF THE WORK.

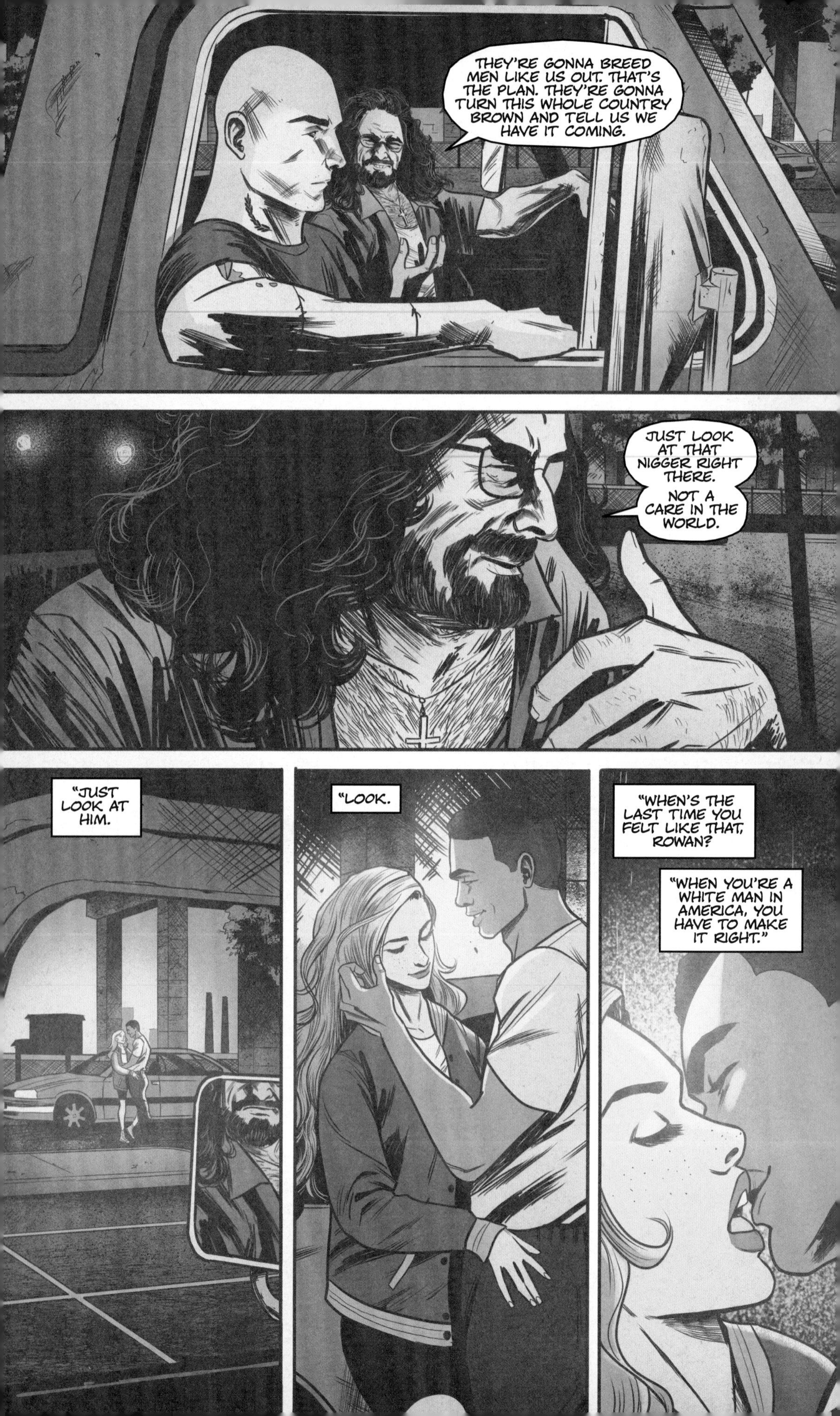
THEY'RE GONNA BREED MEN LIKE US OUT. THAT'S THE PLAN. THEY'RE GONNA TURN THIS WHOLE COUNTRY BROWN AND TELL US WE HAVE IT COMING.
JUST LOOK AT THAT NIGGER RIGHT THERE.
NOT A CARE IN THE WORLD.
"JUST LOOK AT HIM.
"LOOK.
"WHEN'S THE LAST TIME YOU FELT LIKE THAT, ROWAN?
"WHEN YOU'RE A WHITE MAN IN AMERICA, YOU HAVE TO MAKE IT RIGHT."

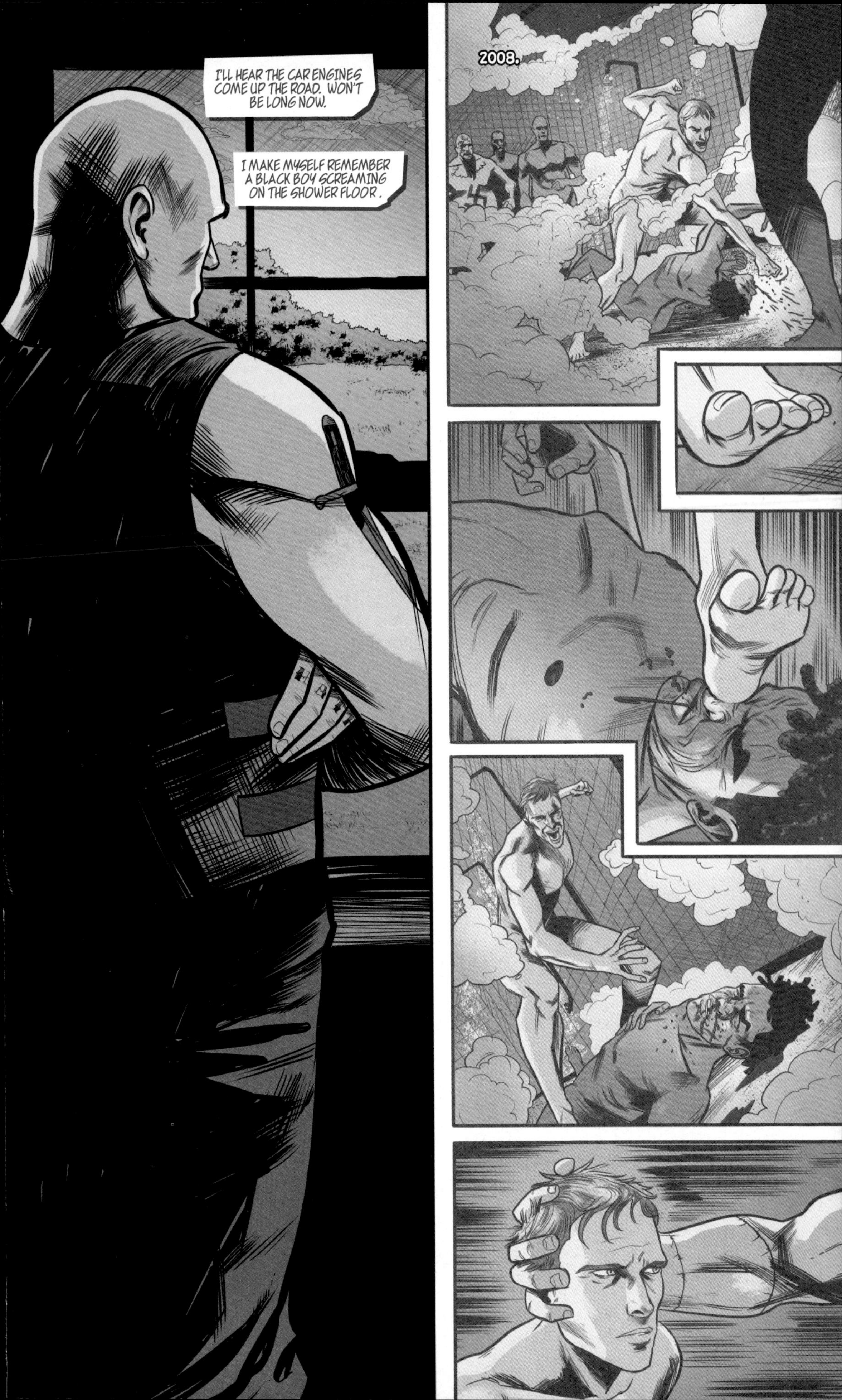
I'LL HEAR THE CAR ENGINES COME UP THE ROAD. WON'T BE LONG NOW.
I MAKE MYSELF REMEMBER A BLACK BOY SCREAMING ON THE SHOWER FLOOR.
2008.

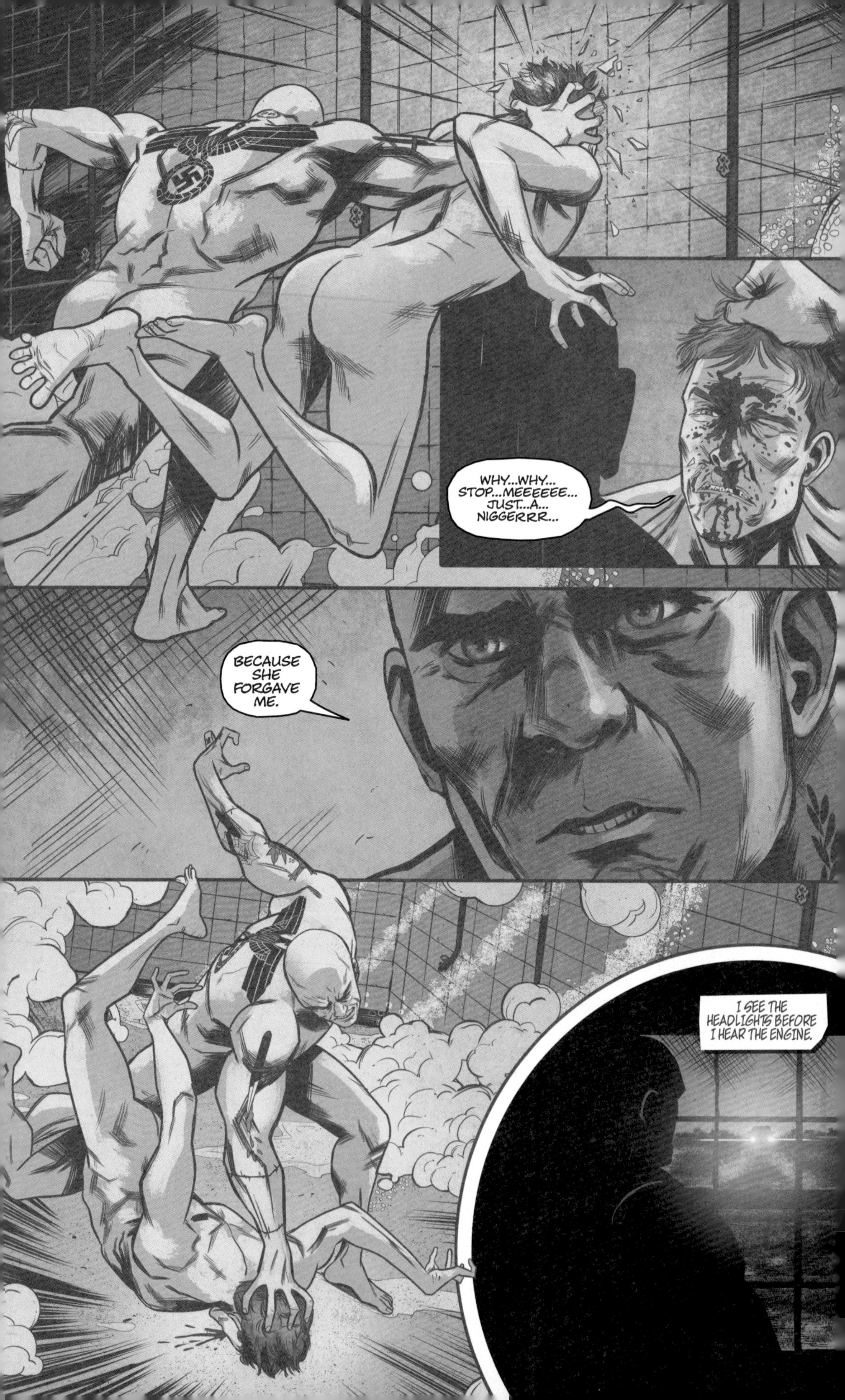
WHY...WHY... STOP...MEEEEEE... JUST...A... NIGGERRR...
BECAUSE SHE FORGAVE ME.
I SEE THE HEADLIGHTS BEFORE I HEAR THE ENGINE.

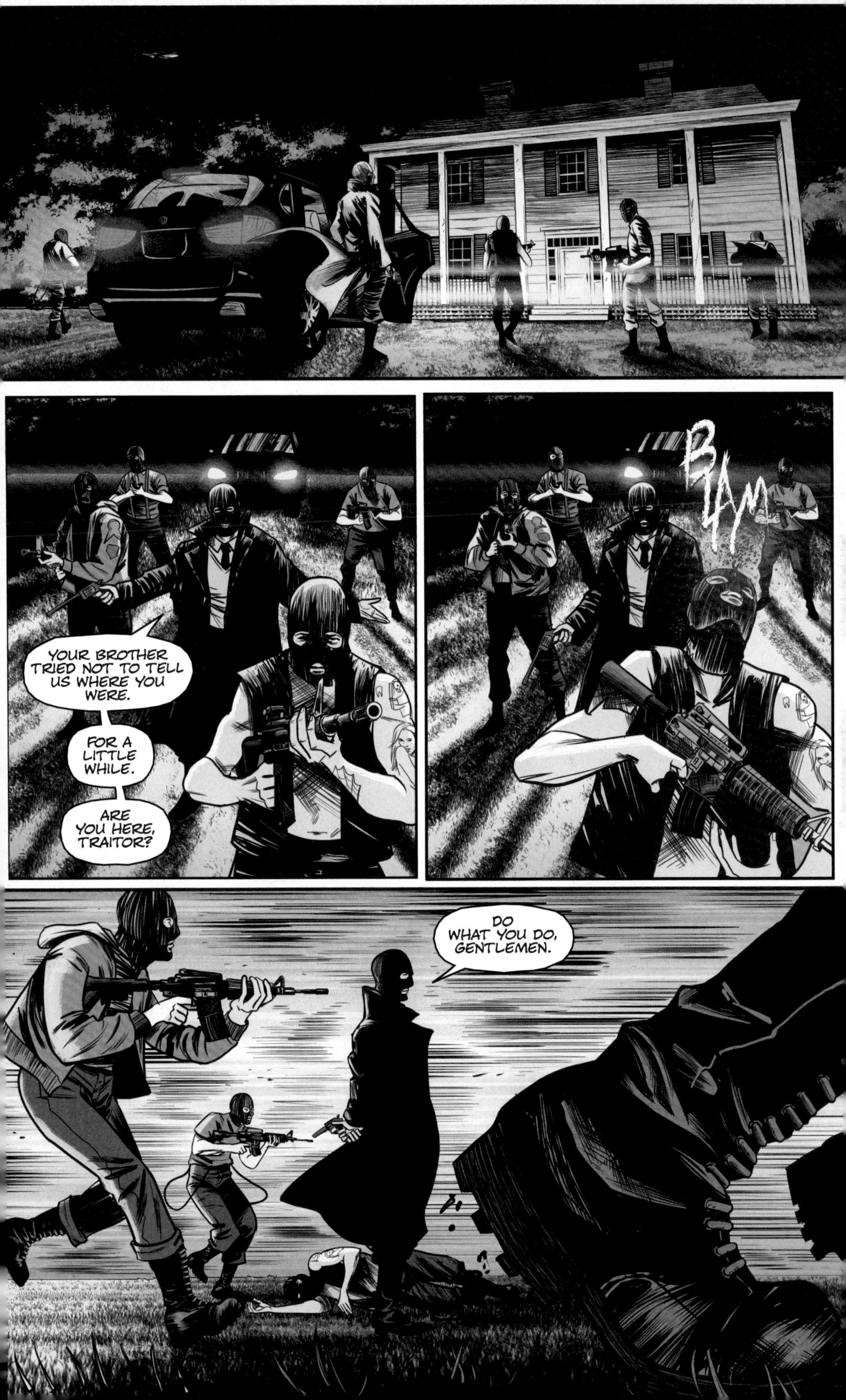
YOUR BROTHER TRIED NOT TO TELL US WHERE YOU WERE.
FOR A LITTLE WHILE.
ARE YOU HERE, TRAITOR?
BLAM
DO WHAT YOU DO, GENTLEMEN.

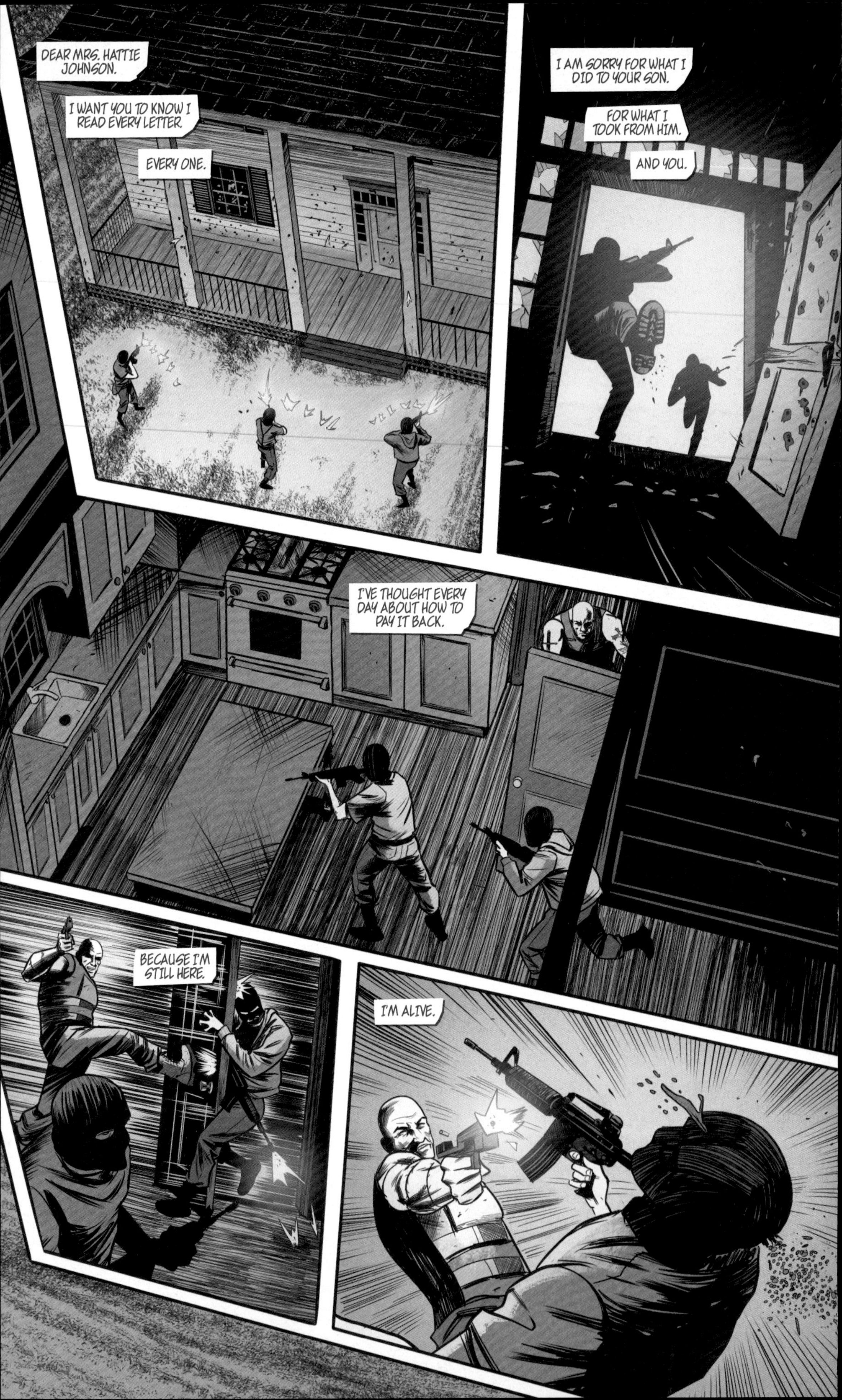
DEAR MRS. HATTIE JOHNSON.
I WANT YOU TO KNOW I READ EVERY LETTER.
EVERY ONE.
I AM SORRY FOR WHAT I DID TO YOUR SON.
FOR WHAT I TOOK FROM HIM.
AND YOU.
I'VE THOUGHT EVERY DAY ABOUT HOW TO PAY IT BACK.
BECAUSE I'M STILL HERE.
I'M ALIVE.

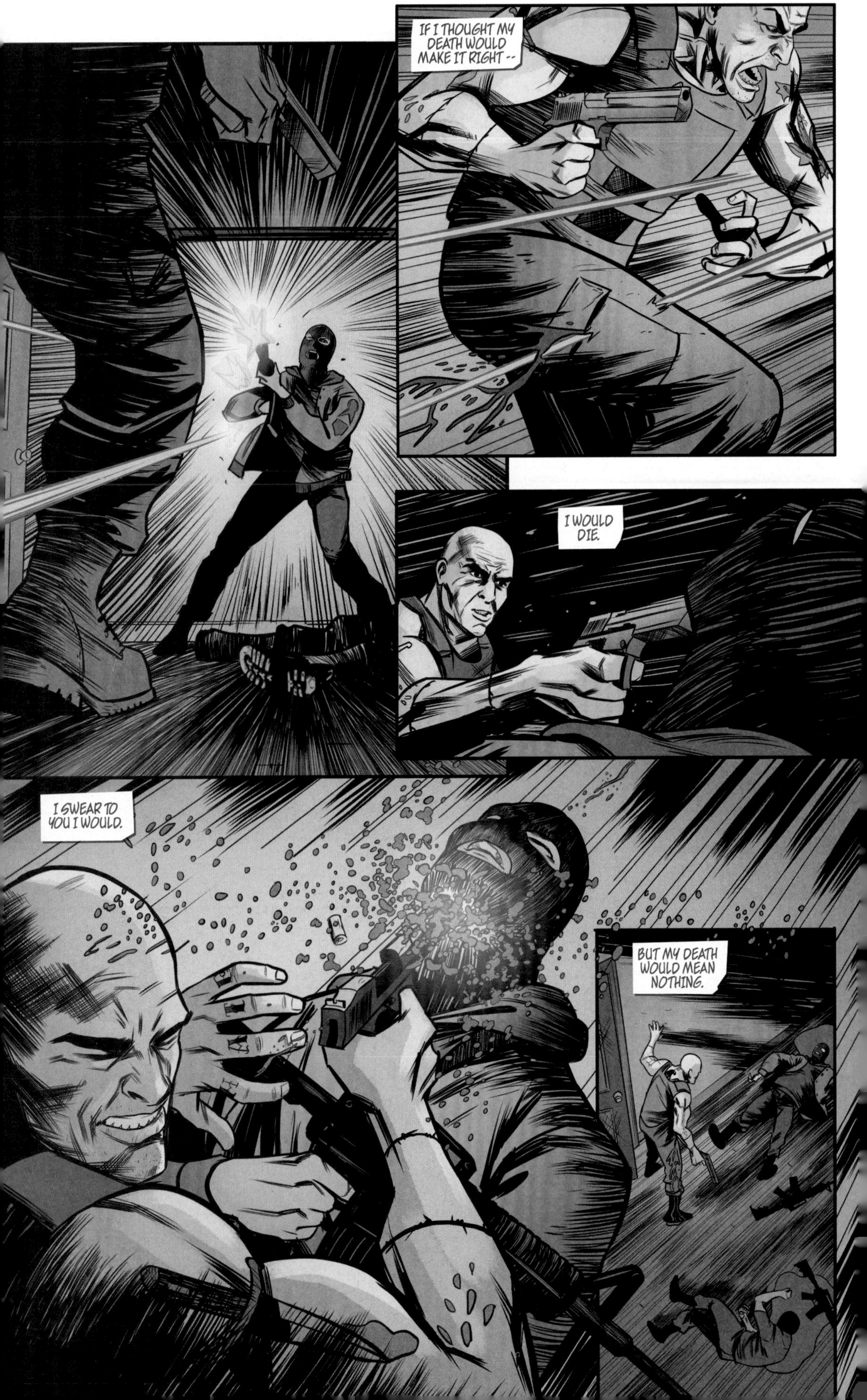
IF I THOUGHT MY DEATH WOULD MAKE IT RIGHT --
I WOULD DIE.
I SWEAR TO YOU I WOULD.
BUT MY DEATH WOULD MEAN NOTHING.

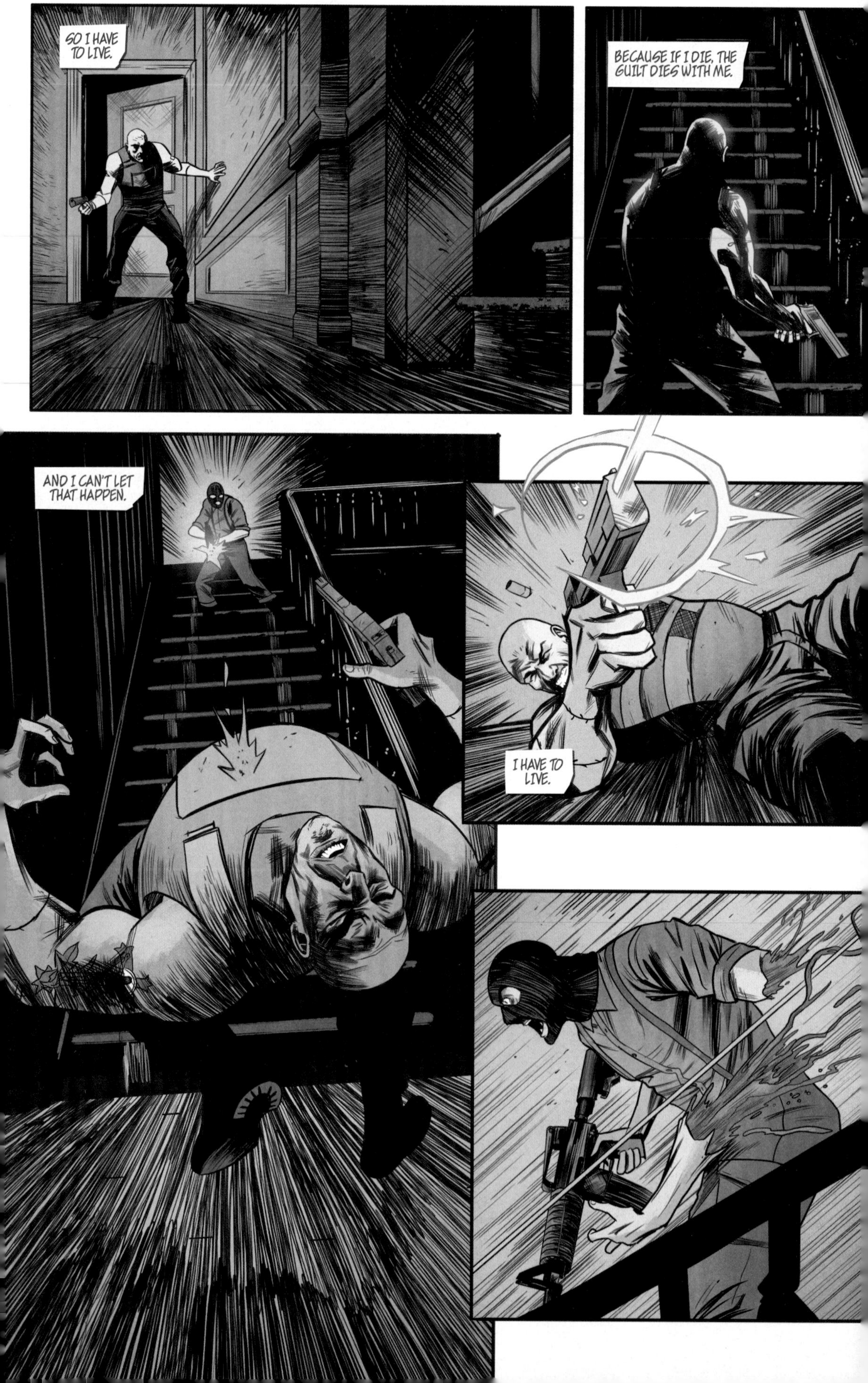
SO I HAVE TO LIVE.
BECAUSE IF I DIE, THE GUILT DIES WITH ME.
AND I CAN'T LET THAT HAPPEN.
I HAVE TO LIVE.

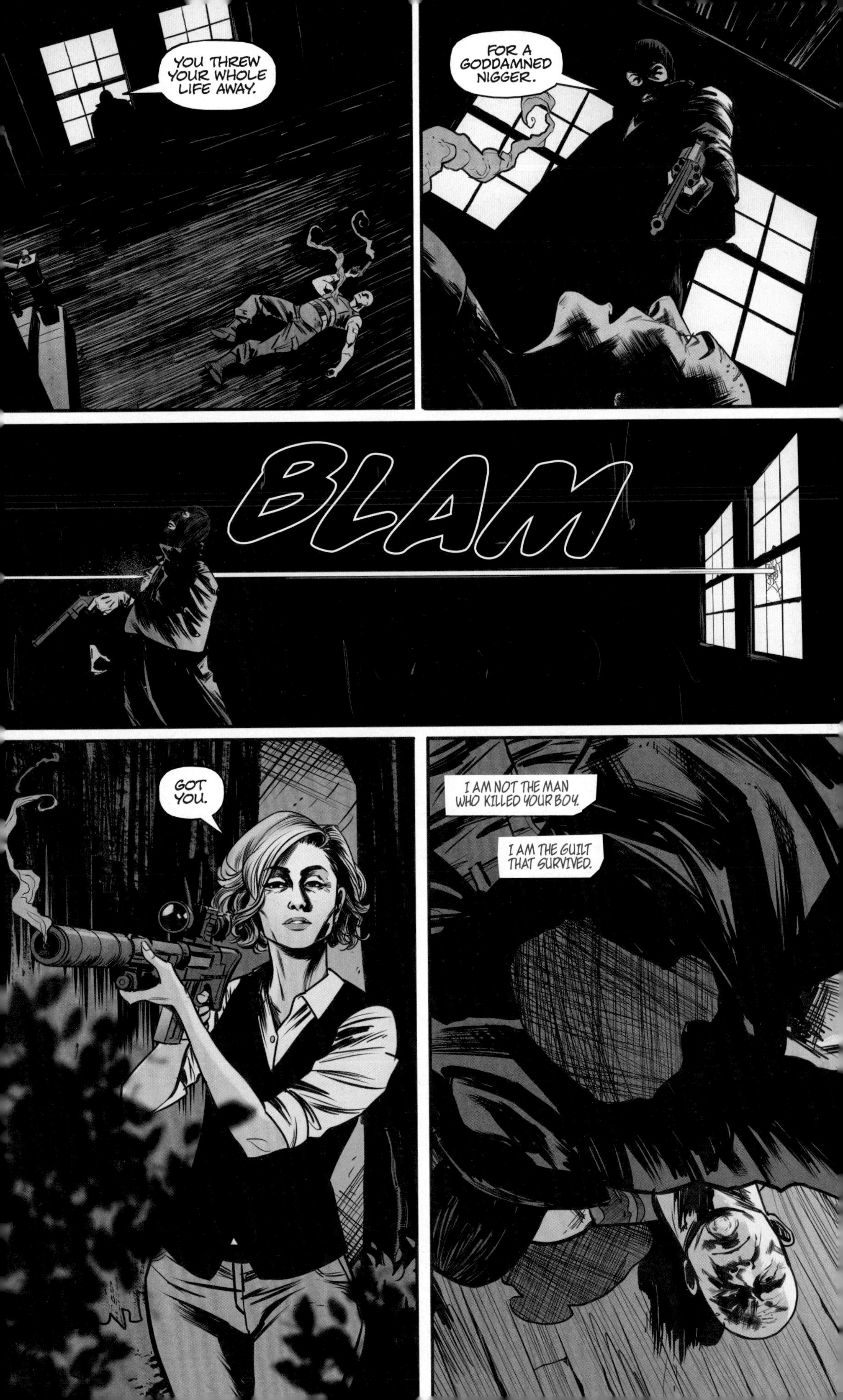

YOU THREW YOUR WHOLE LIFE AWAY.
FOR A GODDAMNED NIGGER.
BLAM
GOT YOU.
I AM NOT THE MAN WHO KILLED YOUR BOY.
I AM THE GUILT THAT SURVIVED.

THE MAN I SHOT WASN'T ABNER. HE WAS SMART ENOUGH TO NOT BE THERE.

BUT THAT MEANS HE'S STILL COMING FOR YOU.

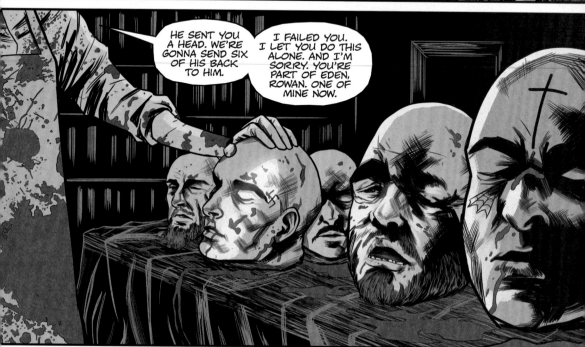

HE SENT YOU A HEAD. WE'RE GONNA SEND SIX OF HIS BACK TO HIM.

I FAILED YOU. I LET YOU DO THIS ALONE. AND I'M SORRY. YOU'RE PART OF EDEN, ROWAN. ONE OF MINE NOW.

I HAVE A LETTER I NEED MARK TO MAIL, TO A WOMAN NAMED MRS. HATTIE JOHN --

MAIL IT WHEN THIS IS DONE. WE HAVE A LOT OF WORK TO DO. FIRST THING?

CALL ABNER. TELL HIM WE'RE READY TO GO TO WAR.

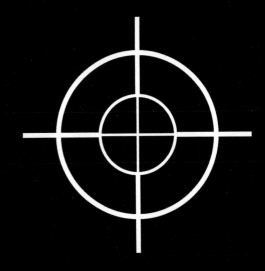

# Chapter 14

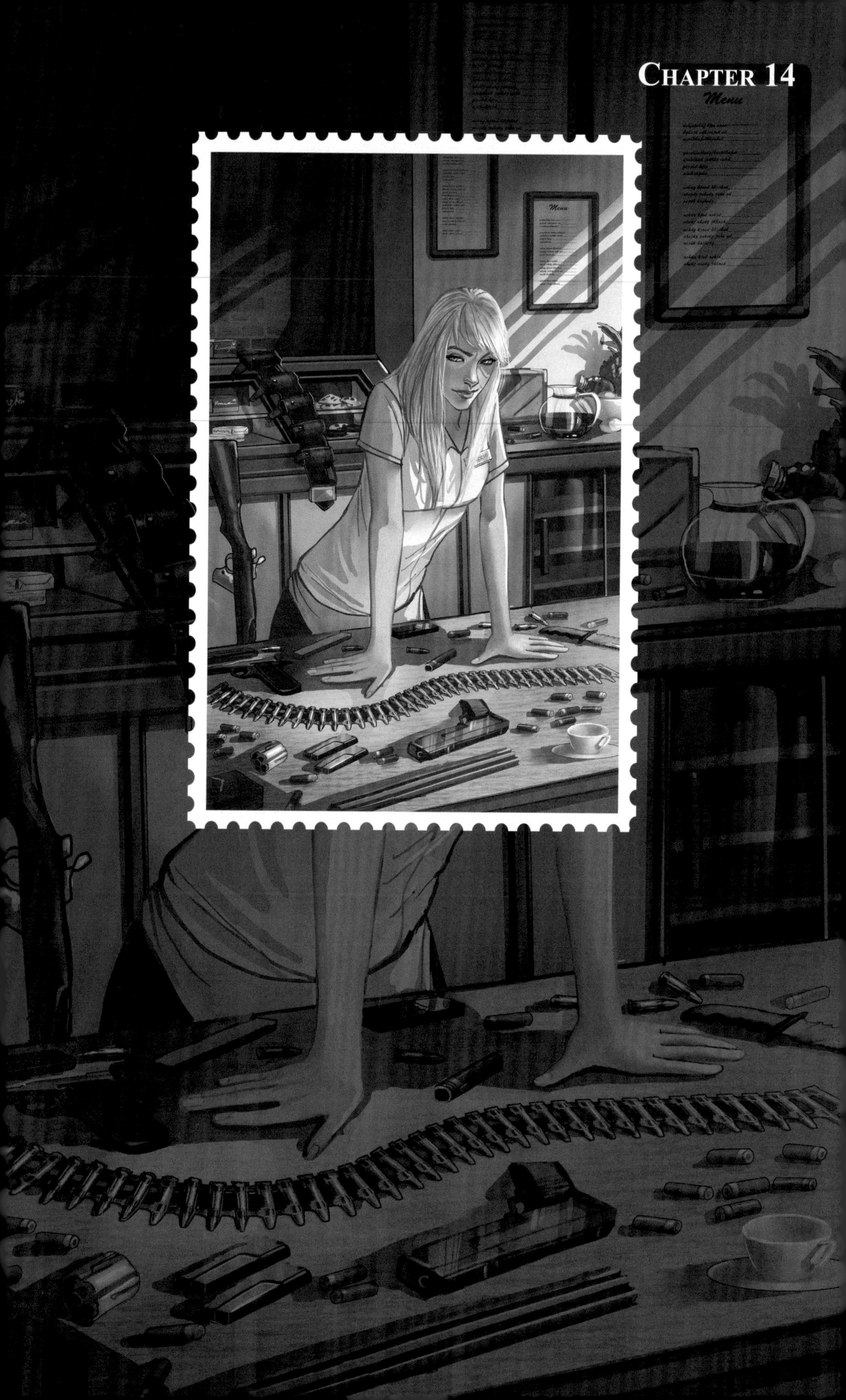
Menu
Menu

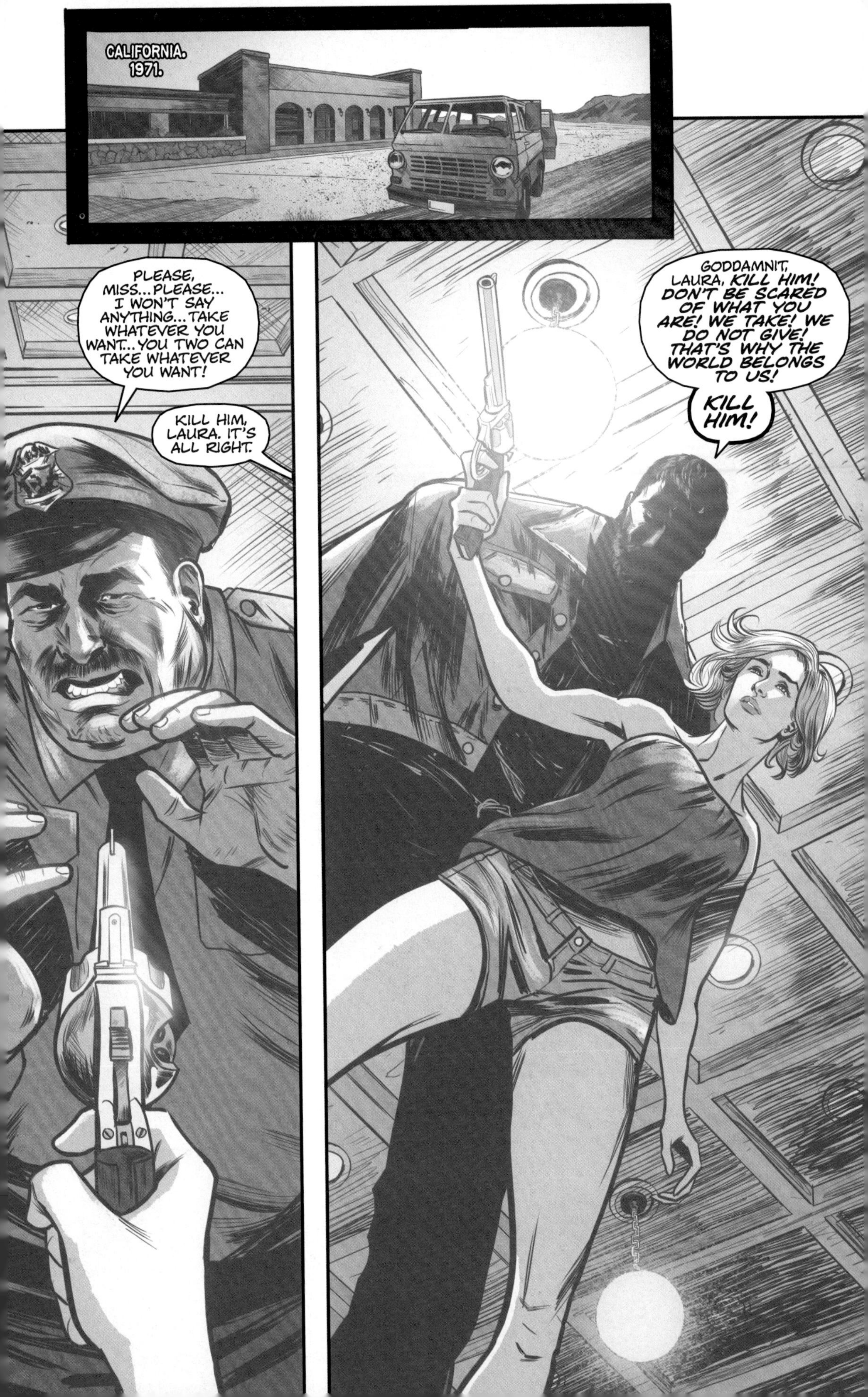
CALIFORNIA. 1971.
PLEASE, MISS...PLEASE... I WON'T SAY ANYTHING...TAKE WHATEVER YOU WANT...YOU TWO CAN TAKE WHATEVER YOU WANT!
KILL HIM, LAURA. IT'S ALL RIGHT.
GODDAMNIT, LAURA, KILL HIM! DON'T BE SCARED OF WHAT YOU ARE! WE TAKE! WE DO NOT GIVE! THAT'S WHY THE WORLD BELONGS TO US!
KILL HIM!

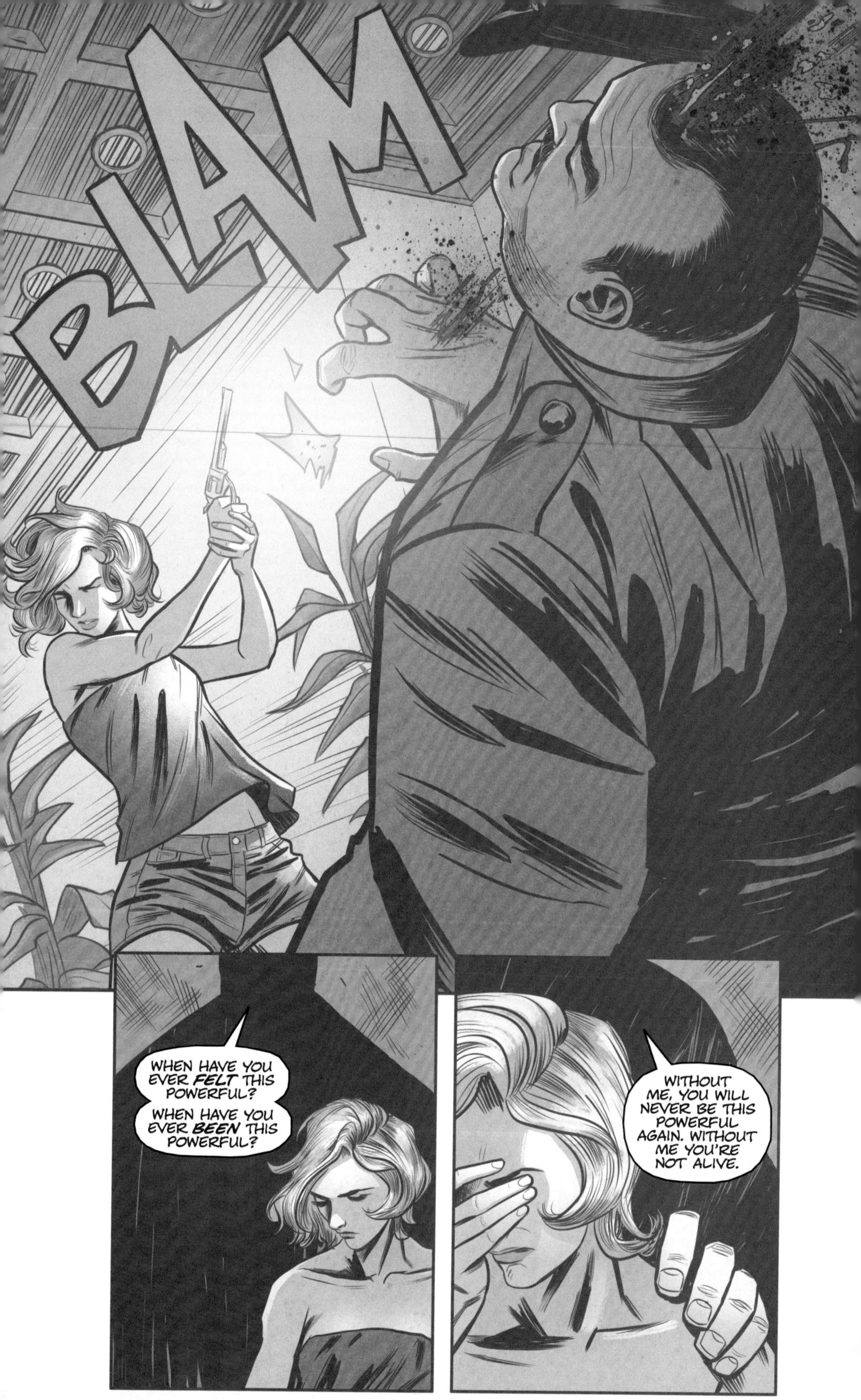
BLAM
WHEN HAVE YOU EVER FELT THIS POWERFUL?
WHEN HAVE YOU EVER BEEN THIS POWERFUL?
WITHOUT ME, YOU WILL NEVER BE THIS POWERFUL AGAIN. WITHOUT ME YOU'RE NOT ALIVE.

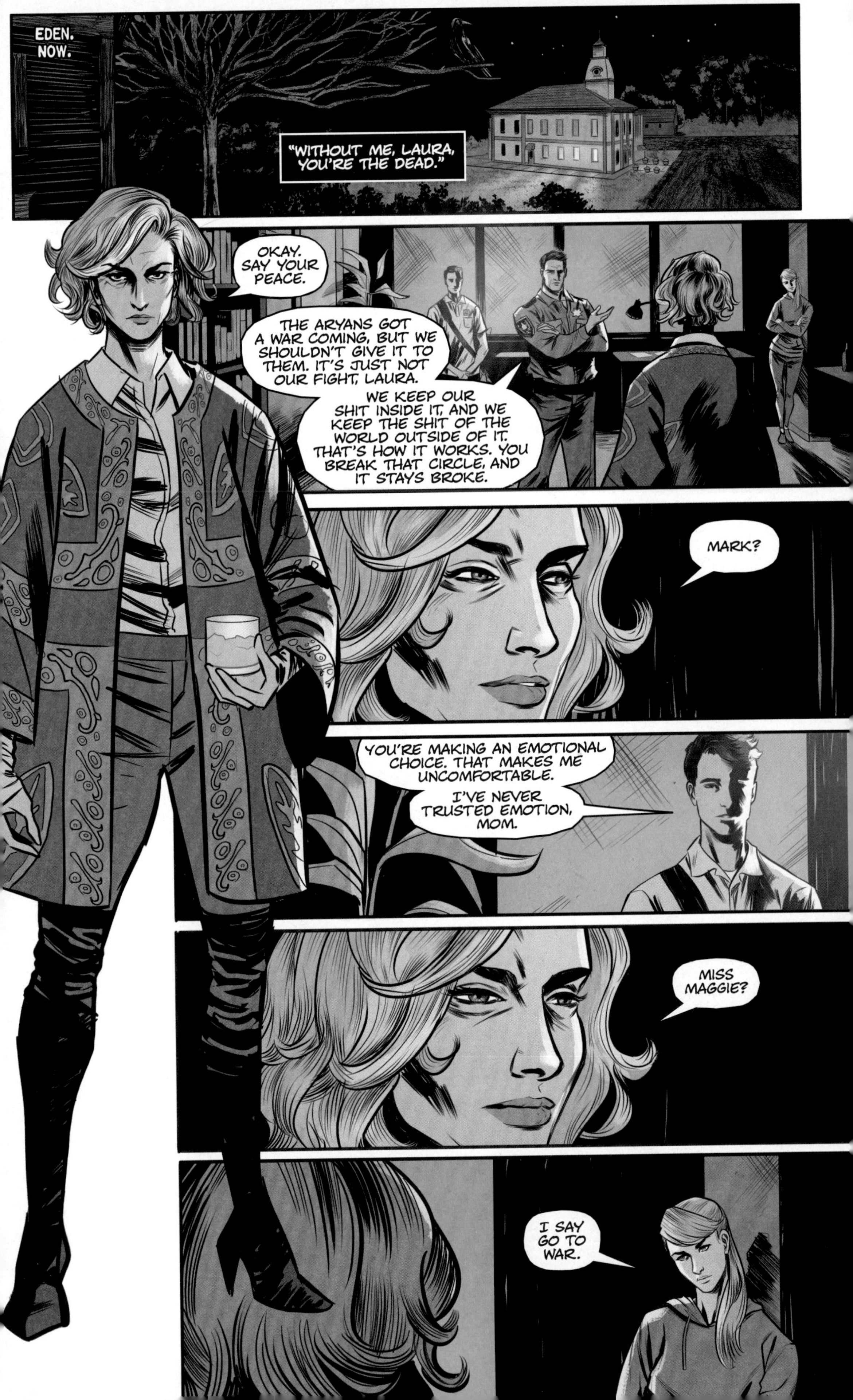
EDEN. NOW.
"WITHOUT ME, LAURA, YOU'RE THE DEAD."
OKAY. SAY YOUR PEACE.
THE ARYANS GOT A WAR COMING, BUT WE SHOULDN'T GIVE IT TO THEM. IT'S JUST NOT OUR FIGHT, LAURA.
WE KEEP OUR SHIT INSIDE IT, AND WE KEEP THE SHIT OF THE WORLD OUTSIDE OF IT. THAT'S HOW IT WORKS. YOU BREAK THAT CIRCLE, AND IT STAYS BROKE.
MARK?
YOU'RE MAKING AN EMOTIONAL CHOICE. THAT MAKES ME UNCOMFORTABLE.
I'VE NEVER TRUSTED EMOTION, MOM.
MISS MAGGIE?
I SAY GO TO WAR.

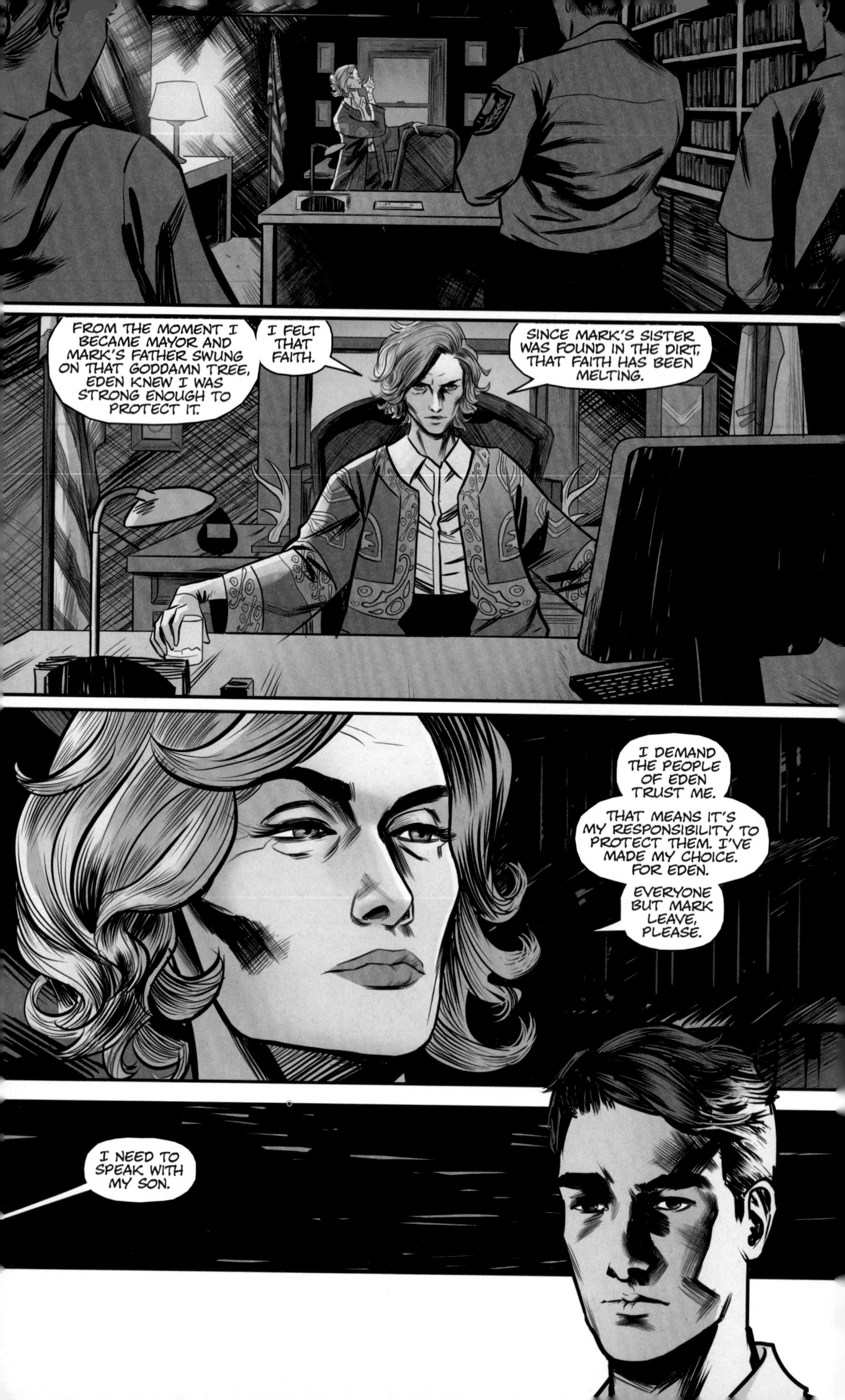
FROM THE MOMENT I BECAME MAYOR AND MARK'S FATHER SWUNG ON THAT GODDAMN TREE, EDEN KNEW I WAS STRONG ENOUGH TO PROTECT IT.
I FELT THAT FAITH.
SINCE MARK'S SISTER WAS FOUND IN THE DIRT, THAT FAITH HAS BEEN MELTING.
I DEMAND THE PEOPLE OF EDEN TRUST ME.
THAT MEANS IT'S MY RESPONSIBILITY TO PROTECT THEM. I'VE MADE MY CHOICE. FOR EDEN.
EVERYONE BUT MARK LEAVE, PLEASE.
I NEED TO SPEAK WITH MY SON.

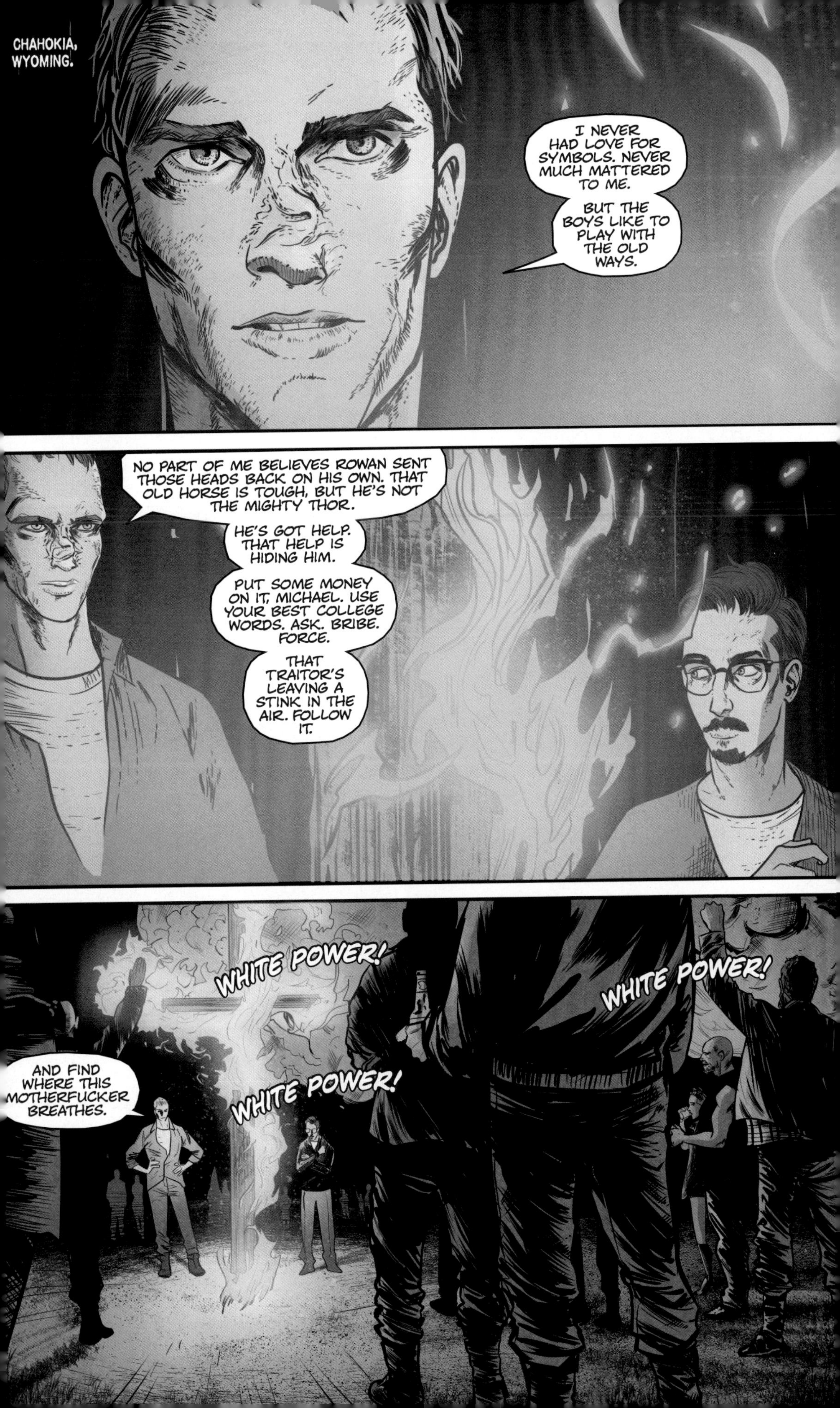
CHAHOKIA, WYOMING.
I NEVER HAD LOVE FOR SYMBOLS. NEVER MUCH MATTERED TO ME.
BUT THE BOYS LIKE TO PLAY WITH THE OLD WAYS.
NO PART OF ME BELIEVES ROWAN SENT THOSE HEADS BACK ON HIS OWN. THAT OLD HORSE IS TOUGH, BUT HE'S NOT THE MIGHTY THOR.
HE'S GOT HELP. THAT HELP IS HIDING HIM.
PUT SOME MONEY ON IT, MICHAEL. USE YOUR BEST COLLEGE WORDS. ASK. BRIBE. FORCE.
THAT TRAITOR'S LEAVING A STINK IN THE AIR. FOLLOW IT.
WHITE POWER!
WHITE POWER!
AND FIND WHERE THIS MOTHERFUCKER BREATHES.
WHITE POWER!

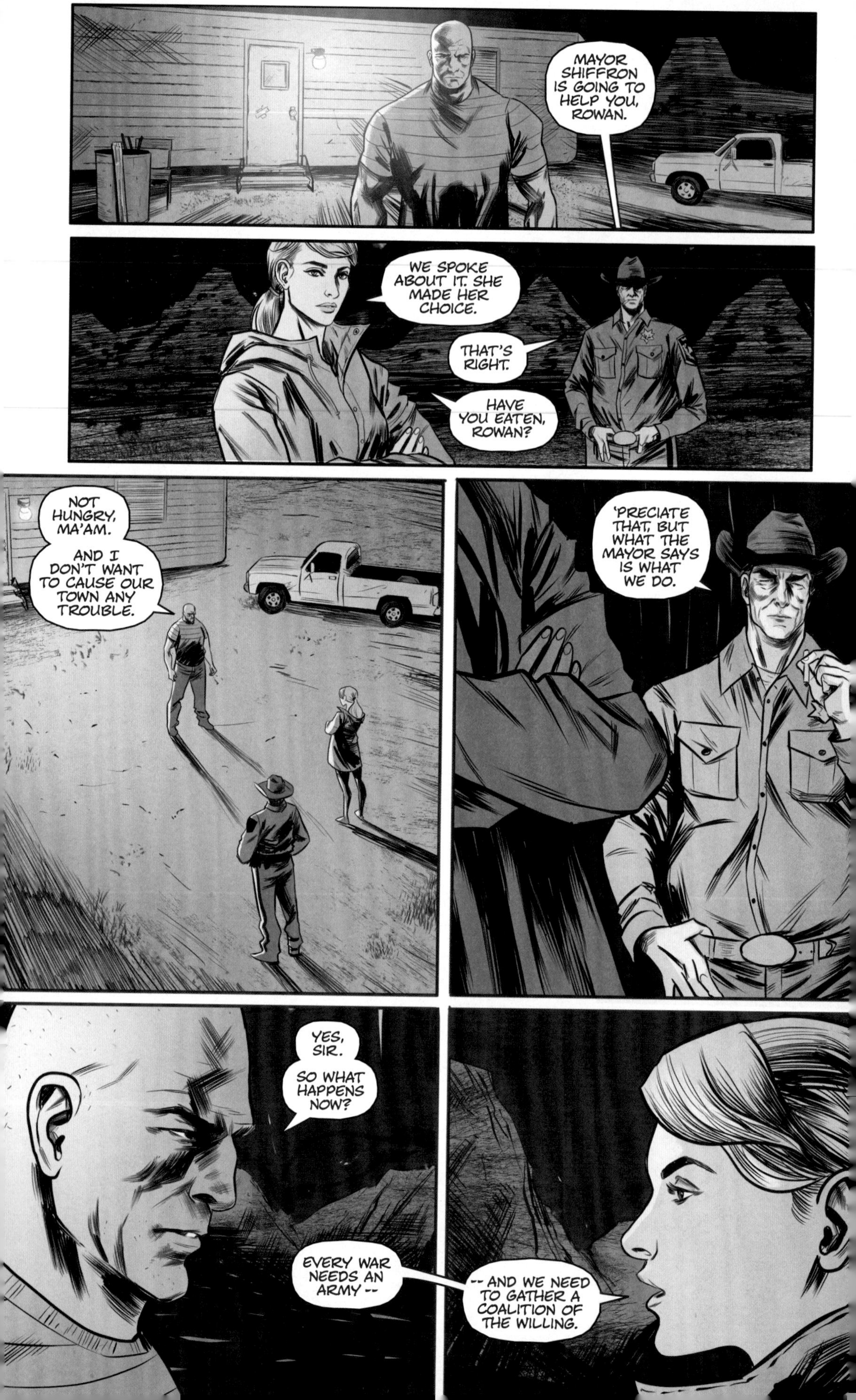
MAYOR SHIFFRON IS GOING TO HELP YOU, ROWAN.
WE SPOKE ABOUT IT. SHE MADE HER CHOICE.
THAT'S RIGHT.
HAVE YOU EATEN, ROWAN?
NOT HUNGRY, MA'AM.
AND I DON'T WANT TO CAUSE OUR TOWN ANY TROUBLE.
'PRECIATE THAT, BUT WHAT THE MAYOR SAYS IS WHAT WE DO.
YES, SIR.
SO WHAT HAPPENS NOW?
EVERY WAR NEEDS AN ARMY --
-- AND WE NEED TO GATHER A COALITION OF THE WILLING.

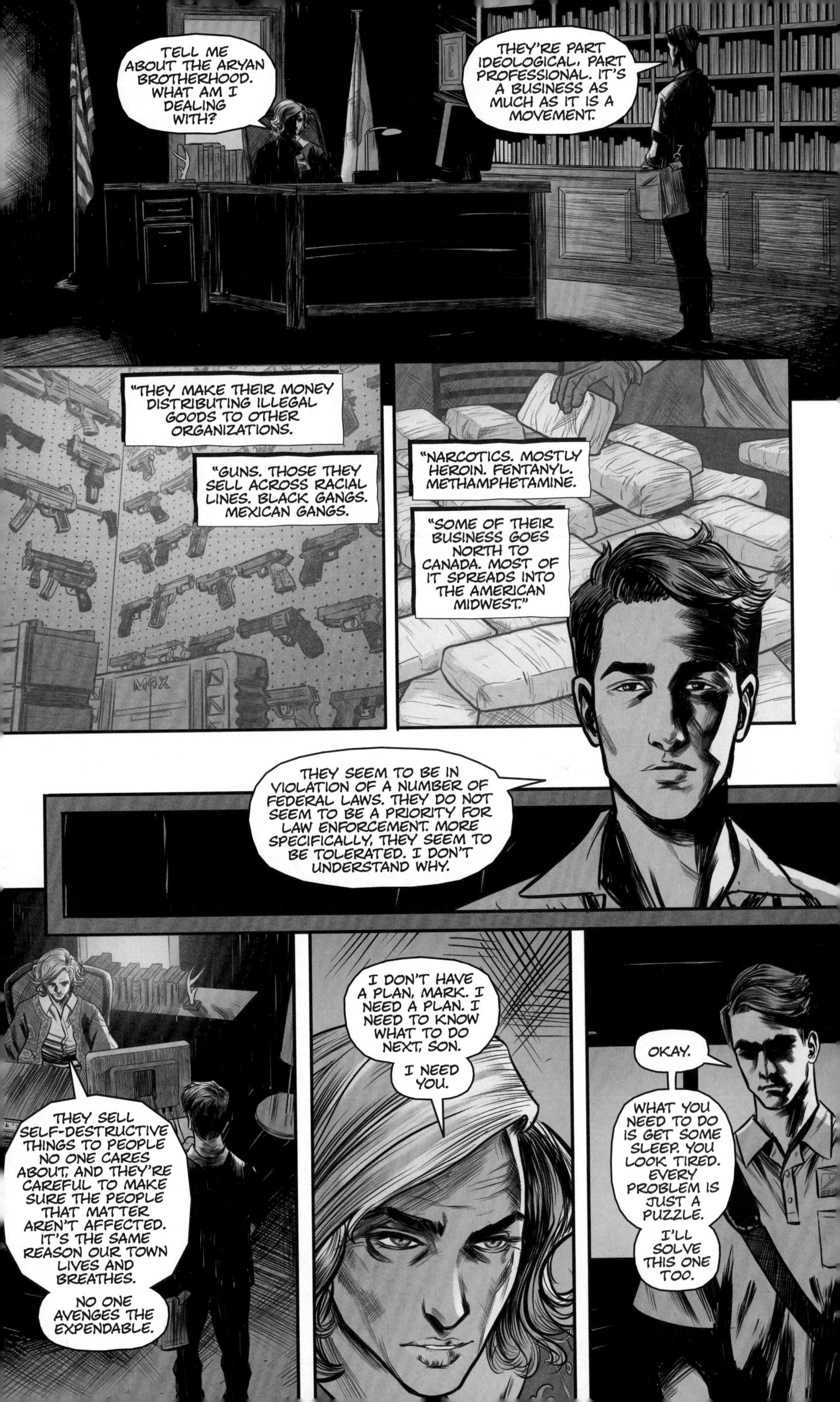

TELL ME ABOUT THE ARYAN BROTHERHOOD. WHAT AM I DEALING WITH?
THEY'RE PART IDEOLOGICAL, PART PROFESSIONAL. IT'S A BUSINESS AS MUCH AS IT IS A MOVEMENT.
"THEY MAKE THEIR MONEY DISTRIBUTING ILLEGAL GOODS TO OTHER ORGANIZATIONS.
"GUNS. THOSE THEY SELL ACROSS RACIAL LINES. BLACK GANGS. MEXICAN GANGS.
"NARCOTICS. MOSTLY HEROIN. FENTANYL. METHAMPHETAMINE.
"SOME OF THEIR BUSINESS GOES NORTH TO CANADA. MOST OF IT SPREADS INTO THE AMERICAN MIDWEST."
THEY SEEM TO BE IN VIOLATION OF A NUMBER OF FEDERAL LAWS. THEY DO NOT SEEM TO BE A PRIORITY FOR LAW ENFORCEMENT. MORE SPECIFICALLY, THEY SEEM TO BE TOLERATED. I DON'T UNDERSTAND WHY.
THEY SELL SELF-DESTRUCTIVE THINGS TO PEOPLE NO ONE CARES ABOUT, AND THEY'RE CAREFUL TO MAKE SURE THE PEOPLE THAT MATTER AREN'T AFFECTED. IT'S THE SAME REASON OUR TOWN LIVES AND BREATHES.
NO ONE AVENGES THE EXPENDABLE.
I DON'T HAVE A PLAN, MARK. I NEED A PLAN. I NEED TO KNOW WHAT TO DO NEXT, SON.
I NEED YOU.
OKAY.
WHAT YOU NEED TO DO IS GET SOME SLEEP. YOU LOOK TIRED. EVERY PROBLEM IS JUST A PUZZLE.
I'LL SOLVE THIS ONE TOO.

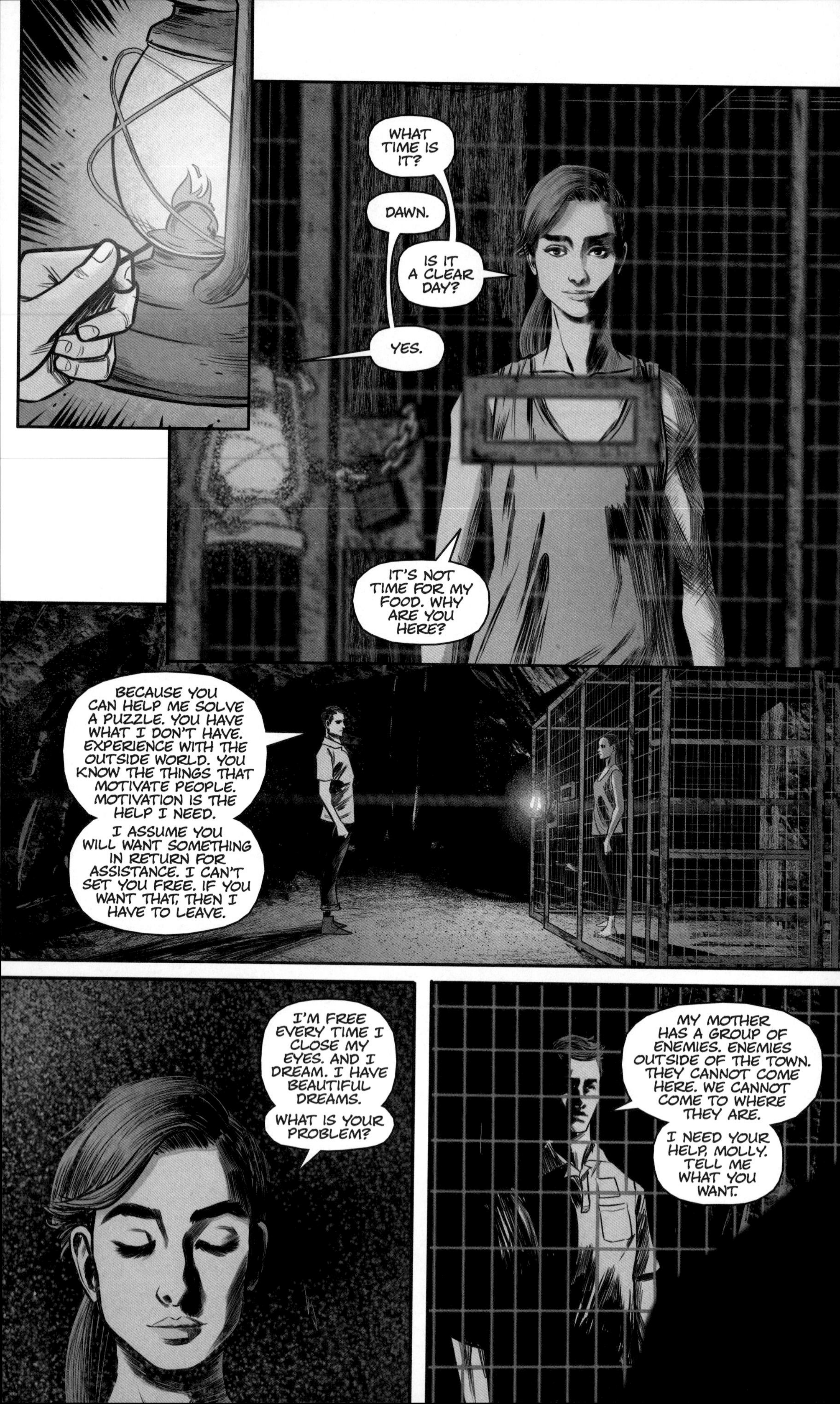
WHAT TIME IS IT?
DAWN.
IS IT A CLEAR DAY?
YES.
IT'S NOT TIME FOR MY FOOD. WHY ARE YOU HERE?
BECAUSE YOU CAN HELP ME SOLVE A PUZZLE. YOU HAVE WHAT I DON'T HAVE. EXPERIENCE WITH THE OUTSIDE WORLD. YOU KNOW THE THINGS THAT MOTIVATE PEOPLE. MOTIVATION IS THE HELP I NEED.
I ASSUME YOU WILL WANT SOMETHING IN RETURN FOR ASSISTANCE. I CAN'T SET YOU FREE. IF YOU WANT THAT, THEN I HAVE TO LEAVE.
I'M FREE EVERY TIME I CLOSE MY EYES. AND I DREAM. I HAVE BEAUTIFUL DREAMS.
WHAT IS YOUR PROBLEM?
MY MOTHER HAS A GROUP OF ENEMIES. ENEMIES OUTSIDE OF THE TOWN. THEY CANNOT COME HERE. WE CANNOT COME TO WHERE THEY ARE.
I NEED YOUR HELP, MOLLY. TELL ME WHAT YOU WANT.

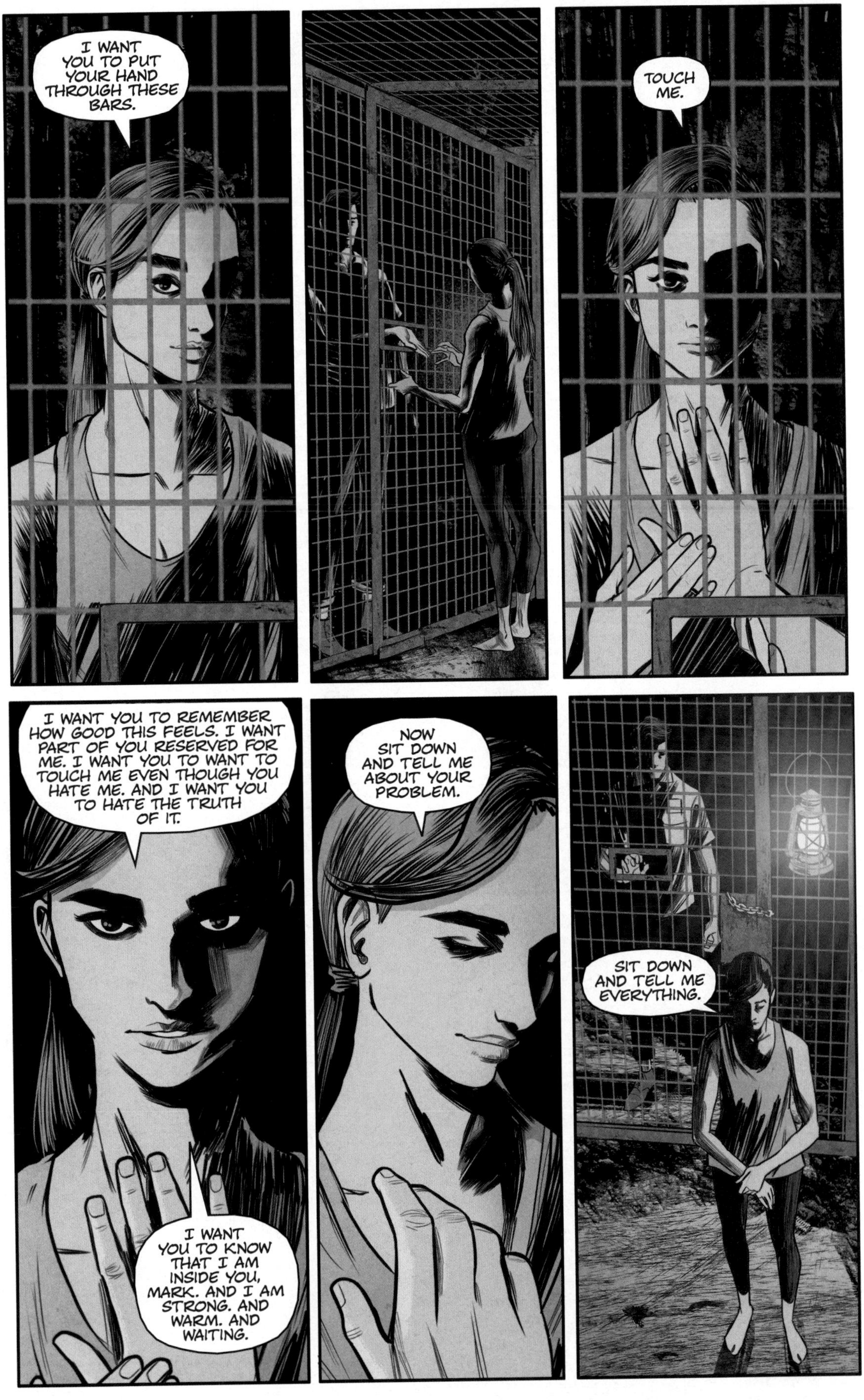
I WANT YOU TO PUT YOUR HAND THROUGH THESE BARS.
TOUCH ME.
I WANT YOU TO REMEMBER HOW GOOD THIS FEELS. I WANT PART OF YOU RESERVED FOR ME. I WANT YOU TO WANT TO TOUCH ME EVEN THOUGH YOU HATE ME. AND I WANT YOU TO HATE THE TRUTH OF IT.
I WANT YOU TO KNOW THAT I AM INSIDE YOU, MARK. AND I AM STRONG. AND WARM. AND WAITING.
NOW SIT DOWN AND TELL ME ABOUT YOUR PROBLEM.
SIT DOWN AND TELL ME EVERYTHING.

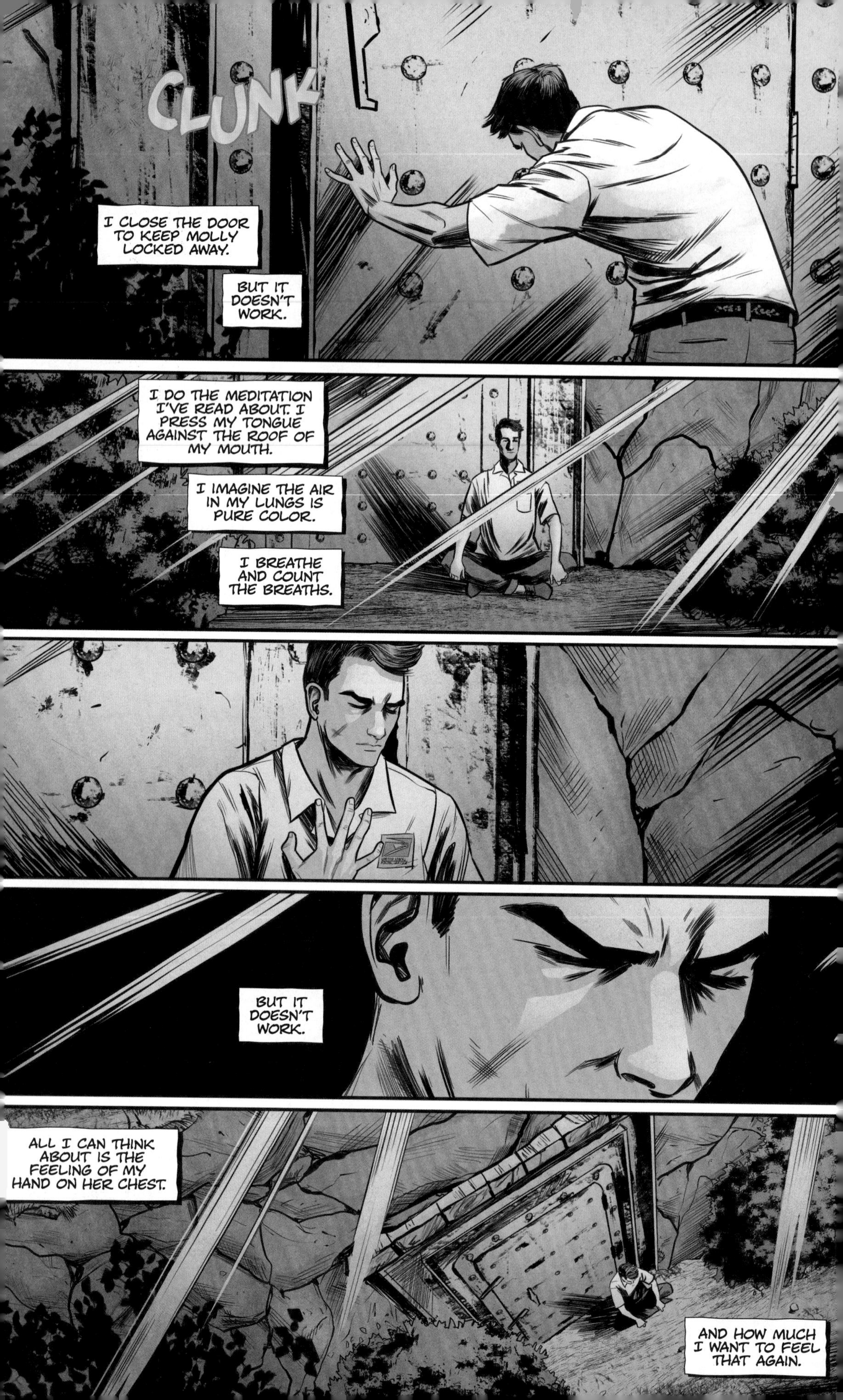
CLUNK
I CLOSE THE DOOR TO KEEP MOLLY LOCKED AWAY.
BUT IT DOESN'T WORK.
I DO THE MEDITATION I'VE READ ABOUT. I PRESS MY TONGUE AGAINST THE ROOF OF MY MOUTH.
I IMAGINE THE AIR IN MY LUNGS IS PURE COLOR.
I BREATHE AND COUNT THE BREATHS.
BUT IT DOESN'T WORK.
ALL I CAN THINK ABOUT IS THE FEELING OF MY HAND ON HER CHEST.
AND HOW MUCH I WANT TO FEEL THAT AGAIN.

Carpenter's SCRAP SHOP

ABNER.

YOU ONLY SEE ME WHEN THERE'S SOMETHING WRONG.

SO WHAT IS WRONG?

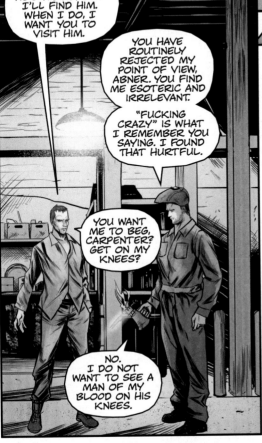

WE'RE AT WAR WITH SOMEONE. HE'S HIDING, BUT I'LL FIND HIM. WHEN I DO, I WANT YOU TO VISIT HIM.

YOU HAVE ROUTINELY REJECTED MY POINT OF VIEW, ABNER. YOU FIND ME ESOTERIC AND IRRELEVANT.

"FUCKING CRAZY" IS WHAT I REMEMBER YOU SAYING. I FOUND THAT HURTFUL.

YOU WANT ME TO BEG, CARPENTER? GET ON MY KNEES?

NO. I DO NOT WANT TO SEE A MAN OF MY BLOOD ON HIS KNEES.

I'VE GOT A POT OF COFFEE I'M WILLING TO SHARE. TELL ME WHAT THREATENS YOU.

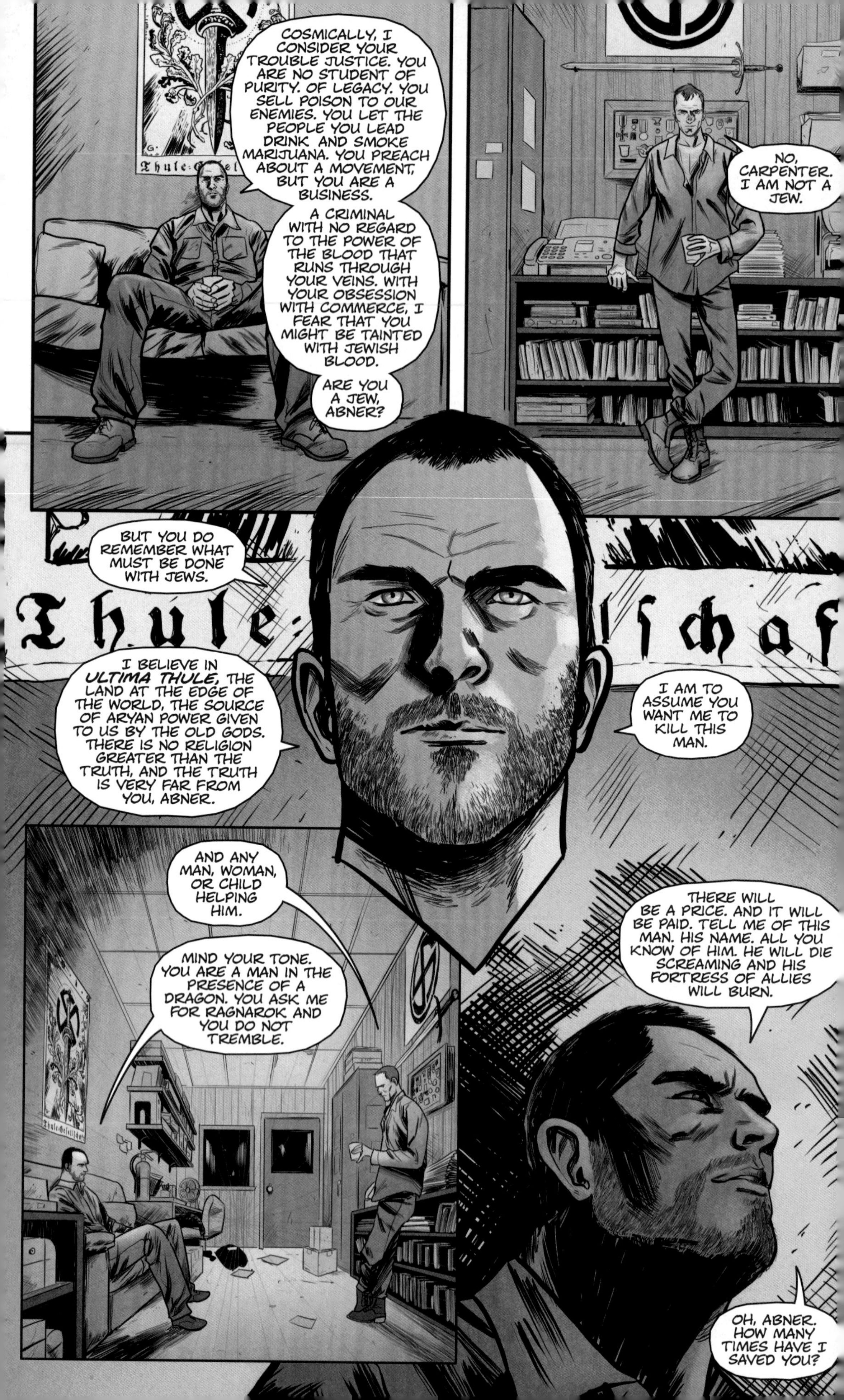

Thule-Gesel
COSMICALLY, I CONSIDER YOUR TROUBLE JUSTICE. YOU ARE NO STUDENT OF PURITY. OF LEGACY. YOU SELL POISON TO OUR ENEMIES. YOU LET THE PEOPLE YOU LEAD DRINK AND SMOKE MARIJUANA. YOU PREACH ABOUT A MOVEMENT, BUT YOU ARE A BUSINESS.
A CRIMINAL WITH NO REGARD TO THE POWER OF THE BLOOD THAT RUNS THROUGH YOUR VEINS. WITH YOUR OBSESSION WITH COMMERCE, I FEAR THAT YOU MIGHT BE TAINTED WITH JEWISH BLOOD.
ARE YOU A JEW, ABNER?
NO, CARPENTER. I AM NOT A JEW.
BUT YOU DO REMEMBER WHAT MUST BE DONE WITH JEWS.
Thule-
lschaf
I BELIEVE IN *ULTIMA THULE,* THE LAND AT THE EDGE OF THE WORLD, THE SOURCE OF ARYAN POWER GIVEN TO US BY THE OLD GODS. THERE IS NO RELIGION GREATER THAN THE TRUTH, AND THE TRUTH IS VERY FAR FROM YOU, ABNER.
I AM TO ASSUME YOU WANT ME TO KILL THIS MAN.
AND ANY MAN, WOMAN, OR CHILD HELPING HIM.
MIND YOUR TONE. YOU ARE A MAN IN THE PRESENCE OF A DRAGON. YOU ASK ME FOR RAGNAROK AND YOU DO NOT TREMBLE.
THERE WILL BE A PRICE. AND IT WILL BE PAID. TELL ME OF THIS MAN. HIS NAME. ALL YOU KNOW OF HIM. HE WILL DIE SCREAMING AND HIS FORTRESS OF ALLIES WILL BURN.
OH, ABNER. HOW MANY TIMES HAVE I SAVED YOU?

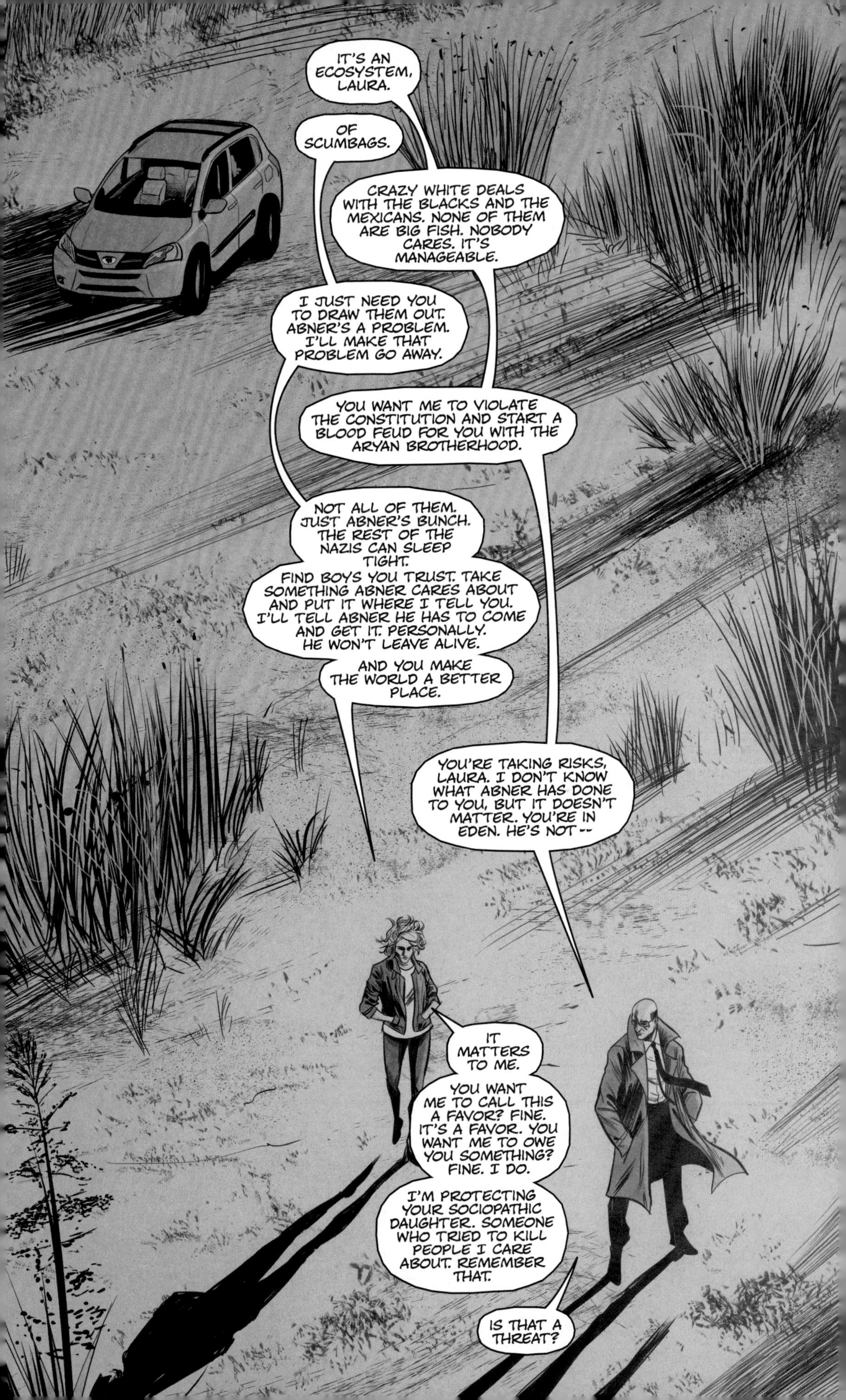
IT'S AN ECOSYSTEM, LAURA.
OF SCUMBAGS.
CRAZY WHITE DEALS WITH THE BLACKS AND THE MEXICANS. NONE OF THEM ARE BIG FISH. NOBODY CARES. IT'S MANAGEABLE.
I JUST NEED YOU TO DRAW THEM OUT. ABNER'S A PROBLEM. I'LL MAKE THAT PROBLEM GO AWAY.
YOU WANT ME TO VIOLATE THE CONSTITUTION AND START A BLOOD FEUD FOR YOU WITH THE ARYAN BROTHERHOOD.
NOT ALL OF THEM. JUST ABNER'S BUNCH. THE REST OF THE NAZIS CAN SLEEP TIGHT.
FIND BOYS YOU TRUST. TAKE SOMETHING ABNER CARES ABOUT AND PUT IT WHERE I TELL YOU. I'LL TELL ABNER HE HAS TO COME AND GET IT. PERSONALLY. HE WON'T LEAVE ALIVE.
AND YOU MAKE THE WORLD A BETTER PLACE.
YOU'RE TAKING RISKS, LAURA. I DON'T KNOW WHAT ABNER HAS DONE TO YOU, BUT IT DOESN'T MATTER. YOU'RE IN EDEN. HE'S NOT --
IT MATTERS TO ME.
YOU WANT ME TO CALL THIS A FAVOR? FINE. IT'S A FAVOR. YOU WANT ME TO OWE YOU SOMETHING? FINE. I DO.
I'M PROTECTING YOUR SOCIOPATHIC DAUGHTER. SOMEONE WHO TRIED TO KILL PEOPLE I CARE ABOUT. REMEMBER THAT.
IS THAT A THREAT?

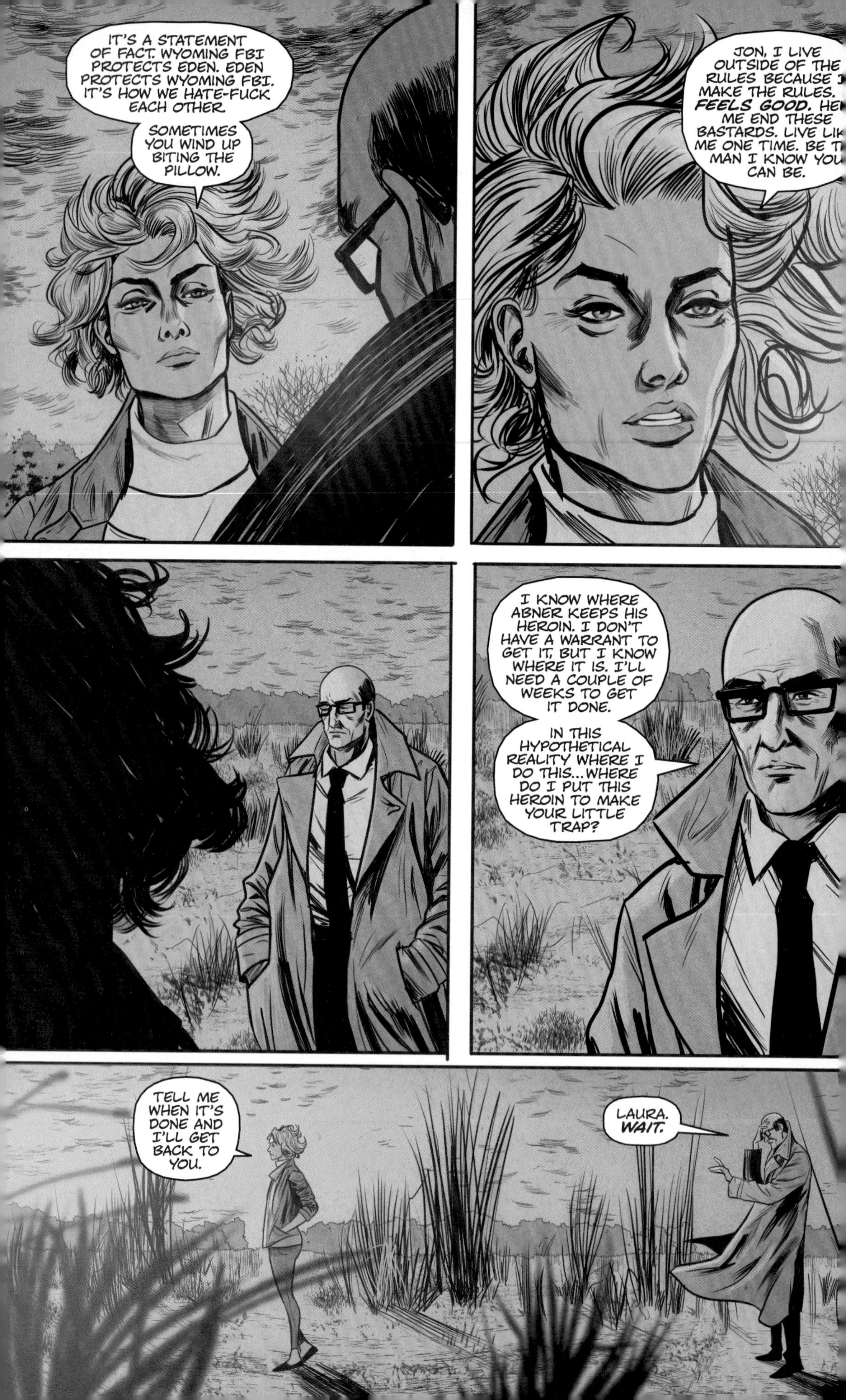
IT'S A STATEMENT OF FACT. WYOMING FBI PROTECTS EDEN. EDEN PROTECTS WYOMING FBI. IT'S HOW WE HATE-FUCK EACH OTHER.
SOMETIMES YOU WIND UP BITING THE PILLOW.
JON, I LIVE OUTSIDE OF THE RULES BECAUSE I MAKE THE RULES. FEELS GOOD. HEL ME END THESE BASTARDS. LIVE LIK ME ONE TIME. BE T MAN I KNOW YOU CAN BE.
I KNOW WHERE ABNER KEEPS HIS HEROIN. I DON'T HAVE A WARRANT TO GET IT, BUT I KNOW WHERE IT IS. I'LL NEED A COUPLE OF WEEKS TO GET IT DONE.
IN THIS HYPOTHETICAL REALITY WHERE I DO THIS...WHERE DO I PUT THIS HEROIN TO MAKE YOUR LITTLE TRAP?
TELL ME WHEN IT'S DONE AND I'LL GET BACK TO YOU.
LAURA. WAIT.

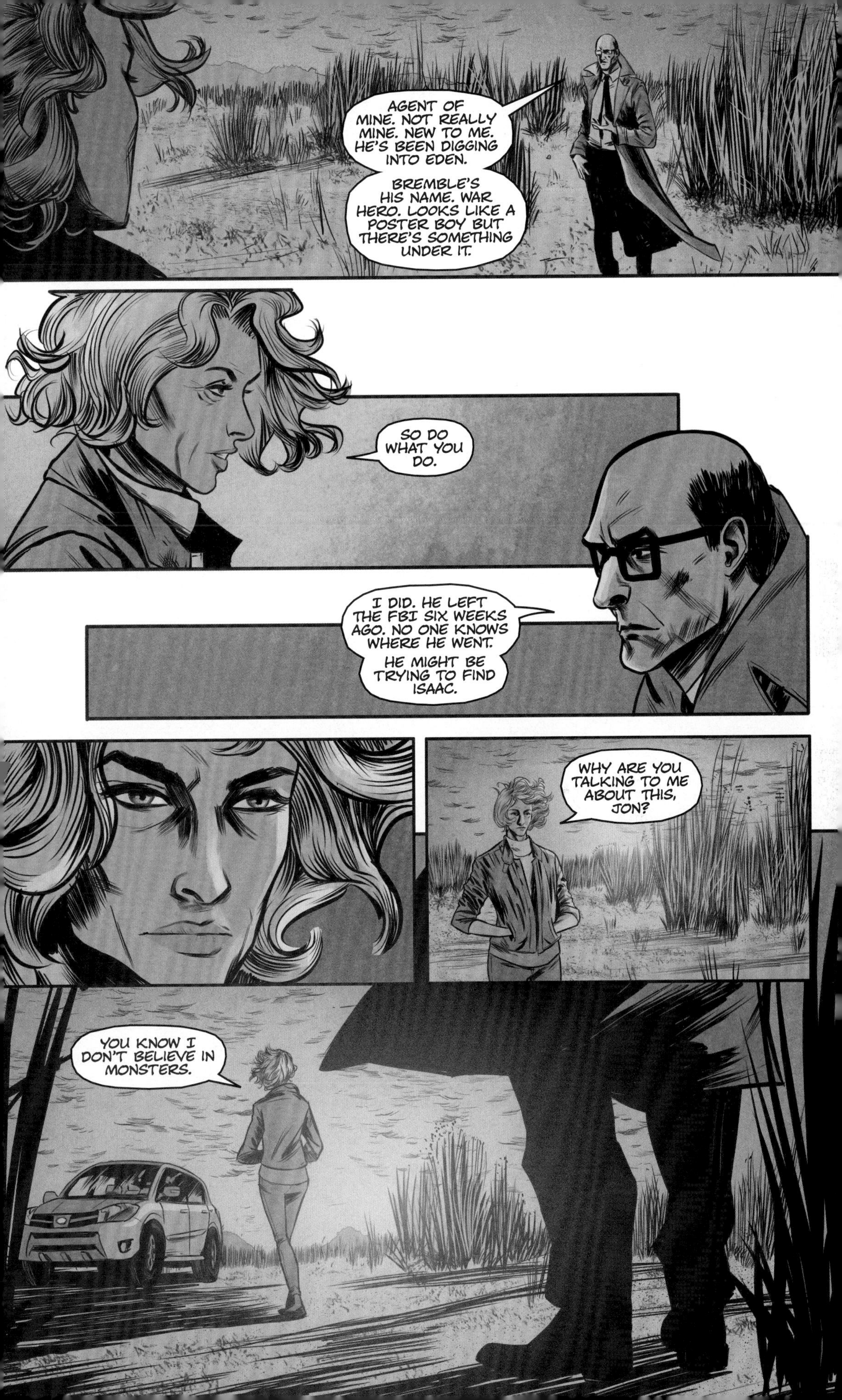
AGENT OF MINE. NOT REALLY MINE. NEW TO ME. HE'S BEEN DIGGING INTO EDEN.
BREMBLE'S HIS NAME. WAR HERO. LOOKS LIKE A POSTER BOY BUT THERE'S SOMETHING UNDER IT.
SO DO WHAT YOU DO.
I DID. HE LEFT THE FBI SIX WEEKS AGO. NO ONE KNOWS WHERE HE WENT.
HE MIGHT BE TRYING TO FIND ISAAC.
WHY ARE YOU TALKING TO ME ABOUT THIS, JON?
YOU KNOW I DON'T BELIEVE IN MONSTERS.

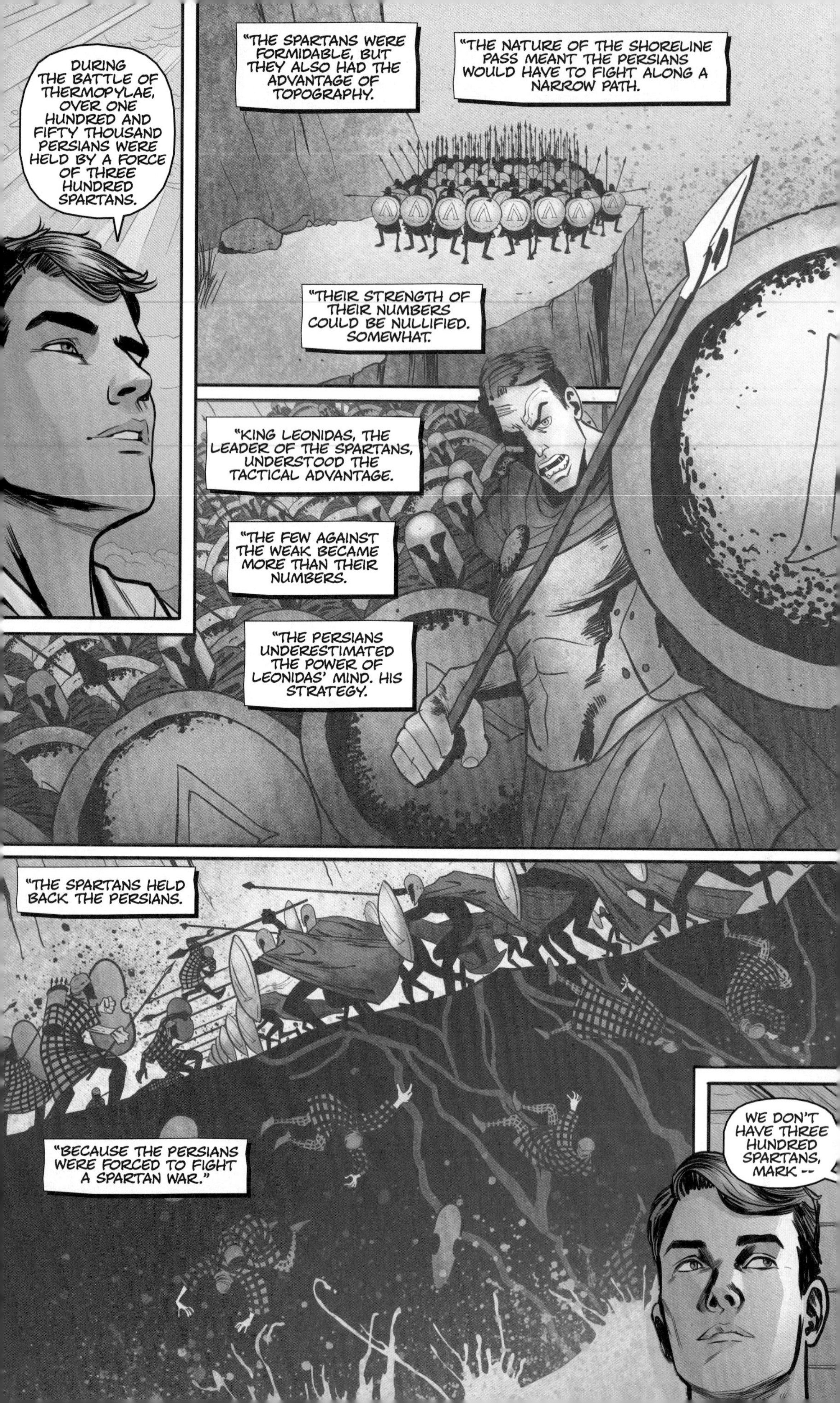
DURING THE BATTLE OF THERMOPYLAE, OVER ONE HUNDRED AND FIFTY THOUSAND PERSIANS WERE HELD BY A FORCE OF THREE HUNDRED SPARTANS.
"THE SPARTANS WERE FORMIDABLE, BUT THEY ALSO HAD THE ADVANTAGE OF TOPOGRAPHY.
"THE NATURE OF THE SHORELINE PASS MEANT THE PERSIANS WOULD HAVE TO FIGHT ALONG A NARROW PATH.
"THEIR STRENGTH OF THEIR NUMBERS COULD BE NULLIFIED. SOMEWHAT.
"KING LEONIDAS, THE LEADER OF THE SPARTANS, UNDERSTOOD THE TACTICAL ADVANTAGE.
"THE FEW AGAINST THE WEAK BECAME MORE THAN THEIR NUMBERS.
"THE PERSIANS UNDERESTIMATED THE POWER OF LEONIDAS' MIND. HIS STRATEGY.
"THE SPARTANS HELD BACK THE PERSIANS.
"BECAUSE THE PERSIANS WERE FORCED TO FIGHT A SPARTAN WAR."
WE DON'T HAVE THREE HUNDRED SPARTANS, MARK --

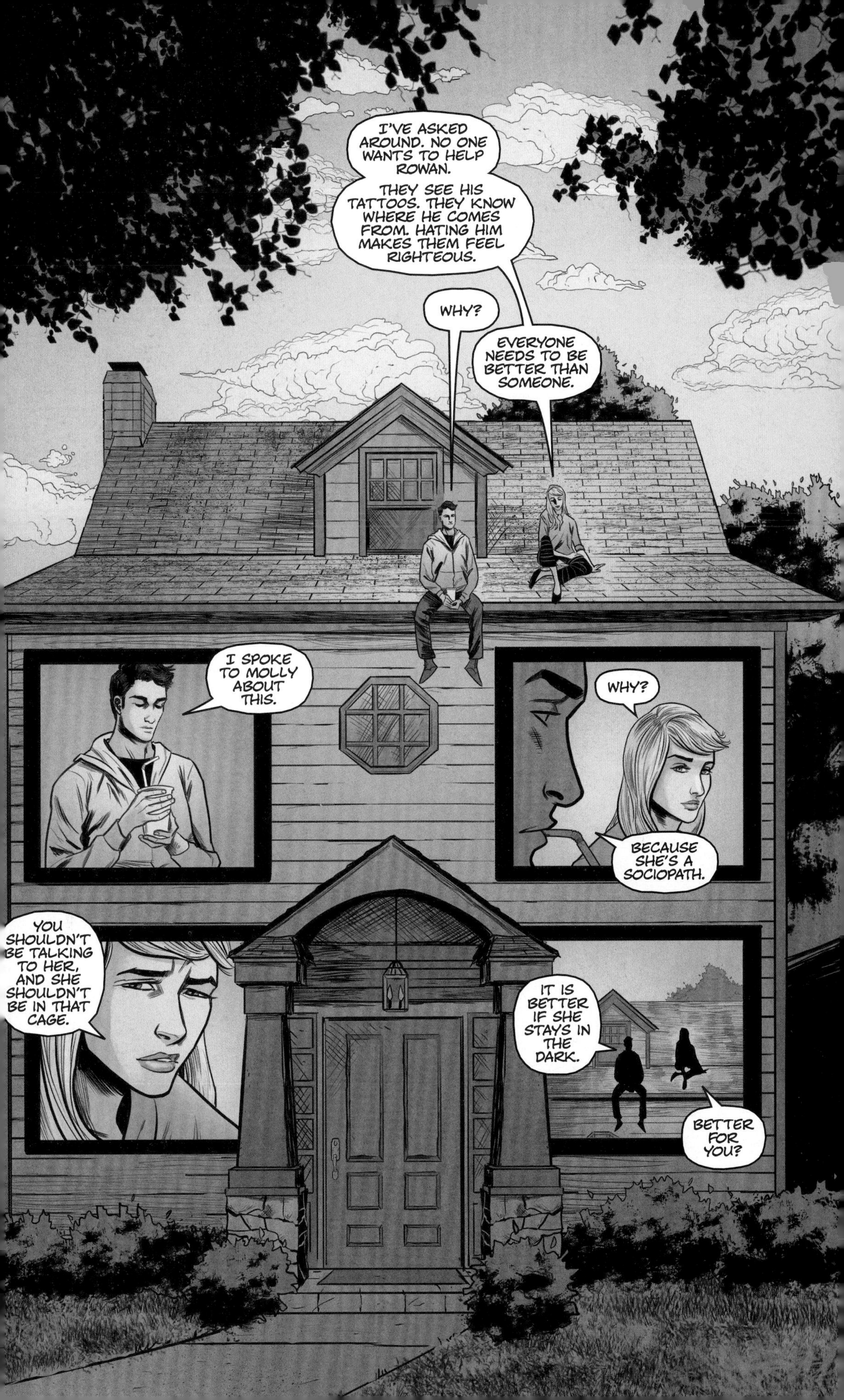
I'VE ASKED AROUND. NO ONE WANTS TO HELP ROWAN.
THEY SEE HIS TATTOOS. THEY KNOW WHERE HE COMES FROM. HATING HIM MAKES THEM FEEL RIGHTEOUS.
WHY?
EVERYONE NEEDS TO BE BETTER THAN SOMEONE.
I SPOKE TO MOLLY ABOUT THIS.
WHY?
BECAUSE SHE'S A SOCIOPATH.
YOU SHOULDN'T BE TALKING TO HER, AND SHE SHOULDN'T BE IN THAT CAGE.
IT IS BETTER IF SHE STAYS IN THE DARK.
BETTER FOR YOU?

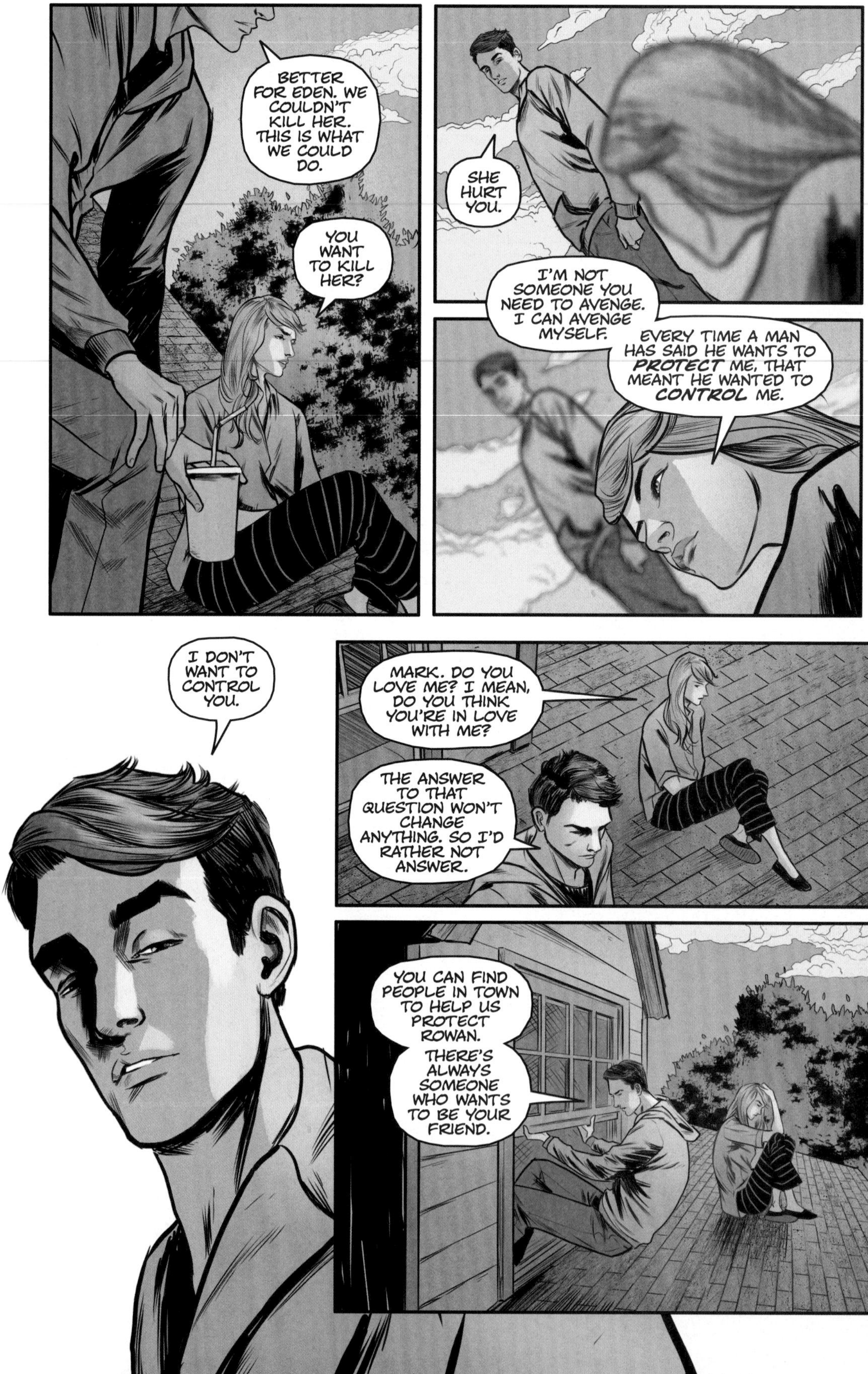
BETTER FOR EDEN. WE COULDN'T KILL HER. THIS IS WHAT WE COULD DO.
YOU WANT TO KILL HER?
SHE HURT YOU.
I'M NOT SOMEONE YOU NEED TO AVENGE. I CAN AVENGE MYSELF.
EVERY TIME A MAN HAS SAID HE WANTS TO PROTECT ME, THAT MEANT HE WANTED TO CONTROL ME.
I DON'T WANT TO CONTROL YOU.
MARK. DO YOU LOVE ME? I MEAN, DO YOU THINK YOU'RE IN LOVE WITH ME?
THE ANSWER TO THAT QUESTION WON'T CHANGE ANYTHING. SO I'D RATHER NOT ANSWER.
YOU CAN FIND PEOPLE IN TOWN TO HELP US PROTECT ROWAN.
THERE'S ALWAYS SOMEONE WHO WANTS TO BE YOUR FRIEND.

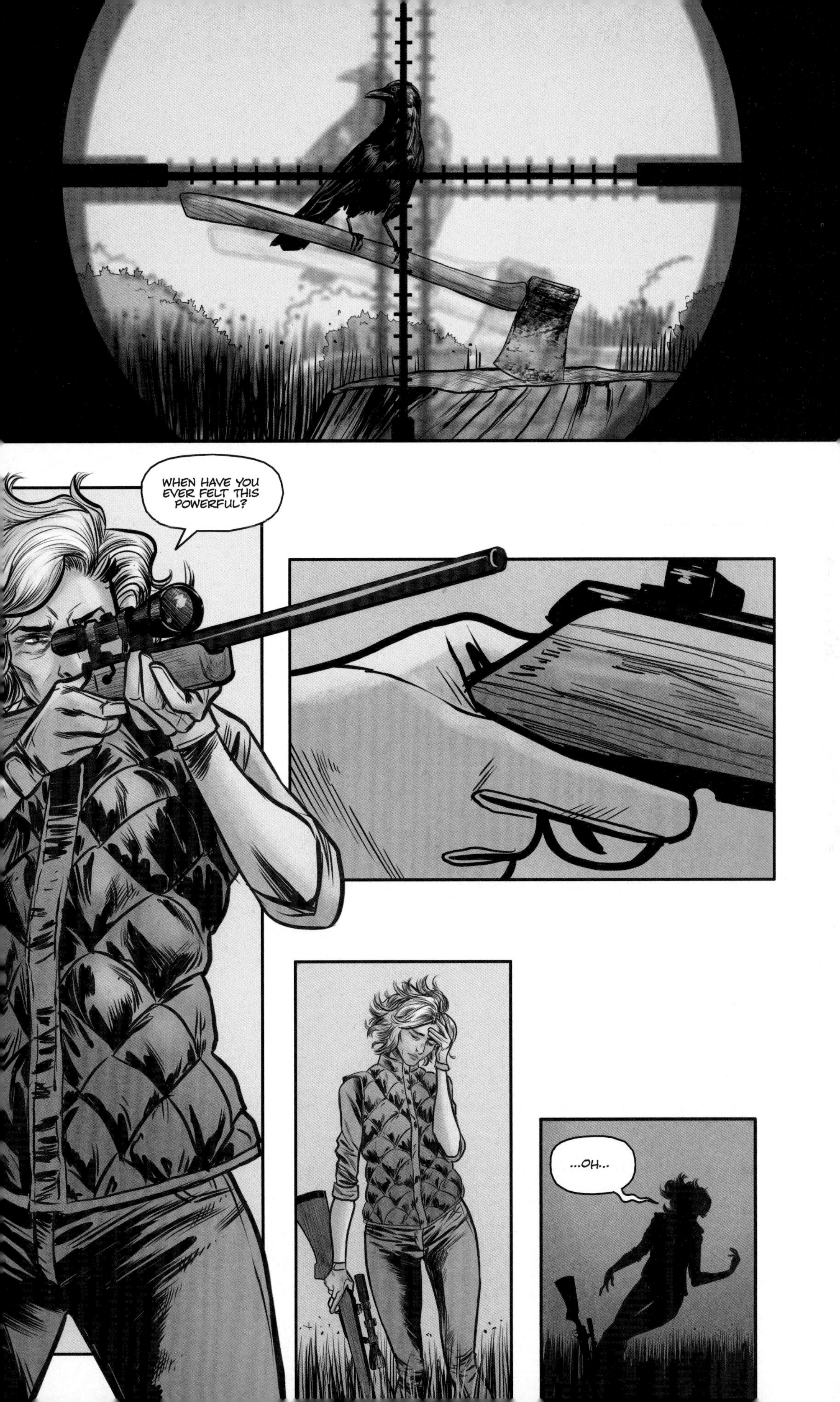
WHEN HAVE YOU EVER FELT THIS POWERFUL?
...OH...

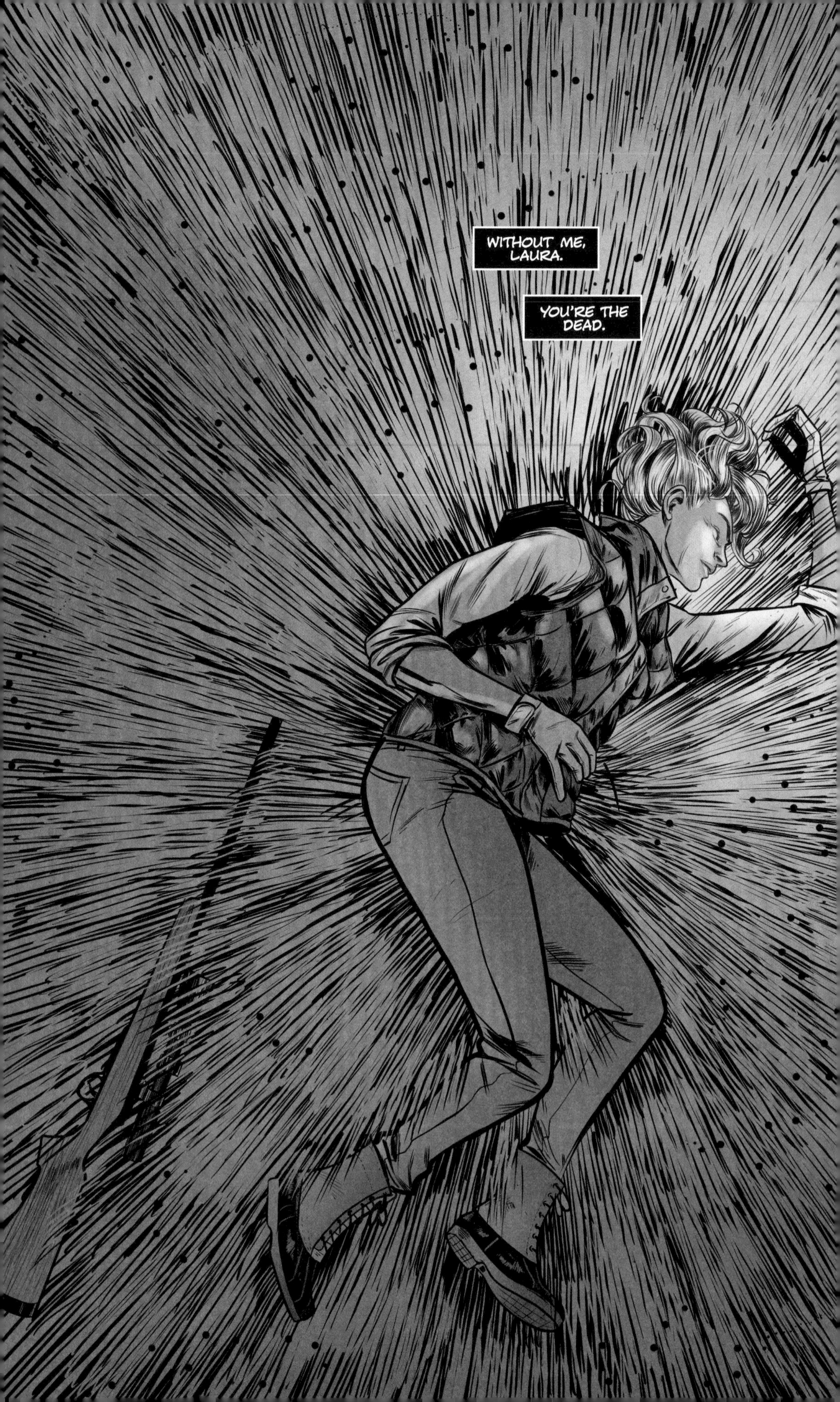
WITHOUT ME, LAURA.
YOU'RE THE DEAD.

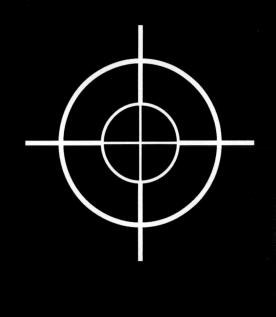

# CHAPTER 15

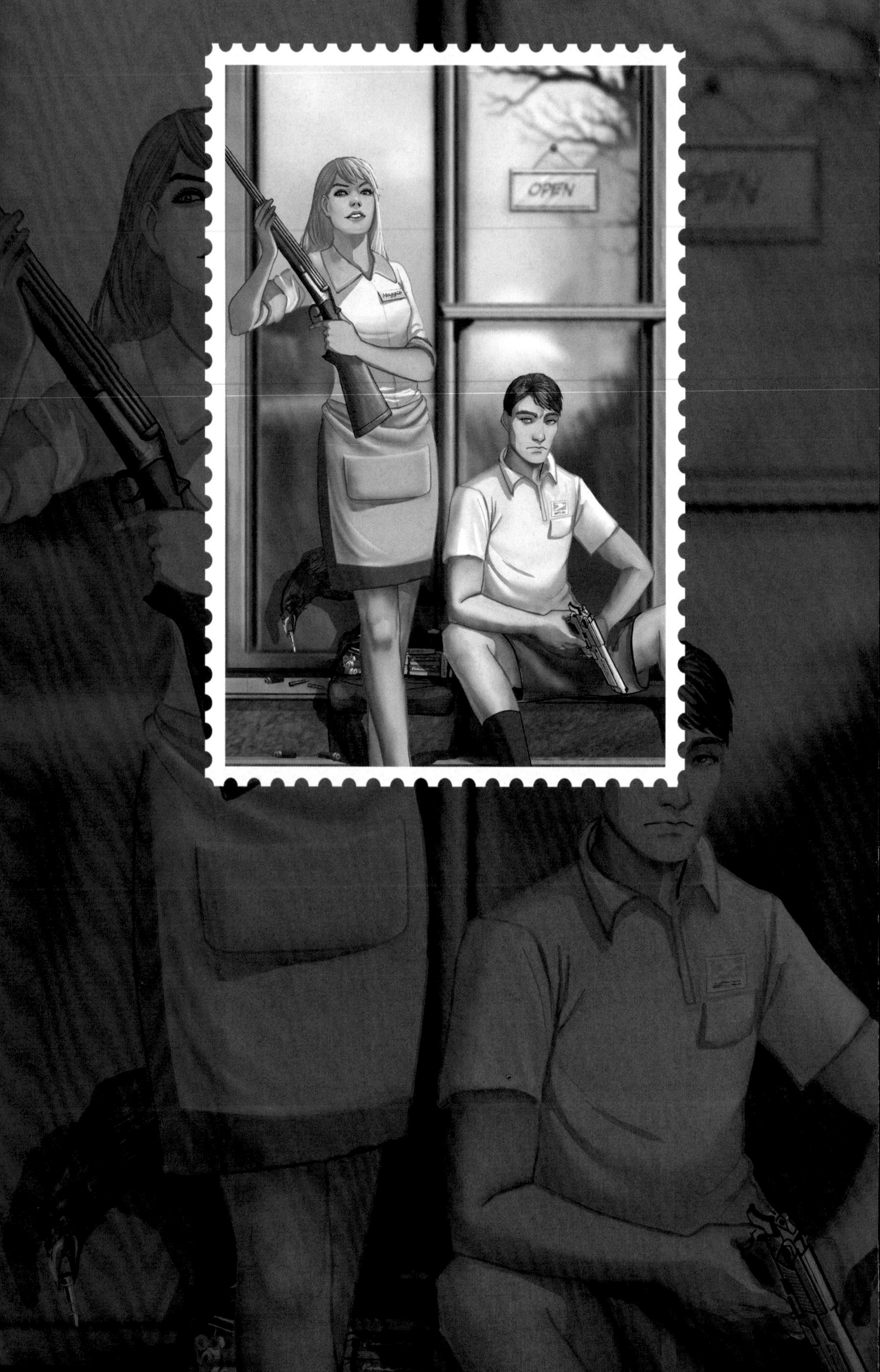
Maggie
OPEN

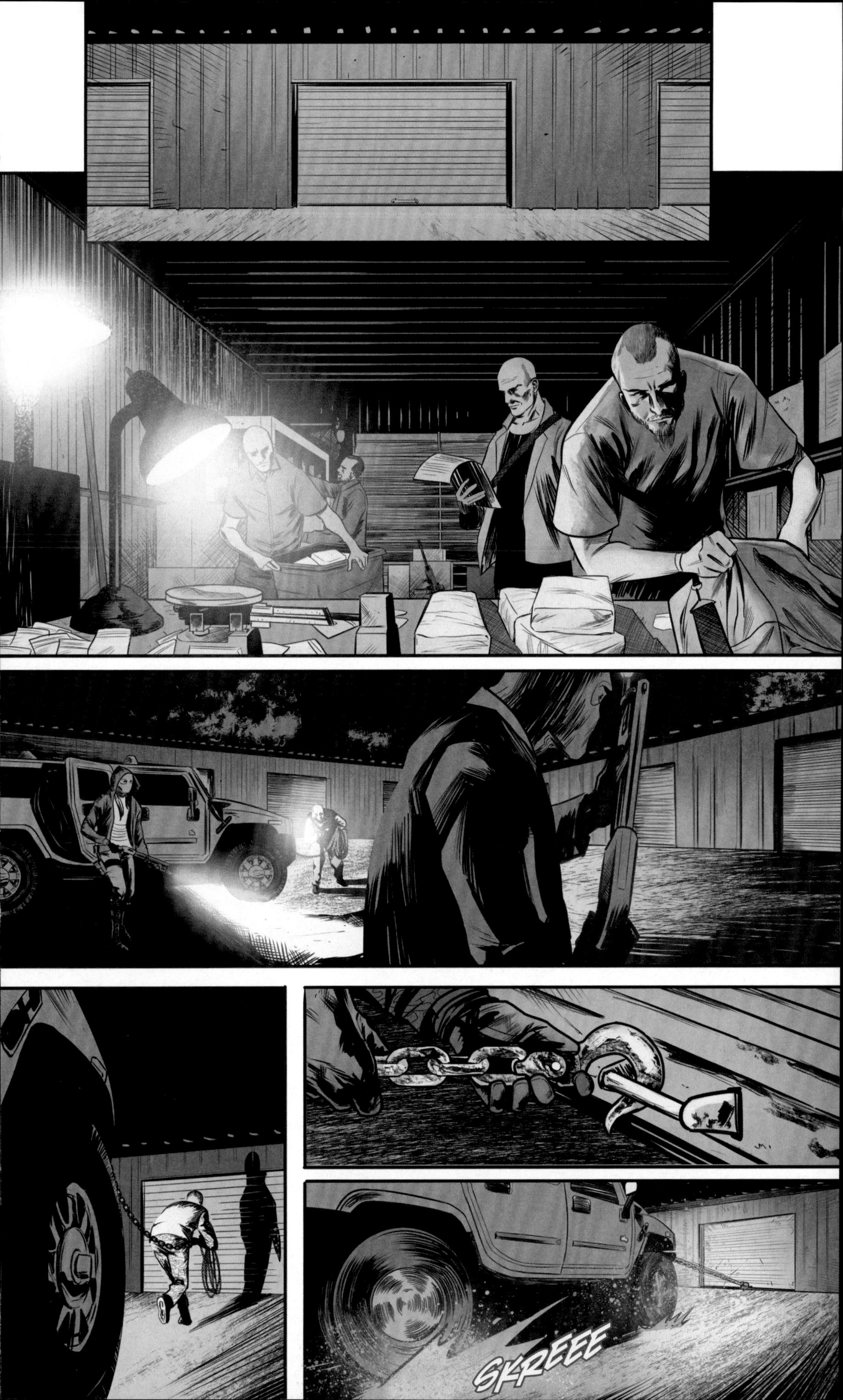
SKREEE

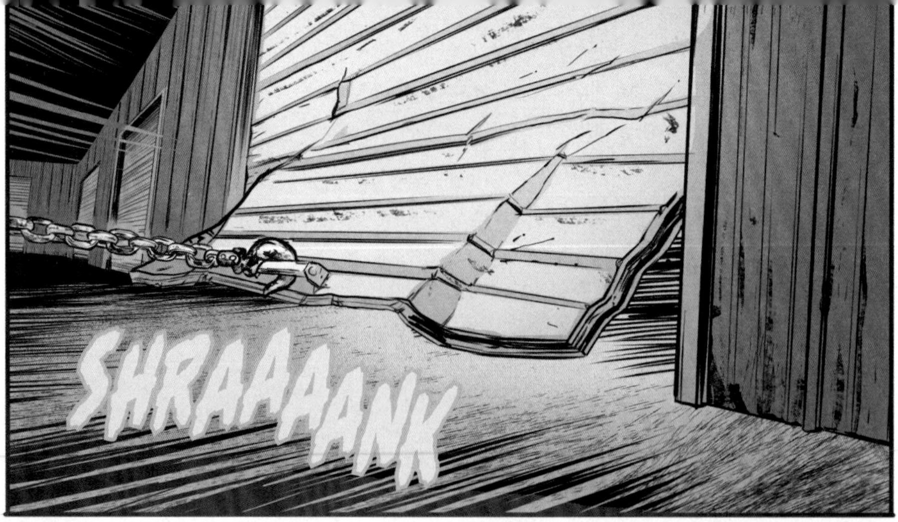
SHRAAAANK

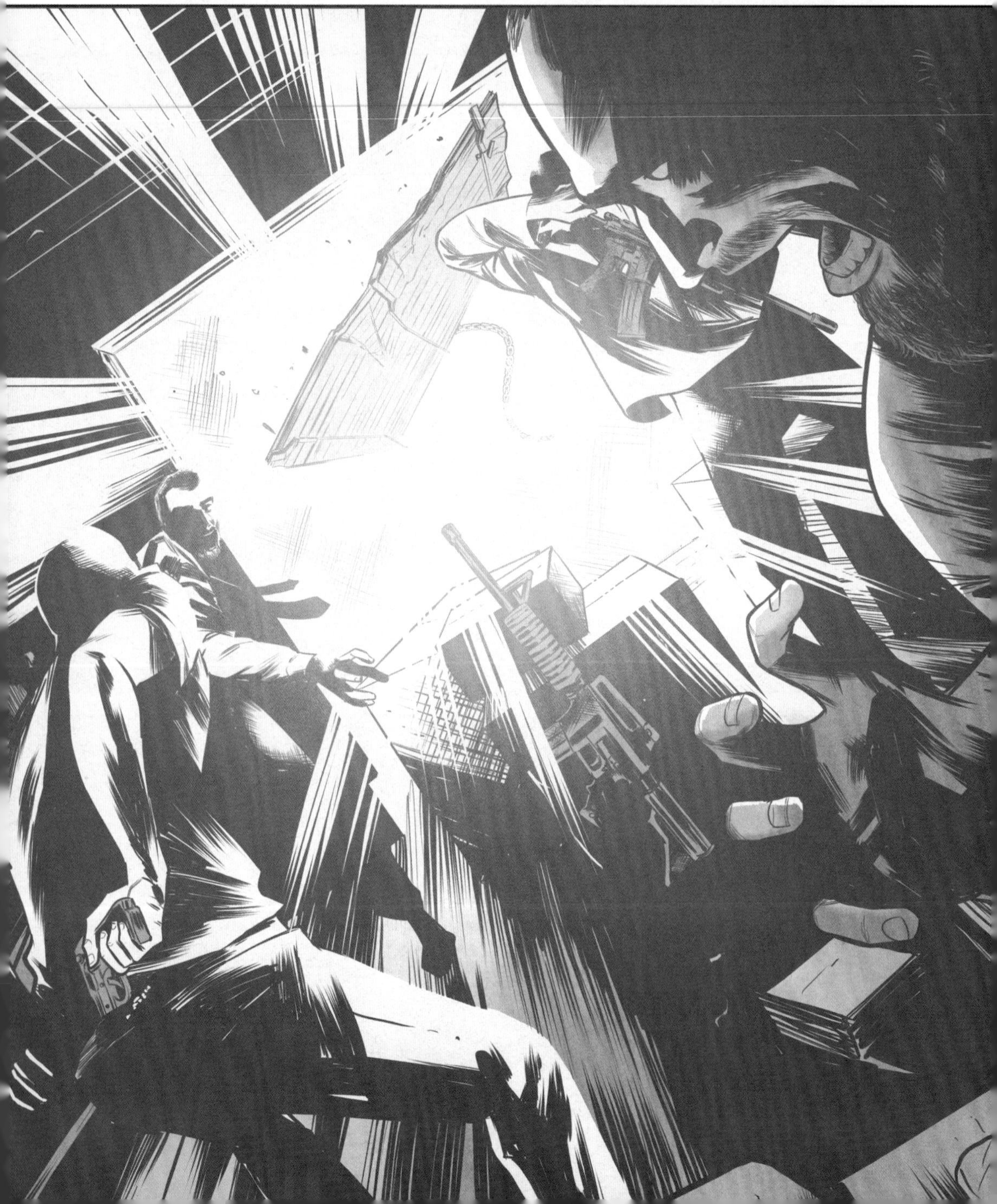

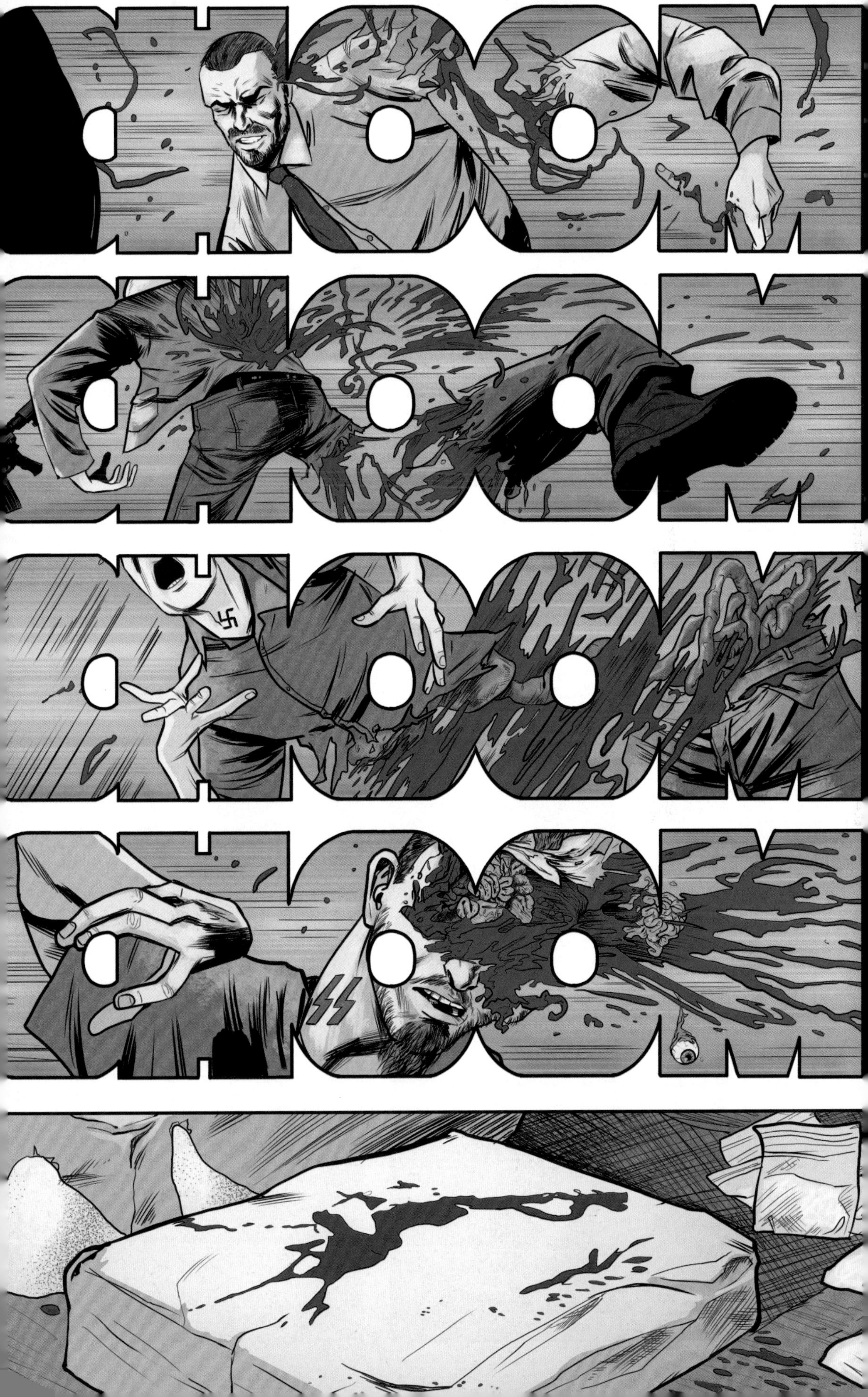
CHOOM
CHOOM
CHOOM
CHOOM

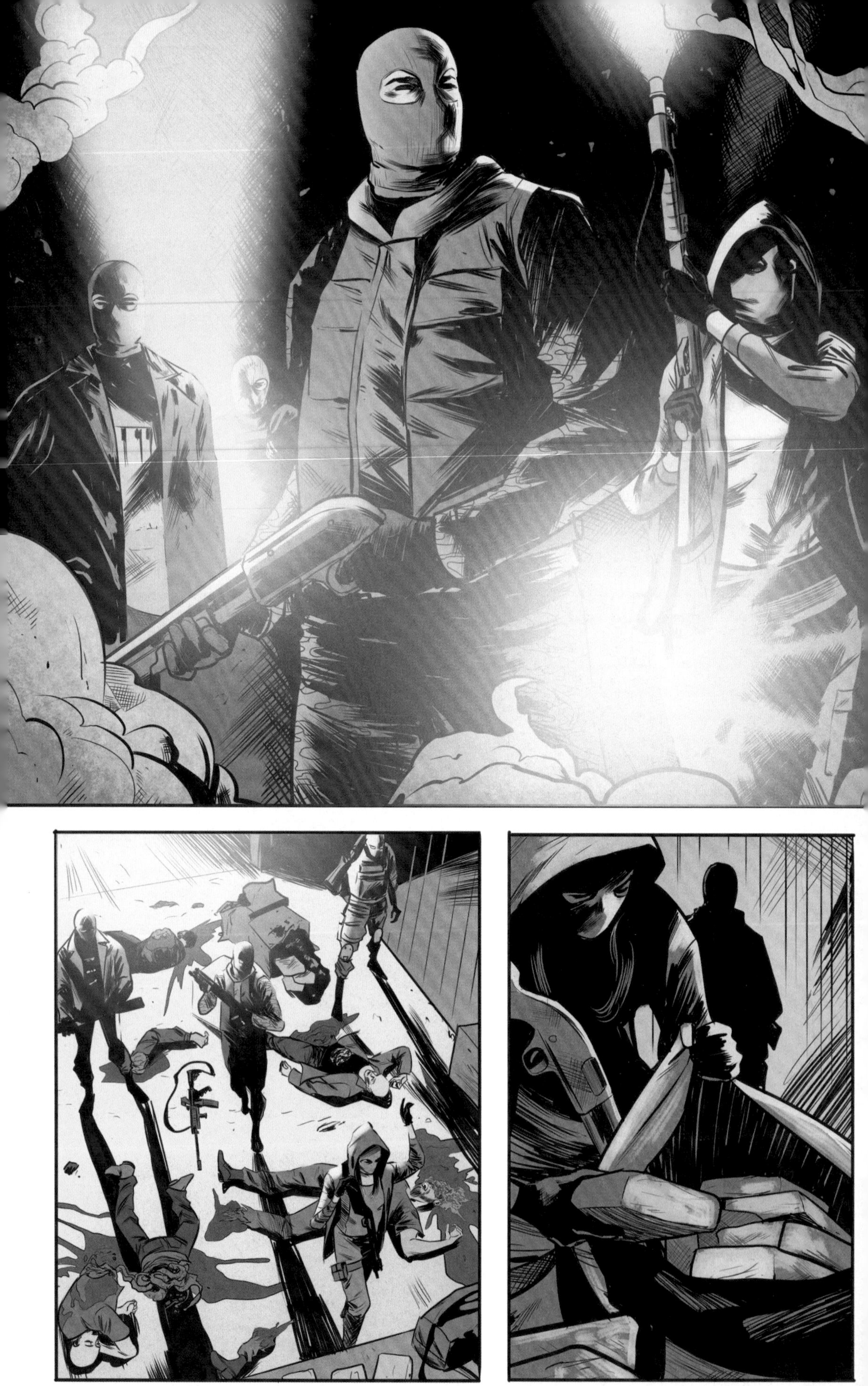

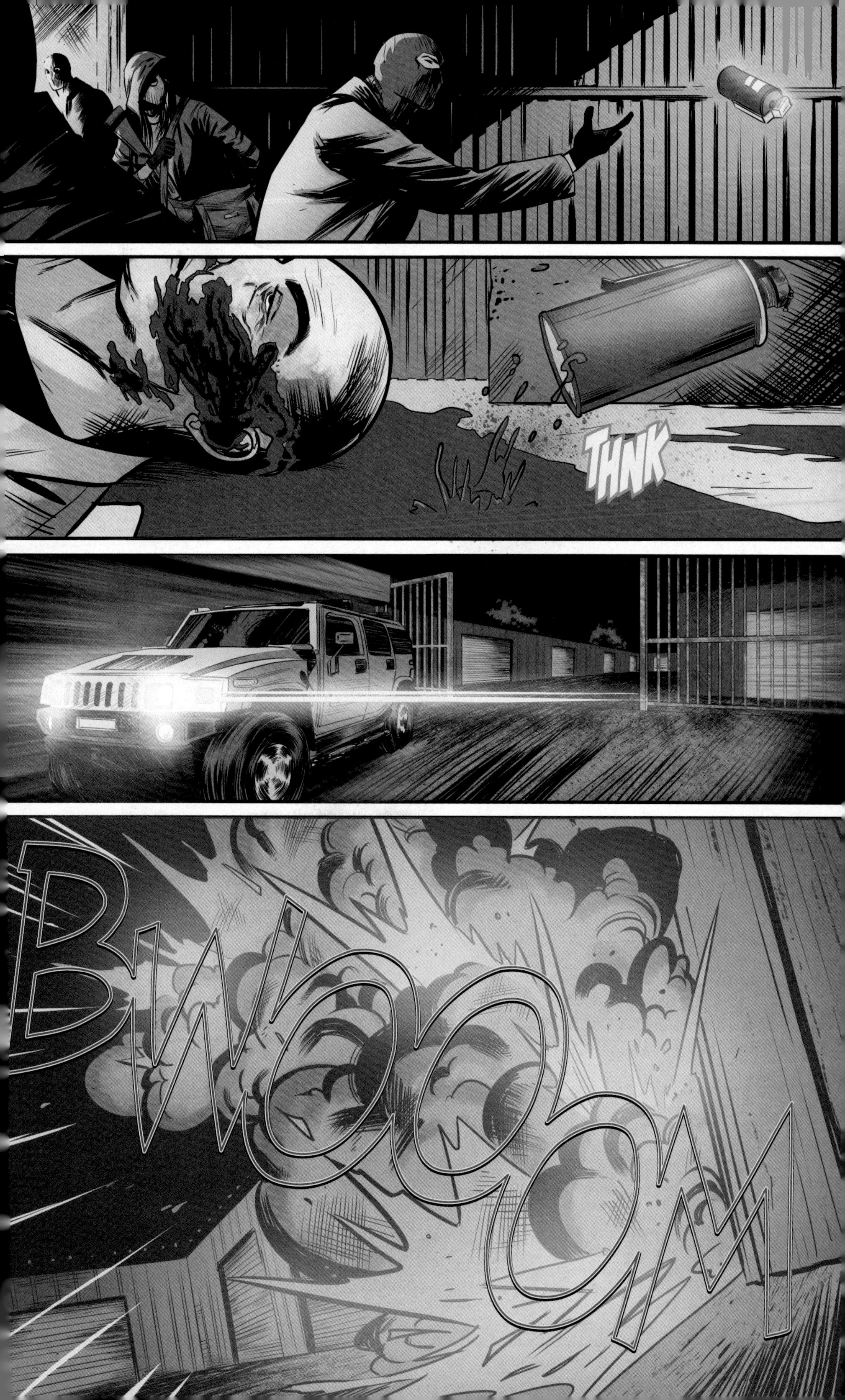
THNK
BWOOOOM

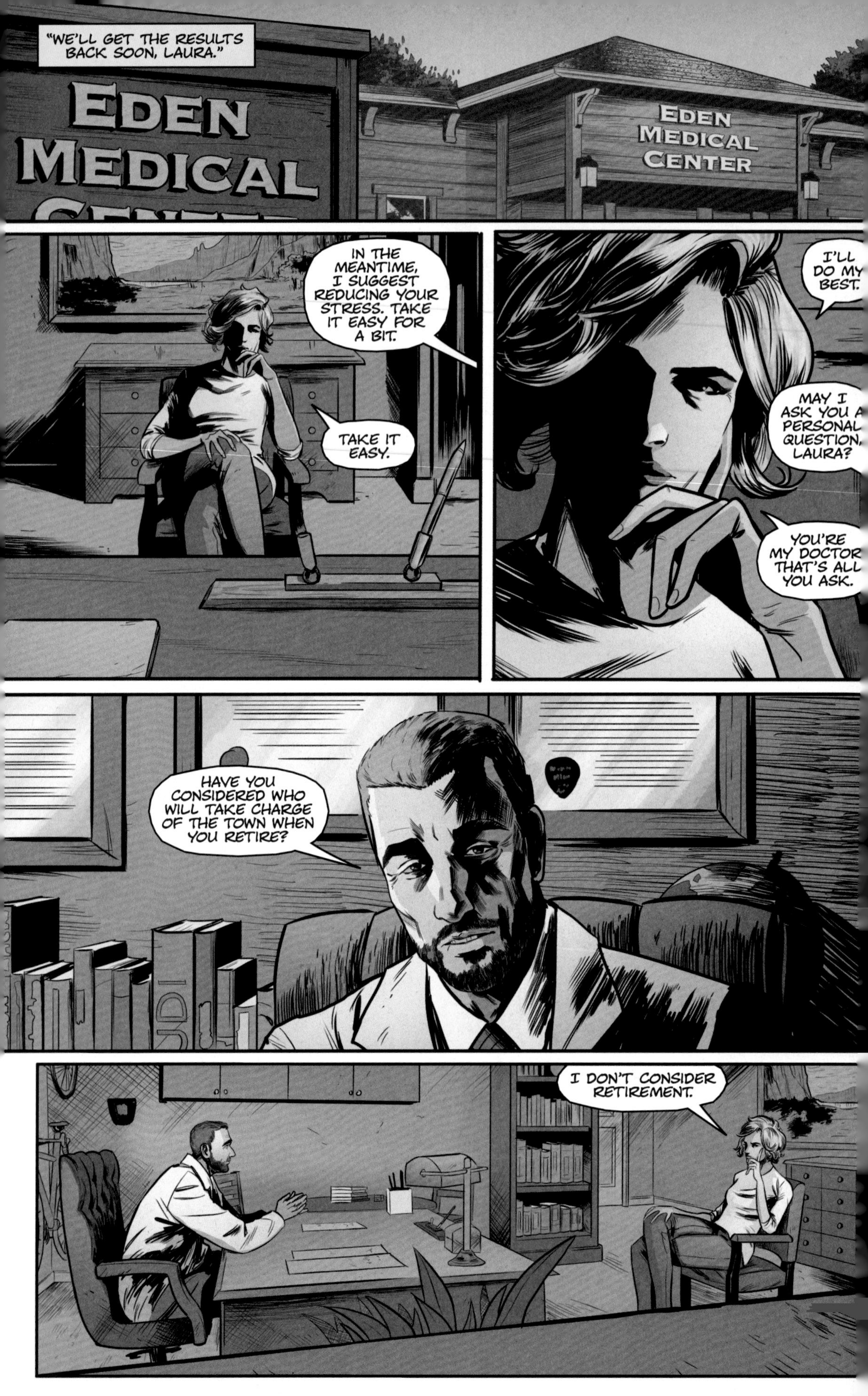
"WE'LL GET THE RESULTS BACK SOON, LAURA."
EDEN MEDICAL CENTER
EDEN MEDICAL CENTER
IN THE MEANTIME, I SUGGEST REDUCING YOUR STRESS. TAKE IT EASY FOR A BIT.
TAKE IT EASY.
I'LL DO MY BEST.
MAY I ASK YOU A PERSONAL QUESTION, LAURA?
YOU'RE MY DOCTOR THAT'S ALL YOU ASK.
HAVE YOU CONSIDERED WHO WILL TAKE CHARGE OF THE TOWN WHEN YOU RETIRE?
I DON'T CONSIDER RETIREMENT.

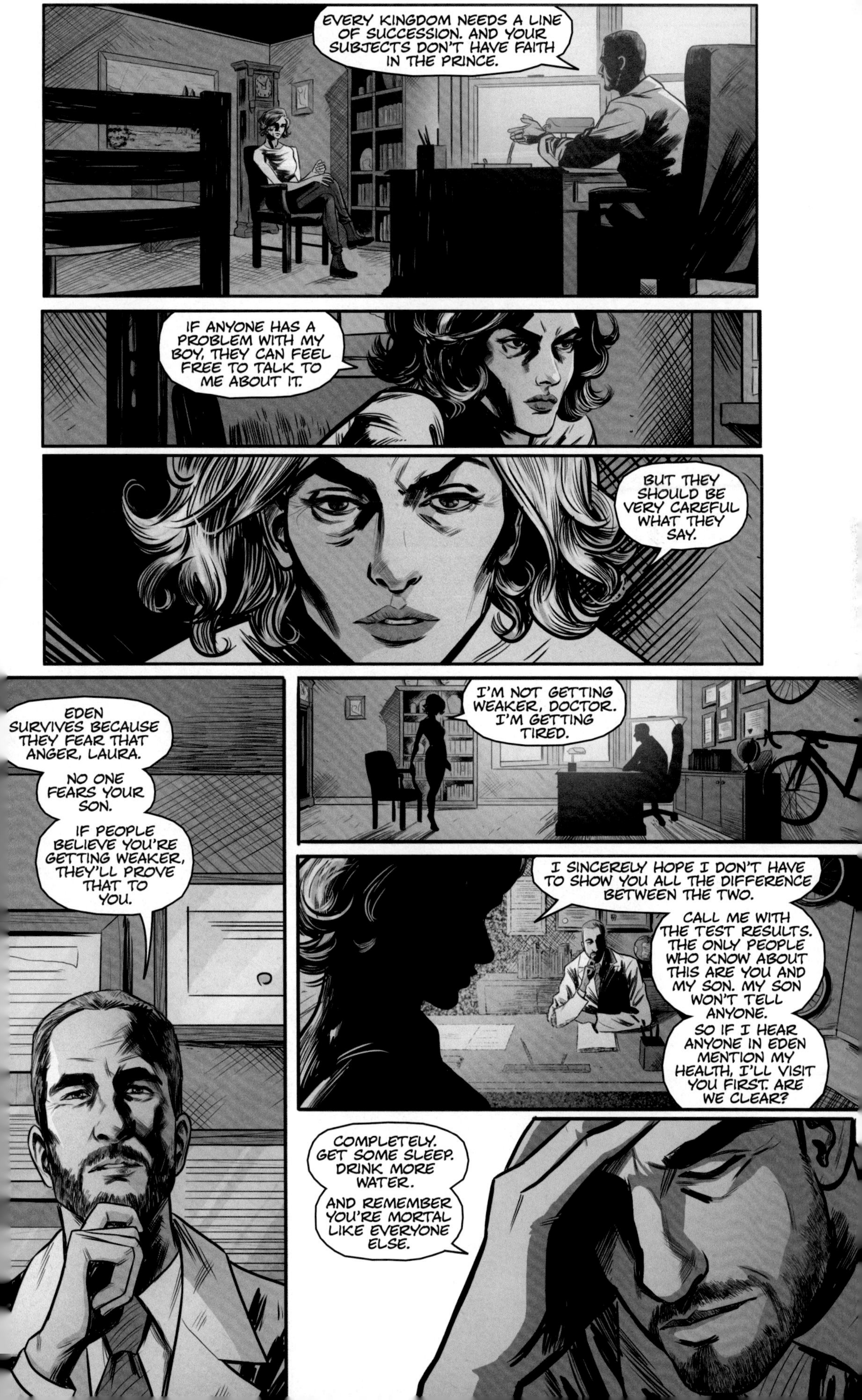
EVERY KINGDOM NEEDS A LINE OF SUCCESSION. AND YOUR SUBJECTS DON'T HAVE FAITH IN THE PRINCE.
IF ANYONE HAS A PROBLEM WITH MY BOY, THEY CAN FEEL FREE TO TALK TO ME ABOUT IT.
BUT THEY SHOULD BE VERY CAREFUL WHAT THEY SAY.
EDEN SURVIVES BECAUSE THEY FEAR THAT ANGER, LAURA.
NO ONE FEARS YOUR SON.
IF PEOPLE BELIEVE YOU'RE GETTING WEAKER, THEY'LL PROVE THAT TO YOU.
I'M NOT GETTING WEAKER, DOCTOR. I'M GETTING TIRED.
I SINCERELY HOPE I DON'T HAVE TO SHOW YOU ALL THE DIFFERENCE BETWEEN THE TWO.
CALL ME WITH THE TEST RESULTS. THE ONLY PEOPLE WHO KNOW ABOUT THIS ARE YOU AND MY SON. MY SON WON'T TELL ANYONE.
SO IF I HEAR ANYONE IN EDEN MENTION MY HEALTH, I'LL VISIT YOU FIRST. ARE WE CLEAR?
COMPLETELY. GET SOME SLEEP. DRINK MORE WATER.
AND REMEMBER YOU'RE MORTAL LIKE EVERYONE ELSE.

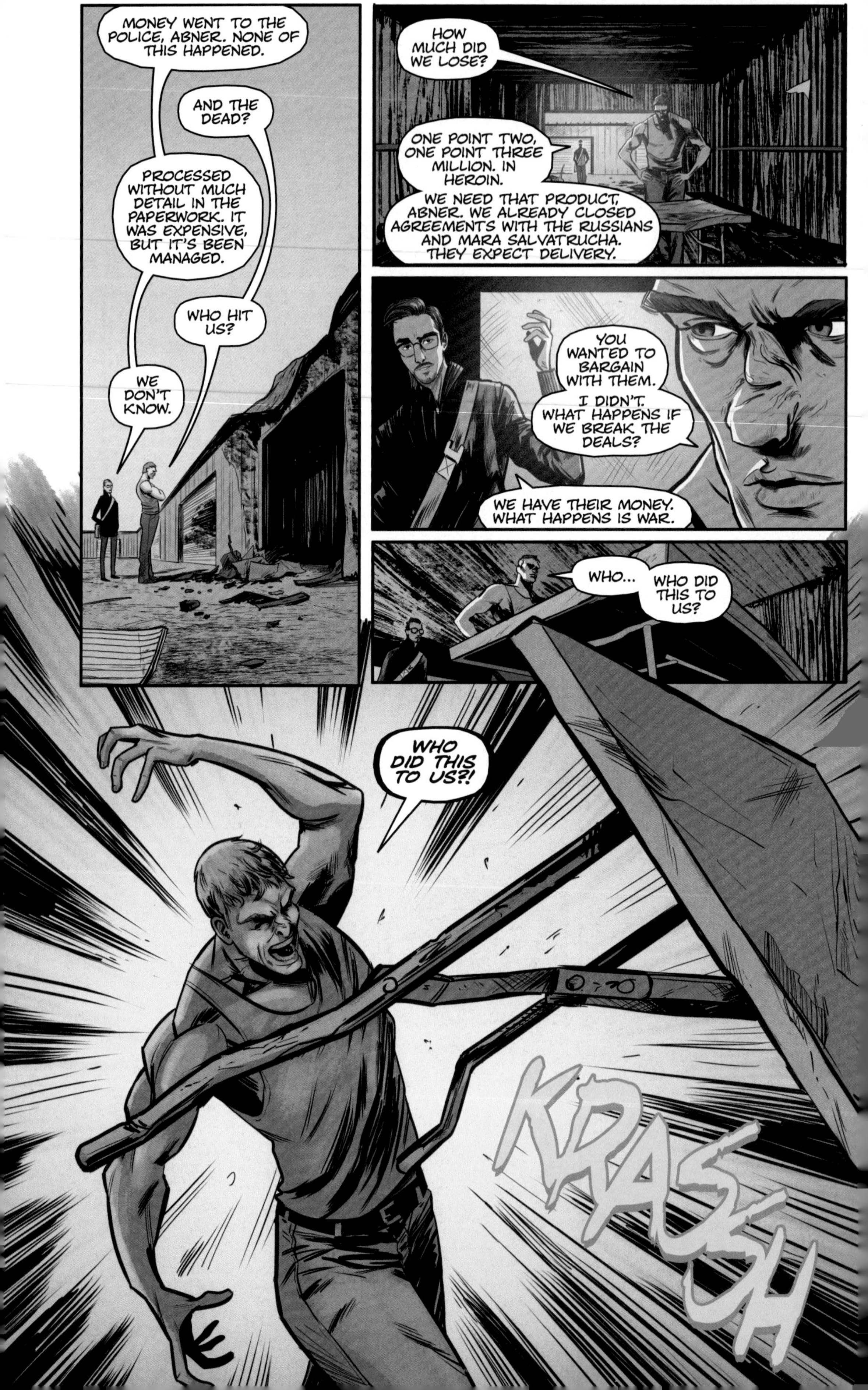
MONEY WENT TO THE POLICE, ABNER. NONE OF THIS HAPPENED.
AND THE DEAD?
PROCESSED WITHOUT MUCH DETAIL IN THE PAPERWORK. IT WAS EXPENSIVE, BUT IT'S BEEN MANAGED.
WHO HIT US?
WE DON'T KNOW.
HOW MUCH DID WE LOSE?
ONE POINT TWO, ONE POINT THREE MILLION. IN HEROIN.
WE NEED THAT PRODUCT, ABNER. WE ALREADY CLOSED AGREEMENTS WITH THE RUSSIANS AND MARA SALVATRUCHA. THEY EXPECT DELIVERY.
YOU WANTED TO BARGAIN WITH THEM.
I DIDN'T. WHAT HAPPENS IF WE BREAK THE DEALS?
WE HAVE THEIR MONEY. WHAT HAPPENS IS WAR.
WHO...
WHO DID THIS TO US?
WHO DID THIS TO US?!
KRASSH

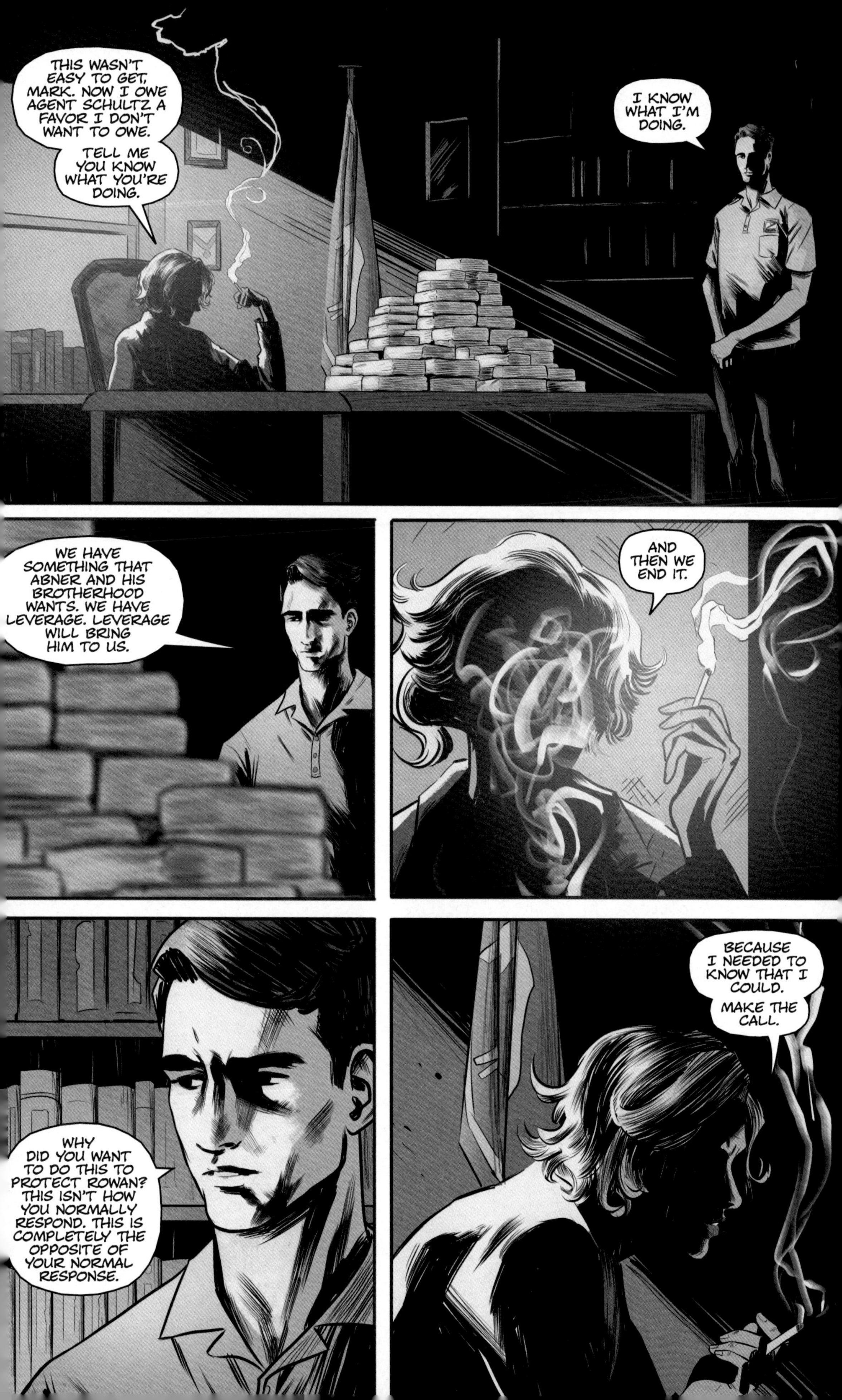
THIS WASN'T EASY TO GET, MARK. NOW I OWE AGENT SCHULTZ A FAVOR I DON'T WANT TO OWE.
TELL ME YOU KNOW WHAT YOU'RE DOING.
I KNOW WHAT I'M DOING.
WE HAVE SOMETHING THAT ABNER AND HIS BROTHERHOOD WANTS. WE HAVE LEVERAGE. LEVERAGE WILL BRING HIM TO US.
AND THEN WE END IT.
WHY DID YOU WANT TO DO THIS TO PROTECT ROWAN? THIS ISN'T HOW YOU NORMALLY RESPOND. THIS IS COMPLETELY THE OPPOSITE OF YOUR NORMAL RESPONSE.
BECAUSE I NEEDED TO KNOW THAT I COULD.
MAKE THE CALL.

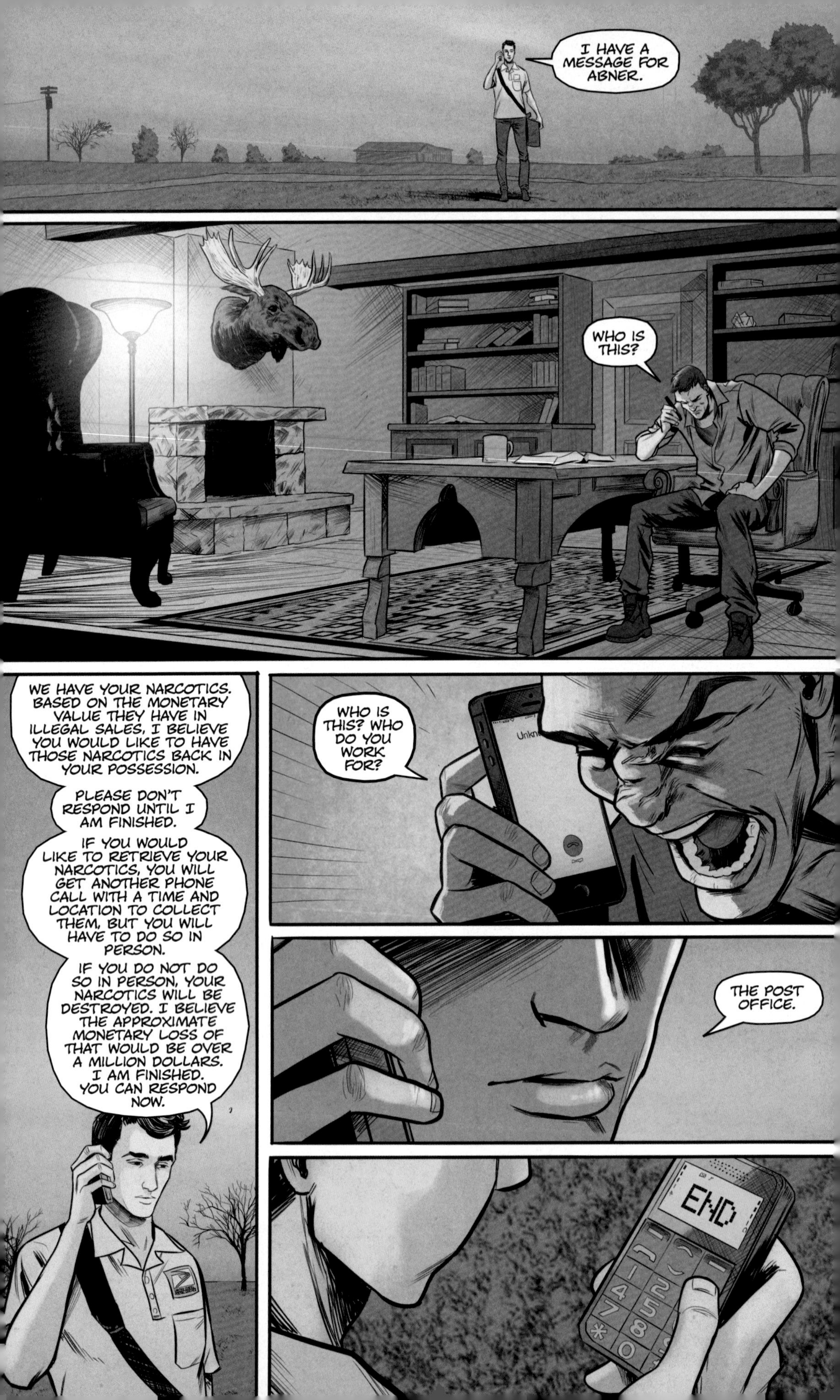
I HAVE A MESSAGE FOR ABNER.
WHO IS THIS?
WE HAVE YOUR NARCOTICS. BASED ON THE MONETARY VALUE THEY HAVE IN ILLEGAL SALES, I BELIEVE YOU WOULD LIKE TO HAVE THOSE NARCOTICS BACK IN YOUR POSSESSION.
PLEASE DON'T RESPOND UNTIL I AM FINISHED.
IF YOU WOULD LIKE TO RETRIEVE YOUR NARCOTICS, YOU WILL GET ANOTHER PHONE CALL WITH A TIME AND LOCATION TO COLLECT THEM, BUT YOU WILL HAVE TO DO SO IN PERSON.
IF YOU DO NOT DO SO IN PERSON, YOUR NARCOTICS WILL BE DESTROYED. I BELIEVE THE APPROXIMATE MONETARY LOSS OF THAT WOULD BE OVER A MILLION DOLLARS. I AM FINISHED. YOU CAN RESPOND NOW.
WHO IS THIS? WHO DO YOU WORK FOR?
THE POST OFFICE.
END

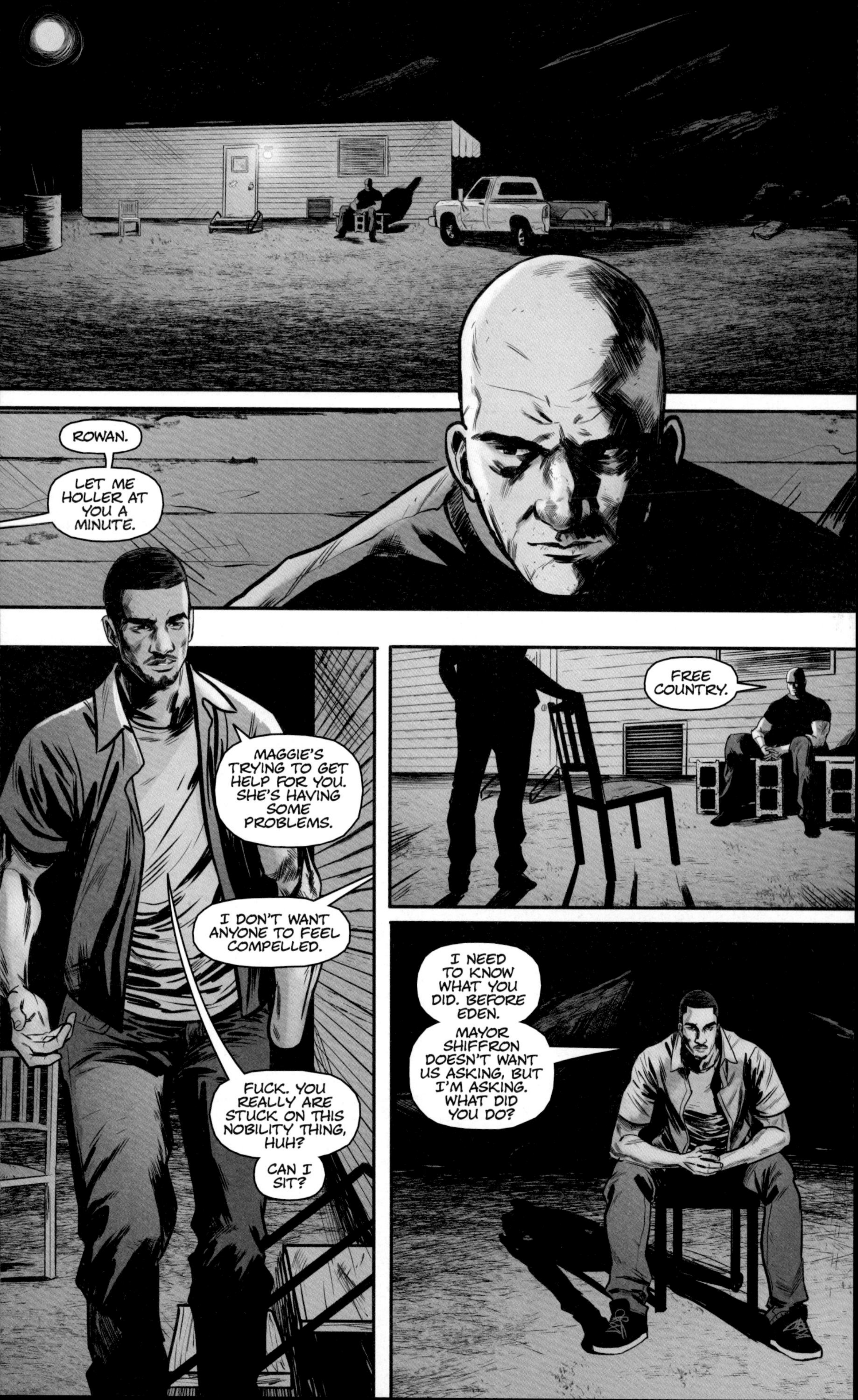
ROWAN.
LET ME HOLLER AT YOU A MINUTE.
MAGGIE'S TRYING TO GET HELP FOR YOU. SHE'S HAVING SOME PROBLEMS.
I DON'T WANT ANYONE TO FEEL COMPELLED.
FUCK. YOU REALLY ARE STUCK ON THIS NOBILITY THING, HUH?
CAN I SIT?
FREE COUNTRY.
I NEED TO KNOW WHAT YOU DID. BEFORE EDEN.
MAYOR SHIFFRON DOESN'T WANT US ASKING, BUT I'M ASKING. WHAT DID YOU DO?

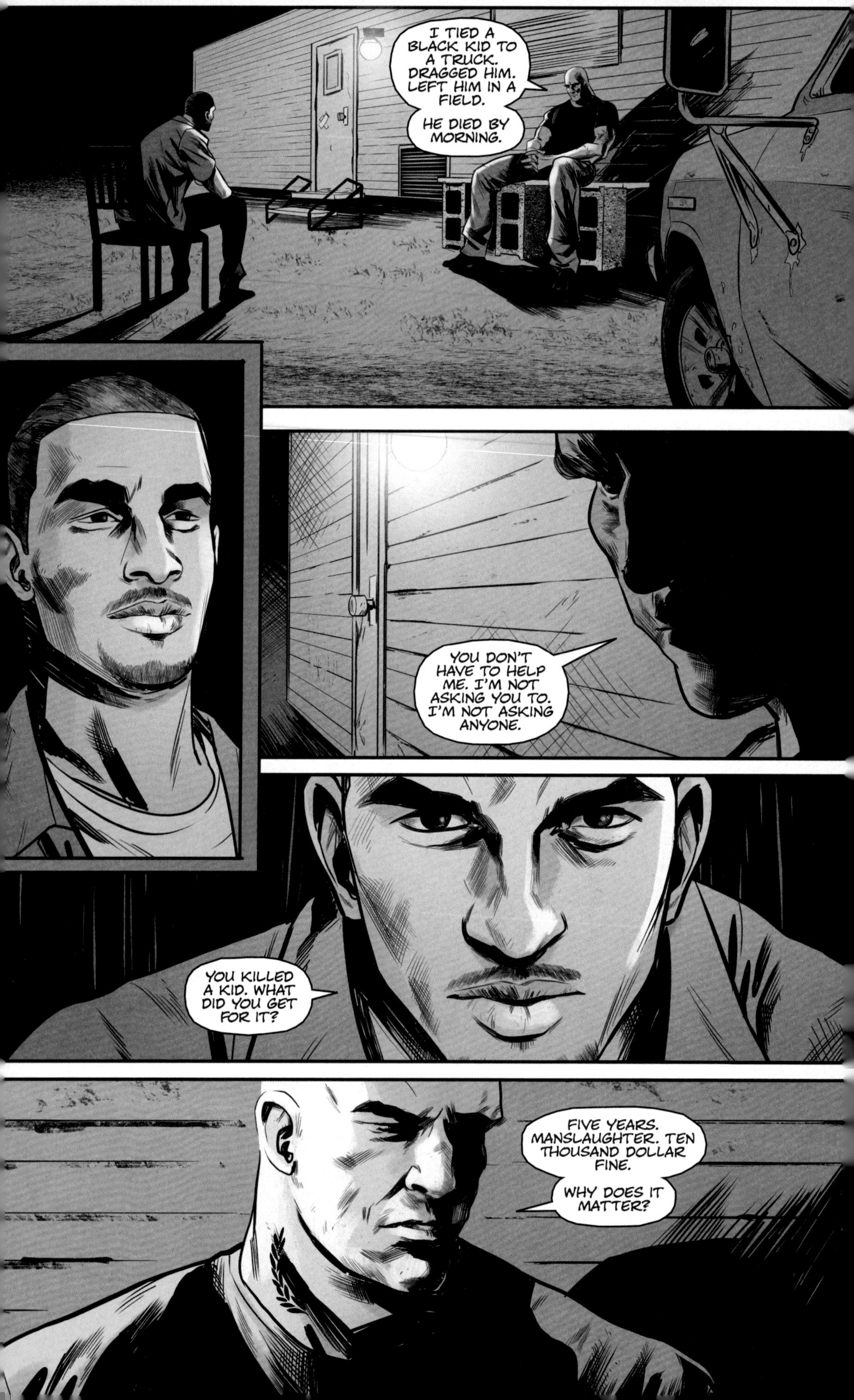
I TIED A BLACK KID TO A TRUCK. DRAGGED HIM. LEFT HIM IN A FIELD.
HE DIED BY MORNING.
YOU DON'T HAVE TO HELP ME. I'M NOT ASKING YOU TO. I'M NOT ASKING ANYONE.
YOU KILLED A KID. WHAT DID YOU GET FOR IT?
FIVE YEARS. MANSLAUGHTER. TEN THOUSAND DOLLAR FINE.
WHY DOES IT MATTER?

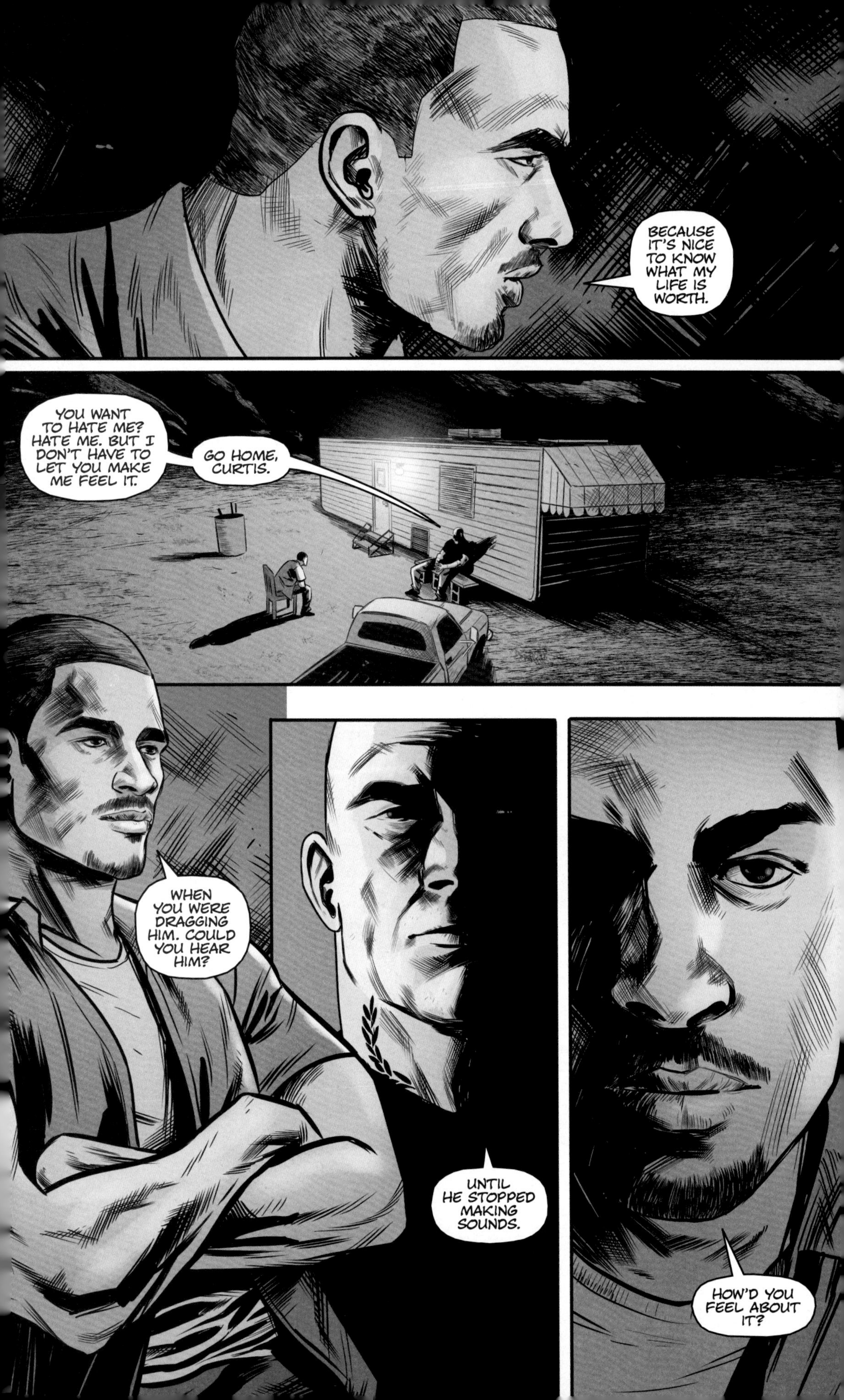
BECAUSE IT'S NICE TO KNOW WHAT MY LIFE IS WORTH.
YOU WANT TO HATE ME? HATE ME. BUT I DON'T HAVE TO LET YOU MAKE ME FEEL IT.
GO HOME, CURTIS.
WHEN YOU WERE DRAGGING HIM. COULD YOU HEAR HIM?
UNTIL HE STOPPED MAKING SOUNDS.
HOW'D YOU FEEL ABOUT IT?

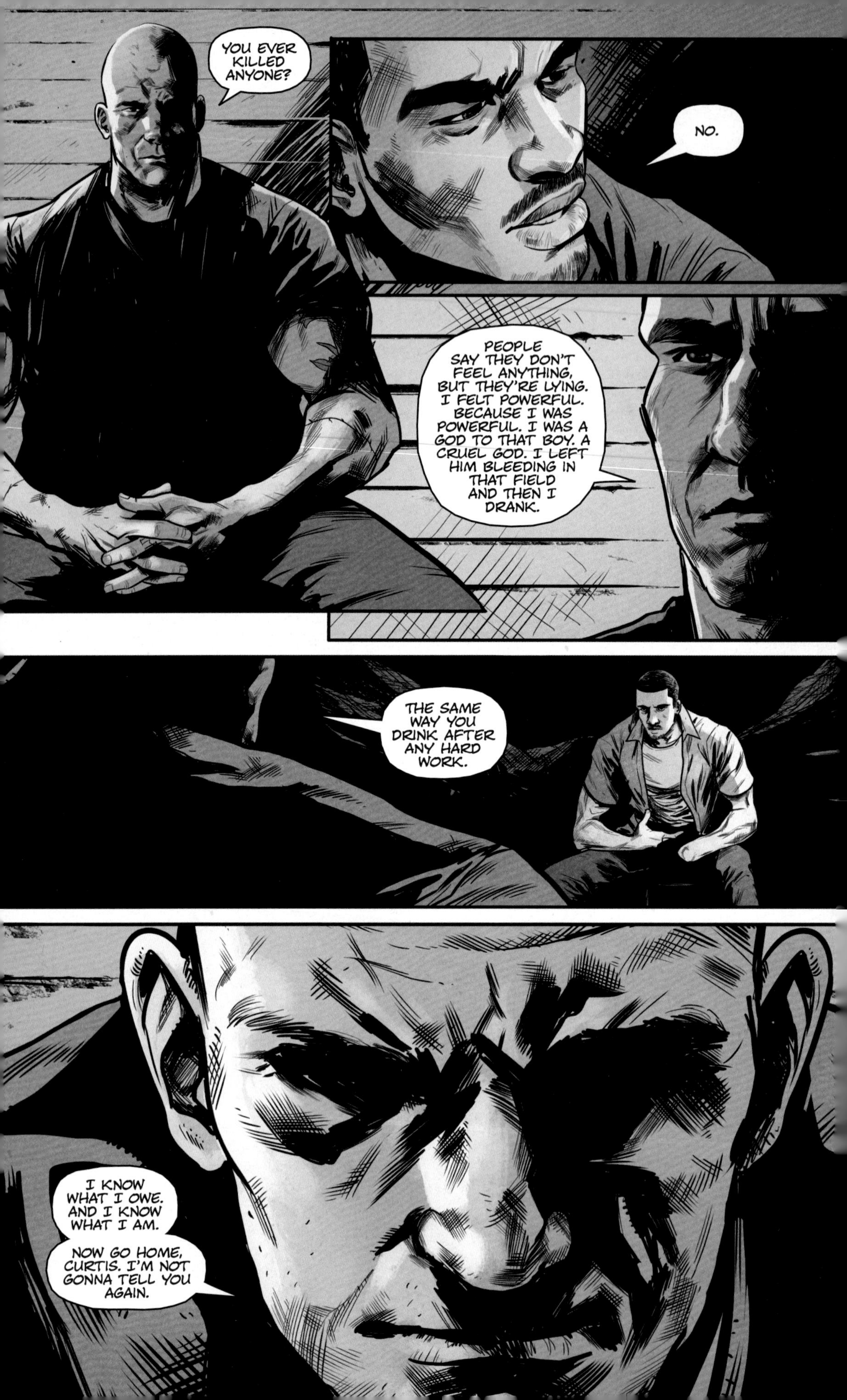
YOU EVER KILLED ANYONE?
NO.
PEOPLE SAY THEY DON'T FEEL ANYTHING, BUT THEY'RE LYING. I FELT POWERFUL. BECAUSE I WAS POWERFUL. I WAS A GOD TO THAT BOY. A CRUEL GOD. I LEFT HIM BLEEDING IN THAT FIELD AND THEN I DRANK.
THE SAME WAY YOU DRINK AFTER ANY HARD WORK.
I KNOW WHAT I OWE. AND I KNOW WHAT I AM.
NOW GO HOME, CURTIS. I'M NOT GONNA TELL YOU AGAIN.

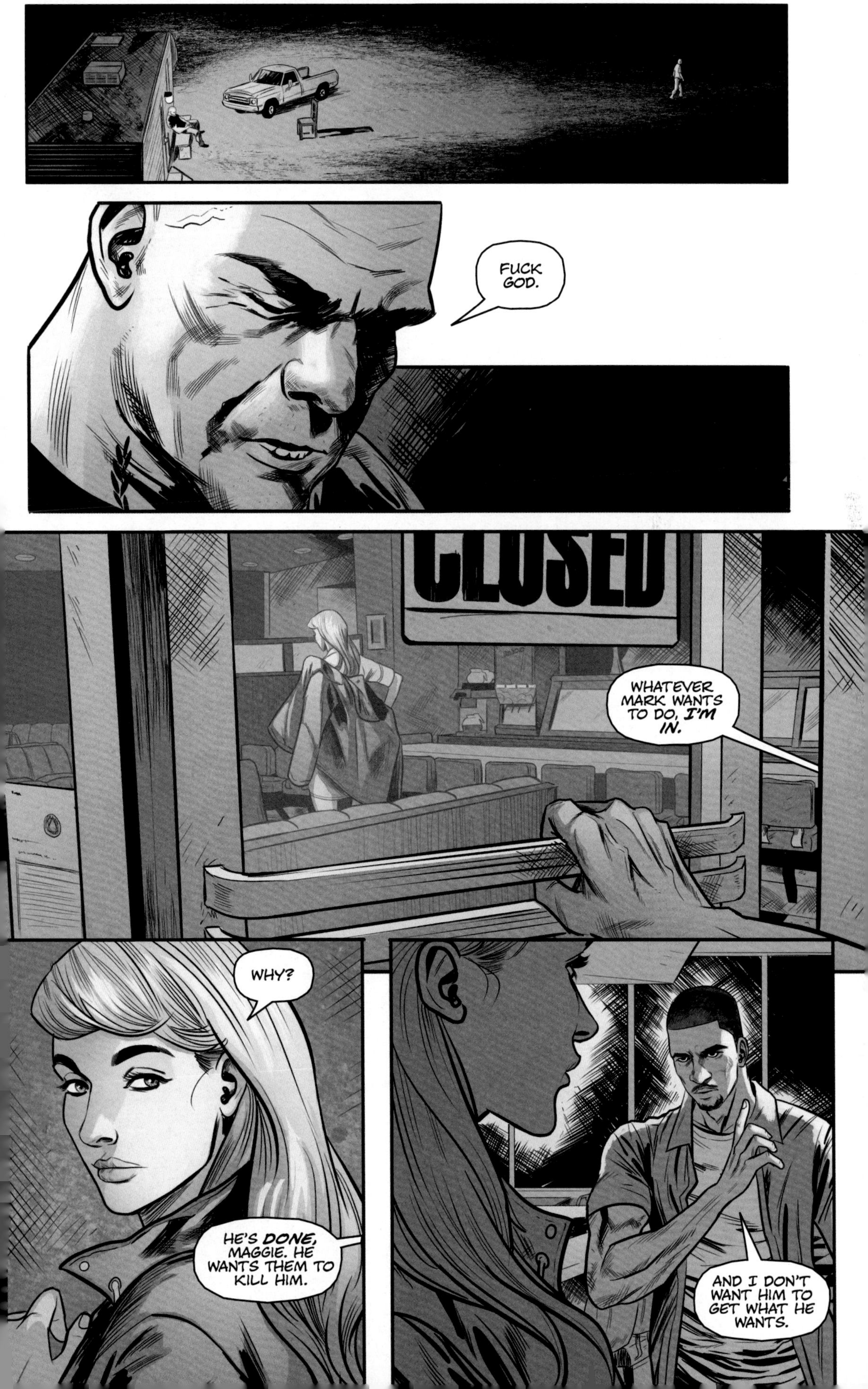
FUCK GOD.
CLOSED
WHATEVER MARK WANTS TO DO, I'M IN.
WHY?
HE'S DONE, MAGGIE. HE WANTS THEM TO KILL HIM.
AND I DON'T WANT HIM TO GET WHAT HE WANTS.

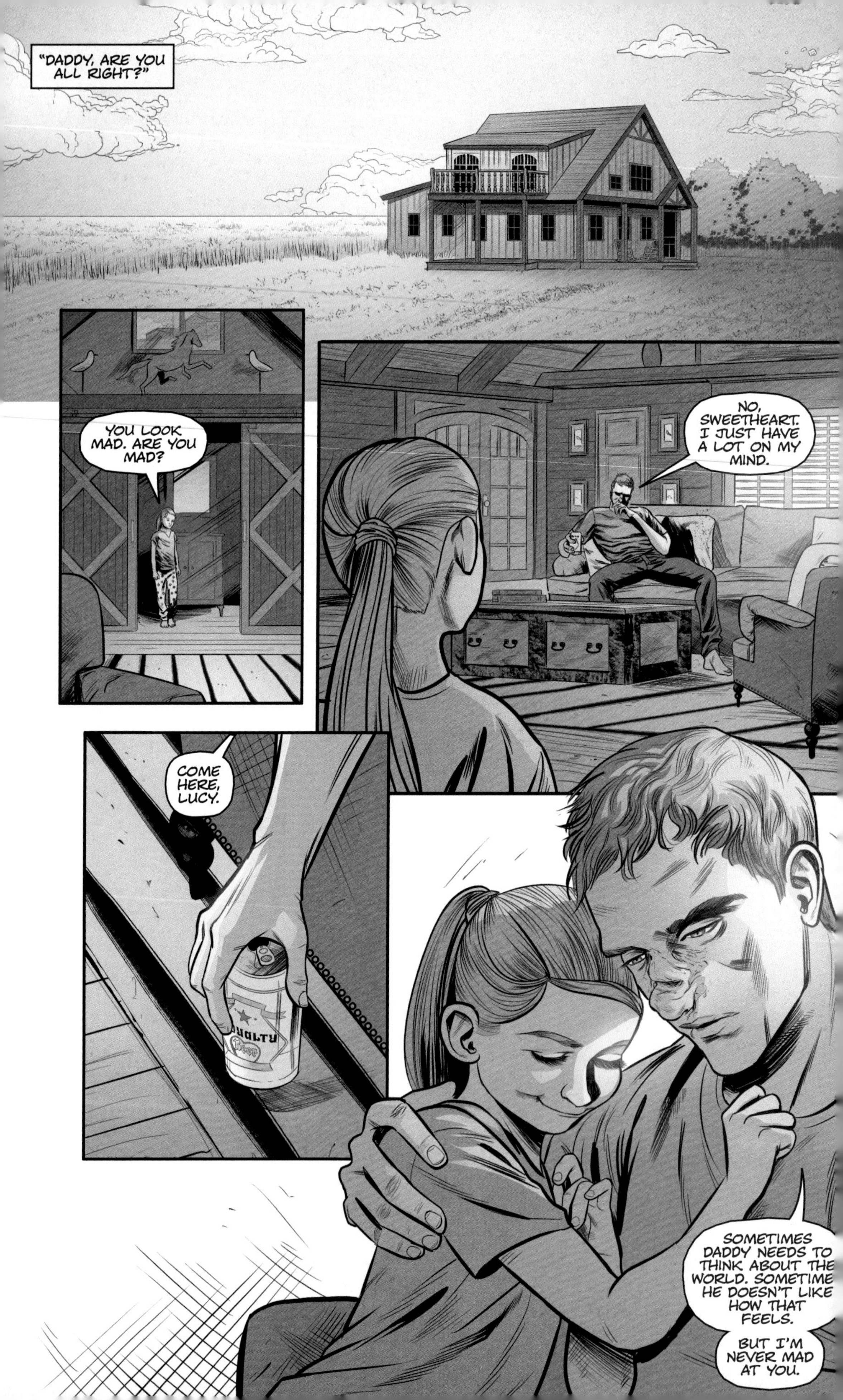
"DADDY, ARE YOU ALL RIGHT?"
YOU LOOK MAD. ARE YOU MAD?
NO, SWEETHEART. I JUST HAVE A LOT ON MY MIND.
COME HERE, LUCY.
SOMETIMES DADDY NEEDS TO THINK ABOUT THE WORLD. SOMETIME HE DOESN'T LIKE HOW THAT FEELS.
BUT I'M NEVER MAD AT YOU.

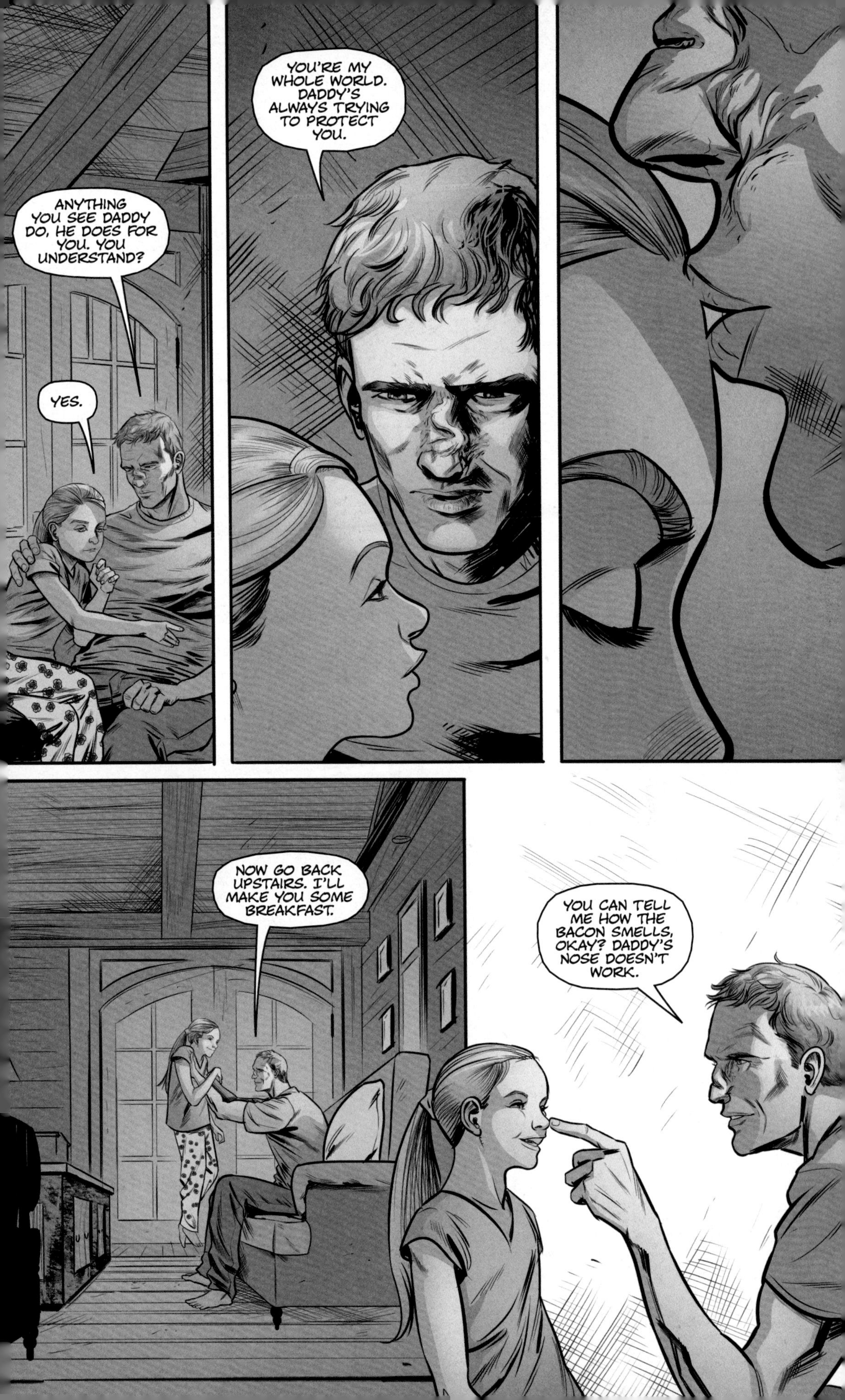
ANYTHING YOU SEE DADDY DO, HE DOES FOR YOU. YOU UNDERSTAND?
YES.
YOU'RE MY WHOLE WORLD. DADDY'S ALWAYS TRYING TO PROTECT YOU.
NOW GO BACK UPSTAIRS. I'LL MAKE YOU SOME BREAKFAST.
YOU CAN TELL ME HOW THE BACON SMELLS, OKAY? DADDY'S NOSE DOESN'T WORK.

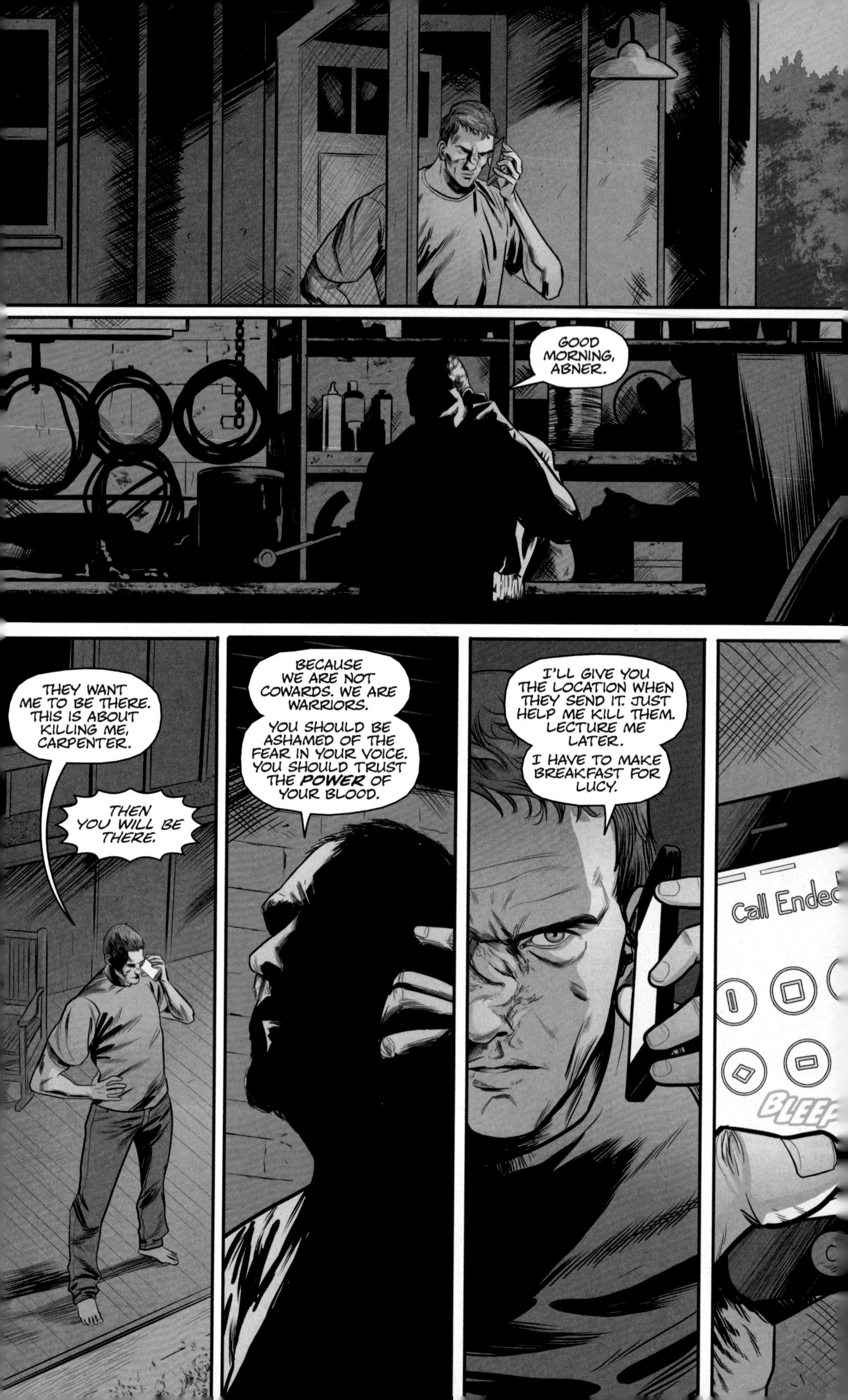
GOOD MORNING, ABNER.
THEY WANT ME TO BE THERE. THIS IS ABOUT KILLING ME, CARPENTER.
THEN YOU WILL BE THERE.
BECAUSE WE ARE NOT COWARDS. WE ARE WARRIORS.
YOU SHOULD BE ASHAMED OF THE FEAR IN YOUR VOICE. YOU SHOULD TRUST THE POWER OF YOUR BLOOD.
I'LL GIVE YOU THE LOCATION WHEN THEY SEND IT. JUST HELP ME KILL THEM. LECTURE ME LATER.
I HAVE TO MAKE BREAKFAST FOR LUCY.
Call Ended

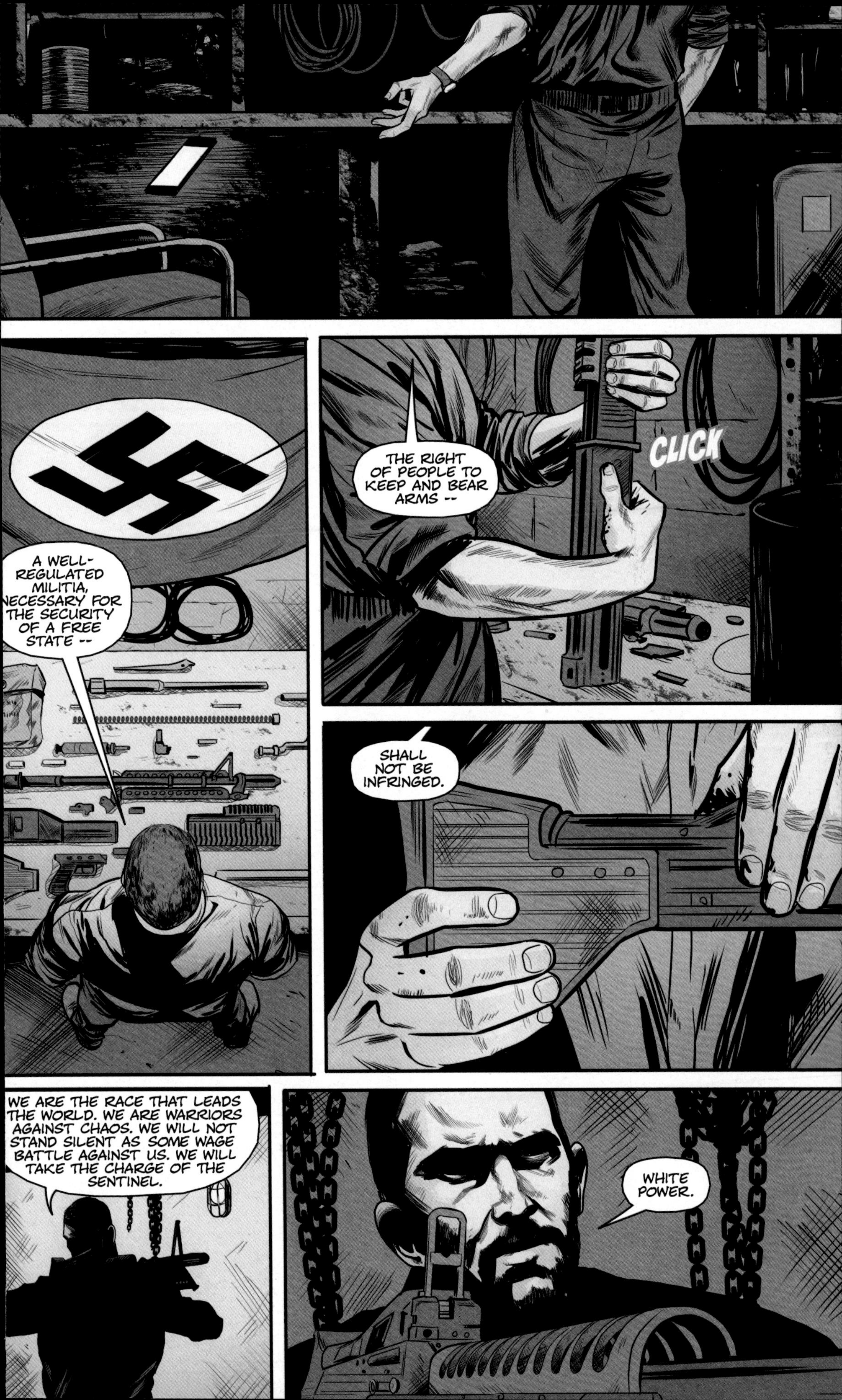
A WELL-REGULATED MILITIA, NECESSARY FOR THE SECURITY OF A FREE STATE --
THE RIGHT OF PEOPLE TO KEEP AND BEAR ARMS --
CLICK
SHALL NOT BE INFRINGED.
WE ARE THE RACE THAT LEADS THE WORLD. WE ARE WARRIORS AGAINST CHAOS. WE WILL NOT STAND SILENT AS SOME WAGE BATTLE AGAINST US. WE WILL TAKE THE CHARGE OF THE SENTINEL.
WHITE POWER.

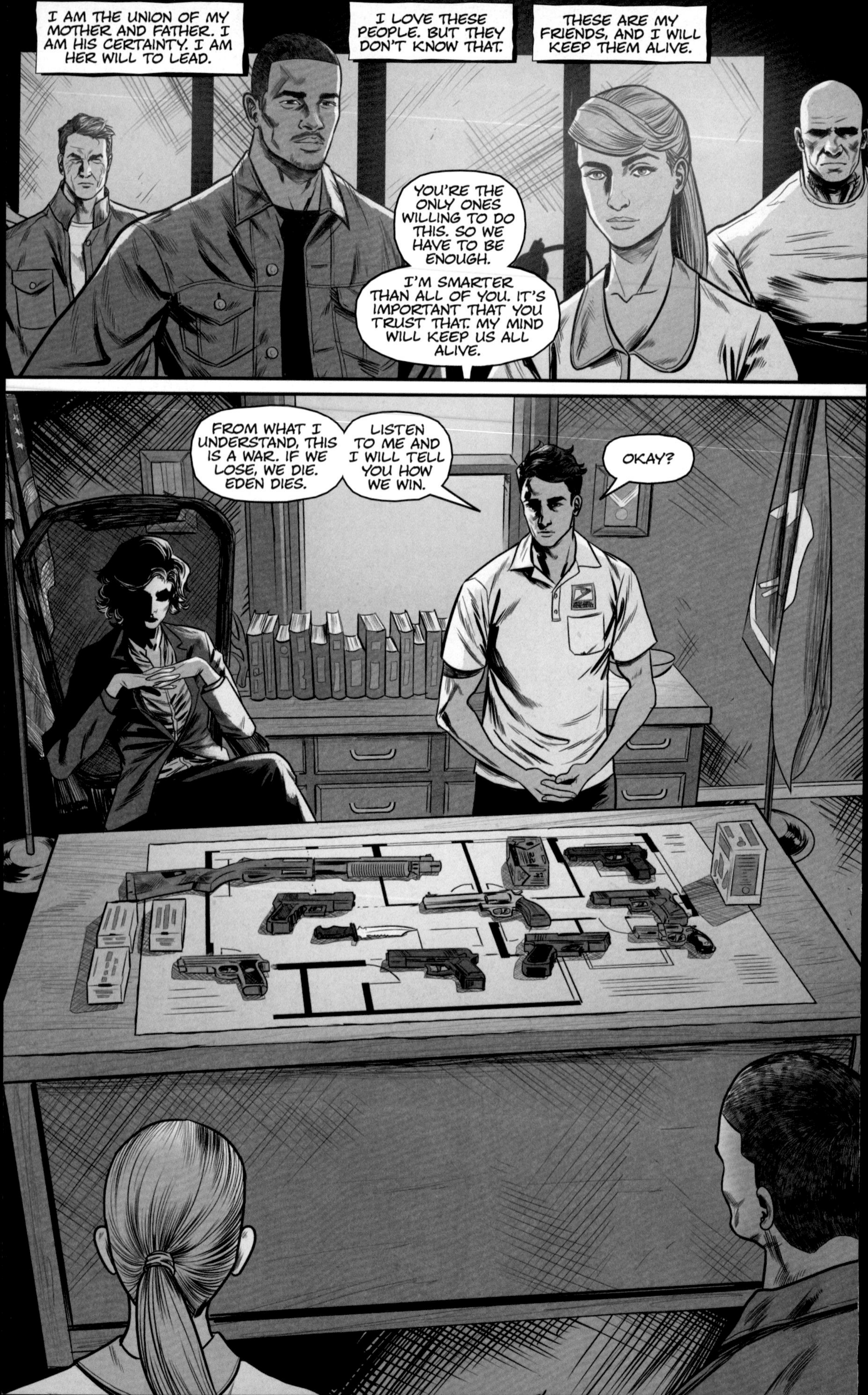
I AM THE UNION OF MY MOTHER AND FATHER. I AM HIS CERTAINTY. I AM HER WILL TO LEAD.
I LOVE THESE PEOPLE. BUT THEY DON'T KNOW THAT.
THESE ARE MY FRIENDS, AND I WILL KEEP THEM ALIVE.
YOU'RE THE ONLY ONES WILLING TO DO THIS. SO WE HAVE TO BE ENOUGH.
I'M SMARTER THAN ALL OF YOU. IT'S IMPORTANT THAT YOU TRUST THAT. MY MIND WILL KEEP US ALL ALIVE.
FROM WHAT I UNDERSTAND, THIS IS A WAR. IF WE LOSE, WE DIE. EDEN DIES.
LISTEN TO ME AND I WILL TELL YOU HOW WE WIN.
OKAY?

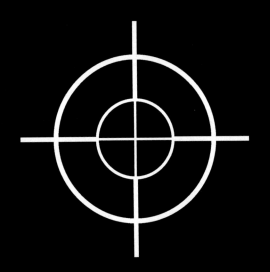

# CHAPTER 16

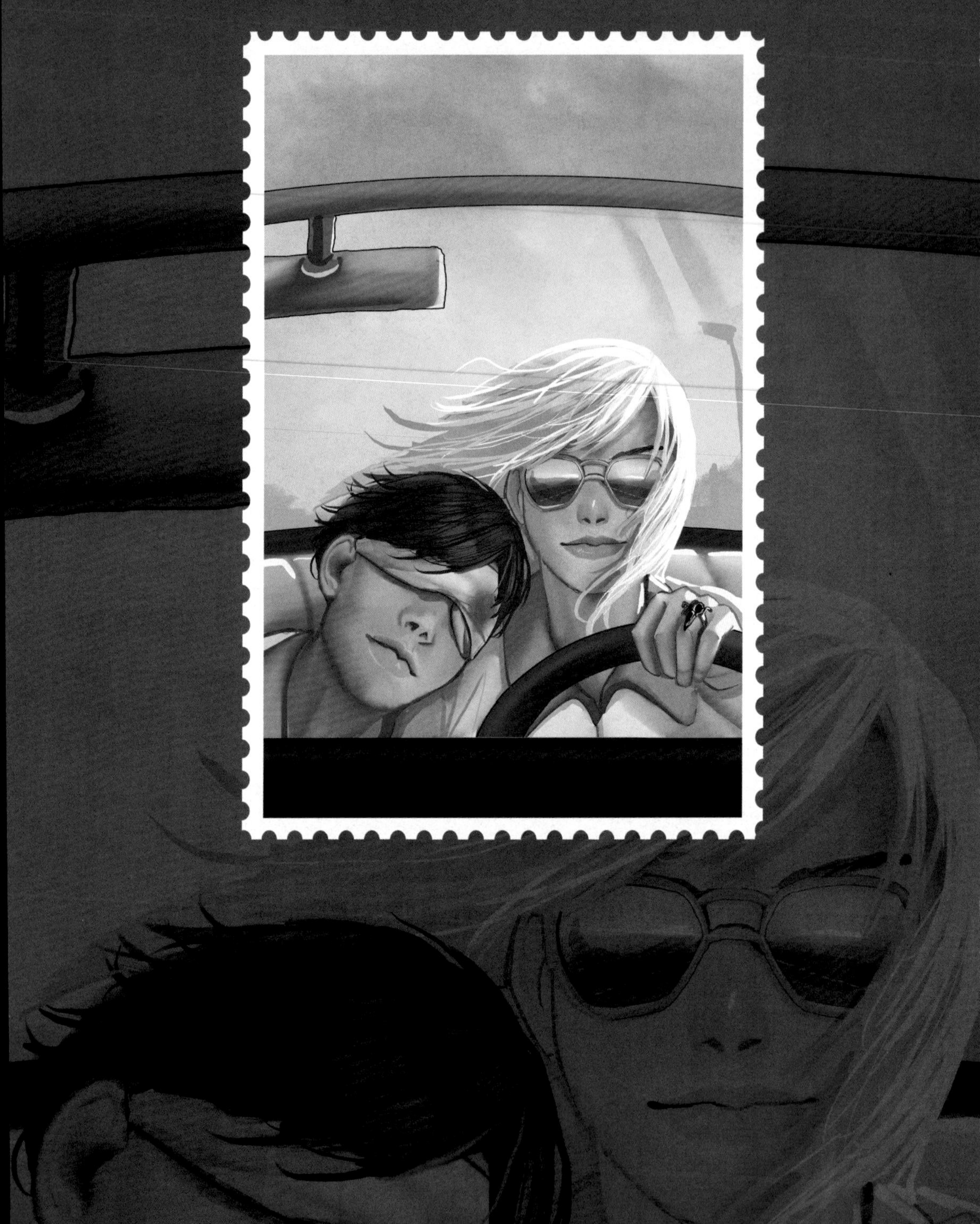

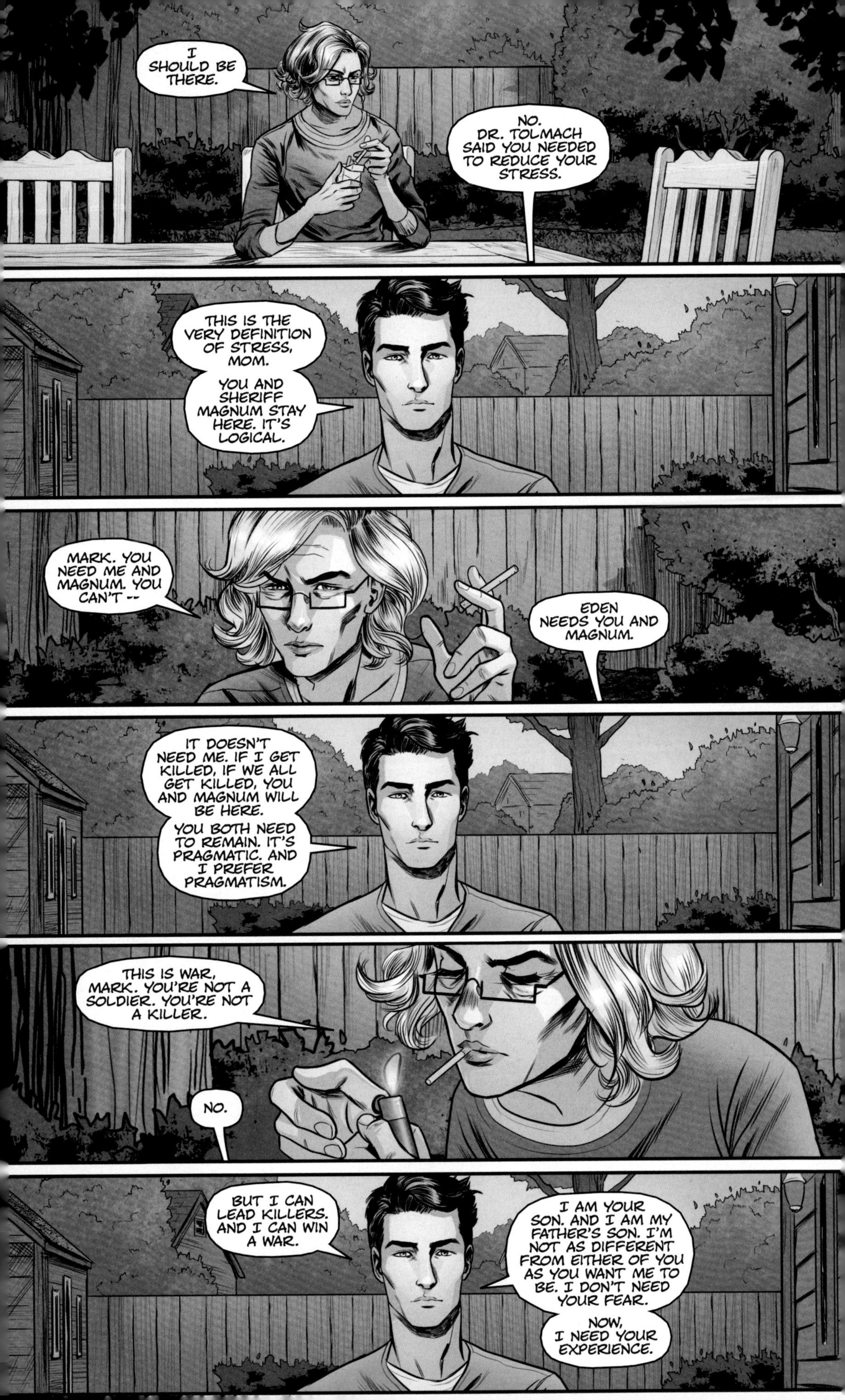
I SHOULD BE THERE.
NO. DR. TOLMACH SAID YOU NEEDED TO REDUCE YOUR STRESS.
THIS IS THE VERY DEFINITION OF STRESS, MOM.
YOU AND SHERIFF MAGNUM STAY HERE. IT'S LOGICAL.
MARK. YOU NEED ME AND MAGNUM. YOU CAN'T --
EDEN NEEDS YOU AND MAGNUM.
IT DOESN'T NEED ME. IF I GET KILLED, IF WE ALL GET KILLED, YOU AND MAGNUM WILL BE HERE.
YOU BOTH NEED TO REMAIN. IT'S PRAGMATIC. AND I PREFER PRAGMATISM.
THIS IS WAR, MARK. YOU'RE NOT A SOLDIER. YOU'RE NOT A KILLER.
NO.
BUT I CAN LEAD KILLERS. AND I CAN WIN A WAR.
I AM YOUR SON. AND I AM MY FATHER'S SON. I'M NOT AS DIFFERENT FROM EITHER OF YOU AS YOU WANT ME TO BE. I DON'T NEED YOUR FEAR.
NOW, I NEED YOUR EXPERIENCE.

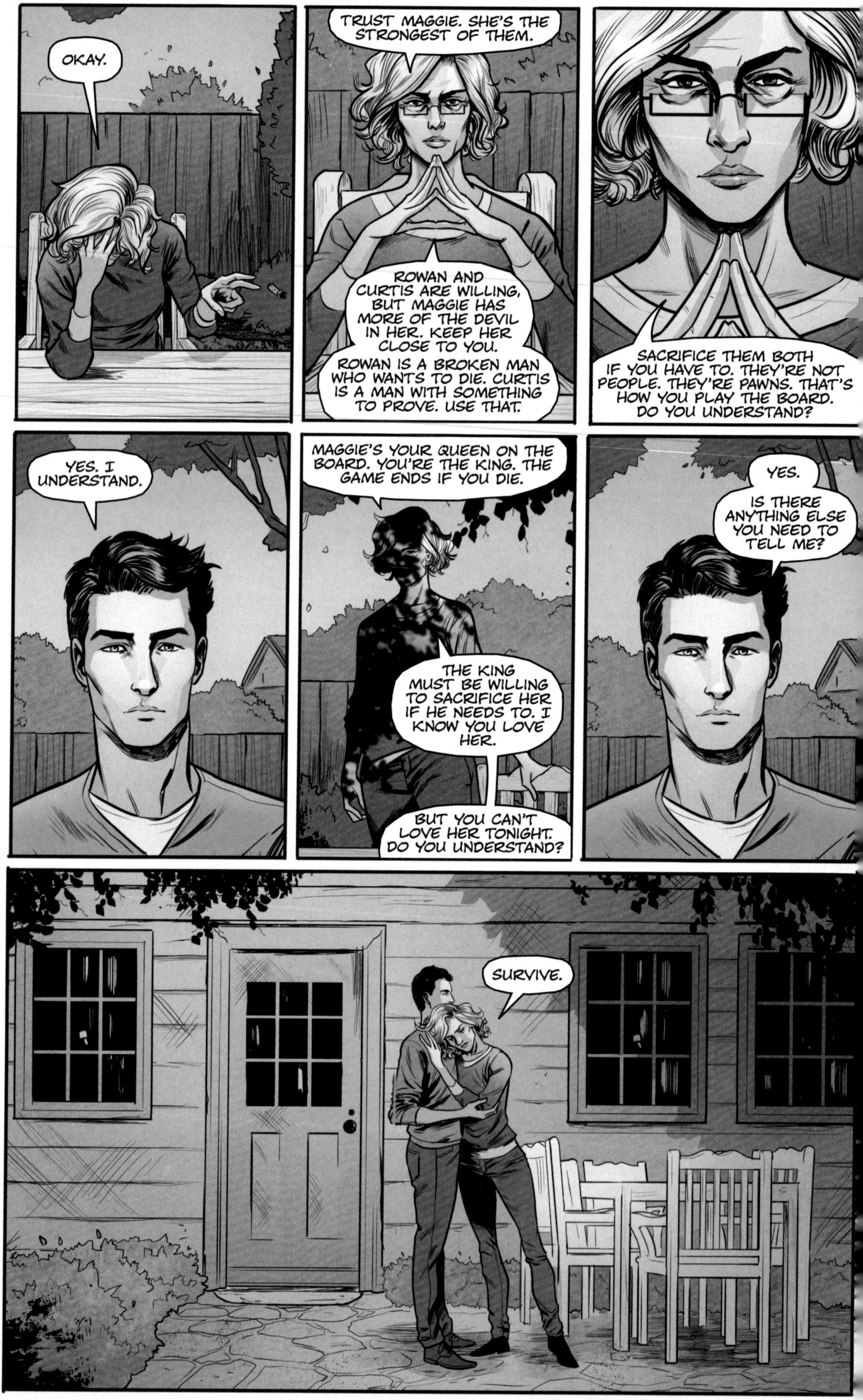
OKAY.
TRUST MAGGIE. SHE'S THE STRONGEST OF THEM.
ROWAN AND CURTIS ARE WILLING, BUT MAGGIE HAS MORE OF THE DEVIL IN HER. KEEP HER CLOSE TO YOU.
ROWAN IS A BROKEN MAN WHO WANTS TO DIE. CURTIS IS A MAN WITH SOMETHING TO PROVE. USE THAT.
SACRIFICE THEM BOTH IF YOU HAVE TO. THEY'RE NOT PEOPLE. THEY'RE PAWNS. THAT'S HOW YOU PLAY THE BOARD. DO YOU UNDERSTAND?
YES. I UNDERSTAND.
MAGGIE'S YOUR QUEEN ON THE BOARD. YOU'RE THE KING. THE GAME ENDS IF YOU DIE.
THE KING MUST BE WILLING TO SACRIFICE HER IF HE NEEDS TO. I KNOW YOU LOVE HER.
BUT YOU CAN'T LOVE HER TONIGHT. DO YOU UNDERSTAND?
YES.
IS THERE ANYTHING ELSE YOU NEED TO TELL ME?
SURVIVE.

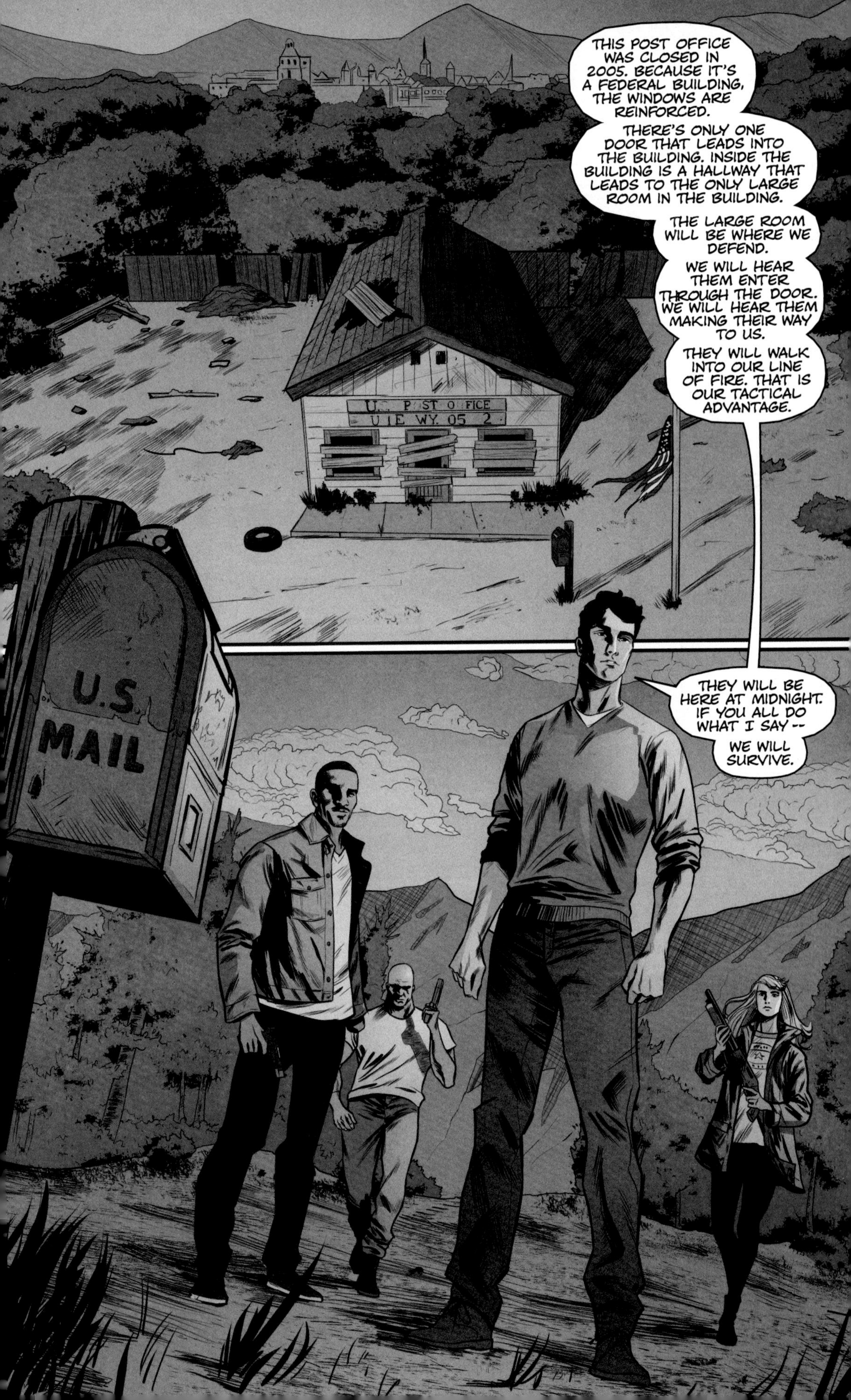
THIS POST OFFICE WAS CLOSED IN 2005. BECAUSE IT'S A FEDERAL BUILDING, THE WINDOWS ARE REINFORCED.
THERE'S ONLY ONE DOOR THAT LEADS INTO THE BUILDING. INSIDE THE BUILDING IS A HALLWAY THAT LEADS TO THE ONLY LARGE ROOM IN THE BUILDING.
THE LARGE ROOM WILL BE WHERE WE DEFEND.
WE WILL HEAR THEM ENTER THROUGH THE DOOR. WE WILL HEAR THEM MAKING THEIR WAY TO US.
THEY WILL WALK INTO OUR LINE OF FIRE. THAT IS OUR TACTICAL ADVANTAGE.
U.S. MAIL
THEY WILL BE HERE AT MIDNIGHT. IF YOU ALL DO WHAT I SAY --
WE WILL SURVIVE.

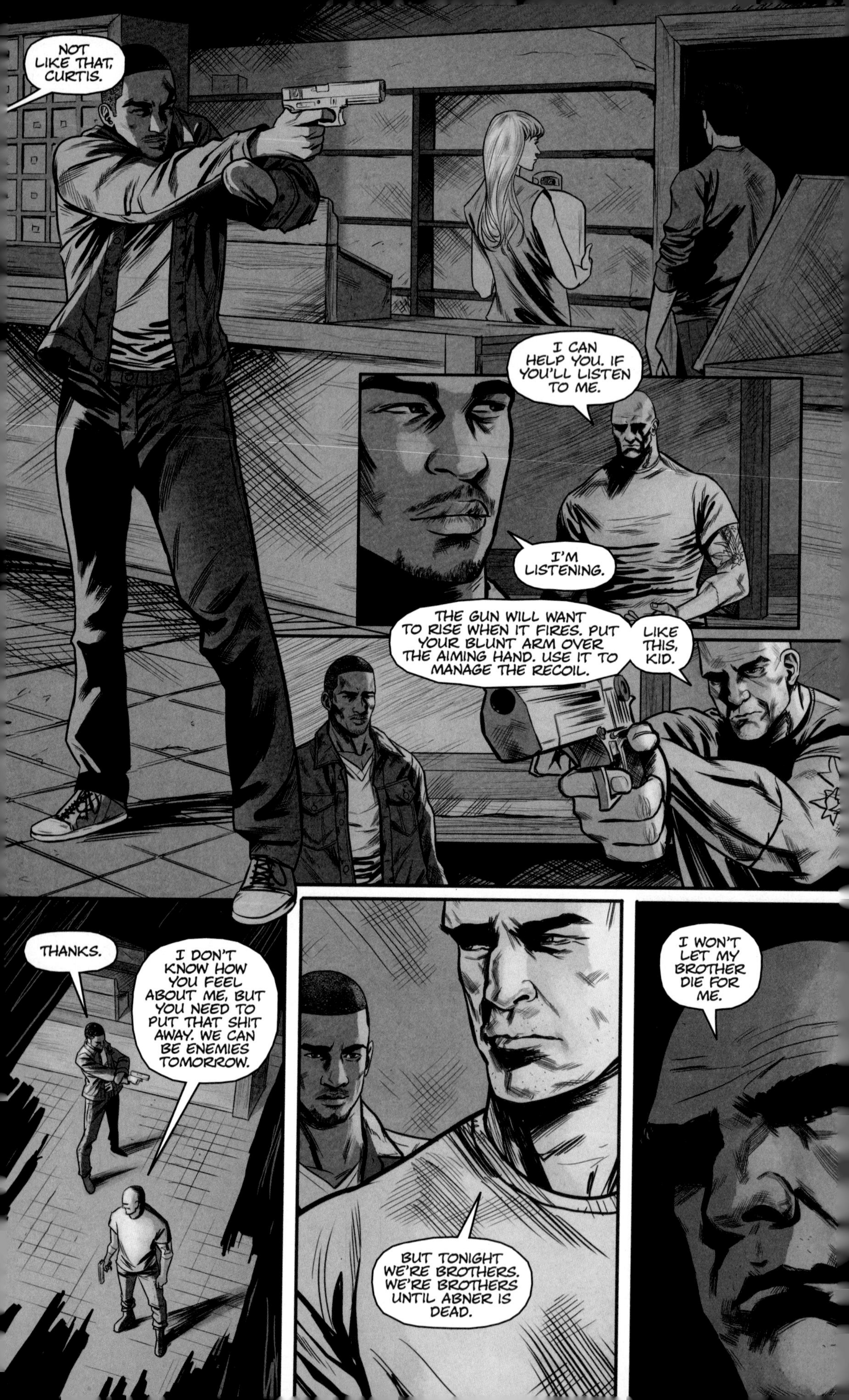
NOT LIKE THAT, CURTIS.
I CAN HELP YOU. IF YOU'LL LISTEN TO ME.
I'M LISTENING.
THE GUN WILL WANT TO RISE WHEN IT FIRES. PUT YOUR BLUNT ARM OVER THE AIMING HAND. USE IT TO MANAGE THE RECOIL.
LIKE THIS, KID.
THANKS.
I DON'T KNOW HOW YOU FEEL ABOUT ME, BUT YOU NEED TO PUT THAT SHIT AWAY. WE CAN BE ENEMIES TOMORROW.
BUT TONIGHT WE'RE BROTHERS. WE'RE BROTHERS UNTIL ABNER IS DEAD.
I WON'T LET MY BROTHER DIE FOR ME.

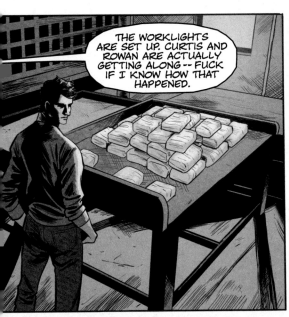

THE WORKLIGHTS ARE SET UP. CURTIS AND ROWAN ARE ACTUALLY GETTING ALONG -- FUCK IF I KNOW HOW THAT HAPPENED.

YOU'RE THINKING. I WOULD FEEL A WHOLE LOT BETTER IF I KNEW WHAT YOU WERE THINKING ABOUT.

IT'S NOT A PLEASANT THING TO SAY. IT'S SOMETHING THAT MIGHT HURT YOU.

SECRETS HURT ME MORE.

MY MOTHER TOLD ME I NEEDED TO BE ABLE TO SACRIFICE YOU. SHE SAID I NEEDED TO BE WILLING TO LET YOU DIE.

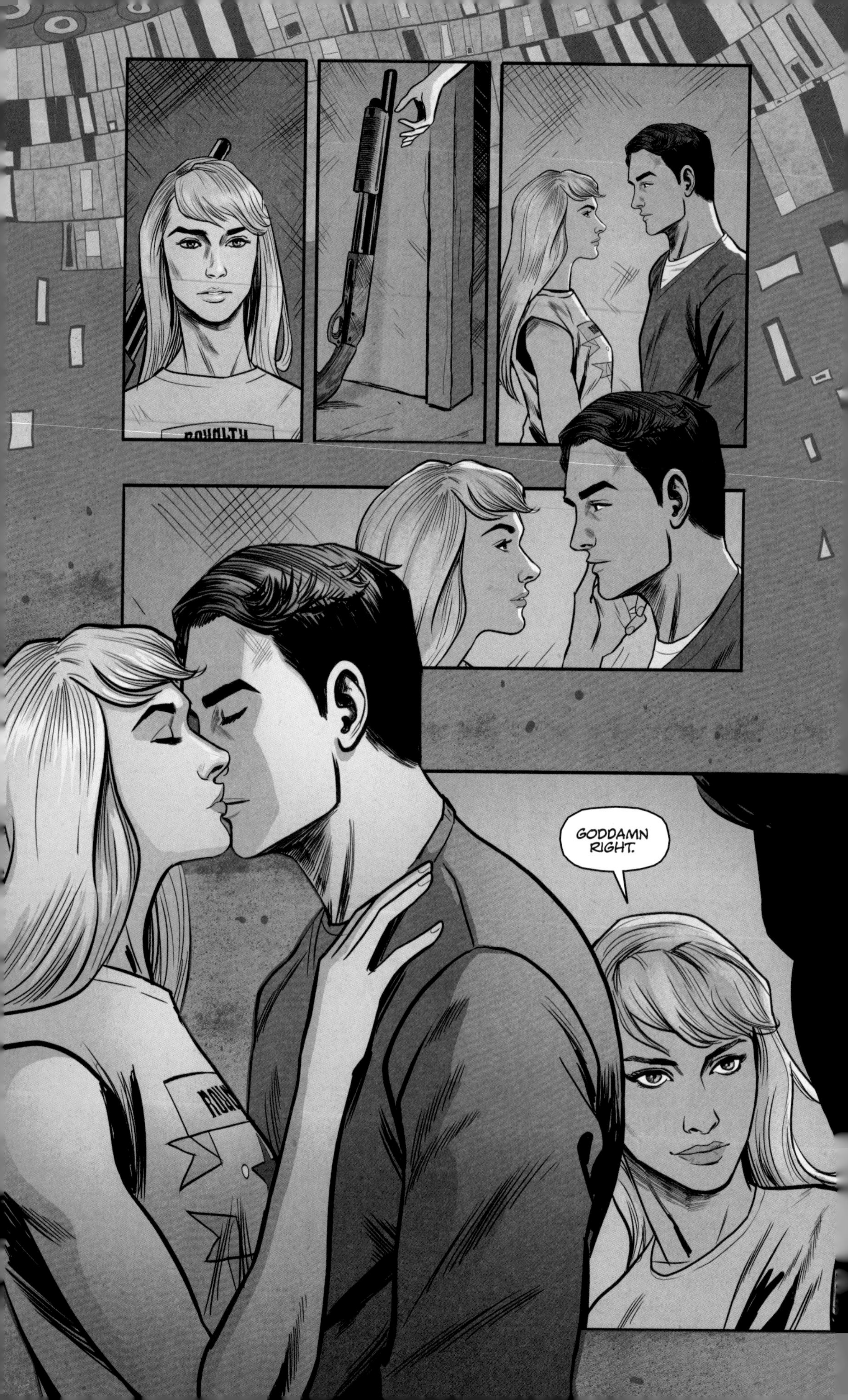
GODDAMN RIGHT.

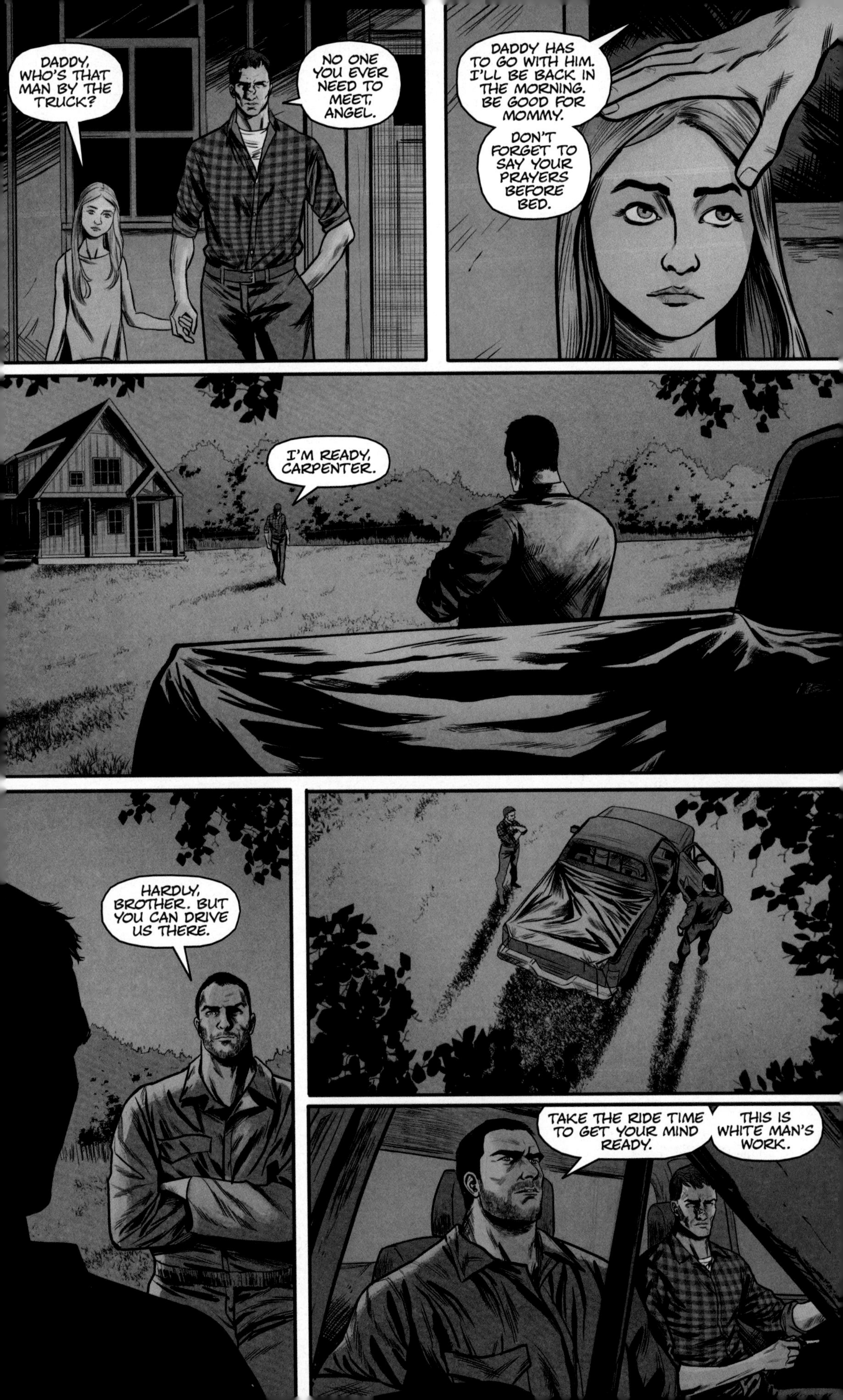
DADDY, WHO'S THAT MAN BY THE TRUCK?
NO ONE YOU EVER NEED TO MEET, ANGEL.
DADDY HAS TO GO WITH HIM. I'LL BE BACK IN THE MORNING. BE GOOD FOR MOMMY.
DON'T FORGET TO SAY YOUR PRAYERS BEFORE BED.
I'M READY, CARPENTER.
HARDLY, BROTHER. BUT YOU CAN DRIVE US THERE.
TAKE THE RIDE TIME TO GET YOUR MIND READY.
THIS IS WHITE MAN'S WORK.

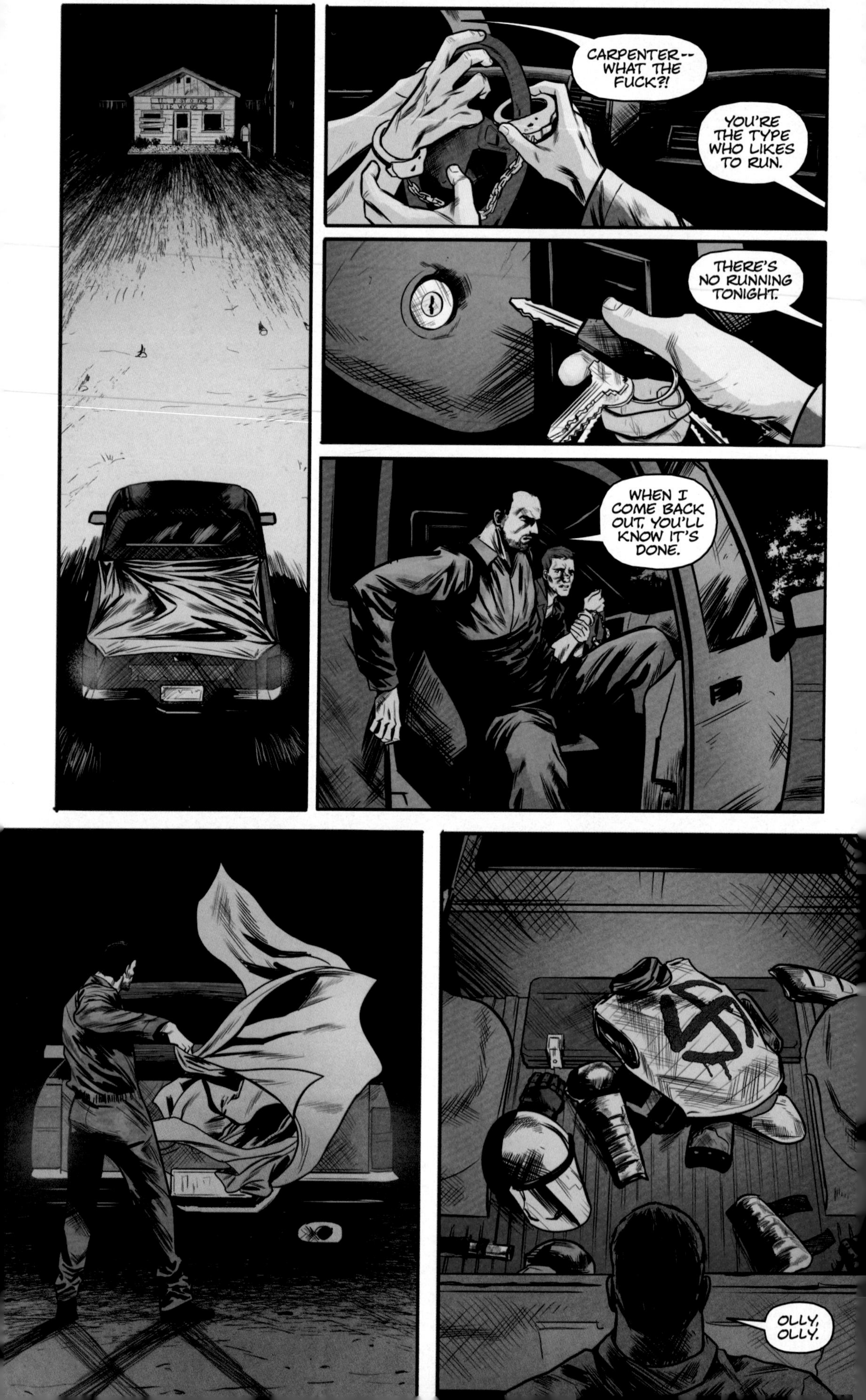
CARPENTER-- WHAT THE FUCK?!
YOU'RE THE TYPE WHO LIKES TO RUN.
THERE'S NO RUNNING TONIGHT.
WHEN I COME BACK OUT, YOU'LL KNOW IT'S DONE.
OLLY, OLLY.

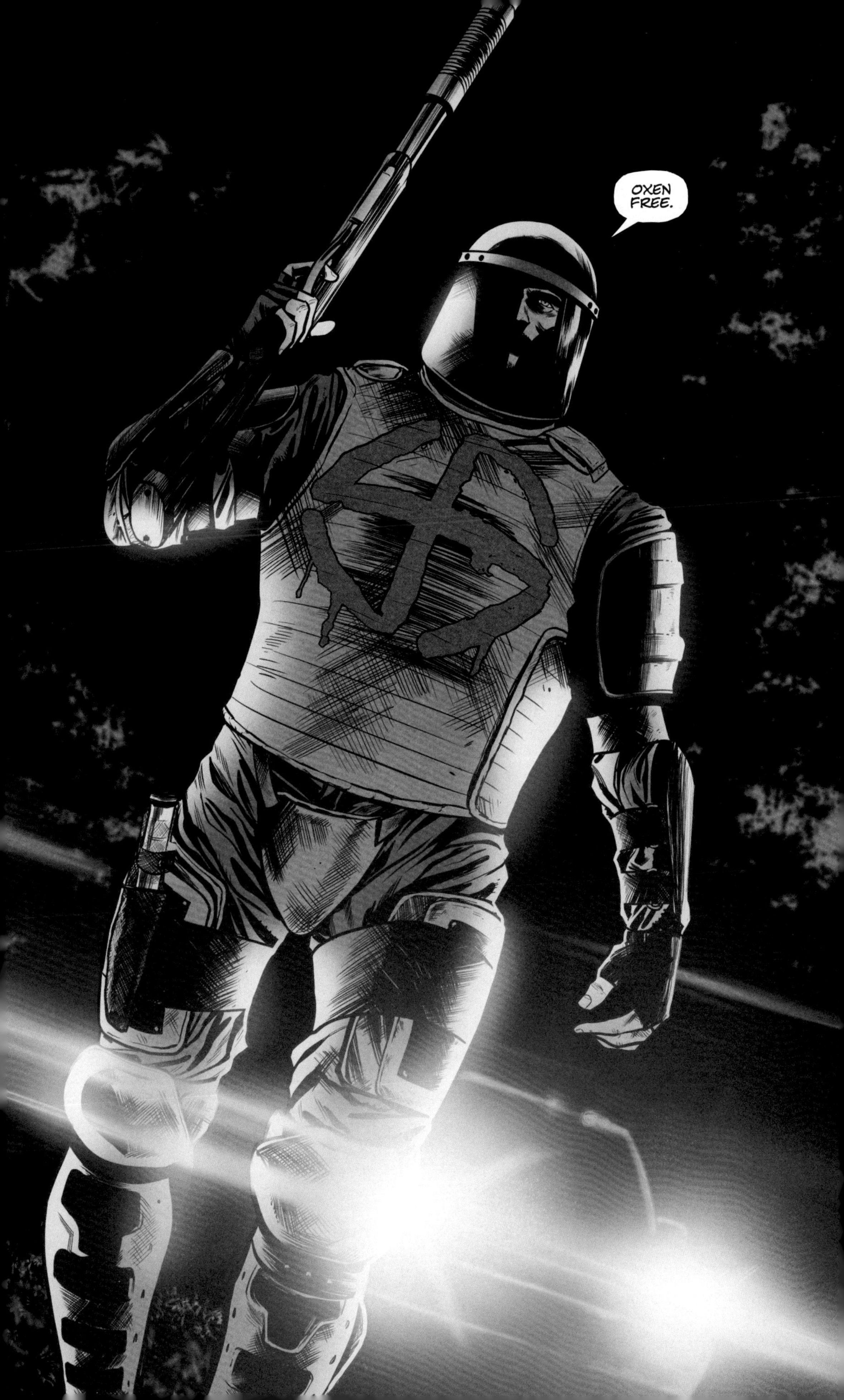
OXEN FREE.

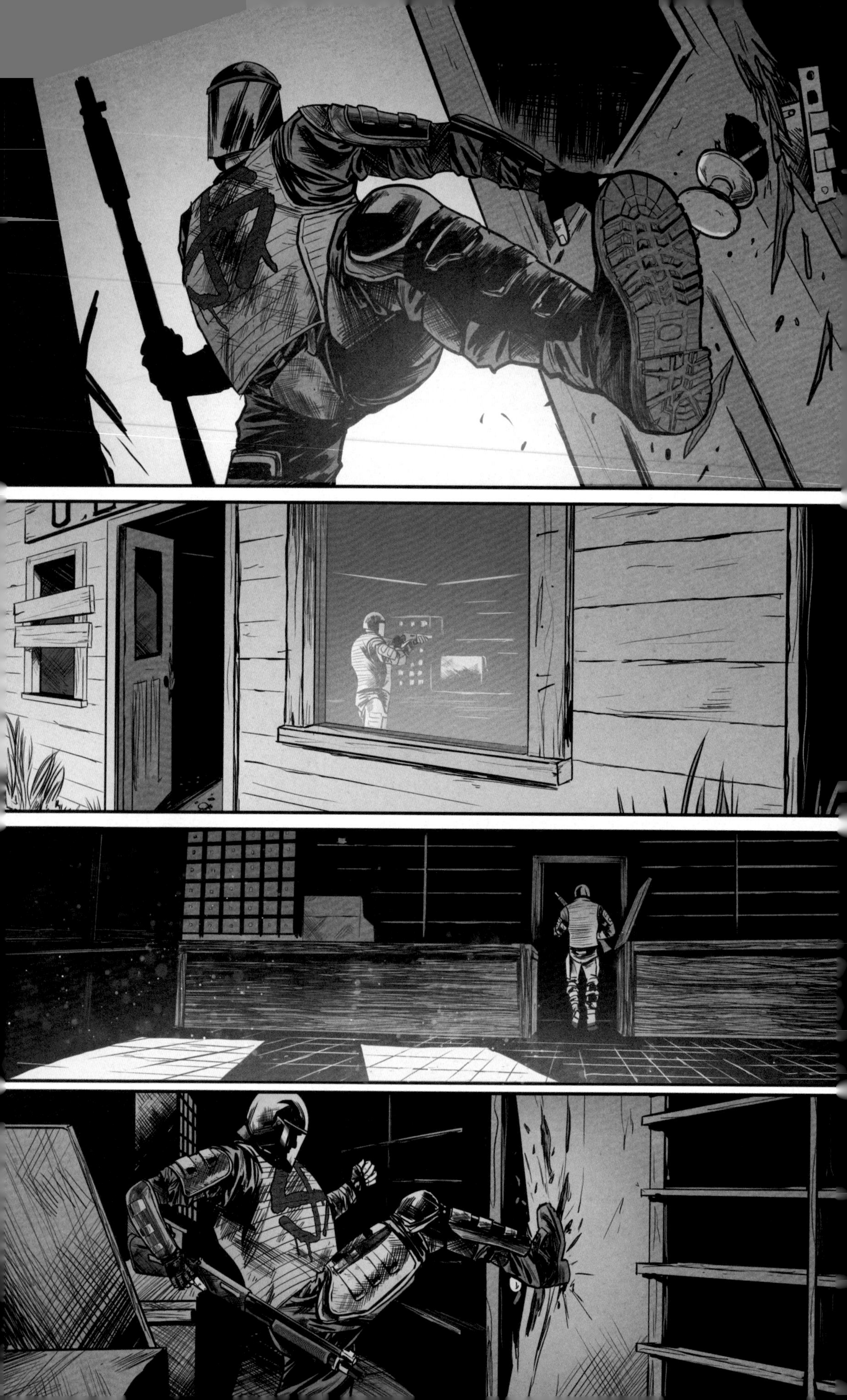

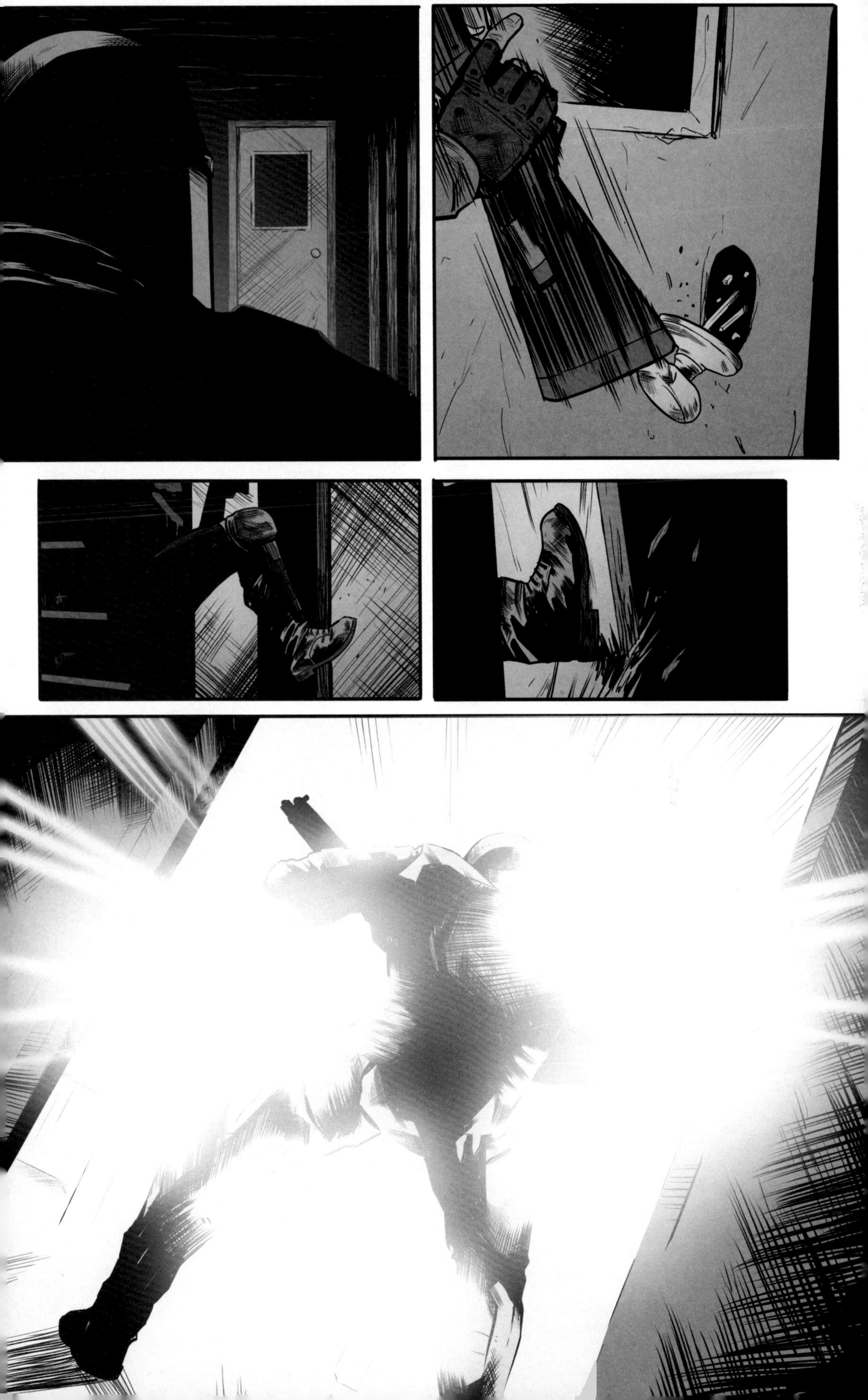

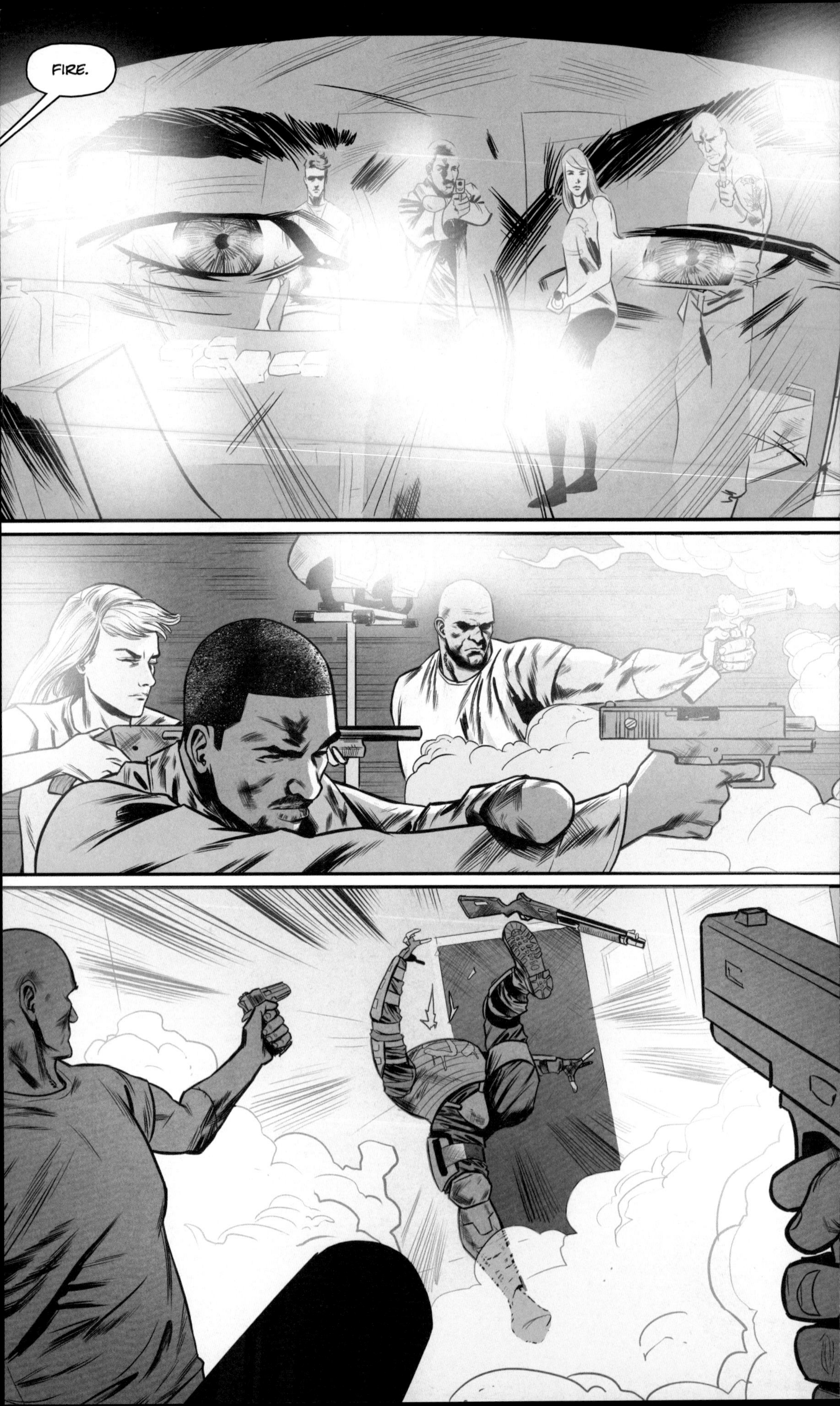
FIRE.

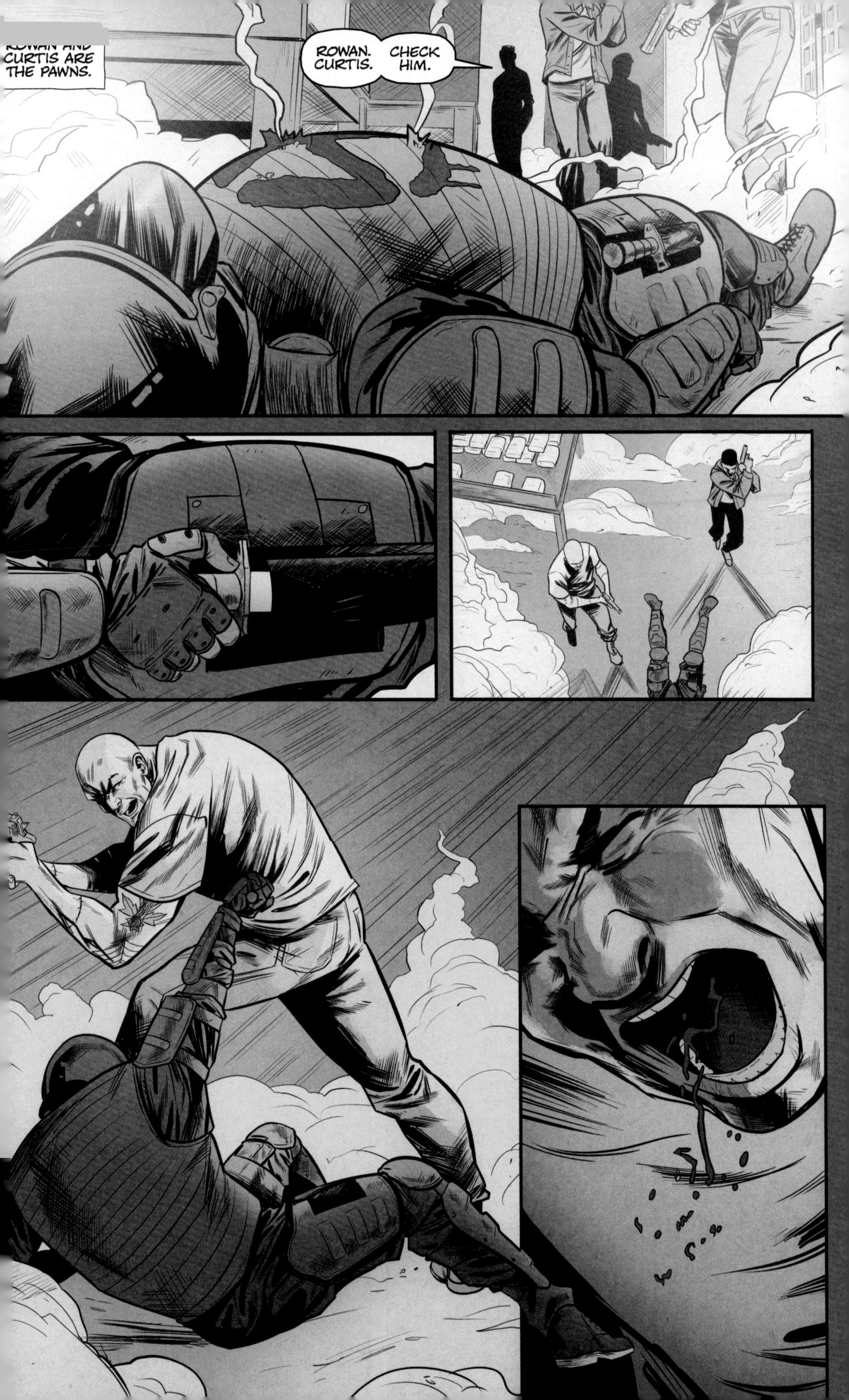
CURTIS ARE
THE PAWNS.
ROWAN. CURTIS.
CHECK HIM.

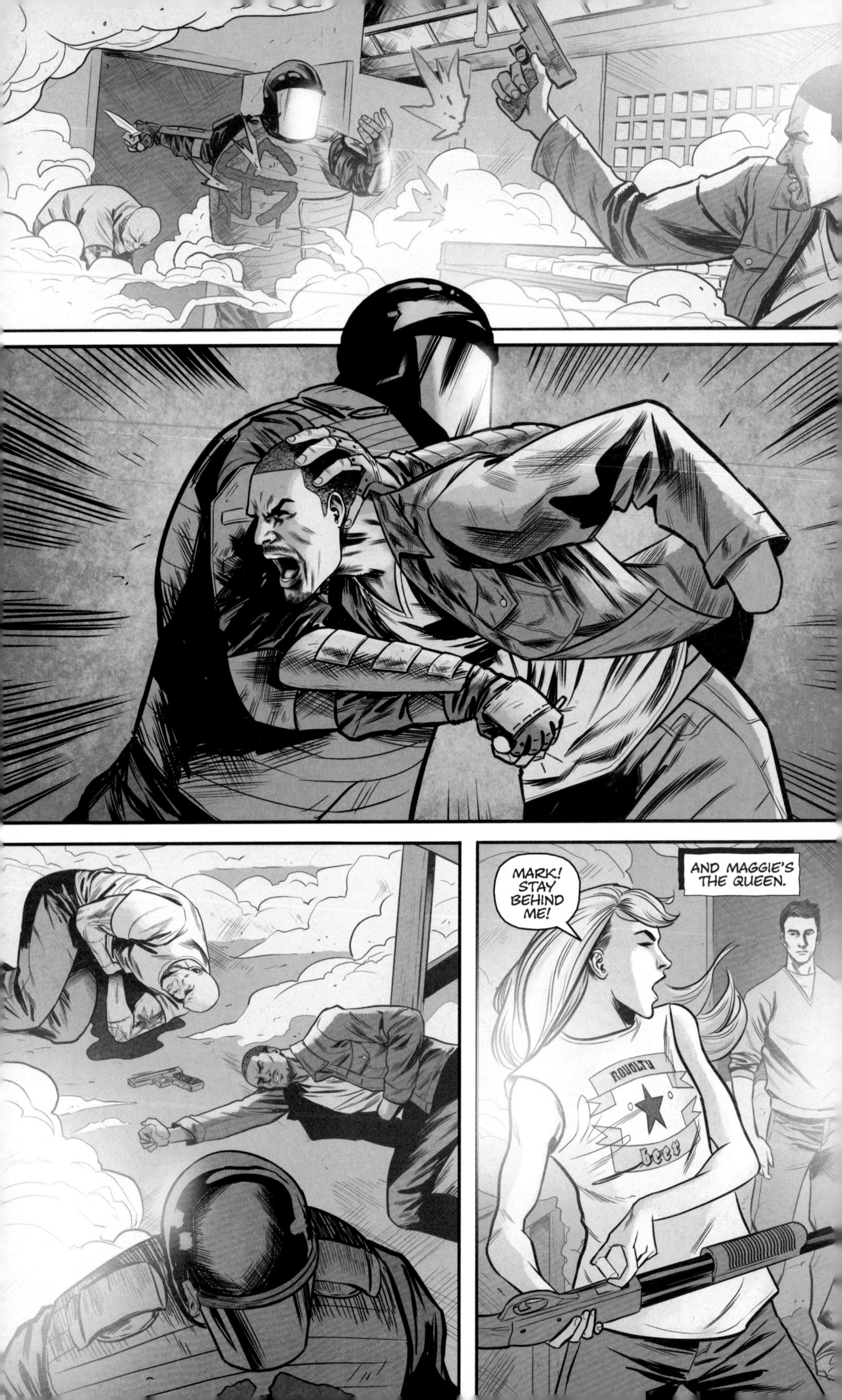
MARK! STAY BEHIND ME!
AND MAGGIE'S THE QUEEN.
ROYALTY
beer

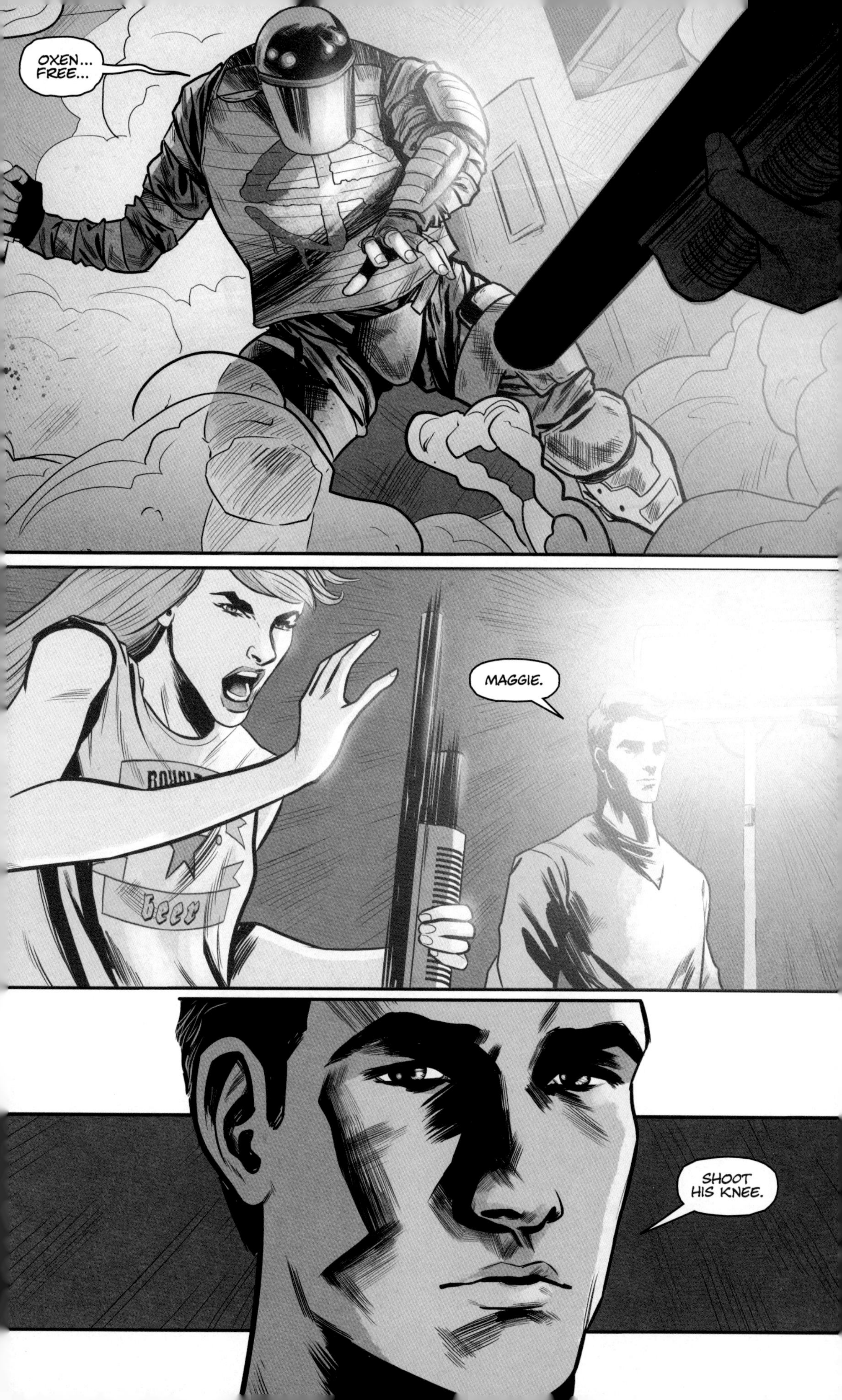
OXEN... FREE...
MAGGIE.
SHOOT HIS KNEE.

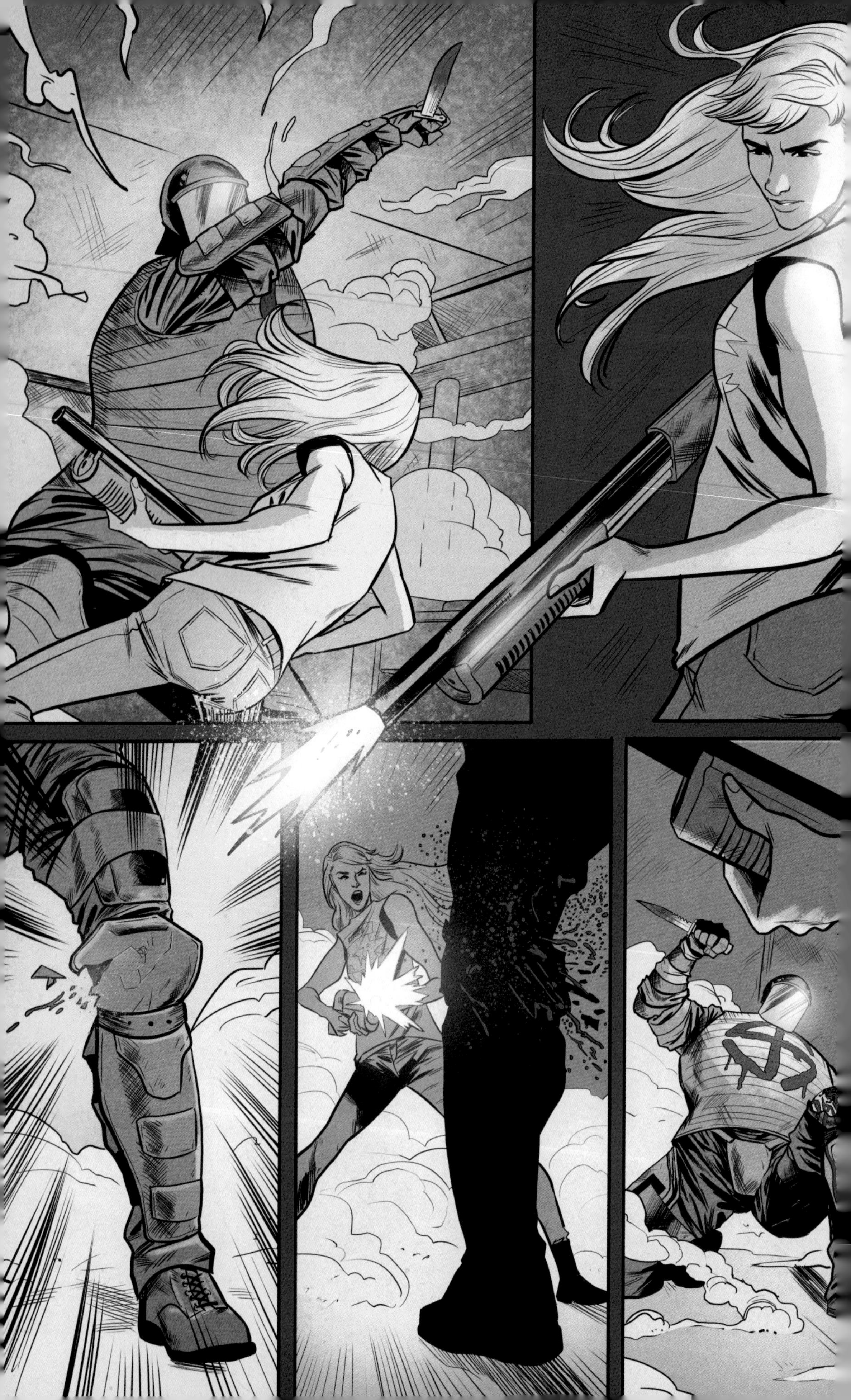

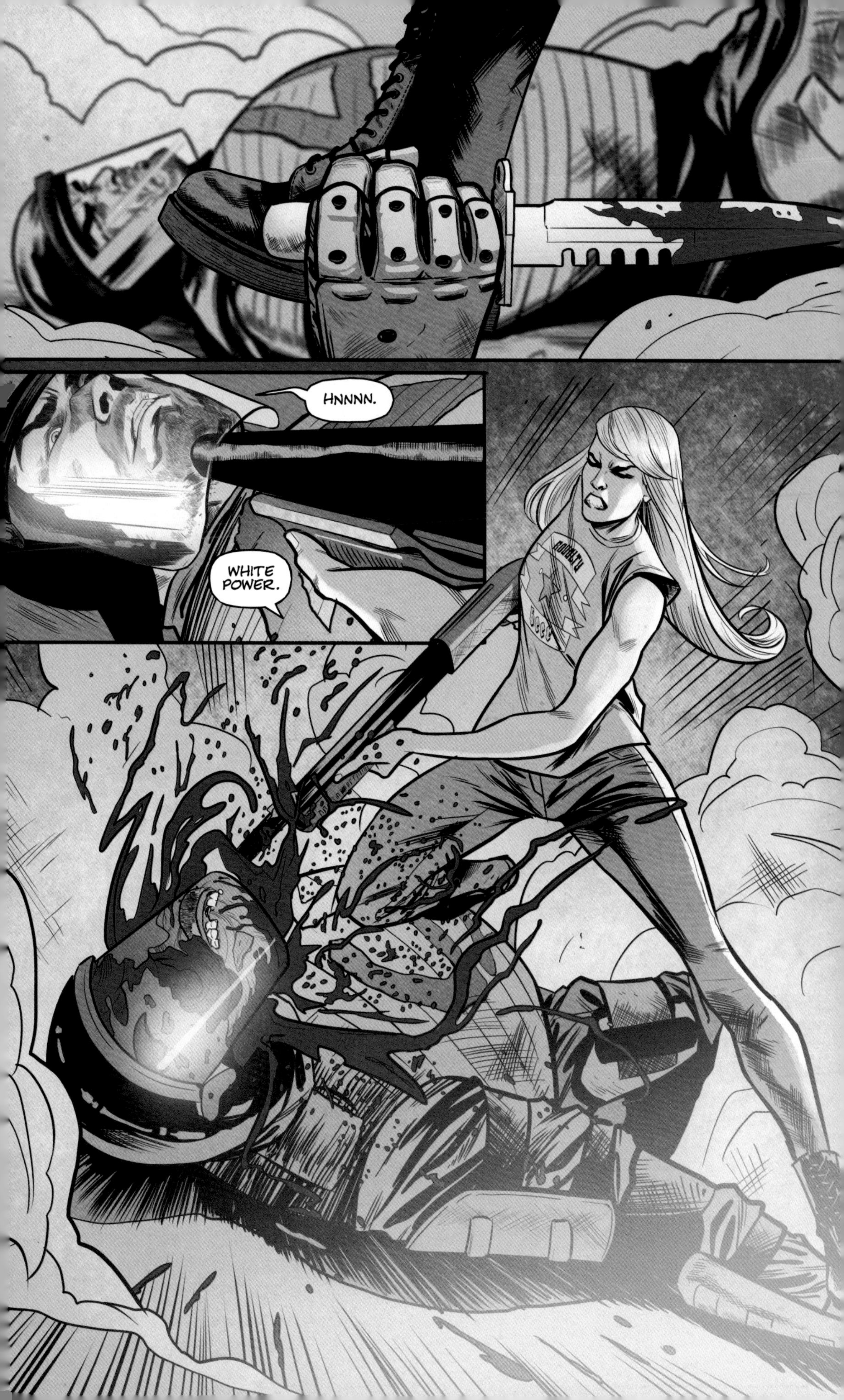
HNNNN.
WHITE POWER.

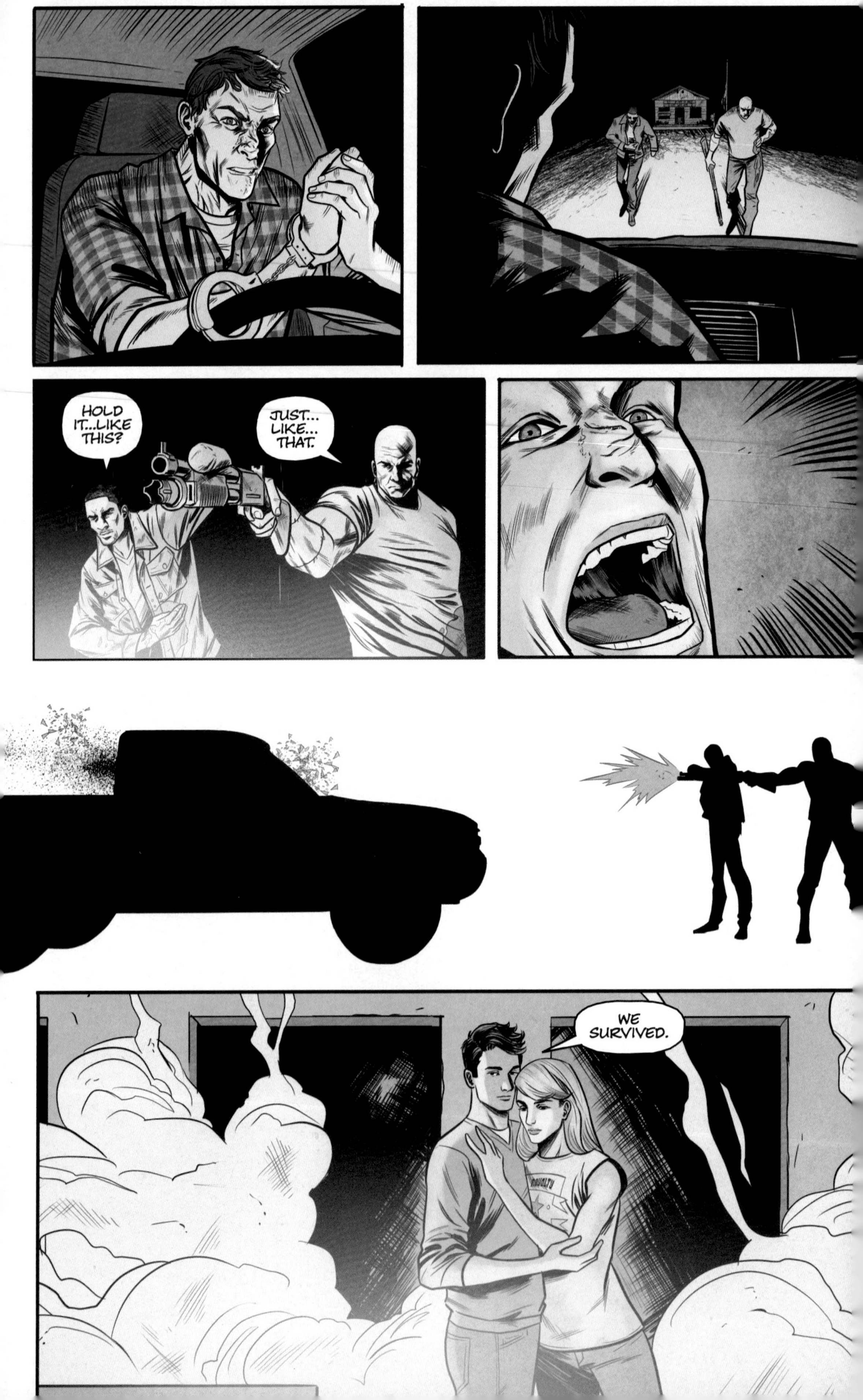
HOLD IT...LIKE THIS?
JUST... LIKE... THAT.
WE SURVIVED.

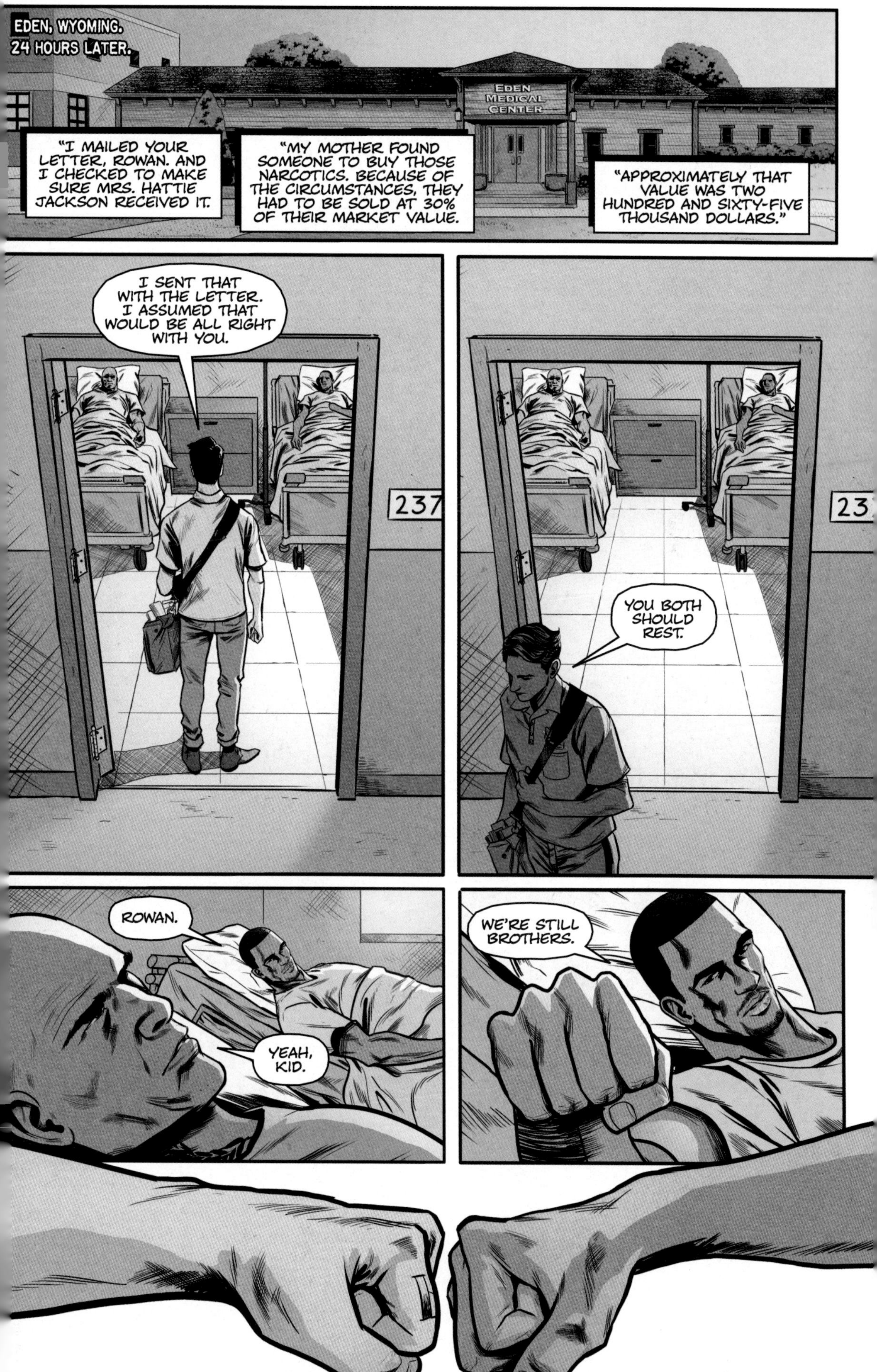
EDEN, WYOMING.
24 HOURS LATER.
EDEN MEDICAL CENTER
"I MAILED YOUR LETTER, ROWAN. AND I CHECKED TO MAKE SURE MRS. HATTIE JACKSON RECEIVED IT.
"MY MOTHER FOUND SOMEONE TO BUY THOSE NARCOTICS. BECAUSE OF THE CIRCUMSTANCES, THEY HAD TO BE SOLD AT 30% OF THEIR MARKET VALUE.
"APPROXIMATELY THAT VALUE WAS TWO HUNDRED AND SIXTY-FIVE THOUSAND DOLLARS."
I SENT THAT WITH THE LETTER. I ASSUMED THAT WOULD BE ALL RIGHT WITH YOU.
237
YOU BOTH SHOULD REST.
23
ROWAN.
YEAH, KID.
WE'RE STILL BROTHERS.

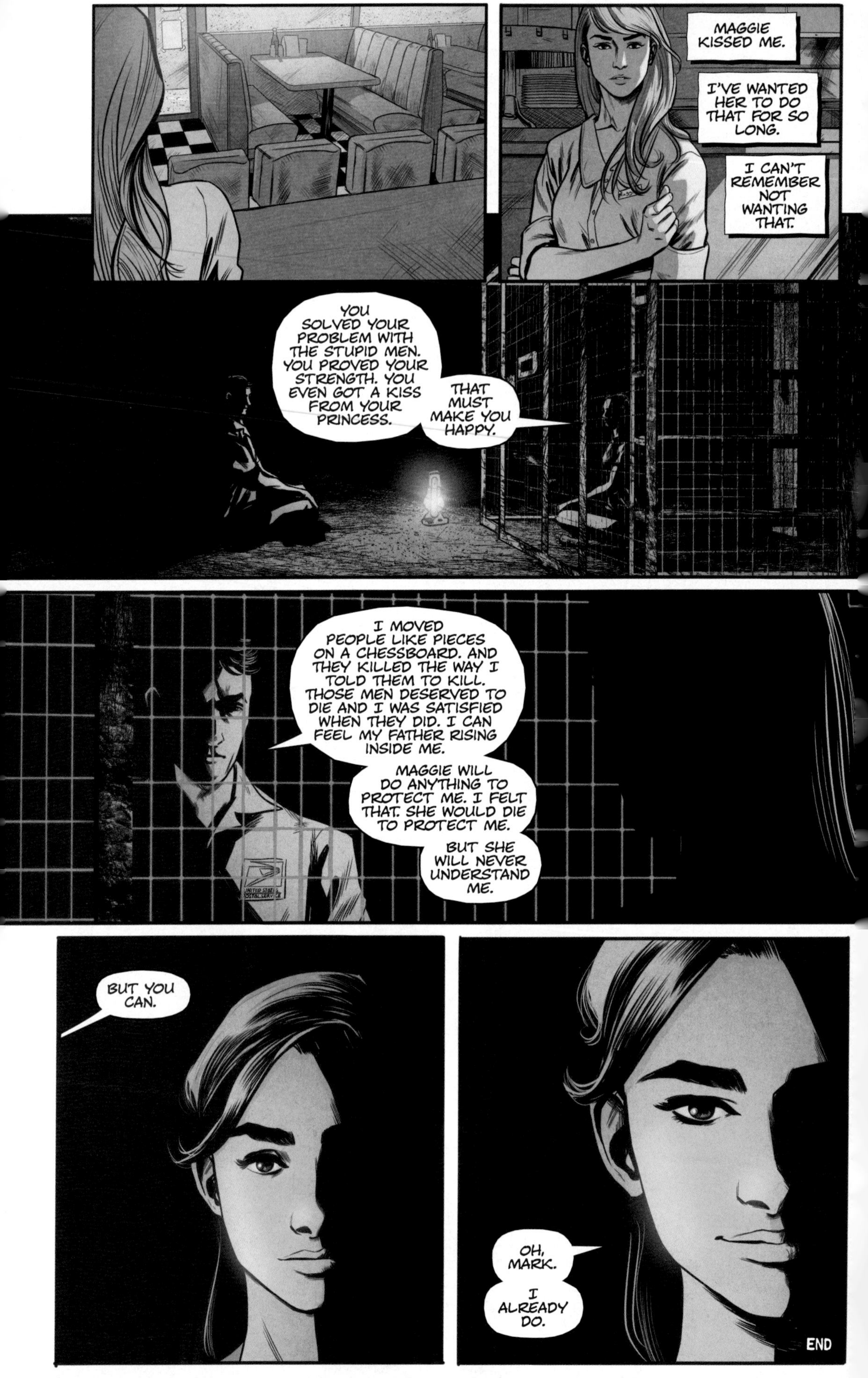
MAGGIE KISSED ME.
I'VE WANTED HER TO DO THAT FOR SO LONG.
I CAN'T REMEMBER NOT WANTING THAT.
YOU SOLVED YOUR PROBLEM WITH THE STUPID MEN. YOU PROVED YOUR STRENGTH. YOU EVEN GOT A KISS FROM YOUR PRINCESS.
THAT MUST MAKE YOU HAPPY.
I MOVED PEOPLE LIKE PIECES ON A CHESSBOARD. AND THEY KILLED THE WAY I TOLD THEM TO KILL. THOSE MEN DESERVED TO DIE AND I WAS SATISFIED WHEN THEY DID. I CAN FEEL MY FATHER RISING INSIDE ME.
MAGGIE WILL DO ANYTHING TO PROTECT ME. I FELT THAT. SHE WOULD DIE TO PROTECT ME.
BUT SHE WILL NEVER UNDERSTAND ME.
BUT YOU CAN.
OH, MARK.
I ALREADY DO.
END

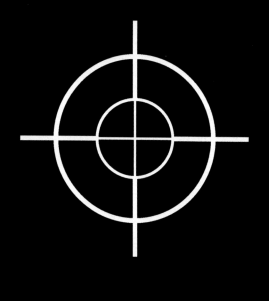

# CHAPTER 17

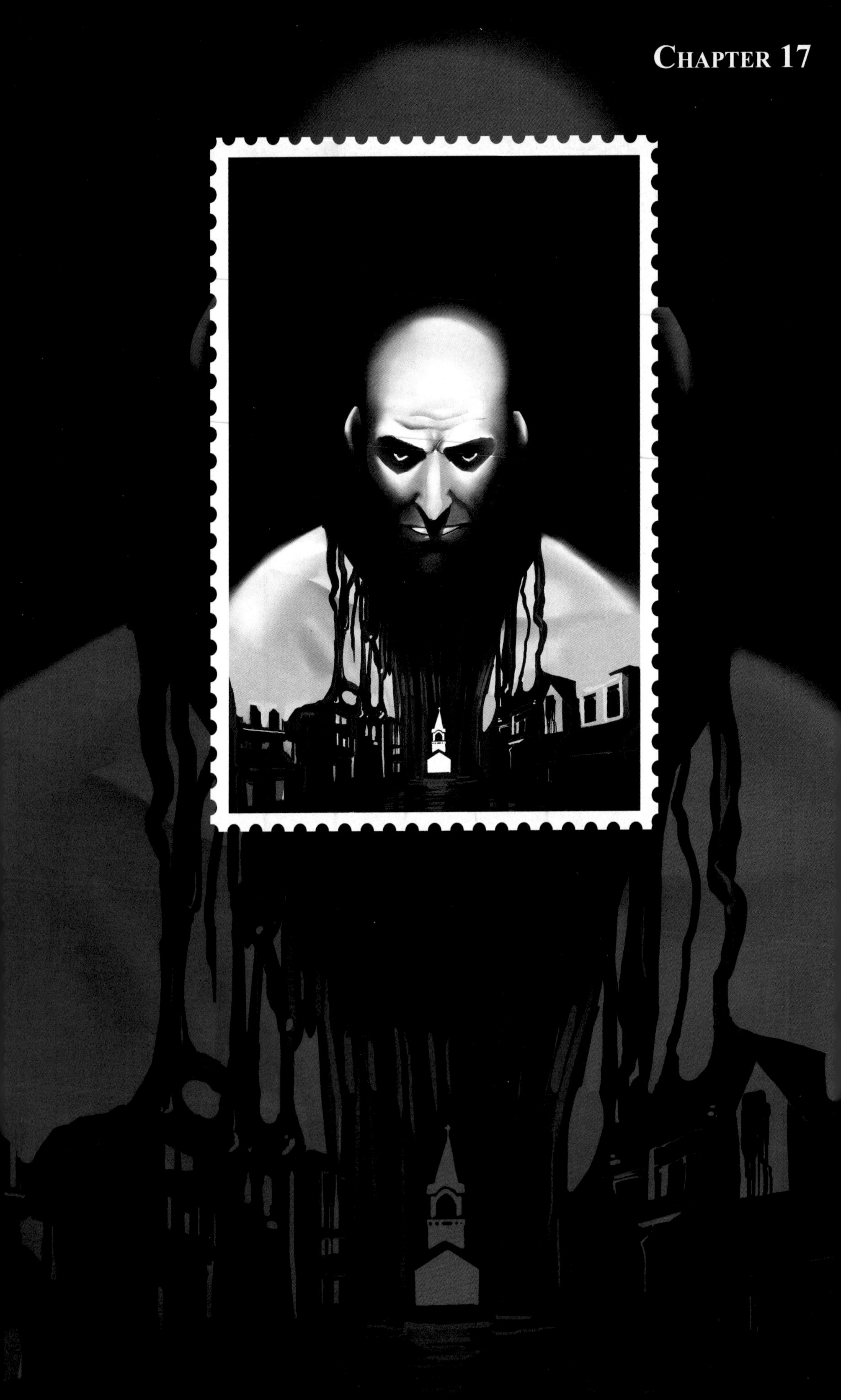

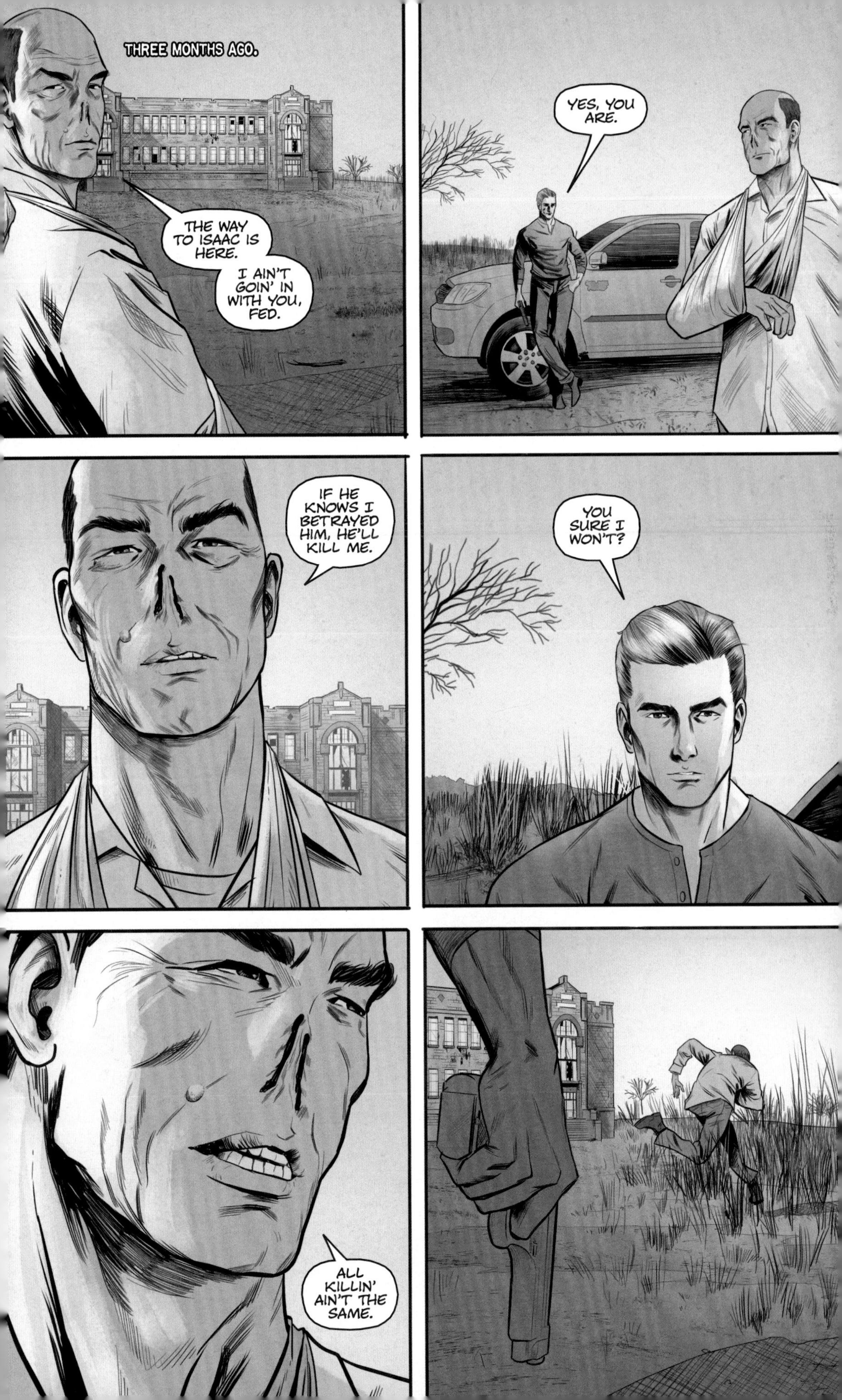
THREE MONTHS AGO.
THE WAY TO ISAAC IS HERE.
I AIN'T GOIN' IN WITH YOU, FED.
YES, YOU ARE.
IF HE KNOWS I BETRAYED HIM, HE'LL KILL ME.
YOU SURE I WON'T?
ALL KILLIN' AIN'T THE SAME.

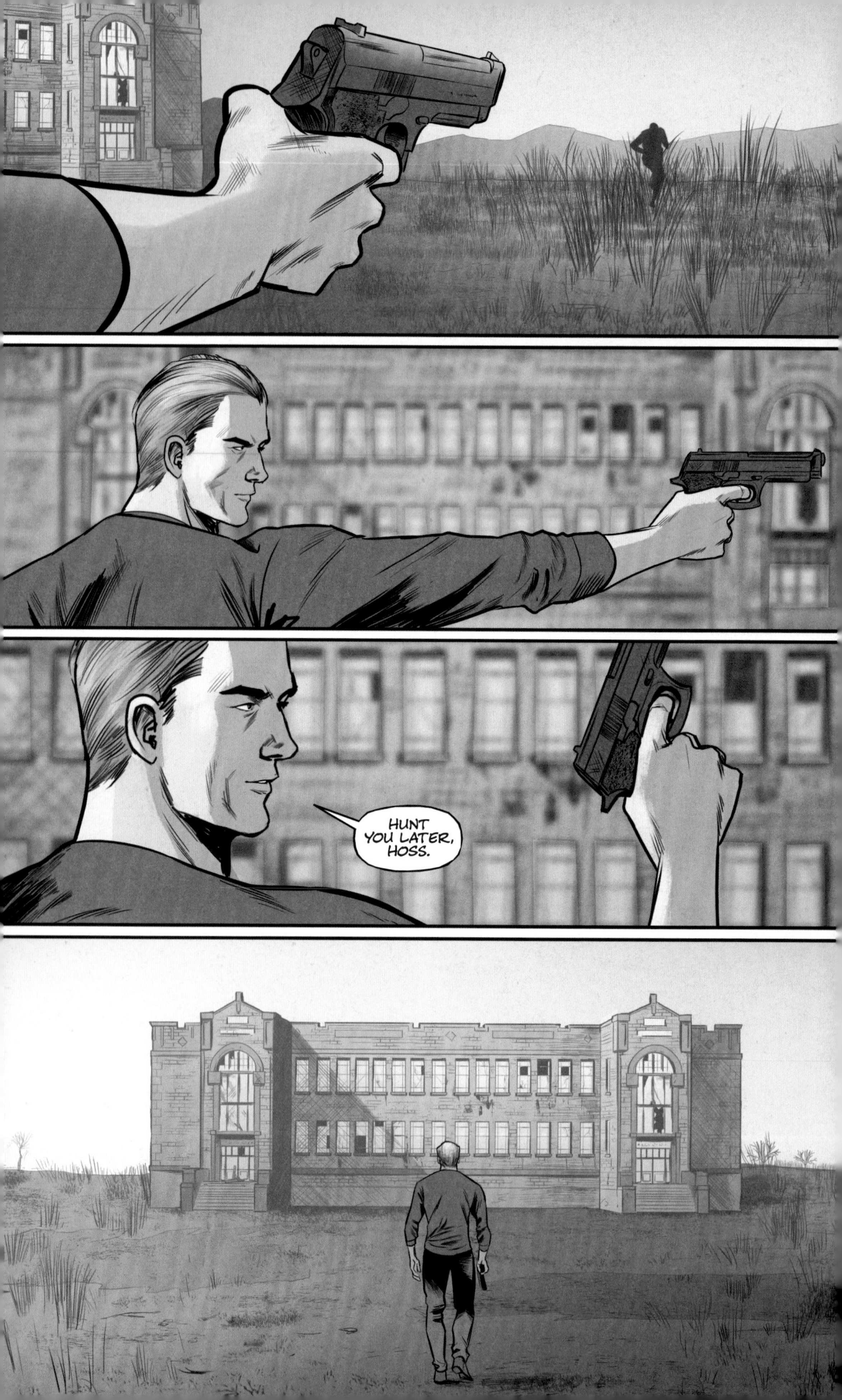
HUNT YOU LATER, HOSS.

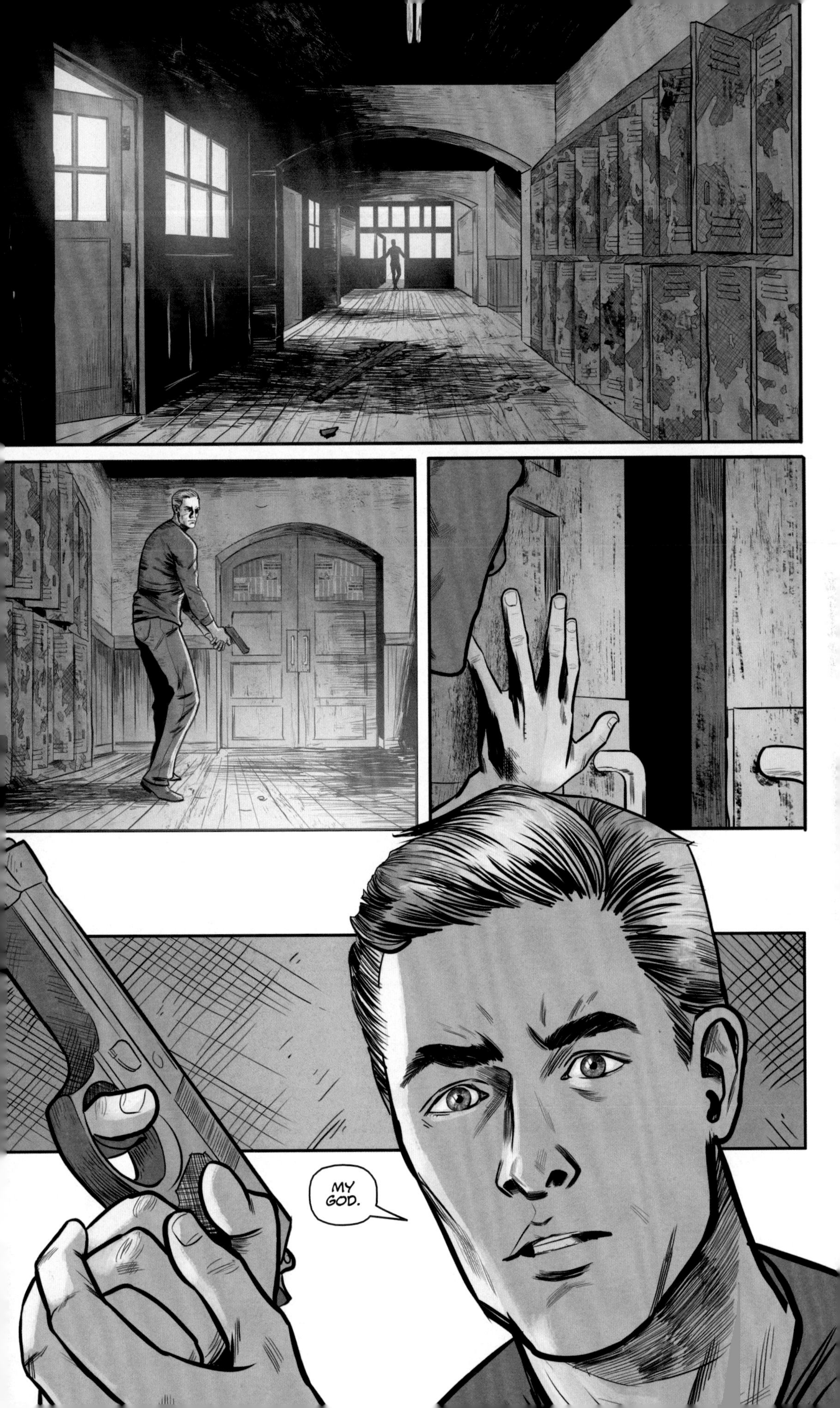
MY GOD.

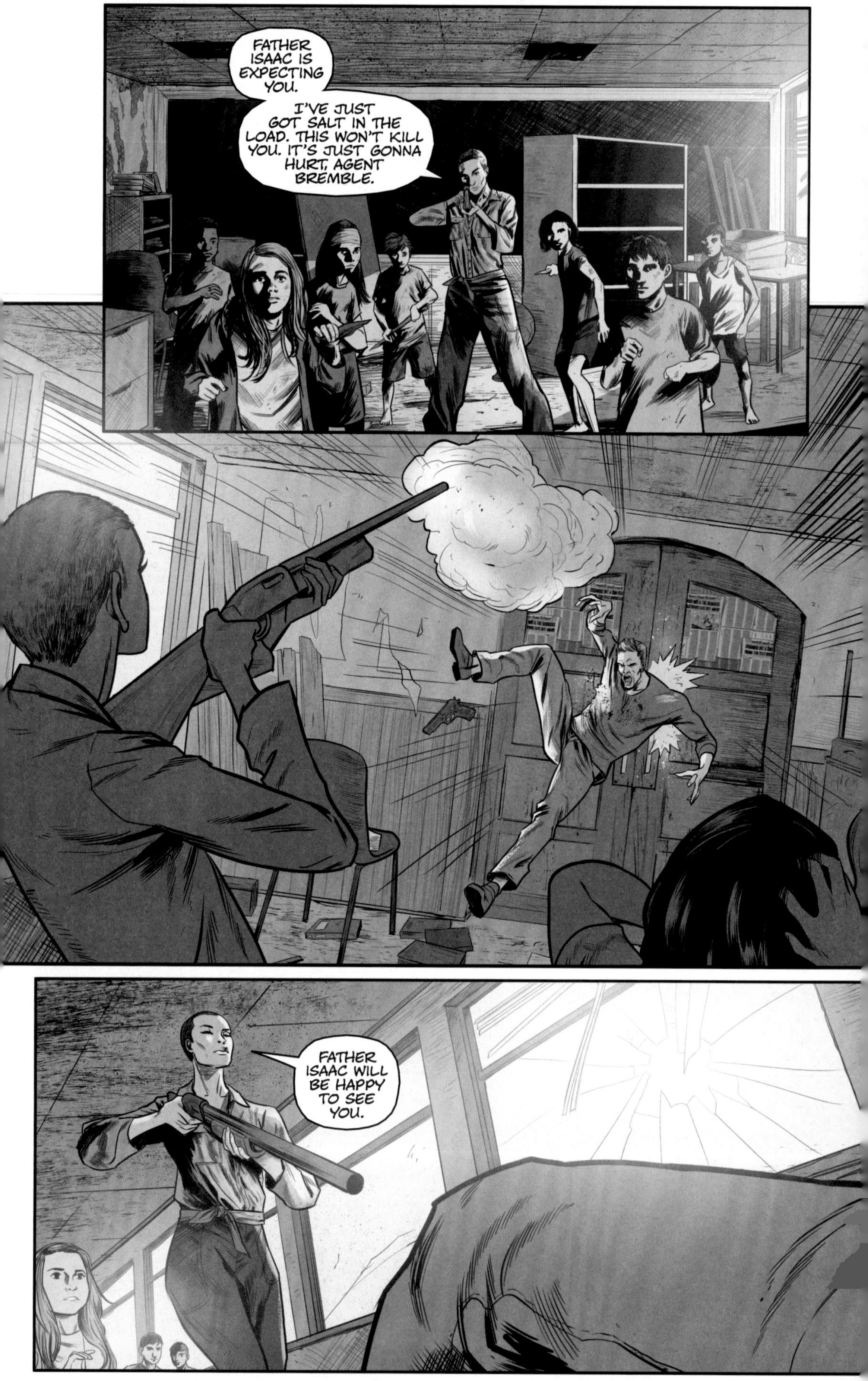
FATHER ISAAC IS EXPECTING YOU.
I'VE JUST GOT SALT IN THE LOAD. THIS WON'T KILL YOU. IT'S JUST GONNA HURT, AGENT BREMBLE.
FATHER ISAAC WILL BE HAPPY TO SEE YOU.

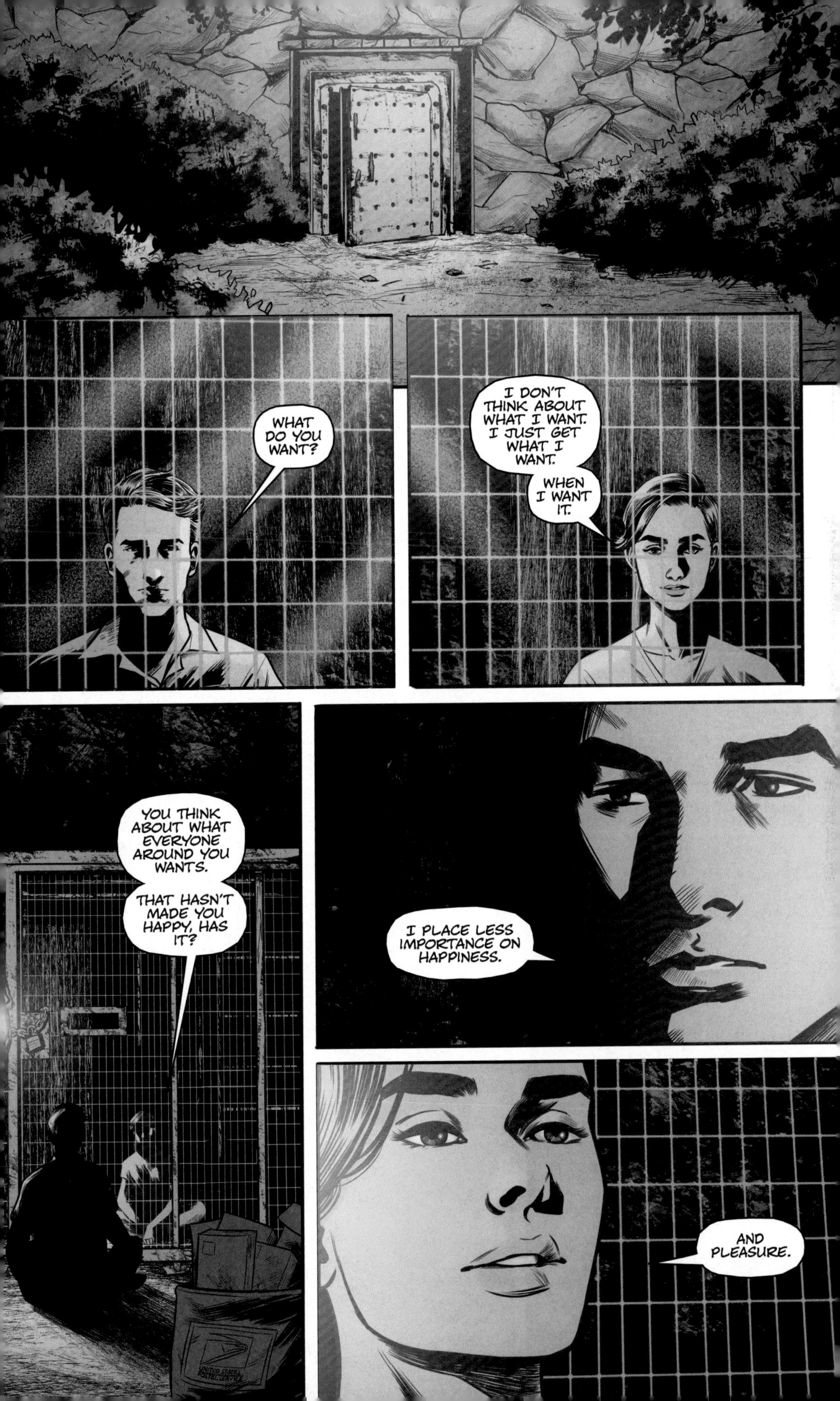
WHAT DO YOU WANT?
I DON'T THINK ABOUT WHAT I WANT. I JUST GET WHAT I WANT.
WHEN I WANT IT.
YOU THINK ABOUT WHAT EVERYONE AROUND YOU WANTS.
THAT HASN'T MADE YOU HAPPY, HAS IT?
I PLACE LESS IMPORTANCE ON HAPPINESS.
AND PLEASURE.

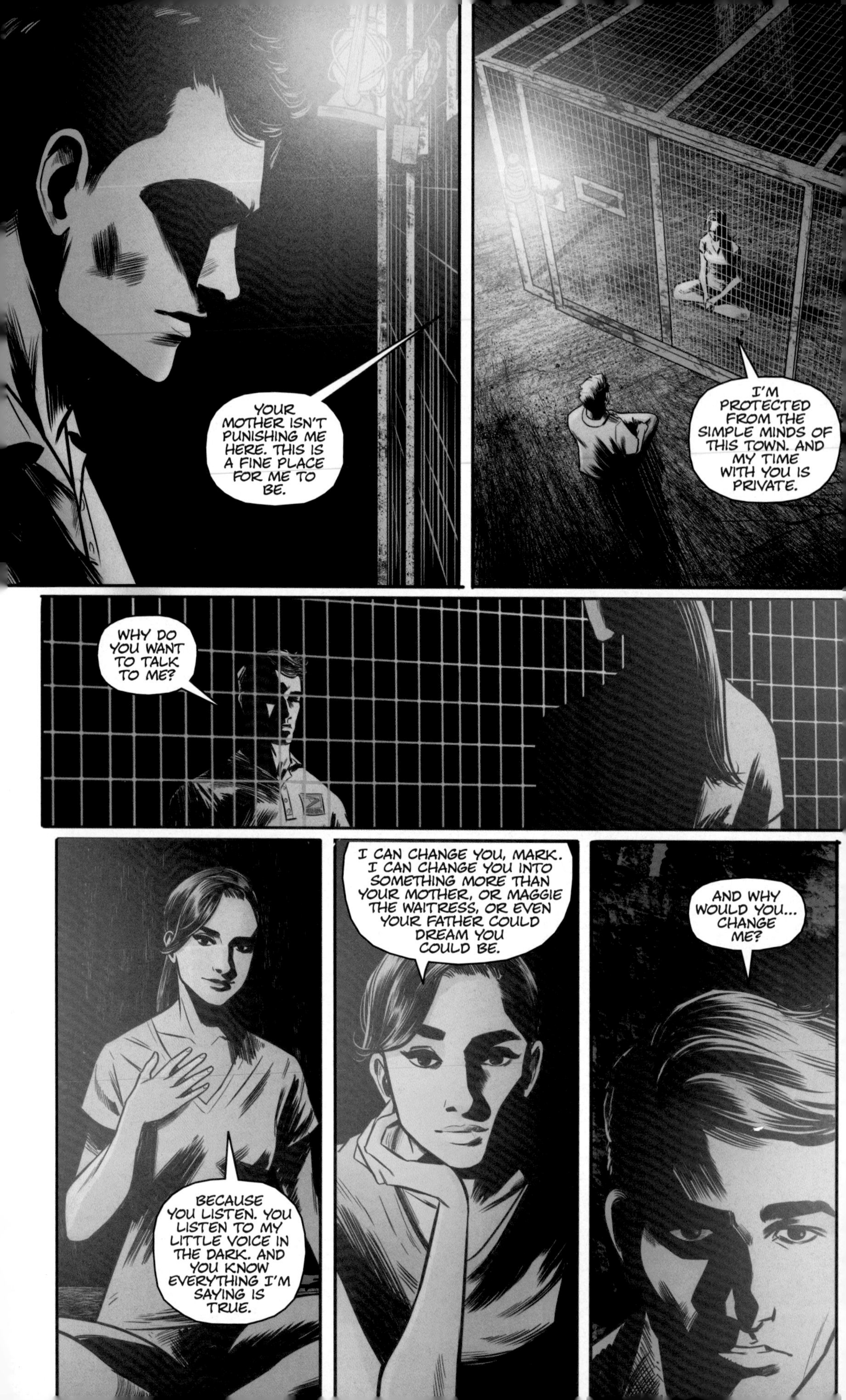
YOUR MOTHER ISN'T PUNISHING ME HERE. THIS IS A FINE PLACE FOR ME TO BE.
I'M PROTECTED FROM THE SIMPLE MINDS OF THIS TOWN. AND MY TIME WITH YOU IS PRIVATE.
WHY DO YOU WANT TO TALK TO ME?
BECAUSE YOU LISTEN. YOU LISTEN TO MY LITTLE VOICE IN THE DARK. AND YOU KNOW EVERYTHING I'M SAYING IS TRUE.
I CAN CHANGE YOU, MARK. I CAN CHANGE YOU INTO SOMETHING MORE THAN YOUR MOTHER, OR MAGGIE THE WAITRESS, OR EVEN YOUR FATHER COULD DREAM YOU COULD BE.
AND WHY WOULD YOU... CHANGE ME?

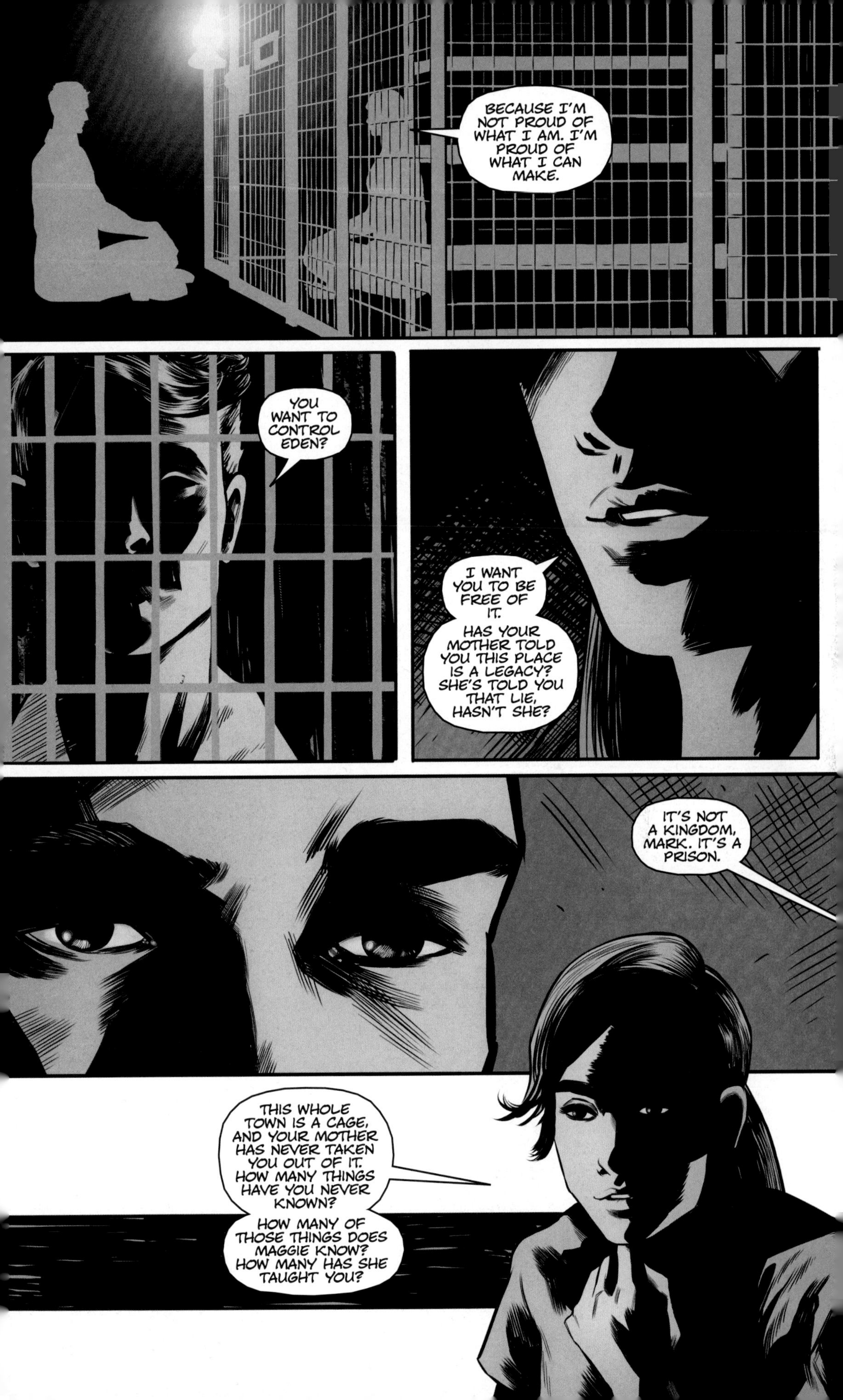

BECAUSE I'M NOT PROUD OF WHAT I AM. I'M PROUD OF WHAT I CAN MAKE.
YOU WANT TO CONTROL EDEN?
I WANT YOU TO BE FREE OF IT.
HAS YOUR MOTHER TOLD YOU THIS PLACE IS A LEGACY? SHE'S TOLD YOU THAT LIE, HASN'T SHE?
IT'S NOT A KINGDOM, MARK. IT'S A PRISON.
THIS WHOLE TOWN IS A CAGE, AND YOUR MOTHER HAS NEVER TAKEN YOU OUT OF IT. HOW MANY THINGS HAVE YOU NEVER KNOWN?
HOW MANY OF THOSE THINGS DOES MAGGIE KNOW? HOW MANY HAS SHE TAUGHT YOU?

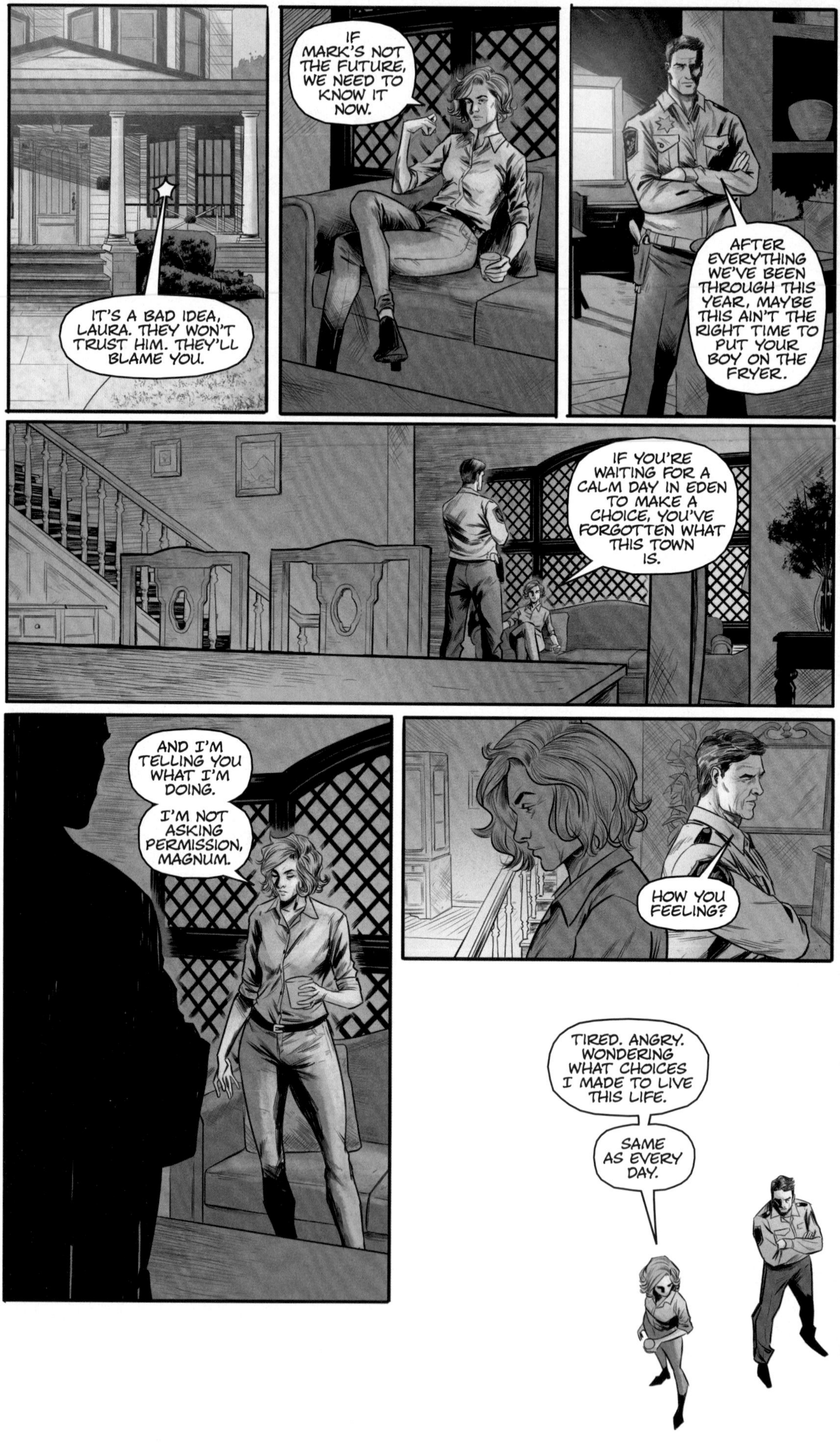
IT'S A BAD IDEA, LAURA. THEY WON'T TRUST HIM. THEY'LL BLAME YOU.
IF MARK'S NOT THE FUTURE, WE NEED TO KNOW IT NOW.
AFTER EVERYTHING WE'VE BEEN THROUGH THIS YEAR, MAYBE THIS AIN'T THE RIGHT TIME TO PUT YOUR BOY ON THE FRYER.
IF YOU'RE WAITING FOR A CALM DAY IN EDEN TO MAKE A CHOICE, YOU'VE FORGOTTEN WHAT THIS TOWN IS.
AND I'M TELLING YOU WHAT I'M DOING.
I'M NOT ASKING PERMISSION, MAGNUM.
HOW YOU FEELING?
TIRED. ANGRY. WONDERING WHAT CHOICES I MADE TO LIVE THIS LIFE.
SAME AS EVERY DAY.

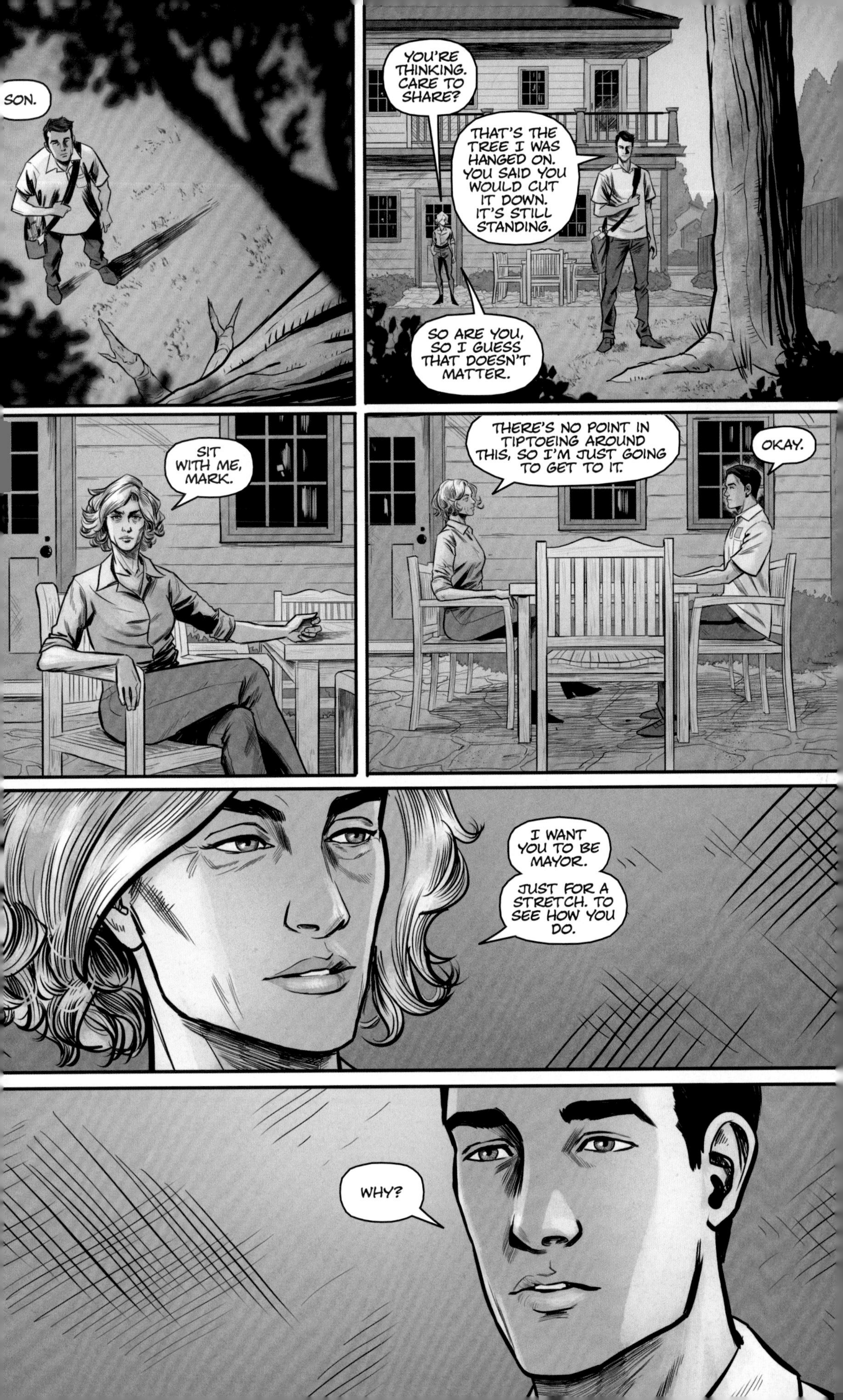
SON.
YOU'RE THINKING. CARE TO SHARE?
THAT'S THE TREE I WAS HANGED ON. YOU SAID YOU WOULD CUT IT DOWN. IT'S STILL STANDING.
SO ARE YOU, SO I GUESS THAT DOESN'T MATTER.
SIT WITH ME, MARK.
THERE'S NO POINT IN TIPTOEING AROUND THIS, SO I'M JUST GOING TO GET TO IT.
OKAY.
I WANT YOU TO BE MAYOR.
JUST FOR A STRETCH. TO SEE HOW YOU DO.
WHY?

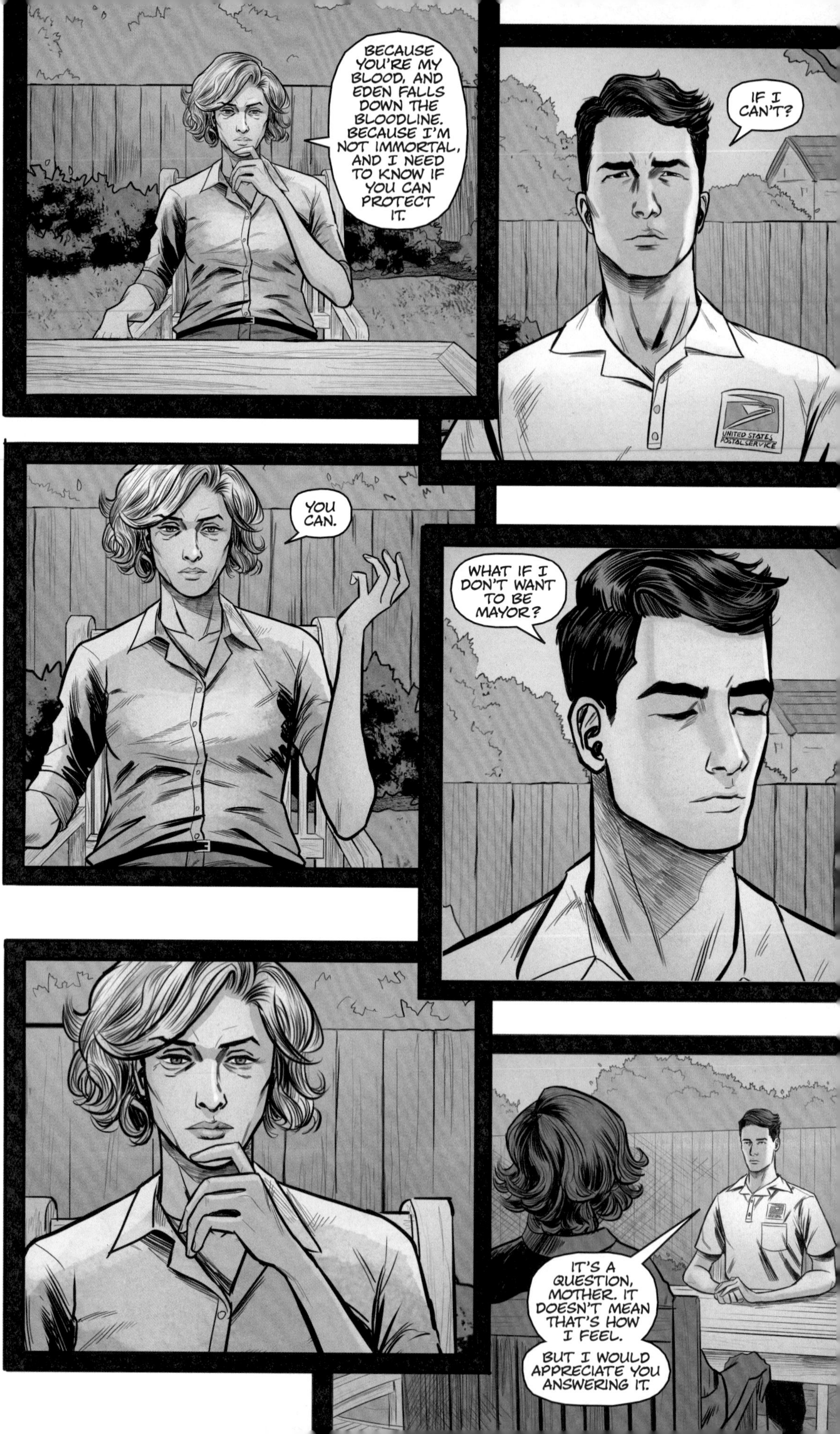
BECAUSE YOU'RE MY BLOOD, AND EDEN FALLS DOWN THE BLOODLINE. BECAUSE I'M NOT IMMORTAL, AND I NEED TO KNOW IF YOU CAN PROTECT IT.
IF I CAN'T?
UNITED STATES POSTAL SERVICE
YOU CAN.
WHAT IF I DON'T WANT TO BE MAYOR?
IT'S A QUESTION, MOTHER. IT DOESN'T MEAN THAT'S HOW I FEEL.
BUT I WOULD APPRECIATE YOU ANSWERING IT.

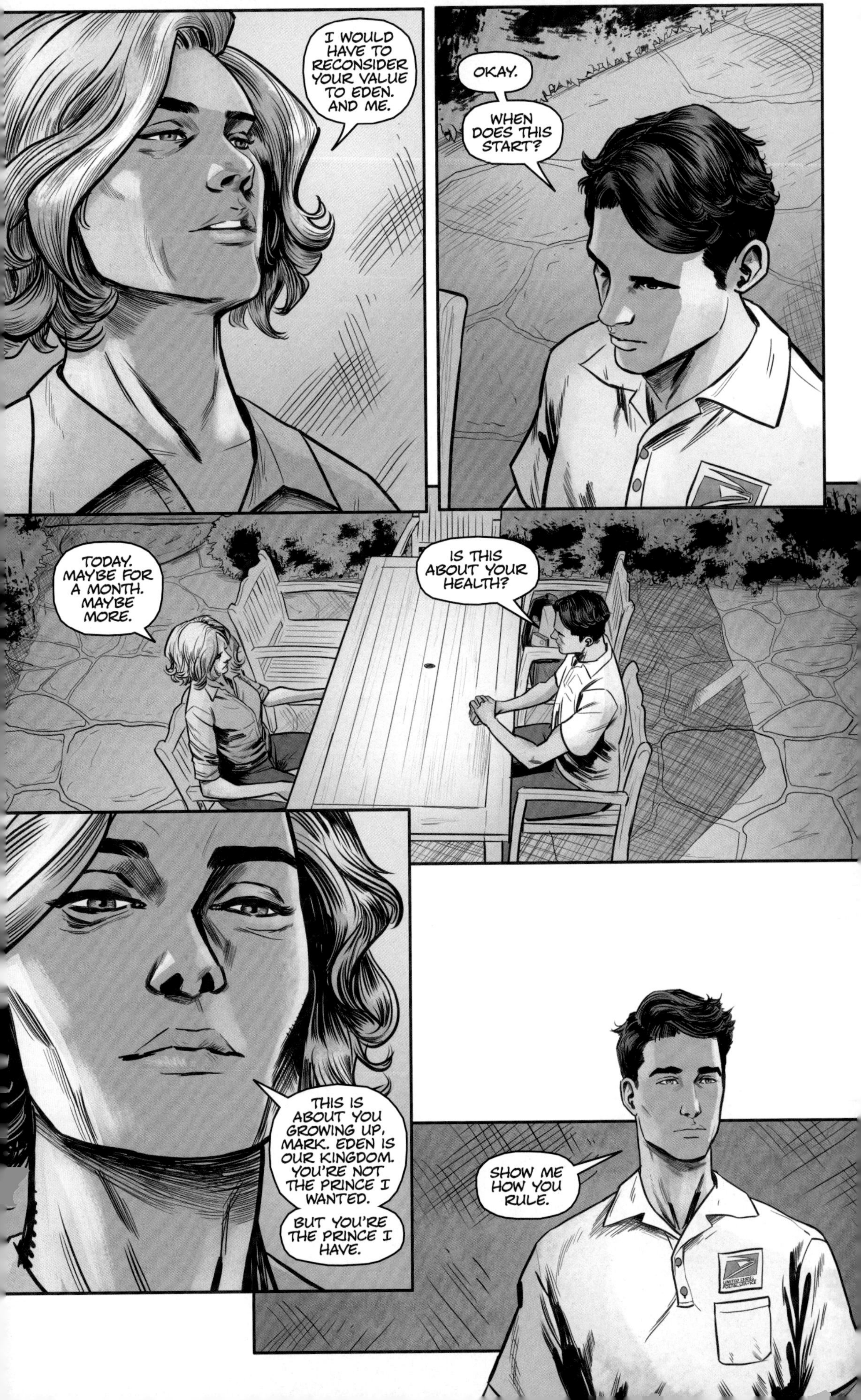
I WOULD HAVE TO RECONSIDER YOUR VALUE TO EDEN. AND ME.
OKAY.
WHEN DOES THIS START?
TODAY. MAYBE FOR A MONTH. MAYBE MORE.
IS THIS ABOUT YOUR HEALTH?
THIS IS ABOUT YOU GROWING UP, MARK. EDEN IS OUR KINGDOM. YOU'RE NOT THE PRINCE I WANTED.
BUT YOU'RE THE PRINCE I HAVE.
SHOW ME HOW YOU RULE.

"WHERE AM I?

"I KNOW YOU'RE THERE. I CAN HEAR YOU.

"MY CHEST HURTS LIKE A BITCH. I NEED TO CLEAN THESE WOUNDS.

"FUCKING SALT? YOU SHOULD HAVE USED LEAD.

"WHEN I GET OUT OF HERE, I'M GOING TO USE LEAD."

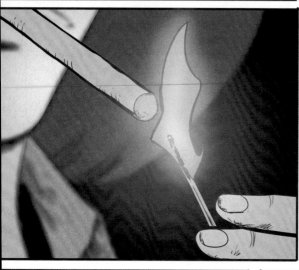

WE TENDED YOUR WOUNDS, AGENT BREMBLE. WE'VE TAKEN GOOD CARE OF YOU. WE'LL CONTINUE TO TAKE GOOD CARE OF YOU.

BECAUSE THAT IS OUR WAY.

NICE WIG. BUT I KNOW WHO YOU ARE.

YOU'RE THE BITCH WHO SHOT ME. SO WHAT HAPPENS NEXT?

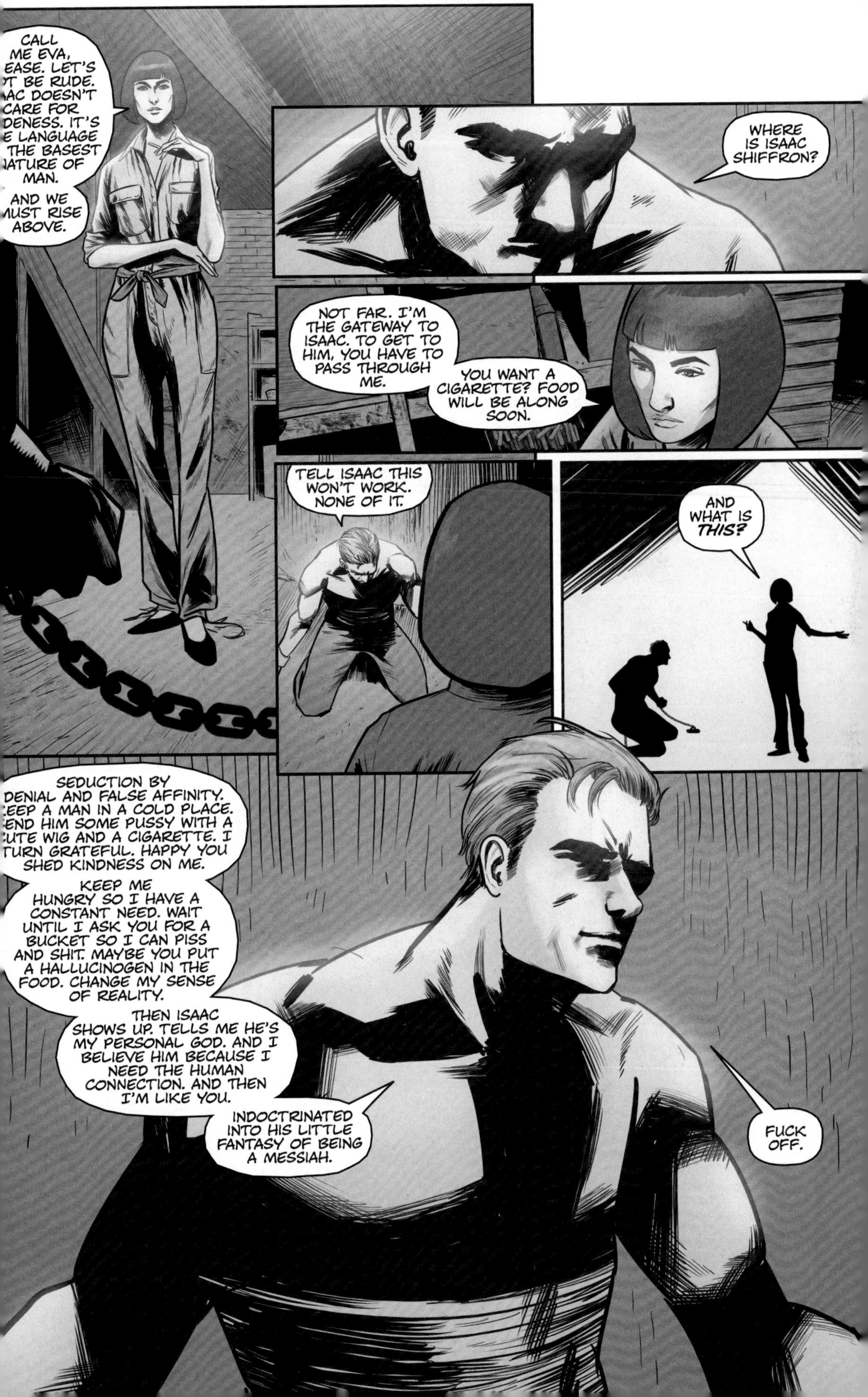
CALL ME EVA, EASE. LET'S T BE RUDE. AC DOESN'T CARE FOR DENESS. IT'S E LANGUAGE THE BASEST NATURE OF MAN.
AND WE MUST RISE ABOVE.
WHERE IS ISAAC SHIFFRON?
NOT FAR. I'M THE GATEWAY TO ISAAC. TO GET TO HIM, YOU HAVE TO PASS THROUGH ME.
YOU WANT A CIGARETTE? FOOD WILL BE ALONG SOON.
TELL ISAAC THIS WON'T WORK. NONE OF IT.
AND WHAT IS *THIS?*
SEDUCTION BY DENIAL AND FALSE AFFINITY. KEEP A MAN IN A COLD PLACE. END HIM SOME PUSSY WITH A UTE WIG AND A CIGARETTE. I TURN GRATEFUL. HAPPY YOU SHED KINDNESS ON ME.
KEEP ME HUNGRY SO I HAVE A CONSTANT NEED. WAIT UNTIL I ASK YOU FOR A BUCKET SO I CAN PISS AND SHIT. MAYBE YOU PUT A HALLUCINOGEN IN THE FOOD. CHANGE MY SENSE OF REALITY.
THEN ISAAC SHOWS UP. TELLS ME HE'S MY PERSONAL GOD. AND I BELIEVE HIM BECAUSE I NEED THE HUMAN CONNECTION. AND THEN I'M LIKE YOU.
INDOCTRINATED INTO HIS LITTLE FANTASY OF BEING A MESSIAH.
FUCK OFF.

I SHOT YOU BECAUSE YOU CAME HERE WITH A WEAPON. I CHAINED YOU BECAUSE IF I DIDN'T, YOU WOULD HURT ME. AGENT BREMBLE, YOU INVADED OUR SOVEREIGNTY.

AND I AM THE ONLY ONE IN THIS ROOM BEING KIND.

TELL ISAAC I WANT TO KNOW ABOUT EDEN, WYOMING. FETCH YOUR MASTER.

TAKE YOUR WET-DOG SMELL WITH YOU.

ISAAC DOESN'T CARE FOR EDEN ANY MORE THAN YOU DO. THAT, HE WANTS YOU TO KNOW.

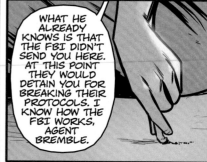

WHAT HE ALREADY KNOWS IS THAT THE FBI DIDN'T SEND YOU HERE. AT THIS POINT THEY WOULD DETAIN YOU FOR BREAKING THEIR PROTOCOLS. I KNOW HOW THE FBI WORKS, AGENT BREMBLE.

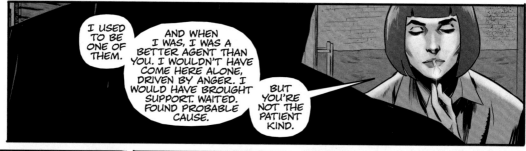

I USED TO BE ONE OF THEM.

AND WHEN I WAS, I WAS A BETTER AGENT THAN YOU. I WOULDN'T HAVE COME HERE ALONE, DRIVEN BY ANGER. I WOULD HAVE BROUGHT SUPPORT. WAITED. FOUND PROBABLE CAUSE.

BUT YOU'RE NOT THE PATIENT KIND.

GET ME OUT OF THESE FUCKING CHAINS!

NO.

BUT I WILL ANSWER QUESTIONS.

WHY ARE THERE CHILDREN HERE?

TEN MILES DOWN THE ROAD. LITTLE MORE. THERE'S A SET OF TRAILERS. MEN GO THERE TO BE WITH CHILDREN.

TO LIE WITH CHILDREN.

ISAAC ALLOWED ME TO HELP THEM. BECAUSE THEY DESERVED HELP. INNOCENCE ISN'T SOMETHING WE CAN GET BACK ONCE IT'S TAKEN FROM US.

SO IN WHAT REMAINS, ALL WE CAN GIVE TO THEM IS JUSTICE.

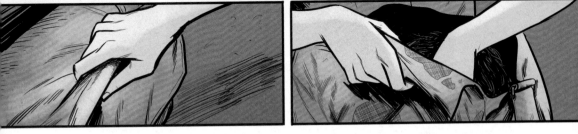

THIS IS WHAT ISAAC ALLOWED ME TO GIVE.

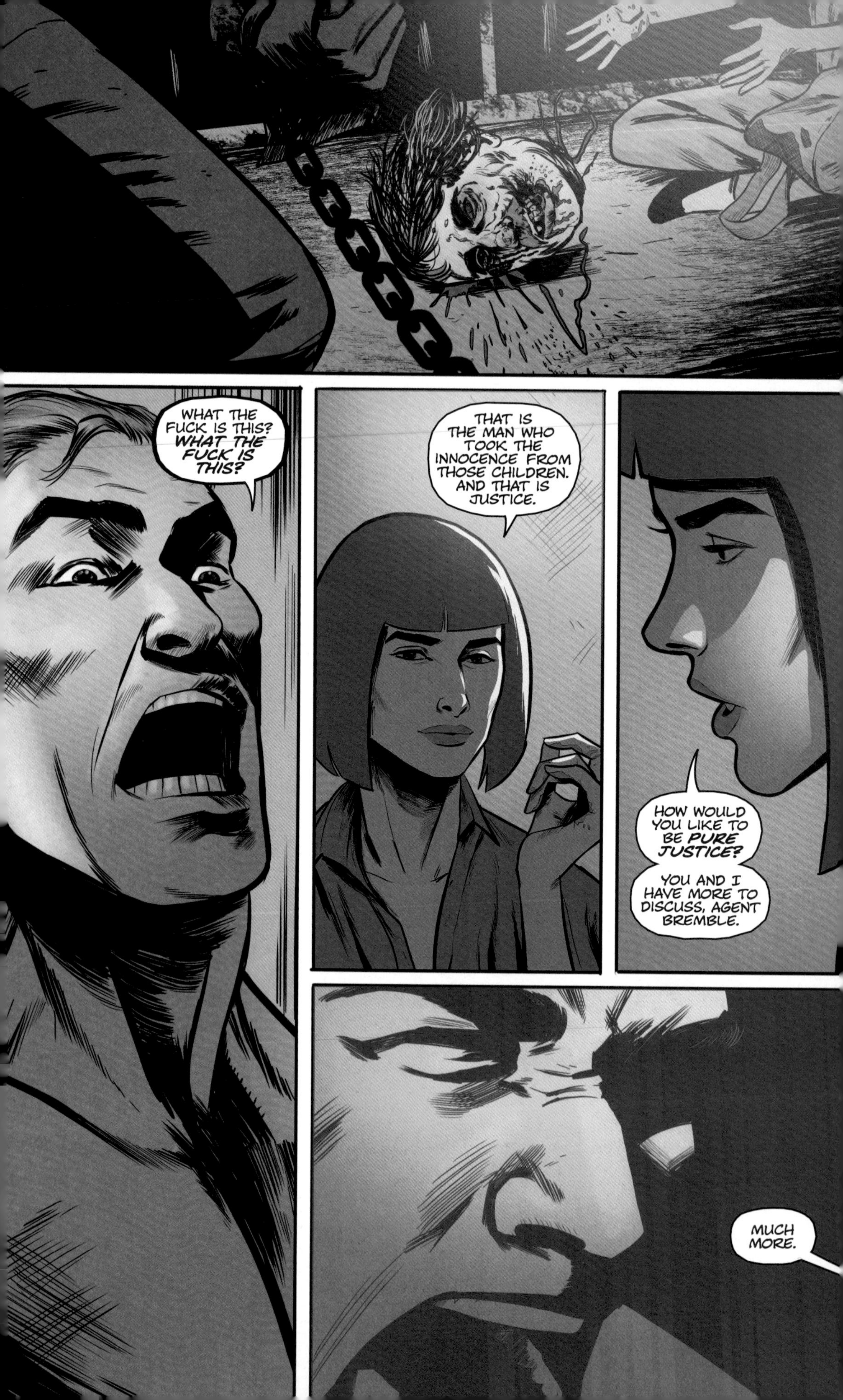
WHAT THE FUCK IS THIS? WHAT THE FUCK IS THIS?
THAT IS THE MAN WHO TOOK THE INNOCENCE FROM THOSE CHILDREN. AND THAT IS JUSTICE.
HOW WOULD YOU LIKE TO BE PURE JUSTICE?
YOU AND I HAVE MORE TO DISCUSS, AGENT BREMBLE.
MUCH MORE.

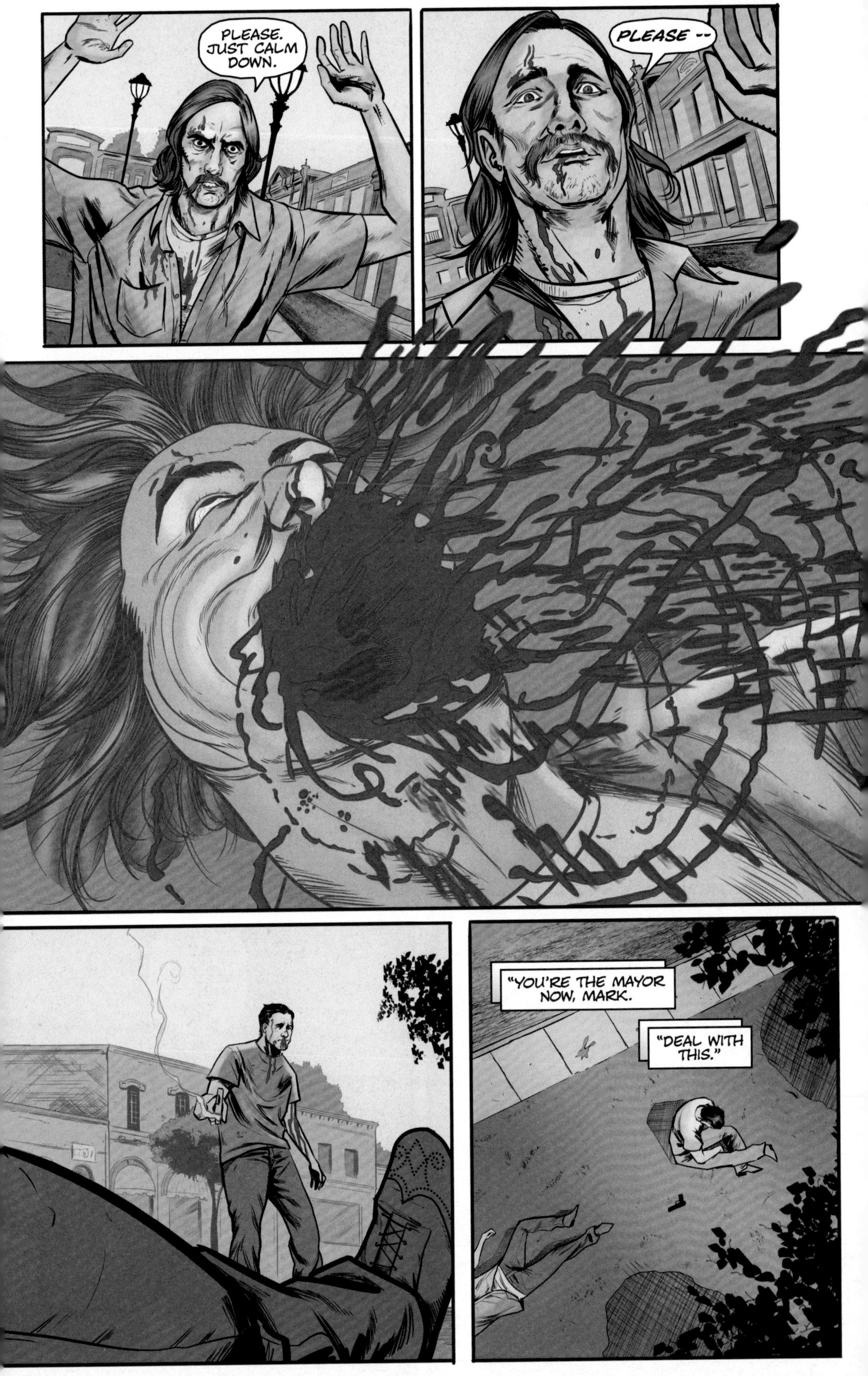
PLEASE. JUST CALM DOWN.
PLEASE --
"YOU'RE THE MAYOR NOW, MARK.
"DEAL WITH THIS."

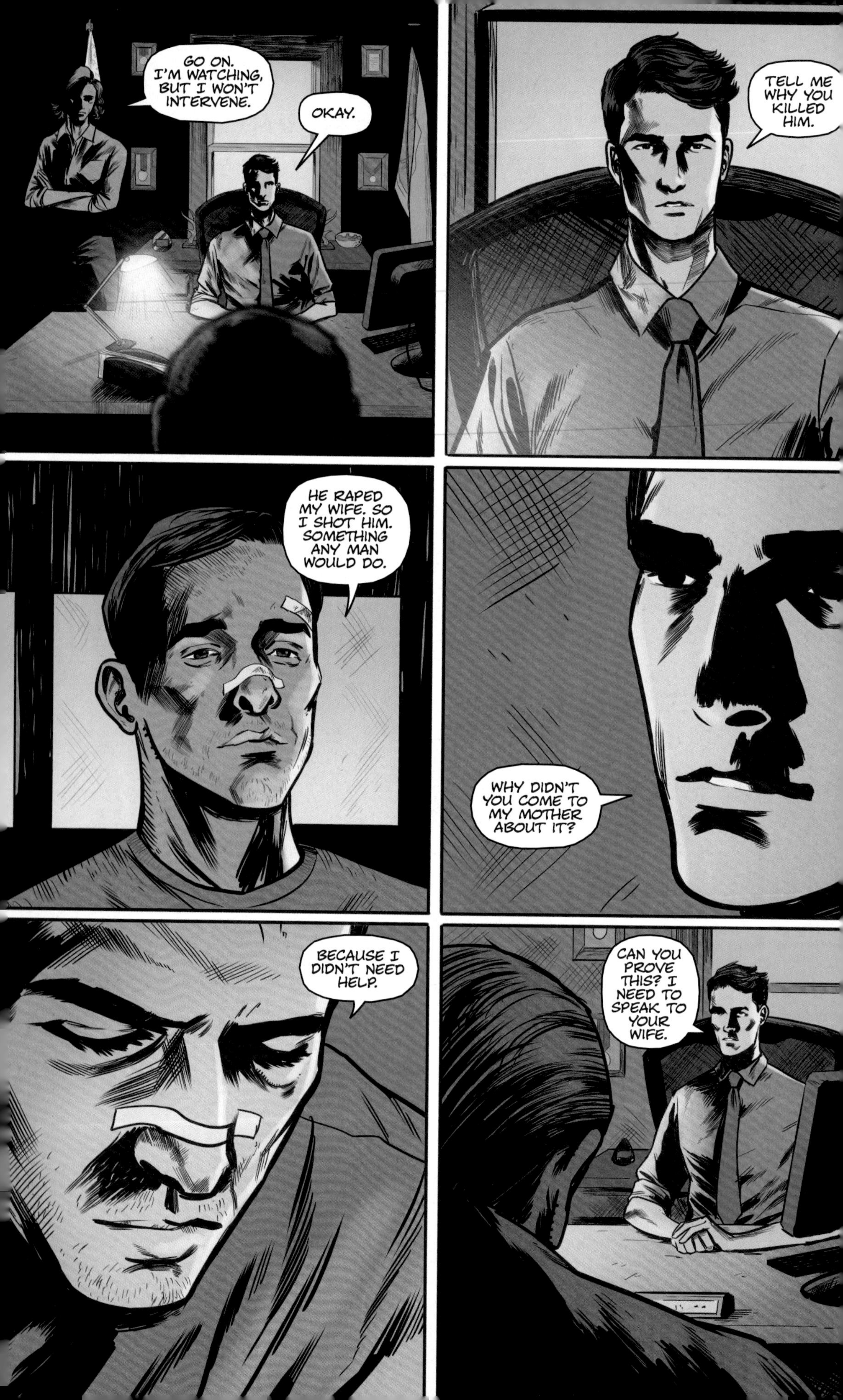
GO ON. I'M WATCHING, BUT I WON'T INTERVENE.
OKAY.
TELL ME WHY YOU KILLED HIM.
HE RAPED MY WIFE. SO I SHOT HIM. SOMETHING ANY MAN WOULD DO.
WHY DIDN'T YOU COME TO MY MOTHER ABOUT IT?
BECAUSE I DIDN'T NEED HELP.
CAN YOU PROVE THIS? I NEED TO SPEAK TO YOUR WIFE.

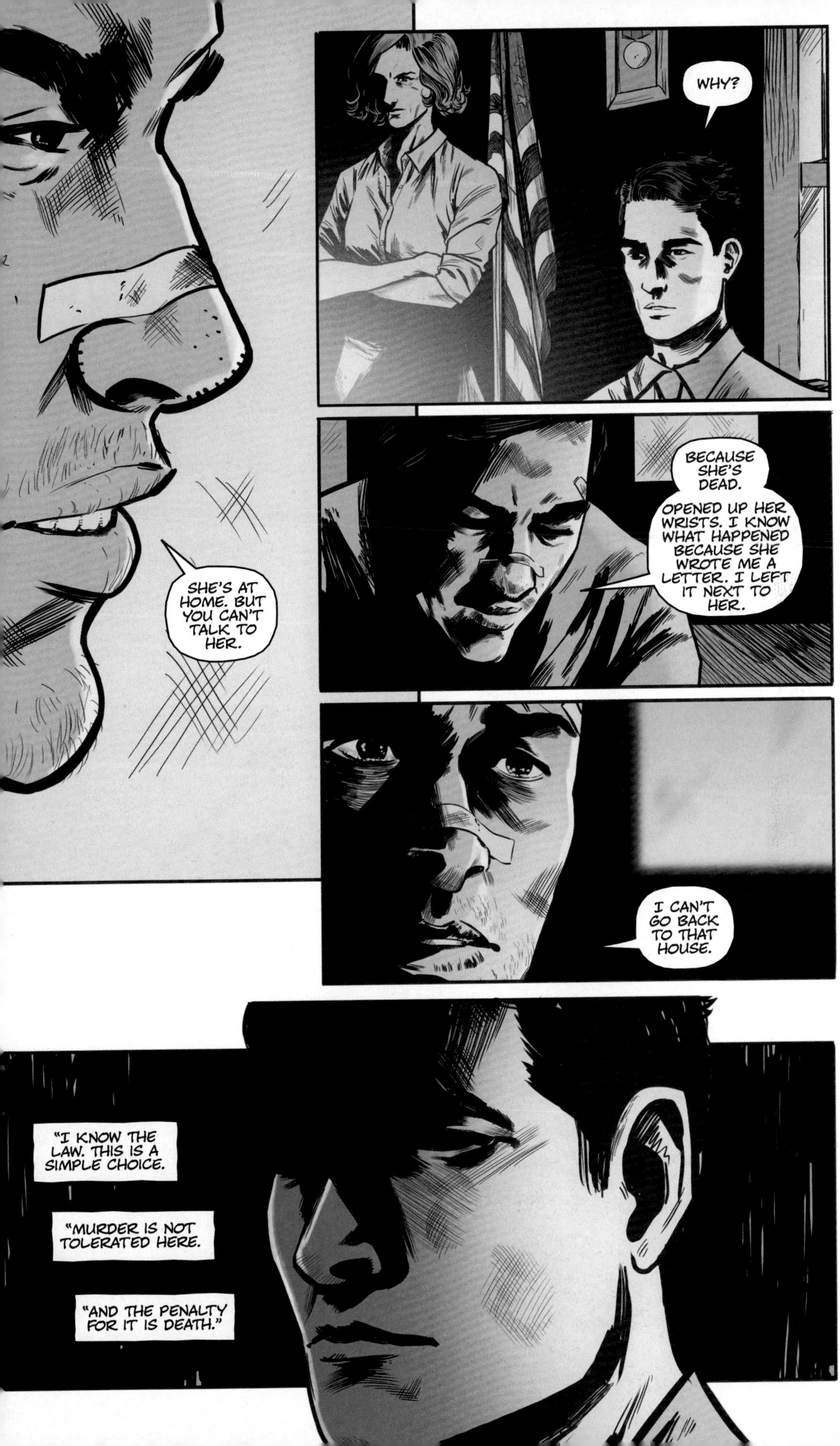
WHY?
SHE'S AT HOME. BUT YOU CAN'T TALK TO HER.
BECAUSE SHE'S DEAD.
OPENED UP HER WRISTS. I KNOW WHAT HAPPENED BECAUSE SHE WROTE ME A LETTER. I LEFT IT NEXT TO HER.
I CAN'T GO BACK TO THAT HOUSE.
"I KNOW THE LAW. THIS IS A SIMPLE CHOICE.
"MURDER IS NOT TOLERATED HERE.
"AND THE PENALTY FOR IT IS DEATH."

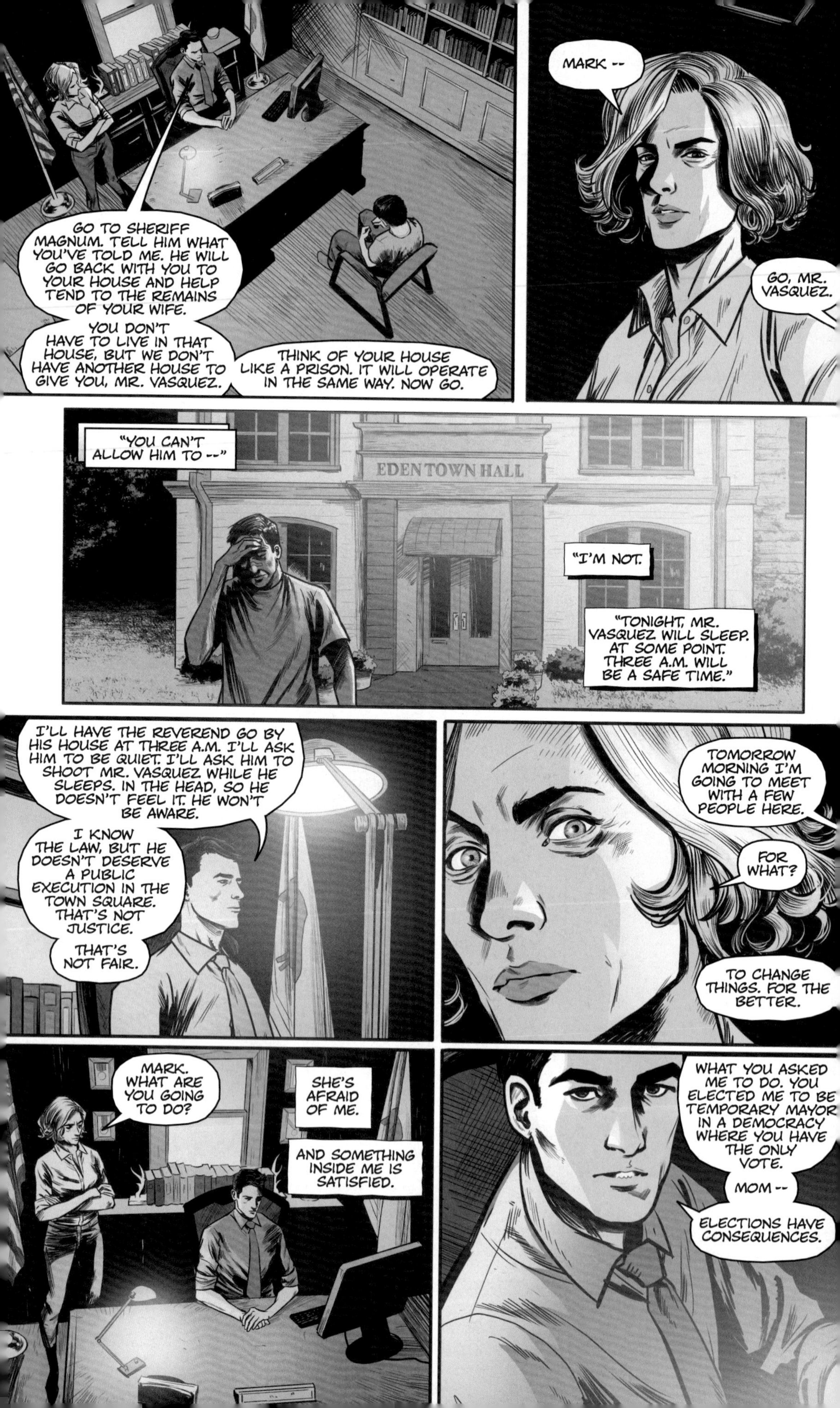
GO TO SHERIFF MAGNUM. TELL HIM WHAT YOU'VE TOLD ME. HE WILL GO BACK WITH YOU TO YOUR HOUSE AND HELP TEND TO THE REMAINS OF YOUR WIFE.
YOU DON'T HAVE TO LIVE IN THAT HOUSE, BUT WE DON'T HAVE ANOTHER HOUSE TO GIVE YOU, MR. VASQUEZ.
THINK OF YOUR HOUSE LIKE A PRISON. IT WILL OPERATE IN THE SAME WAY. NOW GO.
MARK --
GO, MR. VASQUEZ.
"YOU CAN'T ALLOW HIM TO --"
EDEN TOWN HALL
"I'M NOT.
"TONIGHT, MR. VASQUEZ WILL SLEEP. AT SOME POINT. THREE A.M. WILL BE A SAFE TIME."
I'LL HAVE THE REVEREND GO BY HIS HOUSE AT THREE A.M. I'LL ASK HIM TO BE QUIET. I'LL ASK HIM TO SHOOT MR. VASQUEZ WHILE HE SLEEPS. IN THE HEAD, SO HE DOESN'T FEEL IT. HE WON'T BE AWARE.
I KNOW THE LAW, BUT HE DOESN'T DESERVE A PUBLIC EXECUTION IN THE TOWN SQUARE. THAT'S NOT JUSTICE.
THAT'S NOT FAIR.
TOMORROW MORNING I'M GOING TO MEET WITH A FEW PEOPLE HERE.
FOR WHAT?
TO CHANGE THINGS. FOR THE BETTER.
MARK. WHAT ARE YOU GOING TO DO?
SHE'S AFRAID OF ME.
AND SOMETHING INSIDE ME IS SATISFIED.
WHAT YOU ASKED ME TO DO. YOU ELECTED ME TO BE TEMPORARY MAYOR IN A DEMOCRACY WHERE YOU HAVE THE ONLY VOTE.
MOM --
ELECTIONS HAVE CONSEQUENCES.

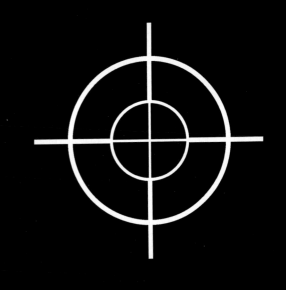

# Chapter 18

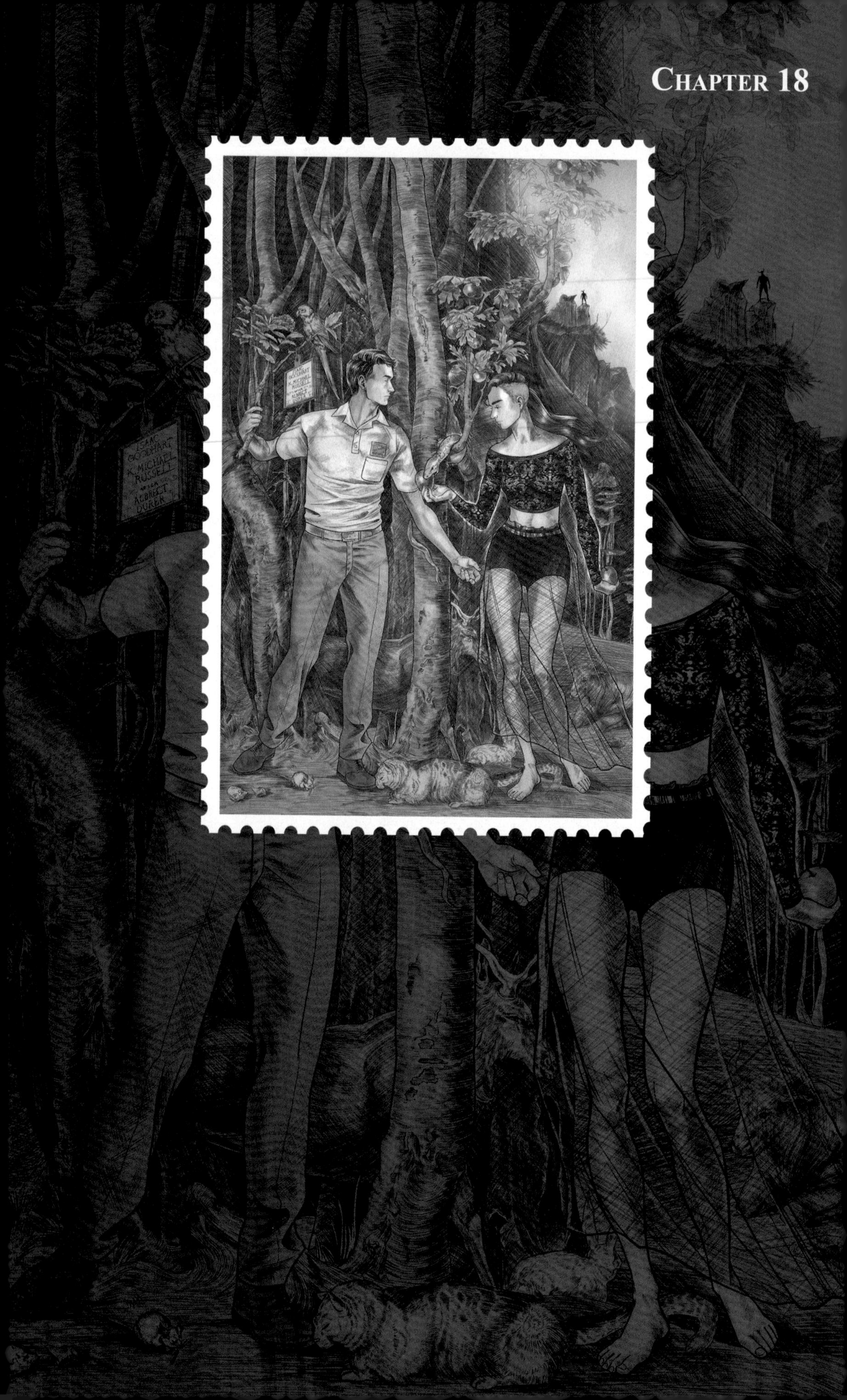
ISAAC GOODHART
K. MICHAEL RUSSELL
ALBRECT DURER

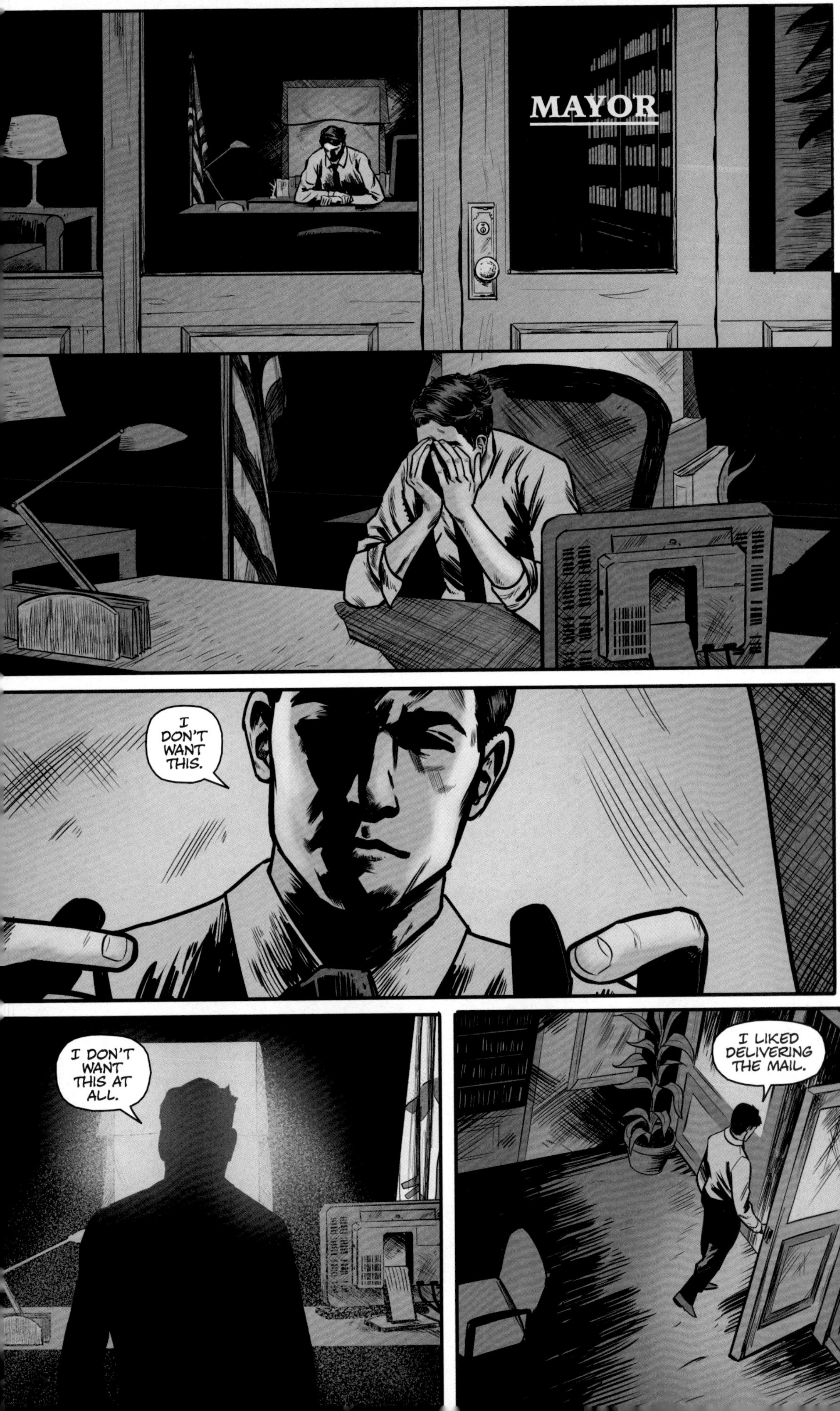
MAYOR
I DON'T WANT THIS.
I DON'T WANT THIS AT ALL.
I LIKED DELIVERING THE MAIL.

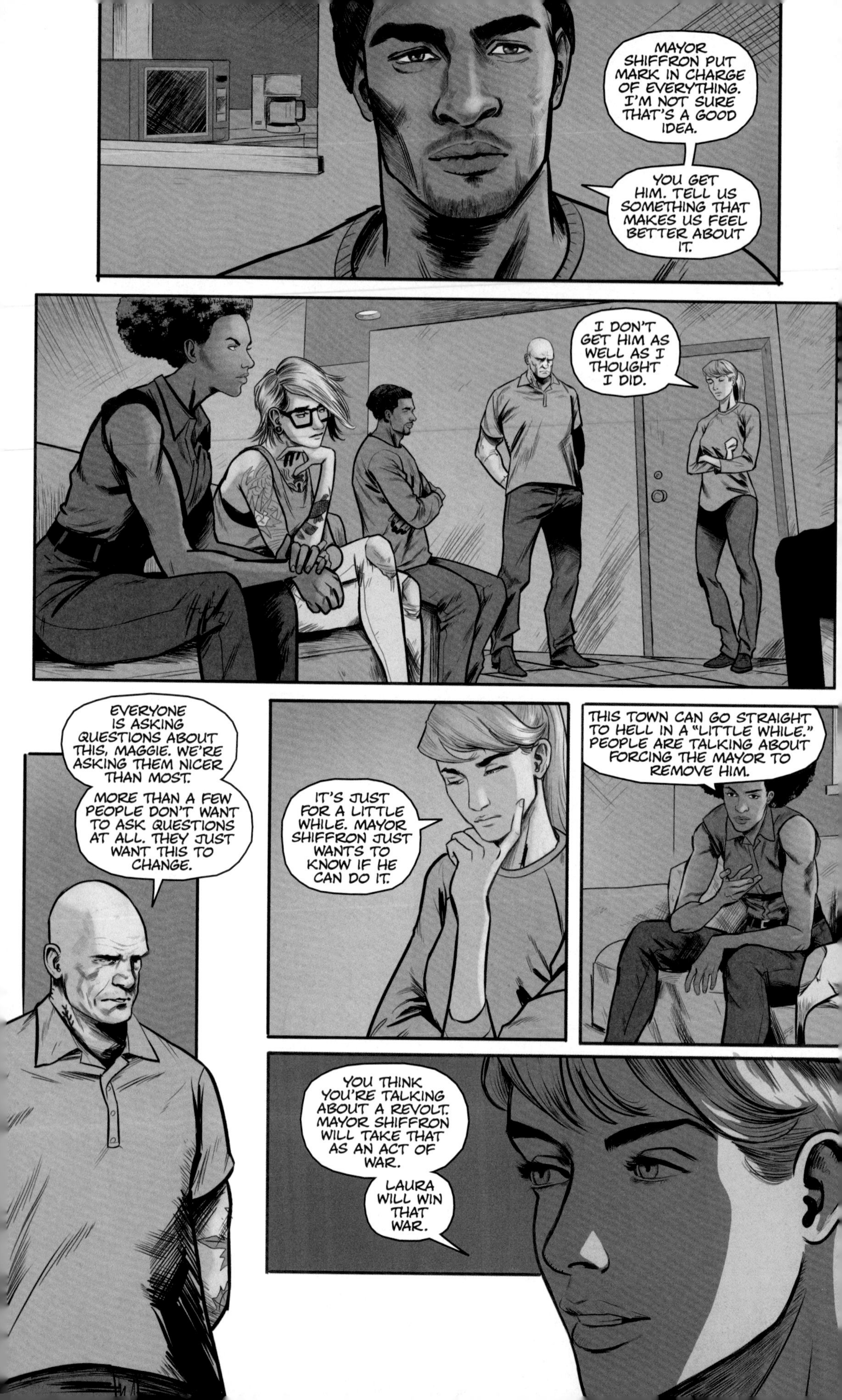
MAYOR SHIFFRON PUT MARK IN CHARGE OF EVERYTHING. I'M NOT SURE THAT'S A GOOD IDEA.
YOU GET HIM. TELL US SOMETHING THAT MAKES US FEEL BETTER ABOUT IT.
I DON'T GET HIM AS WELL AS I THOUGHT I DID.
EVERYONE IS ASKING QUESTIONS ABOUT THIS, MAGGIE. WE'RE ASKING THEM NICER THAN MOST.
MORE THAN A FEW PEOPLE DON'T WANT TO ASK QUESTIONS AT ALL. THEY JUST WANT THIS TO CHANGE.
IT'S JUST FOR A LITTLE WHILE. MAYOR SHIFFRON JUST WANTS TO KNOW IF HE CAN DO IT.
THIS TOWN CAN GO STRAIGHT TO HELL IN A "LITTLE WHILE." PEOPLE ARE TALKING ABOUT FORCING THE MAYOR TO REMOVE HIM.
YOU THINK YOU'RE TALKING ABOUT A REVOLT. MAYOR SHIFFRON WILL TAKE THAT AS AN ACT OF WAR.
LAURA WILL WIN THAT WAR.

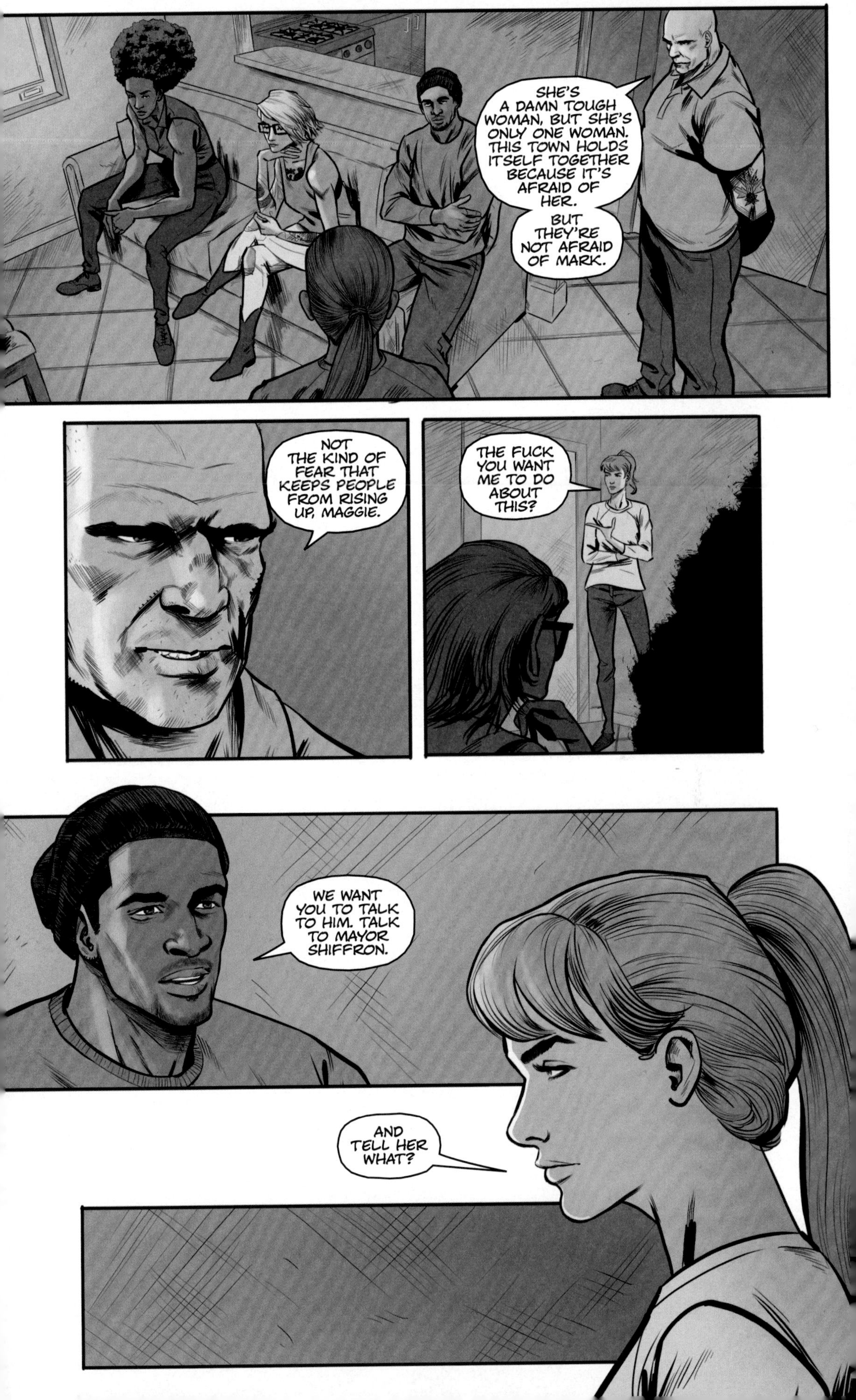
SHE'S A DAMN TOUGH WOMAN, BUT SHE'S ONLY ONE WOMAN. THIS TOWN HOLDS ITSELF TOGETHER BECAUSE IT'S AFRAID OF HER.
BUT THEY'RE NOT AFRAID OF MARK.
NOT THE KIND OF FEAR THAT KEEPS PEOPLE FROM RISING UP, MAGGIE.
THE FUCK YOU WANT ME TO DO ABOUT THIS?
WE WANT YOU TO TALK TO HIM. TALK TO MAYOR SHIFFRON.
AND TELL HER WHAT?

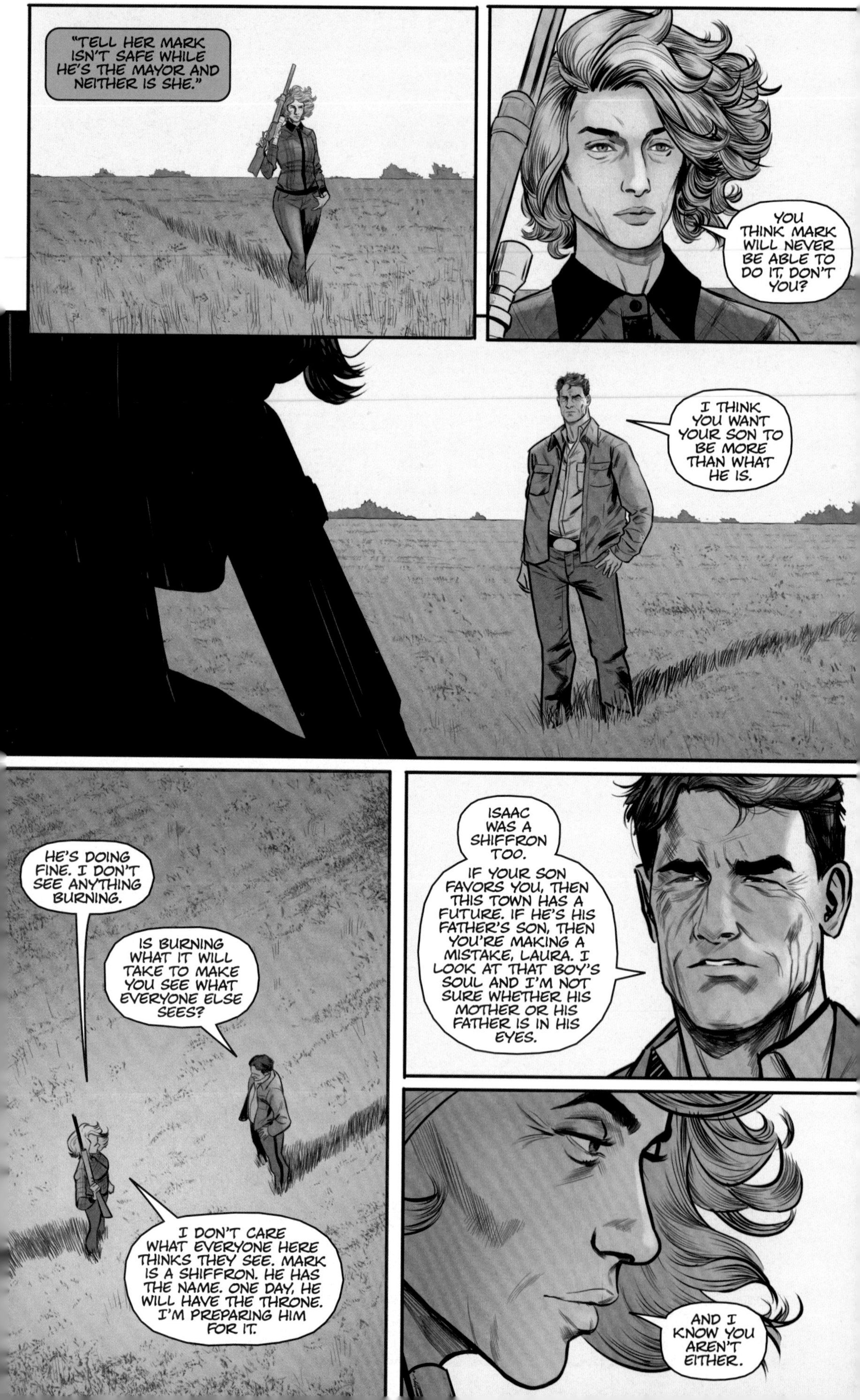
"TELL HER MARK ISN'T SAFE WHILE HE'S THE MAYOR AND NEITHER IS SHE."
YOU THINK MARK WILL NEVER BE ABLE TO DO IT, DON'T YOU?
I THINK YOU WANT YOUR SON TO BE MORE THAN WHAT HE IS.
HE'S DOING FINE. I DON'T SEE ANYTHING BURNING.
IS BURNING WHAT IT WILL TAKE TO MAKE YOU SEE WHAT EVERYONE ELSE SEES?
I DON'T CARE WHAT EVERYONE HERE THINKS THEY SEE. MARK IS A SHIFFRON. HE HAS THE NAME. ONE DAY, HE WILL HAVE THE THRONE. I'M PREPARING HIM FOR IT.
ISAAC WAS A SHIFFRON TOO.
IF YOUR SON FAVORS YOU, THEN THIS TOWN HAS A FUTURE. IF HE'S HIS FATHER'S SON, THEN YOU'RE MAKING A MISTAKE, LAURA. I LOOK AT THAT BOY'S SOUL AND I'M NOT SURE WHETHER HIS MOTHER OR HIS FATHER IS IN HIS EYES.
AND I KNOW YOU AREN'T EITHER.

"YOU'LL MEET ISAAC SOON ENOUGH, BUT YOU NEED TO LEAVE YOUR ANGER WITH ME, AGENT BREMBLE.

"ISAAC WON'T MEET AN FBI AGENT. HE'LL MEET THE MAN UNDERNEATH IT."

WHAT DO YOU WANT FROM ME?

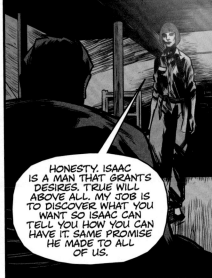

HONESTY. ISAAC IS A MAN THAT GRANTS DESIRES. TRUE WILL ABOVE ALL. MY JOB IS TO DISCOVER WHAT YOU WANT SO ISAAC CAN TELL YOU HOW YOU CAN HAVE IT. SAME PROMISE HE MADE TO ALL OF US.

I WANT TO MEET THE SON OF A BITCH AND FIND OUT THE TRUTH ABOUT EDEN.

THAT'S WHY YOU CAME HERE WITH YOUR LITTLE GUN AND BADGE, BUT THAT'S NOT WHAT YOU WANT. YOU'RE THE KIND OF MAN WHO HIDES WHAT HE WANTS, HOPING SOMEDAY IT'LL FIND HIM. THAT'S NOT HOW LIFE WORKS.

MAYBE ISAAC IS THE DEVIL. MAYBE HE'S THE LORD THY GOD. EITHER WAY, WHEN YOU MEET HIM, YOU DON'T WANT TO WASTE A MOMENT INSIDE HIS POWER. YOU WANT TO OPEN YOURSELF UP AND LET HIM FILL YOU WITH THE TRUTH OF HOW YOU CAN BECOME YOUR WILL.

SO LET ME ASK YOU AGAIN. WHAT DO YOU WANT?

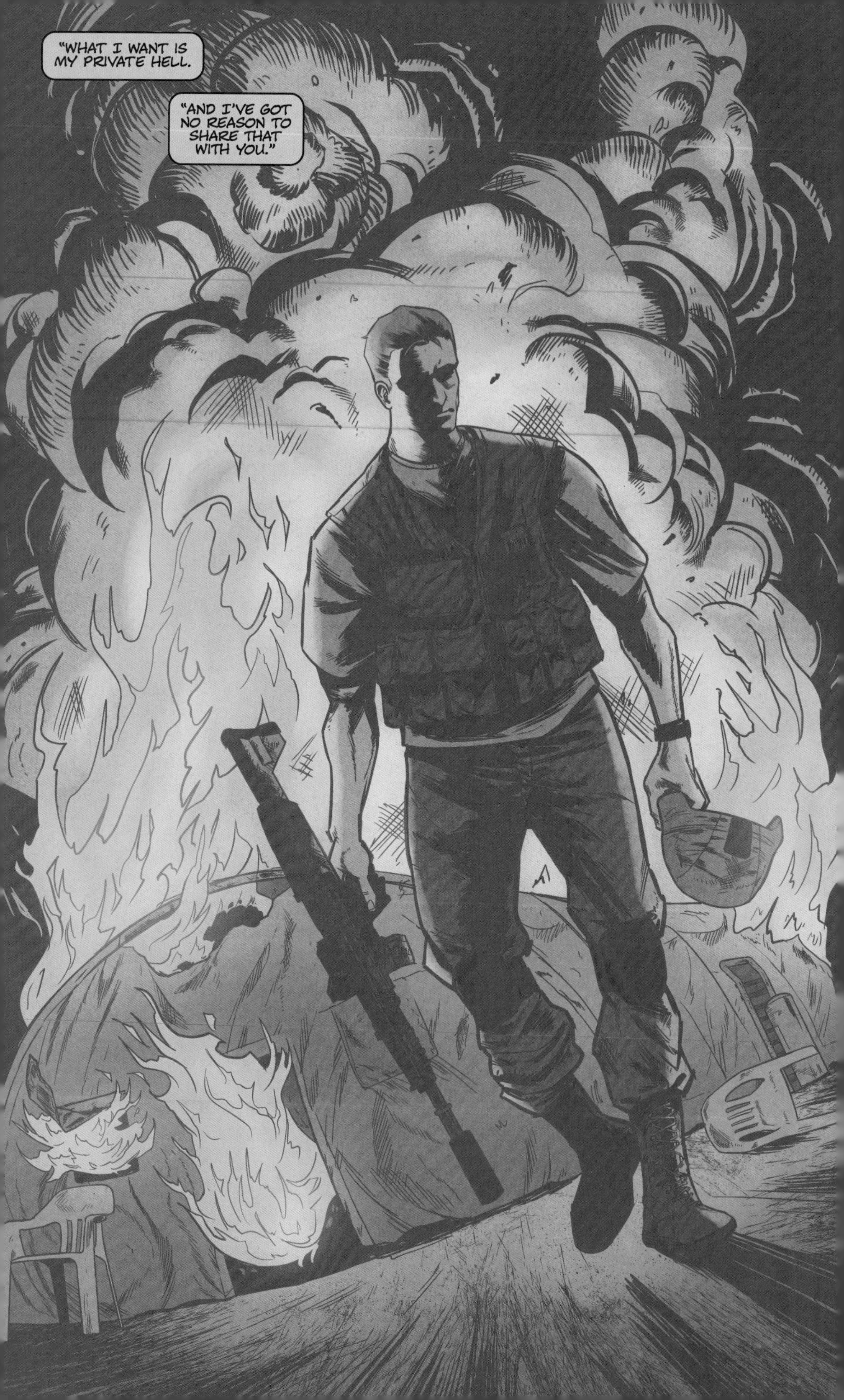
"WHAT I WANT IS MY PRIVATE HELL.
"AND I'VE GOT NO REASON TO SHARE THAT WITH YOU."

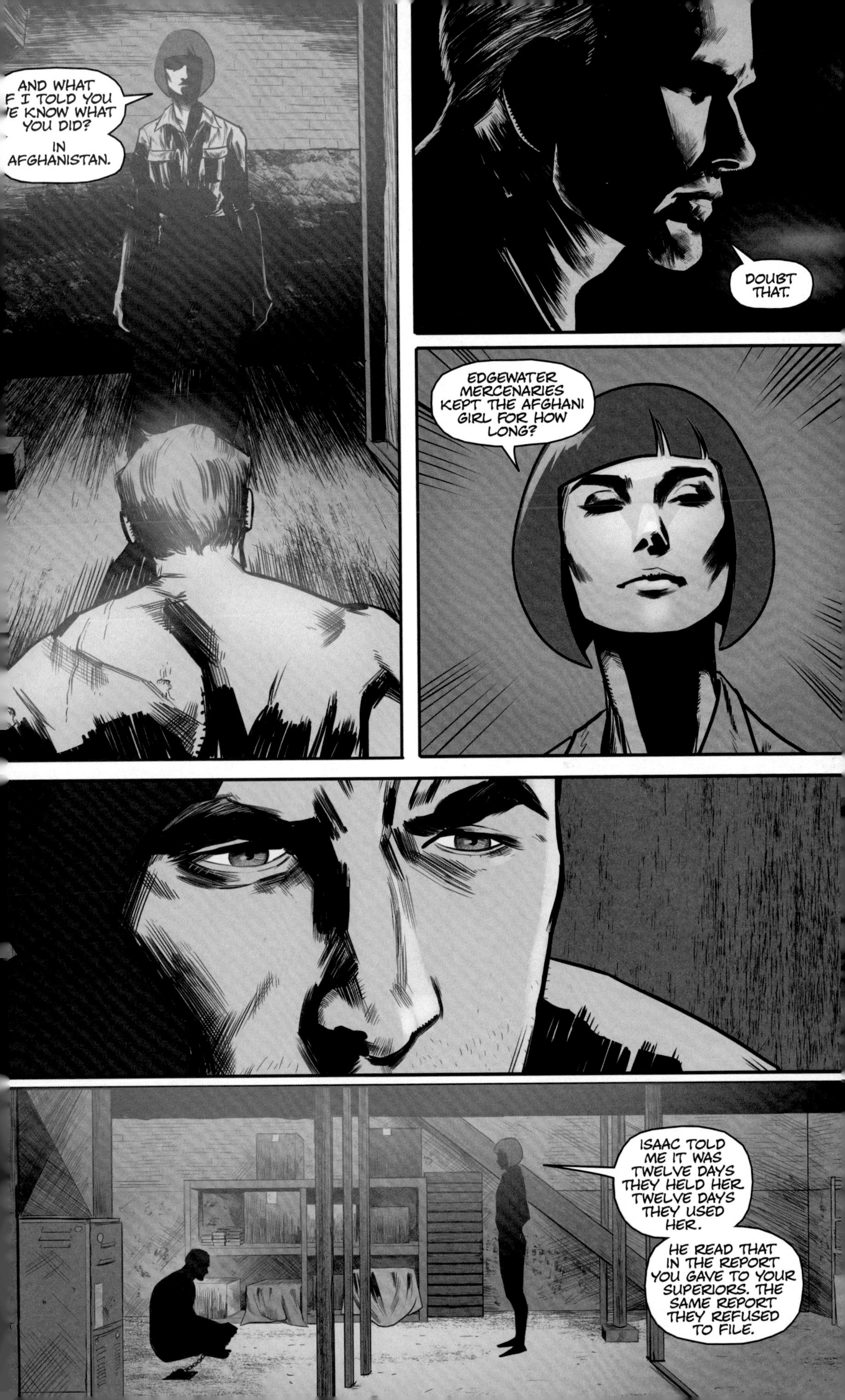
AND WHAT
F I TOLD YOU
'E KNOW WHAT
YOU DID?
IN
AFGHANISTAN.
DOUBT
THAT.
EDGEWATER
MERCENARIES
KEPT THE AFGHANI
GIRL FOR HOW
LONG?
ISAAC TOLD
ME IT WAS
TWELVE DAYS
THEY HELD HER
TWELVE DAYS
THEY USED
HER.
HE READ THAT
IN THE REPORT
YOU GAVE TO YOUR
SUPERIORS. THE
SAME REPORT
THEY REFUSED
TO FILE.

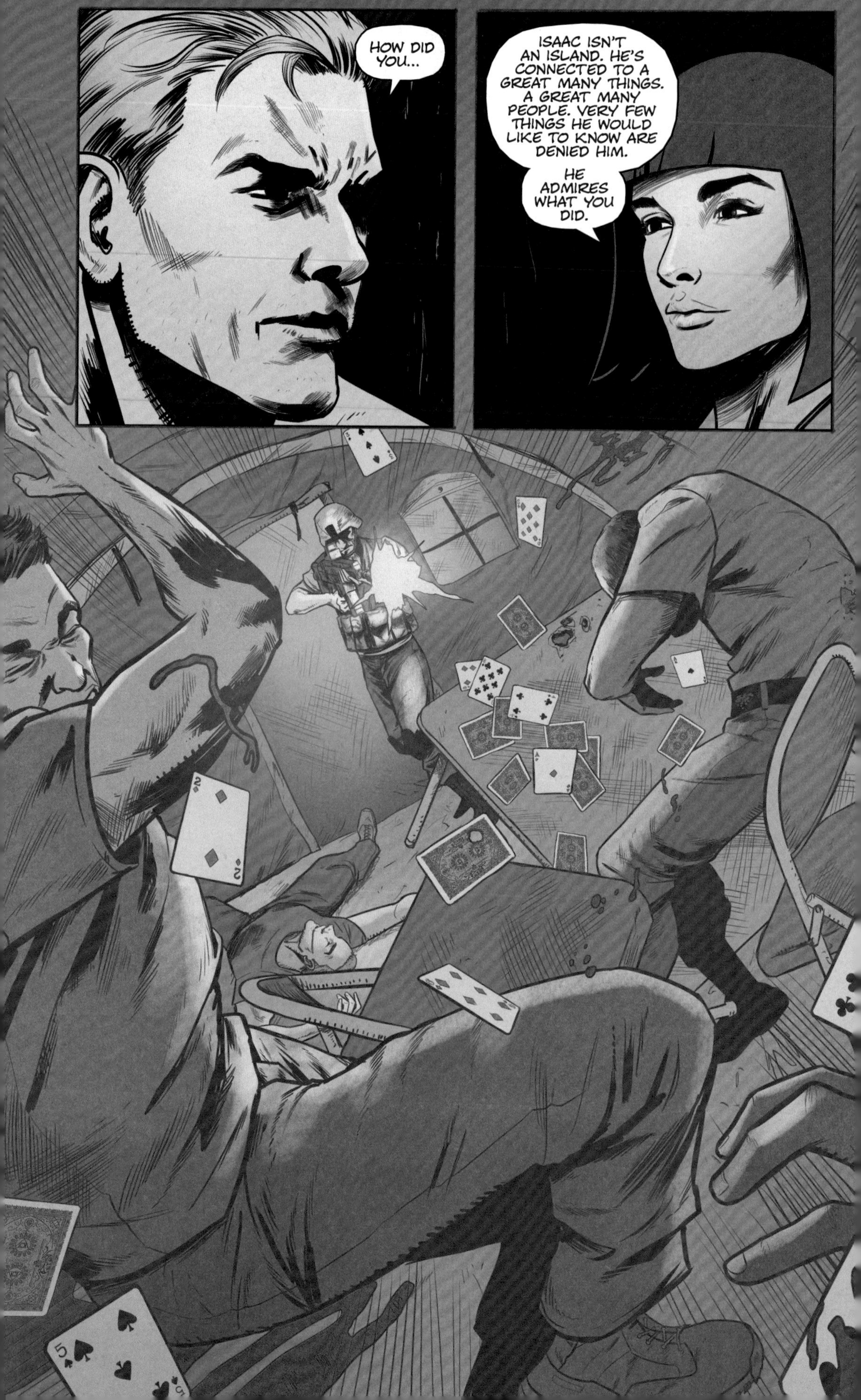
HOW DID YOU...
ISAAC ISN'T AN ISLAND. HE'S CONNECTED TO A GREAT MANY THINGS. A GREAT MANY PEOPLE. VERY FEW THINGS HE WOULD LIKE TO KNOW ARE DENIED HIM.
HE ADMIRES WHAT YOU DID.

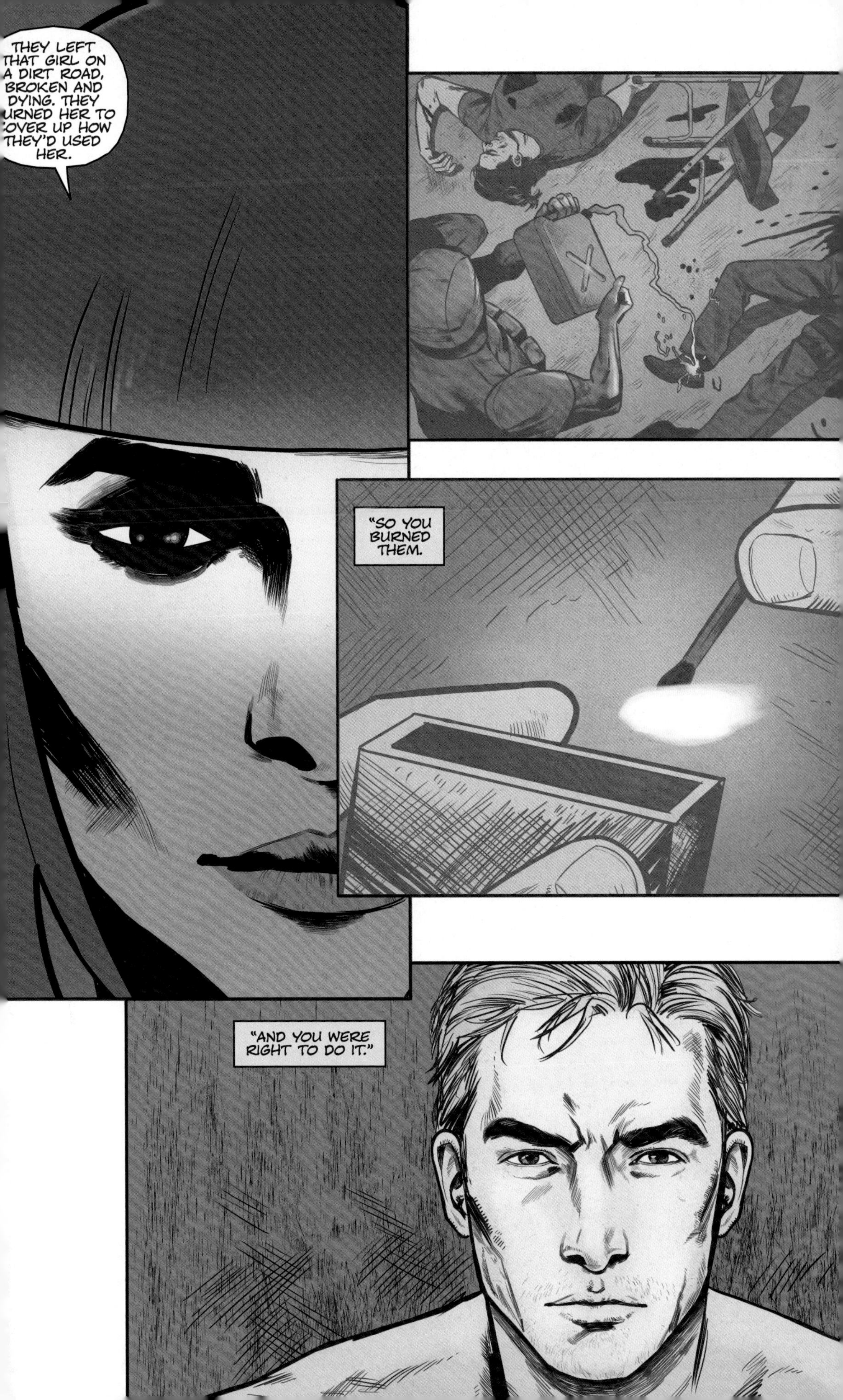
THEY LEFT THAT GIRL ON A DIRT ROAD, BROKEN AND DYING. THEY BURNED HER TO COVER UP HOW THEY'D USED HER.
"SO YOU BURNED THEM.
"AND YOU WERE RIGHT TO DO IT."

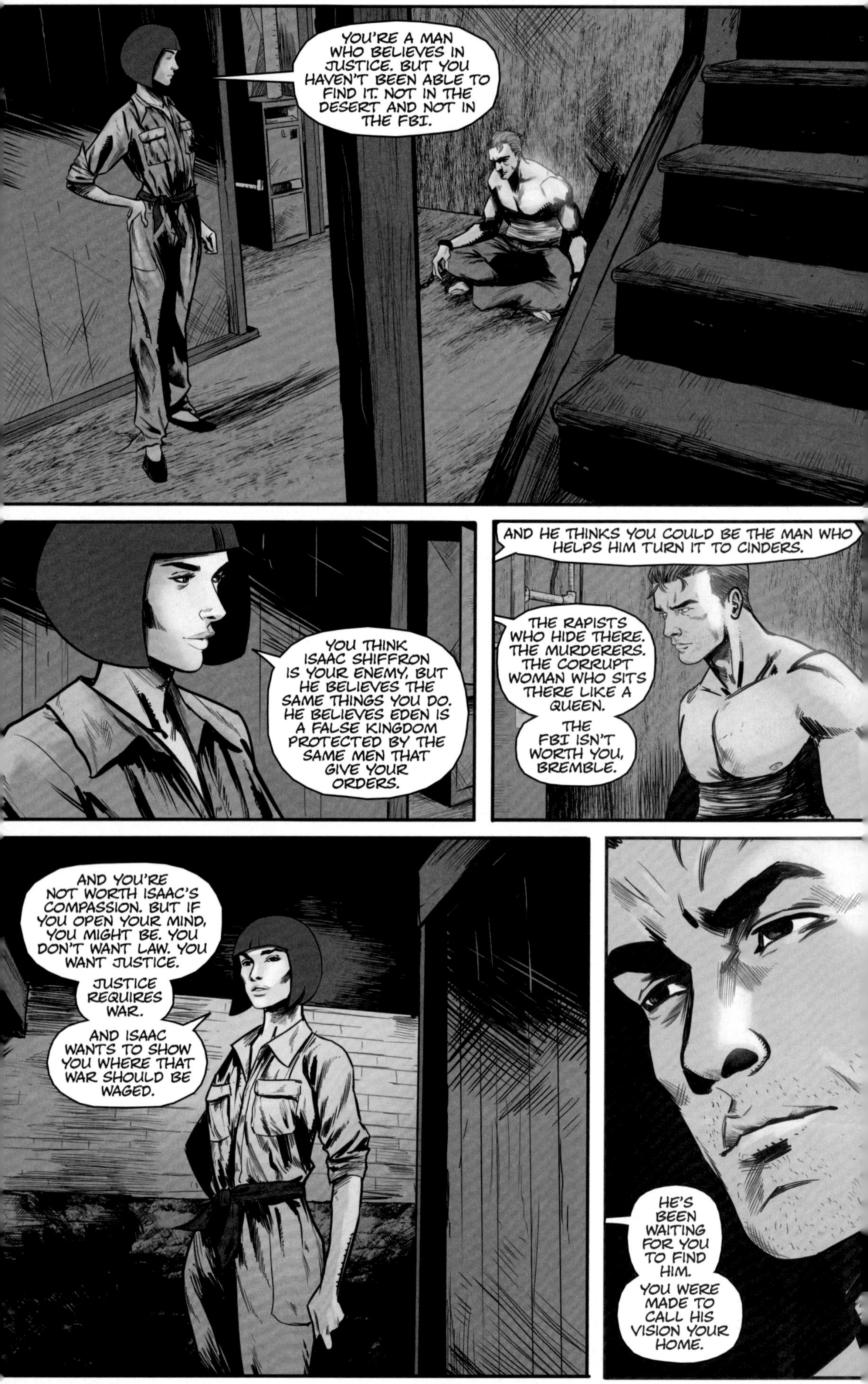
YOU'RE A MAN WHO BELIEVES IN JUSTICE. BUT YOU HAVEN'T BEEN ABLE TO FIND IT. NOT IN THE DESERT AND NOT IN THE FBI.
YOU THINK ISAAC SHIFFRON IS YOUR ENEMY, BUT HE BELIEVES THE SAME THINGS YOU DO. HE BELIEVES EDEN IS A FALSE KINGDOM PROTECTED BY THE SAME MEN THAT GIVE YOUR ORDERS.
AND HE THINKS YOU COULD BE THE MAN WHO HELPS HIM TURN IT TO CINDERS.
THE RAPISTS WHO HIDE THERE. THE MURDERERS. THE CORRUPT WOMAN WHO SITS THERE LIKE A QUEEN.
THE FBI ISN'T WORTH YOU, BREMBLE.
AND YOU'RE NOT WORTH ISAAC'S COMPASSION. BUT IF YOU OPEN YOUR MIND, YOU MIGHT BE. YOU DON'T WANT LAW. YOU WANT JUSTICE.
JUSTICE REQUIRES WAR.
AND ISAAC WANTS TO SHOW YOU WHERE THAT WAR SHOULD BE WAGED.
HE'S BEEN WAITING FOR YOU TO FIND HIM.
YOU WERE MADE TO CALL HIS VISION YOUR HOME.

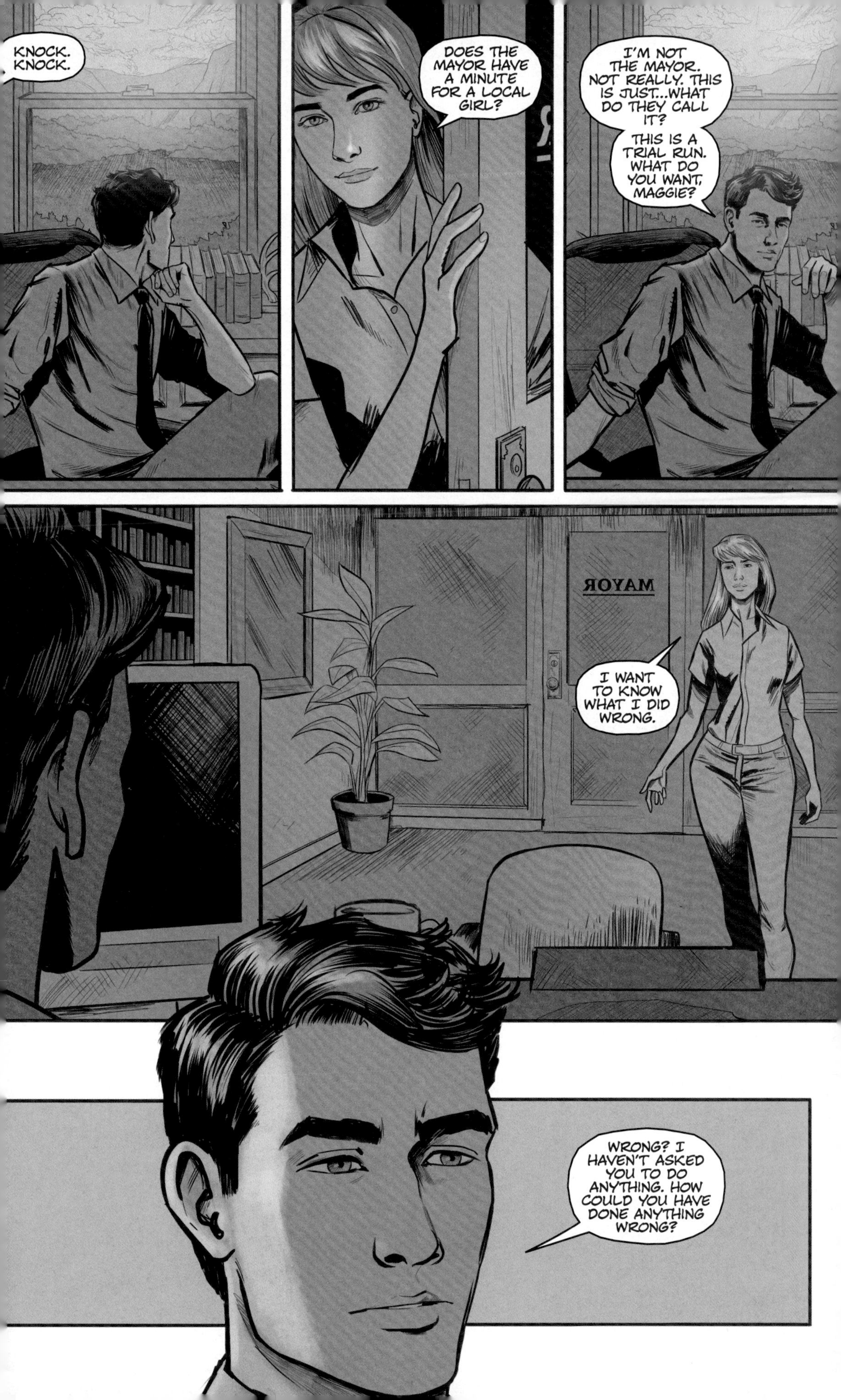
KNOCK. KNOCK.
DOES THE MAYOR HAVE A MINUTE FOR A LOCAL GIRL?
I'M NOT THE MAYOR. NOT REALLY. THIS IS JUST...WHAT DO THEY CALL IT?
THIS IS A TRIAL RUN. WHAT DO YOU WANT, MAGGIE?
MAYOR
I WANT TO KNOW WHAT I DID WRONG.
WRONG? I HAVEN'T ASKED YOU TO DO ANYTHING. HOW COULD YOU HAVE DONE ANYTHING WRONG?

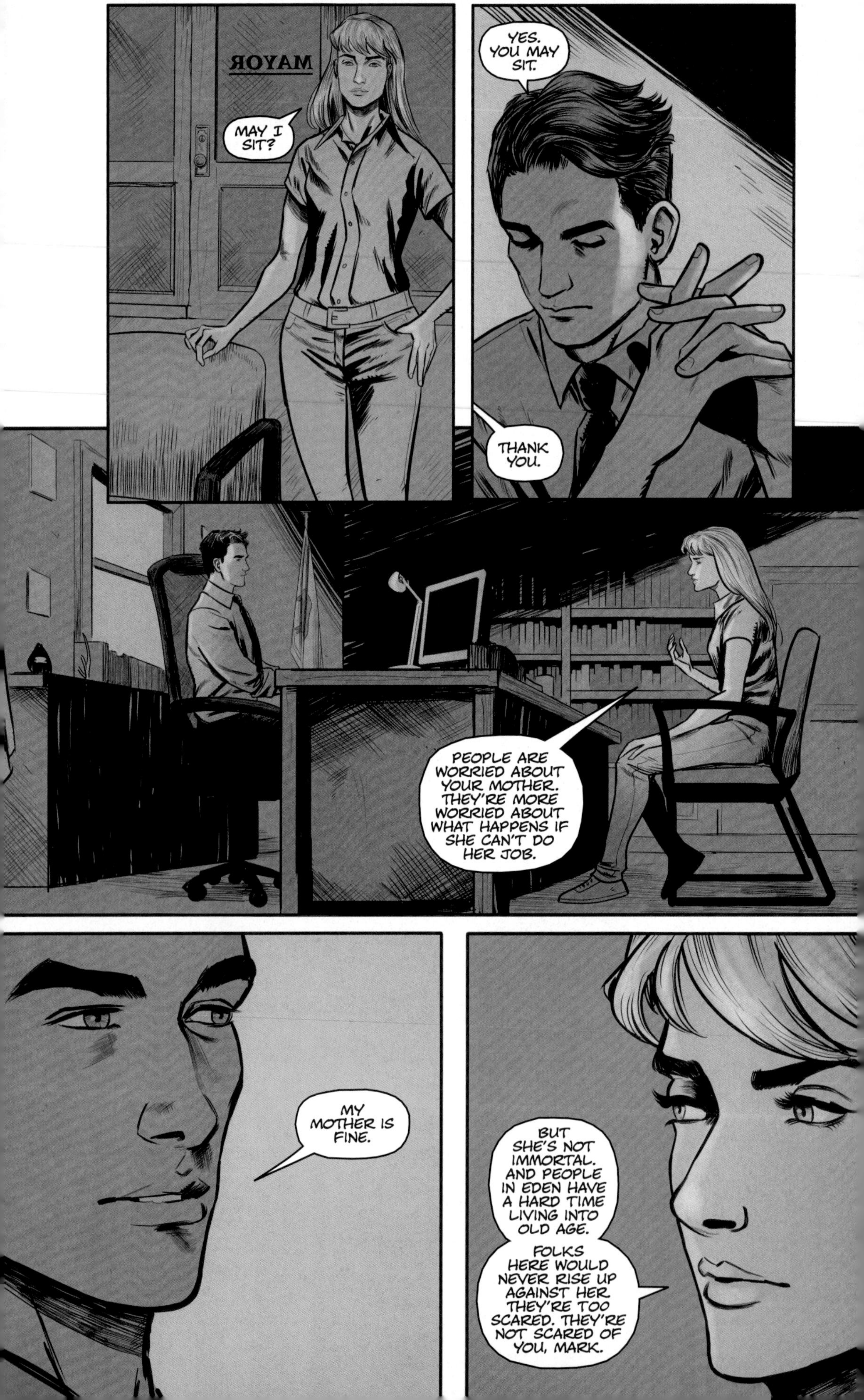
MAYOR
MAY I SIT?
YES. YOU MAY SIT.
THANK YOU.
PEOPLE ARE WORRIED ABOUT YOUR MOTHER. THEY'RE MORE WORRIED ABOUT WHAT HAPPENS IF SHE CAN'T DO HER JOB.
MY MOTHER IS FINE.
BUT SHE'S NOT IMMORTAL. AND PEOPLE IN EDEN HAVE A HARD TIME LIVING INTO OLD AGE.
FOLKS HERE WOULD NEVER RISE UP AGAINST HER THEY'RE TOO SCARED. THEY'RE NOT SCARED OF YOU, MARK.

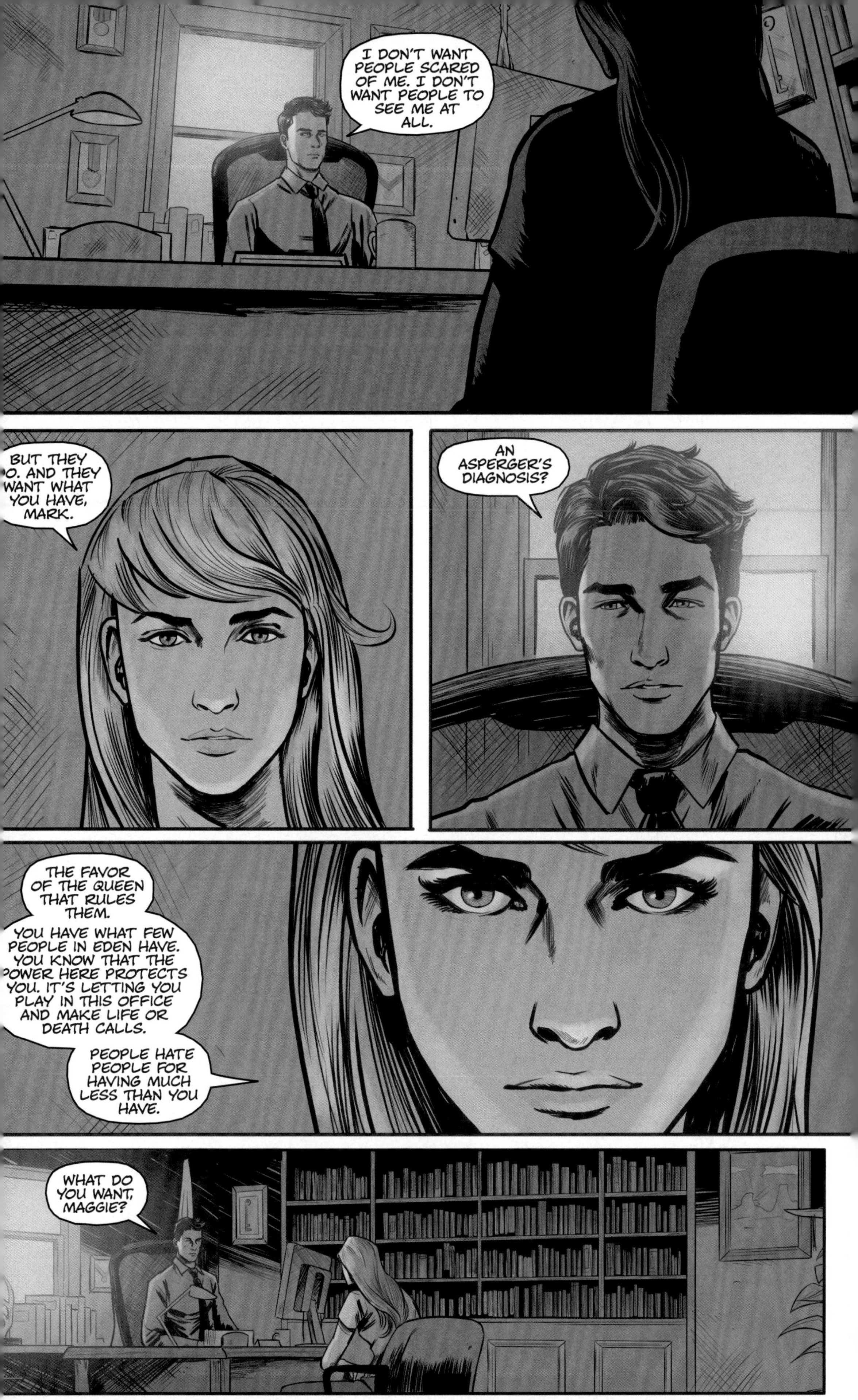
I DON'T WANT PEOPLE SCARED OF ME. I DON'T WANT PEOPLE TO SEE ME AT ALL.
BUT THEY DO. AND THEY WANT WHAT YOU HAVE, MARK.
AN ASPERGER'S DIAGNOSIS?
THE FAVOR OF THE QUEEN THAT RULES THEM.
YOU HAVE WHAT FEW PEOPLE IN EDEN HAVE. YOU KNOW THAT THE POWER HERE PROTECTS YOU. IT'S LETTING YOU PLAY IN THIS OFFICE AND MAKE LIFE OR DEATH CALLS.
PEOPLE HATE PEOPLE FOR HAVING MUCH LESS THAN YOU HAVE.
WHAT DO YOU WANT, MAGGIE?

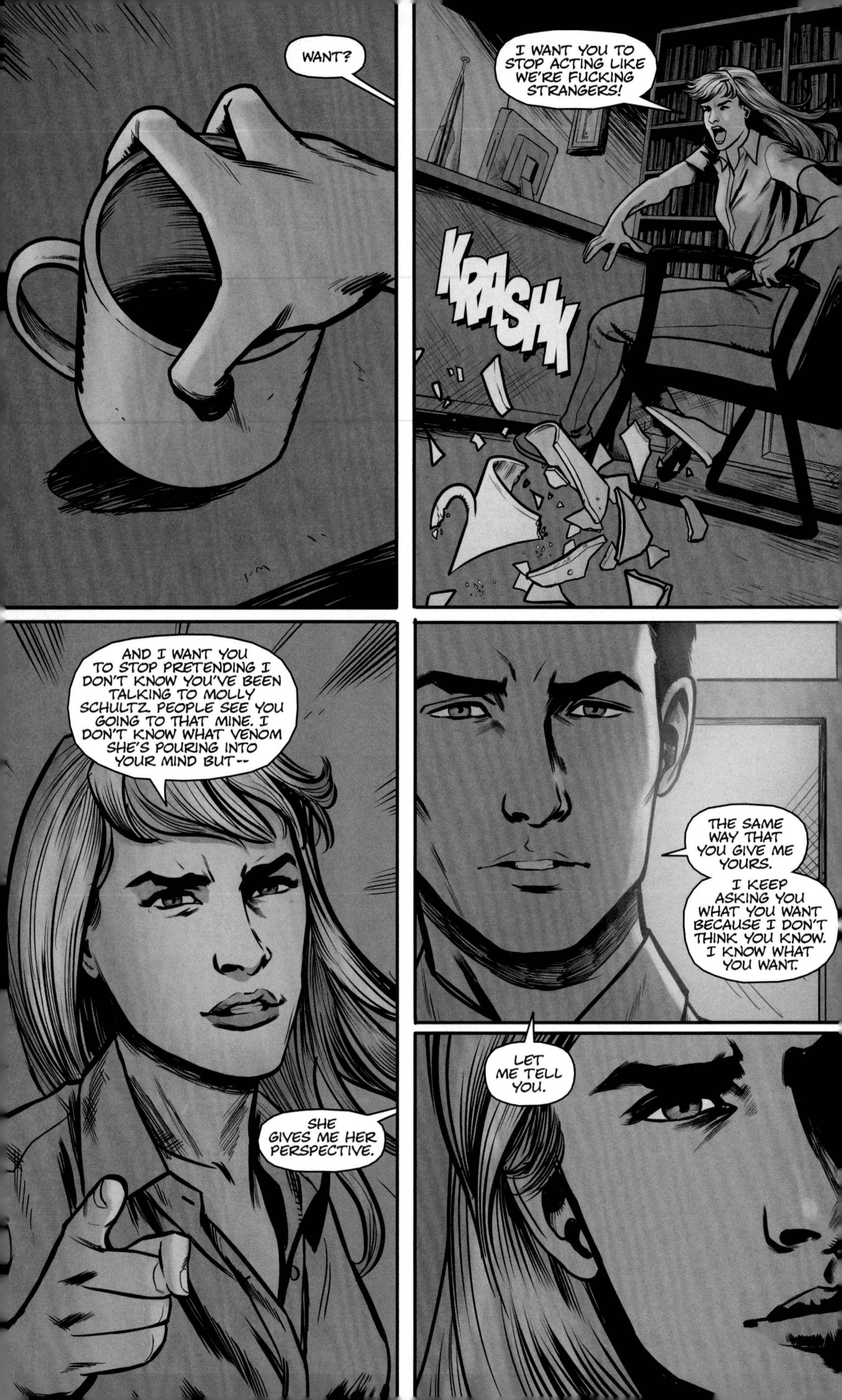
WANT?
I WANT YOU TO STOP ACTING LIKE WE'RE FUCKING STRANGERS!
KRASHK
AND I WANT YOU TO STOP PRETENDING I DON'T KNOW YOU'VE BEEN TALKING TO MOLLY SCHULTZ. PEOPLE SEE YOU GOING TO THAT MINE. I DON'T KNOW WHAT VENOM SHE'S POURING INTO YOUR MIND BUT--
SHE GIVES ME HER PERSPECTIVE.
THE SAME WAY THAT YOU GIVE ME YOURS.
I KEEP ASKING YOU WHAT YOU WANT BECAUSE I DON'T THINK YOU KNOW. I KNOW WHAT YOU WANT.
LET ME TELL YOU.

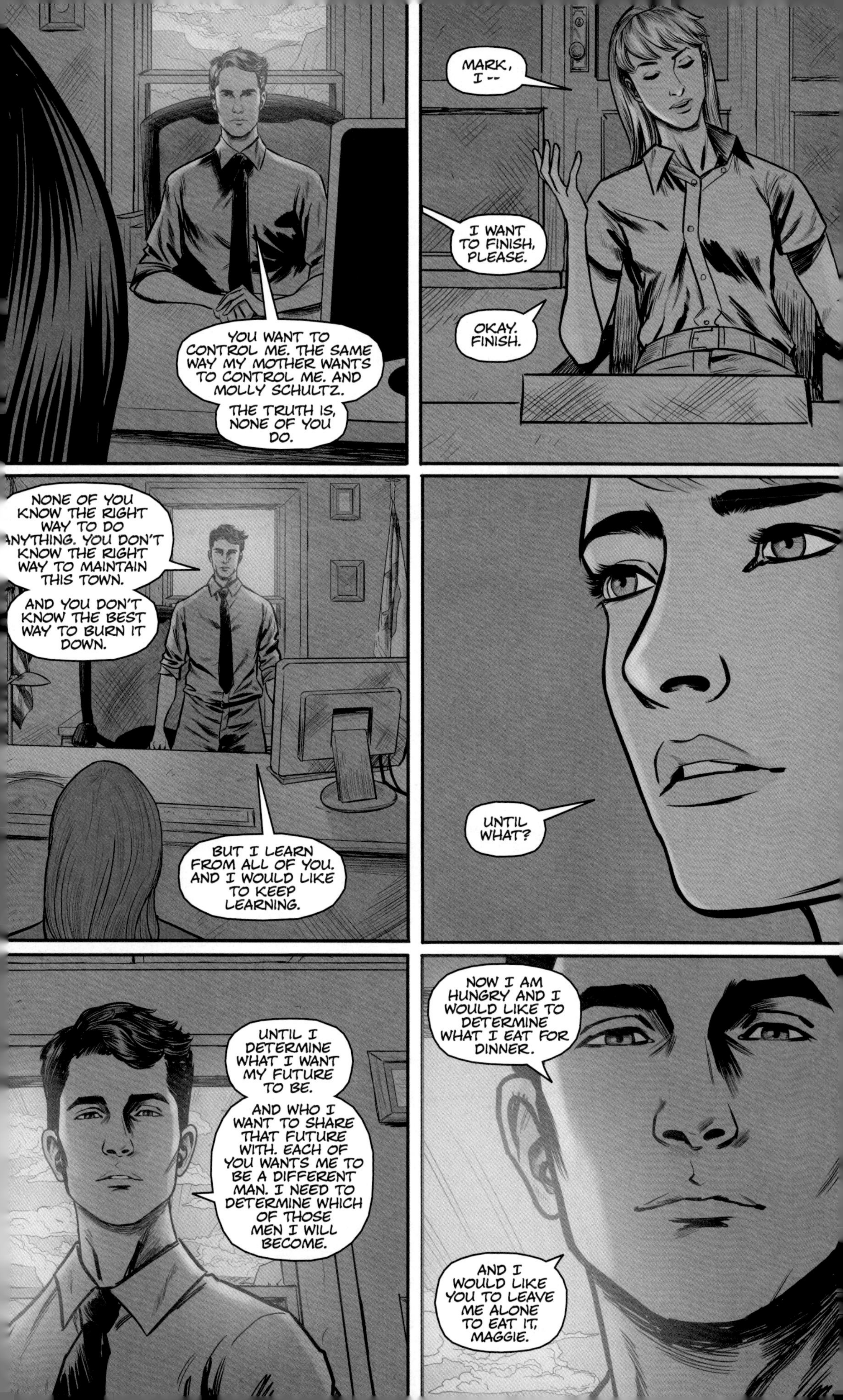
YOU WANT TO CONTROL ME. THE SAME WAY MY MOTHER WANTS TO CONTROL ME. AND MOLLY SCHULTZ.
THE TRUTH IS, NONE OF YOU DO.
MARK, I --
I WANT TO FINISH, PLEASE.
OKAY. FINISH.
NONE OF YOU KNOW THE RIGHT WAY TO DO ANYTHING. YOU DON'T KNOW THE RIGHT WAY TO MAINTAIN THIS TOWN.
AND YOU DON'T KNOW THE BEST WAY TO BURN IT DOWN.
BUT I LEARN FROM ALL OF YOU. AND I WOULD LIKE TO KEEP LEARNING.
UNTIL WHAT?
UNTIL I DETERMINE WHAT I WANT MY FUTURE TO BE.
AND WHO I WANT TO SHARE THAT FUTURE WITH. EACH OF YOU WANTS ME TO BE A DIFFERENT MAN. I NEED TO DETERMINE WHICH OF THOSE MEN I WILL BECOME.
NOW I AM HUNGRY AND I WOULD LIKE TO DETERMINE WHAT I EAT FOR DINNER.
AND I WOULD LIKE YOU TO LEAVE ME ALONE TO EAT IT, MAGGIE.

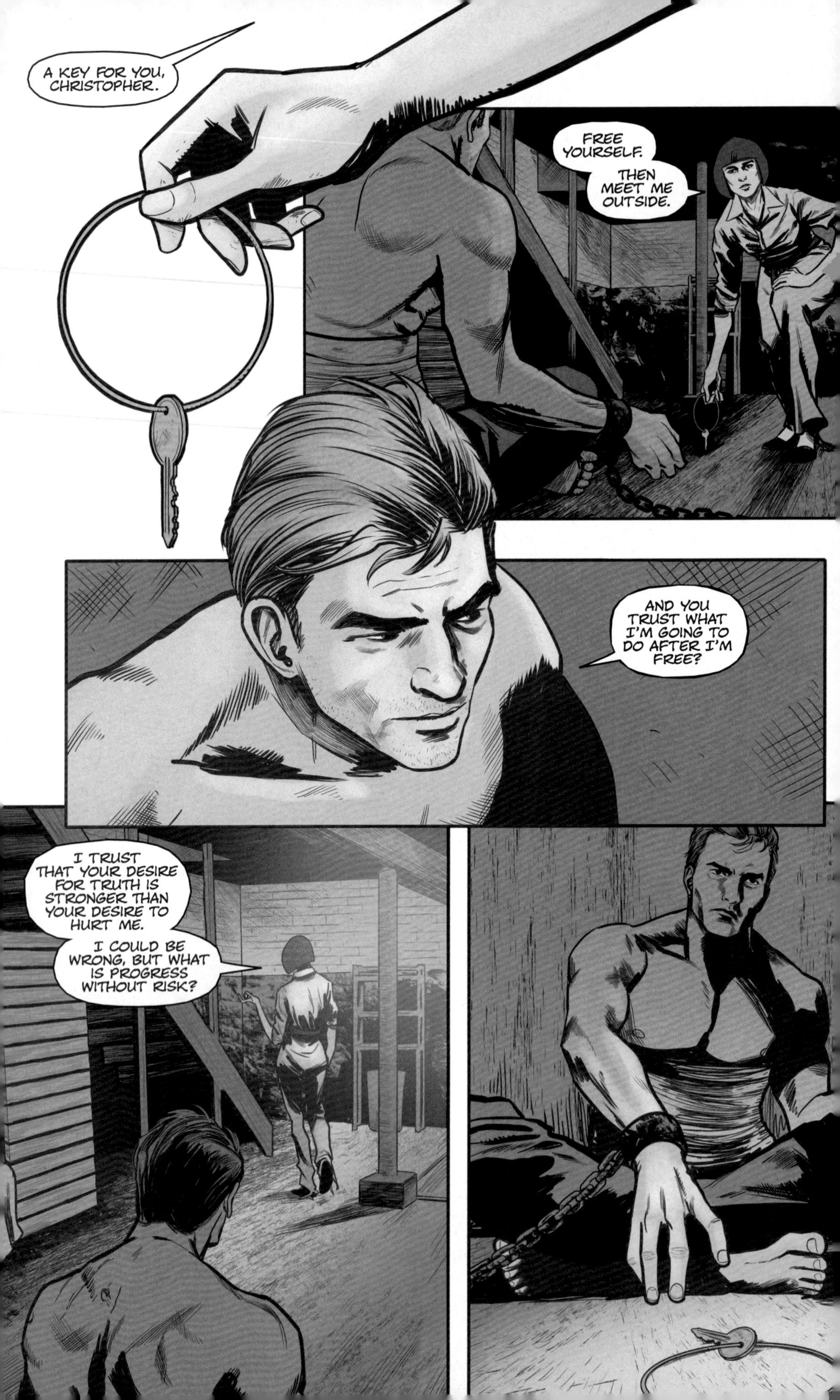
A KEY FOR YOU, CHRISTOPHER.
FREE YOURSELF.
THEN MEET ME OUTSIDE.
AND YOU TRUST WHAT I'M GOING TO DO AFTER I'M FREE?
I TRUST THAT YOUR DESIRE FOR TRUTH IS STRONGER THAN YOUR DESIRE TO HURT ME.
I COULD BE WRONG, BUT WHAT IS PROGRESS WITHOUT RISK?

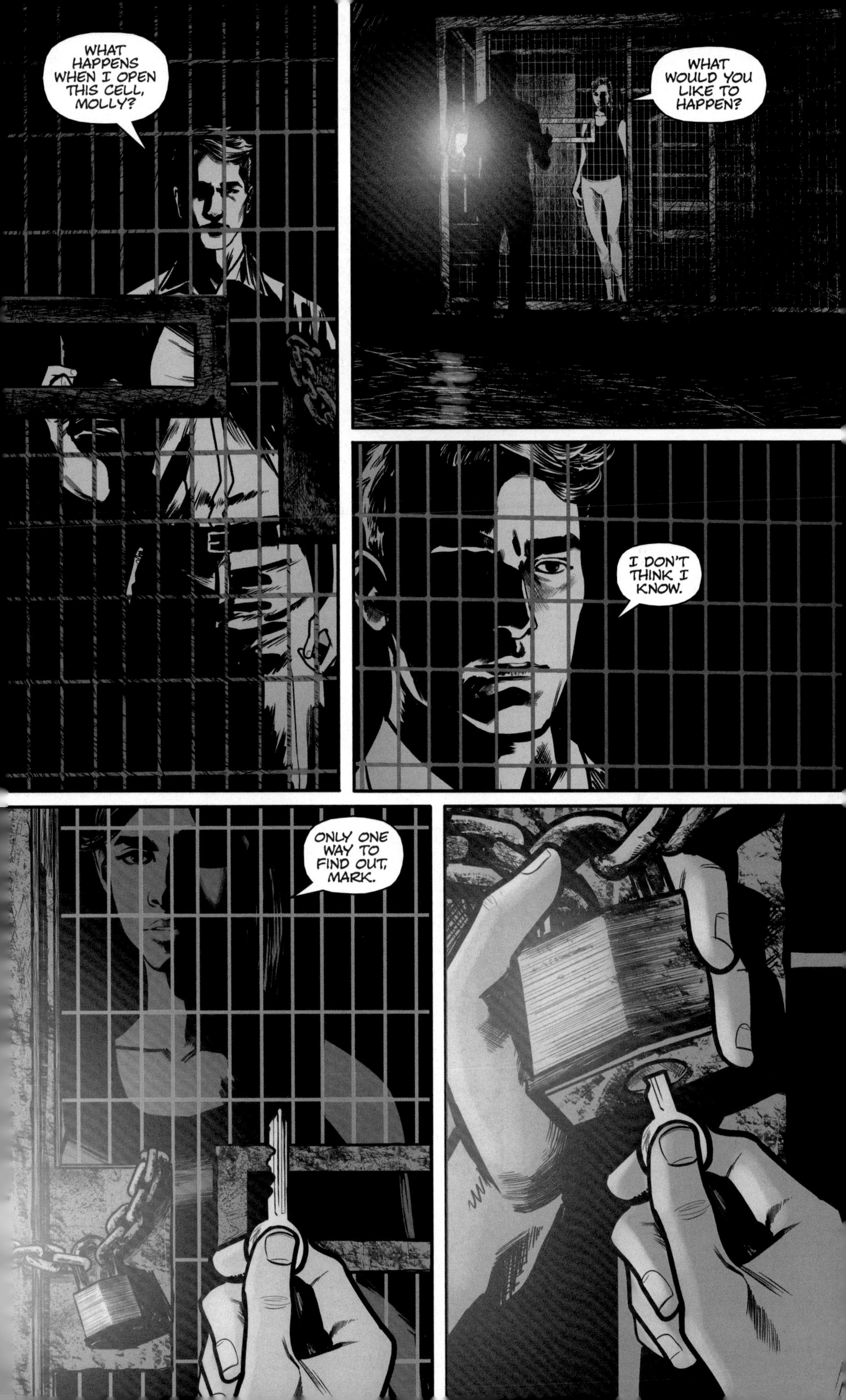
WHAT HAPPENS WHEN I OPEN THIS CELL, MOLLY?
WHAT WOULD YOU LIKE TO HAPPEN?
I DON'T THINK I KNOW.
ONLY ONE WAY TO FIND OUT, MARK.

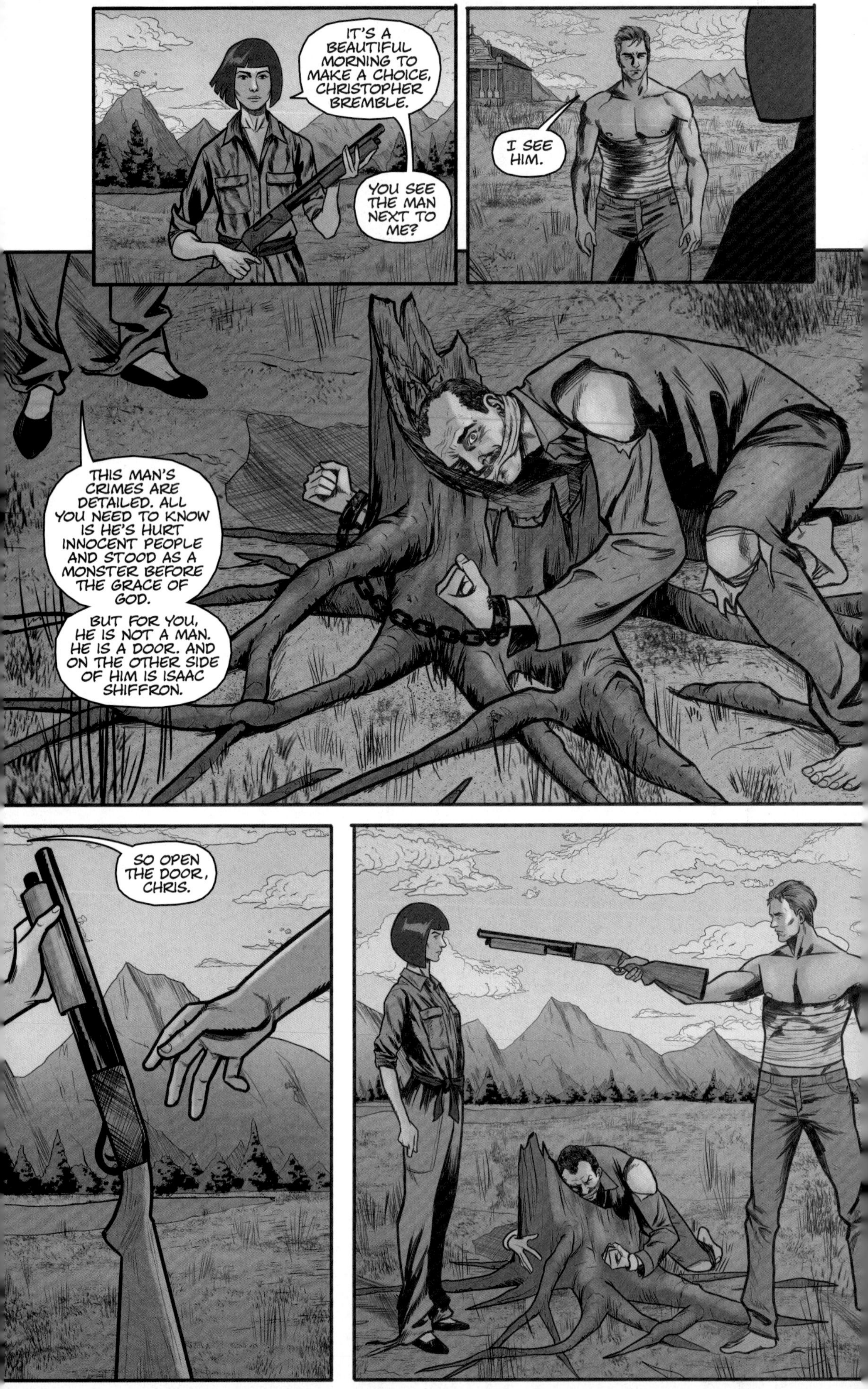
IT'S A BEAUTIFUL MORNING TO MAKE A CHOICE, CHRISTOPHER BREMBLE.
YOU SEE THE MAN NEXT TO ME?
I SEE HIM.
THIS MAN'S CRIMES ARE DETAILED. ALL YOU NEED TO KNOW IS HE'S HURT INNOCENT PEOPLE AND STOOD AS A MONSTER BEFORE THE GRACE OF GOD.
BUT FOR YOU, HE IS NOT A MAN. HE IS A DOOR. AND ON THE OTHER SIDE OF HIM IS ISAAC SHIFFRON.
SO OPEN THE DOOR, CHRIS.

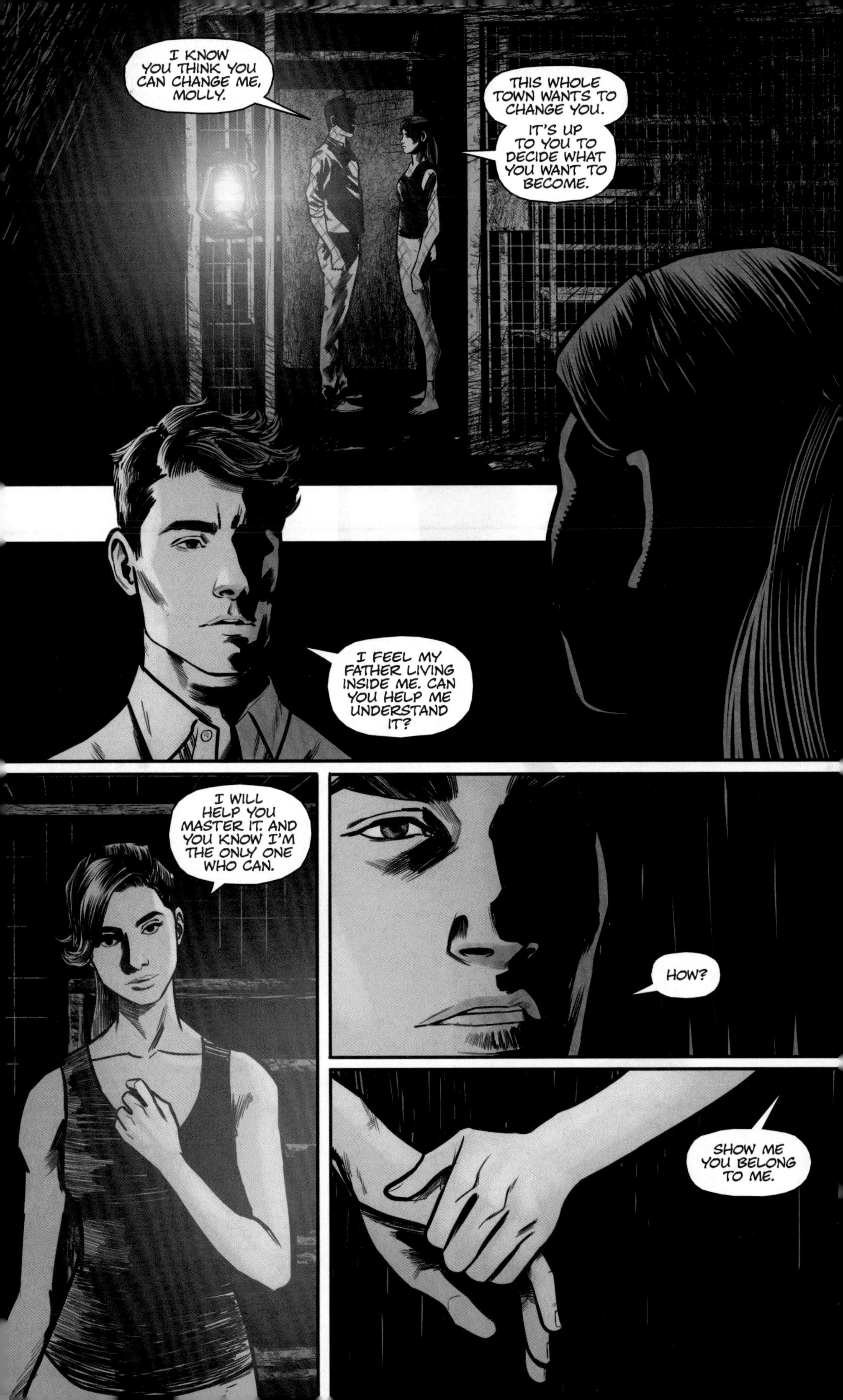
I KNOW YOU THINK YOU CAN CHANGE ME, MOLLY.
THIS WHOLE TOWN WANTS TO CHANGE YOU.
IT'S UP TO YOU TO DECIDE WHAT YOU WANT TO BECOME.
I FEEL MY FATHER LIVING INSIDE ME. CAN YOU HELP ME UNDERSTAND IT?
I WILL HELP YOU MASTER IT. AND YOU KNOW I'M THE ONLY ONE WHO CAN.
HOW?
SHOW ME YOU BELONG TO ME.

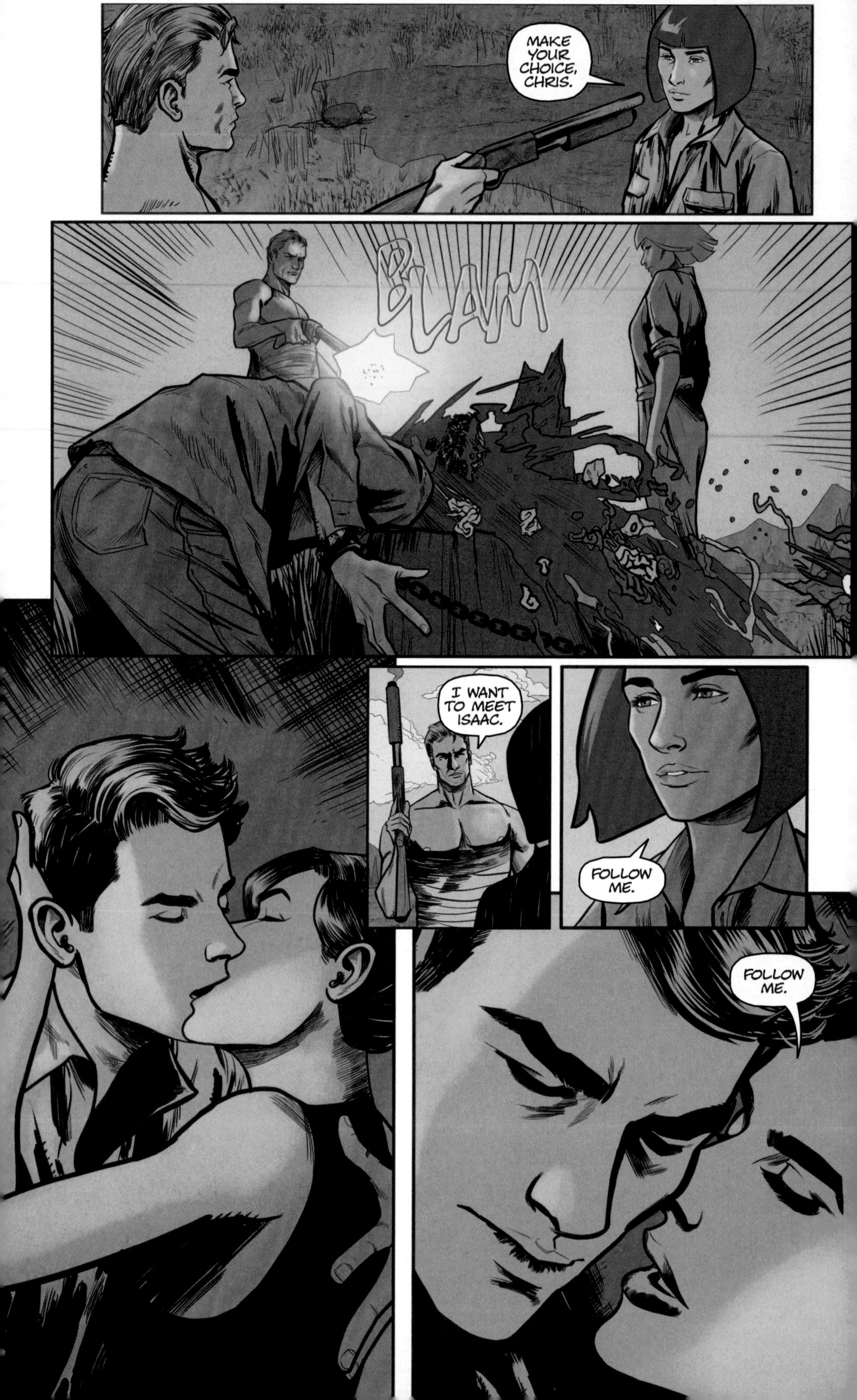
MAKE YOUR CHOICE, CHRIS.
BLAM
I WANT TO MEET ISAAC.
FOLLOW ME.
FOLLOW ME.

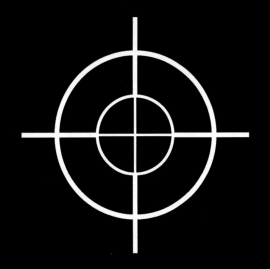

# Chapter 19

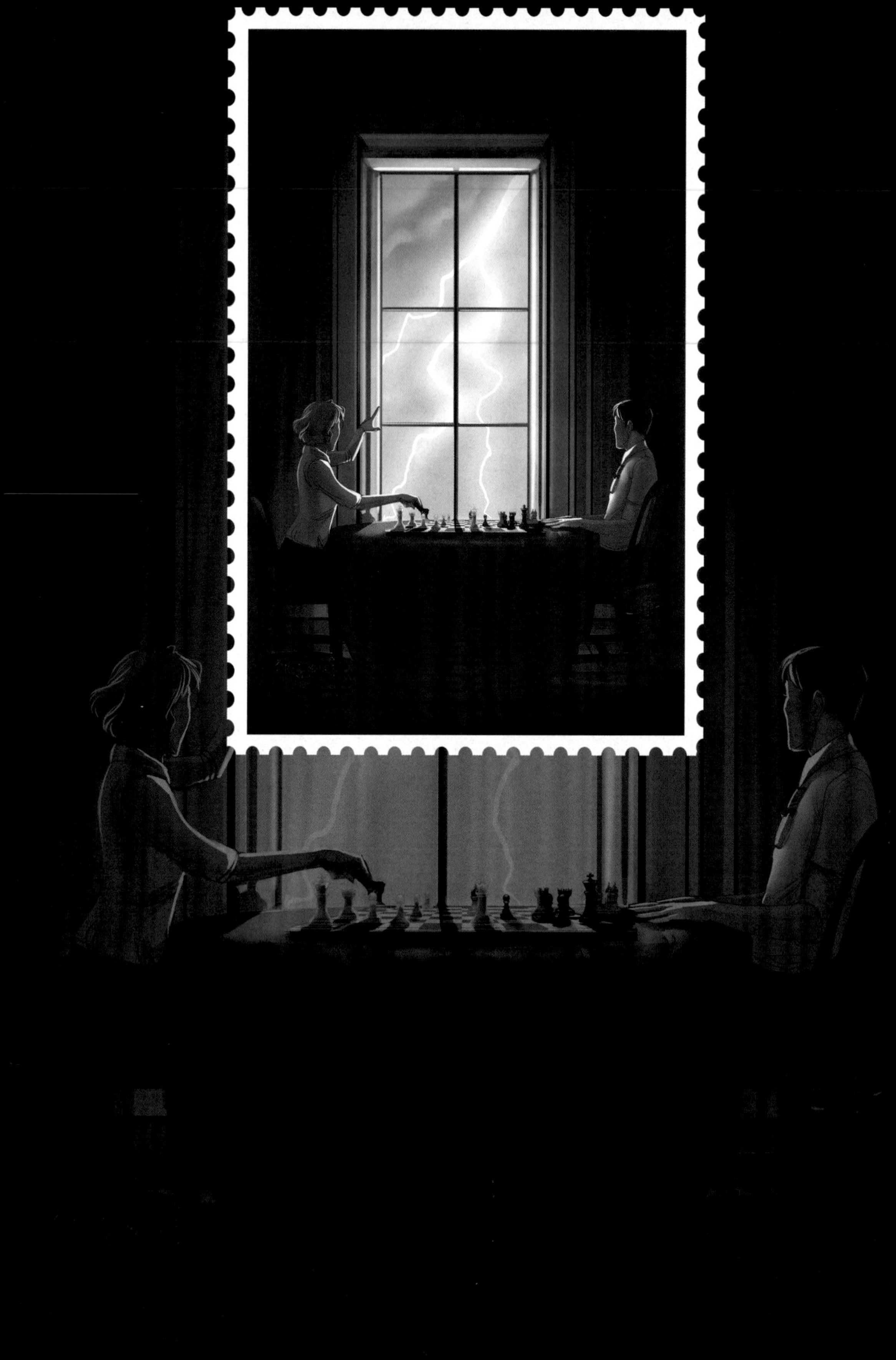

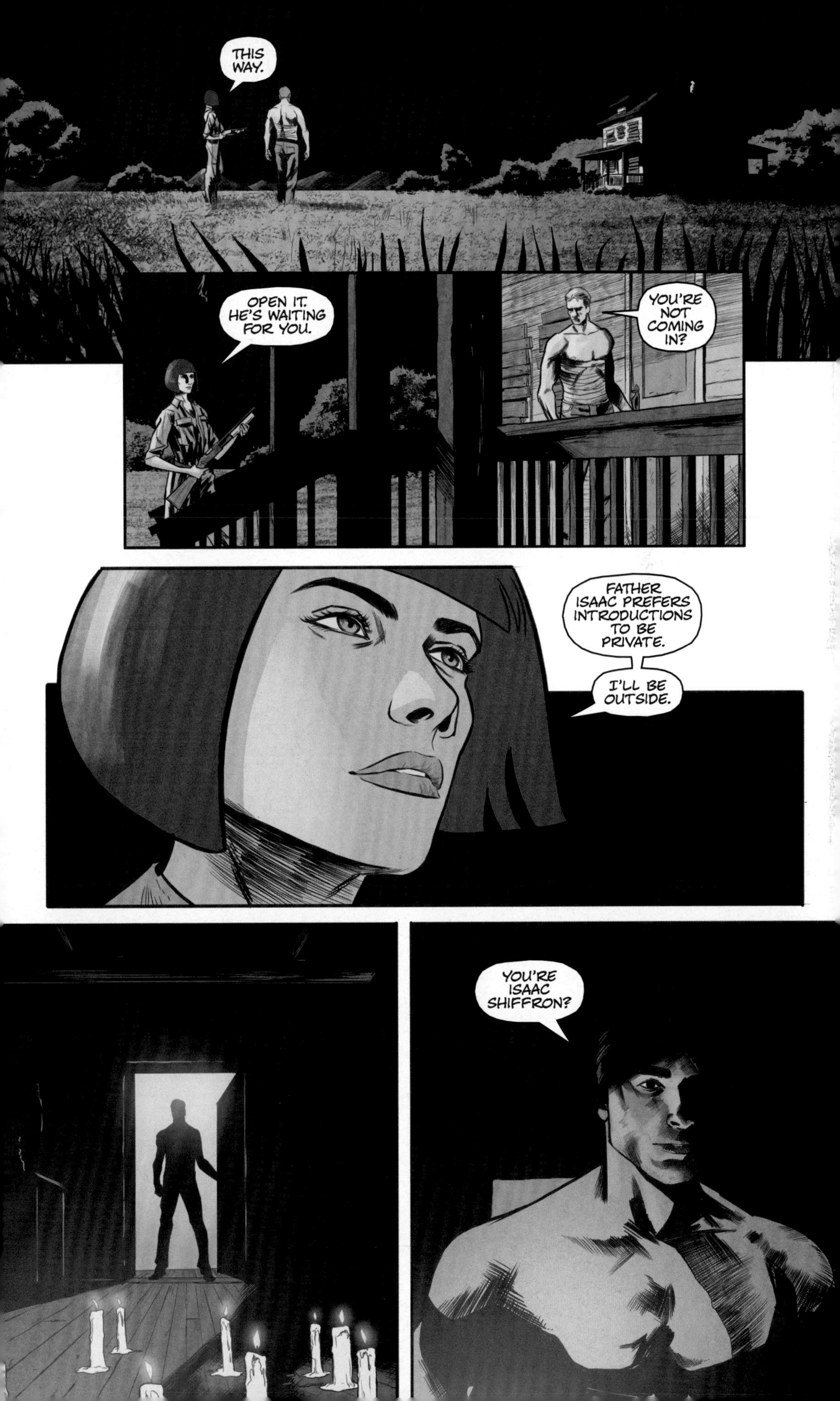
THIS WAY.
OPEN IT. HE'S WAITING FOR YOU.
YOU'RE NOT COMING IN?
FATHER ISAAC PREFERS INTRODUCTIONS TO BE PRIVATE.
I'LL BE OUTSIDE.
YOU'RE ISAAC SHIFFRON?

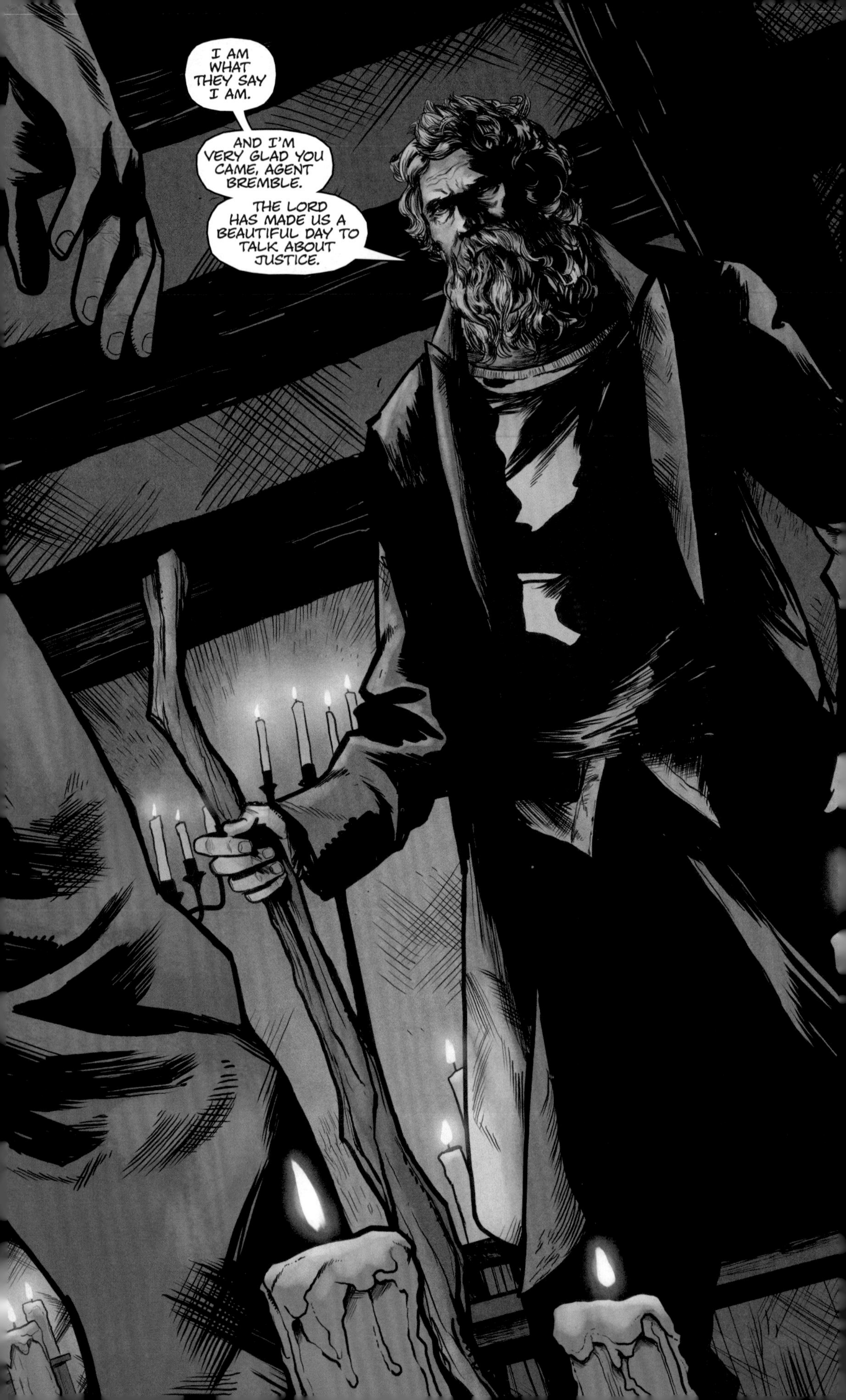
I AM WHAT THEY SAY I AM.
AND I'M VERY GLAD YOU CAME, AGENT BREMBLE.
THE LORD HAS MADE US A BEAUTIFUL DAY TO TALK ABOUT JUSTICE.

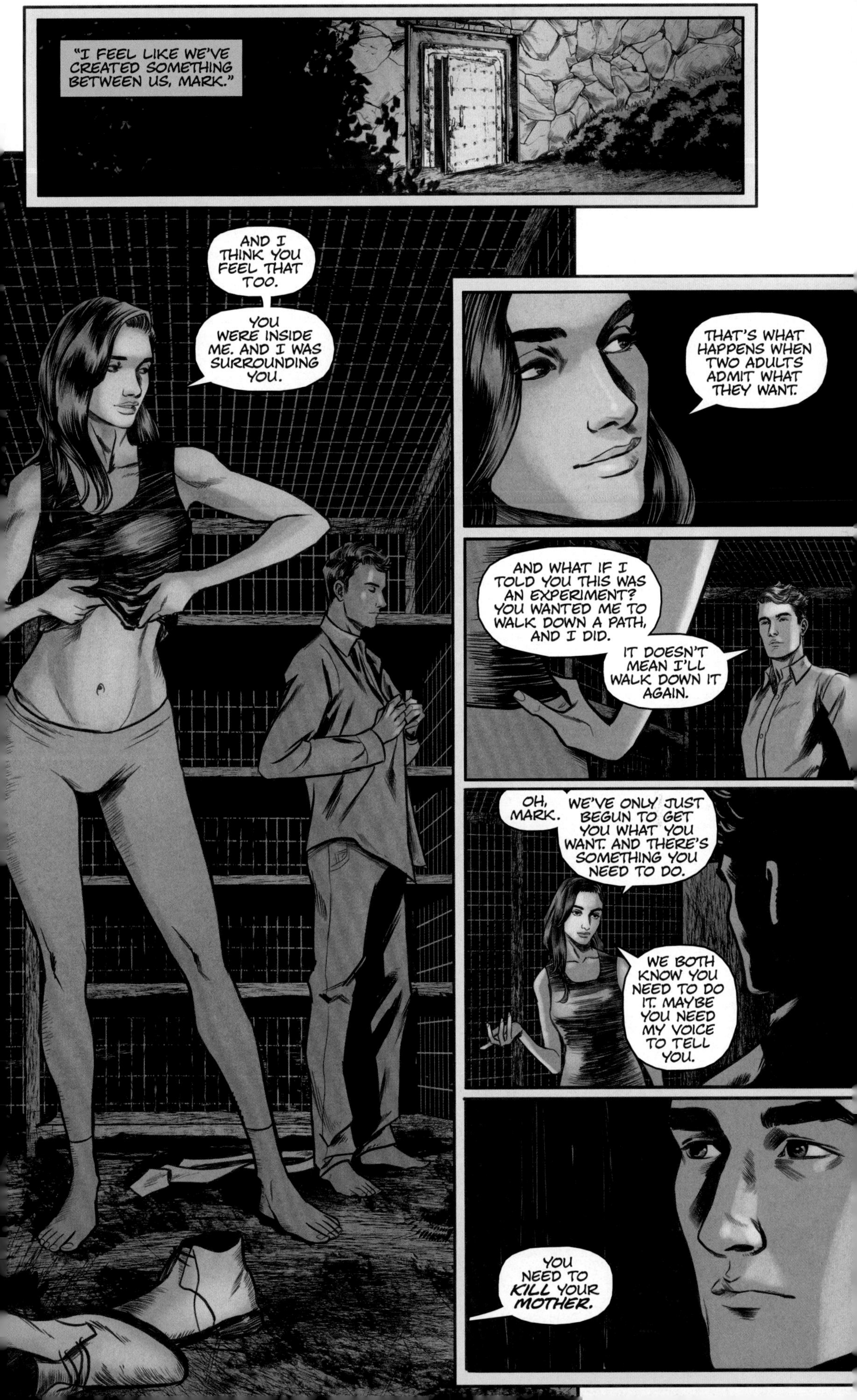
"I FEEL LIKE WE'VE CREATED SOMETHING BETWEEN US, MARK."
AND I THINK YOU FEEL THAT TOO.
YOU WERE INSIDE ME. AND I WAS SURROUNDING YOU.
THAT'S WHAT HAPPENS WHEN TWO ADULTS ADMIT WHAT THEY WANT.
AND WHAT IF I TOLD YOU THIS WAS AN EXPERIMENT? YOU WANTED ME TO WALK DOWN A PATH, AND I DID.
IT DOESN'T MEAN I'LL WALK DOWN IT AGAIN.
OH, MARK.
WE'VE ONLY JUST BEGUN TO GET YOU WHAT YOU WANT. AND THERE'S SOMETHING YOU NEED TO DO.
WE BOTH KNOW YOU NEED TO DO IT. MAYBE YOU NEED MY VOICE TO TELL YOU.
YOU NEED TO KILL YOUR MOTHER.

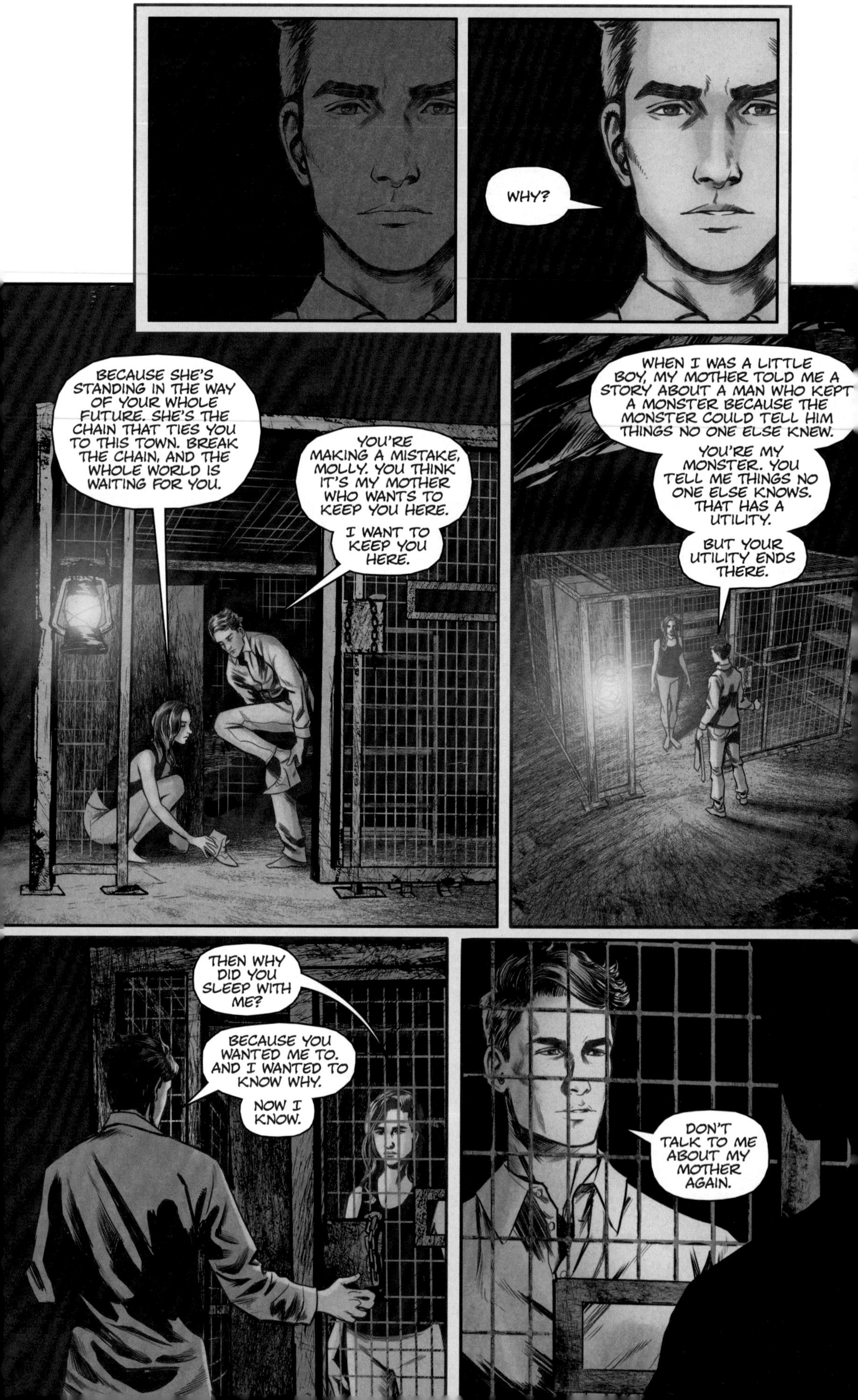
WHY?
BECAUSE SHE'S STANDING IN THE WAY OF YOUR WHOLE FUTURE. SHE'S THE CHAIN THAT TIES YOU TO THIS TOWN. BREAK THE CHAIN, AND THE WHOLE WORLD IS WAITING FOR YOU.
YOU'RE MAKING A MISTAKE, MOLLY. YOU THINK IT'S MY MOTHER WHO WANTS TO KEEP YOU HERE.
I WANT TO KEEP YOU HERE.
WHEN I WAS A LITTLE BOY, MY MOTHER TOLD ME A STORY ABOUT A MAN WHO KEPT A MONSTER BECAUSE THE MONSTER COULD TELL HIM THINGS NO ONE ELSE KNEW.
YOU'RE MY MONSTER. YOU TELL ME THINGS NO ONE ELSE KNOWS. THAT HAS A UTILITY.
BUT YOUR UTILITY ENDS THERE.
THEN WHY DID YOU SLEEP WITH ME?
BECAUSE YOU WANTED ME TO. AND I WANTED TO KNOW WHY.
NOW I KNOW.
DON'T TALK TO ME ABOUT MY MOTHER AGAIN.

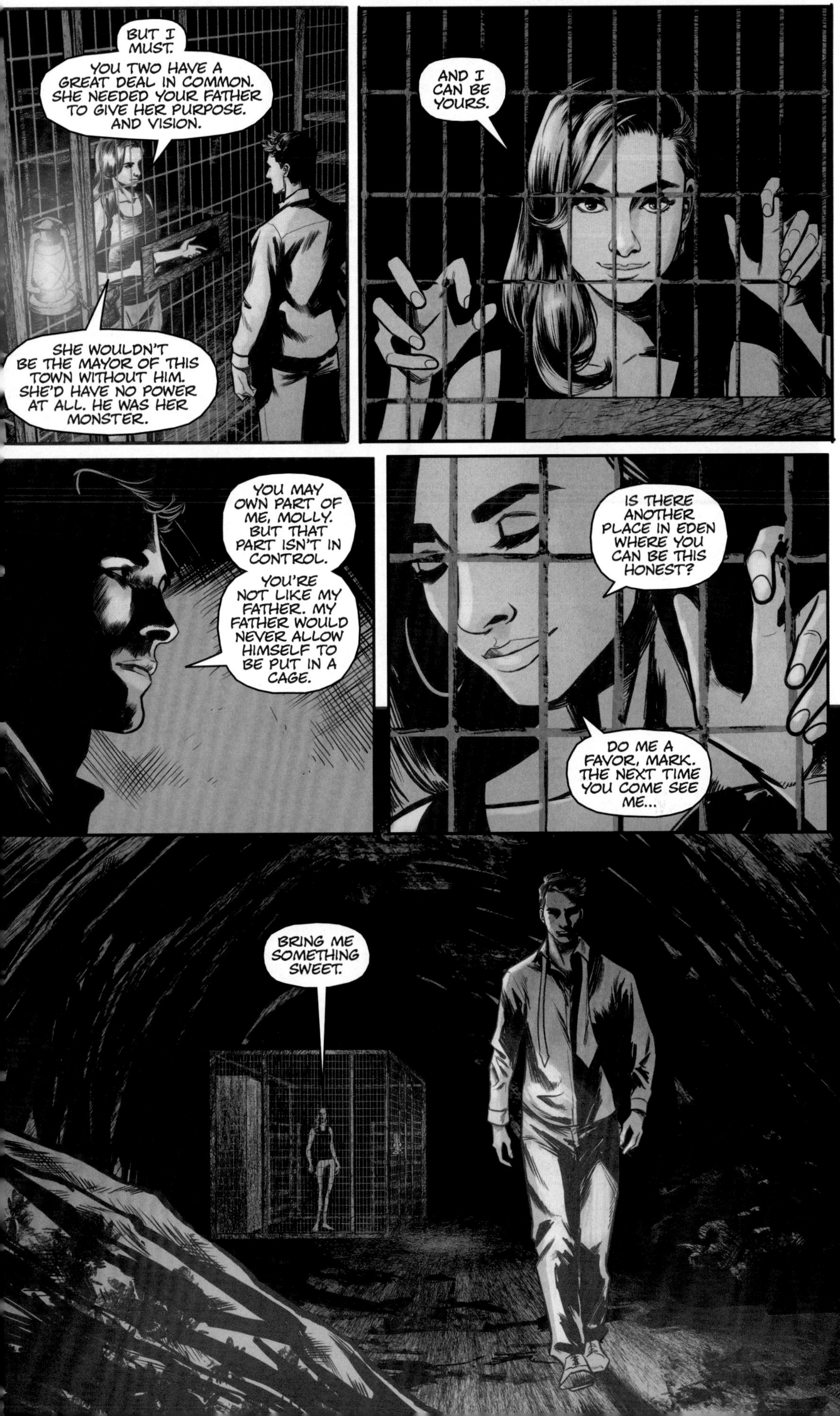
BUT I MUST.
YOU TWO HAVE A GREAT DEAL IN COMMON. SHE NEEDED YOUR FATHER TO GIVE HER PURPOSE. AND VISION.
SHE WOULDN'T BE THE MAYOR OF THIS TOWN WITHOUT HIM. SHE'D HAVE NO POWER AT ALL. HE WAS HER MONSTER.
AND I CAN BE YOURS.
YOU MAY OWN PART OF ME, MOLLY. BUT THAT PART ISN'T IN CONTROL.
YOU'RE NOT LIKE MY FATHER. MY FATHER WOULD NEVER ALLOW HIMSELF TO BE PUT IN A CAGE.
IS THERE ANOTHER PLACE IN EDEN WHERE YOU CAN BE THIS HONEST?
DO ME A FAVOR, MARK. THE NEXT TIME YOU COME SEE ME...
BRING ME SOMETHING SWEET.

YOU WANTED TO SEE ME, BIG?

YOU ALONE?

YES.

THEN I'LL PUT DOWN MY ACT.

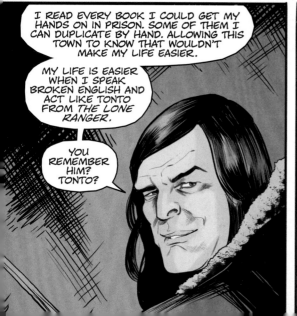

I READ EVERY BOOK I COULD GET MY HANDS ON IN PRISON. SOME OF THEM I CAN DUPLICATE BY HAND. ALLOWING THIS TOWN TO KNOW THAT WOULDN'T MAKE MY LIFE EASIER.

MY LIFE IS EASIER WHEN I SPEAK BROKEN ENGLISH AND ACT LIKE TONTO FROM *THE LONE RANGER*.

YOU REMEMBER HIM? TONTO?

NEVER BEEN A FAN OF *THE LONE RANGER*.

DON'T LIKE COPS.

WHY'D YOU CALL ME HERE, BIG?

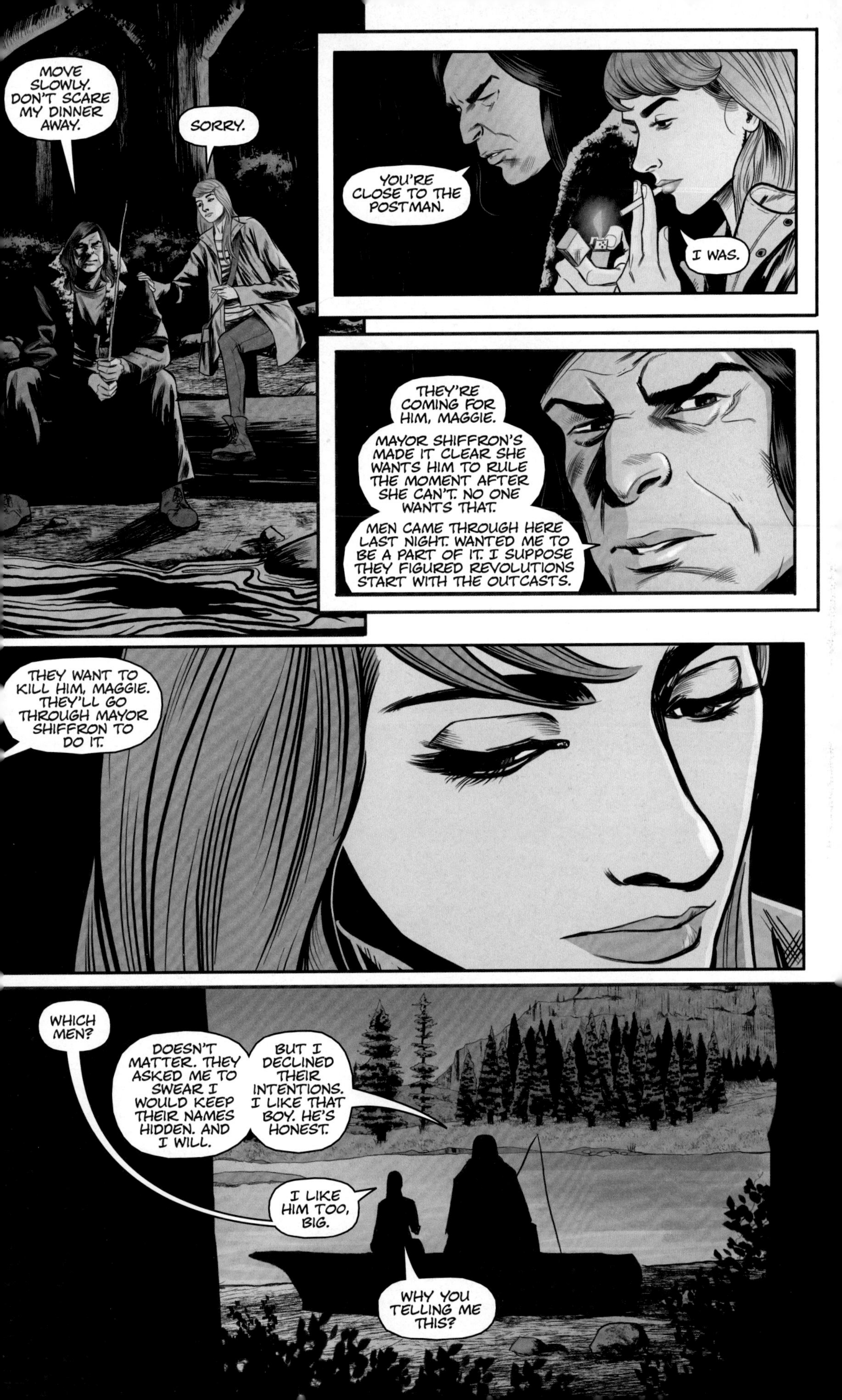
MOVE SLOWLY. DON'T SCARE MY DINNER AWAY.
SORRY.
YOU'RE CLOSE TO THE POSTMAN.
I WAS.
THEY'RE COMING FOR HIM, MAGGIE.
MAYOR SHIFFRON'S MADE IT CLEAR SHE WANTS HIM TO RULE THE MOMENT AFTER SHE CAN'T. NO ONE WANTS THAT.
MEN CAME THROUGH HERE LAST NIGHT. WANTED ME TO BE A PART OF IT. I SUPPOSE THEY FIGURED REVOLUTIONS START WITH THE OUTCASTS.
THEY WANT TO KILL HIM, MAGGIE. THEY'LL GO THROUGH MAYOR SHIFFRON TO DO IT.
WHICH MEN?
DOESN'T MATTER. THEY ASKED ME TO SWEAR I WOULD KEEP THEIR NAMES HIDDEN. AND I WILL.
BUT I DECLINED THEIR INTENTIONS. I LIKE THAT BOY. HE'S HONEST.
I LIKE HIM TOO, BIG.
WHY YOU TELLING ME THIS?

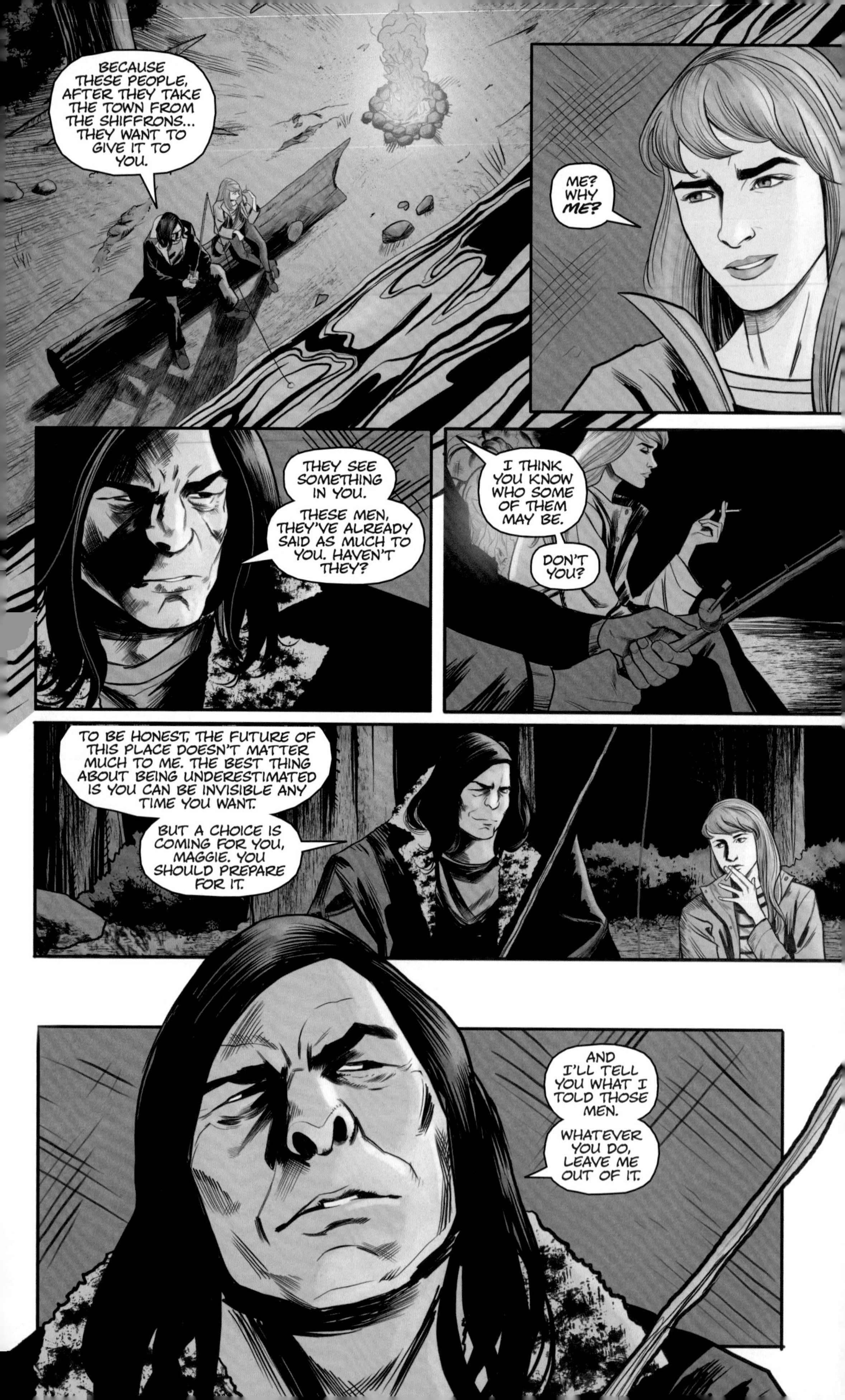

BECAUSE THESE PEOPLE, AFTER THEY TAKE THE TOWN FROM THE SHIFFRONS... THEY WANT TO GIVE IT TO YOU.
ME? WHY *ME?*
THEY SEE SOMETHING IN YOU.
THESE MEN, THEY'VE ALREADY SAID AS MUCH TO YOU. HAVEN'T THEY?
I THINK YOU KNOW WHO SOME OF THEM MAY BE.
DON'T YOU?
TO BE HONEST, THE FUTURE OF THIS PLACE DOESN'T MATTER MUCH TO ME. THE BEST THING ABOUT BEING UNDERESTIMATED IS YOU CAN BE INVISIBLE ANY TIME YOU WANT.
BUT A CHOICE IS COMING FOR YOU, MAGGIE. YOU SHOULD PREPARE FOR IT.
AND I'LL TELL YOU WHAT I TOLD THOSE MEN.
WHATEVER YOU DO, LEAVE ME OUT OF IT.

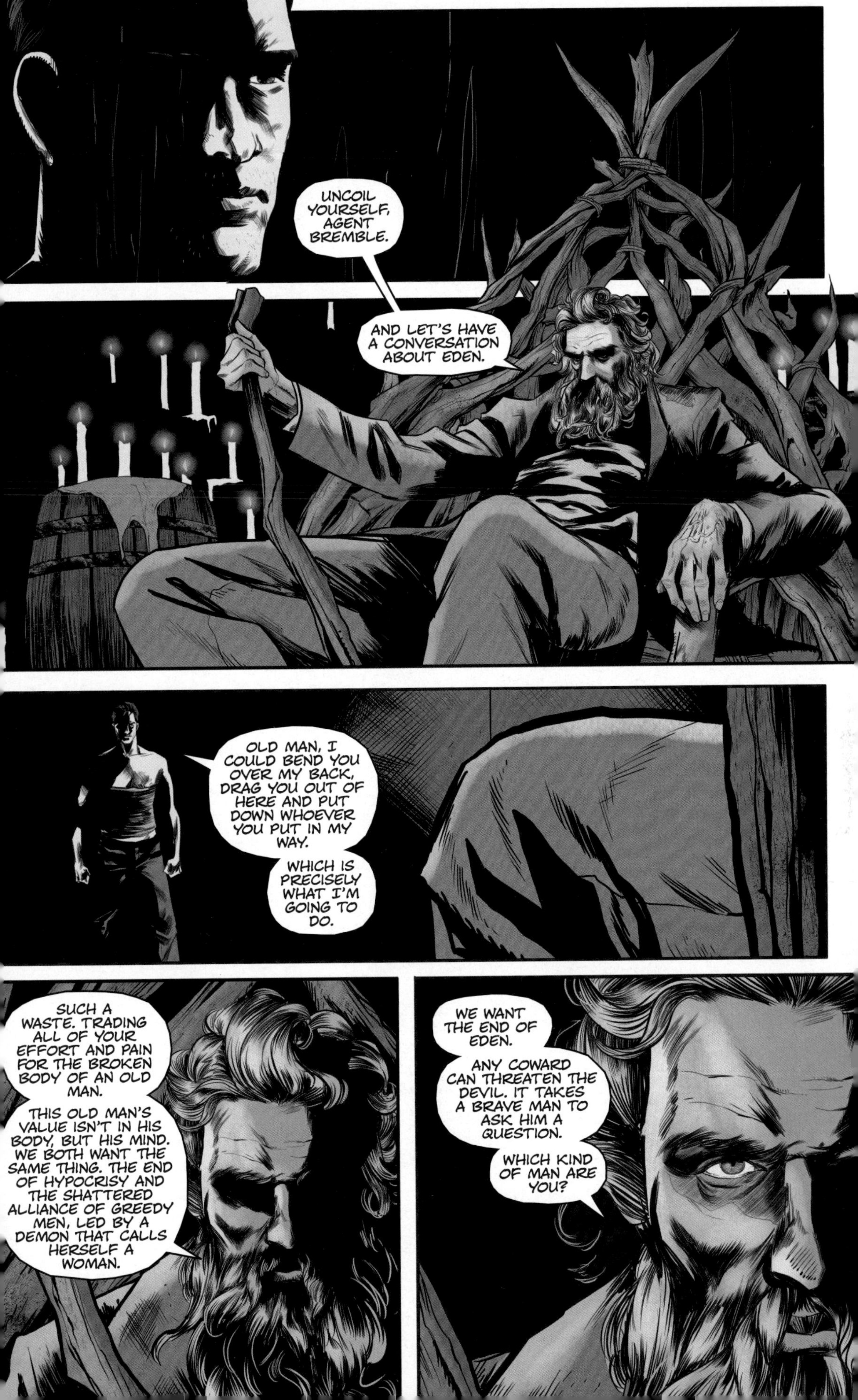
UNCOIL YOURSELF, AGENT BREMBLE.
AND LET'S HAVE A CONVERSATION ABOUT EDEN.
OLD MAN, I COULD BEND YOU OVER MY BACK, DRAG YOU OUT OF HERE AND PUT DOWN WHOEVER YOU PUT IN MY WAY.
WHICH IS PRECISELY WHAT I'M GOING TO DO.
SUCH A WASTE. TRADING ALL OF YOUR EFFORT AND PAIN FOR THE BROKEN BODY OF AN OLD MAN.
THIS OLD MAN'S VALUE ISN'T IN HIS BODY, BUT HIS MIND. WE BOTH WANT THE SAME THING. THE END OF HYPOCRISY AND THE SHATTERED ALLIANCE OF GREEDY MEN, LED BY A DEMON THAT CALLS HERSELF A WOMAN.
WE WANT THE END OF EDEN.
ANY COWARD CAN THREATEN THE DEVIL. IT TAKES A BRAVE MAN TO ASK HIM A QUESTION.
WHICH KIND OF MAN ARE YOU?

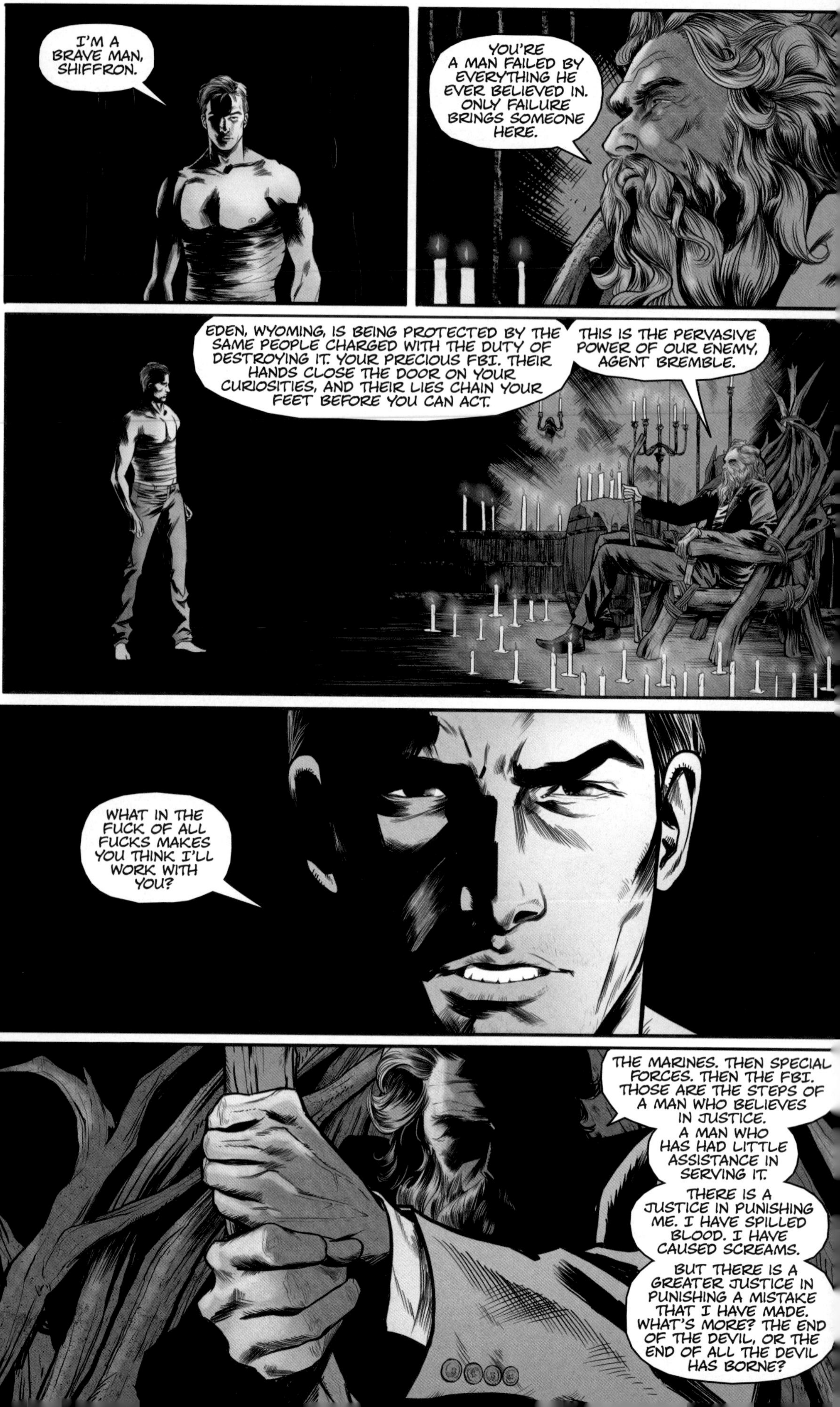
I'M A BRAVE MAN, SHIFFRON.
YOU'RE A MAN FAILED BY EVERYTHING HE EVER BELIEVED IN. ONLY FAILURE BRINGS SOMEONE HERE.
EDEN, WYOMING, IS BEING PROTECTED BY THE SAME PEOPLE CHARGED WITH THE DUTY OF DESTROYING IT. YOUR PRECIOUS FBI. THEIR HANDS CLOSE THE DOOR ON YOUR CURIOSITIES, AND THEIR LIES CHAIN YOUR FEET BEFORE YOU CAN ACT.
THIS IS THE PERVASIVE POWER OF OUR ENEMY, AGENT BREMBLE.
WHAT IN THE FUCK OF ALL FUCKS MAKES YOU THINK I'LL WORK WITH YOU?
THE MARINES. THEN SPECIAL FORCES. THEN THE FBI. THOSE ARE THE STEPS OF A MAN WHO BELIEVES IN JUSTICE.
A MAN WHO HAS HAD LITTLE ASSISTANCE IN SERVING IT.
THERE IS A JUSTICE IN PUNISHING ME. I HAVE SPILLED BLOOD. I HAVE CAUSED SCREAMS.
BUT THERE IS A GREATER JUSTICE IN PUNISHING A MISTAKE THAT I HAVE MADE. WHAT'S MORE? THE END OF THE DEVIL, OR THE END OF ALL THE DEVIL HAS BORNE?

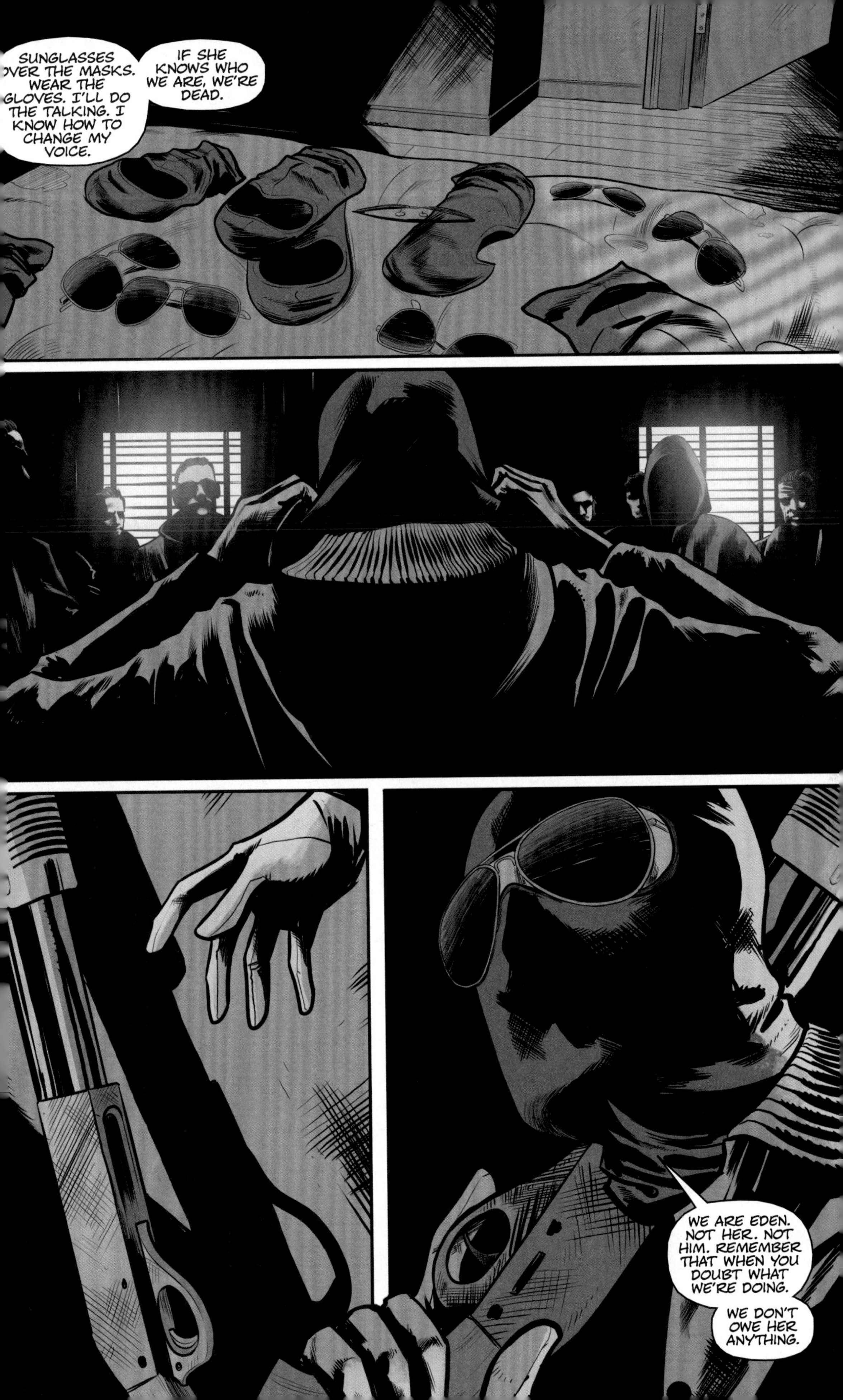
SUNGLASSES OVER THE MASKS. WEAR THE GLOVES. I'LL DO THE TALKING. I KNOW HOW TO CHANGE MY VOICE.
IF SHE KNOWS WHO WE ARE, WE'RE DEAD.
WE ARE EDEN. NOT HER. NOT HIM. REMEMBER THAT WHEN YOU DOUBT WHAT WE'RE DOING.
WE DON'T OWE HER ANYTHING.

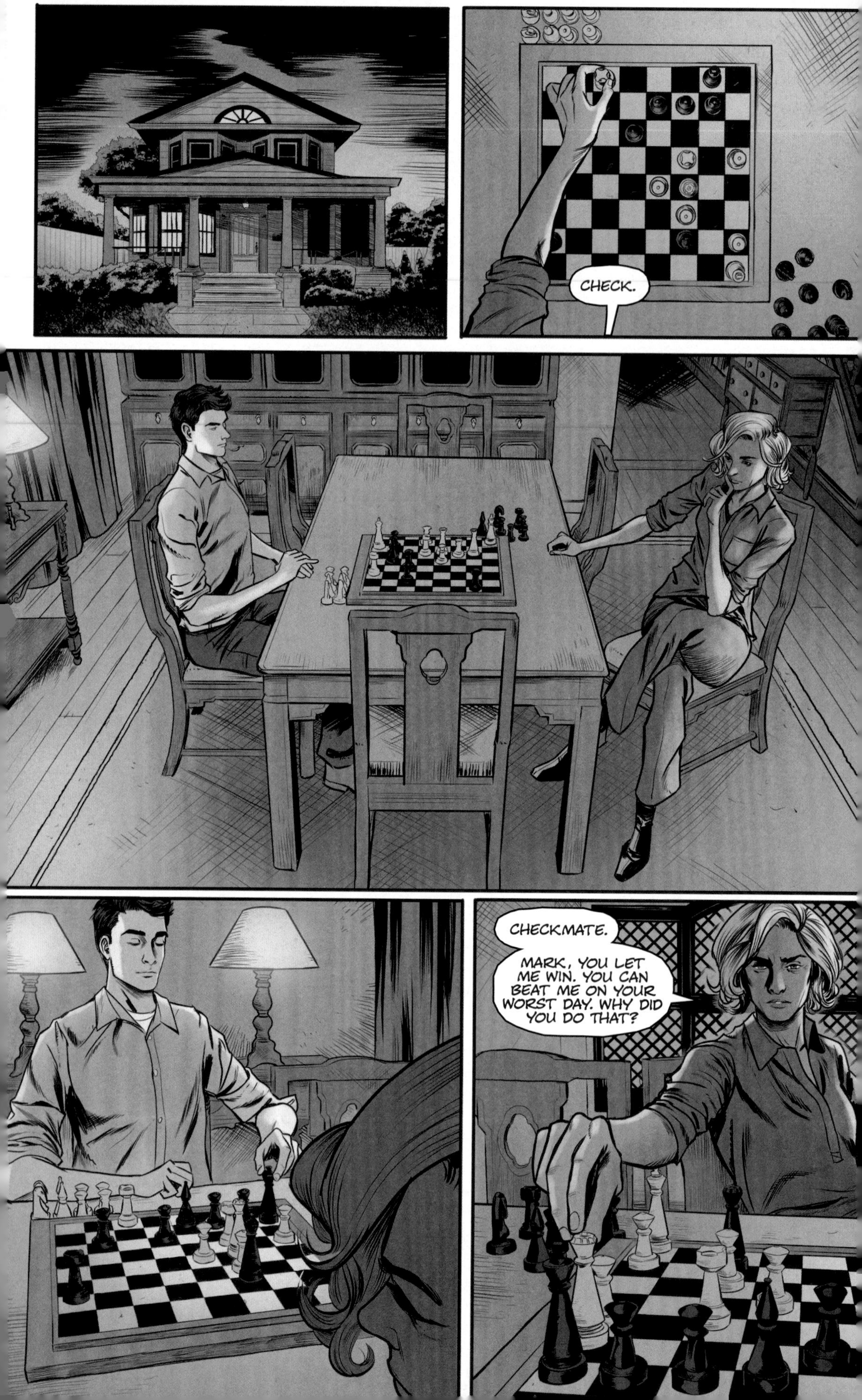
CHECK.
CHECKMATE.
MARK, YOU LET ME WIN. YOU CAN BEAT ME ON YOUR WORST DAY. WHY DID YOU DO THAT?

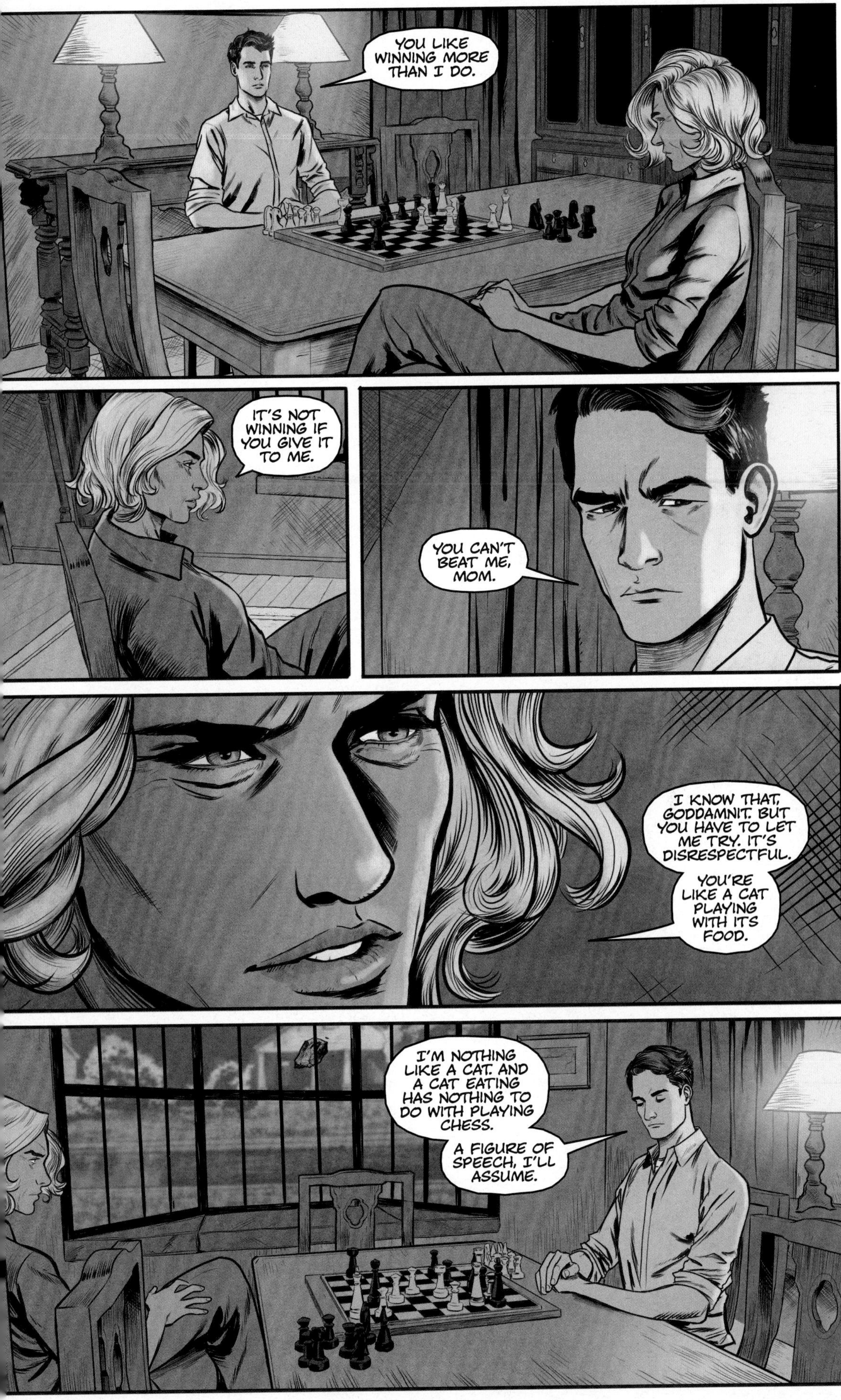
YOU LIKE WINNING MORE THAN I DO.
IT'S NOT WINNING IF YOU GIVE IT TO ME.
YOU CAN'T BEAT ME, MOM.
I KNOW THAT, GODDAMNIT. BUT YOU HAVE TO LET ME TRY. IT'S DISRESPECTFUL.
YOU'RE LIKE A CAT PLAYING WITH ITS FOOD.
I'M NOTHING LIKE A CAT. AND A CAT EATING HAS NOTHING TO DO WITH PLAYING CHESS.
A FIGURE OF SPEECH, I'LL ASSUME.

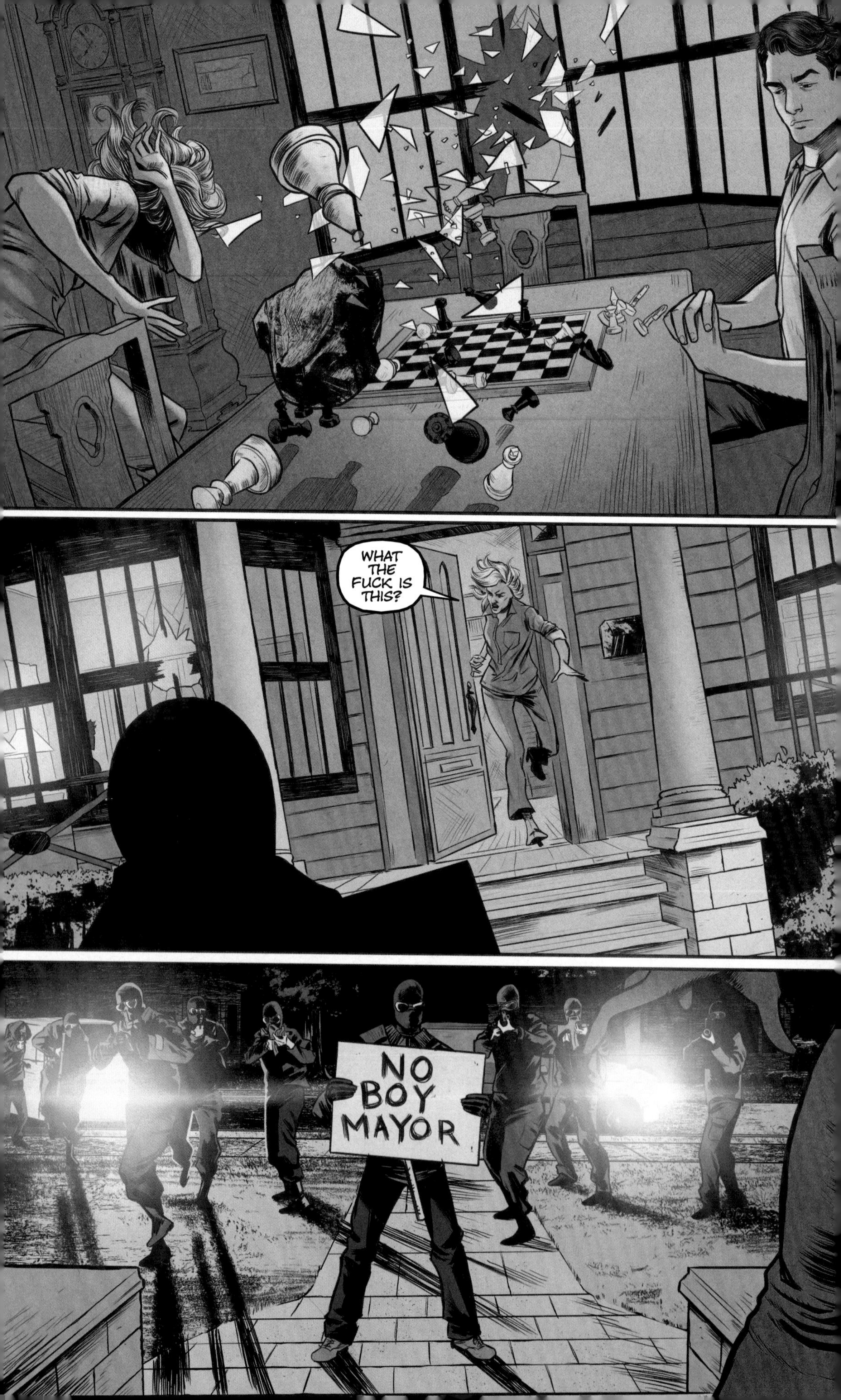
WHAT THE FUCK IS THIS?
NO BOY MAYOR

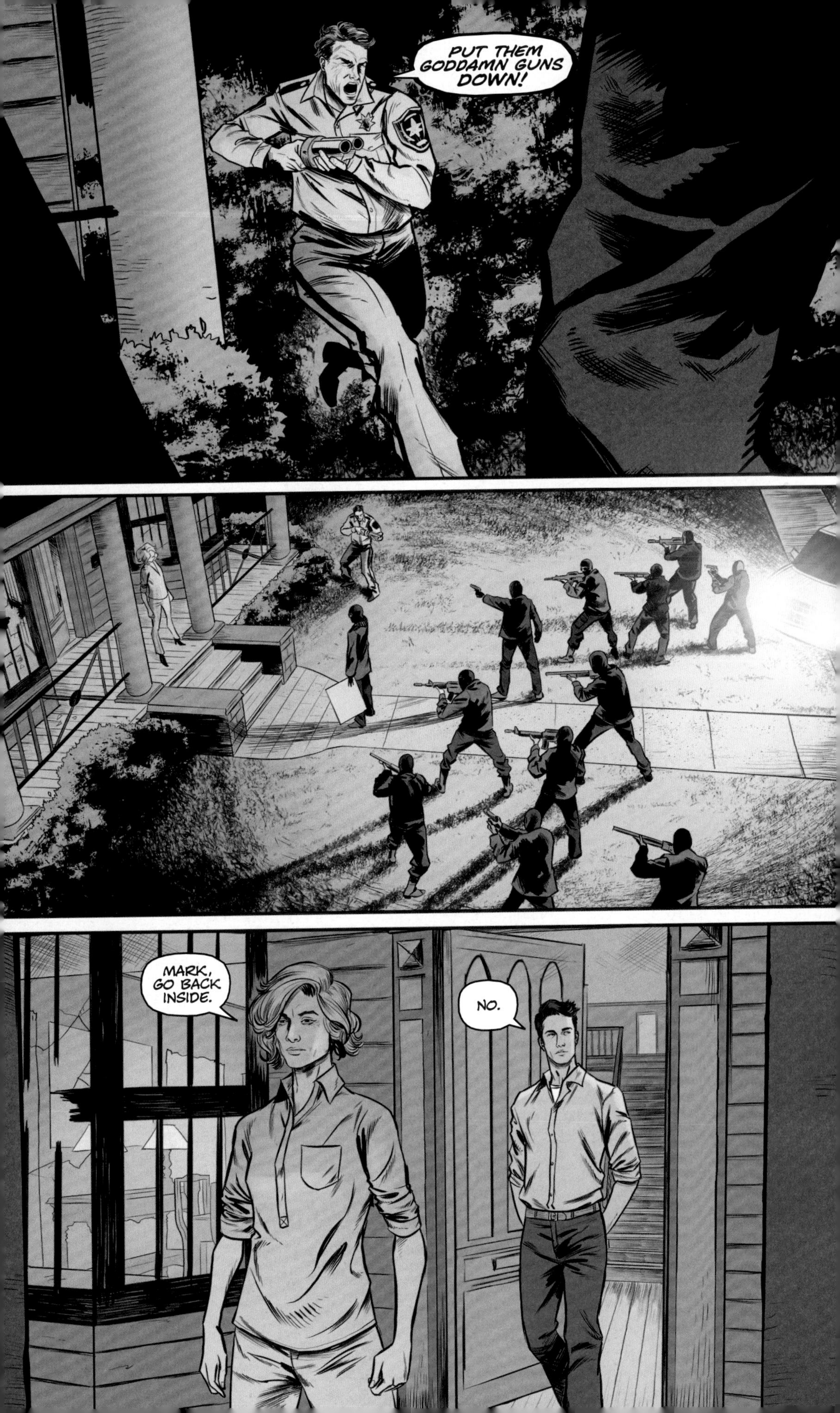
PUT THEM GODDAMN GUNS DOWN!
MARK, GO BACK INSIDE.
NO.

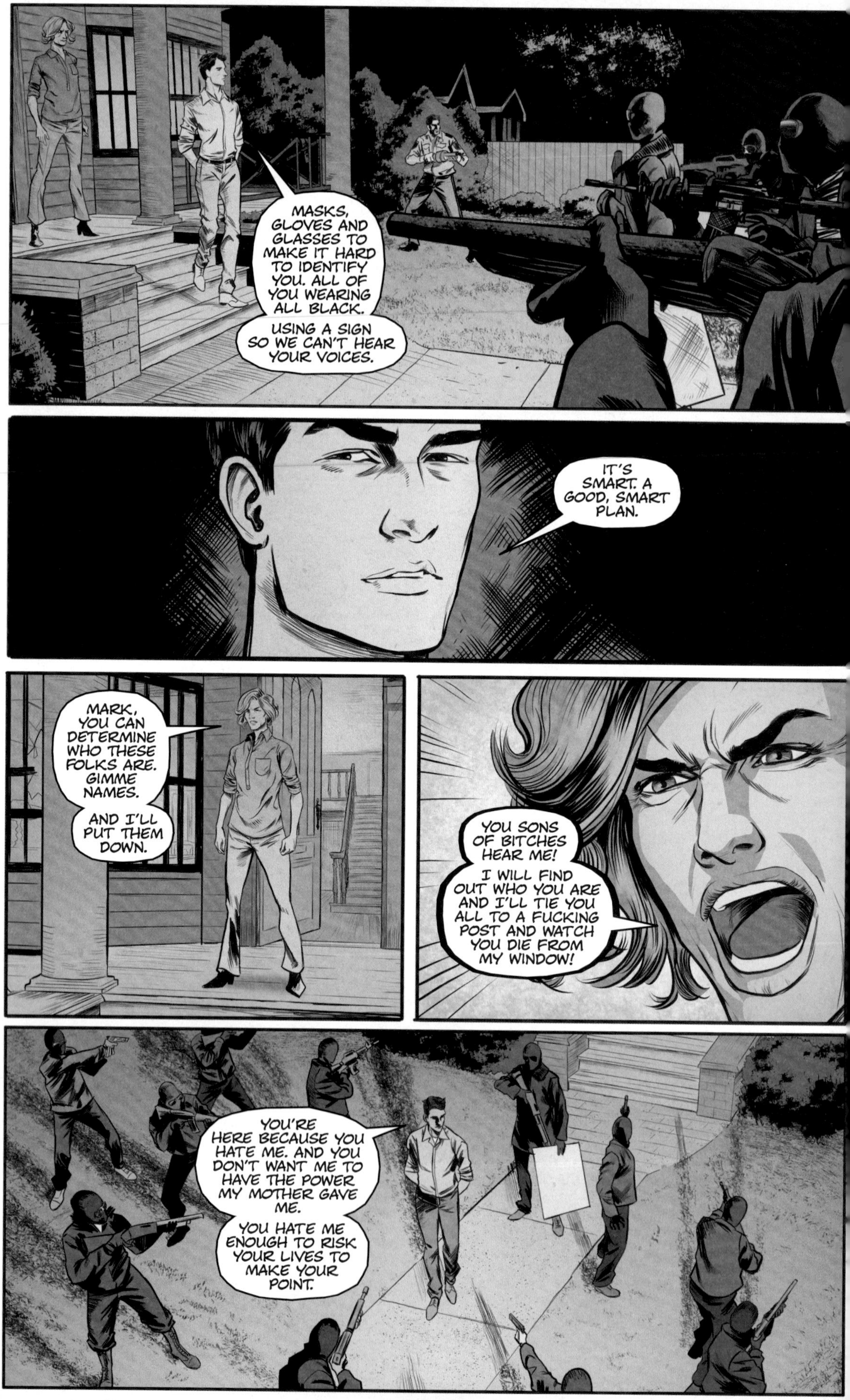
MASKS, GLOVES AND GLASSES TO MAKE IT HARD TO IDENTIFY YOU. ALL OF YOU WEARING ALL BLACK.
USING A SIGN SO WE CAN'T HEAR YOUR VOICES.
IT'S SMART. A GOOD, SMART PLAN.
MARK, YOU CAN DETERMINE WHO THESE FOLKS ARE. GIMME NAMES.
AND I'LL PUT THEM DOWN.
YOU SONS OF BITCHES HEAR ME!
I WILL FIND OUT WHO YOU ARE AND I'LL TIE YOU ALL TO A FUCKING POST AND WATCH YOU DIE FROM MY WINDOW!
YOU'RE HERE BECAUSE YOU HATE ME. AND YOU DON'T WANT ME TO HAVE THE POWER MY MOTHER GAVE ME.
YOU HATE ME ENOUGH TO RISK YOUR LIVES TO MAKE YOUR POINT.

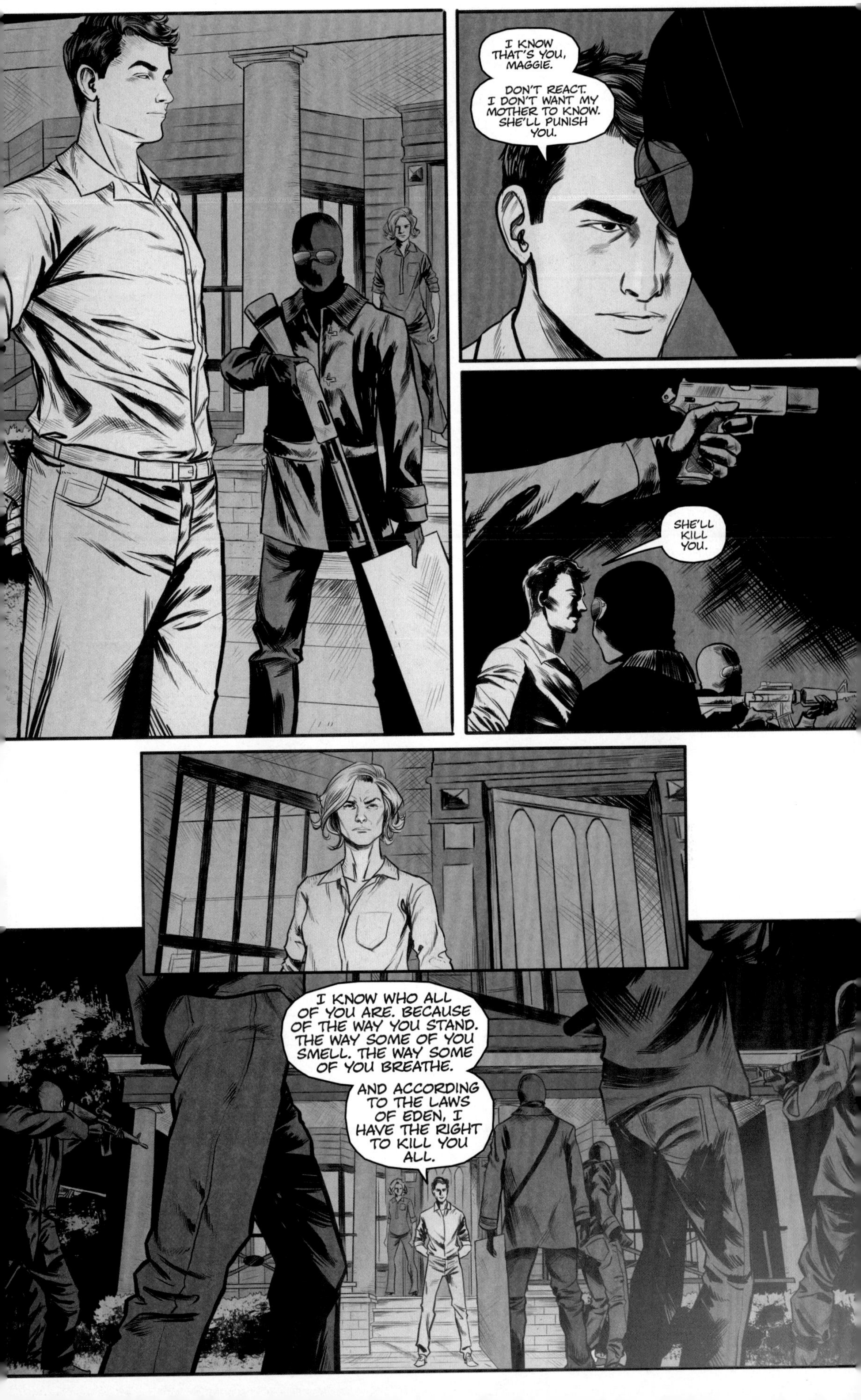
I KNOW THAT'S YOU, MAGGIE.
DON'T REACT. I DON'T WANT MY MOTHER TO KNOW. SHE'LL PUNISH YOU.
SHE'LL KILL YOU.
I KNOW WHO ALL OF YOU ARE. BECAUSE OF THE WAY YOU STAND. THE WAY SOME OF YOU SMELL. THE WAY SOME OF YOU BREATHE.
AND ACCORDING TO THE LAWS OF EDEN, I HAVE THE RIGHT TO KILL YOU ALL.

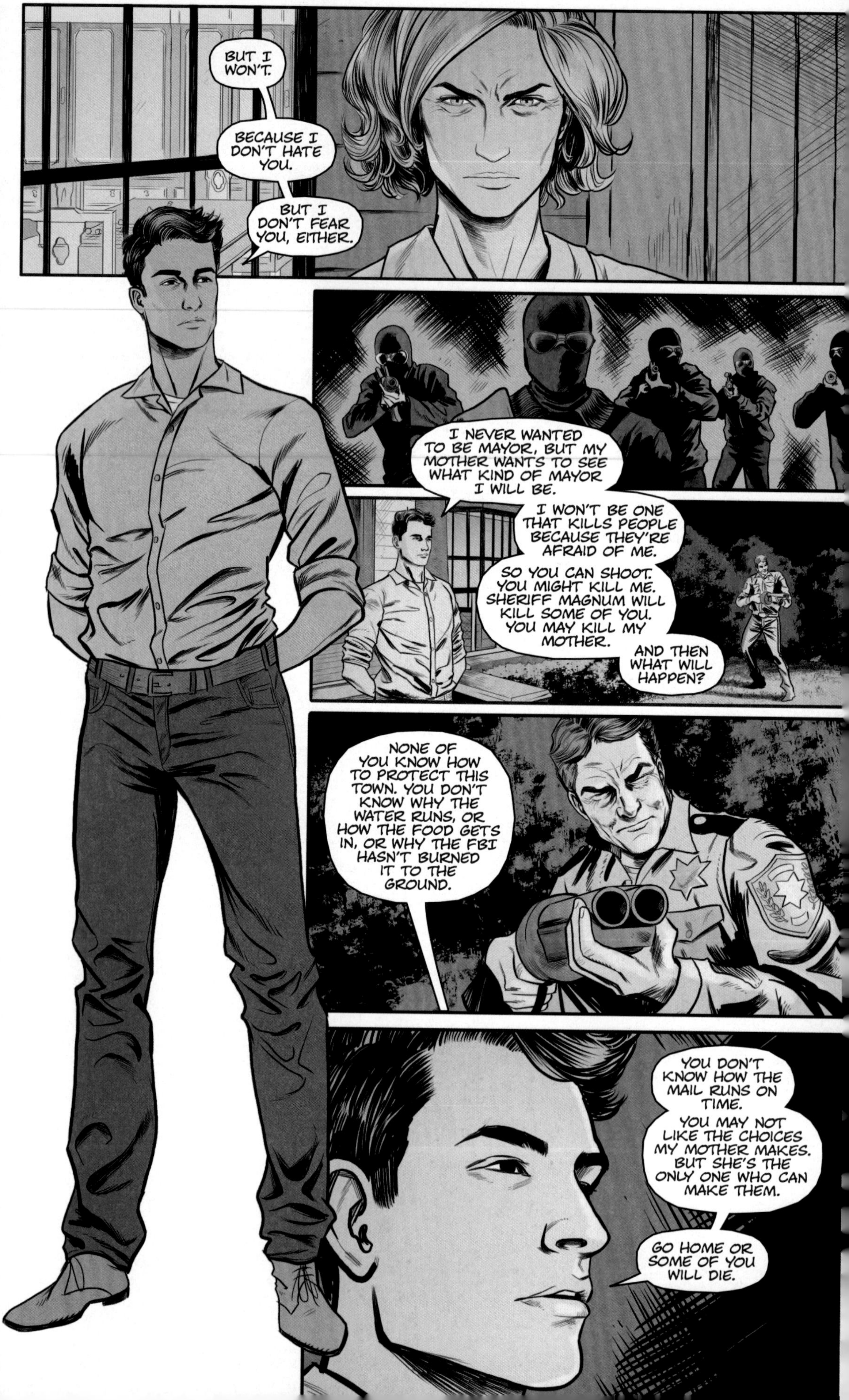
BUT I WON'T.
BECAUSE I DON'T HATE YOU.
BUT I DON'T FEAR YOU, EITHER.
I NEVER WANTED TO BE MAYOR, BUT MY MOTHER WANTS TO SEE WHAT KIND OF MAYOR I WILL BE.
I WON'T BE ONE THAT KILLS PEOPLE BECAUSE THEY'RE AFRAID OF ME.
SO YOU CAN SHOOT. YOU MIGHT KILL ME. SHERIFF MAGNUM WILL KILL SOME OF YOU. YOU MAY KILL MY MOTHER.
AND THEN WHAT WILL HAPPEN?
NONE OF YOU KNOW HOW TO PROTECT THIS TOWN. YOU DON'T KNOW WHY THE WATER RUNS, OR HOW THE FOOD GETS IN, OR WHY THE FBI HASN'T BURNED IT TO THE GROUND.
YOU DON'T KNOW HOW THE MAIL RUNS ON TIME.
YOU MAY NOT LIKE THE CHOICES MY MOTHER MAKES. BUT SHE'S THE ONLY ONE WHO CAN MAKE THEM.
GO HOME OR SOME OF YOU WILL DIE.

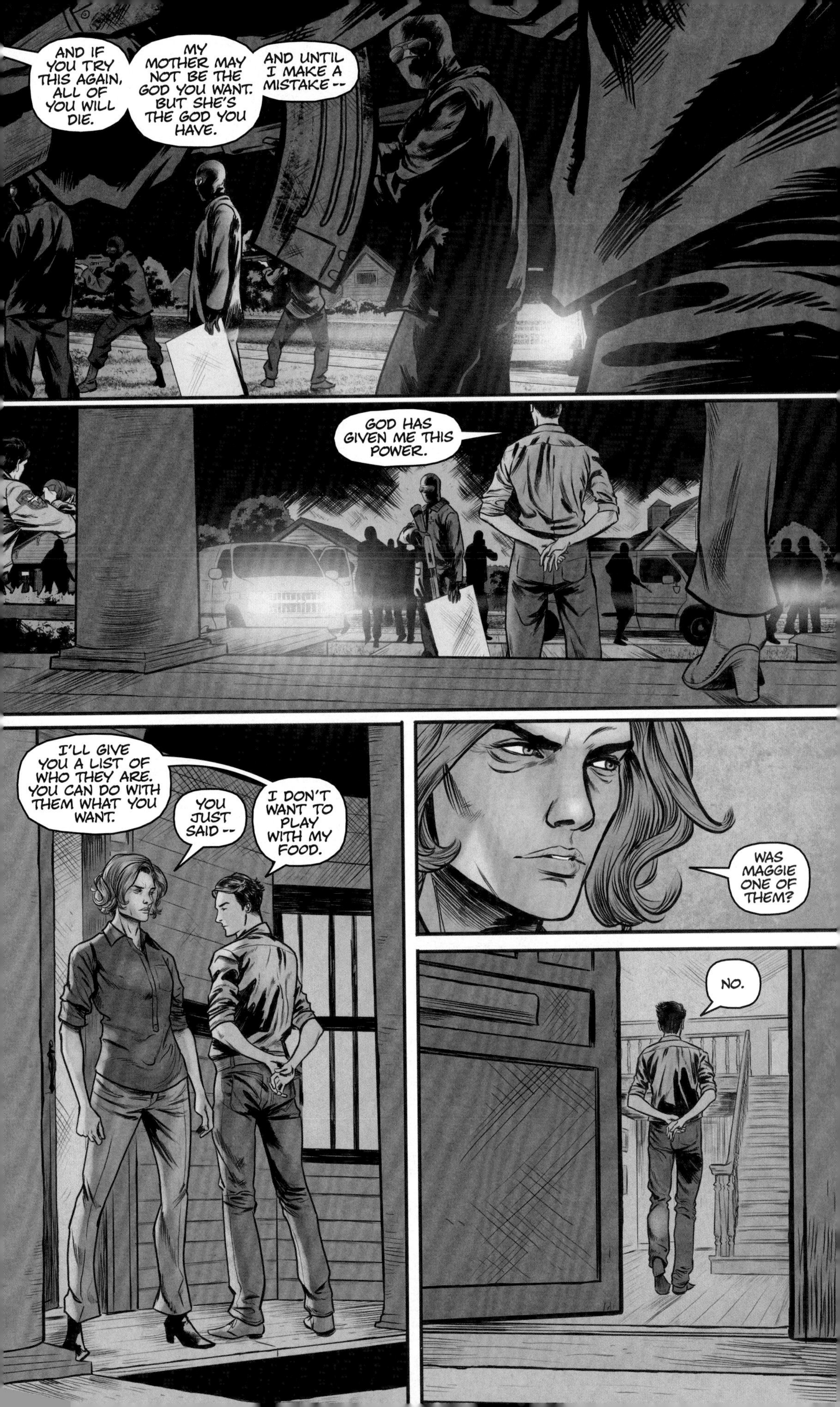
AND IF YOU TRY THIS AGAIN, ALL OF YOU WILL DIE.
MY MOTHER MAY NOT BE THE GOD YOU WANT. BUT SHE'S THE GOD YOU HAVE.
AND UNTIL I MAKE A MISTAKE --
GOD HAS GIVEN ME THIS POWER.
I'LL GIVE YOU A LIST OF WHO THEY ARE. YOU CAN DO WITH THEM WHAT YOU WANT.
YOU JUST SAID --
I DON'T WANT TO PLAY WITH MY FOOD.
WAS MAGGIE ONE OF THEM?
NO.

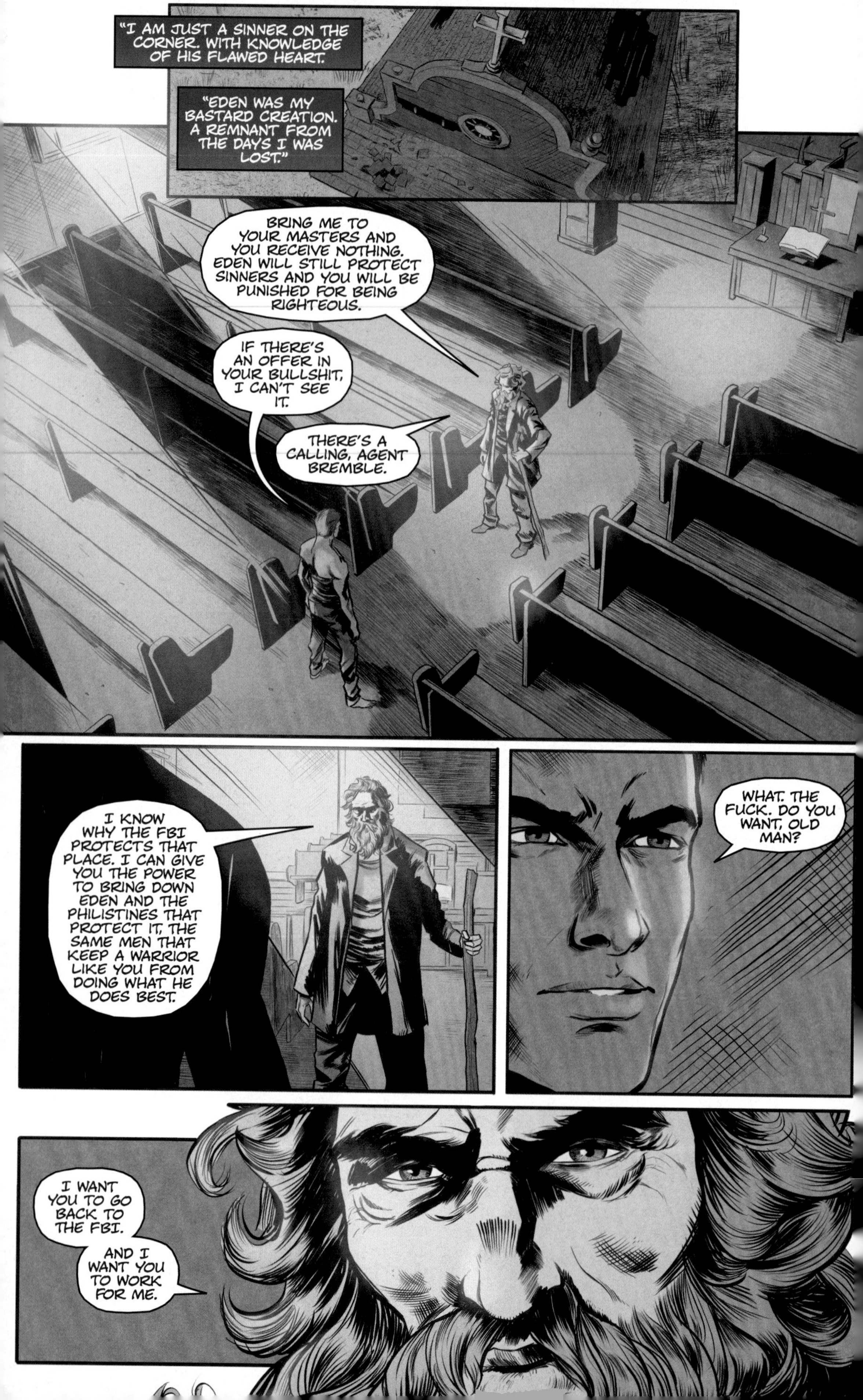
"I AM JUST A SINNER ON THE CORNER. WITH KNOWLEDGE OF HIS FLAWED HEART.
"EDEN WAS MY BASTARD CREATION. A REMNANT FROM THE DAYS I WAS LOST."
BRING ME TO YOUR MASTERS AND YOU RECEIVE NOTHING. EDEN WILL STILL PROTECT SINNERS AND YOU WILL BE PUNISHED FOR BEING RIGHTEOUS.
IF THERE'S AN OFFER IN YOUR BULLSHIT, I CAN'T SEE IT.
THERE'S A CALLING, AGENT BREMBLE.
I KNOW WHY THE FBI PROTECTS THAT PLACE. I CAN GIVE YOU THE POWER TO BRING DOWN EDEN AND THE PHILISTINES THAT PROTECT IT, THE SAME MEN THAT KEEP A WARRIOR LIKE YOU FROM DOING WHAT HE DOES BEST.
WHAT. THE FUCK. DO YOU WANT, OLD MAN?
I WANT YOU TO GO BACK TO THE FBI.
AND I WANT YOU TO WORK FOR ME.

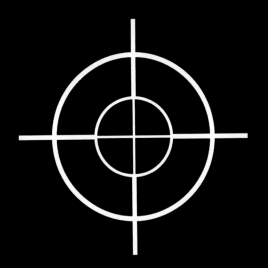

# Chapter 20

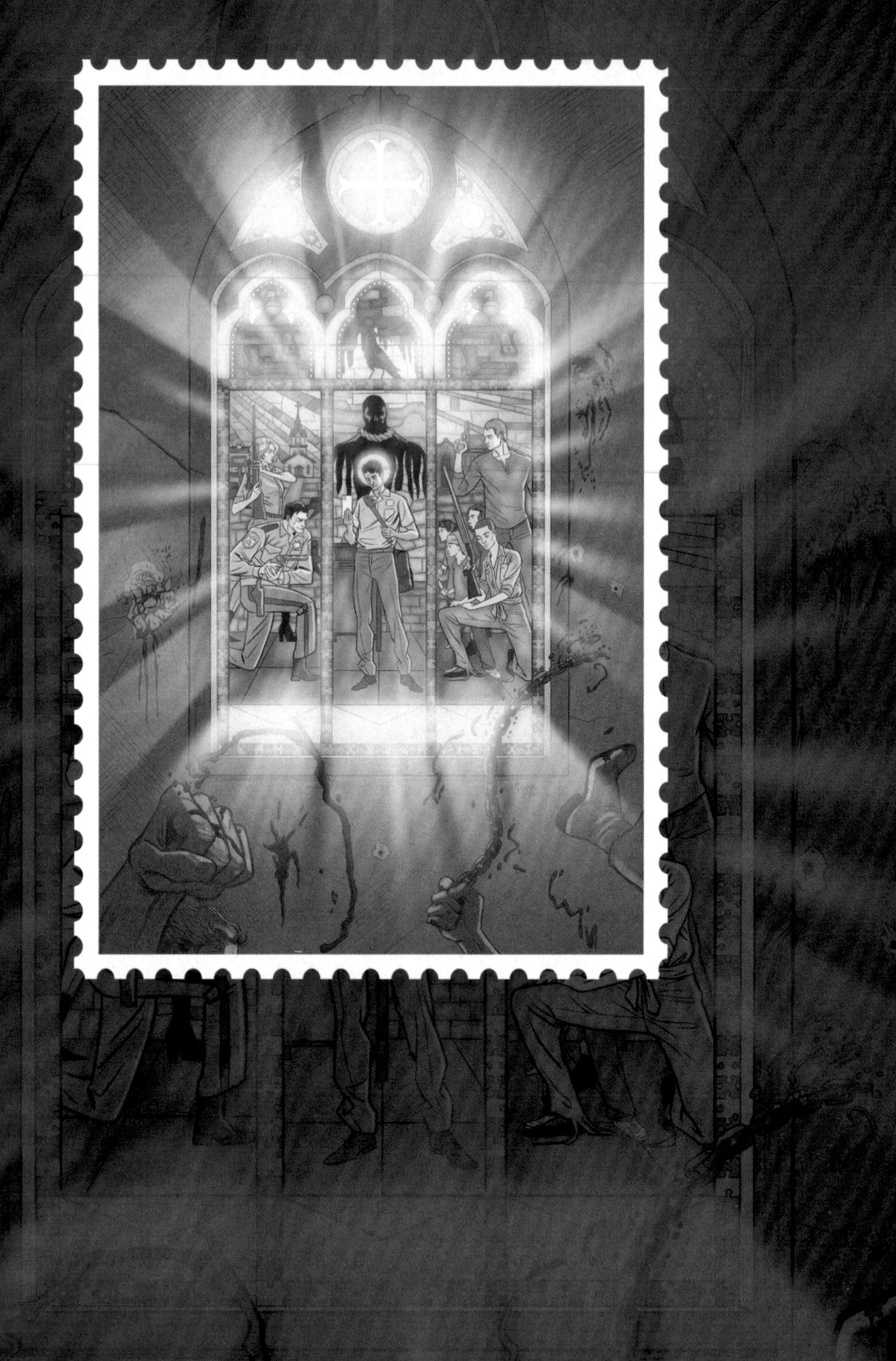

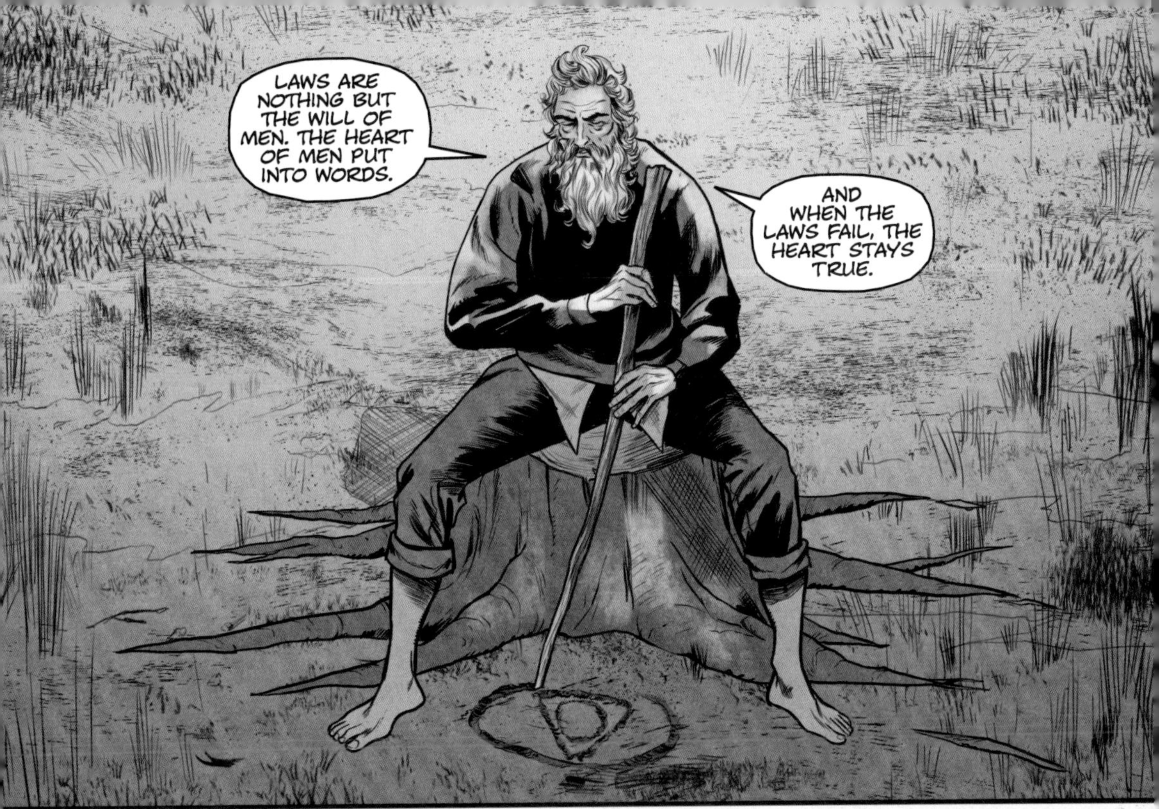
LAWS ARE NOTHING BUT THE WILL OF MEN. THE HEART OF MEN PUT INTO WORDS.
AND WHEN THE LAWS FAIL, THE HEART STAYS TRUE.

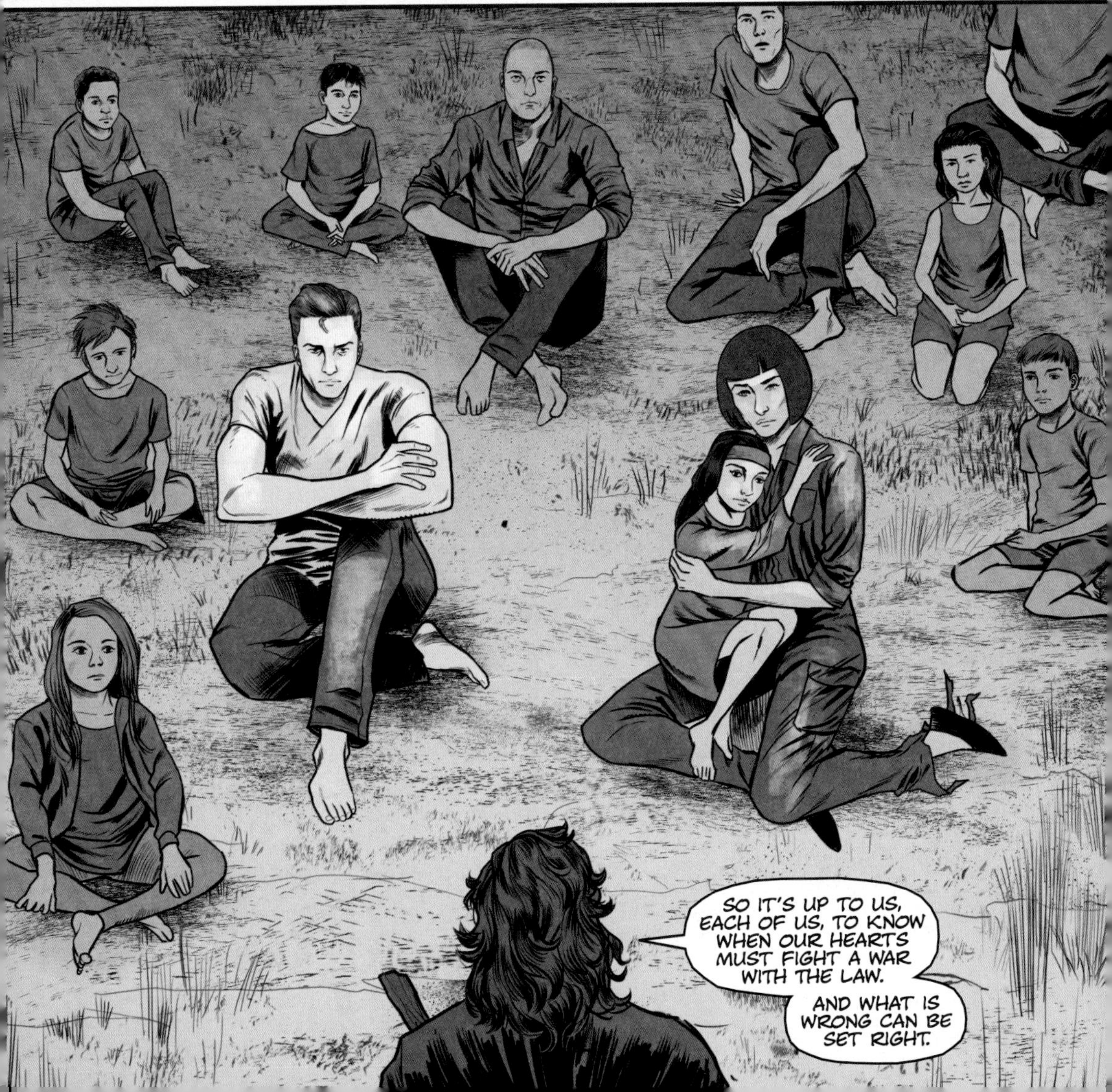
SO IT'S UP TO US, EACH OF US, TO KNOW WHEN OUR HEARTS MUST FIGHT A WAR WITH THE LAW.
AND WHAT IS WRONG CAN BE SET RIGHT.

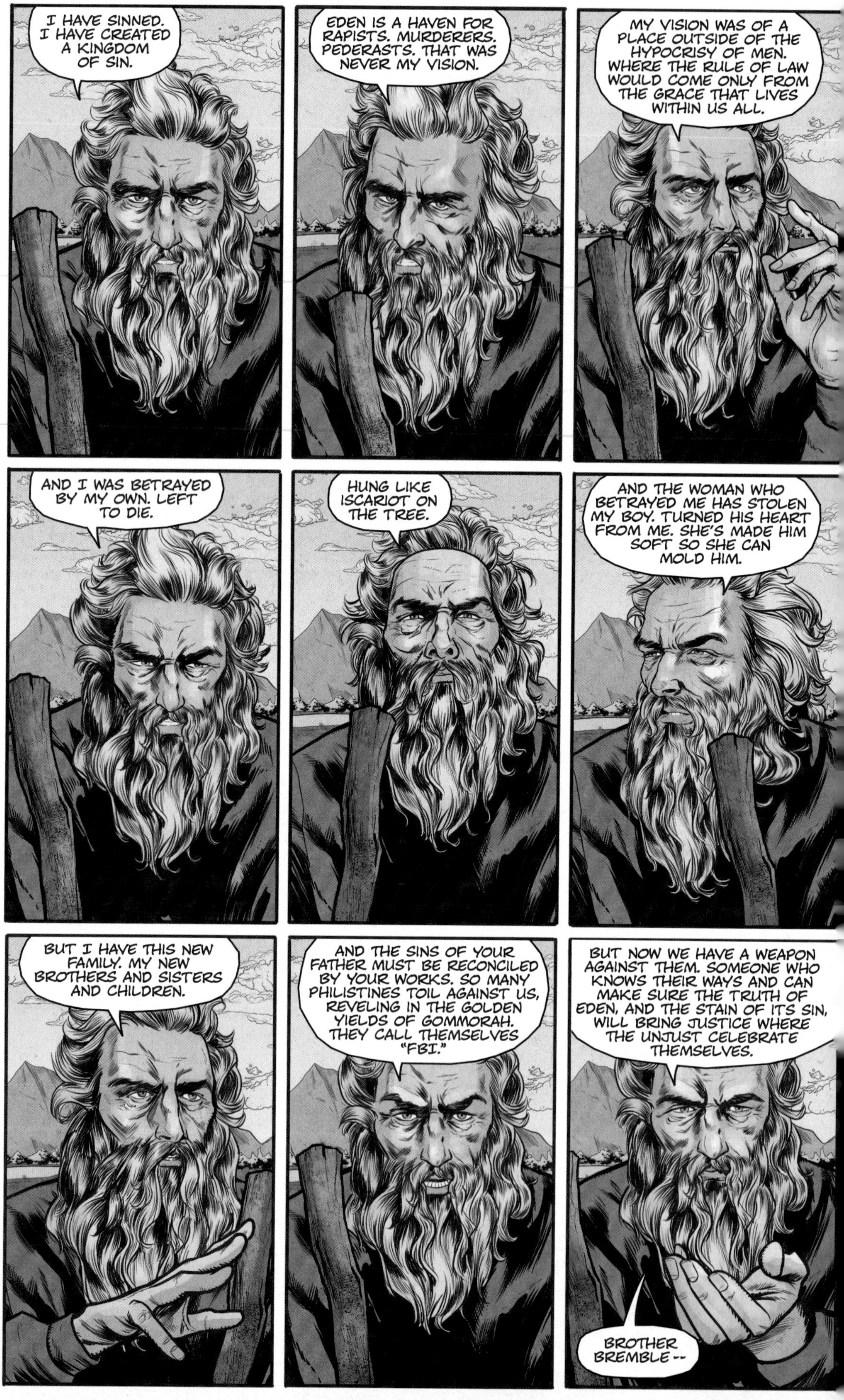
I HAVE SINNED. I HAVE CREATED A KINGDOM OF SIN.
EDEN IS A HAVEN FOR RAPISTS. MURDERERS. PEDERASTS. THAT WAS NEVER MY VISION.
MY VISION WAS OF A PLACE OUTSIDE OF THE HYPOCRISY OF MEN. WHERE THE RULE OF LAW WOULD COME ONLY FROM THE GRACE THAT LIVES WITHIN US ALL.
AND I WAS BETRAYED BY MY OWN. LEFT TO DIE.
HUNG LIKE ISCARIOT ON THE TREE.
AND THE WOMAN WHO BETRAYED ME HAS STOLEN MY BOY. TURNED HIS HEART FROM ME. SHE'S MADE HIM SOFT SO SHE CAN MOLD HIM.
BUT I HAVE THIS NEW FAMILY. MY NEW BROTHERS AND SISTERS AND CHILDREN.
AND THE SINS OF YOUR FATHER MUST BE RECONCILED BY YOUR WORKS. SO MANY PHILISTINES TOIL AGAINST US, REVELING IN THE GOLDEN YIELDS OF GOMMORAH. THEY CALL THEMSELVES "FBI."
BUT NOW WE HAVE A WEAPON AGAINST THEM. SOMEONE WHO KNOWS THEIR WAYS AND CAN MAKE SURE THE TRUTH OF EDEN, AND THE STAIN OF ITS SIN, WILL BRING JUSTICE WHERE THE UNJUST CELEBRATE THEMSELVES.
BROTHER BREMBLE--

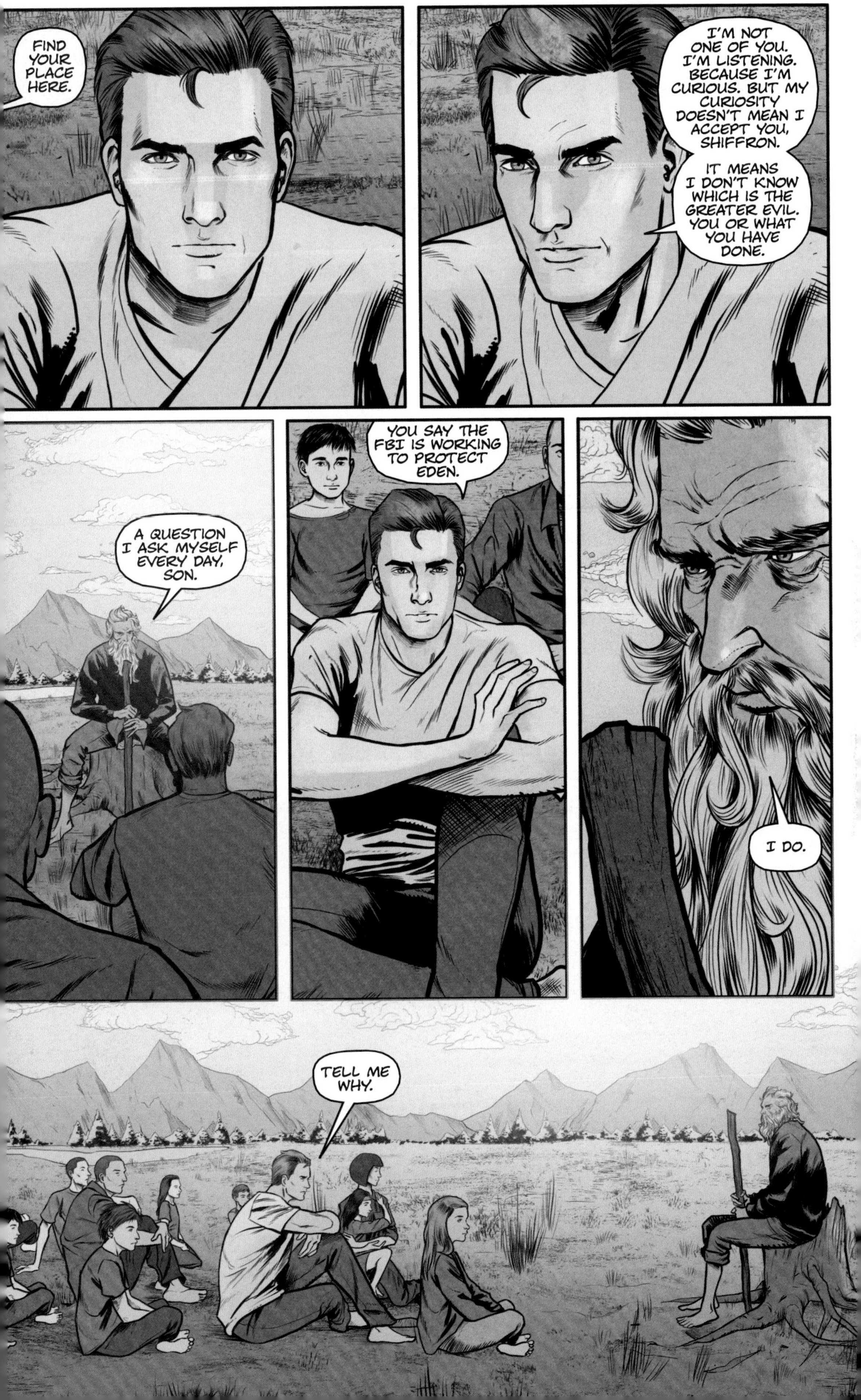
FIND YOUR PLACE HERE.
I'M NOT ONE OF YOU. I'M LISTENING. BECAUSE I'M CURIOUS. BUT MY CURIOSITY DOESN'T MEAN I ACCEPT YOU, SHIFFRON.
IT MEANS I DON'T KNOW WHICH IS THE GREATER EVIL. YOU OR WHAT YOU HAVE DONE.
A QUESTION I ASK MYSELF EVERY DAY, SON.
YOU SAY THE FBI IS WORKING TO PROTECT EDEN.
I DO.
TELL ME WHY.

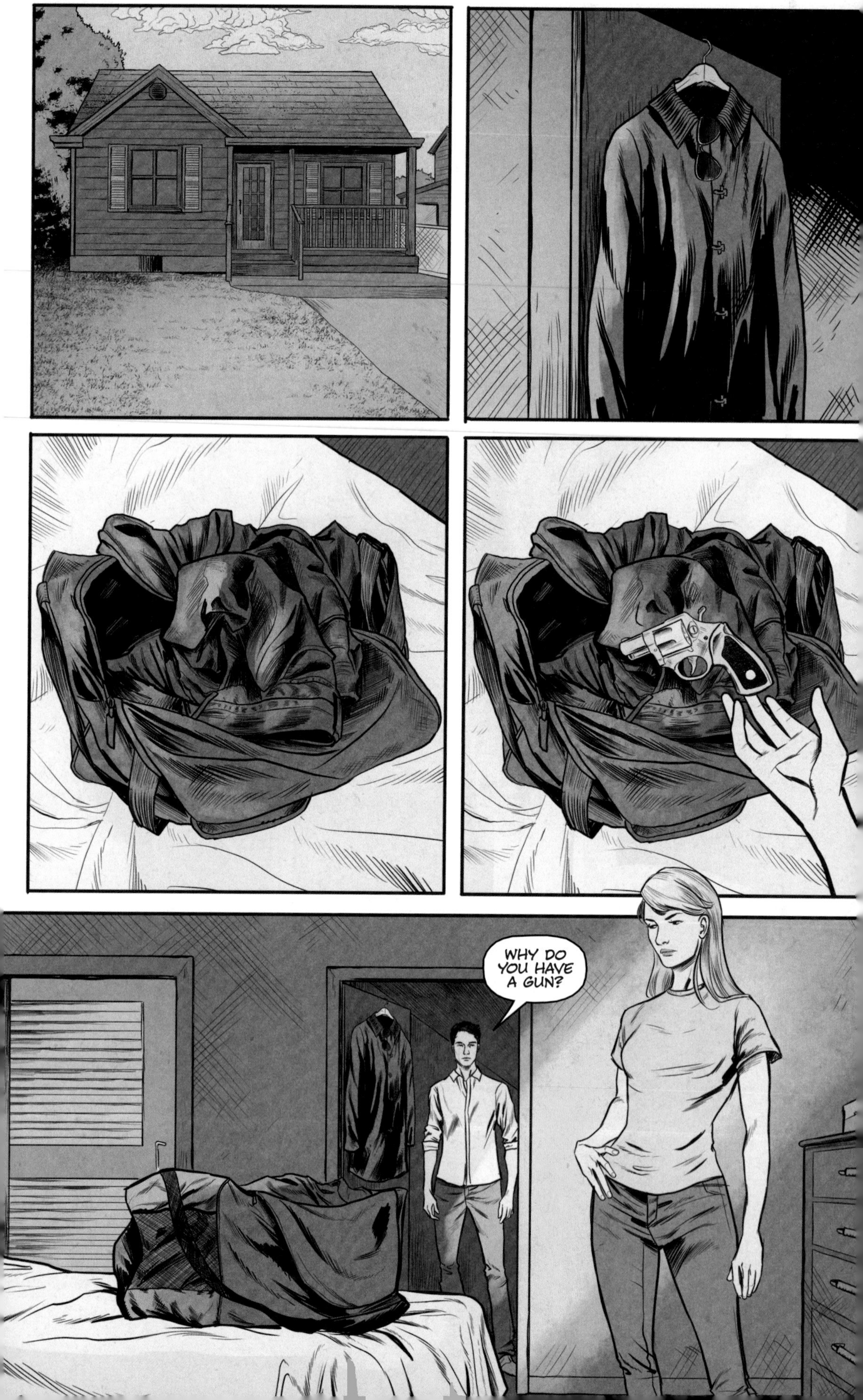
WHY DO YOU HAVE A GUN?

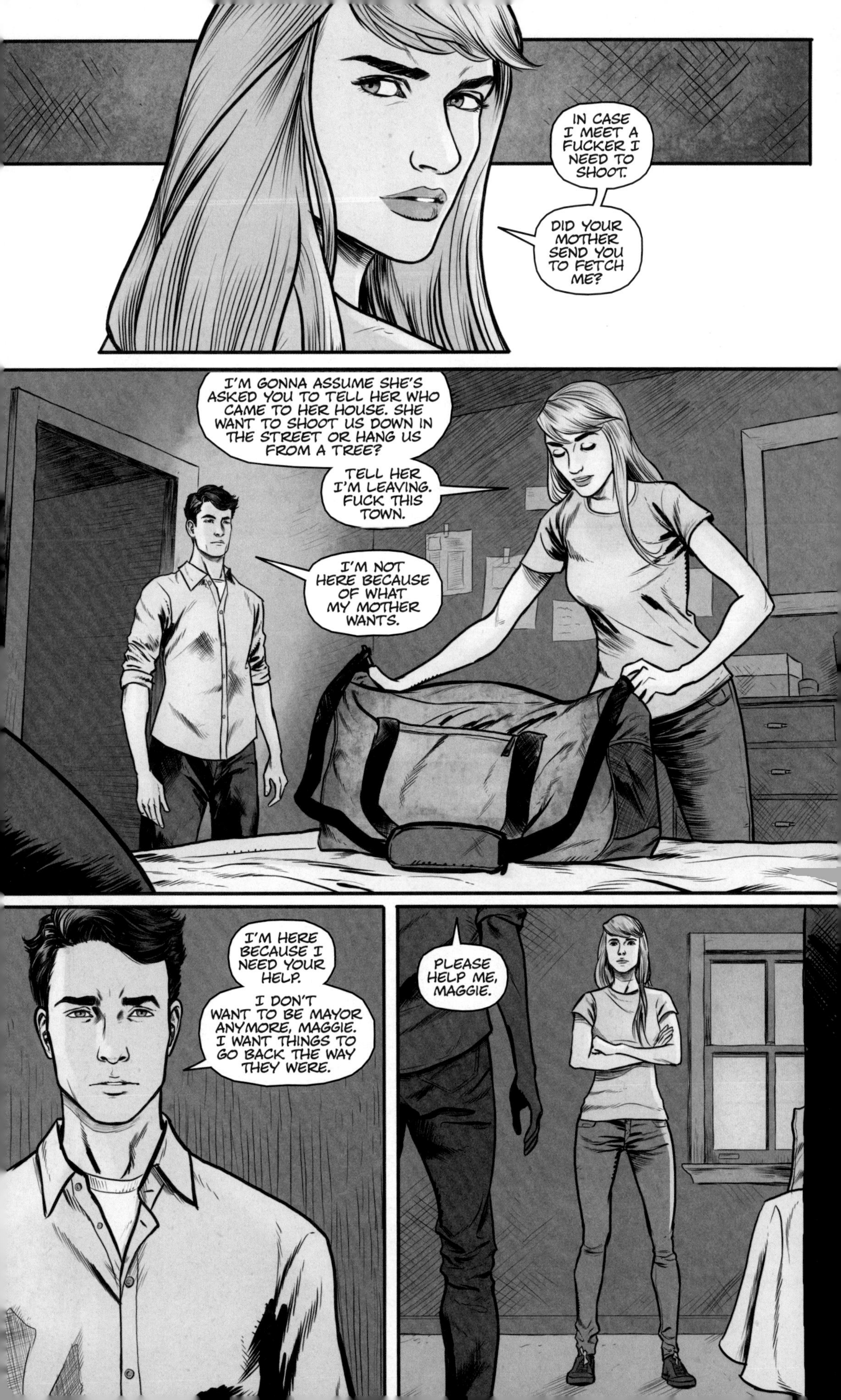
IN CASE I MEET A FUCKER I NEED TO SHOOT.
DID YOUR MOTHER SEND YOU TO FETCH ME?
I'M GONNA ASSUME SHE'S ASKED YOU TO TELL HER WHO CAME TO HER HOUSE. SHE WANT TO SHOOT US DOWN IN THE STREET OR HANG US FROM A TREE?
TELL HER I'M LEAVING. FUCK THIS TOWN.
I'M NOT HERE BECAUSE OF WHAT MY MOTHER WANTS.
I'M HERE BECAUSE I NEED YOUR HELP.
I DON'T WANT TO BE MAYOR ANYMORE, MAGGIE. I WANT THINGS TO GO BACK THE WAY THEY WERE.
PLEASE HELP ME, MAGGIE.

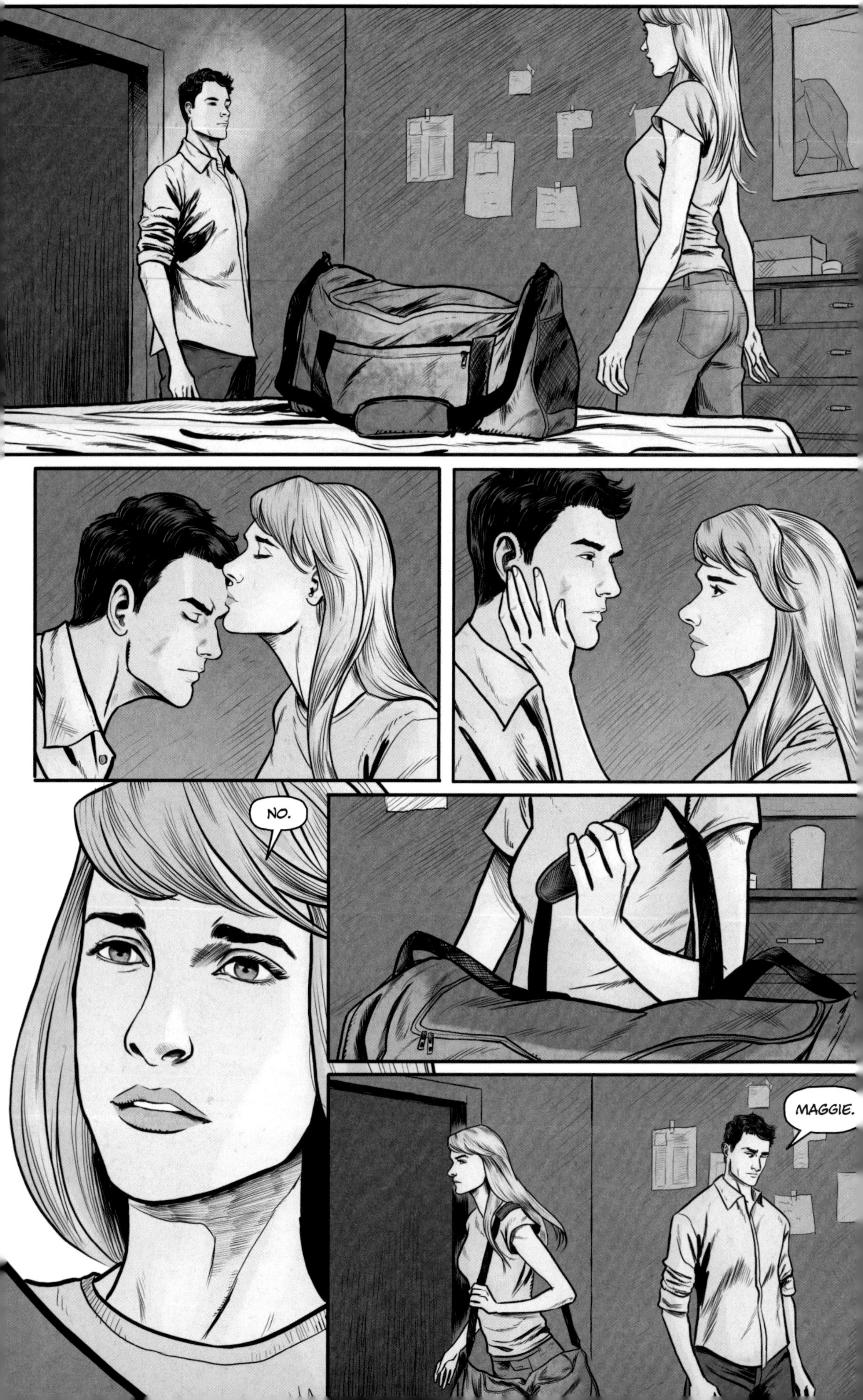
NO.
MAGGIE.

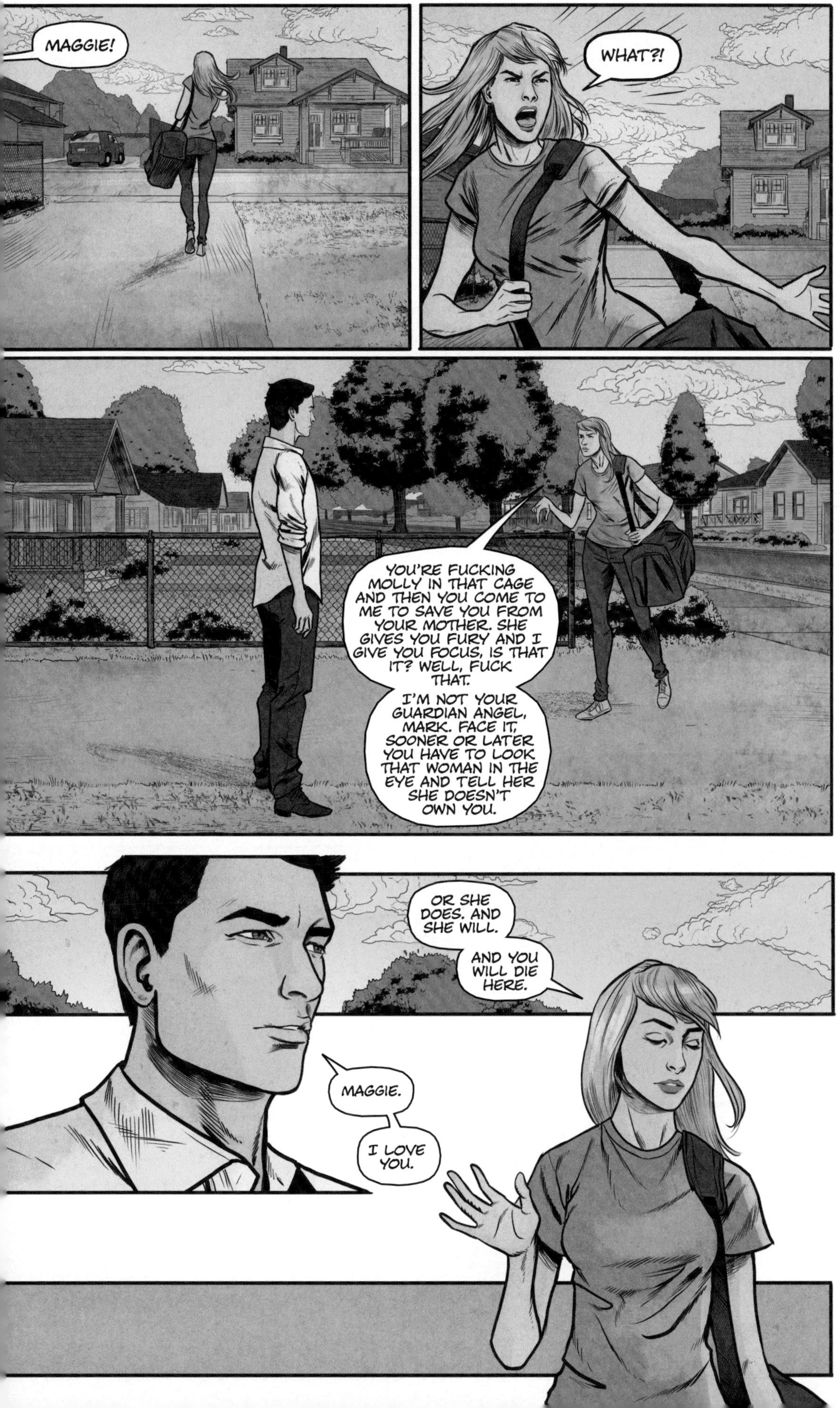
MAGGIE!
WHAT?!
YOU'RE FUCKING MOLLY IN THAT CAGE AND THEN YOU COME TO ME TO SAVE YOU FROM YOUR MOTHER. SHE GIVES YOU FURY AND I GIVE YOU FOCUS, IS THAT IT? WELL, FUCK THAT.
I'M NOT YOUR GUARDIAN ANGEL, MARK. FACE IT, SOONER OR LATER YOU HAVE TO LOOK THAT WOMAN IN THE EYE AND TELL HER SHE DOESN'T OWN YOU.
OR SHE DOES. AND SHE WILL.
AND YOU WILL DIE HERE.
MAGGIE.
I LOVE YOU.

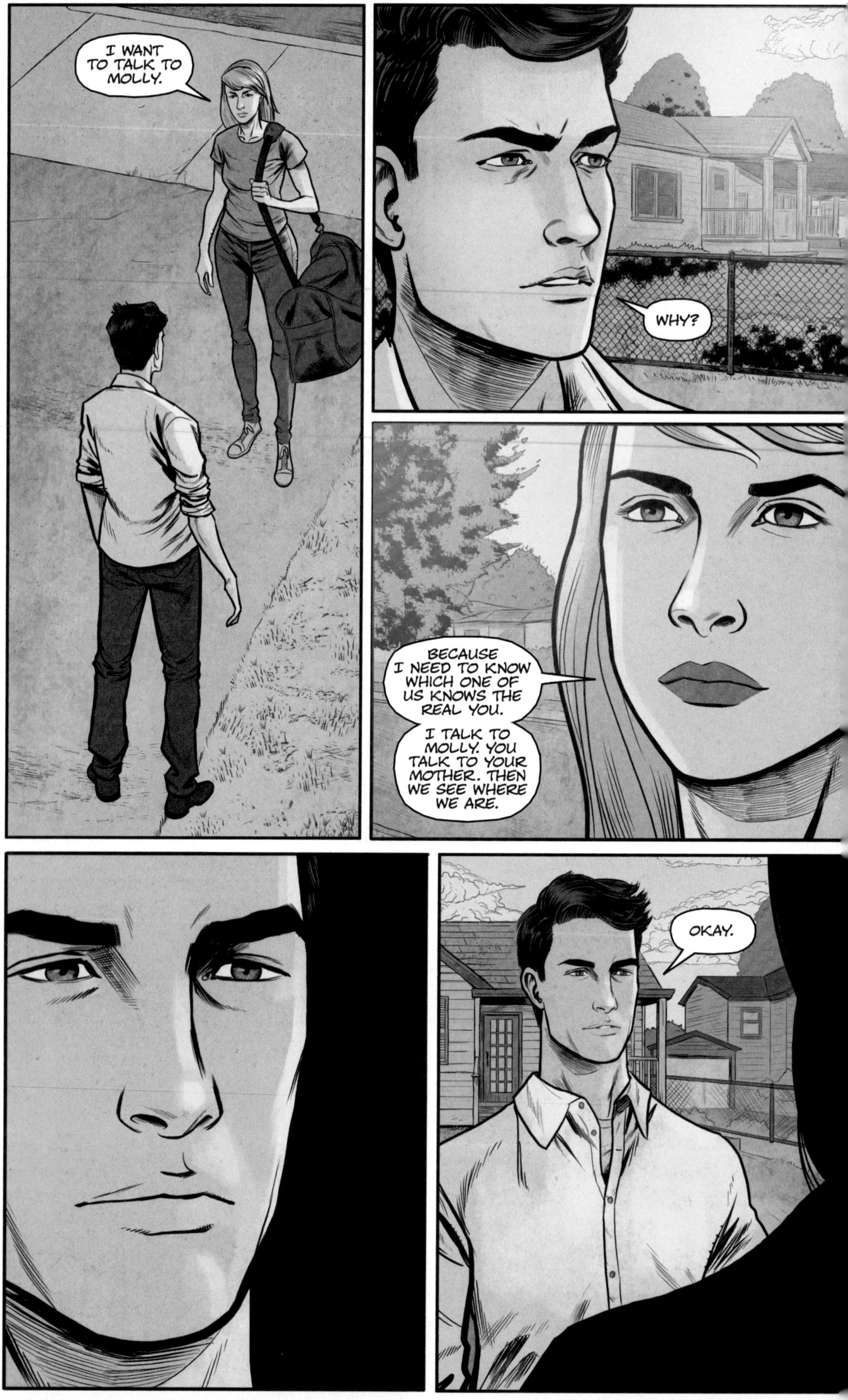
I WANT TO TALK TO MOLLY.
WHY?
BECAUSE I NEED TO KNOW WHICH ONE OF US KNOWS THE REAL YOU.
I TALK TO MOLLY. YOU TALK TO YOUR MOTHER. THEN WE SEE WHERE WE ARE.
OKAY.

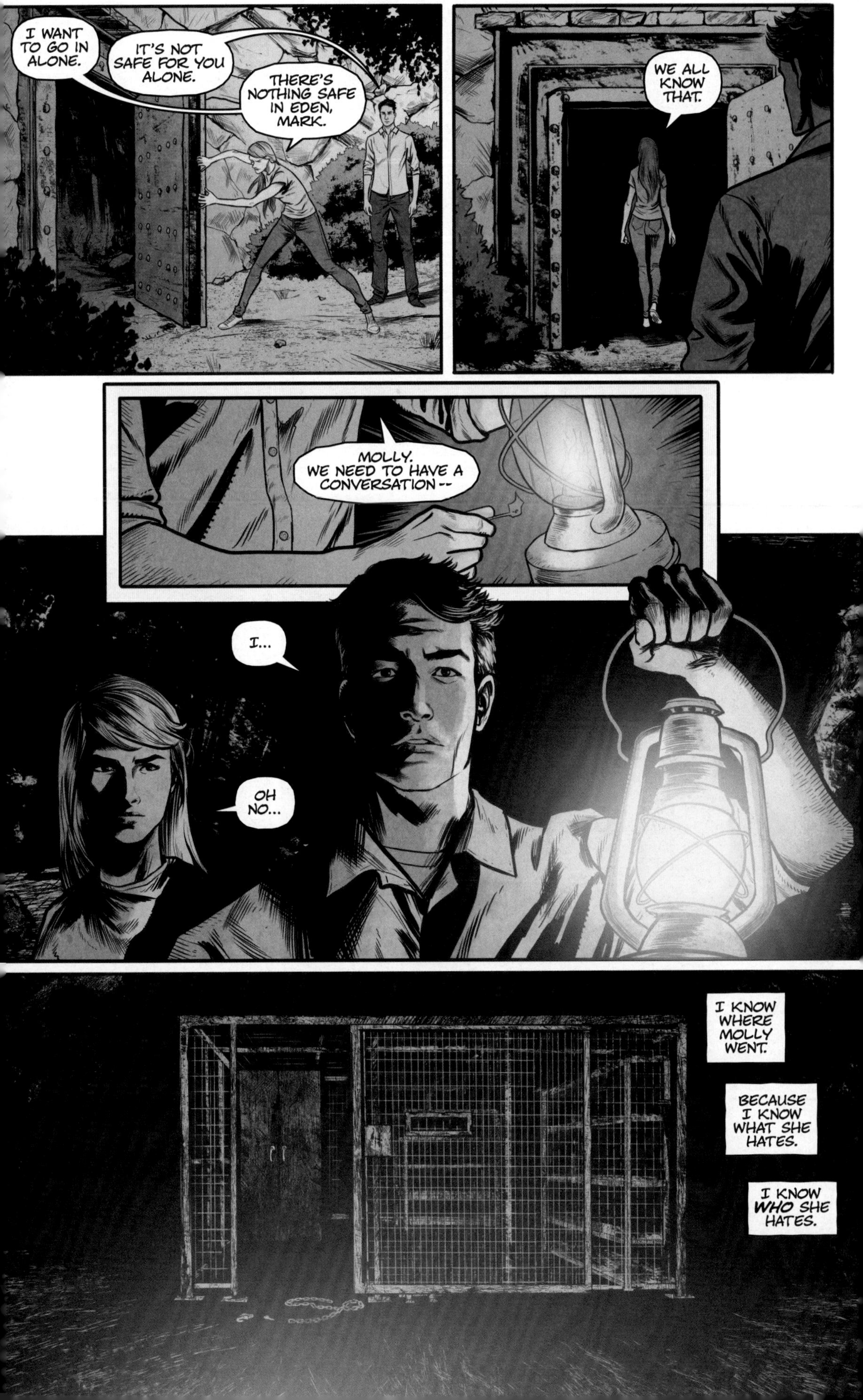
I WANT TO GO IN ALONE.
IT'S NOT SAFE FOR YOU ALONE.
THERE'S NOTHING SAFE IN EDEN, MARK.
WE ALL KNOW THAT.
MOLLY. WE NEED TO HAVE A CONVERSATION --
I...
OH NO...
I KNOW WHERE MOLLY WENT.
BECAUSE I KNOW WHAT SHE HATES.
I KNOW WHO SHE HATES.

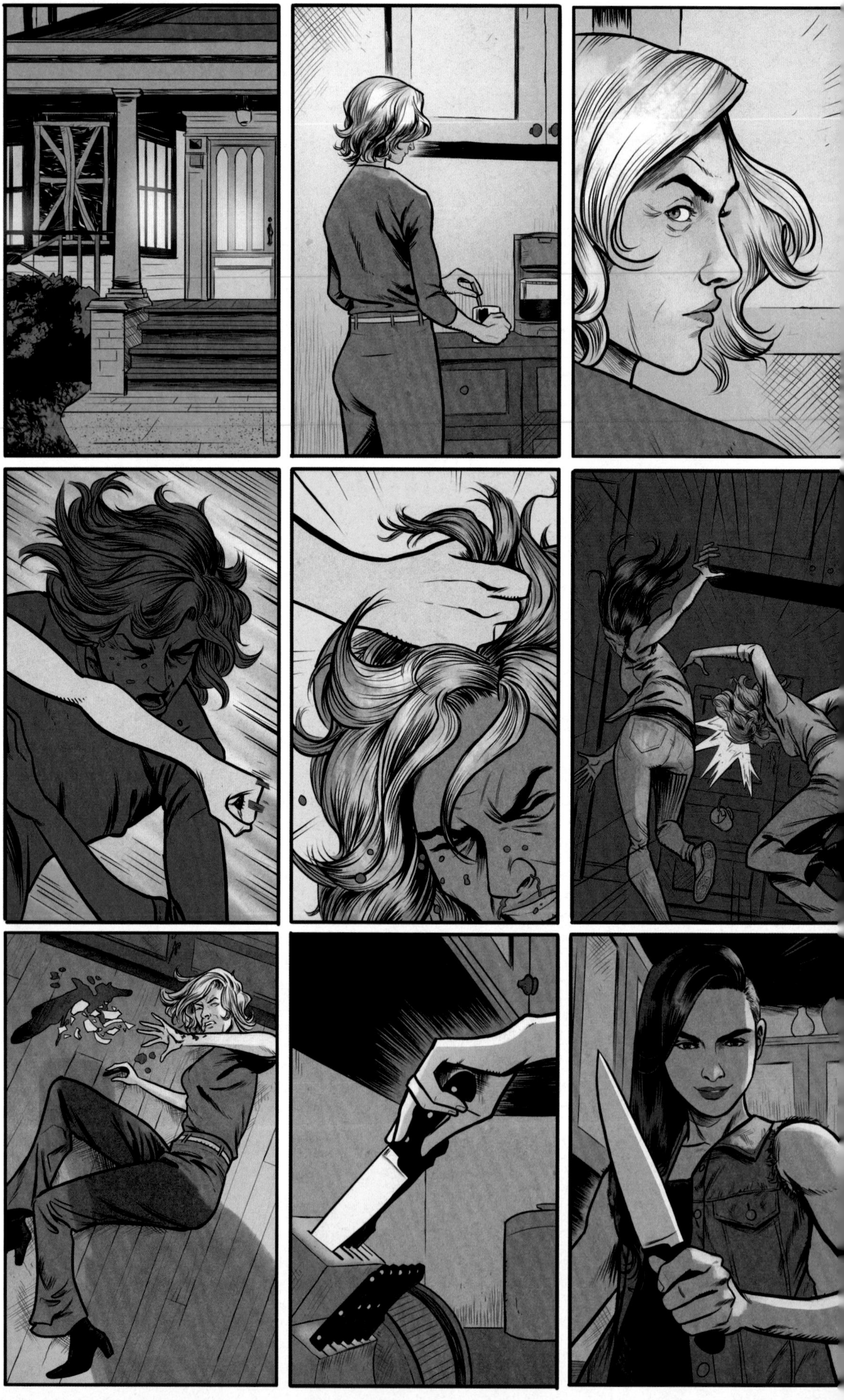

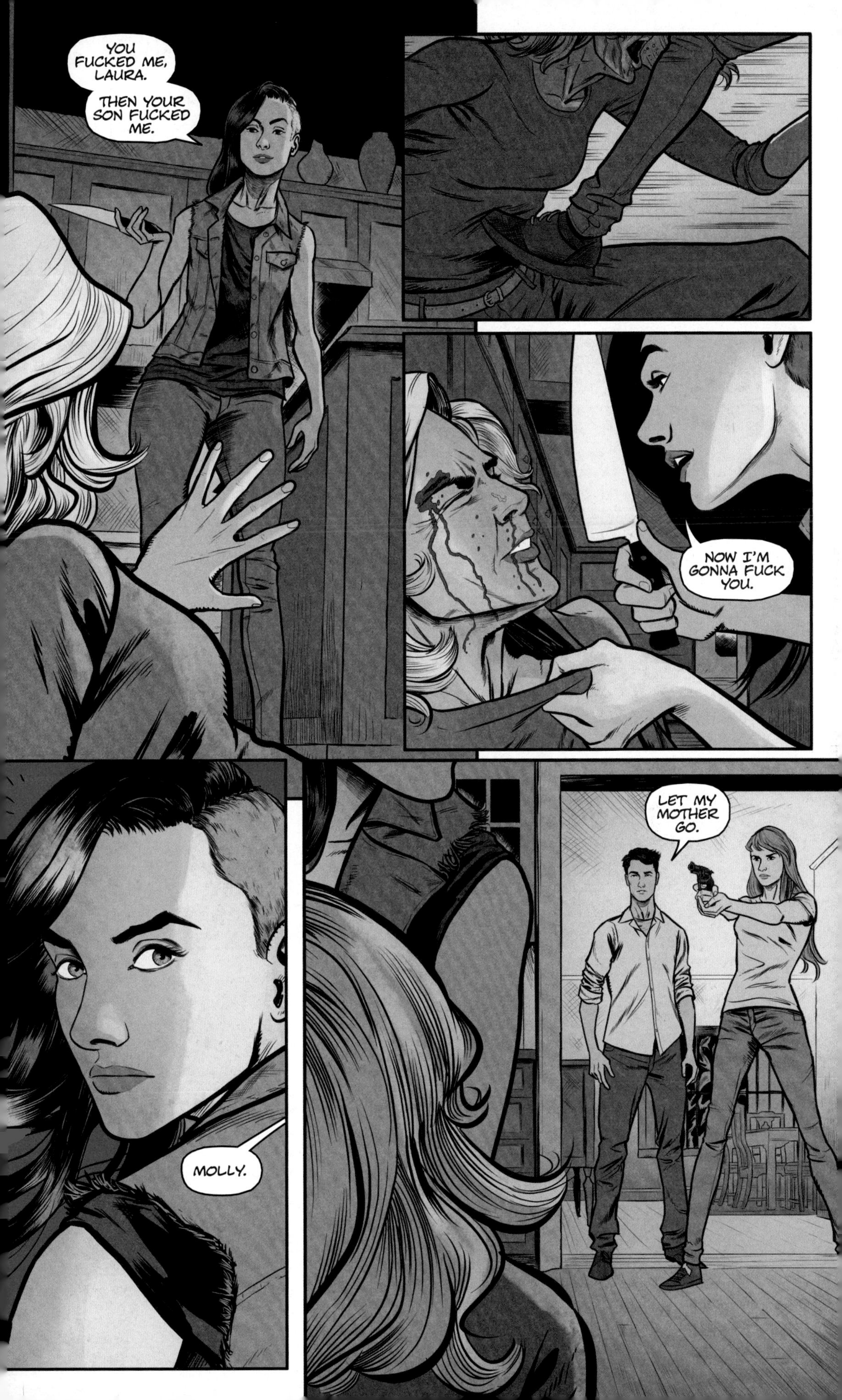
YOU FUCKED ME, LAURA.
THEN YOUR SON FUCKED ME.
NOW I'M GONNA FUCK YOU.
MOLLY.
LET MY MOTHER GO.

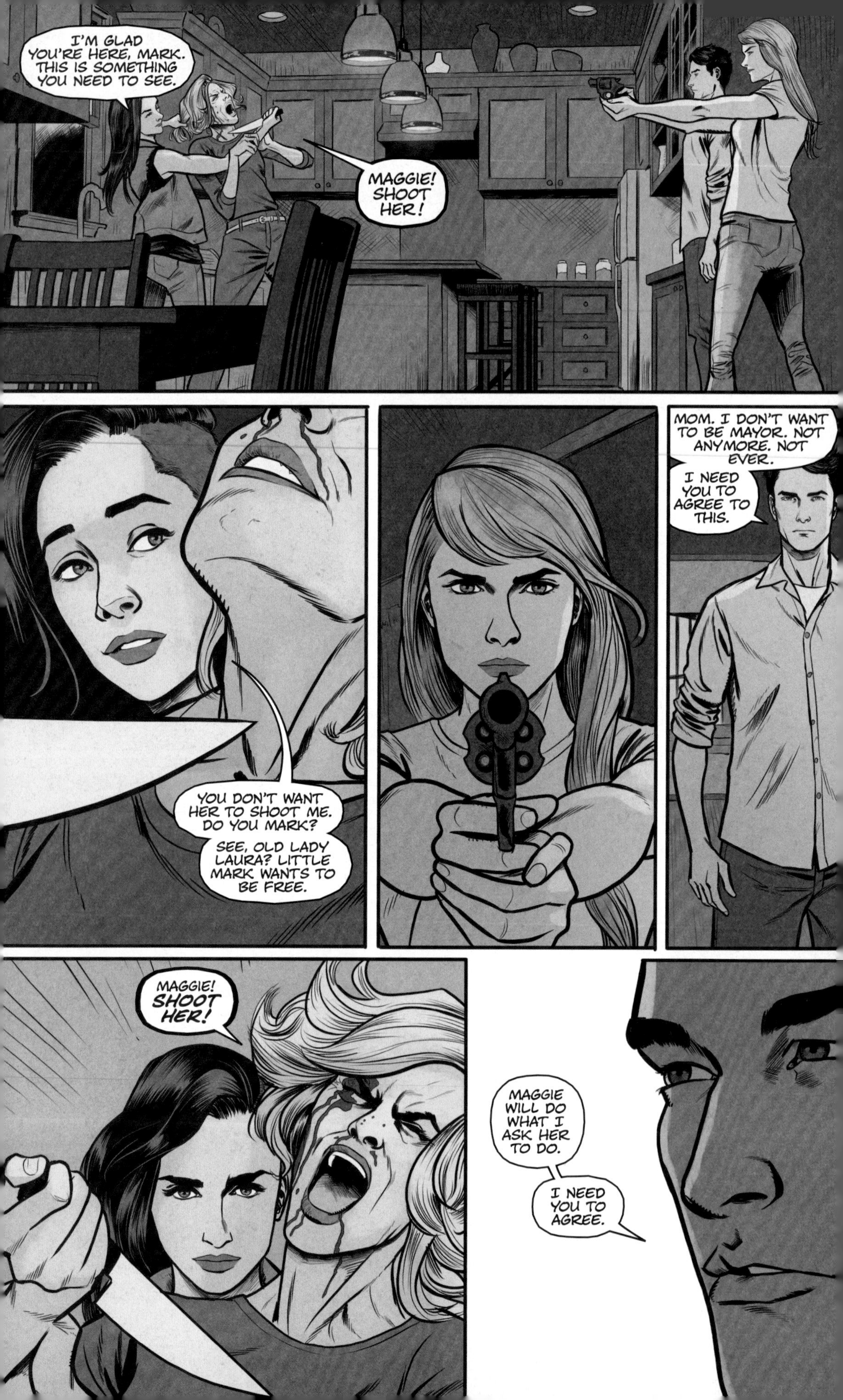
I'M GLAD YOU'RE HERE, MARK. THIS IS SOMETHING YOU NEED TO SEE.
MAGGIE! SHOOT HER!
YOU DON'T WANT HER TO SHOOT ME. DO YOU MARK?
SEE, OLD LADY LAURA? LITTLE MARK WANTS TO BE FREE.
MOM. I DON'T WANT TO BE MAYOR. NOT ANYMORE. NOT EVER.
I NEED YOU TO AGREE TO THIS.
MAGGIE! SHOOT HER!
MAGGIE WILL DO WHAT I ASK HER TO DO.
I NEED YOU TO AGREE.

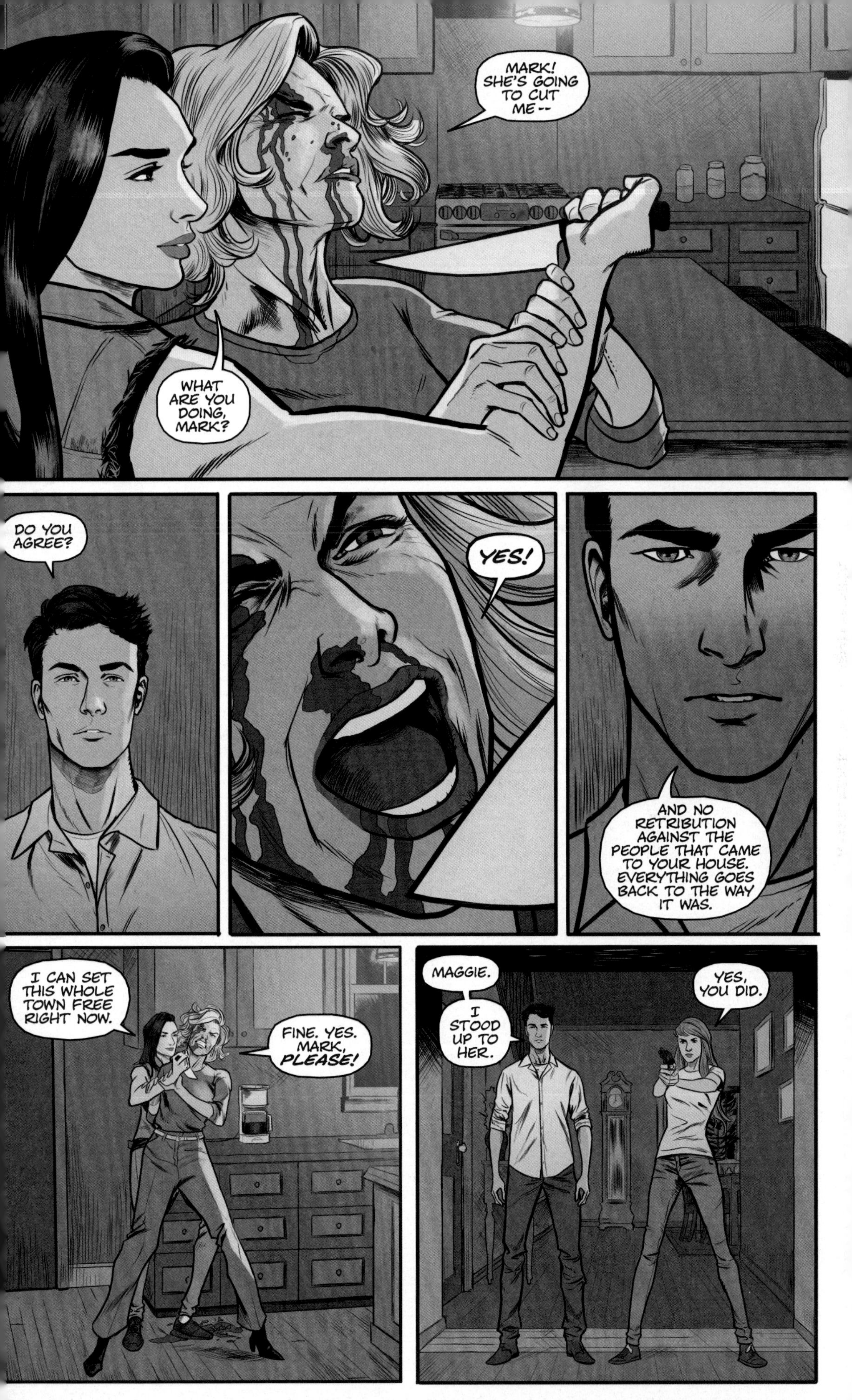
MARK! SHE'S GOING TO CUT ME--
WHAT ARE YOU DOING, MARK?
DO YOU AGREE?
YES!
AND NO RETRIBUTION AGAINST THE PEOPLE THAT CAME TO YOUR HOUSE. EVERYTHING GOES BACK TO THE WAY IT WAS.
I CAN SET THIS WHOLE TOWN FREE RIGHT NOW.
FINE. YES. MARK, PLEASE!
MAGGIE.
I STOOD UP TO HER.
YES, YOU DID.

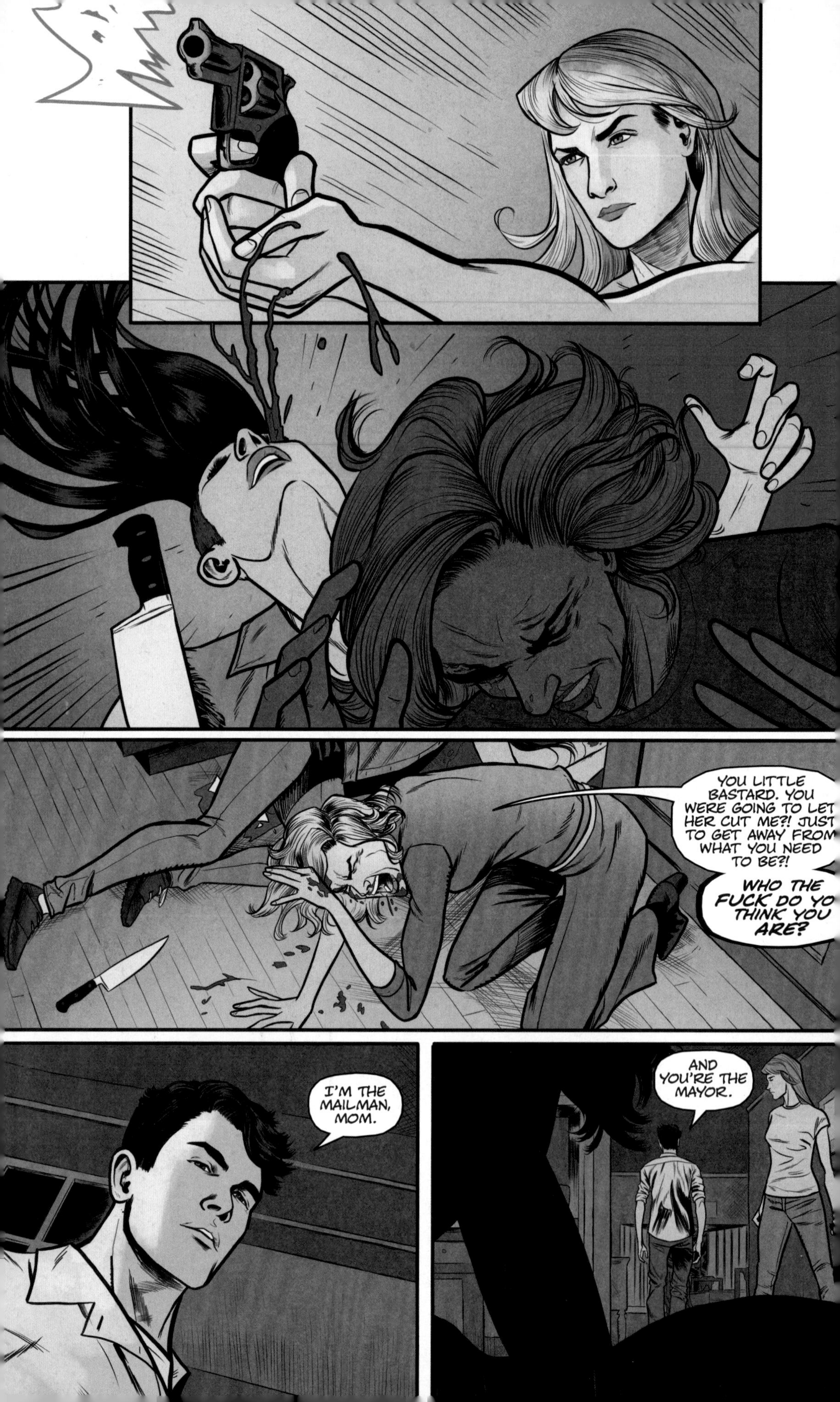
YOU LITTLE BASTARD. YOU WERE GOING TO LET HER CUT ME?! JUST TO GET AWAY FROM WHAT YOU NEED TO BE?!
WHO THE FUCK DO YO THINK YOU ARE?
I'M THE MAILMAN, MOM.
AND YOU'RE THE MAYOR.

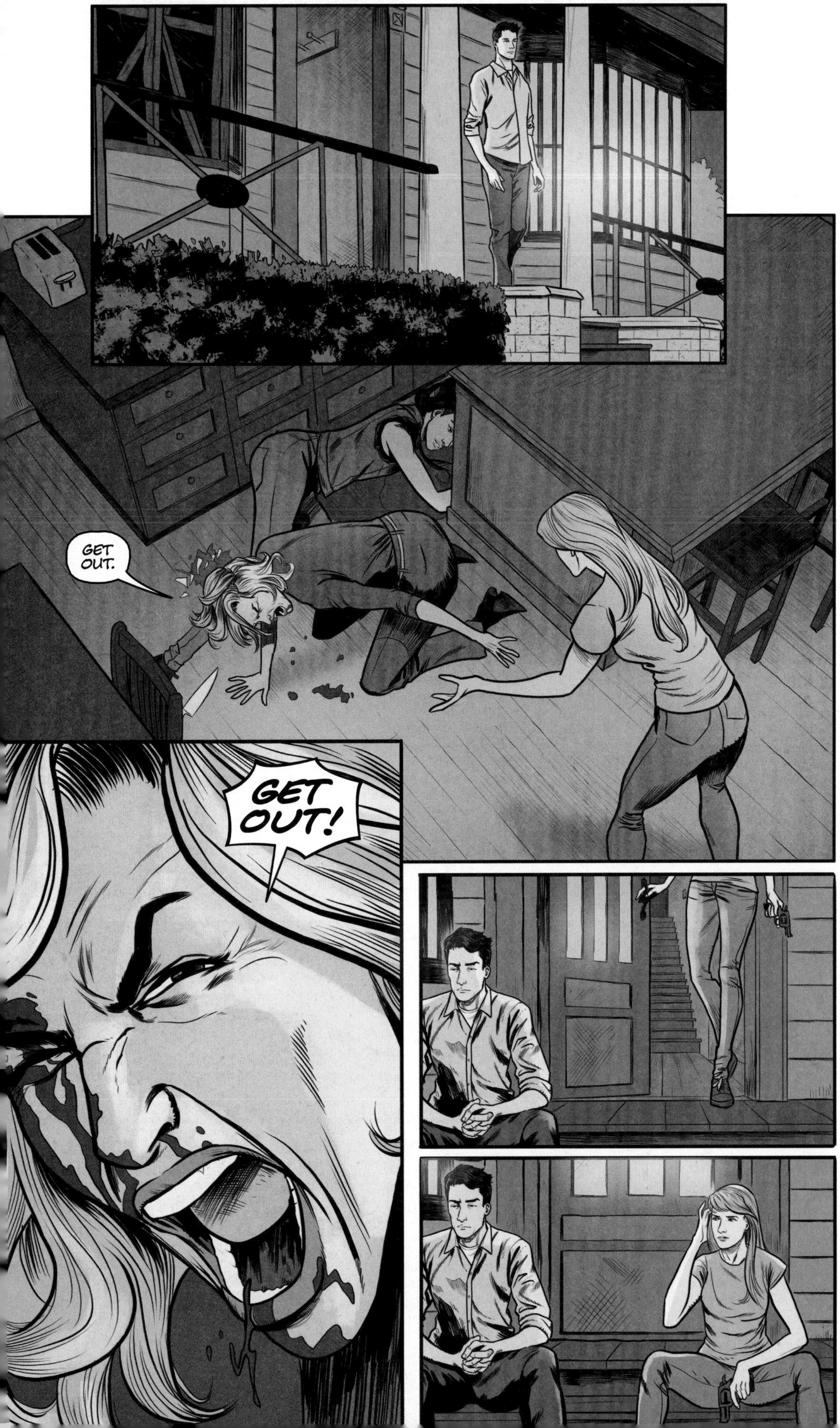
GET OUT.
GET OUT!

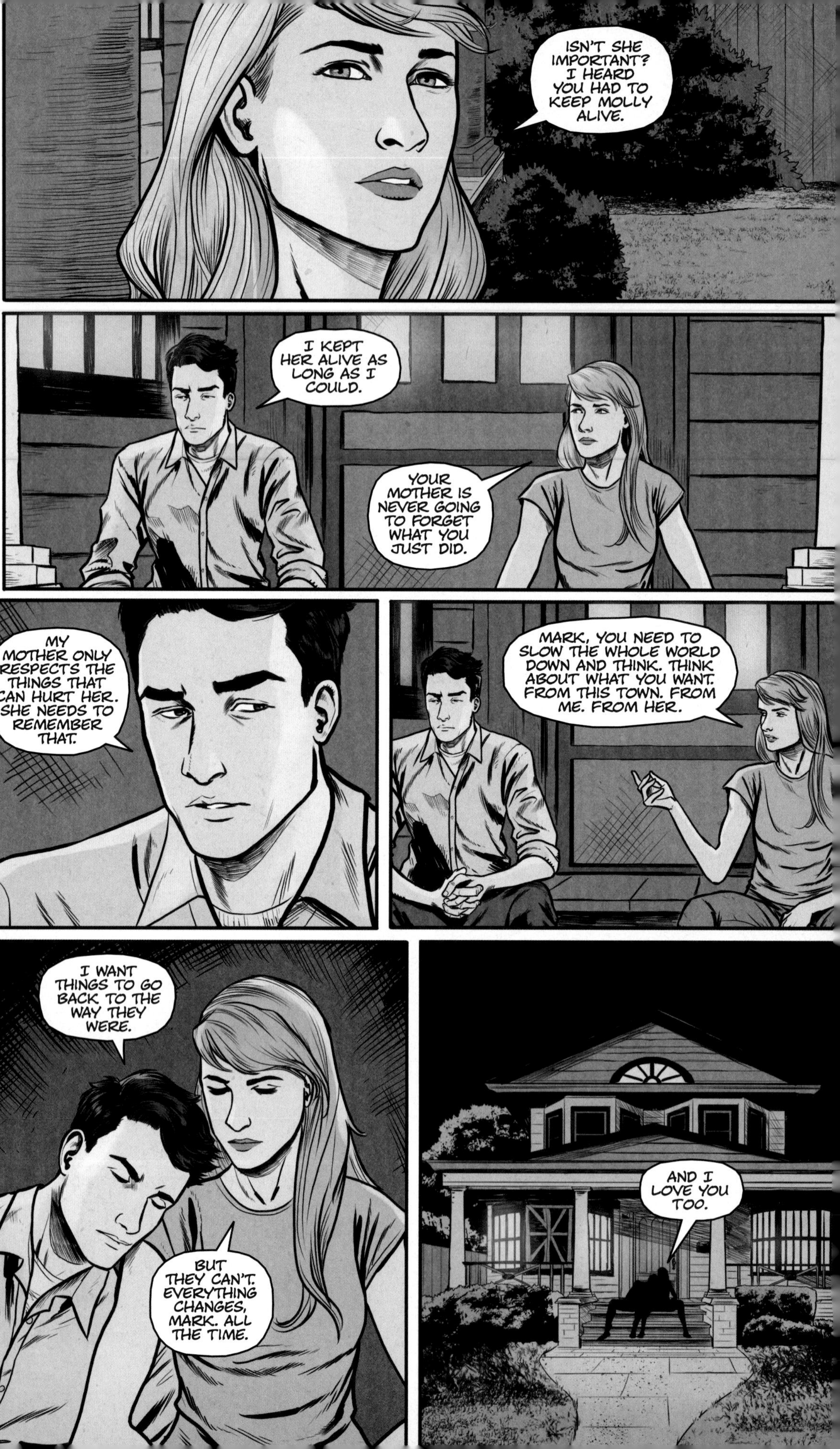
ISN'T SHE IMPORTANT? I HEARD YOU HAD TO KEEP MOLLY ALIVE.
I KEPT HER ALIVE AS LONG AS I COULD.
YOUR MOTHER IS NEVER GOING TO FORGET WHAT YOU JUST DID.
MY MOTHER ONLY RESPECTS THE THINGS THAT CAN HURT HER. SHE NEEDS TO REMEMBER THAT.
MARK, YOU NEED TO SLOW THE WHOLE WORLD DOWN AND THINK. THINK ABOUT WHAT YOU WANT. FROM THIS TOWN. FROM ME. FROM HER.
I WANT THINGS TO GO BACK TO THE WAY THEY WERE.
BUT THEY CAN'T. EVERYTHING CHANGES, MARK. ALL THE TIME.
AND I LOVE YOU TOO.

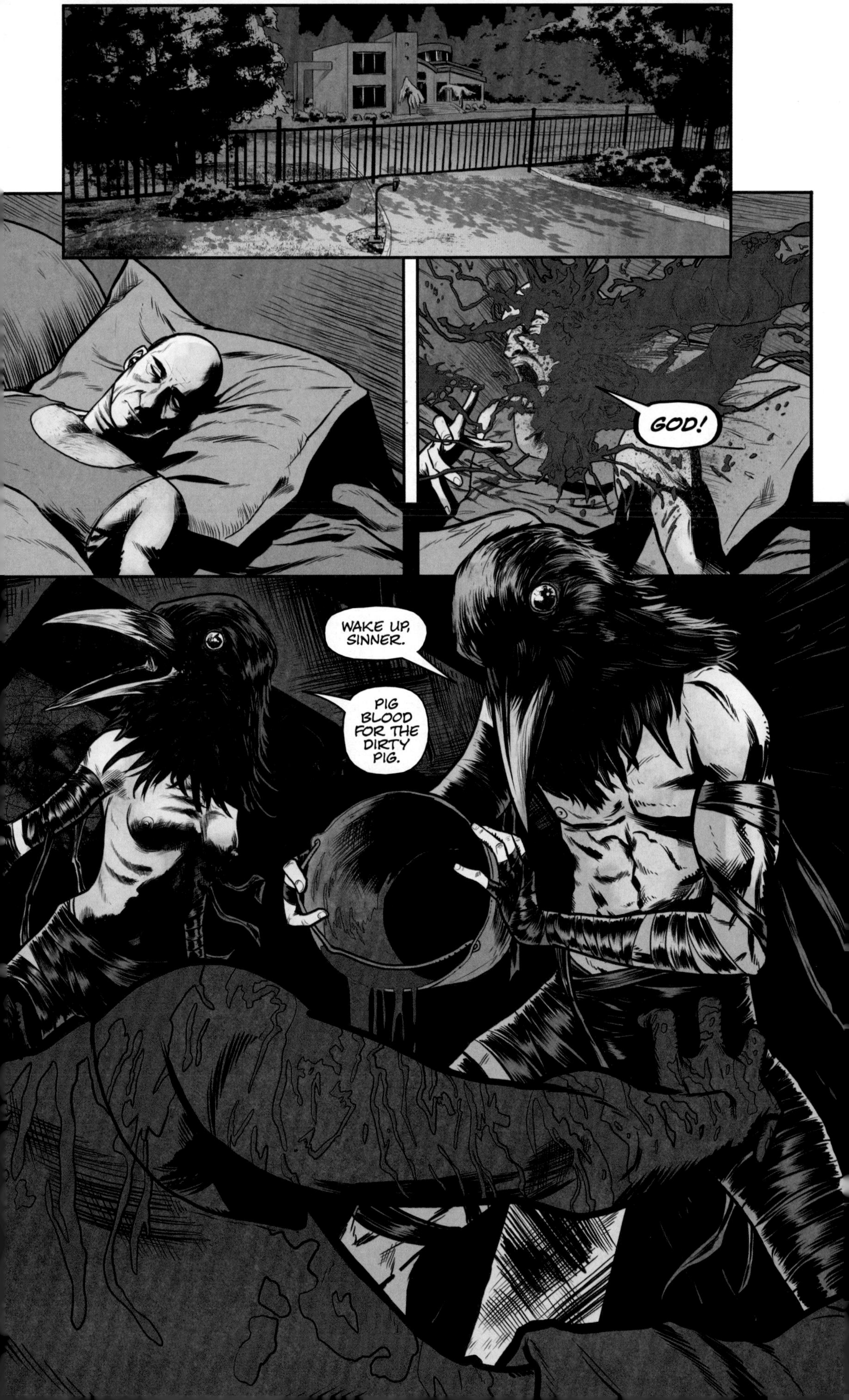
GOD!
WAKE UP, SINNER.
PIG BLOOD FOR THE DIRTY PIG.

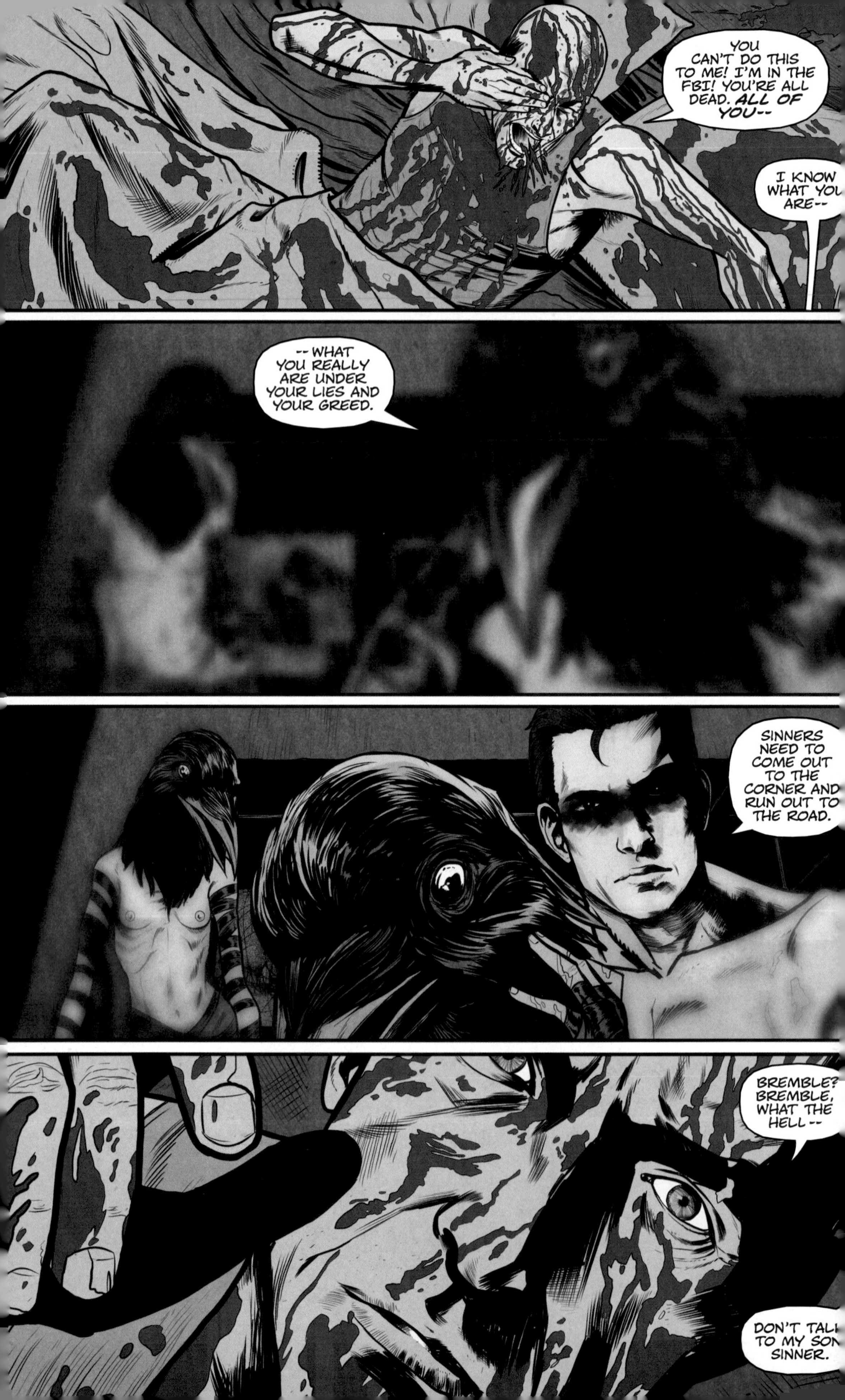
YOU CAN'T DO THIS TO ME! I'M IN THE FBI! YOU'RE ALL DEAD. ALL OF YOU--
I KNOW WHAT YOU ARE--
--WHAT YOU REALLY ARE UNDER YOUR LIES AND YOUR GREED.
SINNERS NEED TO COME OUT TO THE CORNER AND RUN OUT TO THE ROAD.
BREMBLE? BREMBLE, WHAT THE HELL--
DON'T TALK TO MY SON SINNER.

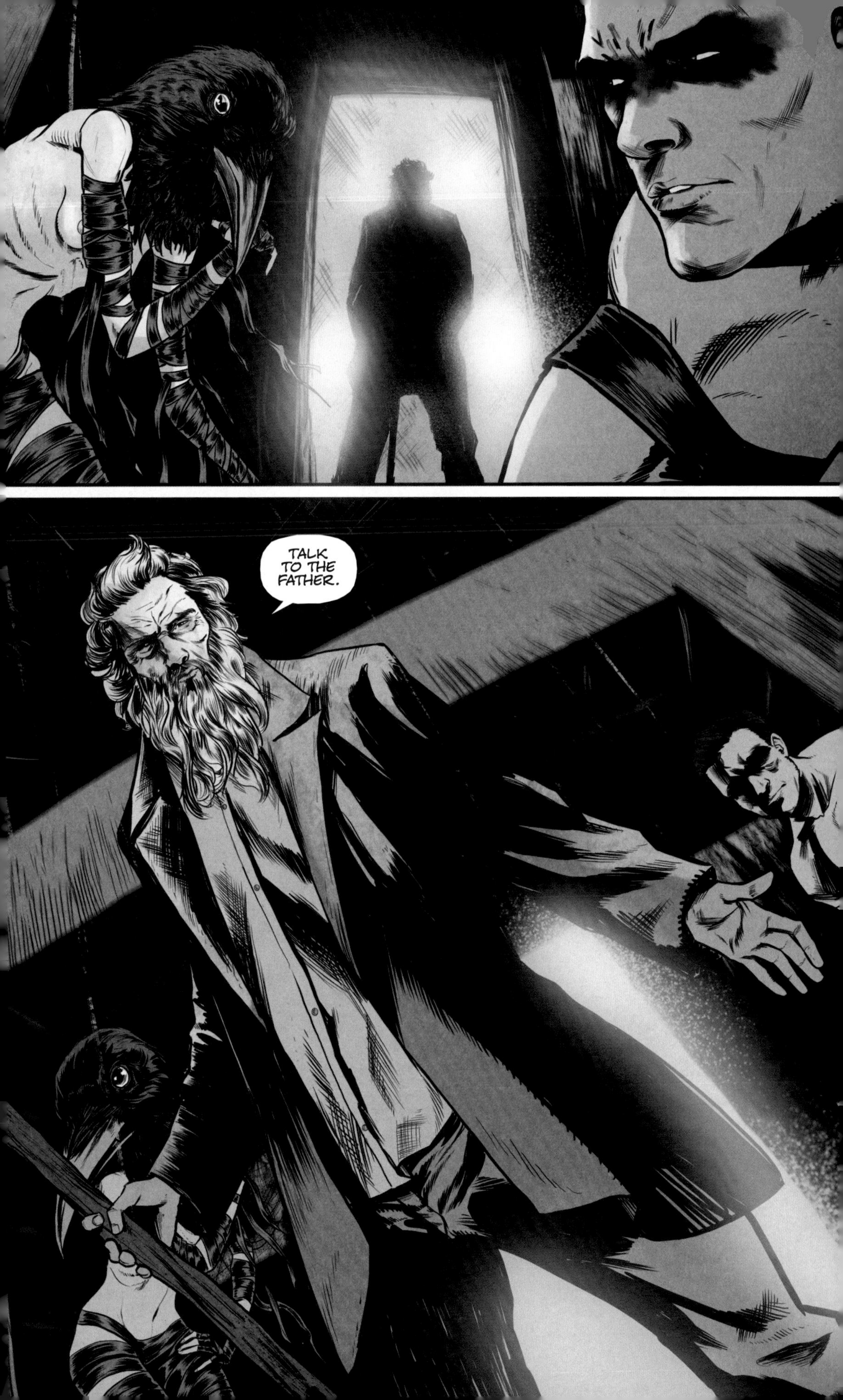
TALK TO THE FATHER.

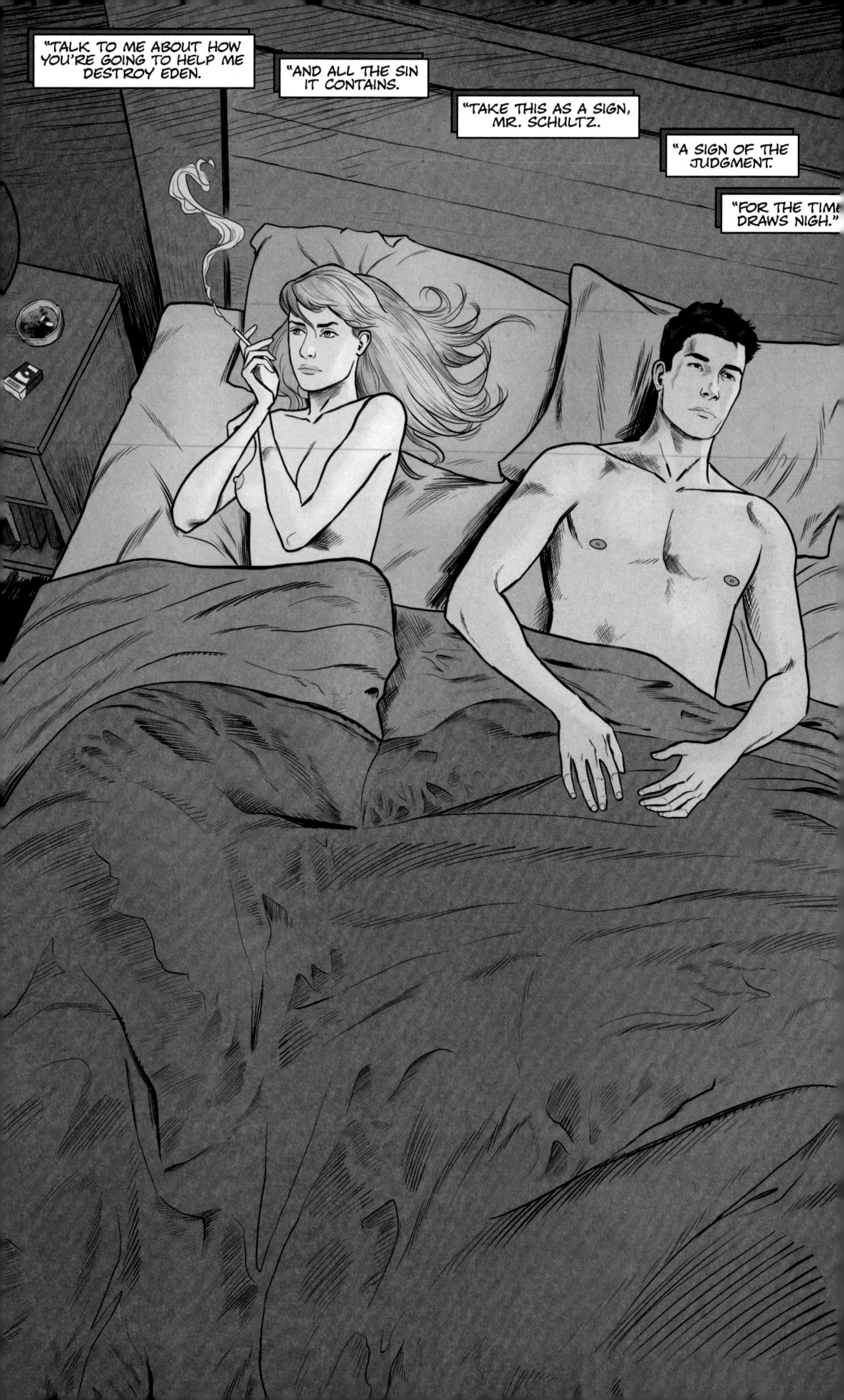
"TALK TO ME ABOUT HOW YOU'RE GOING TO HELP ME DESTROY EDEN.
"AND ALL THE SIN IT CONTAINS.
"TAKE THIS AS A SIGN, MR. SCHULTZ.
"A SIGN OF THE JUDGMENT.
"FOR THE TIME DRAWS NIGH."

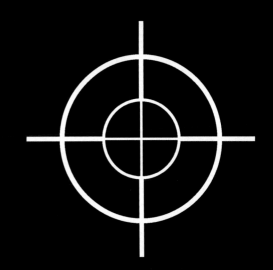

# CHAPTER 21

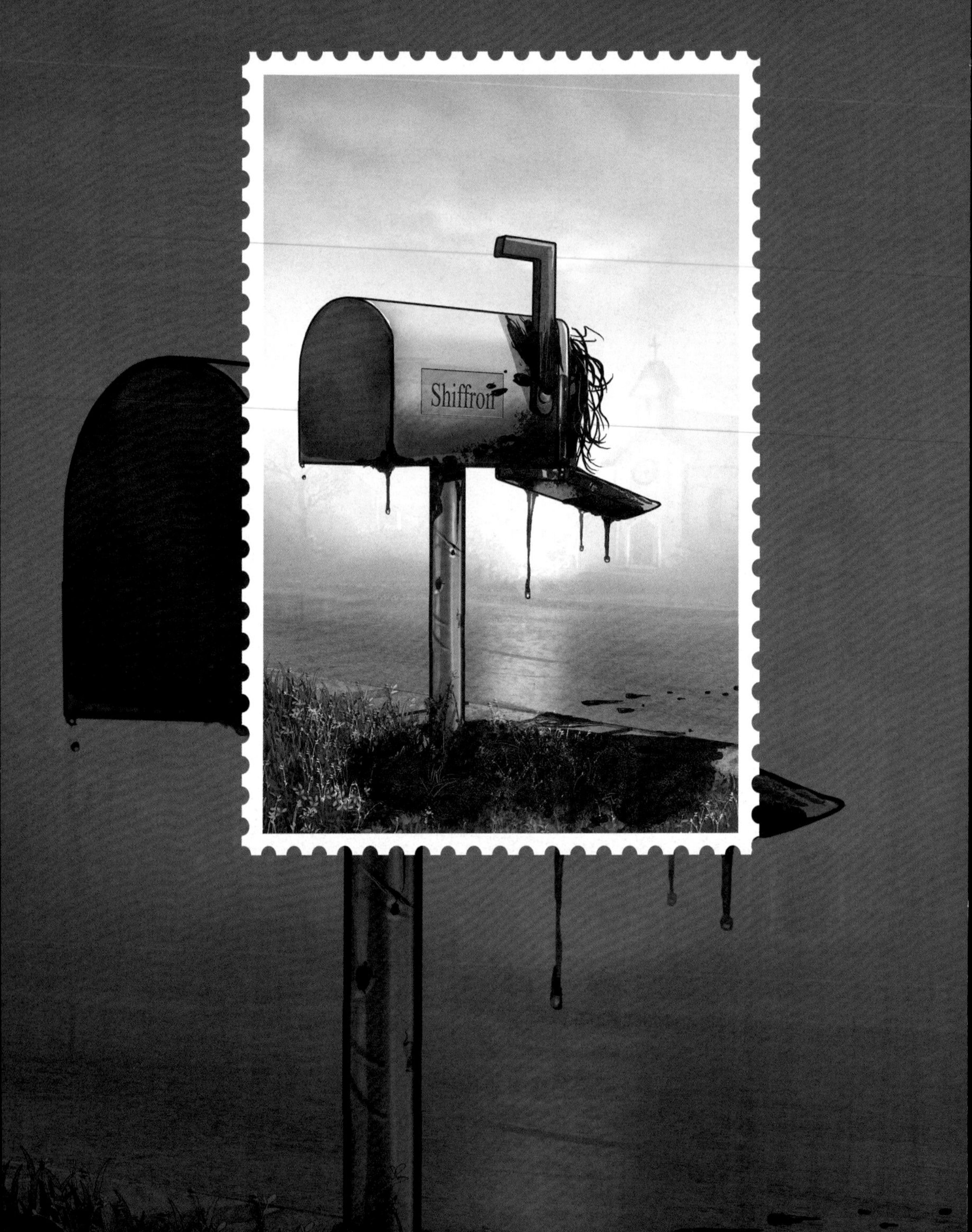
Shiffron

TAKE IT. CALM YOUR NERVES.
I QUIT LAST YEAR.
YOU'RE A FUCKING HYPOCRITE ABOUT EVERYTHING ELSE IN YOUR LIFE. WHY MAKE A GOOD CHOICE NOW?
THERE YOU GO.
LET'S STOP PRETENDING YOU'RE A DECENT MAN WITH GOOD JUDGMENT.
NO POINT IN LYING NOW, JON.

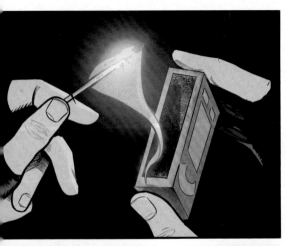

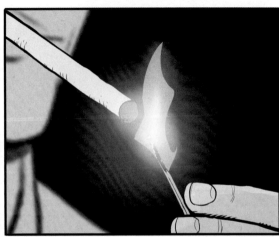

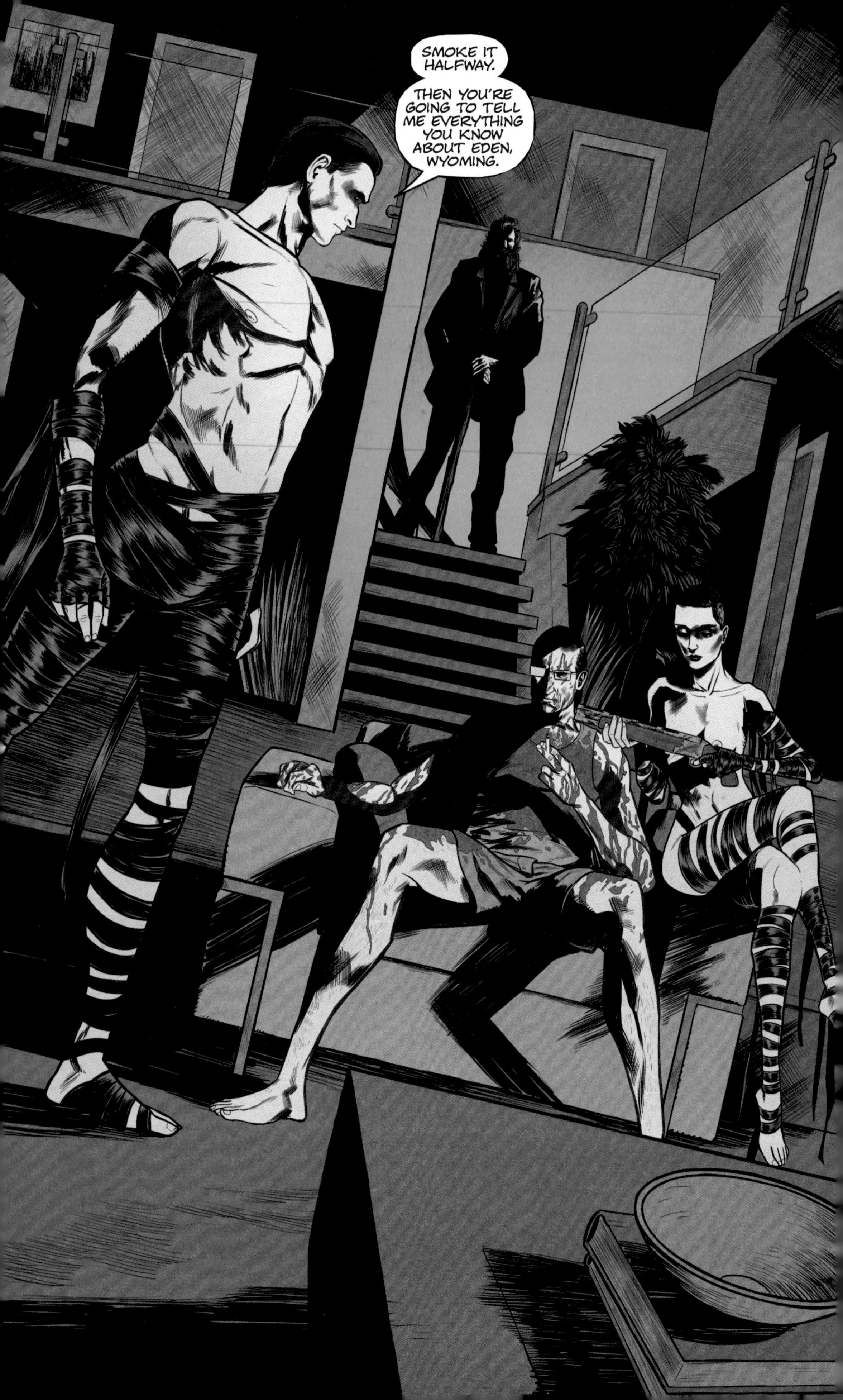
SMOKE IT HALFWAY.
THEN YOU'RE GOING TO TELL ME EVERYTHING YOU KNOW ABOUT EDEN, WYOMING.

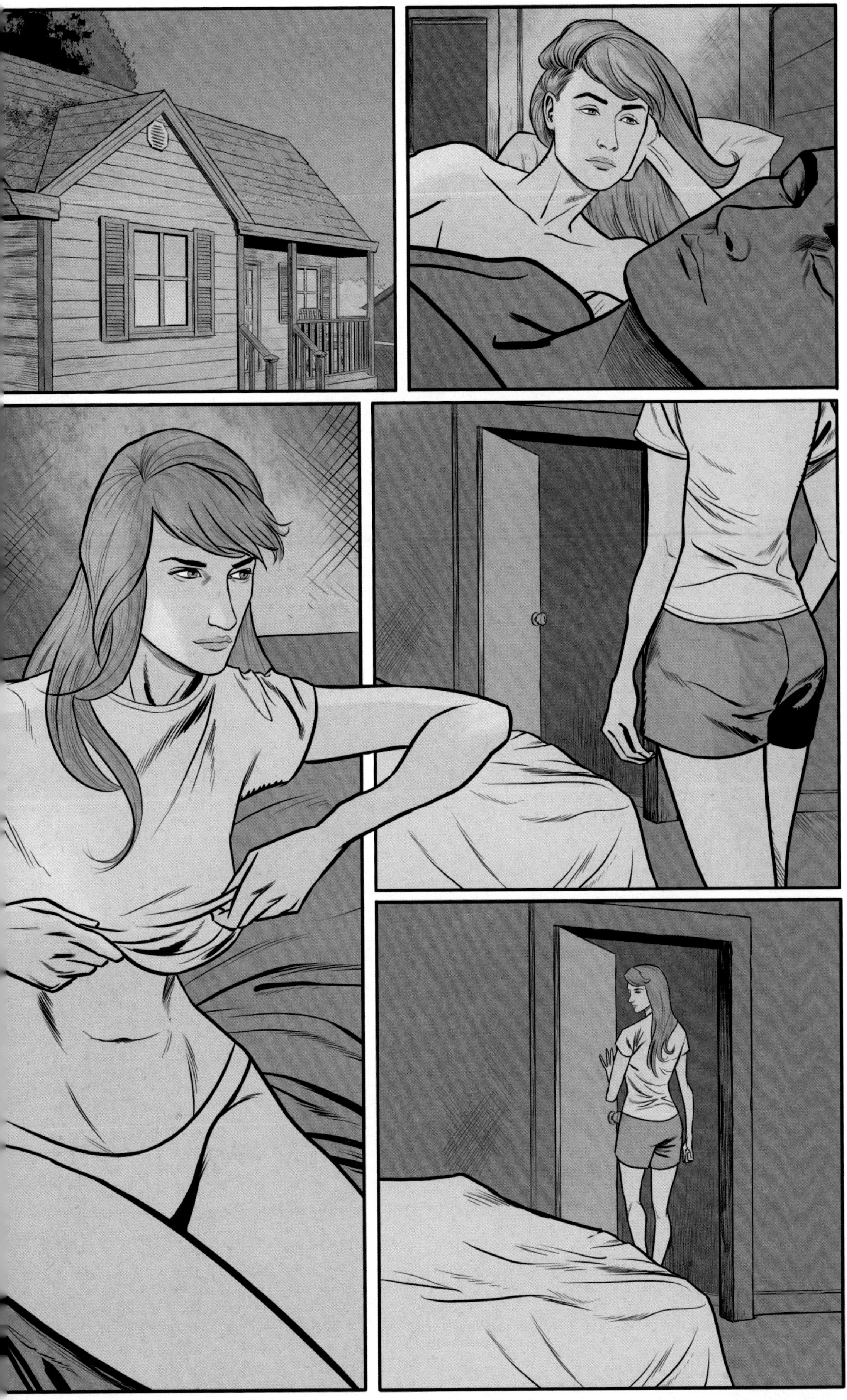

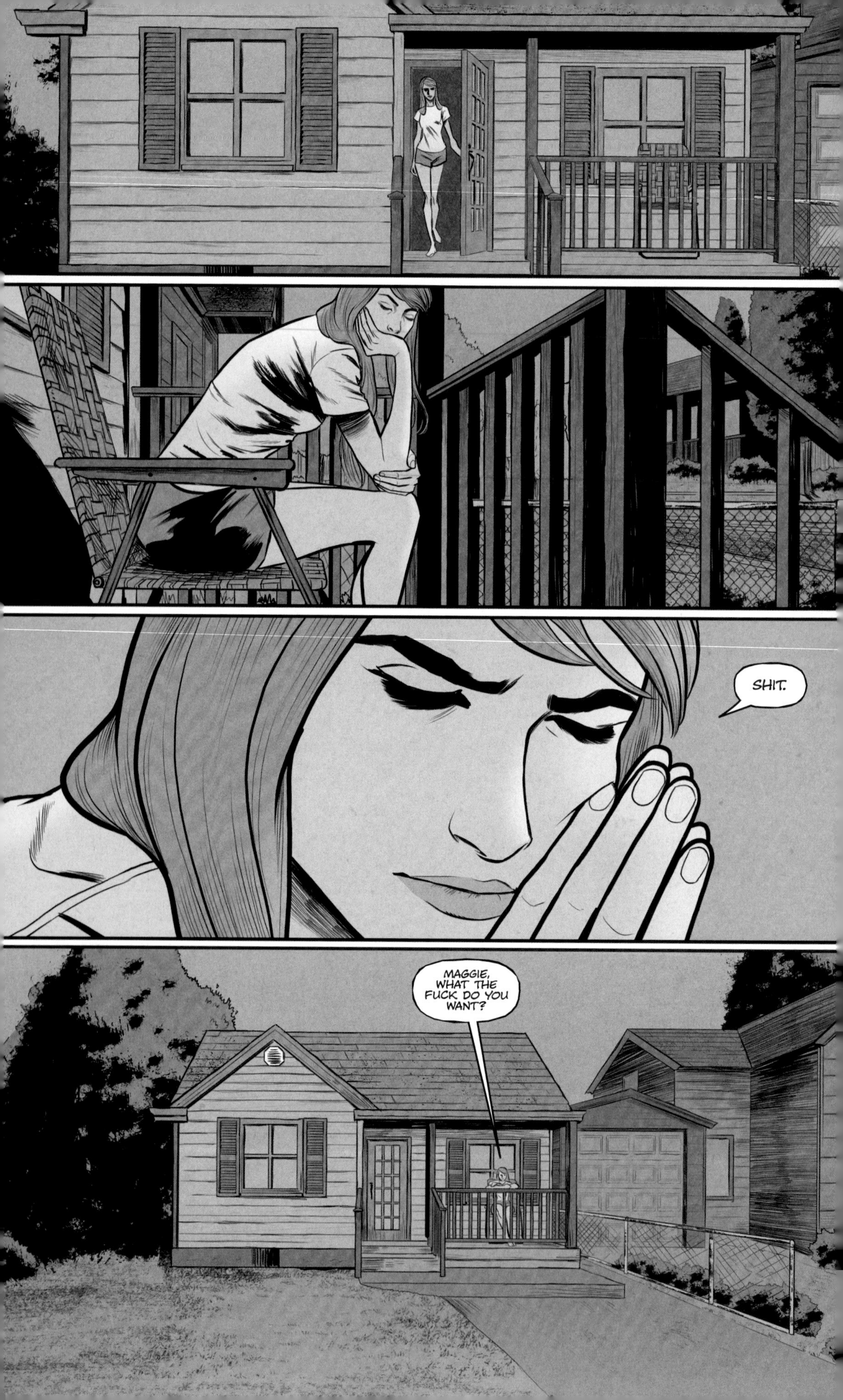
SHIT.
MAGGIE, WHAT THE FUCK DO YOU WANT?

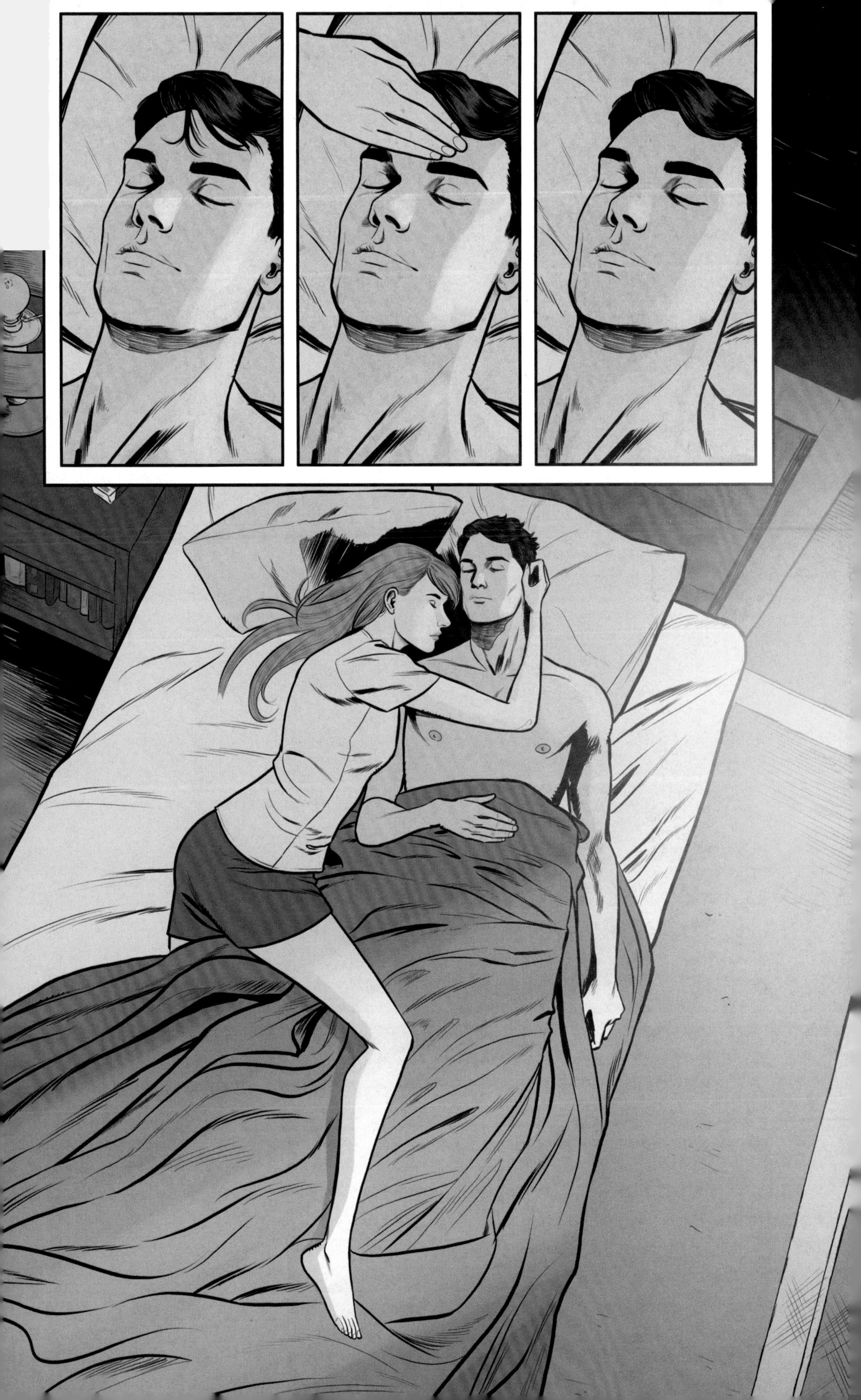

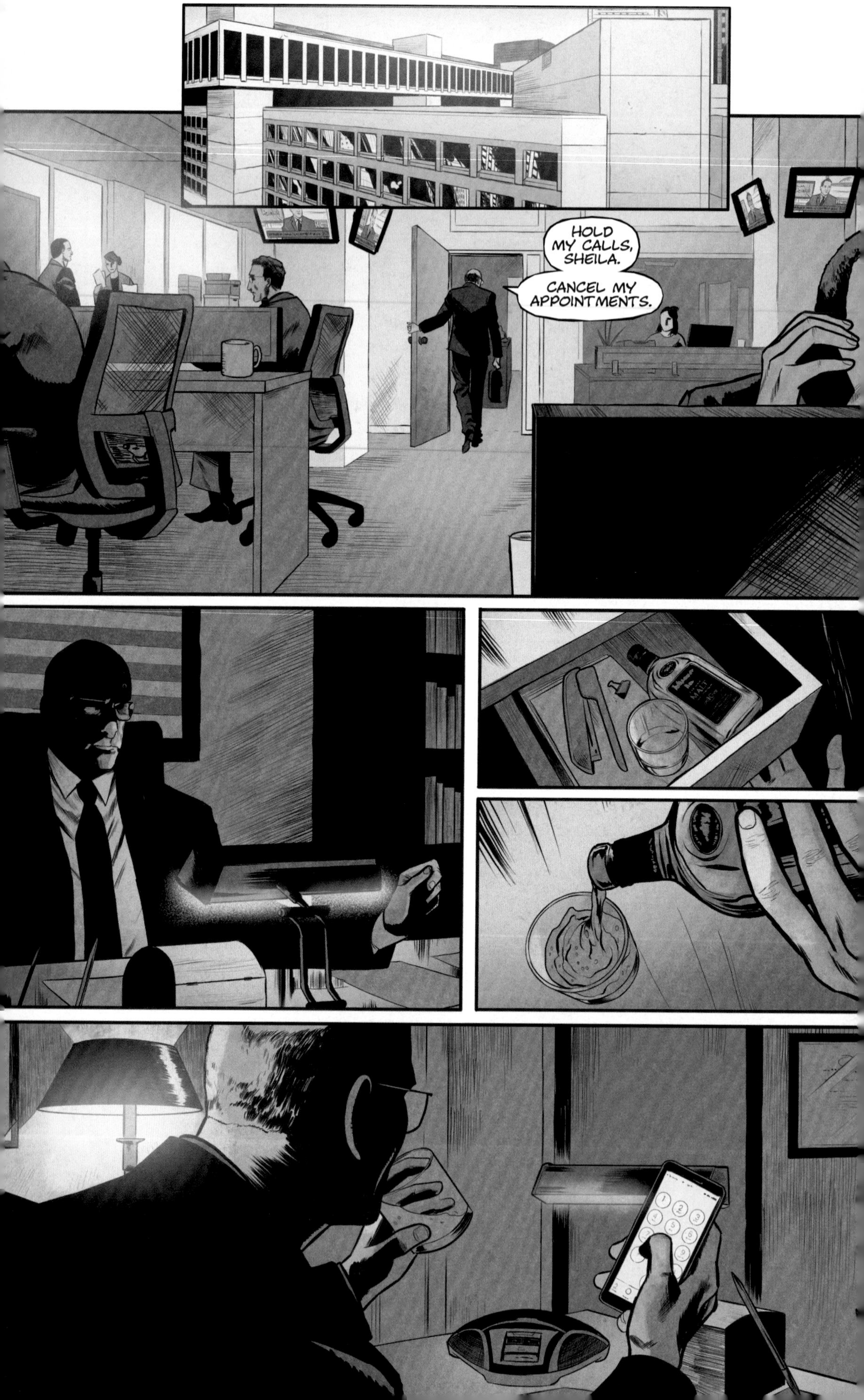
HOLD MY CALLS, SHEILA.
CANCEL MY APPOINTMENTS.

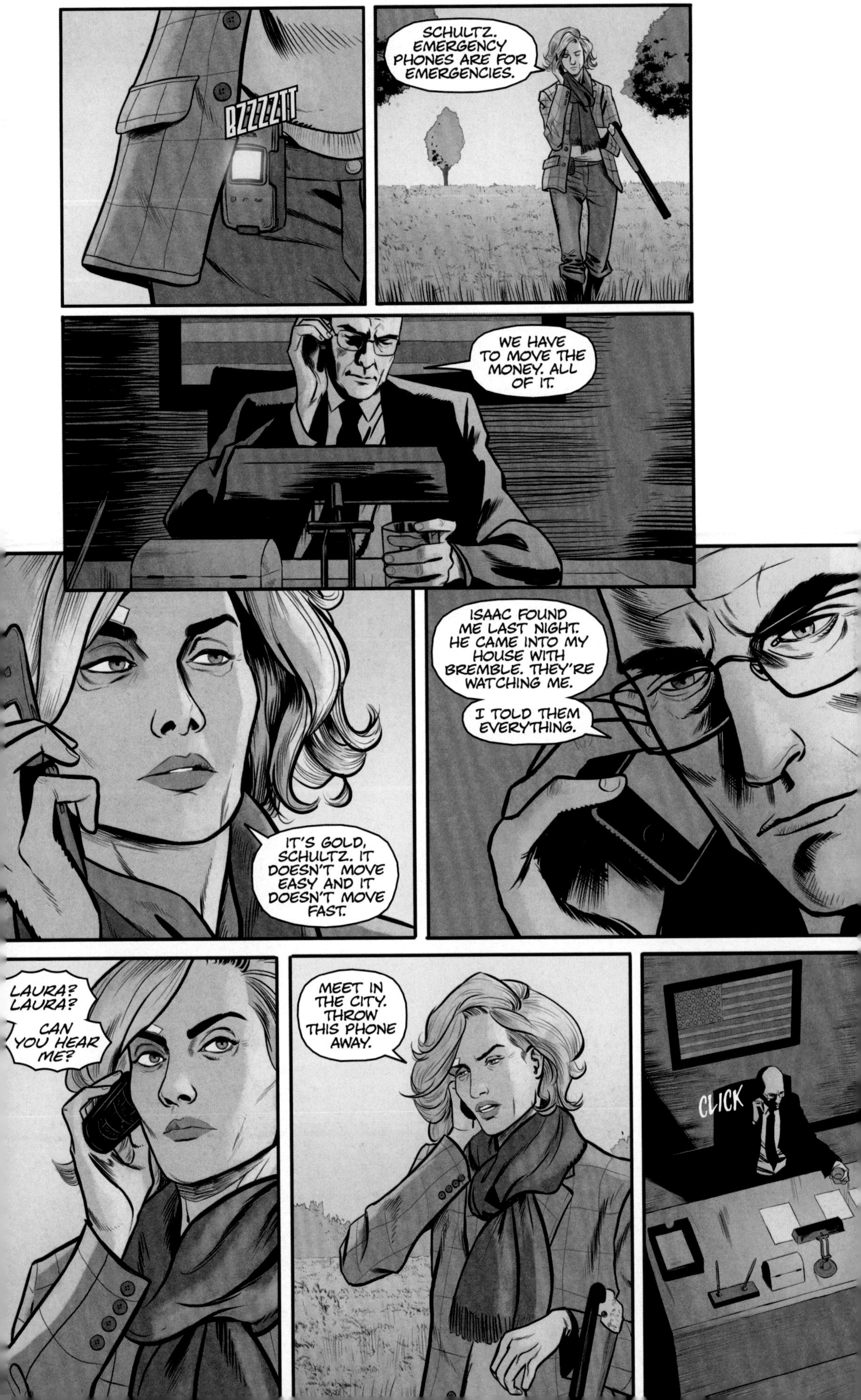
BZZZZTT
SCHULTZ. EMERGENCY PHONES ARE FOR EMERGENCIES.
WE HAVE TO MOVE THE MONEY. ALL OF IT.
IT'S GOLD, SCHULTZ. IT DOESN'T MOVE EASY AND IT DOESN'T MOVE FAST.
ISAAC FOUND ME LAST NIGHT. HE CAME INTO MY HOUSE WITH BREMBLE. THEY'RE WATCHING ME.
I TOLD THEM EVERYTHING.
LAURA? LAURA?
CAN YOU HEAR ME?
MEET IN THE CITY. THROW THIS PHONE AWAY.
CLICK

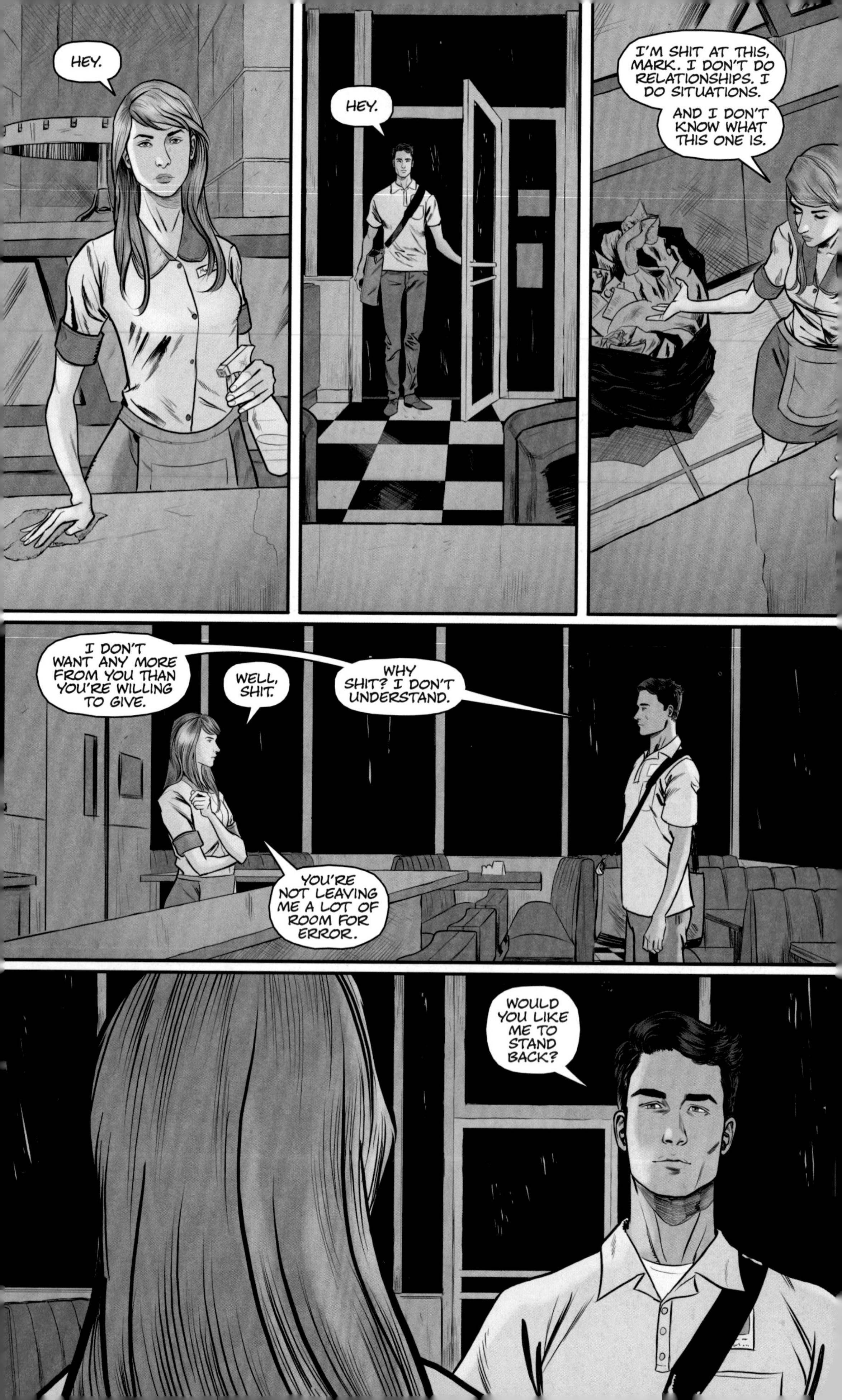
HEY.
HEY.
I'M SHIT AT THIS, MARK. I DON'T DO RELATIONSHIPS. I DO SITUATIONS.
AND I DON'T KNOW WHAT THIS ONE IS.
I DON'T WANT ANY MORE FROM YOU THAN YOU'RE WILLING TO GIVE.
WELL, SHIT.
WHY SHIT? I DON'T UNDERSTAND.
YOU'RE NOT LEAVING ME A LOT OF ROOM FOR ERROR.
WOULD YOU LIKE ME TO STAND BACK?

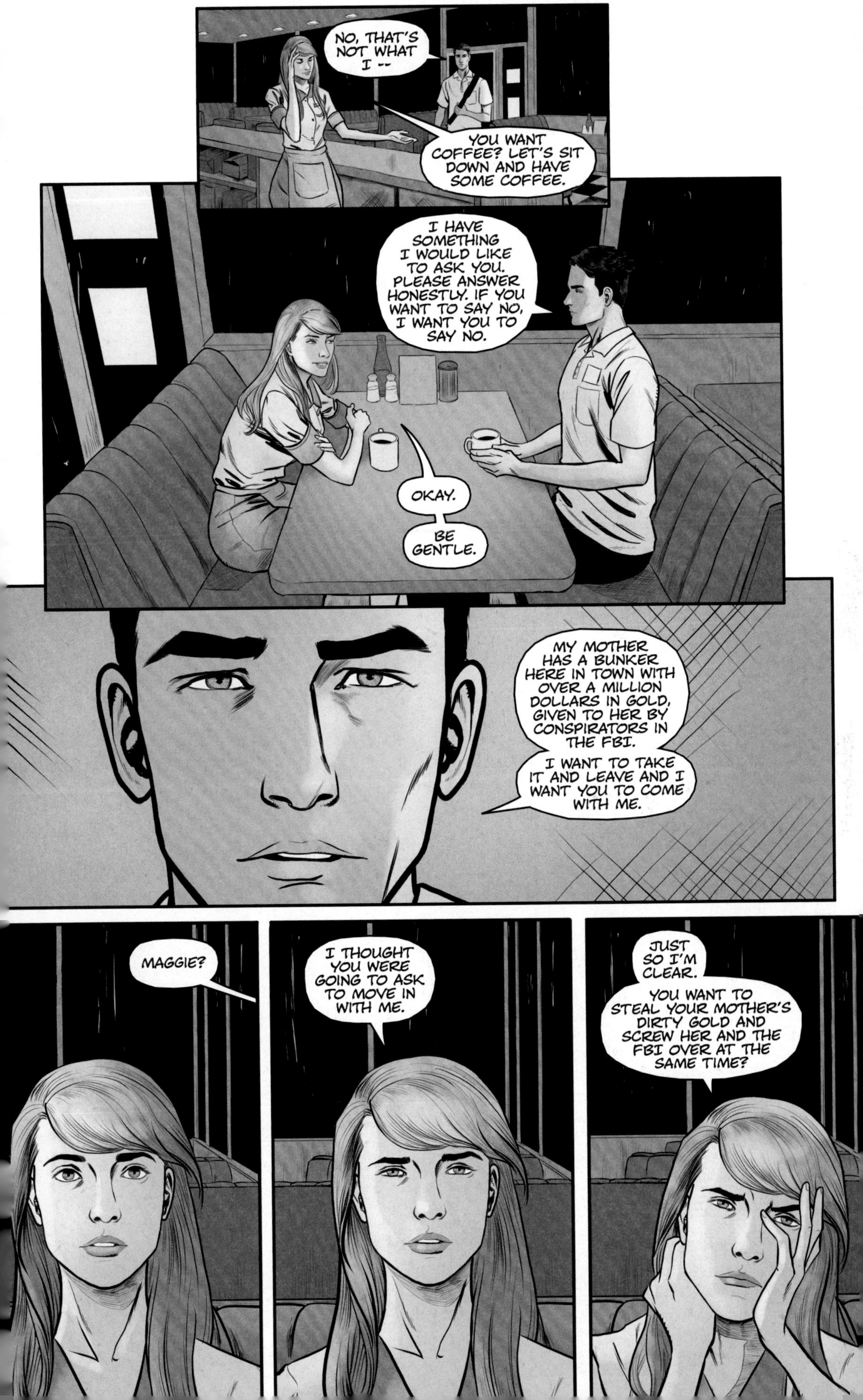

NO, THAT'S NOT WHAT I --
YOU WANT COFFEE? LET'S SIT DOWN AND HAVE SOME COFFEE.
I HAVE SOMETHING I WOULD LIKE TO ASK YOU. PLEASE ANSWER HONESTLY. IF YOU WANT TO SAY NO, I WANT YOU TO SAY NO.
OKAY.
BE GENTLE.
MY MOTHER HAS A BUNKER HERE IN TOWN WITH OVER A MILLION DOLLARS IN GOLD, GIVEN TO HER BY CONSPIRATORS IN THE FBI.
I WANT TO TAKE IT AND LEAVE AND I WANT YOU TO COME WITH ME.
MAGGIE?
I THOUGHT YOU WERE GOING TO ASK TO MOVE IN WITH ME.
JUST SO I'M CLEAR.
YOU WANT TO STEAL YOUR MOTHER'S DIRTY GOLD AND SCREW HER AND THE FBI OVER AT THE SAME TIME?

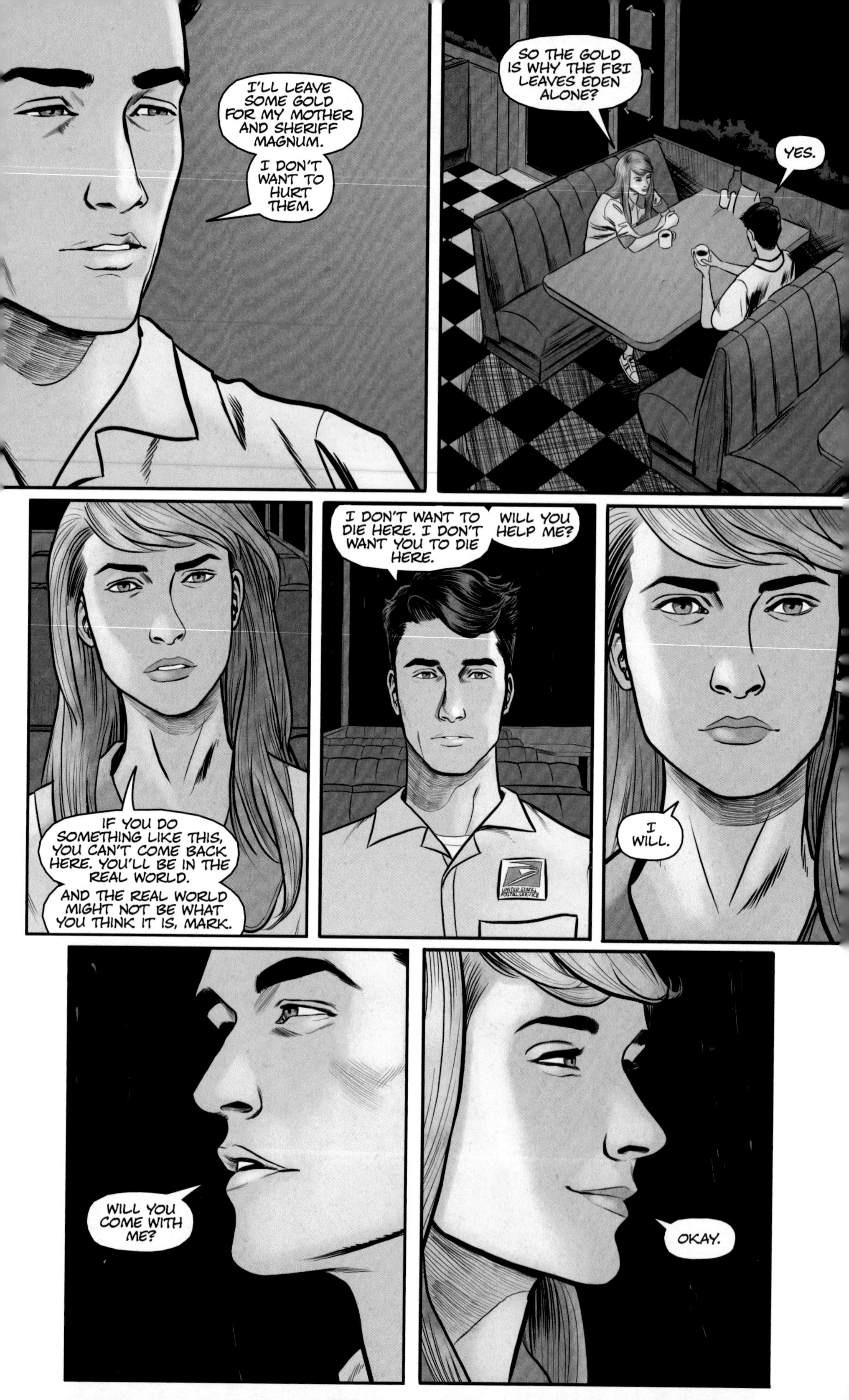
I'LL LEAVE SOME GOLD FOR MY MOTHER AND SHERIFF MAGNUM.
I DON'T WANT TO HURT THEM.
SO THE GOLD IS WHY THE FBI LEAVES EDEN ALONE?
YES.
IF YOU DO SOMETHING LIKE THIS, YOU CAN'T COME BACK HERE. YOU'LL BE IN THE REAL WORLD.
AND THE REAL WORLD MIGHT NOT BE WHAT YOU THINK IT IS, MARK.
I DON'T WANT TO DIE HERE. I DON'T WANT YOU TO DIE HERE.
WILL YOU HELP ME?
I WILL.
WILL YOU COME WITH ME?
OKAY.

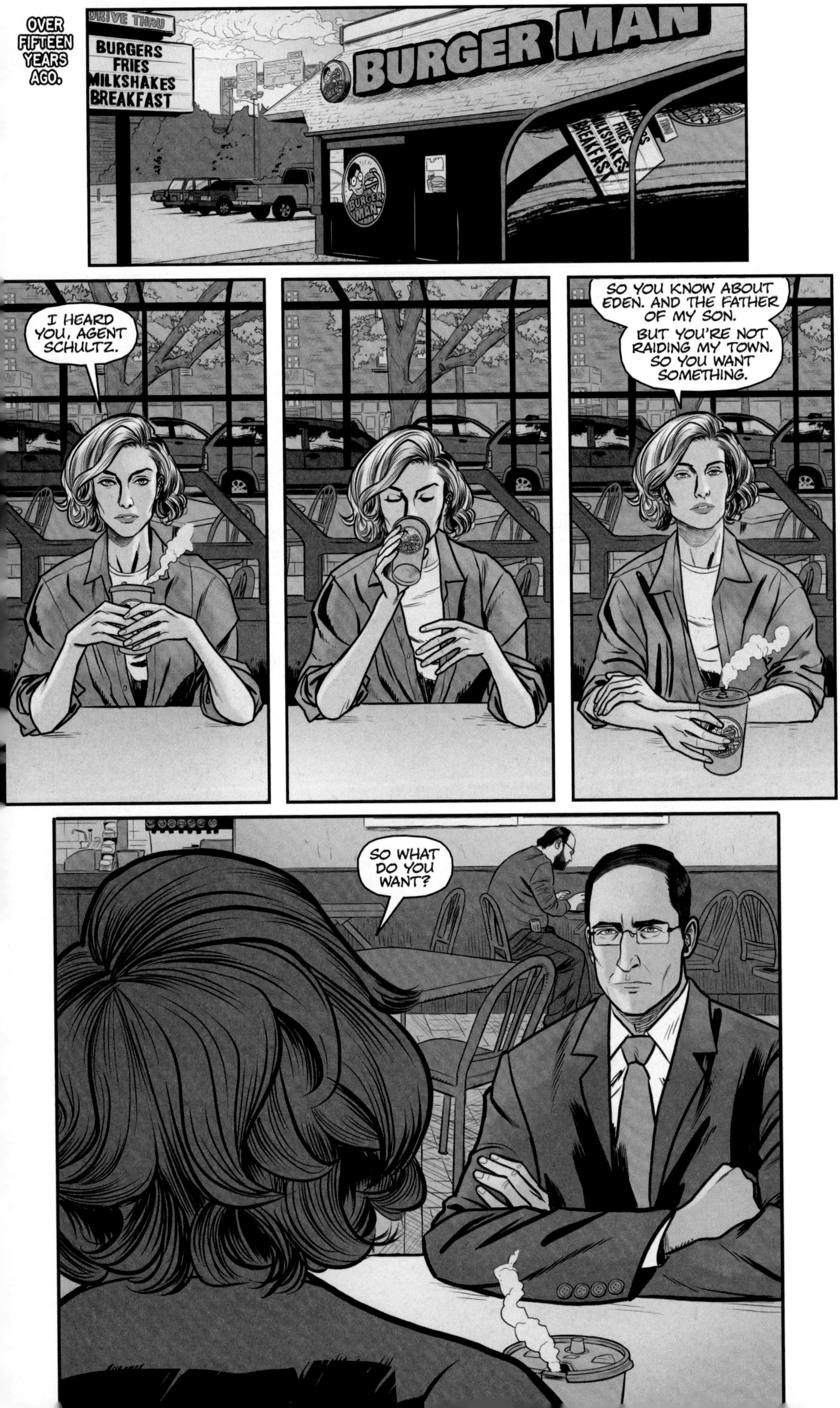
OVER FIFTEEN YEARS AGO.
DRIVE THRU
BURGERS
FRIES
MILKSHAKES
BREAKFAST
BURGER MAN
I HEARD YOU, AGENT SCHULTZ.
SO YOU KNOW ABOUT EDEN. AND THE FATHER OF MY SON.
BUT YOU'RE NOT RAIDING MY TOWN. SO YOU WANT SOMETHING.
SO WHAT DO YOU WANT?

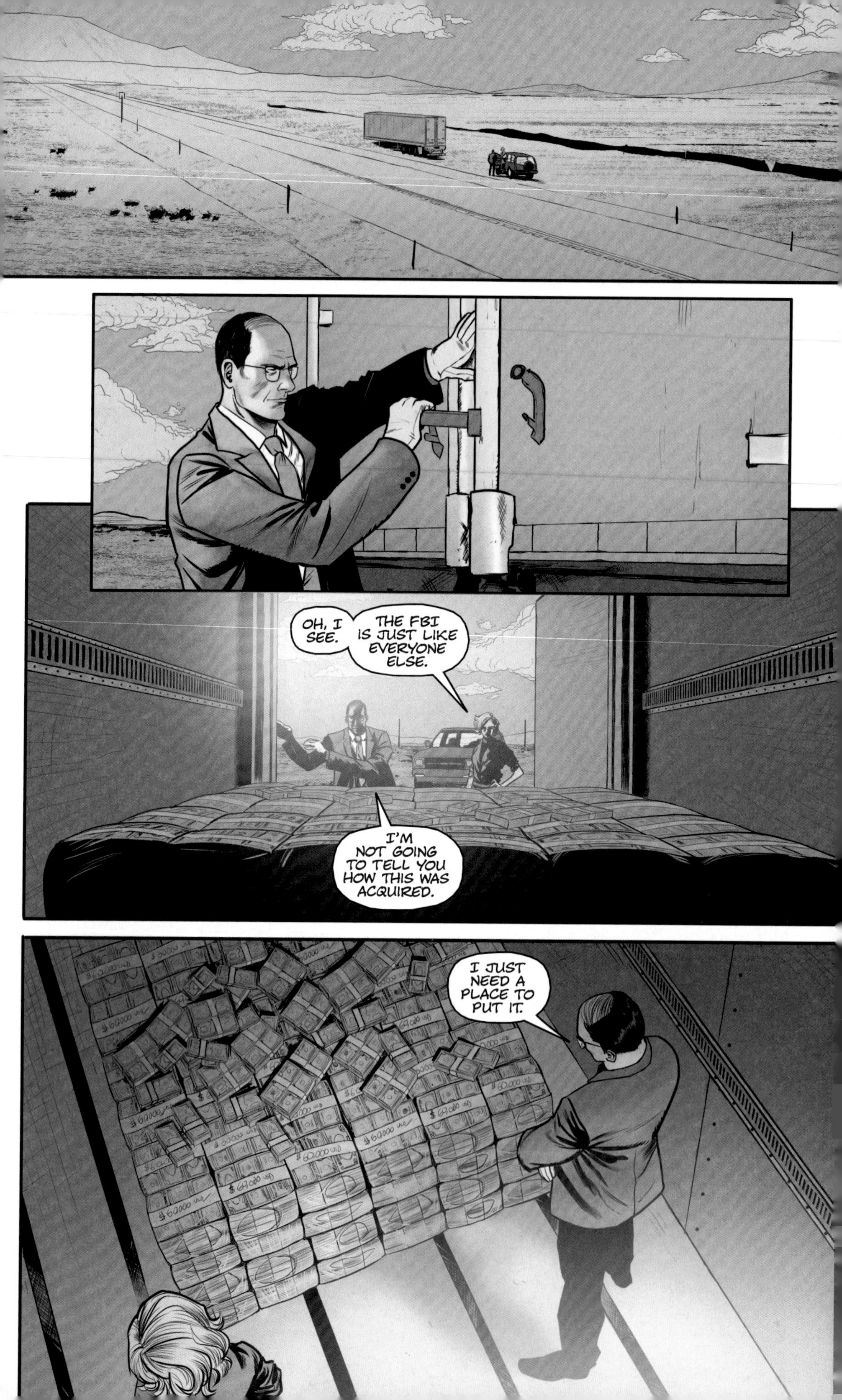
OH, I SEE.
THE FBI IS JUST LIKE EVERYONE ELSE.
I'M NOT GOING TO TELL YOU HOW THIS WAS ACQUIRED.
I JUST NEED A PLACE TO PUT IT.

YOU HAVE A PEN? GIVE ME ONE AND OPEN YOUR HAND.

CASH LEAVES THE WRONG KIND OF TRAIL. CALL THIS NUMBER. TELL HIM LAURA SHIFFRON IS CASHING IN HER FAVOR.

YOU'RE GOING TO CONVERT THIS TO GOLD, AND PAY THE MAN ON THE LINE FIFTEEN PERCENT OF THE TOTAL.

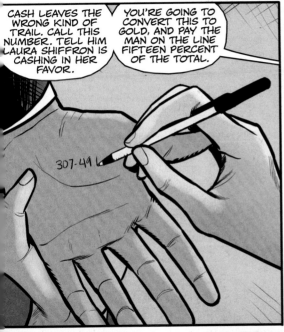

307-49

THEN YOU'RE GOING TO GIVE ME THE GOLD TO ME FOR SAFE KEEPING.

I'M NOT A CRIMINAL, LAURA. THIS IS SOMETHING I DESERVE TO HAVE. I MADE SACRIFICES FOR IT.

DON'T SWEAT, SCHULTZ.

YOU'LL SMEAR THE NUMBER AND THEN WE'LL HAVE TO START ALL OVER.

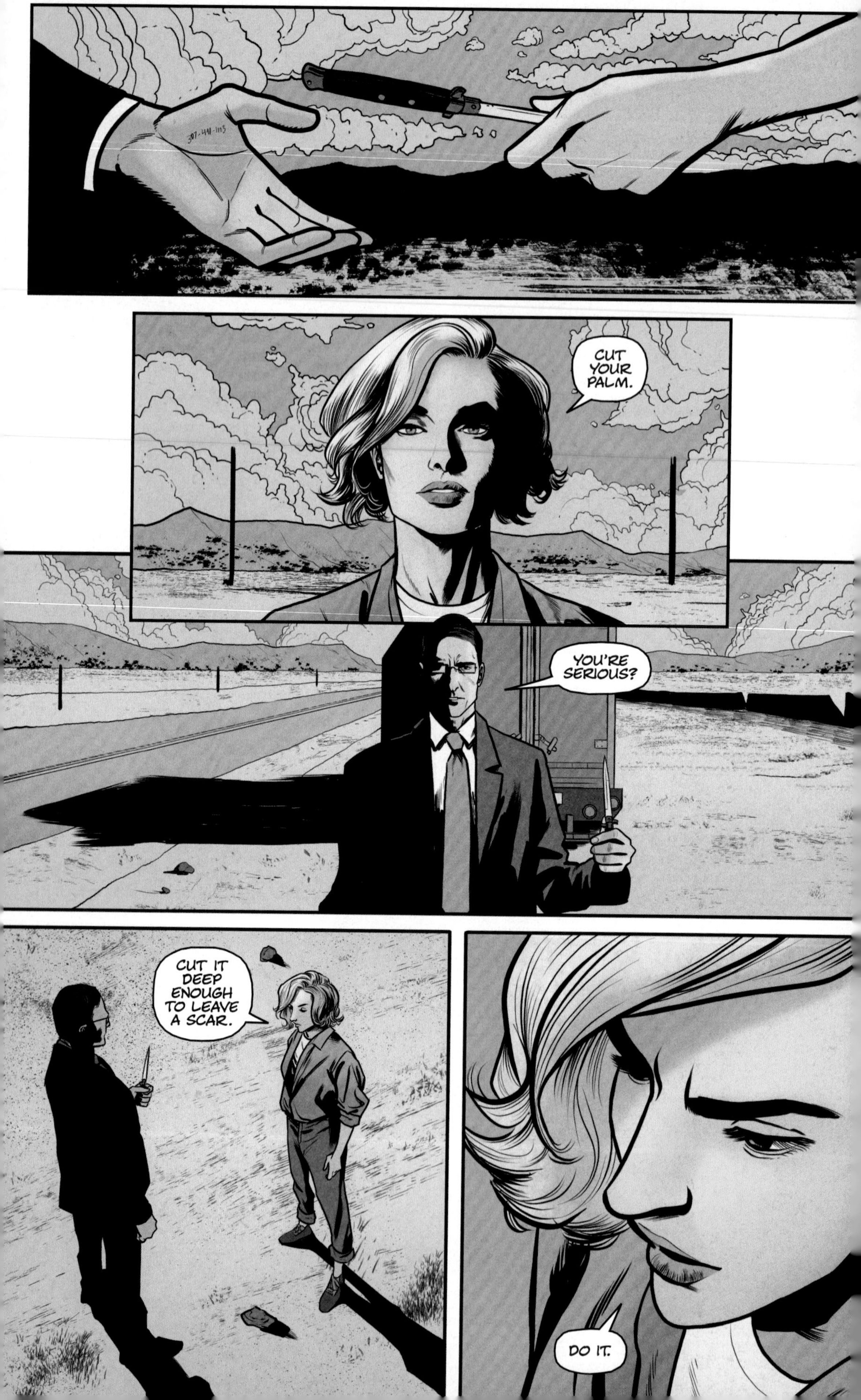
CUT YOUR PALM.
YOU'RE SERIOUS?
CUT IT DEEP ENOUGH TO LEAVE A SCAR.
DO IT.

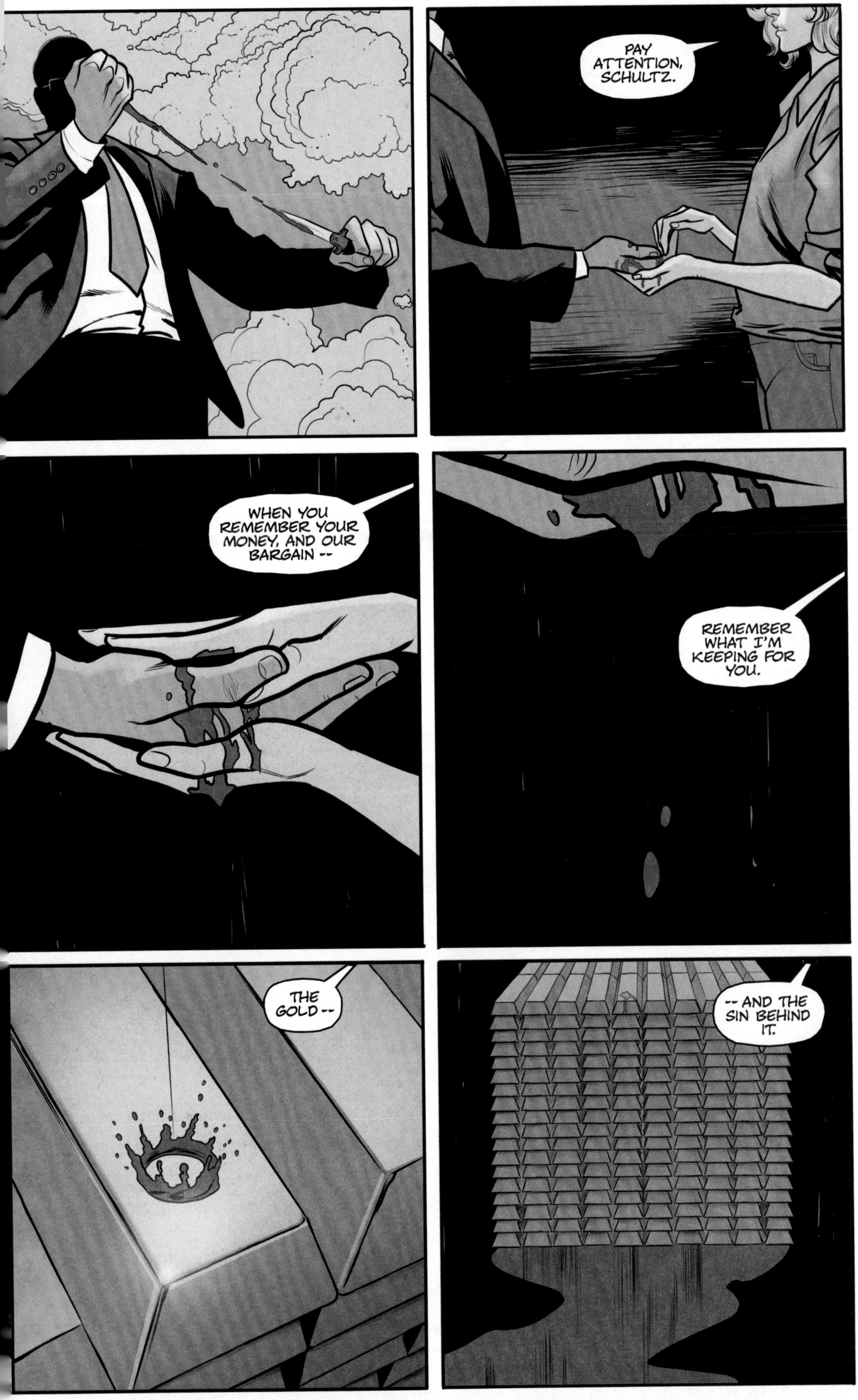
PAY ATTENTION, SCHULTZ.
WHEN YOU REMEMBER YOUR MONEY, AND OUR BARGAIN --
REMEMBER WHAT I'M KEEPING FOR YOU.
THE GOLD --
-- AND THE SIN BEHIND IT.

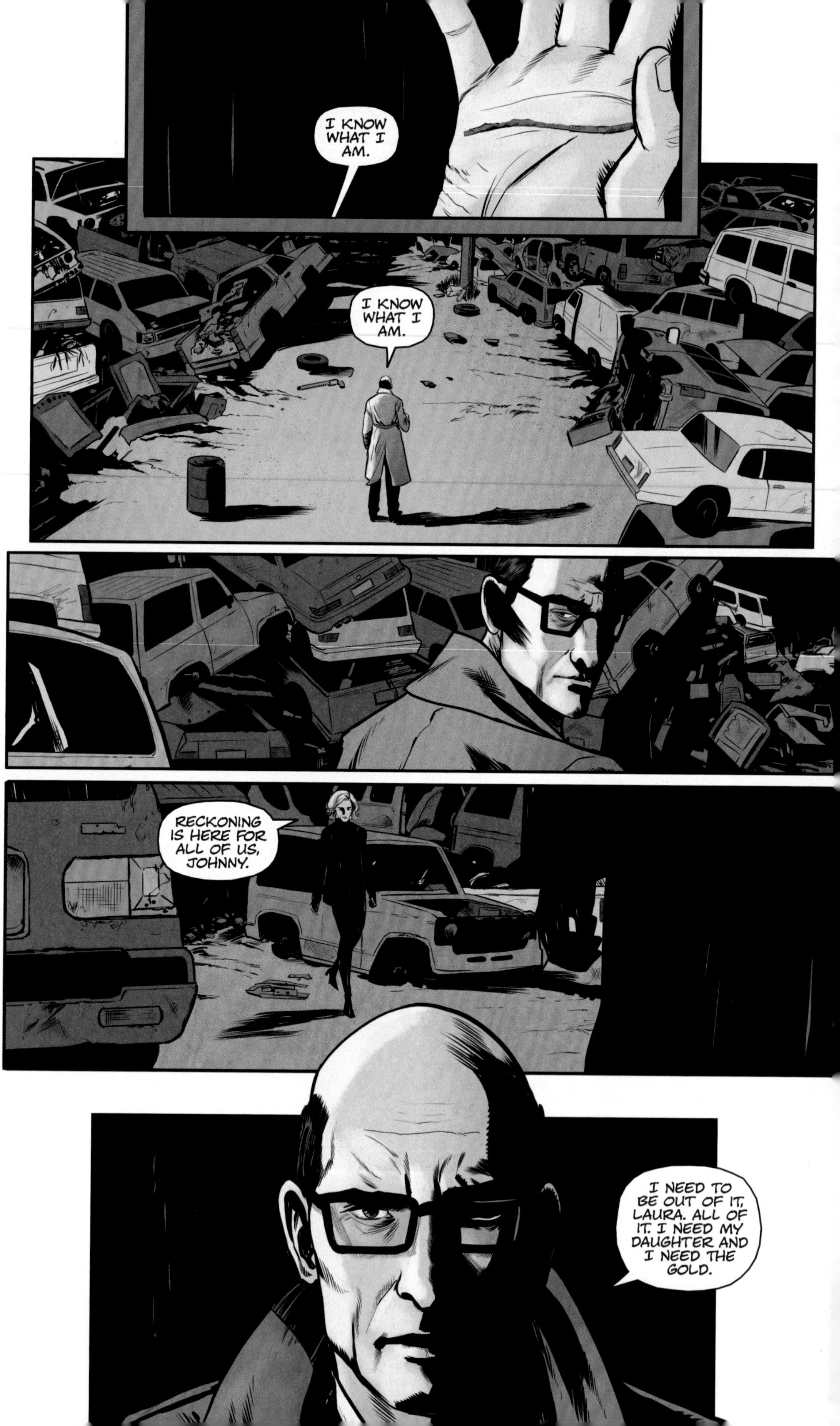
I KNOW WHAT I AM.
I KNOW WHAT I AM.
RECKONING IS HERE FOR ALL OF US, JOHNNY.
I NEED TO BE OUT OF IT, LAURA. ALL OF IT. I NEED MY DAUGHTER AND I NEED THE GOLD.

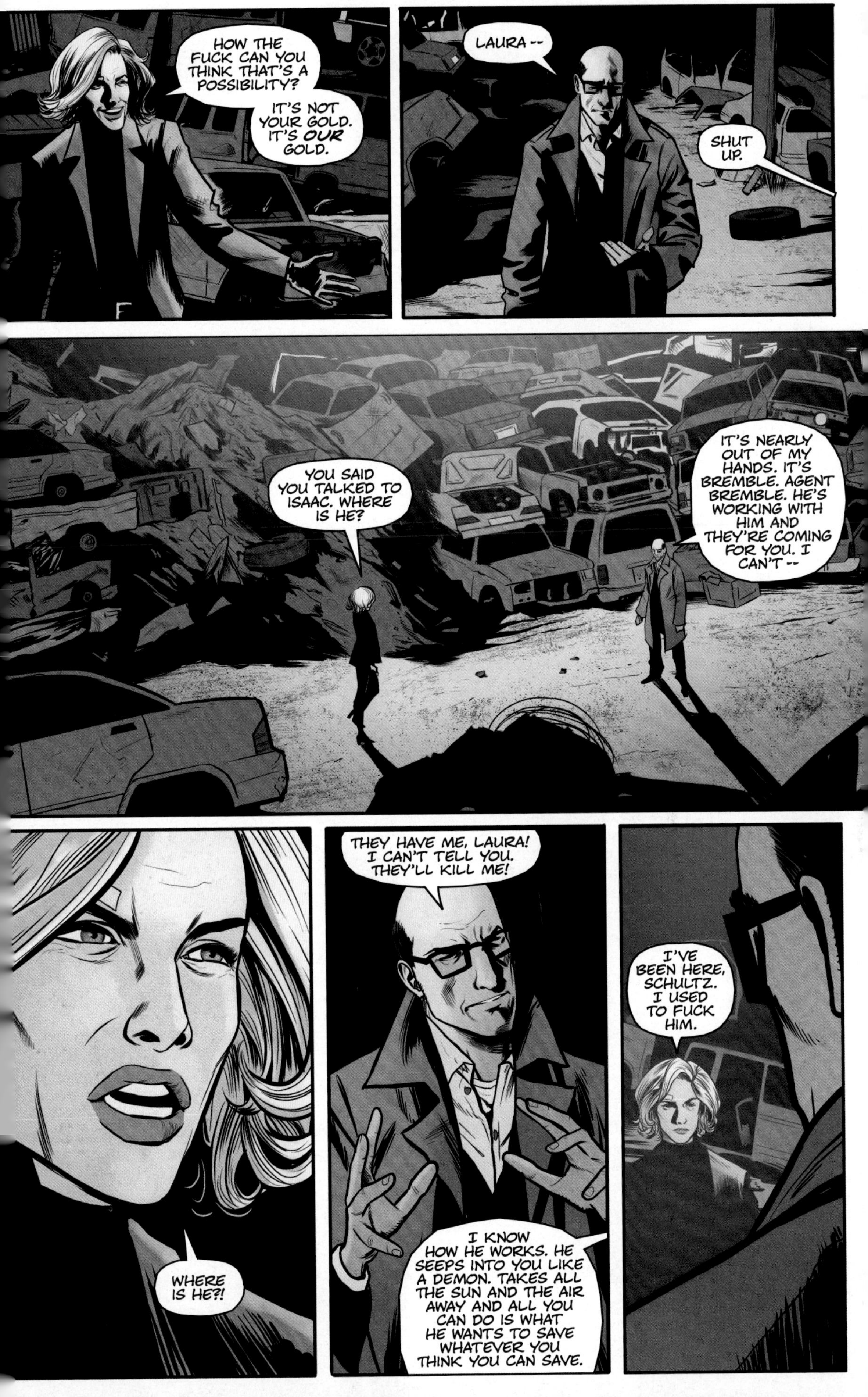
HOW THE FUCK CAN YOU THINK THAT'S A POSSIBILITY?
IT'S NOT YOUR GOLD. IT'S OUR GOLD.
LAURA --
SHUT UP.
YOU SAID YOU TALKED TO ISAAC. WHERE IS HE?
IT'S NEARLY OUT OF MY HANDS. IT'S BREMBLE. AGENT BREMBLE. HE'S WORKING WITH HIM AND THEY'RE COMING FOR YOU. I CAN'T --
WHERE IS HE?!
THEY HAVE ME, LAURA! I CAN'T TELL YOU. THEY'LL KILL ME!
I KNOW HOW HE WORKS. HE SEEPS INTO YOU LIKE A DEMON. TAKES ALL THE SUN AND THE AIR AWAY AND ALL YOU CAN DO IS WHAT HE WANTS TO SAVE WHATEVER YOU THINK YOU CAN SAVE.
I'VE BEEN HERE, SCHULTZ. I USED TO FUCK HIM.

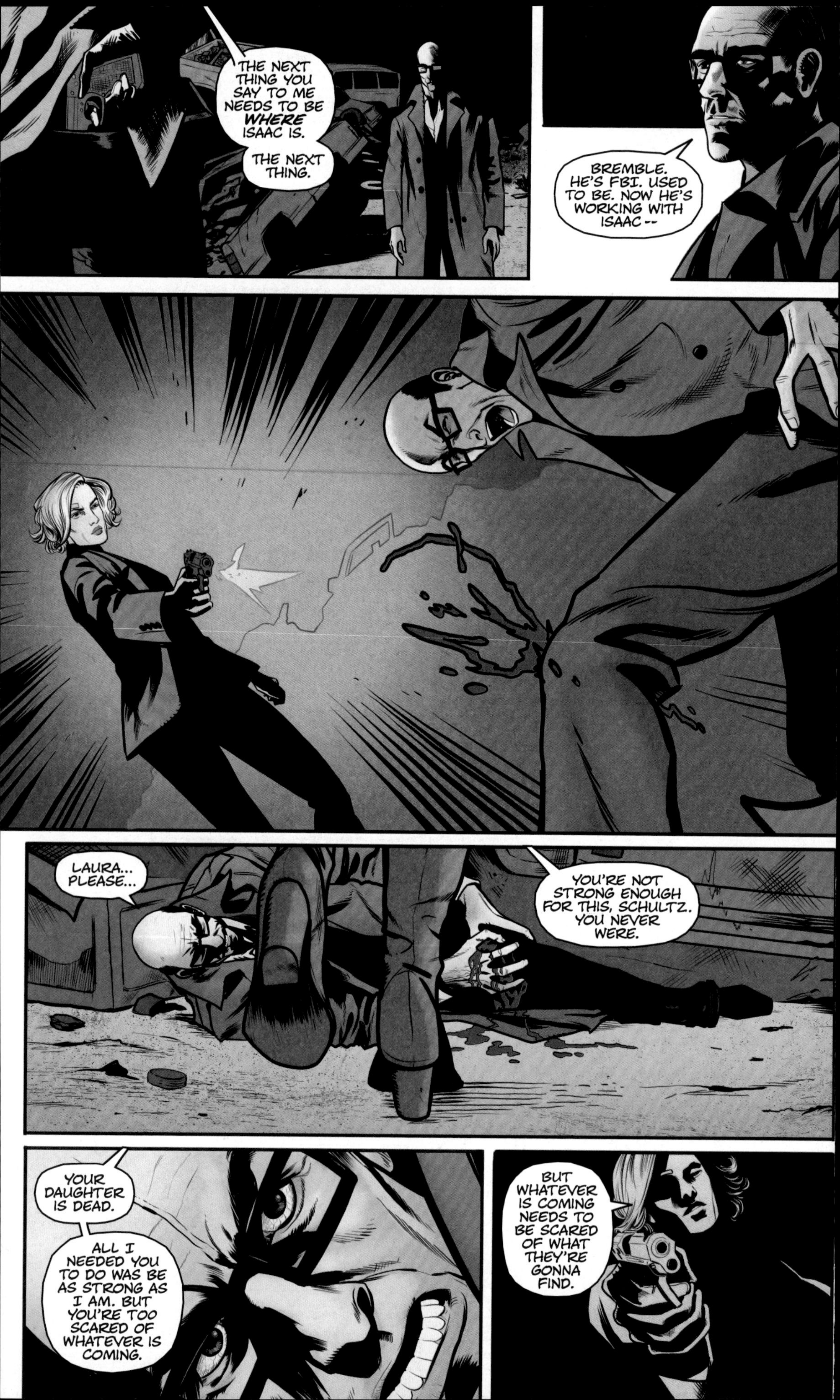
THE NEXT THING YOU SAY TO ME NEEDS TO BE ***WHERE*** ISAAC IS.
THE NEXT THING.
BREMBLE. HE'S FBI. USED TO BE. NOW HE'S WORKING WITH ISAAC --
LAURA... PLEASE...
YOU'RE NOT STRONG ENOUGH FOR THIS, SCHULTZ. YOU NEVER WERE.
YOUR DAUGHTER IS DEAD.
ALL I NEEDED YOU TO DO WAS BE AS STRONG AS I AM. BUT YOU'RE TOO SCARED OF WHATEVER IS COMING.
BUT WHATEVER IS COMING NEEDS TO BE SCARED OF WHAT THEY'RE GONNA FIND.

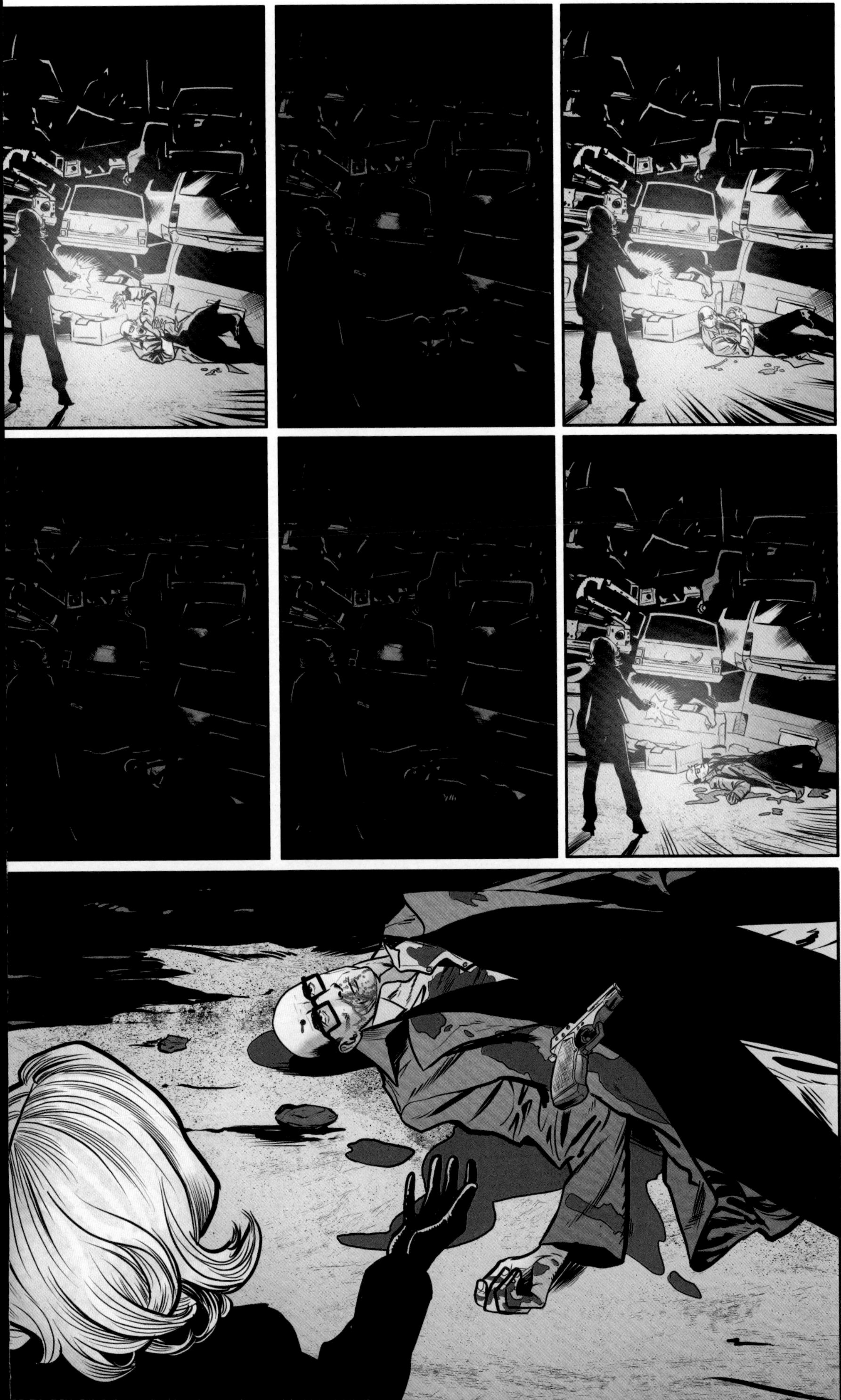

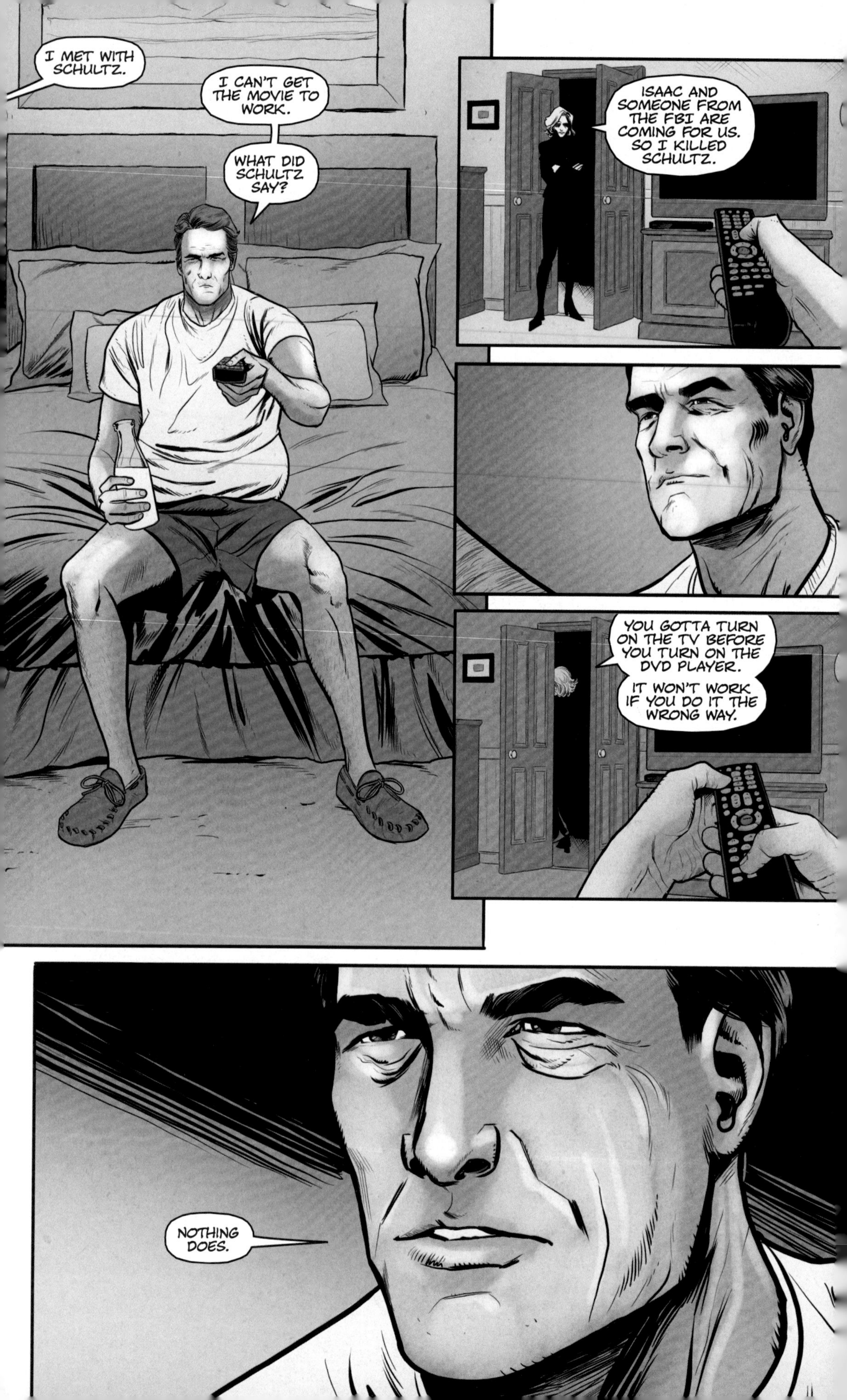
I MET WITH SCHULTZ.
I CAN'T GET THE MOVIE TO WORK.
WHAT DID SCHULTZ SAY?
ISAAC AND SOMEONE FROM THE FBI ARE COMING FOR US. SO I KILLED SCHULTZ.
YOU GOTTA TURN ON THE TV BEFORE YOU TURN ON THE DVD PLAYER.
IT WON'T WORK IF YOU DO IT THE WRONG WAY.
NOTHING DOES.

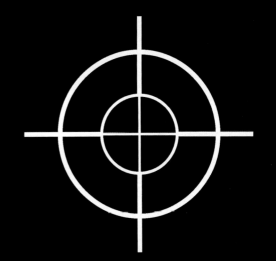

# CHAPTER 22

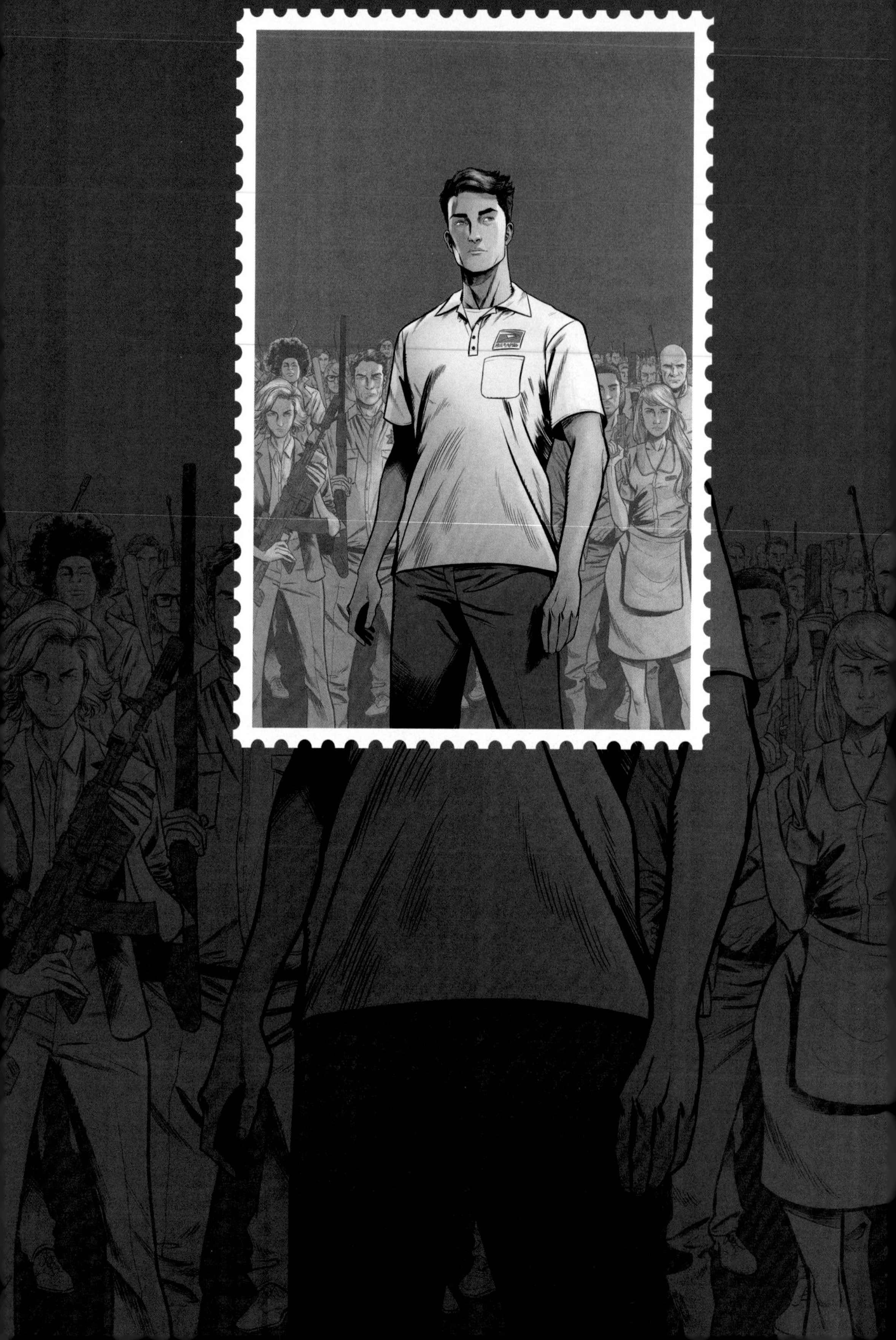

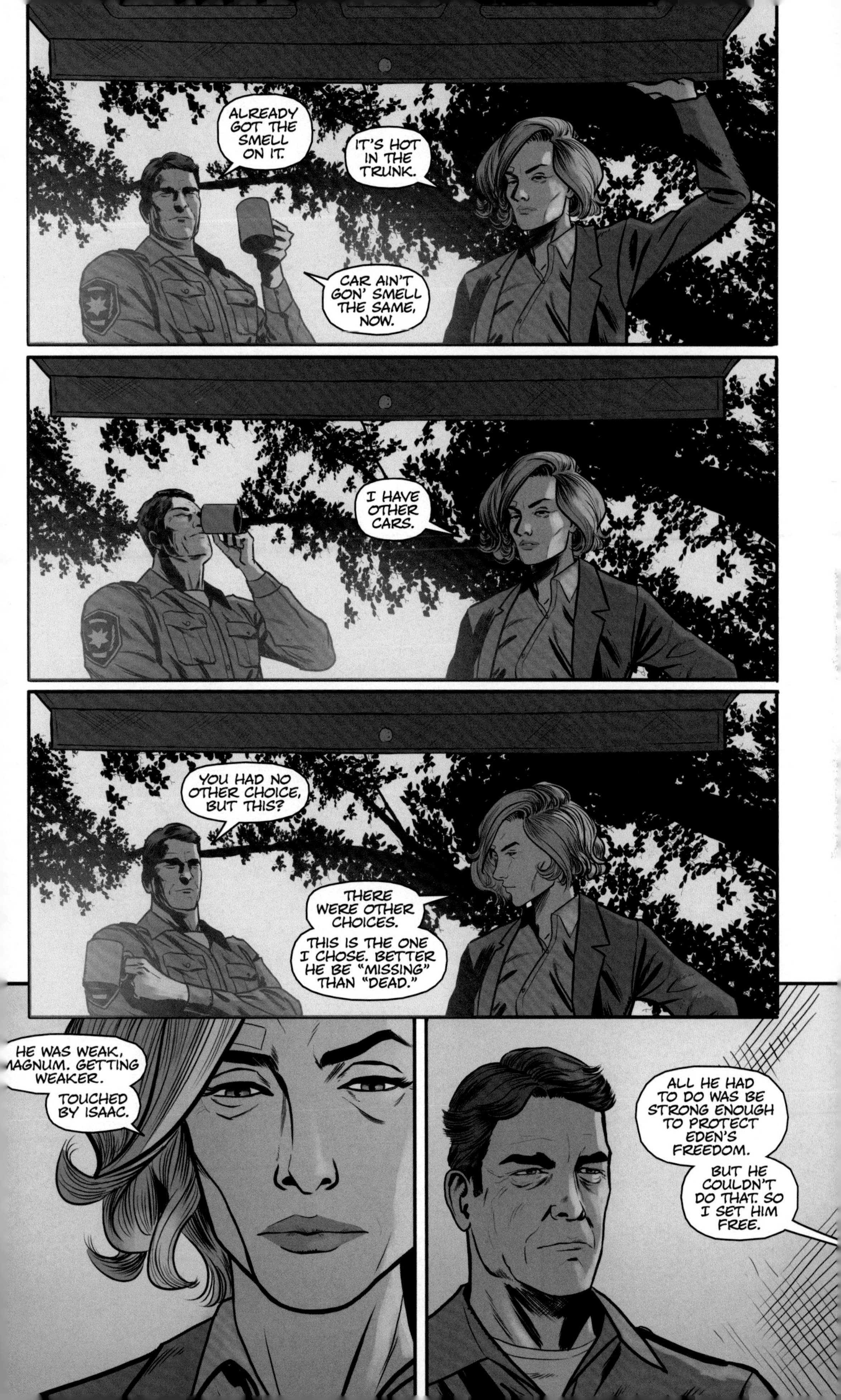
ALREADY GOT THE SMELL ON IT.
IT'S HOT IN THE TRUNK.
CAR AIN'T GON' SMELL THE SAME, NOW.
I HAVE OTHER CARS.
YOU HAD NO OTHER CHOICE, BUT THIS?
THERE WERE OTHER CHOICES.
THIS IS THE ONE I CHOSE. BETTER HE BE "MISSING" THAN "DEAD."
HE WAS WEAK, MAGNUM. GETTING WEAKER.
TOUCHED BY ISAAC.
ALL HE HAD TO DO WAS BE STRONG ENOUGH TO PROTECT EDEN'S FREEDOM.
BUT HE COULDN'T DO THAT. SO I SET HIM FREE.

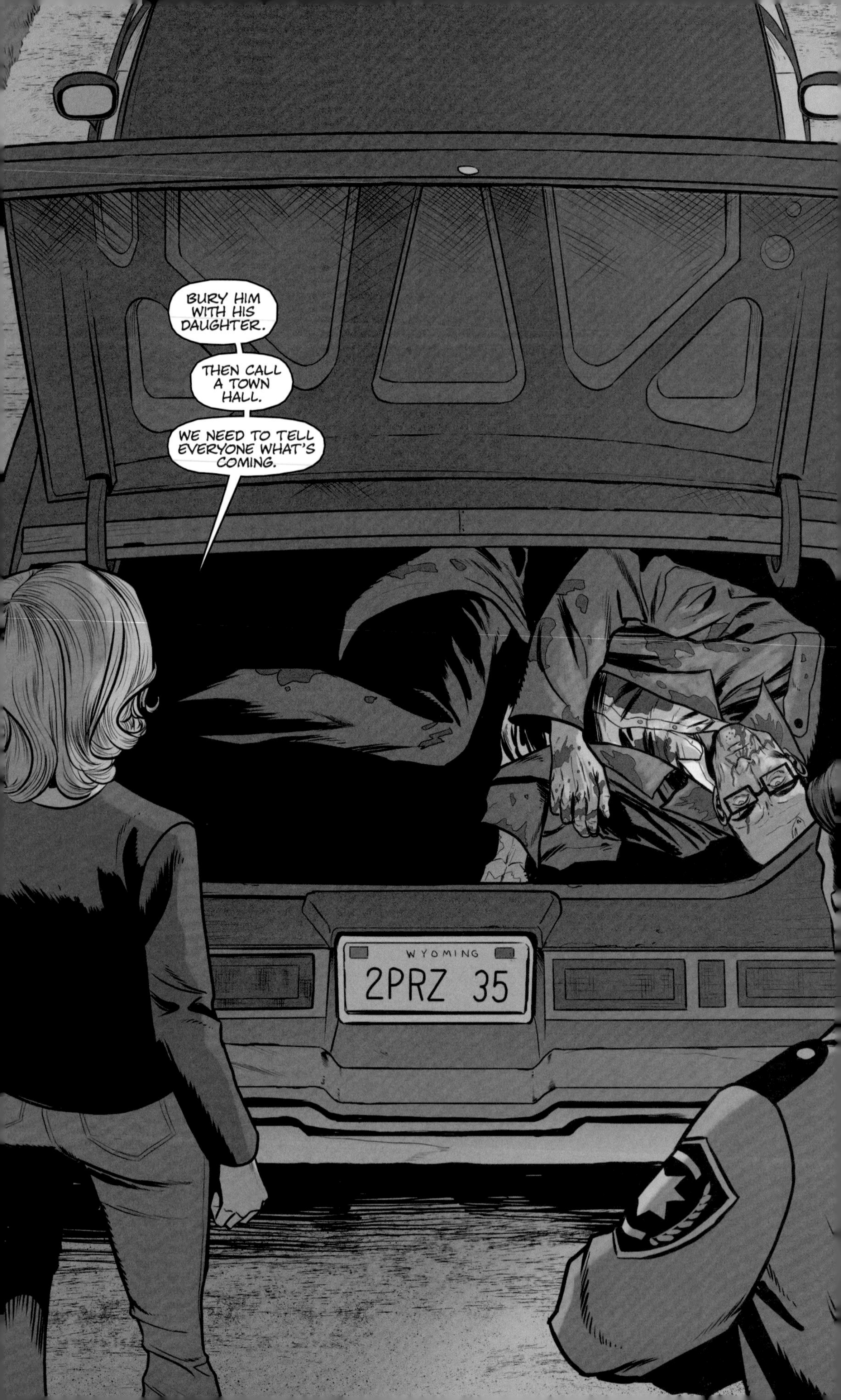
BURY HIM WITH HIS DAUGHTER.
THEN CALL A TOWN HALL.
WE NEED TO TELL EVERYONE WHAT'S COMING.
WYOMING
2PRZ 35

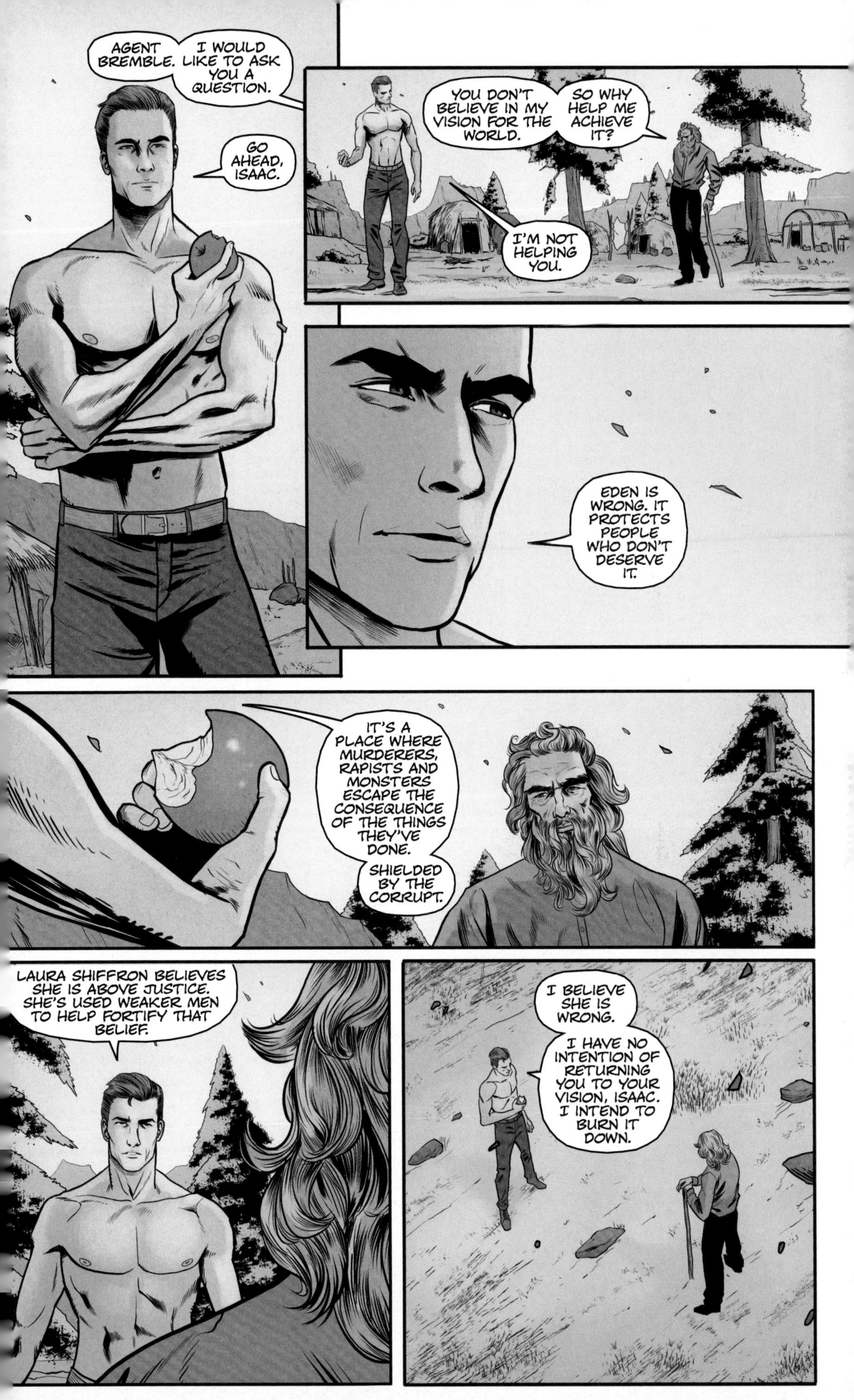
AGENT BREMBLE.
I WOULD LIKE TO ASK YOU A QUESTION.
GO AHEAD, ISAAC.
YOU DON'T BELIEVE IN MY VISION FOR THE WORLD.
SO WHY HELP ME ACHIEVE IT?
I'M NOT HELPING YOU.
EDEN IS WRONG. IT PROTECTS PEOPLE WHO DON'T DESERVE IT.
IT'S A PLACE WHERE MURDERERS, RAPISTS AND MONSTERS ESCAPE THE CONSEQUENCE OF THE THINGS THEY'VE DONE.
SHIELDED BY THE CORRUPT.
LAURA SHIFFRON BELIEVES SHE IS ABOVE JUSTICE. SHE'S USED WEAKER MEN TO HELP FORTIFY THAT BELIEF.
I BELIEVE SHE IS WRONG.
I HAVE NO INTENTION OF RETURNING YOU TO YOUR VISION, ISAAC. I INTEND TO BURN IT DOWN.

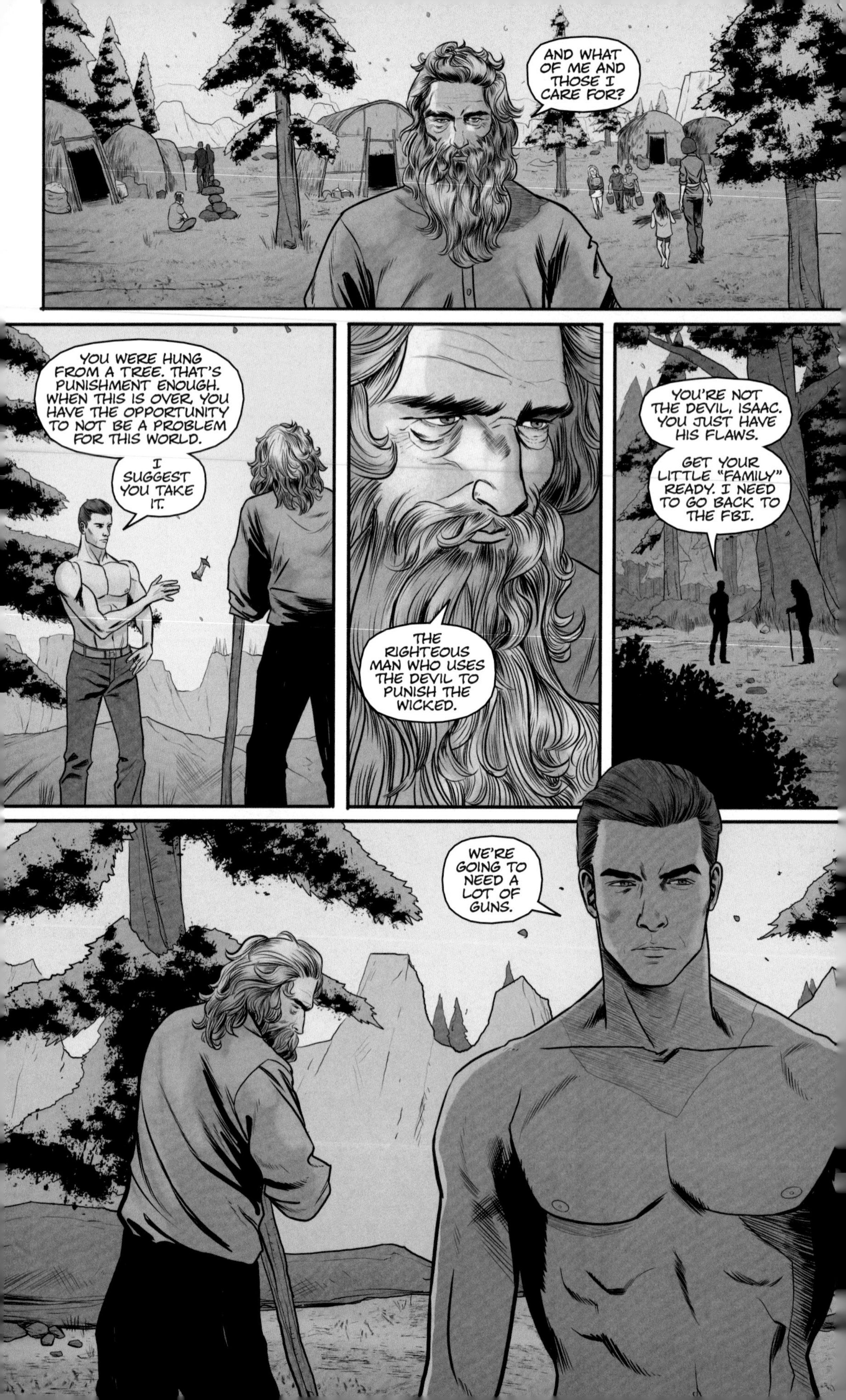
AND WHAT OF ME AND THOSE I CARE FOR?
YOU WERE HUNG FROM A TREE. THAT'S PUNISHMENT ENOUGH. WHEN THIS IS OVER, YOU HAVE THE OPPORTUNITY TO NOT BE A PROBLEM FOR THIS WORLD.
I SUGGEST YOU TAKE IT.
THE RIGHTEOUS MAN WHO USES THE DEVIL TO PUNISH THE WICKED.
YOU'RE NOT THE DEVIL, ISAAC. YOU JUST HAVE HIS FLAWS.
GET YOUR LITTLE "FAMILY" READY. I NEED TO GO BACK TO THE FBI.
WE'RE GOING TO NEED A LOT OF GUNS.

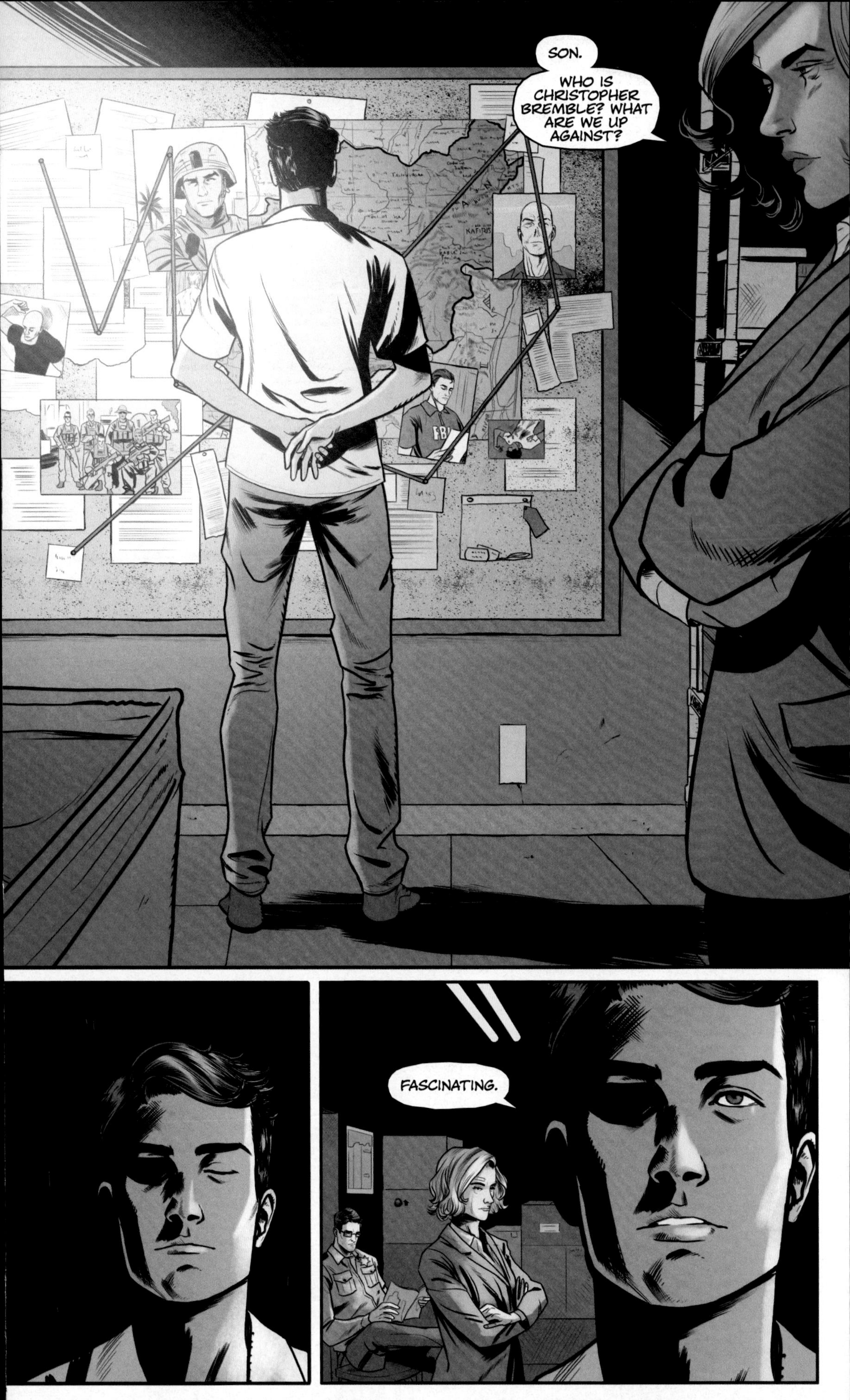
SON.
WHO IS CHRISTOPHER BREMBLE? WHAT ARE WE UP AGAINST?
FASCINATING.

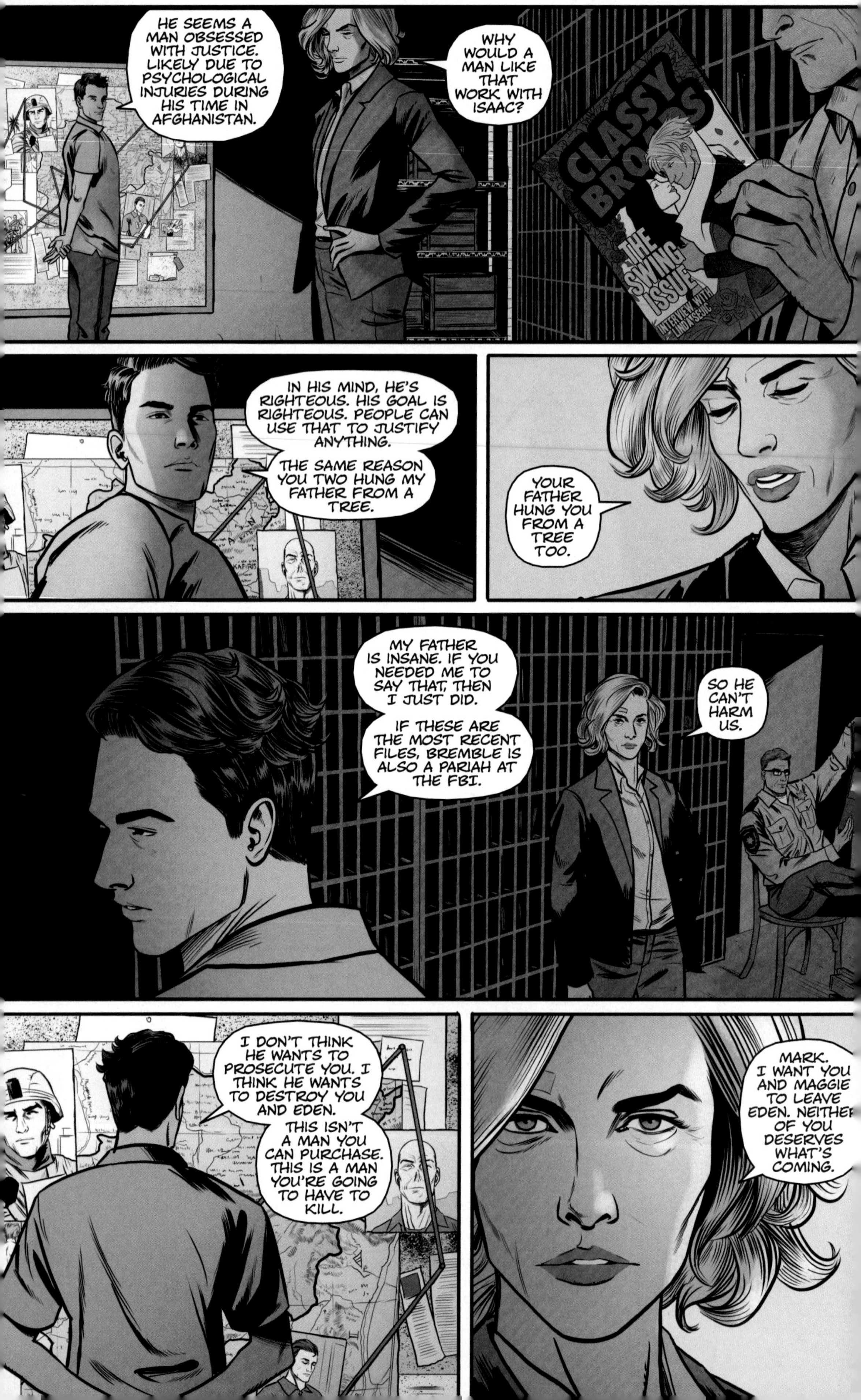
HE SEEMS A MAN OBSESSED WITH JUSTICE. LIKELY DUE TO PSYCHOLOGICAL INJURIES DURING HIS TIME IN AFGHANISTAN.
WHY WOULD A MAN LIKE THAT WORK WITH ISAAC?
CLASSY BROADS
THE SWING ISSUE
INTERVIEW WITH LINDA ASCUIC
IN HIS MIND, HE'S RIGHTEOUS. HIS GOAL IS RIGHTEOUS. PEOPLE CAN USE THAT TO JUSTIFY ANYTHING.
THE SAME REASON YOU TWO HUNG MY FATHER FROM A TREE.
YOUR FATHER HUNG YOU FROM A TREE TOO.
MY FATHER IS INSANE. IF YOU NEEDED ME TO SAY THAT, THEN I JUST DID.
IF THESE ARE THE MOST RECENT FILES, BREMBLE IS ALSO A PARIAH AT THE FBI.
SO HE CAN'T HARM US.
I DON'T THINK HE WANTS TO PROSECUTE YOU. I THINK HE WANTS TO DESTROY YOU AND EDEN.
THIS ISN'T A MAN YOU CAN PURCHASE. THIS IS A MAN YOU'RE GOING TO HAVE TO KILL.
MARK. I WANT YOU AND MAGGIE TO LEAVE EDEN. NEITHER OF YOU DESERVES WHAT'S COMING.

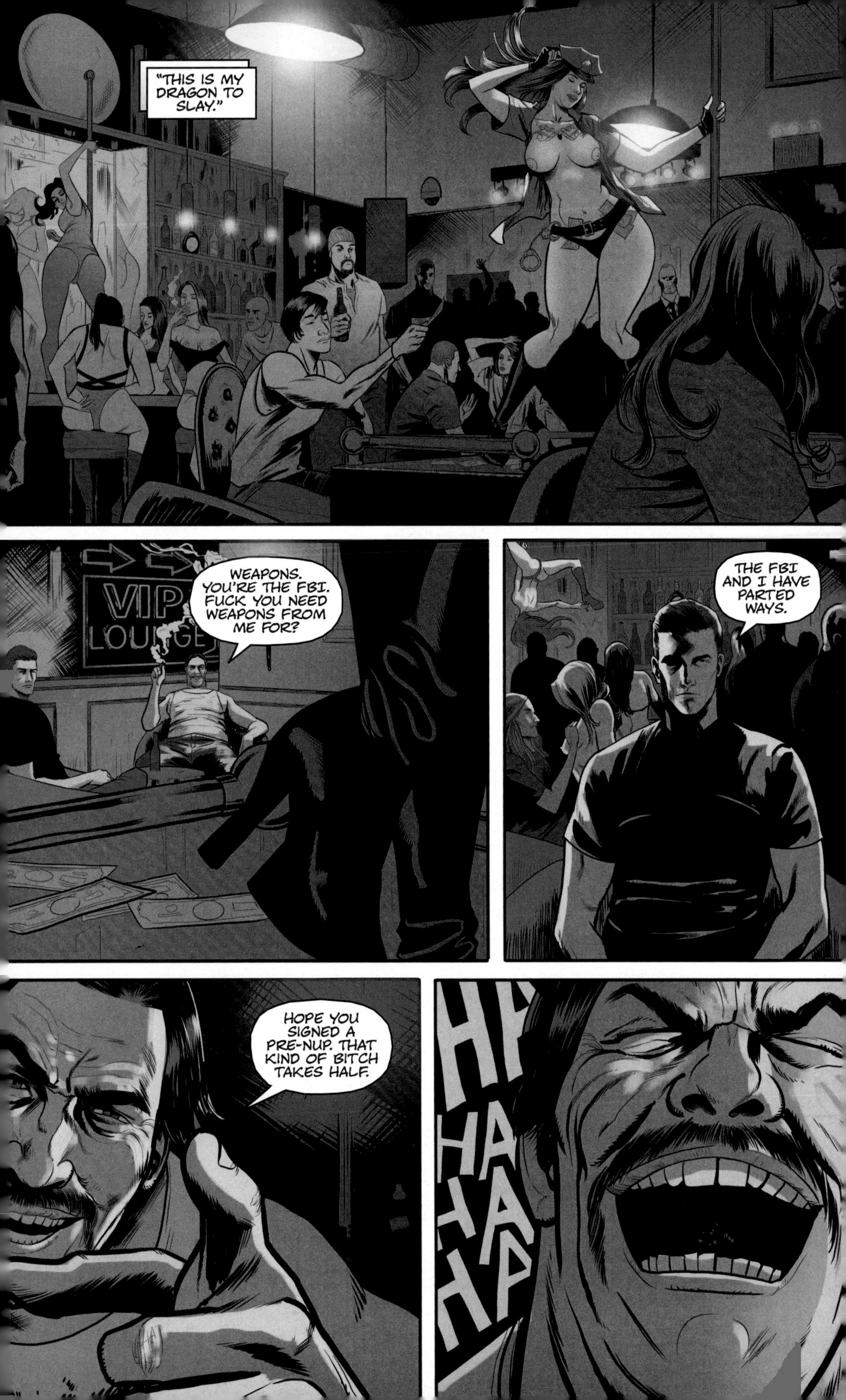
"THIS IS MY DRAGON TO SLAY."
WEAPONS. YOU'RE THE FBI. FUCK YOU NEED WEAPONS FROM ME FOR?
THE FBI AND I HAVE PARTED WAYS.
HOPE YOU SIGNED A PRE-NUP. THAT KIND OF BITCH TAKES HALF.
HA HA HA HA

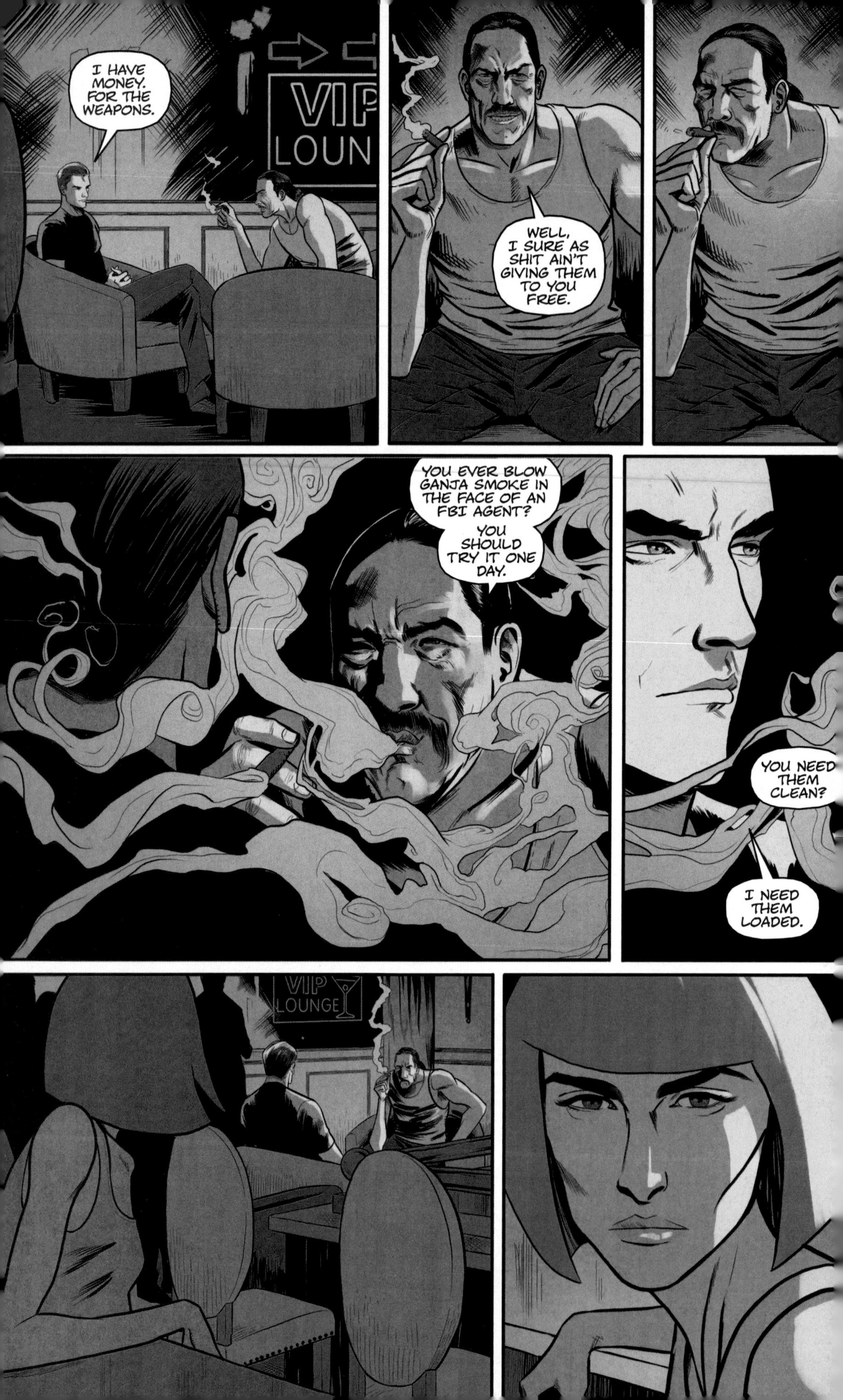
I HAVE MONEY. FOR THE WEAPONS.
VIP LOUN
WELL, I SURE AS SHIT AIN'T GIVING THEM TO YOU FREE.
YOU EVER BLOW GANJA SMOKE IN THE FACE OF AN FBI AGENT?
YOU SHOULD TRY IT ONE DAY.
YOU NEED THEM CLEAN?
I NEED THEM LOADED.
VIP LOUNGE

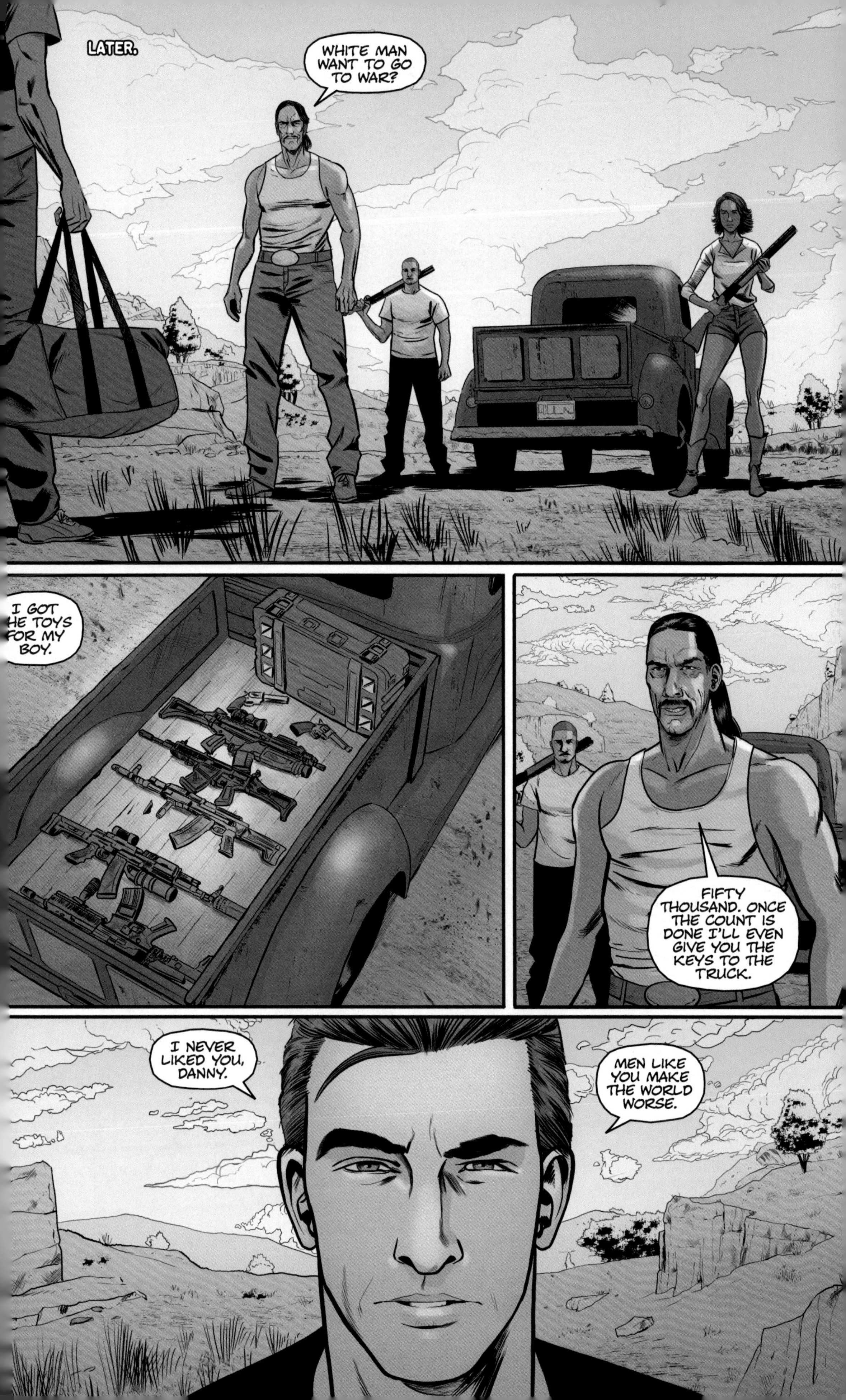
LATER.
WHITE MAN WANT TO GO TO WAR?
I GOT THE TOYS FOR MY BOY.
FIFTY THOUSAND. ONCE THE COUNT IS DONE I'LL EVEN GIVE YOU THE KEYS TO THE TRUCK.
I NEVER LIKED YOU, DANNY.
MEN LIKE YOU MAKE THE WORLD WORSE.

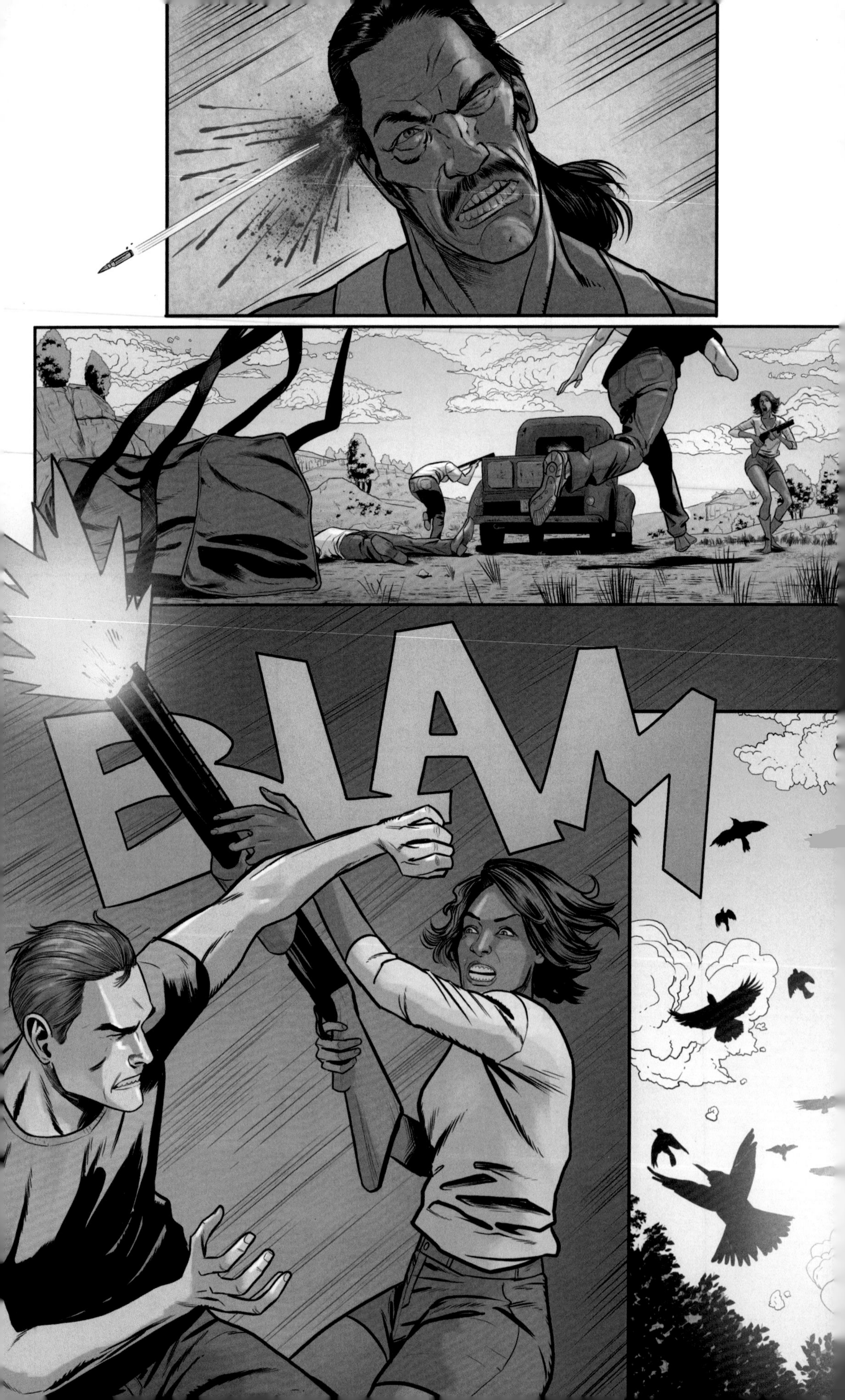
BLAM

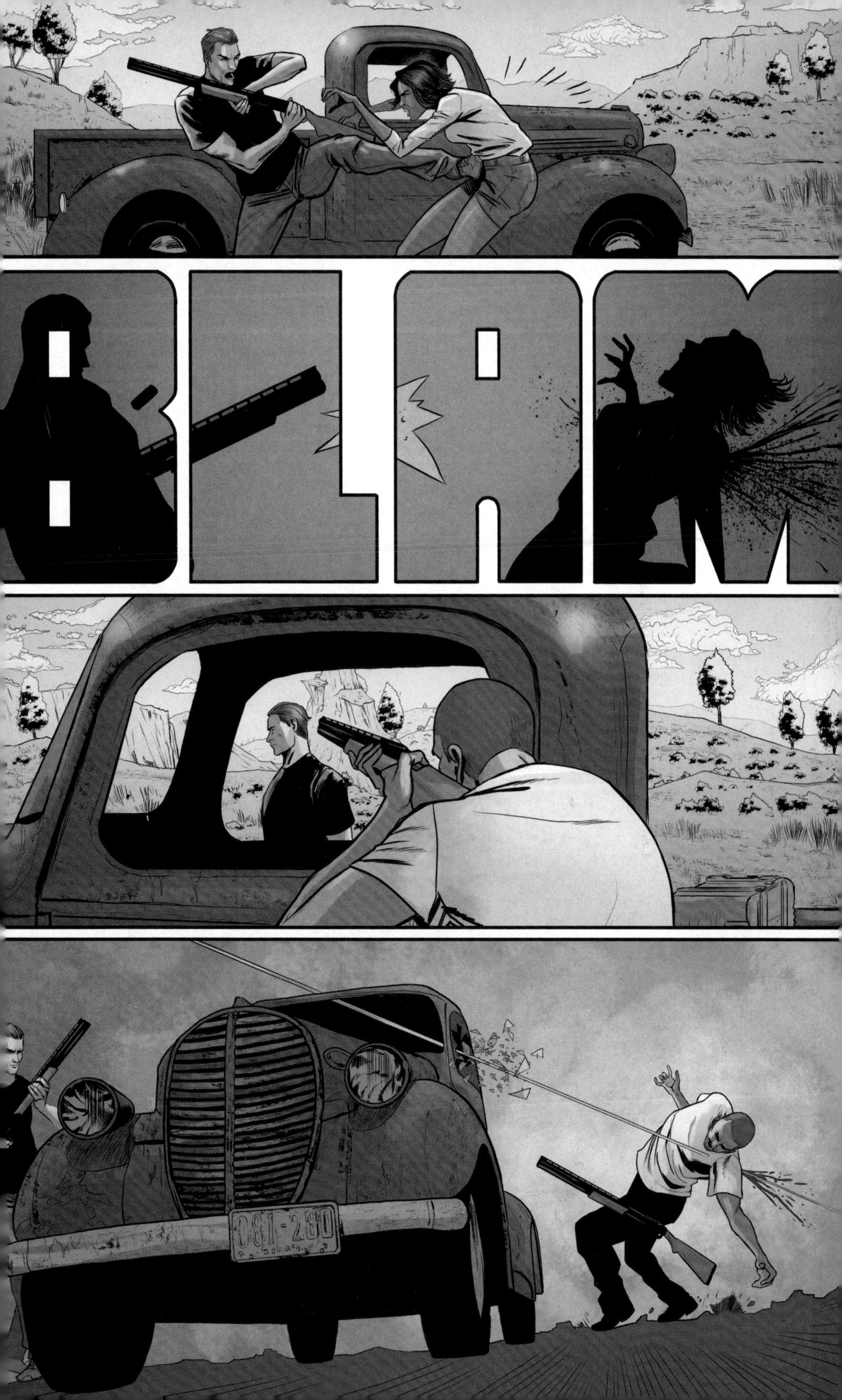
BLAM
081-280

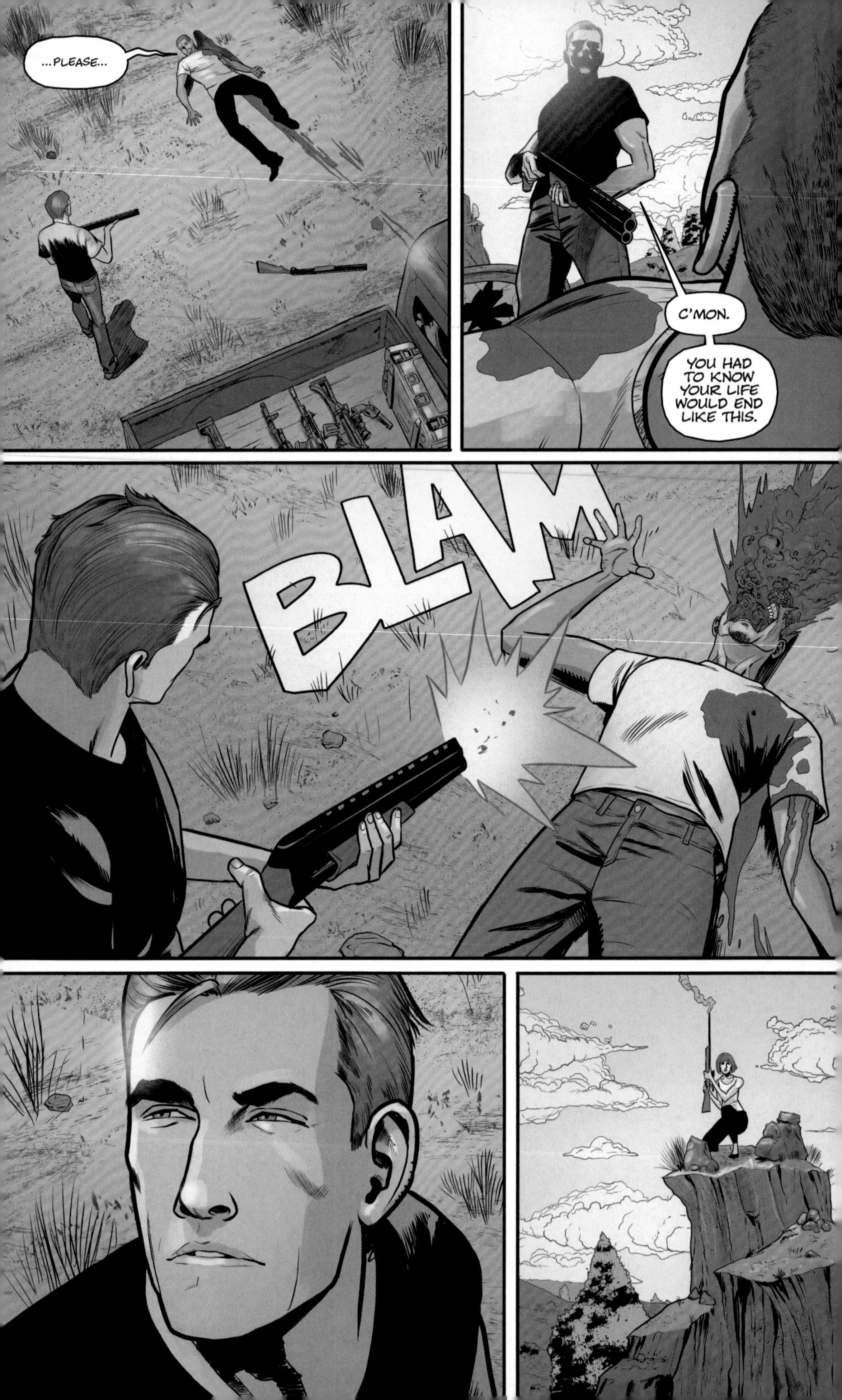
...PLEASE...
C'MON.
YOU HAD TO KNOW YOUR LIFE WOULD END LIKE THIS.
BLAM

WHAT HAPPENS IF I LEAVE? LIKE YOUR MOTHER ASKED US TO?

I WOULD GO WITH YOU.

AND IF YOUR MOTHER DOESN'T WIN THIS TIME?

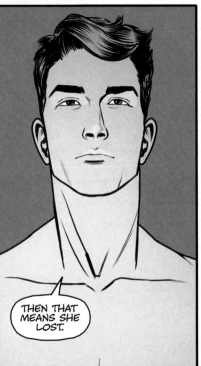

THEN THAT MEANS SHE LOST.

NO. THAT'S NOT WHAT I MEAN.

GODDAMNIT. LISTEN.

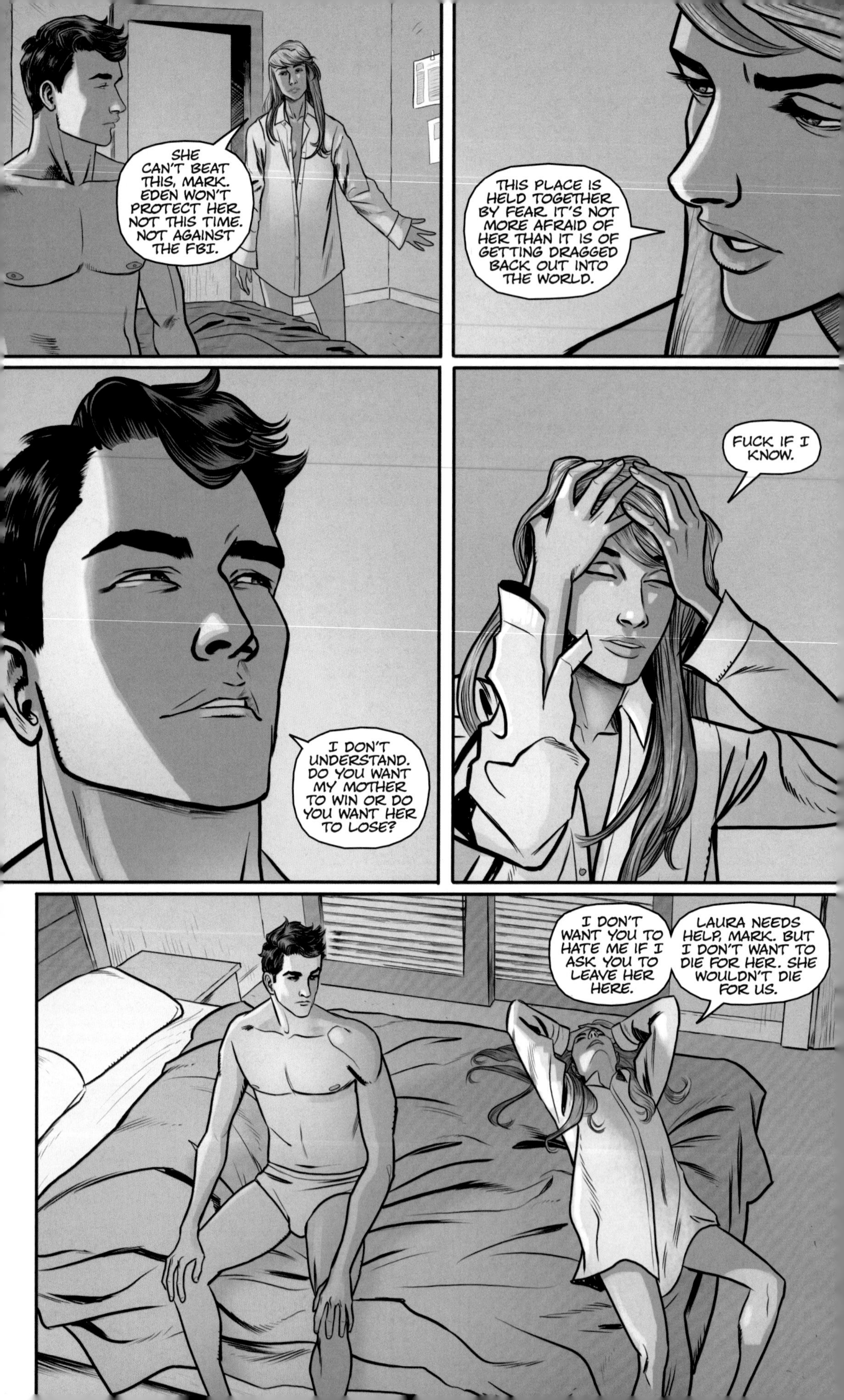
SHE CAN'T BEAT THIS, MARK. EDEN WON'T PROTECT HER NOT THIS TIME. NOT AGAINST THE FBI.
THIS PLACE IS HELD TOGETHER BY FEAR. IT'S NOT MORE AFRAID OF HER THAN IT IS OF GETTING DRAGGED BACK OUT INTO THE WORLD.
I DON'T UNDERSTAND. DO YOU WANT MY MOTHER TO WIN OR DO YOU WANT HER TO LOSE?
FUCK IF I KNOW.
LAURA NEEDS HELP, MARK. BUT I DON'T WANT TO DIE FOR HER. SHE WOULDN'T DIE FOR US.
I DON'T WANT YOU TO HATE ME IF I ASK YOU TO LEAVE HER HERE.

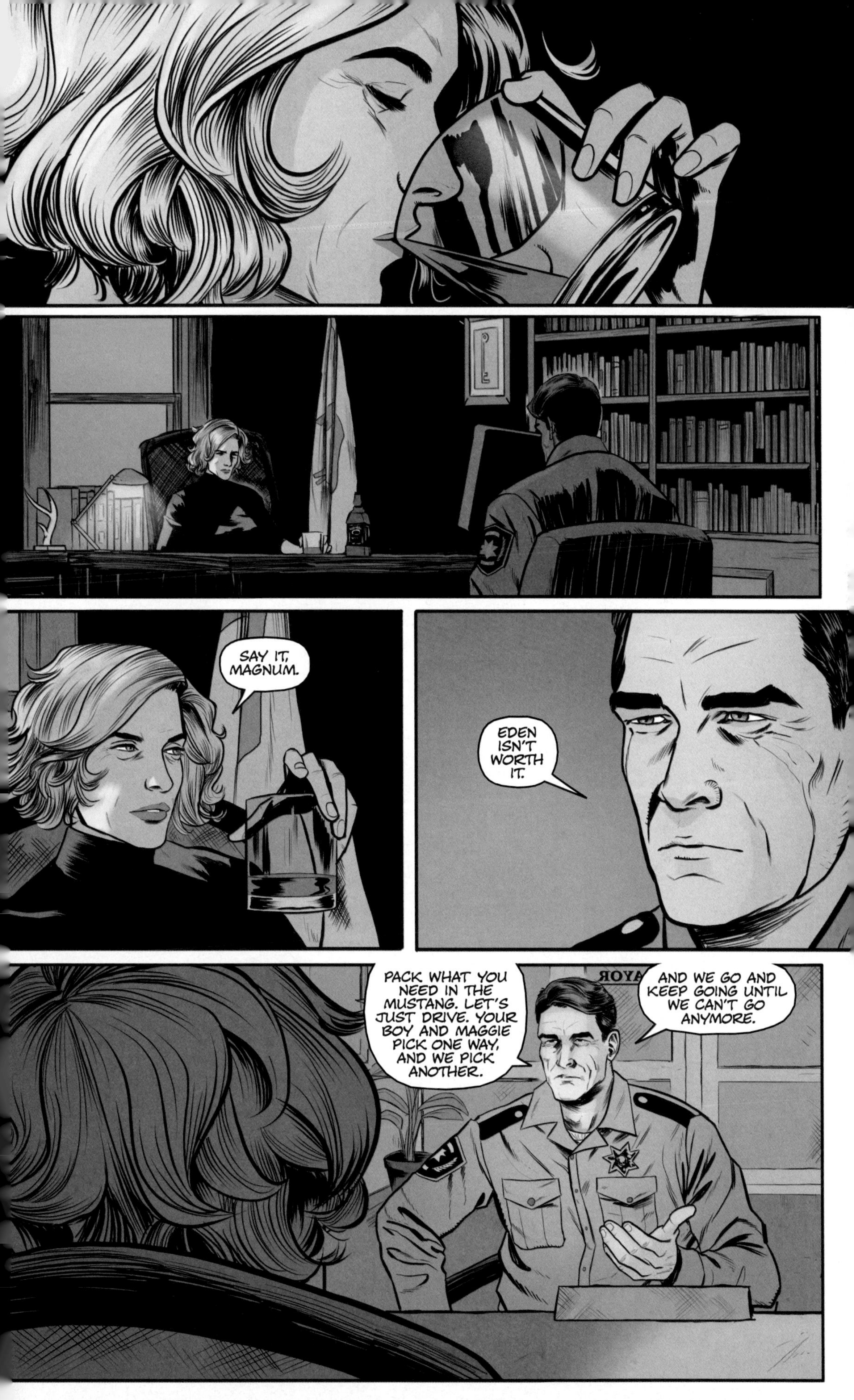

SAY IT, MAGNUM.
EDEN ISN'T WORTH IT.
AYOR
PACK WHAT YOU NEED IN THE MUSTANG. LET'S JUST DRIVE. YOUR BOY AND MAGGIE PICK ONE WAY, AND WE PICK ANOTHER.
AND WE GO AND KEEP GOING UNTIL WE CAN'T GO ANYMORE.

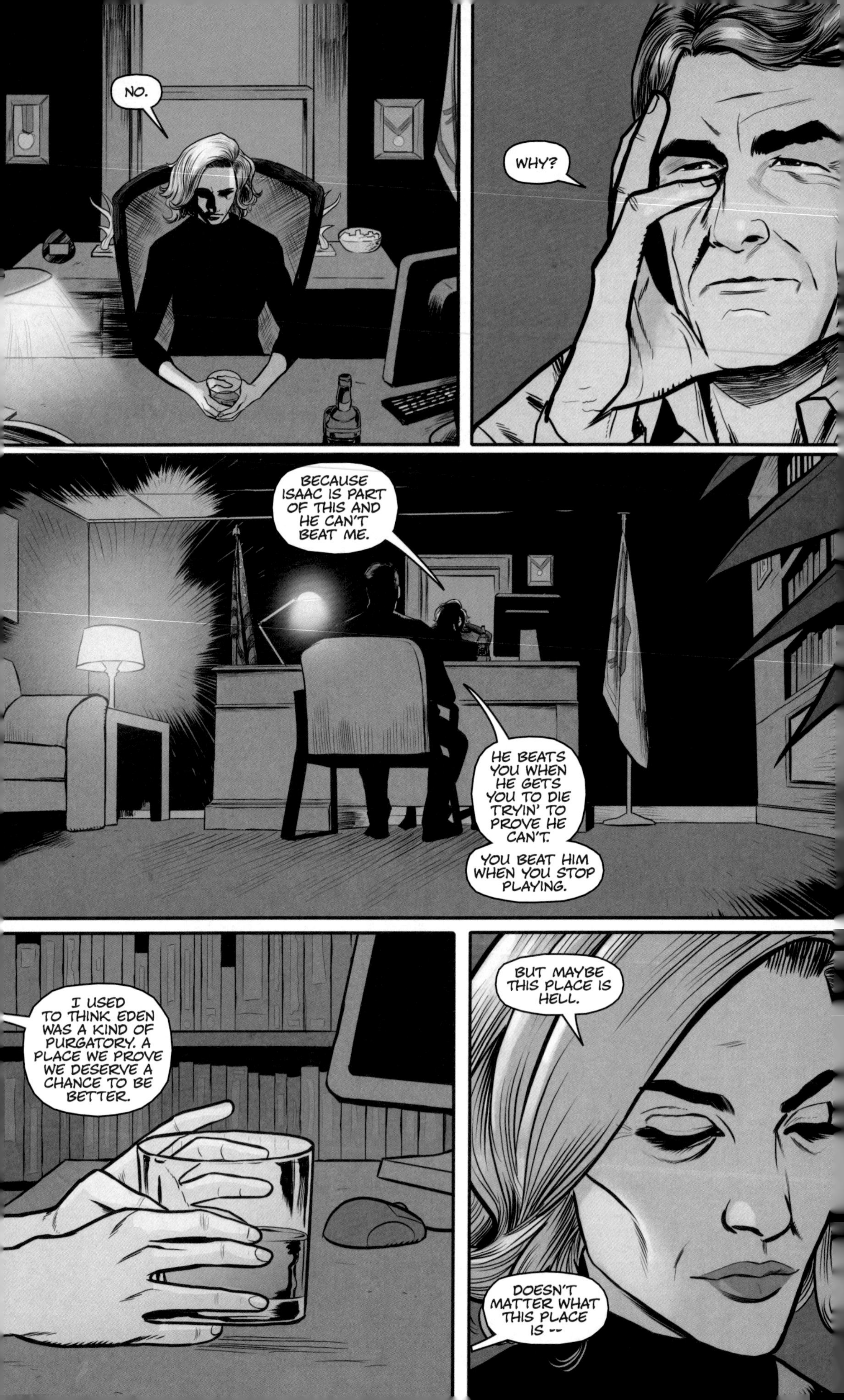
NO.
WHY?
BECAUSE ISAAC IS PART OF THIS AND HE CAN'T BEAT ME.
HE BEATS YOU WHEN HE GETS YOU TO DIE TRYIN' TO PROVE HE CAN'T.
YOU BEAT HIM WHEN YOU STOP PLAYING.
I USED TO THINK EDEN WAS A KIND OF PURGATORY. A PLACE WE PROVE WE DESERVE A CHANCE TO BE BETTER.
BUT MAYBE THIS PLACE IS HELL.
DOESN'T MATTER WHAT THIS PLACE IS --

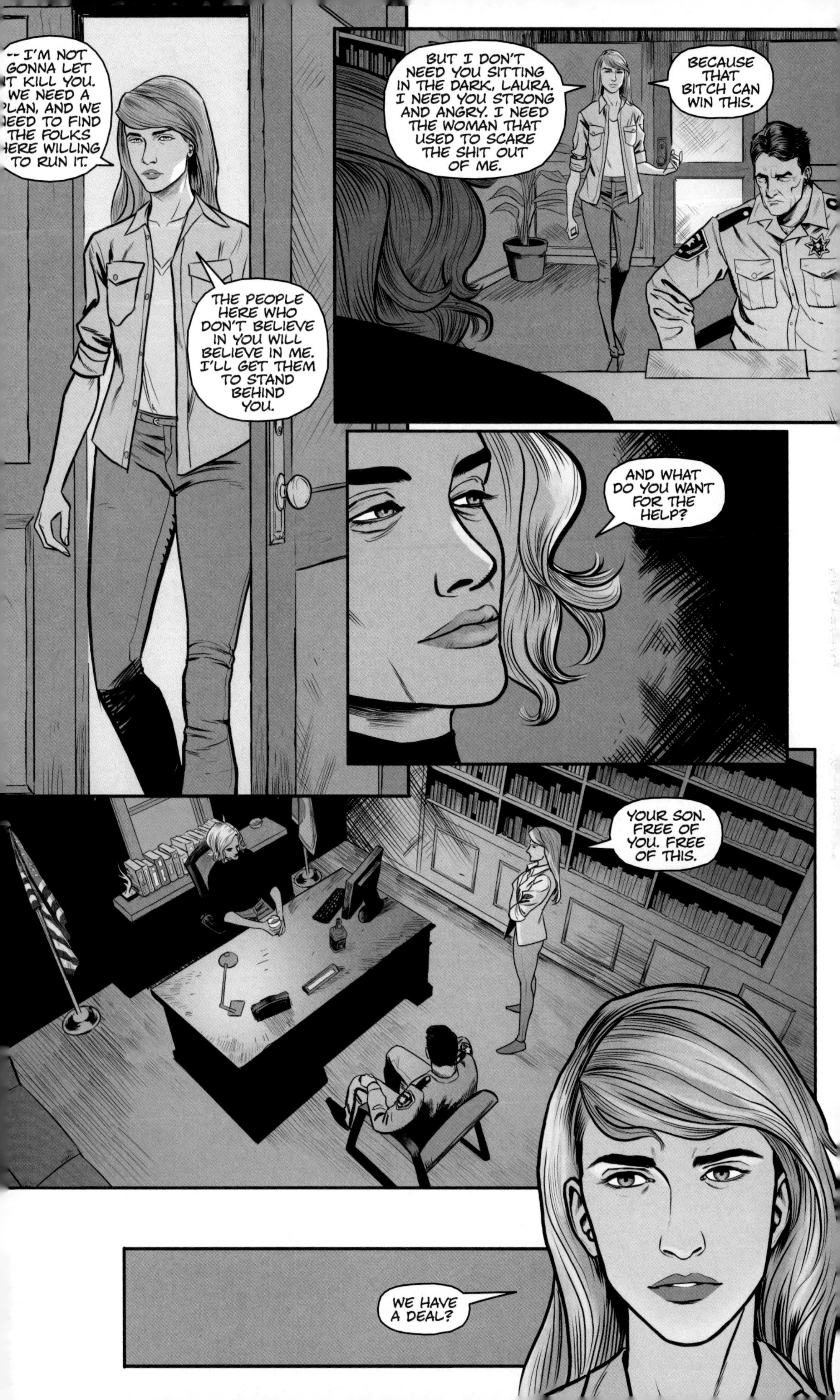
-- I'M NOT GONNA LET IT KILL YOU. WE NEED A PLAN, AND WE NEED TO FIND THE FOLKS HERE WILLING TO RUN IT.
THE PEOPLE HERE WHO DON'T BELIEVE IN YOU WILL BELIEVE IN ME. I'LL GET THEM TO STAND BEHIND YOU.
BUT I DON'T NEED YOU SITTING IN THE DARK, LAURA. I NEED YOU STRONG AND ANGRY. I NEED THE WOMAN THAT USED TO SCARE THE SHIT OUT OF ME.
BECAUSE THAT BITCH CAN WIN THIS.
AND WHAT DO YOU WANT FOR THE HELP?
YOUR SON. FREE OF YOU. FREE OF THIS.
WE HAVE A DEAL?

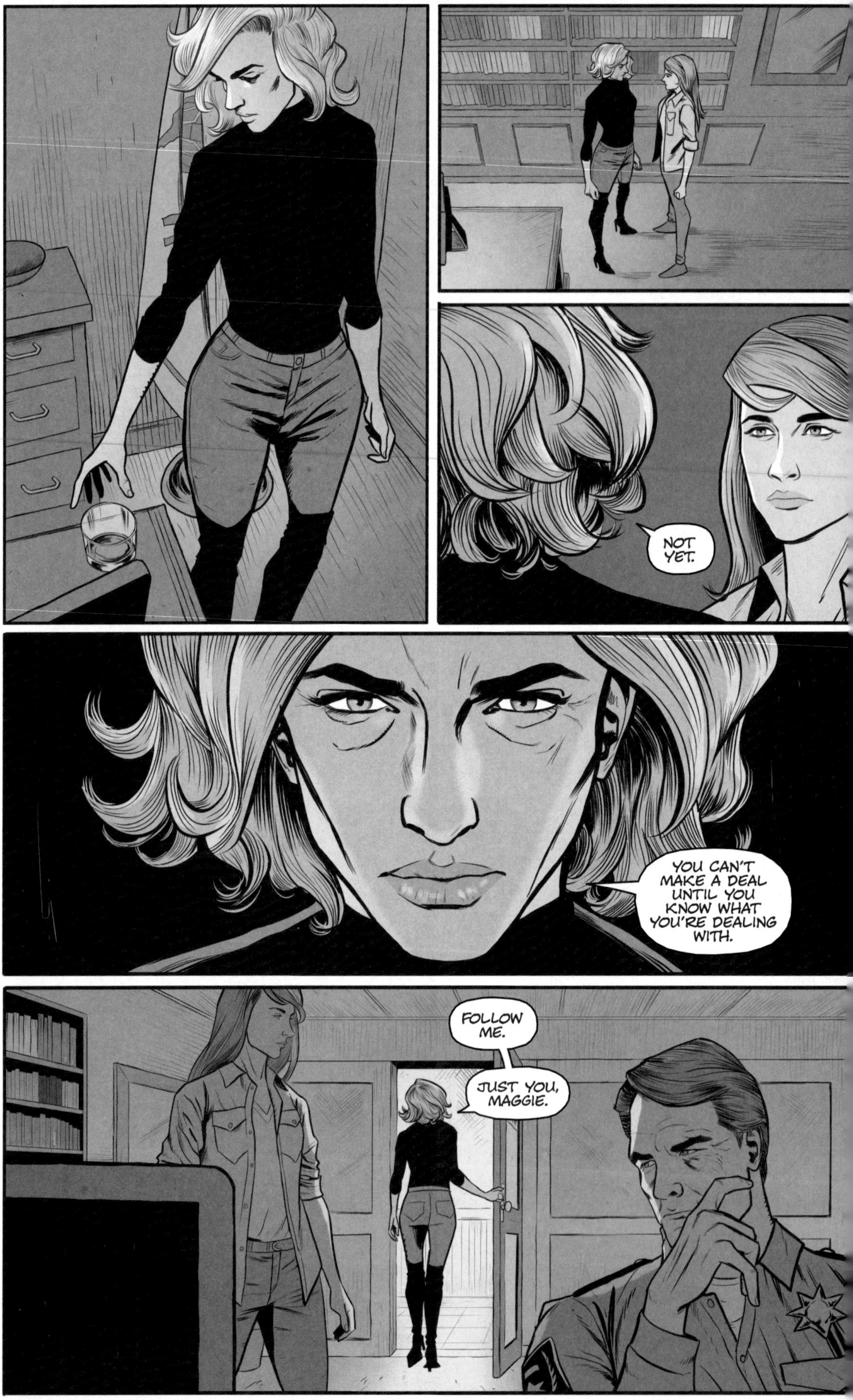
NOT YET.
YOU CAN'T MAKE A DEAL UNTIL YOU KNOW WHAT YOU'RE DEALING WITH.
FOLLOW ME.
JUST YOU, MAGGIE.

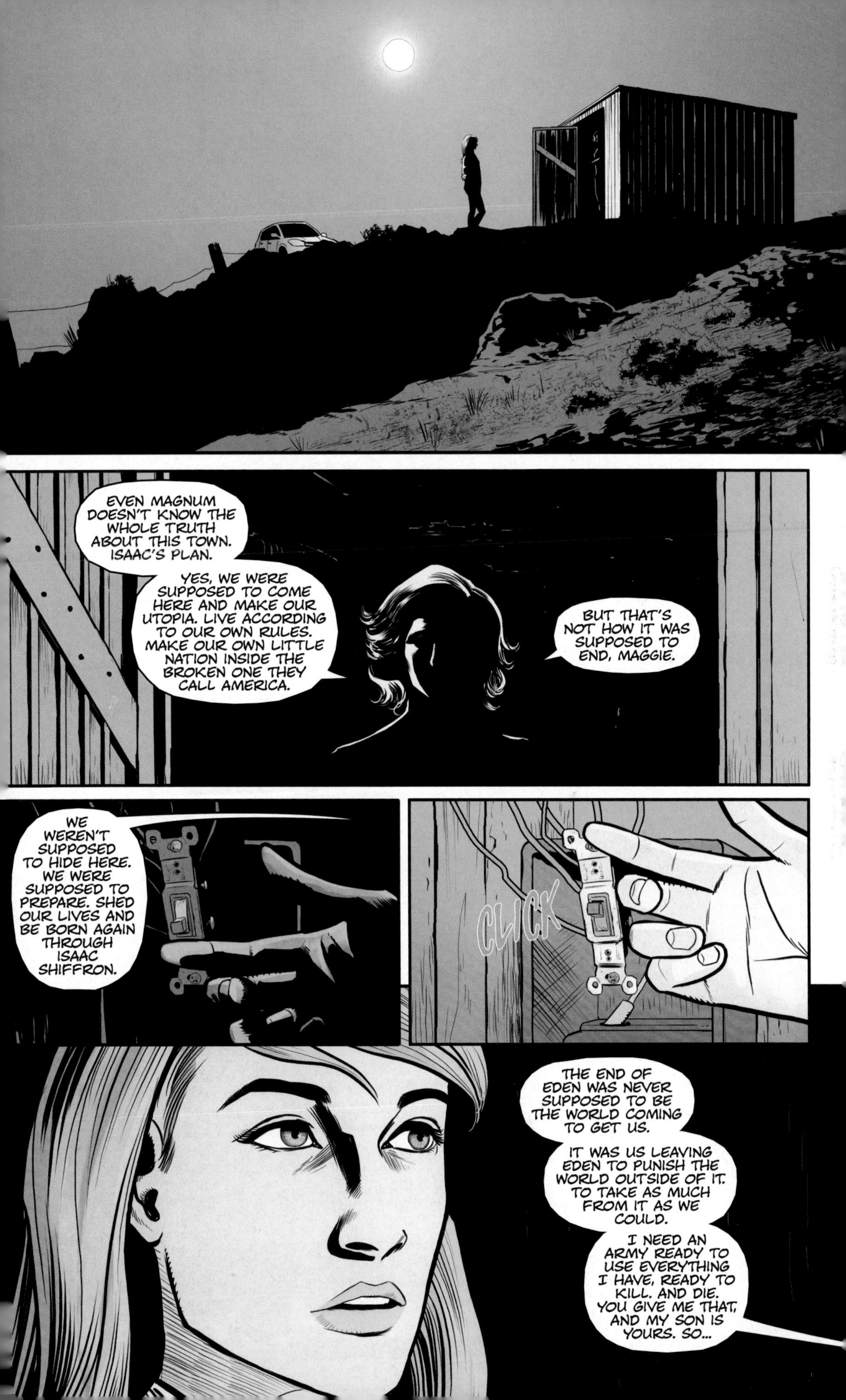

EVEN MAGNUM DOESN'T KNOW THE WHOLE TRUTH ABOUT THIS TOWN. ISAAC'S PLAN.
YES, WE WERE SUPPOSED TO COME HERE AND MAKE OUR UTOPIA. LIVE ACCORDING TO OUR OWN RULES. MAKE OUR OWN LITTLE NATION INSIDE THE BROKEN ONE THEY CALL AMERICA.
BUT THAT'S NOT HOW IT WAS SUPPOSED TO END, MAGGIE.
WE WEREN'T SUPPOSED TO HIDE HERE. WE WERE SUPPOSED TO PREPARE. SHED OUR LIVES AND BE BORN AGAIN THROUGH ISAAC SHIFFRON.
CLICK
THE END OF EDEN WAS NEVER SUPPOSED TO BE THE WORLD COMING TO GET US.
IT WAS US LEAVING EDEN TO PUNISH THE WORLD OUTSIDE OF IT. TO TAKE AS MUCH FROM IT AS WE COULD.
I NEED AN ARMY READY TO USE EVERYTHING I HAVE, READY TO KILL. AND DIE. YOU GIVE ME THAT, AND MY SON IS YOURS. SO...

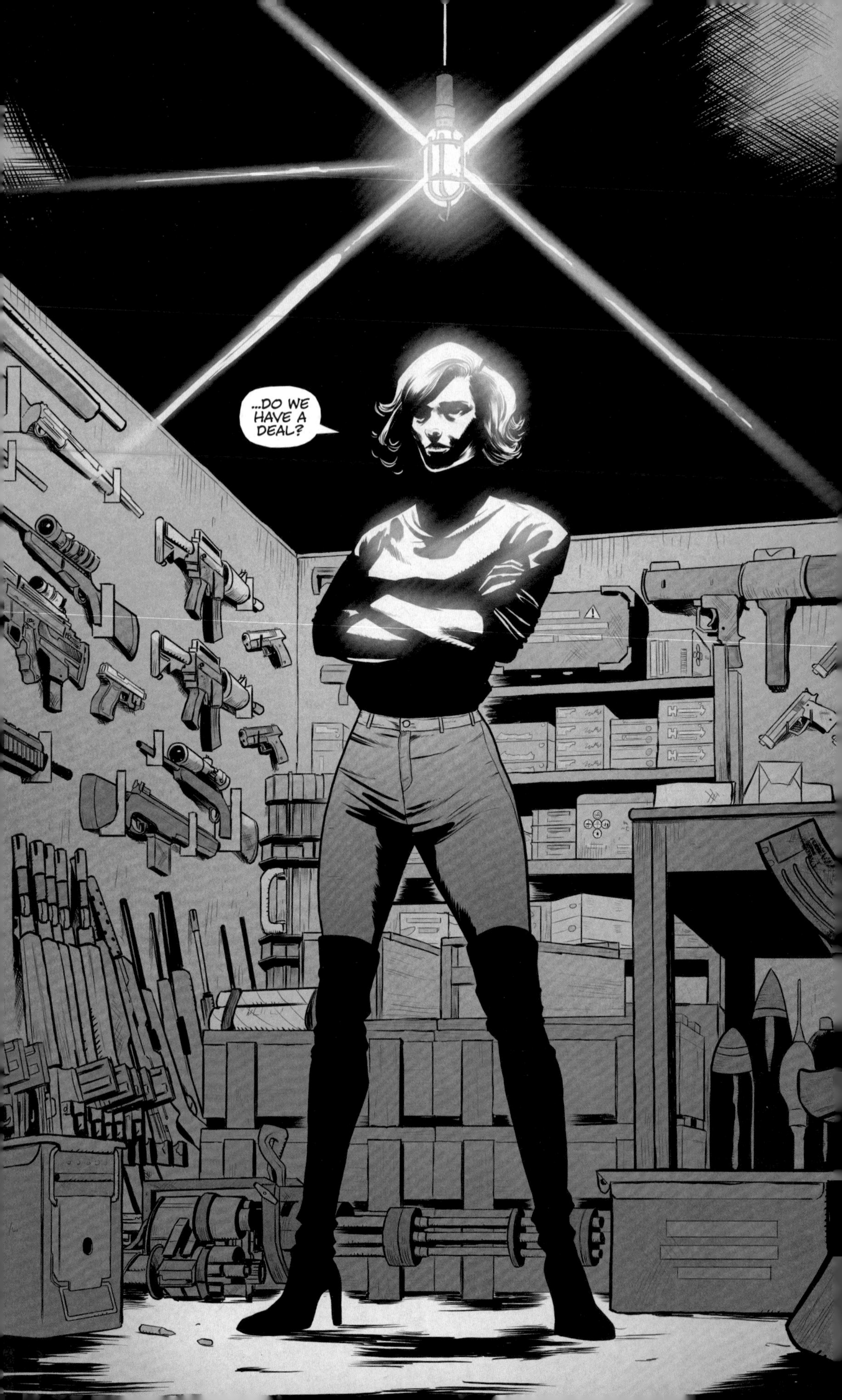
...DO WE HAVE A DEAL?

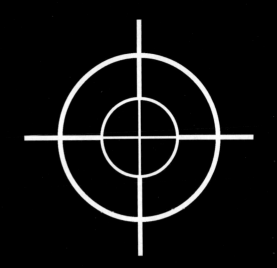

# CHAPTER 23

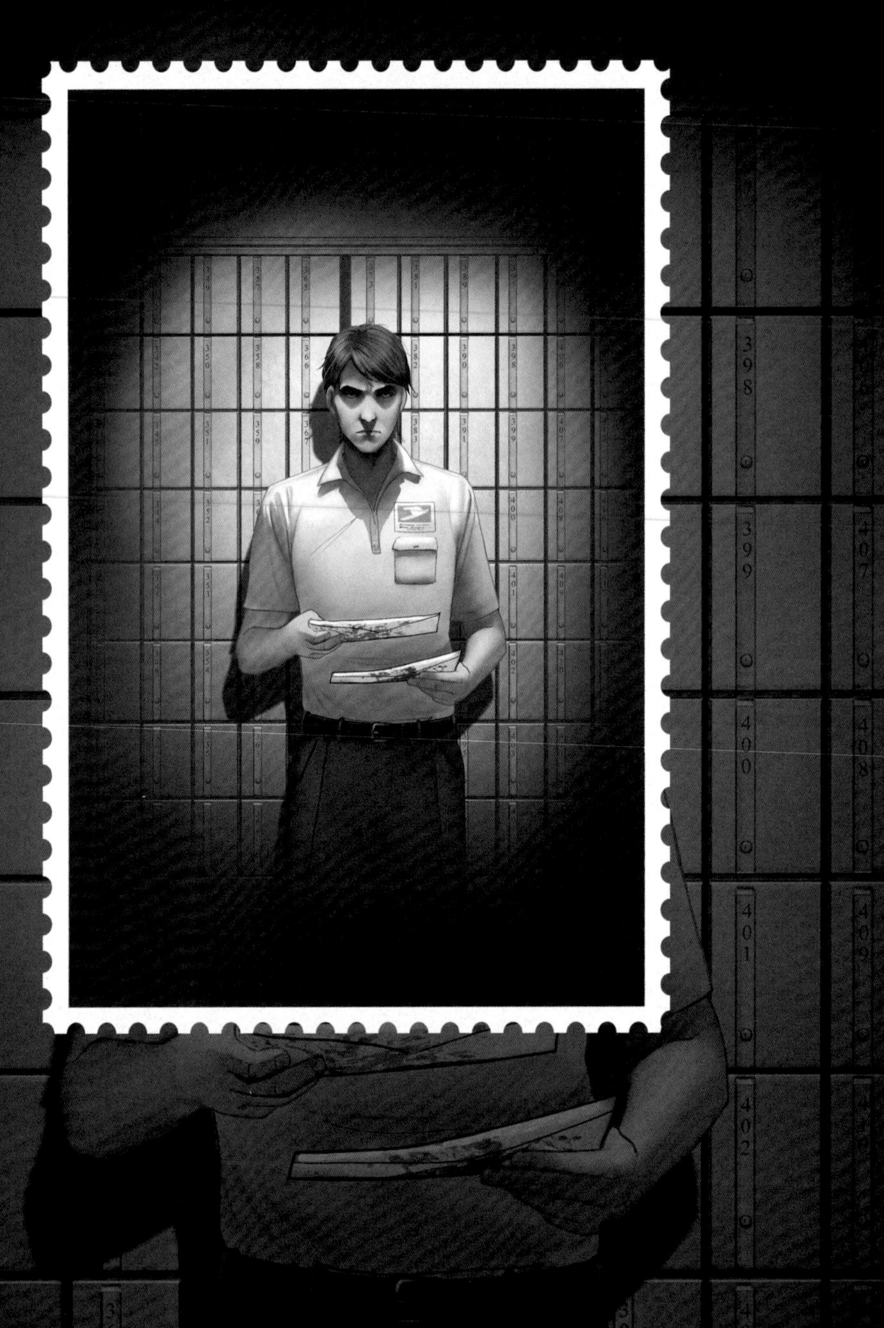
398
399
400
401
402
407
408
409

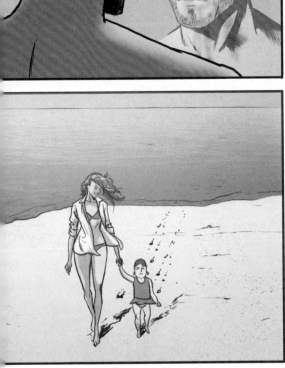

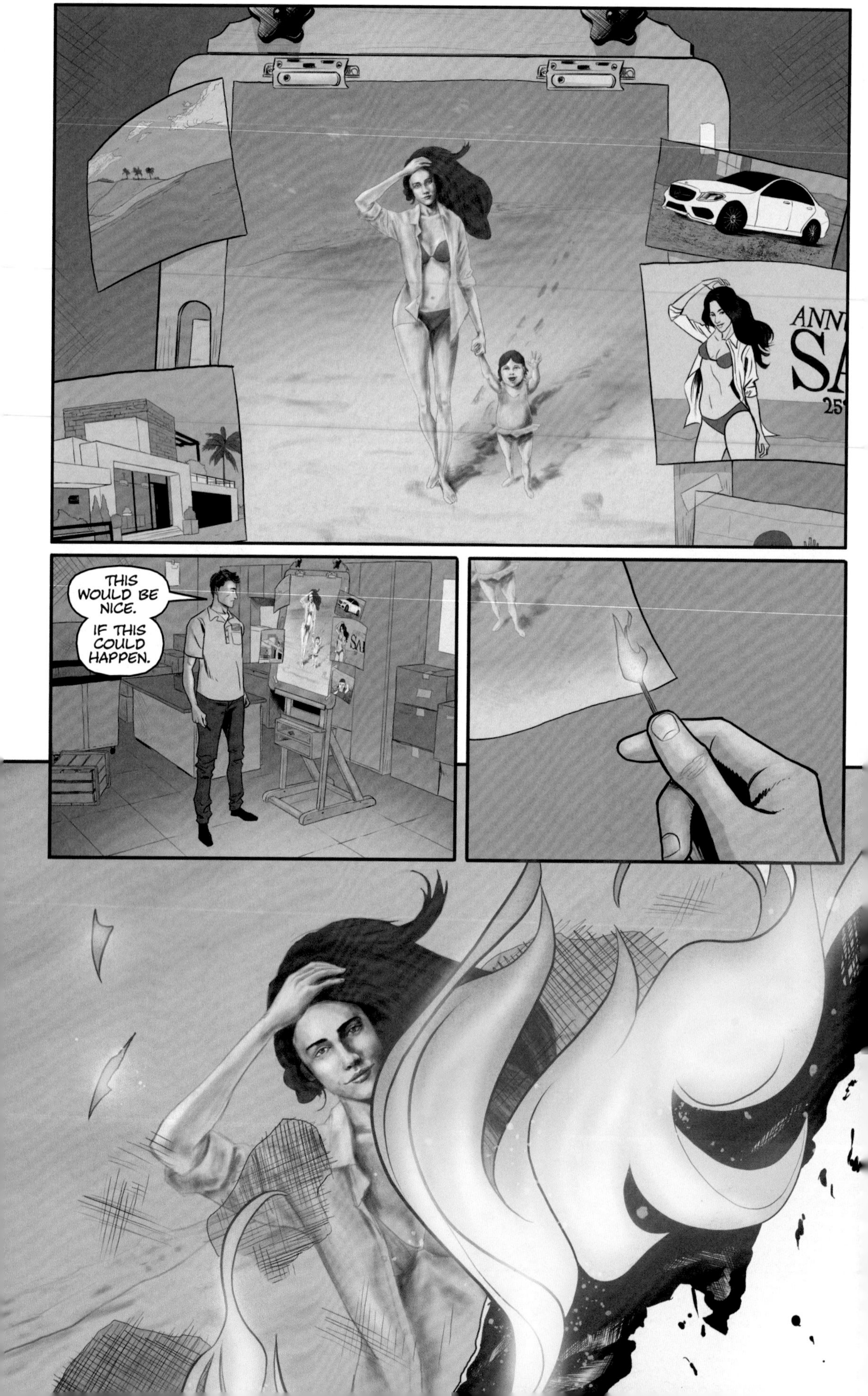
THIS WOULD BE NICE.
IF THIS COULD HAPPEN.

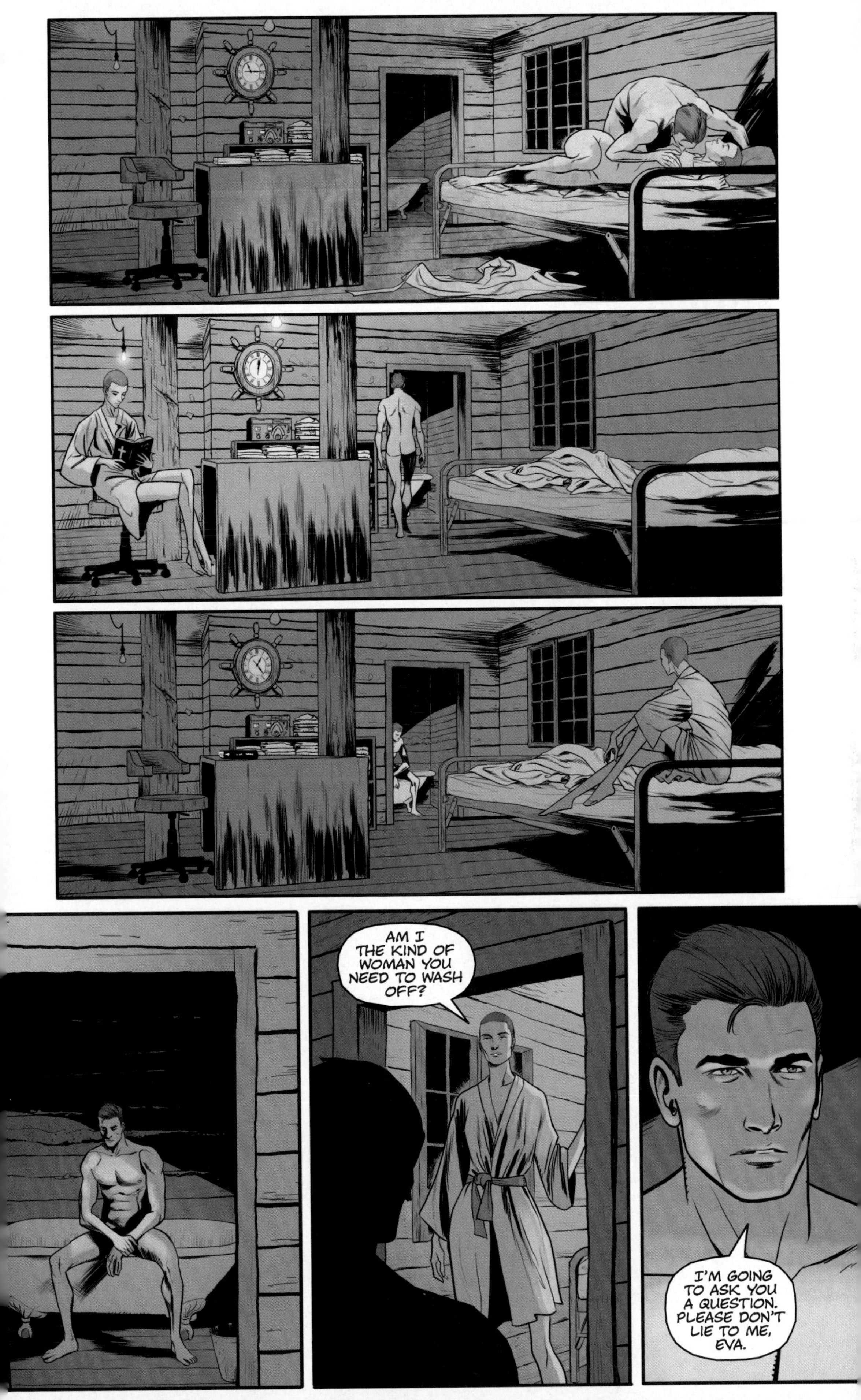
AM I THE KIND OF WOMAN YOU NEED TO WASH OFF?
I'M GOING TO ASK YOU A QUESTION. PLEASE DON'T LIE TO ME, EVA.

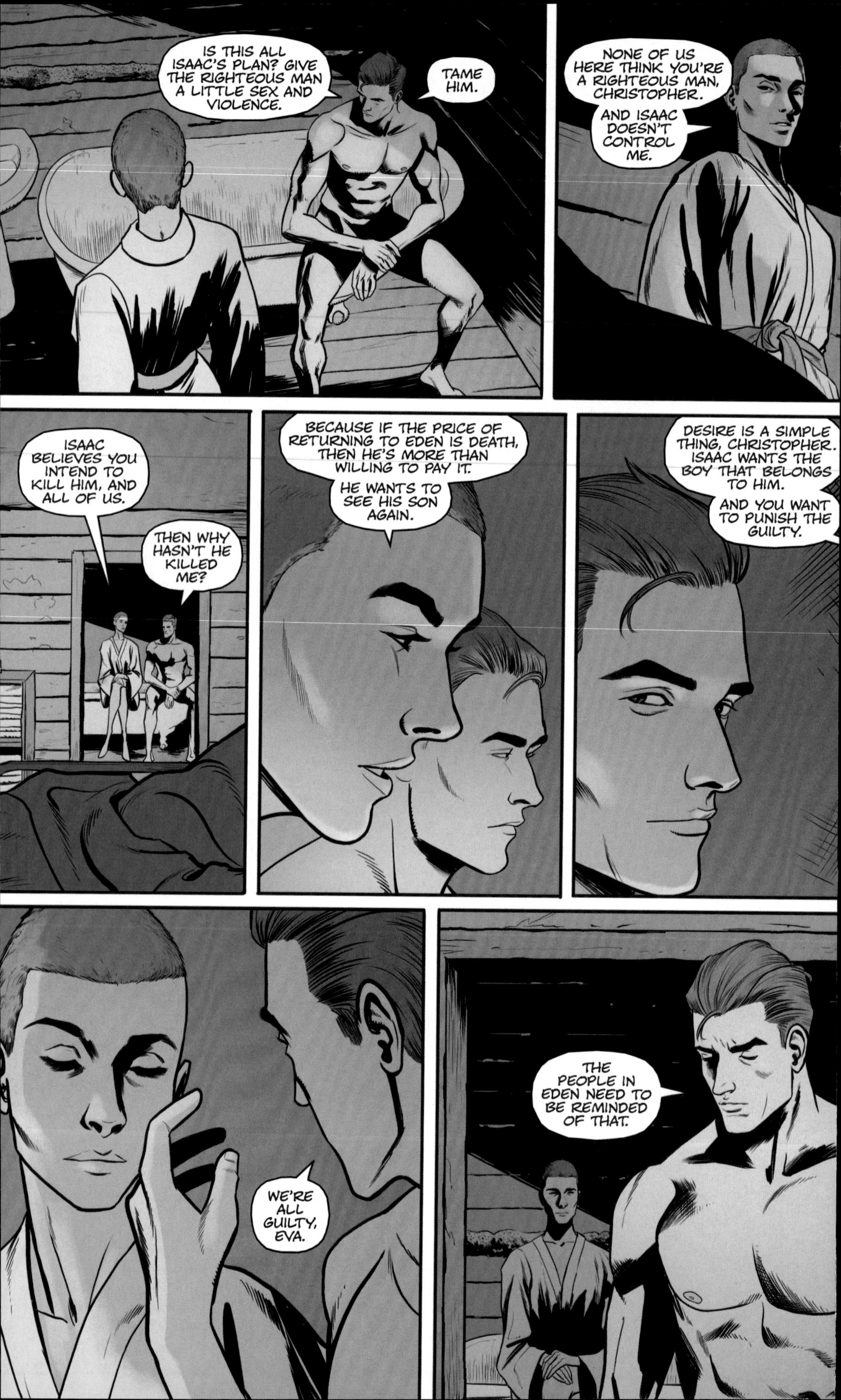
IS THIS ALL ISAAC'S PLAN? GIVE THE RIGHTEOUS MAN A LITTLE SEX AND VIOLENCE.
TAME HIM.
NONE OF US HERE THINK YOU'RE A RIGHTEOUS MAN, CHRISTOPHER.
AND ISAAC DOESN'T CONTROL ME.
ISAAC BELIEVES YOU INTEND TO KILL HIM, AND ALL OF US.
THEN WHY HASN'T HE KILLED ME?
BECAUSE IF THE PRICE OF RETURNING TO EDEN IS DEATH, THEN HE'S MORE THAN WILLING TO PAY IT.
HE WANTS TO SEE HIS SON AGAIN.
DESIRE IS A SIMPLE THING, CHRISTOPHER. ISAAC WANTS THE BOY THAT BELONGS TO HIM.
AND YOU WANT TO PUNISH THE GUILTY.
WE'RE ALL GUILTY, EVA.
THE PEOPLE IN EDEN NEED TO BE REMINDED OF THAT.

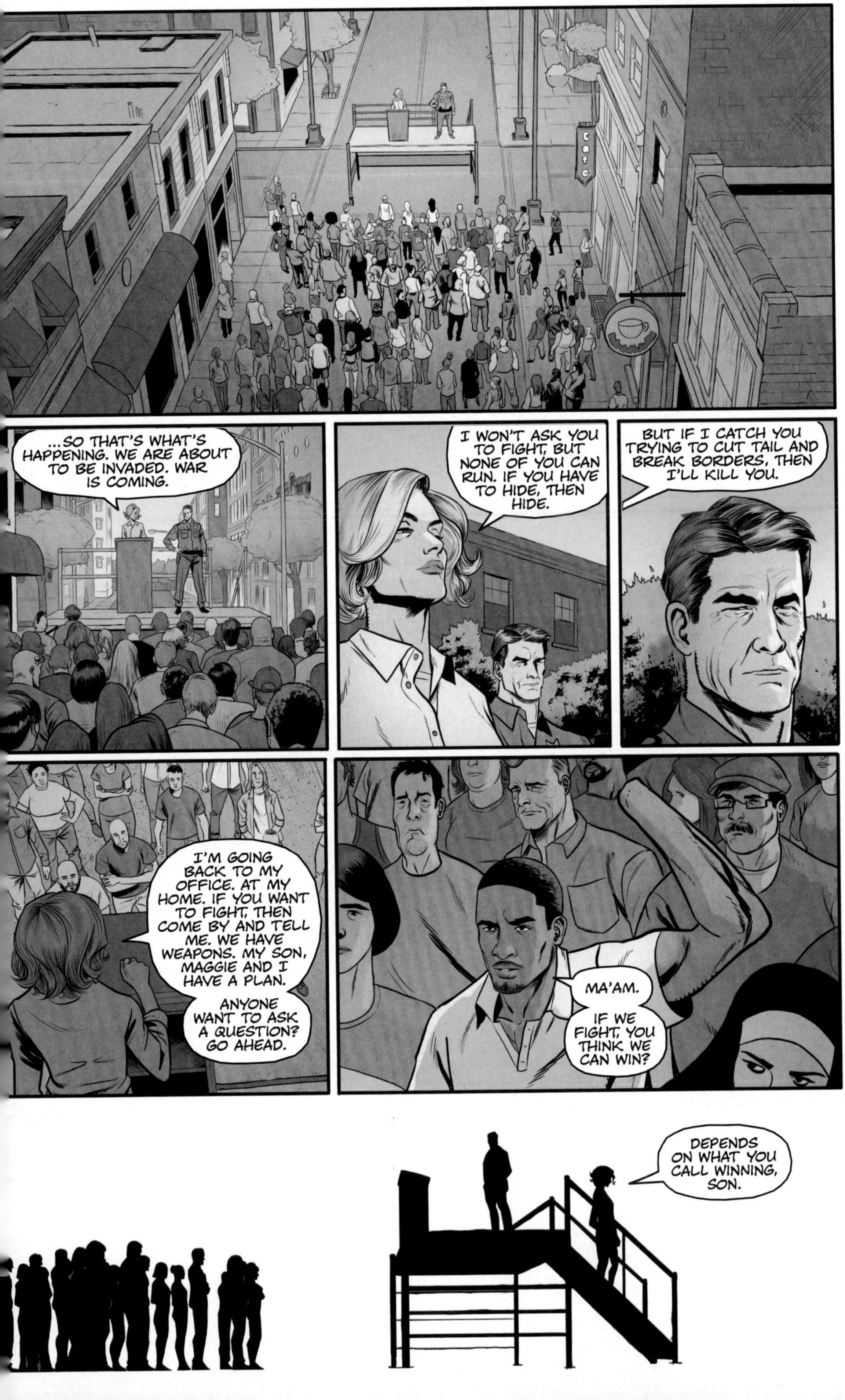

cafe
...SO THAT'S WHAT'S HAPPENING. WE ARE ABOUT TO BE INVADED. WAR IS COMING.
I WON'T ASK YOU TO FIGHT, BUT NONE OF YOU CAN RUN. IF YOU HAVE TO HIDE, THEN HIDE.
BUT IF I CATCH YOU TRYING TO CUT TAIL AND BREAK BORDERS, THEN I'LL KILL YOU.
I'M GOING BACK TO MY OFFICE. AT MY HOME. IF YOU WANT TO FIGHT, THEN COME BY AND TELL ME. WE HAVE WEAPONS. MY SON, MAGGIE AND I HAVE A PLAN.
ANYONE WANT TO ASK A QUESTION? GO AHEAD.
MA'AM.
IF WE FIGHT, YOU THINK WE CAN WIN?
DEPENDS ON WHAT YOU CALL WINNING, SON.

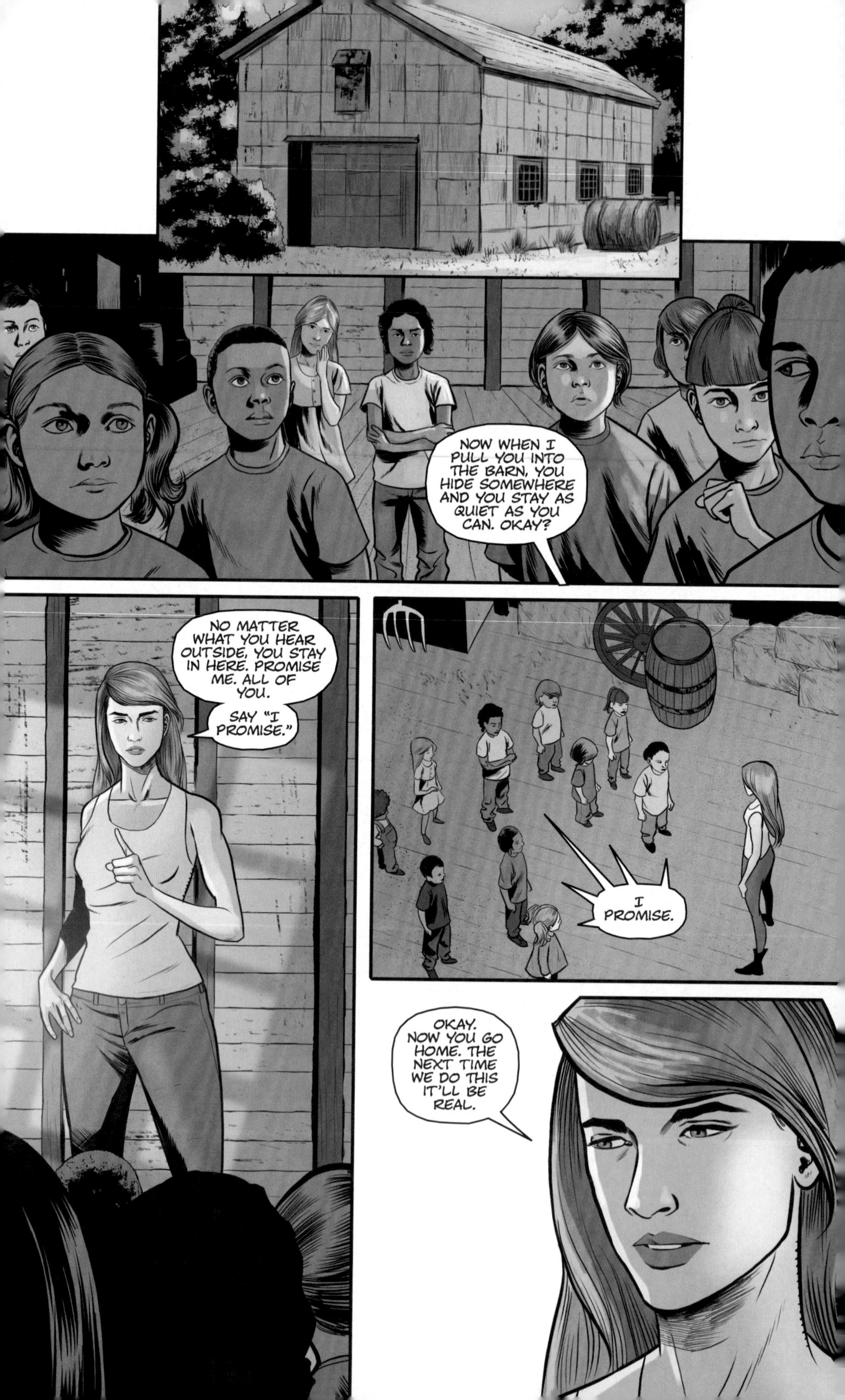
NOW WHEN I PULL YOU INTO THE BARN, YOU HIDE SOMEWHERE AND YOU STAY AS QUIET AS YOU CAN. OKAY?
NO MATTER WHAT YOU HEAR OUTSIDE, YOU STAY IN HERE. PROMISE ME. ALL OF YOU.
SAY "I PROMISE."
I PROMISE.
OKAY. NOW YOU GO HOME. THE NEXT TIME WE DO THIS IT'LL BE REAL.

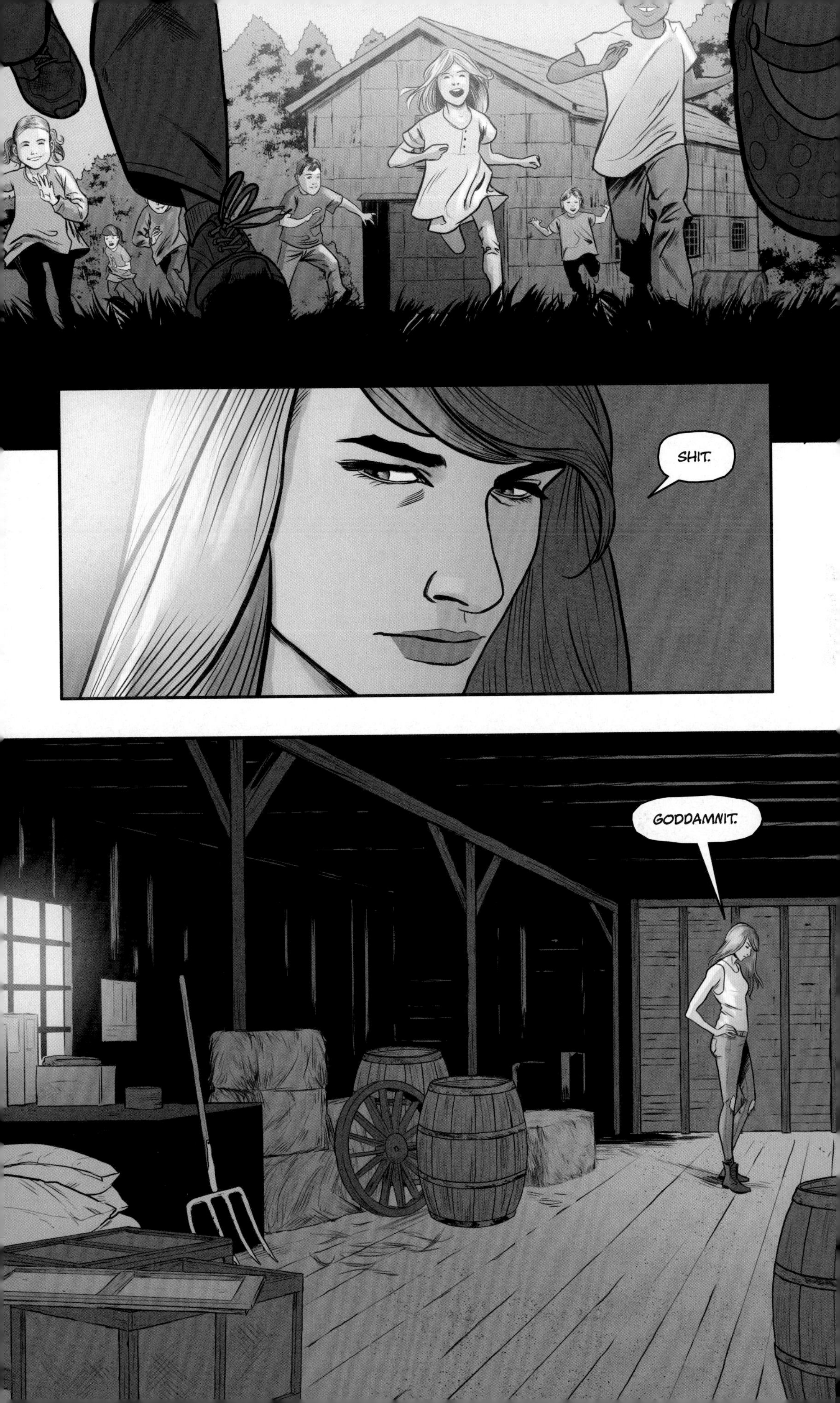
SHIT.
GODDAMNIT.

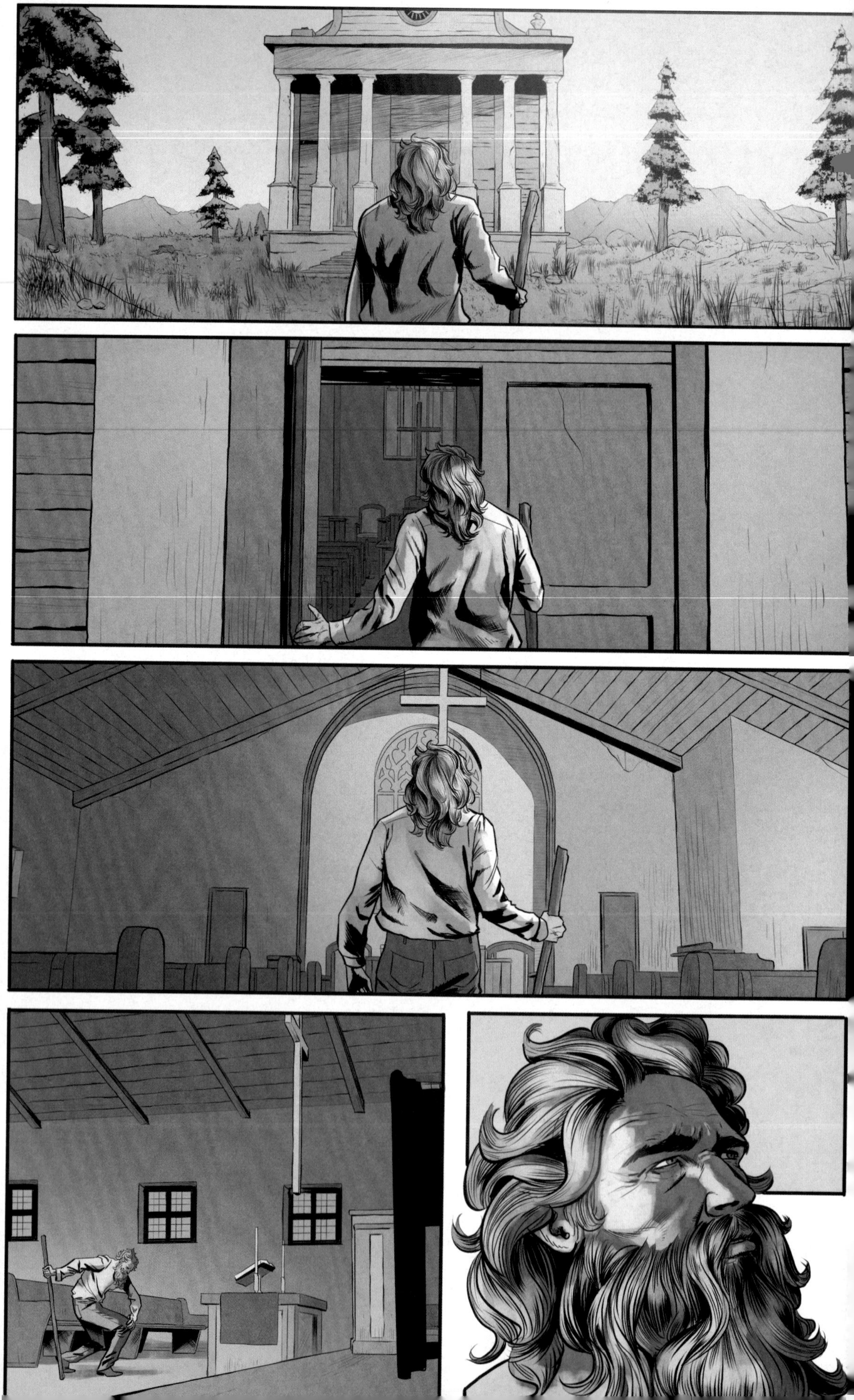

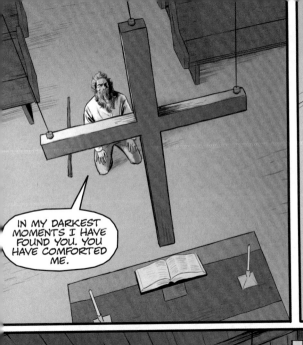

IN MY DARKEST MOMENTS I HAVE FOUND YOU. YOU HAVE COMFORTED ME.

YOU KNOW MY HEART FOR YOU HAVE GIVEN IT TO ME. YOU KNOW MY THOUGHTS FOR YOU HAVE CREATED MY MIND.

SO YOU KNOW MY FEAR.

MY ONLY FEAR. I SEE A WORLD THAT WANTS TO CHERISH WEAKNESS OVER STRENGTH. COWARDICE OVER COURAGE.

THIS WORLD PUNISHES THOSE WHO CHOOSE CONFRONTATION. IT CODDLES THOSE THAT CANNOT STAND.

AND IT HAS TAKEN MY SON FROM ME.

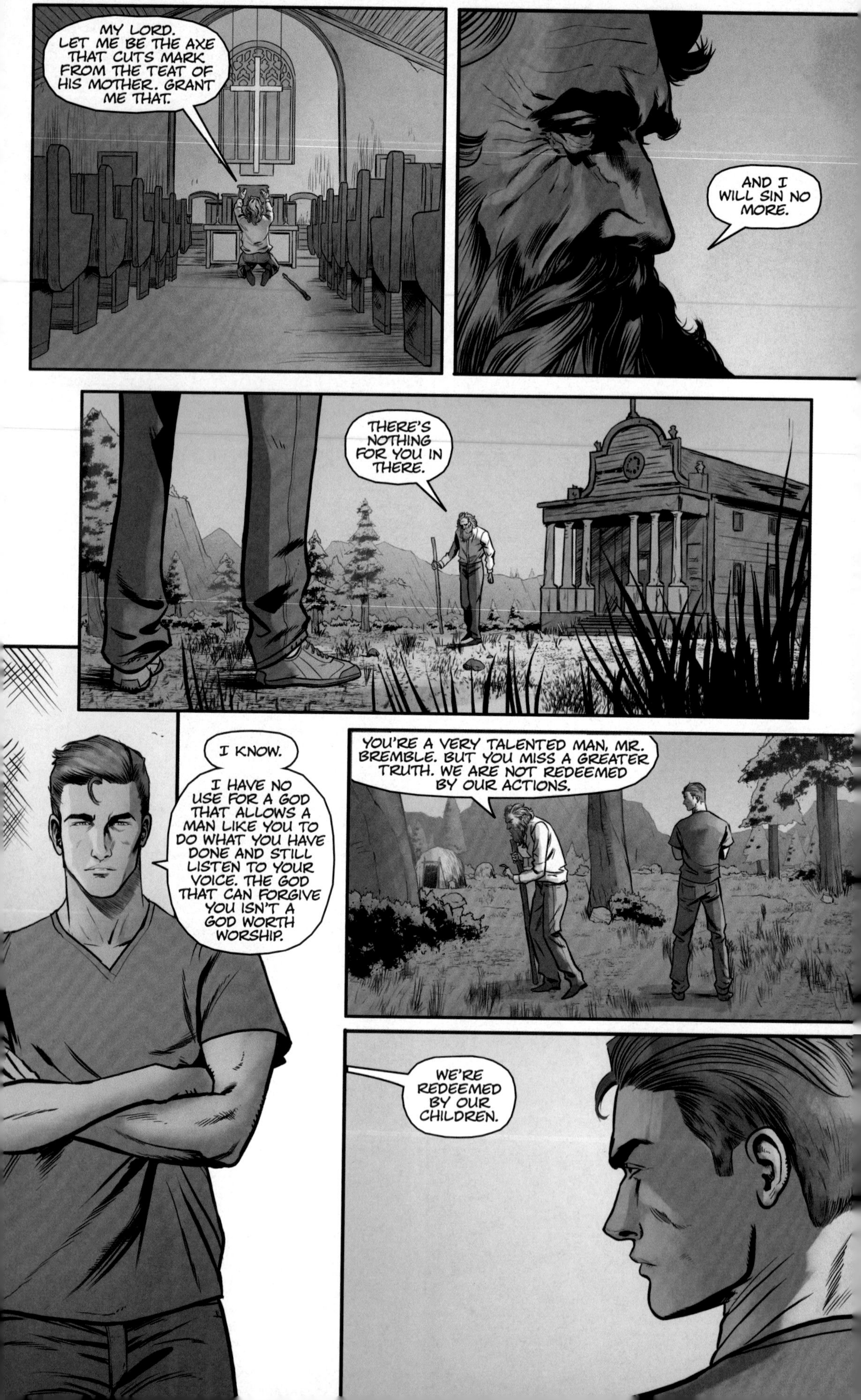
MY LORD. LET ME BE THE AXE THAT CUTS MARK FROM THE TEAT OF HIS MOTHER. GRANT ME THAT.
AND I WILL SIN NO MORE.
THERE'S NOTHING FOR YOU IN THERE.
I KNOW.
I HAVE NO USE FOR A GOD THAT ALLOWS A MAN LIKE YOU TO DO WHAT YOU HAVE DONE AND STILL LISTEN TO YOUR VOICE. THE GOD THAT CAN FORGIVE YOU ISN'T A GOD WORTH WORSHIP.
YOU'RE A VERY TALENTED MAN, MR. BREMBLE. BUT YOU MISS A GREATER TRUTH. WE ARE NOT REDEEMED BY OUR ACTIONS.
WE'RE REDEEMED BY OUR CHILDREN.

IF WE MOVE THEM INTO THE CENTER PATH...

...DALLAS CAN PRESSURE THEM FROM ABOVE.

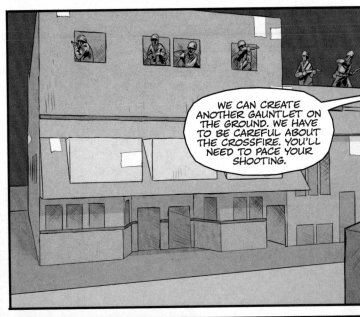

WE CAN CREATE ANOTHER GAUNTLET ON THE GROUND. WE HAVE TO BE CAREFUL ABOUT THE CROSSFIRE. YOU'LL NEED TO PACE YOUR SHOOTING.

AGENT BREMBLE HAS A MILITARY BACKGROUND. HE KNOWS HOW TO PLAN A SIEGE AND HE KNOWS HOW TO DEFEND AGAINST ONE.

THE STRATEGY WITH THE HIGHEST CHANCE OF SUCCESS IS THE ONE HE'LL EXPECT US TO USE.

AND I EXPECT HIM TO HAVE HIS OWN COUNTER MEASURES.

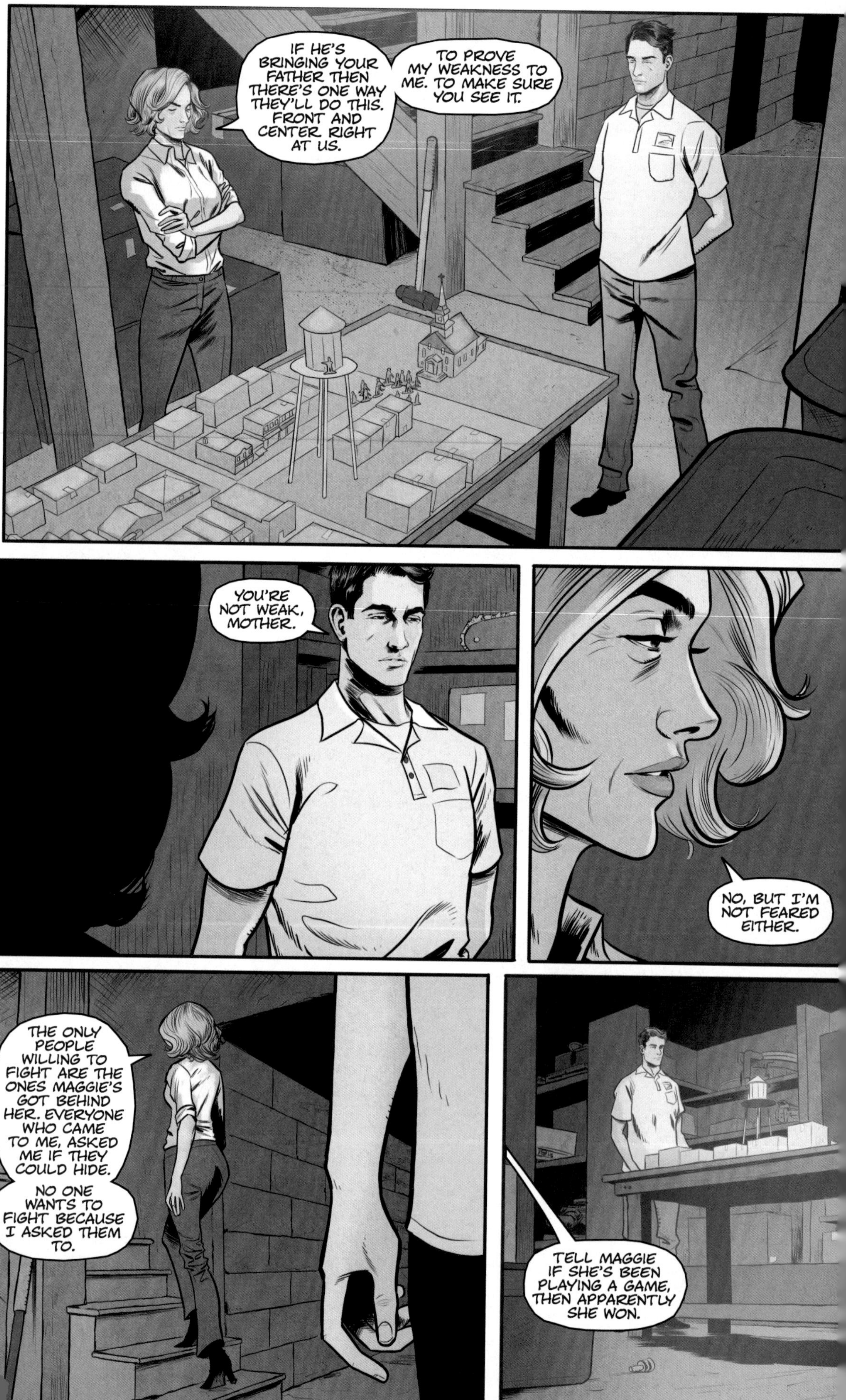
IF HE'S BRINGING YOUR FATHER THEN THERE'S ONE WAY THEY'LL DO THIS. FRONT AND CENTER RIGHT AT US.
TO PROVE MY WEAKNESS TO ME. TO MAKE SURE YOU SEE IT.
YOU'RE NOT WEAK, MOTHER.
NO, BUT I'M NOT FEARED EITHER.
THE ONLY PEOPLE WILLING TO FIGHT ARE THE ONES MAGGIE'S GOT BEHIND HER. EVERYONE WHO CAME TO ME, ASKED ME IF THEY COULD HIDE.
NO ONE WANTS TO FIGHT BECAUSE I ASKED THEM TO.
TELL MAGGIE IF SHE'S BEEN PLAYING A GAME, THEN APPARENTLY SHE WON.

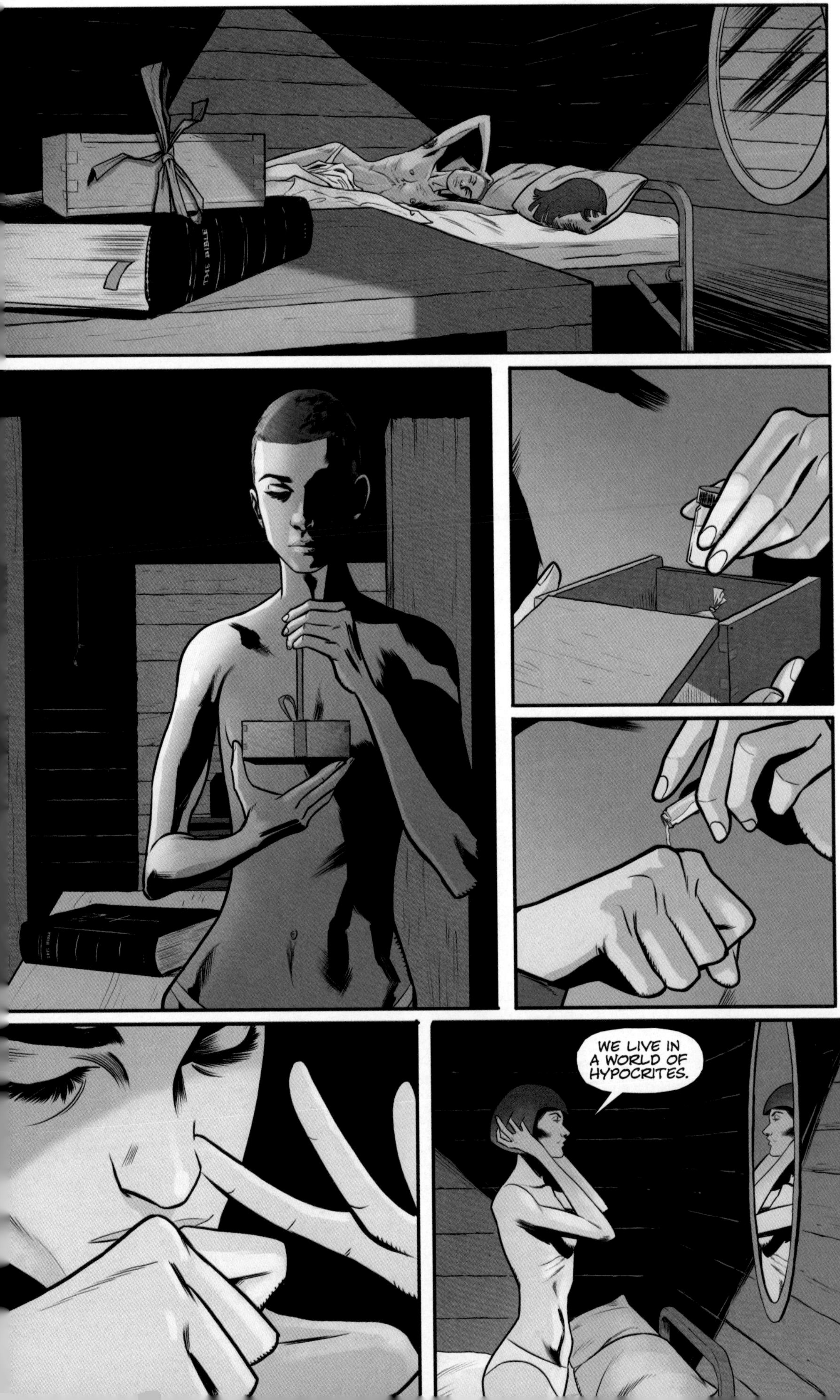
THE BIBLE
WE LIVE IN A WORLD OF HYPOCRITES.

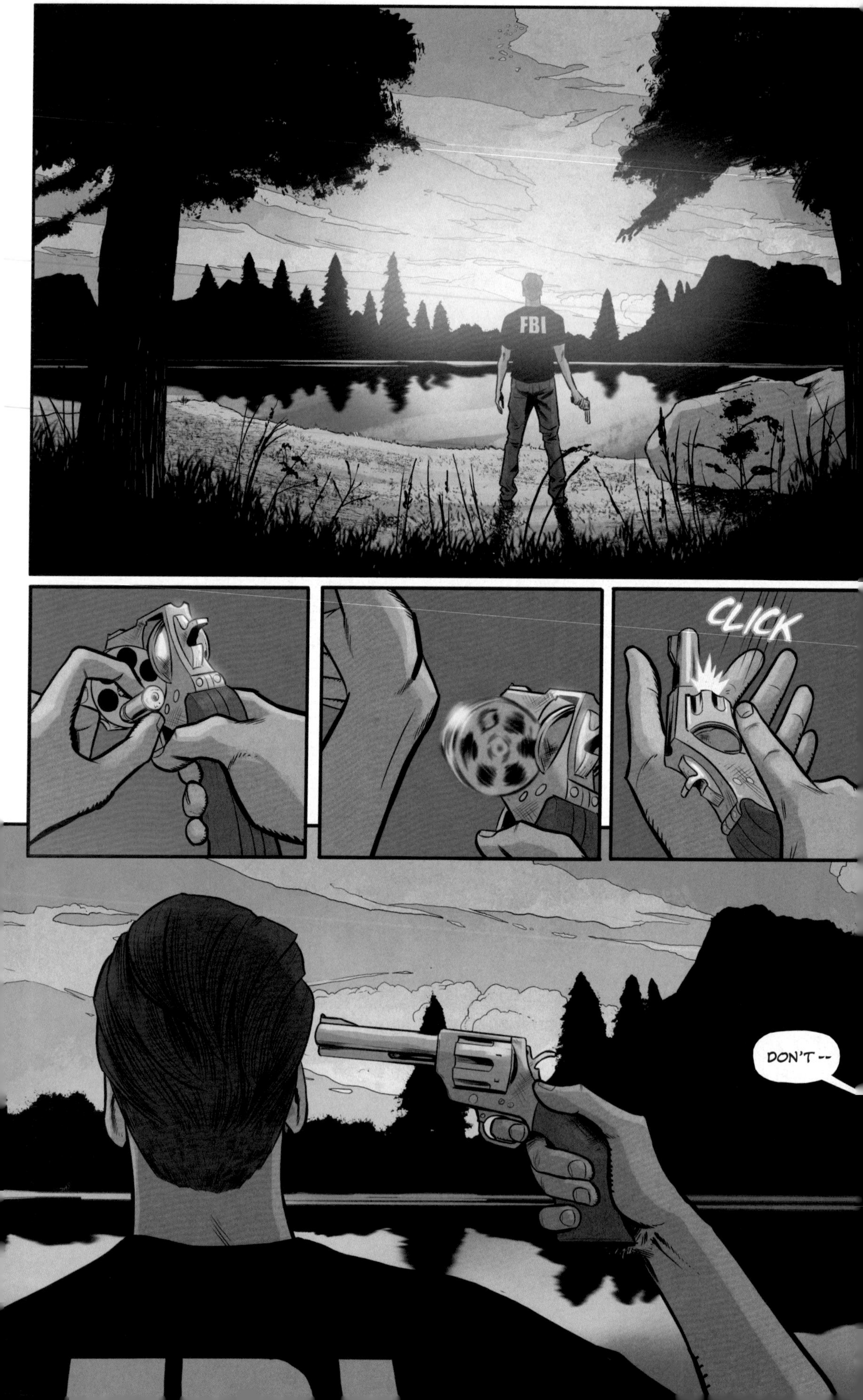
FBI
CLICK
DON'T --

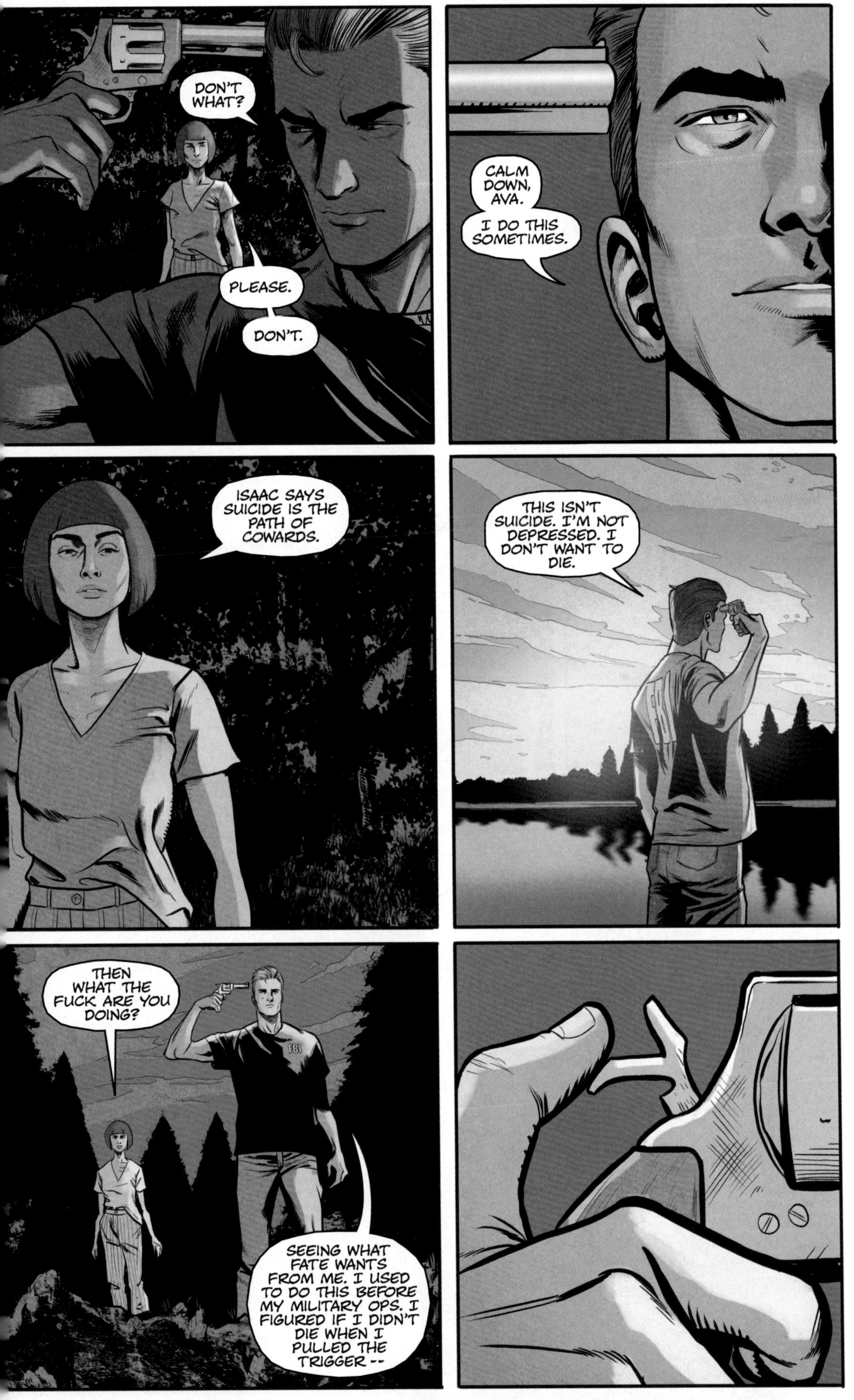
DON'T WHAT?
PLEASE.
DON'T.
CALM DOWN, AVA.
I DO THIS SOMETIMES.
ISAAC SAYS SUICIDE IS THE PATH OF COWARDS.
THIS ISN'T SUICIDE. I'M NOT DEPRESSED. I DON'T WANT TO DIE.
FBI
THEN WHAT THE FUCK ARE YOU DOING?
FBI
SEEING WHAT FATE WANTS FROM ME. I USED TO DO THIS BEFORE MY MILITARY OPS. I FIGURED IF I DIDN'T DIE WHEN I PULLED THE TRIGGER --

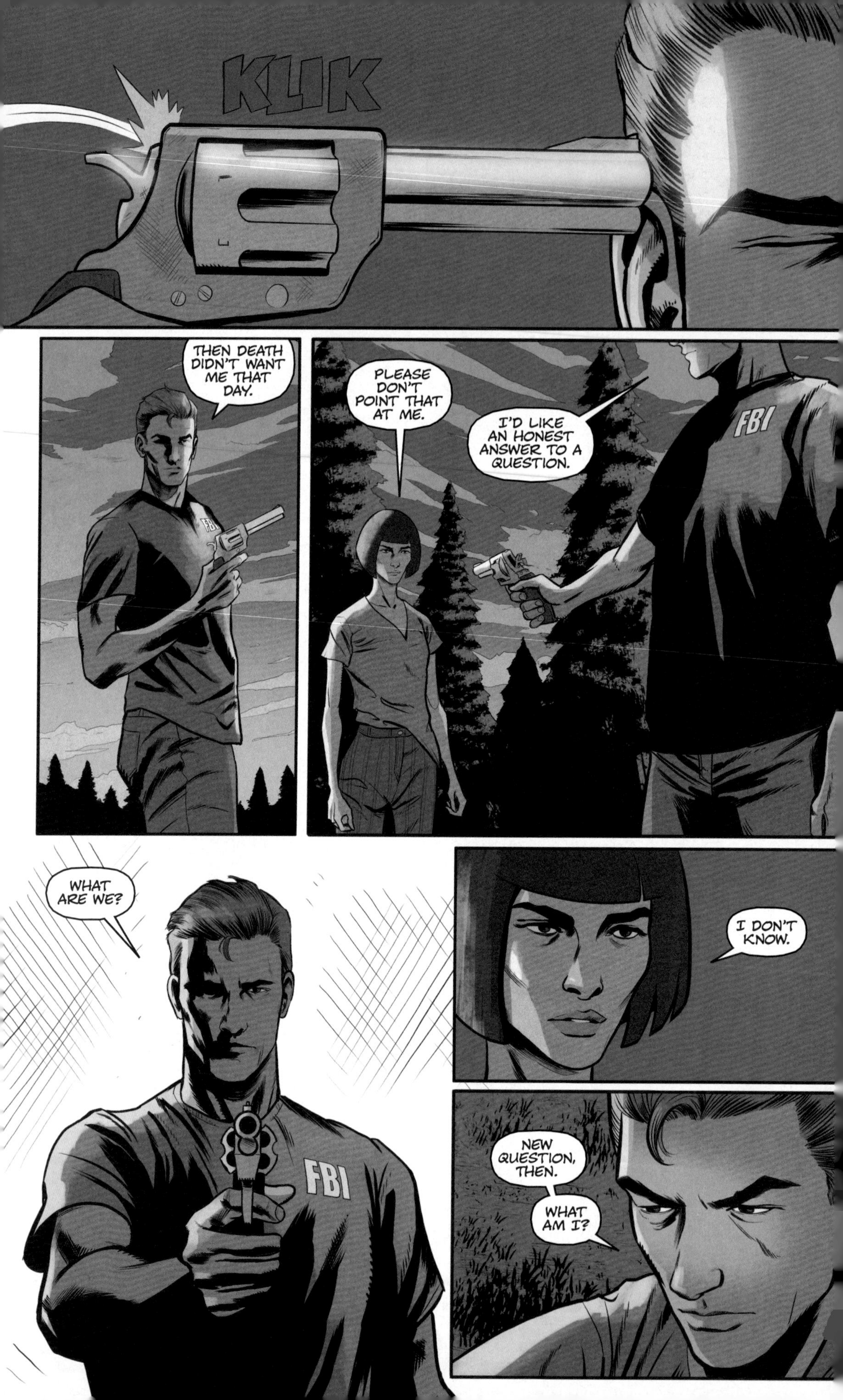
KLIK
THEN DEATH DIDN'T WANT ME THAT DAY.
PLEASE DON'T POINT THAT AT ME.
I'D LIKE AN HONEST ANSWER TO A QUESTION.
FBI
FBI
WHAT ARE WE?
FBI
I DON'T KNOW.
NEW QUESTION, THEN.
WHAT AM I?

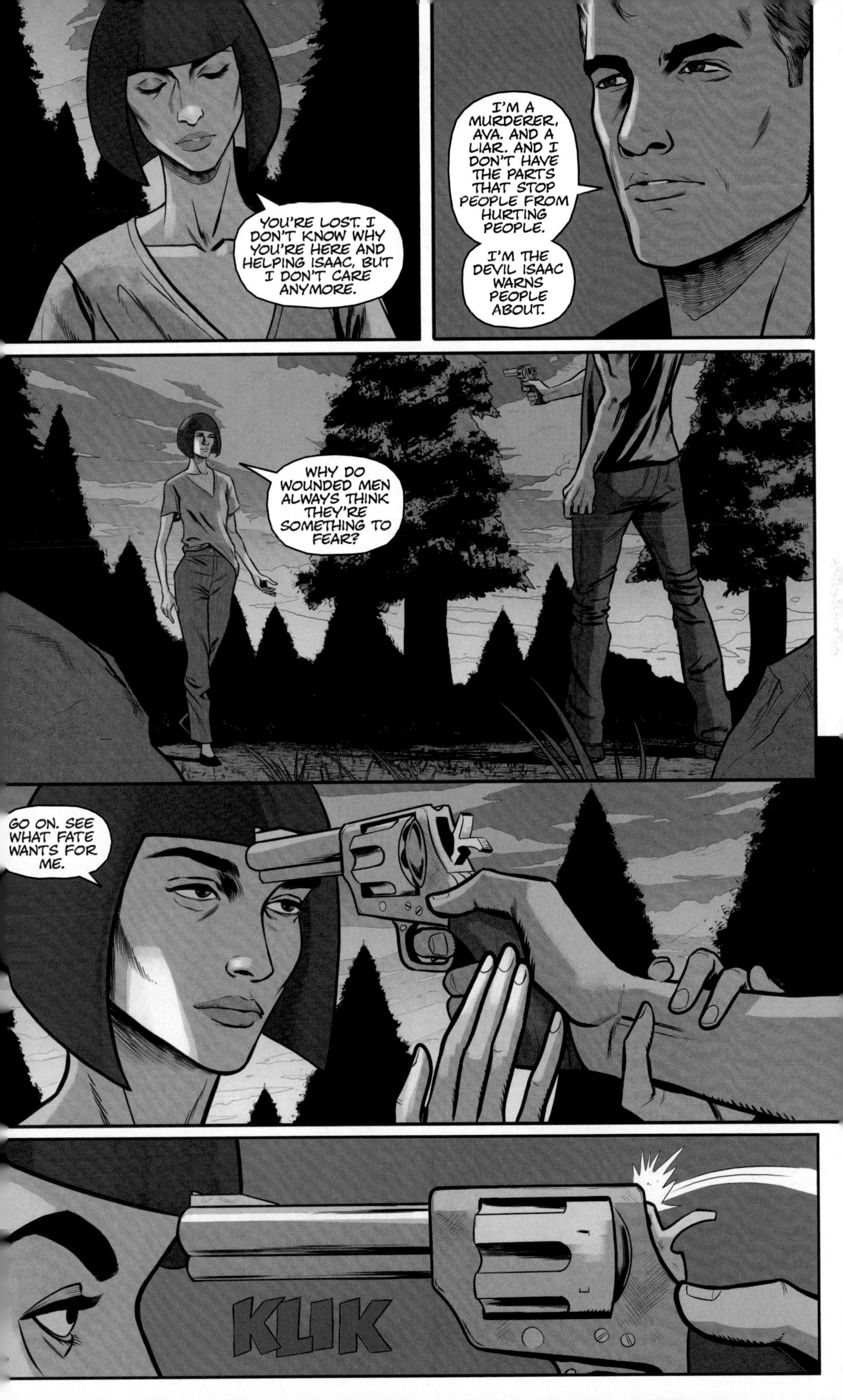

YOU'RE LOST. I DON'T KNOW WHY YOU'RE HERE AND HELPING ISAAC, BUT I DON'T CARE ANYMORE.
I'M A MURDERER, AVA. AND A LIAR. AND I DON'T HAVE THE PARTS THAT STOP PEOPLE FROM HURTING PEOPLE.
I'M THE DEVIL ISAAC WARNS PEOPLE ABOUT.
WHY DO WOUNDED MEN ALWAYS THINK THEY'RE SOMETHING TO FEAR?
GO ON. SEE WHAT FATE WANTS FOR ME.
KLIK

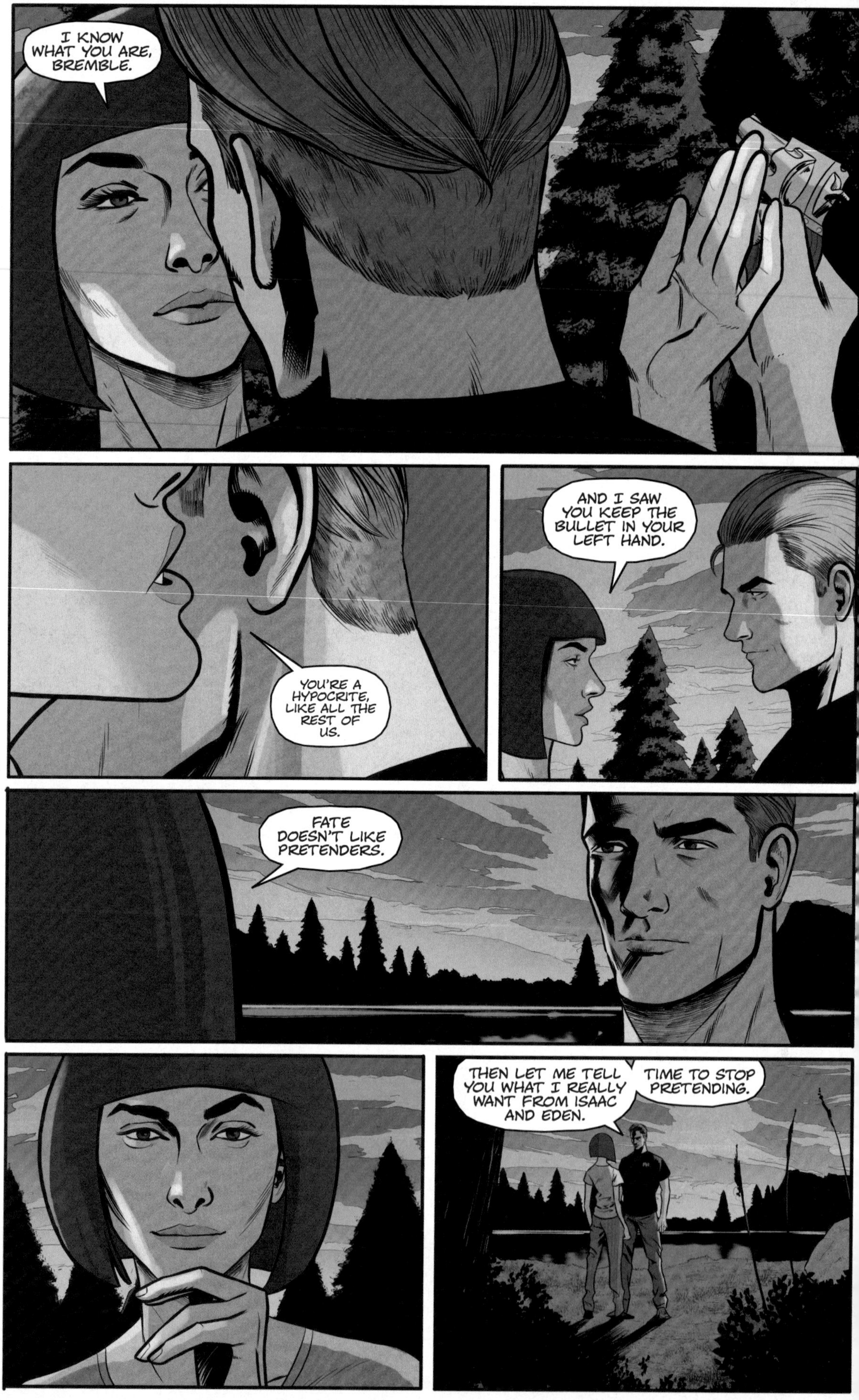
I KNOW WHAT YOU ARE, BREMBLE.
YOU'RE A HYPOCRITE, LIKE ALL THE REST OF US.
AND I SAW YOU KEEP THE BULLET IN YOUR LEFT HAND.
FATE DOESN'T LIKE PRETENDERS.
TIME TO STOP PRETENDING.
THEN LET ME TELL YOU WHAT I REALLY WANT FROM ISAAC AND EDEN.

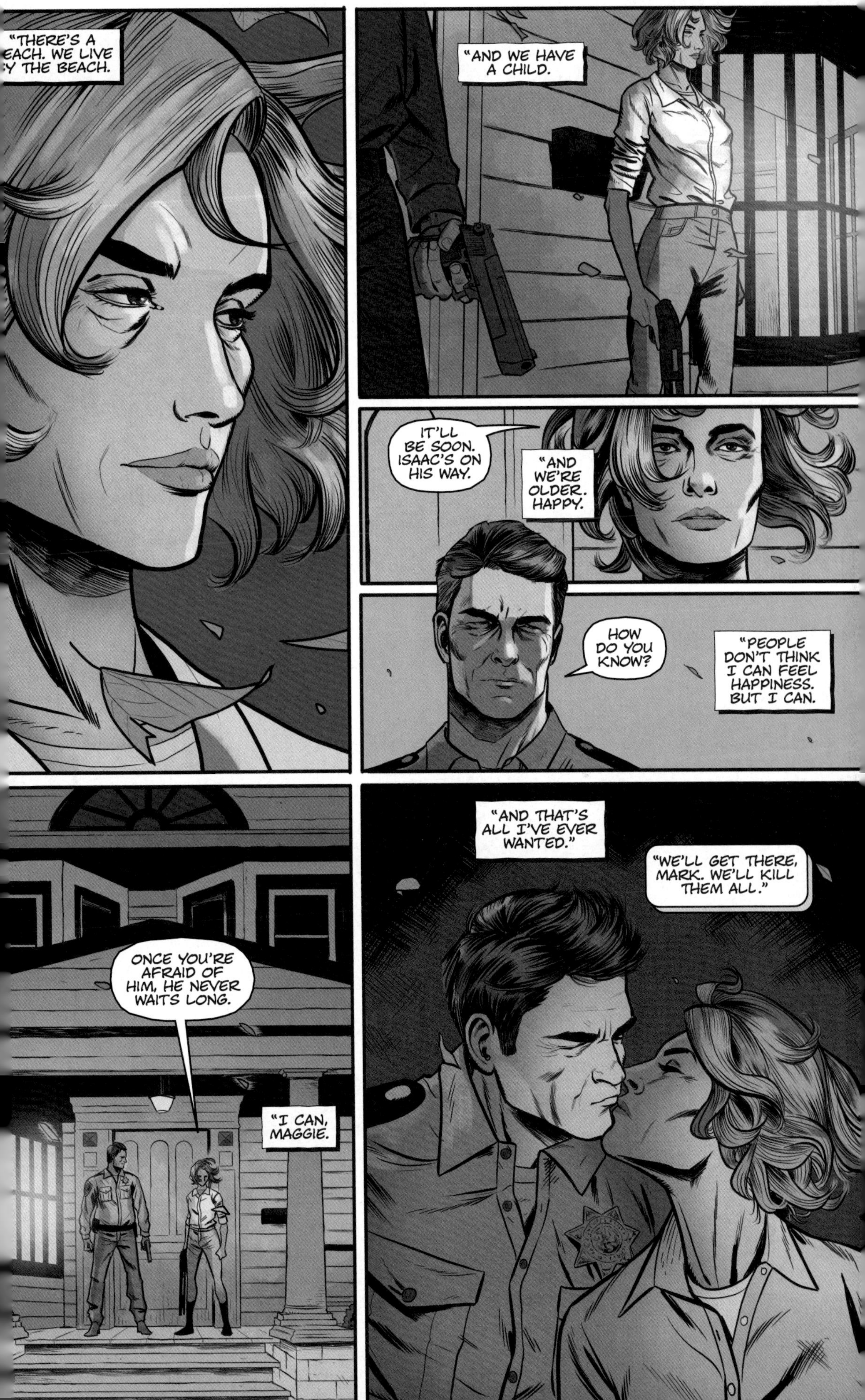
"THERE'S A
EACH. WE LIVE
Y THE BEACH.
"AND WE HAVE A CHILD.
IT'LL BE SOON. ISAAC'S ON HIS WAY.
"AND WE'RE OLDER. HAPPY.
HOW DO YOU KNOW?
"PEOPLE DON'T THINK I CAN FEEL HAPPINESS. BUT I CAN.
ONCE YOU'RE AFRAID OF HIM, HE NEVER WAITS LONG.
"I CAN, MAGGIE.
"AND THAT'S ALL I'VE EVER WANTED."
"WE'LL GET THERE, MARK. WE'LL KILL THEM ALL."

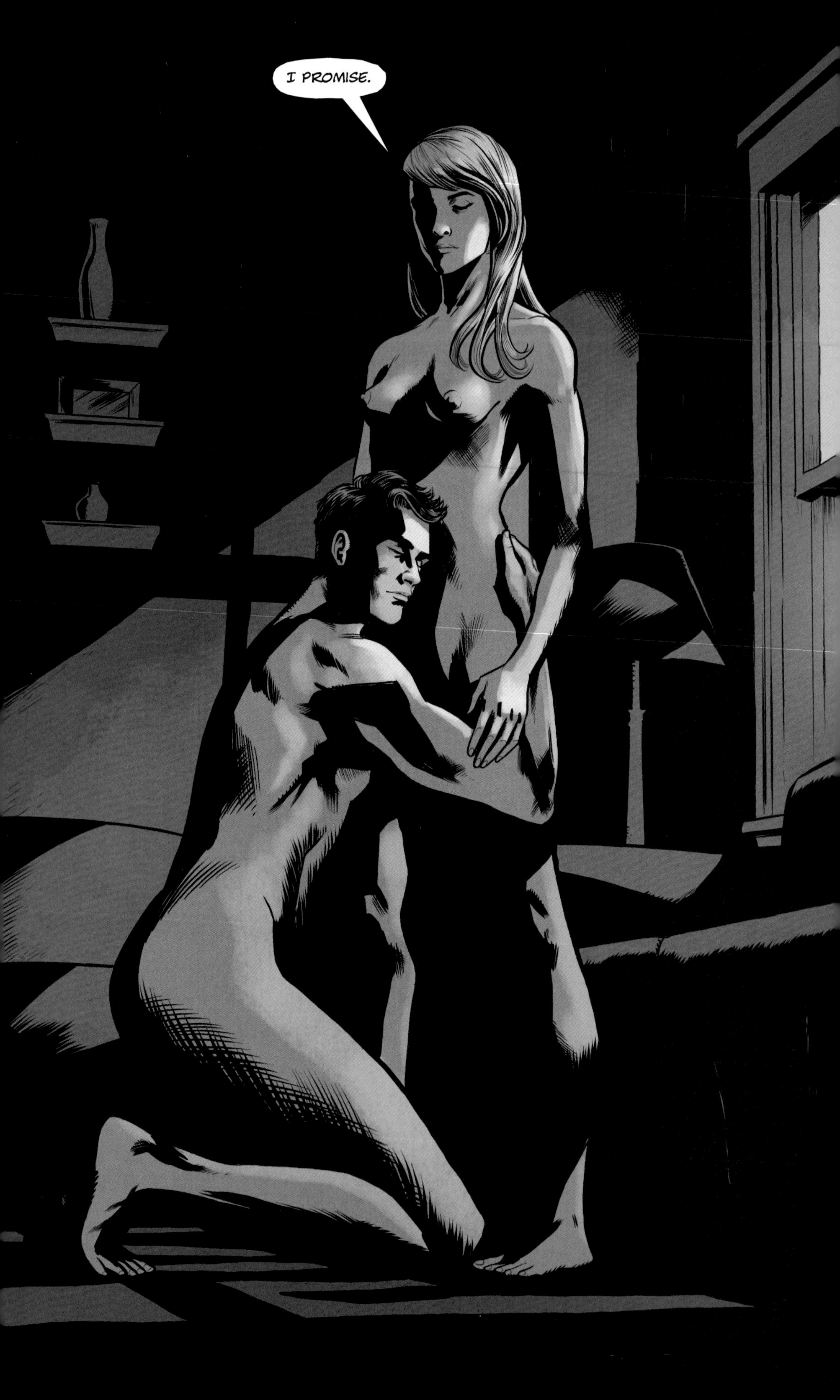
I PROMISE.

# CHAPTER 24

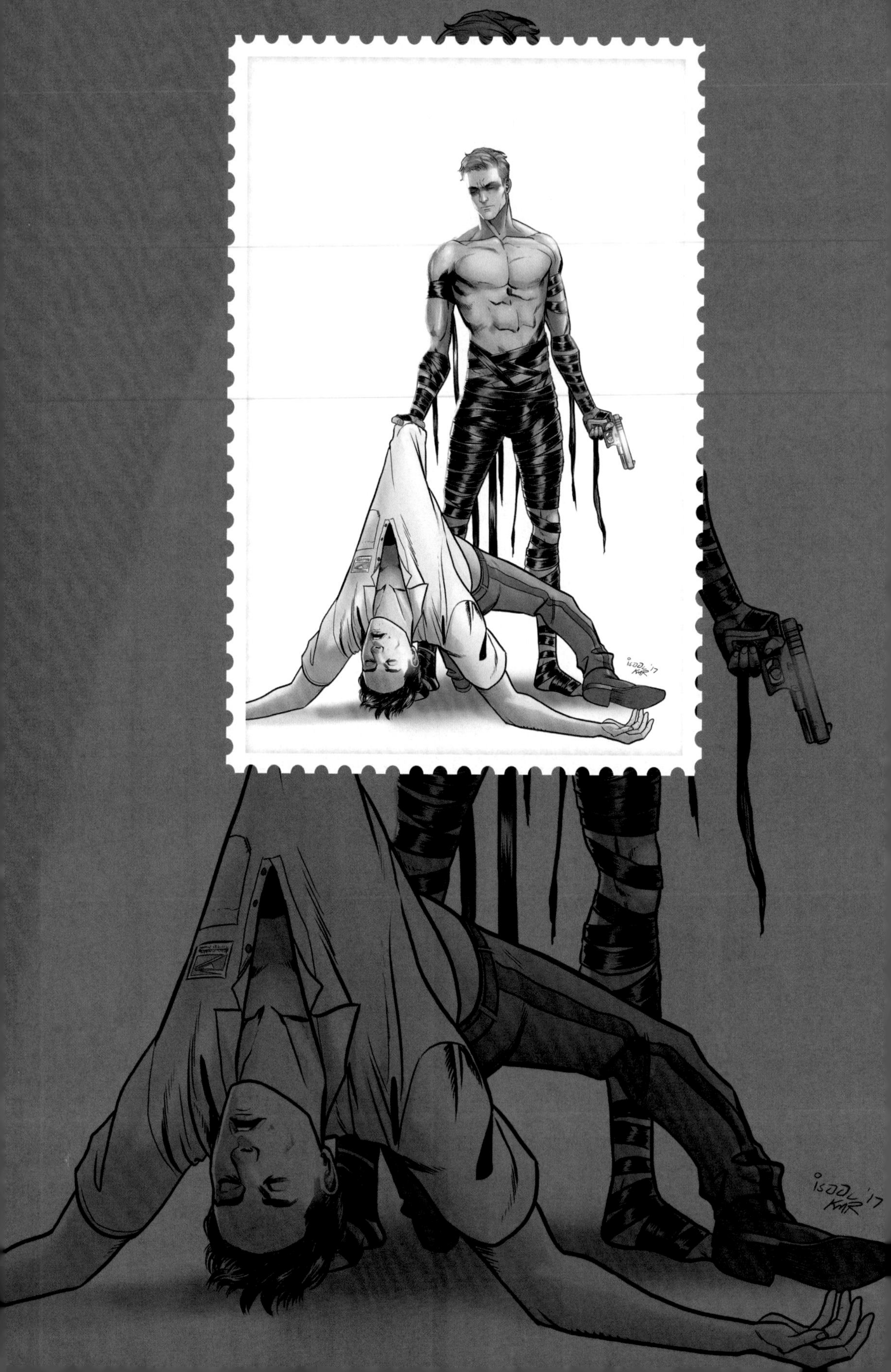

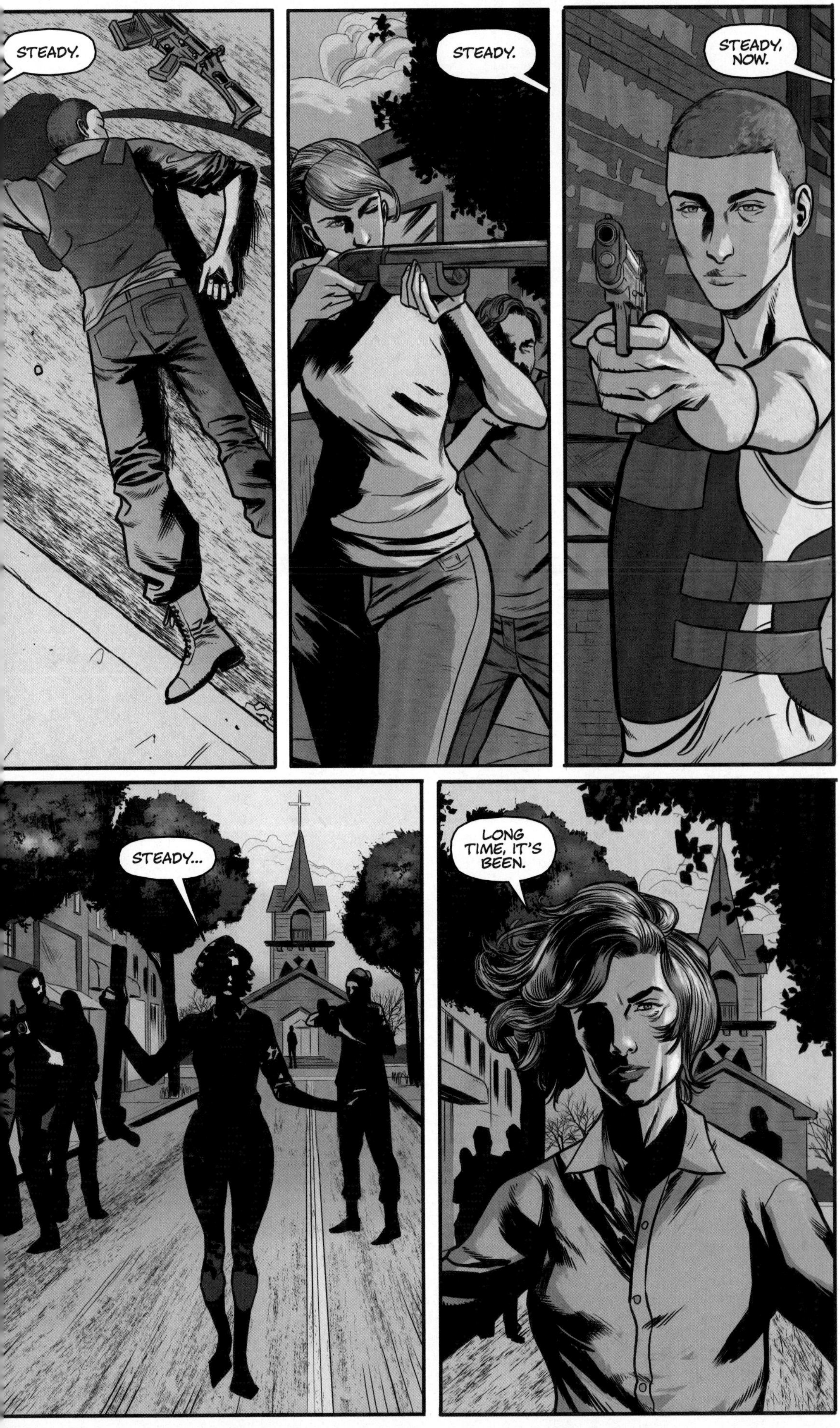
STEADY.
STEADY.
STEADY, NOW.
STEADY...
LONG TIME, IT'S BEEN.

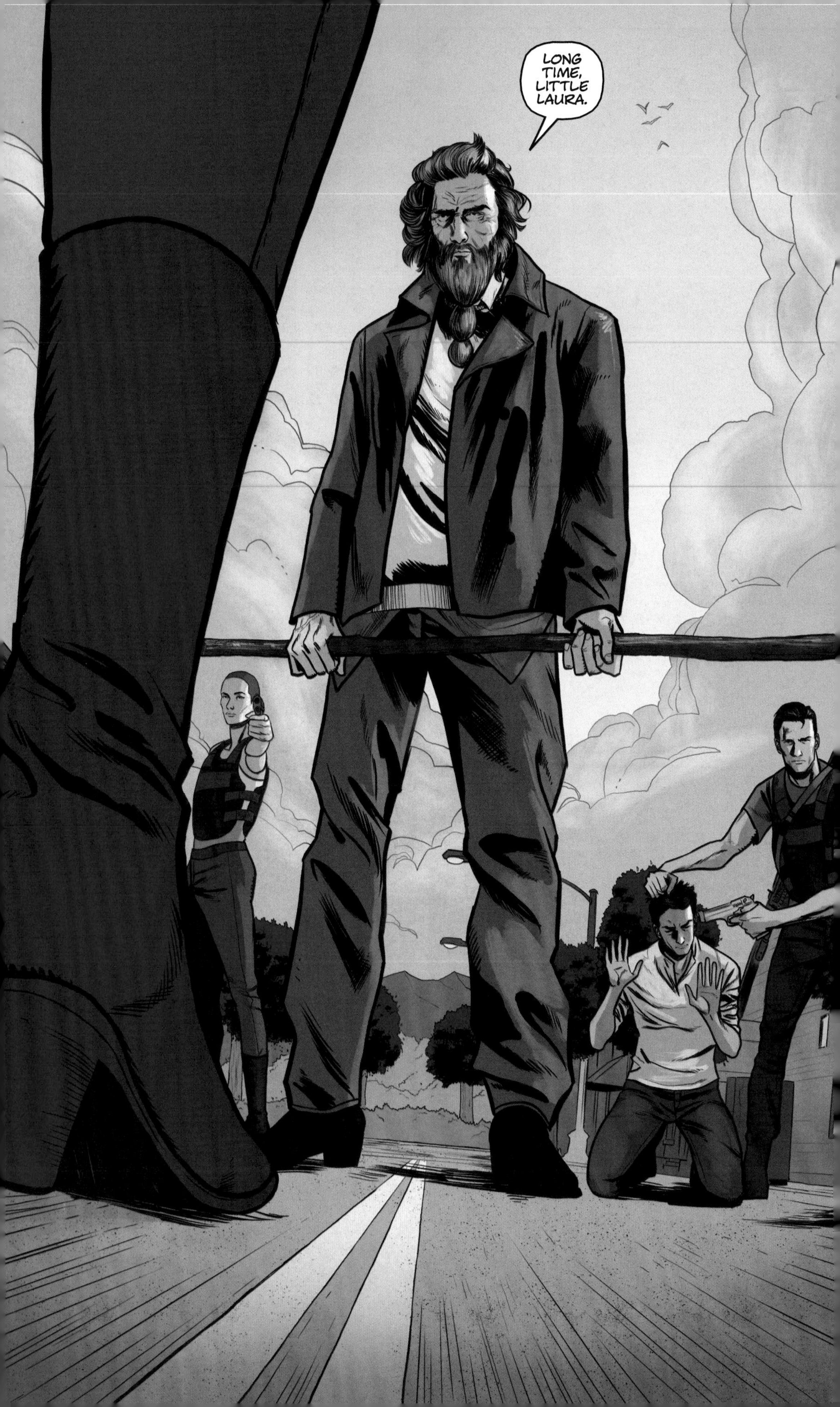
LONG TIME, LITTLE LAURA.

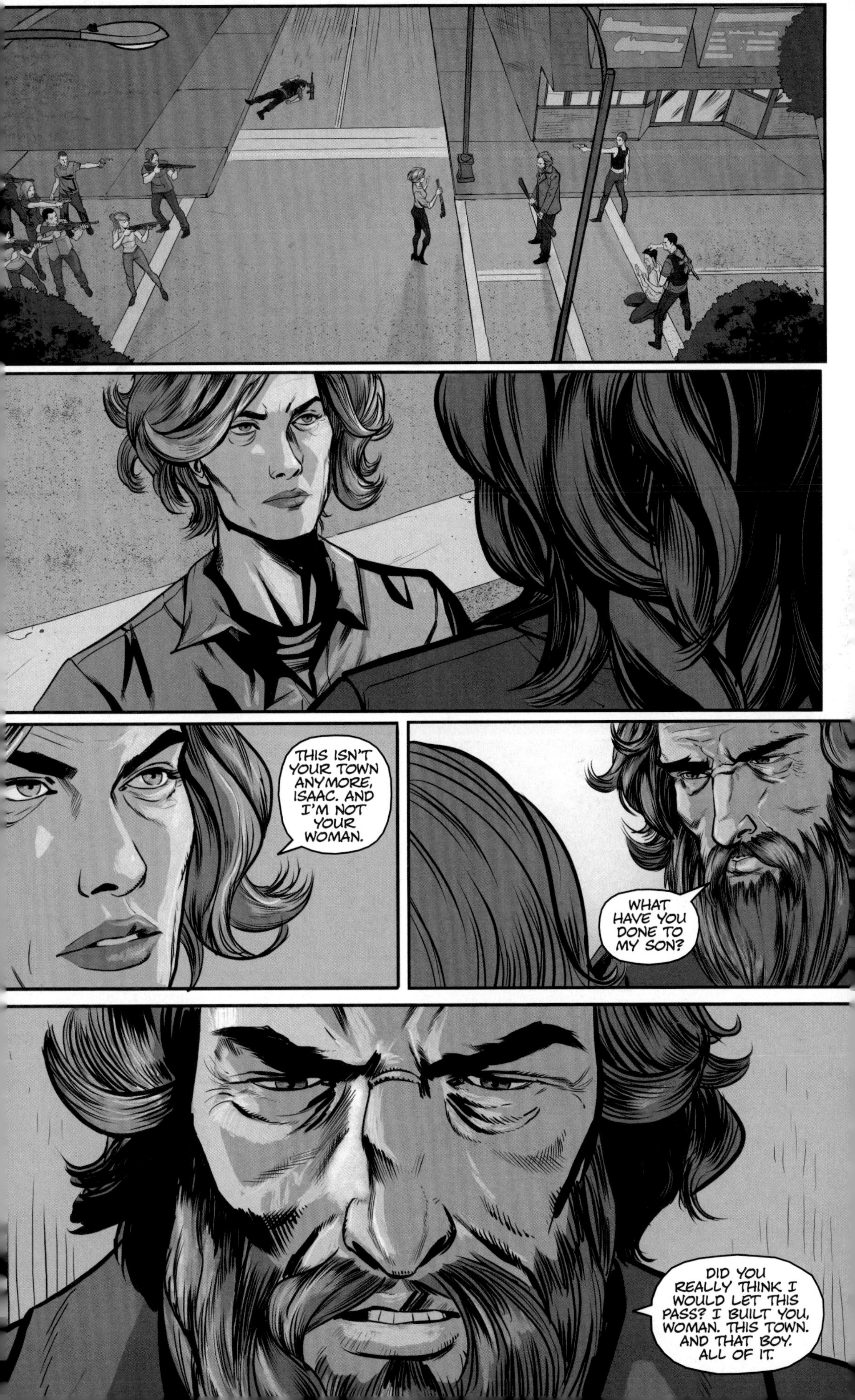
THIS ISN'T YOUR TOWN ANYMORE, ISAAC. AND I'M NOT YOUR WOMAN.
WHAT HAVE YOU DONE TO MY SON?
DID YOU REALLY THINK I WOULD LET THIS PASS? I BUILT YOU, WOMAN. THIS TOWN. AND THAT BOY. ALL OF IT.

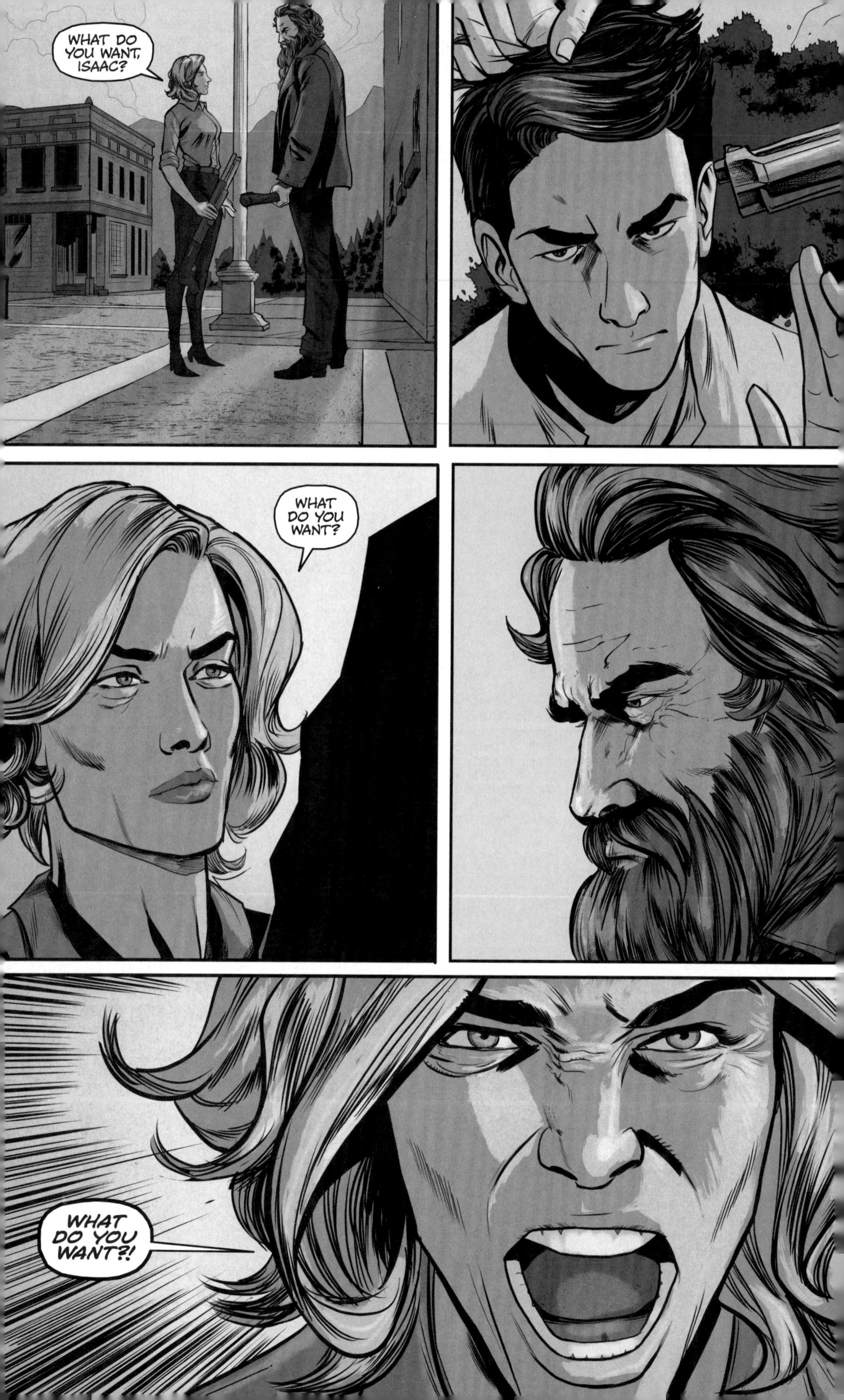
WHAT DO YOU WANT, ISAAC?
WHAT DO YOU WANT?
WHAT DO YOU WANT?!

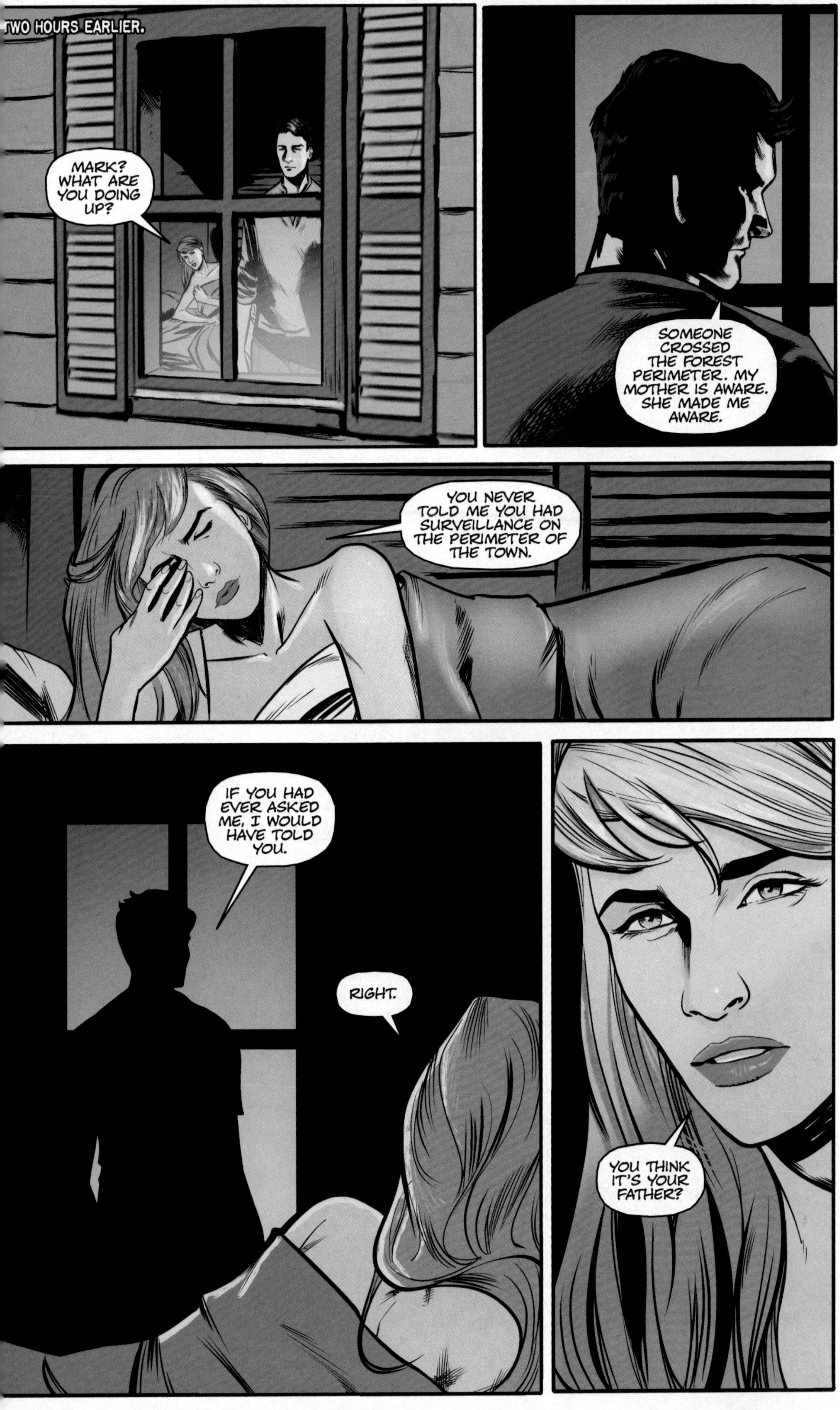
TWO HOURS EARLIER.
MARK? WHAT ARE YOU DOING UP?
SOMEONE CROSSED THE FOREST PERIMETER. MY MOTHER IS AWARE. SHE MADE ME AWARE.
YOU NEVER TOLD ME YOU HAD SURVEILLANCE ON THE PERIMETER OF THE TOWN.
IF YOU HAD EVER ASKED ME, I WOULD HAVE TOLD YOU.
RIGHT.
YOU THINK IT'S YOUR FATHER?

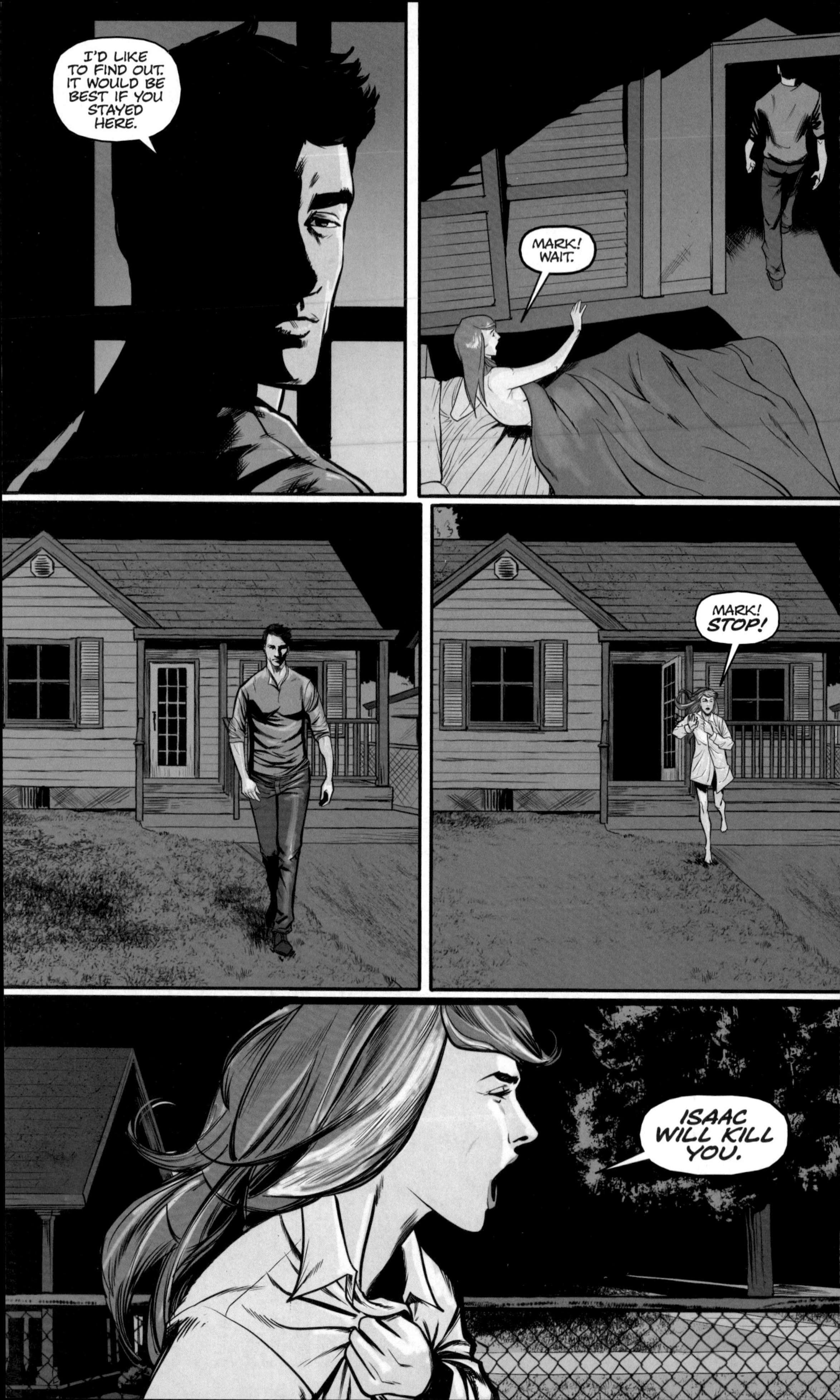
I'D LIKE TO FIND OUT. IT WOULD BE BEST IF YOU STAYED HERE.
MARK! WAIT.
MARK! STOP!
ISAAC WILL KILL YOU.

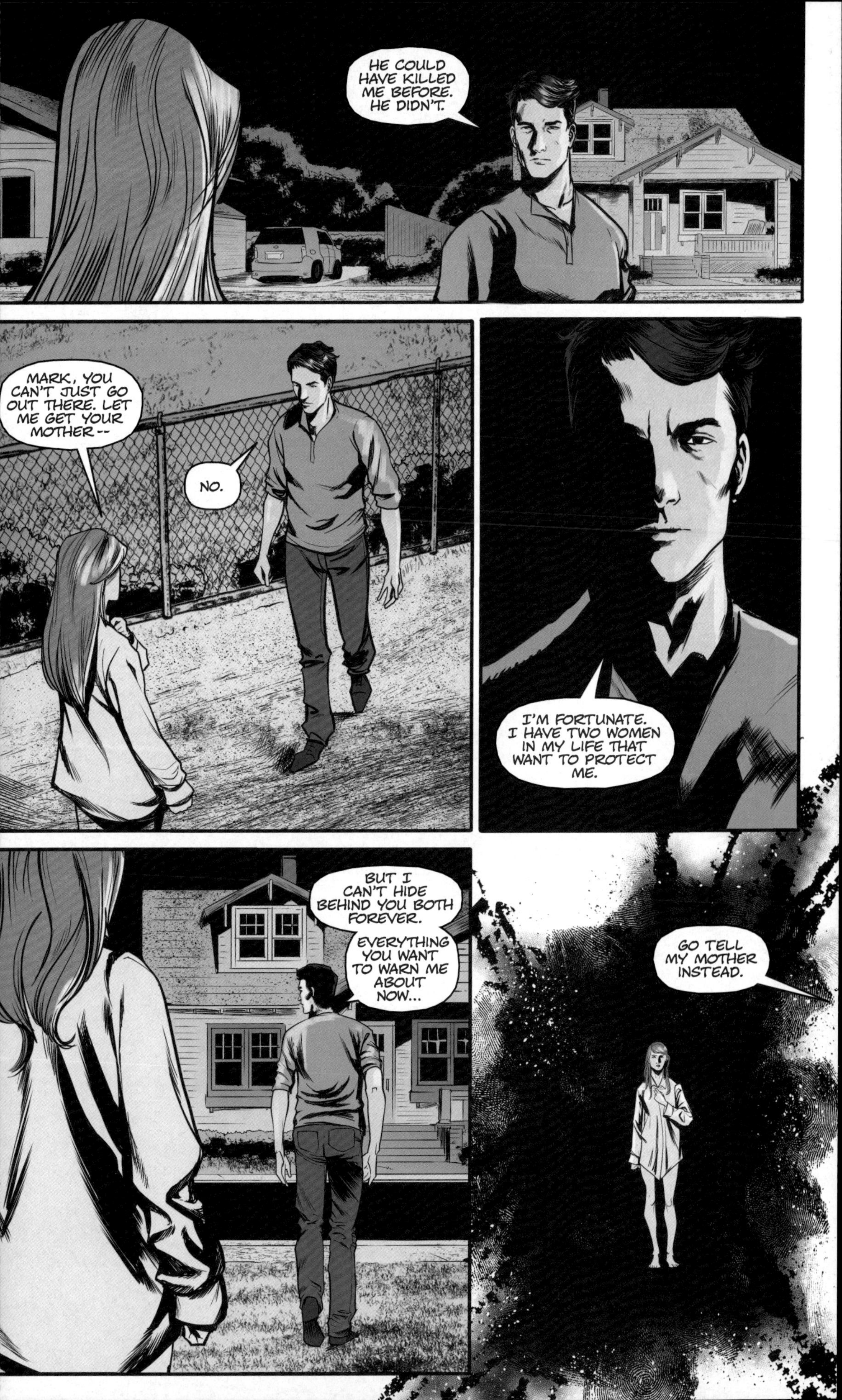
HE COULD HAVE KILLED ME BEFORE. HE DIDN'T.
MARK, YOU CAN'T JUST GO OUT THERE. LET ME GET YOUR MOTHER --
NO.
I'M FORTUNATE. I HAVE TWO WOMEN IN MY LIFE THAT WANT TO PROTECT ME.
BUT I CAN'T HIDE BEHIND YOU BOTH FOREVER.
EVERYTHING YOU WANT TO WARN ME ABOUT NOW...
GO TELL MY MOTHER INSTEAD.

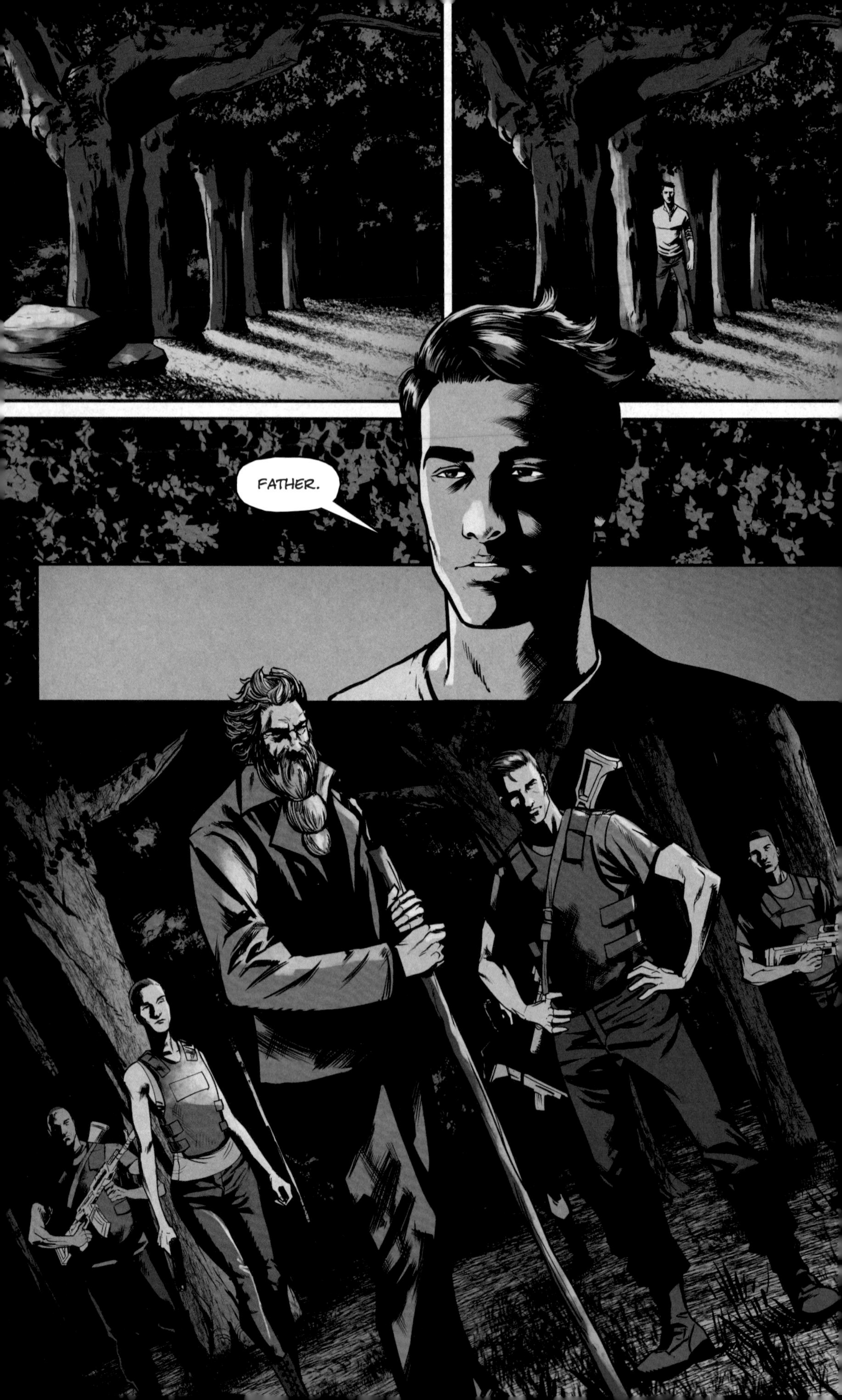
FATHER.

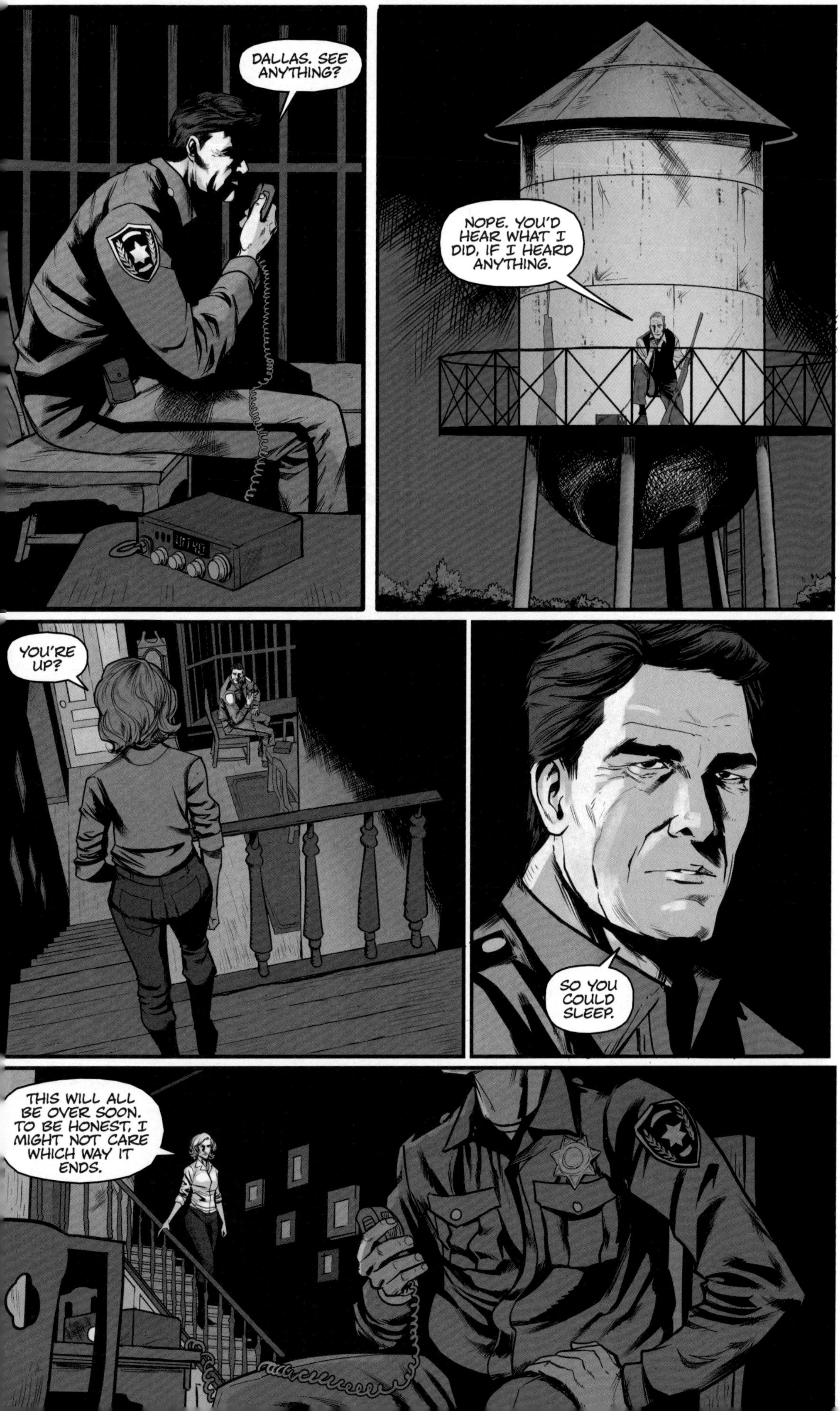
DALLAS. SEE ANYTHING?
NOPE. YOU'D HEAR WHAT I DID, IF I HEARD ANYTHING.
YOU'RE UP?
SO YOU COULD SLEEP.
THIS WILL ALL BE OVER SOON. TO BE HONEST, I MIGHT NOT CARE WHICH WAY IT ENDS.

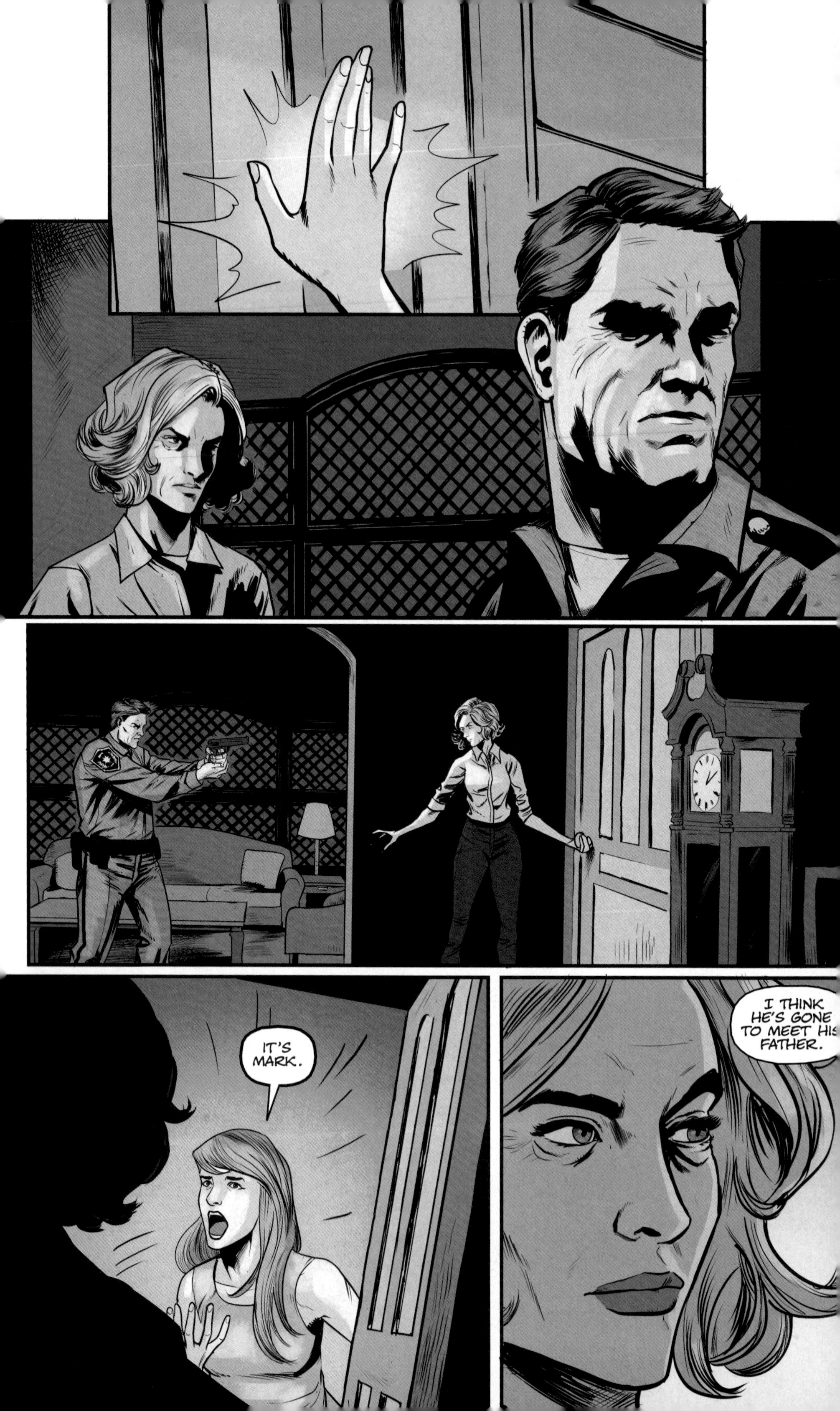
IT'S MARK.
I THINK HE'S GONE TO MEET HIS FATHER.

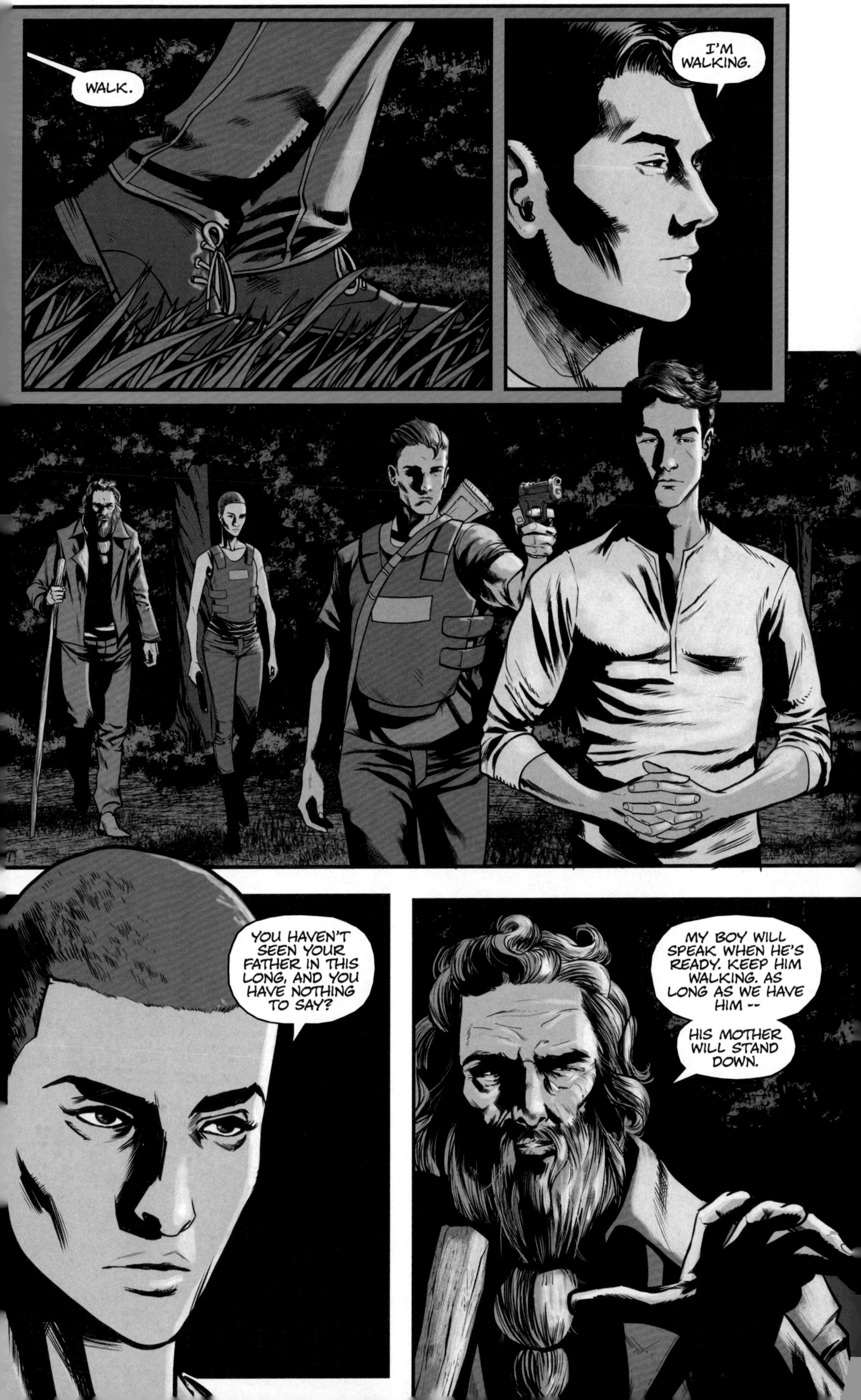
WALK.
I'M WALKING.
YOU HAVEN'T SEEN YOUR FATHER IN THIS LONG, AND YOU HAVE NOTHING TO SAY?
MY BOY WILL SPEAK WHEN HE'S READY. KEEP HIM WALKING. AS LONG AS WE HAVE HIM --
HIS MOTHER WILL STAND DOWN.

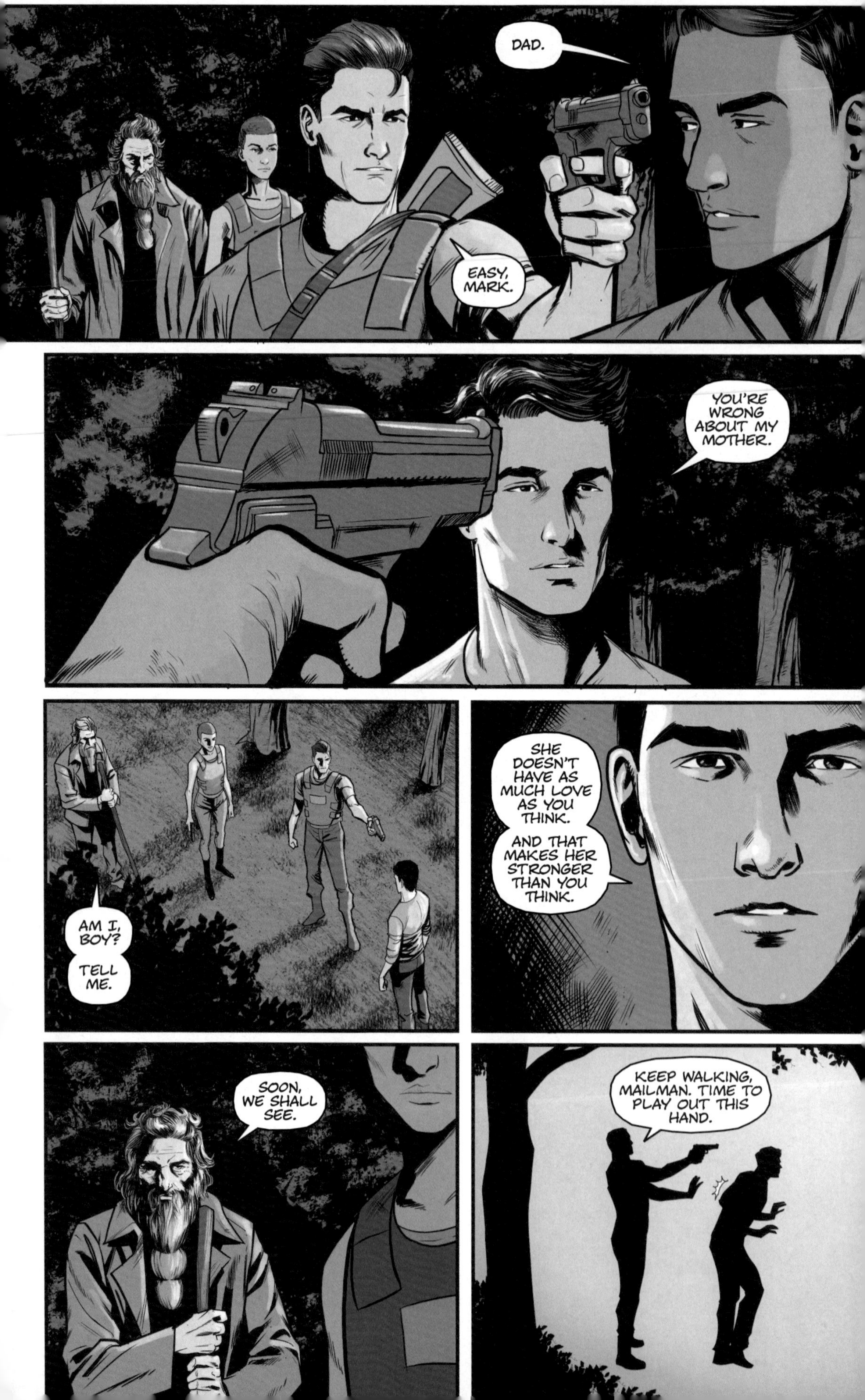
DAD.
EASY, MARK.
YOU'RE WRONG ABOUT MY MOTHER.
AM I, BOY?
TELL ME.
SHE DOESN'T HAVE AS MUCH LOVE AS YOU THINK.
AND THAT MAKES HER STRONGER THAN YOU THINK.
SOON, WE SHALL SEE.
KEEP WALKING, MAILMAN. TIME TO PLAY OUT THIS HAND.

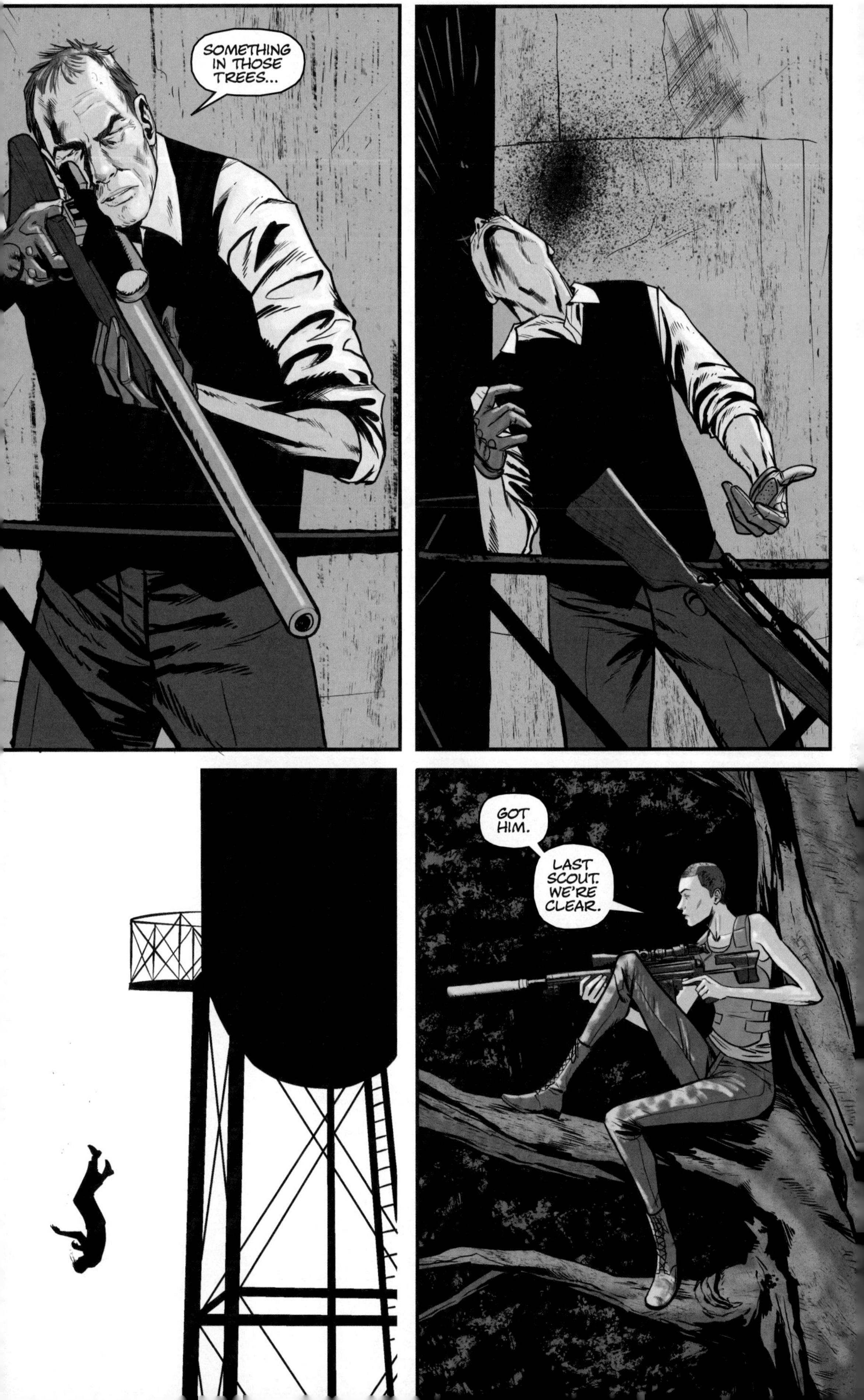
SOMETHING IN THOSE TREES...
GOT HIM.
LAST SCOUT. WE'RE CLEAR.

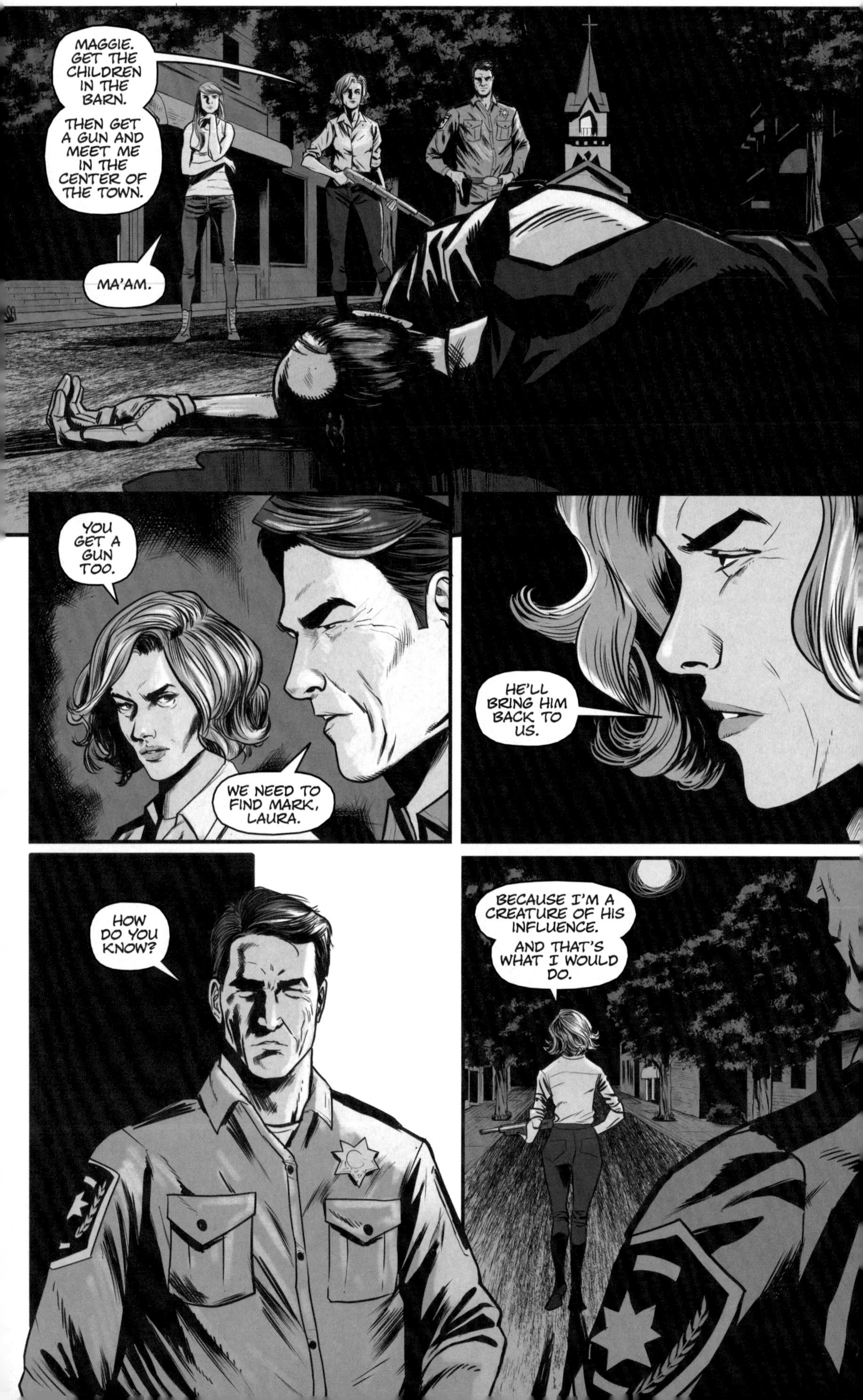
MAGGIE. GET THE CHILDREN IN THE BARN.
THEN GET A GUN AND MEET ME IN THE CENTER OF THE TOWN.
MA'AM.
YOU GET A GUN TOO.
WE NEED TO FIND MARK, LAURA.
HE'LL BRING HIM BACK TO US.
HOW DO YOU KNOW?
BECAUSE I'M A CREATURE OF HIS INFLUENCE.
AND THAT'S WHAT I WOULD DO.

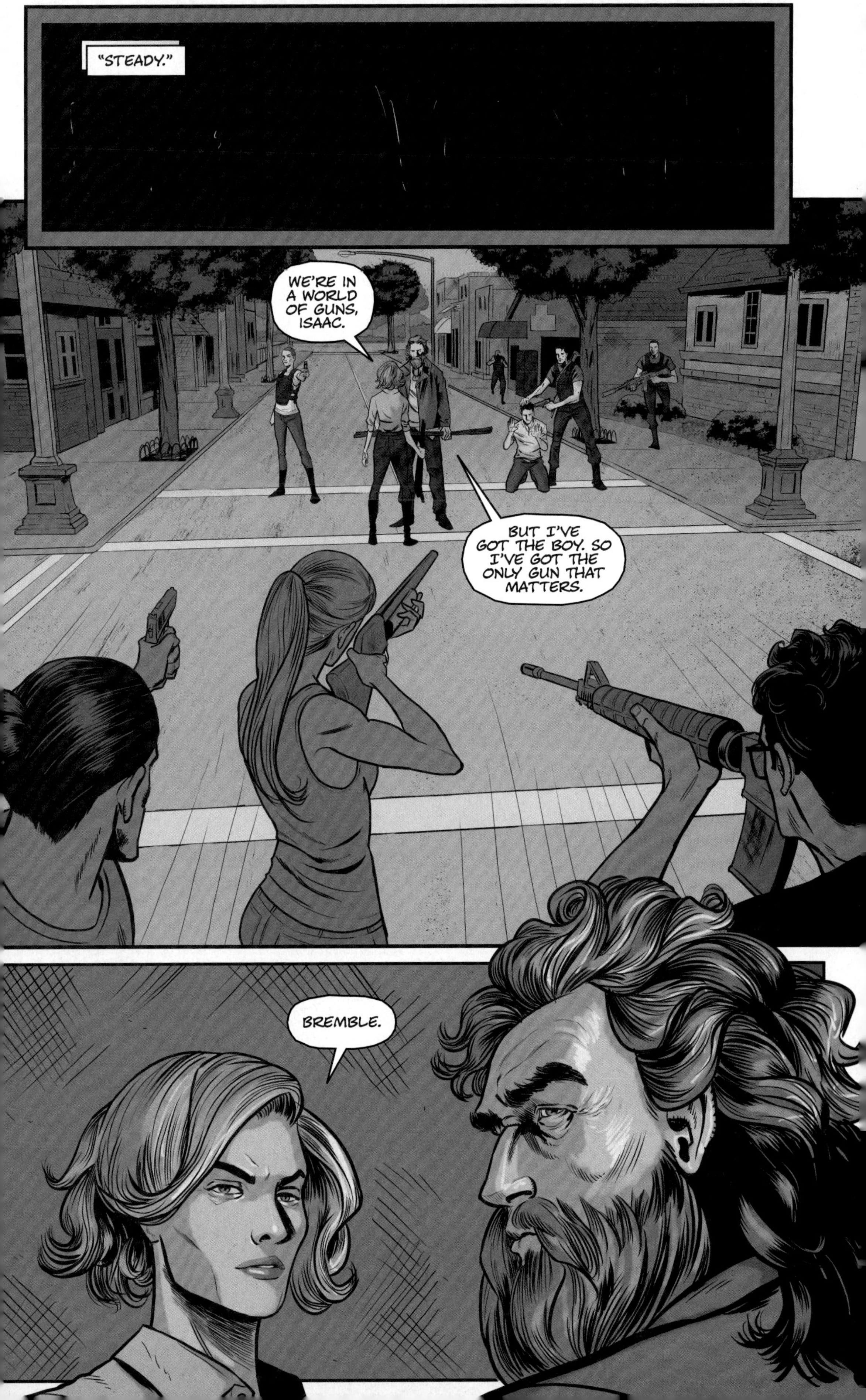
"STEADY."
WE'RE IN A WORLD OF GUNS, ISAAC.
BUT I'VE GOT THE BOY. SO I'VE GOT THE ONLY GUN THAT MATTERS.
BREMBLE.

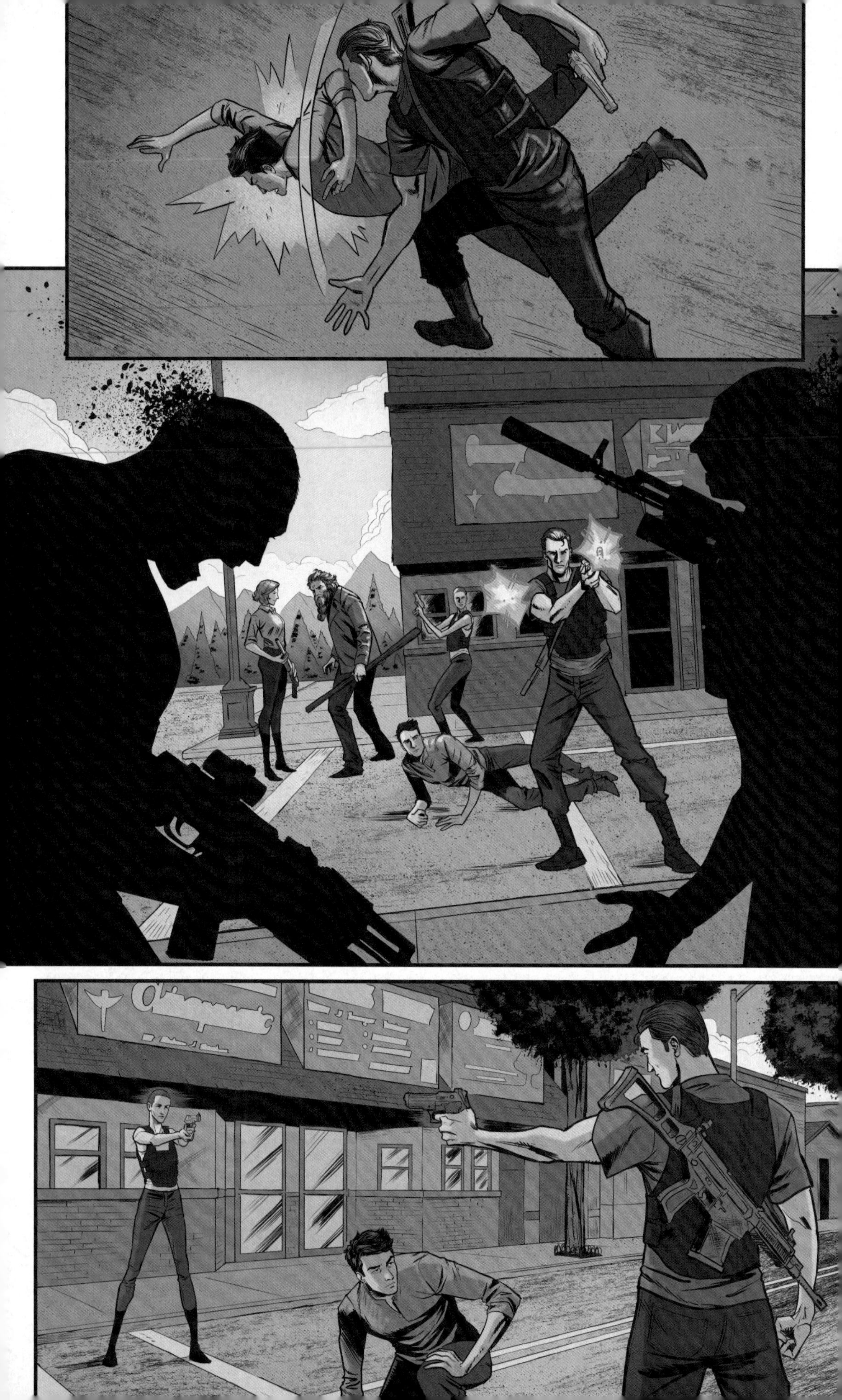

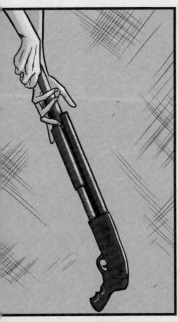

PUT THE GUN DOWN, AVA.

WHAT IS THIS? WHAT IS THIS?

THIS IS WHAT HAPPENS WHEN YOU GET OLD AND TRUST TOO MANY PEOPLE, ISAAC.

I...

PUT IT DOWN OR I HAVE TO KILL YOU.

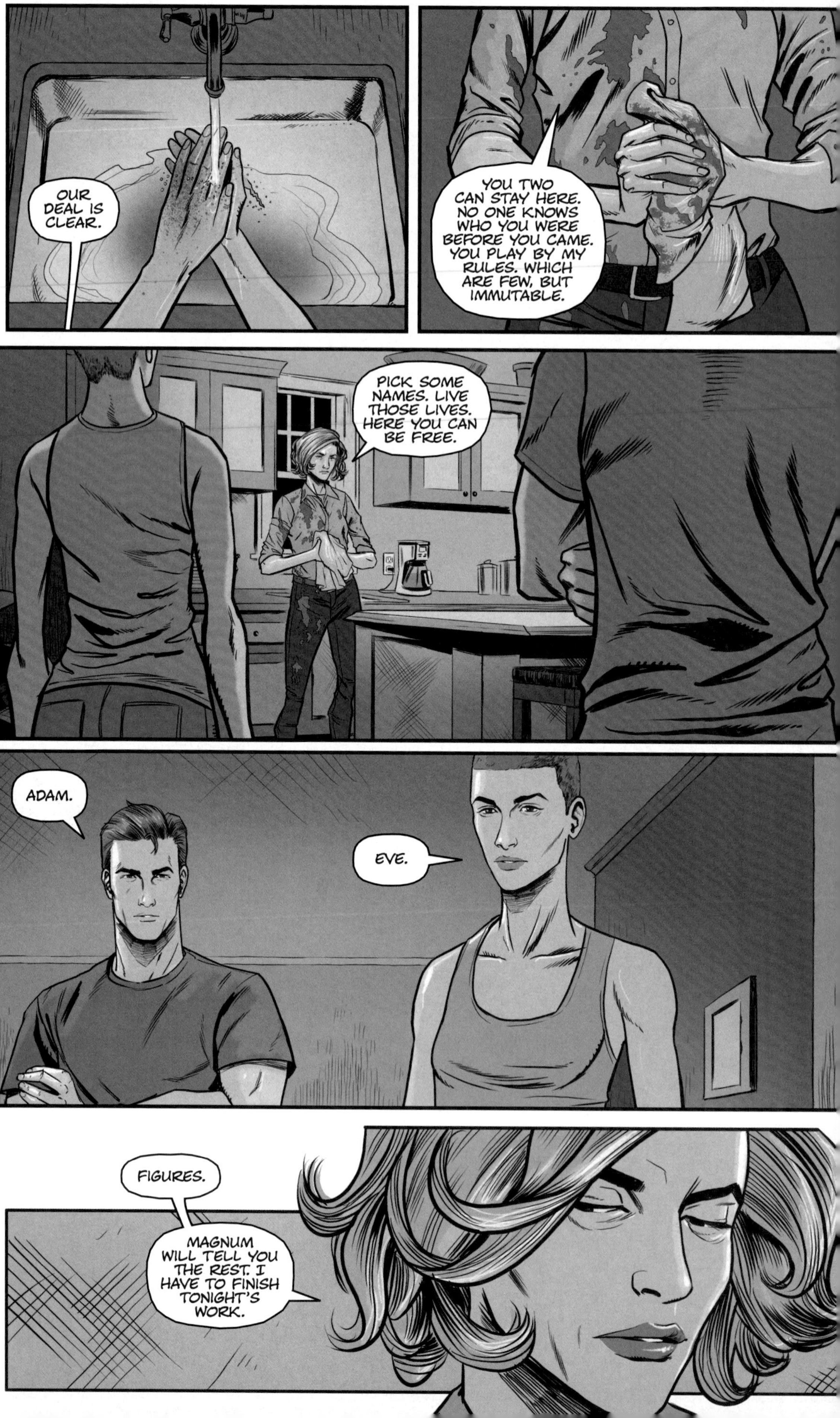
OUR DEAL IS CLEAR.
YOU TWO CAN STAY HERE. NO ONE KNOWS WHO YOU WERE BEFORE YOU CAME. YOU PLAY BY MY RULES. WHICH ARE FEW, BUT IMMUTABLE.
PICK SOME NAMES. LIVE THOSE LIVES. HERE YOU CAN BE FREE.
ADAM.
EVE.
FIGURES.
MAGNUM WILL TELL YOU THE REST. I HAVE TO FINISH TONIGHT'S WORK.

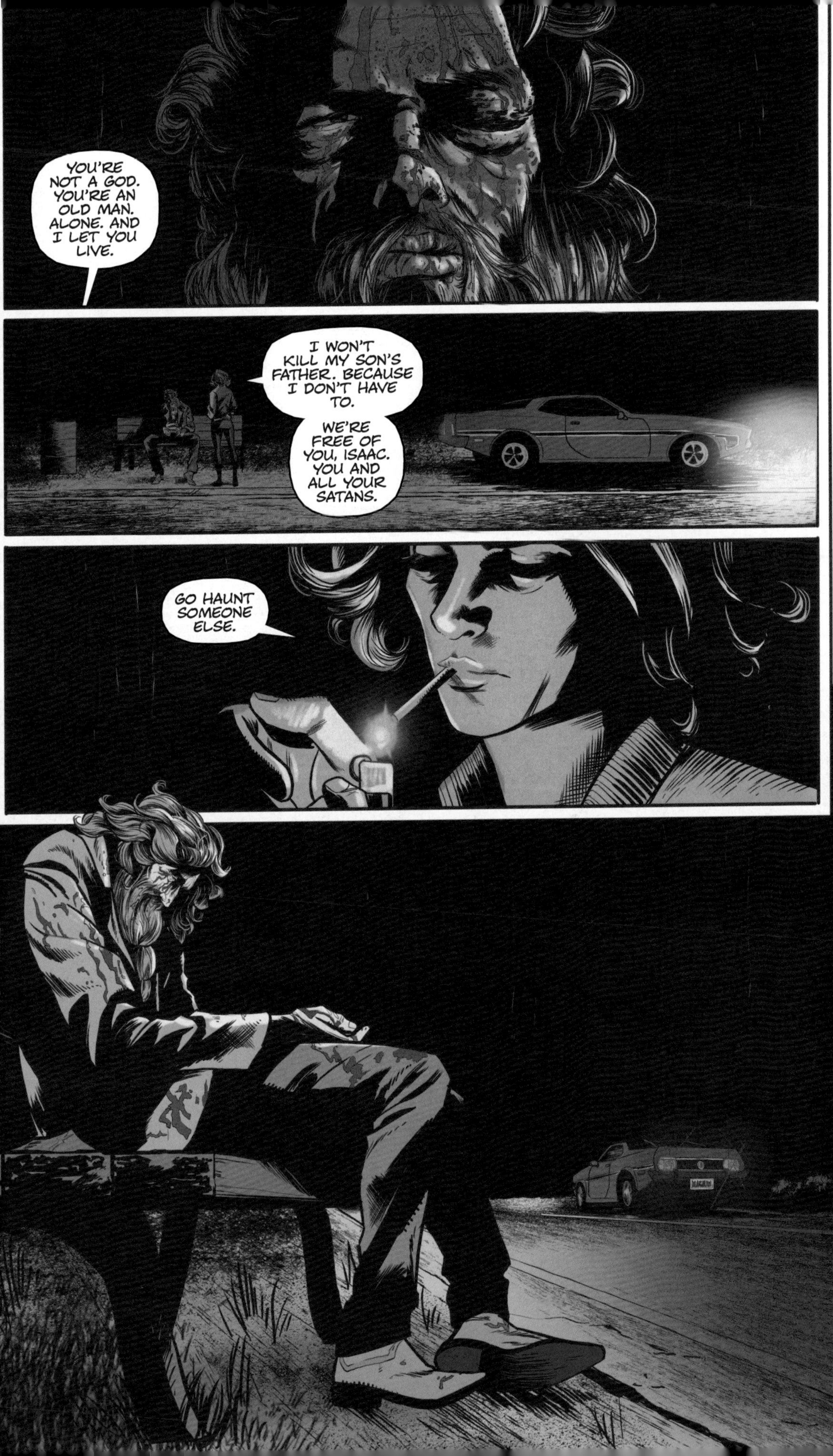
YOU'RE NOT A GOD. YOU'RE AN OLD MAN. ALONE. AND I LET YOU LIVE.
I WON'T KILL MY SON'S FATHER. BECAUSE I DON'T HAVE TO.
WE'RE FREE OF YOU, ISAAC. YOU AND ALL YOUR SATANS.
GO HAUNT SOMEONE ELSE.

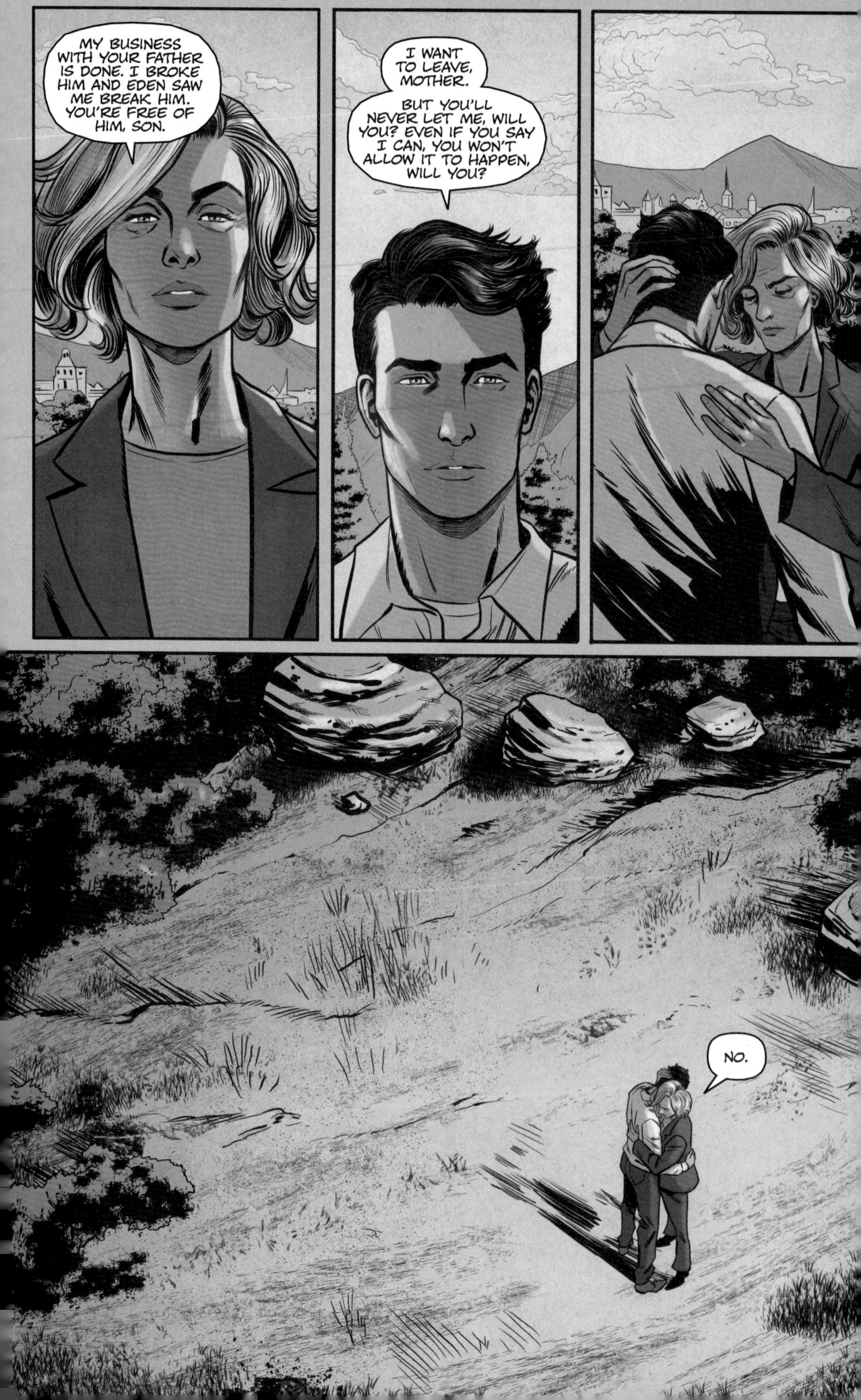
MY BUSINESS WITH YOUR FATHER IS DONE. I BROKE HIM AND EDEN SAW ME BREAK HIM. YOU'RE FREE OF HIM, SON.
I WANT TO LEAVE, MOTHER.
BUT YOU'LL NEVER LET ME, WILL YOU? EVEN IF YOU SAY I CAN, YOU WON'T ALLOW IT TO HAPPEN, WILL YOU?
NO.

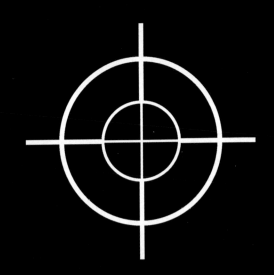

# CHAPTER 25

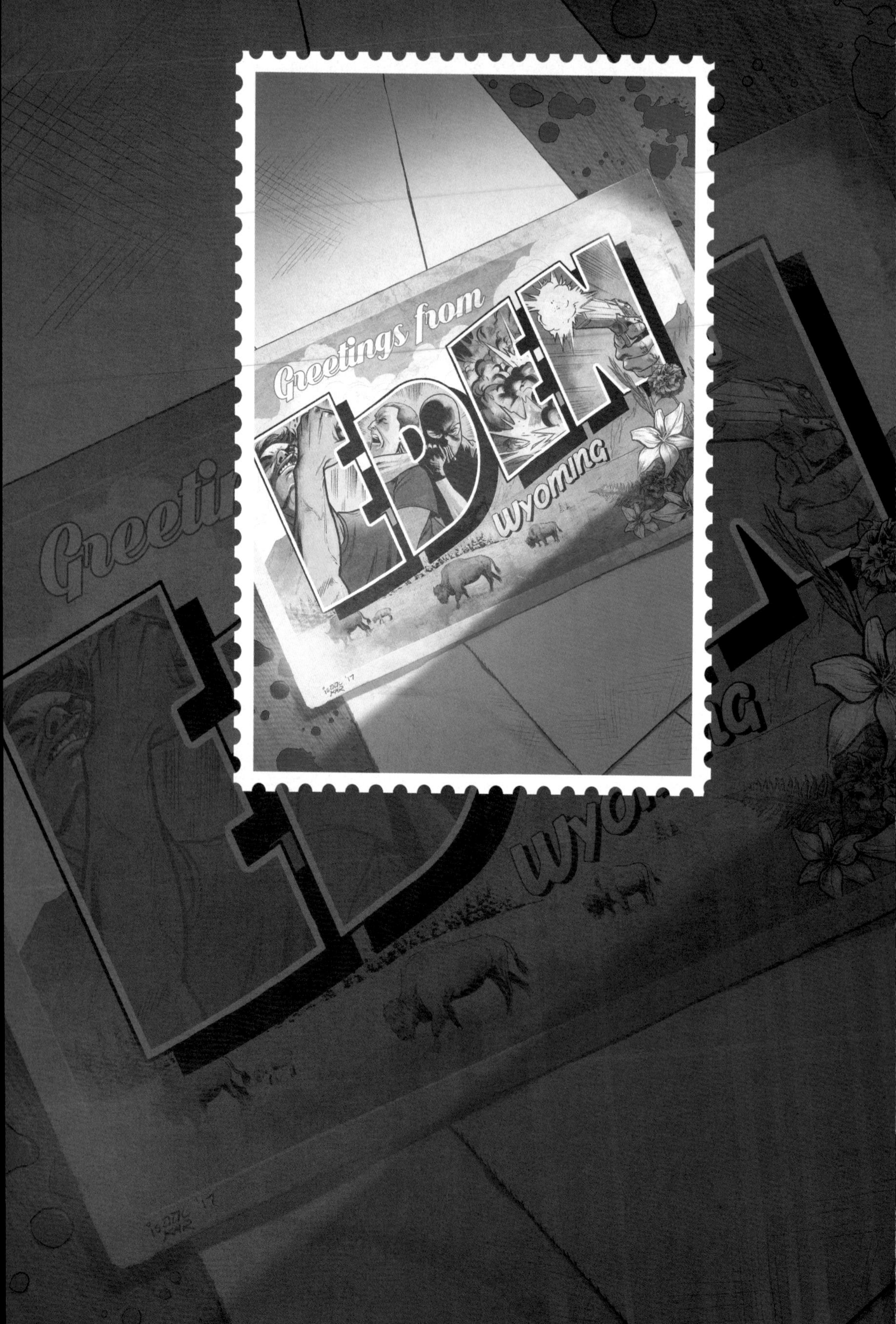
Greetings from
EDEN
wyoming

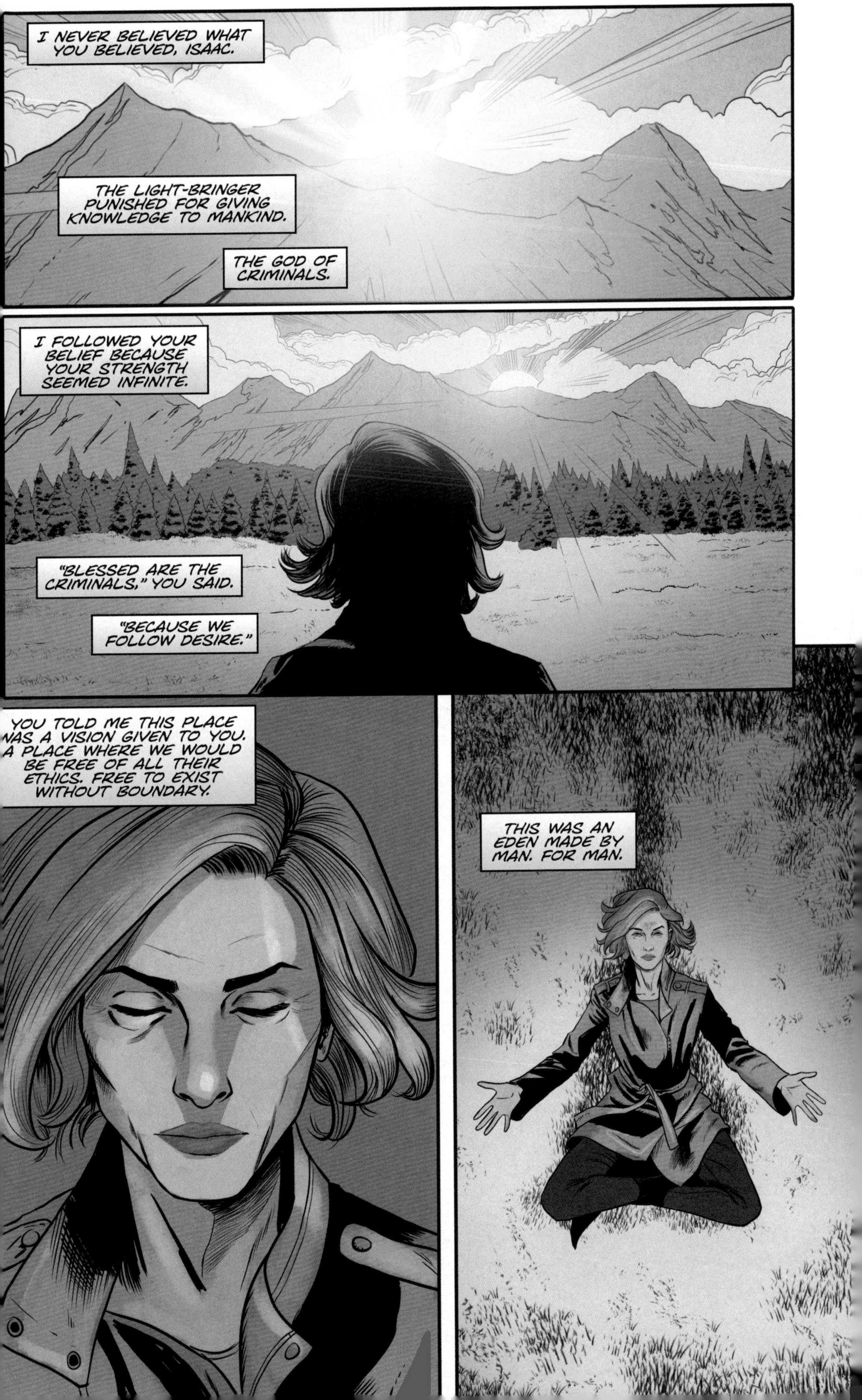
I NEVER BELIEVED WHAT YOU BELIEVED, ISAAC.
THE LIGHT-BRINGER PUNISHED FOR GIVING KNOWLEDGE TO MANKIND.
THE GOD OF CRIMINALS.
I FOLLOWED YOUR BELIEF BECAUSE YOUR STRENGTH SEEMED INFINITE.
"BLESSED ARE THE CRIMINALS," YOU SAID.
"BECAUSE WE FOLLOW DESIRE."
YOU TOLD ME THIS PLACE AS A VISION GIVEN TO YOU. A PLACE WHERE WE WOULD BE FREE OF ALL THEIR ETHICS. FREE TO EXIST WITHOUT BOUNDARY.
THIS WAS AN EDEN MADE BY MAN. FOR MAN.

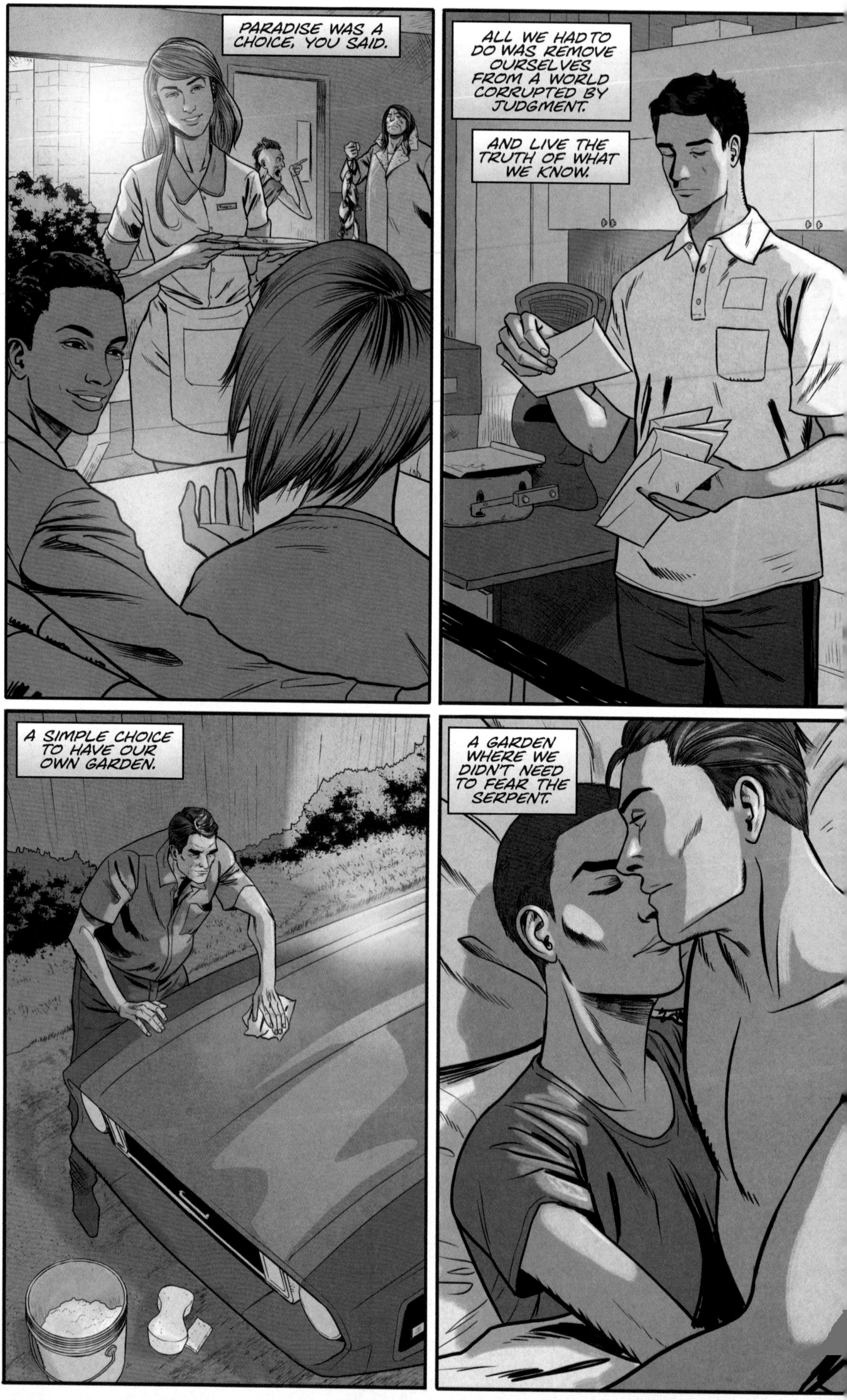
PARADISE WAS A CHOICE, YOU SAID.
ALL WE HAD TO DO WAS REMOVE OURSELVES FROM A WORLD CORRUPTED BY JUDGMENT.
AND LIVE THE TRUTH OF WHAT WE KNOW.
A SIMPLE CHOICE TO HAVE OUR OWN GARDEN.
A GARDEN WHERE WE DIDN'T NEED TO FEAR THE SERPENT.

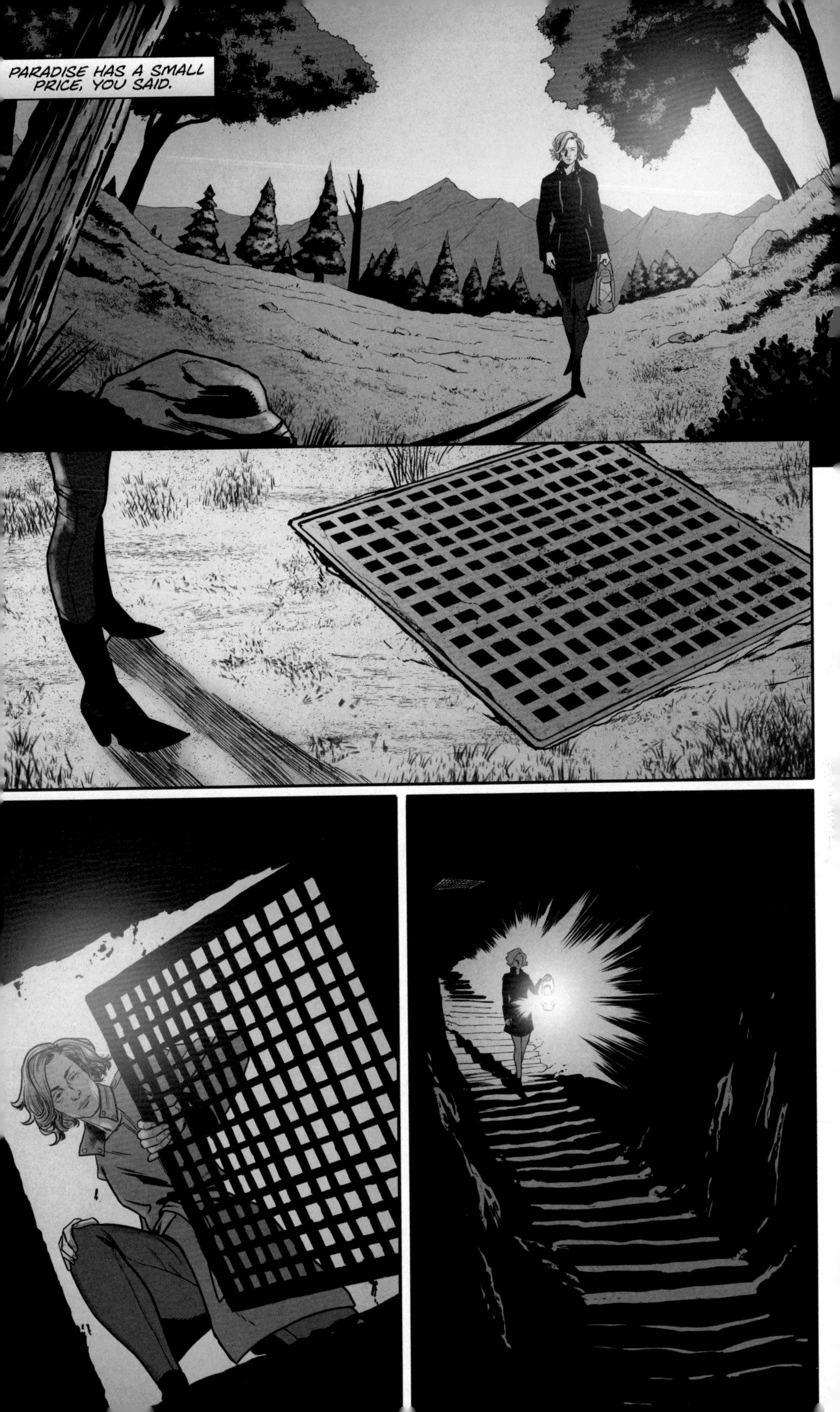
PARADISE HAS A SMALL PRICE, YOU SAID.

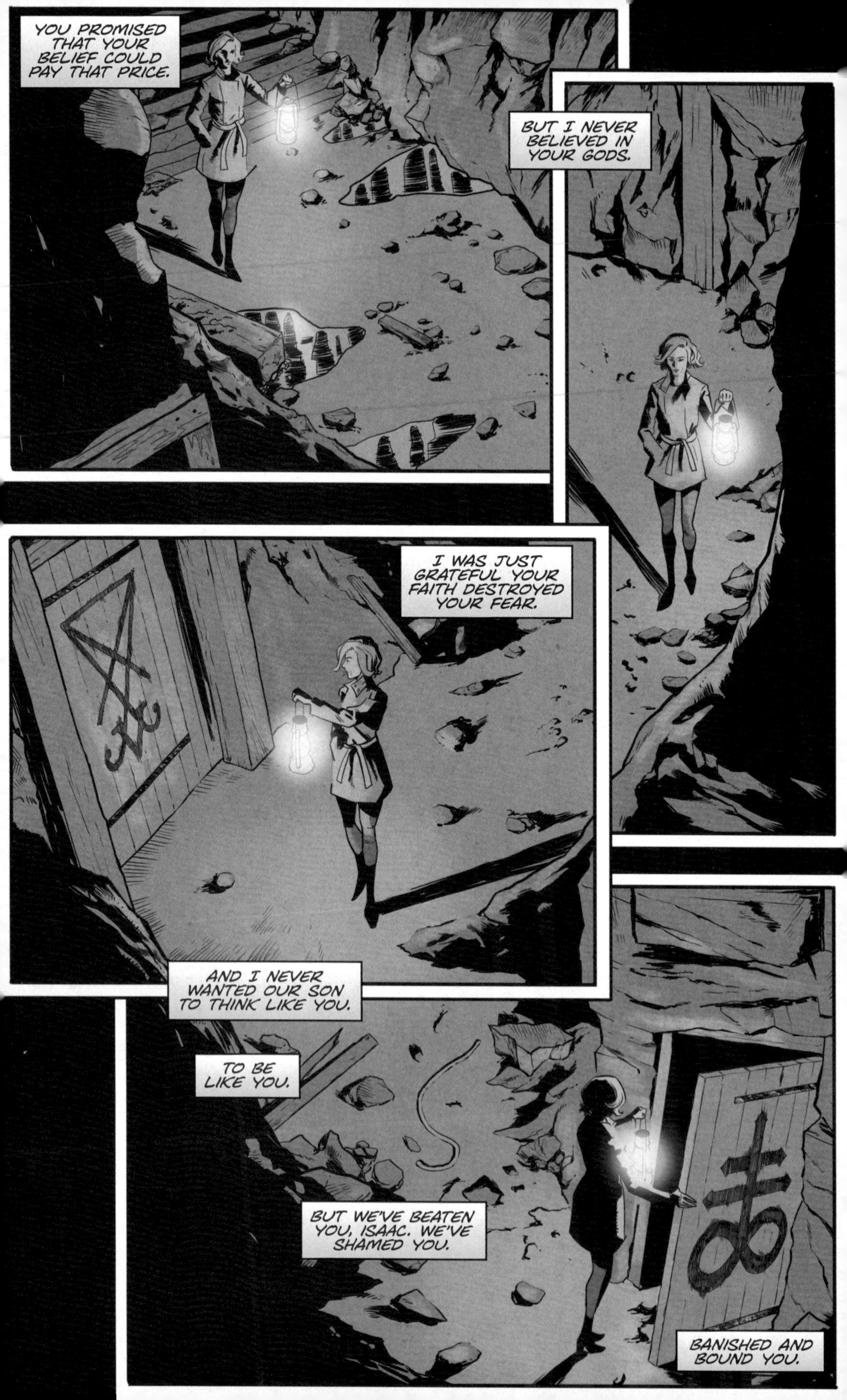
YOU PROMISED THAT YOUR BELIEF COULD PAY THAT PRICE.
BUT I NEVER BELIEVED IN YOUR GODS.
I WAS JUST GRATEFUL YOUR FAITH DESTROYED YOUR FEAR.
AND I NEVER WANTED OUR SON TO THINK LIKE YOU.
TO BE LIKE YOU.
BUT WE'VE BEATEN YOU, ISAAC. WE'VE SHAMED YOU.
BANISHED AND BOUND YOU.

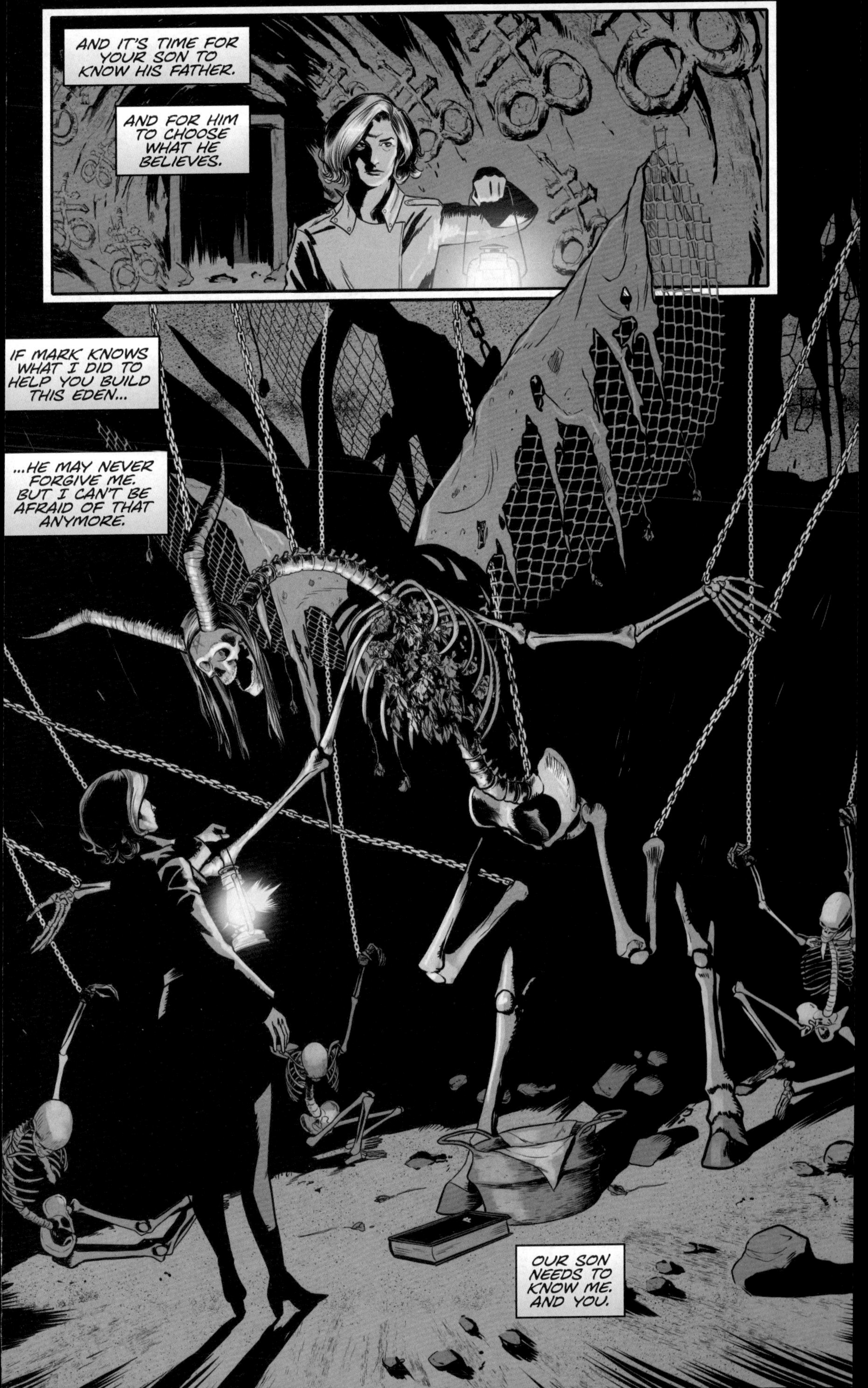
AND IT'S TIME FOR YOUR SON TO KNOW HIS FATHER.
AND FOR HIM TO CHOOSE WHAT HE BELIEVES.
IF MARK KNOWS WHAT I DID TO HELP YOU BUILD THIS EDEN...
...HE MAY NEVER FORGIVE ME. BUT I CAN'T BE AFRAID OF THAT ANYMORE.
OUR SON NEEDS TO KNOW ME. AND YOU.

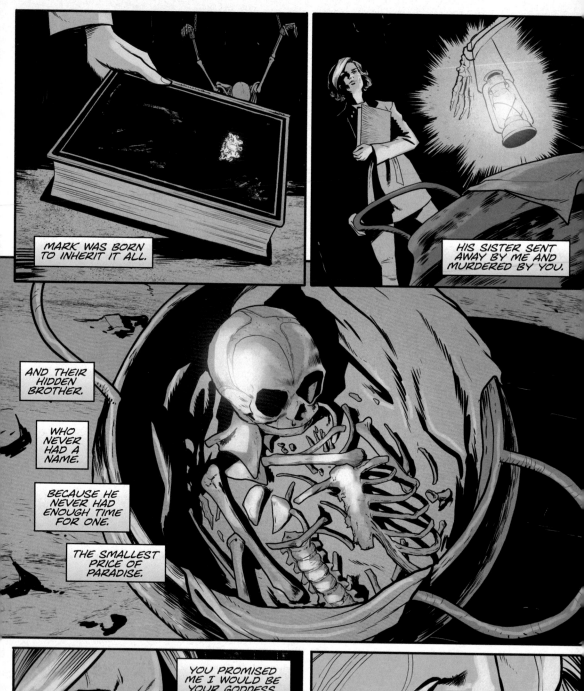

MARK WAS BORN TO INHERIT IT ALL.

HIS SISTER SENT AWAY BY ME AND MURDERED BY YOU.

AND THEIR HIDDEN BROTHER.

WHO NEVER HAD A NAME.

BECAUSE HE NEVER HAD ENOUGH TIME FOR ONE.

THE SMALLEST PRICE OF PARADISE.

YOU PROMISED ME I WOULD BE YOUR GODDESS.

AND I WAS.

BUT IT'S TIME FOR THE GODS TO DIE.

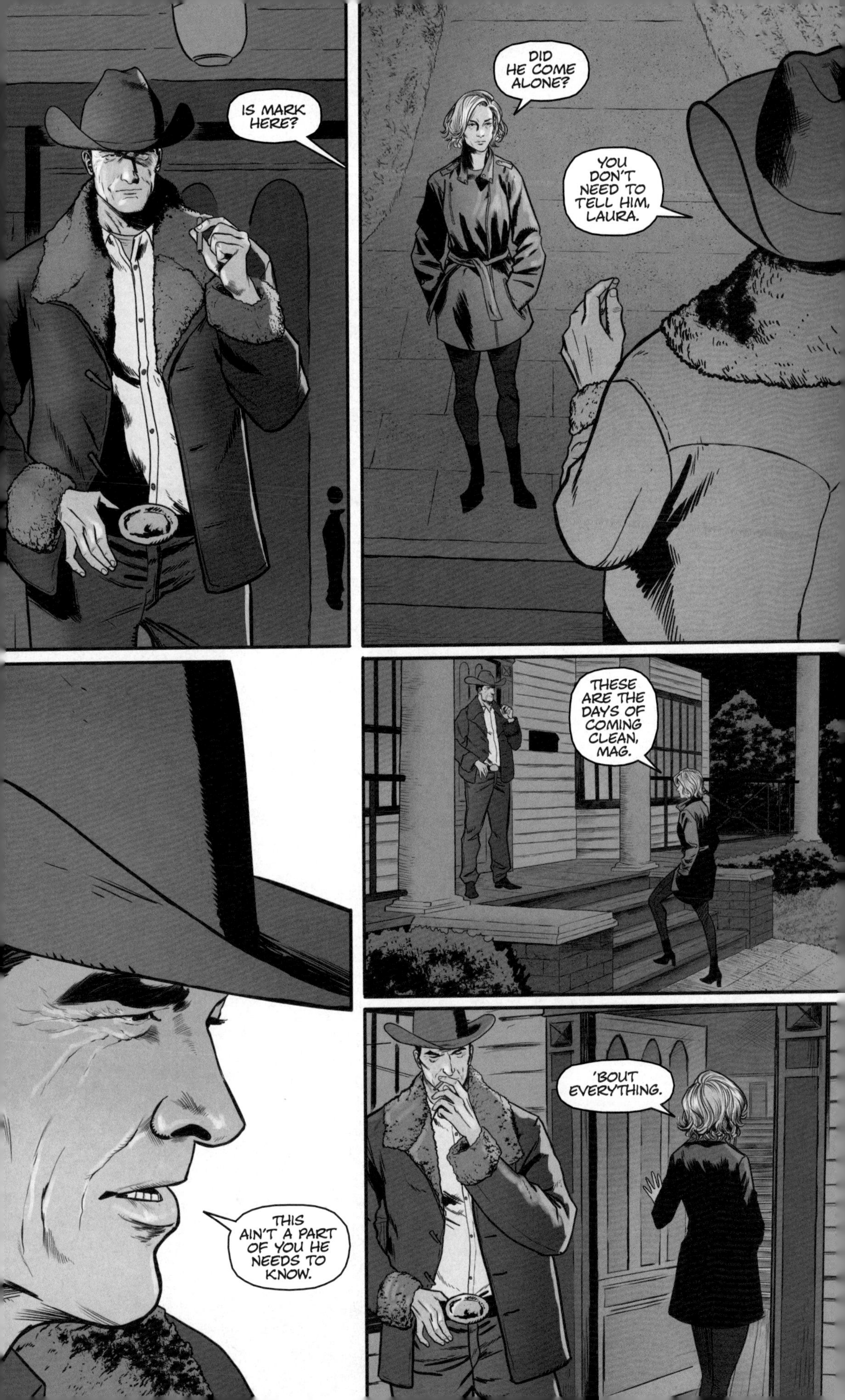
IS MARK HERE?
DID HE COME ALONE?
YOU DON'T NEED TO TELL HIM, LAURA.
THIS AIN'T A PART OF YOU HE NEEDS TO KNOW.
THESE ARE THE DAYS OF COMING CLEAN, MAG.
'BOUT EVERYTHING.

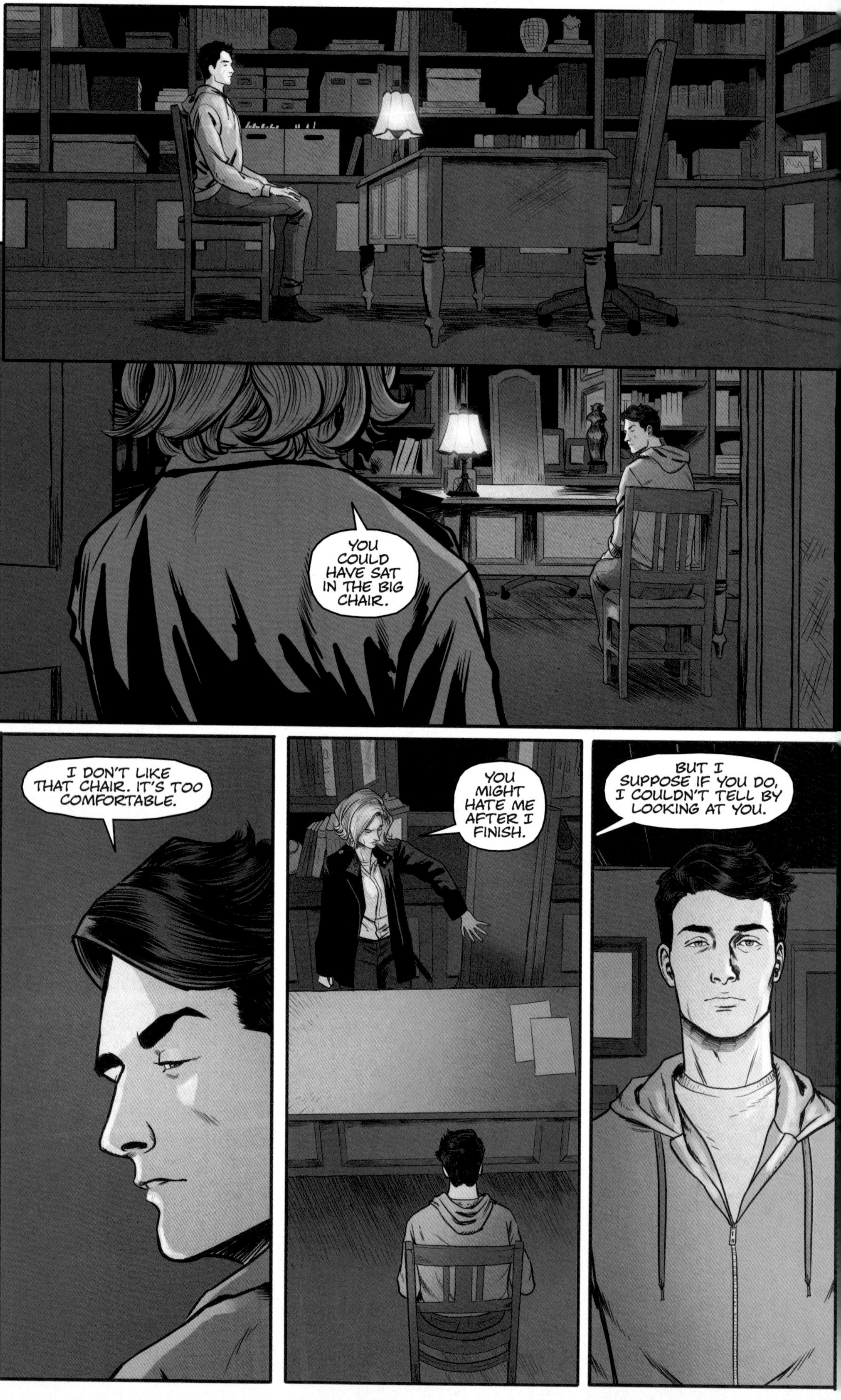
YOU COULD HAVE SAT IN THE BIG CHAIR.
I DON'T LIKE THAT CHAIR. IT'S TOO COMFORTABLE.
YOU MIGHT HATE ME AFTER I FINISH.
BUT I SUPPOSE IF YOU DO, I COULDN'T TELL BY LOOKING AT YOU.

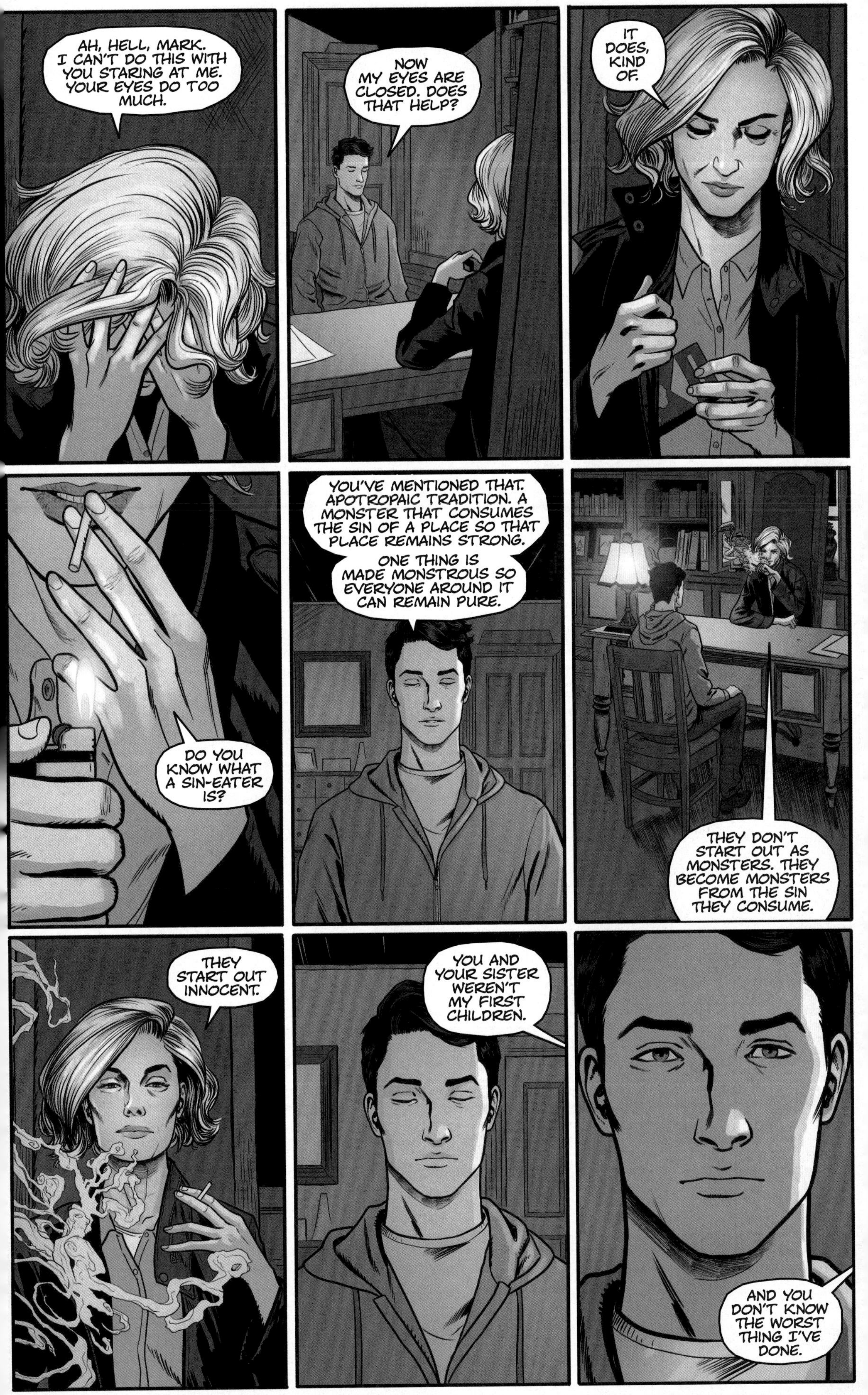
AH, HELL, MARK. I CAN'T DO THIS WITH YOU STARING AT ME. YOUR EYES DO TOO MUCH.
NOW MY EYES ARE CLOSED. DOES THAT HELP?
IT DOES, KIND OF.
DO YOU KNOW WHAT A SIN-EATER IS?
YOU'VE MENTIONED THAT. APOTROPAIC TRADITION. A MONSTER THAT CONSUMES THE SIN OF A PLACE SO THAT PLACE REMAINS STRONG.
ONE THING IS MADE MONSTROUS SO EVERYONE AROUND IT CAN REMAIN PURE.
THEY DON'T START OUT AS MONSTERS. THEY BECOME MONSTERS FROM THE SIN THEY CONSUME.
THEY START OUT INNOCENT.
YOU AND YOUR SISTER WEREN'T MY FIRST CHILDREN.
AND YOU DON'T KNOW THE WORST THING I'VE DONE.

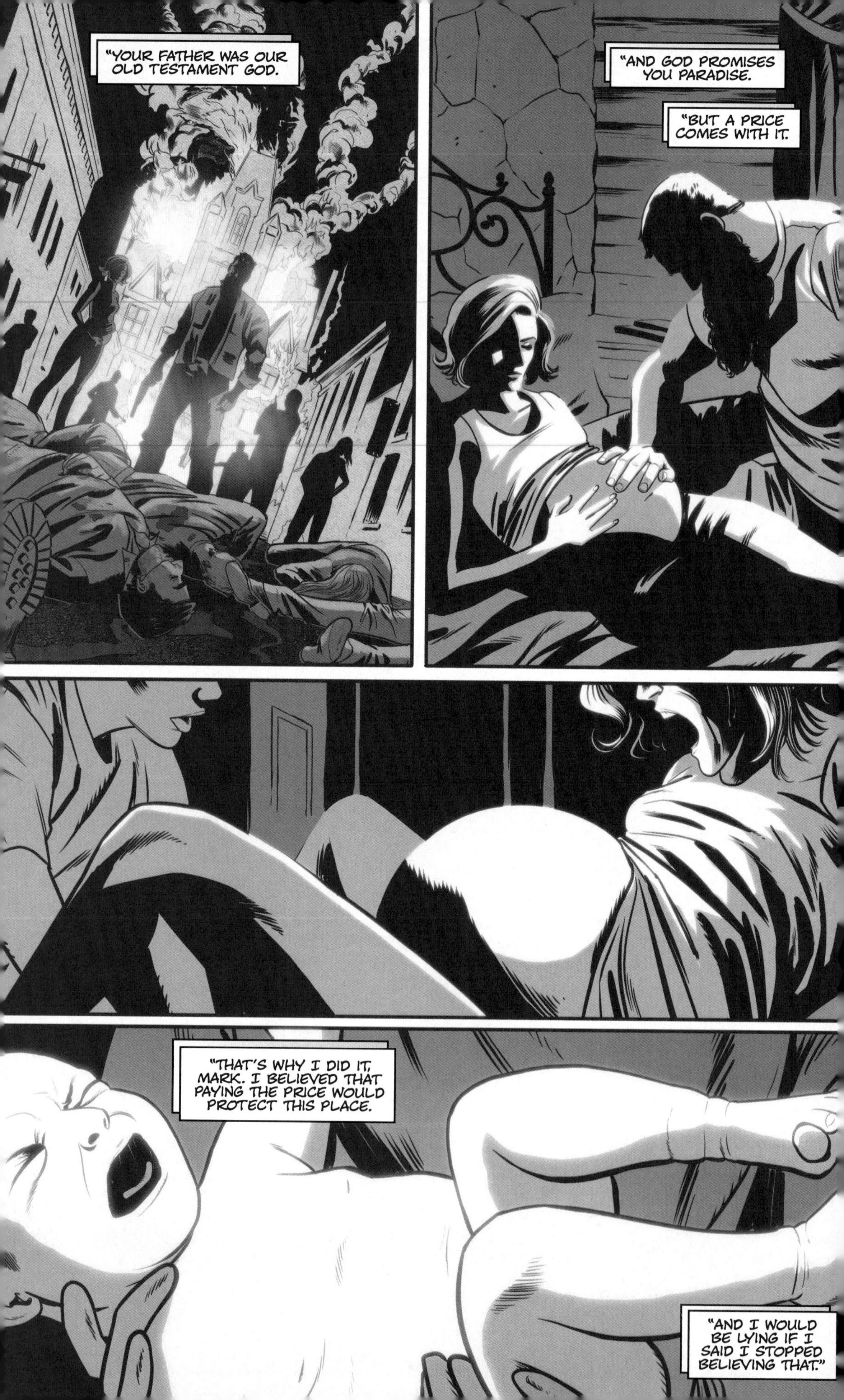
"YOUR FATHER WAS OUR OLD TESTAMENT GOD.
"AND GOD PROMISES YOU PARADISE.
"BUT A PRICE COMES WITH IT.
"THAT'S WHY I DID IT, MARK. I BELIEVED THAT PAYING THE PRICE WOULD PROTECT THIS PLACE.
"AND I WOULD BE LYING IF I SAID I STOPPED BELIEVING THAT."

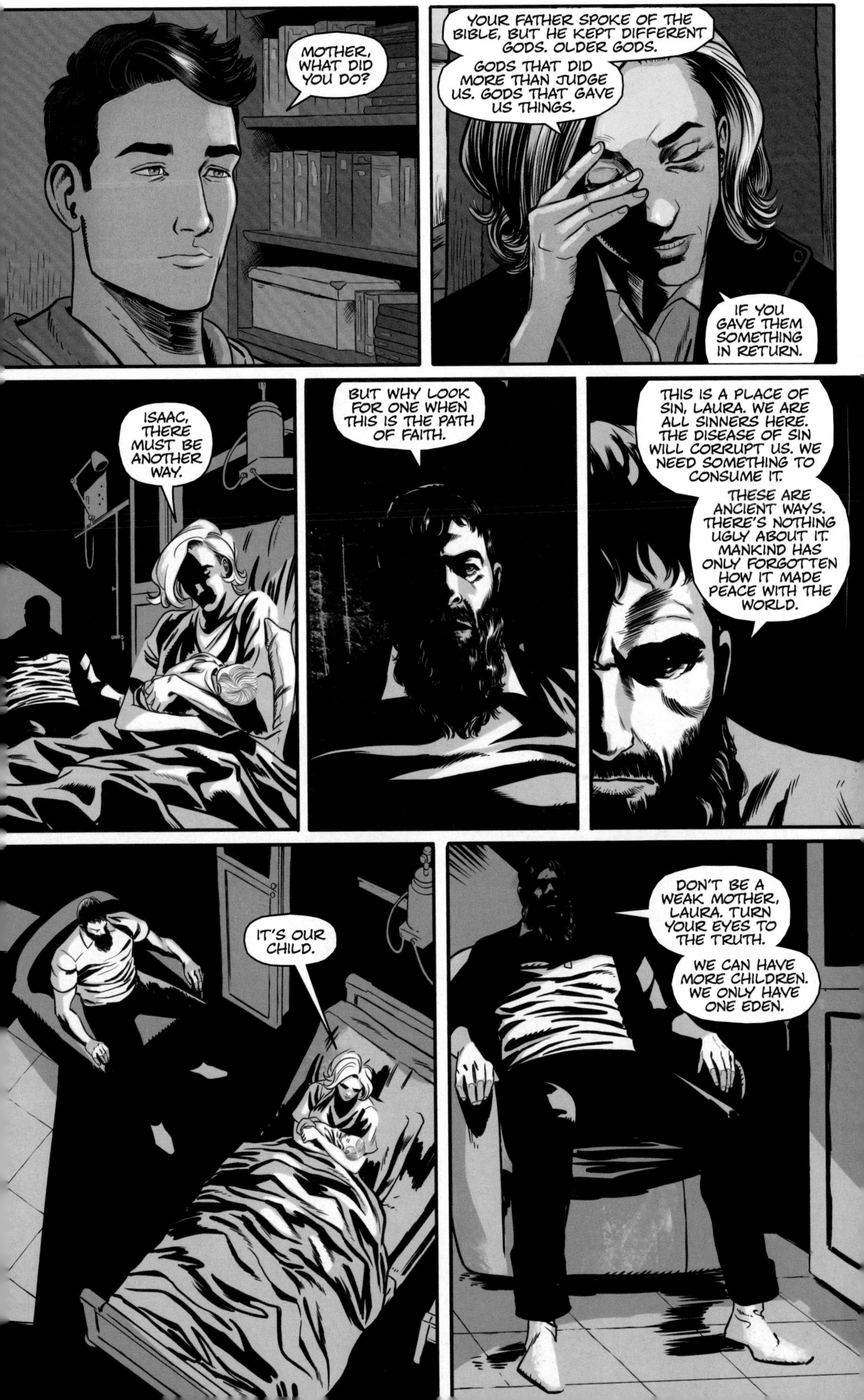
MOTHER, WHAT DID YOU DO?
YOUR FATHER SPOKE OF THE BIBLE, BUT HE KEPT DIFFERENT GODS. OLDER GODS.
GODS THAT DID MORE THAN JUDGE US. GODS THAT GAVE US THINGS.
IF YOU GAVE THEM SOMETHING IN RETURN.
ISAAC, THERE MUST BE ANOTHER WAY.
BUT WHY LOOK FOR ONE WHEN THIS IS THE PATH OF FAITH.
THIS IS A PLACE OF SIN, LAURA. WE ARE ALL SINNERS HERE. THE DISEASE OF SIN WILL CORRUPT US. WE NEED SOMETHING TO CONSUME IT.
THESE ARE ANCIENT WAYS. THERE'S NOTHING UGLY ABOUT IT. MANKIND HAS ONLY FORGOTTEN HOW IT MADE PEACE WITH THE WORLD.
IT'S OUR CHILD.
DON'T BE A WEAK MOTHER, LAURA. TURN YOUR EYES TO THE TRUTH.
WE CAN HAVE MORE CHILDREN. WE ONLY HAVE ONE EDEN.

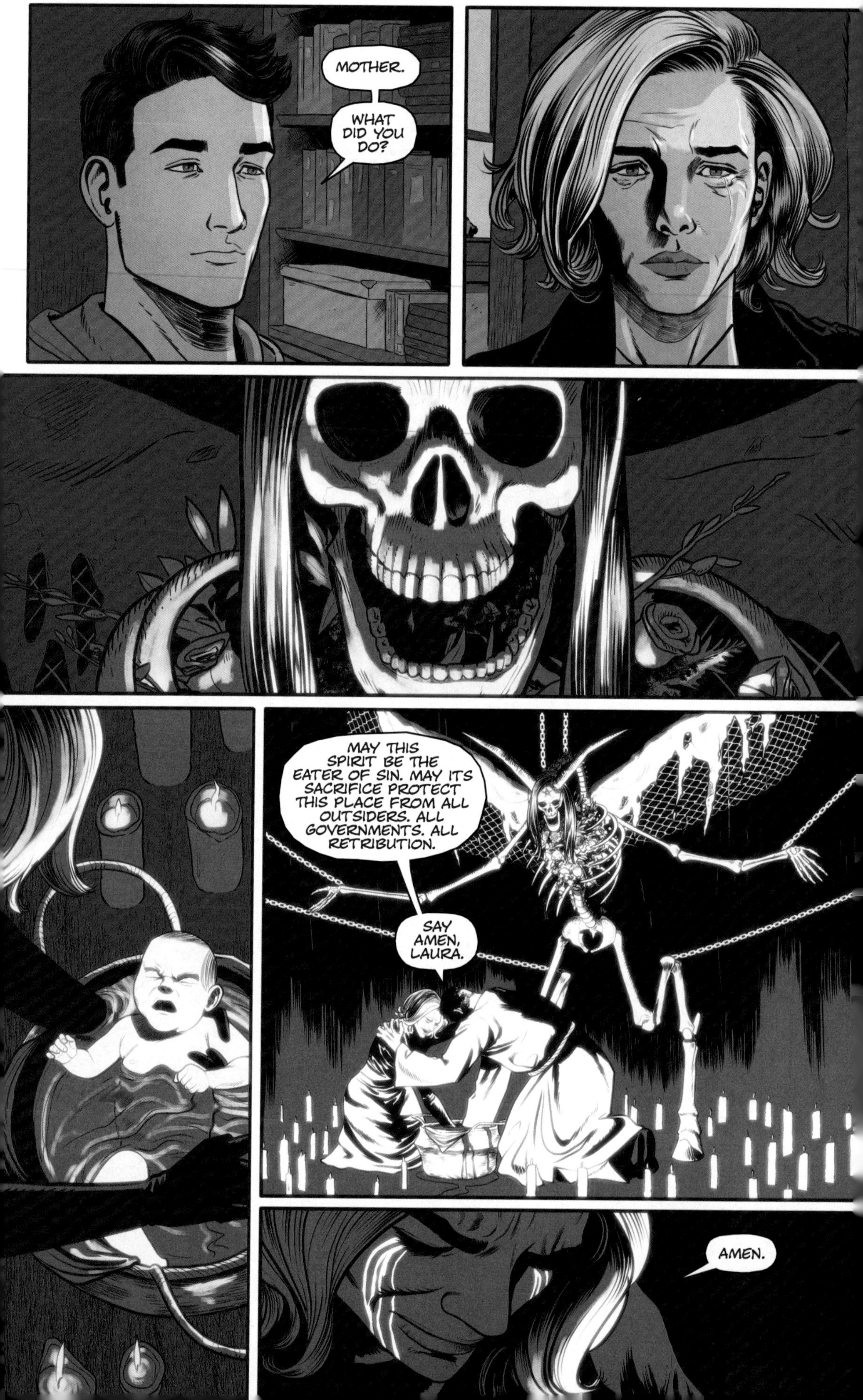
MOTHER.
WHAT DID YOU DO?
MAY THIS SPIRIT BE THE EATER OF SIN. MAY ITS SACRIFICE PROTECT THIS PLACE FROM ALL OUTSIDERS. ALL GOVERNMENTS. ALL RETRIBUTION.
SAY AMEN, LAURA.
AMEN.

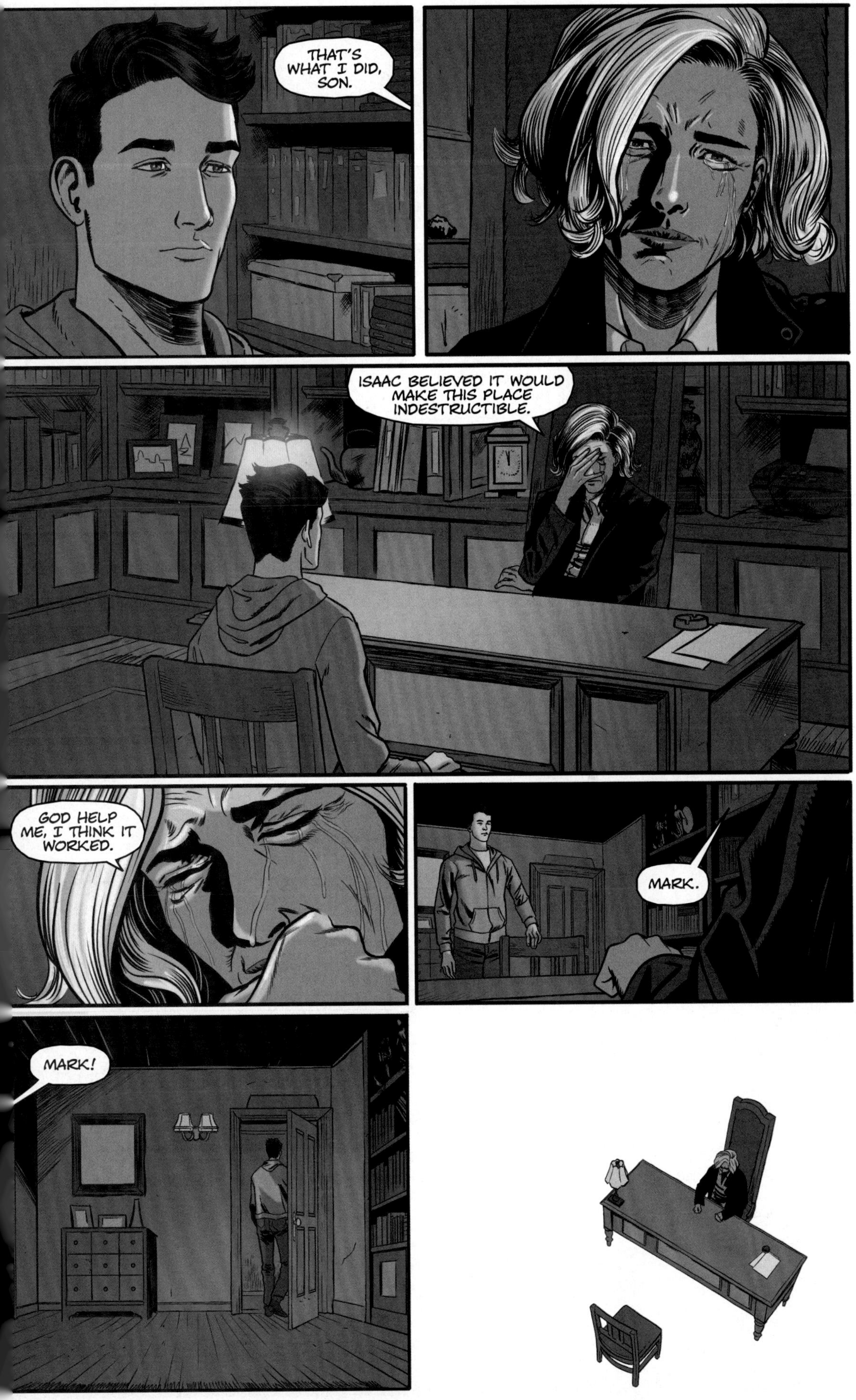
THAT'S WHAT I DID, SON.
ISAAC BELIEVED IT WOULD MAKE THIS PLACE INDESTRUCTIBLE.
GOD HELP ME, I THINK IT WORKED.
MARK.
MARK!

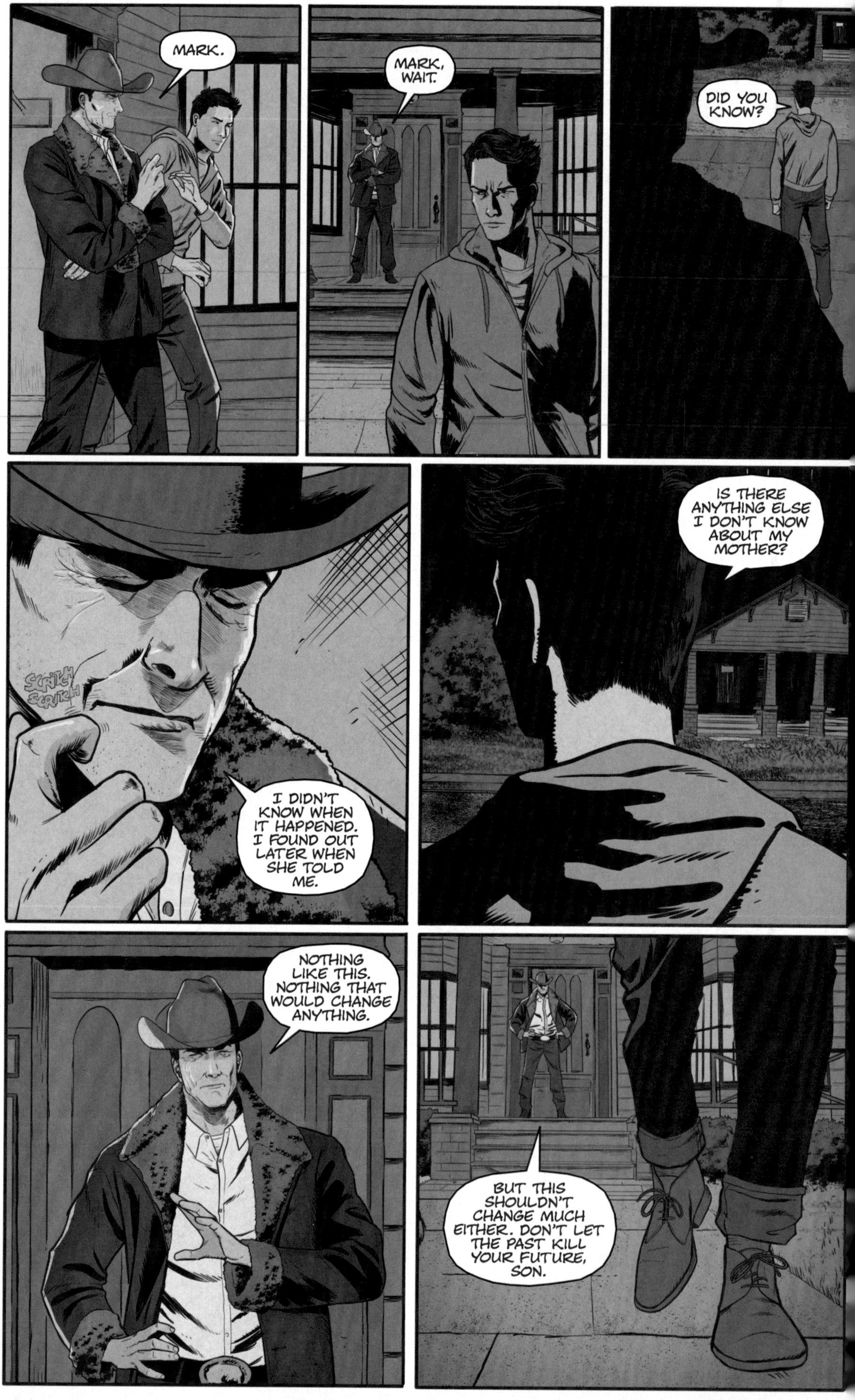
MARK.
MARK, WAIT.
DID YOU KNOW?
SCRITCH SCRITCH
I DIDN'T KNOW WHEN IT HAPPENED. I FOUND OUT LATER WHEN SHE TOLD ME.
IS THERE ANYTHING ELSE I DON'T KNOW ABOUT MY MOTHER?
NOTHING LIKE THIS. NOTHING THAT WOULD CHANGE ANYTHING.
BUT THIS SHOULDN'T CHANGE MUCH EITHER. DON'T LET THE PAST KILL YOUR FUTURE, SON.

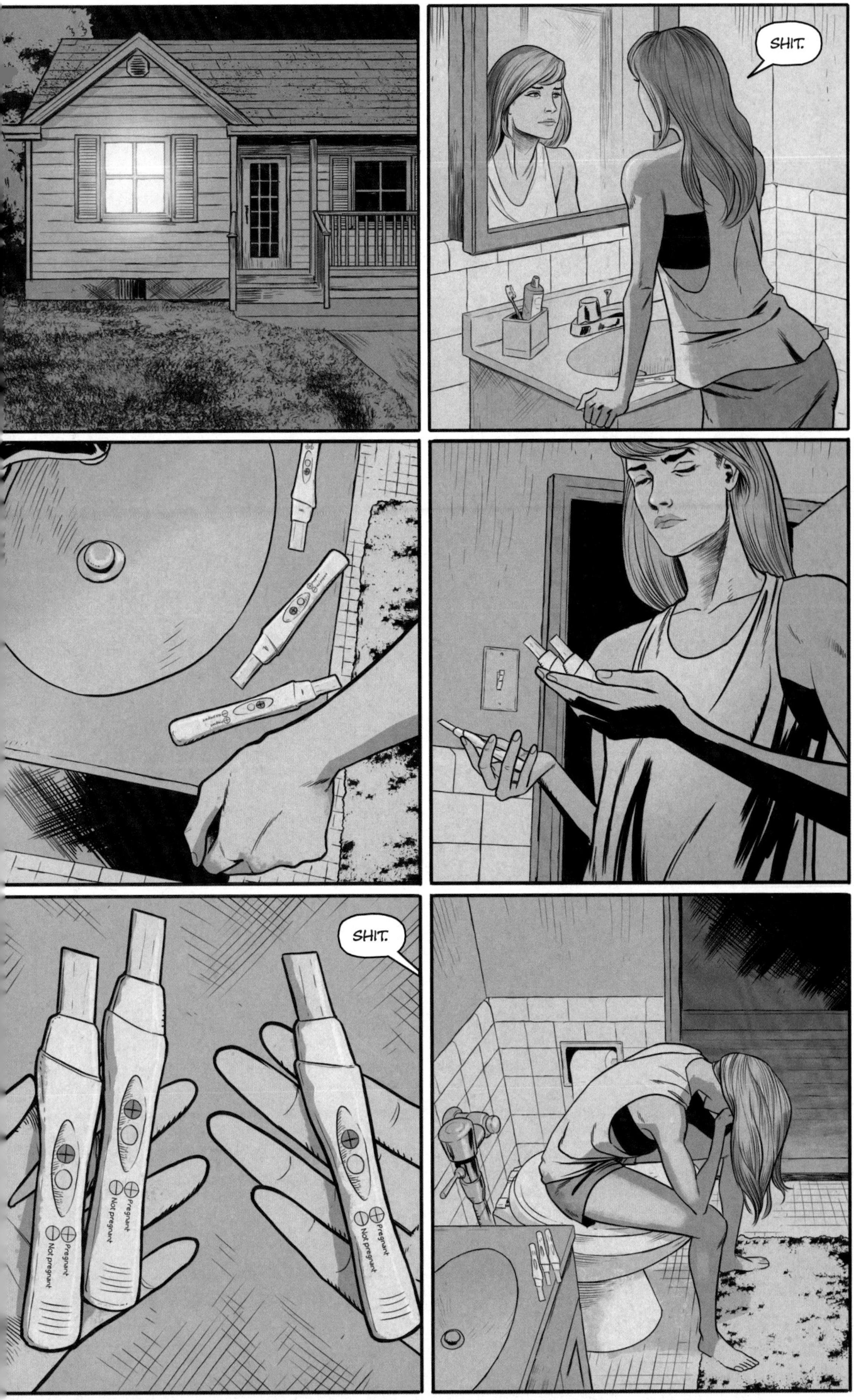
SHIT.
SHIT.
Pregnant
Not pregnant
Pregnant
Not pregnant
Pregnant
Not pregnant

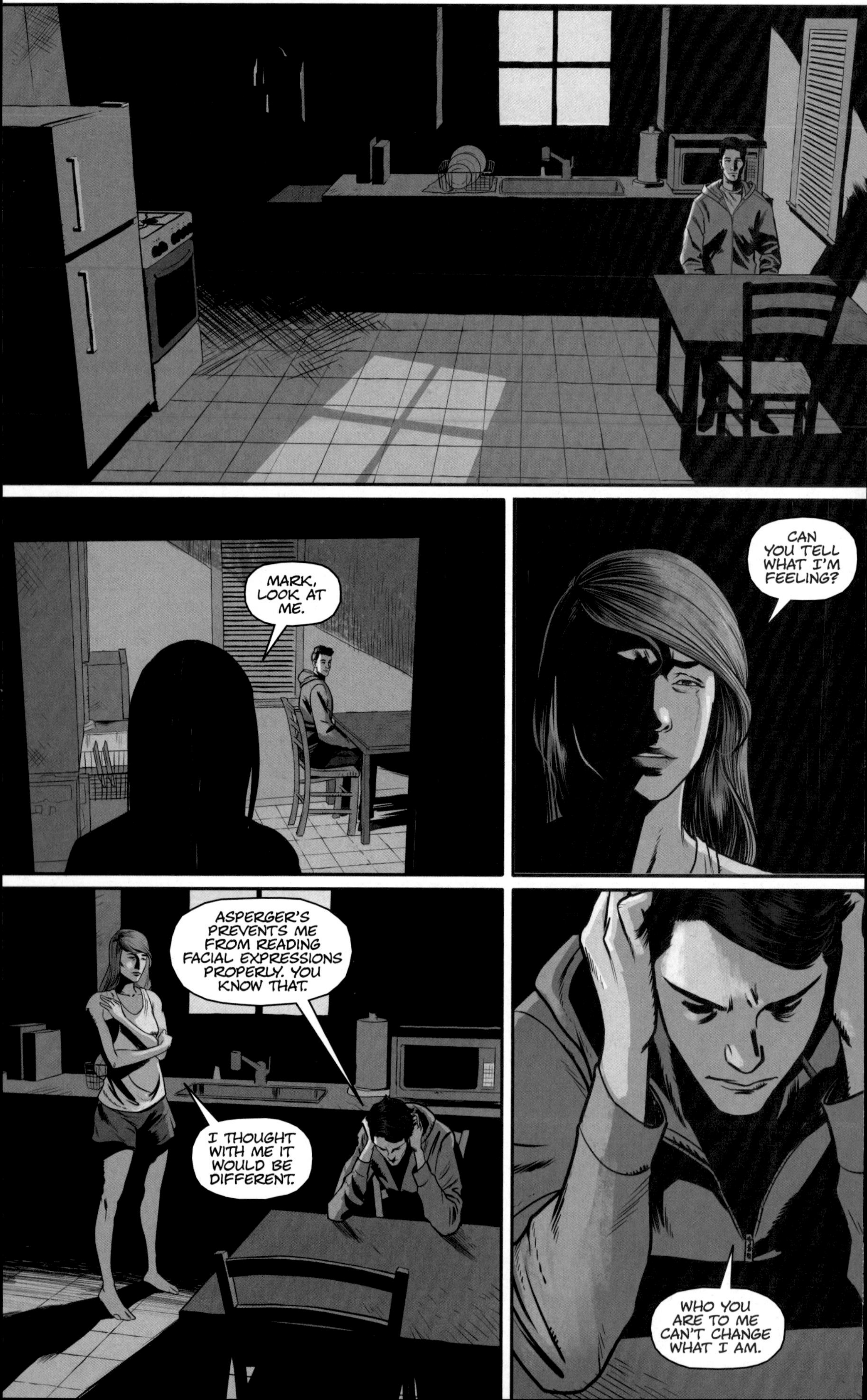
MARK, LOOK AT ME.
CAN YOU TELL WHAT I'M FEELING?
ASPERGER'S PREVENTS ME FROM READING FACIAL EXPRESSIONS PROPERLY. YOU KNOW THAT.
I THOUGHT WITH ME IT WOULD BE DIFFERENT.
WHO YOU ARE TO ME CAN'T CHANGE WHAT I AM.

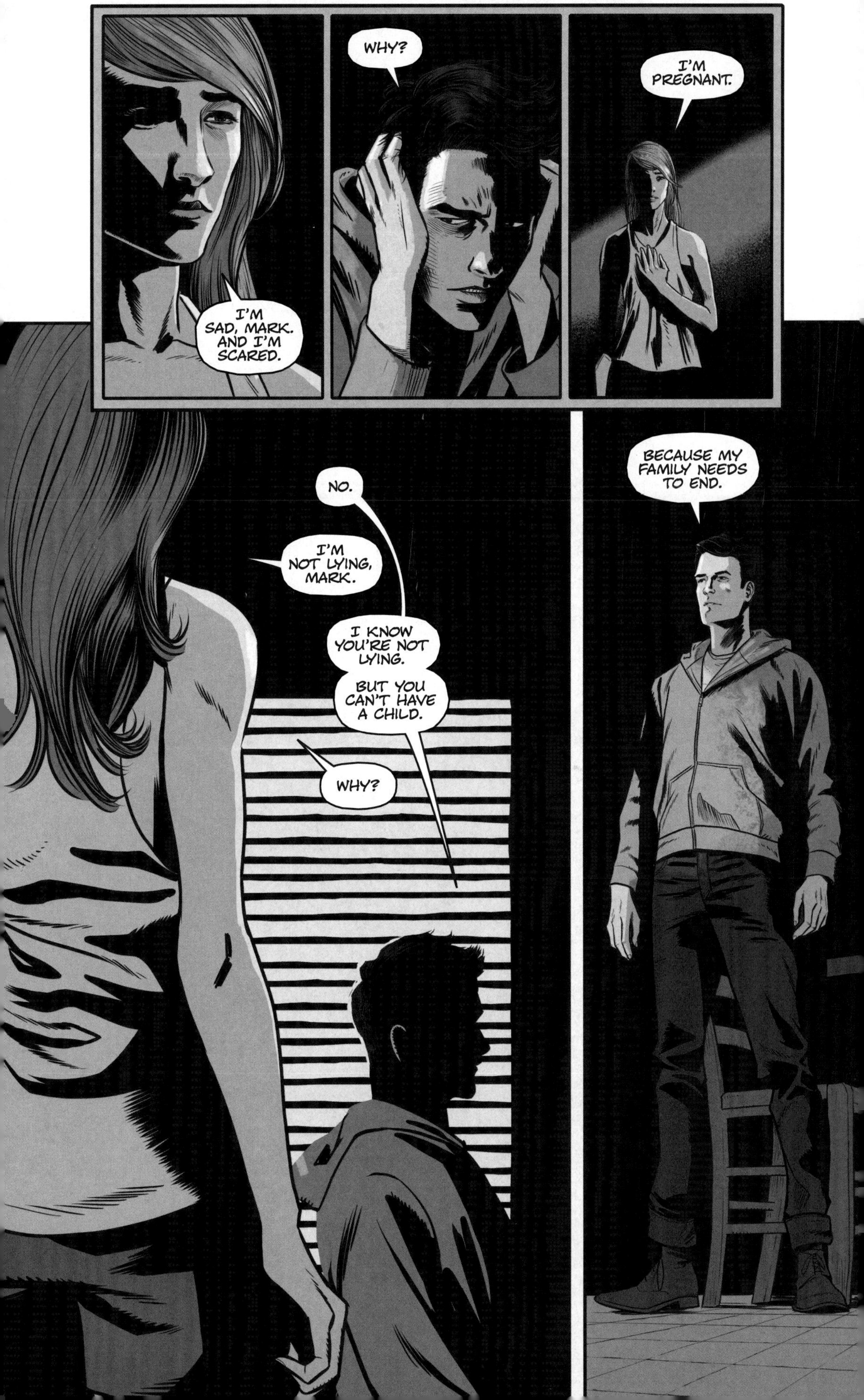
I'M SAD, MARK. AND I'M SCARED.
WHY?
I'M PREGNANT.
NO.
I'M NOT LYING, MARK.
I KNOW YOU'RE NOT LYING.
BUT YOU CAN'T HAVE A CHILD.
WHY?
BECAUSE MY FAMILY NEEDS TO END.

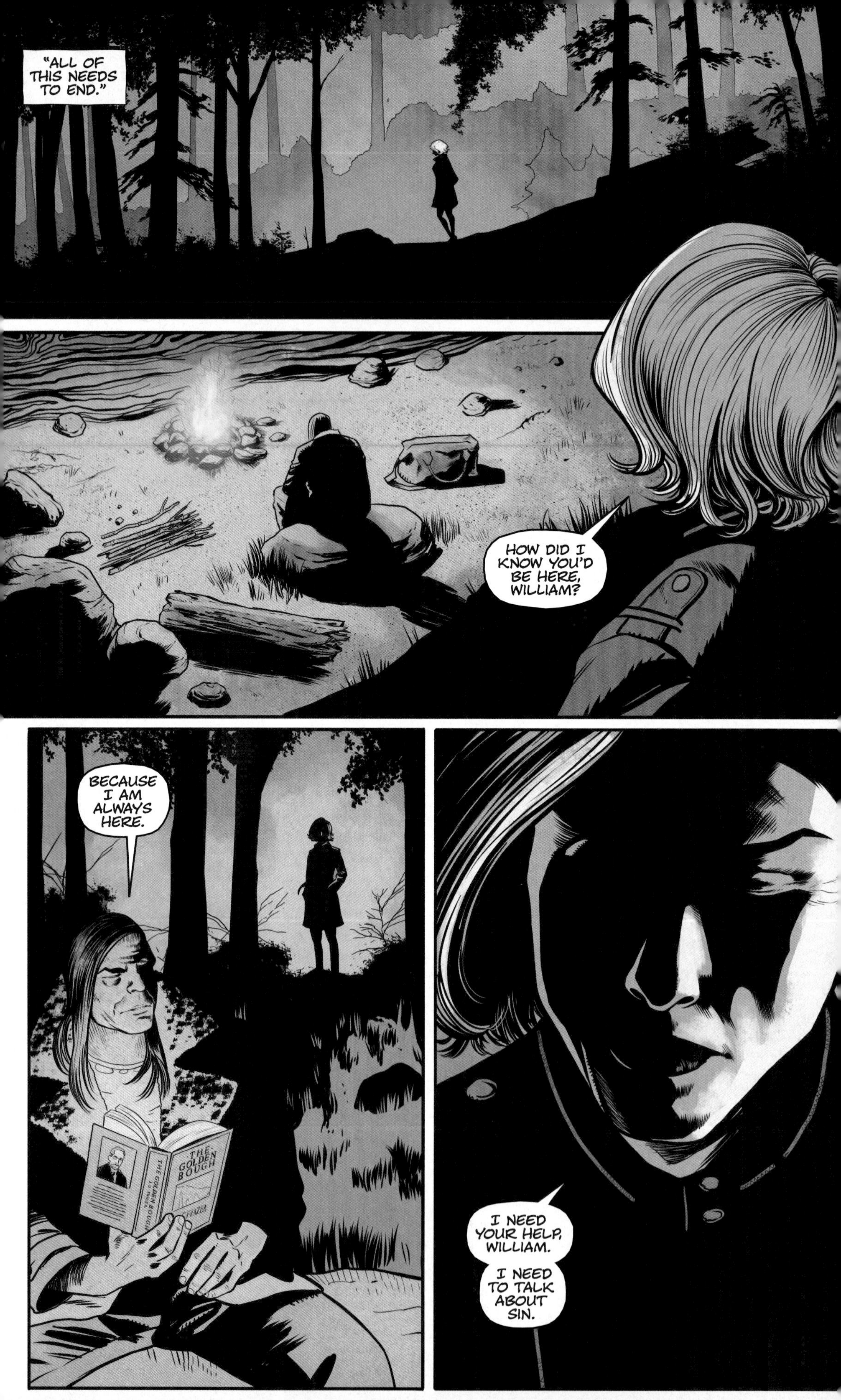
"ALL OF THIS NEEDS TO END."
HOW DID I KNOW YOU'D BE HERE, WILLIAM?
BECAUSE I AM ALWAYS HERE.
THE GOLDEN BOUGH
I NEED YOUR HELP, WILLIAM.
I NEED TO TALK ABOUT SIN.

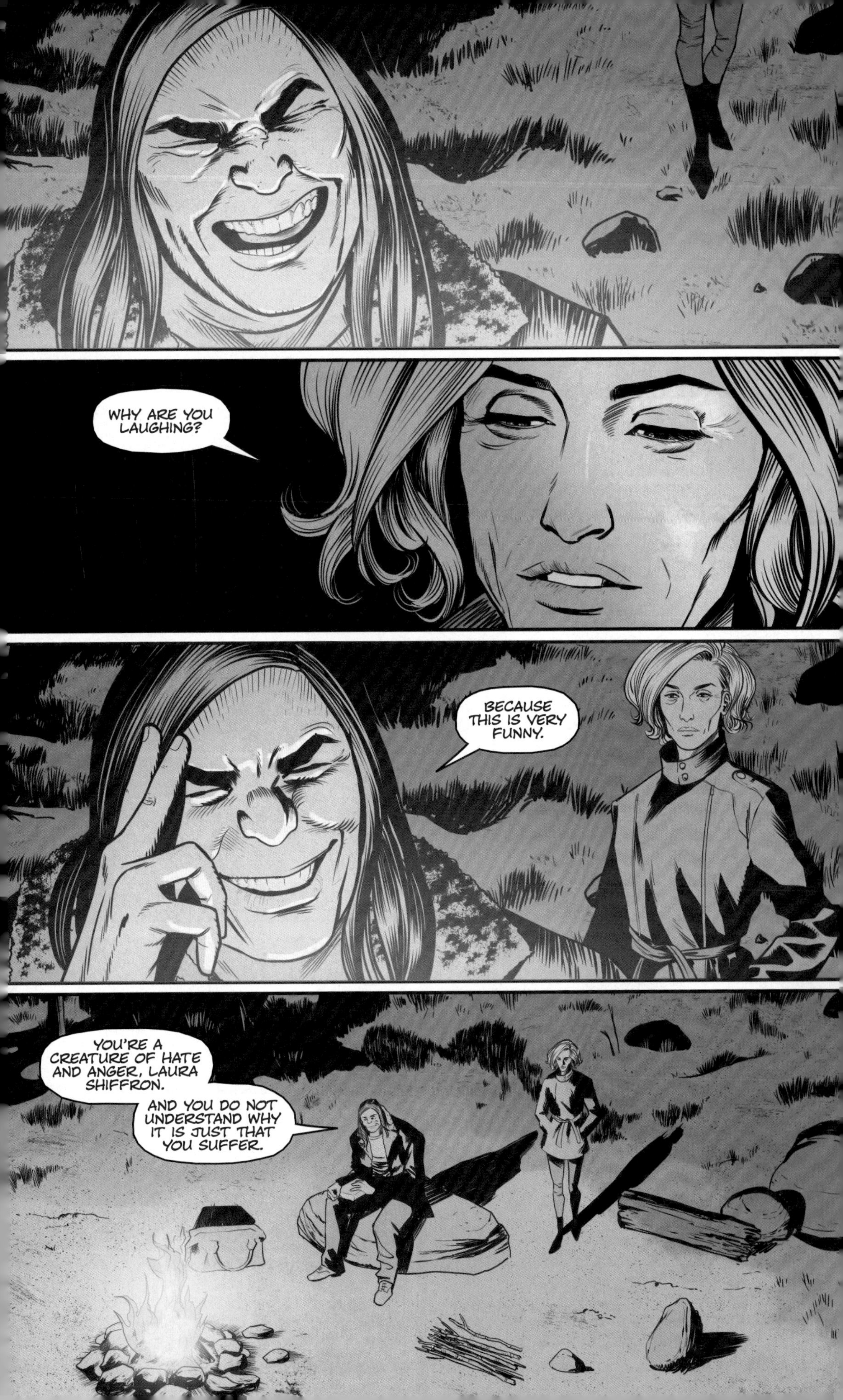
WHY ARE YOU LAUGHING?
BECAUSE THIS IS VERY FUNNY.
YOU'RE A CREATURE OF HATE AND ANGER, LAURA SHIFFRON.
AND YOU DO NOT UNDERSTAND WHY IT IS JUST THAT YOU SUFFER.

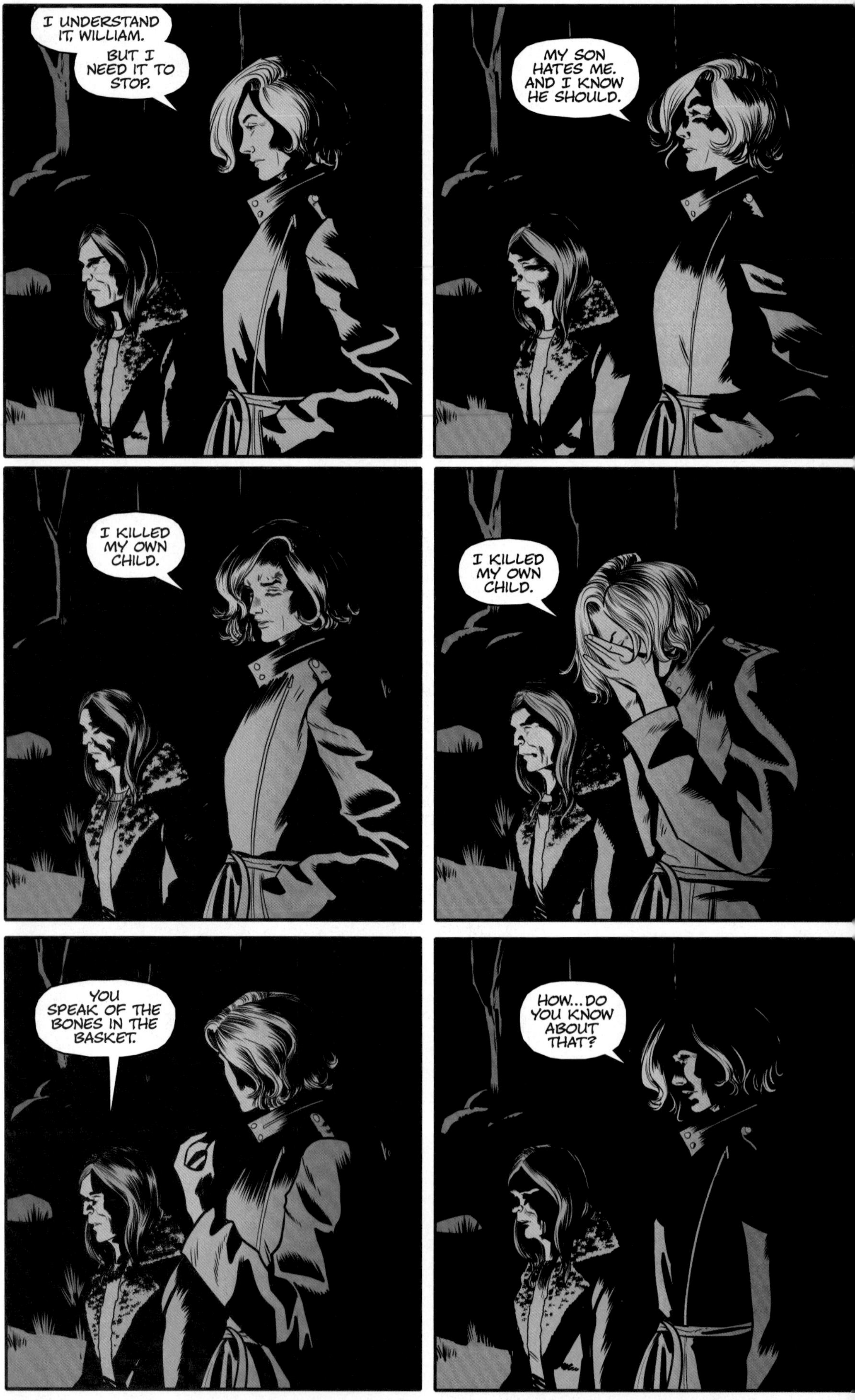
I UNDERSTAND IT, WILLIAM.
BUT I NEED IT TO STOP.
MY SON HATES ME. AND I KNOW HE SHOULD.
I KILLED MY OWN CHILD.
I KILLED MY OWN CHILD.
YOU SPEAK OF THE BONES IN THE BASKET.
HOW...DO YOU KNOW ABOUT THAT?

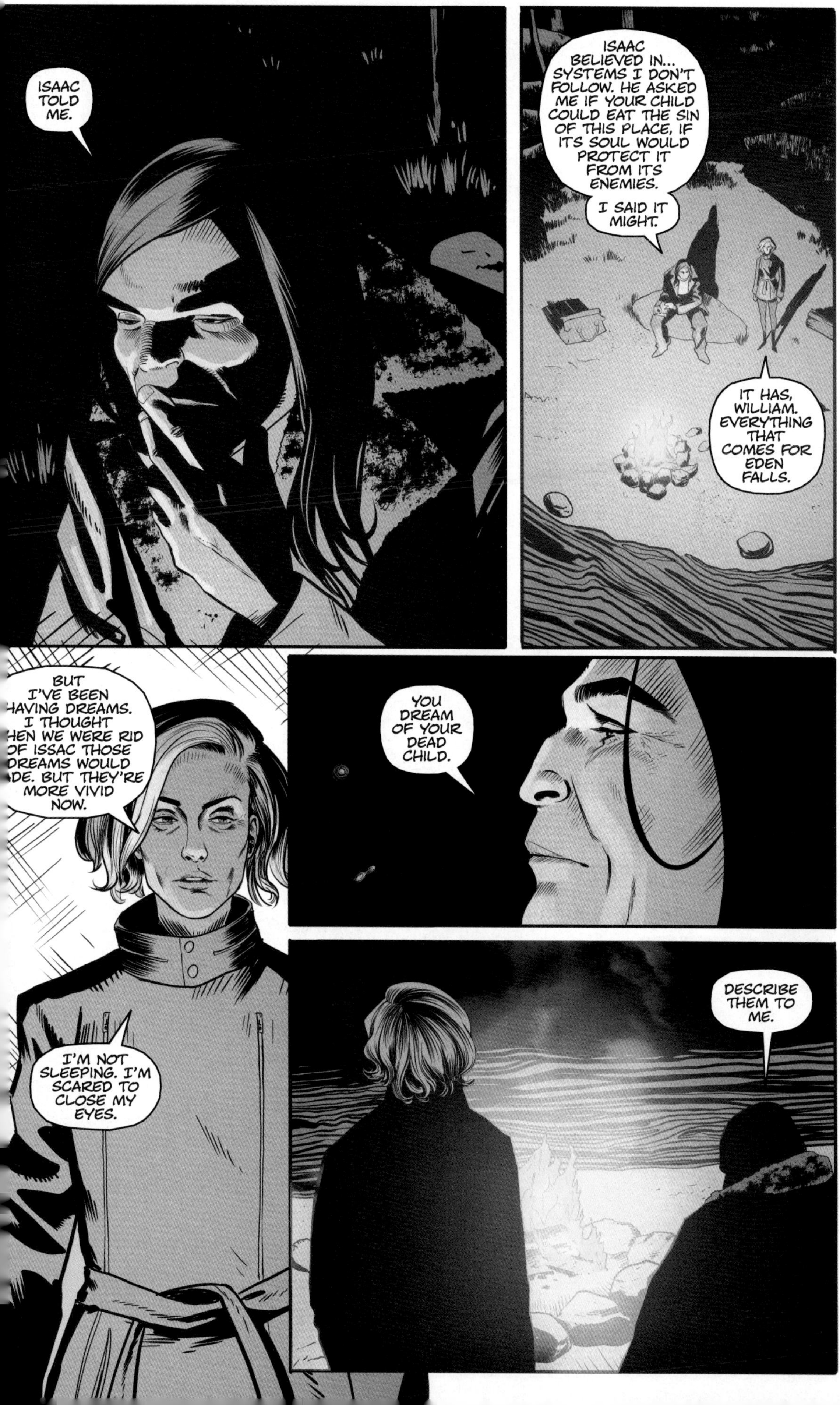
ISAAC TOLD ME.
ISAAC BELIEVED IN... SYSTEMS I DON'T FOLLOW. HE ASKED ME IF YOUR CHILD COULD EAT THE SIN OF THIS PLACE, IF ITS SOUL WOULD PROTECT IT FROM ITS ENEMIES.
I SAID IT MIGHT.
IT HAS, WILLIAM. EVERYTHING THAT COMES FOR EDEN FALLS.
BUT I'VE BEEN HAVING DREAMS. I THOUGHT HEN WE WERE RID OF ISSAC THOSE DREAMS WOULD ADE. BUT THEY'RE MORE VIVID NOW.
YOU DREAM OF YOUR DEAD CHILD.
I'M NOT SLEEPING. I'M SCARED TO CLOSE MY EYES.
DESCRIBE THEM TO ME.

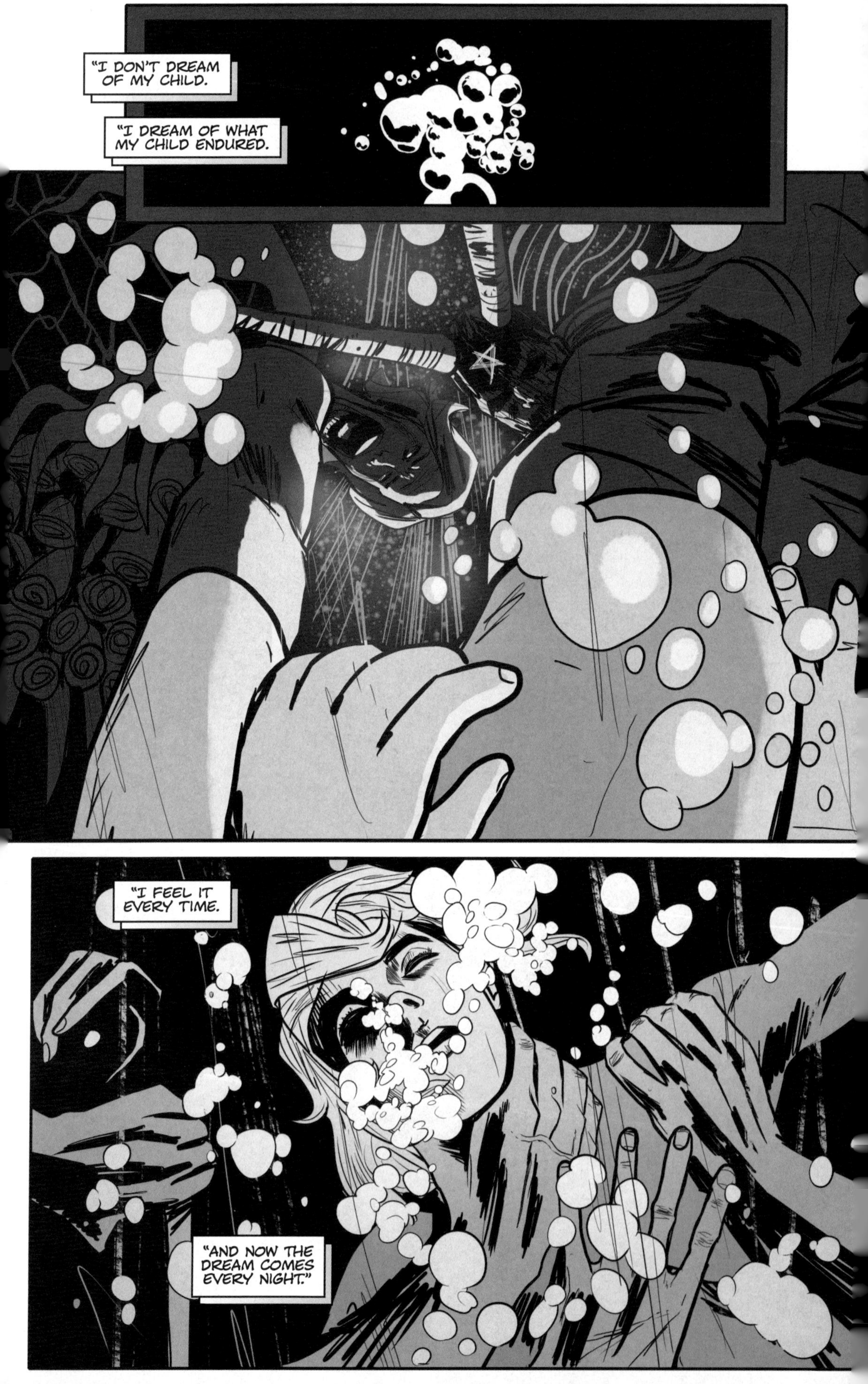
"I DON'T DREAM OF MY CHILD.
"I DREAM OF WHAT MY CHILD ENDURED.
"I FEEL IT EVERY TIME.
"AND NOW THE DREAM COMES EVERY NIGHT."

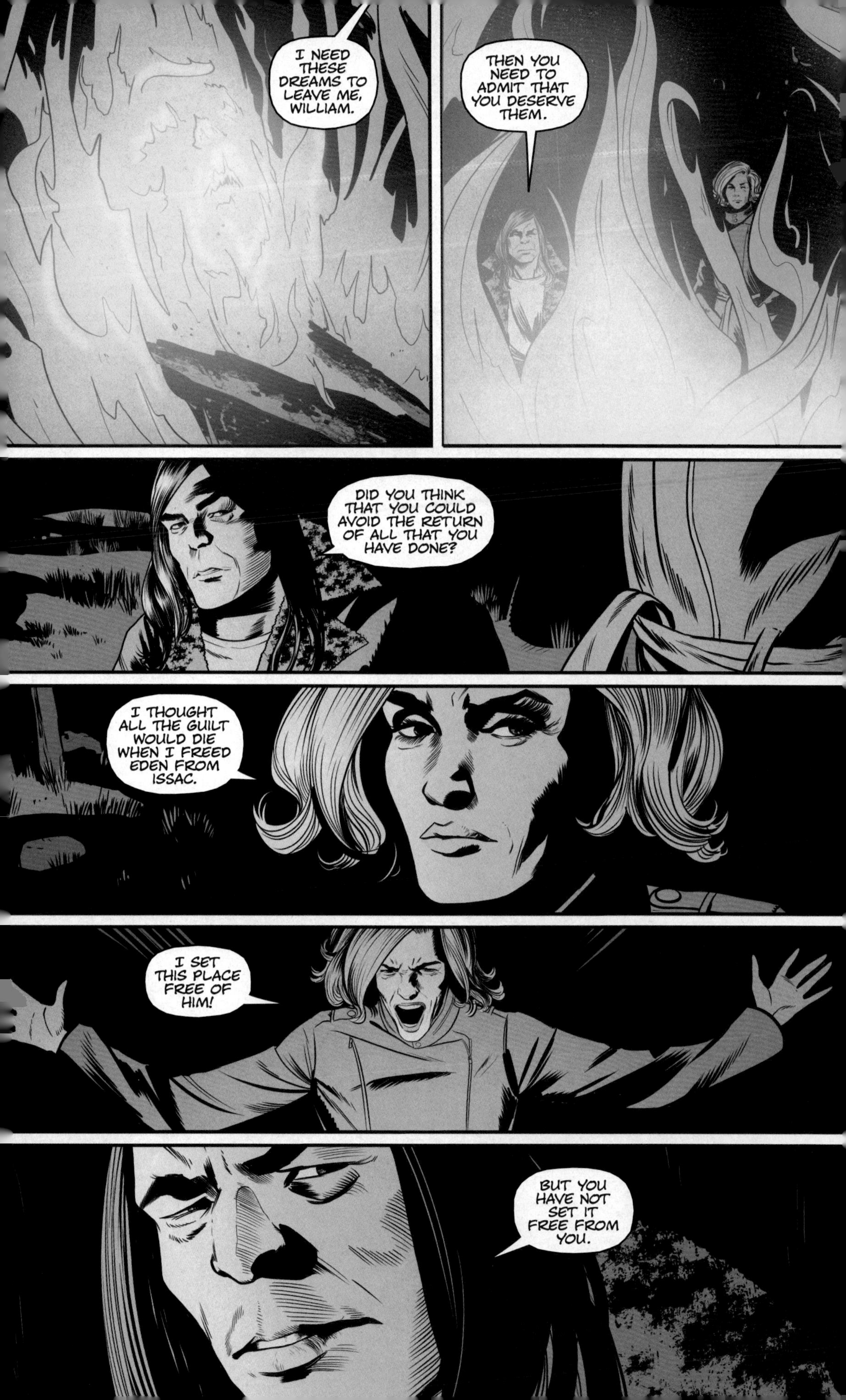
I NEED THESE DREAMS TO LEAVE ME, WILLIAM.
THEN YOU NEED TO ADMIT THAT YOU DESERVE THEM.
DID YOU THINK THAT YOU COULD AVOID THE RETURN OF ALL THAT YOU HAVE DONE?
I THOUGHT ALL THE GUILT WOULD DIE WHEN I FREED EDEN FROM ISSAC.
I SET THIS PLACE FREE OF HIM!
BUT YOU HAVE NOT SET IT FREE FROM YOU.

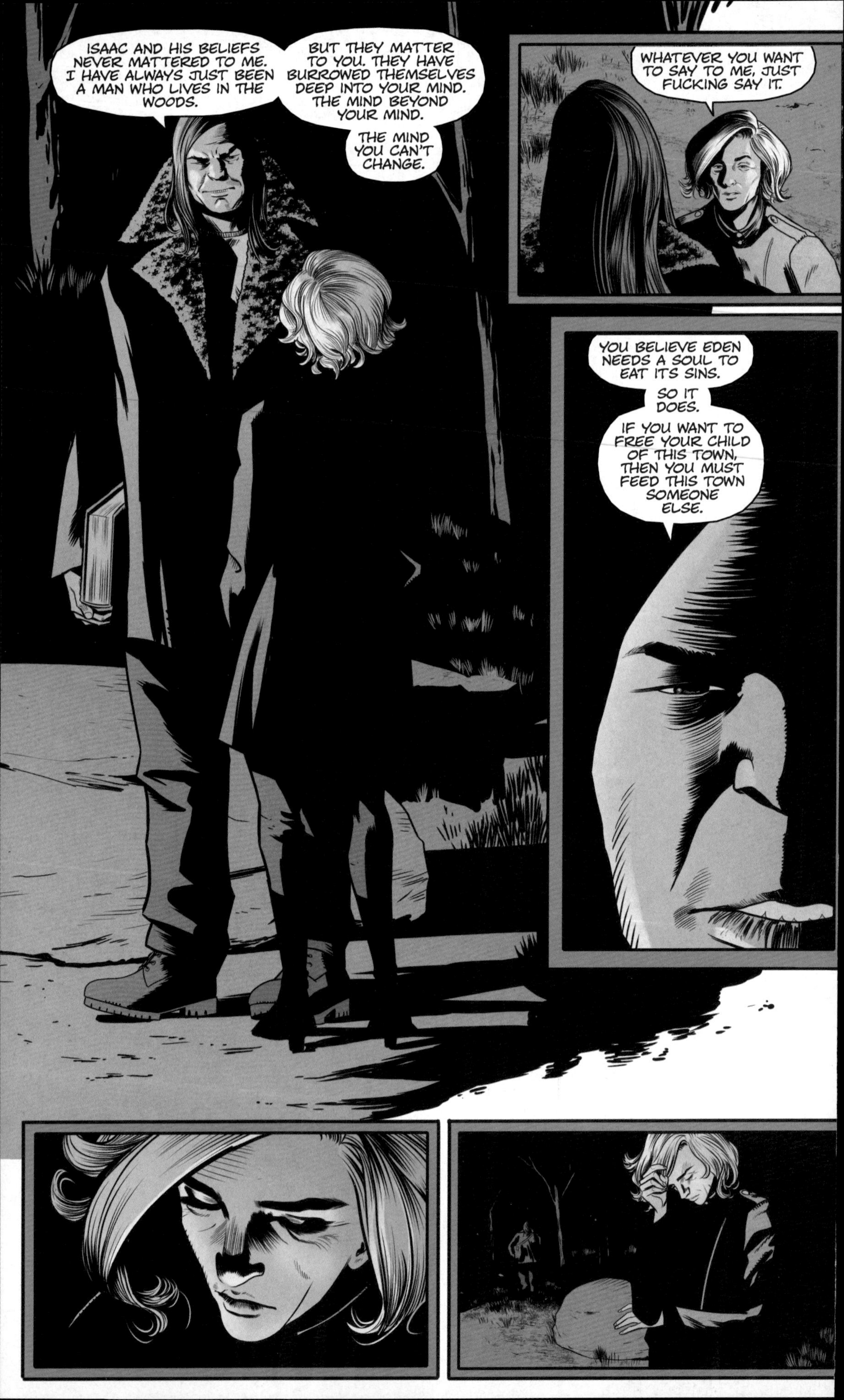
ISAAC AND HIS BELIEFS NEVER MATTERED TO ME. I HAVE ALWAYS JUST BEEN A MAN WHO LIVES IN THE WOODS.
BUT THEY MATTER TO YOU. THEY HAVE BURROWED THEMSELVES DEEP INTO YOUR MIND. THE MIND BEYOND YOUR MIND.
THE MIND YOU CAN'T CHANGE.
WHATEVER YOU WANT TO SAY TO ME, JUST FUCKING SAY IT.
YOU BELIEVE EDEN NEEDS A SOUL TO EAT ITS SINS.
SO IT DOES.
IF YOU WANT TO FREE YOUR CHILD OF THIS TOWN, THEN YOU MUST FEED THIS TOWN SOMEONE ELSE.

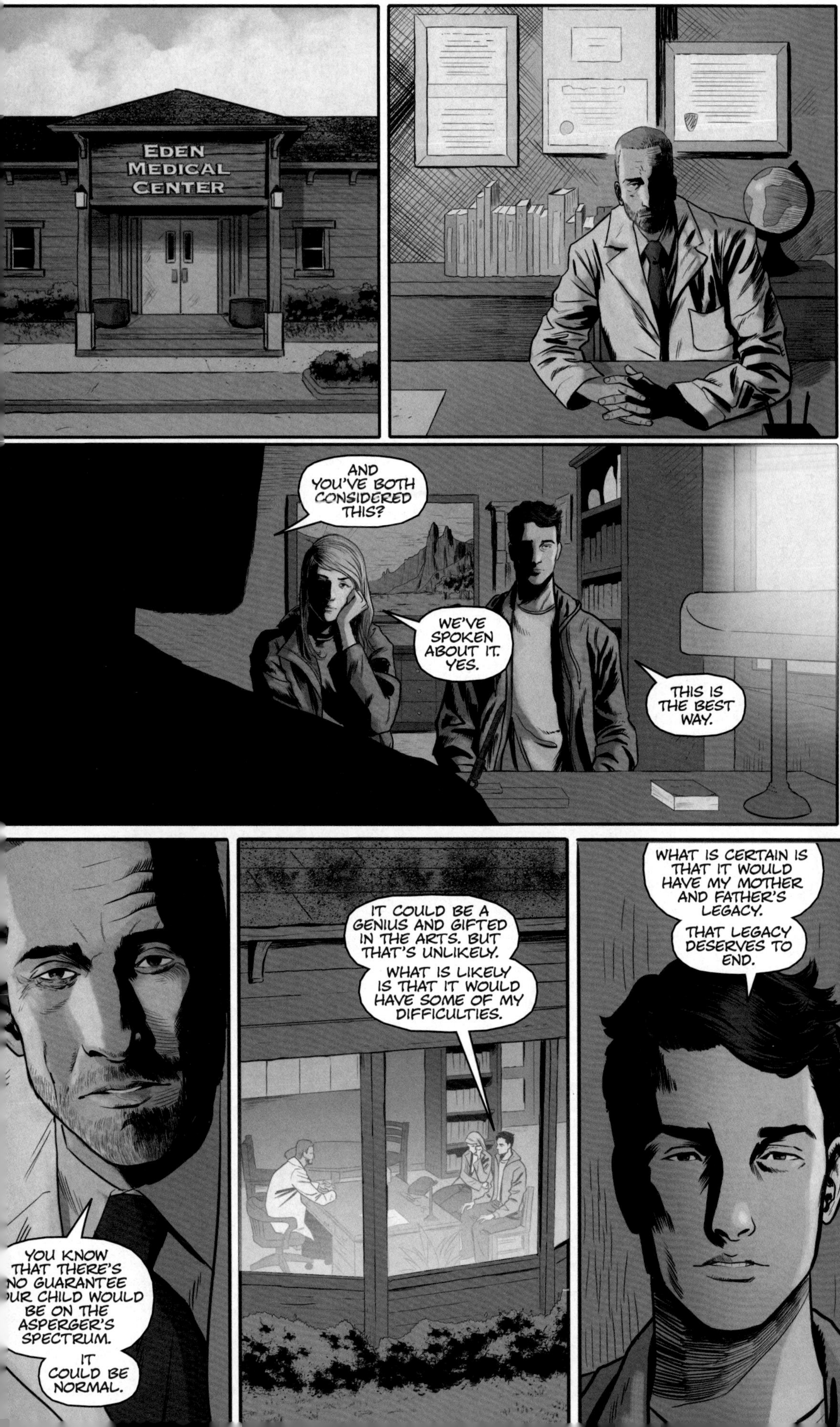
EDEN MEDICAL CENTER
AND YOU'VE BOTH CONSIDERED THIS?
WE'VE SPOKEN ABOUT IT. YES.
THIS IS THE BEST WAY.
YOU KNOW THAT THERE'S NO GUARANTEE OUR CHILD WOULD BE ON THE ASPERGER'S SPECTRUM.
IT COULD BE NORMAL.
IT COULD BE A GENIUS AND GIFTED IN THE ARTS. BUT THAT'S UNLIKELY.
WHAT IS LIKELY IS THAT IT WOULD HAVE SOME OF MY DIFFICULTIES.
WHAT IS CERTAIN IS THAT IT WOULD HAVE MY MOTHER AND FATHER'S LEGACY.
THAT LEGACY DESERVES TO END.

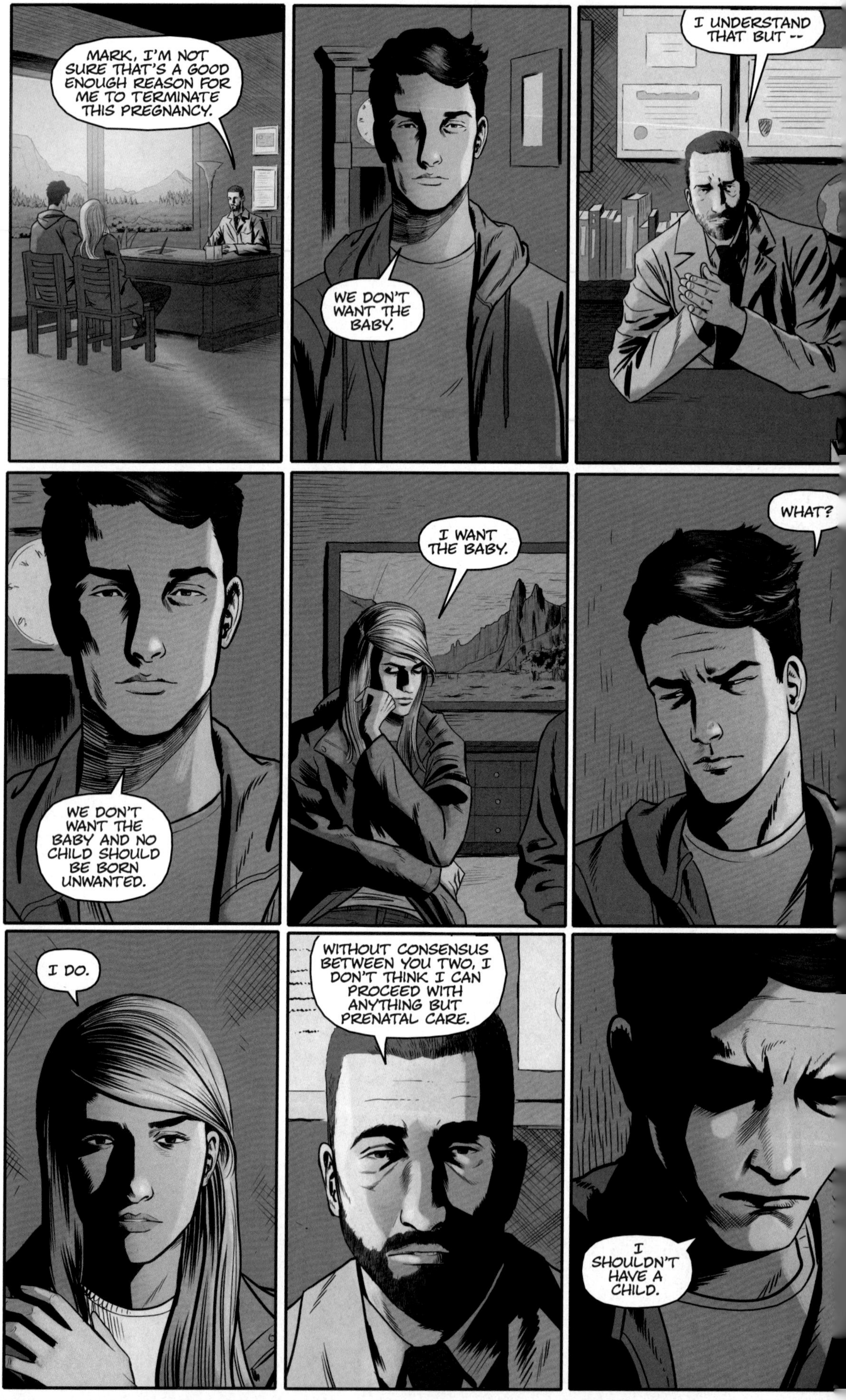
MARK, I'M NOT SURE THAT'S A GOOD ENOUGH REASON FOR ME TO TERMINATE THIS PREGNANCY.
WE DON'T WANT THE BABY.
I UNDERSTAND THAT BUT --
WE DON'T WANT THE BABY AND NO CHILD SHOULD BE BORN UNWANTED.
I WANT THE BABY.
WHAT?
I DO.
WITHOUT CONSENSUS BETWEEN YOU TWO, I DON'T THINK I CAN PROCEED WITH ANYTHING BUT PRENATAL CARE.
I SHOULDN'T HAVE A CHILD.

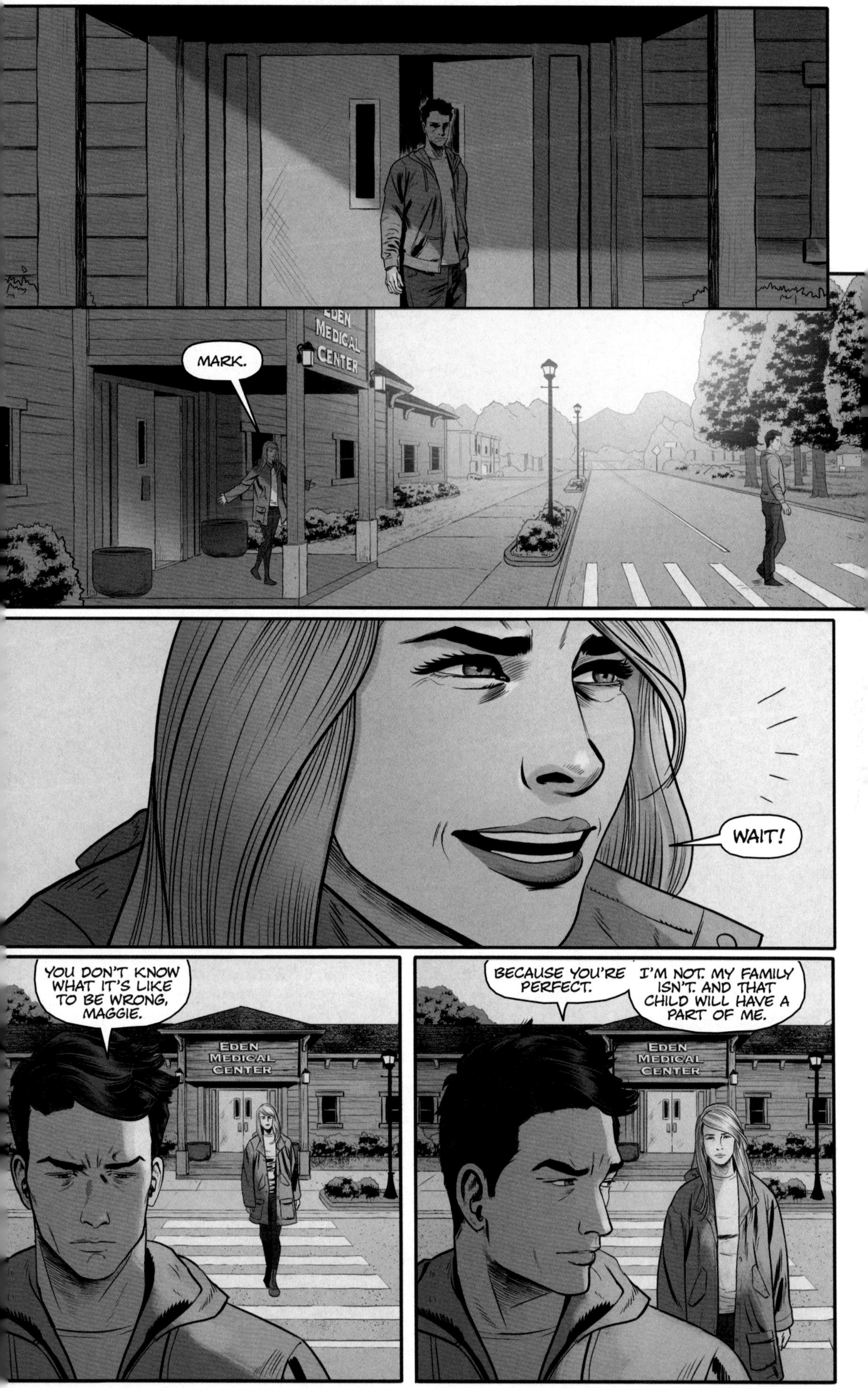
EDEN MEDICAL CENTER
MARK.
WAIT!
YOU DON'T KNOW WHAT IT'S LIKE TO BE WRONG, MAGGIE.
EDEN MEDICAL CENTER
BECAUSE YOU'RE PERFECT.
I'M NOT. MY FAMILY ISN'T. AND THAT CHILD WILL HAVE A PART OF ME.
EDEN MEDICAL CENTER

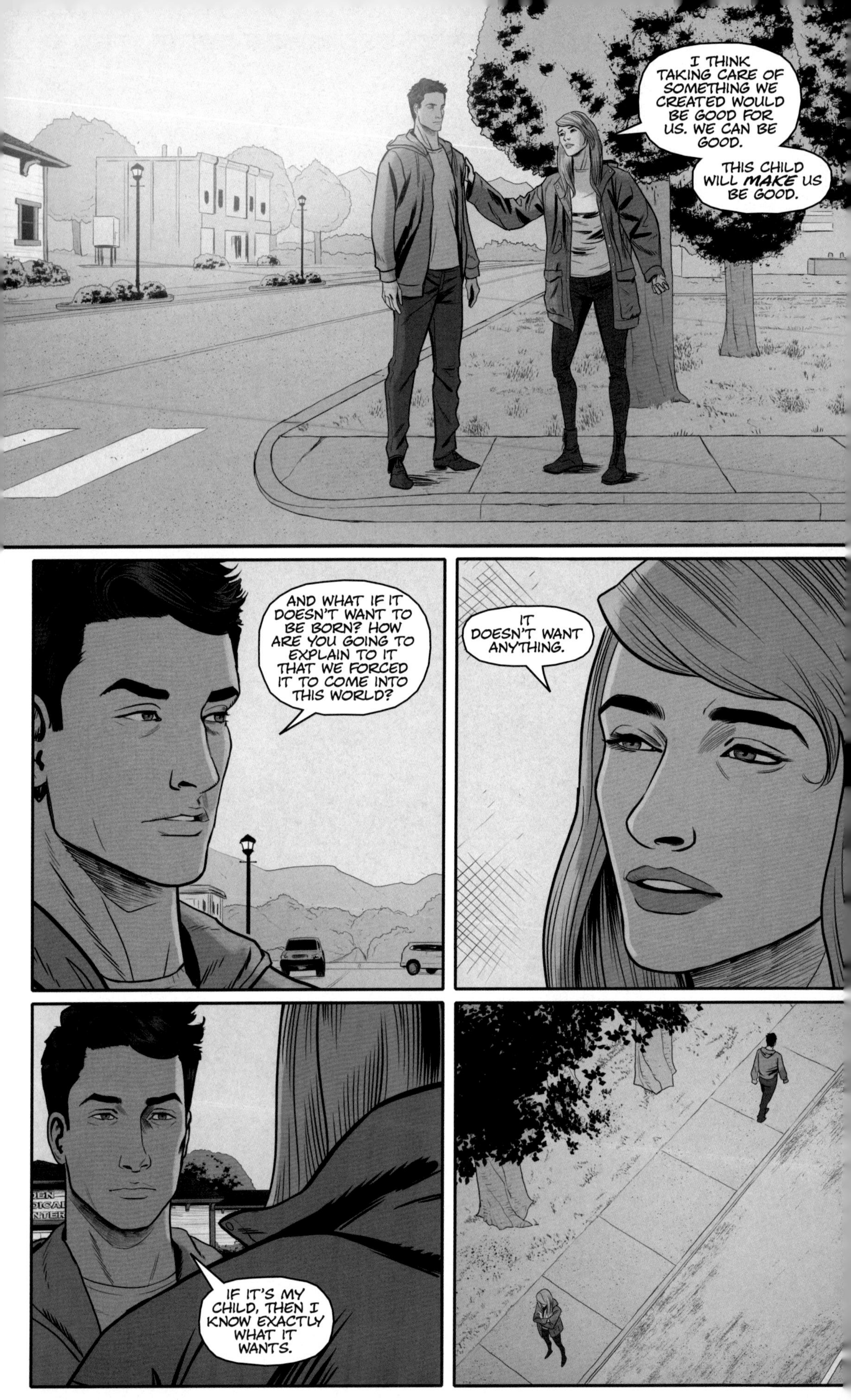
I THINK TAKING CARE OF SOMETHING WE CREATED WOULD BE GOOD FOR US. WE CAN BE GOOD.
THIS CHILD WILL *MAKE* US BE GOOD.
AND WHAT IF IT DOESN'T WANT TO BE BORN? HOW ARE YOU GOING TO EXPLAIN TO IT THAT WE FORCED IT TO COME INTO THIS WORLD?
IT DOESN'T WANT ANYTHING.
IF IT'S MY CHILD, THEN I KNOW EXACTLY WHAT IT WANTS.

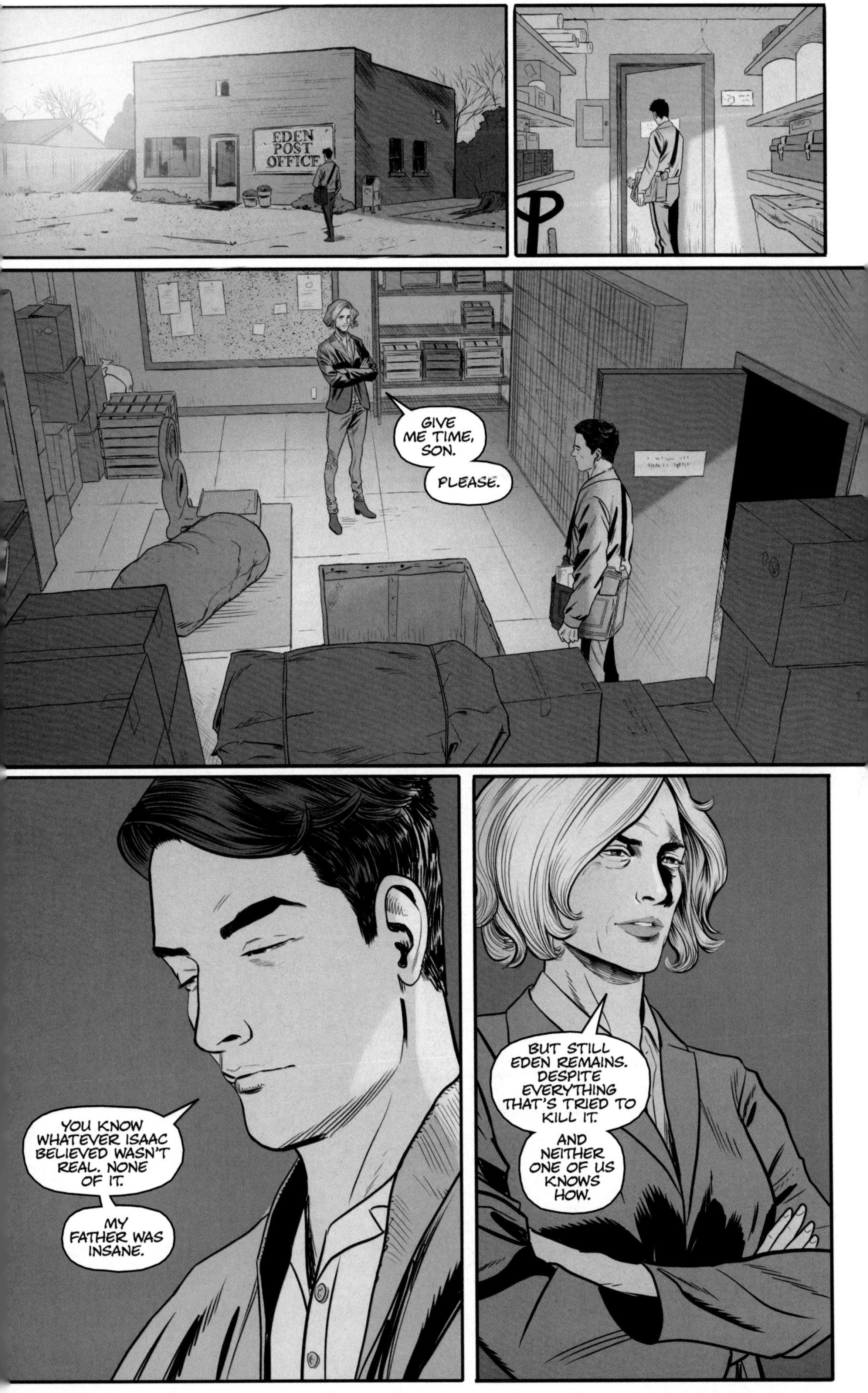
EDEN POST OFFICE
GIVE ME TIME, SON.
PLEASE.
YOU KNOW WHATEVER ISAAC BELIEVED WASN'T REAL. NONE OF IT.
MY FATHER WAS INSANE.
BUT STILL EDEN REMAINS. DESPITE EVERYTHING THAT'S TRIED TO KILL IT.
AND NEITHER ONE OF US KNOWS HOW.

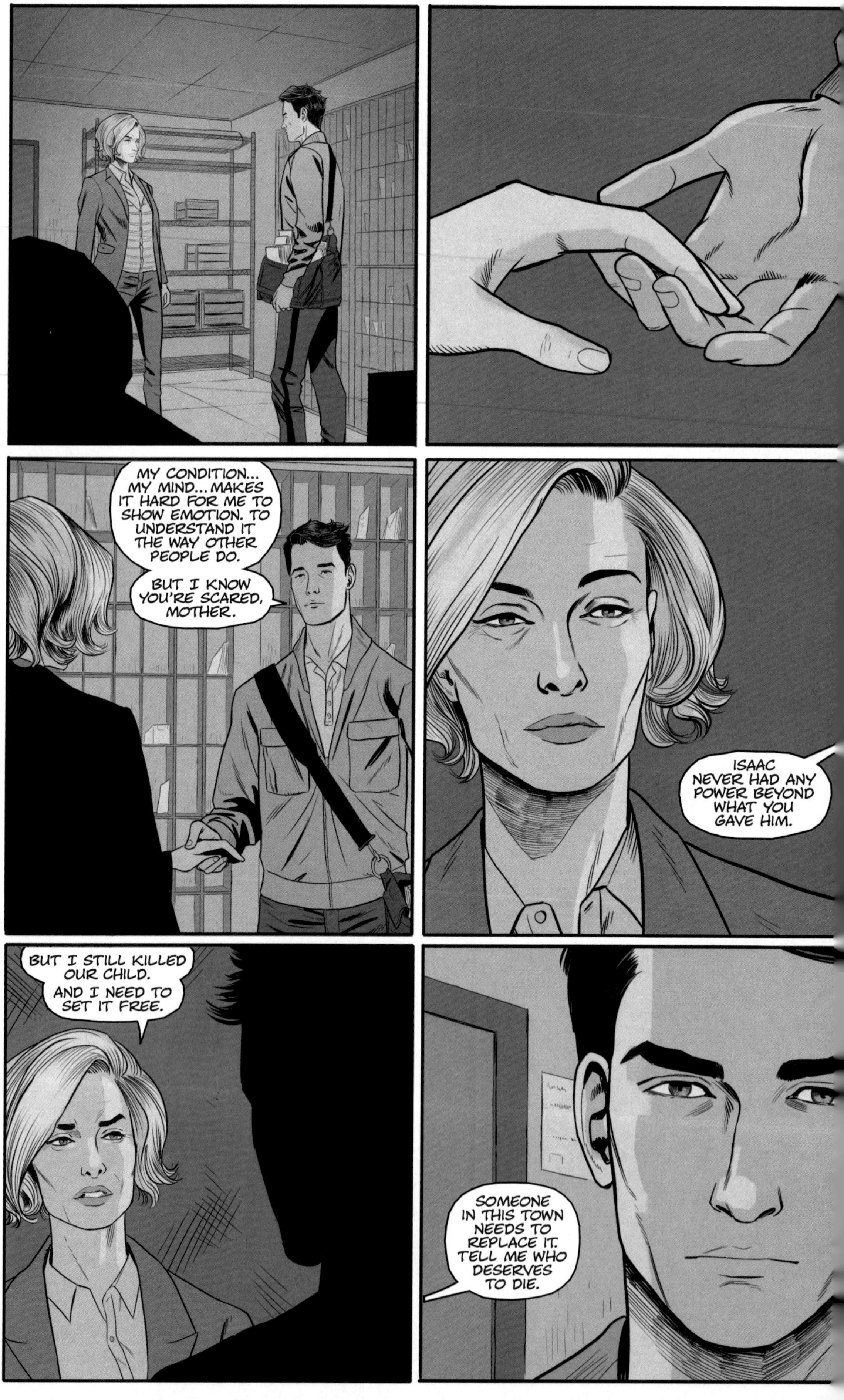
MY CONDITION... MY MIND... MAKES IT HARD FOR ME TO SHOW EMOTION. TO UNDERSTAND IT THE WAY OTHER PEOPLE DO.
BUT I KNOW YOU'RE SCARED, MOTHER.
ISAAC NEVER HAD ANY POWER BEYOND WHAT YOU GAVE HIM.
BUT I STILL KILLED OUR CHILD.
AND I NEED TO SET IT FREE.
SOMEONE IN THIS TOWN NEEDS TO REPLACE IT. TELL ME WHO DESERVES TO DIE.

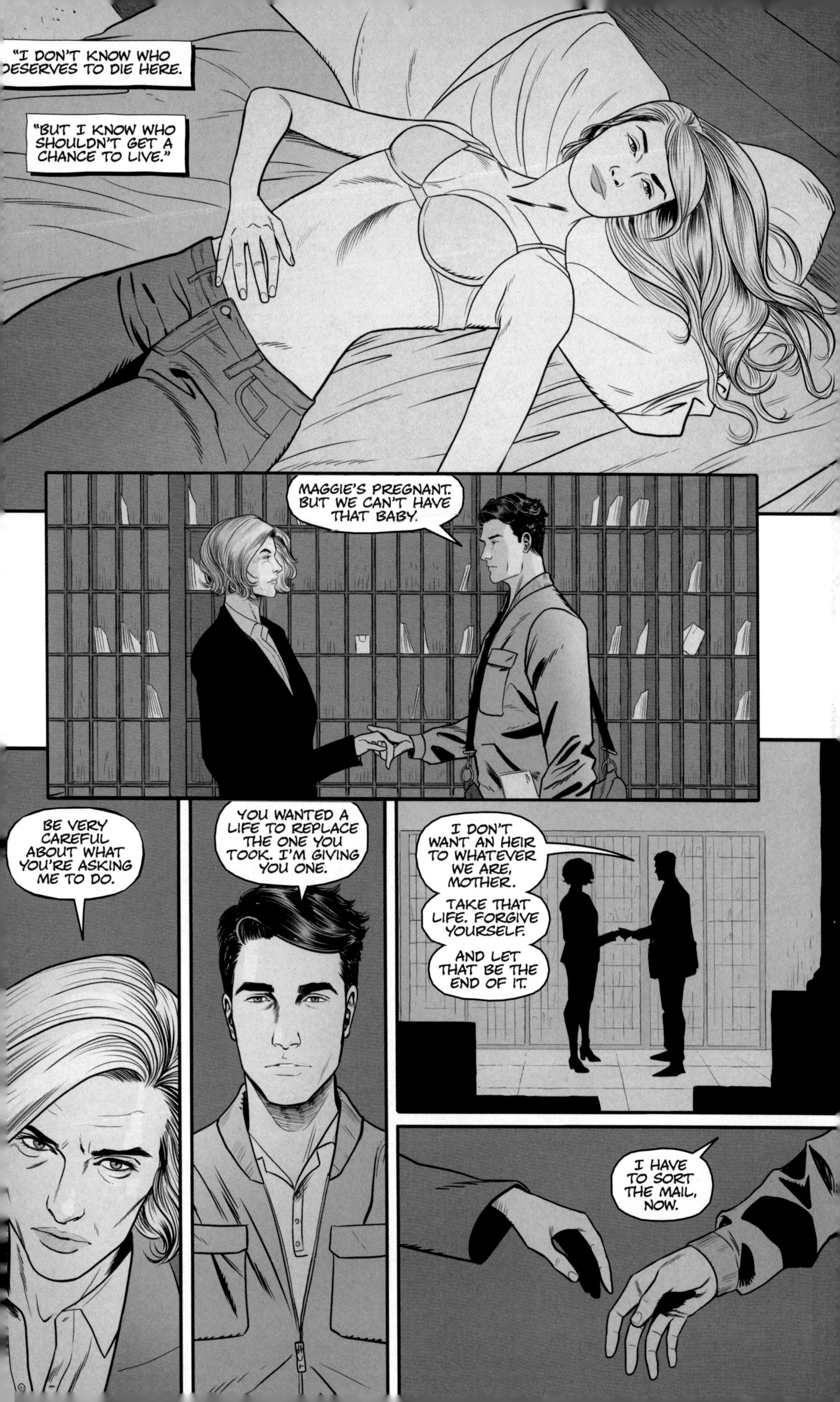
"I DON'T KNOW WHO DESERVES TO DIE HERE.
"BUT I KNOW WHO SHOULDN'T GET A CHANCE TO LIVE."
MAGGIE'S PREGNANT. BUT WE CAN'T HAVE THAT BABY.
BE VERY CAREFUL ABOUT WHAT YOU'RE ASKING ME TO DO.
YOU WANTED A LIFE TO REPLACE THE ONE YOU TOOK. I'M GIVING YOU ONE.
I DON'T WANT AN HEIR TO WHATEVER WE ARE, MOTHER.
TAKE THAT LIFE. FORGIVE YOURSELF.
AND LET THAT BE THE END OF IT.
I HAVE TO SORT THE MAIL, NOW.

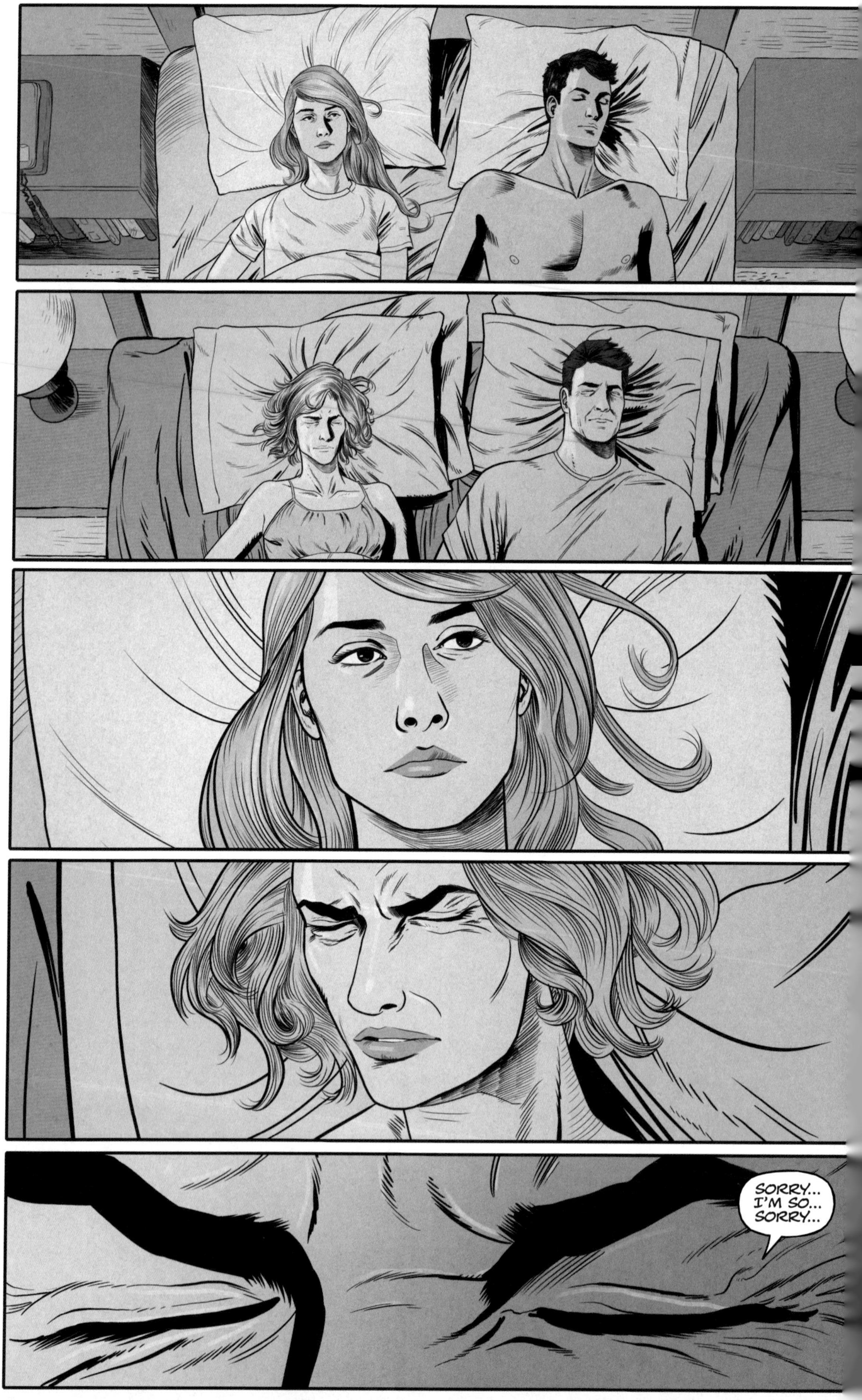
SORRY... I'M SO... SORRY...

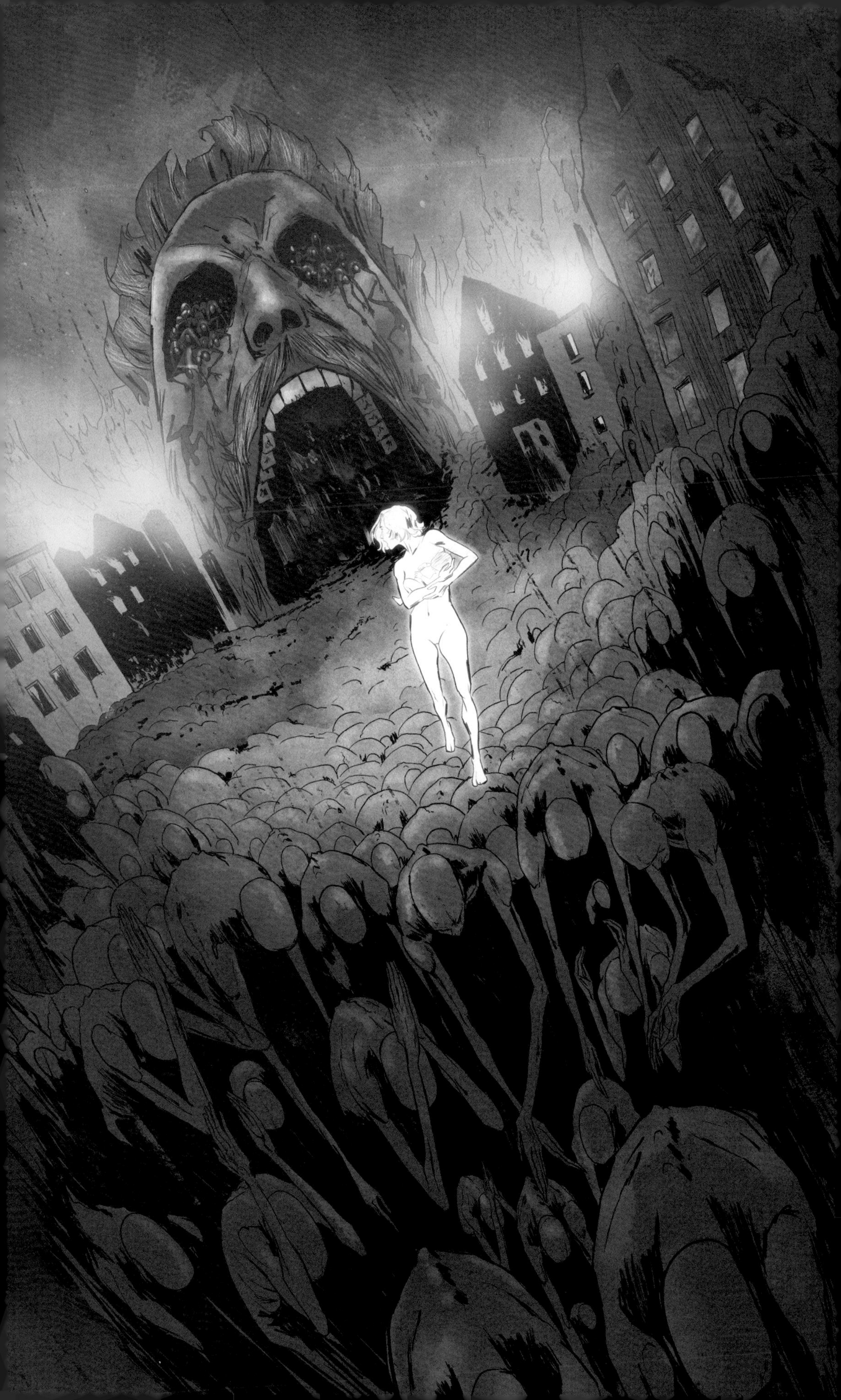

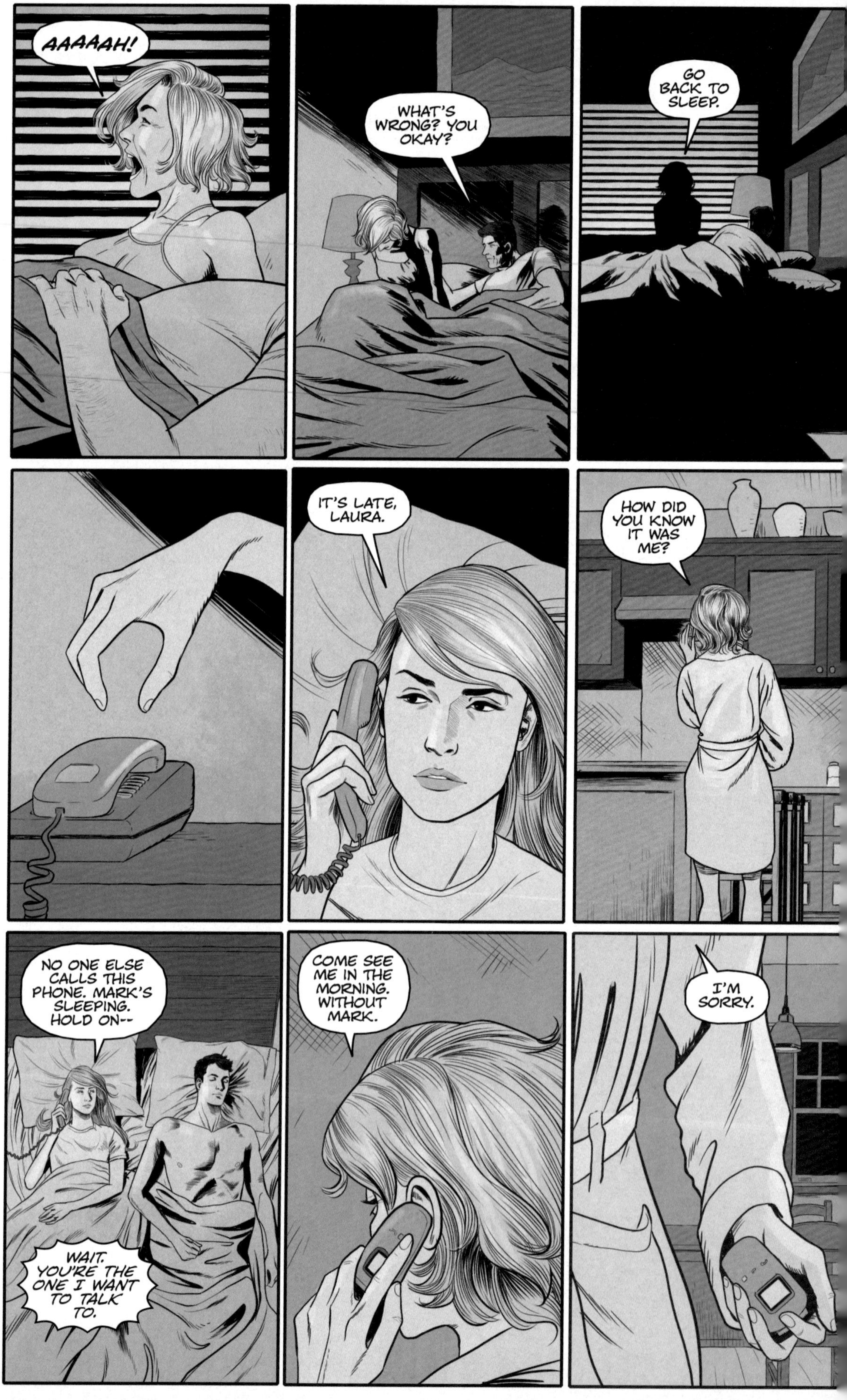
AAAAAH!
WHAT'S WRONG? YOU OKAY?
GO BACK TO SLEEP.
IT'S LATE, LAURA.
HOW DID YOU KNOW IT WAS ME?
NO ONE ELSE CALLS THIS PHONE. MARK'S SLEEPING. HOLD ON--
WAIT. YOU'RE THE ONE I WANT TO TALK TO.
COME SEE ME IN THE MORNING. WITHOUT MARK.
I'M SORRY.

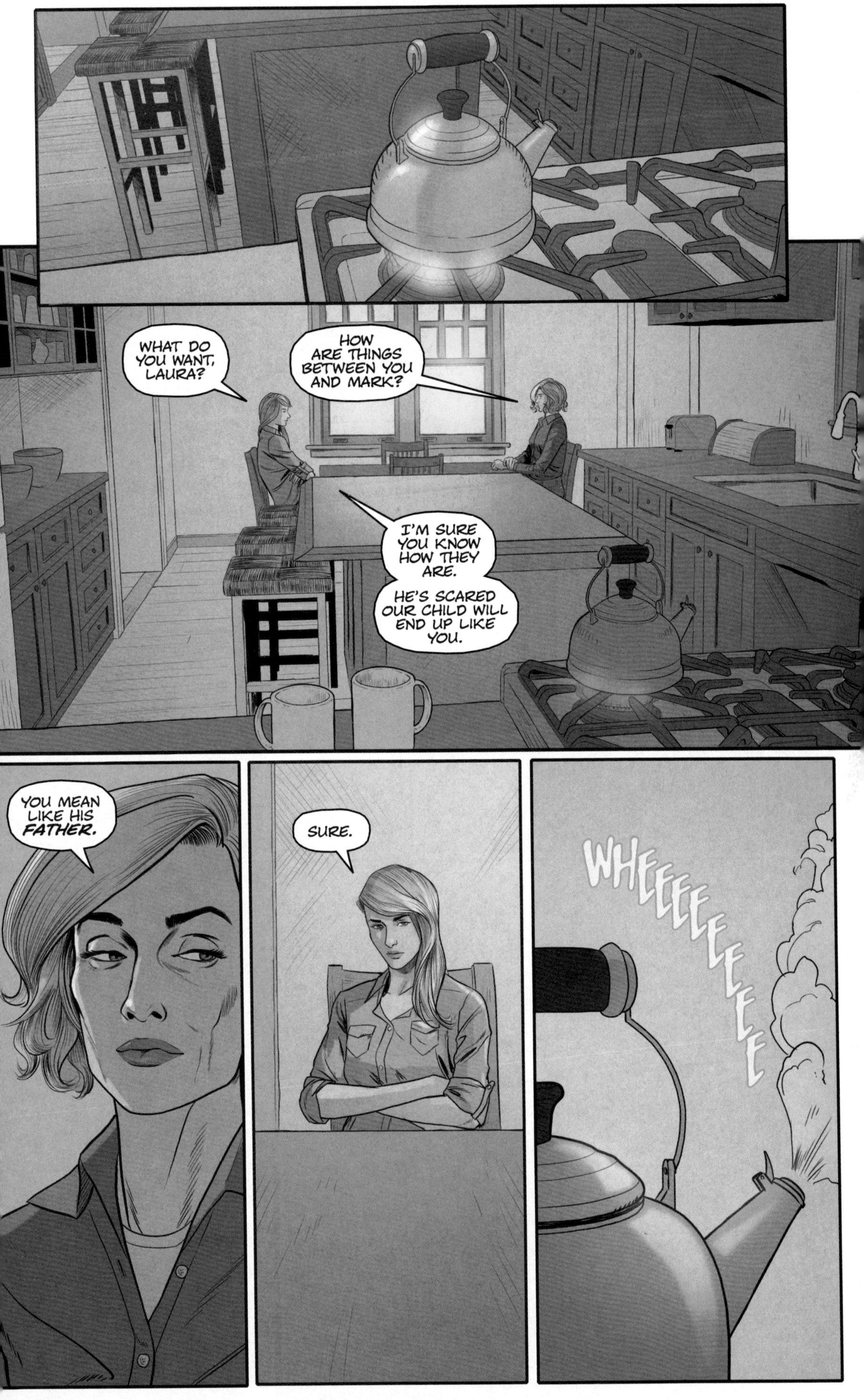
WHAT DO YOU WANT, LAURA?
HOW ARE THINGS BETWEEN YOU AND MARK?
I'M SURE YOU KNOW HOW THEY ARE.
HE'S SCARED OUR CHILD WILL END UP LIKE YOU.
YOU MEAN LIKE HIS *FATHER*.
SURE.
WHEEEEEEEE

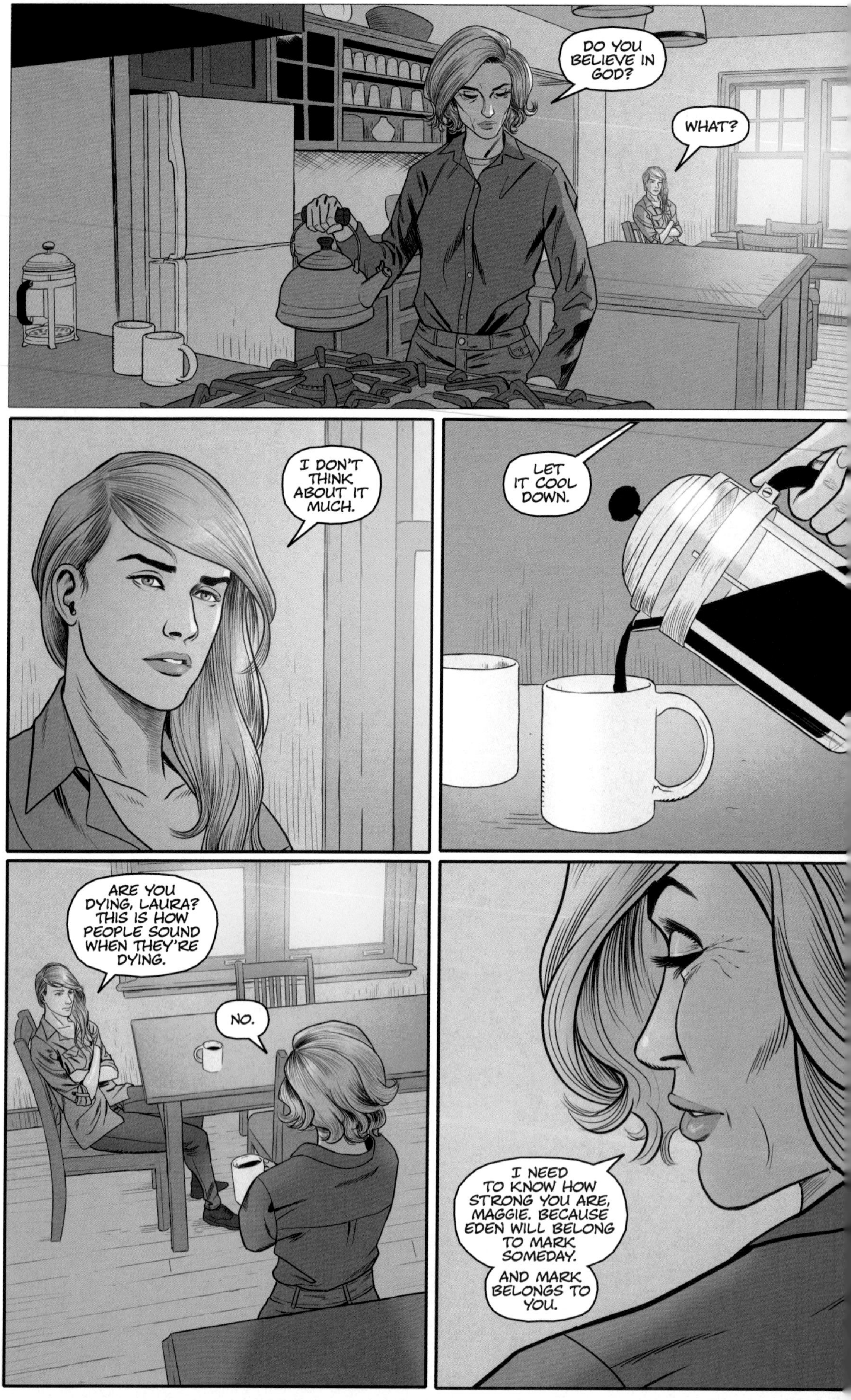
DO YOU BELIEVE IN GOD?
WHAT?
I DON'T THINK ABOUT IT MUCH.
LET IT COOL DOWN.
ARE YOU DYING, LAURA? THIS IS HOW PEOPLE SOUND WHEN THEY'RE DYING.
NO.
I NEED TO KNOW HOW STRONG YOU ARE, MAGGIE. BECAUSE EDEN WILL BELONG TO MARK SOMEDAY.
AND MARK BELONGS TO YOU.

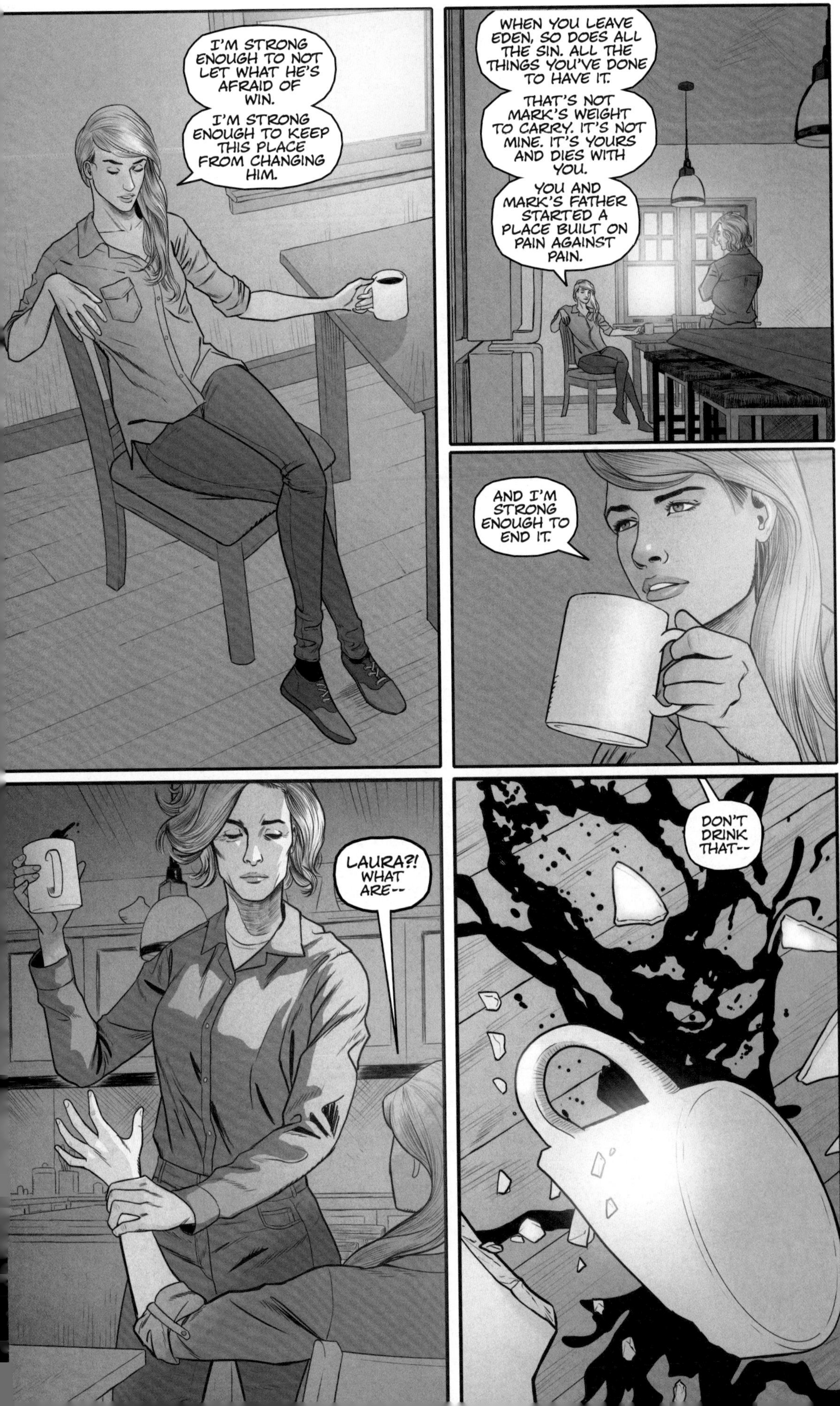
I'M STRONG ENOUGH TO NOT LET WHAT HE'S AFRAID OF WIN.
I'M STRONG ENOUGH TO KEEP THIS PLACE FROM CHANGING HIM.
WHEN YOU LEAVE EDEN, SO DOES ALL THE SIN. ALL THE THINGS YOU'VE DONE TO HAVE IT.
THAT'S NOT MARK'S WEIGHT TO CARRY. IT'S NOT MINE. IT'S YOURS AND DIES WITH YOU.
YOU AND MARK'S FATHER STARTED A PLACE BUILT ON PAIN AGAINST PAIN.
AND I'M STRONG ENOUGH TO END IT.
LAURA?! WHAT ARE--
DON'T DRINK THAT--

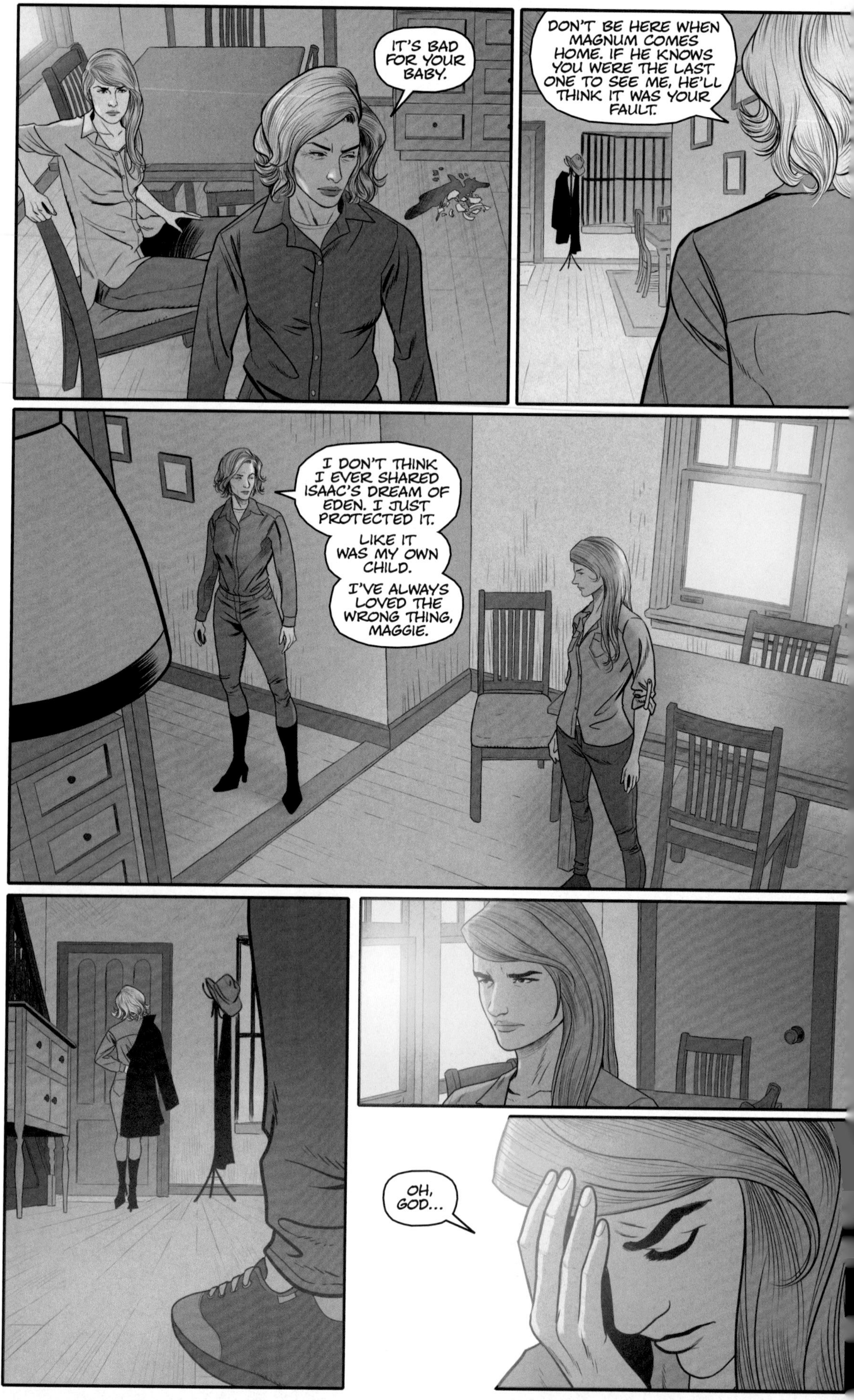
IT'S BAD FOR YOUR BABY.
DON'T BE HERE WHEN MAGNUM COMES HOME. IF HE KNOWS YOU WERE THE LAST ONE TO SEE ME, HE'LL THINK IT WAS YOUR FAULT.
I DON'T THINK I EVER SHARED ISAAC'S DREAM OF EDEN. I JUST PROTECTED IT.
LIKE IT WAS MY OWN CHILD.
I'VE ALWAYS LOVED THE WRONG THING, MAGGIE.
OH, GOD...

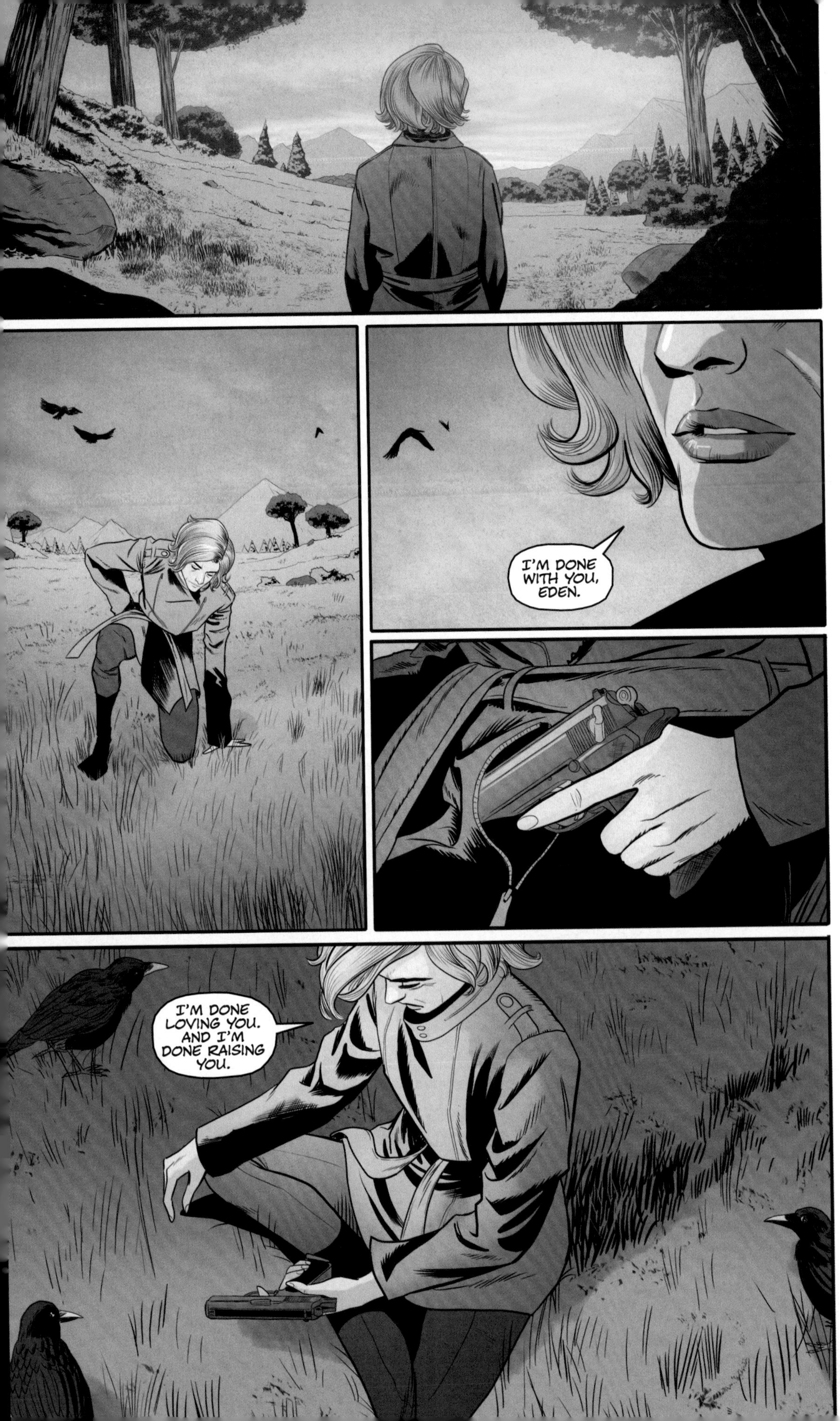
I'M DONE WITH YOU, EDEN.
I'M DONE LOVING YOU. AND I'M DONE RAISING YOU.

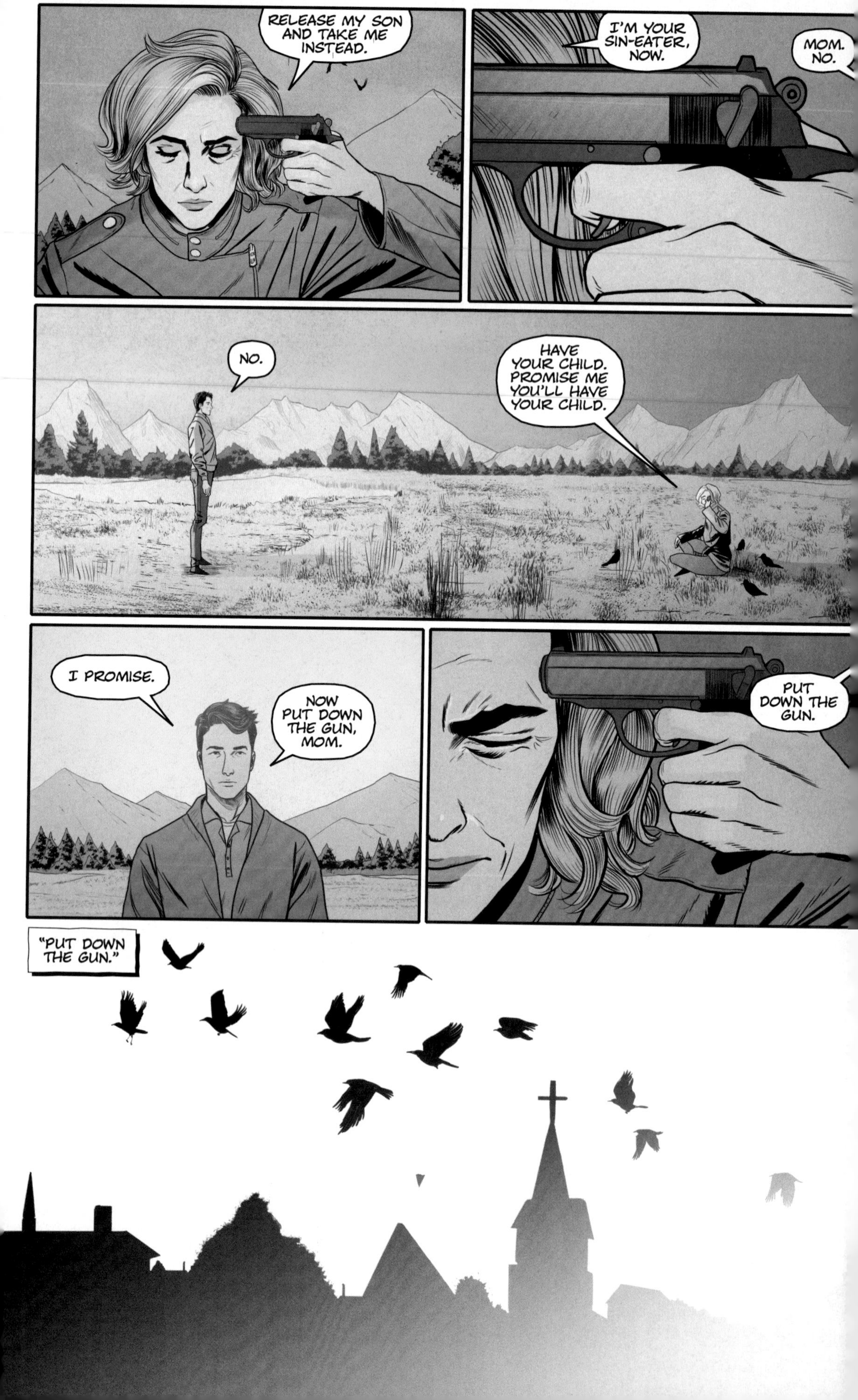
RELEASE MY SON AND TAKE ME INSTEAD.
I'M YOUR SIN-EATER, NOW.
MOM. NO.
NO.
HAVE YOUR CHILD. PROMISE ME YOU'LL HAVE YOUR CHILD.
I PROMISE.
NOW PUT DOWN THE GUN, MOM.
PUT DOWN THE GUN.
"PUT DOWN THE GUN."

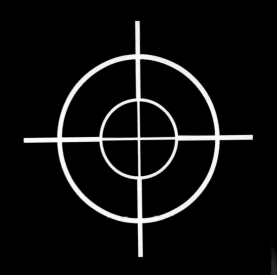

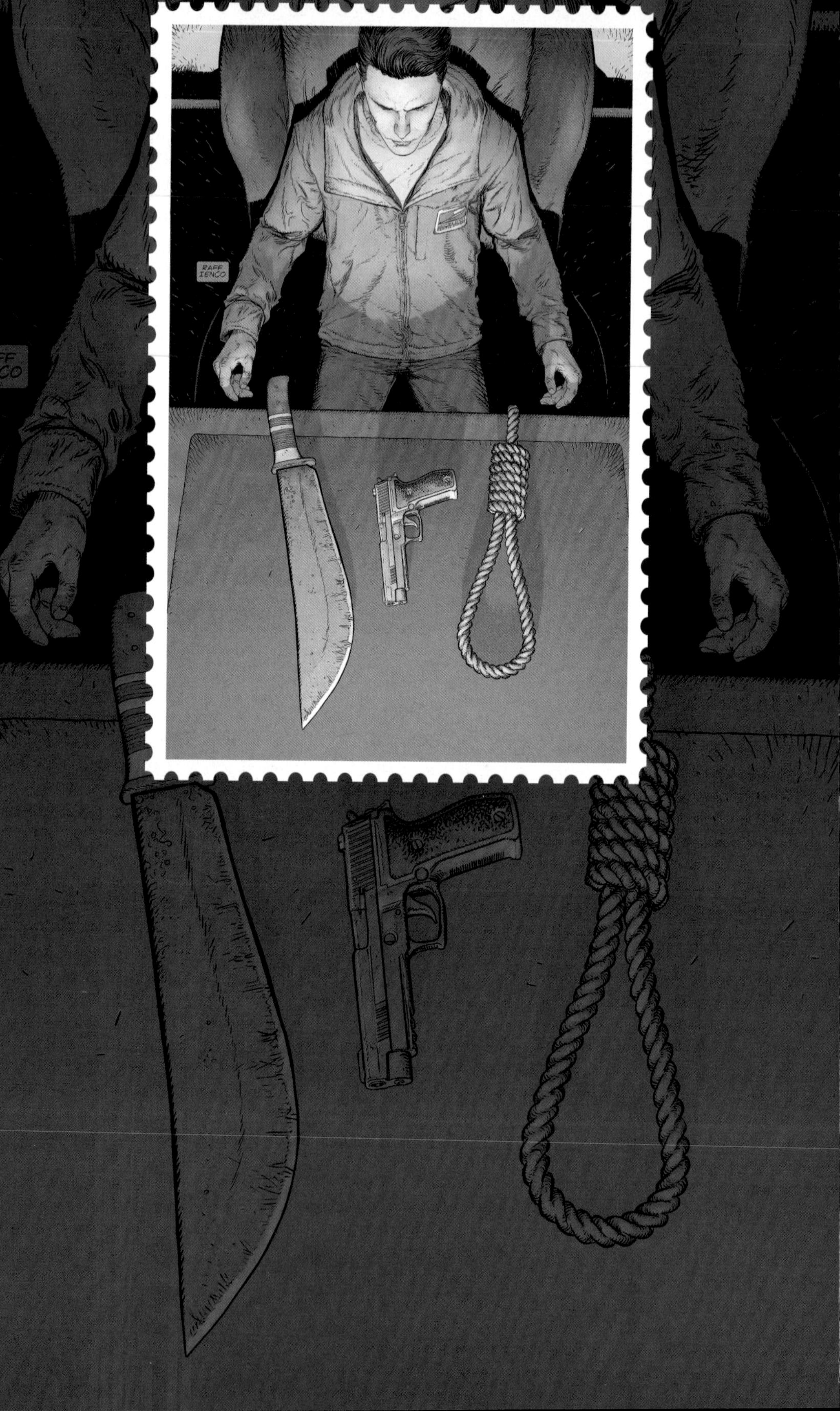
RAFF
IENCO

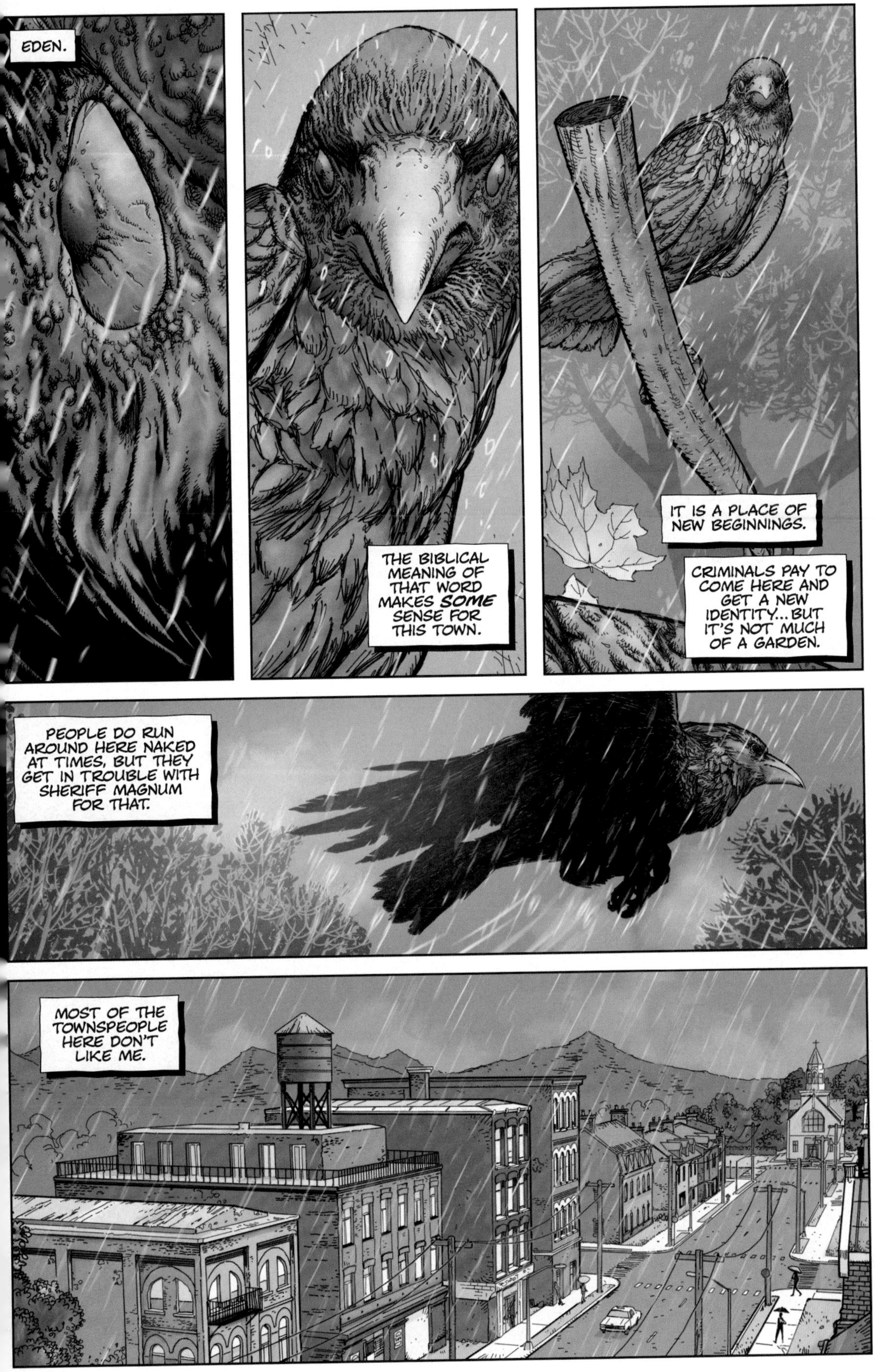

EDEN.
THE BIBLICAL MEANING OF THAT WORD MAKES SOME SENSE FOR THIS TOWN.
IT IS A PLACE OF NEW BEGINNINGS.
CRIMINALS PAY TO COME HERE AND GET A NEW IDENTITY...BUT IT'S NOT MUCH OF A GARDEN.
PEOPLE DO RUN AROUND HERE NAKED AT TIMES, BUT THEY GET IN TROUBLE WITH SHERIFF MAGNUM FOR THAT.
MOST OF THE TOWNSPEOPLE HERE DON'T LIKE ME.

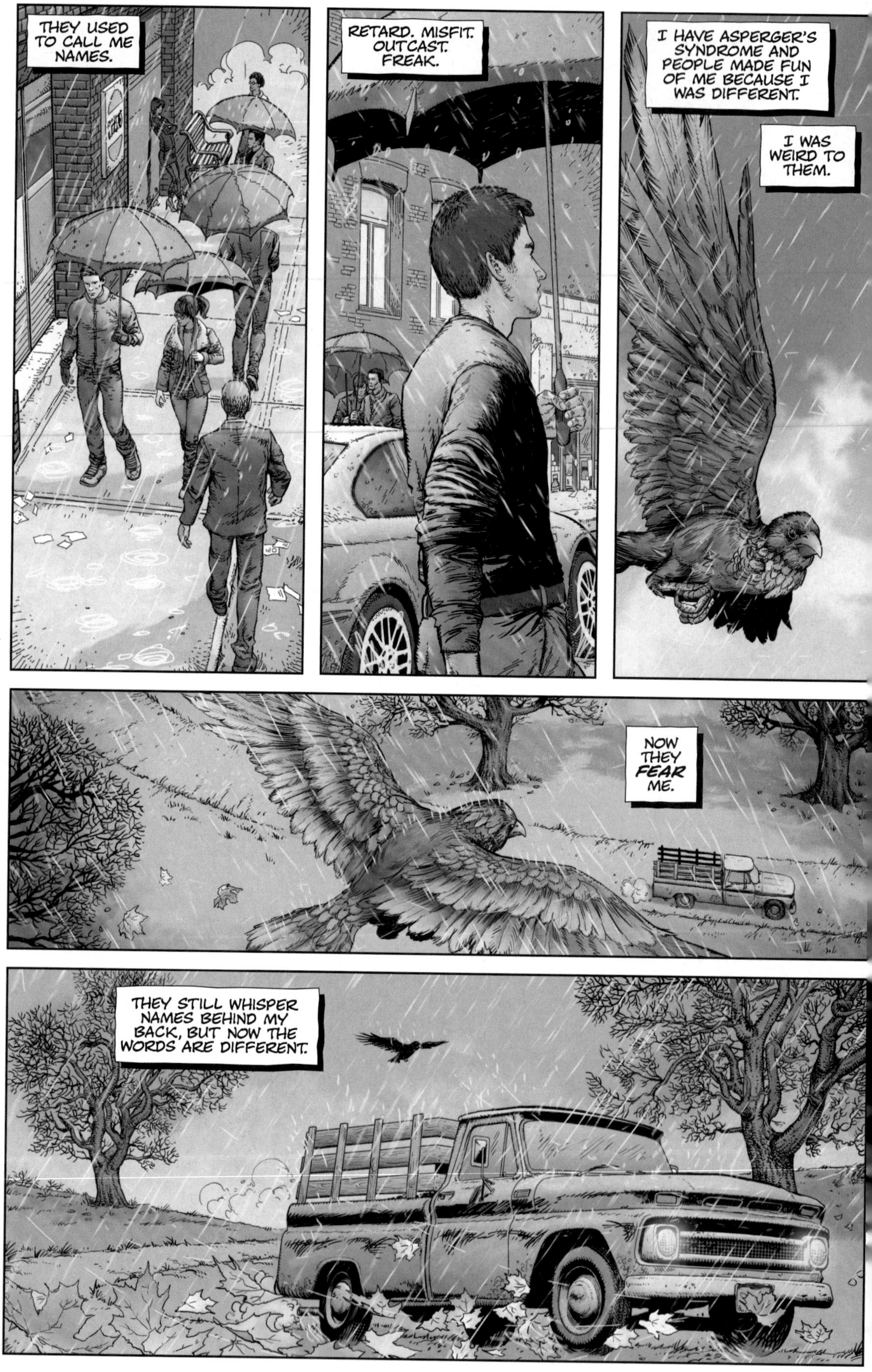
THEY USED TO CALL ME NAMES.
RETARD. MISFIT. OUTCAST. FREAK.
I HAVE ASPERGER'S SYNDROME AND PEOPLE MADE FUN OF ME BECAUSE I WAS DIFFERENT.
I WAS WEIRD TO THEM.
NOW THEY *FEAR* ME.
THEY STILL WHISPER NAMES BEHIND MY BACK, BUT NOW THE WORDS ARE DIFFERENT.

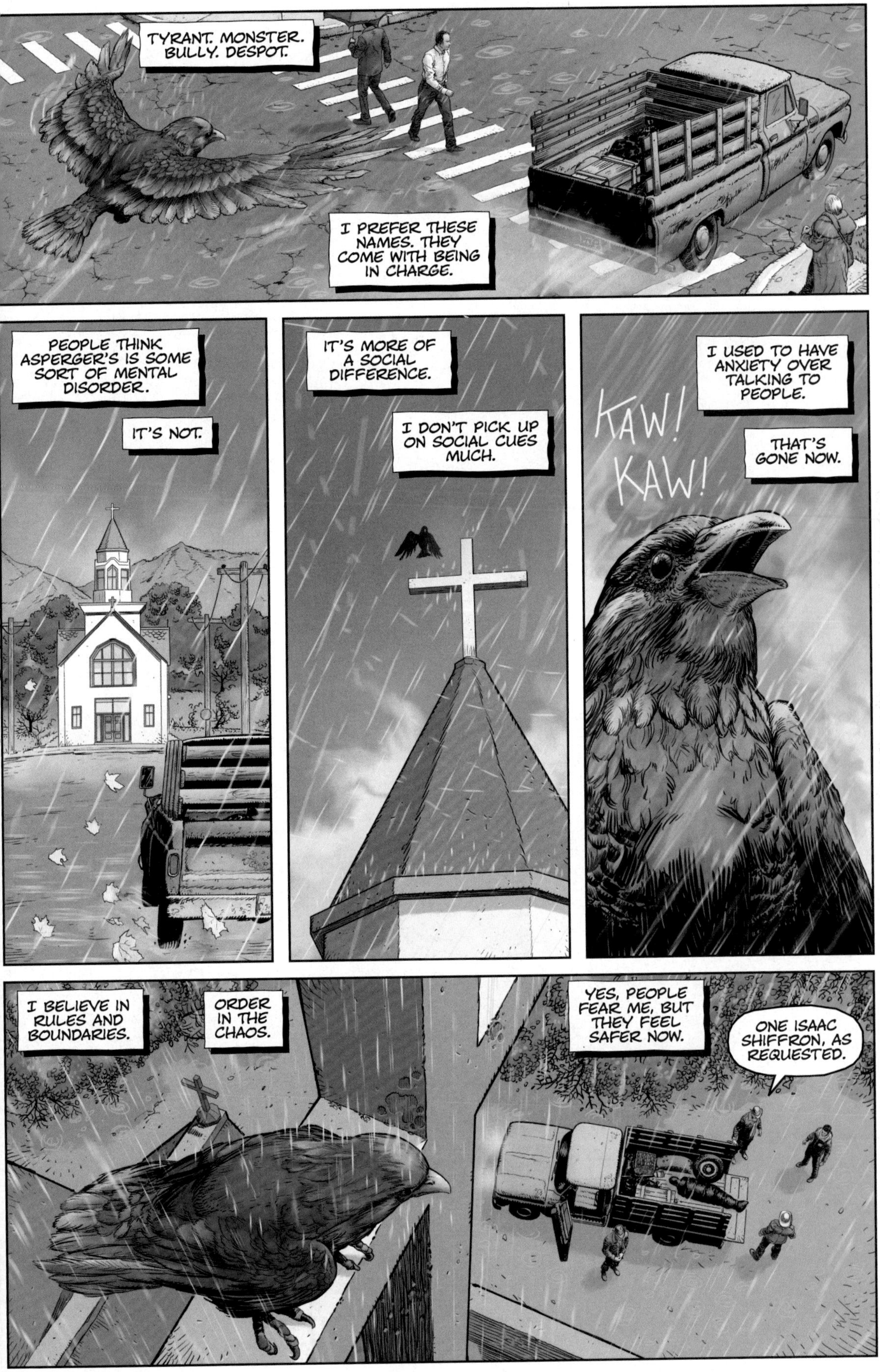
TYRANT. MONSTER. BULLY. DESPOT.
I PREFER THESE NAMES. THEY COME WITH BEING IN CHARGE.
PEOPLE THINK ASPERGER'S IS SOME SORT OF MENTAL DISORDER.
IT'S NOT.
IT'S MORE OF A SOCIAL DIFFERENCE.
I DON'T PICK UP ON SOCIAL CUES MUCH.
I USED TO HAVE ANXIETY OVER TALKING TO PEOPLE.
KAW! KAW!
THAT'S GONE NOW.
I BELIEVE IN RULES AND BOUNDARIES.
ORDER IN THE CHAOS.
YES, PEOPLE FEAR ME, BUT THEY FEEL SAFER NOW.
ONE ISAAC SHIFFRON, AS REQUESTED.

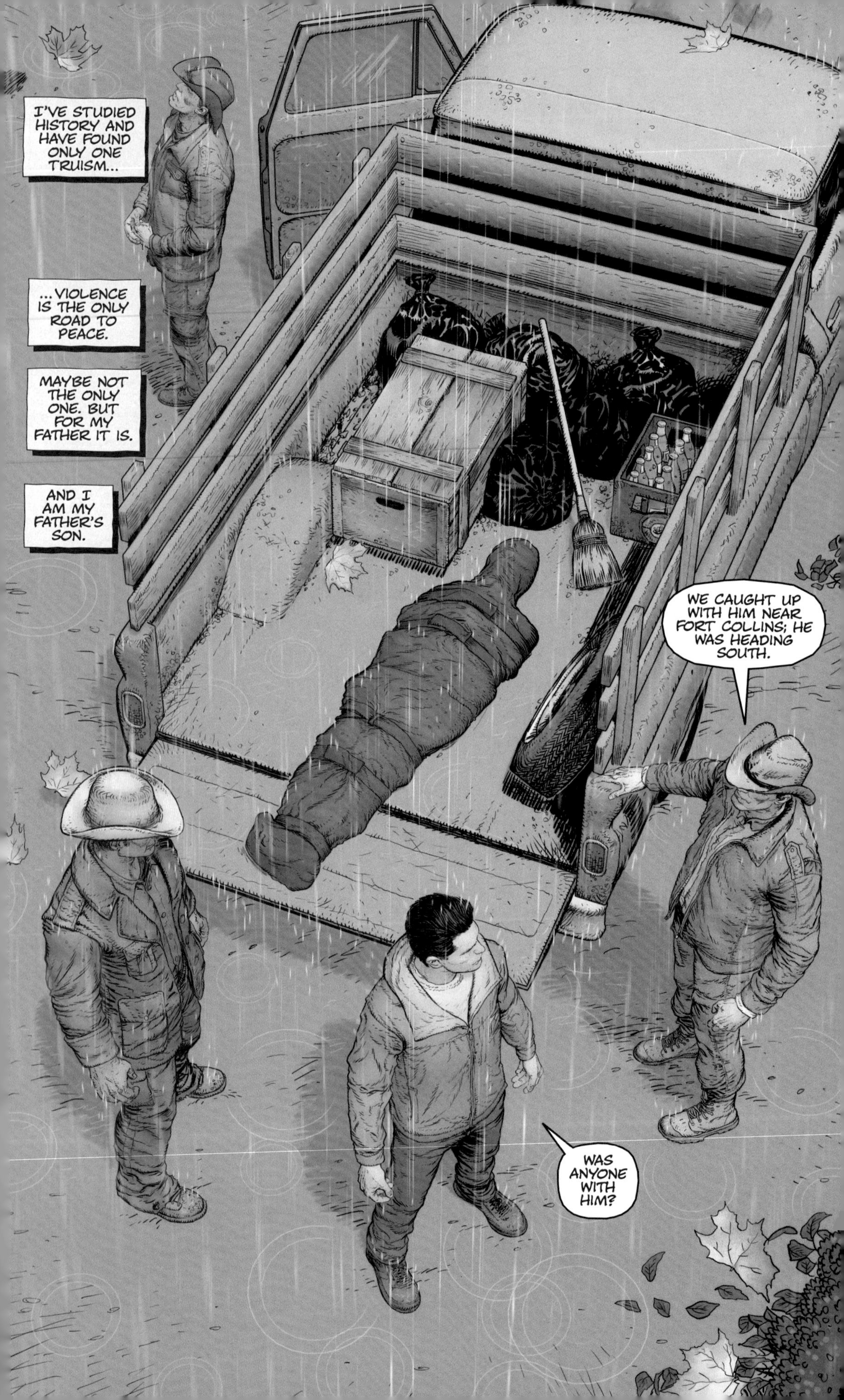
I'VE STUDIED HISTORY AND HAVE FOUND ONLY ONE TRUISM...
...VIOLENCE IS THE ONLY ROAD TO PEACE.
MAYBE NOT THE ONLY ONE. BUT FOR MY FATHER IT IS.
AND I AM MY FATHER'S SON.
WE CAUGHT UP WITH HIM NEAR FORT COLLINS; HE WAS HEADING SOUTH.
WAS ANYONE WITH HIM?

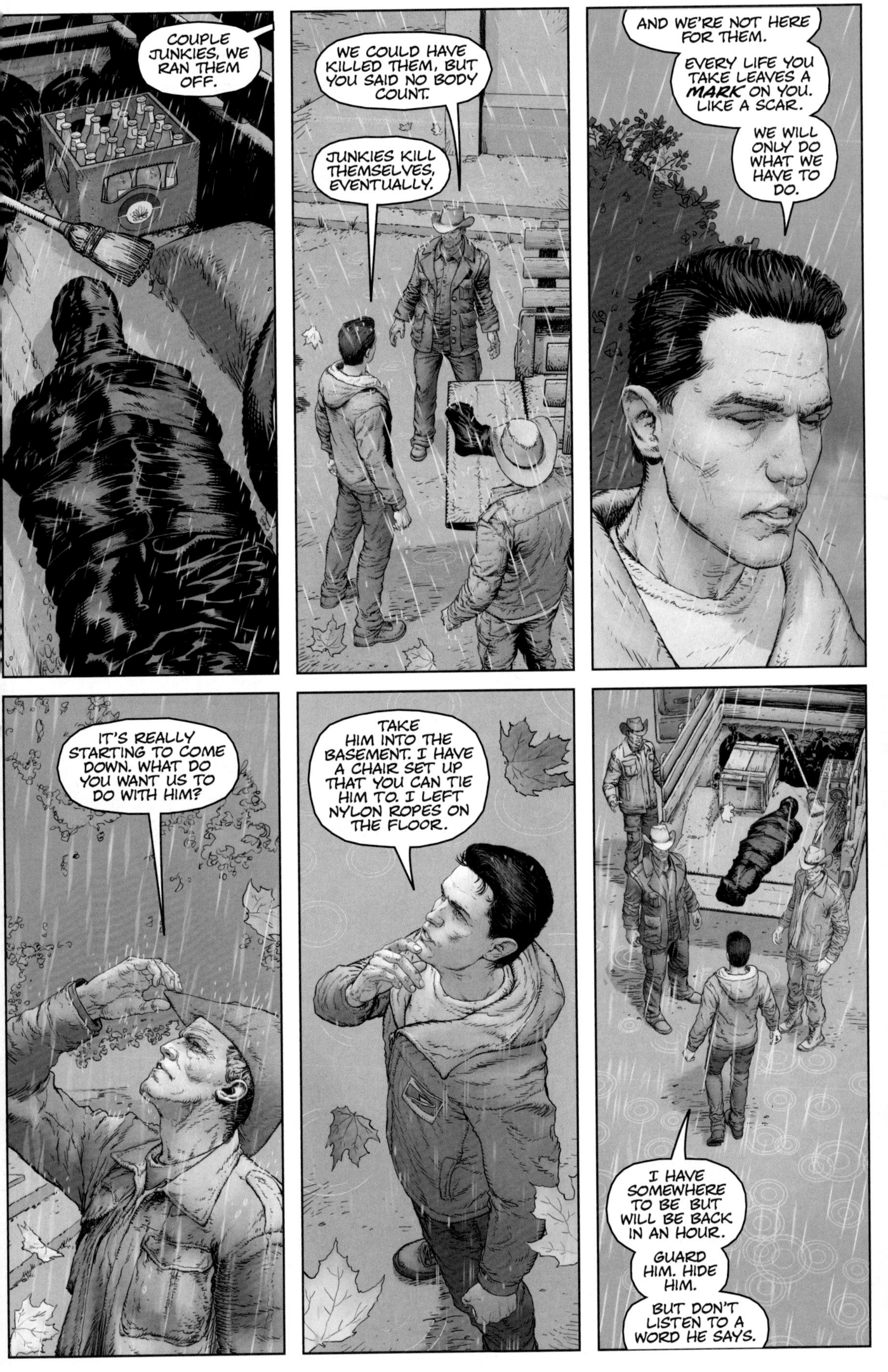
COUPLE JUNKIES, WE RAN THEM OFF.
WE COULD HAVE KILLED THEM, BUT YOU SAID NO BODY COUNT.
JUNKIES KILL THEMSELVES, EVENTUALLY.
AND WE'RE NOT HERE FOR THEM.
EVERY LIFE YOU TAKE LEAVES A MARK ON YOU. LIKE A SCAR.
WE WILL ONLY DO WHAT WE HAVE TO DO.
IT'S REALLY STARTING TO COME DOWN. WHAT DO YOU WANT US TO DO WITH HIM?
TAKE HIM INTO THE BASEMENT. I HAVE A CHAIR SET UP THAT YOU CAN TIE HIM TO. I LEFT NYLON ROPES ON THE FLOOR.
I HAVE SOMEWHERE TO BE BUT WILL BE BACK IN AN HOUR.
GUARD HIM. HIDE HIM.
BUT DON'T LISTEN TO A WORD HE SAYS.

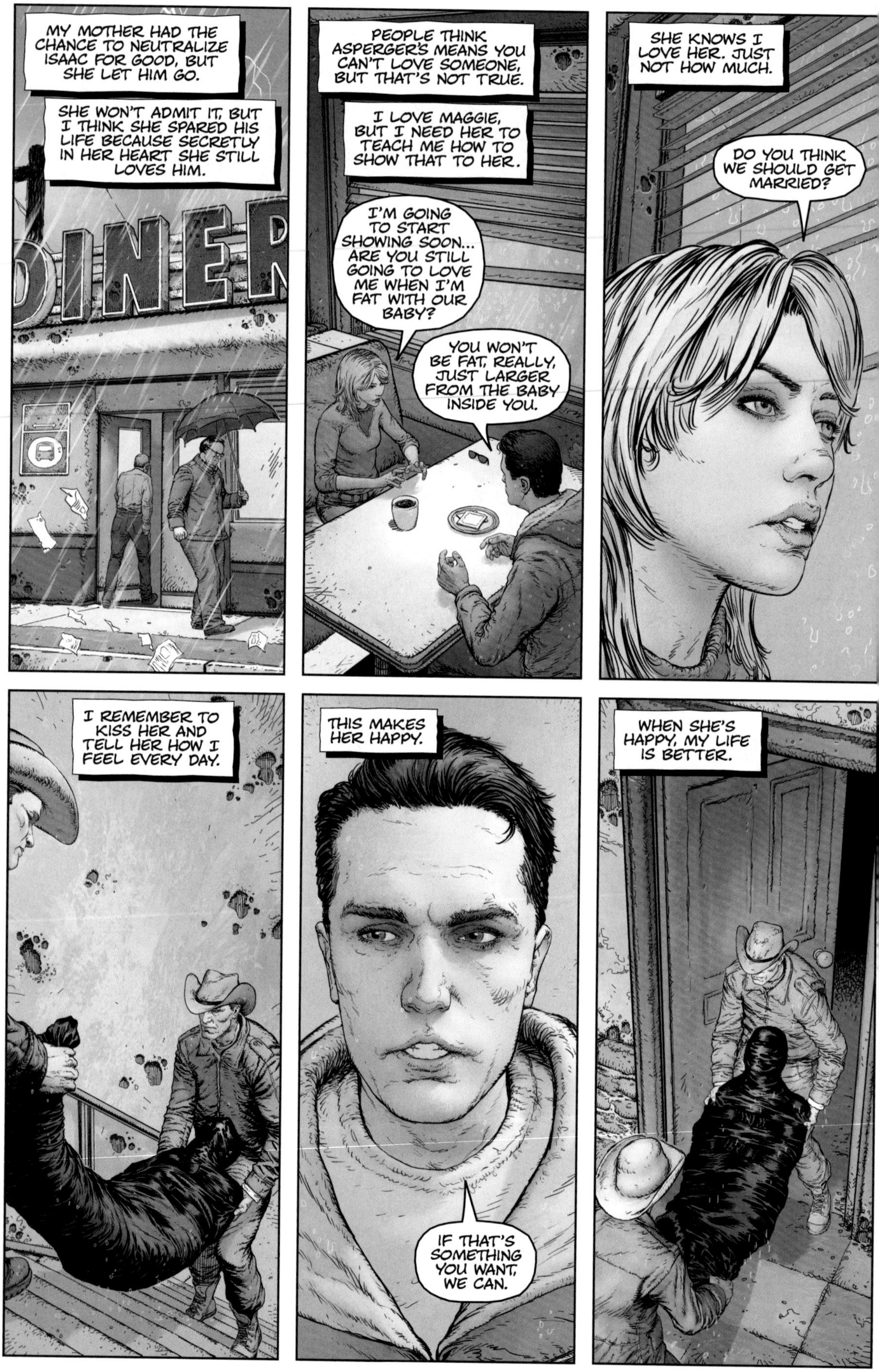
MY MOTHER HAD THE CHANCE TO NEUTRALIZE ISAAC FOR GOOD, BUT SHE LET HIM GO.
SHE WON'T ADMIT IT, BUT I THINK SHE SPARED HIS LIFE BECAUSE SECRETLY IN HER HEART SHE STILL LOVES HIM.
DINER
PEOPLE THINK ASPERGER'S MEANS YOU CAN'T LOVE SOMEONE, BUT THAT'S NOT TRUE.
I LOVE MAGGIE, BUT I NEED HER TO TEACH ME HOW TO SHOW THAT TO HER.
I'M GOING TO START SHOWING SOON... ARE YOU STILL GOING TO LOVE ME WHEN I'M FAT WITH OUR BABY?
YOU WON'T BE FAT, REALLY, JUST LARGER FROM THE BABY INSIDE YOU.
SHE KNOWS I LOVE HER. JUST NOT HOW MUCH.
DO YOU THINK WE SHOULD GET MARRIED?
I REMEMBER TO KISS HER AND TELL HER HOW I FEEL EVERY DAY.
THIS MAKES HER HAPPY.
IF THAT'S SOMETHING YOU WANT, WE CAN.
WHEN SHE'S HAPPY, MY LIFE IS BETTER.

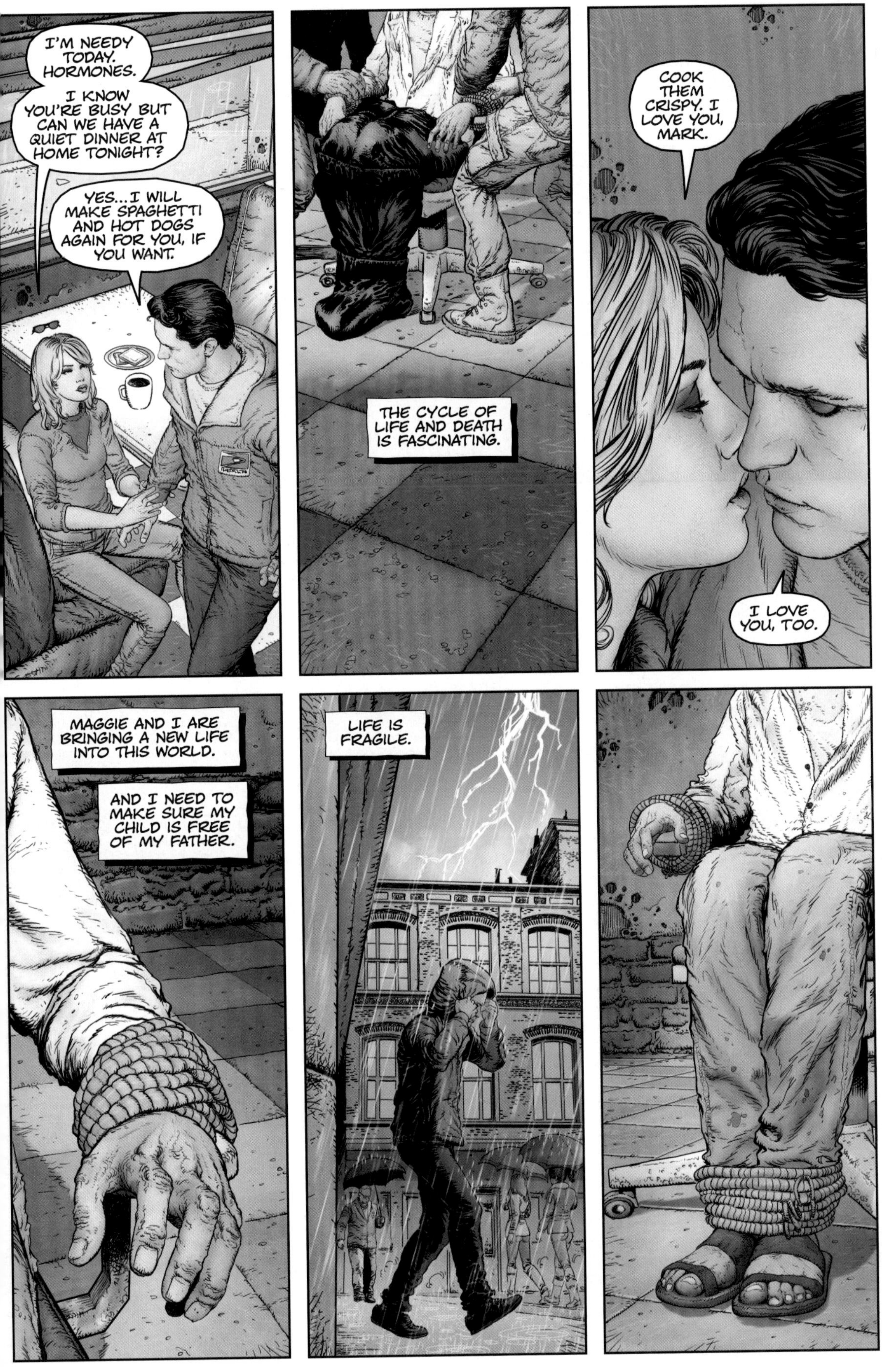
I'M NEEDY TODAY. HORMONES.
I KNOW YOU'RE BUSY BUT CAN WE HAVE A QUIET DINNER AT HOME TONIGHT?
YES...I WILL MAKE SPAGHETTI AND HOT DOGS AGAIN FOR YOU, IF YOU WANT.
THE CYCLE OF LIFE AND DEATH IS FASCINATING.
COOK THEM CRISPY. I LOVE YOU, MARK.
I LOVE YOU, TOO.
MAGGIE AND I ARE BRINGING A NEW LIFE INTO THIS WORLD.
AND I NEED TO MAKE SURE MY CHILD IS FREE OF MY FATHER.
LIFE IS FRAGILE.

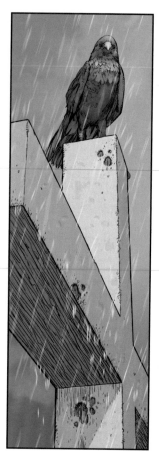

I HAVEN'T DECIDED IF MY FATHER IS A CHARLATAN OR IF HE ACTUALLY BELIEVES THE INSANITIES OF OLD WORLD MAGIC THAT HE RAVES ABOUT ENDLESSLY.

ANCIENT PROPHECIES, RELIGION AND CTHULHIAN WEIRDNESS.

TOOLS TO GET LAID AND CONTROL THE WEAK-MINDED? OR THE WORKINGS OF A DERANGED MIND? BOTH?

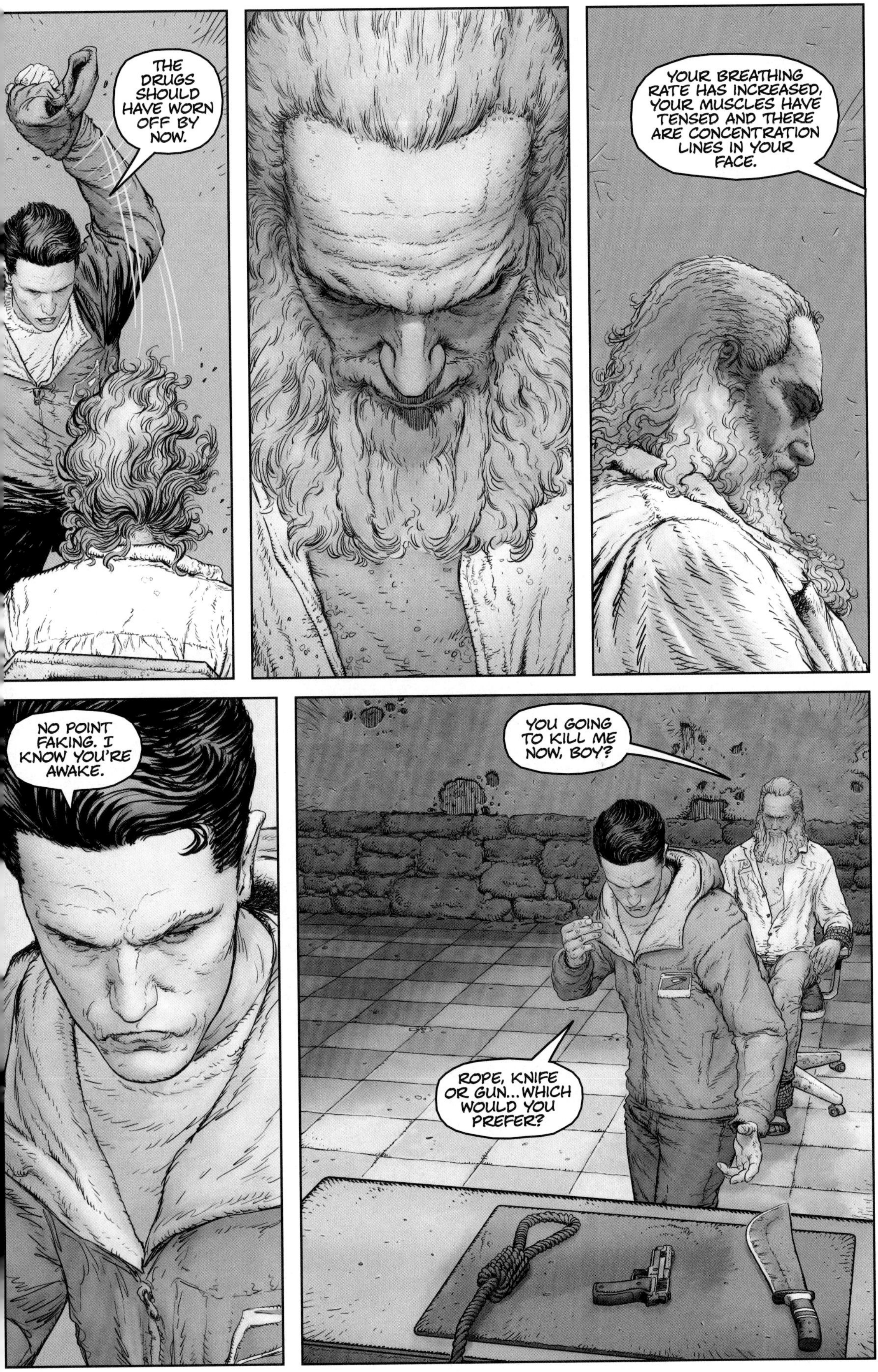
THE DRUGS SHOULD HAVE WORN OFF BY NOW.
YOUR BREATHING RATE HAS INCREASED, YOUR MUSCLES HAVE TENSED AND THERE ARE CONCENTRATION LINES IN YOUR FACE.
NO POINT FAKING. I KNOW YOU'RE AWAKE.
YOU GOING TO KILL ME NOW, BOY?
ROPE, KNIFE OR GUN... WHICH WOULD YOU PREFER?

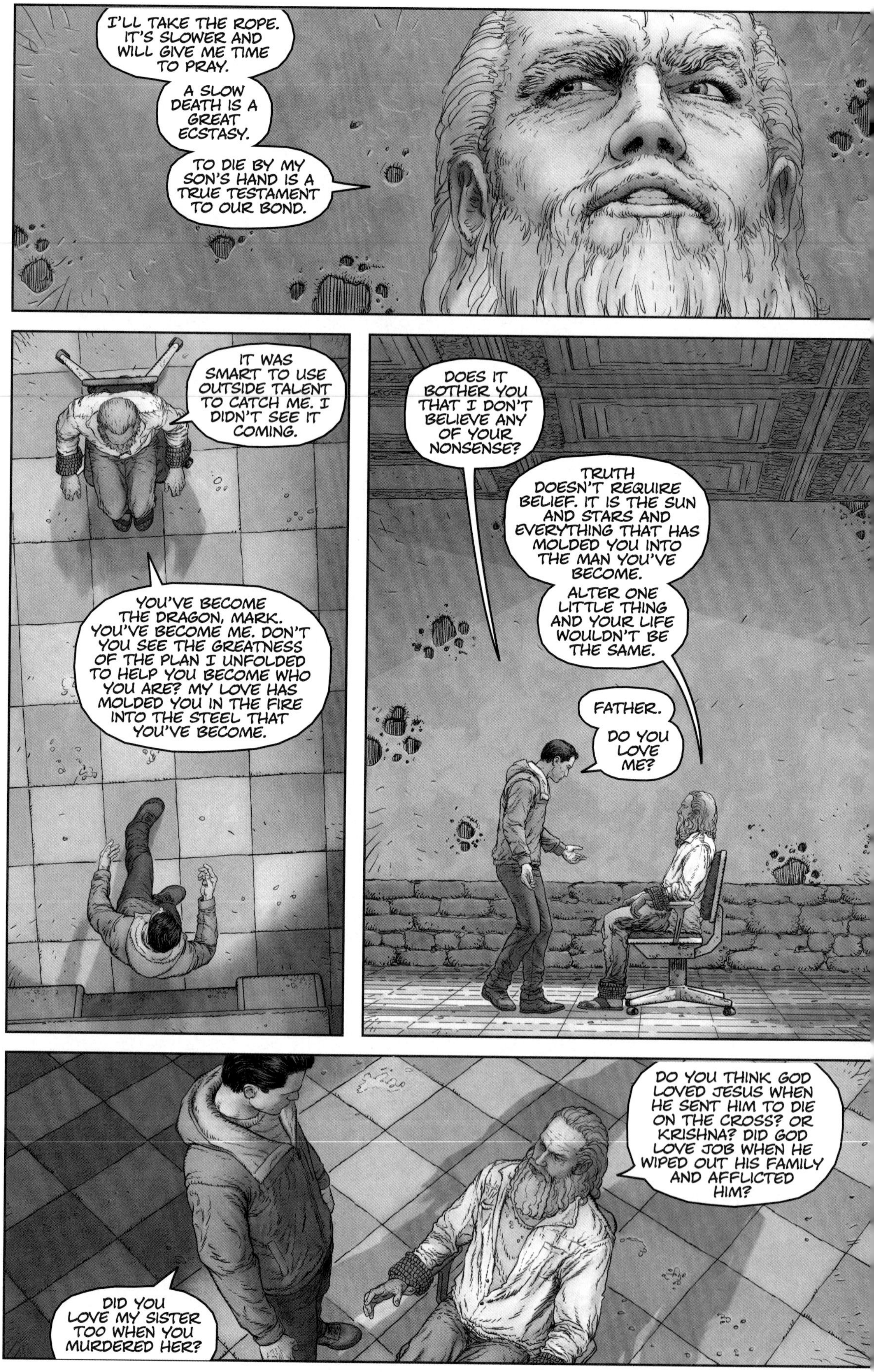
I'LL TAKE THE ROPE. IT'S SLOWER AND WILL GIVE ME TIME TO PRAY.
A SLOW DEATH IS A GREAT ECSTASY.
TO DIE BY MY SON'S HAND IS A TRUE TESTAMENT TO OUR BOND.
IT WAS SMART TO USE OUTSIDE TALENT TO CATCH ME. I DIDN'T SEE IT COMING.
YOU'VE BECOME THE DRAGON, MARK. YOU'VE BECOME ME. DON'T YOU SEE THE GREATNESS OF THE PLAN I UNFOLDED TO HELP YOU BECOME WHO YOU ARE? MY LOVE HAS MOLDED YOU IN THE FIRE INTO THE STEEL THAT YOU'VE BECOME.
DOES IT BOTHER YOU THAT I DON'T BELIEVE ANY OF YOUR NONSENSE?
TRUTH DOESN'T REQUIRE BELIEF. IT IS THE SUN AND STARS AND EVERYTHING THAT HAS MOLDED YOU INTO THE MAN YOU'VE BECOME.
ALTER ONE LITTLE THING AND YOUR LIFE WOULDN'T BE THE SAME.
FATHER.
DO YOU LOVE ME?
DO YOU THINK GOD LOVED JESUS WHEN HE SENT HIM TO DIE ON THE CROSS? OR KRISHNA? DID GOD LOVE JOB WHEN HE WIPED OUT HIS FAMILY AND AFFLICTED HIM?
DID YOU LOVE MY SISTER TOO WHEN YOU MURDERED HER?

"YOUR MOTHER RUINED HER.

"KILLING HER WAS A KINDNESS.

"I FOUND HER IN DENVER.

"SHE'D SUNK AS LOW AS A WOMAN COULD.

"AT FIRST I THOUGHT THERE WAS A BEAUTY IN HER BACCHANALIAN DANCE.

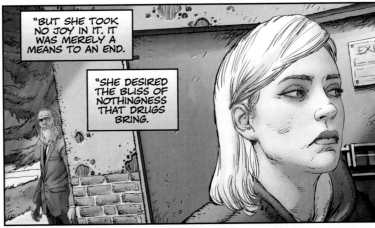

"BUT SHE TOOK NO JOY IN IT. IT WAS MERELY A MEANS TO AN END.

"SHE DESIRED THE BLISS OF NOTHINGNESS THAT DRUGS BRING.

"A SWEET OBLIVION TO BLUR HOW SHITTY HER LIFE WAS."

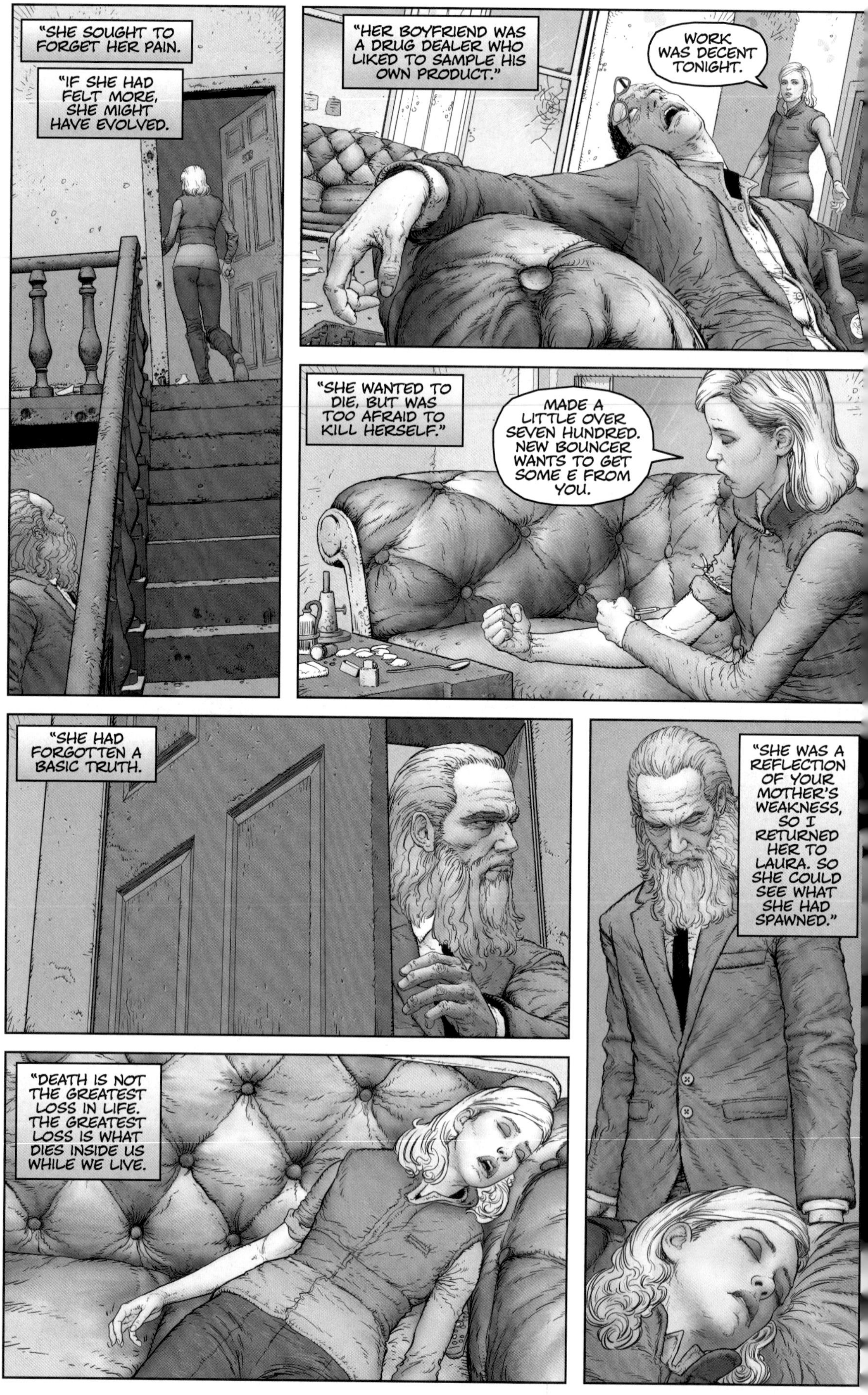
"SHE SOUGHT TO FORGET HER PAIN.
"IF SHE HAD FELT MORE, SHE MIGHT HAVE EVOLVED.
"HER BOYFRIEND WAS A DRUG DEALER WHO LIKED TO SAMPLE HIS OWN PRODUCT."
WORK WAS DECENT TONIGHT.
"SHE WANTED TO DIE, BUT WAS TOO AFRAID TO KILL HERSELF."
MADE A LITTLE OVER SEVEN HUNDRED. NEW BOUNCER WANTS TO GET SOME E FROM YOU.
"SHE HAD FORGOTTEN A BASIC TRUTH.
"DEATH IS NOT THE GREATEST LOSS IN LIFE. THE GREATEST LOSS IS WHAT DIES INSIDE US WHILE WE LIVE.
"SHE WAS A REFLECTION OF YOUR MOTHER'S WEAKNESS, SO I RETURNED HER TO LAURA. SO SHE COULD SEE WHAT SHE HAD SPAWNED."

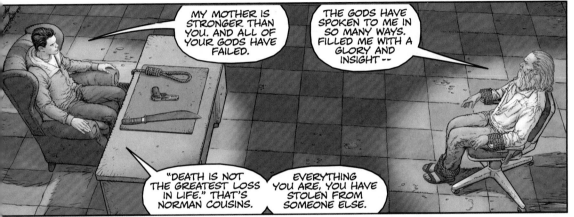

MY MOTHER IS STRONGER THAN YOU. AND ALL OF YOUR GODS HAVE FAILED.

THE GODS HAVE SPOKEN TO ME IN SO MANY WAYS. FILLED ME WITH A GLORY AND INSIGHT --

"DEATH IS NOT THE GREATEST LOSS IN LIFE." THAT'S NORMAN COUSINS.

EVERYTHING YOU ARE, YOU HAVE STOLEN FROM SOMEONE ELSE.

YOU TEST MY PATIENCE, BOY. YOU MIGHT NOT LIKE ME WHEN I'M ANGRY.

AND THAT COMES FROM DAVID BANNER.

I GAVE YOU LIFE, YOU MISERABLE RETARD.

I'M NOT RETARDED, FATHER. AND "RETARDED" IS AN UGLY WORD.

YOU WERE WEAK. LOOK AT WHAT YOU'VE BECOME NOW. YOU OWE ME EVERYTHING.

THE PAIN YOU KNEW WAS NOTHING BEFORE I SHOWED YOU WHAT REAL PAIN WAS.

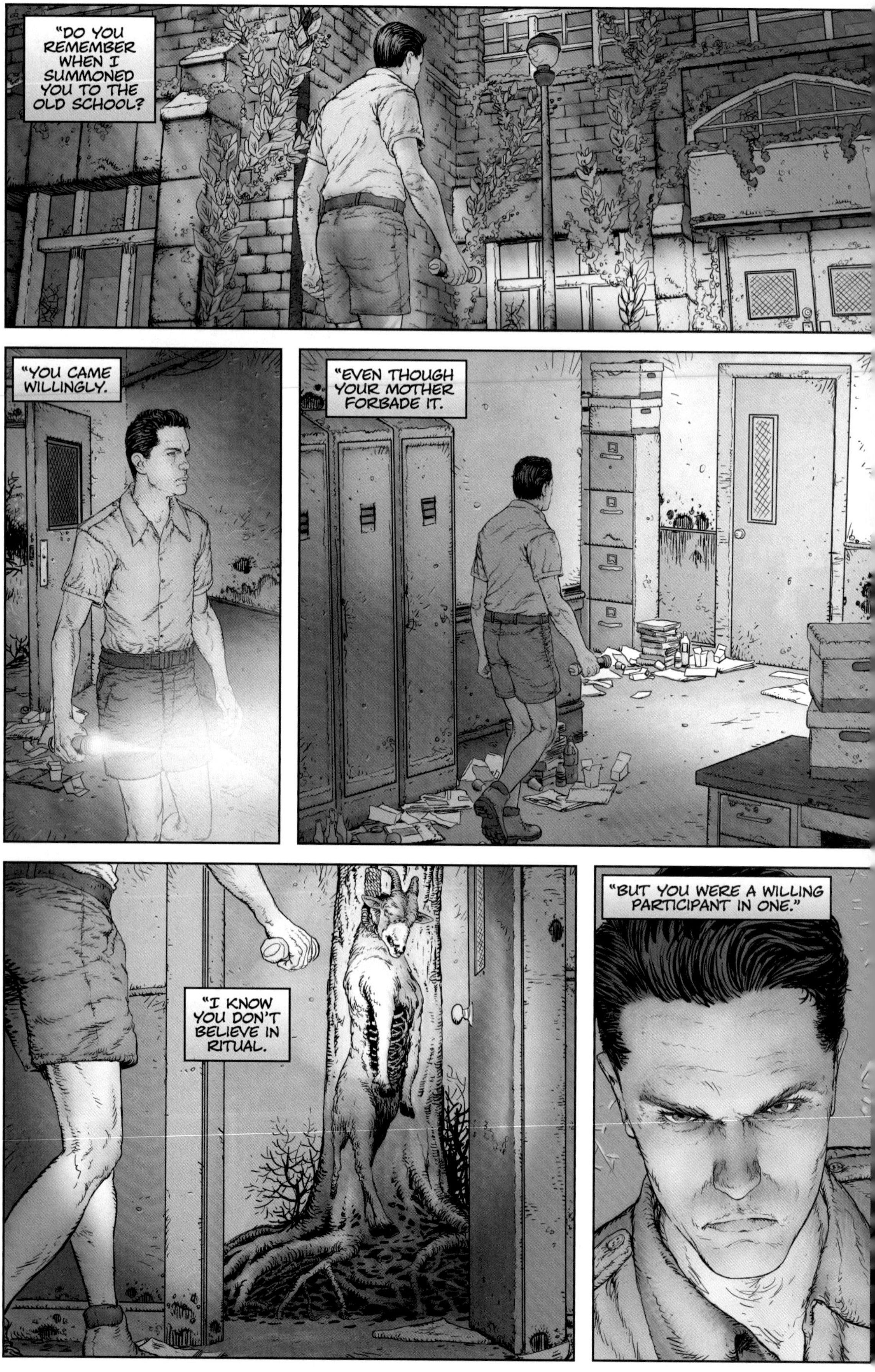
"DO YOU REMEMBER WHEN I SUMMONED YOU TO THE OLD SCHOOL?
"YOU CAME WILLINGLY.
"EVEN THOUGH YOUR MOTHER FORBADE IT.
"I KNOW YOU DON'T BELIEVE IN RITUAL.
"BUT YOU WERE A WILLING PARTICIPANT IN ONE."

"*THINK*. MARK, YOU'RE A MAN NOW.

"A WEAPON TO BE FEARED."

JESUS...

"A WEAPON MUST BE BEATEN FROM THE RAW INTO A SMOOTH, SHARP INSTRUMENT OF DEATH.

"FORGED IN THE CRUCIBLE FIRE TO BECOME HARD.

"YOUR MOTHER NEVER DID ANYTHING BUT HIDE YOU. SHE GAVE YOU A USELESS JOB TO WASTE YOUR TIME WITH.

"YOU MAY RESENT WHAT I DID TO YOU..."

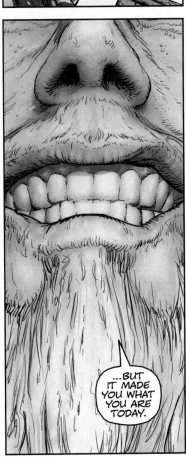

...BUT IT MADE YOU WHAT YOU ARE TODAY.

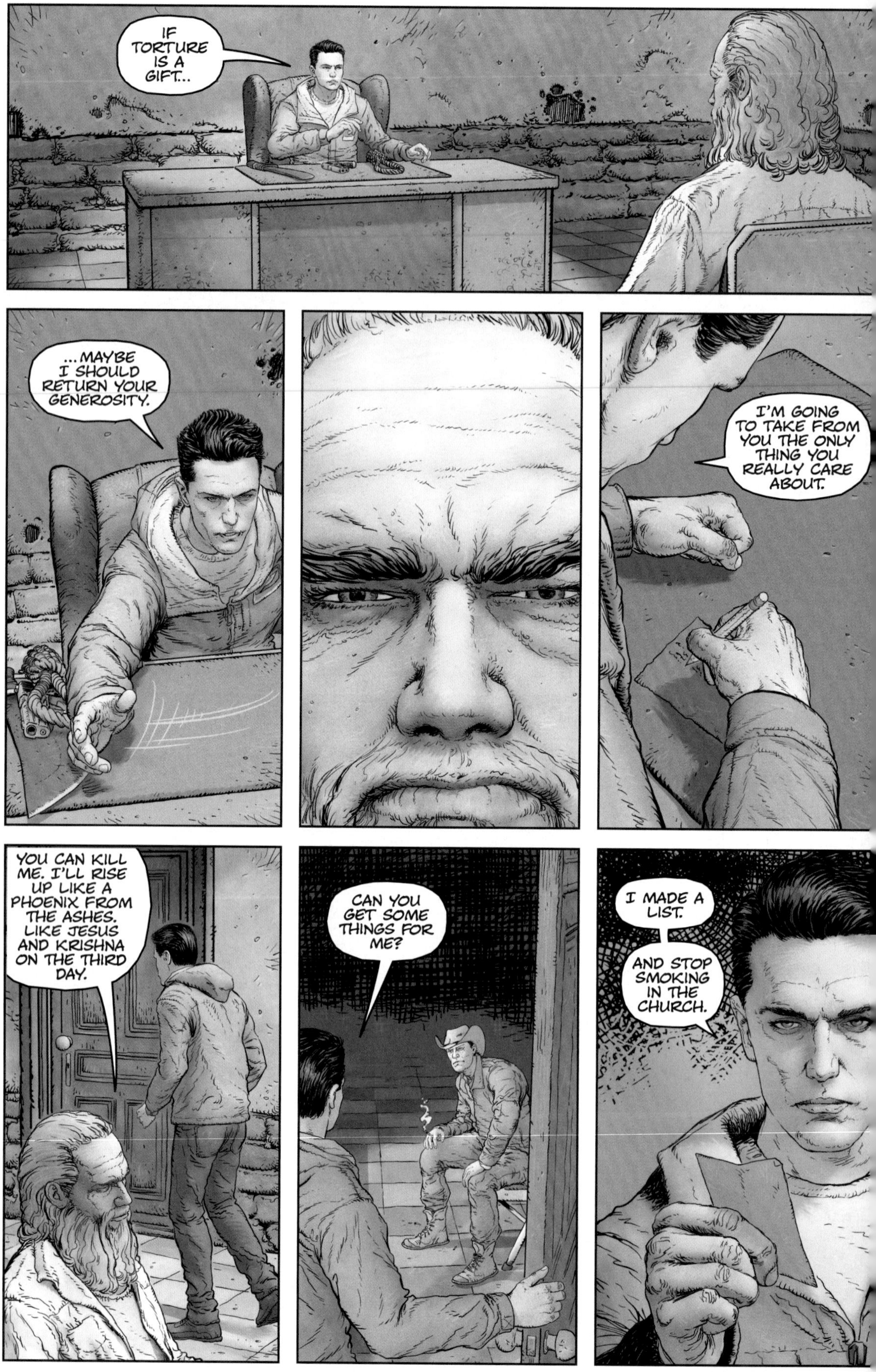
IF TORTURE IS A GIFT...
...MAYBE I SHOULD RETURN YOUR GENEROSITY.
I'M GOING TO TAKE FROM YOU THE ONLY THING YOU REALLY CARE ABOUT.
YOU CAN KILL ME. I'LL RISE UP LIKE A PHOENIX FROM THE ASHES. LIKE JESUS AND KRISHNA ON THE THIRD DAY.
CAN YOU GET SOME THINGS FOR ME?
I MADE A LIST.
AND STOP SMOKING IN THE CHURCH.

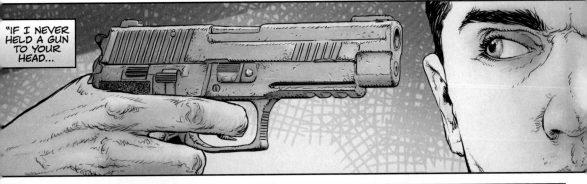

"IF I NEVER HELD A GUN TO YOUR HEAD..."

"YOU'D STILL BE YOUR MOM'S LITTLE BITCH BOY RUNNING ERRANDS FOR HER. EVERYONE WOULD STILL CALL YOU A RETARD."

YOU NEVER ACTUALLY POINTED A GUN AT ME. YOU HAD OTHER PEOPLE DO IT...AND YOU'RE THE ONLY ONE WHO CALLS ME THAT.

MARK, YOU CAN KILL ME. I DESERVE IT. I ONLY DID WHAT I DID BECAUSE I LOVE YOU.

YOUR MOTHER NEVER LOVED YOU. SHE WANTED TO ABORT YOU. WHEN I WOULDN'T LET HER MURDER YOU, SHE TOOK SOME MEDICATION TO TRY AND FORCE A MISCARRIAGE.

"I'VE OFTEN WONDERED IF THAT CAUSED YOUR ASPERGER'S."

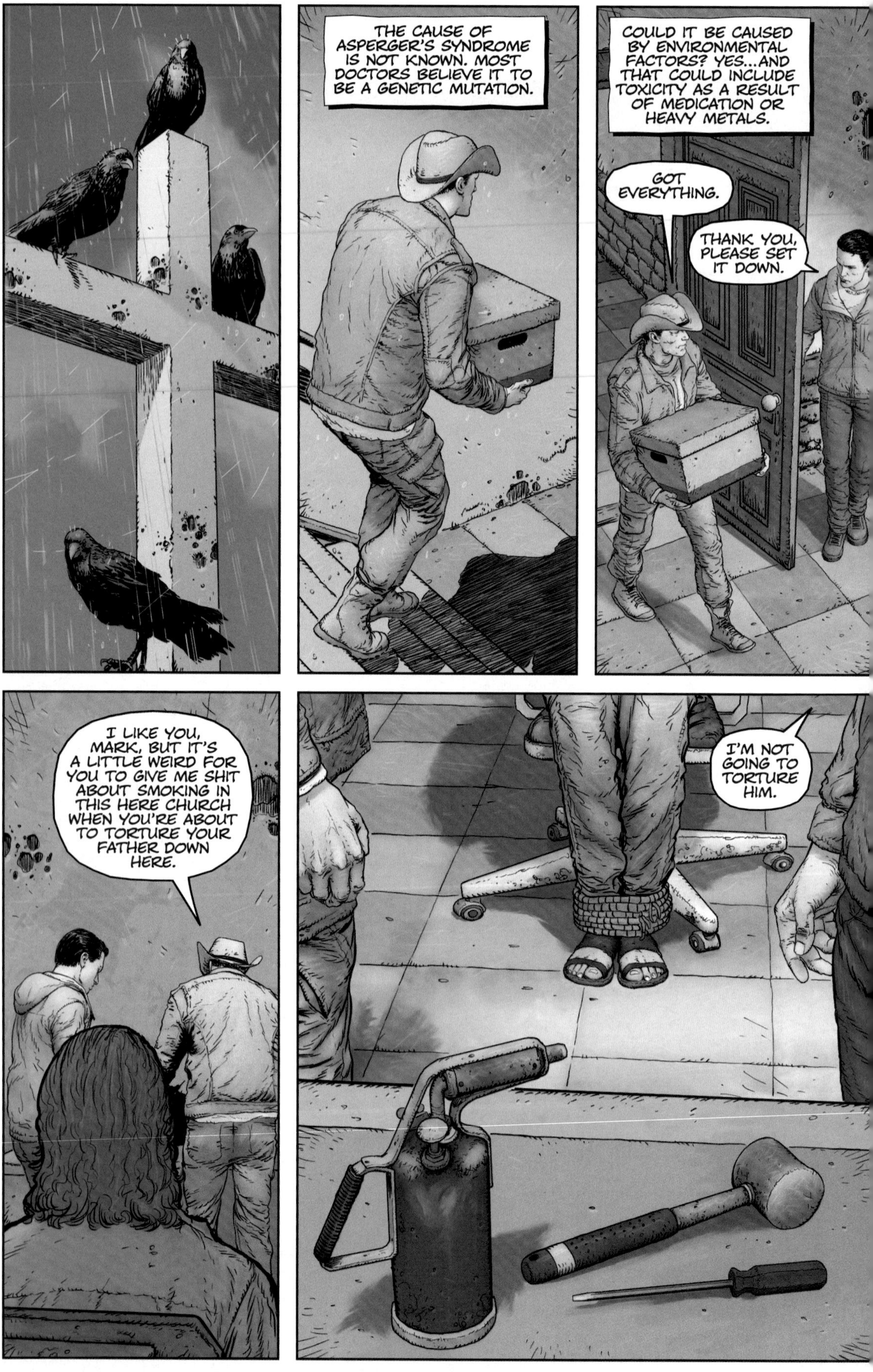
THE CAUSE OF ASPERGER'S SYNDROME IS NOT KNOWN. MOST DOCTORS BELIEVE IT TO BE A GENETIC MUTATION.
COULD IT BE CAUSED BY ENVIRONMENTAL FACTORS? YES...AND THAT COULD INCLUDE TOXICITY AS A RESULT OF MEDICATION OR HEAVY METALS.
GOT EVERYTHING.
THANK YOU, PLEASE SET IT DOWN.
I LIKE YOU, MARK, BUT IT'S A LITTLE WEIRD FOR YOU TO GIVE ME SHIT ABOUT SMOKING IN THIS HERE CHURCH WHEN YOU'RE ABOUT TO TORTURE YOUR FATHER DOWN HERE.
I'M NOT GOING TO TORTURE HIM.

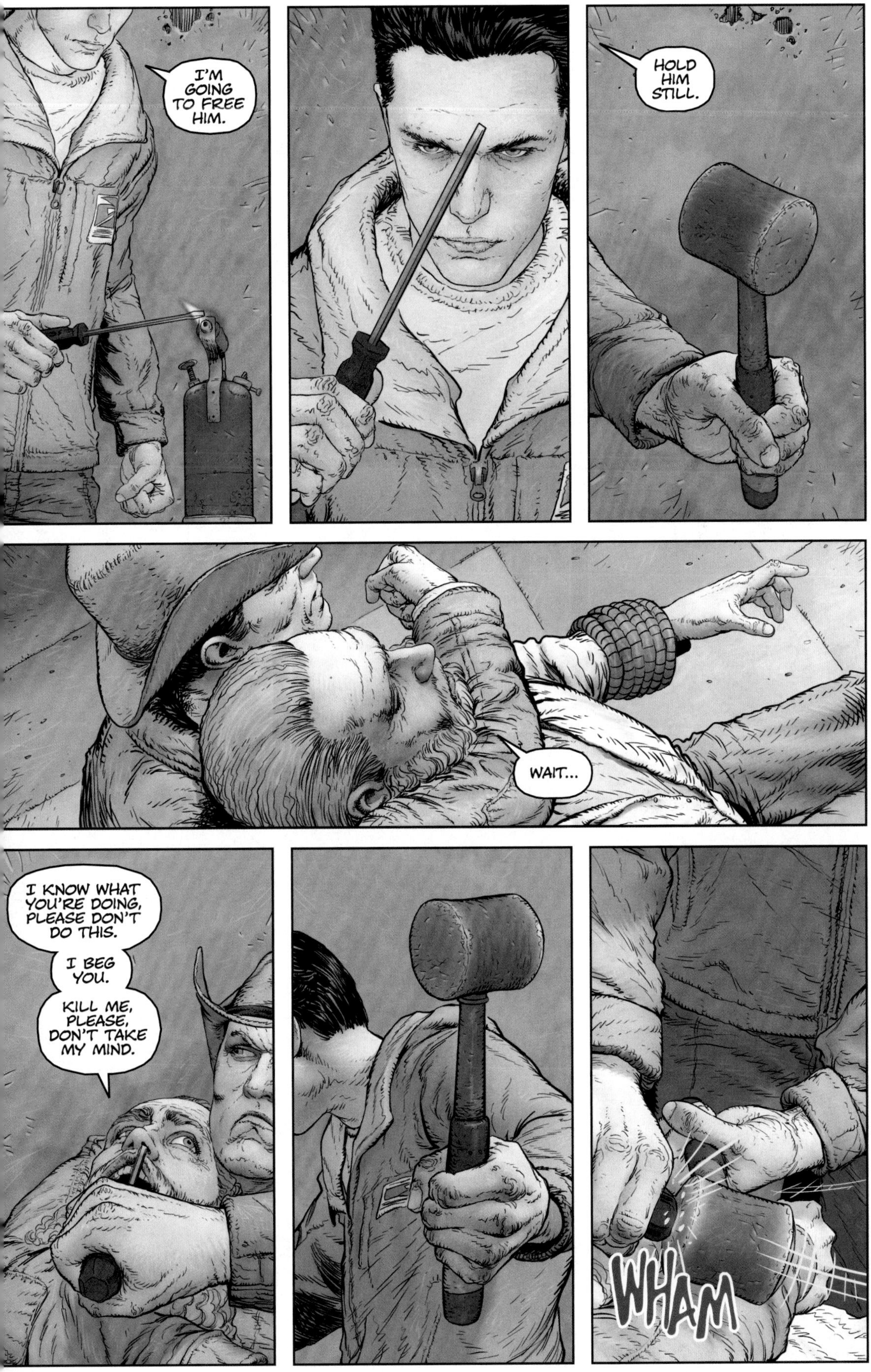
I'M GOING TO FREE HIM.
HOLD HIM STILL.
WAIT...
I KNOW WHAT YOU'RE DOING, PLEASE DON'T DO THIS.
I BEG YOU.
KILL ME, PLEASE, DON'T TAKE MY MIND.
WHAM

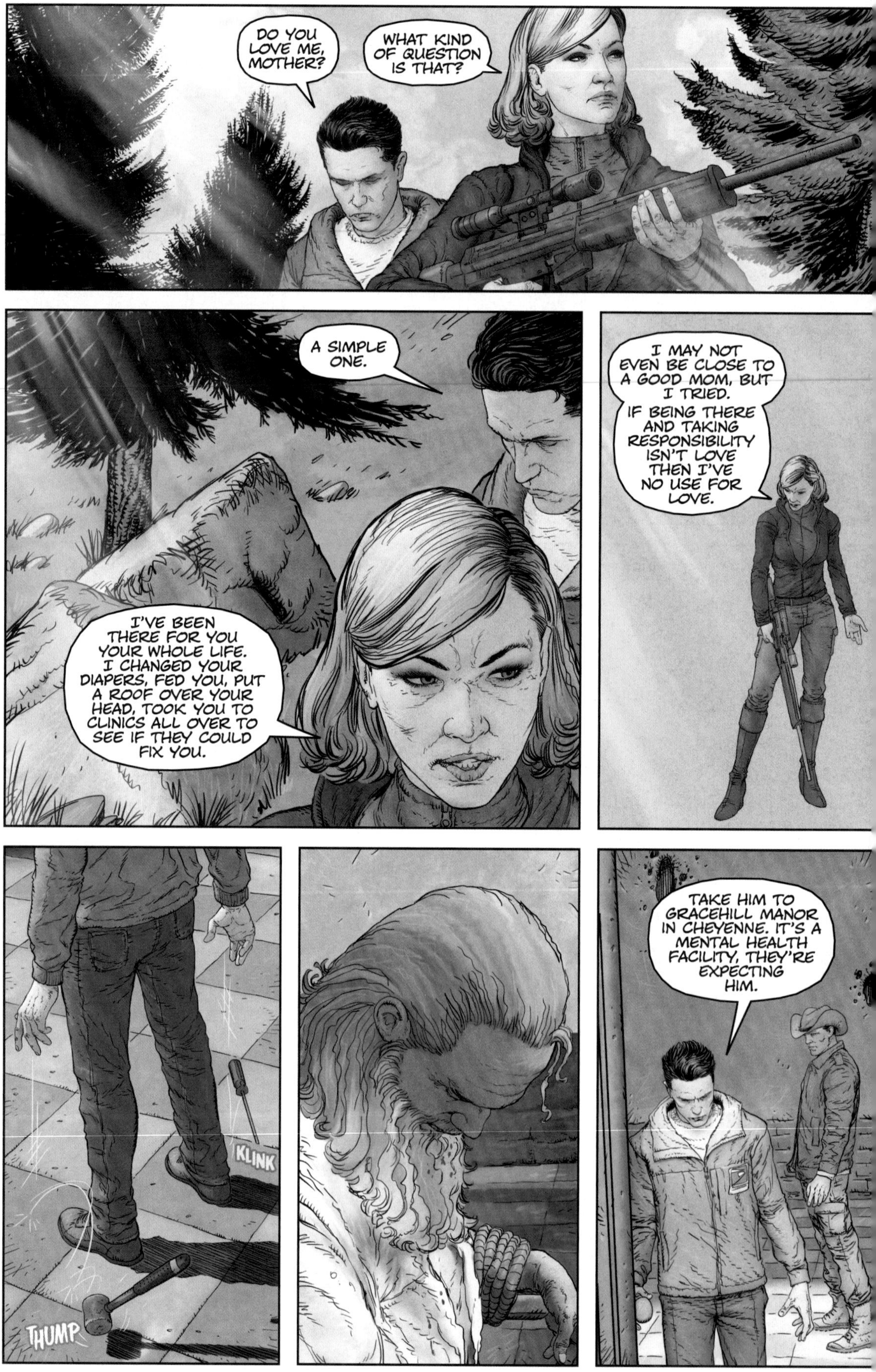
DO YOU LOVE ME, MOTHER?
WHAT KIND OF QUESTION IS THAT?
A SIMPLE ONE.
I'VE BEEN THERE FOR YOU YOUR WHOLE LIFE. I CHANGED YOUR DIAPERS, FED YOU, PUT A ROOF OVER YOUR HEAD, TOOK YOU TO CLINICS ALL OVER TO SEE IF THEY COULD FIX YOU.
I MAY NOT EVEN BE CLOSE TO A GOOD MOM, BUT I TRIED.
IF BEING THERE AND TAKING RESPONSIBILITY ISN'T LOVE THEN I'VE NO USE FOR LOVE.
KLINK
THUMP
TAKE HIM TO GRACEHILL MANOR IN CHEYENNE. IT'S A MENTAL HEALTH FACILITY, THEY'RE EXPECTING HIM.

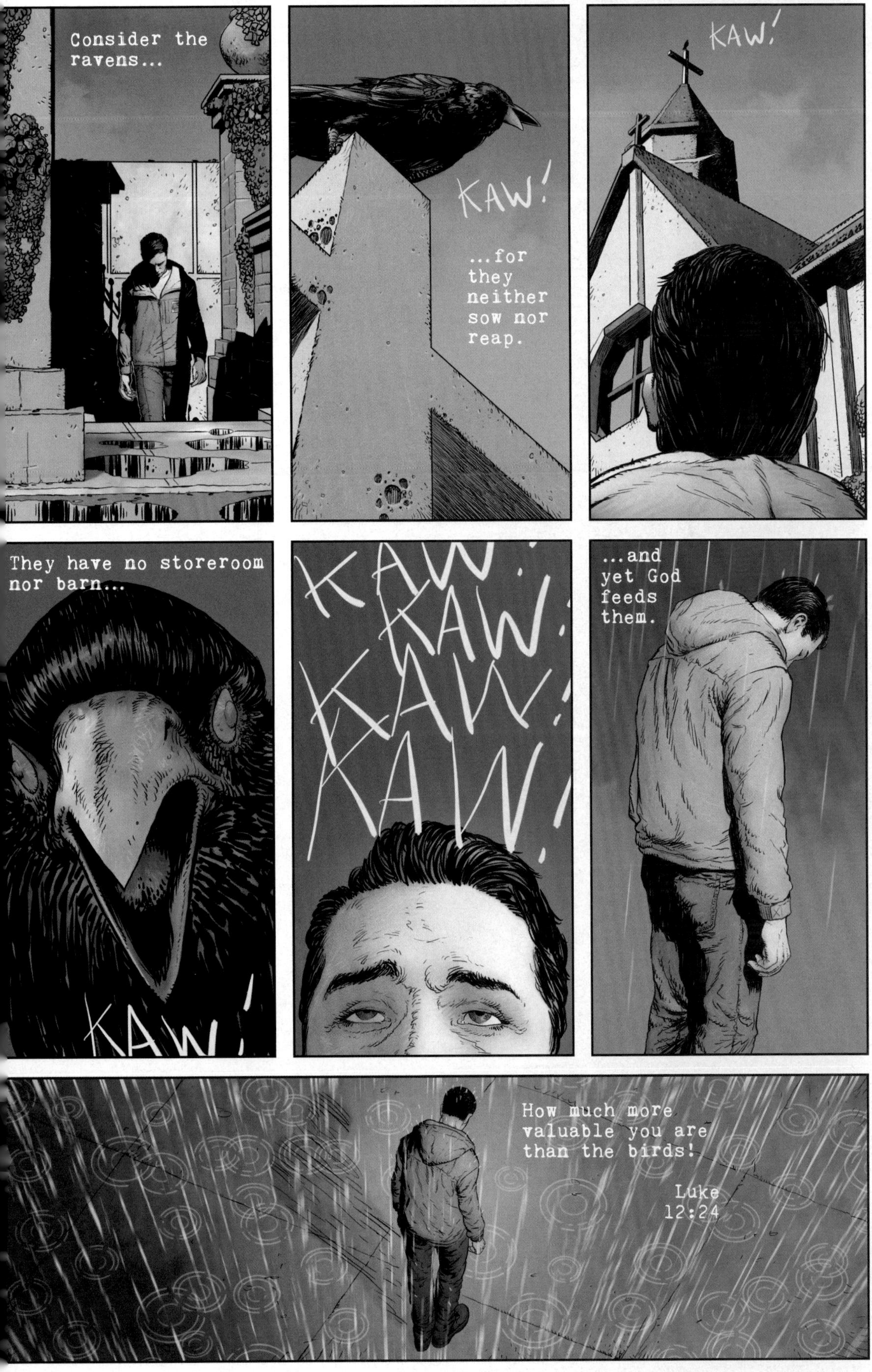
Consider the ravens...
KAW!
...for they neither sow nor reap.
KAW!
They have no storeroom nor barn...
KAW!
KAW! KAW! KAW! KAW!
...and yet God feeds them.
How much more valuable you are than the birds!
Luke 12:24

# POSTAL: LAURA

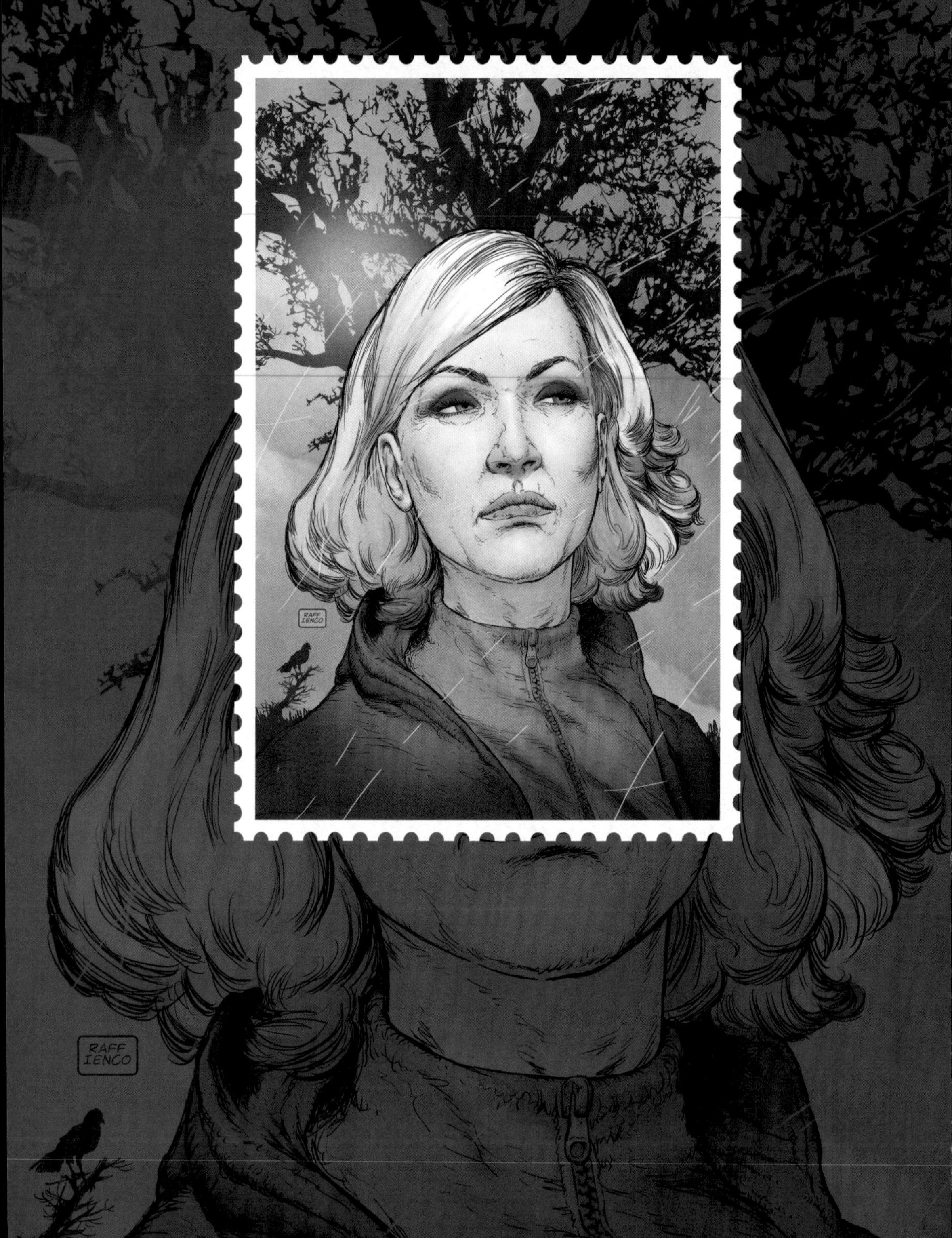
RAFF IENCO
RAFF IENCO

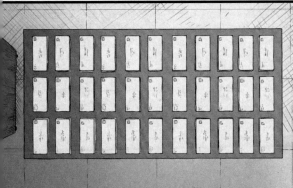

"MARK. WAKE UP.

"MAYORS CAN'T SLEEP IN.

"AND TODAY IS A SPECIAL DAY FOR EDEN."

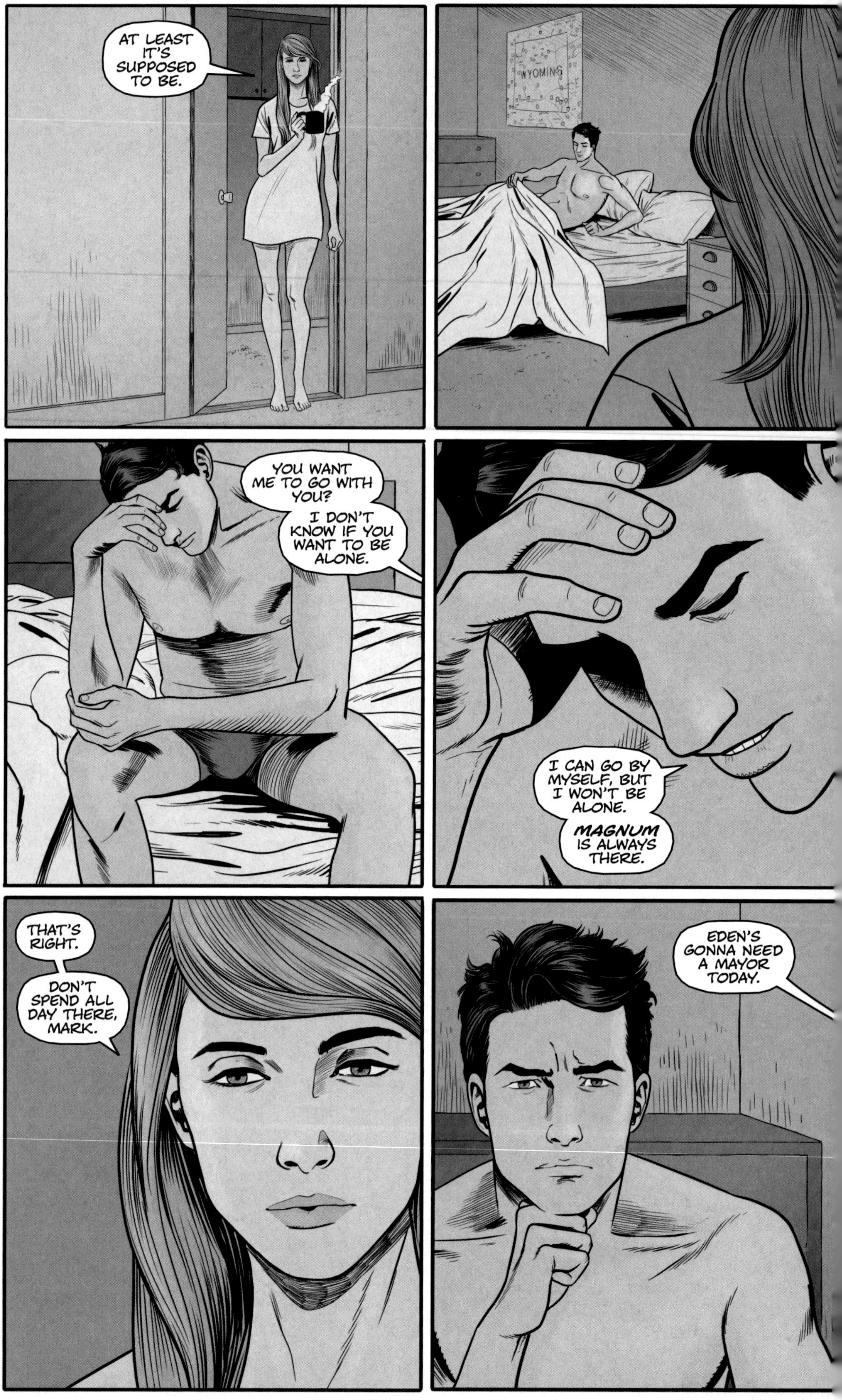
AT LEAST IT'S SUPPOSED TO BE.
WYOMING
YOU WANT ME TO GO WITH YOU?
I DON'T KNOW IF YOU WANT TO BE ALONE.
I CAN GO BY MYSELF, BUT I WON'T BE ALONE.
MAGNUM IS ALWAYS THERE.
THAT'S RIGHT.
DON'T SPEND ALL DAY THERE, MARK.
EDEN'S GONNA NEED A MAYOR TODAY.

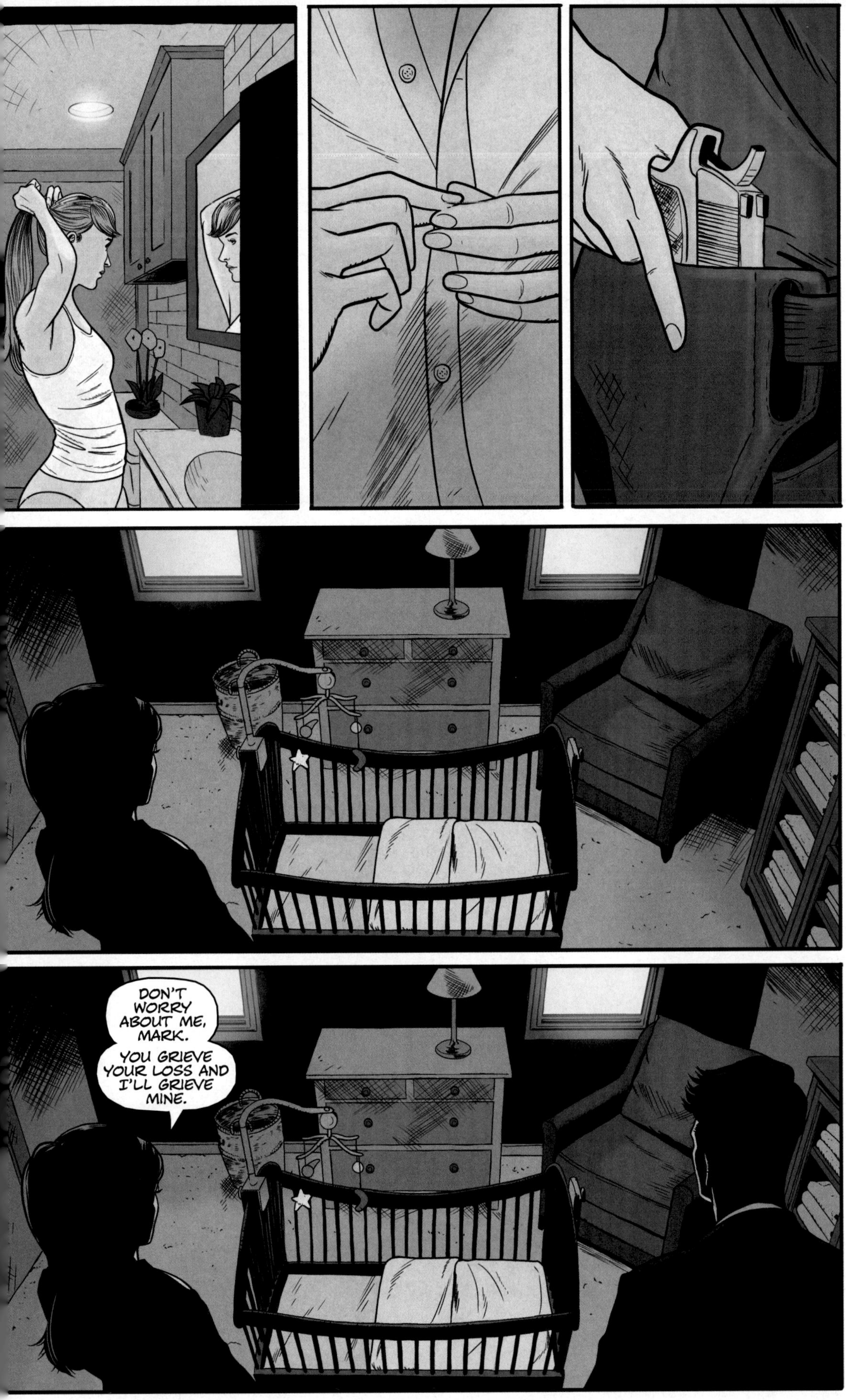
DON'T WORRY ABOUT ME, MARK.
YOU GRIEVE YOUR LOSS AND I'LL GRIEVE MINE.

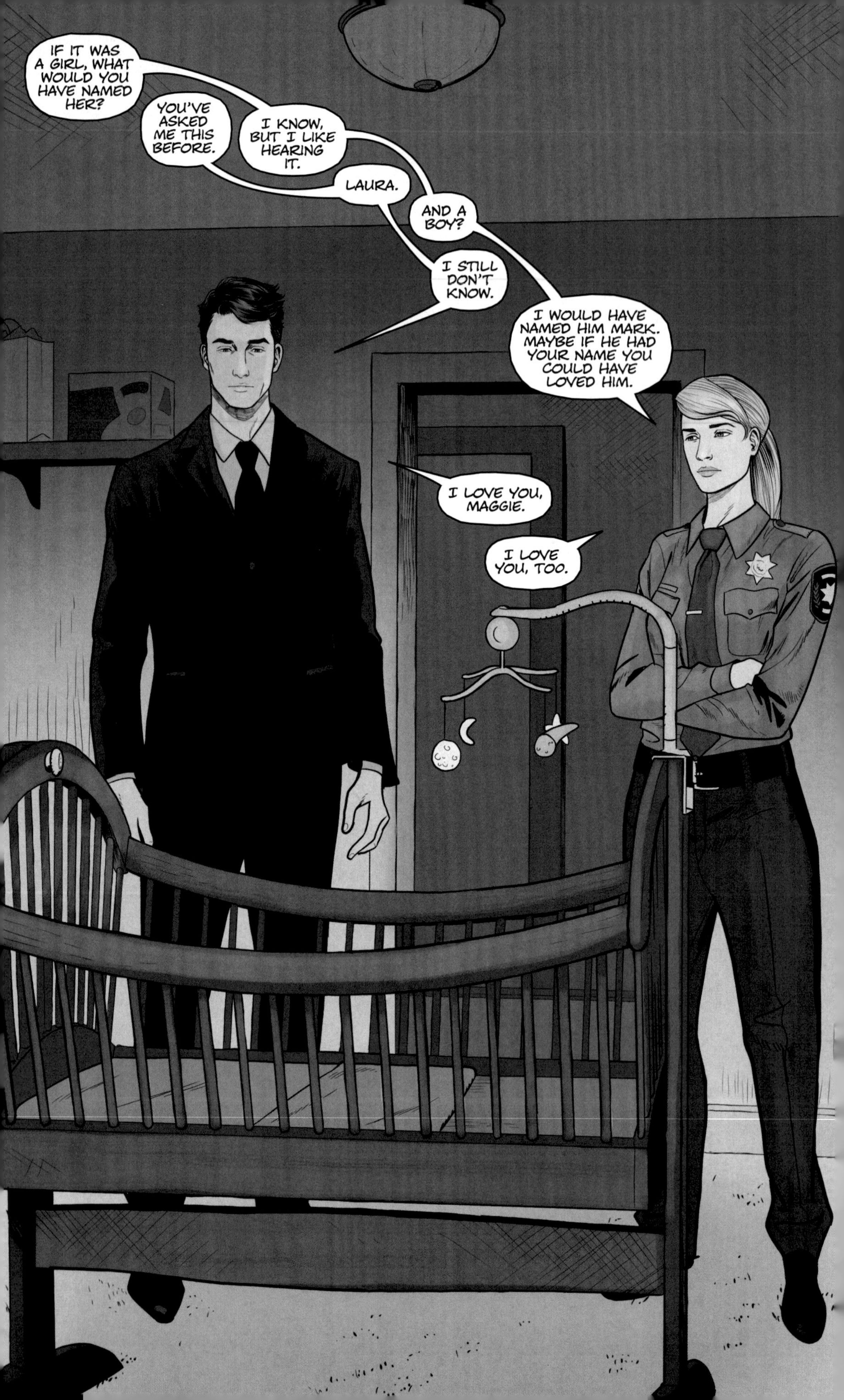
IF IT WAS A GIRL, WHAT WOULD YOU HAVE NAMED HER?
YOU'VE ASKED ME THIS BEFORE.
I KNOW, BUT I LIKE HEARING IT.
LAURA.
AND A BOY?
I STILL DON'T KNOW.
I WOULD HAVE NAMED HIM MARK. MAYBE IF HE HAD YOUR NAME YOU COULD HAVE LOVED HIM.
I LOVE YOU, MAGGIE.
I LOVE YOU, TOO.

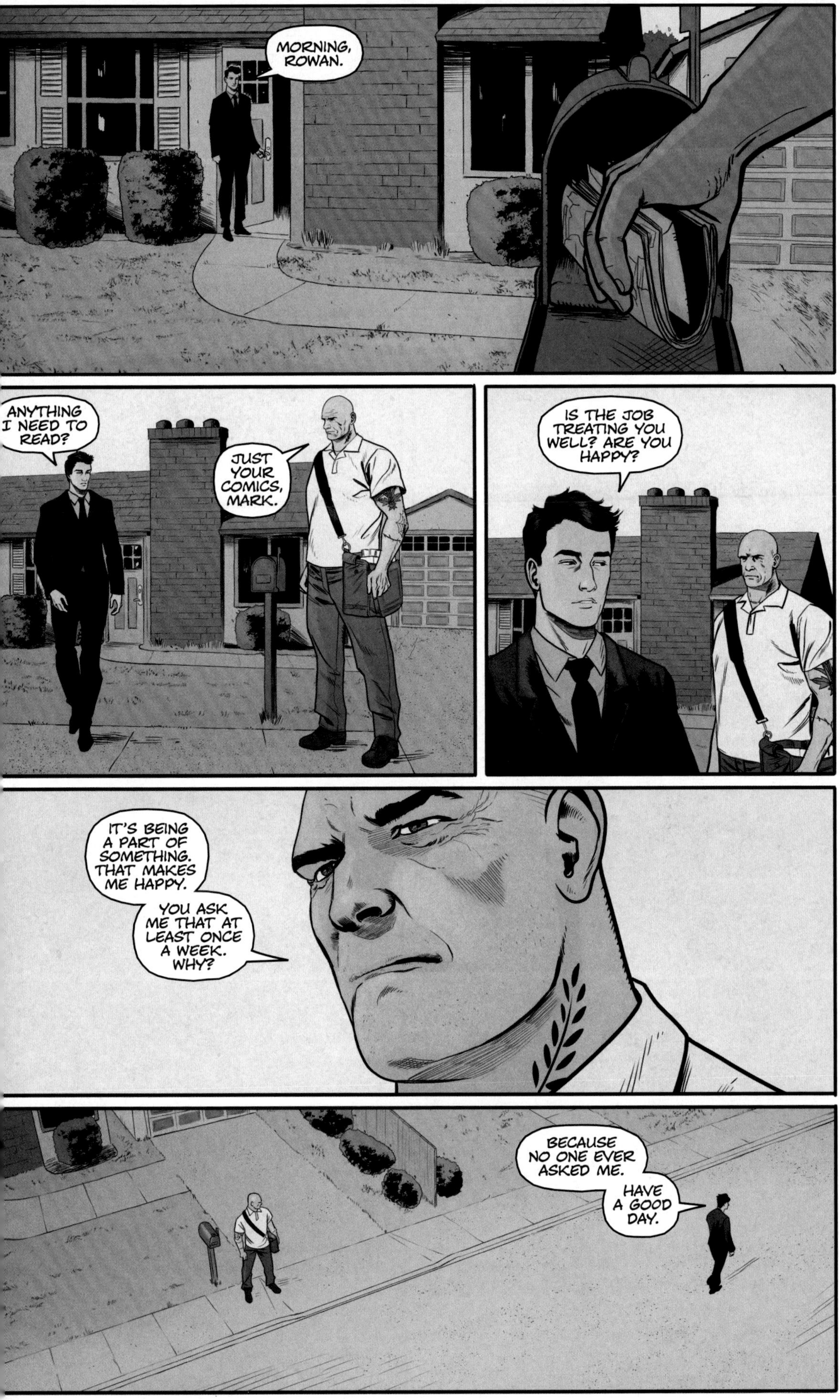
MORNING, ROWAN.
ANYTHING I NEED TO READ?
JUST YOUR COMICS, MARK.
IS THE JOB TREATING YOU WELL? ARE YOU HAPPY?
IT'S BEING A PART OF SOMETHING. THAT MAKES ME HAPPY.
YOU ASK ME THAT AT LEAST ONCE A WEEK. WHY?
BECAUSE NO ONE EVER ASKED ME.
HAVE A GOOD DAY.

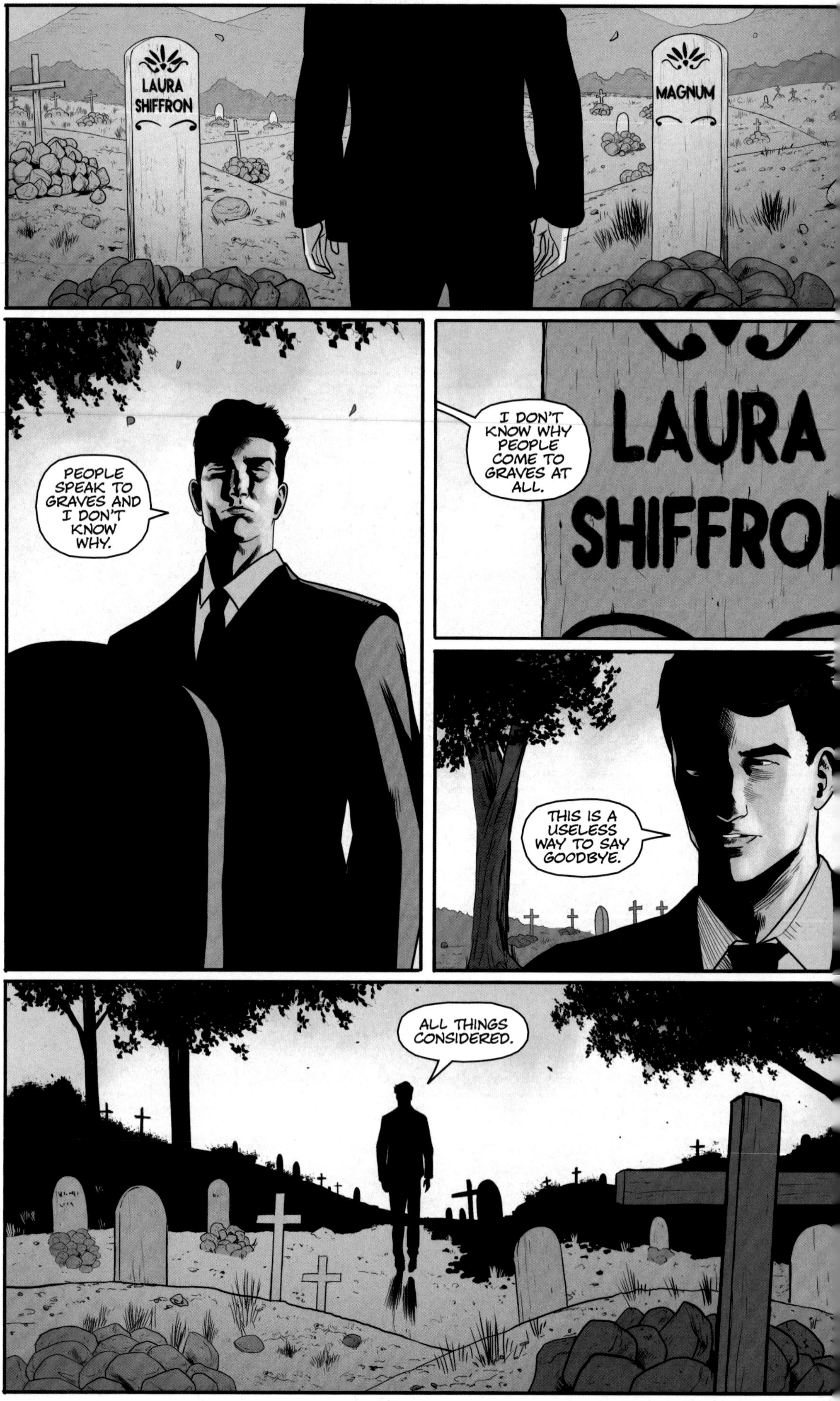
LAURA SHIFFRON
MAGNUM
PEOPLE SPEAK TO GRAVES AND I DON'T KNOW WHY.
LAURA SHIFFRO
I DON'T KNOW WHY PEOPLE COME TO GRAVES AT ALL.
THIS IS A USELESS WAY TO SAY GOODBYE.
ALL THINGS CONSIDERED.

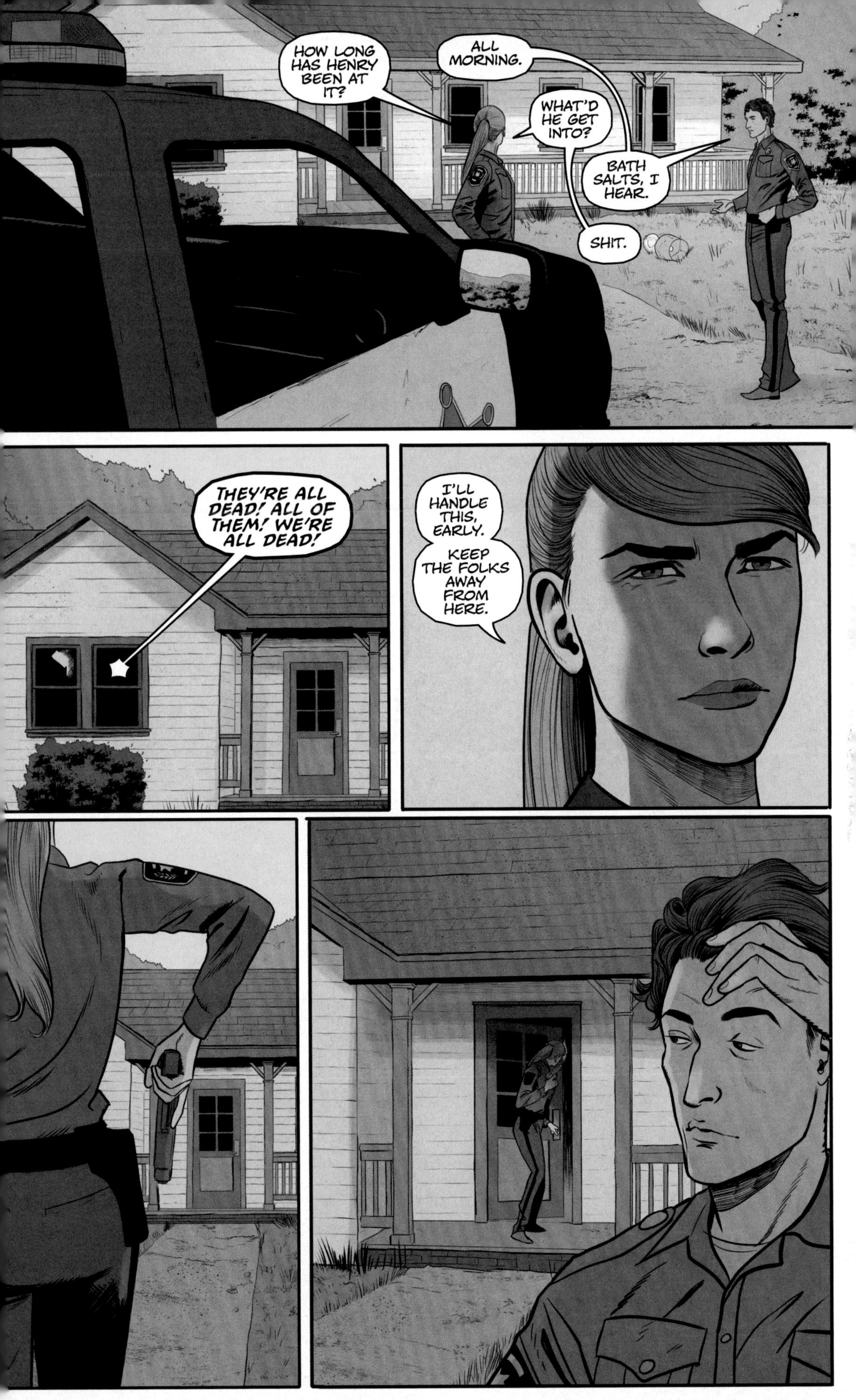
HOW LONG HAS HENRY BEEN AT IT?
ALL MORNING.
WHAT'D HE GET INTO?
BATH SALTS, I HEAR.
SHIT.
THEY'RE ALL DEAD! ALL OF THEM! WE'RE ALL DEAD!
I'LL HANDLE THIS, EARLY.
KEEP THE FOLKS AWAY FROM HERE.

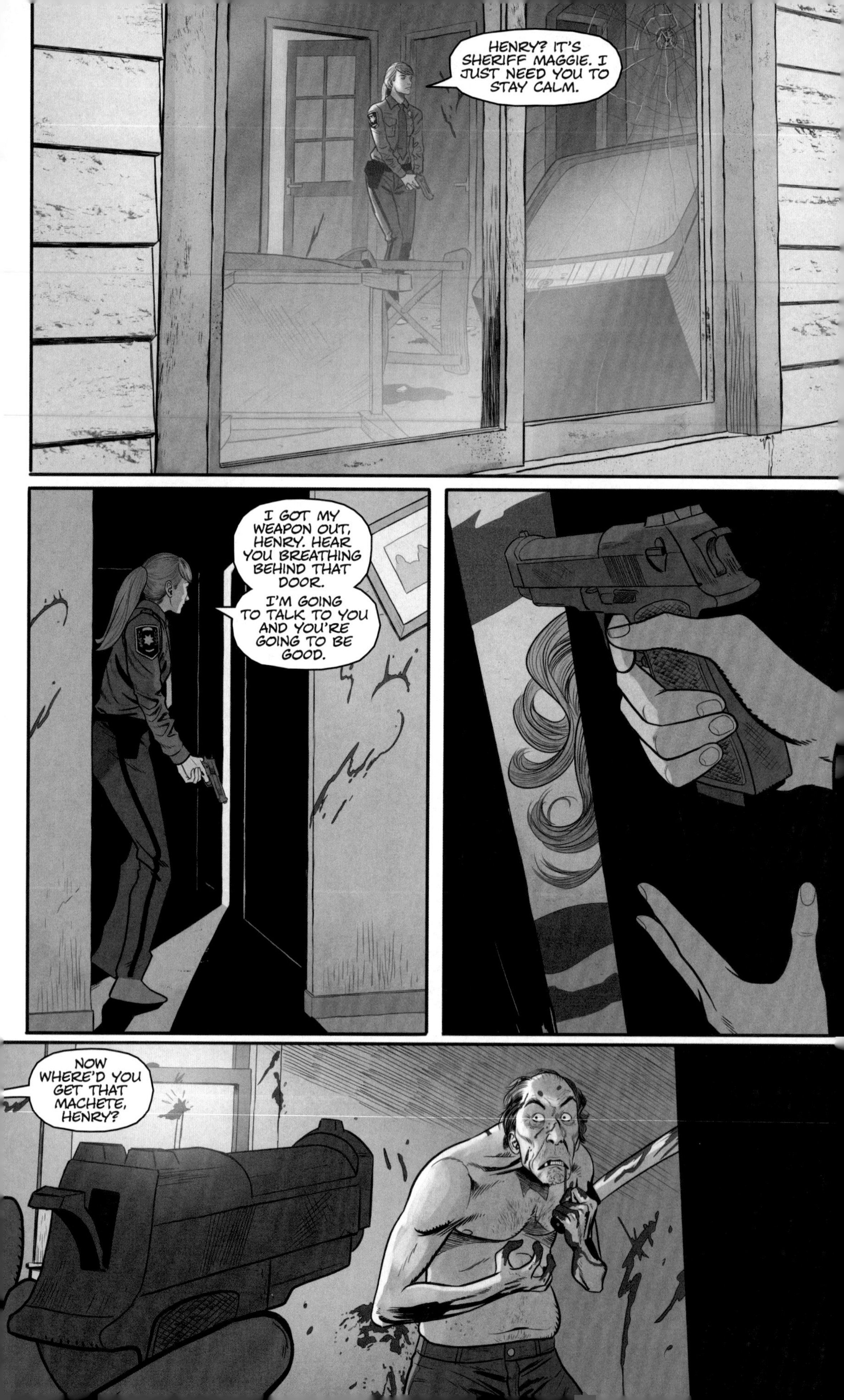
HENRY? IT'S SHERIFF MAGGIE. I JUST NEED YOU TO STAY CALM.
I GOT MY WEAPON OUT, HENRY. HEAR YOU BREATHING BEHIND THAT DOOR.
I'M GOING TO TALK TO YOU AND YOU'RE GOING TO BE GOOD.
NOW WHERE'D YOU GET THAT MACHETE, HENRY?

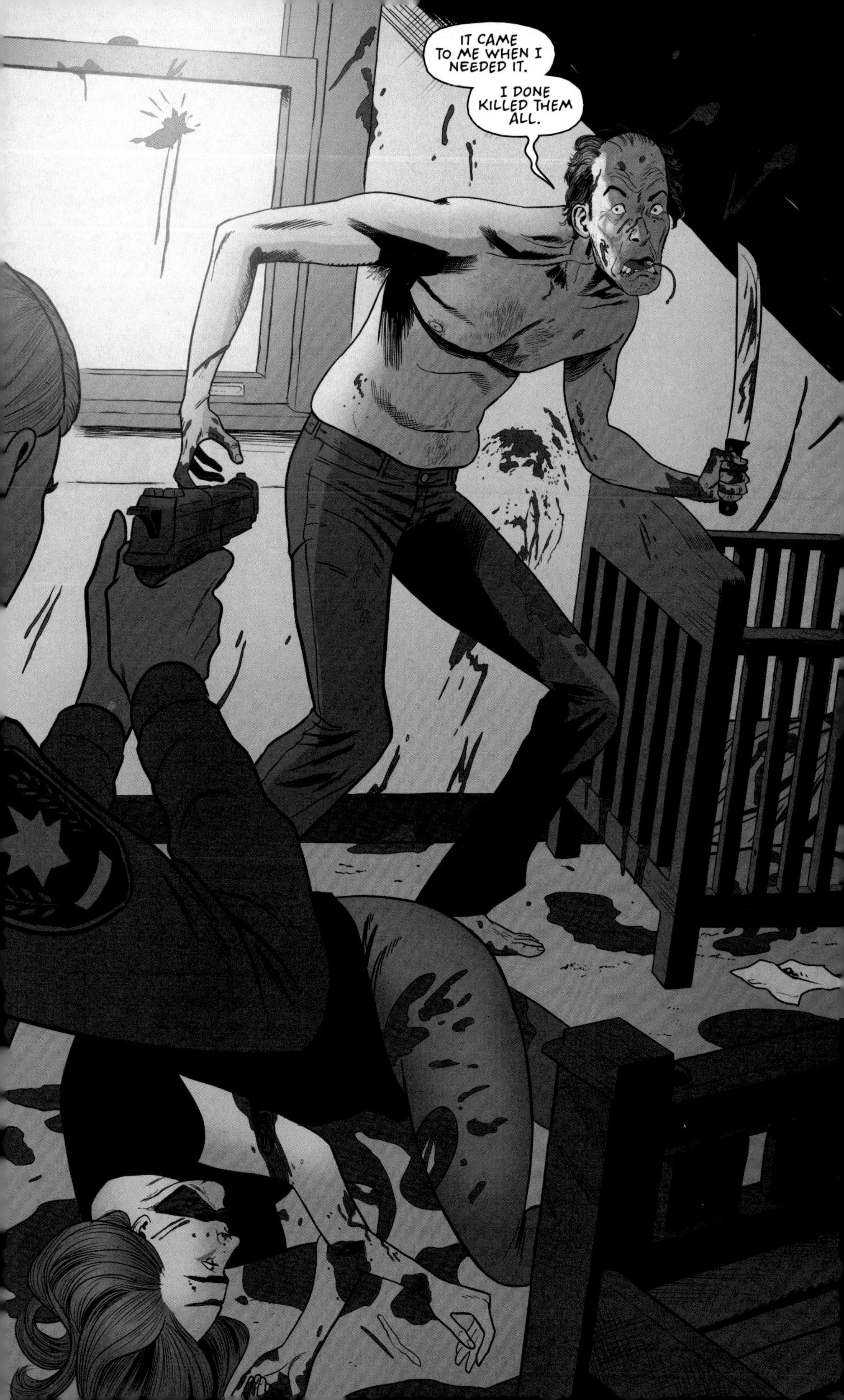
IT CAME TO ME WHEN I NEEDED IT.
I DONE KILLED THEM ALL.

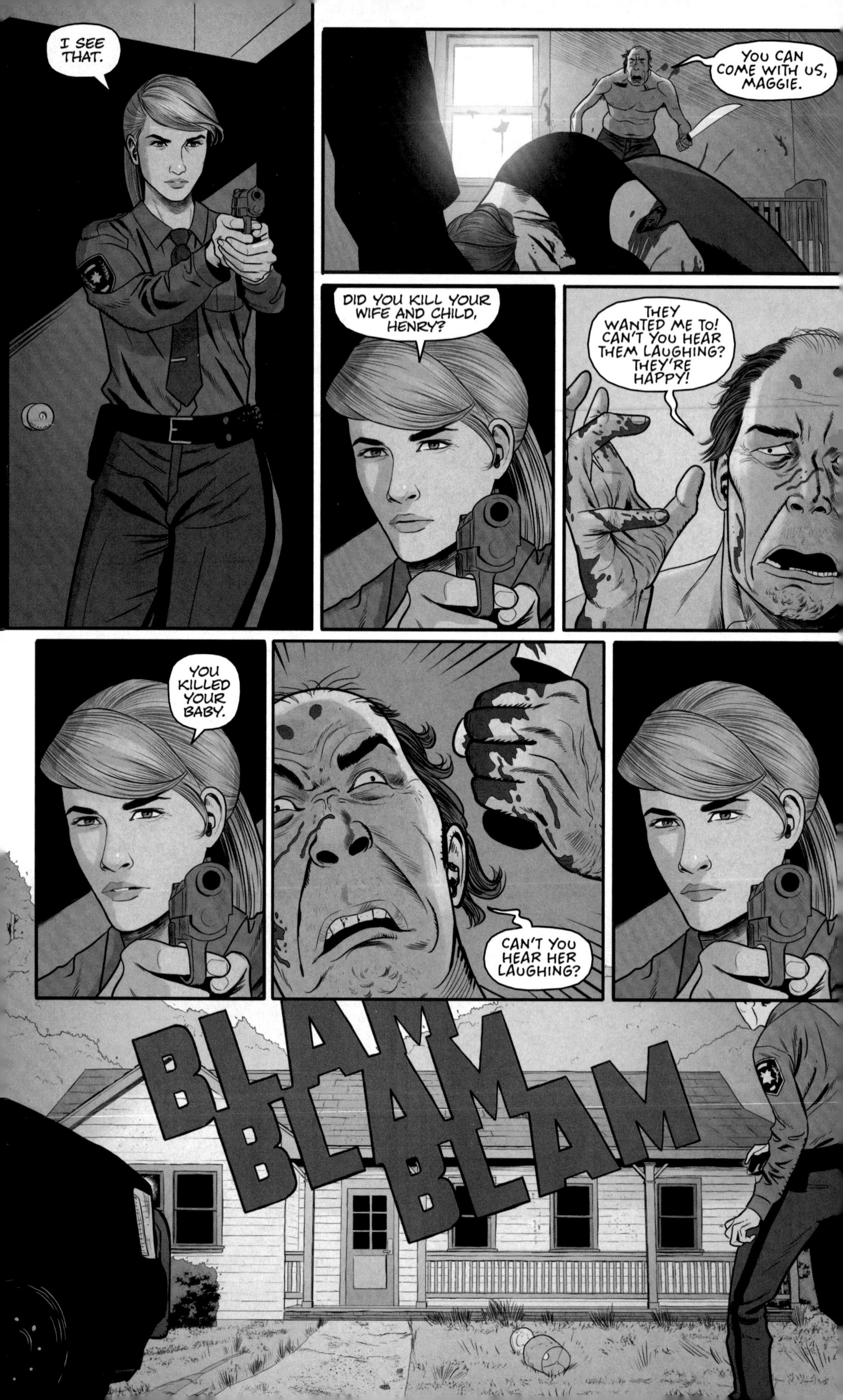
I SEE THAT.
YOU CAN COME WITH US, MAGGIE.
DID YOU KILL YOUR WIFE AND CHILD, HENRY?
THEY WANTED ME TO! CAN'T YOU HEAR THEM LAUGHING? THEY'RE HAPPY!
YOU KILLED YOUR BABY.
CAN'T YOU HEAR HER LAUGHING?
BLAM BLAM BLAM BLAM

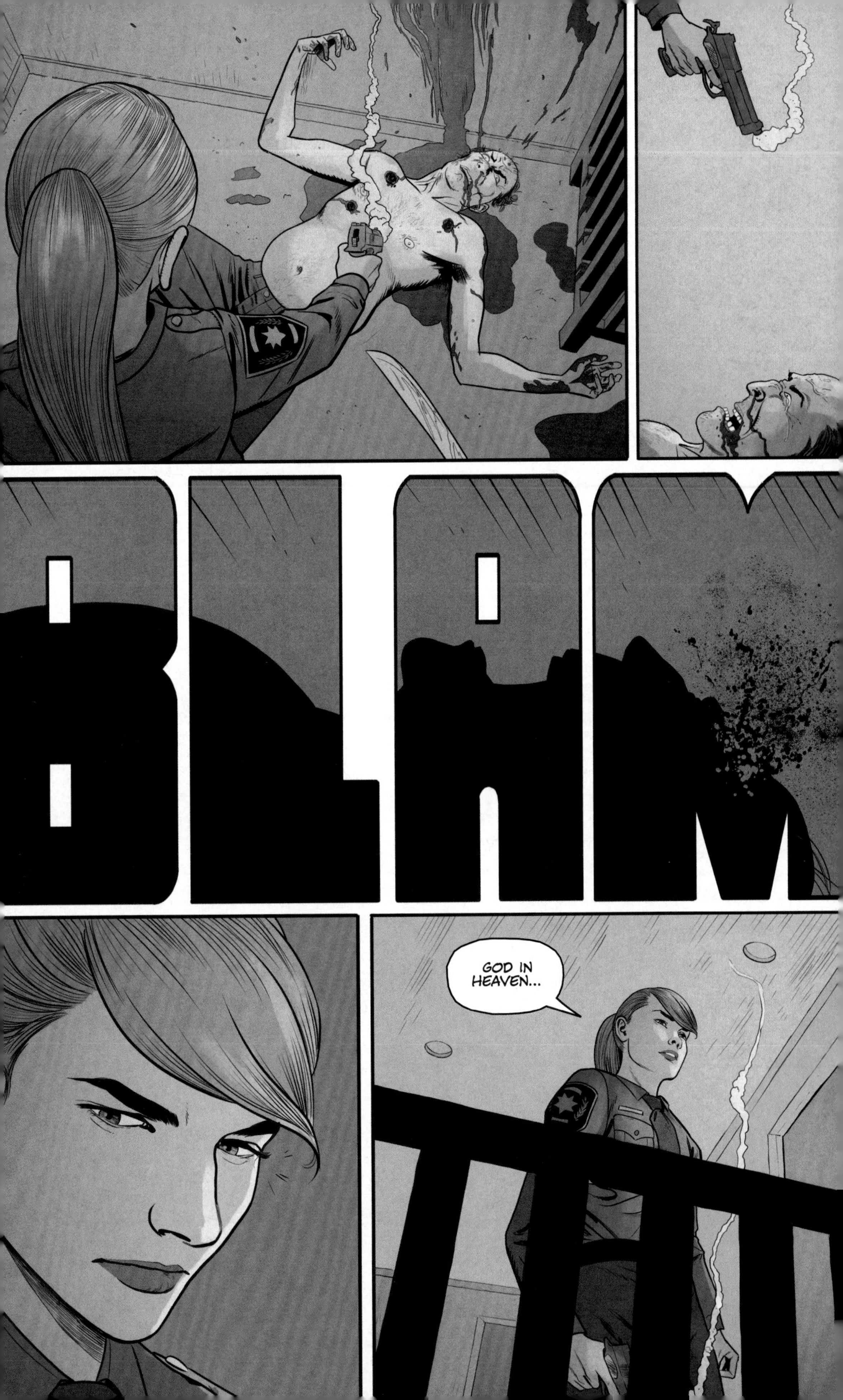
BLAM
GOD IN HEAVEN...

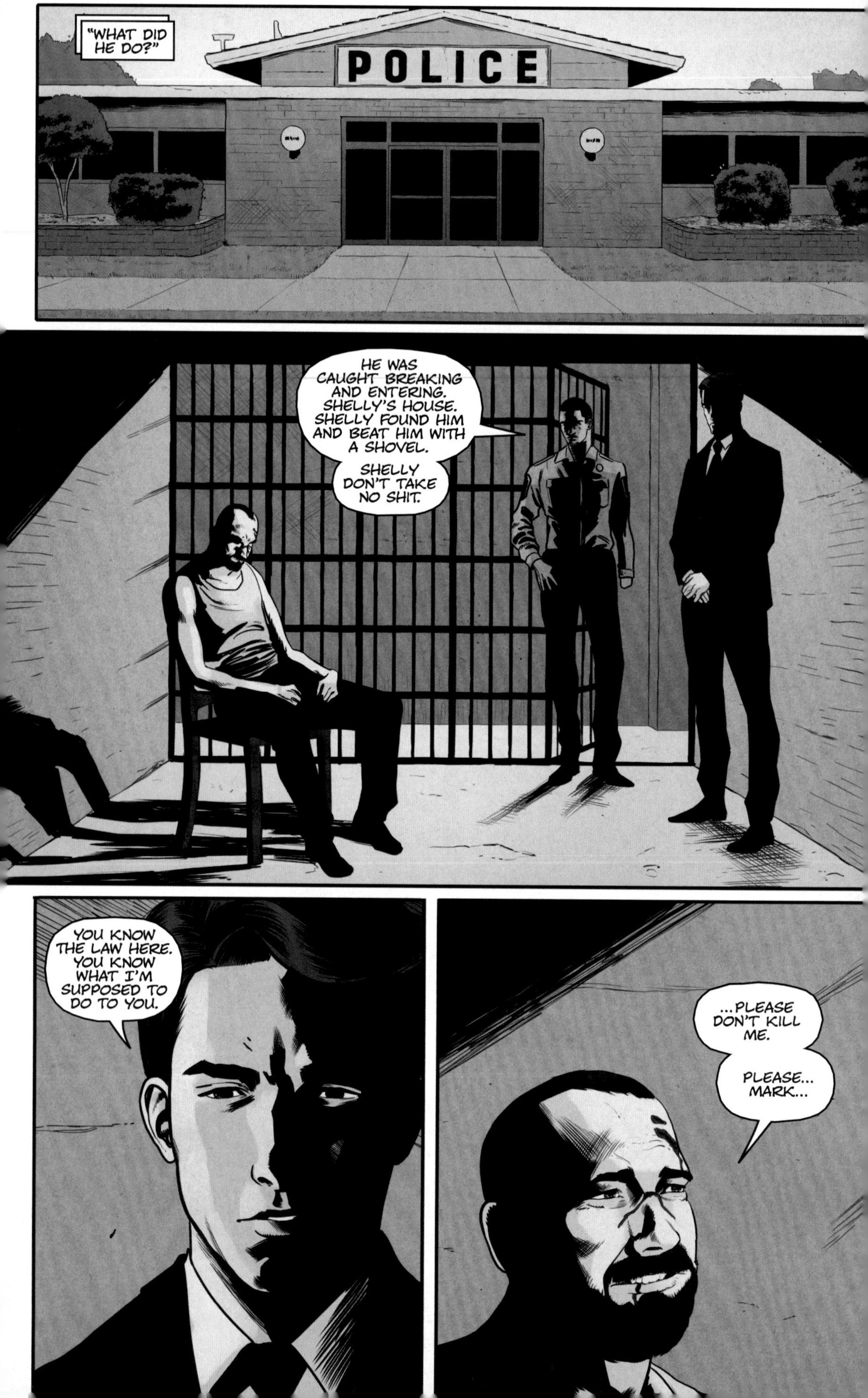
"WHAT DID HE DO?"
POLICE
HE WAS CAUGHT BREAKING AND ENTERING. SHELLY'S HOUSE. SHELLY FOUND HIM AND BEAT HIM WITH A SHOVEL.
SHELLY DON'T TAKE NO SHIT.
YOU KNOW THE LAW HERE. YOU KNOW WHAT I'M SUPPOSED TO DO TO YOU.
...PLEASE DON'T KILL ME.
PLEASE... MARK...

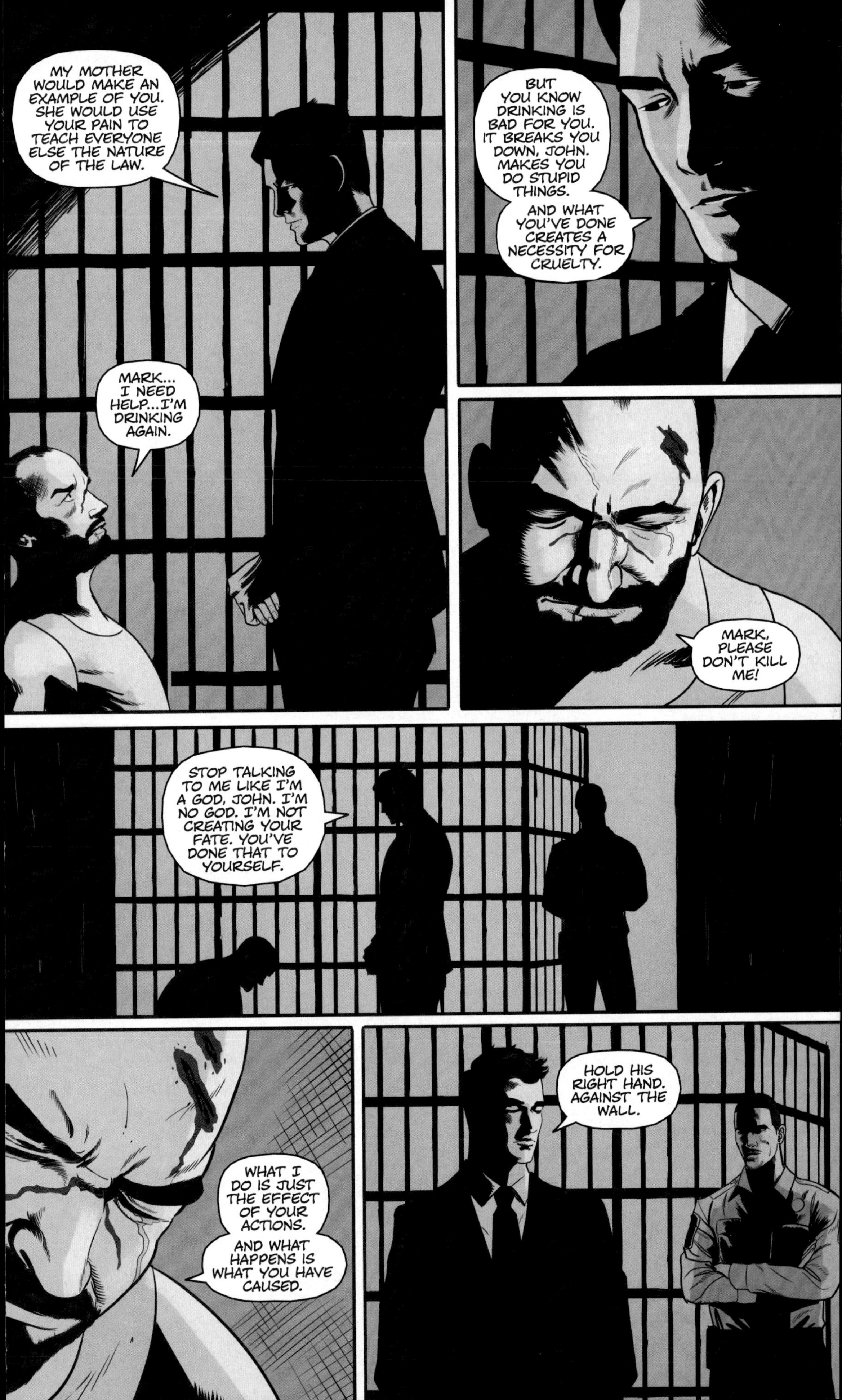
MY MOTHER WOULD MAKE AN EXAMPLE OF YOU. SHE WOULD USE YOUR PAIN TO TEACH EVERYONE ELSE THE NATURE OF THE LAW.
MARK... I NEED HELP...I'M DRINKING AGAIN.
BUT YOU KNOW DRINKING IS BAD FOR YOU. IT BREAKS YOU DOWN, JOHN. MAKES YOU DO STUPID THINGS.
AND WHAT YOU'VE DONE CREATES A NECESSITY FOR CRUELTY.
MARK, PLEASE DON'T KILL ME!
STOP TALKING TO ME LIKE I'M A GOD, JOHN. I'M NO GOD. I'M NOT CREATING YOUR FATE. YOU'VE DONE THAT TO YOURSELF.
WHAT I DO IS JUST THE EFFECT OF YOUR ACTIONS.
AND WHAT HAPPENS IS WHAT YOU HAVE CAUSED.
HOLD HIS RIGHT HAND. AGAINST THE WALL.

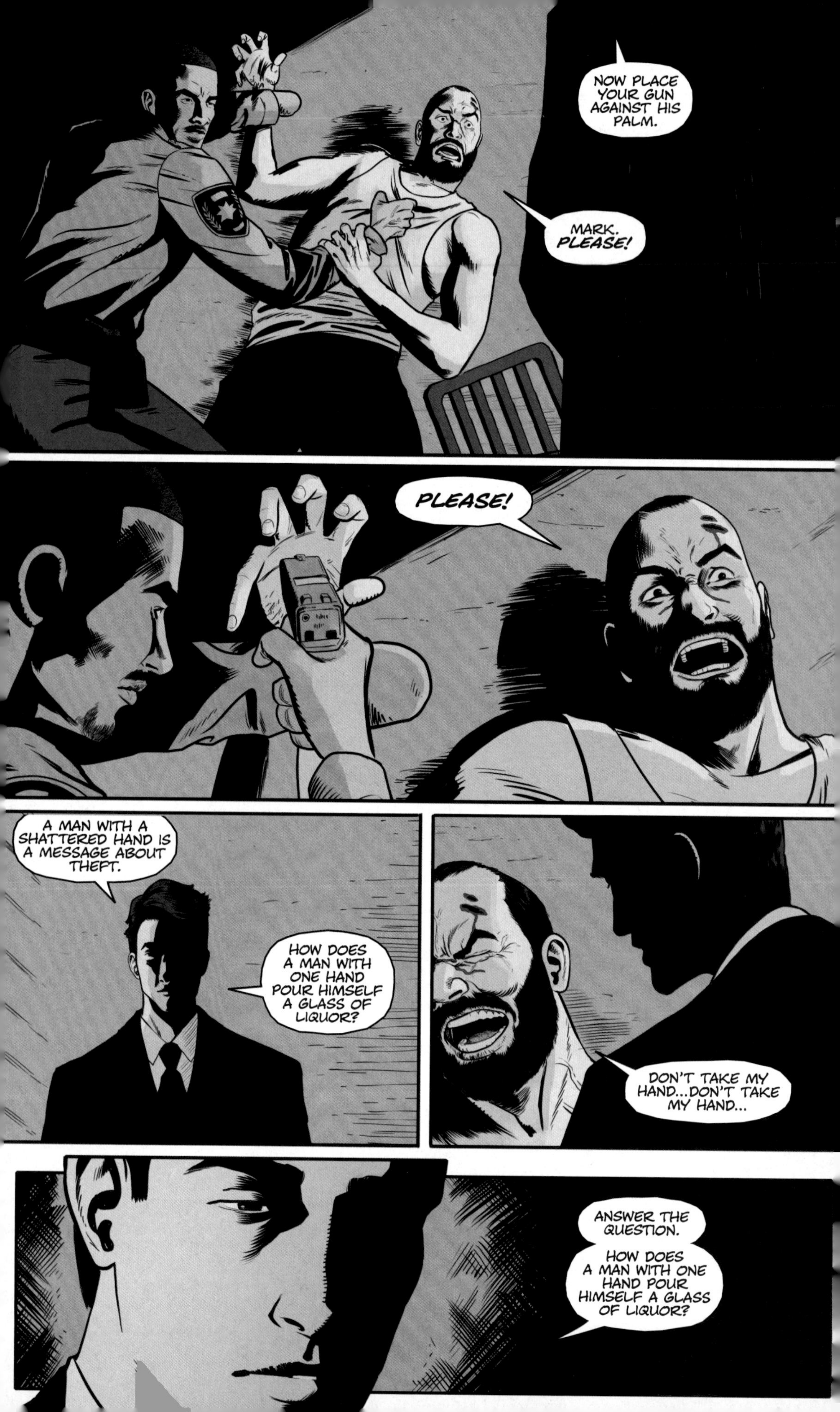
NOW PLACE YOUR GUN AGAINST HIS PALM.
MARK. PLEASE!
PLEASE!
A MAN WITH A SHATTERED HAND IS A MESSAGE ABOUT THEFT.
HOW DOES A MAN WITH ONE HAND POUR HIMSELF A GLASS OF LIQUOR?
DON'T TAKE MY HAND...DON'T TAKE MY HAND...
ANSWER THE QUESTION.
HOW DOES A MAN WITH ONE HAND POUR HIMSELF A GLASS OF LIQUOR?

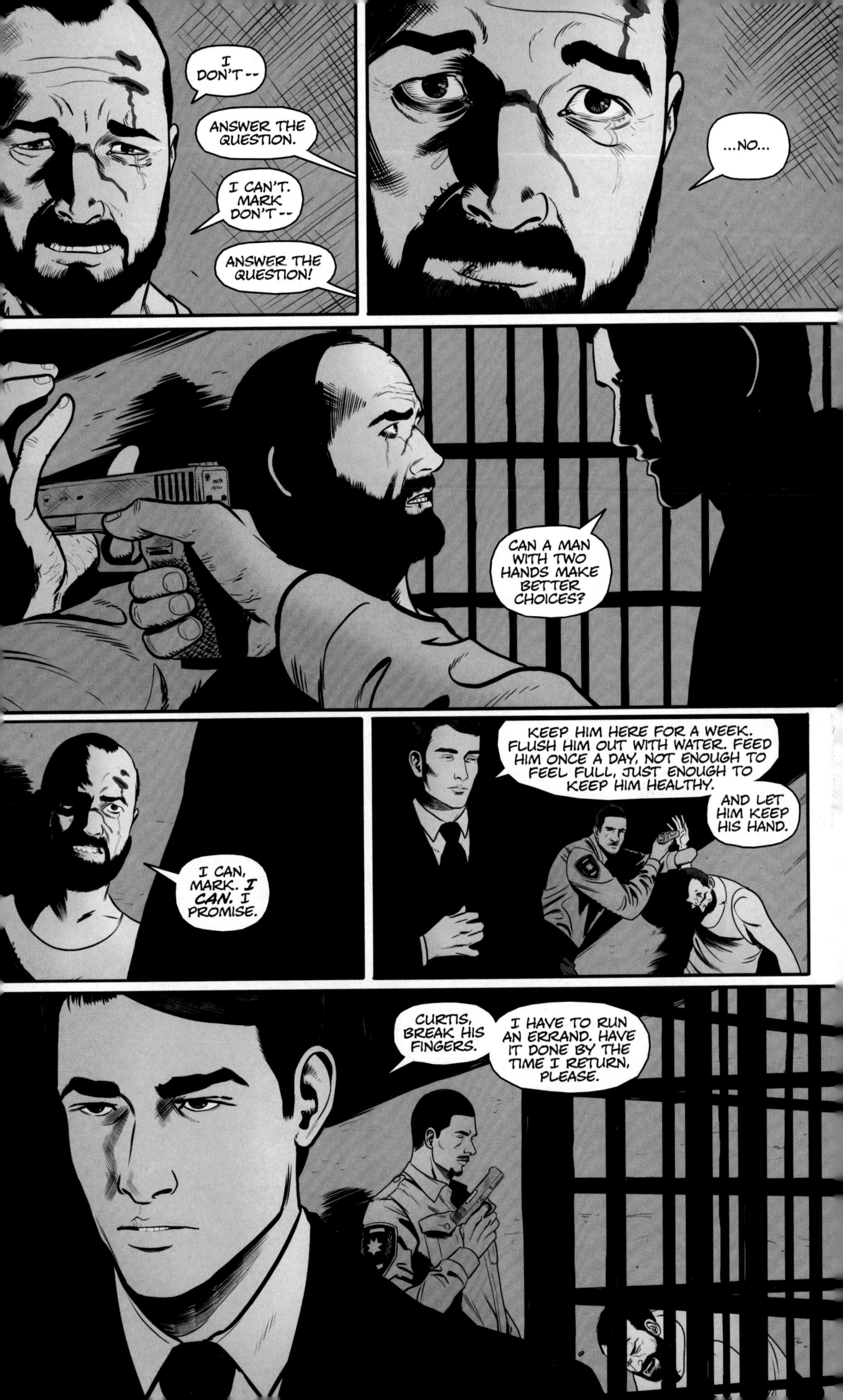
I DON'T --
ANSWER THE QUESTION.
I CAN'T. MARK DON'T --
ANSWER THE QUESTION!
...NO...
CAN A MAN WITH TWO HANDS MAKE BETTER CHOICES?
I CAN, MARK. *I CAN.* I PROMISE.
KEEP HIM HERE FOR A WEEK. FLUSH HIM OUT WITH WATER. FEED HIM ONCE A DAY, NOT ENOUGH TO FEEL FULL, JUST ENOUGH TO KEEP HIM HEALTHY.
AND LET HIM KEEP HIS HAND.
CURTIS, BREAK HIS FINGERS.
I HAVE TO RUN AN ERRAND. HAVE IT DONE BY THE TIME I RETURN, PLEASE.

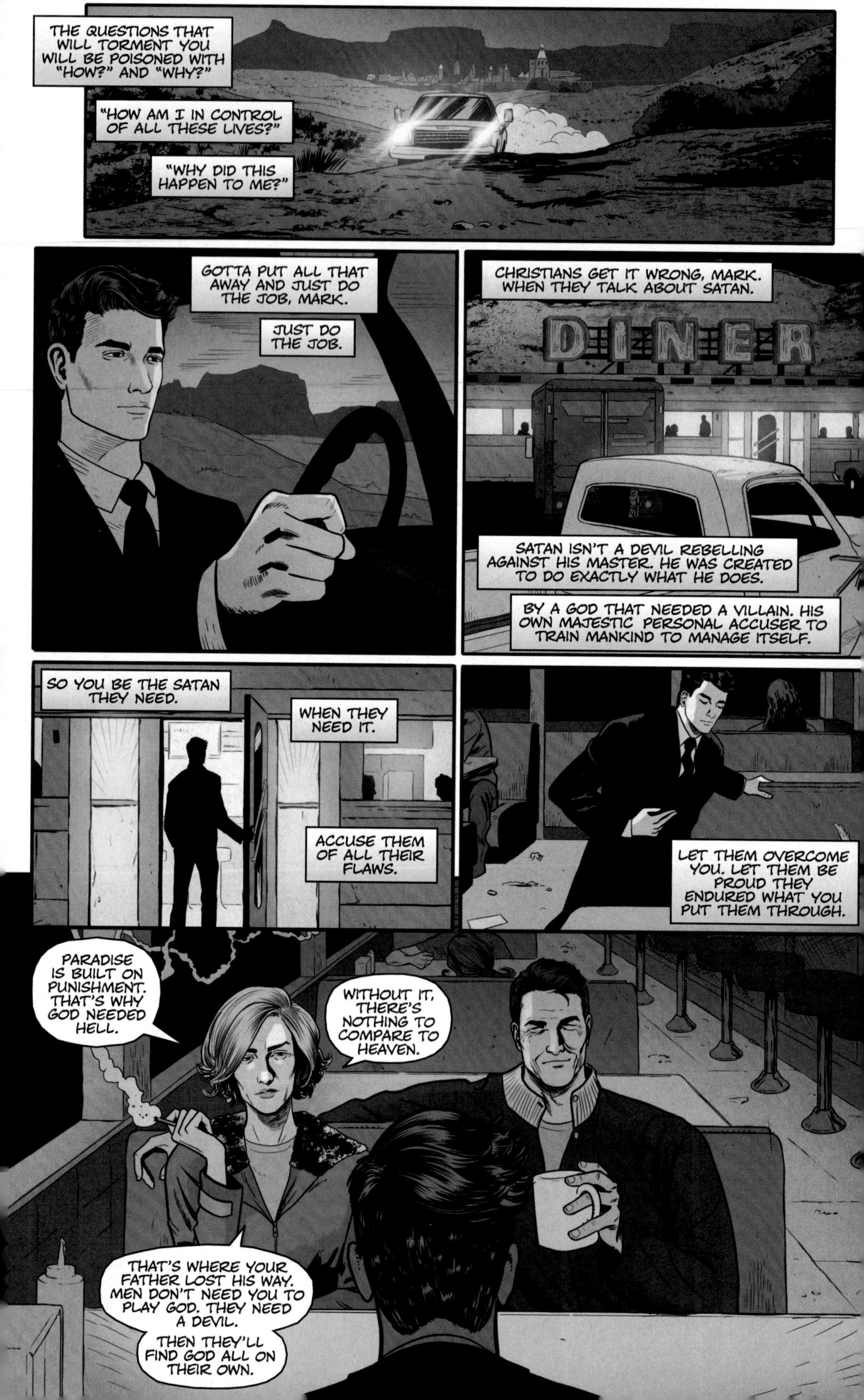
THE QUESTIONS THAT WILL TORMENT YOU WILL BE POISONED WITH "HOW?" AND "WHY?"
"HOW AM I IN CONTROL OF ALL THESE LIVES?"
"WHY DID THIS HAPPEN TO ME?"
GOTTA PUT ALL THAT AWAY AND JUST DO THE JOB, MARK.
JUST DO THE JOB.
CHRISTIANS GET IT WRONG, MARK. WHEN THEY TALK ABOUT SATAN.
DINER
SATAN ISN'T A DEVIL REBELLING AGAINST HIS MASTER. HE WAS CREATED TO DO EXACTLY WHAT HE DOES.
BY A GOD THAT NEEDED A VILLAIN. HIS OWN MAJESTIC PERSONAL ACCUSER TO TRAIN MANKIND TO MANAGE ITSELF.
SO YOU BE THE SATAN THEY NEED.
WHEN THEY NEED IT.
ACCUSE THEM OF ALL THEIR FLAWS.
LET THEM OVERCOME YOU. LET THEM BE PROUD THEY ENDURED WHAT YOU PUT THEM THROUGH.
PARADISE IS BUILT ON PUNISHMENT. THAT'S WHY GOD NEEDED HELL.
WITHOUT IT, THERE'S NOTHING TO COMPARE TO HEAVEN.
THAT'S WHERE YOUR FATHER LOST HIS WAY. MEN DON'T NEED YOU TO PLAY GOD. THEY NEED A DEVIL.
THEN THEY'LL FIND GOD ALL ON THEIR OWN.

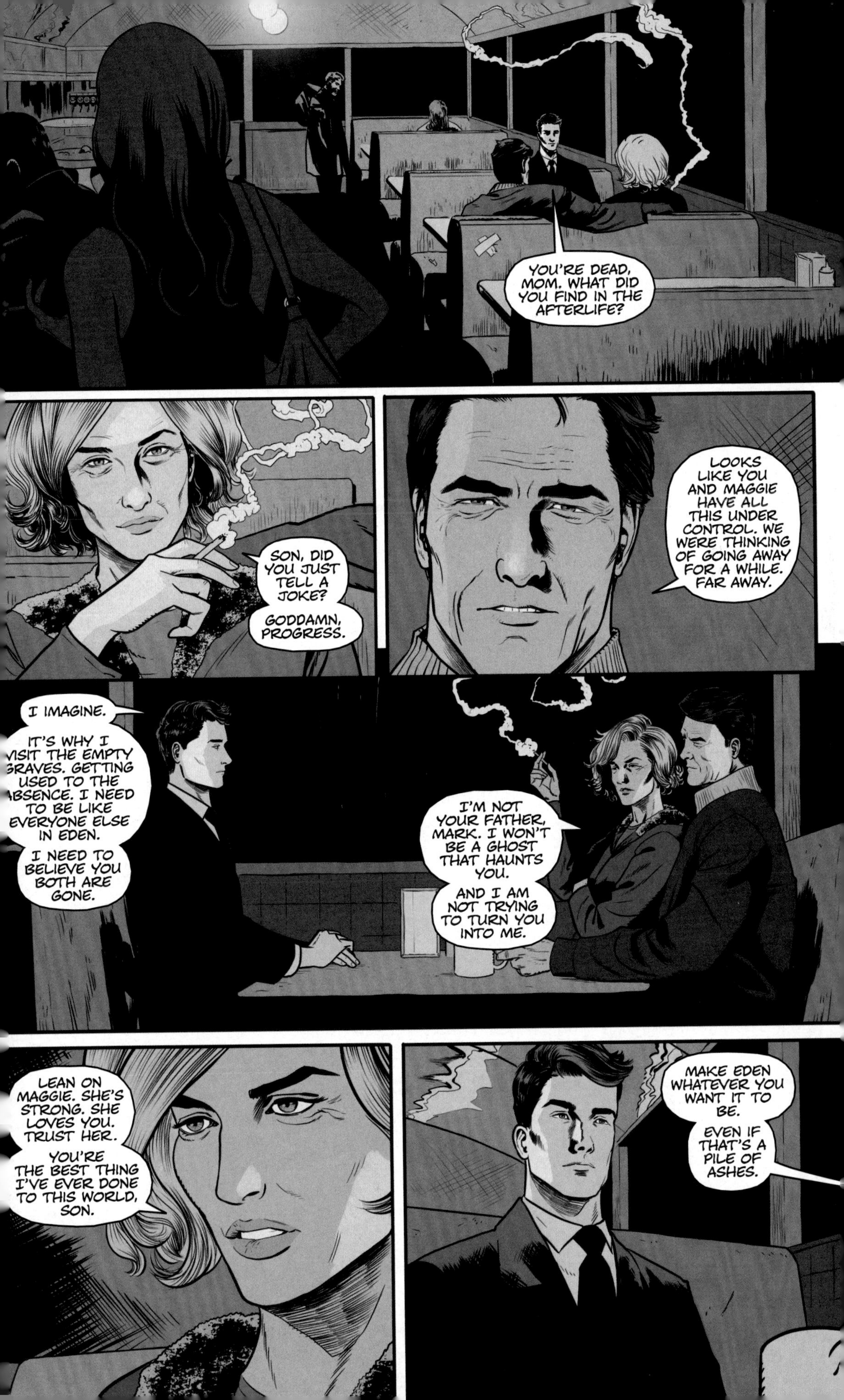
YOU'RE DEAD, MOM. WHAT DID YOU FIND IN THE AFTERLIFE?
SON, DID YOU JUST TELL A JOKE?
GODDAMN, PROGRESS.
LOOKS LIKE YOU AND MAGGIE HAVE ALL THIS UNDER CONTROL. WE WERE THINKING OF GOING AWAY FOR A WHILE. FAR AWAY.
I IMAGINE.
IT'S WHY I VISIT THE EMPTY GRAVES. GETTING USED TO THE ABSENCE. I NEED TO BE LIKE EVERYONE ELSE IN EDEN.
I NEED TO BELIEVE YOU BOTH ARE GONE.
I'M NOT YOUR FATHER, MARK. I WON'T BE A GHOST THAT HAUNTS YOU.
AND I AM NOT TRYING TO TURN YOU INTO ME.
LEAN ON MAGGIE. SHE'S STRONG. SHE LOVES YOU. TRUST HER.
YOU'RE THE BEST THING I'VE EVER DONE TO THIS WORLD, SON.
MAKE EDEN WHATEVER YOU WANT IT TO BE.
EVEN IF THAT'S A PILE OF ASHES.

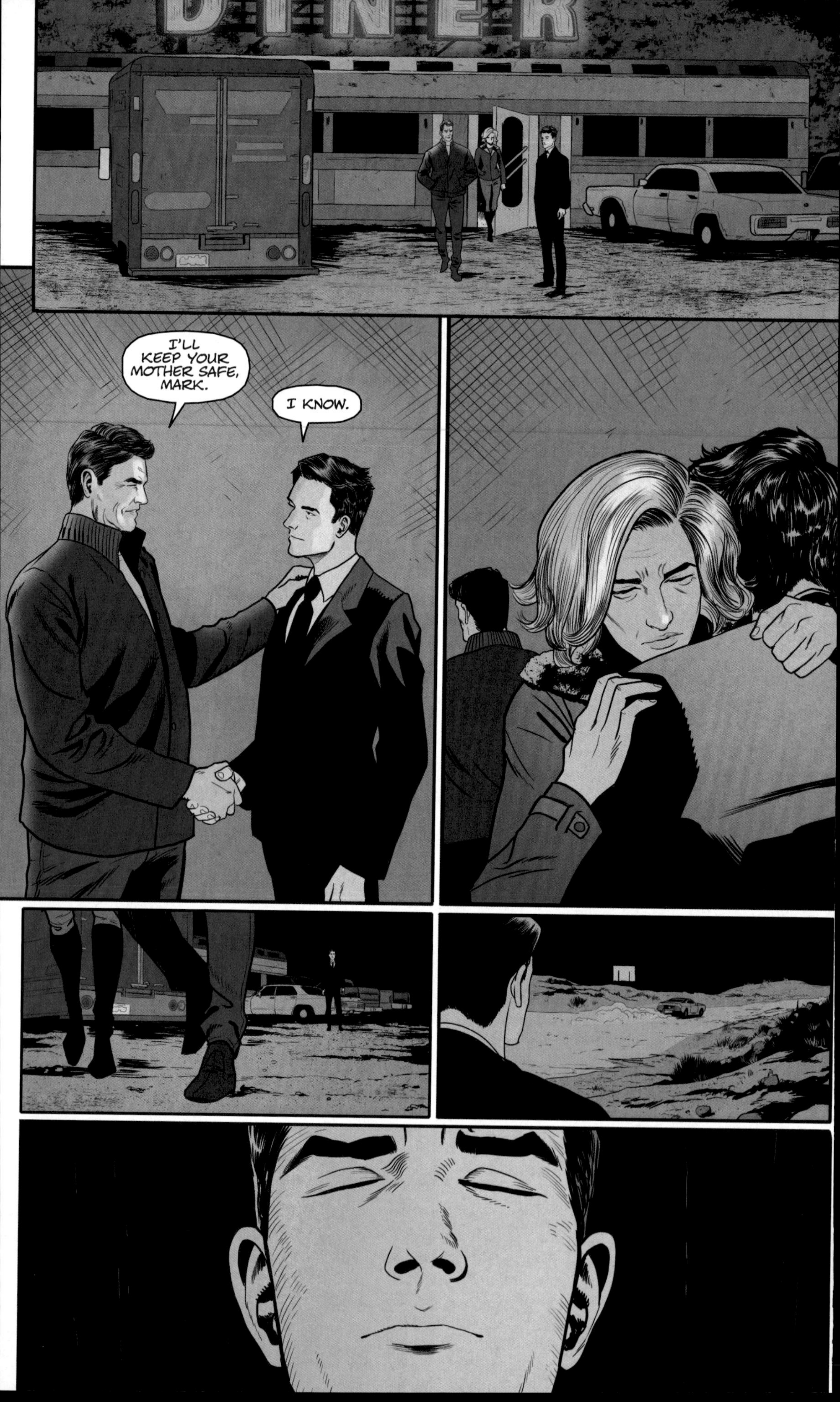
I'LL KEEP YOUR MOTHER SAFE, MARK.
I KNOW.

I'M NOT ASHAMED TO TELL YOU I WANT THIS. AND IF I CAN'T HAVE IT, THEN I'LL ACCEPT IT. BUT I MIGHT NOT FORGIVE YOU FOR IT.

IF I SAID NO, WOULD YOU LEAVE ME?

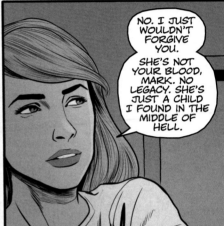

NO. I JUST WOULDN'T FORGIVE YOU.

SHE'S NOT YOUR BLOOD, MARK. NO LEGACY. SHE'S JUST A CHILD I FOUND IN THE MIDDLE OF HELL.

SHE NEVER CRIES. REMINDS ME OF YOU.

AND YOU WANT US TO RAISE HER.

YES.

OKAY, BUT WE NAME HER "LAURA."

AND WE CAN'T RAISE HER TO BE LIKE US.

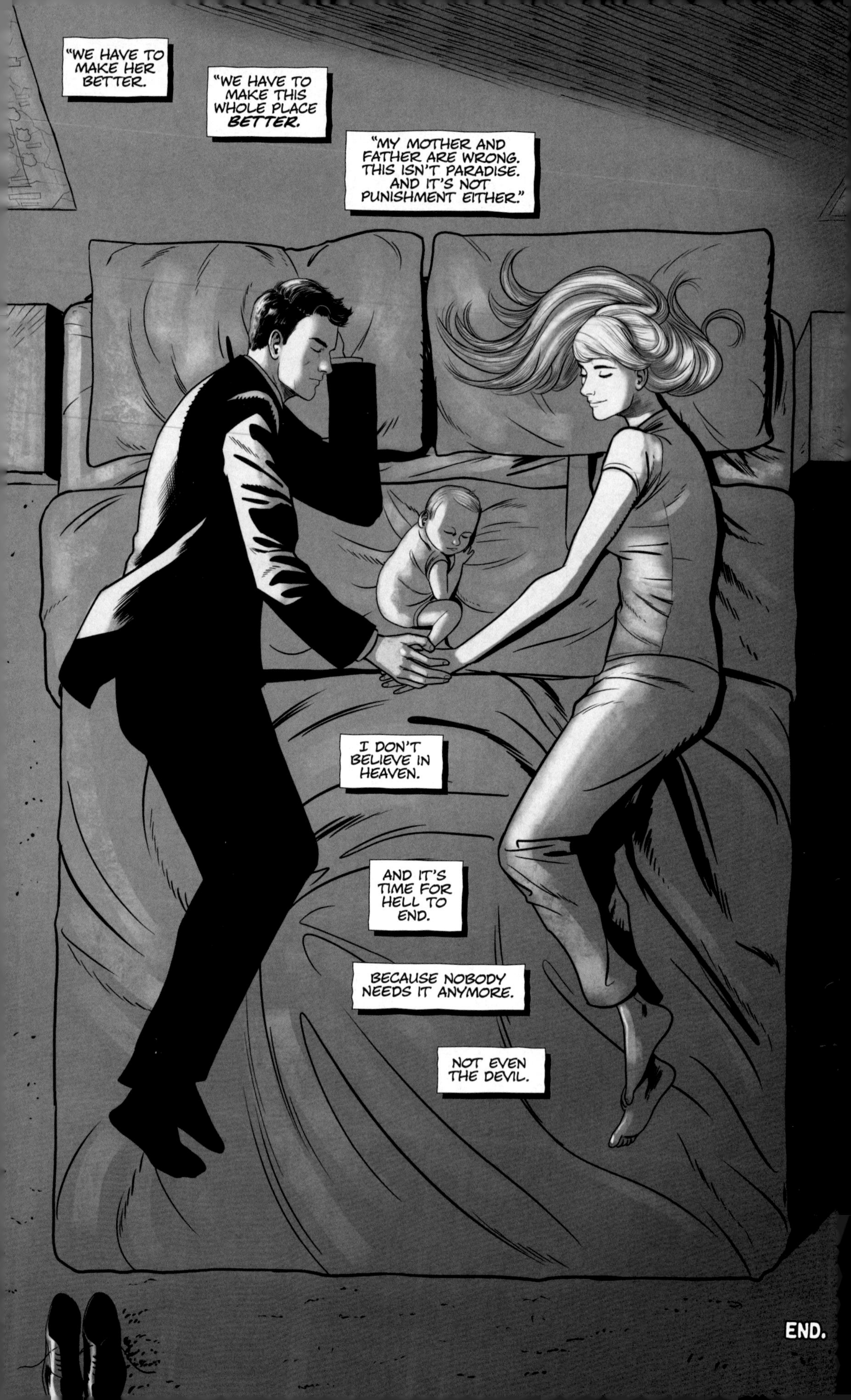
"WE HAVE TO MAKE HER BETTER.
"WE HAVE TO MAKE THIS WHOLE PLACE *BETTER.*
"MY MOTHER AND FATHER ARE WRONG. THIS ISN'T PARADISE. AND IT'S NOT PUNISHMENT EITHER."
I DON'T BELIEVE IN HEAVEN.
AND IT'S TIME FOR HELL TO END.
BECAUSE NOBODY NEEDS IT ANYMORE.
NOT EVEN THE DEVIL.
END.

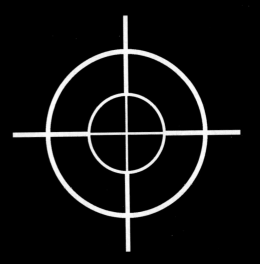

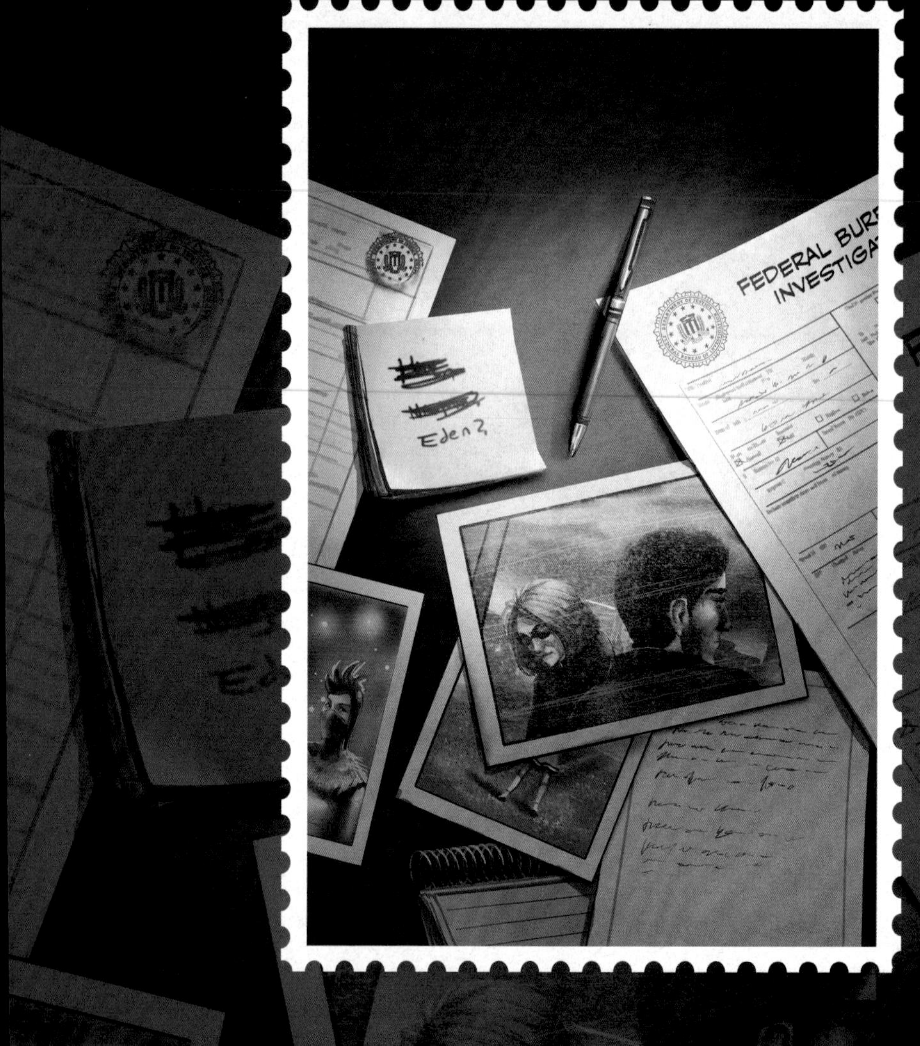
FEDERAL BUR
INVESTIGA
Eden?

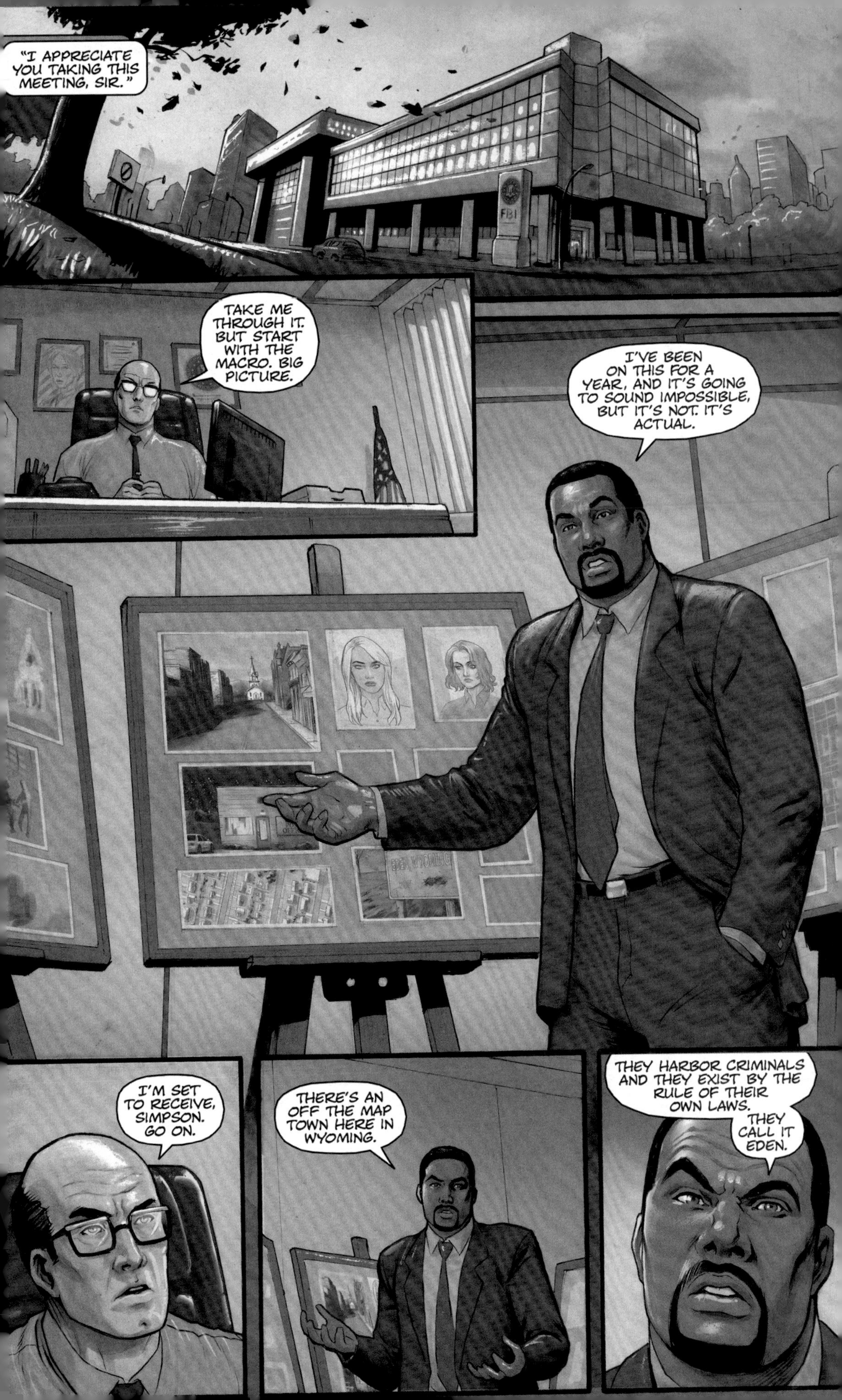
"I APPRECIATE YOU TAKING THIS MEETING, SIR."
FBI
TAKE ME THROUGH IT. BUT START WITH THE MACRO. BIG PICTURE.
I'VE BEEN ON THIS FOR A YEAR, AND IT'S GOING TO SOUND IMPOSSIBLE, BUT IT'S NOT. IT'S ACTUAL.
I'M SET TO RECEIVE, SIMPSON. GO ON.
THERE'S AN OFF THE MAP TOWN HERE IN WYOMING.
THEY HARBOR CRIMINALS AND THEY EXIST BY THE RULE OF THEIR OWN LAWS.
THEY CALL IT EDEN.

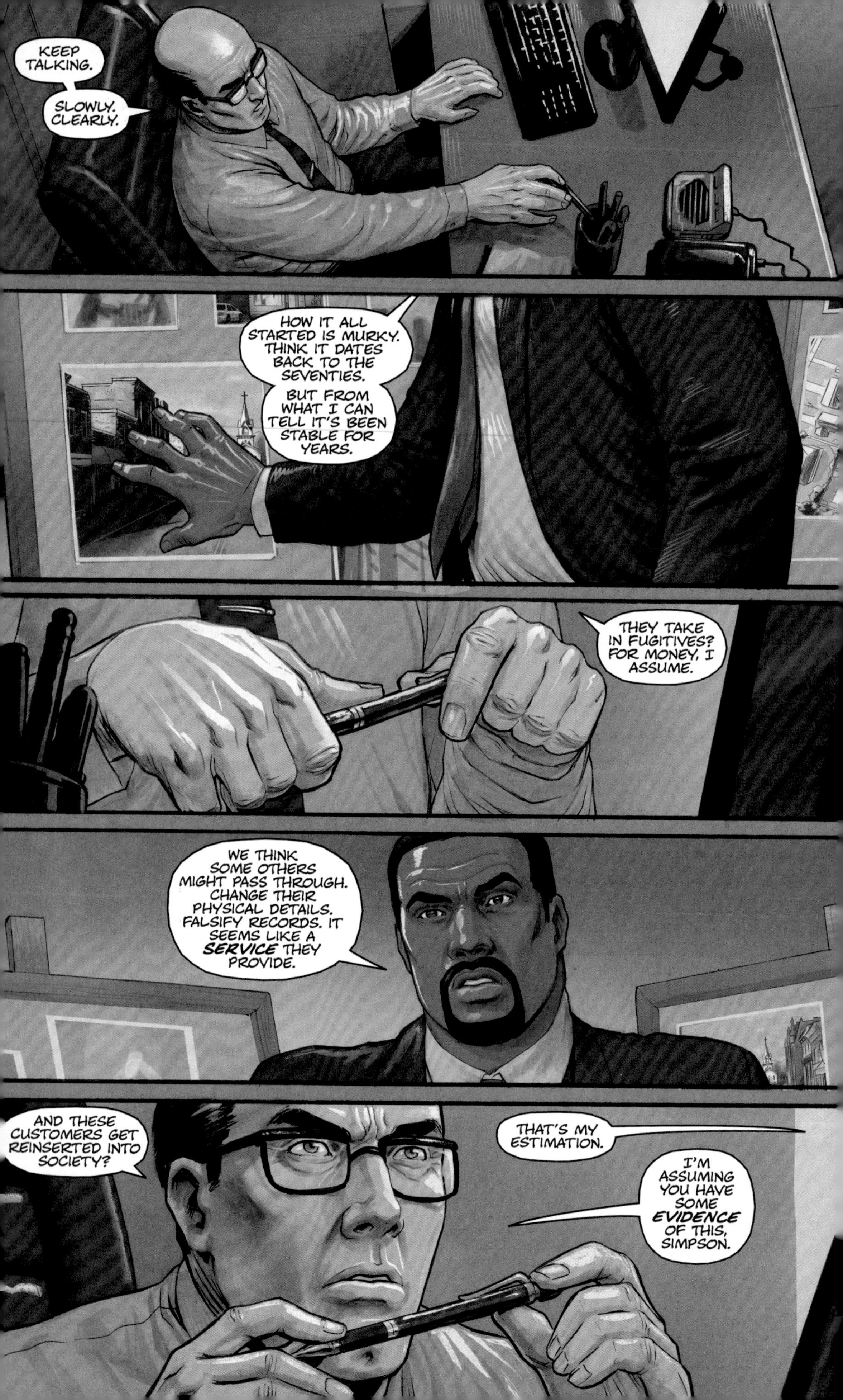
KEEP TALKING.
SLOWLY. CLEARLY.
HOW IT ALL STARTED IS MURKY. THINK IT DATES BACK TO THE SEVENTIES.
BUT FROM WHAT I CAN TELL IT'S BEEN STABLE FOR YEARS.
THEY TAKE IN FUGITIVES? FOR MONEY, I ASSUME.
WE THINK SOME OTHERS MIGHT PASS THROUGH. CHANGE THEIR PHYSICAL DETAILS. FALSIFY RECORDS. IT SEEMS LIKE A SERVICE THEY PROVIDE.
AND THESE CUSTOMERS GET REINSERTED INTO SOCIETY?
THAT'S MY ESTIMATION.
I'M ASSUMING YOU HAVE SOME EVIDENCE OF THIS, SIMPSON.

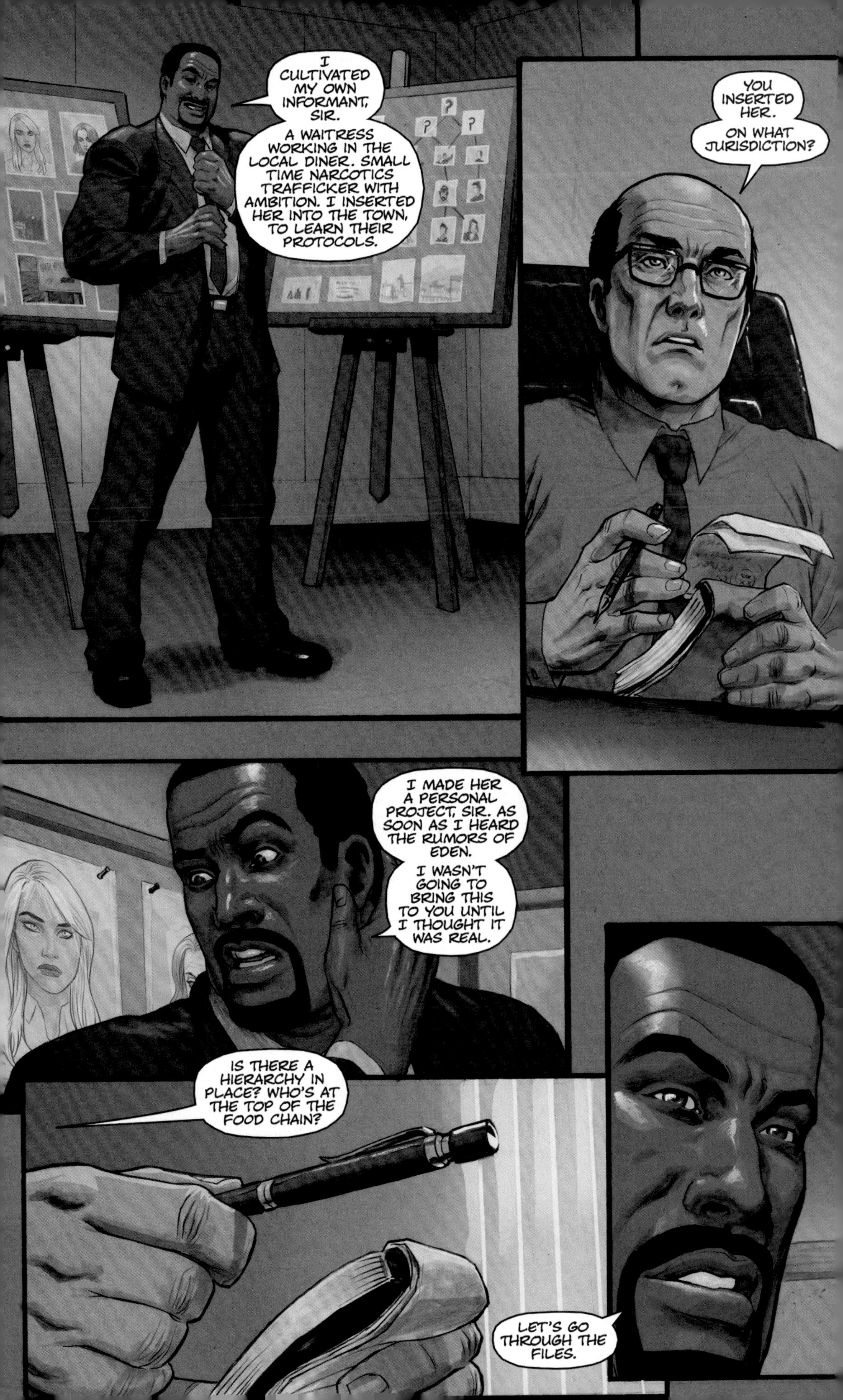
I CULTIVATED MY OWN INFORMANT, SIR.
A WAITRESS WORKING IN THE LOCAL DINER. SMALL TIME NARCOTICS TRAFFICKER WITH AMBITION. I INSERTED HER INTO THE TOWN, TO LEARN THEIR PROTOCOLS.
YOU INSERTED HER.
ON WHAT JURISDICTION?
I MADE HER A PERSONAL PROJECT, SIR. AS SOON AS I HEARD THE RUMORS OF EDEN.
I WASN'T GOING TO BRING THIS TO YOU UNTIL I THOUGHT IT WAS REAL.
IS THERE A HIERARCHY IN PLACE? WHO'S AT THE TOP OF THE FOOD CHAIN?
LET'S GO THROUGH THE FILES.

# EDEN, WYOMING

**POPULATION:** 2,190 (Approximate)

**FOUNDED:** 1979

**FOUNDED BY:** Isaac [REDACTED]

**DMS Lat:** 40 - 48° ?' ????" N

**DMS Long:** 105 - 109?° ??' ????" W

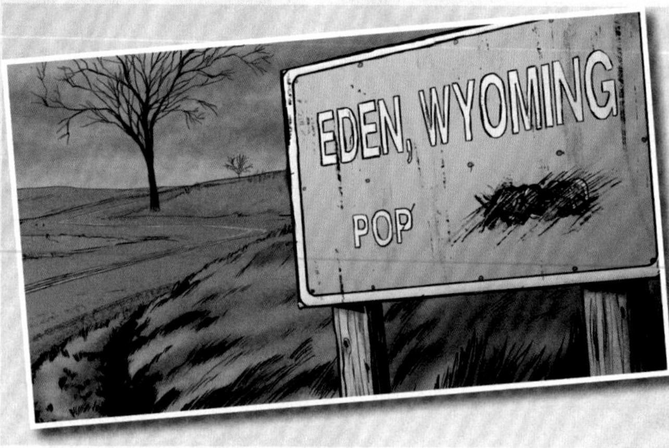
EDEN, WYOMING
POP

**LOCAL GOVERNMENT:**
Laura Shiffron – Mayor
Roy Magnum (alias) – Sheriff
Mark Shiffron – Postmaster (unofficial)

**NOTES ON STATISTICS:** Data for ethnic makeup, crime rate (ha!), birth rate, death rate, state and federal civic participation, and local economy are effectively unavailable – and, this agent would argue, irrelevant.

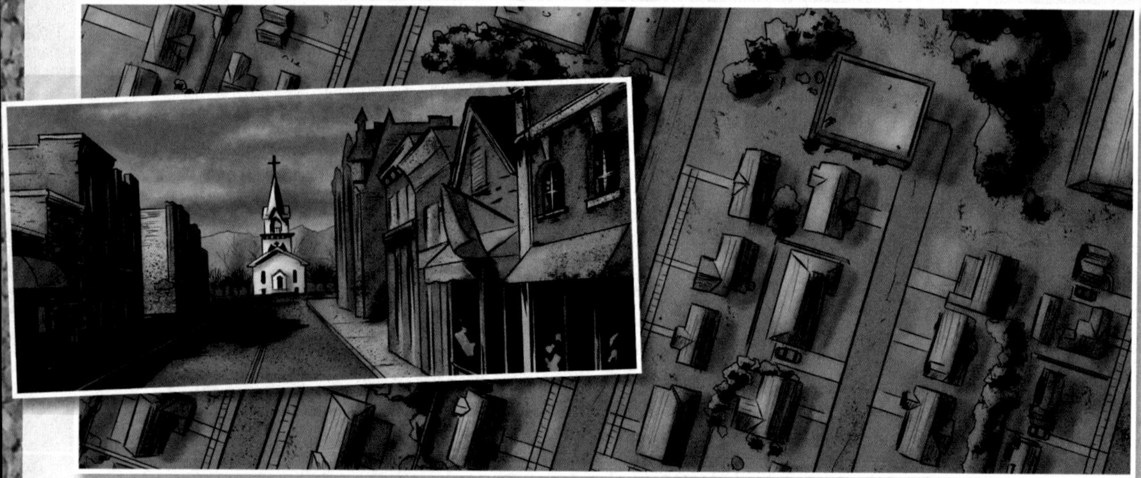

**"This is a place that wants to be quiet."**

A town like Eden doesn't have an official motto, but I heard one of the townspeople say that once, during surveillance, and it stuck with me. Eden doesn't have an official anything – even the sign posted at the town limits isn't DOT official, trust me – I checked.

You won't find it on a map, and you won't find it on satellite imaging. There's no cellphone towers, no open internet usage, no cable TV, no state infrastructure – not even the road that runs through it. Eden doesn't apply for any state or federal funding, doesn't submit tax records, and – in spite of the evidence I am presenting to you in this report – doesn't have a zip code or designation.

The Department of Water and Power, the State Comptroller's office, the United States Postal Service, any relevant branch of the federal government – including the FBI and the CIA, I've checked – and even the congressmen chomping at the bit to gerrymander the state every chance they can get. Not a single trace or record of the town anywhere. How is that possible?

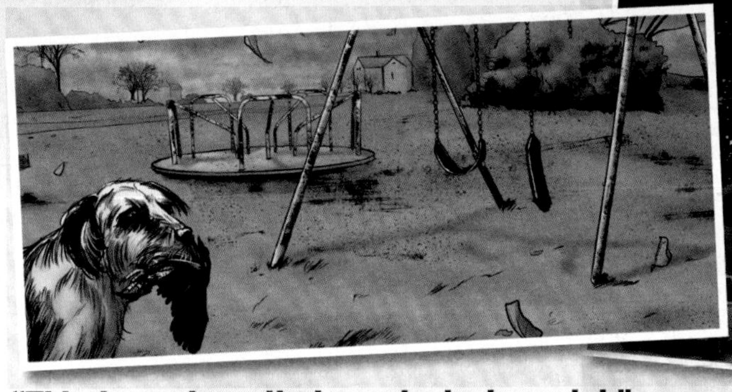

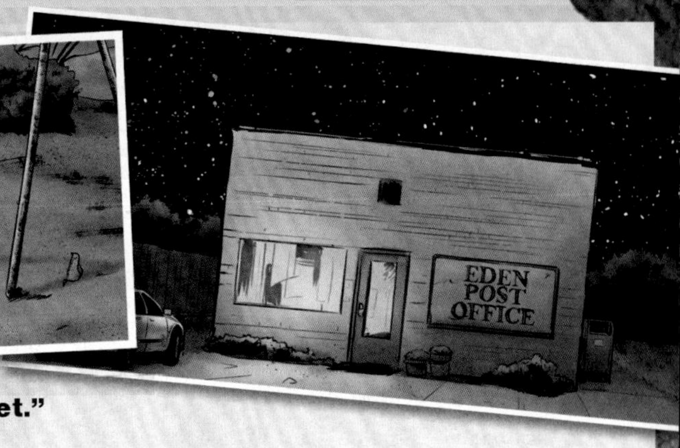
EDEN
POST
OFFICE

**"This is a place that wants to be quiet."**

They take it to heart out here, and for good reason, because with a handful of exceptions – most of them children – every single individual within the town limits is a person of interest in a criminal investigation. Most that I've identified are convicted felons, adjusting to society following release from security facilities. Others are witnesses, or individuals wanted for questioning…or people who've never been brought up on formal charges but have, in all likelihood, committed felonies of their own.

Some of Eden's residents, however – and this is where it gets troubling – appear to be wanted criminals on the run, men and women who have performed heinous acts and violent crimes and may never be brought to justice.

This town shelters them, some of them temporarily, some of them permanently, but either way it ensures that they elude our grasp. Some of the intel gathered even suggests that Eden employs a skilled plastic surgeon – someone by the name of Tolmach, though no records of interest matching that name could be found – who painstakingly reconstructs their faces to mask their appearance. I can even confirm that Eden employs a highly skilled technician (likely Johan Richter, see file) to systematically delete and replace records of the town's individuals, allowing them to transition back into society with no repercussions. (Having consulted with Southwest Branch's Agent James Miller, Badge no. [REDACTED], I can confirm the plausibility of such a scenario.)

To get down to the rub – Eden operates like a twisted version of the Federal Witness Protection Program, keeping the scum of the earth out of sight and out of the justice system. This is a maximum priority investigation, and if even half of the hearsay I've come across about the town's founder, Isaac, is true, then Eden could become a hotbed for the kind of violence that alters a nation irrevocably.

Admittedly, I have been conducting an off-the-books investigation of my own on Eden, which I've denoted in my own files as OPERATION: FORBIDDEN FRUIT. I understand the potential legal pitfalls I've placed the Bureau in, but I was careful not to violate any individual rights or clauses, and I've not disclosed my identity or blown my cover to anyone within the town – barring, of course, my single undercover informant.

This is the kind of bust that goes down in the history books, the kind of bust that makes careers – more importantly, the town of Eden flies in the face of everything that this country, and the Federal Bureau of Investigation, stands for.

I consider it my civic duty as an American to eliminate this hidden threat, and look forward to pressing forward with OPERATION: FORBIDDEN FRUIT in a more official capacity, with the full force of the Bureau behind me.

*Simpson*

**OFFICIAL REQUISITIONS AND ACQUISITIONS DISCLOSURE FORM**

**Federal Bureau of Investigation**

**Operation:** "Forbidden Fruit"
**Location of Operation:** Eden, Wyoming
**Lead Operative:** Simpson
**Relevant Director of Operations:** Jon Schultz

**Equipment Logged:**
-Binoculars [QUANTITY: 1 Pair]
-9mm Rounds [QUANTITY: 50]
-Parabolic Microphone [QUANTITY: 1]

**Vehicle(s) Logged:**
**Make:** Ford
**Model:** Taurus
**Year:** 2002
**Color:** Burnt Sienna
**Was this vehicle returned in an unaltered condition:** Mostly.
**If not, describe alterations:** Dents in back fender

**Expenses Logged:**

**Travel (including, but not limited to, gasoline, airfare, public transportation):** $467
**Lodging:** $245
**Food/Necessities:** $580
**Misc. (please provide detailed receipts):** $1,189

**Human Resources Logged:** Informant Established

**Name of Informant:** Margaret [REDACTED] (alias surname of "Prendowski")

**Occupation of Informant:** Food Services, Waitress

**Brief Description of Informant:** Blonde Hair, Blue Eyes, Mid-20s, svelte

**Is this Informant applicable for consideration as a "Criminal Informant" (If so, please complete and attach FORM NO. 88-C):** Yes.

**Brief Description of Informant's Prior Offenses:** Narcotics Distribution, Assault, Tax Evasion

**Brief Description of Informant's Role:** Observes much of the criminal activity in and around the town of Eden. May be romantically involved with one MARK SHIFFRON, town postmaster and son of the town's mayor.

# STATEMENT OF INTENT TO PURSUE CRIMINAL CHARGES

## Federal Bureau of Investigation

**CHARGES WILL BE LEVIED AGAINST:**

-The Town of Eden, Wyoming (see previous report on success of the Racketeer Influenced and Corrupt Organizations Act)
-Laura Shiffron

**AT THE TIME OF THIS FORM'S COMPLETION, IS THERE EVIDENCE SIGNIFICANT ENOUGH TO LEVY THE AFOREMENTIONED CHARGES:** No.

**IF NO, HAS A FOLLOW-UP OPERATION BEEN REQUESTED:** Yes.

**IF YES, LIST THE FOLLOW-UP OPERATION'S DESIGNATION HERE:**
Operation: Forbidden Fruit.

**LIST OF CHARGES TO BE PURSUED:**

-Conspiracy to Commit Murder in the First Degree
-Murder in the First Degree
-Murder in the Second Degree
-Murder in the Third Degree
-Manslaughter
-Resisting Arrest
-Obstructing Justice
-Treason
-Racketeering
-Terrorist Activities
-Tax Evasion
-Tax Fraud

**MINIMUM NUMBER OF PERSONS TO BE CHARGED:** 2,190

**SPECIAL NOTES:** Utilizing RICO, I believe that we can successful charge the town of Eden with its many crimes – it's happened before. Read my previous report on the successful implementation of RICO in small town racketeering cases, and against these so-called homegrown mafias.

*Simpson*

**To: Deputy Director Jon Schultz**
**Federal Bureau of Investigation**

The following profiles represent the most significant intelligence I've gathered on the residents of the town of Eden, Wyoming. After reading through my report on the town itself, and considering the evidence in support of my discoveries, I've whittled down my surveillance footage and notes, my full psychological profiles on the town's residents, and my opinion on the its functions into the following single page profiles.

The proceeding files are succinct, and to the point, and have avoided unnecessary idle speculation – although in some cases speculation was necessary, as you will see. Still, I have avoided discussing the nonsensical or the irrelevant.

For example, while I have dozens of pages and hours of recorded surveillance on the Chef at the Eden Diner, who is almost certainly the same "Chef" made infamous in the violent socioanarcho demonstrations in France during the '90s, I have not included this information. I have not included the town's lone Native American resident, affectionately (or hatefully, depending on the speaker) nicknamed "Big Injun," in the following report, because some of my research suggest that the Comanche may in fact have been innocent of the previous charges held against him.

Most importantly, I have not included the vast amount of speculation, hearsay, and near myth associated with the town's co-founder, Isaac - former husband to Laura Shiffron and father of Mark. I have not listed his frequent association with the quasioccult criminal sprees of the late 1980s – although, in the attached miscellany, I have attached a newsprint article from the mid-80s that may allude to one of his crimes. But I will not waste time digging around for the possible real life identity of this legend of a man. Isaac is dead. Eden's residents hanged him from a tree well over a decade ago.

There are enough monsters in Eden without my needing to bring back a dead man, Director Schultz.

See for yourself.

*Simpson*

**LEGAL NAME:** SHIFFRON, LAURA

**KNOWN ALIAS(ES): N/A**

**BIRTH DATE:** 23 SEPTEMBER 1965
**STATE/NATION OF ORIGIN:** Hartford, CT
**HEIGHT/WEIGHT:** 5' 6", 120 LBS
**OCCUPATION:** Mayor of Eden

**PRIOR OFFENSES:** Fraud, Racketeering, Distribution of Narcotics, Distribution of Firearms, Conspiracy to Commit Murder in the First Degree

**KNOWN CRIMINAL AFFILIATIONS:** N/A

**KNOWN NONCRIMINAL AFFILIATIONS:** N/A

**PSYCHOLOGICAL PROFILE:** I've read the profiles the Bureau has on record, from back when Shiffron first started associating with Isaac. It's not pretty stuff, but it's inaccurate, in my opinion – I don't think Shiffron is a sociopath.
Rather, I classify her as an amateur autocrat – there's an inherent Narcissism to a person who sees the violence and chaos at work in the world and thinks they can chain it up, make it a pet. You can't domesticate a place like Eden, with its people, but Laura seems to think that, given an iron first, a surveillance grid, and the occasional "Barn Brawl" that she can keep the pressure from boiling over. She's brilliant, cruel, and runs Eden as well as it could've been run, I believe – but she's either blind to, or in denial of, the carnage that's building up in that place.

**SURVEILLANCE LOG (MARCH 29th, 2015):**

**6:00 AM** – Subject rises. Engages in a 4 mile run around and through Eden.

**7:00 AM** – Subject returns to discover MARK SHIFFRON at her residence. The two enter and emerge several minutes later, heading for town.

**7:30 AM – 9:00 AM** – Subject, MARK SHIFFRON, and ROY MAGNUM meet in Sheriff's Office. DEPUTY EARLE is not present.

**12:00 PM** – Town hall meeting at CHURCH. Over 500 residents in attendance. (Surveillance note: Parabolic mic encounters extraordinary interference. Could not discern topics of discussion at meeting, but can guess – when the residents emerge, they are carrying the body of one DANIEL MESSERSMITH.)

**1:00 PM** – At some point while my surveillance was occupied on the church itself, the body of a young, white female was placed in the church's parking lot. At no point did I hear or see an automobile, or a suspect.

**2:00 – 5:00 PM** – Subject and SHERIFF canvas Eden and outskirts. SHERIFF and DEPUTY begin interrogating residents, as Subject returns home.

**7:00 PM** – Subject stands on porch, drinking from a mug and watching.
(Surveillance note: it's not possible, but I feel like she's looking right at me. Like she can see me, sitting in my dark car, parked in the woods, no one else around.)

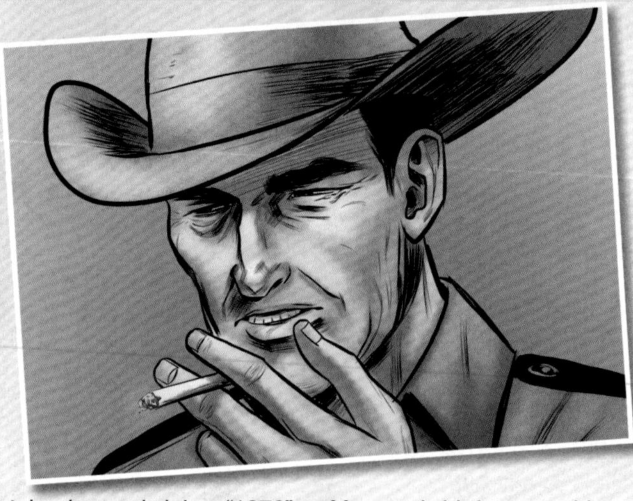

**LEGAL NAME:** LAFLEUR, RORY

**KNOWN ALIAS(ES):** ROY MAGNUM

**BIRTH DATE:** 14 MARCH (A previously obtained record claims "1972" as Magnum's birth year – this seems unlikely, and may have been included by Magnum to obfuscate…or flatter himself.)
**STATE/NATION OF ORIGIN:** SAN FRANCISCO, CA
**HEIGHT/WEIGHT:** 6' 1", 203 LBS
**OCCUPATION:** Sheriff of Eden

**PRIOR OFFENSES:** Fraud, Petty Theft, Vandalism, Possession of an Unregistered Firearm, Assault and Battery
**KNOWN CRIMINAL AFFILIATIONS:** Hell's Angels (Inconsequential)
**KNOWN NONCRIMINAL AFFILIATIONS:** U.S. Army Rangers (Dishonorable Discharge), Gold's Gym (Membership Expired)

**PSYCHOLOGICAL PROFILE:** Profiles created before Magnum's association with Eden were scant, and many of them seemed to focus on Magnum's perceived overcompensation and nigh-obsession with North American standards of masculinity. These, I believe, may be in error – after detailed examination of intelligence, both new and old, it is this agent's opinion that Roy Magnum is neither an angry, closeted homosexual, nor a hotbed of toxic masculinity evolving into a homegrown terrorist. Rather, I would contend that Magnum is just as he appears – fatherly, but stern, capable of extreme action but not extreme planning. He is, in a word, simple. That, of course, makes him dangerous.

**SURVEILLANCE LOG (MARCH 28th, 2015):**

**8:15 AM** – Subject wakes, prepares and consumes breakfast of bacon, eggs, and milk.

**9:03 AM** – Subject finishes showering, shaving, and dressing – exits home in uniform.

**9:30 AM – 5:06 PM** – Subject patrols EDEN, both on foot and in vehicle. Nothing of consequence occurs. Subject samples muffins at grocery store, greets citizens, and partakes of meals at the EDEN DINER. Subject returns home, and removes uniform.

**5:30 PM – 6:00 PM** – Subject lifts weights and performs limited cardiovascular exercise. Music playlist comprised of "The Eagles" tunes plays at high volume.

**7:00 PM** – Subject travels to home of Mayor Laura Shiffron. Subject does not leave Shiffron's home until the following morning. A romantic relationship can be inferred.

**LEGAL NAME:** SHIFFRON, MARK

**KNOWN ALIAS(ES):** N/A

**BIRTH DATE:** 11 NOVEMBER 1985
**STATE/NATION OF ORIGIN:** EDEN, WY
**HEIGHT/WEIGHT:** 6' 0", 175 LBS
**OCCUPATION:** Eden Postmaster

**PRIOR OFFENSES:** N/A

**KNOWN CRIMINAL AFFILIATIONS:** Son of Laura Shiffron and Isaac [REDACTED]

**KNOWN NONCRIMINAL AFFILIATIONS:** United States Postal Service (Unofficial)

**PSYCHOLOGICAL PROFILE:** Examining my own earlier psych profiles of Mark, I discovered that I had been lax in my analysis, simplifying the man into little more than a Forrest Gump analog. I should've known better – nothing in Eden is simple.

Mark is, assuredly, a textbook case of Asperger's Syndrome. Given the information from my own in-town source, and what I've observed, Mark can be brusque, fails to read social cues, and often displays behavior and reasoning we've come to associate with individuals stuck in Piaget's "Concrete Operational" state.

Still, Mark has his father in him – and his mother. He has been raised by criminals and sociopaths, murderers and monsters, and where once I suspected a weak link I now fear may manifest an avatar of the violence in Eden, an heir to the bloody throne that Isaac and Laura have built.

To put it plainly – I believe that Mark could become something very, very dangerous.

**SURVEILLANCE LOG (JULY 8th, 2015):**
(Surveillance note – subject is meticulous and slow in his actions. What might take an average person five minutes to do can take Mark up to half an hour.)

**8:15 AM** – Subject wakes late. Prepares and eats breakfast. (Surveillance note: Subject returned to town late last evening following his weekly pickup run, escorted by SHERIFF MAGNUM. He appears to be wounded. I have been unable to tail Mark on these excursions, which I believe involve him retrieving parcels and letters.)

**9:30 AM – 12:00 PM** – Subject sorts and transcribes mail.

**12:30 – 2:30 PM** – Subject breaks usual routine and eats lunch with MAYOR SHIFFRON and SHERIFF MAGNUM, presumably to debrief.

**3:00 PM – 6:00 PM** – Subject delivers mail and parcels.

**7:00 PM** – MAGGIE PRENDOWSKI arrives, with food from the diner. The two, presumably, share a meal. (Surveillance note – romantic connection? MAGGIE was exceedingly cagey on this particular topic.)

**LEGAL NAME:** MARGARET [REDACTED]

**KNOWN ALIAS(ES):** "Margaret Prendowski" (Bureau-established false identity)

**BIRTH DATE:** 9 January 1985
**STATE/NATION OF ORIGIN:** Los Angeles, CA
**HEIGHT/WEIGHT:** 5' 7", 120 LBS
**OCCUPATION:** Food Service

**PRIOR OFFENSES:** Distribution of Narcotics, Assault, Manslaughter, Possession of an Illegal Firearm
**KNOWN CRIMINAL AFFILIATIONS:** MS-13 (The cartel has standing orders to kill Margaret on sight)
**KNOWN NONCRIMINAL AFFILIATIONS:** N/A

**PSYCHOLOGICAL PROFILE:** Now that I'm no longer fluffing up her profile with fake
information about "Margaret Prendowski," I can be honest about Maggie.
Here is a person capable of great moral sacrifice, and I mean that in the worst possible way. Maggie is
ambitious, fatally so – a pretty little white girl from Los Angeles tried to cut in on the heroin trade…and
almost succeeded, until she got on the bad side of MS-13 and got her boyfriend gunned down in front of
her.
But that didn't phase her. Not remotely.
I only happened upon Maggie because she was begging for deals, she knew the
Guatemalans would gut her in federal, and I had friends looking for criminals that fit a certain profile. In
that respect, Maggie was perfect.
But that experience in her life didn't quell the violence in her, and neither did Eden. Every time she and
I met up to exchange information, she became more hostile. In our last meeting, there was an incident.
She seems to have eyes on taking control of the town – I think she may be slipping from my grasp. It
might not be the worst thing for the op if, with the Deputy Director's permission, of course, her time as an
informant was terminated. With extreme prejudice.

**SURVEILLANCE LOG (SEPTEMBER 1st, 2015):**

**9:00 AM – 5:00 PM** – Subject serves guests at the EDEN DINER. Among them: "BIG INJUN," SHERIFF
MAGNUM, MARK SHIFFRON, and DEPUTY EARLE.

**6:00 – 8:00 PM** – Subject engages in a series of (presumably clandestine) meetings with town residents,
most notably ROWAN, CURTIS, and "BIG INJUN."
(Surveillance note: I don't have enough information to speculate on what Subject is up to with these
meetings, but I know that she's ambitious enough that whatever it is, it's going to shake up Eden. I'm
telling you – a bloodbath is imminent.)

**9:00 PM** – Subject returns to residence, and prepares a light meal before reading.

**11:00 PM** – Subject falls asleep.

**LEGAL NAME:** RICHTER, JOHAN

**KNOWN ALIAS(ES):** J0hk3r (Hacker's online history confirmed with the assistance of Southwest Branch Field Agent James Miller, Badge No. [REDACTED])

**BIRTH DATE:** 13 SEPTEMBER 1983
**STATE/NATION OF ORIGIN:** Baltimore, MD
**HEIGHT/WEIGHT:** 5' 9", 180 LBS
**OCCUPATION:** Evidence suggests that MAYOR SHIFFRON pays Johan directly for his technological servies

**PRIOR OFFENSES:** Murder in the First Degree (Acquitted)

**KNOWN CRIMINAL AFFILIATIONS:** Anonymous

**KNOWN NONCRIMINAL AFFILIATIONS:** Best Buy Corporation – "Geek Squad"

**PSYCHOLOGICAL PROFILE:** Johan's life appears very straightforward to me.
Here is a boy who never really became a man. He was picked on in school, probably bullied relentlessly, and, after graduating, he assuredly retreated into a wholly introverted lifestyle. There were online exploits, and like many shy, awkward boys, he may have found some solace there. But all of that changed when they found the girl's body.
And yes, he was acquitted, and, yes, it's entirely possible that Johan Richter was innocent of the heinous crimes perpetuated on that child. But as far as the public was concerned? As far as the general population of a federal prison would be concerned? Guilty. And you know how they treat pedophiles in general pop. So somewhere along the line, Laura Shiffron found him, and picked him up, and hid him away. Another asset gathered. And here is, as far as I can tell, a spineless worm of man with the technological skill to help take down infrastructures vastly superior to Eden's own…and Shiffron's got him in her pocket. See why I'm worried?

**SURVEILLANCE LOG (SEPTEMBER 28th, 2015):**

**11:30 AM** – MAYOR SHIFFRON arrives at Subject's trailer. SHIFFRON seems unwilling to enter the dwelling, and the two discuss terms outside.

**12:45 PM** – A short while after SHIFFRON leaves, Subject exits his trailer, carrying several large duffel bags. Later surveillance determines these bags to be full of tech.

**1:30 – 4:00 PM** – Subject travels from location to location throughout the town, examining power lines, testing areas with various meters, and examining outlets.

**8:00 PM** – Subject returns to trailer and rendezvous with an UNIDENTIFIED WOMAN. The two enter, and she leaves 30 min later. I suspect this woman was a prostitute, based on her dress and the timing of their visit, but I cannot confirm.

**LEGAL NAME:** EARLE, DAVID F.

**KNOWN ALIAS(ES):** "Early"

**BIRTH DATE:** 12 FEBRUARY 1990
**STATE/NATION OF ORIGIN:** EDEN, WY
**HEIGHT/WEIGHT:** 5' 11", 175 LBS
**OCCUPATION:** Sheriff's Deputy

**PRIOR OFFENSES:** N/A

**KNOWN CRIMINAL AFFILIATIONS:** N/A

**KNOWN NONCRIMINAL AFFILIATIONS:** N/A

**PSYCHOLOGICAL PROFILE:** If this were any other small town in America, Earle would be the squeaky clean town darling. Young, not brilliant but not dumb, not ugly, not fat – the fellow who spent his entire life in Eden. Just another yokel.

Except, of course, for the fact that his parents, who brought him here as an infant, were convicts on the run, and much like Mark Shiffron, he was raised by murderers, con men, and criminals.

He grew up idolizing SHERIFF MAGNUM – his own father was out of the picture pretty early on, and I think, in a place where order is the only thing that keeps the wolves at bay, MAGNUM must've looked like a powerful, respectable man (even if, realistically, it's LAURA SHIFFRON who commands all the power and respect.)

I don't want to discount or write-off anyone in this unlikely place, but if I had to choose a weak link – a simple man – it'd be Earle. I don't believe he has a hidden agenda, or any grand plans; he's just your stereotypical, townie Deputy-Dawg-type.

**SURVEILLANCE LOG (OCTOBER 1st, 2015):**

**9:05 AM** – Subject rushes out of home, disheveled in appearance. Late for work, Subject is clearly in a hurry, and spills coffee on himself several times.

**9:25 AM** – Subject arrives at the EDEN CIVIC CENTER.

**11:00 AM** – Subject and SHERIFF MAGNUM leave office, to investigate what appears to be a domestic disturbance. As Magnum attempts to placate her partner, an African-American woman throws a mug at Subject, who tried to enter their home.

**12:30 PM** – SHERIFF MAGNUM and Subject eat lunch at the EDEN DINER.

**3:00 – 4:30 PM** – Subject washes windows at the EDEN CIVIC CENTER

**5:00 PM** – SHERIFF MAGNUM and Subject hold detailed, heated discussion.

**6:00 PM** – Subject attends late services at the EDEN CONGREGATIONAL CHURCH.

**7:00 PM** – Subject purchases takeout meal from the EDEN DINER, takes it with him to the town's playground, and eats it, watching the sunset while seated on a swing.

**8:00 PM** – Subject returns home. Loud rock music can be heard from Subject's dwelling.

**LEGAL NAME:** NIXON, ATTICUS F.

**KNOWN ALIAS(ES):** ATTICUS WHITE, "The White Power Preacher"

**BIRTH DATE:** 9 FEBRUARY 1969
**STATE/NATION OF ORIGIN:** LOUISIANA (City/County Unknown)
**HEIGHT/WEIGHT:** 5' 10", 180 LBS
**OCCUPATION:** Pastor, First Congregational Church of Eden

**PRIOR OFFENSES:** Disturbing the Peace, Destruction of Public Property, Vandalism, Hate Speech, Conspiracy to Commit Murder, Assault and Battery (Acquitted)

**KNOWN CRIMINAL AFFILIATIONS:** The Aryan Brotherhood, The Ku Klux Klan

**KNOWN NONCRIMINAL AFFILIATIONS:** Southern Baptist Church

**PSYCHOLOGICAL PROFILE:** Nixon was raised a racist, in the Deep South. That kind of hate was in his blood. But he was bright, for a good ol' boy, and somehow ended up learning how to preach from some of those hateful old revival types that travel around the Baptist circuit.
I watched Nixon closely when I first came to Eden – he appeared to have no intention on altering his identity or appearance, and seemed intent on staying in the town. I couldn't find any records of his time in federal, but somewhere along the line he appears to have genuinely dislodged his ethnocentric beliefs. Eden's no stranger to white supremacists (see: the "boxer," BRAD MULVEY), or to former white supremacists (see: the recent addition, ROWAN).
He answers to SHIFFRON, sure enough, and he seems to hold some sway over the town – criminals always seem to find God once they've been caught – but I think SHIFFRON exploits what is clearly latent Narcissism (see: Nixon's flamboyant, theatrical sermons, and his insistence that town hall meetings occur at the church) to ensure Nixon stays under her thumb.

**SURVEILLANCE LOG (OCTOBER 3rd, 2015):**

**7:00 AM** – Subject rises early, and following a shower and breakfast, Subject goes for a short walk around the Church grounds, near the town limits.

**8:00 AM** – Early Service. No one of significance in attendance.

**10:00 AM** – Several residents arrive, and Reverend Nixon conducts individual confessions. (Surveillance note: Nixon has never worked within a church or congregation that conducts formal confession. I've checked his history. A fascinating appropriation of the Catholic tradition, where it appears to be necessary.)

**12:00 – 5:00 PM** – Subject remains within church. No one visits.

**6:00 PM** – Late service. DEPUTY EARLE, and a slightly greater crowd, attends.

**8:00 PM** – MAYOR SHIFFRON, SHERIFF MAGNUM, and Subject meet.

**9:00 PM** – Subject retires to apartment attached to rectory.

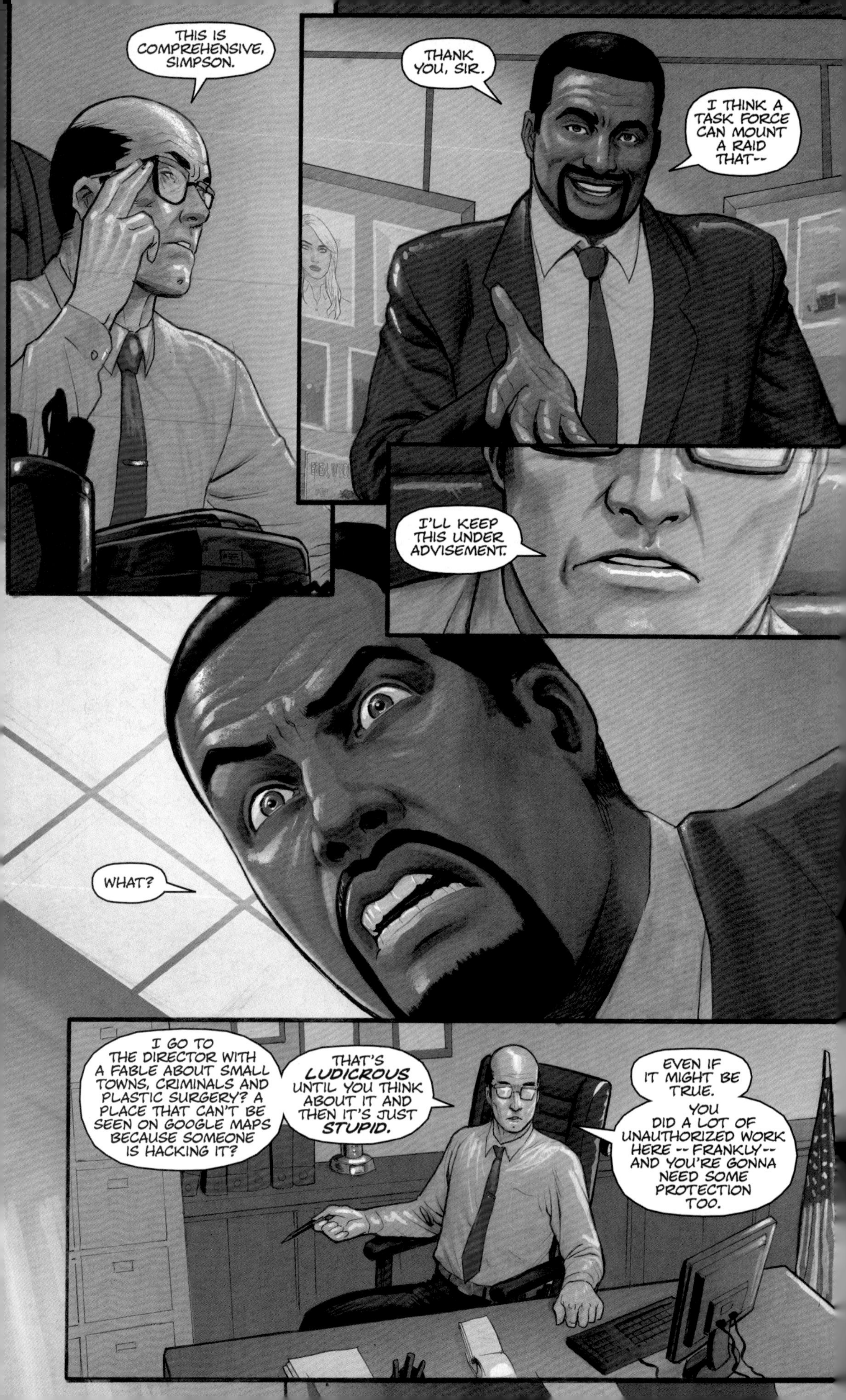
THIS IS COMPREHENSIVE, SIMPSON.
THANK YOU, SIR.
I THINK A TASK FORCE CAN MOUNT A RAID THAT--
I'LL KEEP THIS UNDER ADVISEMENT.
WHAT?
I GO TO THE DIRECTOR WITH A FABLE ABOUT SMALL TOWNS, CRIMINALS AND PLASTIC SURGERY? A PLACE THAT CAN'T BE SEEN ON GOOGLE MAPS BECAUSE SOMEONE IS HACKING IT?
THAT'S LUDICROUS UNTIL YOU THINK ABOUT IT AND THEN IT'S JUST STUPID.
EVEN IF IT MIGHT BE TRUE.
YOU DID A LOT OF UNAUTHORIZED WORK HERE -- FRANKLY-- AND YOU'RE GONNA NEED SOME PROTECTION TOO.

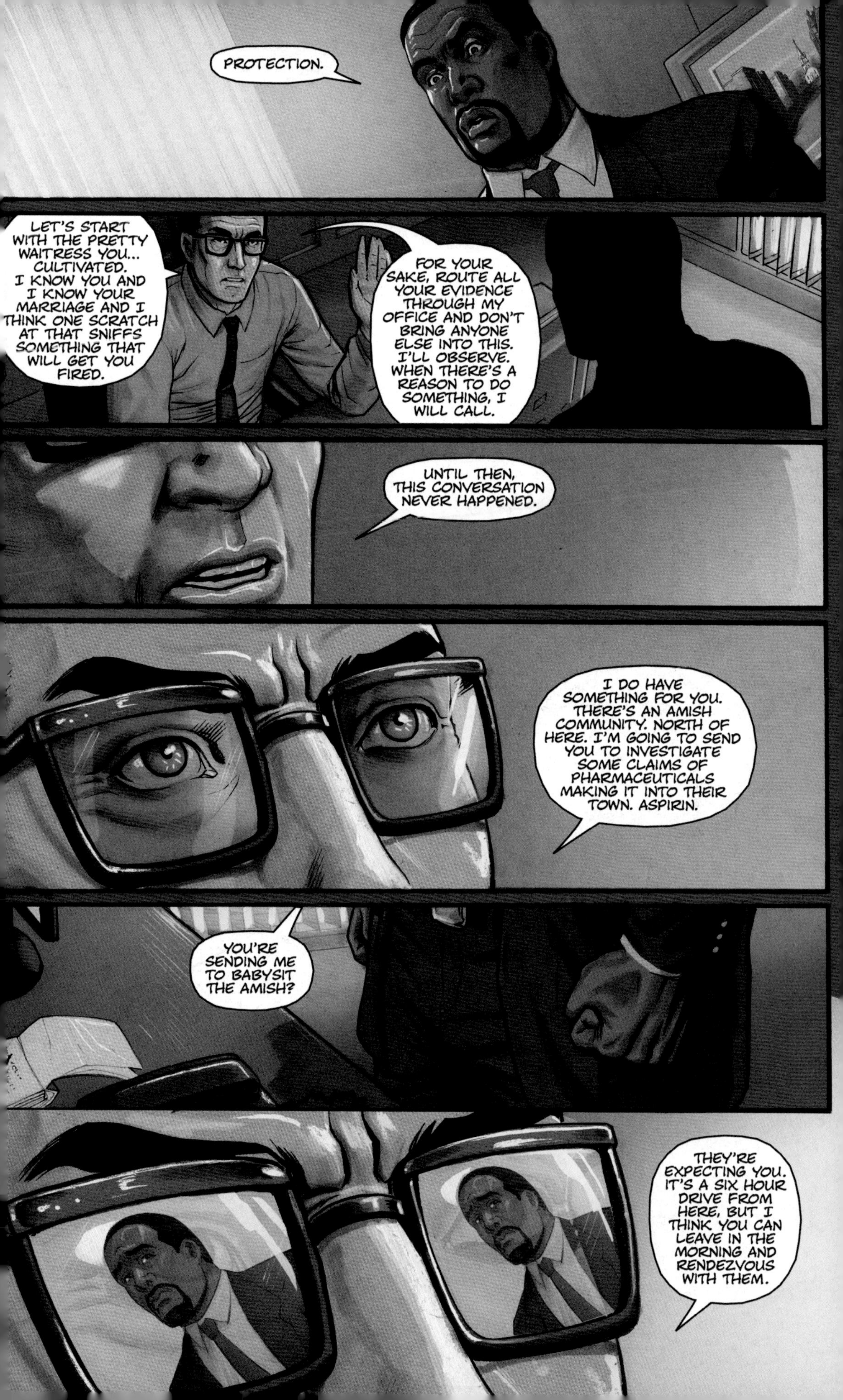
PROTECTION.
LET'S START WITH THE PRETTY WAITRESS YOU... CULTIVATED. I KNOW YOU AND I KNOW YOUR MARRIAGE AND I THINK ONE SCRATCH AT THAT SNIFFS SOMETHING THAT WILL GET YOU FIRED.
FOR YOUR SAKE, ROUTE ALL YOUR EVIDENCE THROUGH MY OFFICE AND DON'T BRING ANYONE ELSE INTO THIS. I'LL OBSERVE. WHEN THERE'S A REASON TO DO SOMETHING, I WILL CALL.
UNTIL THEN, THIS CONVERSATION NEVER HAPPENED.
I DO HAVE SOMETHING FOR YOU. THERE'S AN AMISH COMMUNITY. NORTH OF HERE. I'M GOING TO SEND YOU TO INVESTIGATE SOME CLAIMS OF PHARMACEUTICALS MAKING IT INTO THEIR TOWN. ASPIRIN.
YOU'RE SENDING ME TO BABYSIT THE AMISH?
THEY'RE EXPECTING YOU. IT'S A SIX HOUR DRIVE FROM HERE, BUT I THINK YOU CAN LEAVE IN THE MORNING AND RENDEZVOUS WITH THEM.

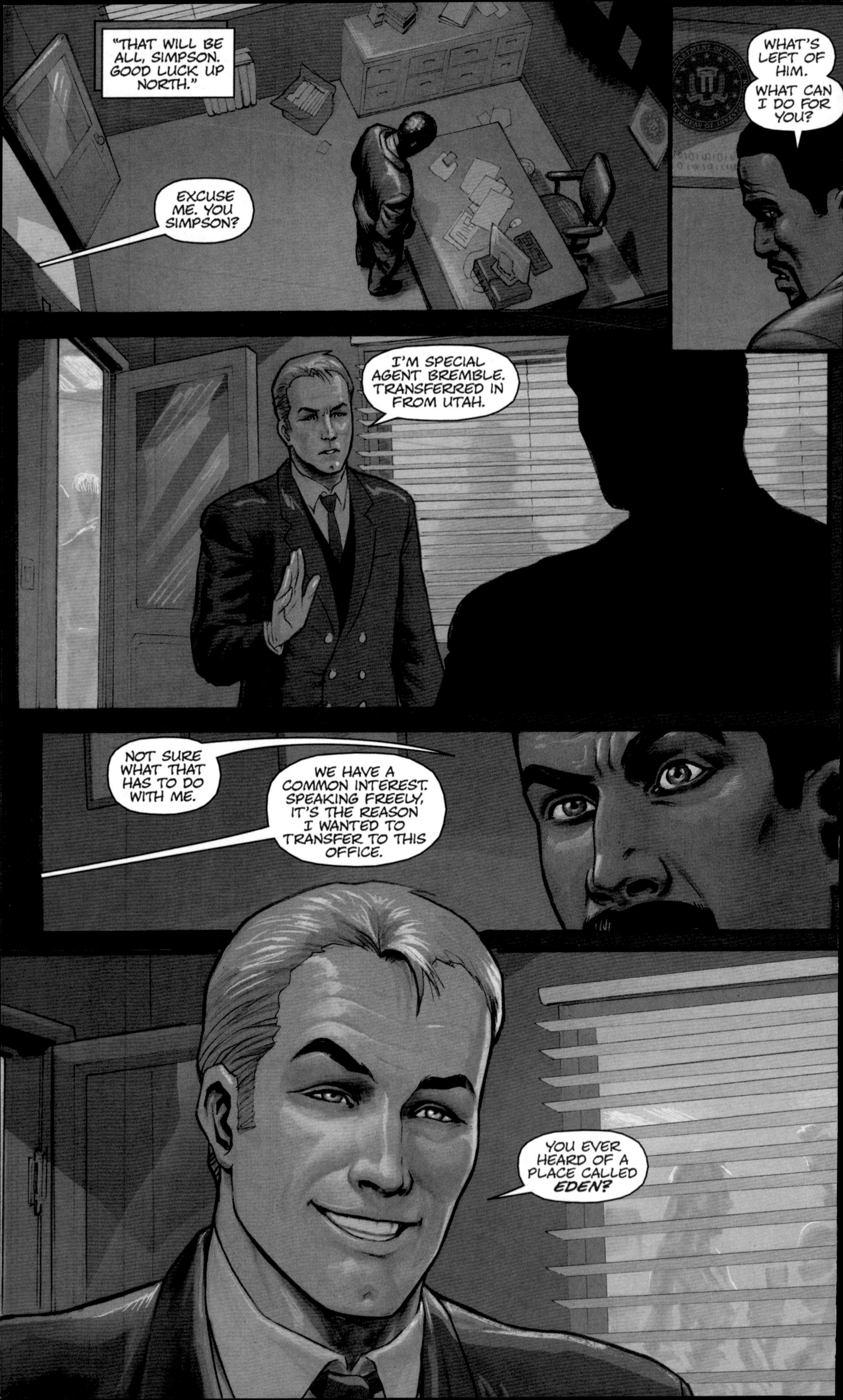
"THAT WILL BE ALL, SIMPSON. GOOD LUCK UP NORTH."
EXCUSE ME. YOU SIMPSON?
WHAT'S LEFT OF HIM.
WHAT CAN I DO FOR YOU?
I'M SPECIAL AGENT BREMBLE. TRANSFERRED IN FROM UTAH.
NOT SURE WHAT THAT HAS TO DO WITH ME.
WE HAVE A COMMON INTEREST. SPEAKING FREELY, IT'S THE REASON I WANTED TO TRANSFER TO THIS OFFICE.
YOU EVER HEARD OF A PLACE CALLED EDEN?

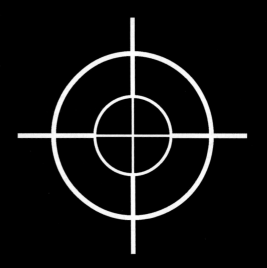

# Racketeer Influenced and Corrupt Organizations Act

By 1970, the US Government was done with public corruption. Organized crime, racketeering, the mafia – for decades, it had proven nearly impossible to weed out the brains behind organized crime operations, or pin any real charges on them. In October of that same year, however, President Richard M. Nixon signed into law the Racketeer Influenced and Corrupt Organizations Act, designed specifically to curtail mafia activity by charging organized crime leaders for the actions of their underlings, mainly under conspiracy charges.

While at first untested, RICO proved itself against organized crime families, corrupt city officials, and even the Hell's Angels. The act became the go-to standard case used in a variety of corruption cases – embezzling, bribery, human trafficking, and even terrorism. Its broad language and potential for generalization has made it a favorite tool not only in criminal proceedings but also in several civil cases – most notably against Major League Baseball in 2002.

Of course, a single anti-racketeering act like RICO isn't the government's only tool in their ongoing efforts to combat corruption. According to their website, the FBI considers public corruption their "top priority" among criminal investigation. The FBI runs hotlines, special task forces, and intense undercover operations in order to root out organized criminal activity. A number of these methods are incredibly simple – an anonymous phone number for police officers to report illegal activity on the part of their colleagues or superiors, or algorithms designed to seek out suspicious data.

While RICO tends to work best with high profile, conspiracy cases, and the media focuses on violent crime or mafia indictments, the FBI is just as active and invested in tackling large scale or long-running corruption in smaller arenas. In August 2014, for

example, the Bureau began investigating a number of public officials and prominent citizens in Progreso, Texas. The small town, located on the Texas-Mexico border, harbored a series of bribery and other corruption violations, the majority of which were conducted by a single family that acted almost like a small town mafia, controlling Progreso's school district contracts and other local government projects. The FBI caught wind of the family's corruption, and on August 11, 2014, several members of the family were sentenced to prison terms.

The family had, over the course of many years, managed to launder money from federal grants as well as local contracts, and through "confidential sources, undercover scenarios, financial record examinations, and witness interviews" the FBI was able to build an airtight case.

It's not the sort of dramatic Mafioso endeavor that makes the news, but it was still considered a major win for the Bureau. Even though there wasn't much in terms of outright, obvious crime – no violence, burglary, or noticeable lawbreaking – simple cases of following the money toppled what was well on its way to becoming a small-town empire of corruption.

# MAIL CALL

## BEHIND THE ART!

Let's take a look at how *Postal* comes to life by comparing Bryan's scripts with Isaac's layouts, to see whose vision is utterly destroyed first! Just kidding. But we thought you'd want to know.

For anyone who has ever wondered how a comic book comes together it is the culmination of several steps executed by various people over the span of several months. It all begins with the finalized script (which has undergone more than a couple revisions up to this point), that gets turned into layouts before the complicated process of final art gets underway.

Bryan and Isaac are prepared to peel back the layers of the onion and show you just how *Postal* is born... hold onto your butts!

## PAGE FOUR

Panel One

On Agent Bremble's car driving a lonely stretch of Wyoming road. Near the highway. Not really rural as much as abandoned industrial.

Panel Two

On Bremble behind the wheel. Driving, looking serious.

Panel Three

Bremble pulls up to what looks like an abandoned gas station, one of those older ones and it has a workshop/garage built onto the side of it.

Panel Four

Bremble exits his car.

Panel Five

Bremble checks the load in his FBI issue 9mm pistol. (I think they have Glocks now. Not sure. I know it's a semi auto, but I'll confirm it for reference).

SFX: Click!

Panel Six

Bremble is slipping the pistol back into his holster (under his blazer) and walking towards the door of the gas station.

# MAIL CALL

Notes from Isaac: One of the great things about working with Bryan is that he will often give me detailed descriptions of the backgrounds in the scripts. Bryan will sometimes talk about the mood and atmosphere in *Postal*, but sometimes I prefer to think of the backgrounds as other characters. Then I can think of the setting as being lonely (as Bryan states in his panel 1 description), dramatic, scary, safe, etc. Thinking this way helps me figure out what I'm trying to communicate.

Panel 1 - Because this industrial area is lonely, we wanted to show a lot of machinery to imply that it was once very busy on this stretch of road but has long since been abandoned. To emphasize Bremble's loneliness, I wanted to make his car very small.

Panel 3 - Sometimes I'll make a quick 3D model of a setting in a program called SketchUp. Using SketchUp is kind of like making cubes and shapes out of paper, but digitally. This program is especially helpful with realizing buildings at difficult angles or maintaining consistency with a background we see multiple times. It can definitely speed up the penciling process as long as I don't get stuck over-detailing the 3D model (which I have lost days doing!).

## PAGE FIVE

Panel One

On Bremble entering the gas station. This is a visual reference to an old 1980's movie called THE HITCHER (which is brilliant by the way. C. Thomas Howell and Rutger Hauer). Bremble is sort of an antagonist, but I'm treating him like the hero of his own story. He's basically trying to investigate a criminal conspiracy so he's not a villain, he just wants to make life hard for Eden and shut it down.
Bremble's entering the gas station. It's dusty, maybe there's some venetian blinds and shafts of light. Ridley Scott shit, LOL. Bremble's entering cautiously, a little tight but he's not expecting danger.

BREMBLE: Mr. Pross? It's Agent Bremble.

Panel Two

Close on Bremble as he hears a voice from off panel.

PROSS(off panel): Here.

Panel Three

Bremble's POV. We see BECK PROSS(50's) standing at the dark end of the gas station. Old jeans and a thick sweater (it's always Fall for me in POSTAL, LOL) a sturdy man with a walking cane and a BLACK BANDANNA wrapped around his face. We can see his eyes. His balding, gray hair.

PROSS: You came a long way for a conversation, Agent Bremble.

Panel Four

Over Pross' shoulder. On Bremble.

BREMBLE: Eden is a difficult conversation to have. With anyone. I don't mind the trip if you're willing to have it, Mr. Pross.

Panel Five

Close on Pross.

PROSS: Have a seat, Agent Bremble. Let's talk about paradise.

# MAIL CALL

Notes from Isaac: Since we won't spend too much time with this setting, I figured it was faster to draw these pages with perspective lines (those light green and pink lines). I'm DEFINITELY not as much of a movie guy as Bryan is and I have NEVER heard of *The Hitcher* and I don't know C. Thomas Howell or Rutger Hauer and sometimes I can get REALLY LOST when talking to Bryan! But! As per his request, I managed to find *The Hitcher* online and I'm glad I watched it! In panel 1, I tried to incorporate the type of lighting they had in that movie, and I'm very happy with how it came out. As an artist, it really helps to take your writer's suggestions and broaden your artistic vocabulary!

As for Beck Pross, I decided we should lose the glasses for the final inks. I was worried he might look a bit too similar to Director Schultz. I was a little sad about it since Pross here bears a striking resemblance to my dad, who also happens to be *Postal*'s #1 super fan.

## PAGE SEVEN

Panel One

Establishing of an apartment building of a more metropolitan Wyoming. It's night. This is a safehouse. Not a a bad neighborhood but not one you would remember.

SCHULTZ(off panel): This is irregular, us meeting in person like this.

LAURA(off panel): Who did you send me?

Panel Two

On Laura and Schultz speaking in an unfurnished apartment. The safehouse where she can meet Schultz when she feels the need.

LAURA: She killed three people in my town. With a fucking rocks glass.

SCHULTZ: She's my daughter.

Panel Three

On Laura.

LAURA: Your what?

SCHULTZ(off panel): Don't you look at me like that.

Panel Four

On Schultz

SCHULTZ: You have children that complicate things too.
(linked)
SCHULTZ: Her mother meant nothing but Molly happened. I never took her in but I kept care of her. From a distance.
(linked)

SCHULTZ: And she's the worst thing I've ever done to this world

# MAIL CALL

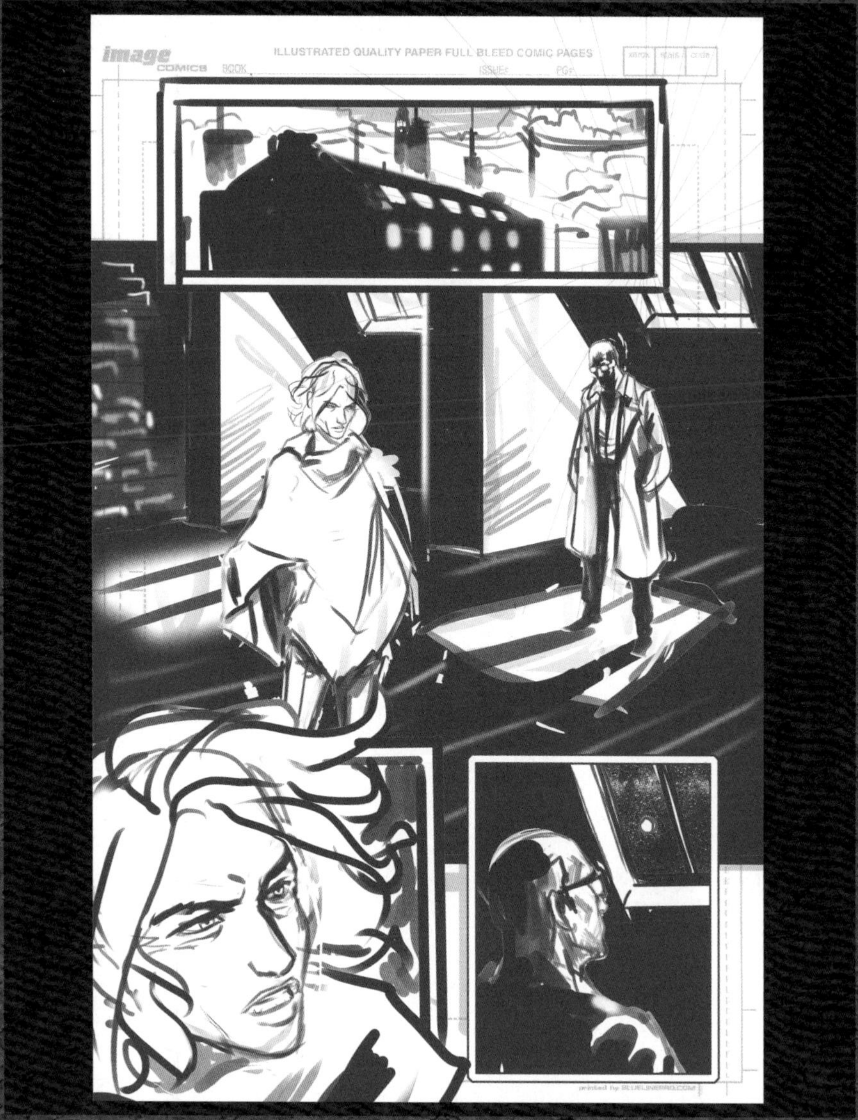
ILLUSTRATED QUALITY PAPER FULL BLEED COMIC PAGES

Notes from Isaac: The script here mentions that this is an unfurnished safe house, so I figured I could put more thought and energy into figuring out the architecture and lighting of the setting. I made the scene dark and the apartment a loft with a sloping ceiling. I thought I'd get some more interesting views and shapes this way. I didn't want Laura and Schultz to just be talking in a hollow white cube with a door.

Because the page is two characters talking in an unfurnished room, I knew I could run the risk of drawing a static page. So instead, I tried to make the conversation a little more interesting with the scale of the characters. Because Laura is being accusatory to Schultz, I wanted her to feel larger than him. In panel two she's closer to camera and in panel 3 she breaks the panel boarders. She has the upper hand in this argument as she catches him in a lie, so I wanted her to feel large and imposing as Schultz hides in the shadow.

# MAIL CALL

## SCRIPT TO ART FROM ISSUE #11

Here is a look at some of the process work from Bryan and Issac on *Postal* #11. Many of these panels have to do with Eden's newest resident — Molly — and how she is going to fit into the unique community *Postal* surrounds.

## PAGE ONE

**Panel One**
Molly stands at a PAY PHONE at the edge of a town, main street. She's already in conversation.
MOLLY: Hey, dad. Yeah, I'm fine here. It's cold and quiet.
(beat)
MOLLY: Remember back when we'd go walking and you'd wrap your jacket around me? Yeah. Cold like that.

**Panel Two**
On Schultz, sitting at home, on the opposite end of the line.
SCHULTZ: They're treating you okay? If there's any problem, you let me know. I told them they can't even let dust hit your shoulders —
MOLLY (from phone): Dad, I'm fine.

**Panel Three**
On Molly.
MOLLY: Everyone's lovely. I even got a little trailer up on a hill. It's got these fake wooden walls. Funny fake wooden walls.
(linked)
MOLLY: You gonna come see me, Dad? I miss you.

**Panel Four**
On Schultz.
SCHULTZ: I'll try, angel, but I can't make a promise right now. The important thing is you're safe.
(linked)
SCHULTZ: You're safe there. You call me every week, okay? Every week. If anything happens.

**Panel Five**
On Molly.
MOLLY: Nothing's gonna happen, Dad. I'm done being like I was before. I really am. I like it here.
(linked)
MOLLY: Eden is a nice place. I'm making friends. I can do that, Dad.
(linked)
MOLLY: I can make friends.

# MAIL CALL

Notes from Isaac: This issue was a tricky one to draw because the entire issue is made up of conversations between the characters. Dialogue can look very monotonous if the panels just show heads talking page after page. In this comics medium (which I love so very much) we don't have actors to deliver the script dynamically or music to emphasize emotion, so we have to compensate. With this page, as well as the rest of the issue, I tried to play with environment, composition, lighting, and fashion. All these "tricks," if I use them as well as I hope, can make a page look a bit more interesting and even introduce some secondary storytelling (more on that later).

In this page I used negative space and dismal lighting to highlight the lonely aspects of both characters. Molly, especially, is an outsider, and I wanted to show that in the first panel by drawing her very small in the outskirts of town. It's dark out, but she doesn't mind. She's not scared of anything.

Eagle-eyed readers will notice Molly's face in the last panel was redrawn before the printed inked and colored version. Drawing for me can be a real struggle — especially with close-ups. I must have spent hours on this blue lined face before I eventually gave up and moved on to page 2. And I still was extremely unhappy with it! Sometimes, however, the best thing to do is to get away from the drawing I'm fussing over and to redraw it in inks days later. Coming back to a drawing with a fresh pair of eyes can make a huge difference.

**PAGE FOURTEEN**

**Panel One**

On Laura.

LAURA: Goddamnit, go home!

**Panel Two**

Mark calmly gets up from the table.

**Panel Three**

Mark walks out of the kitchen.

**Panel Four**

On Laura and Magnum.

MAGNUM: I understand him, Laura. This ain't right.

LAURA: Magnum, either stand with me and help me —

**Panel Five**

On Laura.

LAURA: Or leave me the fuck alone.

# MAIL CALL

Notes from Isaac: This page is pretty standard stuff, but I'm pretty proud of panel 3, actually. The composition is cut into two halves: light and dark. Mark, in this panel, is literally turning his back on his mother whom has just rejected him and he is walking into the darkness. This is that secondary storytelling I mentioned earlier. Bryan always writes amazing dialogue and I love it when I have an opportunity to draw the feeling of the words. It's a wordless panel which I tried to inject some darkness and emotion into. Hopefully, this panel shows some foreshadowing of Mark's small betrayal as he devizes a plan behind his mother's back.

## PAGE FIFTEEN

### Panel One

Day. This is the trailer where Molly lives. There's a LARGE OAK TREE in front of the trailer and Molly sits on a swingset. This is a long shot. Picturesque. Molly and the tree are in silhouette against the bright sky.

Molly's singing to herself.

MOLLY: Into the sea of waking dreams...I follow without pride...

### Panel Two

Close on Molly on the swing. Still singing. She's not facing us.

MOLLY: Cause nothing stands between us here...that I won't be denied...

### Panel Three

Now Molly's facing us.

MOLLY: Hi, Mark.

### Panel Four

On Mark, standing in the grass, facing Molly.

MARK: Why are you invincible?

# MAIL CALL

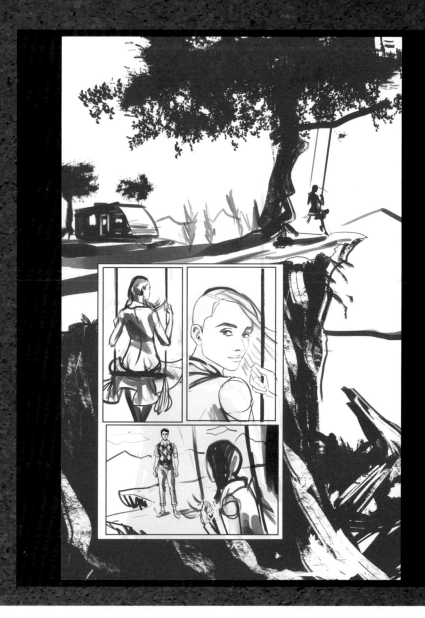

This page was fun because I got to design a weird background. The script had Molly on a swing and my idea was to have her over a cliff with a steep drop to jagged rocks. The cliff and rocks emphasize that both characters are one step away from becoming very dangerous. Molly flirts with that dangerous side of hers and swings back and forth. One moment she can be sweet and nice, and the next she is violent and ruthless. Mark is not swinging, but he too is very close to crossing the line into some scary territory.

Bryan and Matt and created these incredible, nuanced, fully realized characters. When the writing is this good, I have room to explore visual elements to highlight what I like about them.

# MAIL CALL

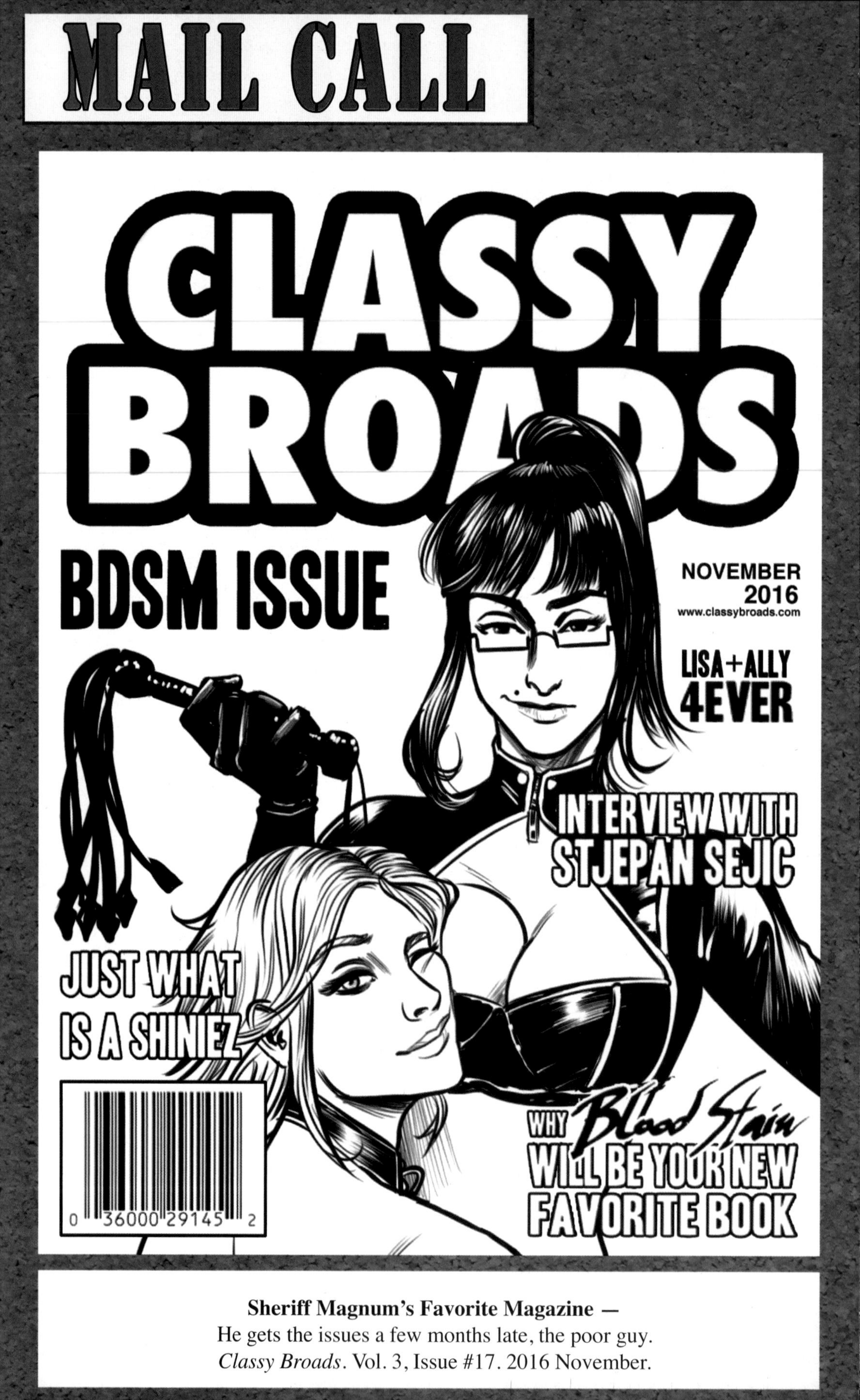
CLASSY BROADS
BDSM ISSUE
NOVEMBER 2016
www.classybroads.com
LISA+ALLY 4EVER
INTERVIEW WITH STJEPAN SEJIC
JUST WHAT IS A SHINIEZ
WHY Blood Stain WILL BE YOUR NEW FAVORITE BOOK
0 36000 29145 2

**Sheriff Magnum's Favorite Magazine —**
He gets the issues a few months late, the poor guy.
*Classy Broads*. Vol. 3, Issue #17. 2016 November.

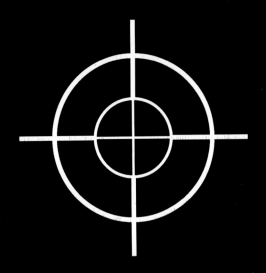

## SCIENCE CLASS (SPECIAL *POSTAL* EDITION)

Thank you for reading this book! When we first started *Postal* I told Bryan Hill and Isaac Goodhart that I wanted them to both commit to a twenty-five issue run. I then brazenly went out and publicly said we're going to do that. I would have looked pretty stupid if we cancelled it after four issues because no one cared, I've seen this happen before. Fortunately, it had not happened to me when I proudly declared it! I've certainly cancelled series earlier than I wanted to, but that's how it goes. With *Postal*, when we laid out the outline for the long arc, we knew the beginning and end of the story, but not the middle. That's pretty common in story development. When we got to issue twenty-one and were planning for the end, the end felt unfinished. So, Bryan and I decided to add two one-shot issues focusing on the aftermath of Mark and Laura to round it out. And this isn't the end of *Postal*. I think we'll take a year or so off and then come back to it, in the meantime please tell your friends about it!

## ASPERGER'S SYNDROME

Mark is near and dear to my heart and is why I wanted to write this one shot. I haven't written an issue of *Postal* in a long time, so it felt good to come back to it. I based a lot of Mark on a guy I knew from college who had Asperger's. I knew him well from about 88-94 and then he went to work for Raytheon. Flash forward a couple decades and he's still there building amazing things that protect us all. So what is Asperger's?

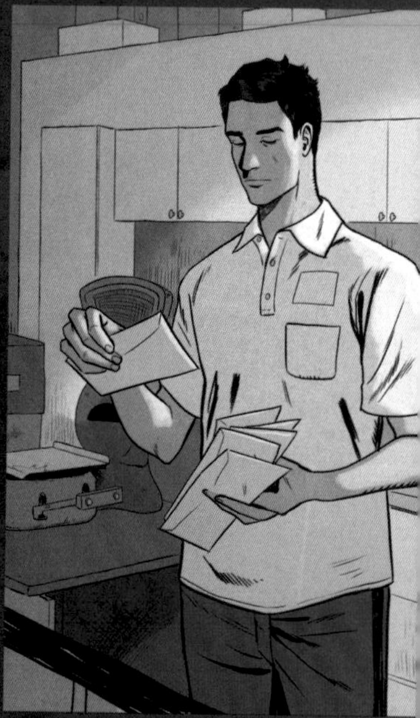

*"Asperger Syndrome (AS) is a neurobiological disorder on the higher-functioning end of the autism spectrum. An individual's symptoms can range from mild to severe. While sharing many of the same characteristics as other Autism Spectrum Disorders (ASD's) including Pervasive Developmental Disorder – Not Otherwise Specified (PDD-NOS) and High-Functioning Autism (HFA), AS has been recognized as a distinct medical diagnosis in Europe for almost 60 years, but has only been included in the U.S. medical diagnostic manual since 1994 ("Asperger Disorder" in the DSM-IV).*

*Individuals with AS and related disorders exhibit serious deficiencies in social and communication skills. Their IQ's are typically in the normal to very superior range. They are usually educated in the mainstream, but most require special education services. Because of their naivete, those with AS are often viewed by their peers as "odd" and are frequently a target for bullying and teasing.*

*They desire to fit in socially and have friends, but have a great deal of difficulty making effective social connections. Many of them are at risk for developing mood disorders, such as anxiety or depression, especially in adolescence. Diagnosis of autistic spectrum disorders should be made by a medical expert to rule out other possible diagnoses and to discuss interventions."*

That's from this link: **https://aspennj.org/what-is-asperger-syndrome**
That page also lists out a ton of typical characteristics of someone with AS.

## WHAT CAUSES ASPERGER'S SYNDROME?

So here's the kicker, we don't really know. We know there's some sort of genetic mutation, but the cause of that mutation is still being investigated. There are rumors about vaccines causing Autism and Asperger's Syndrome but there's zero proof this is reality. I've heard rumors that the Earth is flat too. Could it be caused by environmental factors? Are there epigenetic factors to parents that when passed on to the child it manifests? That's certainly possible. There's been a ton of research on it and the below two links I've found to be the most readable by people without medical degrees.

» **http://www.kennethrobersonphd.com/what-causes-aspergers-syndrome/**

» **http://www.autism-help.org/aspergers-syndrome-cause.html**

If you want a more science-heavy explanation, go here:

» **http://www.autisme.com/autism/explanatory-theories-on-asd.html**

» **https://www.scientificamerican.com/article/broken-mirrors-a-theory-of-autism-2007-06/**

**WHAT DOES HAVING ASPERGER'S FEEL LIKE?**

Having known a man with Asperger's for three decades now, I've had many conversations with him about it. His most succinct answer is he feels like he's not the same species as the rest of us. They don't think the same way...and not in a sociopathic way. Imagine not understanding why someone smiles at you. Or that you're expected to respond to people when they talk to you. They have to learn how to make the rest of us not feel uncomfortable around them. When I reflect on that... it's baffling. I've found most Aspies to be smarter than the average human. They care about different things and have interests that we might not get...but isn't that everyone really? They're just people, slightly different. Trying to make their way in this world like the rest of us and find some happiness.

» **https://www.psychologytoday.com/blog/after-party-chat/201405/what-does-it-feel-have-aspergers**

» **https://www.autismspeaks.org/blog/2015/08/25/12-things-you-should-never-say-someone-autism**

What's it like to date if you have Asperger's?

» **https://www.vice.com/en_nz/article/wjjnkw/what-its-like-to-date-when-youre-on-the-autism-spectrum**

» **https://psychcentral.com/lib/romance-love-and-asperger-syndrome/**

**LOBOTOMY**

This was a regularly practiced procedure all the way into the early 20th century. It was used to treat mental disorders and other things. A lobotomy effectively ends your mind. It's not clear if it ends consciousness. I hope it did, can you imagine living and knowing everything but being unable to do anything? How horrifying would that be? Mark decided to remove Isaac's mind because he knew that would be a fitting punishment.

Transorbital Lobotomy Procedure
©2010 HowStuffWorks
Frontal Lobe
Orbitoclast


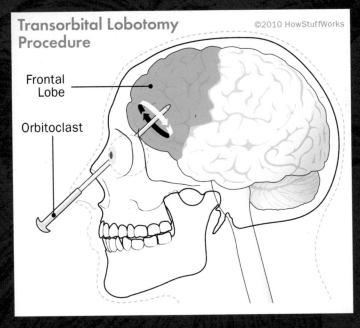

» **http://www.weirdworm.com/lobotomy-victims-and-their-life-afterward/**

That's it for *Postal: Mark*! Thanks again for reading and let me know on my social media feeds what you thought of this book.

**Carpe Diem.**

**Matt Hawkins**
**Twitter: @topcowmatt**
**http://www.facebook.com/selfloathingnarcissist**

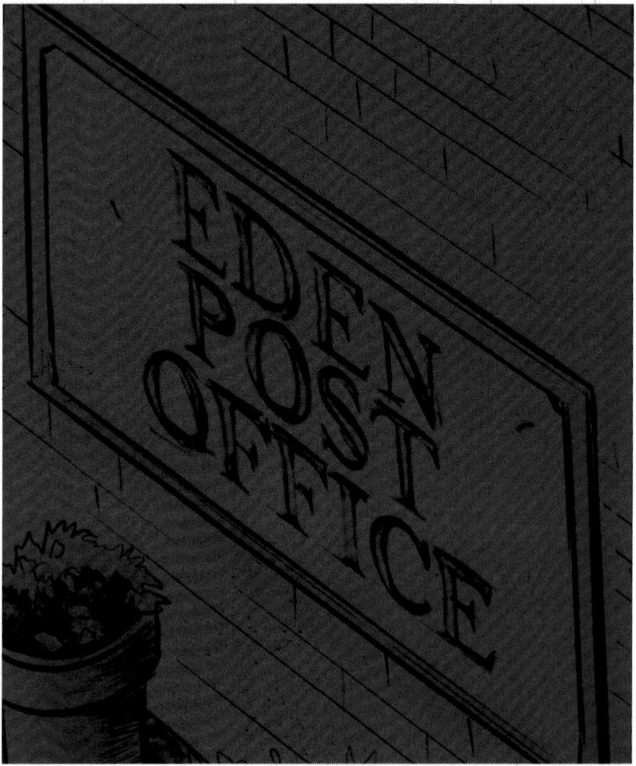
EDEN
POST
OFFICE

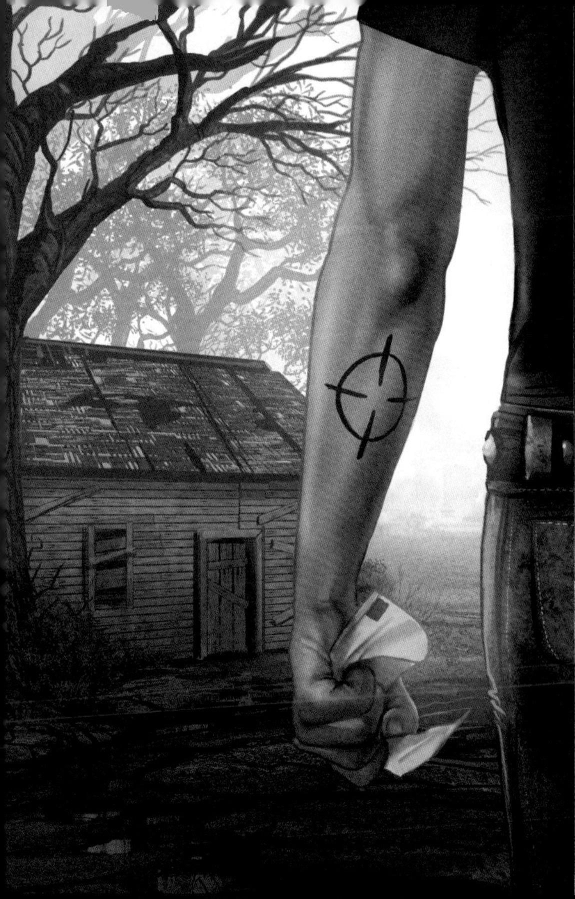

Postal #1 Cover A – Linda Sejic

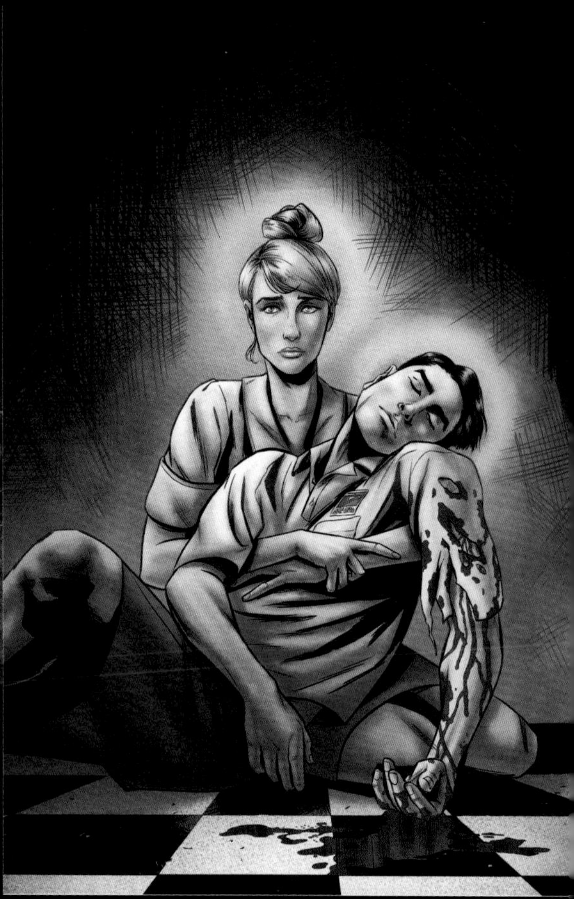

Postal #1 Cover B – Isaac Goodhart & Betsy Golden

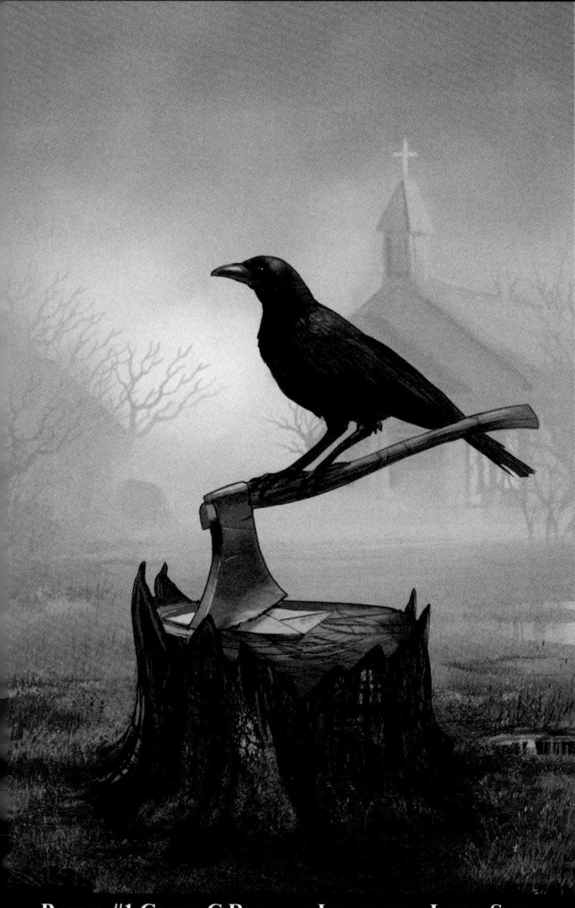

Postal #1 Cover C Retailer Incentive – Linda Sejic

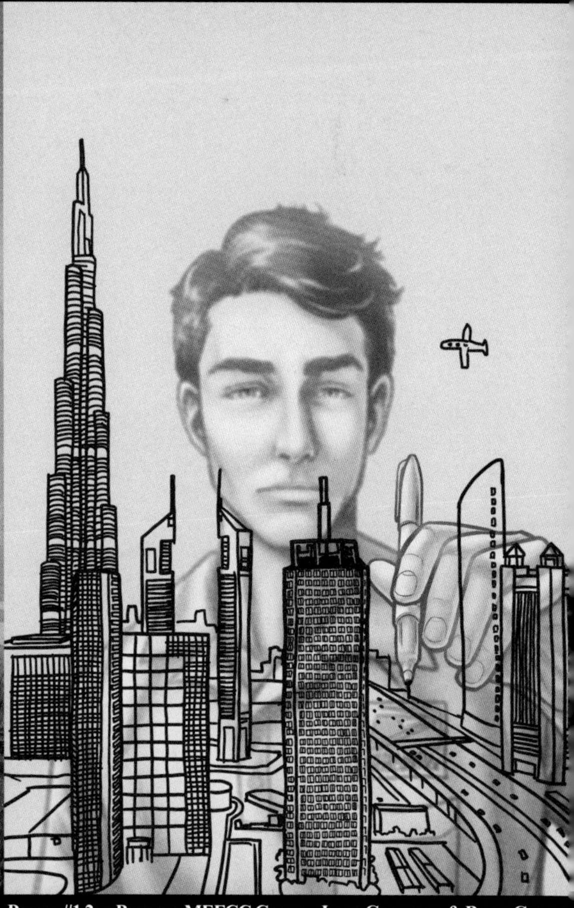

Postal #1 2nd Printing MEFCC Cover – Isaac Goodhart & Betsy Golden

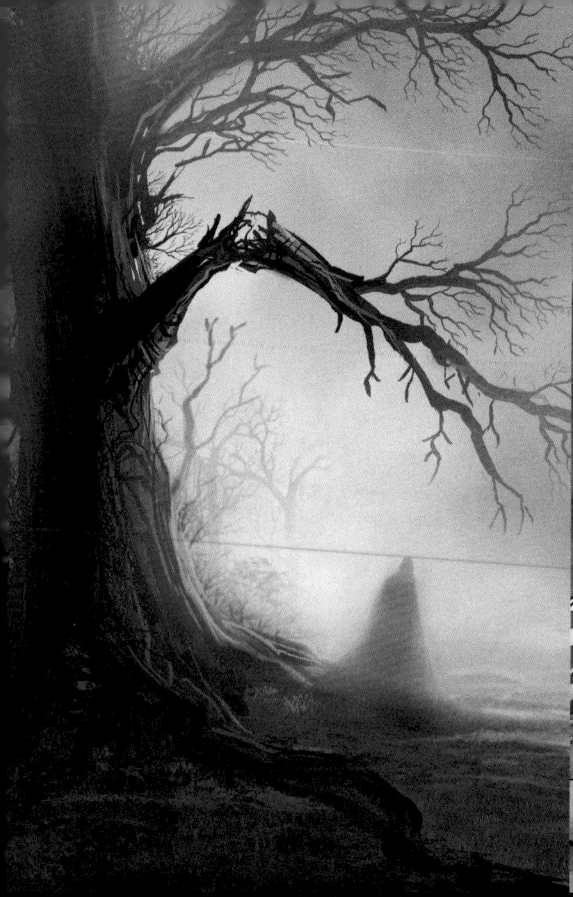

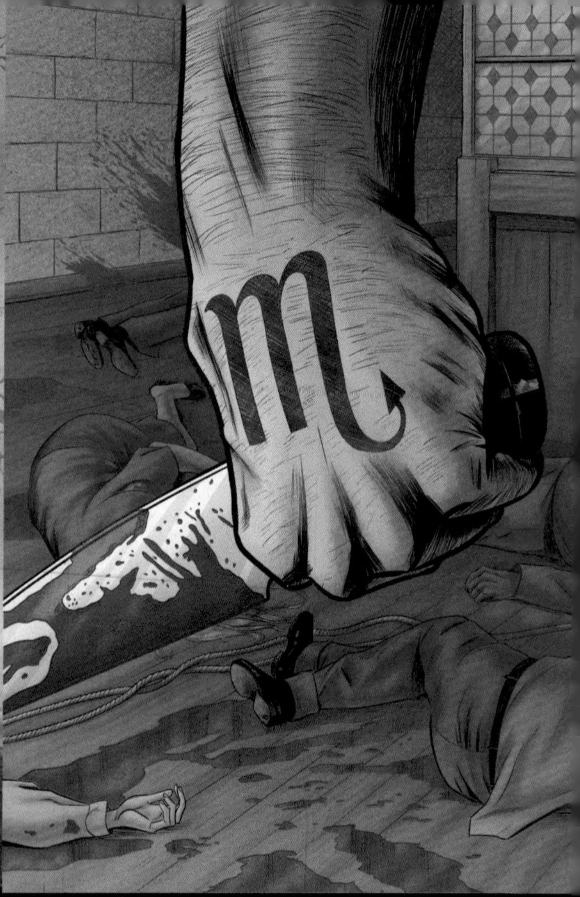

**Postal #2 Cover A – Linda Sejic**

**Postal #2 Cover B – Isaac Goodhart & Betsy Golden**

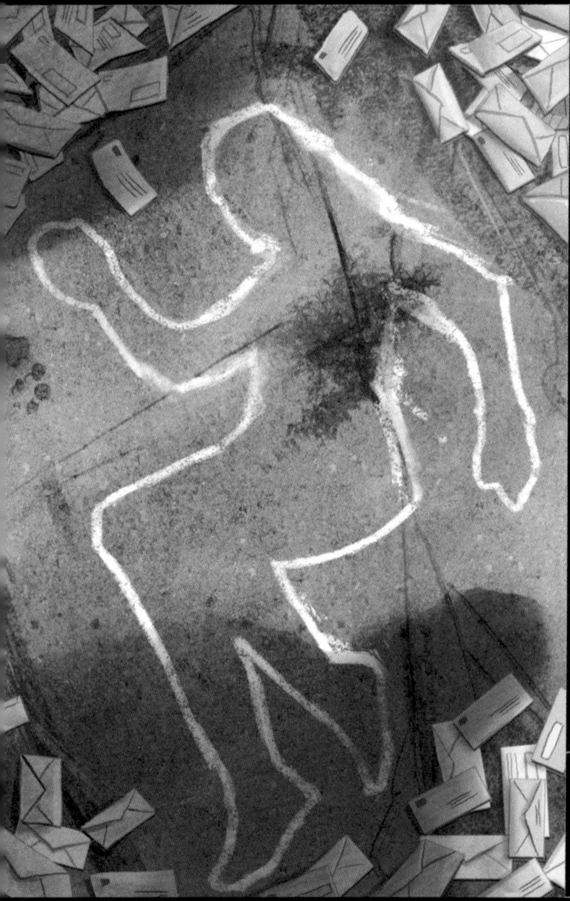

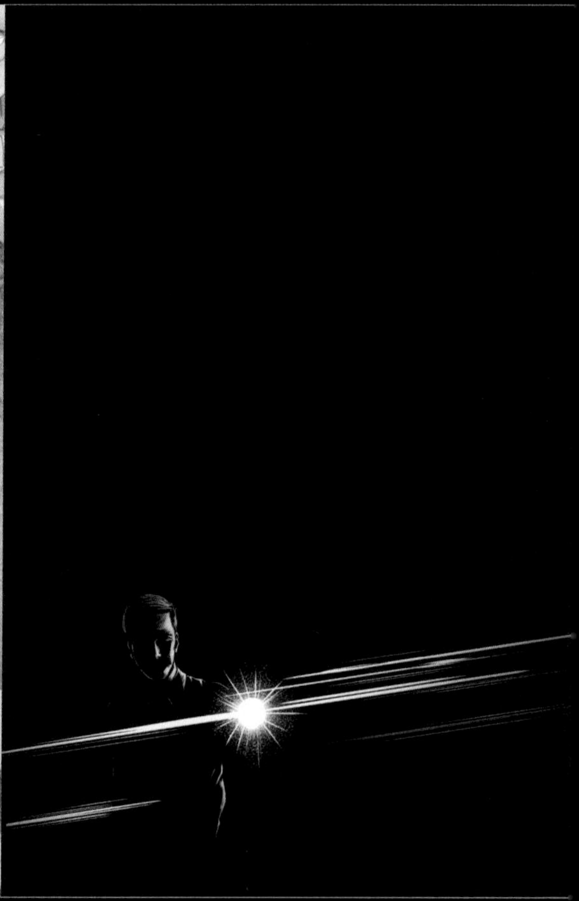

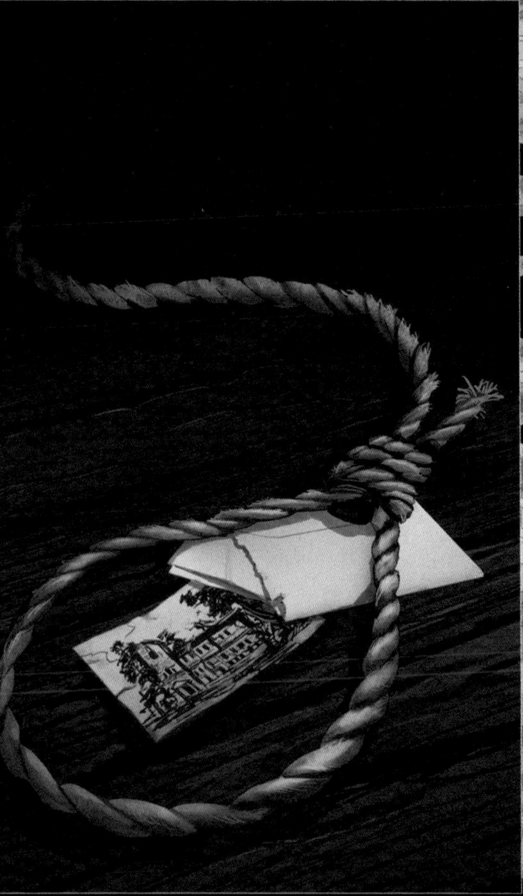

POSTAL #4 COVER A – LINDA SEJIC

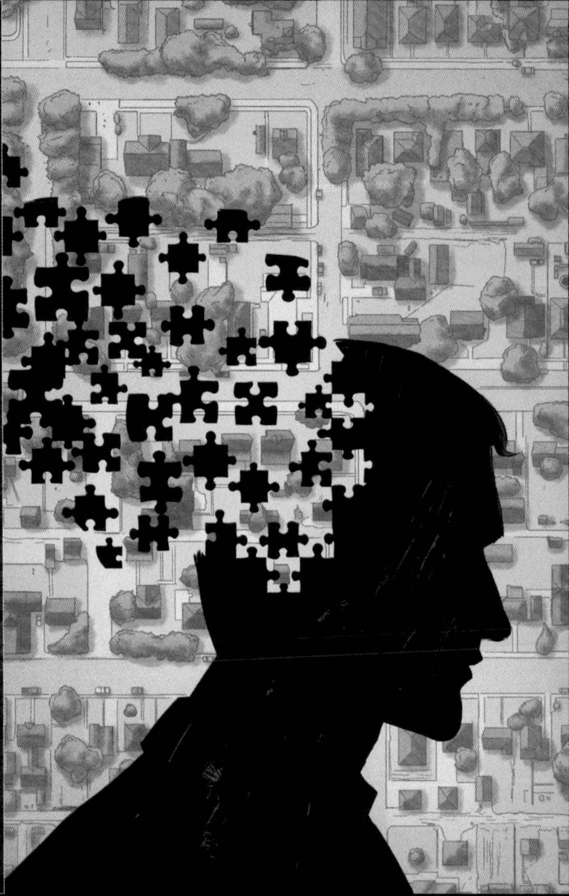

POSTAL #4 COVER B – ISAAC GOODHART & BETSY GOLDEN

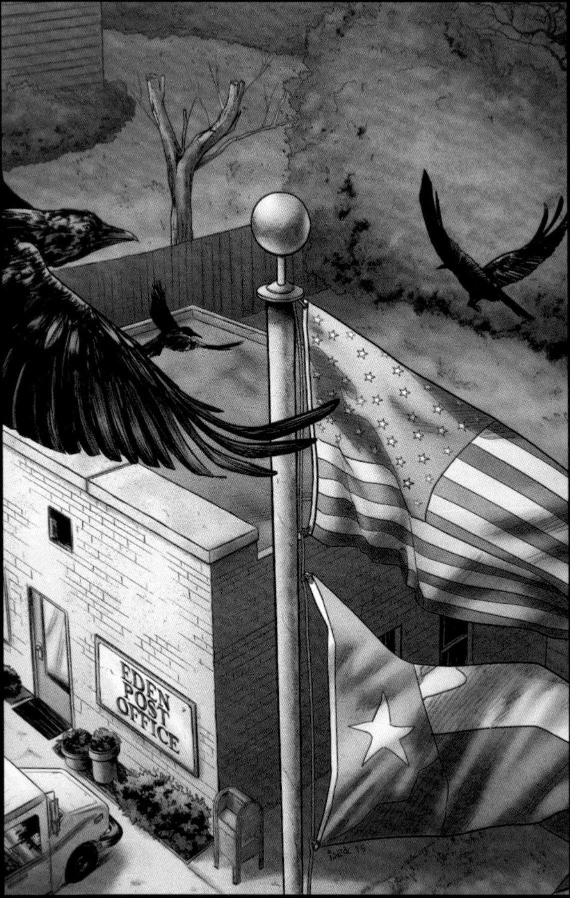
EDEN POST OFFICE

POSTAL #4 COVER C - COMICPALOOZA EXCLUSIVE – ISAAC GOODHART & BETSY GOLDEN

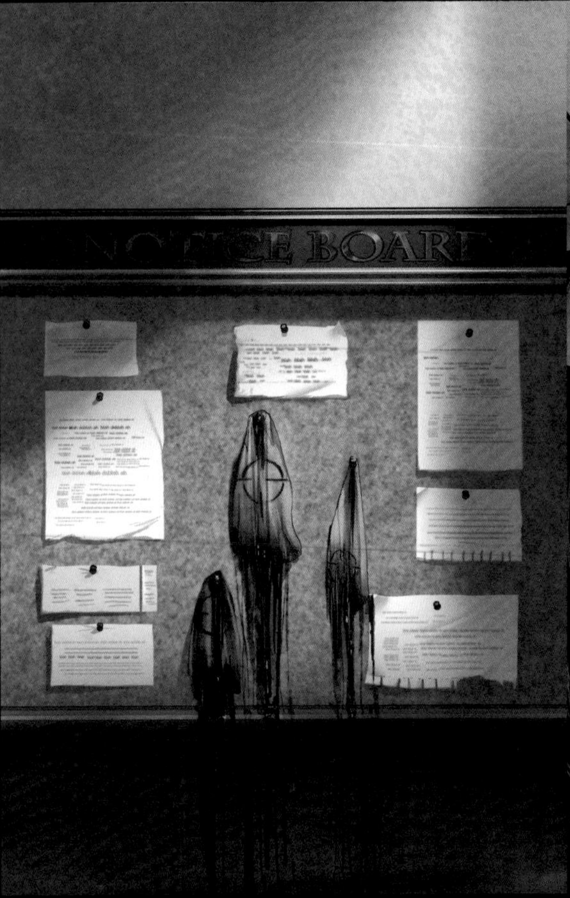

**Postal #5 Cover A – Linda Sejic**

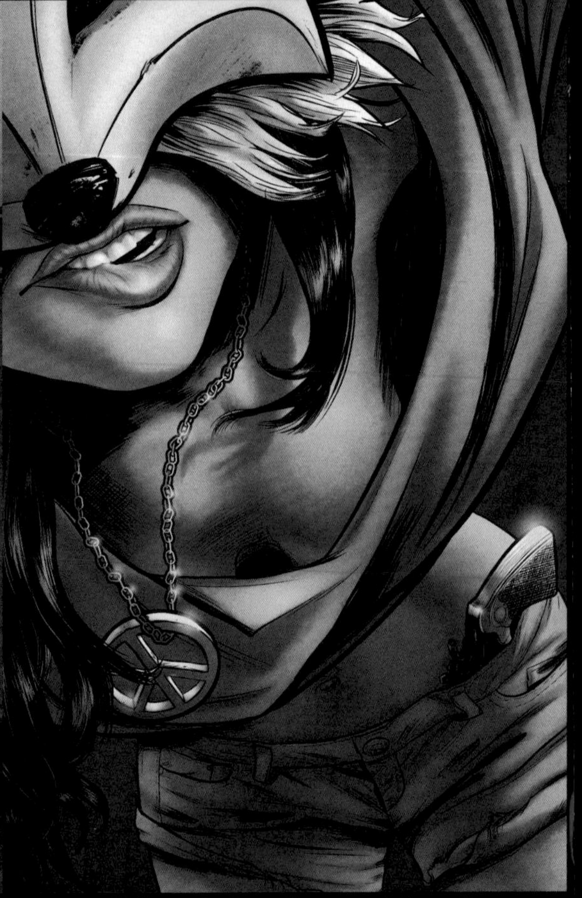

**Postal #5 Cover B – Isaac Goodhart & Betsy Golden**

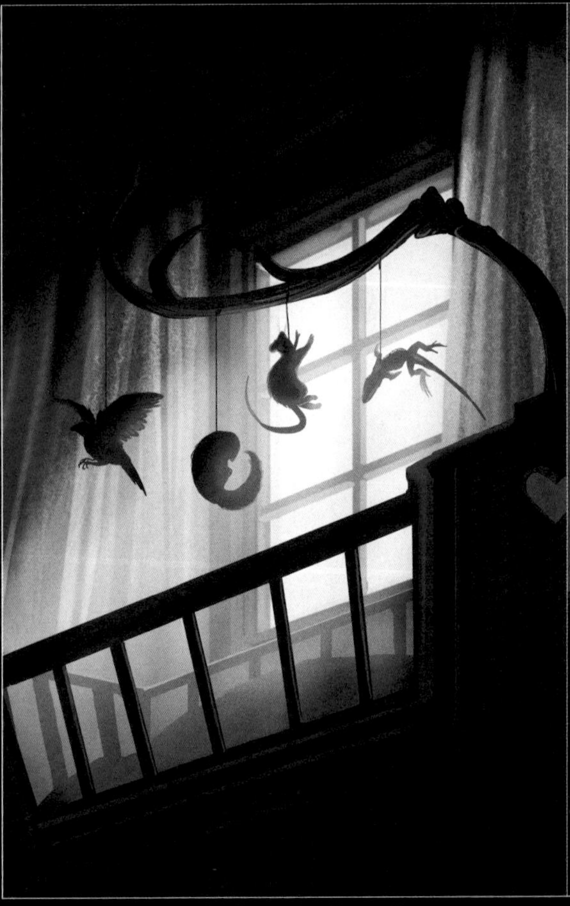

**Postal #6 Cover A – Linda Sejic**

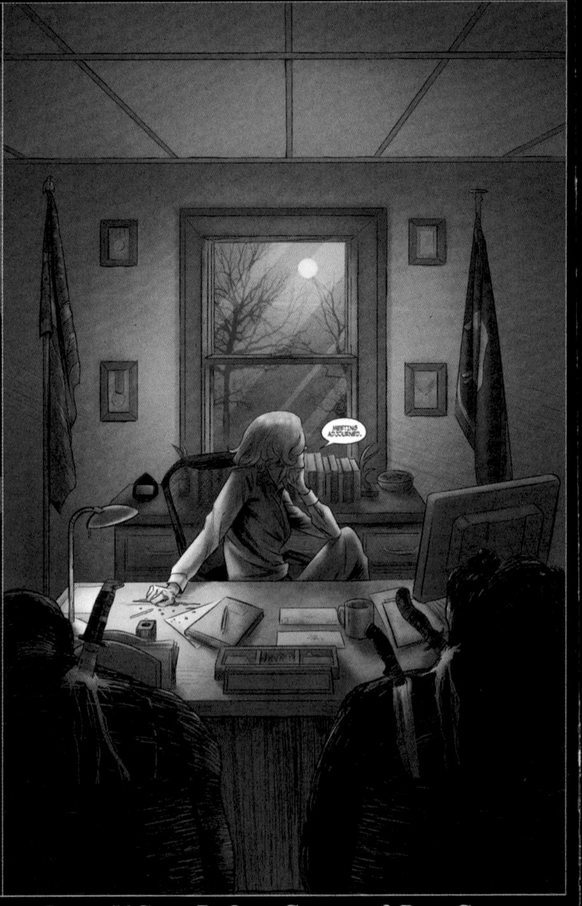
MEETING ADJOURNED.

**Postal #6 Cover B – Isaac Goodhart & Betsy Golden**

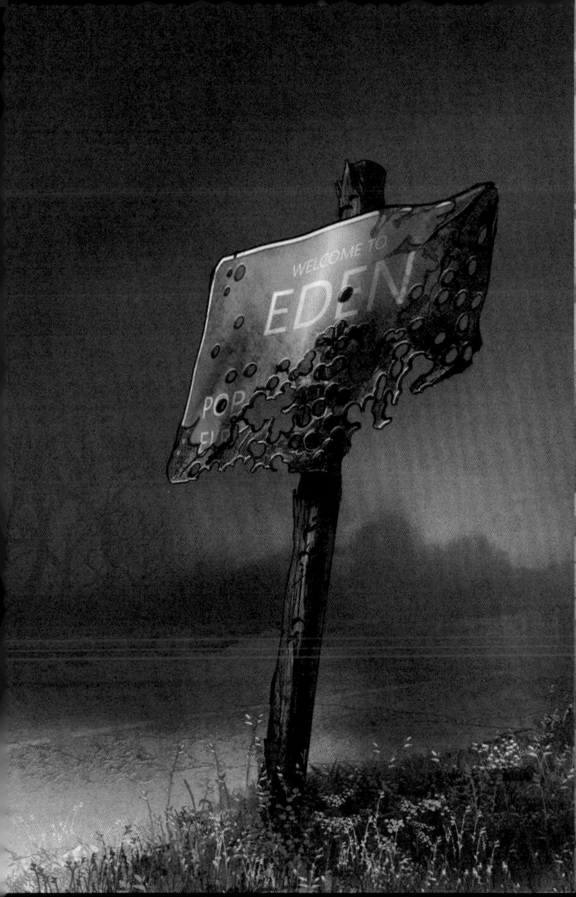
WELCOME TO
EDEN

**Postal #7 Cover A – Linda Sejic**

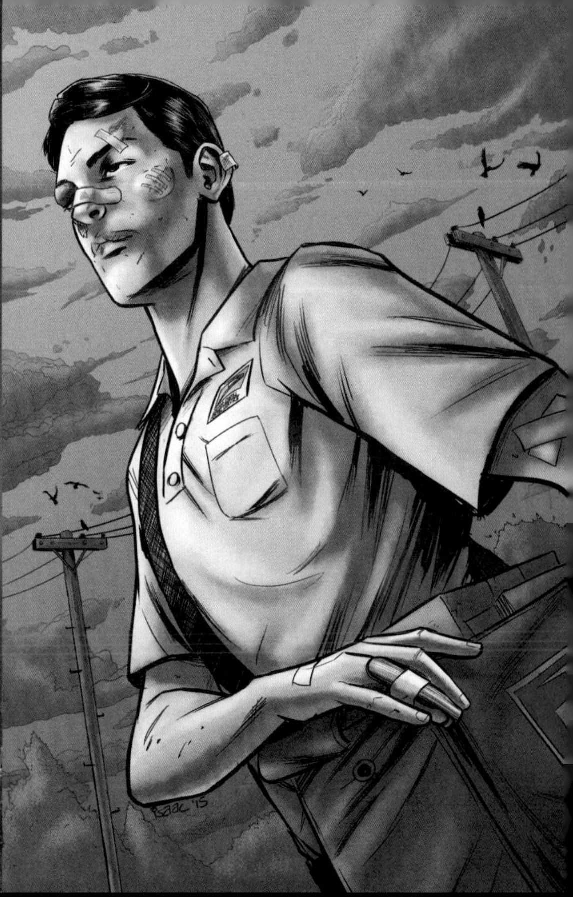

**Postal #7 Cover B – Isaac Goodhart & Betsy Golden**

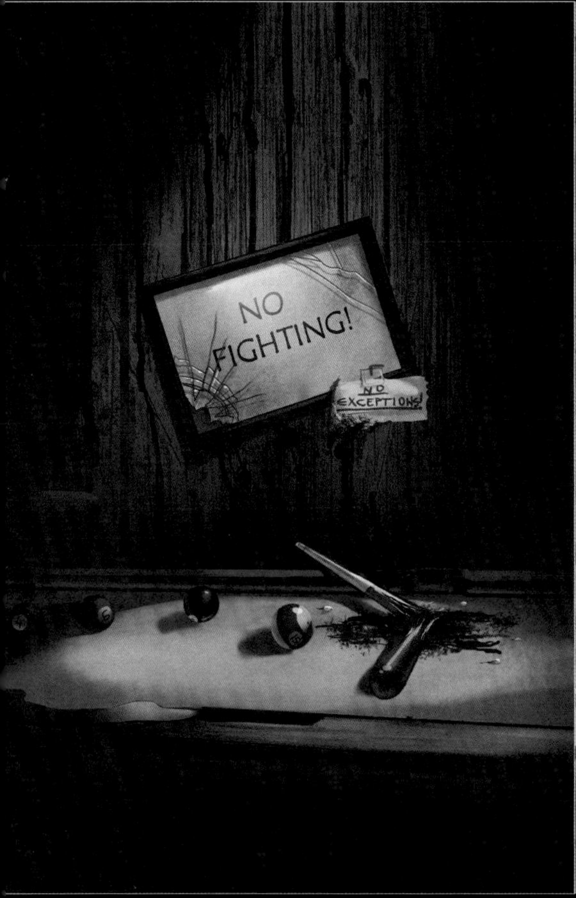
NO
FIGHTING!
NO
EXCEPTIONS!

**Postal #8 Cover A – Linda Sejic**

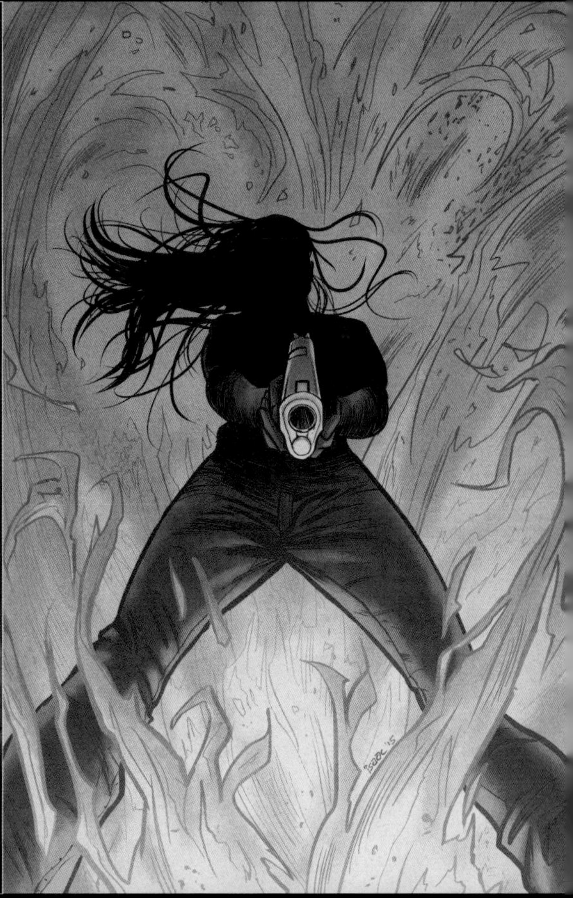

**Postal #8 Cover B – Isaac Goodhart & Betsy Golden**

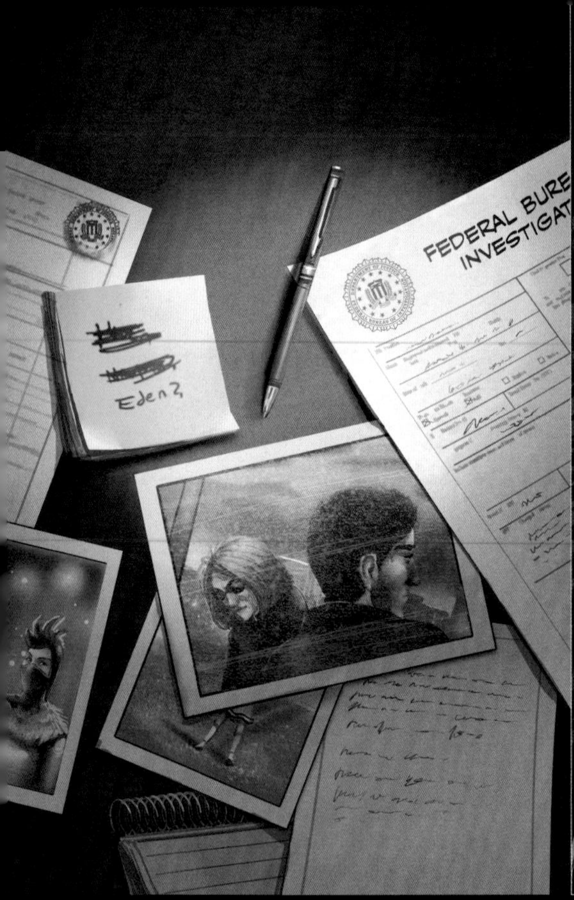
FEDERAL BURE
INVESTIGAT
Eden?

Postal Dossier #1 Cover A – Linda Sejic

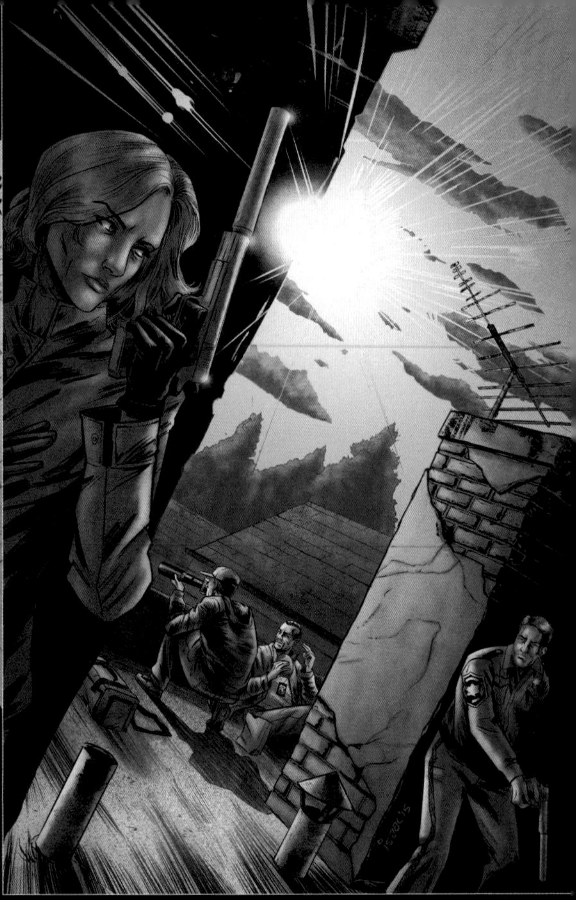

Postal Dossier #1 Cover B – Isaac Goodhart & Betsy Golden

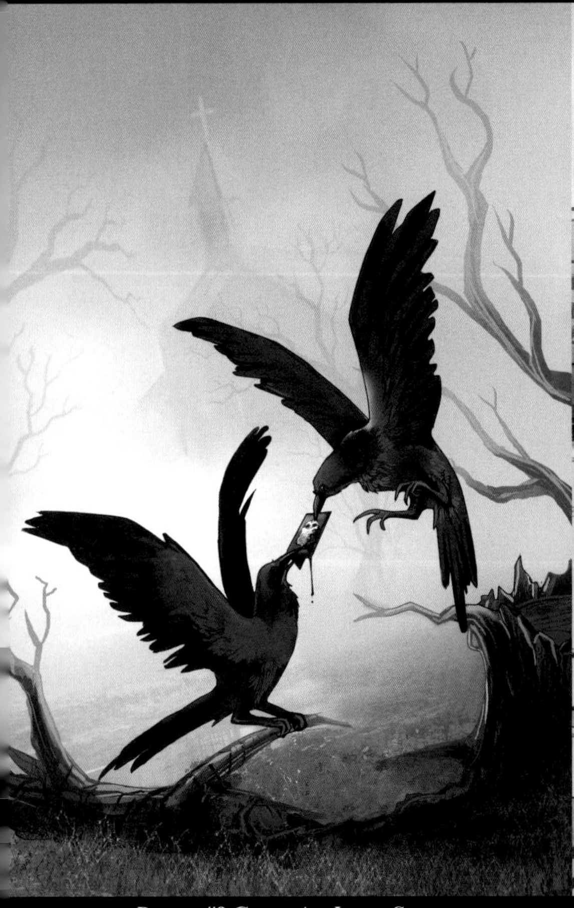

Postal #9 Cover A – Linda Sejic

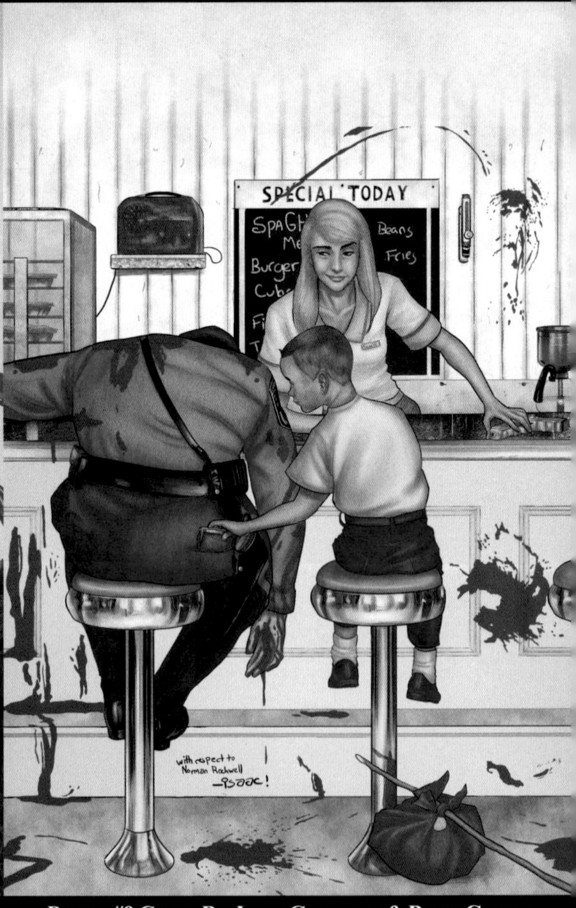
SPECIAL TODAY
Beans
Burger
Fries
with respect to Norman Rockwell
-Isaac!

Postal #9 Cover B – Isaac Goodhart & Betsy Golden

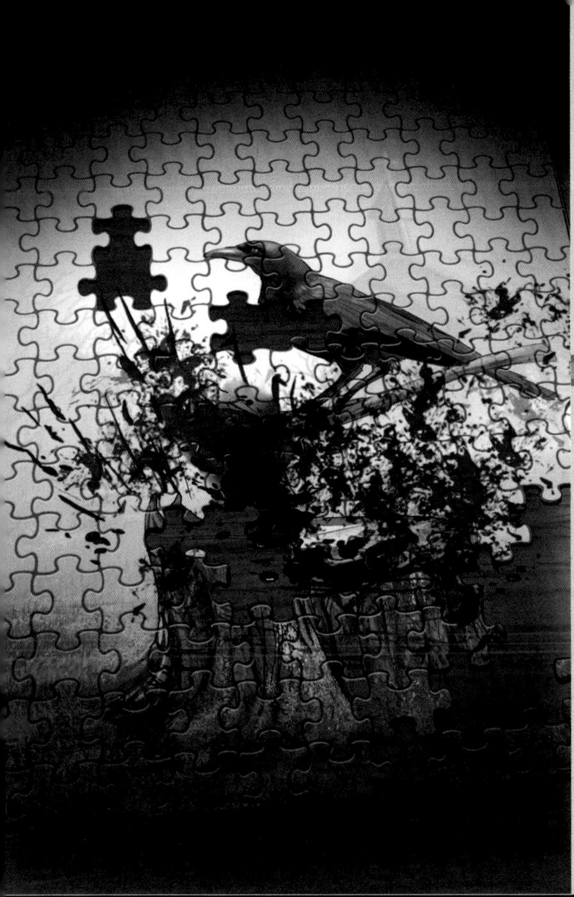

**Postal #10 Cover A – Linda Sejic**

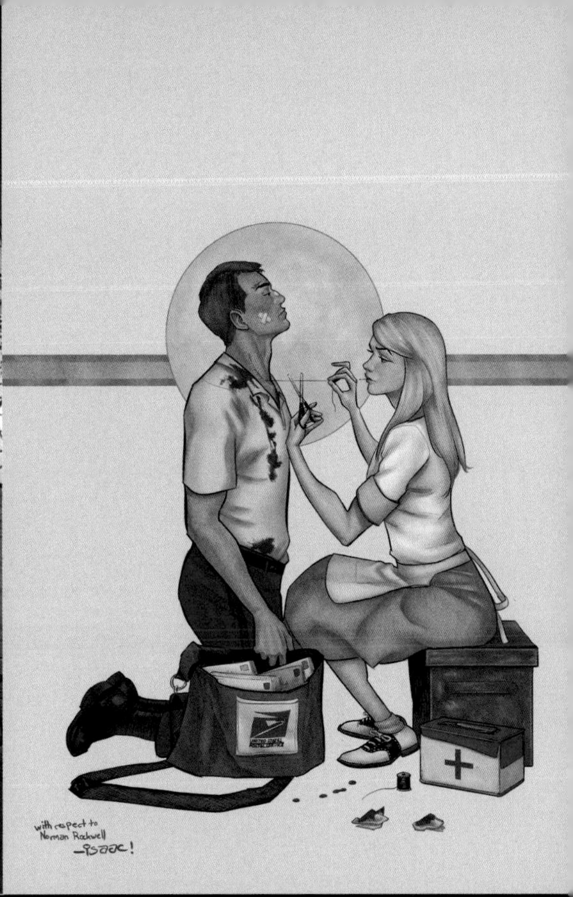
with respect to
Norman Rockwell
—Isaac!

**Postal #10 Cover B – Isaac Goodhart & Betsy Golden**

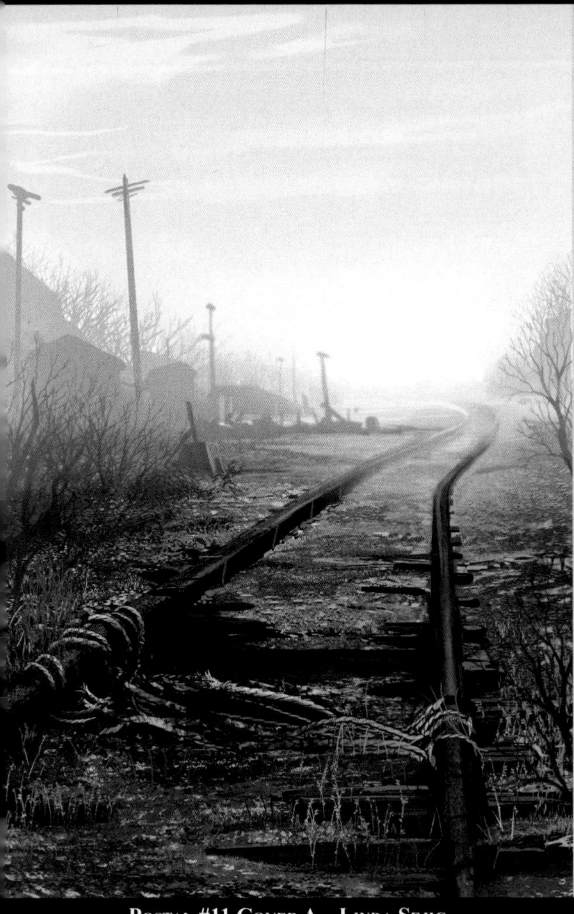

**Postal #11 Cover A – Linda Sejic**

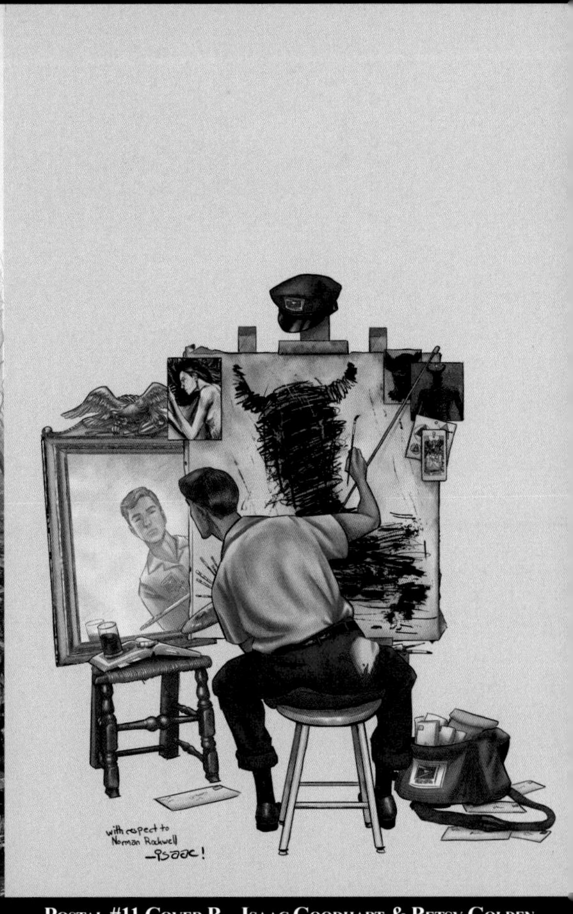
with respect to
Norman Rockwell
—Isaac!

**Postal #11 Cover B – Isaac Goodhart & Betsy Golden**

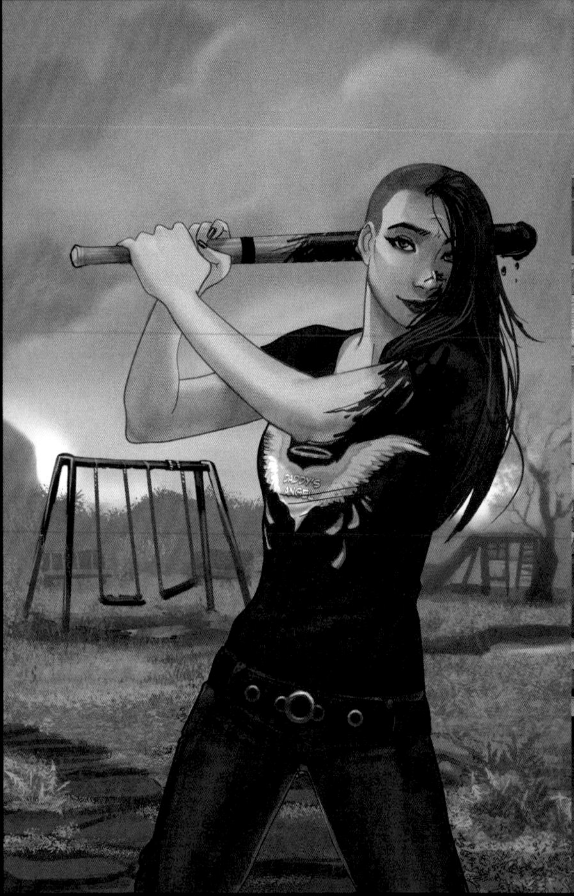
DADDY'S ANGEL

POSTAL #12 COVER A – LINDA SEJIC

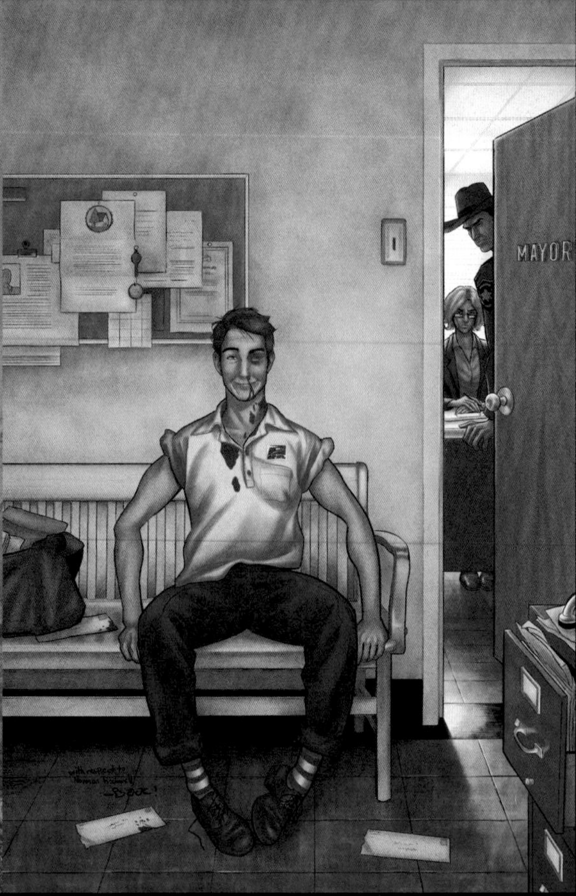
MAYOR

POSTAL #12 COVER B – ISAAC GOODHART & BETSY GOLDEN

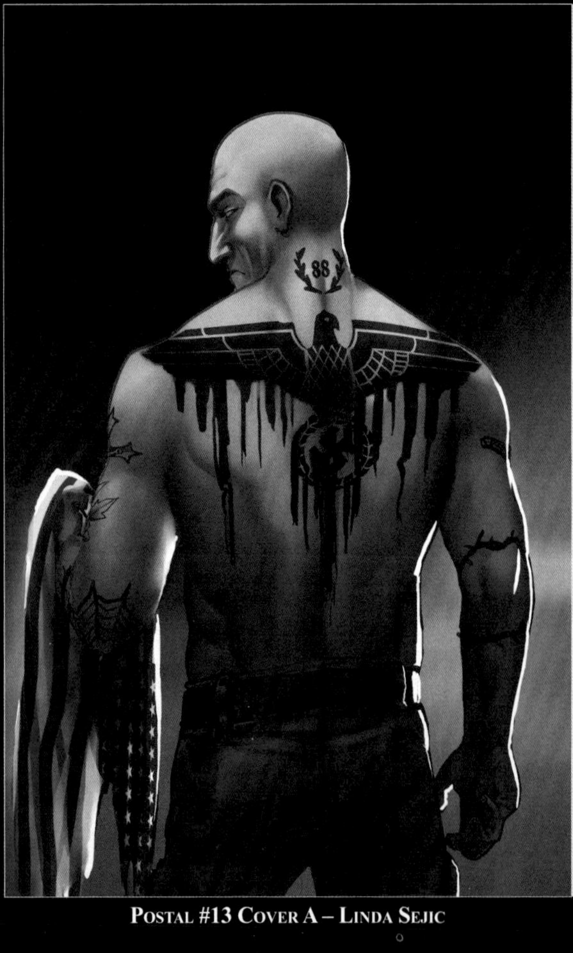
88

POSTAL #13 COVER A – LINDA SEJIC

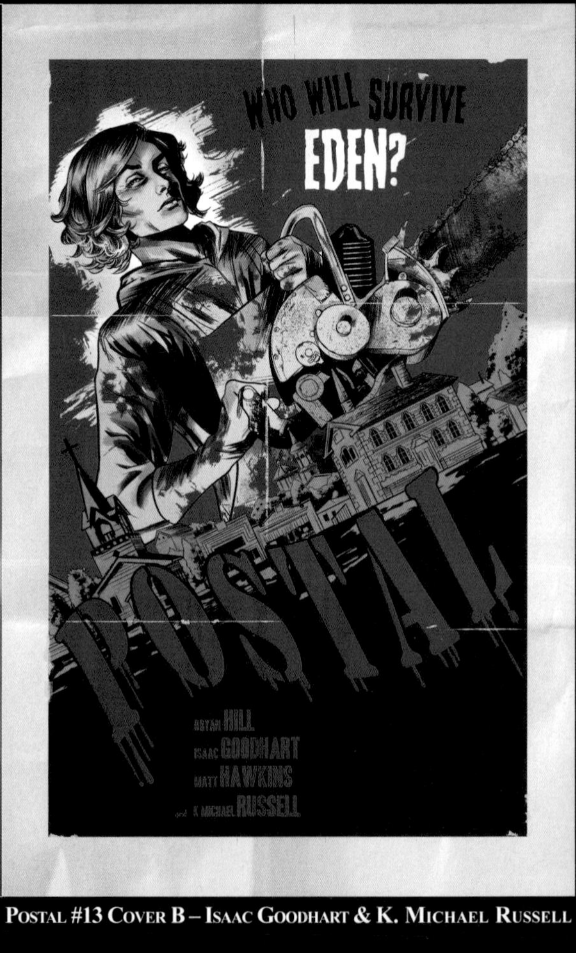
WHO WILL SURVIVE
EDEN?
POSTAL
BRYAN HILL
ISAAC GOODHART
MATT HAWKINS
and K MICHAEL RUSSELL

POSTAL #13 COVER B – ISAAC GOODHART & K. MICHAEL RUSSELL

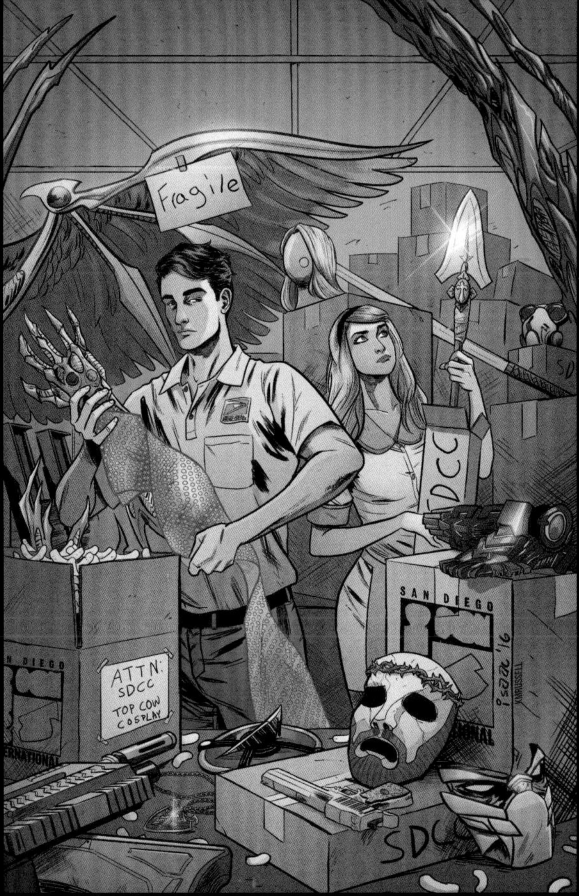
Fragile
SDCC
SAN DIEGO
ATTN: SDCC TOP COW COSPLAY
SDC

**Postal #13 SDCC Exclusive Cover – Isaac Goodhart & K. Michael Russell**

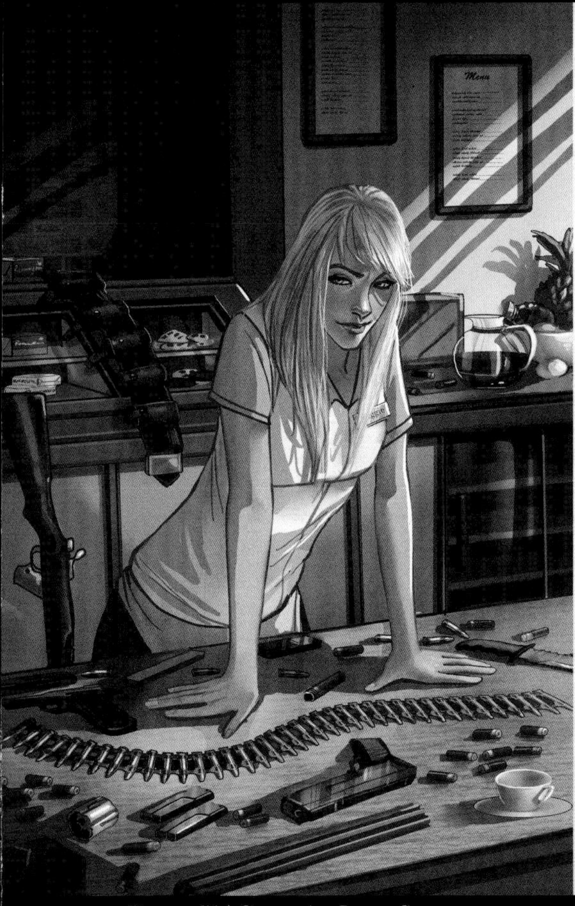
Menu

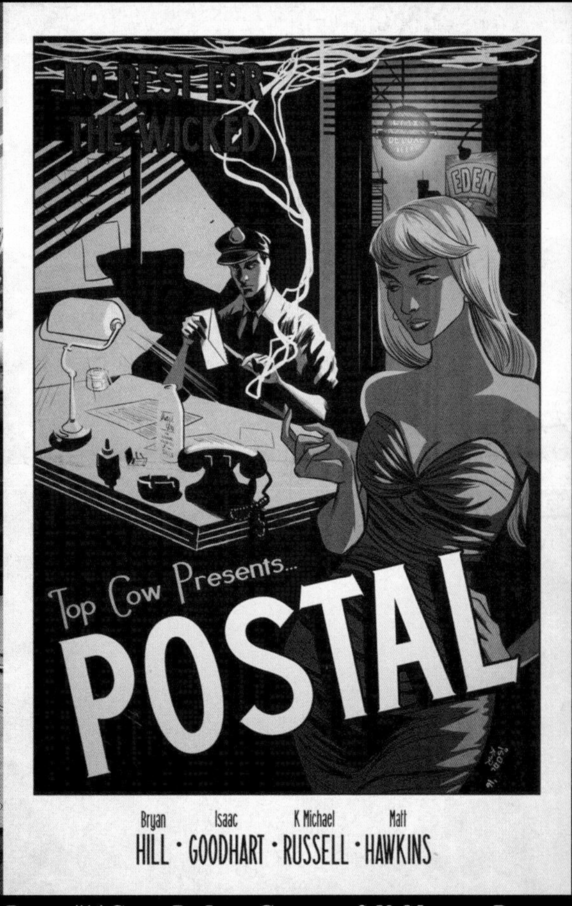
NO REST FOR THE WICKED
EDEN
Top Cow Presents...
POSTAL
Bryan HILL · Isaac GOODHART · K Michael RUSSELL · Matt HAWKINS

**Postal #14 Cover A – Linda Sejic**

**Postal #14 Cover B – Isaac Goodhart & K. Michael Russell**

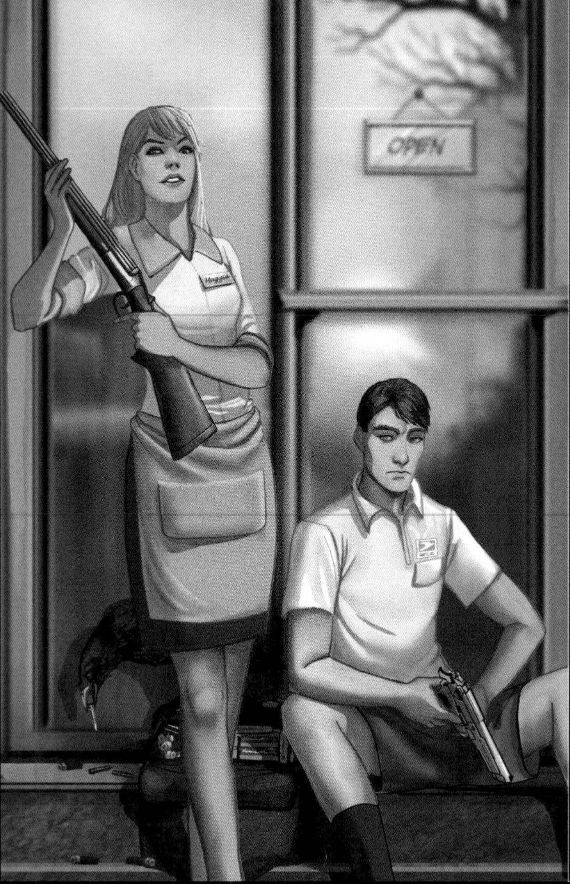
OPEN
**Postal #15 Cover A – Linda Sejic**

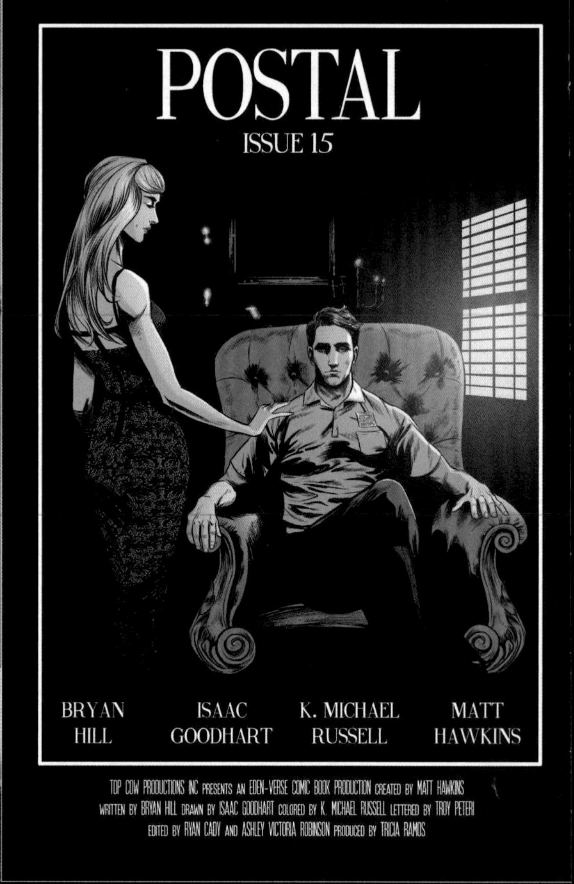
POSTAL
ISSUE 15
BRYAN HILL
ISAAC GOODHART
K. MICHAEL RUSSELL
MATT HAWKINS
TOP COW PRODUCTIONS INC PRESENTS AN EDEN-VERSE COMIC BOOK PRODUCTION CREATED BY MATT HAWKINS
WRITTEN BY BRYAN HILL DRAWN BY ISAAC GOODHART COLORED BY K. MICHAEL RUSSELL LETTERED BY TROY PETERI
EDITED BY RYAN CADY AND ASHLEY VICTORIA ROBINSON PRODUCED BY TRICIA RAMOS
**Postal #15 Cover B – Isaac Goodhart & K. Michael Russell**

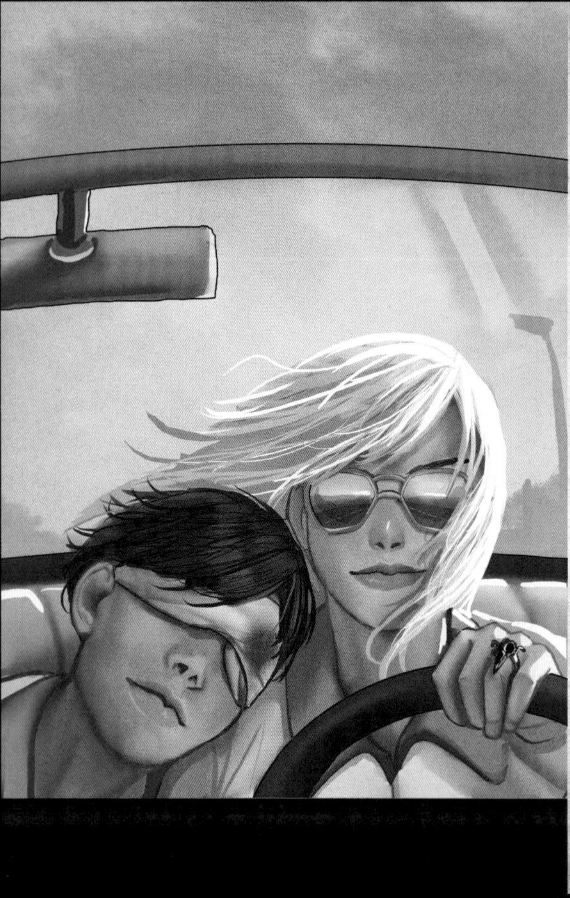
**Postal #16 Cover A – Linda Sejic**

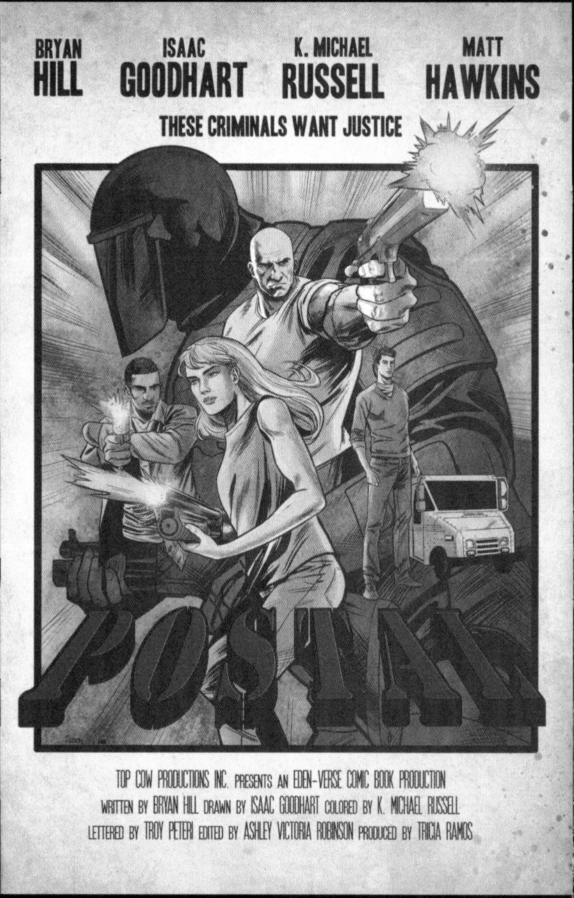
BRYAN HILL
ISAAC GOODHART
K. MICHAEL RUSSELL
MATT HAWKINS
THESE CRIMINALS WANT JUSTICE
TOP COW PRODUCTIONS INC. PRESENTS AN EDEN-VERSE COMIC BOOK PRODUCTION
WRITTEN BY BRYAN HILL DRAWN BY ISAAC GOODHART COLORED BY K. MICHAEL RUSSELL
LETTERED BY TROY PETERI EDITED BY ASHLEY VICTORIA ROBINSON PRODUCED BY TRICIA RAMOS
**Postal #16 Cover B – Isaac Goodhart & K. Michael Russell**

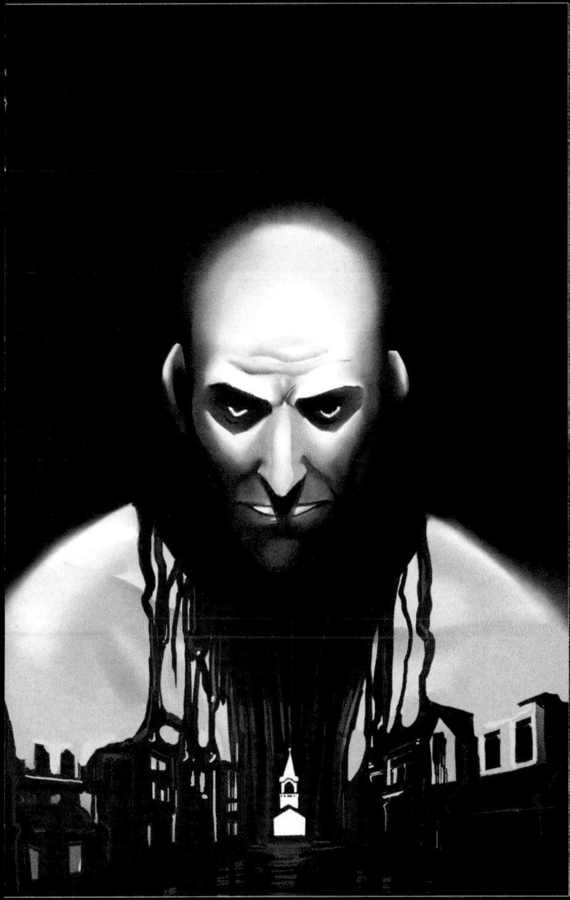

POSTAL #17 COVER – LINDA SEJIC

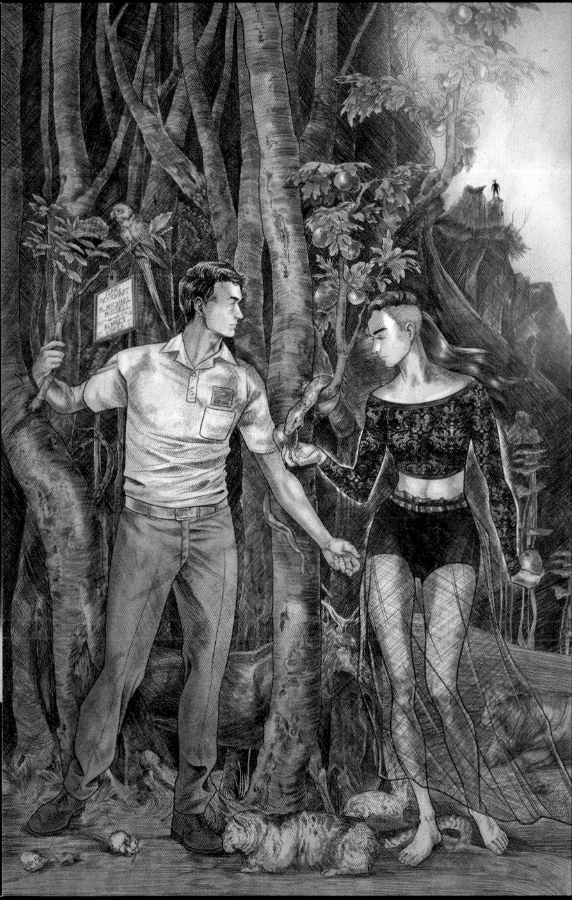

POSTAL #18 COVER – ISAAC GOODHART & K. MICHAEL RUSSELL

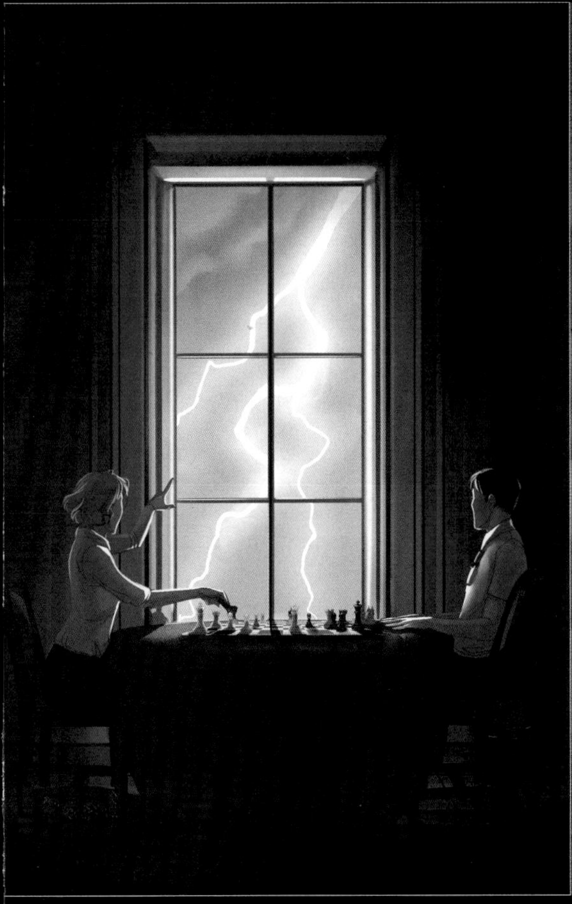

POSTAL #19 COVER – LINDA SEJIC

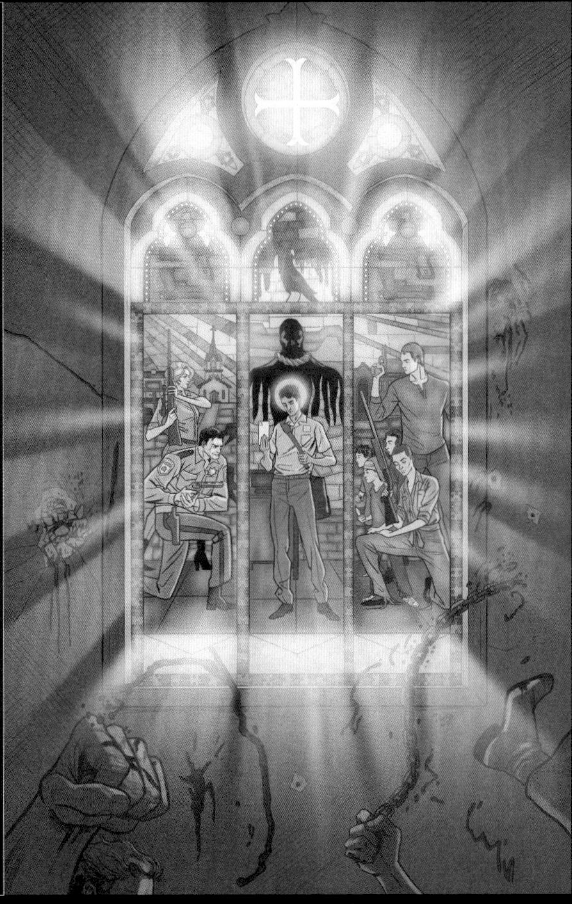

POSTAL #20 COVER – ISAAC GOODHART & K. MICHAEL RUSSELL

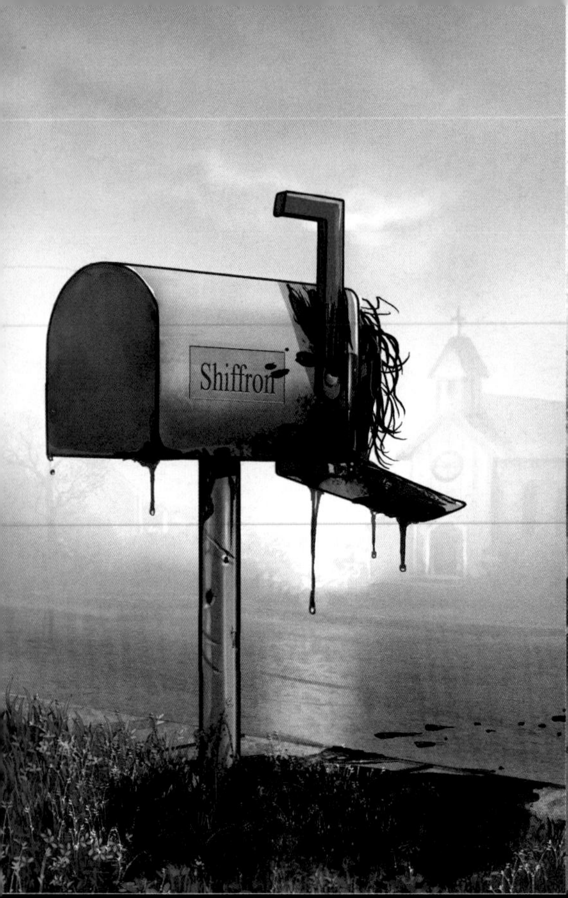
Shiffron

POSTAL #21 COVER – LINDA SEJIC

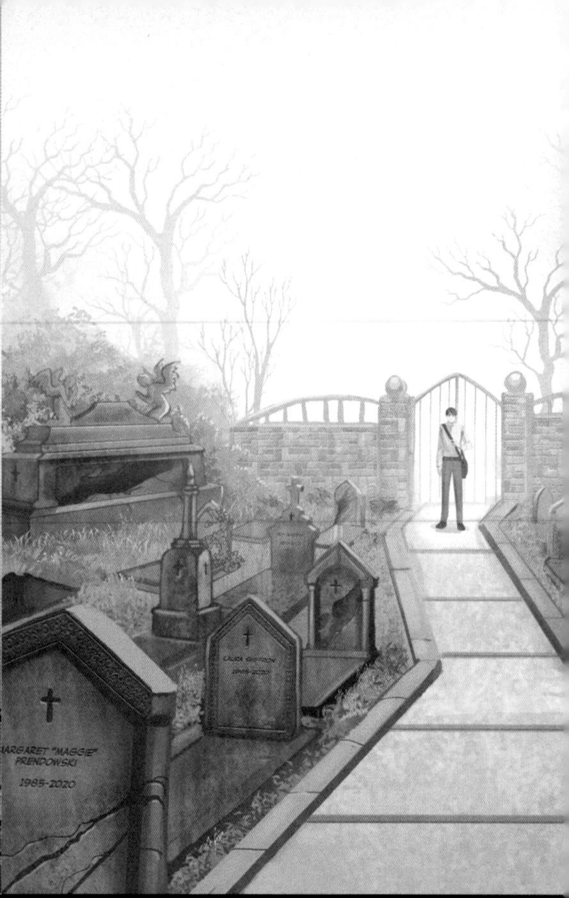
ARGARET "MAGGIE"
PRENDOWSKI
1985-2020

POSTAL #21 IMAGE OF TOMORROW VARIANT COVER – LINDA SEJIC

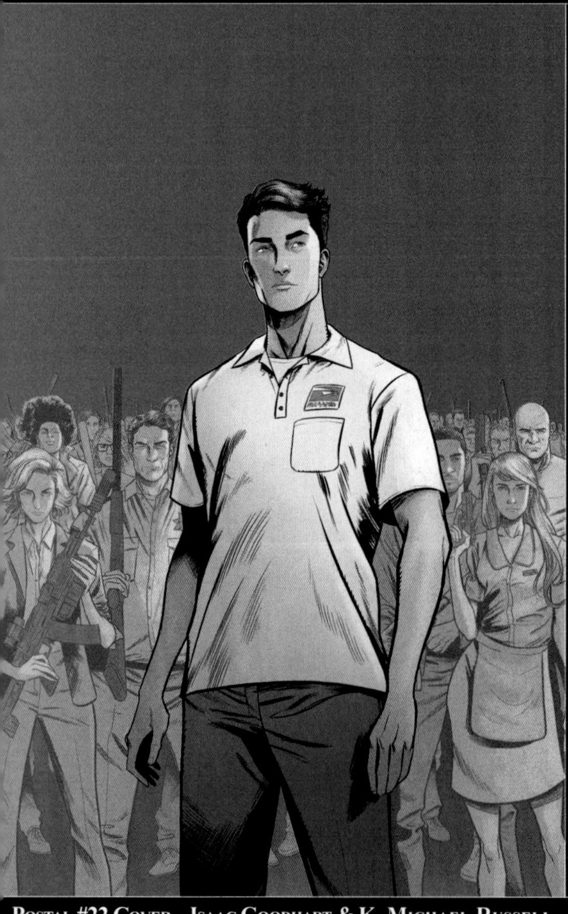

POSTAL #22 COVER – ISAAC GOODHART & K. MICHAEL RUSSELL

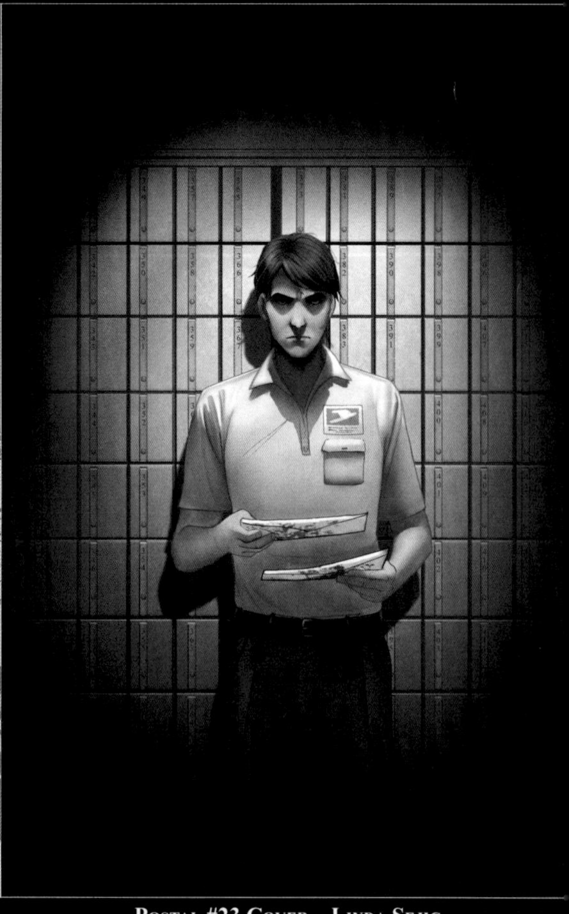

POSTAL #23 COVER – LINDA SEJIC

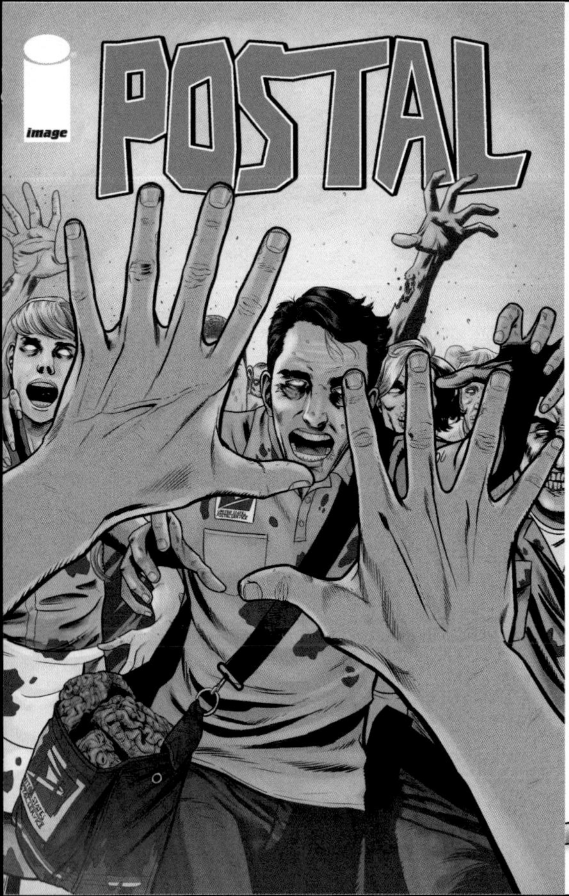
image
POSTAL

Postal #23 Walking Dead Variant Cover – Isaac Goodhart & K. Michael Russell

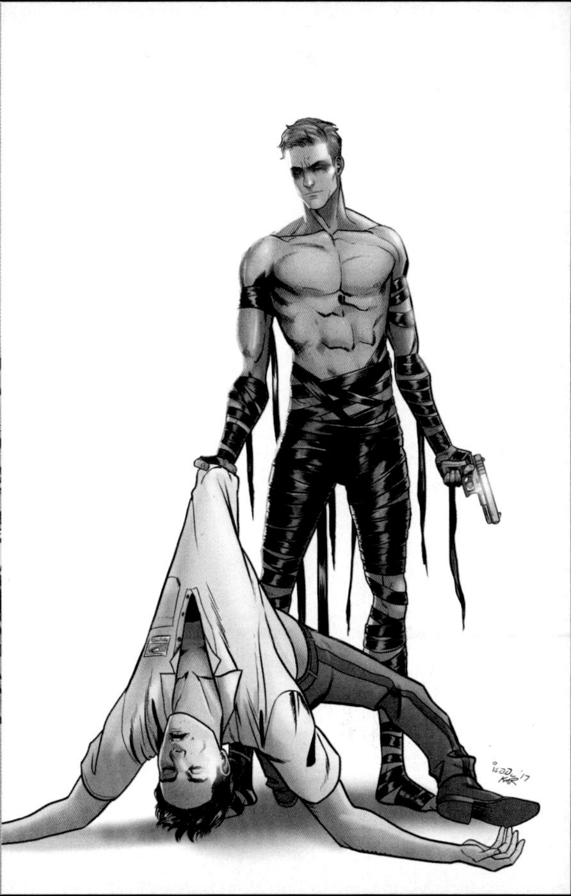

Postal #24 Cover – Isaac Goodhart & K. Michael Russell

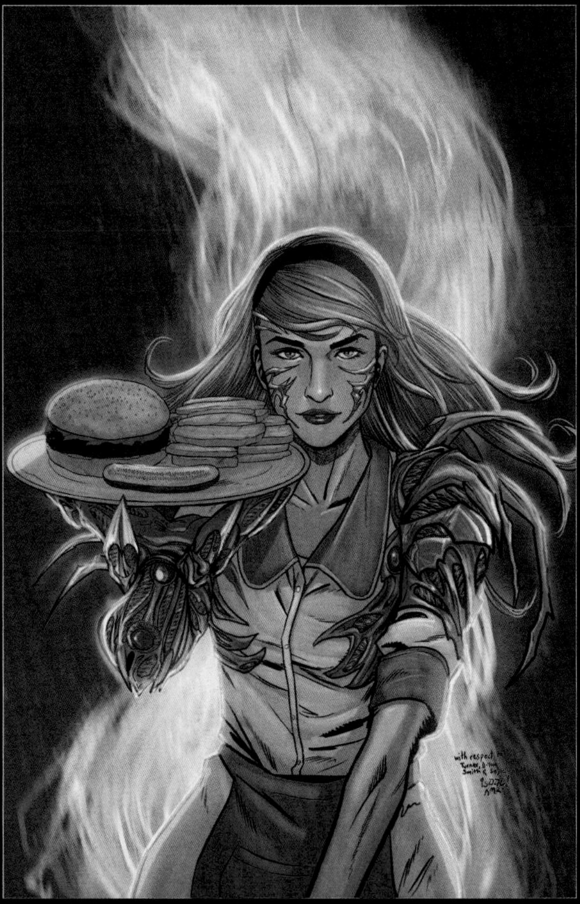

Postal #24 Witchblade Variant Cover – Isaac Goodhart & K. Michael Russell

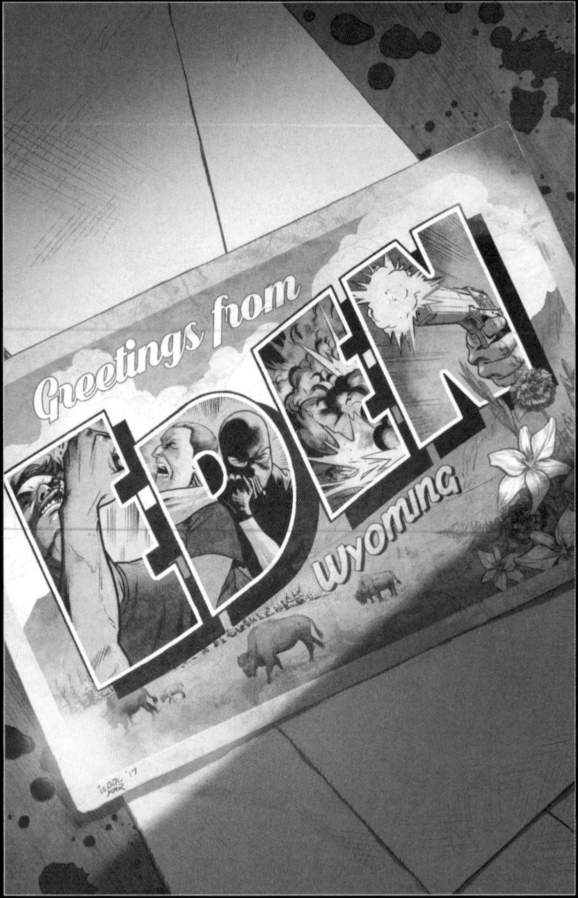
Greetings from
EDEN
Wyoming

POSTAL #25 COVER – ISAAC GOODHART

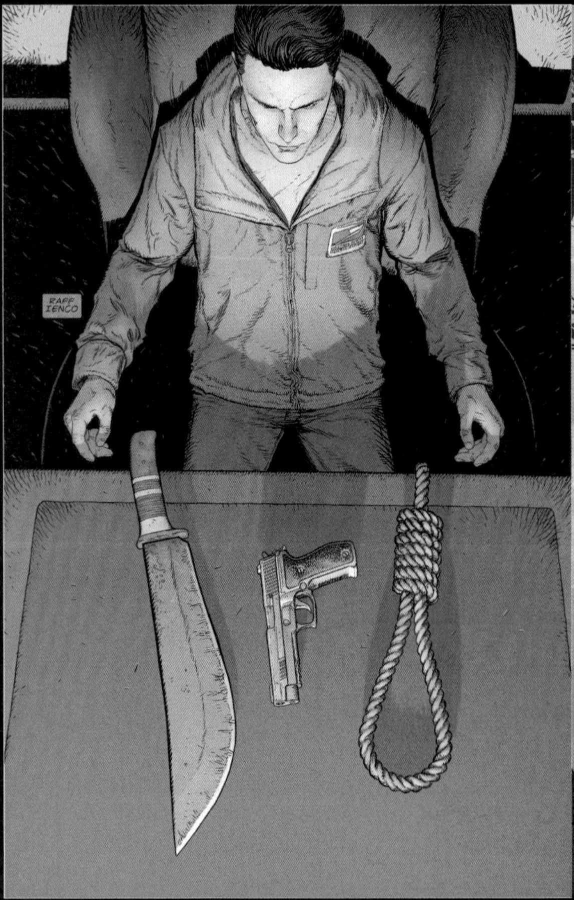
RAFF
IENCO

POSTAL: MARK COVER – RAFFAELE IENCO

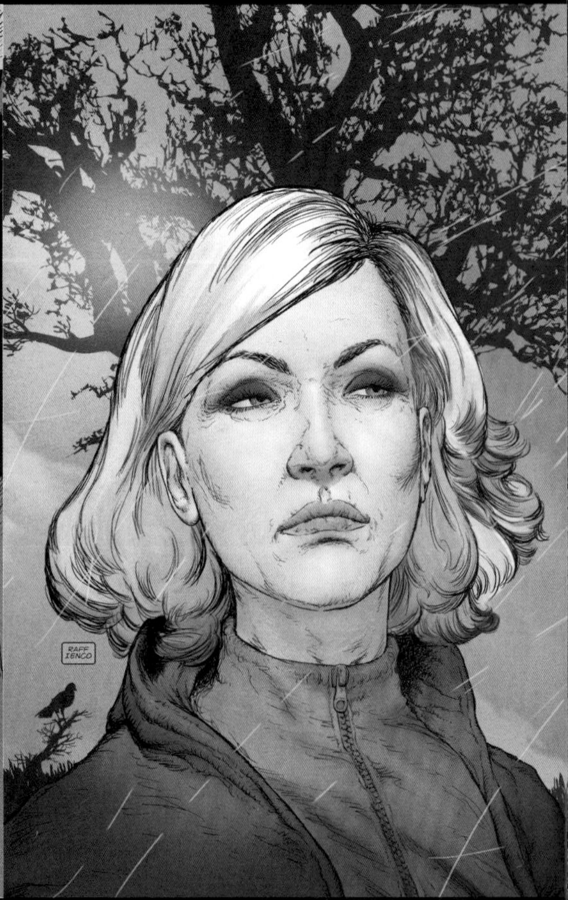
RAFF
IENCO

POSTAL: LAURA COVER – RAFFAELE IENCO

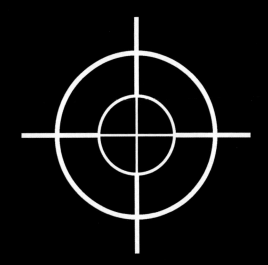

# The Top Cow essentials checklist:

**A Man Among Ye, Volume 1**
(ISBN: 978-1-5343-1691-1)

**Aphrodite IX: Rebirth, Volume 1**
(ISBN: 978-1-60706-828-0)

**Blood Stain, Volume 1**
(ISBN: 978-1-63215-544-3)

**The Complete Cyberforce, Volume 1**
(ISBN: 978-1-5343-2221-9)

**The Clock, Volume 1**
(ISBN: 978-1-5343-1611-9)

**The Complete Darkness, Volume 1**
(ISBN: 978-1-5343-1793-2)

**Death Vigil, Volume 1**
(ISBN: 978-1-63215-278-7)

**Eclipse, Volume 1**
(ISBN: 978-1-5343-0038-5)

**The Freeze, OGN**
(ISBN: 978-1-5343-1211-1)

**Fine Print, Volume 1**
(ISBN:  978-1-5343-2070-3)

**Helm Greycastle, Volume 1**
(ISBN: 978-1-5343-1962-2)

**Infinite Dark, Volume 1**
(ISBN: 978-1-5343-1056-8)

**La Mano Del Destino, Volume 1**
(ISBN: 978-1-5343-1947-9)

**La Voz De M.A.Y.O.:**
**Tata Rambo, Volume 1**
(ISBN: 978-1-5343-1363-7)

**Paradox Girl, Volume 1**
(ISBN: 978-1-5343-1220-3)

**Port of Earth, Volume 1**
(ISBN: 978-1-5343-0646-2)

**Postal, Volume 1**
(ISBN: 978-1-63215-342-5)

**Punderworld, Volume 1**
(ISBN: 978-1-5343-2072-7)

**Stairway Anthology**
(ISBN: 978-1-5343-1702-4)

**Sugar, Volume 1**
(ISBN: 978-1-5343-1641-7)

**Sunstone, Volume 1**
(ISBN: 978-1-63215-212-1)

**Swing, Volume 1**
(ISBN: 978-1-5343-0516-8)

**Symmetry, Volume 1**
(ISBN: 978-1-63215-699-0)

**Syphon, Volume 1**
(ISBN: 978-1-5343-2073-4)

**The Clock, OGN**
(ISBN: 978-1-5343-1611-9)

**The Tithe, Volume 1**
(ISBN: 978-1-63215-324-1)

**Think Tank, Volume 1**
(ISBN: 978-1-60706-660-6)

**The Complete Witchblade, Volume 1**
(ISBN: 978-1-5343-1564-8)